Victor Hugo's ...d love follows
the fortunes of Jean Valjean, an escaped convict determined
to put his criminal past behind him. A miracle of fate turns
Valjean down an honorable path, but his attempts to become a
respected member of the community are constantly put under
threat by the relentless investigations of the dogged policeman
Javert. However, it is not simply for himself that Valjean must
stay free, for he has sworn to protect Cosette, the daughter
of Fantine, a once-beautiful working-class woman driven to
poverty and ruin. As Valjean's story winds itself from a lowly
prison all the way up to the heart-rending drama of the Paris
Uprising of 1832, Hugo expounds with moving eloquence on
the social issues that troubled France in his time and continue
to resound in our own. Called 'one of the half-dozen greatest novels of the world' by Upton Sinclair, *Les Misérables* is a
genuine literary treasure: a vital portrait of a dark world within
the City of Light and a sweeping history of a turbulent age told
through an unforgettable cast of characters.

'Donougher's translation is a magnificent achievement [with]
endnotes which clear up every imaginable doubt or query . . .
[an] almost flawless translation, which brings the full flavour
of one of the greatest novels of the nineteenth century to new
readers in the twenty-first.'
—William Doyle, *The Times Literary Supplement* (London)

PENGUIN CLASSICS  DELUXE EDITION

LES MISÉRABLES

VICTOR HUGO was born in Besançon, France in 1802. In 1822 he published his first collection of poetry and in the same year, he married his childhood friend, Adèle Foucher. In 1831 he published his most famous youthful novel, *Notre-Dame de Paris*. A royalist and conservative as a young man, Hugo later became a committed social democrat and was exiled from France as a result of his political activities. In 1862, he wrote his longest and greatest novel, *Les Misérables*. After his death in 1885, his body lay in state under the Arc de Triomphe before being buried in the Panthéon.

CHRISTINE DONOUGHER is a freelance translator and editor. She has translated numerous books from French and Italian, and won the 1992 Scott Moncrieff Translation Prize for her translation of Sylvie Germain's *The Book of Nights*.

ROBERT TOMBS is Professor of History at St John's College, Cambridge. His most recent book is *That Sweet Enemy: The French and the British from the Sun King to the Present*, co-written with Isabelle Tombs.

VICTOR HUGO
Les Misérables

Translated with Notes by
CHRISTINE DONOUGHER

Introduction by
ROBERT TOMBS

PENGUIN BOOKS

PENGUIN BOOKS

Published by the Penguin Group
Penguin Group (USA) LLC
375 Hudson Street
New York, New York 10014

USA | Canada | UK | Ireland | Australia | New Zealand | India | South Africa | China
penguin.com
A Penguin Random House Company

This translation under the title *The Wretched* published in Penguin Books (UK) 2013
Published in Penguin Books (USA) 2015

ISBN 978-0-14-310756-9

Printed in the United States of America
1 3 5 7 9 10 8 6 4 2

Set in Sabon

Contents

LES MISÉRABLES

Part One: Fantine

Part Two: Cosette

Part Three: Marius

Part Four: The Rue Plumet Idyll and the Rue St-Denis Epic

Part Five: Jean Valjean

Chronology

1802 26 February: Born in Besançon, the third son of an army officer, Léopold-Sigisbert Hugo, who was himself the son of a carpenter.

1811 Following postings to Elba, Paris, Italy and then Paris again, the family moves to Madrid, where the father, now a general, is serving with the Napoleonic army in the war against the British. The young Victor is captivated by the exoticism of Spanish life.

1812 Return to Paris.

1814–18 As a pupil at a Parisian boarding-school and then at the Lycée Louis-le-Grand, writes his first literary essays, poems (on Napoleon) and historical dramas.

1819 Proposes to a childhood friend, Adèle Foucher. Continues to write poetry, and, with his brother Abel, launches a bi-monthly review, royalist in inspiration, entitled *Le Conservateur littéraire*, which runs for fifteen months.

1822 Publishes his first poetry collection, *Odes et poésies diverses*; marries Adèle Foucher. His brother Eugène becomes insane.

1823 Publishes his gory and melodramatic first novel, *Han d'Islande* (*Hans of Iceland*), and collaborates on a new monthly review, *La Muse française*. Birth of his first son, who lives for only three months.

1824 Publishes *Nouvelles Odes*. Birth of a daughter, Léopoldine.

1825 Appointed to the Légion d'Honneur and attends the coronation of the last Bourbon King, Charles X. Travels in eastern France. Discovers Shakespeare.

1826 Publishes a second, equally violent and exotic novel, *Bug-Jargal*, set during the 1791 slave revolt in Santo Domingo. Publishes *Odes et ballades*, which attracts the attention of the leading critic, Sainte-Beuve. Birth of a second son, Charles.

1827 Publishes his drama *Cromwell*, with a long preface that proves the most powerful and influential manifesto of the new Romanticism and the aesthetic revolution it aimed to bring about, in literature as in the theatre. Writes 'Ode à la Colonne de la Place Vendôme'.

1828 Death of his father. A new historical drama *Amy Robsart* fails in the theatre. Birth of another son, François-Victor.

1829 Publishes *Le Dernier jour d'un condamné*, a novel in the form of an interior monologue, whose hero is awaiting execution. Hugo was later to claim it had been intended as an argument against capital punishment.

1830 February: the first night of his new drama *Hernani* becomes known as the 'battle of *Hernani*', as young Romantics in the audience provoke its more staid and reactionary members by their support for the liberties Hugo has taken, politically, morally and artistically. In July, the 'three glorious days' of rioting in Paris force the hated Charles X into exile, to be replaced by Louis-Philippe, the more liberal 'Citizen King'. Hugo withdraws to write *Notre-Dame de Paris*. Birth of a second daughter, Adèle.

1831 16 March: *Notre-Dame de Paris* published.
Publishes one of his best-known poetry collections, *Les Feuilles d'automne*.

1832 Sets up house in what is now the Place des Vosges, in the Marais. His play *Le Roi s'amuse* (later the basis of Verdi's *Rigoletto*) is put on and banned after one performance, reinforcing his new-found liberalism. June insurrection in Paris.

1833 Starts a love affair with an actress, Juliette Drouet, who was to remain his mistress for fifty years.

1835 Publishes another poetry collection, *Les Chants du crépuscule*.

1836 Fails to get elected to the Académie Française. The first of numerous musical versions of *Notre-Dame de Paris* flops.

1837–40 Years of extensive travels, in France, Belgium, Germany and Switzerland.

1841 Elected to the Académie Française.

1843 His daughter Léopoldine and her husband are drowned in a boating accident on the Seine.

1845 Becomes a peer of France, i.e. a member of the French Upper House. Affair with Léonie Biard. Begins *Les Misérables*.

1848 Following the February Revolution in Paris, becomes mayor of the eighth *arrondissement* and is elected in June to the National Constituent Assembly. Launches a newspaper, *L'Événement*, with his sons.
June: involved in suppressing Paris insurrection.
December: Louis-Napoleon Bonaparte elected the first president of the new Republic.

1849 Elected to the new legislative Assembly as a *député* for Paris.

1850 Moves to the political left.

1851 December: Louis-Napoleon seizes power in a *coup d'état*. Hugo tries to organize the popular resistance to him but is forced to leave France secretly and take refuge in Brussels.

1852 His 'expulsion' from France is promulgated. Leaves Belgium and takes up residence in Jersey. Publishes *Napoléon le Petit*, a robust broadside against the illiberal new emperor, Napoleon III, seen as unfit to be compared with his uncle, Napoleon I.

1853 Publishes *Les Châtiments*, a vituperative collection of poems likewise attacking the new regime and the Church. Goes in for 'table-turning' with a medium.

1855 Declares his support for a group of French exiles expelled from Jersey for publishing a letter attacking Queen Victoria. Leaves Jersey for Guernsey.

1856 Publishes another collection of poetry, *Les Contemplations*. Settles into Hauteville House, now a Hugo museum.

1859 Rejects the offer of an amnesty from the emperor. Publishes the first part of *La Légende des siècles*, a vast sequence of poems tracing the historical and spiritual progress of humanity.

1860 Resumes work on *Les Misérables*.

1862 Publishes *Les Misérables*, his longest and finest novel.

1863 Publication of *Victor Hugo raconté par un témoin de sa vie*, a memoir purportedly written by Mme Hugo but usually thought to be the work of its subject. Publishes a set of engravings made after his own drawings.

1866 Publishes *Les Travailleurs de la mer* (*The Toilers of the Sea*), another huge novel, set in and around the Channel Islands.

1869 Publishes *L'Homme qui rit* (*The Laughing Man*), a novel set in seventeenth-century England.

1870 Plants an oak tree dedicated to 'The United States of Europe'. July: war breaks out between France and Prussia.
After learning of serious French setbacks, Hugo travels to Brussels and, following the disastrous defeat at Sedan and the surrender of the emperor, to Paris, where he remains during the Prussian siege. Addresses public appeals in turn to the Germans, the French and Parisians.

1871 Elected to the National Assembly following the armistice but resigns a month later, after strong disagreements with the conservative majority. Sudden death of his son, Charles.
March: the left-wing insurrection of the Paris Commune breaks out, and is crushed in May. Writes *L'Année terrible*.

Hugo moves back to Brussels, where he offers asylum to refugee Communards. Expelled from Belgium by the authorities. Returns to Paris.

1873 Death of his last son, François-Victor. His mentally unstable daughter, Adèle (the subject of François Truffaut's film *L'Histoire d'Adèle H.*), is by now in an asylum.

1874 Publishes his last novel, *Quatre-Vingt Treize* (*'93*), a story set in Brittany during the Revolutionary Terror.

1876 Becomes a member of the Senate.

1877 Publishes the second part of *La Légende des siècles*, and a collection of sixty-eight poems celebrating his grandchildren, *L'Art d'être grand-père*. Finally publishes his *Histoire d'un crime*, his account of Louis-Napoleon's *coup d'état*.

1883 Death of Juliette Drouet. Publishes third and final part of *La Légende*.

1885 22 May: Dies of pneumonia.

His coffin is displayed beneath the Arc de Triomphe before a state funeral in the Panthéon.

Introduction

I want to destroy human inevitability; I condemn slavery, I chase out poverty, I instruct ignorance, I treat illness, I light up the night, I hate hatred. That is what I am and that is why I have written *Les Misérables*. As I see it, *Les Misérables* is nothing other than a book having fraternity as its foundation and progress as its summit.

Victor Hugo, 1862[1]

On 4 March 1861, the world's most famous political exile boarded the ferry from St Peter's Port, Guernsey, in the British Channel Islands, to Weymouth in England with the voluminous and nearly completed manuscript of *Les Misérables* in a waterproof bag. Victor-Marie Hugo was on the way to the battlefield of Waterloo to finish the book. He was one of those bushy-bearded nineteenth-century monsters of egotism, energy and creativity. Several contemporaries compared him with that other domineering genius, Wagner. Tolstoy bracketed him with Dostoevsky. In British terms, one would have to think of him as Dickens, Tennyson and Carlyle rolled into one: the greatest popular novelist, the greatest modern poet ('Alas!' said André Gide), and the irrepressible conscience of the nation. But there is no Anglophone equivalent of the political career he added to this, as a crusading enemy of the death penalty, an implacable opponent of tyranny, a parliamentarian under three different regimes and a patriotic bard. He tried out every permutation of nineteenth-century French politics, starting as an arch-conservative and finishing as a left-wing hero. Romantic artists saw themselves as the prophets and guides of humanity: none more so than Hugo. Like some of the other geniuses with whom he was compared – perhaps more comprehensively than most – he was a danger to those around him, blighting the lives of most of his family, and an incorrigible and insatiable sex-pest specializing in vulnerable women amenable to his fame, money and patriarchal authority.

Born in 1802, he was the third son of the daughter of a Breton sea captain and of a tough soldier in Napoleon's army, who was doing very well out of the Revolutionary and Napoleonic Wars, ending a general and a count. Victor was brought up largely by his mother, who, like most French people, finally came to prefer a restored Bourbon dynasty to the endless upheavals of revolution and war. In 1814, as Allied armies marched on Paris, Napoleon abdicated, and the Bourbon King Louis XVIII (brother of the guillotined Louis XVI) returned. But the ex-emperor soon tired of his little realm on the island of Elba, where spies reported he was putting on weight. He sailed with 900 men and landed near Cannes on 1 March 1815. He was acclaimed by the army and a large minority – perhaps one in three – of the country, especially the bureaucracy and the army, including Hugo's father. But the Allied powers had learned that they could not trust Napoleon, and prepared to fight. Napoleon's chief of police predicted that he would win two battles and lose the third. He did win – or partially win – at Ligny, against the Prussians, and at Quatre-Bras, against Wellington's Anglo-Dutch army. The third was Waterloo, a turning point in French and European history – and fundamental to the plot of *Les Misérables*. So Louis XVIII returned to reign over a bitterly divided country, and was duly succeeded by his brother Charles X in 1825. Hugo evokes these touchy years of division: 'Whether one said "regicides" or "voters", "enemies" or "allies", "Napoleon" or "Buonaparte" – this could divide two men more than any abyss' (p. 109).

Victor Hugo came to prominence during the 1820s as a brilliant young royalist poet, proclaiming that poetry required 'monarchist ideas and religious beliefs', and happy to turn out odes on royal occasions and denounce 'Buonaparte' in verse. As a leading figure in the new French Romantic movement and yet one loyal to the Bourbons, he was in favour with the government. Romanticism, however, brought notoriety and friction with a conservative artistic establishment. Hugo wrote disturbing and controversial novels. He proclaimed himself a great admirer of – and perhaps by implication successor to – Shakespeare, 'the leading poet of all time', who had transcended the 'absurd pseudo-Aristotelian' traditions of the French classical theatre, of which patriots were so proud. Shakespeare's boundless imagination and willingness to ignore convention were, for Hugo, 'the torrent that has burst its banks', the precursor of modern Romanticism.[2] Hugo's own torrential work would also break literary boundaries. His collision with the establishment came in the political as well as the artistic realm. In 1827 he wrote a floridly patriotic ode: 'À la Colonne de la Place Vendôme' – Napoleon's memorial column in Paris. In this he seemed to threaten a new 'dawning of the sun of Austerlitz' to re-establish France's greatness. Although the poem was careful not to criticize the Bourbons directly, any praise of Napoleon was provocative. Hugo's new-found admiration for Napoleon was linked to his rediscovery of his estranged father after his mother's death, and of his family's claim to nobility, conferred by the emperor – all fictionalized (and, like so much in Les Misérables, idealized) in the story of Marius Pontmercy.

Sharper clashes with the establishment came over his plays. Marion de Lorme (1829) was banned, largely for its hostile portrayal of Louis XIII. Hugo had a personal audience with Charles X, who refused to allow its performance but tried to buy him off with an increased royal pension, which he disdainfully and publicly refused.[3] Hugo's next innovation, Hernani, was described by critics as an amalgam of Spanish Romanticism and Shakespeare (it had echoes of Romeo and Juliet). It opened at the Théâtre Français, the prestigious state theatre, in March 1830. The first week became a battle between defenders of the French classical tradition of Corneille and Racine, who jeered and blew whistles, and Hugo's friends (he issued wads of free tickets), who cheered his lines and heckled the hecklers. Critics hated Hugo's ostentatious flouting of classical proprieties: unorthodox versification, unpoetic language, vulgar characters and violence on stage. A female character calls her lover 'my lion' (the actress insisted on changing it to 'my lord'); bandits are put on stage; disrespectful words are addressed to a king; a noblewoman is portrayed 'without dignity or modesty'; and dialogue is naturalistic. As Hugo saw it, classicists wanted art to improve and idealize reality, while he insisted it should 'paint life', with its confusion of the good, the bad and the absurd.[4] In retrospect, this clash took on political significance as a cultural rebellion against the Bourbon regime, only months before it was overthrown by a popular revolution in the streets of Paris in July 1830. This revolution delayed the completion of Hugo's first great popular success as a novelist, Notre-Dame de Paris (1831) – The Hunchback of Notre-Dame.

The revolution brought to power the compromise 'July Monarchy' of King Louis-Philippe, a parliamentary system on British lines, with a limited electorate. It won the support of many leading intellectuals. They included the political philosopher Alexis de Tocqueville, the painter Eugène Delacroix, the historian François Guizot (who became its dominant political figure) and Hugo. He gives a sympathetic if critical pen-portrait of Louis-Philippe, with whom he was on excellent terms, in Les Misérables. He would, wrote Hugo, have been 'ranked among the most illustrious rulers in history if he had cared a little for glory ... His great failing was this: he was modest in the name of France' (pp. 748, 749). Yet the king's caution in foreign policy, if it brought him the hatred of nationalists, won the support of much of the public, who feared a return to the turmoil of the Revolutionary and Napoleonic years. At the time, Hugo himself, now a tax-paying, property-owning father of four, seems to have shared these views. But, for its first five years, the July Monarchy had to fight for survival against both left and right, in a Europe which seemed on the verge of another cataclysm.[5] Revolts broke out in Belgium, Poland and Italy, which French Republicans, Bonapartists and socialists (overlapping categories) supported enthusiastically and wanted France to join in with. Some were willing to use insurrection and assassination to reignite the revolution begun in 1830. Louis-Philippe was the target of eight attempts on his life. Some revolutionaries aimed at another international conflagration, like the Revolutionary Wars of the 1790s, in which French armies would forcibly liberate the peoples of Europe. The left, proclaimed one of its leading spokesmen, 'have no fear of a European war'. This was the feverish atmosphere of the Republican underground, which Hugo portrayed in the 'Friends of the ABC', led by the clear-eyed fanatic Enjolras, 'a charming young man, capable of being fearsome. Of angelic beauty, he ... had a sacerdotal and war-like nature, at odds with his boyishness' (p. 585).

A terrible cholera outbreak in 1832 killed 18,000 people in Paris, including the tough prime minister, Casimir Périer, and an opposition leader, the former Napoleonic hero, General Maximilien Lamarque. The latter's funeral procession on 5 June 1832 provided the occasion for a rebellion planned by Republican secret societies, possibly with support from Bonapartists and 'Carlists' (supporters of the ex-king Charles X).[6] When the shooting started, thousands of young Parisian workers joined in, and about 200 barricades were thrown up. The rising was eventually defeated by the army and the part-time National Guard, who lost at least 150 men, while the insurgents lost roughly the same.[7] Hugo disapproved of this 'riot', as did several leading Republicans – 'Follies drowned in blood,' he noted. 'We shall have a republic one day, and when it comes of its own volition, it will be good ... We must be patient [and] not permit ruffians to daub our flag with red ... They make the republic a bogeyman ... we should speak a little less of Robespierre and a little more of Washington.'[8] But three decades later he was to rehabilitate and immortalize this minor tragedy in one of the climactic scenes in Les Misérables.

This then was the turbulent period – between 1815 and 1833 – within which *Les Misérables* was set. Now begins the period during which it was written. The first hint may go back to 1839, when Hugo visited the *bagne* at Toulon as part of his interest in the treatment of criminals. He was, by this time, a celebrated and successful poet, playwright and novelist. He was elected in 1841 to the Académie Française, the pinnacle of the intellectual establishment, and in 1845 given a peerage by Louis-Philippe, with a seat in the upper chamber. The 1840s was a decade for socially conscious literature in France, as in England: works by George Sand, Balzac, Eugène Sue and Félix Pyat match those by Dickens, Charlotte Brontë, Disraeli, Carlyle and Elizabeth Gaskell. Hugo began writing his own social novel, provisionally titled *Jean Tréjean* (later Vlajean, and finally Valjean), on 17 November 1845, and retitled *Les Misères* by 1848, when most of the book was in draft. Hugo had earlier sketched out the main story round Valjean, Cosette and Marius, and then added depth, detail and secondary characters, usually working on several episodes at once.[9] Masses of classical and historical allusions give this humble contemporary story a universal significance as part of the great spiritual drama of history, in which humanity moves towards fulfilment – a central Romantic vision. Completion, however, was decisively delayed in the aftermath of another revolution, and, in consequence, the final version was to take on a very different form. In February 1848, the July Monarchy was suddenly overthrown in the streets of Paris, as part of the 'Springtime of the Peoples' that brought regimes crashing down across Europe at a time of severe economic and political crisis. Hugo vainly urged a regency to try to save the monarchy, but the Parisian crowd demanded a democratic republic. This Second Republic was to be racked by economic and political conflict, in which Hugo was caught up.

He was elected to the new National Constituent Assembly in June 1848 as a representative for Paris. Almost at once, tensions erupted in the capital's worst violence yet, the 'June Days', which began as demonstrations by unemployed workers and grew into a full-scale insurrection, with half the city barricaded. The rising was eventually crushed by the full force of the army, with thousands of deaths and mass arrests. Hugo's private jottings clearly show his ideas concerning what he would later call *les misérables*. They were, in some circumstances, the 'noble and worthy people', but they could be 'perverted and misled' by extremists and turned into a destructive and anarchic mob. During the February Revolution they had been 'ardent, good, generous, full of respectful love for every noble thing', but by June 'the same people' had become 'bitter, discontented, unjust, suspicious', some of them 'dreaming of pillage, massacre and arson'. They had been demoralized, he thought, by 'inactivity, laziness, organized fecklessness . . . Handouts that corrupt the heart rather than wages that satisfy it.' Hugo actively opposed the June rebellion as an Assembly 'Representative of the People', going so far as to accompany the military in attacking a barricade. In his private notebooks, he tells a story of young prostitutes standing on top of barricades, lifting up their skirts to taunt the soldiers, and being shot down – for him a potent symbol of the depravity and cruelty on both sides. During the fighting, a soldier was killed in the courtyard of his house. He summed up the struggle as 'on one side, the despair of the people, on the other, the despair of society'. But he had no doubt about which side he was on: 'Saving civilization, as Paris did in June, could almost be said to have saved the life of the human race.' As always, he consoled himself with a vision of Progress: 'we are living in a furnace [but] the statue of the Future will emerge, and it needed such a conflagration to cast such a bronze.'[10] It has been plausibly argued that the psychological stress of the June violence, and his own part in it, was a turning point in his life.[11] Nevertheless, the appearance of Les Misères was announced as imminent by his son in July. In fact, there was to be a gap of twelve years before writing resumed.

The June Days signalled the failure of Republicanism, whose support was limited to an urban minority in a largely rural society. When a president was elected in December 1848, the Republicans were trounced by Louis-Napoleon Bonaparte, the emperor's nephew, who won more than three times as many votes as all the other candidates combined. Hugo, who had family and intellectual links to the Bonapartist tradition, was at first warily hopeful, but he soon turned against Louis-Napoleon as a threat to freedom and the Republic. Both critics and admirers of Hugo have suspected a mixture of motives, including disappointed ambition. Hugo was not alone among politicians in expecting that Louis-Napoleon, an adept flatterer, intended to listen to their advice, and who felt both personal resentment and political outrage when he followed his own populist strategy. This culminated in a military coup in December 1851, in which the established political class – royalist and Republican, and including, of course, Representative Hugo – was forcibly and contemptuously ejected from power. Failing in various fumbling attempts to rouse resistance, Assembly members found themselves under temporary arrest or expelled from France. Hugo left for Brussels. Popular resistance in the countryside was crushed, and thousands arrested and transported. The final blow was that the electorate overwhelmingly endorsed the coup in a plebiscite, and Bonaparte explained that he had 'acted illegally to ensure justice'. The Republic was formally replaced by the Second Empire of Napoleon III in 1852 – endorsed by another plebiscite – as the economy grew and Napoleon increased both his power and his popularity. In the eyes of Hugo and other exiles, the corrupted people had proved unworthy of their destiny:

> Great nation, at this time you can enjoy,
> While in the dark men suffer, weep and die,
> ... Illuminations, games and fun galore:
> Your wages as this wretched fellow's whore![12]

The 1851 coup transformed Hugo's life and his political role. From defender of law and order against the mob in June 1848, he became an upholder of Republicanism as a sacred creed, a denouncer of dictatorship, and an implacable, even hysterical, enemy of Napoleon III personally. He went into exile and rejected an amnesty, remaining outside France, mainly in the Channel Islands, until the Second Empire collapsed, in September 1870, due to a disastrous war against Prussia. Hugo pilloried the new emperor in two works of literary and political fury, a book-length pamphlet, *Napoléon-le-Petit* (1852), and a volume of savage political verses, *Les Châtiments* (1853) – 'punishments'. These were international best-sellers and circulated illegally in France.

Hugo spent eighteen of his most superhumanly productive years in exile, and became a world-wide celebrity. Another great poet, Tennyson, later paid a brotherly tribute to

> Victor in Drama, Victor in Romance,
> Cloud-weaver of phantasmal hopes and fears,
> French of the French, and Lord of human tears ...
> As yet unbroken, Stormy voice of France![13]

He invented a new religion (still practised in Vietnam), and experimented with spiritualism, in order to communicate with other great men (Napoleon I indicated his approval of Hugo's opposition to his nephew, and Shakespeare dictated a new play). He also shared many of the Anglophobic prejudices common in France, refused to learn English and visited as little of Britain as possible. About 100 of the most militant exiles – 'hairy, hunchbacked and obtuse', according to Hugo's long-suffering lover Juliette Drouet[14] – gathered round him in Jersey, under the surveillance of the French vice-consul and the Royal Navy. But after one exile published rude remarks about Queen Victoria, several dozen were expelled, really as a sop to the French government, by now Britain's ally in the Crimean War. Hugo simply moved to Guernsey, another of the islands. 'I find exile better and better,' he wrote in November 1855. 'I shall perhaps die in exile, but I shall die greater.'[15]

He wrote vast quantities of poetry and visionary literature, and two novels, one set in the Channel Islands, the other in a fantasy Britain inhabited by characters such as Gwynplaine, Dea and Lord Linnaeus Clancharlie. Meanwhile, his son François-Victor translated the complete works of Shakespeare, to which Hugo contributed a book-length introduction. Hugo, like most of the disillusioned French left, backed away from militaristic nationalism, which had been hijacked by Napoleon III. He turned to pacifism, continued to campaign against the death penalty and dreamed of a united Europe that would inevitably have Paris as its capital – 'Before it has a people, Europe has a city.' Above all, he remained as the 'unbroken voice' of resistance to Napoleon III:

> If we're but a thousand, count me in,
> If only a hundred, there I'll be.
> If ten stand firm, I'll be the tenth
> And if there's only one, it will be me![16]

Work on Les Misérables was delayed by other writings and by tough financial negotiations with publishers. It was resumed on 27 April 1860: 'Today I have taken Les Misérables out of the manuscript box.' It took two weeks to reread the text, and seven months to 'penetrate the work with meditation and light' and create 'absolute unity between what I wrote thirteen years ago and what I am going to write today'.[17] On 30 December the final writing began. Now were added the great digressive sections to give breadth and what Hugo saw as the huge untidy complexity of reality – what he called the 'foliage' – to the basic narrative branches: the fresco of the year 1817, the analyses of Paris, its criminal underworld and its sewers, the Revolutionary 'Friends of the ABC', the battle of Waterloo, and even more episodes not used in the final version. Also, Part Five was written, which included the dramatic climax of the barricade and Marius's rescue by Jean Valjean.[18] The myth-making description of the barricade, drawing on history but otherwise entirely a product of Hugo's imagination, dramatized a new form of urban fighting, for barricades had only become familiar in Paris in the late 1820s. In Les Misérables, the barricade of 1832, described both as a symbolic object and as the group of people defending it, provides the link between the battle of Waterloo and the future revolution of 1848, whose barricades are evoked in the novel as having drawn on lessons learned in 1832.[19]

The book was almost finished when Hugo left Guernsey in March 1861 to do his final piece of research at Waterloo: 'I shall say no more than a word on the subject in my book, but I want that word to be accurate.'[20] The subject was the battle itself, and he wanted to go and experience the very place where, as he saw it, the march of Progress had temporarily gone astray before resuming in a new direction. He stumbled on the bullet-scarred farm of Hougoumont, resonant of his own name:

> Hougomont was a fateful place, the initial obstruction, the first resistance encountered at Waterloo by that great tree-feller of Europe whose name was Napoleon: the first knot under the fall of his axe . . .
> The tumult of battle is still in this courtyard; the horror is visible; the confusion of the fighting is frozen here; it lives on, the dying continues; it was yesterday. (p. 278)

This was not his first literary excursion to what, in a famous poem in *Les Châtiments*, 'The Expiation', he had called the 'morne plaine', the 'dismal plain', of Waterloo. That had been part of his bitter attack on Bonapartism, presenting Napoleon's defeat as punishment for his seizure of power in 1799, with, as his final humiliation, the vulgar exploitation of his heroic legend by his crooked nephew and his cronies. Now, in *Les Misérables*, his 'word' on the subject of Waterloo ran to more than fifty pages. It was this section that had the greatest immediate impact on the public, and created a legendary version of the battle that dominated the French popular memory thereafter.[21] In the novel, it also acts as a vital link in the story of Marius and Cosette. Hugo knew that a bravura battle scene would boost the prospects of publishing success. In June, the month of the battle, he wrote the final words at Waterloo itself, and then celebrated in his accustomed manner with a maidservant at the inn, named Hélène, who made him think of a Rubens: '*Helena nuda* . . . Anniversary of Waterloo. Battle won.'[22]

He had 'won' Waterloo in two ways. First, he portrayed it as a moral victory for the French: defeat had been nothing but the consequence of circumstances, from rain that delayed victory over Wellington and allowed the arrival of the Prussians, to the existence of a hidden sunken lane that destroyed a French cavalry charge. For Hugo, such circumstances were providential: God had ended the reign of the individual genius.[23] The 'undistinguished' British victory was ridiculed by General Cambronne's immortal (and perhaps apocryphal) shout of 'Merde!' 'The man who won the battle of Waterloo was Cambronne,' insists Hugo. 'To hurl such a verbal thunderbolt at the bombshells that are killing you is to be victorious!' Second, Hugo 'won' Waterloo by detaching it from the Bonapartist legend, and attaching it to the Revolution and the Republic, whose soldiers, he insisted, had fought and died heroically there. Cambronne hurls his 'word of titanic disdain ... not only at Europe in the name of the Empire – that would be of little consequence – he hurls it at the past in the name of the Revolution' (p. 313). This was important for Hugo, because of his fundamental belief in the onward march of Progress, and also because he thought it was vital for the Republican party to show its patriotism, and not allow Napoleon III a monopoly of nationalism. Some Republican writers had tried to debunk Waterloo: 'What a mistake for a party to denationalize itself!' he wrote. 'That is a mistake I shall never make.'[24] The glorious defeat of Waterloo begins, for Hugo, a new historical era, in which Republican revolution, of which the barricade of 1832 is a prophetic sign, will one day triumph.

The circumstances in which he began *Les Misérables* in Paris were in most ways very different from those in which he finished it sixteen years later at Waterloo, but in one way similar: he began and ended with sexual adventure, a constant part of his life. In July 1845 he had been caught *in flagrante delicto* with Léonie Biard by a commissaire of police sent by her husband. Hugo became the butt of indignant or derisive comment, and Léonie was imprisoned for adultery. Her enforced absence gave him both time to write and a theme: society's cruelty to vulnerable women, in the character of Fantine.[25]

Most of the story had been written before it acquired, in about 1853, its final strange and significant title: *Les Misérables*. Hugo considered this untranslatable, and it was kept for the first and subsequent English editions. The closest English rendering is 'the wretches' or 'the wretched', conveying both pity and condemnation: 'there is a point where the poor and the wicked become mixed up and lumped together in the one fateful word: the wretched. Whose fault is this?' (p. 671).

This duality was a central theme of the book, and a crucial issue in political and social debate of the 1840s. Those on the left – of whom Hugo was broadly speaking one – saw future progress as linked with the emancipation of the People. Liberty, Equality and Fraternity had been the watchwords of their version of French history since 1789, the year of the fall of the Bastille and the Declaration of the Rights of Man and the Citizen. But the Revolution had spun out of control into civil war, violence and persecution, and France was still living in the shadow of that other Revolution, that of the Terror of the 1790s – 'the savage beast', in Louis-Philippe's words, that liked to 'dip its muzzle in blood'.[26] Even convinced Republicans, such as the great historian Jules Michelet, were well aware of the burden: 'Human blood has a terrible power against those who have spilt it . . . The terrorists have done us immense and lasting harm. Were you to go to the last cottage in the furthest country of Europe, you would meet that memory and that curse.'[27]

So there was no more urgent question than revolution. When was it legitimate to use violence in an 'insurrection' that was not merely a destructive 'riot'? How could revolution be made to serve Civilization rather than Barbarism? When would 'the people' be its noble, patriotic self, rather than a debased and destructive 'mob' which is 'traitor to the people'? (p. 945). And how could one tell which was which? We have seen how Hugo was confronted painfully with this dilemma in June 1848, when he had sided with 'Civilization' against the mob. The problem, and the words used to analyse it, are discussed obsessively by Hugo in Les Misérables, as they were by contemporaries. One 1840s sociologist defined 'the labouring classes' and the 'dangerous classes' as different entities. Phrenologists saw criminal tendencies as biological. A leading politician, Adolphe Thiers, made a notorious distinction in 1851 between 'the People' and 'the vile multitude' that has 'delivered over to every tyrant the liberty of every Republic'.[28] For Hugo, with his genuine compassion for the downtrodden, sweeping dismissals of the masses were unacceptable. Yet, in his mind, there seemed to be no clear divide between 'people' and 'mob' but a mere linguistic distinction: 'Clear-sighted today, the instinct of the masses may be blurred tomorrow' (p. 945). All that distinguished 'insurrection' from 'riot' was the outcome – insurrection was 'forward-moving' (p. 946). This was hardly a clear road-map to the enlightened future.

Hugo's solution relates not to sociology or ideology but to morality. When inspired and educated to do good, they were 'the people'; when debased and corrupted, they were 'the mob'. This is one of the fundamental themes of Les Misérables, which he described as 'a sort of social epic'. Hugo struggled for years with the problem of popular vice and virtue. He was criticized in a left-wing newspaper in 1841 for using the term populace, derogatory in French, in his acceptance speech to the Académie, and he had responded with some embarrassment by insisting that 'there is a gilded populace as well as a ragged populace', the former marked by 'selfishness and idleness', the latter by 'envy and fecklessness' – a comment he would paraphrase in Les Misérables. In a debate in the National Assembly in July 1849, in the aftermath of the terrible June 1848 revolt, he struggled again with the meaning of misère and misérable: 'La misère is not suffering; it is not merely poverty;

it is a nameless thing that I have tried to define . . . Suffering cannot disappear, but *la misère* must disappear. There will always be unfortunates, but it is possible that there will be no more *misérables*.'[29] The problem for Hugo, and for many of his contemporaries, was in diagnosing and treating what seemed a new, and above all an urban, malady: poverty, instability, and social breakdown, creating an uncertain and constantly changing frontier between poverty and crime, in which the real *misérables* were those who became predatory and dangerous to society. Hugo personifies the distinction in the contrast between Jean Valjean, the redeemed convict, and the elder Thénardiers, irredeemable because cruel and vicious by choice.

In the background is the looming nightmare of the *bagne*, presented as the epitome of the brutality both of the *misérable* and of the state, an institution whose cruelty aggravates the viciousness it punishes. It was the descendant of the Old Regime's galley slavery – the slaves remained, without the galleys – in which the worst criminals who escaped a death sentence, identified by their red tunics, were sentenced to forced labour in the main naval ports under military discipline. The *bagne* was an old-fashioned punishment, with no ambition to make prisoners repent, as nineteenth-century reformers hoped to do by exhortation and solitary confinement: 'at Toulon we worked hard, that's true', recalled one old lag, 'but we drank a lot, and we could talk and laugh to our heart's content.'[30] Jean Valjean spends nineteen years in the *bagne* at Toulon for stealing a loaf – the proverbial crime of the poor – and then for trying to escape. He is turned from a victim to a brute by his treatment, and by his stigmatization as released *galérien*, forced to carry a yellow passport, and shunned by the law-abiding. Society, in the person of the policeman Javert, tries obsessively to thrust him back into that horror. When he and the innocent Cosette are walking in Paris, they see a chain gang of condemned men being dragged off to the *bagne*, 'the seven circles of hell in procession', of which Hugo gives a long description mingling pity and disgust at men whose lack of remorse is treated only by indiscriminate beating. 'Father, are they men?' asks Cosette. 'Sometimes,' answers Valjean, knowing that his own humanity had been saved only by a chance encounter with the saintly bishop of Digne, who treated him as a brother, but knowing, too, that the taint of the *bagne* is indelible, that he was 'dragging the invisible but heavy chain of perpetual infamy' (p. 803).

The contrast between Hugo's visceral opposition to the June 1848 revolt and his romanticization of the 1832 revolt in *Les Misérables* seems flagrant. It is usually explained by his move to the left following the Bonapartist overthrow of the Republic in 1851 – he had, after all, supported the regime against which the 1832 revolt had been aimed. Yet there are clear consistencies in his view throughout. The core idea is of *misérables* who can either be inspired to heroism (as in February 1848) or fall into depravity (as in June 1848): 'This multitude can be made sublime . . . These bare feet, bare arms, rags, this benightedness, degradation, darkness may be used for the conquest of the ideal' (p. 535). Moreover, as we have seen, he justifies revolt by its outcome – whether it was 'forward-moving'. Identical actions, whether by rebels or by governments, are therefore good or bad according to their progressive potential: 'The same cannon aimed at the crowd, on the tenth of August is in the wrong, and on the fourteenth of Vendémiaire in the right' (p. 945).[31] But ultimately, even failed and illegitimate conflict can advance the march of History and cast that bronze statue of the Future. And, of course, Hugo's barricade heroes are middle-class idealists, not a hungry mob – though, in fact, those who fought on the barricades in 1832 were overwhelmingly young workers.[32]

Les Misérables was not, of course, merely a fictionalized political treatise, even though critics as distinguished as Gustave Flaubert criticized Hugo's characters as artificial mouthpieces for his ideas, and his dialogue as stagey. But a treatise could never have had the lasting popular success of *Les Misérables*. Hugo put into the story a passion that came from his deep personal involvement in the eventful history of the time – 'I am a son of this century.'[33] Intimate autobiographical elements run through the story at many levels. Some are obvious. Marius Pontmercy's life – son of a Bonapartist officer, brought up by a Legitimist family, converted to Bonapartism and Republicanism – parallels that of the son of General Hugo. The brave young revolutionaries of the 'Friends of the ABC' provide Hugo with the wonderful opportunity of 'describing himself seven times over'.[34] He puts into Jean Valjean, a different alter ego, his humanitarian impulses, and perhaps a vague desire for escape into obscurity and self-sacrifice. There are many hidden personal clues too: names, places, dates – such as 16 February 1833 – 'Marius and Cosette's wedding night' (p. 1219) – which was the date of Hugo's first night with the actress Juliette Drouet, when 'I awoke to love', and which began a liaison that lasted for fifty years. On 7 September 1832, Jean Valjean is asked to give away his beloved adopted daughter Cosette in marriage; on 7 September 1843 Hugo had learned that his daughter Léopoldine had been drowned. At one level, the novel is a vast attempt by Hugo to make sense of his own life and its passing, in a Paris that was disappearing during his exile, as he often emphasizes. The final words, at Valjean's anonymous grave, with its fading inscription, poignantly sum up this transience. The mingling of individual stories and great historical events, with Hugo's massive ego at the centre, gives the book its power.

From the time of its publication, if not even before, it was a huge best-seller, building on Hugo's literary and political fame: 150,000 volumes were sold in France alone in a year. Its impact had been prepared by an international advertising campaign, which he, a keen man of business, had fed with press releases, announcing 'the social and historical drama of the nineteenth century', and spurred on by tricks of the trade, such as dividing the initial print-run into several 'editions', to suggest runaway sales. Within a few months there were also dozens of pirated editions. His biggest market was, of course, in France, whose government would take a dim view of one of its most prominent enemies praising revolt on the barricades. Yet the barricade was, for Hugo, 'the heart of the subject', and he expected it would be a large part of the book's attraction. So, to prevent 'the present abominable regime' from banning the book, he told his Belgian publisher to 'emphasize Waterloo': 'Bring out the national aspect of the book, pluck at French heart-strings . . . make it impossible for them to seize it by saying that it's *the battle of Waterloo now won by France, etc.*'[35] In Britain, where patriotic sentiment was less obviously a motive, Hugo's defiance of Napoleon III, who was regarded as a potential enemy as well as a domestic oppressor, must have provided a substitute. The London *Evening Star* reported within days of publication of the first part (*Fantine*) that '*The Miserables* of Victor Hugo [is] in the hands of all those who are able to purchase it and little circulating libraries have taken as many as fifty copies each.'[36]

Yet the political, historical and patriotic messages of *Les Misérables* are only a small part of its attraction. The 'Lord of human tears' was at least the equal of his contemporary Dickens as an impresario of emotion. Cosette's sufferings at the hands of the Thénardiers – nastier than Fagin – are at least as harrowing as Oliver Twist's ordeal in the workhouse. Fantine's fate is as horrible as that of Nancy. Javert is as grimly representative of a heartless society as Quilp or Bumble. Jean Valjean is as movingly selfless as Mr Peggoty and his death is as pathetic as that of Little Nell. Gavroche is as indomitable as the Artful Dodger, and much funnier. Hugo had a similar emotional impact on generations of readers as Dickens, and Cosette became as familiar to generations of French children as a character in a fairy tale.

Like that of Dickens, Hugo's solution to wickedness and cruelty is humanitarian, not administrative – they shared a suspicion of reformers. Both believed in inevitable Progress, but, in the meantime, their remedy for social evils is simple goodness. Both have drawn the fire of critics impatient with what they see as self-indulgent sentimentality. One contemporary joked that Dickens put his trust in 'the immense spiritual power of the Christmas turkey'.[37] Hugo's trust is in the redeeming power of love, both charitable and erotic. Jean Valjean is redeemed by an act of Christian charity, in turn rescues Cosette by human kindness, and saves Marius for love of Cosette. The *misérable*, once corrupted by the inhumanity of the *bagne*, is no longer a brute, but a saint: 'No doubt, in the shadows, some immense angel stood with wings outspread, awaiting his soul' (p. 1304). Marius and Cosette, too, are saved by their love for each other: 'If at this point in her life Cosette had fallen in love with a dissolute and not very scrupulous man it would have been her ruin . . . There is no half way with love. It means either ruin or salvation . . . Of all things God has made, the human heart is the one that sheds the most light and alas! the most darkness. God willed that the love Cosette encountered was a love that saves' (p. 903). Even poor Éponine Thénardier is partly redeemed by her infatuation for Marius, which costs her her life. Much of the message of *Les Misérables* is therefore broadly Christian – that of the non-sectarian Romantic religiosity of the first half of the nineteenth century, which after 1848 came to seem increasingly old-fashioned, indeed pernicious, among the avant-garde, though clearly not among the reading public. The book was banned by the Vatican and burned in Spain, which Hugo believed was because there was 'a bishop who is kind, sincere, humble, fraternal, who has wit as well as gentleness . . . that is why *Les Misérables* is an infamous book'.[38] Jean Valjean, by experiencing love and discovering his conscience, points the way for Everyman.

Given Hugo's sexual proclivities, his idealization of the asexual love of a serious young man and a naive young woman – 'that ineffable first embrace between two virginities in the realm of the ideal. Two swans meeting on the Jungfrau' (p. 904) – is not the least oddity of the novel. In reading his rhapsodies to purity, his declarations of respect for the modesty of young girls, his awe at the conjugal bedroom ('The soul goes into spiritual contemplation before this sanctuary where the celebration of love occurs'), it would take a heart of stone not to laugh, as Oscar Wilde might have said. 'The down on the peach, the bloom on the plum, the prismatic snow crystal, the powdery butterfly-wing, are coarse things beside that chastity that does not even know it is chaste' (p. 1081). But real hypocrisy has a clear conscience, and there is no reason to doubt the authenticity of Hugo's emotions.

More serious is the dangerous vacuity of his political Romanticism.

He was aware, as we have seen, of the horrors of civil war, and of the dangers of popular violence. Yet all this is wiped away by insisting on the long-term beneficence of Revolution, Progress and Providence: 'Revolutions have a strong arm and a good hand, they strike hard and have the luck of the draw. Even incomplete, even bastardized and mongrelized and reduced to the state of minor revolution like the 1830 Revolution, they are nearly always left with enough providential far-sightedness to make it impossible they should ever come amiss.' All revolutionaries, and all revolutions, are unconsciously working together towards making 'a paradise . . . of this world', and aiming 'through fear and trembling if need be, to force the human race towards paradise' (p. 767). Then Hugo allows himself an easy let-out: 'Neither despotism nor terrorism. We want the gentle incline towards progress. God sees to that' (p. 768).

In 1870, Napoleon III became a prisoner of the Prussians after the disastrous battle of Sedan, and his regime collapsed. Hugo returned in triumph to France, his long and stubborn dissidence vindicated at a stroke by the military defeat of another Napoleon, and by another Republican revolution in Paris. The capital was soon besieged by the German armies, and Hugo, dressed in a military shako, became a hero to some and an irritation to others with his grandiose proclamations of Republican patriotism, his long-winded addresses to the German People, urging them to go away, his unrealistic calls to win a war that was irretrievably lost, and his predictions of Europe-wide revolution. One of his many female votaries was a militant schoolmistress and poet, Louise Michel, inspired by *Les Misérables* to call herself 'Enjolras': he doubtless admired the implacable dedication of a woman who would later fight for the Paris Commune, survive a penal colony and be named 'the Red Virgin'; and she consented to take her clothes off for the master.[39] Thus he whiled away the tedium of being under siege. In January 1871, Paris finally surrendered when its food stocks (eked out by horsemeat, animals from the zoo and even rats) finally reached the verge of famine. In February, Hugo was elected by the Parisians, alongside other Republican heroes, to a new National Assembly, with over 200,000 votes. But he walked out in March as a patriotic protest against acceptance of defeat.

Albert Camus, who saw as much conflict as Hugo, said: 'I abhor comfortable violence. I abhor those whose words go further than their deeds.'[40] Hugo's crowd-pleasing heroics in 1870, and his glorification in the 1860s of a futile insurrection he had condemned in 1832, fit this bill. His was feeding a Romantic patriotic culture of revolt, what has been called the 'revolutionary passion play', with its familiar rituals of barricade-building and grandiose oratory. No other work of literature gives such an important place to the barricade as *Les Misérables*, gives it such a leading role, or more completely replaces reality with myth.[41] It all came to a disastrous end in May 1871, 'like some appalling level-crossing accident that occurs at the end of a school outing to the seaside'.[42] The revolutionary Paris Commune was crushed in a week of barricade fighting, destruction, arson and slaughter. This was the culmination of what Hugo aptly called *l'année terrible*. He kept out of the fight, like all the leading Republican figures, and remained a powerless onlooker from the safety of Brussels. It was a struggle between two parties he could neither identify with or even understand: a radical workers' insurrection and a conservative National Assembly determined to stamp it out: 'this Commune is as stupid as the Assembly is vicious.'[43] His response was a series of poems, stuffed with erudite allusions, lamenting the violence and barbarism committed by both sides 'in this hurricane that passes / Mixing up everything, good, evil, heroes, bandits'. One of the most famous of these poems recalls the bravado of Gavroche: a boy of twelve about to be summarily executed with a group of rebels, who asks the soldiers to let him go and give his watch to his mother; but, to their astonishment, he returns voluntarily to face the firing squad: 'Stupid death was ashamed and the officer spared him.'[44] Hugo's courageous sympathy for Communard refugees caused trouble: a Brussels mob attacked his house shouting (he noted) 'Death to Victor Hugo! Death to Jean Valjean!' He shouted back 'Vous êtes des misérables!'[45]

Arguably, the catastrophe of 1871 removed the romance of the barricades from politics and confined it to fantasy: 'the last great uprising . . . the one which created the most fear and shed the most blood . . . formed the ultimate exorcism of a violence which had been an inseparable part of French public life since the eighteenth century . . . In this Paris in flames, the French Revolution bade farewell to history.' The reign of the orators ended.[46] Yet the myth of insurrection, the intoxication of courageous revolt against the odds, aiming to sweep away injustice in a day, still retains its magnetism, whether as escapism (as in the musical version of 'Les Mis') or even in reality, as in the 'Arab Spring', so reminiscent of the 'Springtime of the Peoples' of 1848.

Hugo was now one of the father figures of the Republican party, which finally won power peacefully during the course of the 1870s as 'the government that divides us least'. He became a senator in 1876. His defence of liberty, and perhaps above all his defiance of Napoleon III, ensured his place, literally, in the Republican Panthéon, where his body now lies. He died on 22 May 1885. His state funeral, attended by huge crowds of Parisians, was one of the great public ceremonies of the later nineteenth century, and itself a source of myth – such as a supposed explosion of what a Catholic newspaper called 'abominable outrages' behind the bushes in the Avenue Victor Hugo.[47] Hugo had insisted on being carried on a pauper's hearse – a quintessential Hugolian gesture that summed up his life: for his admirers, it identified him eternally with *les misérables*; for his critics, it was a final piece of sanctimonious gesture politics.

His real memorial, almost as controversial, is his mighty literary oeuvre, a third of it published posthumously. Some found his death a kind of release. The poet Stéphane Mallarmé thought it meant that French poetry could now evolve: and he wrote a great, if ambivalent, tribute to Hugo's importance: 'Hugo, in his mysterious task, boiled all of prose, philosophy, eloquence, history down to verse, and, since he *was* verse, personally, he confiscated from anyone who thinks, discourses, or narrates almost the right to speak.'[48] *Les Misérables* epitomizes this boiling down of philosophy, history and politics into poetry. It stands as a massive monolith, the greatest as well as the biggest of French Romantic novels, containing one of the longest sentences and some of the longest digressions in French fiction, as if, notes Graham Robb, Hugo (who was worried by illness and premonitions of death) felt that this was 'his last chance to say everything'.[49] It is greatly exceeded in size among classic works only by Proust's *À la Recherche du temps perdu*, almost its opposite as social observation. As a fresco of post-Revolutionary France, *Les Misérables* far outdistances earlier models, such as Eugène Sue's *Les Mystères de Paris* (1842–3), in literary power, intellectual sophistication and subtlety of observation. It provides an intimate view of how people saw and experienced their society not only by what Hugo deliberately described, but also for what he could not help but describe unconsciously, and even by what he failed to understand.[50] Yet it is not its value as a historical document that makes *Les Misérables* still compelling enough to be the core of one the most popular modern musicals, attracting thousands who are uninterested in the ideas and politics of the nineteenth century. For millions of readers in many languages over 150 years, and now for thousands of film- and theatre-goers, the attraction of *Les Misérables* lies in the emotional power of its story of love, redemption and sacrifice.

Robert Tombs, 2013

NOTES

All translations, except those taken from the main text
or otherwise referenced, are the introducer's own.

1. Letter, 1862, in Hubert de Phalèse, *Dictionnaire des Misérables* (Paris: Nizet, 1994), p. 88
2. Victor Hugo, *Oeuvres Complètes: théâtre: vol. 1* (Paris: Albin Michel, 1922), pp. 19, 20, 25, 32, 50
3. Graham Robb, *Victor Hugo* (London: Picador, 1997), pp. 144–5
4. Hugo, *Oeuvres Complètes: théâtre: vol. 1*, pp. 714, 719, 726, 15, 20
5. See Munro Price, *The Perilous Crown: France between Revolutions, 1814–1848* (London: Macmillan, 2007)
6. Jeanne Gilmore, *La République clandestine, 1818–1848* (Paris: Aubier, 1997), pp. 168–70
7. Thomas Bouchet, *Le Roi et les barricades: une histoire des 5 et 6 juin 1832* (Paris: Seli Arslan, 2000), pp. 34, 68–9
8. Victor Hugo, *Choses vues: souvenirs, journaux, cahiers, 1830–1846*, ed. H. Juin (Paris: Gallimard, 1972), pp. 133–4
9. René Journet, Introduction to *Les Misérables* (Paris: Garnier-Flammarion, 1967), vol. I, pp. 16–17; Jean-Bertrand Barrère, ed., *Un Carnet des Misérables, octobre–décembre 1860* (Paris: Minard, 1965), p. 20
10. Victor Hugo, *Choses vues: souvenirs, journaux, cahiers, 1847–1848*, ed. H. Juin (Paris: Gallimard, 1972), pp. 332–3, 336, 344, 346, 347
11. Robb, *Victor Hugo*, pp. 269–76
12. 'Applaudissement', *Les Châtiments* (1853)
13. Alfred Tennyson, 'To Victor Hugo', *Ballads and Other Poems* (London: C. Kegan Paul & Co., 1880), p. 165 (a sonnet first published in 1877 in a slightly different version)
14. Robb, *Victor Hugo*, p. 330
15. Jean-Bertrand Barrère, *Victor Hugo à l'oeuvre: le poète en exil et en voyage* (Paris: Klincksieck, 1965), p. 23
16. 'Ultima verba', *Les Châtiments*
17. Barrère, *Un Carnet*, pp. 5–6
18. Journet, Introduction, p. 17; and see Bernard Leuilliot, *Victor Hugo publie Les Misérables* (Paris: Klincksieck, 1970)
19. Thomas Bouchet, 'La Barricade des *Misérables*', in Alain Corbin and Jean-Marie Mayeur, eds., *La Barricade* (Paris: Publications de la Sorbonne, 1997), pp. 125–35
20. Robb, *Victor Hugo*, p. 374
21. Jean-Marc Largeaud, *Napoléon et Waterloo: la défaite glorieuse de 1815 à nos jours* (Paris: Boutique de l'Histoire, 2006), pp. 308–9
22. Robb, *Victor Hugo*, p. 375
23. Barrère, *Un Carnet*, p. 9
24. Largeaud, *Napoléon et Waterloo*, p. 306
25. Ibid., pp. 253–4
26. Guy Antonetti, *Louis-Philippe* (Paris: Fayard, 1994), p. 897
27. François Furet, *Revolutionary France, 1770–1880* (Oxford: Blackwell, 1992), p 374

28. J. P. T. Bury and R. P. Tombs, *Thiers 1797–1877: A Political Life* (London: Allen & Unwin, 1986), p. 126
29. Louis Chevalier, *Classes laborieuses et classes dangereuses à Paris pendant la première moitié du XIXe siècle* (Paris: Plon, 1958), pp. 92, 94, 96–7
30. Michelle Perrot, *Les Ombres de l'histoire: Crime et châtiment au XIXe siècle* (Paris: Flammarion, 2001), p. 166
31. The reference is to the 10 August 1792 overthrow of the monarchy, and the failed Vendémiaire (October 1795) royalist uprising against the Republic.
32. Bouchet, *Le Roi et les barricades*, pp. 69–72
33. 'Amis, un dernier mot!', *Les Feuilles d' automne*
34. Robb, *Victor Hugo*, p. 69
35. Leuilliot, *Victor Hugo publie*, pp. 302–3
36. Robb, *Victor Hugo*, p. 378
37. [Margaret Oliphant], 'Charles Dickens', *Blackwood's Edinburgh Magazine*, June 1871, p. 677
38. Phalèse, *Dictionnaire*, p. 91
39. Victor Hugo, *Choses vues: souvenirs, journaux, cahiers, 1870–1885*, ed. H. Juin (Paris: Gallimard, 1972), pp. 87, 88, 466
40. Albert Camus, 'Première réponse à Emmanuel d'Astier de la Vigerie', quoted in Renee Winegarten, 'Victor Hugo: On the Legacy of Myth', *Encounter* (Sept.–Oct. 1987), p. 35
41. Bouchet, 'La Barricade des *Misérables*', p. 125
42. Richard Cobb, *Tour de France* (London: Duckworth, 1976), p. 129
43. *Choses vues: 1870–1885*, p. 164
44. 'Juin, XI: Sur une barricade au milieu des pavés', *L'Année terrible* (written 27 June 1871)
45. *Choses vues: 1870–1885*, p. 176
46. Furet, *Revolutionary France*, p. 506; Martin P. Johnson, *The Paradise of Association: Political Culture and Popular Organizations in the Paris Commune of 1871* (Ann Arbor: University of Michigan Press, 1996), p. 287
47. Robb, *Victor Hugo*, p. 528
48. Denis Hollier, ed., *A New History of French Literature* (Cambridge, Mass.: Harvard University Press, 1989), p. 798
49. Robb, *Victor Hugo*, p. 374
50. Chevalier, *Classes laborieuses et classes dangereuses*, pp. 88–91

Further Reading

The starting-point is Graham Robb's vivid biography, *Victor Hugo* (London: Picador, 1997). The detailed political setting of *Les Misérables* is provided by Munro Price, *The Perilous Crown: France between Revolutions, 1814–1848* (London: Macmillan, 2007), and the broader context by Robert Tombs, *France 1814–1914* (London: Longman, 1996), and Peter McPhee, *A Social History of France, 1789–1914* (London: Palgrave Macmillan, 2004).

The social world from which Jean Valjean and his fellow wretches emerged is presented magisterially by Olwen H. Hufton, *The Poor of Eighteenth-Century France, 1750–1789* (Oxford: Clarendon, 1974), and colourfully by Richard Cobb, *The Police and the People: French Popular Protest, 1789–1820* (Oxford: Oxford University Press, 1970); see also André Gueslin, *Gens pauvres, Pauvres gens dans la France du XIXe siècle* (Paris: Aubier, 1998).

Paris, the main focus of *Les Misérables*, is put under the microscope by Philip Mansel, *Paris Between Empires, 1814–1852* (London: John Murray, 2001). A broader portrayal of the city's whole history is Colin Jones's *Paris: Biography of a City* (London: Allen Lane, 2004). Patrice Higonnet takes us briskly through the city's mythology in *Paris: Capital of the World* (Cambridge, Mass.: Harvard University Press, 2002); for the city's literary images, see Christopher Prendergast, *Paris and the Nineteenth Century: Writing the City* (Oxford: Wiley-Blackwell, 1995). *Paris au temps des Misérables de Victor Hugo* (Paris: Paris-Musées, 2008) provides paintings, photographs, and maps showing the places where the action happens.

Contemporary ideas about the social underworld of Paris are analysed in a classic work by Louis Chevalier, *Classes laborieuses et classes dangereuses à Paris pendant la première moitié du XIXe siècle* (Paris: Plon, 1958), which discusses *Les Misérables* specifically, and is available in an English edition. The criminal world and attempts to control and punish it are discussed by Clive Emsley, *Policing and its Context, 1750–1870* (London: Macmillan, 1983), a comparison of

France and Britain. A study of crime and punishment by one of France's leading social historians is Michelle Perrot, *Les Ombres de l'histoire: Crime et châtiment au XIXe siècle* (Paris: Flammarion, 2001).

Hugo's literary and cultural milieu is surveyed by F. W. J. Hemmings, *Culture and Society in France, 1789–1848* (Leicester: Leicester University Press, 1987), and by James Smith Allen, *Popular French Romanticism: Authors, Readers, and Books in the 19th Century* (New York: Syracuse University Press, 1981). A detailed study is D. G. Charlton, ed., *The French Romantics* (2 vols, Cambridge: Cambridge University Press, 1984). The longer perspective is analysed chronologically and thematically in Denis Hollier, ed., *A New History of French Literature* (Cambridge, Mass.: Harvard University Press, 1989).

The political underworld of 'the Friends of the ABC' is put in context by Pamela Pilbeam, in *The 1830 Revolution in France* (London: Macmillan, 1991) and *Republicanism in Nineteenth Century France, 1814–1871* (London: Macmillan, 1995). The crucial nationalist theme is fully analysed in Philippe Darriulat, *Les Patriotes: la gauche républicaine et la nation, 1830–1870* (Paris: Le Seuil, 2001), essential to understanding the mind-set of people like Marius and Enjolras.

A lively account of insurrection is Jill Harsin, *Barricades: The War of the Streets in Revolutionary Paris, 1830–1848* (Houndmills: Palgrave, 2002), and a major analytical study is Alain Corbin and Jean-Marie Mayeur, eds., *La Barricade* (Paris: Publications de la Sorbonne, 1997). The dramatic events of June 1832 are fully analysed in Thomas Bouchet, *Le Roi et les barricades: une histoire des 5 et 6 juin 1832* (Paris: Seli Arslan, 2000), which includes a chapter on *Les Misérables*. A factor in the 1832 insurrection, omitted by Hugo, was the preceding cholera epidemic, discussed by Catherine J. Kudlick, *Cholera in Post-Revolutionary Paris: A Cultural History* (Berkeley: University of California Press, 1996). The best view from the other side of the barricades is still Louis Girard, *La Garde nationale, 1814–1871* (Paris: Plon, 1964).

The 1848 Revolution, the Second Republic and the June Days, in which Hugo was involved, are explained from the grass-roots perspective by Mark Traugott, *Armies of the Poor: Determinants of Working-Class Participation in the Parisian Insurrection of June 1848* (Princeton: Princeton University Press, 1985); and for its vast, Europe-wide context, see Dieter Dowe et al., eds., *Europe in 1848: Revolution and Reform* (New York and Oxford: Berghahn, 2001). On the last of the revolutions in which Hugo was involved, see Robert Tombs, *The Paris Commune 1871* (London: Longman, 1999).

The cultural importance of Waterloo is laid out by Jean-Marc Largeaud, *Napoléon et Waterloo: la défaite glorieuse de 1815 à nos jours* (Paris: Boutique de l'Histoire, 2006). The important Bonapartist thread in *Les Misérables* is put in context by Sudhir Hazareesingh, *The Legend of Napoleon* (London: Granta, 2004), and by Natalie Petiteau, *Napoléon: de la mythologie à l'histoire* (Paris: Le Seuil, 1999). The *coup d'état* of 1851 and the ensuing Second Empire, which changed Hugo's life and his novel, are clearly summarized by James F. McMillan, *Napoleon III* (London: Longman, 1991), and Alain Plessis, *The Rise and Fall of the Second Empire, 1852–1871* (Cambridge: Cambridge University Press, 1985). On the popularity of Napoleon III, which so disgusted Hugo, see Bernard Ménager, *Les Napoléon du peuple* (Paris: Aubier, 1988).

Hugo's grandiose funeral is fully analysed by Avner Ben-Amos in Pierre Nora, ed., *Les Lieux de mémoire*, vol. I (Paris: Gallimard, 1984), pp. 473–522.

Hugo's own jottings on personal and public events, sometimes fragmentary, sometimes detailed, are published as *Choses vues: souvenirs, journaux, cahiers*, edited by Hubert Juin, in several volumes, by Gallimard.

Note on the Translation

Les Misérables is one of the great crusading novels for social reform, inspired by a deep sense of social injustice, a missionary zeal to expose that injustice, and a huge energy to advocate the benefits of righting wrong and of cultivating the fulfilment of human potential. It is addressed to all and speaks in a language intended to be understood by all. It combines rhetorical grandeur and poetic lyricism, such as might be found in parts of the Bible, with the heart-stopping suspense narrative of the action-packed mass-market thriller, and even the farcical humour of the sitcom.

First published in 1862, and rooted in one of the most turbulent periods of French history, when the country occupied a central position on the world stage, it remains contemporary and universal in its message. This translation attempts to convey both that historical particularity and that contemporary relevance, that 'Frenchness' and that universality, while striving to avoid both unconvincing pastiche and modern intrusions.

Central to the themes of *Les Misérables* is the dignity of the individual. Embedded in the French language and in the French idiom, to a far greater extent than in English, is a recognition of that dignity in the way that the individual is addressed. For this reason I have retained formal titles in French: monsieur l'abbé, monsieur le président etc., and I have footnoted key moments in the text when the formal 'vous' or the informal 'tu' form of the verb are used to dramatic effect.

I have also footnoted other points of linguistic significance – puns, quotations and literary references – while glosses on the historical background and other references are to be found in the endnotes.

Hugo himself footnoted his own text, largely in the section devoted to 'slang', and in some instances quite extensively, presenting the slang used by the criminal fraternity as a grotesquely arcane language foreign to the ordinary French citizen. Having considered how early-nineteenth-century Parisian slang might be translated to achieve the same effect without introducing unwanted echoes of a different culture and without seeming unnecessarily contrived, I decided, in the end, that the most authentic solution was also to treat it as a foreign language, and to translate only Hugo's footnote 'translation', which is included so that readers – even those without any knowledge of French – can see the gulf between the two.

Where characters speak in slang or in dialect, it is invariably signalled by Hugo; otherwise they speak in standard French, not in a substandard or class-distinctive form of the language. This seems to me central to the educative aspirations of this novel and important to preserve in the translation.

A key word in *Les Misérables* that poses particular problems for the translator is the dread prison sentence, *le bagne.*

The *bagne* was not only a place – the arsenal prison, and in particular, in the case of *Les Misérables*, the one at Toulon – but also a brutal regime of punishment. Prisoners were condemned to hard labour, kept in chains from the beginning to the end of their sentence, and subjected to extremely harsh treatment and appalling living conditions. They were housed, when the arsenal prisons first came into being in 1748, on decommissioned galleys and, later, on other vessels.

Although the need for land-based accommodation at Toulon was addressed by the authorities as early as 1777, prison hulks continued to be used until the arsenal prison was finally closed down in 1873. In 1783, only thirteen years before Jean Valjean would have been sent there, sixty per cent of the prisoners were housed on the hulks. (A fascinating and detailed account of this subject, based on archive documents, is given by the Académie du Var in *Le Bagne de Toulon 1748–1873*, published by Éditions Autres Temps, 2010.)

It is for this reason, and because of the English term's naval associations and the similarly fearsome resonance it has in the popular imagination, that I have chosen to translate *le bagne* as 'the prison hulks'. (See also my note on the account that Jean Valjean gives of himself to the bishop of Digne, under the entry *I'm an ex-convict . . . from Toulon*, p. 1312).

The extent to which Hugo wove reality into his work is remarkable, lending a documentary authority to his fiction, and the endnotes will, I hope, illuminate this aspect of Hugo's writing. In this respect the resources of the internet have proved invaluable, and I am immensely grateful to the countless contributors of information to the web who have enormously facilitated the task of the translator and annotator of such a work as this. I am sure that Hugo would have greatly approved of this democratization of knowledge.

I imagine, too, he would in the same spirit have embraced today's abbreviated modes of communication, if the story of an exchange of telegrams with his English publisher is to be believed. Wishing to know how sales of the translation of *Les Misérables* were going, he is supposed to have sent the message: '?' – to which came the equally pithy reply: '!'

Finally, I am very grateful to Sue Phillpott for the close attention with which she copyedited my translation and for the many useful suggestions that she made, and to Stephen Ryan for his meticulous proofreading.

Christine Donougher, 2013

LES MISÉRABLES

As long as through the workings of laws and customs there exists a damnation-by-society artificially creating hells in the very midst of civilization and complicating destiny, which is divine, with a man-made fate; as long as the three problems of the age are not resolved: the debasement of men through proletarianization, the moral degradation of women through hunger, and the blighting of children by keeping them in darkness; as long as in certain strata social suffocation is possible; in other words and from an even broader perspective, as long as there are ignorance and poverty on earth, books of this kind may serve some purpose.

Victor Hugo, Hauteville House, 1 January 1862

PART ONE

FANTINE

BOOK ONE
A GOOD MAN

I
Monsieur Myriel

In 1815, Charles-François-Bienvenu Myriel was bishop of Digne. He was an old man of about seventy-five. He had been bishop of Digne since 1806.

If only for the sake of being accurate in every particular, although this circumstance in no way impinges on the basic substance of what we are about to relate, it may be worth mentioning here the rumours and gossip circulating about him at the time of his arrival in the diocese. True or false, what is said about men often figures as large in their lives, and above all in the fate that befalls them, as what they do. Monsieur Myriel was the son of a councillor in the parliament at Aix – judicial aristocracy. It was reported that his father, intending that his son should inherit his position, had married him off very young, aged eighteen or twenty, a fairly common practice among parliamentary families. This marriage, it was said, did not prevent Charles Myriel from being much talked about. He was good-looking, though rather short in stature, elegant, charming, witty. His entire early life was devoted to fashionable society and amorous intrigue. The Revolution came. Events moved fast. Decimated, driven out, hunted down, the parliamentary families scattered. During the very first days of the Revolution, Monsieur Charles Myriel emigrated to Italy. There, his wife died of a chest ailment that had long afflicted her. They had no children. What then happened to Monsieur Myriel? The collapse in France of the old world, the downfall of his own family, the tragic spectacles of '93, perhaps even more terrifying for the émigrés watching from afar with magnifying horror – did these give rise in him to thoughts of renunciation and solitude? Was he, in the midst of one of those distractions and attachments that filled his existence, suddenly dealt one of those mysterious and terrible blows that by striking at the heart sometimes fell a man who would be left unshaken by public catastrophes that strike at his way of life and his fortune? No one could have said. All anyone knew was that when he returned from Italy he was a priest.

In 1804 Monsieur Myriel was parish priest of Brignolles. He was already old, and lived a very secluded life.

Around the time of the coronation some parish matter, no one quite knows what any more, took him to Paris. Among other influential individuals that he applied to on behalf of his parishioners was Cardinal Fesch. The worthy priest happened to be waiting in the antechamber one day when the emperor had come to visit his uncle. As Napoleon was on his way out, realizing he was being observed with some curiosity by this elderly gentleman, his majesty turned round and said abruptly, 'What good fellow is this, staring at me?'

'Sire,' said Monsieur Myriel, 'in this fellow you see goodness, in the man before me I see greatness. There's advantage to both of us.'

That same evening the emperor enquired of the cardinal the name of the priest, and some time afterwards Monsieur Myriel was very surprised to learn he had been appointed bishop of Digne.

Anyway, what truth was there in the stories told of Monsieur Myriel's early life? No one could tell. Few families had known the Myriel family before the Revolution.

Monsieur Myriel had to undergo the fate of every newcomer to a small town where there are plenty of tongues given to wagging and very few minds given to reflection. He had to be subjected to it although he was a bishop and because he was a bishop. But the rumours his name was associated with were after all perhaps just that: rumours, idle gossip, talk, empty words, not even words – *palabres*, in the muscular language of the south.

Be that as it may, after Monsieur Myriel had been living in Digne and serving as bishop for nine years, all this tittle-tattle, these topics of conversation that give small towns and small-minded people something to talk about, had been thoroughly forgotten. No one would have dared mention them, no one would even have dared call them to mind.

Monsieur Myriel had arrived in Digne accompanied by a spinster, Mademoiselle Baptistine, who was his sister and ten years his junior.

Their only domestic help was a woman of the same age as Mademoiselle Baptistine called Madame Magloire, who, having been 'monsieur le curé's servant', now acquired the dual status of Mademoiselle's maid and Monseigneur's housekeeper.*

Mademoiselle Baptistine was long, pale, slight and meek. She was the perfect incarnation of the word 'respectable', for apparently a woman must be motherly to be venerable. She had never been pretty.

* As a simple parish priest Monsieur Myriel would have been addressed as *monsieur le curé*; as bishop he is now *Monseigneur*.

Her whole life, which had been simply a succession of good deeds, had ultimately conferred on her a sort of paleness and brightness, and with advancing years she had gained what might be called the beauty of goodness. What had been thinness in her youth became transparency in her maturity, and this diaphanous quality revealed the angel. She was more of an essence than a virgin. Physically, she seemed to be made of shadow with hardly enough of a body to have any sexual identity: a little substance containing a glimmer of light, her big eyes always downcast, an excuse for a soul to remain on earth.

Madame Magloire was a busy, fat, round, little white-haired old woman, always out of breath, firstly because of her busyness and then because of her asthma.

On his arrival, Monsieur Myriel was installed in the episcopal palace with the honours dictated by imperial decree whereby a bishop ranks immediately below a brigadier. The mayor and the president of the local judiciary first called on him, and he in turn made his first call on the general and the police chief.

His installation complete, the town waited to see what the bishop would do.

II

Monsieur Myriel Becomes Monseigneur Bienvenu

The episcopal palace of Digne was next door to the hospital.

The palace was an immense and handsome residence, built of stone at the beginning of the last century by Monseigneur Henri Puget, doctor of theology at the Faculty of Paris and abbot of Simore, who had been bishop of Digne in 1712. A veritable baronial hall, was this palace. Everything about it was grand: the bishop's apartments, the drawing rooms, the bedchambers, the very spacious court of honour with covered walks and arcades in the old Florentine style, the gardens planted with magnificent trees. In the dining room, a long and splendid gallery on the ground floor looking out over the gardens, Monseigneur Henri Puget had on the twenty-ninth of July 1714 held a ceremonial banquet for Monseigneurs Charles Brûlart de Genlis, prince-archbishop of Embrun; Antoine de Mesgrigny of the Capuchin Order, bishop of Grasse; Philippe de Vendôme, grand prior of France, abbot of St-Honoré de Lérins; François de Berton de Crillon, baron-bishop of Vence; César de Sabran de Forcalquier, seigneur-bishop of Glandève; and Jean Soanen, Oratorian priest, chaplain in ordinary to the king, seigneur-bishop of Senez. The portraits of these seven reverend figures adorned this room, and that memorable date, the twenty-ninth of July 1714, was engraved in letters of gold on a white marble table.

The hospital was a single-storey, low, narrow building with a small garden.

Three days after his arrival the bishop visited the hospital. At the end of his visit he left an invitation for the director to call on him.

'Monsieur le directeur de l'hôpital, how many patients have you at present?' he said.

'Twenty-six, Monseigneur.'

'That was the number I counted,' said the bishop.

'The beds are very close to each other,' the director added.

'That's what I observed.'

'The wards are no bigger than small bedrooms, and it's hard to keep them aired.'

'That's what I would think.'

'And then, when there is a ray of sunshine, the garden's very small for those convalescing.'

'That's what I said to myself.'

'In the event of an epidemic – we've had typhus this year, we had miliary fever two years ago, a hundred patients sometimes – we just don't know what to do.'

'That was the thought that occurred to me.'

'There's no point in complaining, Monseigneur,' said the director. 'We must accept things as they are.'

This conversation took place in the gallery dining room on the ground floor. The bishop remained silent for a moment, then suddenly turned to the director of the hospital.

'Monsieur,' he said, 'how many beds do you think would fit into this room alone?'

'Monseigneur's dining room?' exclaimed the director in amazement.

The bishop glanced around the room and appeared to be estimating measurements and making calculations.

'Twenty beds easily!' he said as though talking to himself. Then raising his voice, 'Now, I tell you what, monsieur le directeur de l'hôpital, obviously something's wrong here. You have twenty-six people in five or six small rooms. There are three of us here and we have room for sixty. Something's wrong, I tell you. You're in my house and I'm in yours. You give me back my house. This is where you belong.'

The following day the twenty-six paupers were moved into the bishop's palace and the bishop was installed in the hospital.

Monsieur Myriel was not a man of means, his family having been ruined by the Revolution. His sister had a life annuity of five hundred

8

francs, which was enough to meet her personal expenses at the presbytery. As bishop, Monsieur Myriel received from the state a salary of fifteen thousand francs. On the very day he took up residence in the hospital building, he determined once and for all the way in which this sum was to be used. We transcribe here a note made in his own hand:

Note to regulate my household expenditure:

For the seminary school:	1,500 francs
Congregation of the Mission:	100 francs
For the Lazarists of Montdidier:	100 francs
Seminary of Foreign Missions of Paris:	200 francs
Congregation of the Holy Spirit:	150 francs
Religious foundations in the Holy Land:	100 francs
Societies for Maternal Charity:	300 francs
An extra payment, for that of Arles:	50 francs
In aid of the improvement of prisons:	400 francs
In aid of the comfort and release of prisoners:	500 francs
To obtain the release of family men imprisoned for debt:	1,000 francs
To supplement the salary of diocesan teachers in need:	2,000 francs
Public granary of the Hautes-Alpes:	100 francs
Congregation of the Ladies of Digne, Manosque and Sisteron, for the free education of girls in need:	1,500 francs
For the poor:	6,000 francs
My personal expenses:	1,000 francs
Total:	15,000 francs

Throughout the entire time that he occupied the see of Digne, Monsieur Myriel made no alteration to this arrangement. As we have seen, he referred to it as 'regulating his household expenditure'.

The arrangement was accepted with total acquiescence by Mademoiselle Baptistine. For this saintly spinster, the Monseigneur of Digne was both brother and bishop, naturally dear to her and ecclesiastically her superior. She quite simply loved and venerated him. When he spoke, she deferred. When he acted, she approved. Their only servant, Madame

Magloire, grumbled a little. The bishop had set aside for himself, it may have been noticed, only one thousand francs, which, added to Mademoiselle Baptistine's income, amounted to a total of fifteen hundred francs a year. Both old women and the old man lived on these fifteen hundred francs.

And thanks to Madame Magloire's unfailing thrift and Mademoiselle Baptistine's clever management, whenever a village priest came to Digne the bishop still found the means to entertain him.

One day after he had been in Digne some three months the bishop said, 'And with all that I still haven't enough!'

'I dare say you haven't!' exclaimed Madame Magloire. 'Monseigneur hasn't even claimed the allowance the *département** owes him for the expense of a carriage in town and of visiting the diocese. That's what bishops used to do in the past.'

'Well, I declare!' said the bishop. 'You're quite right, Madame Magloire.'

And he submitted his claim.

Some time afterwards the general council, taking his request into consideration, voted him an annual sum of three thousand francs that was registered as 'Allowance awarded to the bishop for carriage expenses, mail-coach expenses, and the expense of pastoral visits'.

This provoked a great outcry among the local bourgeoisie, and at the time a senator of the Empire, former member of the Council of Five Hundred who had supported the 18th Brumaire and been given a magnificent senatorial estate near the town of Digne, privately wrote to Monsieur Bigot de Préameneu, the minister of public worship, an angry note on the subject, from which we quote the following lines verbatim:

'Carriage expenses? What for in a town of fewer than four thousand inhabitants? The expense of pastoral visits? What good are these visits in the first place? And how can a mail-coach get about in these mountainous parts? There are no roads. You can only travel on horseback. Even the bridge over the Durance at Château-Arnoux can barely support ox-carts. These priests are all the same: greedy and miserly. This one pretended to be the good apostle when he first came here. Now he behaves just like the rest. He has to have a carriage and travel by post-chaise. He has to have luxury like the bishops of old. Oh, this priestly rabble! Things will be put right, Your Excellency, only when the emperor has delivered us from the clergy. Down with the pope!' (Relations with Rome were not good.) 'For my part, I am all for Caesar.' Et cetera, et cetera.

* The division of post-Revolutionary France into newly created administrative areas called *départements* came into effect in 1790.

Madame Magloire, on the other hand, was delighted. 'Well,' said she to Mademoiselle Baptistine, 'Monseigneur put everyone else first but he had to come round to himself eventually. He's taken care of all his charities. These three thousand francs are for us! At last!'

That same evening the bishop wrote out and handed to his sister a memorandum worded as follows:

Carriage allowance and allowance for pastoral visits:

To provide meat broth for the hospital patients:	1,500 francs
For the Society for Maternal Charity of Aix:	250 francs
For the Society for Maternal Charity of Draguignan:	250 francs
For the benefit of foundlings:	500 francs
For the benefit of orphans:	500 francs
Total:	3,000 francs

Such was Monsieur Myriel's budget.

As for episcopal emoluments – fees for marriage banns, dispensations, private baptisms, sermons, benedictions of churches and chapels, marriages, et cetera – the bishop was all the more assiduous in extracting them from the wealthy because he gave them to the poor.

After a while, offerings of money poured in. The haves and the have-nots came knocking at Monsieur Myriel's door, the latter in search of the alms brought to him by the former. In less than a year the bishop had become the treasurer for all charitable donations and the dispenser of funds for all cases of financial distress. Considerable sums of money passed through his hands but nothing could induce him to make any change in his lifestyle or to add the least extra to his barest needs.

Far from it. As there is always more poverty below than fellow feeling above, everything was given away, so to speak, in advance of receipt. It was like water on dry ground: no matter how much money he received, he never had any. So he would stint himself.

It being the custom for bishops to state their baptismal names at the head of their episcopal decrees and pastoral letters, the local poor, with a kind of affectionate instinct, had selected from the bishop's various names and first names the one that held some meaning for them, and they never called him anything but Monseigneur Bienvenu*. We will follow their example, and thus refer to him where appropriate. Besides, this designation pleased him.

* 'Bienvenu' means 'Welcome'.

'I like the name,' he said. 'Bienvenu compensates for Monseigneur.'

We would not say that the portrait we have presented here is one that seems very likely; all we say is that it is very like.

III
For a Good Bishop, a Demanding Bishopric

Even though he had converted his carriage into alms, the bishop made his pastoral visits nonetheless. The diocese of Digne is a punishing one. There are very few plains, a great many mountains, hardly any roads, as we saw earlier. Thirty-two parishes, forty-one vicariates and two hundred and eighty-five chapels of ease. To visit all these is quite a task. The bishop managed it. He went on foot to places nearby, travelled by cart on the plain, and on a donkey in the mountains. The two elderly women accompanied him. When the trip was too much for them, he went alone.

One day he arrived in Senez, an ancient episcopal town, riding an ass. His resources, which were very depleted at that time, did not allow him any better turn-out. The mayor came to welcome him at the gates of the town and watched, scandalized, as he dismounted from his ass. Some of the townsfolk around him were laughing. 'Monsieur le maire,' said the bishop, 'and honourable citizens, I see I shock you. You think it very arrogant of a poor priest to ride on a mount which was that of Jesus Christ. I have done so out of necessity, I assure you, and not vanity.'

On his visits he was kind and indulgent, and did not so much preach as chat. He placed no virtue beyond reach. He never went looking very far for his arguments and his exemplars. To the inhabitants of one village he would cite the example of the neighbouring one.

In districts where they treated the destitute harshly he would say, 'Look at the people of Briançon! They've granted to the poor, to widows and orphans the right to mow their meadows three days before everyone else. When their houses are falling down they rebuild them at no cost. Consequently, it's a place blessed by God. There's not been a single person guilty of murder for a whole century.'

To the villages bent on gain and on bringing in the harvest he said, 'Look at the people of Embrun! If at harvest time the father of a family has his sons serving in the army and his daughters in service in town, and he happens to be ill and unable to work, the parish priest asks the congregation to pray for him. And after mass on Sunday all the people in the village – men, women and children – go to the poor man's field and do his harvesting for him, and bring back the straw and the grain to his granary.'

To families divided by questions of money and inheritance he said, 'Look at the mountain folk of Dévoluy, a landscape so wild that not once in fifty years has the nightingale been heard. Well, when the father of a family dies, the boys go off to seek their fortunes, leaving the property to the girls that they may find husbands.'

To those areas that were inclined to go to law and where the farmers ruined themselves paying duty on legal documents he said, 'Look at the good countryfolk of the Queyras valley! They number three thousand souls. My God! It's like a little republic. Both judge and bailiff are unknown there. The mayor does everything. He shares out the tax levy, taxes each person fairly, settles disputes free of charge, divides estates without remuneration, gives judgements at no cost. And he's obeyed, because he's a good man among simple folk.'

To villages where he found no schoolmaster, again he cited the people of Queyras. 'Do you know what they do?' he said. 'Since a little village of a dozen or so dwellings can't always support a teacher, they have schoolmasters paid by the whole valley who make the round of the villages, spending a week in this one, ten days in that, giving instruction. These teachers go to the country markets, where I've seen them. You can tell them by the quill pens they wear in their hat bands. Those who teach just reading have one quill. Those who teach reading and arithmetic have two. And those who teach reading, arithmetic and Latin have three quills. But what a shame to be uneducated! Do what the people of Queyras do!'

This is the way he talked, seriously and like a father, inventing parables in the absence of examples, going directly to the point with few fine words and many illustrations, which was Jesus Christ's eloquence exactly, assured and persuasive.

IV
Deeds to Match Words

His conversation was affable and cheerful. He was sociable with the two old women who spent their lives with him. When he laughed it was the laugh of a schoolboy.

Madame Magloire liked to call him 'Your Highness'. One day he rose from his armchair and went to his bookcase to fetch a book. This book was on one of the top shelves. As the bishop was rather small in stature he could not reach it. 'Madame Magloire,' he said, 'bring me a chair. My Highness falls short of that shelf.'

One of his distant relatives, Madame la Comtesse de Lô, rarely let pass an opportunity when he was present to run through the list of what she called 'the expectations' of her three sons. She had several very elderly relatives close to death, and her sons were their natural heirs. The youngest of the three was to come into a good hundred thousand francs a year from his great-aunt, the second was to inherit the title of duke from his uncle, the eldest was to succeed to his grandfather's peerage. The bishop usually listened in silence to this harmless and forgivable maternal swanking. On one occasion, however, he appeared to be more thoughtful than usual as Madame de Lô rehearsed once again the details of all these inheritances and all these 'expectations'.

She broke off, saying impatiently, 'For heaven's sake, cousin! What is it you're thinking about?'

'I'm thinking,' replied the bishop, 'of something curious to be found, I believe, in St Augustine: "Place your hope in him who has no successor."'

On another occasion, when he received a letter announcing the death of a local dignitary that included a full-page list of not only the dead man's credentials but also the feudal and noble qualifications of all his relatives, he exclaimed, 'What a broad back death has! What a remarkable load of titles is blithely heaped on it, and what a sense of humour men must have to use the grave like this to flatter themselves!'

He was sometimes capable of gentle mockery that almost always had a serious significance. Once, during Lent, a young vicar came to Digne and preached in the cathedral. He was quite eloquent. The subject of his sermon was charity. He urged the rich to give to the poor so as to avoid going to hell, which he depicted in the most dreadful terms he could, and to get to paradise, which he represented as desirable and delightful. Among his audience was a somewhat tight-fisted retired wealthy merchant named Monsieur Géborand, who had amassed half a million in the manufacture of coarse cloth, serge, caddis and felt caps. Monsieur Géborand had never in his life been charitable to any poor unfortunate. After that sermon it was noticed he gave one sou every Sunday to the old beggar-women at the cathedral door. They had to share it between six of them. One day the bishop saw him making his donation and said to his sister with a smile, 'There's Monsieur Géborand buying one sou's worth of paradise.'

When charity was at stake he was not to be discouraged even by a refusal, and on such occasions he found words that gave pause for thought. Once he was collecting for the poor in one of the town's salons. The Marquis de Champtercier was there. A rich and mean old man, he contrived to be both ultra-royalist and ultra-Voltairian. Such a type did exist. When the bishop came to him, touching his arm, he said, 'Monsieur le marquis, you must give me something.'

The marquis turned round and responded drily, 'Monseigneur, I have my own poor.'

'Give them to me,' replied the bishop.

One day he preached the following sermon in the cathedral:

'Beloved brethren, my good friends, there are thirteen hundred and twenty thousand peasant dwellings in France that have only three openings, eighteen hundred and seventeen thousand that have but two, the door and one window, and finally three hundred and forty-six thousand hovels that have just the one – the door. And this is because of something called "the door and window tax". Put poor families, old women and young children in those buildings, and see the fevers and illnesses you get! Alas! While God gives men fresh air, the law sells it to them! I'm not accusing the law but I thank God. In Isère, in the Var, in the two Alpes – Hautes and Basses – the peasants don't even have wheelbarrows, the men carry the manure on their backs. They have no candles, they burn resinous sticks and bits of rope dipped in pitch. That's the state of affairs throughout the Dauphiné highlands. They make bread for six months at a time. They bake it with dried cow dung. In the winter they break this bread with an axe and soak it for twenty-four hours in order to be able to eat it.

'My brethren, have pity! See the suffering around you!'

Born a Provençal, he had readily familiarized himself with all the southern dialects. He would say, '*Eh bé! moussu, sès sagé?*'* as in the lower Languedoc, '*Onté anaras passa?*'† as in the lower Alps, '*Puerte un bouen moutu embe un bouen froumage grase*',‡ as in the upper Dauphiné. This pleased people and had contributed in no small way to his gaining acceptance by all. Both in a thatched cottage and up in the mountains he was perfectly at home. He could say the most noble things in the most unrefined language. Speaking everyone's language, he found his way into everyone's soul.

Furthermore, he was the same with everybody, whatever their social status.

He would not condemn anything without due consideration or without taking circumstances into account. He would say, 'Let's see how the wrong-doing was arrived at.'

Being, as he described himself with a smile, an ex-sinner, there was

* 'Now then, monsieur, are you being sensible?'
† 'Where have you been?'
‡ 'I've come with a good sheep and a good creamy cheese.'

nothing off-puttingly doctrinaire about him, and he professed quite openly, and without the frown of the ferociously virtuous, beliefs that may be summed up thus:

'Man exists in the flesh, which is at once his burden and his temptation. He drags it around with him and gives in to it.

'He must be vigilant, keep it in check, repress it, and yield to it only in the last extremity. Yielding to it may still be wrong but in that case the wrong-doing is venial. In so falling he falls on his knees, and it may end in prayer.

'To be a saint is the exception. To be a good man is the rule. Err, weaken and sin, but be among the good.

'To sin as little as possible, that is the law of mankind. Not to sin at all is the angel's dream. Everything earthly is subject to sin. Sin is a gravitational force.'

When he saw everyone condemning very loudly and being very quick to express indignation, 'Oh my,' he would say with a smile, 'this looks like being a great crime that everyone commits. Here we have hypocrisies in fright, hurrying to protest and to take cover.'

He was forbearing towards women and the poor on whom the burden of human society falls. He said, 'The failings of women, children and servants, of the feeble, the destitute and the ignorant, are the fault of their husbands, fathers and masters, of the strong, the rich and the learned.'

He also said, 'Teach those who are ignorant as much as you can. Society is to blame for not giving free education. It's responsible for the darkness it produces. In any benighted soul – that's where sin will be committed. It's not he who commits the sin that's to blame but he who causes the darkness to prevail.'

As we can see, he had his own peculiar way of judging things. I suspect he had taken it from the Gospels.

One day he heard in a salon the story of a criminal case that was going to come to trial. Some poor wretch in desperate straits, out of love for a woman and the child she had borne him, had coined counterfeit money. At that time counterfeiting was still punishable by death. The woman had been caught passing off the first fake coin made by the man. She was detained, but there was evidence only against her. She alone could incriminate her lover and ruin him by confessing. She denied the accusation. She was pressed. She persisted in her denial. At this point the crown prosecutor had an idea. He alleged an infidelity on the part of the lover and by means of cunningly presented fragments of letters succeeded in persuading the poor woman she had a rival and that this man was deceiving her. Provoked by jealousy she denounced her lover, confessed all, proved all. It was the man's undoing. He was shortly to be tried at Aix with his accomplice. It was this that was being talked of, and everyone was marvelling at the magistrate's ingenuity. By bringing jealousy into play he had used anger to elicit the truth. He had brought about the justice of revenge. The bishop listened to all of this in silence.

When the discussion came to a close he asked, 'Where are this man and woman to face judgement?'

'At the court of assizes.'

He went on, 'And where will the crown prosecutor face judgement?'

A tragic incident occurred at Digne. A man was condemned to death for murder. Not really educated but not completely uneducated, this poor wretch had been a fairground entertainer and a public letter-writer. The trial was the talk of the town. On the eve of the day set for the condemned man's execution the prison chaplain fell ill. A priest was needed to attend the criminal in his final moments. They sent for the parish priest. Apparently he refused to come, saying, 'It's nothing to do with me. I can't take on the responsibility of dealing with that charlatan, I too am unwell. In any case it's not my job.'

This response was reported to the bishop, who said, 'Monsieur le curé is right. It's not his job. It's mine.'

He went straight to the prison and down into the 'charlatan's' cell, called him by name, took him by the hand, and spoke to him. He spent the whole day and the whole night with him, forgetting about food and sleep, praying to God for the condemned man's soul, and asking the man to pray for his. He told him the best truths, which are the simplest ones. He was father, brother, friend to him, bishop only in blessing him. He taught him everything, sustaining and comforting him. This man was about to die in despair. Death was an abyss to him. As he stood trembling on that macabre threshold he recoiled in horror. He was not ignorant enough to be totally unaffected. Deeply traumatic, his condemnation had, as it were, rent here and there the screen dividing us from the mystery of things and what we call life. He kept looking beyond this world through these fateful chinks and saw only darkness. The bishop enabled him to see light.

When they came to fetch the poor man the following day the bishop was there. He went with him. He appeared before the crowd in his purple mozzetta with his episcopal cross round his neck, alongside that trussed-up criminal.

He climbed into the tumbril with him, he climbed on to the scaffold with him.

So crushed and despondent the previous day, the man facing death was radiant. He felt his soul had been reconciled and his trust was in God. The bishop embraced him and as the blade was about to drop said to him, 'He whom man slays God restores to life. He who is cast out by his brothers returns to the Father. Pray, believe, enter into life! The Father is there.'

When he came down from the scaffold there was something in his expression that made the crowd draw aside. It could not be said which gave greater cause for wonder, his pallor or his serenity. Coming home to the humble dwelling he would refer to with a smile as his palace, he said to his sister, 'I have just been officiating as bishop.'

As the most sublime things are often those least understood, there were people in town who, commenting on the bishop's conduct, said, 'It's affectation.' Actually, it was only in the salons this was said. The ordinary people, who see no harm in saintly deeds, were touched and felt admiration.

As for the bishop, it was a shock to him to have seen the guillotine, and it took him a long time to get over it.

There is something nightmarish about the scaffold when it is standing there ready. It is possible to feel a certain indifference about the death penalty, not to declare yourself, to say yes and no, so long as you have not seen a guillotine with your own eyes. But if you do come across one, it has a violent impact. You are forced to make a decision, to take sides, for or against. Some, like de Maistre, admire it. For others, like Beccaria, it is abhorrent. The guillotine is the law made concrete. Its name is retribution. It is not neutral and does not allow you to remain neutral. Whoever sees it shudders with the most mysterious of shudders. All social problems raise question marks around this blade. The scaffold is not a structure. The scaffold is not a machine. The scaffold is not an inert contraption made of wood, iron and rope. It is as though it were some kind of being with its own sinister initiative. To all appearances this wooden construction can see, this machine can hear, this contraption can understand, this wood, this iron and this rope have a will of their own. Its presence casts the soul into a ghastly trance in which the scaffold appears terrifying and involved in what it is doing. The scaffold is the executioner's accomplice. It devours. It eats flesh. It drinks blood. The scaffold is a kind of monster put together by the judge and the carpenter, a spectre that seems to live by some dreadful life force created out of all the death it has inflicted.

So it left a deep and horrible impression. The day after the execution and for many days afterwards the bishop seemed devastated. Gone was that almost fierce serenity he had had at the fateful moment. The phantom of social justice haunted him. He who generally returned from everything he did with such radiant satisfaction seemed to reproach himself. At times he talked to himself and muttered lugubrious monologues under his breath.

This is one which his sister overheard one evening and recorded:

'I didn't realize it was so monstrous. It's wrong to be so deeply absorbed in divine law that you become unaware of human law. Death depends on God alone. By what right do men meddle with this matter of destiny?'

With the passage of time these impressions diminished and probably faded away. Nevertheless, it was observed that from then on the bishop avoided crossing the square on which executions took place.

Monsieur Myriel could be summoned at any hour to the bedside of the sick and the dying. He was not unaware that this was his most important duty and his most important work. Widowed and orphaned families had no need to ask, he came of his own accord. He had the understanding to sit quietly with the man who had lost the wife he loved, with the mother who had lost her child. Just as he knew when to remain silent, so also he knew when to speak. O wonderful comforter! He did not try to blot out sorrow through oblivion but to magnify and dignify it through hope. He said, 'Mind which way you look at the dead. Don't think of what perishes. Look hard. You'll see the living light of your dear departed up there in heaven.' He knew that faith is healing. He sought to counsel and calm the disconsolate by pointing to the resigned, and to transform the grief that dwells on the grave by teaching the grief that dwells on a star.

V
Monseigneur Bienvenu Made His Cassocks Last Far Too Long

Monsieur Myriel's private life was filled with the same thoughts as his public life. To anyone able to see it at close hand the voluntary poverty in which the bishop of Digne lived would have been a dignified and charming spectacle.

Like all old men and most thinkers, he slept little. This brief sleep was a deep sleep. In the morning he meditated for an hour, then said mass, either at the cathedral or in his private chapel. Once he had said mass, he breakfasted on rye bread dipped in milk from his own cows. Then he worked.

A bishop is a very busy man. Every day he has to see the diocesan secretary, generally a canon, and nearly every day his vicars-general.

He has congregations to supervise, privileges to grant, a whole library full of ecclesiastical publications to study – prayer books, diocesan catechisms, books of hours, et cetera – newsletters to write, sermons to approve, parish priests and mayors to bring together, a clerical correspondence, an administrative correspondence, with the state on the one hand and the holy see on the other, countless matters to be dealt with.

Whatever time was left to him by these countless matters, his religious services and his breviary, he gave first of all to the needy, the sick and the bereaved. Whatever time was left to him by the bereaved, the sick and the needy, he devoted to work. Sometimes he dug the soil in his garden, sometimes he read or wrote. For both these kinds of work he had just one word: he called this 'gardening'. 'The mind is a garden,' he used to say.

At midday he had his lunch. Lunch was the same as breakfast.

At around two o'clock, when the weather was fine, he would go for a walk in the countryside or in town, often entering the humblest dwellings. He was to be seen walking by himself entirely absorbed in his thoughts, with his eyes on the ground, leaning on his long walking-stick, dressed in his very warm purple quilted coat, purple stockings and heavy shoes, and wearing his flat hat with three gold-braided tassels dangling from its three corners.

There was celebration wherever he appeared. He seemed to bring something bright and warming with him as he went by. Children and old folk came out on the doorstep for the bishop as if for the sun. He gave his blessing and they blessed him. Anyone in need of anything was directed to his house.

He would stop here and there, talk to the little boys and girls and smile at their mothers. As long as he had money he visited the poor. When he had none left he visited the rich.

Since he made his cassocks last a very long time and did not want anyone to notice, he never went into town without his purple quilted coat. This was a little uncomfortable in summer.

At half-past eight in the evening he had supper with his sister, with Madame Magloire standing behind them and serving them at table. Nothing could be more frugal than this meal. If, however, the bishop had one of his parish priests to supper Madame Magloire took advantage of the opportunity to serve Monseigneur some excellent lake-water fish or some choice game from the mountains. Every parish priest was an excuse for a good meal. The bishop did not interfere. Otherwise, his usual meal consisted only of boiled vegetables and soup with oil.

Consequently it was said in town: 'When the bishop does not dine like a parish priest, he dines like a Trappist monk.'

After supper he would chat for half an hour with Mademoiselle Baptistine and Madame Magloire, then retire to his own room and begin writing again, sometimes on loose pages, sometimes in the margin of a folio volume. He was well read and somewhat erudite. He has left five or six rather curious manuscripts – among others, a dissertation on the verse from Genesis: 'In the beginning the spirit of God moved upon the face of the waters.' He compares this verse with three texts: the Arabic version that says, 'The winds of God blew'; Flavius Josephus, who says, 'A wind from on high came down upon the earth'; and finally Onkelos paraphrased it in Chaldaic as 'A wind emanating from God blew upon the face of the waters.' In another dissertation he examines the theological works of Hugo, bishop of Ptolemais, great-great-uncle of the author of this book, and establishes that the various tracts published during the last century under the pseudonym of Barleycourt are to be attributed to this bishop.

Sometimes in the middle of reading, no matter what the book he had in his hand might be, he would suddenly fall into a deep meditation, emerging from it only to write a few lines on the actual pages of the book. These lines often have no connection whatsoever with the book that contains them. We have now before our eyes a note written by him in the margin of a quarto volume entitled *Correspondence of Lord Germain with Generals Clinton, Cornwallis and the Admirals of the American Station* (Versailles, Poinçot, Bookseller, and Paris, Pissot, Bookseller, Quai des Augustins).

This is the note:

'Oh, you who are!

'Ecclesiastes names you Almighty, the Maccabees name you Creator, the Epistle to the Ephesians names you Freedom, Baruch names you Immensity, the Psalms name you Wisdom and Truth, John names you Light, the Book of Kings names you Lord, Exodus names you Providence. Leviticus, Sanctity. Esdras, Justice. Creation names you God. Mankind names you Father. But Solomon names you Mercy, and of all your names this is the most beautiful.'

About nine o'clock in the evening the two women would retire and go up to their rooms on the first floor, leaving him alone on the ground floor until morning.

At this point we need to give an accurate idea of the bishop of Digne's accommodation.

VI
Under Whose Protection He Placed His House

The house where he lived consisted, as we have said, of a ground floor and a first floor – three rooms on the ground floor, three on the first, with an attic above. Behind the house was a garden of some quarter of an acre. The two women occupied the first floor. The bishop slept downstairs. The first room, which opened on to the street, served as his dining room, the second was his bedroom, and the third his private chapel. There was no way out of this chapel except through the bedroom, or out of the bedroom except through the dining room. At the far end of the chapel was a separate alcove with a bed in it for the use of guests. The bishop would offer this bed to priests brought to Digne by the needs of their rural parishes or on other business.

The hospital pharmacy, a small building added to the house and extending into the garden, had been turned into a kitchen and storeroom.

There was also in the garden an outbuilding, formerly the old hospital kitchen, where the bishop kept two cows. However much milk they gave, he invariably sent half of it every morning to the patients in the hospital. 'I'm paying my tithes,' he said.

His bedroom was quite big and quite difficult to heat in winter. As wood is extremely expensive in Digne he came up with the idea of having a wooden partition installed in the cowshed to create a separate closet. Here he spent his evenings when it was very cold. He called it his winter drawing room.

This drawing room had no other furniture than a square whitewood table and four straw-bottomed chairs, as in the dining room. The dining room also boasted an old sideboard painted with pink distemper. Out of a similar sideboard, appropriately draped with white cloths and imitation lace, the bishop had fashioned the altar that graced his chapel.

His wealthy penitents and the pious women of Digne had often contributed to a fund to pay for the expense of a new altar for Monseigneur's chapel. Every time this happened he had taken the money and given it to the poor. 'The most beautiful of altars,' he said, 'is the soul of one comforted in their distress who thanks God.'

There were two straw-bottomed chairs with kneelers in his chapel, and an armchair, also straw-bottomed, in his bedroom. When he happened to have seven or eight guests at the same time – the prefect, or the general, or the officers of the regiment in garrison, or several pupils from the seminary school – someone had to go and fetch the chairs from the winter drawing room in the cowshed, the chairs with kneelers from the chapel and the armchair from the bedroom. As many as eleven chairs could be thus assembled for visitors. With every new arrival a room was emptied of furniture.

It sometimes happened they were twelve in all. The bishop then disguised the awkwardness of the situation by standing in front of the chimney if it was winter or suggesting a stroll in the garden if it was summer.

There was yet another chair in the alcove but the straw bottom was half giving way and it was balanced on only three legs, which meant it could only be used propped up against the wall. Mademoiselle Baptistine also had in her room a very large bergère of wood that had once been gilt, and upholstered in a flower-patterned Peking silk. But this bergère had to be brought up to the first floor through the window as the staircase was too narrow. So it could not be included among the furniture available when needed.

Mademoiselle Baptistine's ambition had been to buy a suite of drawing-room furniture, including a sofa, in yellow rose-patterned Utrecht velvet and mahogany, with swan-neck carving. But this would have cost five hundred francs at least, and seeing that she had been able to save up only forty-two francs and ten sous in five years, she eventually gave up the idea. Anyway, who ever attains their ideal?

Nothing could be simpler to visualize than the bishop's bedroom. A french window opening on to the garden, with the bed facing it, a hospital bed, iron-framed with a green serge canopy. Close to the bed, behind a curtain, the toilet articles that still betrayed the old stylish ways of the man of the world. Two doors, one by the fireplace leading to the chapel, the other by the bookcase leading to the dining room. The bookcase, a large glass-fronted cabinet full of books. The fireplace, with a wooden mantel painted to look like marble, usually without a fire. In the fireplace a pair of andirons decorated with two garlanded vases and flutings once silver-plated, which was a kind of episcopal luxury. Above, where a mirror would normally be hung, a crucifix made of copper with the silver plating worn off, set against threadbare black velvet in a wooden frame that had lost its gilt. By the french window, a large table with an inkstand laden with a jumble of papers and some thick volumes. In front of the table, the straw-bottomed armchair. In front of the bed, a chair with kneeler, borrowed from the chapel.

Hanging on the wall on either side of the bed were two portraits in oval frames. Small gilt inscriptions on the plain cloth background, beside these heads, indicated that one of the portraits was of Abbé de Chaliot, bishop of St-Claude; the other of Abbé Tourteau, vicar-general of Agde, abbot of Grand-Champ of the Cistercian Order in the diocese of Chartres. When the bishop took over this room from the hospital patients he found these portraits in it and had left them there. They were priests, probably benefactors – two reasons why he should respect them. All he knew about these two individuals was that they had been appointed – the one to his bishopric, the other to his living – by the king, on the same day, the twenty-seventh of April 1785. The bishop discovered this information, written in faded ink on a little square of paper yellowed with age and attached with four blobs of sealing-wax to the back of the portrait of the abbot of Grand-Champ, when Madame Magloire took the pictures down to shake the dust off them.

He had a very old window curtain of coarse woollen cloth that eventually became so old that to avoid the expense of a new one Madame Magloire was obliged to sew a large patch right in the middle of it. This patch was in the shape of a cross. The bishop often remarked on it. 'How well that looks!' he would say.

All the rooms in the house without exception, on the ground floor as well as the first floor, were whitewashed, which is a common practice in barracks and hospitals.

However, as we shall see, underneath the whitewashed paper Madame Magloire had recently discovered paintings that decorated Mademoiselle Baptistine's room. Before it was a hospital this house had been the town council building. Hence the decoration. The bedroom floors were of red brick, washed every week, with a woven straw mat before every bed. Indeed, this place, looked after by two women, was immaculately clean from top to bottom. This was the sole luxury the bishop allowed. He said, 'It takes nothing from the poor.'

It must be acknowledged, though, that of his former possessions he was still left with six silver forks and spoons and a large soup ladle that for Madame Magloire were a daily joy to see gleaming splendidly on the white linen tablecloth. And as we are painting a portrait of the bishop of Digne just as he was, we must add that he had more than once been heard to say, 'It would be hard to give up eating off silver.'

To this silverware must be added two large candlesticks of solid silver that he had inherited from a great-aunt. These candlesticks held two wax candles and usually stood on the bishop's mantelpiece. When he had someone to dinner Madame Magloire would light the two candles and set the candlesticks on the table.

In the bishop's own bedroom, at the head of his bed, was a small cupboard in which Madame Magloire locked away the six silver forks and spoons and the large ladle every evening. It has to be said, the key was never removed.

A little spoiled by the rather ugly outhouses mentioned above, the garden consisted of four paths that formed a cross radiating from a drainage well. Another path ran all the way round the garden and along the white wall that enclosed it. These paths marked out four square plots edged with box. In three of these Madame Magloire grew vegetables. In the fourth the bishop had planted flowers. Here and there were a few fruit trees.

Madame Magloire had once said to him with a sort of gentle mockery, 'Monseigneur is always one for putting everything to good use but this is a waste of a plot. It would be more useful to have salads here than bunches of flowers.'

'Madame Magloire,' replied the bishop, 'you're mistaken. The beautiful is just as useful as the useful.' He added after a pause, 'Perhaps more so.'

This plot, consisting of three or four flowerbeds, occupied the bishop almost as much as his books. He would gladly spend an hour or two at them, pruning, weeding and making holes in the ground here and there, in which he put seeds. He was not as hostile to insects as a gardener might have wished. Indeed, he had no botanical pretensions at all. He knew nothing of groups and solidism. He was not in the least concerned with deciding between Tournefort and the natural method. He did not favour utricles over cotyledons, or Jussieu over Linnaeus. He did not study plants. He loved flowers. He had a great deal of respect for the learned. He had even more respect for the uneducated. And without ever failing in his respect for both, he watered his flowerbeds every summer evening with a green tin watering-can.

The house had not a single door that could be locked. The door of the dining room which, as we have said, opened directly on to the cathedral square had formerly been fitted with locks and bolts like a prison door. The bishop had all these iron fittings removed, and day or night this door was always left on the latch. No matter what time it was, anyone that called by had only to push it open. At first the two women had fretted greatly about this door that was never locked, but the bishop of Digne said to them, 'Have bolts fitted to your rooms if you like.' They ended up sharing his trustfulness, or at least behaving as if they did. Madame Magloire alone had frights from time to time. As for the bishop, an explanation of his thinking, or at least a clue to it, can be found in a few lines he wrote in the margin of a bible. 'There is a subtle distinction to be made: the doctor's door should never be shut, the priest's door should always be open.'

On another book, entitled *Philosophy of Medical Science*, he had written this note: 'Am not I a physician like them? I too have my patients. In the first place, I have theirs, whom they call the sick. And then I have mine, whom I call those in distress.'

Elsewhere he wrote: 'Don't ask the name of anyone that asks you for shelter. It is especially the person whose name is a burden to him that has need of shelter.'

It so happened that a well-meaning priest – the parish priest of Couloubroux or Pompierry, I don't remember which – one day took it upon himself, probably at Madame Magloire's instigation, to ask whether Monseigneur was quite sure he was not acting a little unwisely in leaving his door open day and night to anyone that might choose to enter, and whether he did not after all fear some harm might come to those in a house so poorly guarded. The bishop touched him on the shoulder with gentle solemnity and said, '*Nisi Dominus custodierit domum, in vanum vigilant qui custodiunt eam.*'* Then he spoke of something else.

He was fond of saying, 'There's the bravery of the priest as well as the bravery of a colonel of dragoons. Only,' he added, 'ours must be a bravery of peace.'

VII
Cravatte

This is the right place to recount an event we must not fail to mention, because it is one of those that best illustrate what kind of man the bishop of Digne was.

After the rout of Gaspard Bès's gang that had infested the Ollioules gorges, one of his lieutenants, Cravatte, took refuge in the mountains. With his outlaws, the remnants of Gaspard Bès's band, he went into hiding for a while in the county of Nice, then made his way to Piedmont, and suddenly reappeared in France in the vicinity of Barcelonnette. He was first seen at Jauziers, then at Tuiles. He hid in the caves of Joug-de-l'Aigle, and from there would descend on the hamlets and villages following the course of the Ubaye and the Ubayette. He even ventured as far as Embrun, entered the cathedral one night and ransacked the sacristy. His depredations were the despair of the locality. The gendarmerie were sent after him, but to no avail. He always escaped. Sometimes he put up a fight. He was a bold wretch.

* Psalm 127, 'Except the Lord build the house, they labour in vain that build it.'

The bishop turned up on his pastoral round in the middle of this terror. At Chastelar the mayor came out to meet him and urged him to turn back. Cravatte had control of the mountains as far as Arche and beyond. It was dangerous even with an escort, which only meant needlessly putting three or four poor gendarmes at risk.

'Which is why,' said the bishop, 'I intend to go without an escort.'

'Are you serious, Monseigneur?' exclaimed the mayor.

'So serious that I don't want a single gendarme and I'm leaving within the hour.'

'Leaving?'

'Leaving.'

'Alone?'

'Alone.'

'Monseigneur! You can't do that.'

'Up in the mountains,' said the bishop, 'is the smallest of humble communities, which I haven't visited for three years. They're my dear friends. Gentle and honest shepherds. They own one goat out of every thirty they tend. They make very pretty woollen cords of various colours, and they play mountain airs on little six-hole flutes. They need someone to tell them about the good Lord from time to time. What would they think of a bishop who was scared? What would they think if I didn't go to them?'

'But the brigands, Monseigneur! What if you were to run into the brigands!'

'Well,' said the bishop, 'I've been thinking about that. You're right. I may run into them. They too need someone to tell them about the good Lord.'

'But Monseigneur, they're a gang! A pack of wolves!'

'Monsieur le maire, it may be that this very pack of wolves is the flock Jesus is placing in my pastoral care. Who understands the ways of providence?'

'Monseigneur, they'll rob you.'

'I have nothing.'

'They'll kill you.'

'A harmless old priest mumbling his prayers as he goes by? Bah! What for?'

'Oh, my goodness! If you were to run into them!'

'I'd ask them to give to my poor.'

'For heaven's sake, don't go, Monseigneur! You're endangering your life!'

'But if that's the only objection, monsieur le maire,' said the bishop, 'I'm not in this world to protect my life but to protect souls.'

There was no way of stopping him. He set out, accompanied only by a child who offered to serve as his guide. His stubborn determination caused a stir among the local people and greatly alarmed them.

He would take with him neither his sister nor Madame Magloire. He crossed the mountain on a mule, encountered no one, and came safe and sound to his 'good friends' the shepherds. He remained with them for a fortnight, preaching, administering the sacraments, teaching, edifying. When he was soon to depart he resolved to sing a solemn *Te Deum*. He told the parish priest. But how was it to be done? No episcopal vestments! All that could be placed at his disposal was a lowly village sacristy with a few old chasubles of threadbare damask trimmed with imitation braid.

'Bah!' said the bishop. 'Let's proclaim our *Te Deum* from the pulpit anyway. Something will turn up.'

A search of the local churches was made. All the finery of these humble parishes put together would not have provided suitable vestments for one cathedral chorister.

While they were in this quandary a large chest was brought and left in the presbytery for the bishop by two unknown horsemen who immediately rode off again. The chest was opened. It contained a cope of cloth-of-gold, a mitre ornamented with diamonds, an archbishop's cross, a magnificent crosier, all the pontifical vestments stolen a month previously from the treasury of Notre-Dame d'Embrun. In the chest was a piece of paper with these words written on it: 'From Cravatte to Monseigneur Bienvenu.'

'Did I not say something would turn up?' said the bishop. Then he added with a smile, 'To him who is satisfied with a priest's surplice, God sends the cope of an archbishop.'

'Monseigneur,' murmured the parish priest, nodding with a smile, 'God . . . or the devil.'

The bishop looked steadily at the priest and corrected him with authority, 'God!'

When he returned to Chastelar, and all along the way, people came to see him out of curiosity. He found Mademoiselle Baptistine and Madame Magloire waiting for him at the presbytery in Chastelar, and he said to his sister, 'Well, I was right, wasn't I? The poor priest went to visit those poor mountain-dwellers empty-handed, and he comes home with his hands full. I set out with only my trust in God. I'm bringing back a cathedral's treasury.'

And that evening before he went to bed he said, 'Never fear robbers or murderers. Those are dangers that come from without. Small dangers. Let us fear ourselves. Prejudices are the real robbers. Vices are the real murderers. The great dangers are within us. Never mind what endangers our life or our purse! Let's be mindful only of what endangers our soul.'

Then turning to his sister, 'Sister, no priest should ever guard himself against his fellow man. Whatever his fellow man does, God allows it. Let us simply pray to God when we believe some danger threatens us. And pray not for ourselves but that our brother may not fall into sin on our account.'

That apart, his life was usually uneventful. We relate what we know of, but generally he spent his life always doing the same things at the same time of day. One month of his year was like one hour of his day.

As to what became of the cathedral of Embrun 'treasure', being questioned on that subject would embarrass us. Very handsome indeed were those things, very tempting, and very good to steal for the benefit of the poor. Anyway, they were already stolen. The job was half done. The theft only needed to be redirected and helped a little on its way to reach the poor. However, we are not making any assertions in this regard. Only a rather obscure note was found among the bishop's papers that may have some bearing on the matter. It is worded as follows: 'The question is, whether it should revert to the cathedral or the hospital.'

VIII
After-Drinking Philosophy

The senator we have spoken of earlier was a calculating man who had made his way regardless of all those obstacles he would have encountered that we call conscience, solemn oath, justice, duty. He had moved straight towards his goal without once faltering in the pursuit of his career and his self-interest. He was a former prosecutor, with a weakness for success, not at all a wicked man, doing all the little favours he could for his sons, sons-in-law, relations, even friends, having wisely taken from life its good aspects, its good opportunities, its strokes of good luck. Anything else seemed rather foolish to him. He was witty and just sufficiently well read to consider himself a disciple of Epicurus while in reality being only a product of Pigault-Lebrun. He joked readily and pleasantly about things infinite and everlasting, and about 'the dear bishop's nonsense'. Sometimes he even joked about these, with a kindly authority, when Monsieur Myriel himself was there listening.

Some semi-official ceremony or other meant that Comte *** (this senator) and Monsieur Myriel were both dinner guests of the prefect. When it came to dessert, the senator, a little merry though still dignified, cried, 'Dash it, monsieur l'évêque, let's have a chat! It's hard for a senator and a bishop to look at each other without winking. We're both augurs. I'm going to be honest with you: I have my philosophy.'

'Quite right too,' replied the bishop. 'As you make your philosophical bed, so must you lie in it. Yours is the bed of purple, monsieur le sénateur.'

Encouraged, the senator went on, 'Let's be good-natured about this.'

'Devilish good-natured, even,' said the bishop.

'I tell you,' continued the senator, 'the Marquis d'Argens, Pyrrho, Hobbes and Monsieur Naigeon are no scoundrels. All the philosophers I have in my library are gilt-edged.'

'Like yourself, monsieur le comte,' the bishop interposed.

The senator went on: 'I hate Diderot. He's an ideologue, a ranter and a revolutionary, who basically believes in God and is more sanctimonious than Voltaire. Voltaire scoffed at Needham, and he was wrong. For Needham's eels prove that God is unnecessary. A drop of vinegar in a spoonful of flour paste replaces the *fiat lux**. Suppose the drop were larger and the spoonful bigger, and there you have the world. Man is the eel. So what use is the Eternal Father? The Jehovah hypothesis bores me, monsieur l'évêque. All it can do is produce people of no substance, who ring hollow. Down with the great Whole that drives me to distraction! Long live Nothingness that leaves me alone! Between you and me, and to come clean and confess to my pastor as one should, I admit I have common sense. I'm not mad about this Jesus of yours who's constantly preaching self-denial and sacrifice. A miser's counsel to the poverty-stricken. Self-denial! Why? Sacrifice! For what? I don't see any wolf sacrificing itself for the sake of another wolf's happiness. So let's stick with nature. We hold pride of place. Let's have the superior philosophy. What's the point of being on top if you can't see further than the end of other people's noses? Let's enjoy life. Life is all. The idea that man has another future elsewhere, up above, down below, wherever – I don't believe a single word of it. Oh! I'm told to make sacrifices and be self-denying, I must beware of everything I do, I have to worry about good and evil, right and wrong, the *fas* and the *nefas*†. Why? Because I shall be called to account for my actions. When? After my death. What a charming fantasy! After my death it will take a lot of cunning to nab me. Just you make a disembodied hand grab a handful of dust. Let's speak the

* An allusion to Genesis 1:3: 'Dixitque Deus fiat lux et facta lux est' ('And God said, Let there be light: and there was light').

† Latin: *fas*, that which is in accordance with divine law; and *nefas*, that which is contrary to it.

truth, we who are among the initiated and have lifted Isis' skirt: there is neither good nor evil, there's vegetation. Let us seek out reality, delve deep, dig to the bottom, damn it! You have to sniff out the truth, burrow underground and snatch it up. Then it gives you exquisite pleasure. Then you become strong and you laugh. I've got my feet on the ground. Monsieur l'évêque, the immortality of man is wishful thinking. Oh! what a delightful promise! Believe it if you will! What an assurance Adam has been given! We're souls, we're going to become angels, we'll have blue wings on our shoulder blades. Help me out here: isn't it Tertullian who says that the blessed will migrate from star to star? Very well. We shall be grasshoppers among the stars. And then we shall see God. Blah, blah, blah. All these paradises are just twaddle! God is a monstrous piece of nonsense. I wouldn't say so in *Le Moniteur*, of course, but I whisper it among friends. *Inter pocula.** To sacrifice the world for paradise is to let go the substance for the shadow. Be taken in by the everlasting? I'm not such a fool! I'm nothing. I call myself Monsieur le Comte of Nothingness, senator. Did I exist before my birth? No. Shall I exist after my death? No. What am I? A little dust bound together by an organism. What am I to do on this earth? I have the choice: to suffer, or to enjoy myself. Where will suffering get me? To non-existence. But I shall have suffered. Where will enjoyment get me? To non-existence. But I shall have enjoyed myself. My choice is made. Of necessity, it is either eat or be eaten. I shall eat. Better to be the tooth than the grass. Such is my wisdom. After that, however long you manage to keep going, the grave-digger is there, the Panthéon for some of us, but all end up in the great hole in the ground. The End. *Finis.* Total elimination. This is the vanishing-point. Death is final, believe me. I laugh at the idea of there being anyone who has anything to tell me on this subject. Nursery make-believe – the bogeyman for children, Jehovah for adults. No, our future is darkness. Beyond the tomb there's nothing but equal non-existences. Whether you were Sardanapalus or Vincent de Paul, it makes no difference. That's the truth of the matter. So above all, live your life. Make use of your self while it's yours. Monsieur l'évêque, I tell you truly, I have my philosophy and I have my philosophers. I don't allow myself to be inveigled by humbug. Of course, there must be something for those at the bottom of society, the barefoot tramps, the ones living on a pittance, the wretched poor. They're given legends to swallow, chimeras, the soul, immortality, paradise, the stars. They chew on that. They put it on their dry crusts. Whoever has nothing has the

* Latin: 'In one's cups'.

31

good Lord. That's the very least he deserves. I've no objection to that but I keep Monsieur Naigeon for myself. The good Lord is good enough for the populace.'

The bishop clapped his hands.

'Well said!' he exclaimed. 'What an excellent and truly marvellous thing that kind of materialism is! It takes more than wanting to come by it. But when you do, ah, you're no longer fooled. You don't stupidly allow yourself to be exiled like Cato, or stoned like Stephen, or burned alive like Joan of Arc. Those that do manage to avail themselves of this admirable materialism have the pleasure of feeling irresponsible and of thinking they can gobble up everything without worrying – positions, sinecures, distinctions, power whether honestly or dishonestly come by, lucrative retractions, advantageous betrayals, delectable compromises with their conscience – and that they shall go to their graves having digested the lot. How satisfying! I don't say this for your sake, monsieur le sénateur. However, I can only congratulate you. You fine gentlemen, as you say, have a philosophy of your own, for yourselves. An exquisite, refined philosophy available only to the rich, to be served up in all kinds of ways, wonderfully adding relish to the pleasures of life. This philosophy is extracted from the hidden depths and unearthed by expert seekers. But you are kindly princes and you don't mind that belief in God should be the philosophy of the people, rather in the same way that goose stuffed with chestnuts is the truffled turkey of the poor.'

IX
The Brother as Described by His Sister

To give some idea of the bishop of Digne's domestic arrangements and of the way those two saintly women subordinated their actions, thoughts, even their instincts, easily frightened as they were, to the habits and wishes of the bishop without his even having to take the trouble to say anything to convey them, we can do no better than to transcribe at this point a letter from Mademoiselle Baptistine to her childhood friend Madame la Vicomtesse de Boischevron. We have the letter in our hands.

Digne, 16th December, 18—

My dear madame,

Not a day passes that we do not speak of you. This is something of a habit of ours but there is yet another reason for it. Just imagine, while washing and dusting the ceilings and walls, Madame Magloire has made

32

some discoveries. Our two bedrooms with old whitewashed paper on the walls would now not discredit a château like yours. Madame Magloire has pulled off all the paper. There was something underneath. My drawing room, containing no furniture, that we use for hanging out the linen after it has been washed, is fifteen foot high by eighteen foot square, with what was once a painted gilded ceiling with beams like yours. It was concealed under baize from the days when this was the hospital. Would you believe, wooden coffering from our grandmothers' day. But you should see my room! Under at least ten layers of paper pasted over them, Madame Magloire has discovered some paintings that without being good are passable. Of Telemachus being knighted by Minerva, and of him again in the gardens. The name escapes me. You know, where Roman ladies would go, on just one night. What shall I say? I have Romans, men, women [an illegible word here]*, and all the rest. Madame Magloire has cleaned it all up, and this summer she is going to have some slight damage repaired, and the whole thing revarnished, and the room will be a veritable museum. She has also found in a corner of the attic two old-fashioned wooden console tables. It would have cost us twelve francs to have them regilded but it is much better to give the money to the poor. In any case they are very ugly, and I would far rather have a round mahogany table.

I am just as happy as ever. My brother is so good. He gives all he has to the poor and the sick. Life is very difficult. The winters are hard in this part of the world, and we really have to do something for those in need. We are fairly well provided with heat and lighting. You see, such things are great luxuries.

My brother has his own ways. In conversation, he says this is how a bishop should be. Would you believe, the door of our house is never locked. Anyone can walk in, straight into my brother's rooms. He is not afraid of anything, even at night. That is his form of bravery, he says.

He does not want me or Madame Magloire to fear for his safety. He exposes himself to all kinds of danger and he does not even want us to look as if we notice. We must be understanding.

He goes out in the rain, walks in the wet, travels in winter. He is not afraid of the dark or of dangerous roads or of whom he might encounter.

Last year he went off by himself into a region of robbers. He would not take us with him. He was away for a fortnight. When he came back nothing had happened to him. We thought he was dead, and he was in fine fettle. And he said, 'Look how I've been robbed!' And he opened up a trunk full of all the treasure belonging to the cathedral of Embrun, which the robbers had given him.

* The comment in brackets is Hugo's.

33

Coming home on that occasion, after I had gone five miles out of town with some of his other friends to meet him, I could not help scolding him a little, taking care to speak only when the carriage was rattling so no one else could hear.

At first I used to say to myself, 'There is no danger that deters him, he's impossible.' I have ended up getting used to it now. I gesture to Madame Magloire not to cross him. He takes whatever risks he wants to. I go off with Madame Magloire, retire to my room, pray for him and fall asleep. My mind's at rest because I know if anything were to happen to him that would be the end of me. I would be on my way to the good Lord with my brother and my bishop. It was much more difficult for Madame Magloire to come to terms with what she calls his recklessness. But now we have got into the habit of it. We both pray, the two of us are frightened, and we fall asleep. The devil could enter this house and no one would stop him. After all, what do we fear in this house? There is always someone with us whose strength is greatest. The devil may visit us but the good Lord dwells here.

For me that is enough. My brother has no need even to say a word to me now. I understand him without his speaking, and we place ourselves in the hands of Providence.

That is how it must be with a man who has greatness of spirit.

I asked my brother for the information you wanted about the De Faux family. You know how he knows everything and remembers things, because he is still a true royalist. They really are a very old Norman family from the Caen district. Going back five hundred years, there was a Raoul de Faux, a Jean de Faux and a Thomas de Faux, who were noblemen, one of them the seigneur de Rochefort. The last of them was Guy-Étienne-Alexandre, who was a regimental commander and something or other in the Brittany light cavalry. His daughter Marie-Louise married Adrien-Charles de Gramont, son of Louis Duc de Gramont, peer of France, colonel of the French guards and lieutenant-general of the armed forces. The name is written Faux, Fauq and Faoucq.

Dear madame, commend us to the prayers of your saintly relative the cardinal. As for your dear Sylvanie, she is quite right not to use up any of the brief time she spends with you in writing to me. She is in good health, works as you will have her do, and still loves me. That is all I want. You have conveyed her kind regards. That gives me pleasure. My health is not too bad and yet I grow thinner every day. Farewell, I've run out of paper and so must leave you. With very best wishes,

Baptistine

P.S. Your sister-in-law is still here with her young family. Your great-nephew is charming. Do you know he will soon be five years old?

Yesterday he saw a horse go by that had had knee-guards put on, and he said, 'What's wrong with his knees?' That child is so sweet!

His little brother pulls an old broom round the house like a cart and says, 'Gee up!'

As can be seen from this letter, with that special genius that women have of understanding a man better than he understands himself these two women were able to conform to the bishop's ways.

Despite his unfailingly gentle and ingenuous manner, the bishop of Digne sometimes did things that were grand, bold and magnificent without appearing to be at all aware of it. It made them fearful, but they did not interfere. Sometimes Madame Magloire tried to remonstrate beforehand but never during or afterwards. They never by so much as a gesture intervened in any action once he had embarked on it. At certain times, without needing to be told, when he was probably not even conscious of it himself – so completely unpretentious was he – in some way they sensed he was acting as a bishop. Then they were no more than two shadows in the house. They served him self-effacingly, and if to obey meant to disappear, they disappeared. With an admirable delicacy of instinct they realized that some shows of concern may be unwelcome. So even when believing him to be in danger, they understood, I will not say his thinking, but his nature, to the extent that they no longer sought to protect him. They entrusted him to God.

Moreover, as we have just read, Baptistine used to say the death of her brother would be the death of her. Madame Magloire did not say so, but she knew it.

X
The Bishop in the Presence of an Unknown Light

Shortly after the date of the letter cited in the pages above he did something even more dangerous, as the whole town would have it, than his mountain excursion through bandit territory.

In the countryside near Digne lived a man all by himself. This man was – let us straight away utter the dread word – a former member of the Convention. His name was G.

In the little world of Digne, Member of the Convention G was spoken of with a kind of horror. A member of the Convention! Can you imagine! That went back to the days when all forms of respect were abandoned and everyone was addressed as 'citizen'. This man was almost a monster. He did not vote for the king's death, but little short of it. He was all but a regicide. He had done terrible things. How was it that on the return of our lawful rulers the man had not been prosecuted by a criminal court? He need not have had his head cut off, if you like, there must be clemency, agreed – but a good life-long banishment, as an example, for goodness' sake! Et cetera, et cetera. Besides, he was an atheist like all the rest of those people.

The cackling of geese with regard to the vulture!

But was G actually a vulture? Yes, to judge by the unsociable nature of his solitude. Not having voted for the death of the king, he had not been included in the edicts of exile and had been able to remain in France.

He dwelt at three-quarters of an hour's distance from the town, far from any hamlet, far from any road, in a remote spot, heaven knows where, in a very wild valley. It was said he had some kind of small-holding there, a bolt-hole, a retreat. No neighbours, not even passers-by. Since he had been living in this valley the path that led there had become overgrown. People spoke about that place as if it were the home of an executioner.

However, the bishop would reflect and from time to time gaze at the horizon where a clump of trees marked the old member of the Convention's valley, and he would say, 'There's an isolated soul out there.'

And deep in his own mind he added, 'I owe him a visit.'

But let us admit, this idea, on the face of it a natural one, after a moment's reflection appeared to him outlandish and impossible, almost repellent. For he basically shared the general impression, and the member of the Convention inspired in him, without his being clearly conscious of it, that feeling bordering as it were on hatred and so well expressed by the word 'aversion'.

Still, should his sheep's scab cause the shepherd to recoil? No. But what a sheep!

The good bishop felt confused. Sometimes he would start off in that direction, then return.

Finally there came a day when news spread through town that some sort of young shepherd who made himself useful to the member of the Convention in his lair had come to fetch a doctor: the old villain was dying, he had creeping paralysis, and would not survive the night. 'Thank God!' some people added.

The bishop took his staff, put on his overcoat because of his rather too threadbare cassock we have already referred to, and also because of the evening breeze that was bound to freshen before long, and set out.

The sun was sinking and almost touching the horizon when the bishop arrived in that shunned place. He realized with a certain pounding of his heart that he was close to the den. He strode across a ditch, came through a fence, lifted a barrier, entered an ill-tended vegetable garden, advanced a few steps quite boldly and all at once on the far side of the neglected plot behind some tall brambles he saw the lair.

It was a very low-built hut, stark, small and clean, with a vine attached to the front of it.

In front of the door in an old chair on wheels, the peasant's armchair, sat a man with white hair smiling at the sun.

By the old man stood a young boy, the shepherd lad. He was offering the old man a bowl of milk.

While the bishop watched, the old man spoke aloud. 'Thank you,' he said, 'I don't need anything more.' And his smile turned from the sun to rest on the child.

The bishop moved forward. At the sound of his footsteps the seated old man looked round and his face expressed all the surprise a man is capable of after a long life.

'This is the first time since I've been here,' he said, 'that anyone has come to my house. Who are you, monsieur?'

The bishop answered, 'My name is Bienvenu Myriel.'

'Bienvenu Myriel? I've heard that name. Are you the man the people call Monseigneur Bienvenu?'

'I am.'

The old man resumed with a half-smile, 'In that case you're my bishop?'

'Indeed.'

'Come in, monsieur.'

The member of the Convention offered his hand to the bishop but the bishop did not take it. All he said was, 'I'm glad to see I was misinformed. You certainly don't look ill to me.'

'Monsieur,' replied the old man, 'I'm going to get better.' He paused and said, 'I shall be dead in three hours' time.' Then he went on, 'I'm something of a doctor. I know how the end comes. Yesterday only my feet were cold. Today the chill is in my knees. Now I feel it rising to my waist. When it reaches my heart, I shall cease to be. Isn't the sun splendid? I had myself wheeled out here to take a last look at things. You can talk to me, it doesn't tire me. You do well to come and watch a man who's going to die. It's right there should be witnesses to that moment. We all have our own little fancies – I'd like to have lasted till dawn. But I know I have barely three hours left. It'll be dark. Anyway, what difference does it make! Dying is a simple matter. There's no need for daylight. Very well then. I shall die by starlight.'

The old man turned to the shepherd.

'You get to bed. You stayed up with me all last night. You're tired.'
The young lad went inside.

The old man's eyes followed him, and as though talking to himself he added, 'While he sleeps I shall die. Our two forms of rest can be good company for each other.'

The bishop was not affected by this as might have been expected. He did not think there was any sense of God in this manner of dying. To tell the whole truth, for the little inconsistencies of the great-hearted need to be signalled like everything else: he who was so quick to laugh at His Highness, when the occasion arose, was rather shocked not to be addressed as Monseigneur and was almost tempted to reply 'citizen'. He had an inclination to be ungraciously familiar, which was common enough in doctors and priests but not typical of him. After all, this man, this member of the Convention, this representative of the people, had been one of the mighty of this world. For perhaps the first time in his life the bishop felt in the mood to be stern.

Meanwhile, the member of the Convention had been looking at him with unassuming friendliness in which might have been discerned the appropriate humility in one so close to his return to dust.

Although he generally guarded against curiosity – as he saw it, bordering on sin – the bishop for his part could not help studying the member of the Convention with an attentiveness that, seeing it did not spring from sympathy, his conscience would probably have reproached him for had it been directed at any other man. A member of the Convention struck him as being something of an outlaw, beyond even the laws of charity.

Composed, almost straight-backed, with a ringing voice, G was one of those great octogenarians that leave the physiologist amazed. The Revolution produced many of these men suited to the age. You could sense that this old man was a man who had stood the test. So near to his end, he had preserved all the signs of good health. In his clear gaze, his firm voice, the robust movement of his shoulders there was cause enough to perplex death. Azrael, the Mohammedan angel of the sepulchre, would have turned back and thought he had come to the wrong door. G seemed to be dying because that was what he wanted. There was freedom in his dying. Only his legs were immobile. By them the shades held fast to him. His feet were lifeless and cold, and his head was alive with all the power of life and appeared in full brightness. At this solemn moment G resembled the king in that oriental tale who is made of flesh above and of marble below.

There was a rock. The bishop sat on it. He began without preamble.

'I congratulate you,' he said in a tone of reproof. 'At least you didn't vote for the king's death.'

The member of the Convention did not seem to notice the bitter implication underlying the words 'at least'. He answered. The smile had completely disappeared from his face.

'Don't congratulate me unduly, monsieur. I did vote for the end of the tyrant.'

This was austereness of tone confronting sternness of tone.

'What do you mean?' said the bishop.

'I mean, man has a tyrant. Ignorance. I voted for the end of that tyrant. That tyrant begot royalty, which is authority falsely understood, while science is authority rightly understood. Man should be governed only by science.'

'And conscience,' added the bishop.

'It's the same thing. Conscience is the quantity of innate science we have within us.'

Monseigneur Bienvenu listened, somewhat surprised, to this language that was very new to him.

The member of the Convention went on, 'So far as Louis XVI was concerned, I said no. I didn't think I had the right to kill a man but I felt it my duty to exterminate evil. I voted for the end of the tyrant. That's to say, the end of prostitution for women, the end of slavery for men, the end of benightedness for children. In voting for the Republic, that's what I voted for. I voted for fraternity, reconciliation, a new dawn. I assisted in the overthrow of prejudice and error. The collapse of prejudice and error creates light. We brought down the old world, and the old world, that vessel of misery, in being overturned on the human race, has become an urn of joy.'

'Not unmixed joy,' said the bishop.

'You could say clouded joy, and now after that disastrous return of the past called 1814, vanished joy! Alas! the work wasn't finished, I admit: we destroyed the old order in its deeds, we were not able entirely to abolish it in its thoughts. To put an end to abuses is not enough, attitudes must change. The mill has gone, the wind is still there.'

'You've brought about destruction. Destruction can be useful but I distrust destruction compounded with anger.'

'Justice has its anger, monsieur l'évêque, and the anger of justice is an element of progress. In any case, and whatever anyone may say, the French Revolution is the greatest step forward taken by the human race since the advent of Christ. Unfinished, maybe, but sublime. It has worked out all the unknowns in the social equation. It has tempered minds, calmed, appeased, enlightened. It has sent tides of civilization sweeping across the earth. It has been a good thing. The French Revolution is the consecration of humanity.'

The bishop could not refrain from murmuring, 'Oh yes? And 1793!'

The member of the Convention straightened up in his chair with almost lugubrious solemnity, and in so far as a dying man is capable of crying out, he cried out, 'Ah, there you are! 1793! I was expecting to hear that. A cloud gathered for fifteen hundred years. At the end of fifteen centuries it burst. And you put the thunderbolt on trial.'

Without perhaps admitting it to himself, the bishop felt that something within him was extinguished. Nevertheless, he put on a brave face. He replied, 'The judge speaks in the name of justice. The priest speaks in the name of pity, which is nothing but a higher form of justice. A thunderbolt must not be misplaced.' And gazing steadily at the member of the Convention he added, 'Louis XVII?'

The Convention member reached out his hand and seized the bishop by the arm. 'Louis XVII! Come now! Who is it that you mourn? Is it the innocent child? In that case, very well, I mourn with you. Is it the royal child? I need to think about that. For me, Cartouche's brother, an innocent child hanged by the arms until dead in Place de Grève for the sole crime of being the brother of Cartouche, is no less cause for sorrow than Louis XV's grandson, an innocent child martyred in the tower of the Temple prison for the sole crime of being the grandson of Louis XV.'

'Monsieur,' said the bishop, 'I don't like this association of these names.'

'Cartouche? Louis XV? Which of them do you speak for?'

There was a moment's silence. The bishop almost regretted having come and yet he felt vaguely and strangely unsettled.

The member of the Convention went on: 'Ah, monsieur le prêtre, you don't like the plainness of truth. Christ did. He seized a rod and cleared the Temple. His scourge replete with flashes of lightning was a rough speaker of truths. When he cried *Sinite parvulos**, he made no distinction between little children. He'd have had no misgiving in seeing a kinship between the heir of Barabbas and the heir of Herod. Innocence, monsieur, is its own crown. Innocence has nothing to do with being royal. It's just as majestic in rags as in the fleur-de-lys.'

'That's true,' said the bishop in a quiet voice.

'I cannot let the matter drop,' continued Member of the Convention G. 'You mentioned Louis XVII. Let's be clear. Shall we weep for

---

* 'Suffer the little children': Matthew 19:14.

every innocent, every martyr, every child, the lowly as well as the exalted? I'm with you. But then, as I said, we must go back further than '93 and our tears must start before Louis XVII. I'll weep with you over the children of kings as long as you weep with me over the youngsters of the people.'

'I weep for all,' said the bishop.

'Equally!' cried G. 'And if the balance must tip one way or the other, let it be on the side of the people. They've been suffering for longer.'

There was another silence. It was the member of the Convention who broke it. He raised himself on one elbow, pinched his cheek between his thumb and his crooked forefinger, as you unconsciously do when you question and judge, and with his eyes filled with all the energies of a man close to death, he challenged the bishop. It was like an explosion.

'Yes, monsieur, it's a long time that the people have been suffering. And besides, that's not all – why do you come here to question me and talk to me about Louis XVII? I don't know you. Ever since I've been in this part of the world I've lived alone in this enclave, never setting foot outside, seeing no one but that child who helps me. It's true, your name has vaguely come to my knowledge, spoken of not too badly, I have to say, but that doesn't mean anything. Clever individuals have so many ways of deceiving the honest man of the people. By the way, I didn't hear the sound of your carriage, you no doubt left it over there, behind the trees where the road divides. I just don't know you. You told me you were the bishop, but that doesn't tell me anything about your moral character. So I repeat my question. Who are you? You're a bishop. That's to say, a prince of the Church, one of those gilded, emblazoned men of means who have fat stipends – the bishopric of Digne, fifteen thousand francs fixed salary, ten thousand in additional income, total: twenty-five thousand francs – who have kitchens, who have liveried servants, who live well, who eat moorhen on Friday, who go parading around in a ceremonial coach with a footman in front, a footman behind, who have palaces, who keep their own carriage in the name of Jesus Christ who went barefoot! You're a cleric; revenues, palaces, horses, servants, a good table, all the pleasures of life – you have that just like the rest of them. And like the rest of them, you enjoy it, well and good, but that's either saying too much or not enough. It doesn't shed any light for me on the intrinsic and essential worth of someone who comes to me with the probable intention of bringing me wisdom. Who am I speaking to? Who are you?'

41

The bishop hung his head and replied, '*Vermis sum*.*'

'An earthworm in a carriage?' muttered the member of the Convention.

It was the turn of the member of the Convention to be human and of the bishop to be humble.

The bishop replied quietly, 'Maybe so. But explain to me how my carriage, standing near by behind those trees, my good table and the moorhens I eat on Fridays, my twenty-five thousand francs' income, my palace and my footmen prove that we are not bound to be merciful and that '93 was not pitiless.'

The member of the Convention wiped his hand across his brow as though to brush away a cloud.

'Before answering,' he said, 'I beg your pardon. I behaved badly just now. You're in my home, you're my guest. I owe it to you to be courteous. You're debating my ideas and I should confine myself to attacking your arguments. Your wealth and your pleasures are advantages I hold against you in the debate, but it's good manners not to exploit them. I promise not to resort to doing so again.'

'Thank you,' said the bishop.

G continued: 'Let's return to that explanation you were asking for. Where were we? What were you saying? That '93 was pitiless?'

'Pitiless, yes,' said the bishop. 'What do you think of Marat clapping his hands at the guillotine?'

'What do you think of Bossuet singing the *Te Deum* to celebrate the *dragonnades*?'

The retort was a harsh one, but it found its mark with the sureness of a steel-tipped blade. The bishop winced. He had no answer but he was offended by this reference to Bossuet. The best of minds have their idols and sometimes feel vaguely hurt by logic's want of respect.

The member of the Convention began to pant. The asthma that affects the man close to death, mingling with his last gasps, broke his voice. Yet there was still a perfect lucidity of spirit in his eyes. He went on: 'Let's say a few more words about this and that, by all means. Leaving aside the Revolution, which taken as a whole is a tremendous assertion of humanity, '93 is, alas! a response. You consider it pitiless – but what of the entire monarchy, monsieur? Carrier is a villain, but what do you call Montrevel? Fouquier-Tinville is a scoundrel, but what's your opinion of Lamoignon-Bâville? Maillard is dreadful,

---

* Psalm 22:6: 'Ego autem sum vermis, et non homo; opprobrium hominum, et abjectio plebis', 'But I am a worm, and no man: a reproach of men and despised of the people.'

but Saulx-Tavannes, if you please? Père Duchêne is vicious, but how would you describe Père Letellier? Jourdan-Coupe-Tête is a monster, but a lesser one than the Marquis de Louvois. Monsieur, monsieur, I feel sorry for archduchess and queen Marie-Antoinette, but I also feel sorry for that poor Huguenot woman who, in 1685, under Louis the Great, monsieur, while nursing her child was tied to a stake, naked to the waist, and the child taken from her. Her breast was swollen with milk and her heart with anguish. Pale and famished, the child close to dying saw that breast and cried. And giving the woman the choice between the death of her child and the death of her conscience the executioner said to that nursing mother, "Recant!" What do you say to that Tantalus torture being applied to a mother? Just remember this, monsieur, the French Revolution had its reasons. Its anger will be forgiven by the future. It has resulted in a better world. Out of its most terrible deeds comes a cherishing of humankind. I won't go on. I'll stop there, I have the winning hand. Besides, I'm dying.'

And ceasing to gaze at the bishop, the member of the Convention concluded his argument with these few calm words: 'Yes, the brutalities of progress are called revolutions. When they are over, what we recognize is this: the human race has had a rough time, but it has advanced.'

The member of the Convention did not suspect that he had taken by storm the bishop's every successive inner retrenchment, one after the other. However, there remained yet one more, and from this retrenchment, the last redoubt of Monseigneur Bienvenu's resistance, came this reply in which nearly all his original asperity returned.

'Progress must believe in God. Good cannot be served by the ungodly. The atheist is a bad guide for the human race.'

The old representative of the people did not reply. A tremor went through him. He looked up at the sky and a tear slowly gathered in that upturned gaze. The tear, filling his eye, trickled down his pallid cheek, and talking to himself in an undertone, his gaze lost in the remote depths, he said almost stammering, 'O you the ideal! You alone exist!'

The bishop experienced a sort of inexpressible turmoil.

After a pause the old man raised a finger skywards and said, 'The infinite exists. It is there. If the infinite had no selfhood, selfhood would set a limit upon it; it would not be infinite. In other words there would be no such thing. Yet exist it does. So it has a self. That selfhood of the infinite is God.'

The dying man delivered these last words in a loud voice and with a shiver of ecstasy, as if he could see someone. After he had spoken, his eyes closed. The effort had exhausted him. It was obvious he had just lived the few hours of life left to him within the space of a minute.

43

What he had just said had brought him closer to the presence of death. His end was near.

The bishop realized this; time was running out, it was as a priest that he had come. From extreme coldness he had passed by degrees to extreme emotion. He looked at those closed eyes, he took that icy wrinkled old hand in his and bent over the dying man.

'This moment belongs to God. Do you not think it would be a pity if we were to have met in vain?'

The member of the Convention opened his eyes again. A gravity in which there was sorrow was imprinted on his countenance.

'Monsieur l'évêque,' said he with a slowness that perhaps owed more to his dignity of soul than his failing strength, 'I've spent my life in meditation, study and contemplation. I was sixty years of age when my country called me and bid me become involved in its affairs. I obeyed. There were abuses, I fought against them. There were tyrannies, I destroyed them. There were rights and principles, I proclaimed and upheld them. The territory was invaded, I defended it. France was threatened, I was prepared to die for her. I was not rich. I am poor. I was one of the rulers of the state: the vaults of the treasury were so full of coin, its walls, about to burst with the pressure of gold and silver, had to be reinforced; I used to dine in Rue de l'Arbre-Sec for twenty-two sous. I've helped the oppressed, I've comforted those who were suffering. I've torn the cloth from the altar, it's true, but I did so to bind the wounds of my country. I've always supported the onward march of the human race towards the light, and I've sometimes resisted ruthless progress. I have on occasion protected my own adversaries, your people. And there is at Peteghem, in Flanders, at the very spot where the Merovingian kings had their summer palace, an Urbanist convent, the abbey of Ste-Claire de Beaulieu, which I saved in 1793. I've done my duty to the best of my ability and whatever good I was able to do. After which I was pursued, hounded, persecuted, vilified, mocked, decried, cursed, ostracized. For quite some years now, white-haired as I am, I've been conscious that a great many people think they have the right to despise me. The poor ignorant mob sees me as damned. And I accept without hating anyone this isolation of hatred. I'm now eighty-six years old. I'm about to die. What is it you want of me?'

'Your blessing,' said the bishop. And he knelt down.

When the bishop looked up again the member of the Convention's expression had become majestic. He had just breathed his last.

The bishop returned home, deeply absorbed in who knows what thoughts. He spent the whole night in prayer. The next day a few good people of an inquisitive nature attempted to speak to him about

Member of the Convention G. He simply pointed heavenward. From then on, his kindness towards the humble and the unfortunate and his fellow-feeling for them increased.

Any reference to 'that old villain G' caused him to fall into a peculiar abstraction. No one could say that the passing of that soul before his own, and the reflection of that great conscience on his own, did not somehow contribute to his approach to perfection.

That 'pastoral visit' naturally gave rise to a good deal of murmuring among all the little local cliques.

'Was that the proper place for a bishop, at the bedside of a dying man such as he? There was obviously no prospect of any conversion. All those Revolutionaries are relapsed heretics. So why go there? What did he go to see? He must have been very curious to witness a soul carried off by the devil.'

One day a dowager of that impertinent breed that considers itself witty came out with this sarcastic remark, 'Monseigneur, people are wondering when Your Grace will be wearing the red cap!'

'Oh! now there's a colour that covers a multitude of sins,' replied the bishop. 'Fortunately those who despise it in a cap respect it in a hat.'

XI
One Reservation

We would be in great danger of deceiving ourselves if we were to conclude from this that Monseigneur Bienvenu was 'a philosopher bishop' or 'a patriot parish priest'. His encounter, we might almost call it a convergence, with Member of the Convention G left him with a sort of wonder that made him yet more kindly. That is all.

Although Monseigneur Bienvenu could not have been less of a politician, this is perhaps the place to outline very briefly what his position was with regard to the events of that time, assuming that Monseigneur Bienvenu ever thought of having a position.

So let us go back a few years.

Some time after Monsieur Myriel was raised to the episcopacy the emperor had made him a baron of the Empire, at the same time as several other bishops. The arrest of the pope took place, as we all know, on the night of the fifth to the sixth of July 1809. Monsieur Myriel was summoned by Napoleon to the synod of bishops of France and Italy, convened in Paris thereafter. This synod was held at Notre-Dame and met for the first time on the fifteenth of June 1811, under the presidency of Cardinal Fesch. Monsieur Myriel was one of the ninety-five bishops who attended it. But he was present only at one sitting and at three or four private discussions. Bishop of a mountain diocese, living in rural simplicity so close to nature, he apparently introduced among these eminent men ideas that altered the temperature of the assembly. He very soon came back to Digne. He was asked about his speedy return and he replied, 'I disturbed them. The air from outside reached them through me. I had the effect of an open door on them.'

On another occasion he said, 'What can you expect? Those gentlemen are princes. I'm just a poor country bishop.'

The fact is that he caused offence. Among other strange things, one evening when he was at the house of one of his most distinguished colleagues he is supposed to have let slip the remark: 'Such beautiful clocks! Such beautiful carpets! Such beautiful liveries! They must be very disturbing. Oh, I wouldn't want to have all these luxuries crying constantly in my ears, "There are people who are hungry! There are people who are cold! There are poor people! There are poor people!"'

Let us say, by the way, that hatred of luxury would not be an intelligent hatred. It is a hatred that would imply hatred of the arts. Nevertheless, other than for official and ceremonial purposes, luxury among churchmen is a transgression. It would seem to reveal habits of little true charitableness. A wealthy priest is a contradiction in terms. The priest ought to remain close to the poor. Now, is it possible to be constantly in contact, night and day, with every hardship, every adversity, every want, without getting a little of that saintly poverty on oneself, like the dust of honest toil? Is it imaginable for a man to be near a brazier and not be warm? Is it imaginable for a workman to be labouring constantly at a furnace and to have neither a singed hair, nor a blackened nail, nor a drop of sweat, nor a speck of ash on his face? The first proof of charity in a priest, in a bishop especially, is poverty.

This is no doubt what the bishop of Digne thought.

It would be mistaken to think, however, that on certain delicate issues he shared what we shall call the 'ideas of the century'. He was little involved in the theological quarrels of the day and remained silent on matters regarding the Church and the state. But had he been strongly pressed, we probably would have found he was rather more ultramontane than Gallican. Since we are presenting a portrait and do not wish to conceal anything, we are compelled to add that he had no sympathy for Napoleon in his decline. From 1813 he supported or applauded every demonstration of opposition. The bishop refused to see him on his way through France after his return from the island of Elba, and declined to ordain that public prayers be said for the emperor in his diocese during the Hundred Days.

Apart from his sister, Mademoiselle Baptistine, the bishop had two brothers, one a general, the other a prefect. He wrote quite frequently to both of them. He was for a while censorious towards the former, because while holding a command in Provence at the time of the landing at Cannes the general had led twelve hundred men in pursuit of the emperor like someone who wanted to let him escape. His correspondence remained more affectionate with the other brother, the former prefect, an honest and decent man who lived in retirement in Paris, on Rue Cassette.

So Monseigneur Bienvenu too had his hour of partisan feeling, his hour of bitterness, his dark cloud. The passions of the day created a passing shadow in this noble and gentle spirit devoted to things eternal. Certainly, such a man would have done well not to have any political opinions. Let there be no misunderstanding of what we think: we do not confuse what are called 'political opinions' with the grand aspiration for progress, with the sublime, patriotic, democratic, humane faith, which today ought to be the very foundation of all generous understanding. Without delving into questions only indirectly connected with the subject of this book, we simply say this: it would have been a fine thing if Monseigneur Bienvenu had not been a royalist and if his gaze had never for one moment been directed away from that serene contemplation of those three pure lights – truth, justice and charity – that are distinctly visible shining above the stormy comings and goings of human affairs.

While granting it was not for political office that God created Monseigneur Bienvenu, we might have understood and admired in him protest in the name of legality and liberty, proud opposition, legitimate but perilous resistance to the all-powerful Napoleon. But what pleases us in the treatment of those on their way up is less pleasing in the treatment of those on their way down. We approve of fighting only so long as there is danger, and in any case only those who fought in the first instance have the right to be exterminators at the last. He who has not been a persistent opponent in times of prosperity should remain silent when the downfall comes. Challenging success gives the only legitimacy to prosecuting failure. For our own part, when Providence intervenes, let it strike where it will. The year 1812 starts to disarm us. In 1813 the cowardly breach of silence on the part of a reticent legislative body emboldened by catastrophe was worthy of nothing but indignation, and it was wrong to applaud it. In 1814, confronted with those treacherous marshals, with that Senate going from one baseness to the next, disparaging the once deified, with that idolatry in retreat spitting on its idol, it was a moral obligation to avert one's gaze. In

1815, when ultimate disaster was in the air, when France shuddered at its sinister approach, when Waterloo could be dimly discerned lying in wait for Napoleon, there was nothing derisory about the mournful cheers from the army and from the people for the man destined to fall. And with all due reservation with regard to the despot, a man of such sensibility as the bishop of Digne should not perhaps have failed to recognize what was noble and affecting in the close embrace of a great nation and a great man on the brink of ruin.

With this one shortcoming, he was in all things just, sincere, fair, intelligent, humble and worthy, doing good and being kind, which is another way of doing good. He was a priest, a man of wisdom and humanity. It must be said that even in that political opinion for which we have just criticized him, and which we are inclined to judge almost severely, he was tolerant and easy-going, more so perhaps than the person who writes these words.

The doorkeeper at the town hall had been given this position by the emperor. He was an elderly non-commissioned officer of the Old Guard, awarded the Legion of Honour at Austerlitz, as Bonapartist as the eagle. This poor fellow occasionally came out with some ill-considered remarks that the law of the day deemed seditious talk. After the imperial profile disappeared from the Legion of Honour he never wore his 'regimentals', as he used to say, so that he would not have to wear his cross. He had himself solemnly removed the imperial effigy from the cross Napoleon had given him, which left a hole, and he would not put anything in its place. 'I'd sooner die,' he said, 'than wear the three toads over my heart!' He had a readiness to mock Louis XVIII aloud. 'Gouty old man in his English gaiters! Let him go to Prussia in his pig-tailed wig!' he would say, delighted to unite in the same denunciation the two things he most detested, Prussia and England. As a result he ended up losing his position. There he was, with no livelihood, out on the street with his wife and children. The bishop sent for him, mildly scolded him and made him verger of the cathedral.

Monsieur Myriel was a true pastor, a friend to everyone in the diocese.

Over the course of nine years Monseigneur Bienvenu had by his saintly deeds and kindly ways filled the town of Digne with a sort of affectionate and filial veneration. Even his attitude towards Napoleon had been accepted and tacitly pardoned, so to speak, by the people, his flock of frail good-hearted souls who adored their emperor but loved their bishop.

Monseigneur Bienvenu's Isolation

A bishop is nearly always surrounded by a troop of minor clerics, like a bunch of young officers around a general. They are what the delightful St Francis of Sales calls somewhere 'beardless boy-priests'. Every profession has its aspiring apprentices who form the retinue of those who have already risen. No power is without its entourage, no fortune without its courtiers. Those seeking a future flurry around present splendour. Every archbishop has his general staff. Every bishop of the slightest influence has about him his patrol squad of cherubim-seminarists that do their rounds of the episcopal palace, maintaining order, and mount guard around Monseigneur's smile. To please a bishop is to get your foot on the ladder for a subdeaconry. A man must make his way. An apostle is not above a sinecure.

Just as elsewhere there are bigwigs, in the Church there are big mitres. These are the bishops who enjoy royal favour, who are astute, wealthy, with a good income and a place in society, who doubtless know how to pray but also how to crave favours. None too scrupulous about turning the whole diocese, represented in their person, into a hanger-on, point of contact between the sacristy and the Church's higher echelons, they are more holders of church livings than priests, more ecclesiastical dignitaries than bishops. Happy those who come within their orbit! Being persons of influence, they shower on those around them, on the zealous and the favoured, and on all that youthful willingness to please, rich parishes, prebends, archdeaconries, chaplaincies and cathedral appointments in the expectation of episcopal honours. As they advance themselves, they cause their satellites to progress also. It is an entire solar system on the move. Their radiance spreads its purple glow over their suite. Their prosperity is dispersed in nice little preferments to those in its orbit. The larger the patron's diocese, the richer his favourite's living. And then, there is Rome. A bishop who manages to become an archbishop, an archbishop who manages to become a cardinal, takes you along with him as a conclavist. You are admitted to the Rota, you receive the pallium, and then you are an auditor, then a chamberlain, then a monsignor; and from Your Grace to Your Eminence is only one step, and between Your Eminence and Your Holiness there is but the smoke of a ballot. Every skullcap may dream of the papal crown. Nowadays the priest is the only man who may properly become king. And what a king! The supreme king. So what a hotbed of aspirations is a seminary! How many blushing choristers, how many young priests, like Perrette with her pot of milk, build castles in the air! How quick ambition is to call itself vocation, in good faith perhaps, deceiving itself in its sanctimonious complacency – who can tell?

Humble, poor, untypical, Monseigneur Bienvenu was not one of the big mitres. This was obvious from the complete absence of young priests about him. We have seen that he 'did not get on' in Paris. Not one clerical future dreamed of grafting itself on to this solitary old man. Not a single sprouting ambition was so foolish as to grow in his shade. His canons and vicars-general were good-hearted old men, of rather humble origin like him, like him cut off in this diocese that led to no cardinalship – with this difference in their resemblance to their bishop: they were finished, he was fulfilled. So well did they sense the impossibility of prospering with Monseigneur Bienvenu that no sooner had the young men ordained by him left the seminary than they would obtain a recommendation to the archbishop of Aix or of Auch and be off very quickly. For after all, we say it again, a man wants to be brought on. A saint who lives an excessively self-denying life makes a dangerous neighbour. He might pass on to you through infectiousness an incurable poverty, a stiffening of those joints useful for self-advancement, and in short more self-denial than you want. And people flee this contagious virtue. Hence the isolation of Monseigneur Bienvenu. We live in a dismal society. Succeed – that is the lesson drip-dripping down from the corruption at the top.

Let it be said in passing, success is a fairly hideous thing. Its false resemblance to merit deceives men. For the masses, success has almost the same profile as supremacy. Success, talent's seeming double, has a dupe: history. Juvenal and Tacitus alone decry it. In our day, a more or less official philosophy has joined its household staff, wears the livery of success, and runs its antechamber. Principle of success: prosperity implies capability. Win the lottery and you are a clever man. Whoever wins is respected. Be born lucky, that is all. If luck is yours, the rest will follow. Be fortunate and you will be thought great. Leaving aside five or six outstanding exceptions who are the glory of their age, contemporary admiration is mere short-sightedness. Gilding is gold. Being a nonentity is no obstacle, as long as you make a name for yourself. The undistinguished is an old Narcissus who adores himself and celebrates the undistinguished. The great genius that makes a man a Moses, an Aeschylus, a Dante, a Michelangelo or a Napoleon, the multitude is quick to recognize by acclamation in any Tom, Dick or Harry who achieves whatever his goal might be. Let a notary transform himself into a deputy, let a spurious Corneille write *Tiridate*, let a eunuch manage to acquire a harem, let a military Prudhomme accidentally win the decisive battle of an era, let an apothecary invent cardboard soles for the Sambre-et-Meuse army and out of this cardboard sold as leather build up for himself an income of four hundred thousand francs, let a pedlar espouse usury and beget seven or eight millions, of which he is the father and usury the mother; let a preacher become bishop by virtue of droning on, let the steward of a good family be so rich on retiring from service that he is made minister of finance – men call this Genius, just as they call Mousqueton's face Beauty and Claudius' bull neck Majesty. They mistake for the constellations in the infinity of space the star-shaped footprints left by ducks in the soft wetland mud.

XIII
What He Believed

We need not go into the bishop of Digne's orthodoxy in terms of Church doctrine. In the presence of such a soul, we are inclined to feel nothing but respect. The good man's conscience must be taken at his word. In any case we recognize that, given a certain disposition, all the glories of human virtue may develop in a person with beliefs different from our own.

What did he think of this dogma, or that mystery? These secrets of the inner self are known only to the grave, where souls go bared. What we are sure of is that for him the difficulties of faith were never resolved by hypocrisy. There is no possibility of corruption in a diamond. He believed as much as he could. *Credo in patrem**! he often exclaimed. And he drew from good works all the satisfaction that conscience needs, a satisfaction that whispers to you, 'You're with God!'

What we do feel bound to point out is that outside, as it were, and beyond his faith the bishop possessed a surfeit of love. It was because of this, *quia multum amavit*†, that he was criticized by 'serious-minded men', 'responsible individuals' and 'reasonable people', favourite expressions in our sad world where egotism takes its cue from pedantry. What was this surfeit of love? It was a serene benevolence, flowing over mankind as we have already mentioned, and on occasion extending even to things. He lived without scorn. He was kind to God's creation. Every man, even the best of men, has within him a

* 'I believe in the Father'.
† An allusion to Luke 7:47, 'Her sins, which are many, are forgiven; *for she loved much.*'

thoughtless callousness reserved for animals. The bishop of Digne did not have this callousness, typical in fact of many priests. He did not go as far as the Brahmin, but he seemed to have meditated on this text from Ecclesiastes: 'Who knows where the spirit of the beast goes?' Physical unsightlinesses, aberrations of instinct, did not disturb him and did not offend him. He was moved almost to pity by them. He seemed thoughtfully to seek the cause, explanation or excuse for them beyond the visible world. At times it seemed as if he were asking God to go easier on them. He examined without anger, and with the eye of a linguist deciphering a palimpsest, the great chaos that still exists in nature. This study sometimes elicited strange words from him. He was in his garden one morning. He thought he was alone but his sister was walking behind him and he did not see her. All of a sudden he paused and gazed at something on the ground. It was a horrible large, black, hairy spider. His sister heard him say, 'Poor creature! It's not to blame!'

Why not relate these childish expressions of almost divine goodness? Infantile if you will, but these sublime infantilisms were those of St Francis of Assisi and Marcus Aurelius. One day he sprained his ankle trying not to step on an ant.

Such was the life of this good man. Sometimes he fell asleep in his garden and then he was as venerable as could be.

If the stories told about him in his youth and even in his maturity were to be believed, Monseigneur Bienvenu had in the past been a passionate, perhaps violent man. His universal kindness was not so much a natural instinct as the result of a strong conviction that had penetrated his heart through the filter of life, a conviction slowly instilled in him, thought by thought. For as drops of water may wear holes in a rock, so it is with character. These grooves are indelible. These formations are indestructible.

In 1815, as we have already said, he was close on seventy-five but looked no more than sixty. He was not tall. He was a little overweight, and to combat this he gladly went on long walks. He was sure-footed and only very slightly stooped, not that we presume to draw any conclusion from this detail. Gregory XVI at the age of eighty was upright and smiling, which did not prevent him from being a bad bishop. Monseigneur Bienvenu was what in common parlance is called a 'good-looking man', but his face was so kindly people forgot about his good looks.

When he chatted with that childish gaiety that was one of his charms and of which we have already spoken, people felt at ease in his company. His entire being seemed to exude joy. His fresh, ruddy complexion, the full set of fine white teeth he still had, which showed when he smiled, gave him that open and easy-going manner which, in a grown man, prompts the remark, 'He's a good lad', and in an old man, 'He's a good fellow.' This, it will be recalled, was the effect he produced on Napoleon. To begin with, and to anyone seeing him for the first time, he was not much more than that, a 'good fellow'. But if you were to remain for a few hours in his company, and ever saw him pensive, the 'good fellow' was gradually transfigured, becoming somehow imposing. His broad, earnest forehead to which his white hair lent nobility was ennobled also by reflection. Majesty emanated from this goodness, while the goodness radiated without ceasing. You experienced something of the emotion you might feel if you saw a smiling angel slowly unfold its wings without ceasing to smile. Respect, an ineffable respect, gradually overcame you and made your heart swell, and you felt that you had before you one of those strong, proven, forgiving souls whose magnanimity is so great it cannot be other than gentle.

As we have seen, every day of his life was filled with prayer, celebrating religious rites, alms-giving, consoling the afflicted, cultivating a patch of land, fraternity, frugality, hospitality, self-denial, trust, study, work. And 'filled' is the appropriate word. The bishop's day was indeed quite full to the brim – of good thoughts, good words and good deeds. Nevertheless, it was not complete if cold or rainy weather prevented him from spending an hour or two in his garden before going to bed at night, after the two women had retired. It seemed to be a kind of ritual for him to prepare for sleep with some contemplative thought in the presence of the spectacular wonders of the nocturnal sky. Sometimes, even quite late at night, if the two elderly women were not asleep they would hear him strolling along the garden paths. There he was, by himself, meditative, peaceful, worshipful, comparing the serenity of his heart with the serenity of the heavens, stirred in the darkness by the visible splendour of the constellations and the invisible splendour of God, opening his soul to thoughts descending from the Unknown. At such moments, offering up his heart when nocturnal flowers offer up their perfume, like a lighted lamp in the middle of the starry night, shining in ecstasy amid the universal radiance of creation, he himself probably could not have said what was happening in his spirit. He felt something soar out of him and something descend upon him. Mysterious exchanges between the chasms of the soul and the chasms of the universe!

He thought of the greatness and presence of God; of the strange mystery of eternity to come and, stranger still, the mystery of past eternity; of all the infinities reaching out before his eyes in every direction. And without seeking to comprehend the incomprehensible, he gazed on it. He did not study God, he yielded to the radiance of God. He considered these magnificent conjunctions of atoms that lend appearances to matter, reveal forces by putting them into effect, create individuality within unity, proportion within the continuum of space, the numberless within the infinite; and produce beauty through light. There is a continuous binding and loosening of these conjunctions. Hence, life and death.

He would sit on a wooden bench with his back against a ramshackle trellis and gaze at the stars through the silhouetted shapes of his puny and stunted fruit trees. He cherished this quarter of an acre, so poorly planted, so cluttered with sheds and tumbledown outhouses, and was content with it.

What further need had this old man who divided the little free time there was in his life between gardening during the day and contemplation at night? Was not this small enclosure, with the heavens for a ceiling, enough for him to be able to worship God in his most delightful works and his most sublime works, each in turn? Was not all here, in fact – what more could anyone wish for? A little garden in which to stroll and boundless space for dreaming. At his feet, what a man may grow and pick, and above his head, what he may study and meditate on: a few flowers in the ground and all the stars in the firmament.

XIV
What He Thought

One last word.

Since details of this kind might give the bishop of Digne, particularly at the present time, a somewhat 'pantheistic' cast, to use a currently fashionable term, and lead to the belief, whether to his credit or discredit, that he entertained one of those personal philosophies peculiar to our century that sometimes germinate in solitary spirits, developing and growing until they replace religion, this we insist on: not one of those who knew Monseigneur Bienvenu would have considered themselves entitled to think anything of the sort. What illuminated this man was the heart. His wisdom was constituted of the light that comes from there.

No abstract theories, many practical deeds. Abstruse speculations have something dizzying about them. Nothing suggests that he ventured into apocalyptic speculations. The apostle may be bold but the bishop must be timid. He would probably have had qualms about exploring too deeply certain problems reserved, as it were, for great revolutionary minds. There is an inviolable horror at the portals of the enigma. Those dark openings stand there gaping, but something tells you, one of life's passers-by, not to enter. Woe to whoever goes in there! Geniuses, in the uncharted depths of abstraction and pure speculation, placed so to speak above all doctrines, propose their ideas to God. Their prayer daringly invites discussion. Their adoration is questioning. This is direct religion, full of anxiety and responsibility for whoever attempts its challenges.

Human thought knows no boundary. At its peril it analyses and explores its own bedazzlement. One might almost say that in a splendid reaction, of sorts, it thereby dazzles nature. The mysterious world that surrounds us returns what it receives. The contemplators are probably contemplated. However that may be, there are on earth men – are they men? – who perceive distinctly, on dreamings' far horizons, the heights of the Absolute and behold the awesome sight of the infinite mountain. Monseigneur Bienvenu was not one of these men. Monseigneur Bienvenu was no genius. He would have feared those sublime peaks from which some, even the very great among them such as Swedenborg and Pascal, have slipped into insanity. Certainly, these powerful conceits have their moral usefulness and by these arduous paths one may approach ideal perfection. But he took the shorter path: the Gospel.

He did not attempt to impart to his chasuble the folds of Elijah's mantle. He cast no future light on the mysterious uncertainty of events. He did not seek to condense the lustre of things into a burning flame. There was nothing of the prophet and nothing of the mage about him. This humble soul loved, that's all.

It is probable he invested in prayer a superhuman level of aspiration, but it is no more possible to pray too much than it is to love too much; and if it were a heresy to pray beyond the texts, St Teresa and St Jerome would be heretics.

He felt for whatever suffers and expiates. The universe seemed to him an immense sickness. He was aware of fever everywhere, everywhere he heard the sound of suffering, and without seeking to understand the mystery he strove to dress the wound. The fearful spectacle of created things fostered compassion in him. His sole concern was to find for himself and to inspire in others the best way to pity and comfort. What exists was for this good and exceptional priest a permanent cause of a sorrow seeking to console.

There are men who toil to extract gold. He toiled to extract pity. Universal wretchedness was his mine. Suffering everywhere was but an opportunity for kindness always. 'Love one another': he declared this to be wholly sufficient, wished for nothing more, and herein lay his entire doctrine.

One day the man who considered himself a 'philosopher', that senator mentioned above, said to the bishop, 'Just look at the spectacle the world presents: everyone at war with everyone else; the mightiest is the most canny. Your "Love one another" is an absurdity.'

'Well,' replied Monseigneur Bienvenu without arguing, 'if it is an absurdity, the soul ought to wrap itself up inside it like the pearl in the oyster.' So did he wrap himself up in it, and lived his life there, absolutely content to do so, leaving aside the stupendous questions that lure and appal, the limitless perspectives of abstraction, the precipices of metaphysics; all those profundities converging, for the apostle, in God; for the atheist, in nothingness: destiny, good and evil, the warring of human beings against each other, man's consciousness, the pensive somnambulism of animals, transformation by death, the compendium of existences contained in the tomb, the incomprehensible grafting of successive loves on the enduring self, essence, substance, Being and Non-being, the soul, nature, freedom, necessity. Unscalable problems, dangerous obscurities on which the gigantic archangels of the human mind turn their attention. Dreadful abysses that Lucretius, Manu, St Paul and Dante contemplate with that blazing eye, gazing intently on the infinite, and there seeming to bring stars into being.

Monseigneur Bienvenu was simply a man who noted the mysterious questions from the outside, but without studying them, without debating them and without troubling his own mind over them, and who had in his soul a serious respect for the unknown.

BOOK TWO
THE FALL

I
The Evening after a Day's Walking

Early in the month of October 1815, about an hour before sunset, a man travelling on foot entered the little town of Digne. The few inhabitants who were at their windows or at the doors of their houses at the time viewed this wayfarer with a kind of unease. It would be hard to come across a more wretched-looking passer-by. He was a man of average height, stocky and robust, in the prime of life. He might have been forty-six or forty-eight years old. A cap with its leather peak pulled down partly concealed his weather-beaten face streaming with sweat. His shirt of coarse yellow cloth, fastened at the neck with a small silver anchor, revealed a glimpse of his hairy chest. He wore a rolled-up neckerchief, threadbare blue drill trousers with one knee faded to white and a hole in the other, a ragged old grey overall patched on one elbow with a bit of green cloth sewn on with twine, a soldier's knapsack on his back that was stuffed full, firmly buckled and brand-new; a huge knotted stick in his hand, hobnailed shoes on his stockingless feet, a shaven head and a long beard.

The sweat, the heat, the journey on foot, the dust, added an indefinable disreputability to this shabby outfit.

His head was shaven yet bristling, for his hair had begun to grow a little and looked as if it had not been cut for some time.

No one knew him. He was obviously just someone passing through. Where did he come from? The south. The coast, perhaps. For he came into Digne by the same route that seven months earlier had witnessed the passage of the emperor Napoleon on his way from Cannes to Paris. This man must have been walking all day. He looked very tired. Some women down in the old part of town had seen him stop under the trees on Boulevard Gassendi and drink at the fountain that stands at the end of the parade. He must have been very thirsty, for the children who followed him saw him stop again two hundred paces further on to drink at the fountain in the market-place.

When he came to the corner of Rue Poichevert he turned left and made for the town hall. He went inside, then emerged a quarter of an hour later. A gendarme was seated near the doorway on the stone bench that General Drouot had climbed on to, on the fourth of March, to read out to the dismayed crowd of Digne's inhabitants the Gulf of Juan proclamation. The man pulled off his cap and bowed humbly to the gendarme.

Without responding to his bow, the gendarme watched him closely, following him with his gaze for a while, then entered the town hall.

In those days there was at Digne a fine inn called the Croix-de-Colbas. The landlord of this inn was a certain Jacquin Labarre, a man respected in the town for being related to another Labarre who was innkeeper of the Trois-Dauphins at Grenoble and had served in the Guides corps. At the time of the emperor's landing there were many rumours circulating locally about this Trois-Dauphins inn. The story was that General Bertrand, disguised as a carter, had made frequent trips there during the month of January, distributing Legion of Honour crosses to soldiers and fistfuls of gold napoleons to respectable citizens. The fact is that when the emperor entered Grenoble he refused to be put up in the prefectural residence. He thanked the mayor, saying, 'I'm going to stay with a good man I know.' And he had gone to the Trois-Dauphins. The glory of this Labarre of the Trois-Dauphins was reflected on to the Labarre of the Croix-de-Colbas a hundred miles away. People in the town said of him, 'He's the cousin of the one at Grenoble.'

The man made his way towards this inn, which was the best there was in that part of the world. He entered the kitchen, which gave directly on to the street. All the ovens were lit. A huge fire blazed cheerfully in the fireplace. The host, who was also the cook, was very busy, to-ing and fro-ing between the hearth and his saucepans, overseeing an excellent dinner intended for some carters who could be heard laughing and talking loudly in an adjoining room. Anyone who has ever travelled knows that none enjoy better fare than carters. A fat marmot, flanked by white partridges and black grouse, was turning on a long spit in front of the fire. Cooking on the range were two large carp from Lake Lauzet and a trout from Lake Alloz.

Hearing the door open and a newcomer enter, the host said without looking up from his cooking range, 'What would monsieur be wanting?'

'Food and lodging,' said the man.

'Nothing easier,' replied the host. At that moment he looked round, took in the traveller's appearance with a single glance and added, '– if it's paid for.'

The man drew a large leather purse from the pocket of his overall and replied, 'I have money.'

'In that case we're at your service,' said the host.

The man put his purse back in his pocket, removed his knapsack, put it on the ground by the door, kept his stick in his hand, and went and sat on a low stool close to the fire. Digne is in the mountains. October evenings are cold there.

Meanwhile, the host went back and forth, observing the traveller.

'Will dinner be ready soon?' said the man.

'Shortly,' replied the landlord.

While the newcomer was warming himself with his back turned, the worthy host Jacquin Labarre drew a pencil from his pocket, then tore off the corner of an old newspaper left lying on a small table by the window. In the blank margin he wrote a line or two, folded it without sealing it and handed this scrap of paper to a youngster who apparently served him as both kitchen help and errand boy. The landlord whispered a word in the kitchen lad's ear and the youngster went running off in the direction of the town hall.

The traveller had seen nothing of all this.

Once again he enquired, 'Will dinner be ready soon?'

'Shortly,' said the host.

The child returned. He brought back the piece of paper. The host unfolded it eagerly, like someone expecting a reply. He appeared to read with close attention, then nodded, and remained thoughtful for a moment. Eventually he took a step towards the traveller, who looked deep in somewhat troubled thought.

'Monsieur,' he said, 'I can't give you a room.'

The man half rose from his seat.

'What! Are you afraid I won't pay? Do you want me to pay in advance? I have money, I tell you.'

'It's not that.'

'What then?'

'You have money—'

'Yes,' said the man.

'But I,' said the host, 'have no room.'

The man answered calmly, 'Put me in the stable.'

'I can't.'

'Why not?'

'The horses take up all the space.'

'Very well,' replied the man, 'a corner in the loft then. A bale of hay. We'll see about it after dinner.'

'I can't serve you dinner.'

This declaration, made in a measured but firm tone, sounded serious to the stranger. He stood up.

'But I'm starving. I've been on the road since sunrise. I've walked thirty miles. I can pay. I want to eat.'

'I have nothing,' said the landlord.

The man burst out laughing and turned towards the fireplace and the cooking range. 'Nothing! And what's all that?'

'I've already taken orders for all that.'

'From whom?'

'The carters.'

'How many are they?'

'Twelve.'

'There's enough food there for twenty.'

'They've ordered the whole lot and paid for it in advance.'

The man sat down again and said without raising his voice, 'I'm here at the inn, I'm hungry, and I'm staying.'

Then the host bent down to his ear and said in a tone that made him start, 'Be on your way!'

The traveller was leaning forward at that moment and poking some brands in the fire with the iron tip of his staff. He whipped round and as he opened his mouth to reply the host gazed steadily at him and added, still in a low voice, 'Look, enough of this talk. Do you want me to tell you what your name is? Your name's Jean Valjean. Now do you want me to tell you who you are? When I saw you come in I suspected something. I sent a message to the town hall and this was the reply I received. Can you read?'

So saying, he held out to the stranger the piece of paper, now unfolded, that had just made the journey from the inn to the town hall, and from the town hall back to the inn. The man glanced at it.

After a pause the landlord went on, 'I make a habit of being polite to everyone. Be on your way!'*

The man bowed his head, picked up the knapsack he had set on the ground and went away.

He followed the main street. He walked on aimlessly, keeping close to the houses, like a man humiliated and dejected. Not once did he turn round. Had he done so he would have seen the innkeeper of the Croix-de-Colbas standing on his threshold, surrounded by all the travellers at his inn and all the passers-by in the street, talking animat-

---

* The landlord's politeness resides in continuing to address Jean Valjean using the *vous* form of the verb.

edly and pointing at him, and he could have told from the group's expressions of suspicion and fear that before long his arrival would be the talk of the whole town.

He saw nothing of all this. The oppressed do not look behind them. They know only too well the ill fate that dogs them.

He kept walking like this for some time, on and on, following at random streets unknown to him, forgetting his weariness, as is the way with those who are despondent. Suddenly he felt extremely hungry. Darkness was falling. He looked about him to see if he could not find some shelter.

The grand hotel had closed its doors to him. He sought some very humble tavern, some very lowly doss-house.

As it happened there was a light shining at the end of the street. A pine branch hanging from an iron bracket was outlined against the pale twilight sky. He made his way there.

It was indeed a tavern. The tavern in Rue de Chaffaut.

The traveller paused for a moment and looked through the window into the tavern's low-ceilinged room, lit by a small lamp on a table and by a big fire in the hearth. A few men were drinking around it. The landlord was warming himself at it. Above the flames simmered an iron pot, suspended from a hook.

There are two doors to this tavern, which is also an inn of sorts. One opens on to the street, the other on to a small yard filled with manure. The traveller dared not enter by the street door. He slipped into the yard, paused again, then raised the latch timidly and pushed open the door.

'Who goes there?' said the master.

'Someone who'd like some supper and a bed.'

'You've come to the right place. There's supper and a bed here.'

He entered. All the people drinking turned round. The lamp lit him from one side, the fire from the other. They studied him for a while as he took off his knapsack.

The host said to him, 'There's a fire here. Supper's cooking in the pot. Come and warm yourself, comrade.'

He went and sat close to the hearth. He stretched out his feet, aching with tiredness, in front of the fire. An appetizing smell came from the pot. All that could be seen of his face under his pulled-down cap took on a vague air of well-being, mingled with that other very poignant expression imparted by the habit of suffering.

Moreover, this was a strong, determined, sad face, with a strange cast of countenance. It started off looking humble and ended up

61

seeming hard. His eyes gleamed beneath his eyebrows like fire in the undergrowth.

However, one of the men sitting at a table was a fishmonger who before coming into the tavern in Rue de Chaffaut had been to stable his horse at Labarre's. As chance would have it he had that very morning encountered this sinister-looking stranger on the road between Bras d'Asse and – I have forgotten the name . . . I think it was Escoublon. Now, as he passed by, the man, who already looked very tired, had asked the fishmonger to let him ride behind him on his horse. To which the fishmonger's only reply had been to quicken his pace. This fishmonger had half an hour earlier been among the group in the company of Jacquin Labarre and had himself related to the people at the Croix-de-Colbas his unpleasant encounter of that morning. From where he sat he signalled discreetly to the tavern-keeper. The tavern-keeper went over to him. They exchanged a few quiet words. Once again the man had become deeply absorbed.

The tavern-keeper returned to the fireplace, clapped his hand on the man's shoulder and said to him, 'You're going to make yourself scarce!'*

The stranger turned round and replied quietly, 'Ah! You know?'

'Yes.'

'I was turned away from the other inn.'

'And you're being thrown out of this one.'

'Where do you expect me to go?'

'Somewhere else.'

The man took his stick and his knapsack and left.

As he came out some children who had followed him from the Croix-de-Colbas, and who seemed to be waiting for him, threw stones at him. He turned round angrily and threatened them with his stick. The children scattered like a flock of birds.

He passed in front of the prison. At the door there was an iron chain hanging down, attached to a bell. He rang the bell.

A grille opened.

'Turnkey,' he said, respectfully removing his cap, 'would you kindly let me in and give me a lodging for the night?'

A voice replied, 'A prison's not a hotel. Get yourself arrested. Then you'll be let in.'

The grille closed again.

He came into a little street where there are many gardens. Some

---

* The tavern-keeper here uses the *tu* form of the verb in addressing Jean Valjean: 'Tu vas t'en aller d'ici.' There is a poignancy in Jean Valjean's continuing to address the tavern-keeper as 'vous': 'Ah! vous savez?'

have only hedges around them, which makes the street more attractive. Among these gardens and hedges he saw a small single-storey house with a light in the window. He looked through the window as he had at the tavern. Inside was a large whitewashed room that had a bed with a chintz bedspread over it and a cradle in one corner, a few wooden chairs, and a double-barrelled gun hanging on the wall. A table was laid in the centre of the room. A copper lamp shed light on the coarse white linen tablecloth, the pewter jug gleaming like silver and filled with wine, and the steaming brown soup tureen. At this table sat a man of about forty with an open and cheerful face, dandling a small child on his knees. Close by, a very young woman was nursing another child. The father was laughing, the child was laughing, the mother was smiling.

The stranger stood musing for a moment before this heartwarming and comforting scene. What was going on inside him? Only he could have said. It is likely that he thought this happy home would be hospitable, and that in a place where he saw so much well-being he would find perhaps a little pity.

He gave a faint little tap on the window-pane.

No one heard.

He knocked again.

He heard the woman say, 'Husband, I think someone's knocking.'

'No,' replied the husband.

He knocked a third time.

The husband rose, took the lamp, went to the door and opened it.

He was a tall man, half peasant-farmer, half artisan. He wore a huge leather apron that came right up to his left shoulder, and bulging round his middle with a hammer, a red handkerchief, a powder-horn, all kinds of objects tucked into the belt used as a pocket. He tilted his head back, with his shirt spread wide open baring his white bull neck. He had thick eyebrows, enormous black whiskers, prominent eyes, a muzzle-like jaw, and overlying all this that air of being a man in his own home, which is something no words can convey.

'Forgive me, monsieur,' said the traveller. 'In exchange for payment, could you give me a plate of soup and a corner where I could sleep in that shed there in the garden? Could you, monsieur? In exchange for payment?'

'Who are you?' asked the master of the house.

The man replied, 'I've come from Puy-Moisson. I've been walking all day. I've done thirty-six miles. Could you? For payment?'

'I wouldn't refuse lodging to any respectable person who would pay me,' said the peasant. 'But why don't you go to an inn?'

'There's no room.'

'Bah! Impossible. There's no fair today, and it's not market day. Have you been to Labarre?'

'Yes.'

'Well?'

The traveller replied with confusion, 'I don't know, he had no room for me.'

'Have you been to what's-his-name in Rue de Chaffaut?'

The stranger's confusion increased. He stammered, 'He had no room for me either.'

The peasant's face took on an expression of suspicion. He looked the newcomer up and down, and abruptly exclaimed with a kind of shudder, 'Would you be the man?'

He took another look at the stranger, stepped back three paces, placed the lamp on the table, and took down his gun from the wall.

Meanwhile, at the words the peasant had spoken – 'Would you be the man?' – the woman had risen, picked up both children in her arms and rushed to take refuge behind her husband, staring at the stranger in terror, her bosom uncovered and with fear in her eyes, murmuring quietly, *'Tso-maraude*.'*

All this happened in less time than it takes to imagine it. Having stared at the man for a few moments the way you stare at a viper, the master of the house came to the door again and said, 'Clear off!'

'For pity's sake, a glass of water,' said the man.

'Over my dead body!' said the peasant.

Then he slammed the door and the man heard him slide two large bolts. A moment later the window shutter closed and the sound of an iron bar being inserted was audible from outside.

It was getting darker. The cold Alpine wind was blowing. In the fading daylight the stranger noticed in one of the gardens that lined the street a kind of hut that seemed to be made of clods of turf. He walked resolutely through a wooden gate and found himself in the garden. He went over to the hut. It had a very low, narrow opening for a doorway, and it looked like those sheds that road labourers build for themselves by the side of the road. No doubt he thought it was actually a road-mender's hut. He was suffering from cold and hunger. Hunger he was resigned to, but this at least was shelter from the cold. This sort of shed is not usually occupied at night. He threw himself flat on his stomach and crept into the hut. It was warm inside and he found a reasonably good bed of straw. He lay for a moment stretched

* Hugo's footnote: Dialect of the French Alps, meaning 'stray cat'.

out on this bed, incapable of any movement, so exhausted was he. Then, as the knapsack on his back felt uncomfortable and as it would do for a pillow, he started unbuckling one of the straps. At that moment he heard a ferocious growl. He looked up. The head of an enormous mastiff loomed out of the darkness in the entrance to the hut.

It was a dog's kennel.

He was himself strong and fearsome. He armed himself with his stick, used his knapsack for a shield, and exited from the kennel as best he could, not without worsening the tears in his ragged clothes.

He also exited from the garden, but backwards, obliged to keep the dog at bay by resorting to that manoeuvre with his stick that masters of this type of fencing call 'the covered rose'.

When he had got through the gate, not without difficulty, and found himself in the street again, alone, homeless, with no roof over his head, no shelter, driven out even from that bed of straw and that miserable kennel, he collapsed on a stone rather than sat on it, and apparently a passer-by heard him cry out, 'I'm not even a dog!'

Soon he stood up and started walking again. He left the town, hoping to find some tree or haystack in the fields where he could take shelter.

So for a while he trudged on, the whole time with his head bowed. When he felt that he was far from all human habitation he looked up and gazed around him. He was in a field. Before him was one of those low hills covered with close-cropped stubble that after the harvest look like shaved heads.

The horizon was pitch-black. It was not only the darkness of night but very low cloud that seemed to rest on the hill itself and, mounting, to fill the whole sky. However, as the moon was about to rise and there still remained a lingering glow of twilight overhead, these clouds formed a kind of pale vault high in the sky that cast a luminous reflection on to the earth.

So the earth was lighter than the sky, which is a peculiarly sinister effect, and the hill, squat and dwarfish in shape, appeared indistinct and pallid against the gloomy horizon. The whole effect was ugly, small, dismal and closed-in. Nothing in the field or on the hill but a misshapen tree, rustling in its writhings a few steps away from the traveller.

This man was obviously very far from having those discerning habits of mind and soul that make a person sensitive to the mysterious aspects of things. Nevertheless, there was something in that sky, that hill, that plain and that tree, something so profoundly desolate that after standing there motionless for a moment, lost in thought, he suddenly turned round and walked back. There are moments when nature seems hostile.

He retraced his steps. The gates of Digne were closed. Digne, which had withstood sieges during the wars of religion, was still surrounded in 1815 by ancient walls flanked by square towers that have since been demolished. He slipped through a gap and re-entered the town.

It might have been eight o'clock in the evening. Since the streets were unfamiliar to him, he resumed his aimless wandering.

This brought him to the Prefecture, then to the seminary. As he walked past the cathedral, crossing the square in front of it, he shook his fist at it.

At the corner of this square is a printing works. Here were first printed the proclamations to the army issued by the emperor and the Imperial Guard, which were brought from the island of Elba and dictated by Napoleon himself.

Utterly worn out and his hopes exhausted, he lay down on the stone bench that stands at the door of this printing house.

At that moment an old lady came out of the church. She saw the man lying in the dark. 'What are you doing there, my friend?' she said.

He answered harshly and angrily, 'As you can see, good lady, I'm going to sleep here.'

The good lady in question, who fully deserved to be so called, was Madame la Marquise de R.

'On this bench?' she said.

'I've had a wooden mattress for nineteen years,' said the man. 'Now I have a stone mattress.'

'You were a soldier?'

'Yes, good lady. A soldier.'

'Why don't you go to an inn?'

'Because I have no money.'

'Unfortunately,' said Madame de R, 'I have only four sous in my purse.'

'Give them to me anyway.'

The man took the four sous.

Madame de R continued, 'You can't pay for lodgings at an inn with so little. But have you actually tried? You can't possibly spend the night here. You must be cold and hungry. Someone might give you a bed out of charity.'

'I've knocked at every door.'

66

'Well?'

'I've been turned away everywhere.'

The 'good lady' touched the man's arm and pointed out to him on the far side of the square a small, low-roofed house that stood beside the episcopal palace.

'You've knocked at every door?' she said.

'Yes.'

'Have you knocked at that one?'

'No.'

'Knock there.'

II
Wisdom Is Advised to Be Prudent

That evening, after he had taken a walk in town, the bishop of Digne remained closeted in his room until rather late. He was busy at his great work on 'Duty', which sadly was never completed. He was carefully analysing everything the Church Fathers and Doctors have said on this important subject. His book was divided into two parts: first, the duties of all, second, the duties of the individual, each according to his station. The duties of all are the highest duties, of which there are four. St Matthew identifies them: duties to God (Matthew 6), to oneself (5:29, 30), to one's neighbour (7:12), to animals (6:20, 25). As for the other duties, the bishop had found them identified and laid down elsewhere: to sovereigns and subjects, in the Epistle to the Romans; to magistrates, wives, mothers and young men, by St Peter; to husbands, fathers, children and servants, in the Epistle to the Ephesians; to the faithful, in the Epistle to the Hebrews; to virgins, in the Epistle to the Corinthians. He was laboriously combining all these precepts into a harmonious spiritual ensemble that he wanted to offer his readers.

At eight o'clock he was still at work, writing rather awkwardly on little squares of paper with a large book open on his lap, when Madame Magloire came in as usual to get the silverware from the cupboard by his bed. A moment later, aware that the table was set and that he might be keeping his sister waiting, the bishop closed his book, rose from his desk, and went into the dining room.

The dining room was rectangular, with a fireplace and (as we have said) a door opening on to the street and a window overlooking the garden.

Madame Magloire had indeed almost finished setting the table.

While busy at her task she chatted to Mademoiselle Baptistine.

A lamp stood on the table. The table was close to the hearth. Quite a good fire was going.

You can easily picture these two women, both over sixty years of age: Madame Magloire, small, plump, bright; Mademoiselle Baptistine, gentle, slight, frail, a little taller than her brother, dressed in a silk gown of brownish purple, a colour fashionable in 1806 when she bought it in Paris, that she was still getting some wear out of. To put it crudely, in terms that have the merit of conveying in a word an idea hardly to be expressed in less than a page, Madame Magloire looked like a peasant and Mademoiselle Baptistine like a lady. Madame Magloire wore a white ruched cap, a small gold cross round her neck, the only piece of women's jewellery in the house; a very white shawl tucked into a gown of homespun black cloth with short wide sleeves, a red-and-green chequered apron tied round the waist with a green ribbon, and a bib of the same fabric attached at the upper corners with two pins; heavy shoes and yellow stockings on her feet, like the women of Marseille. Mademoiselle Baptistine's gown was cut to the patterns of 1806, with a high waist, narrow skirt, shoulder-capped sleeves, tape ties and buttons. She concealed her grey hair under a curled wig in the so-called *à l'enfant* style*. Madame Magloire looked intelligent, brisk and good-hearted. The unequally upturned corners of her mouth and an upper lip that was fuller than the lower one gave a suggestion of brusqueness and bossiness to her appearance. So long as Monseigneur remained silent she spoke to him firmly with a mixture of respect and boldness, but as soon as Monseigneur began to speak, as we have seen, she meekly obeyed like her mistress. Mademoiselle Baptistine did not even speak. She confined herself to obeying and trying to please him. She had never been pretty, even when young. She had big, bulging blue eyes and a long hooked nose, but as we said at the beginning her whole face, her whole person, emanated an ineffable goodness. She was always destined for goodness, but faith, hope and charity, those three virtues that gently nurture the soul, had gradually promoted goodness to saintliness. She was but a lamb by nature; religion had made an angel of her. Poor sainted virgin! Now fondly remembered!

Mademoiselle Baptistine so often related what happened at the bishop's residence that evening that there are several people still alive who remember her account of it in every detail.

When the bishop came in, Madame Magloire was talking with some animation. She was speaking to Mademoiselle Baptistine about

---

* A hairstyle of some simplicity (*enfant* meaning 'child') invented for Marie-Antoinette by her hairdresser when her hair started thinning after childbirth.

a favourite topic of hers, one with which the bishop was familiar. And that was the front-door latch.

Apparently, while doing a little shopping for supper, Madame Magloire had heard rumours in various places. There was talk of some sinister-looking individual prowling around; according to which, some suspicious vagrant had turned up, he was bound to be somewhere in the town, and there could well be some nasty encounters in store for those who might take it into their heads to go home late that night. And the police were not to be relied on, given that the prefect and the mayor did not get on and tried to discredit each other by provoking incidents. So it was up to law-abiding folk to do the work of the police and to protect themselves, and they should make sure they closed up properly, and bolted and barred their houses, and locked their doors securely.

Madame Magloire emphasized those last words. But the bishop had been rather cold in his room and when he came in he sat down in front of the fireplace to warm himself, and in any case he was thinking of something else. He did not respond to the pointed remark Madame Magloire had just made. She repeated it. Then, wanting to satisfy Madame Magloire without upsetting her brother, Mademoiselle Baptistine timidly ventured, 'Did you hear what Madame Magloire was saying, brother?'

'I did vaguely hear something,' replied the bishop. Then half turning in his chair, placing both hands on his knees and with his amiable and readily cheerful face lit from below by the fire, looking up at the old servant he said, 'Now then, what's the matter? What's the matter? We're in some great danger, are we?'

So Madame Magloire told the whole story all over again, unintentionally exaggerating a little. It would seem that a gypsy, a tramp, some sort of dangerous beggar, was at this moment in town. He had turned up at the inn looking for lodgings but Jacquin Labarre had sent him away. He was seen coming along Boulevard Gassendi and roaming the streets at dusk. A desperado with a terrible face.

'Really?' said the bishop.

This willingness to question her encouraged Madame Magloire. She thought it suggested the bishop was about to become alarmed. She continued triumphantly, 'Yes, Monseigneur. That's the way it is. Something terrible will happen in town tonight. Everyone says so. What with the police not to be relied on' (something worth repeating). 'Honestly, living up here in the mountains and not even having streetlights at night! You go out – well, it's pitch-black! And, Monseigneur, I say and Mademoiselle here too says—'

'I say nothing,' his sister broke in. 'Whatever my brother does is done as it should be.'

Madame Magloire carried on as if no protest had been made. 'We say this house isn't at all safe, that with Monseigneur's permission I'll go and tell Paulin Musebois the locksmith to come and put the old bolts back on the door – we have them right here, it'll only take a minute – and I say bolts are needed, Monseigneur, if only for tonight, for nothing's more terrible, I say, than a door with a latch that can be opened from the outside by anyone that happens to pass by, what with it being Monseigneur's habit always to say come in – not that anyone needs to ask permission, God help us, even in the middle of the night!'

At that moment someone rapped at the door quite violently.

'Come in,' said the bishop.

III
The Heroism of Passive Obedience

The door opened.

It burst wide open as though someone had pushed it with energy and determination.

A man came in.

We already know the man. He was the traveller we saw earlier, wandering about in search of shelter.

He entered, took one step forward, and halted, leaving the door open behind him. He had his knapsack on his shoulder, his staff in his hand, a boorish, insolent, weary and violent expression in his eyes. The fire in the hearth lighted him. He looked dreadful. This was a sinister apparition.

Madame Magloire had not even the strength to utter a cry. She trembled and stood there gaping. Mademoiselle Baptistine turned round, saw the man who came in, and half started up in terror, then slowly turning her head back towards the hearth she began to observe her brother and her face became once more profoundly calm and serene.

The bishop eyed the man with tranquillity.

As he opened his mouth – no doubt to ask the newcomer what he wanted – the man rested both hands on his staff, took stock of the old man and the two women in turn, and without waiting for the bishop to speak said in a loud voice, 'Listen. My name's Jean Valjean. I'm an ex-convict. I've spent nineteen years in chains. I was freed four days ago and I'm on my way to Pontarlier, which is my destination. Four days I've been walking from Toulon. I've done thirty-six miles on foot today. When I arrived here this evening, I went to an inn. They turned me away because of my yellow passport that I'd shown at the town hall – I had to. I went to another inn. They said to me: "Clear off!" The same everywhere. No one would have me. I went to the prison, the turnkey wouldn't let me in. I was in a dog kennel. The dog bit me and chased me away as if it were a man. It seemed to know who I was. I went out into the countryside to sleep under the stars. There were no stars. I thought it would rain, and there was no good Lord to prevent the rain. I came back into town to shelter in a doorway. Out there, in the square, I was lying down to sleep on a stone bench. A woman pointed out your house and told me, "Knock there!" I knocked. What is this place? Is it an inn? I have money, my savings. One hundred and nine francs fifteen sous that I earned for the nineteen years' work I did on the chain gang. I'll pay. Why shouldn't I? I have money. I'm very tired, thirty-six miles on foot, and I'm hungry. Will you let me stay?'

'Madame Magloire,' said the bishop, 'will you set another place.'

The man took three steps and moved towards the lamp that was on the table. 'Wait,' he said, as if he had not properly understood, 'you've got me wrong. Did you hear? I'm an ex-convict. Sentenced to hard labour. I come from the prison hulks.'

He drew from his pocket a large sheet of yellow paper, which he unfolded. 'Here's my passport. Yellow, as you see. It serves to get me driven out everywhere I go. Do you want to read it? I can read. I learned in the hulks. They have a school there for those that want to learn. Listen, this is what they put on my passport: "Jean Valjean, freed convict, native of—" – that's of no interest to you – "has served nineteen years in chains. Five years for theft with breaking and entering. Fourteen years for trying to escape four times. This man is very dangerous." There! Everyone has thrown me out. Will you people let me stay? Is this an inn? Will you give me something to eat and a place to sleep? Have you a stable?'

'Madame Magloire,' said the bishop, 'you will put clean sheets on the bed in the alcove.'

We have already described the nature of both women's obedience. Madame Magloire left the room to carry out these instructions.

The bishop turned to the man. 'Sit down, monsieur, and warm yourself. We're going to have supper in a while and a bed will be made up for you while you eat.'

Now the man understood completely. The expression on his face, till now sullen and obdurate, reflected stupefaction, doubt, joy, and became extraordinary. He began stammering like a lunatic.

'Really? You mean you're letting me stay? You're not turning me away? An ex-convict! You call me monsieur! You treat me with respect! "Clear off, you dog!" is what I'm always told. I thought you would surely turn me away. That's why I told you at once who I am. Oh, she was a good soul, that woman who directed me here! I'm going to eat tonight! A bed! A bed with a mattress and sheets! Like everyone else! A bed! It's nineteen years since I slept in a bed! You really don't want me to go! What fine people you are! In any case, I have money. I'll pay well. Forgive me, innkeeper, what's your name? I'll pay anything you ask. You're a good man. You're an innkeeper, aren't you?'

'I'm a priest who lives here,' replied the bishop.

'A priest!' said the man. 'Oh, a good honest priest! So you're not asking any money of me? The parish priest, are you? Of this big church? Well, how stupid of me! Of course! I hadn't noticed your skull-cap.'

While speaking, he had dropped his knapsack and staff in a corner, then put his passport back in his pocket, and sat down. Mademoiselle Baptistine observed him kindly.

He continued. 'You're human, monsieur le curé. You've no contempt. A good priest, that's a very good thing. So there's no need for me to pay you?'

'No,' said the bishop, 'keep your money. You have how much? Did you not say one hundred and nine francs?'

'And fifteen sous,' the man added.

'One hundred and nine francs and fifteen sous. And how long did it take you to earn that?'

'Nineteen years.'

'Nineteen years!' The bishop sighed deeply.

The man went on, 'I still have all my money. In the past four days I've spent only twenty-five sous, which I earned by helping unload some wagons at Grasse. Seeing as you're a churchman, I'm going to tell you, we had a chaplain in the hulks. And one day I saw a bishop. Monseigneur is what they call him. He was the bishop of La Majore at Marseille. He's the priest who's above the parish priests. You know, I'm sorry, I put it badly, but for me it's so remote! You understand, for the likes of us! He said mass in the middle of the hulks, on an altar, he had a pointed thing, made of gold, on his head. It glittered in the mid-day sun. We were lined up on three sides, with cannons facing us, fuses lit. We couldn't see very well. He spoke but he was too far away, we couldn't hear. That's what a bishop is.'

While he was speaking the bishop went and shut the door that had been left wide open.

Madame Magloire returned. She brought a place setting that she put on the table.

'Madame Magloire,' said the bishop, 'put that place setting as near the fire as possible.' And turning to his guest, 'The night wind is bitter in the Alps. You must be cold, monsieur.'

Each time he uttered that word 'monsieur', in his mildly serious and educated voice, the man's face lit up. 'Monsieur' to a convict is like a glass of water to one of the shipwrecked survivors of the *Medusa*. Ignominy thirsts for respect.

'This lamp doesn't give much light,' said the bishop.

Madame Magloire understood, and went to fetch the two silver candlesticks from the mantelpiece in Monseigneur's bedroom and placed the lighted candles on the table.

'Monsieur le curé,' said the man, 'you're good-hearted. You don't treat me with contempt. You invite me into your home. You light your candles for me. Yet I've made no secret of where I come from and what a wretch I am.'

The bishop, sitting beside him, gently touched his hand. 'You didn't have to tell me who you were. This isn't my house, it's the house of Jesus Christ. This door does not ask whoever enters whether he has a name but whether he is in distress. You're in distress, you're hungry and thirsty: you're welcome here. And don't thank me, don't say I'm inviting you into my home. No one is at home here except whoever needs a refuge. I tell you, a passing visitor, this is your home more than mine. Everything here is yours. Why should I need to know your name? Besides, even before you told me, I already knew your name.'

The man eyes widened in astonishment. 'Really? You knew me by name?'

'Yes,' replied the bishop, 'by the name of "Brother".'

'Listen, monsieur le curé,' exclaimed the man, 'I was very hungry when I first came in, but you're so good I don't know what state I'm in now. My hunger's gone.'

The bishop looked at him and said, 'You've suffered a great deal?'

'Oh, the red jacket, the ball and chain, a plank to sleep on, the heat, the cold, the hard labour, the chain gang, the beatings! The double-chain punishment for no reason. Solitary confinement for one wrong word. Even sick in bed with the chain! Dogs, dogs are better off! Nineteen years! I'm forty-six. And now a yellow passport. There you have it.'

'Yes,' said the bishop, 'you come from a place of sorrow. Listen. There will be more joy in heaven over the tearful face of a repentant sinner than over the white robes of a hundred virtuous men. If you come away from that place of sorrow with thoughts of hatred and anger against mankind, you're deserving of pity. If you come away with benevolent thoughts, of kindness and peace, you're worth more than any of us.'

In the meantime Madame Magloire had served supper: soup made with water, oil, bread and salt, a little bacon, a piece of mutton, some figs, fresh cheese, and a large loaf of rye bread. She had on her own initiative added to the bishop's ordinary fare a bottle of aged Mauves wine.

The bishop's face suddenly took on that expression of geniality typical of those of a hospitable nature. 'Take your seats!' he said cheerfully. As was his custom when he had a guest at his evening meal, he sat the man on his right. Mademoiselle Baptistine sat on his left, perfectly calm and natural.

The bishop said grace, then as usual served the soup himself.

The man began to eat voraciously.

All at once the bishop said, 'But I think there's something missing from this table.'

Madame Magloire had indeed put out only the three place settings that were absolutely necessary. Now, it was the custom of the house when the bishop had anyone to supper to lay out on the tablecloth, in innocent display, all six sets of silverware. This gracious semblance of luxury was a kind of childishness full of charm in that sweetly austere household where poverty was elevated to the level of dignity.

Madame Magloire understood his remark, left the room without a word, and a moment later the three sets of silverware requested by the bishop were gleaming on the tablecloth, symmetrically arranged before each of the three at table.

IV
About the Cheese Dairies of Pontarlier

Now to give an idea of what occurred at that table, we could do no better than to transcribe here a passage from one of Mademoiselle Baptistine's letters to Madame de Boischevron, in which the conversation between the ex-convict and the bishop is related in ingenuous detail.

... This man paid no attention to anyone. He ate ravenously. However, after supper he said, 'Monsieur le curé, all this is still far too good for me, yet I must say the carters who wouldn't let me eat with them keep a better table than the good Lord's servant does.'

Between ourselves, this remark rather shocked me.

My brother replied, 'Their work is harder than mine.'

74

'No,' replied the man, 'they have more money. You're poor. I can see that. You may not even have your own parish. Do you actually have a parish? Now, if the good Lord were just, you certainly ought to!'

'The good Lord is more than just,' said my brother. A moment later he added, 'Monsieur Jean Valjean, it's Pontarlier you're headed for?'

'Under obligation to follow a fixed route.' I think that's what the man said. Then he went on, 'I must be on my way by daybreak tomorrow. It's no easy journey. While the nights are cold, the days are hot.'

'That's a good place you're going to,' said my brother. 'During the Revolution my family lost everything. I took refuge in Franche-Comté at first and for a while earned my living there by the sweat of my brow. I was willing enough. I found plenty of work. It's only a matter of choosing. There are paper mills, tanneries, distilleries, big watch-making factories, steel mills, copper works, at least twenty iron foundries, four of which – at Lods, Châtillon, Audincourt and Beure – are of a very considerable size . . .'

I think I am not mistaken in saying those are the names my brother mentioned, then he broke off and addressed me.

'My dear sister, have we not relatives in those parts?'

I replied, 'We did have some, among them Monsieur de Lucenet, who was captain of the gates at Pontarlier before the Revolution.'

'Yes,' replied my brother, 'but in '93 a man no longer had relatives, he had only his own pair of hands. I worked. In the Pontarlier region where you're going, Monsieur Valjean, they have an industry that goes back a very long way, and is quite fascinating, sister. It's their cheese dairies, which they call *fruitières*.'

Then, while encouraging the man to eat, my brother explained to him in great detail what these *fruitières* of Pontarlier were like. That there were two types: the big estates that belong to the rich, and where there are forty or fifty cows that produce seven or eight thousand cheeses every summer, and the co-operative *fruitières* that belong to the poor. These are the peasant-farmers at medium altitude who farm their cows jointly and share their produce. They hire a cheese-maker, whom they call the *grurin*. The *grurin* collects the milk from the joint contributors three times a day, and marks the quantities on a double-entry tally. It's towards the end of April that the work of the cheese dairies begins. And it's towards the middle of June that the cheese-makers take their cows up to the mountain pastures.

The man's spirits revived as he ate. My brother served him that good Mauves wine he does not drink himself because he says it is an expensive wine. My brother told him all these details with that relaxed cheerfulness you know he has, combining his words with thoughtfulness towards me.

He kept coming back to this honest job of *grurin*, as if, without saying so directly and without forcing this advice on him, he hoped the man would understand that it would offer him sanctuary. One thing struck me. This man was what I have told you. Well, apart from a few remarks about Jesus when he came in, my brother did not say a single word throughout the whole meal, or the entire evening, that might remind the man of what he was, or impress on him who my brother was. It was certainly an opportunity, on the face of it, for a bit of a sermon and for the bishop to impress himself on the ex-convict and leave his mark. It might have seemed to anyone else that now was the time, when he had the poor wretch right there, to nourish his soul as well as his body, and to voice either some censure leavened with moral instruction and advice, or a little pity with an exhortation to behave better in the future. My brother did not even ask him where he came from or about his past. For in his past lay his wrong-doing, and my brother seemed to avoid anything that might remind him of it. So much so that at one point, when my brother was talking about the mountain-dwellers of Pontarlier who have pleasant work close to heaven – and are happy, he added, because they are innocent – he stopped short, fearing there might be something to cause the man offence in this remark he had let slip. Having reflected on it, I believe I understand what was in my brother's heart. Doubtless he thought this man, who is called Jean Valjean, was only too well aware of his wretchedness. That the best thing was to distract him from it and, by behaving normally towards him, to make him think, if only for a moment, that he was like any other person. Is that not a real understanding of charity? Is there not, dear madame, something truly evangelical in such delicacy that refrains from sermonizing, moralizing and criticizing? And when a man has a sore point, is not the ultimate pity not to touch on it at all? It seemed to me this might have been my brother's inward thought. In any case, what I can say is that if he did have all these thoughts there was no way of telling, even for me. He was throughout no different from the way he is every evening, and he took his supper with this Jean Valjean in the same spirit and in the same manner as he would have taken his supper with Monsieur Gédéon Le Prévost or our local parish priest.

Towards the end of the meal, when we were eating the figs, there was a knock at the door. It was Madame Gerbaud with her little one in her arms. My brother kissed the child on the forehead and borrowed fifteen sous that I had on me to give to Madame Gerbaud. The man did not pay much attention in the meantime. He had stopped talking and looked very tired. Once poor old Madame Gerbaud had left, my brother said grace, then he turned to the man and said, 'You must be in much need of your bed.' Madame Magloire very quickly cleared the table. I understood we were supposed to retire to let this traveller sleep, and we both went upstairs. However, a moment later I sent Madame Magloire to take down for the man's bed a roe-deer skin from the Black Forest that I have in my room. The nights are freezing and it keeps you warm. It's a pity the skin is an old one, it's losing all its fur. My brother bought it while he was in Germany, at Tottlingen, close to the source of the Danube, as well as the little ivory-handled knife I use at table.

Madame Magloire came back upstairs almost immediately. We said our prayers in the room where we hang the laundry to dry, and then we went each to her own room without exchanging another word.

V

Tranquillity

After bidding his sister goodnight, Monseigneur Bienvenu took one of the two silver candlesticks from the table, handed the other to his guest and said to him, 'I'll show you to your room, monsieur.'

The man followed him.

As may have been noted from what was said above, the house was so arranged that to get to and from the chapel, where the alcove was, you had to pass through the bishop's bedroom.

Just as they passed through it, Madame Magloire was putting away the silverware in the bedside cupboard. This was the last task she performed every evening before going to bed.

The bishop installed his guest in the alcove. A bed had been made up there with clean white sheets. The man set the candlestick down on the small table.

'Well, I wish you goodnight,' said the bishop. 'Tomorrow morning before you set out, you shall have a cup of warm milk straight from our own cows.'

'Thank you, monsieur l'abbé,' said the man.

Hardly had he uttered these peaceful words than all of a sudden and without transition something strange came over him that, had they witnessed it, would have chilled the two sainted women with horror. Even to this day it is difficult for us to explain what was prompting him at that moment. Did he mean to convey a warning or issue a threat? Was he simply obeying an instinctive impulse of some sort, obscure even to himself? He turned abruptly to the old man, folded his arms and fixing his host with a fierce gaze he cried in a hoarse voice, 'I don't believe it! You take me in and give me a bed, right next to you, like this!'

He broke off, and added with a laugh that had something

monstrous about it, 'Have you really given this proper consideration? How do you know I'm not a murderer?'

The bishop looked up at the ceiling and replied, 'That's the concern of the good Lord.'

Then solemnly, and moving his lips like someone praying or talking to himself, he raised the two fingers of his right hand and blessed the man, who did not bow, and without turning his head and without looking back, he went to his room.

When the alcove was in use a big serge curtain, drawn across from one side of the chapel to the other, concealed the altar. The bishop knelt as he passed in front of this curtain and said a brief prayer. A moment later he was in his garden, strolling, musing, contemplating, his heart and soul wholly absorbed in those great mysterious things that God reveals at night to eyes that remain open.

As for the man, he truly was so tired that he did not even make the most of those clean white sheets. He snuffed out his candle with his nostril, the way convicts do, and dropping on to the bed fully dressed, immediately fell into a deep sleep.

Midnight struck as the bishop returned from the garden to his room.

A few minutes later the entire little household was asleep.

VI
Jean Valjean

In the middle of the night Jean Valjean woke up.

Jean Valjean came from a poor peasant family in Brie. As a child he had not learned to read. When he reached manhood he became a tree-pruner at Faverolles. His mother's name was Jeanne Mathieu. His father was called Jean Valjean or Vlajean – a nickname, probably, and a contraction of 'Voilà Jean'*.

Jean Valjean was a thoughtful individual without being gloomy, which is typical of those who are by nature affectionate. On the whole, however, Jean Valjean was, in appearance at least, a rather dozy and unremarkable creature. He had lost his father and mother at a very early age. His mother had died of milk fever that was not properly treated. His father, a tree-pruner like himself, was killed falling from a tree. Jean Valjean was left with only a widowed sister older than himself, who had seven children, boys and girls. This sister had brought up Jean Valjean and as long as she still had her husband she

---

* 'There's Jean'.

housed and fed her younger brother. The husband died. The eldest of the seven children was eight years old, the youngest, one.

Jean Valjean had just reached the age of twenty-five. He took the father's place, and he in turn supported the sister who had brought him up. This was done as a matter of course, as a duty, even a little churlishly, on the part of Jean Valjean. And so his youth was spent doing hard and ill-paid work. He was never known to have had any local 'sweetheart'. He had no time for being in love.

He would come home tired in the evening and eat his soup without uttering a word. His sister, mother Jeanne, often took the best part of his meal from his bowl as he ate – the piece of meat, the slice of bacon, the heart of the cabbage – to give to one of her children. Hunched over the table with his head almost in his soup, his long hair falling around his bowl and covering his eyes while he ate, he appeared not to notice and did nothing to stop her.

There was at Faverolles not far from the Valjeans' cottage, on the other side of the lane, a farmer's wife named Marie-Claude. The Valjean children, who were always hungry, sometimes used to go to Marie-Claude to ask for a pint of milk, supposedly for their mother, which they would drink behind a hedge or in some corner of the street, snatching the jug from each other, and they drank so quickly the little girls would spill it on their pinafores and down their little necks. If their mother had known about this cadging, she would have punished the culprits severely. Gruff and grumbling, Jean Valjean paid Marie-Claude for the pint of milk behind their mother's back, and the children were not punished.

He earned twenty-four sous a day in the pruning season and also hired himself out as hay-maker, labourer, farmhand, odd-job man. He did whatever he could. His sister worked also, but how to manage with seven young children? A sorry band they were, little by little engulfed, crushed, by poverty. Then came one hard winter. Jean had no work. The family had no bread. No bread. Literally. And seven children!

One Sunday evening Maubert Isabeau, baker on the church square at Faverolles, was getting ready for bed when he heard a violent smashing of his shuttered shop window. He arrived in time to see an arm reach inside a hole punched through the shutter and the window-pane. The arm grabbed a loaf of bread and made off with it. Isabeau rushed outside. The thief was running away as fast as his legs could carry him. Isabeau ran after him and caught him. The thief had thrown away the loaf but his arm was still bleeding. It was Jean Valjean.

This took place in 1795. Jean Valjean was brought before the law courts of the day for 'theft with breaking and entering an occupied house at night'. He had a shotgun and was a better shot with it than any marksman in the world, for he was a bit of a poacher. This went against him. There is a legitimate prejudice against poachers. The poacher, like the smuggler, is very much akin to the brigand. However, let us say in passing, there is still a gulf between this breed of men and the hideous urban murderer. The poacher lives in the forest, the smuggler lives in the mountains or on the sea. Towns produce vicious men because they produce corrupted men. The mountains, the sea, the forest produce men of the wild; they develop the wildness in them, but often without destroying their humanity.

Jean Valjean was found guilty. The terms of the Penal Code were mandatory. There are in our civilization dread moments; these are the times when the ruling of the penal system spells perdition. What a fateful moment it is when society distances itself and irredeemably casts adrift a thinking being! Jean Valjean was condemned to five years' hard labour.

On the twenty-second of April 1796 there were celebrations in Paris for the victory at Montenotte, won by the general-in-chief of the army in Italy who, in the message dated the second of Floréal in the year IV, sent by the Directory to the Five Hundred, is named as Buona-Parte. On that same day a great chain gang was put in irons at Bicêtre. Jean Valjean was part of that gang. A former turnkey at the prison, now close on ninety, still recalls perfectly the wretch who was chained to the end of the fourth line in the north corner of the courtyard. He was sitting on the ground like all the others. He seemed to have no understanding of his situation except that it was horrible. It is likely that amid the confused notions of a poor man knowing nothing, he also discerned something excessive in it. As the bolt was riveted into his iron collar with heavy hammer blows behind his head, he wept; his tears choked him, they prevented him from speaking, all he managed to say every now and then was 'I was a tree-pruner at Faverolles.' Then, still sobbing, he would raise his right hand and lower it seven times in progression, as though touching seven heads of unequal height one after the other, and from this gesture it was surmised that whatever he had done, he had done to clothe and feed seven young children.

He left for Toulon. He arrived there after twenty-seven days travelling on a cart with a chain round his neck. At Toulon he was clothed in the red jacket. Everything that had been his life till then was obliterated, his name included. He was not even Jean Valjean any more, he was number 24601. What became of his sister? What became of the seven children? Who is responsible for them? What becomes of the handful of leaves on the young tree sawn off at the base?

It is always the same story. Those poor mortals, those creatures of God, left with no means of support, no guide, no refuge, wandered off aimlessly – who knows? perhaps went their separate ways – and eventually disappeared in that cold fog where lone destinies founder, those dismal shadows where so many unfortunate individuals come to grief in the doleful progress of mankind. They left the area. The clock-tower of what had been their village forgot them. The boundary of what had been their land forgot them. After a few years in prison Jean Valjean himself forgot them. In that heart where there had been an open wound there was now a scar. That is all. In all the time he spent at Toulon he only once heard any word of his sister. It was, I believe, towards the end of the fourth year of his captivity. How the news reached him, I do not know. Someone who had known them back home had seen his sister. She was in Paris. She lived in a back street near St-Sulpice, Rue du Gindre. She had only one child with her, a little boy, the youngest. Where were the other six? She herself may not have known. Every morning she went to a printing works at 3 Rue du Sabot where she was a sheet-folder and -stitcher. She had to be there at six in the morning, well before daylight in winter. In the same building as the print shop was a school and to this school she took her little boy, who was seven years old. But as she started at the printer's at six and the school did not open until seven, the child had to wait an hour in the courtyard for the school to open – an hour out in the open in winter! They would not let the child come into the print shop because he got in the way, they said. Those on their way to work in the morning would see this poor little creature sitting on the pavement, unable to stay awake, and often sleeping in the dark, hunkered down and bent over his lunch-box. When it rained an old woman, the door-keeper, would take pity on him and let him into her cubicle that contained only a pallet, a spinning-wheel and two wooden chairs, and the little one would sleep there in a corner, hugging the cat for warmth. At seven o'clock the school opened and he would go in. This is what Jean Valjean was told. Someone spoke of it one day: it was moment-ary, a brief flash, like a window suddenly opened on the fate of his loved ones, then everything closed up again. That was the last he ever heard of them. No further news ever reached him. He never again saw them, or met them. Nor shall we again encounter them throughout the rest of this sad story.

Towards the end of that fourth year it was Jean Valjean's turn to escape. His comrades helped him, as is the way in that woeful place. He escaped. For two days he roamed the countryside in freedom, if it can be called freedom to be hunted, to be constantly looking over your shoulder, starting at the slightest sound, afraid of everything – a smoking chimney, a man going by, a dog barking, a galloping horse, the striking of the hour, daylight because the eye can see, darkness because it cannot, the highway, the path, a bush, sleep. On the evening of the second day he was recaptured. He had neither eaten nor slept for thirty-six hours. The naval court condemned him for this offence to an additional three years, which made eight. In the sixth year it was again his turn to escape. He took his turn but could not make good his escape. He had failed to turn up at roll-call. The cannon was fired, and at night the patrol found him hiding under the keel of a vessel under construction. He resisted the guards who seized him. Escape and rebellion. This infraction under the terms of the special code incurred an additional five years, with two years of the double chain. Thirteen years. In the tenth year his turn came round again, and again he tried. He was no more successful than before. Three years for this fresh attempt. Sixteen years. Finally, it was, I think, during his thirteenth year that he made his last attempt and succeeded only in getting caught after four hours' absence. Three years for those four hours. Nineteen years. In October 1815 he was released. He had gone in there in 1796 for breaking a pane of glass and stealing a loaf of bread.

A brief parenthesis here. This is the second time in his studies of the penal issue and the doom meted out by the law that the author of this book has come across the theft of a loaf of bread as the starting-point in ruining a life. Claude Gueux stole a loaf of bread. Jean Valjean stole a loaf of bread. According to one English statistic, the primary cause of four out of five thefts in London is hunger.

Jean Valjean went into the prison hulks sobbing and trembling. He came out emotionless. He went in despairing. He came out dour.

What had happened inside that soul?

VII
Inside Despair

Let us try to describe it.

It is surely incumbent on society to examine these things, since it is society that creates them.

He was, as we have said, an uneducated man, but he was no fool. There was the light of natural intelligence in him. Hardship, which sheds a light of its own, increased the little illumination there was in that soul. Under the rod, in chains, in solitary confinement, in exhaustion, under the burning sun of penal servitude, on the convict's plank bed, he turned in on himself and reflected.

He set himself up as a court of justice.

He began by sitting in judgement on himself.

He recognized that he was not an innocent man unjustly punished. He admitted that he had committed a drastic and reprehensible deed. That he probably would not have been refused the loaf of bread, had he asked for it. That in any case it would have been better to wait, and rely on pity or work to obtain it. That it is not an utterly conclusive argument to say, 'Can hunger be kept waiting?' That in the first place it is very rare for anyone literally to die of hunger, and anyway, regrettably or not, human beings are so constituted that they are capable of suffering a great deal for a long time, morally and physically, without dying. That patience was necessary. That it would have been better even for those poor little children. That it was an act of madness for a miserable wretch such as he to take on the whole of society and to imagine that theft was a way out of poverty. That under any circumstances the gateway that led to criminality was a bad escape route from poverty. In short, he had done wrong.

Then he asked himself the following:

Whether he was the only one at fault in his fateful story. Whether, firstly, it was not a serious matter that, hard-working as he was, he had no work, conscientious as he was, he had no bread. And whether, after he confessed to the crime he had committed, the punishment had not been harsh and disproportionate. Whether there had not been greater wrong perpetrated by the law through the penalty inflicted than by the culprit through his offence. Whether one of the scalepans had not been overladen, the one that weighed expiation. Whether the excessively heavy penalty did not cancel out the offence, and did not result in reversing the situation, in replacing the delinquent's offence with the offence of repression, in making the guilty man the victim, and the debtor the creditor, and in ultimately vindicating the one who had broken the law. Whether this penalty, compounded with successive supplementary sentences for the attempted escapes, did not end up becoming some kind of assault of the strong against the weak, a crime of society against the individual, a crime that recommenced every day, a crime that went on for nineteen years.

He wondered whether human society could possibly be entitled to inflict on its members both its unconscionable improvidence on the one hand and its ruthless providence on the other; and to trap a poor man for ever between want and excess, want of work and excess of punishment.

Whether it was not outrageous that society should treat in this manner precisely those least favoured by the chance distribution of assets, and consequently those most deserving of care.

Having raised and answered these questions, he passed judgement on society, and condemned it.

He condemned it to his hatred.

He held it responsible for the fate he suffered and told himself that he might not hesitate to make it answerable one day. He determined that there was no proportionality between the wrong he had done and the wrong done to him. Lastly, he concluded that his punishment was not strictly speaking a miscarriage of justice, but it was most certainly iniquitous.

Anger may be foolish and absurd. It is possible to be unjustifiably incensed. A man is outraged only when, one way or another, he is basically in the right. Jean Valjean felt outraged.

After all, human society had done him nothing but harm. This angry face that it calls Justice, and that it presents to those it smites, was the only one he had ever seen. The only reason other people had ever laid a finger on him was to hurt him. He had had no physical contact with anyone that had not been a blow struck against him. Never, since childhood, since his mother, his sister, had he ever encountered a friendly word, a look of kindness. With every succeeding injury, he had gradually come to the firm belief that life is a war, and in this war he was the vanquished. He had no other weapon than his hatred. He resolved to hone it in prison and take it with him when he left.

There was at Toulon a school for convicts run by the Ignorantine friars, where the basics were taught to any of those poor wretches willing to learn. He was one of the willing. He went to school at the age of forty and learned to read, write and count. He felt that to strengthen his intelligence was to strengthen his hatred. In certain cases, education and enlightenment may serve to extend the scope of evil.

It is sad to say that, having passed judgement on the society that had been his undoing, he passed judgement on the providence that had created that society, and this providence too he condemned.

So during those nineteen years of torture and slavery, this soul both rose and fell. Light penetrated it on the one side, darkness on the other.

As we have seen, Jean Valjean was not a bad person by nature. He was still good when he arrived at the prison. There, he condemned society and felt he was becoming wicked. There, he condemned providence and felt he was becoming ungodly.

At this point it is hard not to pause for reflection.

Does human nature change so thoroughly and so radically? Can the human being created good by God be made wicked by man? Can the soul be completely remade by fate and, being ill-fated, become ill-natured? Can the heart grow deformed and develop incurable uglinesses and infirmities under the pressure of inordinate misfortune, like the spine under too low a vault? Is there not in every human soul, was there not in the soul of Jean Valjean in particular, an original spark, a divine element, incorruptible in this world, immortal in the next, which goodness is capable of nurturing, stoking, kindling, fanning into a glorious blaze of brilliance, and which evil can never wholly extinguish?

Grave and perplexing questions, to the latter of which any physiologist would probably have answered no, without hesitation, had he seen this sullen convict in Toulon at moments of rest, which for Jean Valjean were moments for rumination: seated, with his arms folded on the bar of some capstan and the end of his chain stuffed into his pocket to prevent it from dragging; serious, silent and thoughtful, one ostracized by the legal system who looked with anger on his fellow men; one doomed by civilization who looked with rancour on heaven.

Certainly – and we would not wish to disguise the fact – the physiologist observing this would have seen before him a wretchedness beyond salvation. He might perhaps have pitied this sick man of the law's making, but he would not even have attempted any treatment. He would have averted his gaze from the cavernous depths he had glimpsed in this soul; and the word 'Hope!', albeit written by the finger of God on the brow of every man, he, like Dante at the portals of hell, would have banished from this existence.

Was the state of his soul, which we have tried to analyse, as perfectly plain to Jean Valjean as we have tried to portray it to our readers? Did Jean Valjean see distinctly after their development, and had he seen distinctly as they developed, all the elements of which his moral wretchedness consisted? Had this rough and uneducated man a true understanding of the chain of thought that had led him step by step, up and down, to the dismal prospect that had for so many years already constituted the inner horizon of his spirit? Was he fully conscious of everything that had gone on inside him and everything stirring within him? This we would not dare to say. Indeed, we believe not. There was too much ignorance in Jean Valjean for there not to remain a great deal of confusion, even after so much misery. At times he did not rightly know what he felt. Jean Valjean was in darkness. He suffered in darkness. He hated in darkness. He might be said to have made his way by hatred. He was used to living in this darkness, groping like a blind man, a dreamer. Only, every now and again there came all at once, from within him or from without, a surge of anger, an intensification of suffering, a pale flash of lightning that lit up his whole soul and suddenly made visible all around him, in front and behind, by the glimmerings of a ghastly brightness, the frightful precipices and bleak perspectives of his destiny.

After the lightning, darkness would fall again. And where was he? He could no longer tell.

It is in the nature of such punishment – in which what prevails is the pitiless, in other words, the brutalizing – to transform a man little by little, by a kind of stupid transfiguration, into a wild beast, sometimes a ferocious beast.

Jean Valjean's persistent attempts at escape alone would suffice to prove this strange working of the law on the human soul. Completely useless and foolish as these attempts were, Jean Valjean would have kept on making them as often as the opportunity presented itself without for one moment considering the outcome or his previous experience. He escaped impetuously like the wolf that finds the cage open. Instinct told him, 'Flee!' Reason would have said, 'Stay!' But in the face of so strong a temptation, reason disappeared. All that remained was instinct. The beast alone acted. When he was recaptured the further punishments inflicted on him only served to make him wilder still.

One detail we must not fail to mention is that he possessed a physical strength far exceeding that any of other inmate of the prison hulks. Paying out a cable or winding a capstan, Jean Valjean could take the strain of four men. He sometimes lifted and supported enormous weights on his back and in cases of necessity acted as a substitute for that implement known as a *cric**, in the past called an *orgueil*, from which incidentally the name of Rue Montorgueil, near the central market in Paris, derives. His comrades had nicknamed him Jean-le-Cric. Once, when repairs were being made to the balcony of Toulon's city hall, one of Puget's splendid caryatids that support the balcony became dislodged and almost fell. Jean Valjean, who happened to be there, took the caryatid's weight on his shoulder, giving the workmen time to get there.

His litheness was even greater than his robustness. Certain convicts, perpetually dreaming of escape, in the end become truly expert

* A jack.

in combining strength and agility. It is an expertise in the muscles. A whole mysterious discipline of statics is daily practised by prisoners, those who are eternally envious of flies and birds. To climb a sheer surface and find purchase where it was almost impossible to see any protrusion was child's play to Jean Valjean. Given the corner of a wall, by tensing his back and his thighs, fitting his elbows and heels into any unevenness in the stone, he could hoist himself as if by magic to the third floor. Sometimes he climbed right up on to the roof of the prison in this way.

He did not say much. He did not laugh. It took some very strong emotion to wring from him once or twice a year that lugubrious laughter of the convict that sounds like an echo of the devil's laughter. By the look of him, his gaze seemed forever to dwell on something terrible.

He was indeed preoccupied.

Through the morbid perceptions of a deficient nature and a defeated mind, he had an obscure feeling that some monstrous thing bore down on him. In that dim and pallid half-light in which he skulked, every time he craned his neck and tried to look up he perceived with terror and rage combined, stacked in layer upon layer above him, rising with dreadful steepness as far as the eye could see, a frightful accumulation, as it were, of things, laws, prejudices, men and deeds, whose contours he could not distinguish, whose mass terrified him, and which was nothing other than that monumental pyramid we call 'civilization'. In this swarming shapeless mass he could pick out here and there, now close to him, now far away on inaccessible levels, some grouping, some brightly illuminated detail: here, the prison warder and his rod; there, the gendarme and his sabre; beyond, the mitred archbishop; right at the top, like a sort of sun, the crowned and dazzling emperor. It seemed to him that these distant splendours, far from dispelling his darkness, made it blacker and more dismal. Laws, prejudices, deeds, men, things – all this came and went above him, observing the complicated and mysterious movement God imparts to civilization, trampling and crushing him with an indefinable calm in its cruelty and an inexorability in its indifference. Souls foundering in the worst possible plight, poor wretches lost in the lowest depths of this limbo where no one looks any more, the law's outcasts feel individually burdened with the whole weight of this human society, so forbidding to anyone outside it, so appalling to anyone at the bottom of it.

In this situation Jean Valjean pondered. What could be the nature of his reflections?

If the grain of millet beneath the millstone were capable of thinking, it would no doubt have thought as Jean Valjean did.

All these things, realities full of phantasma, phantasmagoria full of realities, had eventually created in him an inner state of a kind that was almost indescribable.

At times in the midst of his penal labour, he would pause, then fall to thinking. His reason, at once more mature and more confused than in the past, would rebel. Everything that had happened to him seemed absurd. Everything that surrounded him seemed impossible. He said to himself, 'This is a dream.' He would gaze at the prison warder standing a few paces away; the prison warder seemed a spectre. Suddenly the spectre would beat him with his rod.

The natural world hardly existed for him. It would almost be true to say that for Jean Valjean there was no sun, no fine summer days, or radiant sky, or fresh April dawns. It was some basement dinginess that normally lit his soul.

In conclusion, to sum up what can be summed up and translated into concrete results in all that we have just mentioned, we shall simply remark that thanks to the way prison had moulded him Jean Valjean, the inoffensive tree-pruner from Faverolles, the dreadful felon of Toulon, had after nineteen years become capable of two kinds of misdeed. First, a swift unthinking kind, full of impulsiveness, entirely instinctive, a reprisal of sorts for the wrong done to him. Second, a grave and serious kind, consciously considered and planned with the mistaken notions such adversity can instil. His premeditations went through three successive phases, a progress of which only natures of a certain quality are capable: rationalization, resolve, determination. His motives were outrage that had become a habit of mind, the bitterness in his heart, a deep sense of the iniquities he had suffered, the impulse to react, even against the good, the innocent and the just, if there be any. The point of departure and of arrival in all his thinking was his hatred of human law; a hatred that if not arrested in its development by some providential occurrence becomes within a given time hatred of society, then hatred of the human race, then hatred of creation, and is reflected in an ill-defined, constant and brutal desire to inflict harm on no matter whom, on any living creature.

As we can see, it was not without reason that Jean Valjean's passport described him as *a very dangerous man*.

Year by year, this soul had hardened slowly but inexorably. The hard-hearted are dry-eyed. When he left prison he had not shed a tear for nineteen years.

The Deep and the Dark

Man overboard!

So what? The ship does not stop. The wind blows, this woeful vessel has a course it is compelled to keep. It passes on.

The man disappears, then reappears, he sinks and rises to the surface again, he calls for help, his arms reach out. No one hears. The ship, shuddering under the gale, is entirely concentrated on its handling, the crew and the passengers do not even see the man in the water. His pathetic head is but a speck in the enormity of the waves.

He utters desperate cries in the troughs. What a ghostly vision that retreating sail is! He watches and watches in panic. It grows distant, it dims, it dwindles. He was there only a moment ago, he was one of the crew, he went to and fro on the deck with the others, he had his share of fresh air and sunlight, he was alive. Now what has happened? He has slipped, he has fallen, it is gone.

He is in the monstrous waters. He has nothing underfoot any more but shifting and treacherousness. The billows torn and chopped by the wind surround him hideously, the heavings of the deep overwhelm him, all the watery raggedness thrashes round his head; a mob of waves spews over him, blurred openings half devour him. Every time he goes under he glimpses precipices filled with darkness, frightful alien vegetations seize him, bind his feet, draw him towards them. He feels that he is becoming the deep, he is part of the spume, the waves toss him from one to another, he drinks bitterness, the craven ocean is furiously intent on drowning him, hugeness toys with him as he perishes. It seems as if all this water were hatred.

Nevertheless he puts up a fight. He tries to defend himself. He tries to keep above the water, he strives, he swims. He, this puny force, immediately exhausted, combats the inexhaustible.

Where, then, is the ship? Over there. Barely visible in the pale obscurity of the horizon.

The wind gusts. All the spray beats down on him. He looks up and sees only the lividness of the clouds. He is a dying witness to the immense frenzy of the sea. He is tormented by this craziness. He hears noises unknown to man that seem to come from beyond the earth and from some dreadful untold outer region.

There are birds in the clouds, just as there are angels above human tribulations. But what can they do for him? They fly, sing and soar, while he draws his dying breath.

He feels simultaneously buried by those two infinities, the ocean and the sky: the one is a tomb, the other a shroud.

Darkness falls. He has been swimming for hours, he has no strength left. That ship, that distant thing in which there were men, has vanished. He is alone in the tremendous twilight chasm; he sinks, he stiffens, he writhes, he senses beneath him the huge undulations of the invisible, he calls out.

Of men there are none. Where is God?

He shouts. Someone! Someone! He keeps on shouting. Nothing on the horizon. Nothing in the heavens.

He implores the expanse, the waves, the seaweed, the rocks. They are deaf. He beseeches the tempest. The insensate tempest obeys only the infinite.

Around him darkness, mist, loneliness, churning and mindless tumult, the endless billowing of untamed waters. Within him horror and weariness. Beneath him the downward drop. Nothing to hold on to. He imagines the corpse's murky fortunes in the unbounded gloom. The bottomless cold paralyses him. His hands clench and close and seize on nothing. Unavailing winds, clouds, waterspouts, breezes, stars! What can he do? The despairing man gives up, he who is weary opts to die, he relinquishes, he surrenders, he lets go, and there he is for evermore, buffeted in the dismal depths of perdition.

O implacable march of human societies! The men and souls lost along the way! Ocean in which all who are dropped by the law sink! Dire failure of rescue! O moral death!

The sea is the inexorable social darkness into which the penal system casts its damned. The sea is immense wretchedness.

The soul cut adrift in these fathomless deeps may become a corpse. Who will resuscitate it?

IX
New Woes

When the time came to leave the prison hulks, when Jean Valjean heard in his ear those strange words, 'You're free!' – it was an improbable and unbelievable moment. A brilliant ray of light, real light, the light of the living, suddenly penetrated him. But it was not long before this ray dimmed. Jean Valjean had been dazzled by the idea of liberty. He had believed in a new life. He very quickly saw what kind of liberty it was to which a yellow passport is given.

And with this realization came much bitterness. He had calculated that his earnings during his time in the prison hulks ought to have amounted to one hundred and seventy-one francs. It is fair to add that he had forgotten to include in his calculations the compulsory days of rest on Sundays and public holidays that over nineteen years resulted in a reduction of about twenty-four francs. Be that as it may, his earnings had been reduced by various local levies to the sum of one hundred and nine francs fifteen sous, which was counted out to him on his release.

He did not understand any of this and believed he had been wronged. Let us say the word: robbed.

The day after he was freed he saw some men unloading bales outside an orange-flower distillery in Grasse. He offered his services. The job needed to be done quickly, he was accepted. He set to work. He was quick-witted, robust and deft. He gave of his best. The foreman seemed pleased. While he was working a gendarme came by, noticed him, and asked for his papers. He had to show the yellow passport. Jean Valjean then went back to work. A little earlier he had asked one of the workmen what their daily rate for this job was. The reply was 'Thirty sous.' Come evening, as he had to be on his way again the following day, he presented himself to the foreman of the distillery and asked to be paid. Without a word the foreman gave him twenty-five sous. He protested. 'That's good enough for you,' he was told. He insisted. The foreman looked him straight in the eye and said, 'You want to end up back in clink?'

Again he felt robbed.

By reducing his savings, society, the state, had robbed him in a big way. Now it was the turn of the individual to rob him in a small way.

Release is not freedom. You are let out of prison, but you continue to serve your sentence.

That is what happened to him at Grasse. We have seen what sort of reception he got at Digne.

X
The Man Awakened

So as the cathedral clock struck two in the morning, Jean Valjean awoke.

What wakened him was that his bed was too comfortable. It was nearly twenty years since he had lain in a bed, and although he had not undressed it was too novel a sensation not to disturb his sleep.

He had slept more than four hours. His tiredness had passed. He was not used to taking many hours' rest.

He opened his eyes and stared for a moment into the darkness around him, then closed them again to go back to sleep.

When it has been a hectic day with many varied sensations, when things are on your mind, you fall asleep, but you do not go back to sleep. Sleep comes more easily than it returns. This is what happened to Jean Valjean. He could not get to sleep again and he fell to thinking.

He was at one of those moments when the thoughts in his mind were unclear. There was a kind of indistinct welter in his brain. His old memories and his very recent memories swirled in a jumble and overlapped chaotically, losing their formal identity, becoming disproportionately magnified, then suddenly disappearing altogether, as in disturbed and muddy waters. Many thoughts occurred to him, but there was one that kept coming to the fore and driving out all the others. What that thought was, we shall say at once: he had noticed the six sets of silverware and the ladle that Madame Magloire had placed on the table.

Those six sets of silver preyed on him. They were right there. A few paces away. Just as he was passing through the next room to reach the one where he was now, the old servant had been putting them away in a small cupboard at the head of the bed. He had taken careful note of that cupboard. On the right, as you entered from the dining room. They were solid silver. Antique silverware. With the ladle they would fetch at least two hundred francs. Double what he had earned in nineteen years. It is true he would have earned more if 'the authorities hadn't robbed him'.

He wavered for a whole hour, and there was certainly some element of conflict in his vacillations. Three o'clock struck. He opened his eyes again, suddenly sat bolt upright, reached out his arm and felt for his knapsack which he had thrown into the corner of the alcove, then swung his legs over and put his feet on the ground. And so, almost without knowing how, he found himself sitting on the side of his bed.

He remained for a while brooding in this position, which might have suggested something sinister to anyone seeing him like this in the dark, the only soul awake in that sleeping household. All at once he bent down, took off his shoes and quietly placed them on the mat beside the bed. Then he resumed his pensive attitude and once again sat motionless.

Throughout these dreadful ruminations the thoughts we referred to above were in constant ferment in his brain, coming and going and returning again, and in a way oppressing him. And then without knowing why, and with the involuntary obsessiveness of idle fancy, he thought too about a convict named Brevet, whom he had known in the prison hulks and whose trousers had been held up by a single brace of knitted cotton. The chequered pattern of that brace kept coming back into his mind.

He remained in this quandary and might have remained so indefinitely until daybreak had the clock not struck – the quarter-hour or the half-hour. It was as if that stroke said to him, 'Get on with it!'

He stood up, hesitated yet a moment, and listened. All was quiet in the house. Then walking gingerly he went directly to the window, which he could see. It was not a very dark night. There was a full moon with large clouds driven by the wind coursing across it. This created alternating darkness and light outside, eclipses then brightnesses, and inside a kind of half-light. This half-light, sufficient for a person to find his way by, and intermittent on account of the clouds, was like that sort of leaden wanness that comes in through a basement window with passers-by coming and going in front of it. When he reached the window Jean Valjean examined it. There were no bars on it, it opened on to the garden and was simply fastened with a small latch, according to local custom. He opened it, but as a rush of biting cold air came into the room he immediately shut it again. He observed the garden with that attentive gaze that does not so much look as study. The garden was enclosed by a fairly low white wall, easy to climb. Beyond the wall at the bottom of the garden he could discern regularly spaced-out tree-tops, which indicated that the wall separated the garden from a tree-lined avenue or lane.

Having taken this quick glance, he shook himself like a man who has made up his mind, strode to his alcove, grabbed his knapsack, opened it, rummaged in it, pulled out something that he placed on the bed, stuffed his shoes into one of the pockets, closed it all up again, shouldered the knapsack; put on his cap and pulled the peak down over his eyes, felt for his staff, went and placed it in the corner by the window; then returned to the bed, and resolutely seized the object he had laid on it. It looked like a short iron bar sharpened at one end like a spear.

It would have been hard to determine in the darkness for what purpose that length of iron could have been designed. Perhaps it was a lever? Perhaps it was a club?

In the daytime it would have been recognizable as none other than a miner's candlestick. At that time convicts were sometimes employed in quarrying stone from the high hills around Toulon, and it was not unusual for them to have miners' tools at their disposal. Miners' candlesticks are of solid iron with the lower end tapering to a point by means of which they are jammed into the rock.

He took this candlestick in his right hand and, holding his breath

93

and softening his footsteps, made for the door to the adjoining room, the bishop's room, as we know. When he reached this door he found it ajar. The bishop had not closed it.

XI
What He Does

Jean Valjean listened. Not a sound.

He pushed the door.

He pushed it gently with his finger, with that furtive and circumspect delicacy of a cat that wants to come in.

The door yielded to the pressure with a scarcely perceptible and silent movement, which enlarged the opening a little.

He waited a moment, then pushed the door a second time, more boldly.

It continued to yield in silence. The opening was now wide enough for him to get through. But there was a little table near the door, at an awkward angle to it, barring the way.

Jean Valjean saw the difficulty. It was absolutely imperative for the opening to be made even wider.

He steeled himself and pushed the door a third time, more energetically than before. This time a hinge that needed oiling emitted a sudden lengthy screech in the darkness.

Jean Valjean quailed. The noise of that hinge rang in his ear with something of the tremendous stridency of the trumpet on the Day of Judgement.

In his fanciful exaggerations of that first instant he almost imagined the hinge had become animate and all at once acquired a dreadful life force, and that it was barking like a dog to alert everyone and waken those who were asleep.

He paused, trembling, panic-stricken, and from tip-toe dropped flat on his feet. He heard the arteries in his temples thudding like two sledgehammers and the breath expelled from his chest sounded to him like wind issuing from a cave. He thought it impossible that the horrible din of that grating hinge would not have disturbed the whole household, like an earthquake tremor. The door he had pushed had taken fright and called out. The old man was going to get up, the two old women were going to cry for help, people would come running. Within a quarter of an hour the town would be in uproar and the gendarmerie mobilized. For a moment he thought he was doomed.

He stood where he was, petrified, like the statue of salt, not daring to move. Several minutes went by. The door was now wide open. He ventured to peer into the room. Nothing had stirred. He listened. All was still in the house. The noise of the rusty hinge had not wakened anyone.

The first danger was past, but there was still a frightful tumult inside him. Yet he did not retreat. Even when he thought he was doomed, he had not retreated. His one concern now was to get it over with quickly. He took a step forward and entered the room.

In this room there was perfect calm. Discernible here and there were ill-defined, vague forms that in daylight were papers scattered on a table, open folios, volumes piled on a stool, an armchair heaped with clothing, a kneeler, but at that hour were no more than shadowy corners and pale patches. Jean Valjean advanced cautiously, taking care not to bump into the furniture. He could hear at the far end of the room the sleeping bishop's calm and regular breathing.

He came to a sudden halt. He was by the bed. He had reached it sooner than he expected.

Nature sometimes marries her dramatic effects and visual displays to our actions with a kind of sombre, intelligent appropriateness, as if wanting to make us think. For nearly half an hour a large cloud had covered the sky. At the very moment that Jean Valjean paused at the foot of the bed, that cloud parted as though on purpose and a shaft of moonlight shining through the long window suddenly illuminated the bishop's pale face. He was sleeping peacefully. Because of the cold nights in the Basses-Alpes he was in bed almost fully clothed, in a brown woollen garment that covered his arms to the wrists. His head rested on the pillow in the abandon of sleep. His hand on which he wore the pastoral ring, a hand that was the author of so many good deeds and saintly acts, was left dangling over the side of the bed. His whole face was lit up with an indefinable expression of satisfaction, hope and bliss. More than a smile, it was almost a radiance. There was on his brow the mystical reflection of an unseen light. In sleep the souls of the just contemplate a mysterious heaven.

A reflection of that heaven fell on the bishop.

It was at the same time a luminous transparency, for that heaven was within him. That heaven was his conscience.

When the moonbeam superimposed itself, so to speak, on that inward radiance the sleeping bishop appeared as if in glory. Yet it was a vision that remained soft and veiled in an ineffable half-light. That moon in the sky, that hush upon nature, that undisturbed garden and that great peacefulness in the house, the hour, the moment, the silence, added some solemn and inexpressible quality to this sage's venerable repose, and surrounded with a kind of serene and majestic aureole that white hair and those closed eyes, that face in which all was hope and all was trustfulness, that old man's head in childlike sleep.

There was almost something divine about this man in his unconscious awesomeness.

Jean Valjean meanwhile was in shadow, standing motionless with his iron candlestick in his hand, terrified of this radiant elder. He had never seen anything like it. This trustfulness appalled him. The moral world has no greater spectacle than this: a troubled and uneasy conscience on the brink of an evil action, contemplating the sleep of a good man.

There was in that sleep, in that separateness, with one such as he near by, an element of the sublime of which he was vaguely but compellingly aware.

No one could have said what was going on inside him, not even he himself. To try to conceive of it, we have to imagine that which is most violent in the presence of that which is most gentle. Even on his face nothing could be discerned with certainty. It was a sort of haggard amazement. He saw. That was all. But what was he thinking? It was impossible to tell. What was obvious was that he was emotionally affected and confused. But what was the nature of his emotion?

He did not take his eyes off the old man. The only thing clearly evident from his attitude and the expression on his face was a strange indecision. He seemed to be hovering between two abysses – that of perdition and that of salvation. He looked as if he were about to crush that skull or kiss that hand.

After a few minutes his left arm rose slowly to his brow and he took off his cap, then just as slowly his arm fell again and Jean Valjean resumed his contemplation with his cap in his left hand, his candlestick in his right, the hair on his feral head bristling.

The bishop slept on in profound peacefulness beneath that terrifying gaze.

A reflection of the moon picked out faintly above the fireplace the crucifix, which seemed to open its arms to both of them, with a blessing for one, forgiveness for the other.

Jean Valjean abruptly replaced his cap on his head, then without looking at the bishop walked rapidly past the bed straight to the cupboard he saw, indistinctly, standing by the head of it. He raised his iron candlestick as though to force the lock. The key was in it. He opened the cupboard. The first thing that met his eyes was the basket of silverware. He took it, and throwing caution to the wind strode across the room not worrying about the noise, reached the door, re-entered the chapel, opened the window, seized his staff, climbed over the ground-floor window-sill, put the silver into his knapsack, threw away the basket, crossed the garden, leapt over the wall like a tiger, and fled.

XII
The Bishop at Work

The next day at sunrise Monseigneur Bienvenu was strolling in his garden. Madame Magloire came running up to him in a frenzy.

'Monseigneur, Monseigneur!' she exclaimed. 'Does Your Highness know where the silverware basket is?'

'Yes,' replied the bishop.

'Blessed be the Lord Jesus!' she said. 'I didn't know what had become of it.'

The bishop had just found the basket in a flowerbed. He handed it to Madame Magloire.

'Here it is.'

'Well?' she said. 'It's empty! What about the silverware?'

'Ah,' replied the bishop. 'So it's the silverware you're worried about? I don't know where that is.'

'Good Lord Almighty! It's been stolen! The man who was here last night has stolen it!'

In a twinkling, with all that spirited old girl's spryness, Madame Magloire ran to the chapel, entered the alcove and returned to the bishop. The bishop had just bent down and was woefully examining a plant, a Guillons cochlearia, which the basket had damaged as it fell into the flowerbed. He straightened up at Madame Magloire's cry.

'Monseigneur, the man's gone! The silver's been stolen!'

As she uttered this exclamation, her eyes fell on a corner of the garden where there were signs of the wall having been climbed. The coping was damaged.

'Look! That's how he got out. He jumped down into Ruelle Coche-filet. Oh, the wicked fellow! He's stolen our silver!'

The bishop remained silent for a moment, then raised his solemn gaze and said quietly to Madame Magloire, 'Now was that silver ours in the first place?'

Madame Magloire was left speechless. There was another silence, then the bishop went on, 'Madame Magloire, I've been wrongfully keeping that silver for a long time. It belonged to the poor. And what was that man? Obviously one of the poor.'

'Dear Jesus!' said Madame Magloire. 'It's not for me, or Mademoiselle. It makes no difference to us. But it's for Monseigneur. What's Monseigneur to eat with now?'

The bishop gazed at her with an expression of amazement. 'Ah, come now! Haven't we some pewter cutlery?'

Madame Magloire shrugged. 'Pewter has a smell.'

'Tin cutlery, then.'

Madame Magloire gave a meaningful grimace.

'Tin leaves a taste in your mouth.'

'Very well,' said the bishop, 'wooden cutlery.'

A few moments later he was having breakfast at the very table where Jean Valjean had sat the previous evening. As he breakfasted Monseigneur Bienvenu remarked cheerfully to his sister, who said nothing, and to Madame Magloire, who muttered to herself, that there is absolutely no need even for a wooden fork or spoon to dip a piece of bread in a cup of milk.

'Really, the very idea', Madame Magloire was saying as she bustled about, 'of allowing a man like that into your house! And letting him stay the night with you! It's lucky all he did was steal! Lord! it makes you shudder to think of it!'

As brother and sister were about to leave the table there was a knock at the door.

'Come in,' said the bishop.

The door opened. An extraordinary, violent group appeared on the threshold. Three men were holding a fourth by the scruff of his neck. The three men were gendarmes, the other was Jean Valjean.

A sergeant of the gendarmerie, who seemed to be in command of the group, stood close to the door. He entered and approached the bishop, giving a military salute.

'Monseigneur,' he said.

At this word Jean Valjean, glum and dejected-looking, lifted his head in amazement.

'Monseigneur?' he murmured. 'So he's not the parish priest?'

'Silence!' said the gendarme. 'This is Monseigneur, the bishop.'

In the meantime Monseigneur Bienvenu had stepped forward as quickly as his great age allowed.

'Ah! There you are!' he exclaimed, looking at Jean Valjean. 'I'm glad to see you. Now, look here, I gave you those candlesticks as well, they're silver like the rest and you'll certainly be able to get two hundred francs for them. Why didn't you take them with your forks and spoons?'

Jean Valjean's eyes widened, and he stared at the venerable bishop with an expression no human tongue can describe.

'Monseigneur,' said the sergeant, 'what this man said is true, then? We ran into him. He looked like someone leaving town. We stopped him to see. He had this silver . . .'

'And he told you,' the bishop broke in with a smile, 'that it was given to him by an old buffer of a priest in whose house he'd spent the night? I see the situation. And you brought him back here? There's been a misunderstanding.'

'You mean, we can let him go?' said the sergeant.

'Undoubtedly,' replied the bishop.

The gendarmes released Jean Valjean, who backed away.

'Is it true they're letting me go?' he said in an almost inarticulate voice and as if he were talking in his sleep.

'Yes, we're letting you go, didn't you hear?' said one of the gendarmes.

'My friend,' said the bishop, 'before you go, here are your candlesticks. Take them.'

He went over to the fireplace, took the two silver candlesticks, and brought them to Jean Valjean. The two women watched him without a word, without making a move, without a glance that might upset the bishop.

Jean Valjean trembled in every limb. He took the two candlesticks automatically, looking bewildered.

'Now,' said the bishop, 'go in peace. By the way, if ever you come back, my friend, there's no need to pass through the garden. You can always enter and leave by the street door. It's left on the latch day and night.'

Then turning to the gendarmes he said, 'You may go, gentlemen.'

The gendarmes left.

Jean Valjean was like a man about to faint.

The bishop went up to him and said quietly, 'Don't forget, never forget, you promised to use this money to become an honest man.'

Jean Valjean, who had no recollection of having made any promise, remained dumbfounded. The bishop had dwelled on these words as he said them. He went on with a kind of solemnity, 'Jean Valjean, my brother, you're no longer owned by evil but by good. It's your soul I'm buying. I'm redeeming it from dark thoughts and the spirit of perdition, and I'm giving it to God.'

XIII
Petit-Gervais

Jean Valjean left the town as though he were escaping. He set off through the countryside walking as fast as he could, following the roads and paths that appeared in front of him without noticing that he kept retracing his steps. He wandered about like this all morning, without having eaten and without feeling hungry. He was prey to a host of new sensations. He felt a kind of rage, he knew not against whom. He would have been unable to say whether he felt touched or humiliated. He was overcome at times with an unfamiliar susceptibility to emotion, which he fought against, resisting it with the hardening of his heart over the last twenty years. Being in this state tired him. He saw with dismay the disintegration within him of that sort of appalling calm that the injustice of his misfortune had bestowed on him. He wondered what would replace it. At times he truly would have preferred to be in prison with the gendarmes, and for things not to have turned out like this. It would have been less disturbing. Although the season was fairly far advanced, here and there in the hedgerows were still a few late flowers, whose scent as he walked past them brought back childhood memories. It was so long since he was last visited by them that these memories were almost unbearable.

Inexpressible thoughts gathered inside him like this, all day long.

As the sun set in the evening, casting a long shadow on the ground even from the smallest pebble, Jean Valjean was sitting behind a bush on a vast russet plain that was absolutely deserted. There was nothing on the horizon except the Alps. Not even the spire of a distant village. Jean Valjean was probably some nine miles from Digne. A path that cut across the plain passed within a few paces of the bush.

In the midst of these reflections that would have contributed in no small way to making his raggedness look terrifying to anyone who might have encountered him, he heard a joyful sound.

He looked round and saw coming along the path a little Savoyard, about ten years old, singing, with his hurdy-gurdy at his side and his marmot cage on his back. One of those sweet, blithe little lads who go from place to place, with their knees showing through the holes in their trousers.

Singing all the while, the young lad interrupted his progress from time to time to play knuckle-bones with a few coins he had in his hand – probably his entire fortune. This small change included one forty-sou piece.

The child drew up beside the bush without noticing Jean Valjean and tossed up his handful of coins, all of which he had until then caught quite deftly on the back of his hand.

This time the forty-sou piece escaped him, and went rolling into the undergrowth till it reached Jean Valjean.

Jean Valjean put his foot over it.

The child meanwhile had been watching where his coin went, and saw this.

Unabashed, he walked straight up to the man.

It was a totally isolated spot. As far as the eye could see, there was no one either on the plain or on the path. The only sound to be heard were the faint little cries of a flock of migratory birds flying through the sky at an immense height. The child stood with his back to the sun, which threaded his hair with gold, and with a blood-red glow dyed crimson the savage face of Jean Valjean.

'Monsieur, my coin?' said the little Savoyard with that childish trustfulness that is a blend of ignorance and innocence.

'What's your name?' said Jean Valjean.

'Petit-Gervais, monsieur.'

'Go away,' said Jean Valjean.

'Monsieur,' said the child, 'give me back my coin.'

Jean Valjean lowered his head and said nothing.

The child repeated, 'My coin, monsieur!'

Jean Valjean's eyes remained fixed on the ground.

'My coin!' cried the child. 'My silver coin! My money!'

Jean Valjean seemed not to hear. The child grasped him by the collar of his shirt and shook him. And at the same time he did his utmost to shift the big hobnailed shoe standing on his treasure.

'I want my coin! My forty-sou coin!'

The child wept. Jean Valjean lifted his head. He was still seated. He was bleary-eyed. He observed the child with a kind of amazement, then he reached for his staff and cried in a terrible voice, 'Who is it?'

'Me, monsieur,' replied the child. 'Petit-Gervais! Me! Me! Please give me back my forty sous! Please move your foot, monsieur!' Then, though very small, annoyed, and becoming almost threatening: 'I say, will you move your foot? Go on, move your foot, will you!'

'Ah! You again!' said Jean Valjean. And suddenly rising to his full height with his foot still covering the silver coin, he added, 'Get lost, will you!'

The terrified child stared at him, then began to tremble from head to foot, and after a few seconds of stupefied paralysis took to his heels, running away as fast as his legs could carry him, not daring to look back or to cry out.

However, some way off he was forced to stop for want of breath, and in his distractedness Jean Valjean heard the child sobbing.

A few moments later the child had vanished.

The sun had set.

Darkness gathered round Jean Valjean. He had eaten nothing all day. He was probably feverish.

He remained standing, his position unchanged since the child fled. At long and irregular intervals his chest rose with his indrawn breath. His gaze, focused ten or twelve paces in front of him, seemed to be studying intently the shape of an old blue earthenware shard lying in the grass. All at once he shuddered, suddenly aware of the evening chill.

He settled his cap more firmly on his brow, unconsciously pulled his shirt closed and buttoned it up, took a step forward and bent down to pick up his staff.

At that moment he caught sight of the forty-sou coin, which his foot had half buried in the ground, glinting among the stones. The effect was seismic.

'What's that?' he said to himself.

He fell back three paces, then stopped, unable to tear his gaze from that spot his foot had been trampling a moment before, as though the thing gleaming there in the dusk were an eye riveted on him.

After a few moments he darted towards the silver coin, seized it, and straightening up again began to gaze into the distance across the plain, looking towards the horizon in every direction, standing there quivering like a frightened wild animal seeking a refuge.

He saw nothing. Darkness was falling, the plain was cold and indistinct, great purple mists were rising in the twilight glow.

'Ah!' he said and struck out rapidly in a certain direction, the one taken by the child when he disappeared. After about thirty paces he paused, looked about him and saw nothing.

Then he shouted with all his might, 'Petit-Gervais! Petit-Gervais!'

He fell silent and waited.

There was no reply.

The landscape was bleak and deserted. He was surrounded by unbounded space. There was nothing around him but a shadowy darkness in which his gaze was lost, and a silence in which his voice was lost.

An icy north wind blew and gave a sort of lugubrious vitality to things around him. The bushes flailed their skinny little limbs with incredible fury. They looked threatening, as if they were pursuing someone.

He set off again, walking, then began to run, and from time to time he stopped and shouted into that solitude in the most rending and most disconsolate voice ever to be heard: 'Petit-Gervais! Petit-Gervais!'

If the child had heard it he would surely have been frightened and have taken good care not to show himself. But the child was no doubt already far away.

He met a priest on horseback. He went up to him and said, 'Monsieur le curé, have you seen a child go by?'

'No,' said the priest.

'One by the name of Petit-Gervais?'

'I've not seen anyone.'

He drew two five-franc pieces from his purse and handed them to the priest.

'Monsieur le curé, take this for your poor. Monsieur le curé, he's a little lad, about ten years old, with a marmot, I think, and a hurdy-gurdy. One of those wandering Savoyards, you know?'

'I haven't seen him.'

'Petit-Gervais? He's not from one of the villages hereabouts? Can you tell me?'

'From what you say, my friend, the child's a little stranger. They pass through. We don't know them.'

Jean Valjean seized another two five-franc coins and thrust them at the priest.

'For your poor,' he said. Then he added wildly, 'Monsieur l'abbé, have me arrested. I'm a thief.'

The priest dug in his spurs and rode off, very scared.

Jean Valjean started running again in the direction he had first taken.

And so he went on for quite a long way, looking round, calling, shouting, but he met no one. Two or three times he ran across the plain towards something that looked like a person lying down or crouching but turned out to be just low-lying shrubs or rocks. Eventually, at a place where three paths met, he came to a halt. The moon had risen. He peered into the distance and called out one last time, 'Petit-Gervais! Petit-Gervais!' His cry died in the mist without even raising an echo. He murmured again, but in a faint and almost inarticulate voice, 'Petit-Gervais!' That was his final effort. His legs suddenly gave way beneath him as though all at once some invisible power had crushed him with the weight of his own bad conscience. He collapsed on a large stone, exhausted, with his hands in his hair and his face in his lap, and he cried, 'I'm a wretch!'

Then his heart burst and he began to weep. It was the first time he had wept in nineteen years.

When Jean Valjean left the bishop's house he was, as we have seen, in what was to him an entirely different mental universe. He could not understand what was going on inside him. He hardened himself against the old man's angelic deed and gentle words.

'You promised to become an honest man. I'm buying your soul. I'm redeeming it from the spirit of iniquity and giving it to the good Lord.'

This kept coming back to him. This heavenly kindness he countered with pride – the fortress of evil, as it were, within us. He had the indistinct feeling that this priest's forgiveness was the greatest assault and most tremendous attack he had ever experienced. That if he resisted this clemency the hardening of his heart would be definitive. That if he yielded he would be obliged to renounce that hatred with which the deeds of other men had filled his soul over so many years, a hatred he relished. That this time he had to vanquish or be vanquished, and that the battle had been joined, a colossal and decisive battle, between his own wickedness and that man's goodness.

Among all these glimmers of understanding he reeled like a drunken man. As he walked on wild-eyed, had he any clear perception of what his experience in Digne might lead to? Did he hear all those mysterious murmurs that caution or badger the spirit at certain moments in life? Did a voice whisper in his ear that what he had just lived through was the key moment of his existence? For him there was no middle ground any more: after this, if he were not to be the best of men, he would be the worst. To put it another way, he would now have to rise higher than the bishop or fall lower than the convict. If he wished to become good, he would have to be an angel. If he wished to remain wicked, he would have to be a monster.

Here again those questions need to be asked that we have already raised elsewhere: did he amid the confusion of his thoughts have any inkling of all this? Certainly, as we have said, understanding is schooled by adversity. However, it is doubtful that Jean Valjean was capable of unravelling all that we are suggesting. If these ideas occurred to him he glimpsed rather than saw them, and they succeeded only in casting him into a state of unbearable and almost painful perplexity. As too bright a light would have hurt his eyes on emerging from the dark, so the bishop hurt his soul when he came out of that perverse place of darkness called penal servitude. The future life, the potential life, now offered to him filled him with trepidation and anxiety. He did not really know where he was any more. Like an owl that might suddenly see the sun rise, the convict had been dazzled and, so to speak, blinded by virtue.

What was certain, what he was sure of, was that he was no longer the same man, he was completely changed within, it was no longer in his power to act as though the bishop had not spoken to him, had not touched him.

In this state of mind he had encountered Petit-Gervais and robbed him of his forty sous. Why? He could certainly not have explained it. Was it `a lingering effect and a final exertion, as it were, of the evil thoughts he had brought with him from prison, a residual impulse, the result of what in statics is called momentum? It was that, and it was also perhaps not even so much as that. Let us put it in simple terms: it was not he who stole. It was not the man; it was the beast that out of habit and instinct had stupidly put his foot on that money while the thinking mind was grappling with so many new and unprecedented obsessions.

When the thinking mind came to its senses again and saw what the brute had done, Jean Valjean recoiled in anguish and uttered a cry of horror.

This was because by stealing money from that child he had done something of which he was no longer capable – a strange phenomenon that was possible only in his present situation.

Be that as it may, this last bad deed had a decisive effect on him. It cut through the chaos in his mind and dispersed it, setting the dark impenetrabilities on one side and light on the other, and it acted on his soul in the state it was then as certain chemical agents act on a cloudy solution by precipitating one element and clarifying the other.

First of all, even before any self-searching or reflection, in a panic, like someone trying to run away, he did his utmost to find the child to give him back his money. Then when he realized this was futile, impossible, he halted in despair. The moment when he cried out, 'I'm a wretch!' he had just seen himself for what he was. And already he was so divorced from himself that he felt that he was no more than a ghost. And that standing there before him, in flesh and blood, with that shirt on his back, with his staff in his hand, with the knapsack he was carrying packed with stolen objects, with his face grim and determined and his mind filled with heinous plans, was the ghastly convicted felon Jean Valjean.

Overwhelming affliction, we have noted, had made him something of a visionary. This, then, was in the nature of a vision. He actually saw this Jean Valjean, this sinister face, before him. He was almost starting to wonder who the man was, and was horrified by him.

His brain was experiencing one of those turbulent and yet

dreadfully calm moments when introspection is so profound that it absorbs reality. You no longer see the objects around you, and you see the images in your mind as if they were outside yourself.

So he beheld himself, as it were, face to face, and at the same time he saw in mysterious depth beyond this hallucination a kind of light which he initially took for a blazing torch. Looking more closely at this light that appeared to his conscience, he realized it had a human form, and that this torch was the bishop.

His conscience considered in turn each of the two men placed before it: the bishop and Jean Valjean. It took no less a person than the former to be the undoing of the latter. By one of those singular effects peculiar to transports of this kind, as his trance-like delirium continued, in his eyes the bishop grew in stature and brilliance while Jean Valjean shrank and faded. There came a point when he was no more than a shadow. All of a sudden he vanished. The bishop alone remained. He filled this wretched man's entire soul with a magnificent radiance.

Jean Valjean wept for a long time. He wept burning tears, he sobbed, more defenceless than a woman, more frightened than a child.

As he wept his mind was flooded with light, an extraordinary light, a light at once ravishing and terrible. His past life, his first misdeed, his long expiation, his outward brutalization, his inward hardening, his release celebrated with so many plans of vengeance, what had happened to him at the bishop's house, the latest thing he had done – stealing forty sous from a child, a crime all the more craven and all the more monstrous coming after the bishop's pardon – all this came back to him, he saw it clearly, and with a clarity such as he had never seen before. He beheld his life and it looked horrible, he beheld his soul and it looked dreadful. Yet this life and this soul were bathed in a gentle light. He thought he saw Satan by the light of Paradise.

How long did he weep like this? What did he do after he had wept? Where did he go? This was never known. One thing only seems to have been established: that same night, the coach driver who did the Grenoble post run in those days and arrived in Digne at about three o'clock in the morning, as he came down the street where the bishop lived, saw a man who looked as if he was praying, kneeling on the ground in the darkness at Monseigneur Bienvenu's front door.

BOOK THREE
IN THE YEAR 1817

I

The Year 1817

Eighteen hundred and seventeen is the year that Louis XVIII described, with a royal self-assurance not lacking in pride, as the twenty-second of his reign. It is the year when Monsieur Bruguière de Sorsum was famous. All the wig-makers' shops, hoping that the 'royal bird' style of powdered wig would make a comeback, were painted blue with the fleur-de-lys. It was the time when, as churchwarden, Comte Lynch sat in the front pew of St-Germain-des-Prés every Sunday wearing the robes of the French peerage, with his Legion of Honour and his long nose, and that majesty of profile characteristic of a man who has performed a brilliant deed. The brilliant deed performed by Monsieur Lynch was this: having as mayor of Bordeaux, on the twelfth of March 1814, surrendered the city a little too promptly to Monsieur le Duc d'Angoulême. Hence his peerage. In 1817 it was the fashion for little boys of between four and six years of age to be enveloped in huge morocco-leather caps with ear-flaps, quite similar to Eskimo headwear. The French army was dressed in white, Austrian-style; regiments were called legions, and instead of numbers they bore the names of *départements*. Napoleon was on St Helena, and as England refused to provide him with green cloth he was having his old coats turned. In 1817 Pellegrini sang, Mademoiselle Bigottini danced, Potier ruled the stage, Odry did not yet exist. Madame Saqui was stepping into the shoes of Forioso. There were still Prussians in France, Monsieur Delalot was a prominent figure. Legitimacy had recently asserted itself by cutting off the hand, then the head, of Pleignier, Carbonneau and Tolleron. Grand Chamberlain Prince de Talleyrand and minister of finance designate Abbé Louis laughed like two soothsayers catching each other's eye: on the fourteenth of July 1790, both of them had celebrated mass in the Champ de Mars for the Feast of the Federation, Talleyrand officiating as bishop and Louis serving as deacon. In 1817, in the side avenues of this same Champ de Mars, great wooden pillars, painted blue with traces of gilded eagles and bees on them, were to be seen lying in the rain, rotting in the grass. These were the columns that two years earlier had supported the emperor's dais in the Champ de

Mai. They were blackened in places, scorched by the camp fires of the Austrians bivouacked near the Gros-Caillou district of Paris. Two or three of these columns had disappeared in their camp fires and warmed the *kaiserlicks*' big hands. The remarkable thing about the Champ de Mai was that it was held in the month of June in the Champ de Mars. In the year 1817 two things were popular: the Touquet edition of Voltaire and the Charter-engraved snuff-box. The latest sensation in Paris was the murder committed by Dautun, who had thrown his brother's head into the fountain at the Marché aux Fleurs. The Ministry of Naval Affairs had opened an investigation into the doomed frigate *Medusa*, which was to cover Chaumareix with shame and Géricault with glory. Colonel Selves went to Egypt, there to become Suleiman Pasha. The Palais des Thermes, in Rue de La Harpe, was used as a cooper's shop. The little wooden cabin that had served Messier, the naval astronomer under Louis XVI, as an observatory could still be seen on the flat roof of the Hôtel de Cluny's octagonal tower. In her boudoir furnished with sky-blue satin stools the Duchesse de Duras read to three or four friends her unpublished *Ourika*. The Ns were scraped off the Louvre. The Pont d'Austerlitz abdicated and took the name Pont du Jardin du Roi – a twofold riddle, disguising both the Pont d'Austerlitz and the Jardin des Plantes. Bringing to his close reading of Horace a particular interest in heroes who become emperors and clog-makers who become dauphins, Louis XVIII had two causes for concern: Napoleon and Mathurin Bruneau. The French Academy set as the subject for its prize competition 'The Happiness to be Attained through Study'. Monsieur Bellart was professionally eloquent. Seen preparing to follow in his footsteps was advocate-general-to-be de Broë, destined to be lampooned by Paul-Louis Courier. There was a pseudo-Chateaubriand named Marchangy, anticipating a pseudo-Marchangy named d'Arlincourt. *Claire d'Albe* and *Malek-Adel* were literary masterpieces, and Madame Cottin was declared the leading writer of the age. The Institute allowed the Academician Napoleon Bonaparte to be struck off its list of members. A royal decree established Angoulême as the site of a naval academy, for with the Duc d'Angoulême being grand admiral, obviously the city of Angoulême was entitled as a matter of course to all the distinctions of a seaport; otherwise, the monarchic principle would have been undermined. The question was raised in the Council of Ministers whether the vignettes of acrobatics that adorned Franconi's advertising posters and attracted throngs of street urchins should be tolerated. Monsieur Paer, author of *Agnese*, a fellow with a square face and a wart on his cheek, directed the Marquise de Sassenay's small private concerts in

Rue de la Ville-l'Évêque. All young girls sang 'L'Ermite de St-Avelle', words by Edmond Géraud. *Le Nain Jaune* became *Le Miroir*. The Café Lemblin favoured the emperor, as opposed to the Café Valois which favoured the Bourbons. Already watched from the shadows by Louvel, the Duc de Berry had just been married to a princess of Sicily. It had been a year since Madame de Staël died. Mademoiselle Mars was booed by members of the royal guard. Newspapers of substance were all very lightweight. Their format was small but they had great freedom of expression. *Le Constitutionnel* was constitutional. *La Minerve* called Chateaubriand 'Chateaubriant'. That prompted much laughter among the bourgeoisie at the expense of the great writer. In suborned newspapers time-serving journalists jeered at those exiled in 1815: David was now devoid of talent, Arnault of wit, Carnot of integrity; Soult had not won a single battle. It is true that Napoleon had lost his military genius. Everybody knows that letters sent to an exile through the post rarely reach their destination, with the police making it their sacred duty to intercept them. This is nothing new. Descartes complained of it during his banishment. Now, when David in a Belgian newspaper expressed some vexation at not having received letters that had been written to him, this was seen as cause for amusement by the royalist rags, which took the opportunity to mock the exile. Whether one said 'regicides' or 'voters', 'enemies' or 'allies', 'Napoleon' or 'Buonaparte' – this could divide two men more than any abyss. All right-minded people agreed that King Louis XVIII, hailed as 'the immortal author of the Charter', had put an end for ever to the era of revolutions. In the open space on the Pont-Neuf the word 'Redivivus'* was carved on the pedestal awaiting the statue of Henri IV. At 4 Rue Thérèse, Monsieur Piet launched his secret conclave dedicated to consolidating the monarchy. In moments of crisis the leaders of the right would say, 'We must write to Bacot.' Messieurs Canuel, O'Mahony and De Chappedelaine were devising – not without the approval of Monsieur – what was later to become 'the Riverside Conspiracy'. The Black Pin had a conspiracy of its own. Delaverderie made contact with Trogoff. Monsieur Decazes, who was something of a liberal, held sway. At 27 Rue St-Dominique, Chateaubriand stood at his window every morning in leggings and slippers, his grey hair in a madras head scarf, staring into a mirror and with a complete set of dentist's instruments laid out before him cleaning his splendid teeth while dictating to his secretary Monsieur Pilorge drafts of 'The Monarchy according to the Charter'. The leading critics rated Lafon

---

* Latin: 'Restored' or 'that lives again'.

above Talma. Monsieur de Féletz signed himself 'A'. Monsieur Hoffmann signed himself 'Z'. Charles Nodier wrote *Thérèse Aubert*. Divorce was abolished. The lycées were called 'colleges'. College students, their collars trimmed with a gold fleur-de-lys, came to blows over the king of Rome. The palace's police spies reported to Her Royal Highness Madame the ubiquitously displayed portrait of Monsieur le Duc d'Orléans, in which – very unfortunately – he cut a better figure in his uniform as colonel-general of the hussars than Monsieur le Duc de Berry in his uniform as colonel-general of the dragoons. The city of Paris had the dome of Les Invalides regilded at its own expense. Serious-minded men wondered what Monsieur de Trinquelague would do in this or that event. Monsieur Clausel de Montals was at odds with Monsieur Clausel de Coussergues on a number of points. Monsieur de Salaberry was not pleased. The actor Picard, who was a member of the Academy to which the actor Molière had not been able to gain membership, had *Les Deux Philibert* staged at the Odéon on the front of which 'THE EMPRESS THEATRE' was still clearly legible, although the letters had been stripped off. People took sides for or against Cugnet de Montarlot. Fabvier was seditious, Bavoux revolutionary. The bookseller Pélicier published an edition of Voltaire under the title *Works by Voltaire of the French Academy*. 'It attracts buyers,' said this candid editor. The general opinion was that Monsieur Charles Loyson would be the genius of the century. He was beginning to be the subject of envy – an indication of success. And these lines were written about him: 'Even when Loyson flies, you can tell he has feet.'*

As Cardinal Fesch refused to resign, Monsieur de Pins, archbishop of Amasie, administered the diocese of Lyon. The dispute between Switzerland and France over the valley of Dappes was sparked by a report by Captain, later General, Dufour. Unrecognized, Saint-Simon was working on his sublime dream. At the Academy of Sciences there was a famous Fourier who has been forgotten by posterity, and in some garret or other a little-known Fourier whom future generations will remember. Lord Byron was beginning to make his name. A note to a poem by Millevoye introduced him to France as 'a certain Lord Baron'. David d'Angers was demonstrating his skill at working in

---

* Hugo is playing on a well known line of verse from *Les Fastes; ou les Usages de l'Année*, canto I, by the poet and Academician Antoine-Marin Lemierre (1733–93): 'Même quand l'oiseau marche on sent qu'il a des ailes' ('Even when the bird walks you can tell it has wings'), with *Loyson* and *l'oiseau* a close homophone.

marble. Abbé Carron was singing the praises, to a small gathering of seminarists in Cul-de-sac des Feuillantines, of an unknown priest named Félicité-Robert, later to become Lamennais. A thing that emitted smoke and splashed about on the Seine, making a noise like a dog paddling, went to and fro past the windows of the Tuileries, between the Pont Royal and the Pont Louis XV. It was a contraption of not much use, some sort of plaything, the fantasy of an impractical inventor, a chimera – a steamboat. Parisians stared at this piece of futility with indifference. Monsieur de Vaublanc, reformer of the Institut by *coup d'état*, royal decree and change of guard, and distinguished creator of several Academicians – having created them, failed to become one himself. The Faubourg St-Germain and the Pavillon de Marsan wanted Monsieur Delavau for prefect of police because of his loyalty. Dupuytren and Récamier had an argument in the amphitheatre at the School of Medicine and threatened to come to blows over the divinity of Jesus Christ. With one eye on Genesis and the other on nature, Cuvier did his best to please religious reactionaries by reconciling fossils with biblical texts and using mastodons to give credit to Moses. Monsieur François de Neufchâteau, admirable promoter of Parmentier's memory, made countless efforts to have *pomme de terre* pronounced *parmentière*, and was utterly unsuccessful. Abbé Grégoire, former bishop, former member of the Convention, former senator, in the royalist polemical vocabulary had been downgraded to 'infamous Grégoire'. That word 'downgraded' was denounced as a neologism by Monsieur Royer-Collard.

Under the third arch of the Pont d'Iéna you could still distinguish by its whiteness the new stone used to fill the hole for explosives that Blücher had made two years earlier to blow up the bridge. The law prosecuted a man who at the sight of the Comte d'Artois entering Notre-Dame had said out loud, 'Oh, for the days when I used to see Bonaparte and Talma going into the Bal-Sauvage arm in arm!' Seditious talk. Six months in prison. Traitors were brazen. Men who had defected to the enemy on the eve of battle made no secret of their reward, and went about shamelessly in the light of day with their cynically acquired riches and honours. In the indecency of their paid abjectness deserters from Ligny and Quatre-Bras nakedly displayed their devotion to the monarchy, forgetting what is written on the wall in public conveniences in England: 'Please adjust your dress before leaving.'

This, in no particular order, is what confusedly survives of that now forgotten year 1817. History neglects nearly all these details, and cannot do otherwise: it would be overwhelmed by their infinitude.

Yet these details, wrongly called trivial – there is no trivial fact in the affairs of man, no trivial leaf in the vegetable world – do serve a purpose. The features of the years are what the face of the century is composed of.

It was in this year, 1817, that four young Parisians 'had a great lark'.

II

Two Foursomes

One of these Parisians came from Toulouse, another from Limoges, the third from Cahors and the fourth from Montauban. But they were students, and to say student is another way of saying Parisian: to study in Paris is to be born in Paris.

They were unexceptional young men – everyone has seen their type: four average specimens, neither good nor bad, learned nor ignorant, geniuses nor fools, with the handsome looks of that delightful spring-time we call the age of twenty. They were four ordinary Oscars, for at that time Arthurs did not yet exist. 'Burn for him the perfumes of Araby!' exclaimed the love song. 'Oscar approaches, Oscar, I shall see him!' Ossian had left his mark, the fashionable was Scandinavian and Caledonian. The pure English style would not prevail until later, and the first of the Arthurs, Wellington, had only just won the battle of Waterloo.

The names of these particular Oscars were Félix Tholomyès, from Toulouse, Listolier from Cahors, Fameuil from Limoges, and lastly Blachevelle from Montauban. Naturally, each of them had his mistress. Blachevelle loved Favourite, so named because she had been in England. Listolier adored Dahlia, who had taken as her *nom de guerre* the name of a flower. Fameuil idolized Zéphine, short for Joséphine. Tholomyès had Fantine, known as the Blonde because of her beautiful hair, the colour of sunlight.

Favourite, Dahlia, Zéphine and Fantine were four lovely young women, sweet-smelling and radiant, still with an air of the seamstress about them, not having entirely forsaken their sewing-needles, giddy with their love affairs but still with a lingering serenity of work on their faces, and in their souls that bloom of innocence that survives a woman's first fall. There was one of the four they called 'the baby' because she was the youngest, and one they called 'the old lady'. The old lady was twenty-three. To be quite candid, the first three were more experienced, more reckless and more pitched into the tumult of life than Fantine the Blonde, who was still cherishing her first illusion.

Dahlia, Zéphine, and especially Favourite, could not have said the same. There was already more than one episode in their stories, which had only just begun, and the lover whose name was Adolph in the first chapter turned out to be Alphonse in the second and Gustave in the third. Poverty and love of finery are two disastrous counsellors. One scolds and the other flatters, and beautiful young girls of humble origin have both whispering in their ears, one on either side. These ill-protected souls pay heed. That is how they come to be fallen women and to have stones thrown at them. They are oppressed by the splendour of all that is snow-white and unattainable. Alas! what if the Jungfrau were hungry?

Dahlia and Zéphine were admirers of Favourite because she had been to England. She was living on her own very early in life. Her father was a churlish old mathematics teacher, full of himself, unmarried, running round town giving private lessons despite his age. As a young man this teacher had one day seen a chambermaid catch her dress on a fender. He fell in love as a consequence of that chance incident. Favourite was the result. She would run into her father from time to time, who would nod to her. One morning a nunnish-looking old woman came to see her at home and said, 'You don't know me, mademoiselle?' 'No.' 'I'm your mother.' Then the old woman helped herself to food and drink, had a mattress she owned delivered there, and moved in. This peevish and sanctimonious mother never spoke to Favourite, let hours go by without uttering a word, ate enough to feed four, morning, noon and night, and would go down to chat in the porter's lodge, where she spoke ill of her daughter.

What had drawn Dahlia to Listolier, and possibly to others, to idleness, was having excessively pretty pink nails. How could she put nails like that to work? The girl who wants to remain virtuous must have no pity for her hands. As for Zéphine, she had conquered Fameuil by the saucily caressive way she had of saying, 'Yes, monsieur.'

The young men were chums, the young girls were friends. Such loves are always matched by such friendships.

It is one thing to be virtuous and another to be philosophical. The proof of this being that, with all due reservations about such irregular relationships, Favourite, Zéphine and Dahlia were philosophical young women and Fantine a virtuous one.

Virtuous? some will say. And what about Tholomyès? Solomon would reply that love constitutes virtue. We will confine ourselves to saying that Fantine's love was a first love, an exclusive love, a true love.

She alone of the four was on intimate terms with one man only.*

Fantine was one of those creatures born, so to speak, of the common people. She emerged from the most unfathomable depths of social obscurity, bearing on her brow the mark of anonymity and of unknown origins. She was born at Montreuil-sur-Mer. Of what parents? Who can say? She had never been known to have father or mother. She was called Fantine. Why Fantine? She had never been called by any other name. At the time of her birth the Directory was still in existence. No family name, since she had no family; and no baptismal name, since the Church was gone. She was called whatever took the fancy of whoever it was that first came across her as a very small child, running barefoot in the street. She accepted a name the way she accepted moisture from the clouds on her forehead when it rained. She was called 'little Fantine'. That is all anyone knew about her. Such was this human being's start in life. At the age of ten Fantine left town and went into domestic service with some local farmers. At fifteen she came to Paris 'to seek her fortune'. Fantine was beautiful, and remained chaste as long as she could. She was a lovely blonde with splendid teeth. She had gold and pearls for her dowry, but her gold was her head of hair and her pearls were in her mouth.

She worked to keep herself alive. Then, also to keep herself alive, she loved, for the heart has its own hunger.

She loved Tholomyès.

A conquest for him, for her the love of her life. The streets of the Latin quarter, thronged with students and grisettes, saw the beginning of this liaison. In that maze of streets on the Panthéon hill, the scene of the making and unmaking of so many intrigues, Fantine had long evaded Tholomyès but in such a way as to keep running into him. There is a way of avoiding someone that is very like seeking that person out. In short, the shepherd won his shepherdess.

Blachevelle, Listolier and Fameuil formed a kind of group of which Tholomyès was the leader. He was the joker.

Tholomyès was the classic perpetual student. He was rich. He had an income of four thousand francs. Four thousand francs! A glorious scandal on Mont Ste-Geneviève! Tholomyès was a thirty-year-old pleasure-seeker, and badly preserved. He was wrinkled and toothless, and he was beginning to show signs of baldness, he himself saying of

* Intimacy here being expressed by the use of the *tu* form: 'Elle . . . ne fût tutoyée que par un seul.'

it unsentimentally, 'Cock-of-the-walk at thirty, coot at forty.' His digestion was poor, and one of his eyes had started watering. But as his youthfulness burned out, his light-heartedness was ignited. He replaced his teeth with buffooneries, his hair with mirth, his health with irony, and in his weeping eye there was always laughter. He was a wreck, but flourishing. Upping sticks long before its time, his youth beat an orderly retreat with gales of laughter, and no one noticed. He had a play rejected at the Vaudeville. He wrote the odd undistinguished poem. Moreover, he was sceptical about everything in a superior way – a great strength in the eyes of the weak. So, being ironic and bald, he was their leader. Is it possible that irony comes from the English word 'iron'?

One day Tholomyès took the other three aside, made sure he had their full attention and said, 'Fantine, Dahlia, Zéphine and Favourite have been asking us for nearly a year to give them a surprise. We've made a solemn promise to do so. They're always talking about it, especially to me. Just as the old women in Naples cry to St Januarius, "Faccia gialluta, fa o miracolo!" – "Yellow face, perform your miracle!" – so our beauties keep saying, "Tholomyès, when are you going to deliver your surprise?" At the same time our parents keep writing to us. Attacked on both sides. I think the time has come. Let's talk.'

At this point Tholomyès lowered his voice and mysteriously described something so amusing that a huge enthusiastic guffaw emerged simultaneously from the mouths of all four of them and Blachevelle cried, 'That's a great idea!'

Finding themselves outside a smoke-filled bar, they went inside, and the rest of their confabulations were shrouded in obscurity.

The result of this shadowy conspiracy was a brilliant outing that took place the following Sunday, to which the four young men invited the four young women.

III
Haphazard Pairings

It is hard nowadays to picture what a country outing for students and grisettes was like forty-five years ago. Paris no longer has the same surroundings. The face of what might be called outer-Parisian life has completely changed in the last half-century. Where there was once the *coucou**, there is now the railway carriage. Where there was once the

---

* Lumbering, box-shaped, brightly painted carriages with benches, for up to twelve passengers and used mostly by the poorer classes.

old barge, there is now the steamboat. Today people talk of Fécamp as in the past they spoke of St-Cloud. Paris of 1862 is a city with all of France for its outskirts.

The four couples conscientiously performed all the country-excursion rituals possible at that time. The holiday season was just beginning and it was a warm, bright summer's day. Favourite, the only one of the girls who knew how to write, in the name of all four had written the following to Tholomyès the day before: 'An early start is a good start.' That is why they rose at five o'clock in the morning. Then they took the passenger barge to St-Cloud, looked at the dry fountain and cried, 'It must look splendid when there's water!' They breakfasted at the Tête-Noire, before Castaing had yet been there. They treated themselves to a game of ring-throwing among the rows of trees by the large pond, went up the Lantern of Diogenes, played roulette for macaroons on the Pont de Sèvres, picked flowers at Puteaux, bought reed-pipes at Neuilly, ate apple turnovers wherever they went, were perfectly happy.

The young girls chirruped and chattered like fugitive songbirds. It was bliss. Now and again they gave the young men little slaps. Morning-of-life's ecstasy! Delightful years! Dragonflies' wings all aquiver! Oh, no matter who you may be, don't you remember? Have you walked through the bushes, holding aside the branches for the pretty face following behind you? Have you slid, on a slope wet with rain, laughing, with a woman you love catching you by the hand and crying, 'Oh, my brand-new ankle-boots! Just look at the state of them!'

Let us say at once, this good-humoured party was spared the vex-atious joy of a shower, although Favourite, sounding authoritative and maternal, had said as they set out, 'The slugs are out on the paths – a sign of rain, my dears.'

All four were exceedingly pretty. Monsieur le Chevalier de Labouïsse, famous at that time as a good old classic poet who had his Éléonore, was strolling under the chestnut trees of St-Cloud that day when he saw them pass by at about ten o'clock in the morning and exclaimed, 'There's one too many,' thinking of the Graces. Favourite, Blachevelle's girl, the twenty-three-year-old, the old lady, ran ahead beneath the great green boughs, jumping ditches, deliriously leaping over bushes, and presided over this merry-making with the spiritedness of a young faun. Zéphine and Dahlia, whose beauty happened to be such that they set each other off to advantage and complemented each other, were never apart, more out of flirtatious instinct than friendship; and clinging to each other, they struck English poses. The first keepsakes had just started to appear; melancholy was the incoming fashion for women as, later, Byronism was for men, and hairstyles for the tender sex were beginning to have a weeping look about them. Zéphine and Dahlia had their hair dressed in ringlets. Listolier and Fameuil, engaged in a discussion about their professors, explained to Fantine the difference between Monsieur Delvincourt and Monsieur Blondeau.

Blachevelle looked as if he had been created for the sole purpose of carrying on his arm, that Sunday, Favourite's Ternaux shawl, patterned at one end only.

Tholomyès followed behind, dominating the group. He was very cheerful but you could sense the controlling force in him. There was dictatorship in his jollity. His principal ornament was a pair of nankeen bell-bottomed trousers with footstraps of braided copper. He had in his hand a strong cane walking-stick that had cost two hundred francs and, since he denied himself nothing, a strange thing called a cigar in his mouth. Holding nothing sacred, he smoked.

'That Tholomyès is amazing!' said the others, in awe. 'What trousers! What energy!'

As for Fantine, she was the essence of joy. Her splendid teeth had evidently been provided by God for a purpose – laughter. She preferred to carry in her hand her little straw hat with its long white ribbons, rather than wear it on her head. Her thick blonde hair, inclined to fan out and easily falling loose, and which she had to keep pinning up again, seemed made for Galatea's flight under the willows. Her rosy lips babbled with delight. The voluptuously turned-up corners of her mouth, as in the ancient masks of Erigone, seemed to encourage the bold. But above this exuberance in the lower part of her face her long shadowy eyelashes were discreetly cast down, like a call to order. There was something ineffably charming and resplendent about her entire outfit. She wore a dress of mauve *barège**, little reddish-brown shoes cross-laced over her fine, white lacy stockings; and that Marseille invention, a type of muslin spencer whose name, *canezou*, a corruption of the words *quinze août* as pronounced on the Canebière, evokes sunny weather, a hot climate, and the south. The other three, less bashful as we have already said, were simply bare-fleshed in low-cut dresses, which in summer, beneath flower-covered hats, looks very charming and flirtatious. But beside their provocative attire, blonde Fantine's *canezou*, with its transparencies, its suggestiveness and its modesty, at once concealing and revealing, seemed an alluring contrivance of decency; and the famous Court of Love, presided over by

* A light gauzy wool fabric, originally made in Barèges in south-western France.

117

the Vicomtesse de Cette with her sea-green eyes, might have awarded the prize for flirtatiousness to this *canezou*, competing for modesty. The simplest is sometimes the canniest. It can happen.

Stunning to look at, with a delicate profile, eyes of deep blue, fleshy eyelids, small arched feet, beautifully turned wrists and ankles, a white complexion showing here and there the azure-tinted branching of the veins, fresh young cheeks, the sturdy neck of Aeginetan Junos, strong and supple in the nape; shoulders that might have been modelled by Coustou, with a voluptuous dimple in the middle visible through the muslin; gaiety tempered with dreaminess, sculptural and exquisite – such was Fantine. And discernible beneath these trappings and ribbons was a statue, and within this statue a soul.

Fantine was beautiful without really being aware of it. Those rare visionaries, mysterious high priests of the beautiful who silently compare everything with perfection, would have glimpsed in this young working girl, through the transparency of her Parisian grace, the sacred euphony of antiquity. This child of obscurity was an aristocrat. She was beautiful in both aspects, style and rhythm. Style is the form the ideal takes, and rhythm its movement.

We have said that Fantine was joyfulness. Fantine was also demureness.

To any observer who might have studied her closely, what emanated from her through all that giddiness of youth, of the season and of her love affair, was an invincible expression of reserve and modesty. She remained a little astonished. This chaste astonishment is the subtle difference that distinguishes Psyche from Venus. Fantine had the long, slender white fingers of the vestal virgin who stirs the ashes of the sacred fire with a golden pin. Although she would have refused Tholomyès nothing, as we shall see only too clearly, her face in repose was supremely virginal. A grave and almost austere dignity suddenly overcame her at certain times, and there was nothing more singular and disturbing than to see her gaiety so quickly subside and introversion succeed her exuberance, without any transition. This abrupt seriousness, sometimes of a pronounced severity, resembled the disdain of a goddess. Her brow, nose and chin presented that balance of line, quite distinct from balance of proportion, from which the harmony of the face derives. In that very telling space that separates the base of the nose from the upper lip, she had a slight and charming hollow, the mysterious sign of chastity that made Barbarossa fall in love with a Diana found in the excavations at Iconium.

Love may very well be a transgression. Fantine was the innocence that survives transgression.

IV
Tholomyès Is So Happy, He Sings a Spanish Song

That whole day was dawn, from morning till night. All nature seemed to be on holiday and filled with gladness. The flowerbeds of St-Cloud perfumed the air. The breeze on the Seine softly stirred the leaves. Branches waved in the wind. Bees plundered the jasmine. A whole artistic colony of butterflies frolicked among the yarrow, clover and wild oats. In the king of France's majestic park there were vagabonds aplenty: the birds.

The four joyous couples revelled in the sunshine, amid these fields, flowers, trees.

And in this shared paradise, talking, singing, running, dancing, chasing butterflies, gathering bindweed, getting their pink lacy stockings wet in the tall grass, radiant, flighty, meaning no harm, every girl received a little randomly the kisses of every man, with the exception of Fantine. Remote in her abstracted, shy, dreamy resistance, she was in love.

'You always have that look about you,' said Favourite.

Such is true joy. This gallivanting of happy couples has a deep affinity with life and with nature, and elicits from everything fondness and light. Once upon a time there was a fairy who created the fields and forests specially for those in love. Hence the eternal truancy of lovers, who are forever escaping to the countryside and will go on doing so as long as lovers and countryside continue to exist. Hence the popularity of springtime among thinkers. The nobleman and the lowly paid worker, duke and upstart, courtiers and townsfolk, as they used to say in the old days, all are vassals of this fairy. People laugh, they seek each other out, and there is in the air a sublime brilliance. What a difference being in love makes! Notaries' clerks are gods. And the little shrieks, the chasing through the grass, the chance to put an arm around a waist, those sweet nothings that are music to the ear, the adoration declared in the way a single syllable is uttered, those cherries plucked from one mouth to another – all this becomes part of the coruscating heavenly radiance. Beautiful young women are sweetly lavish of themselves. They think this will never end. Philosophers, poets, painters, observe these raptures and do not know what to make of them, so bedazzled are they. 'The departure for Cythera!' cries Watteau. Lancret, painter of the lower classes, observes his commoners going off into the blue. Diderot opens his arms to all these dalliances, and d'Urfé introduces Druids among them.

After breakfast the four couples went to what was then called the King's Square to see a plant recently arrived from India, whose name escapes us at present, which at that time was drawing the whole of Paris to St-Cloud. It was a bizarre yet attractive long-stemmed shrub with countless branches of thread-like slenderness, tangled and leafless, and covered with a million tiny white rosettes, which made the shrub look like a head of hair spangled with flowers. There was always an admiring crowd around it.

After viewing the shrub Tholomyès exclaimed, 'Donkey-rides on me!' And having agreed a price with the owner of the donkeys, they rode back by way of Vanves and Issy. At Issy an incident occurred. By chance the park, confiscated land at that time owned by the army supplier Bourguin, happened to be wide open. They went through the gates, visited the model of an anchorite in his grotto, tried the mysterious distorting effects of the famous chamber of mirrors, a lewd trap worthy of some millionaire satyr or Turcaret metamorphosed into Priapus. Vigorously they set in motion the big net swing attached to the two chestnut trees extolled by Abbé de Bernis. And while swinging the girls in it, one after the other, which amid general laughter created all the billowing skirts Greuze might have wished to see, Tholomyès from Toulouse, who had a touch of the Spaniard about him (Toulouse being related to Tolosa), sang to a melancholy tune the old Galician song probably inspired by some lovely maiden flying through the air on a rope hung between two trees:

> Soy de Badajoz,
> Amor me llama,
> Toda mi alma,
> Es en mi ojos,
> Porque enseñas,
> A tus piernas.

Fantine alone refused to go on the swing.

'I don't like people putting on airs like that,' Favourite muttered tartly.

Their donkeys gave way to a fresh delight: they crossed the Seine in a boat, and from Passy arrived at the Étoile gate on foot. Let us not forget they had been up since five o'clock that morning, but – Bah! 'There's no such thing as tiredness on Sundays,' as Favourite would say, 'on Sundays tiredness has the day off.' At about three o'clock the four gleefully terrified couples were rattling down on the coaster ride, a curious structure which then stood on the Beaujon heights and whose serpentine loops could be seen outlined above the trees on the Champs-Élysées.

From time to time Favourite cried out, 'What about the surprise? I want the surprise.'

'Patience,' replied Tholomyès.

V
At Bombarda's

When they had exhausted the delights of the coaster ride, their thoughts turned to eating. And the radiant party of eight, somewhat tired at last, fetched up at Bombarda's tavern, a subsidiary establishment set up on the Champs-Élysées by Bombarda, the owner of the famous restaurant whose sign then hung in the Rue de Rivoli, near the Passage Delorme.

A large but ugly room with an alcove containing a bed at the back of it (given how crowded the tavern was on a Sunday, they had no choice but to accept this accommodation); two windows affording a view of the embankment and the river through the elm trees; a magnificent August sunbeam glancing across the windows; two tables: on one, a triumphant pile of posies mingled with ladies' and gents' hats; at the other, the four couples seated round a festive clutter of dishes, plates, glasses and bottles, jugs of beer along with flasks of wine. Not much orderliness on the table, some disorderliness underneath it.

'The noise they made under the table, / drumming their feet – a terrible din! It was unbearable,' says Molière.

This was where the pastoral idyll that began at five o'clock in the morning had got to by half-past four in the afternoon. The sun was setting, appetites had been satisfied.

Thronging and full of sunshine, the Champs-Élysées were all light and dust, two things that constitute Elysian glory. Those whinnying marbles the Marly horses reared up in a golden cloud. There was a to-ing and fro-ing of carriages. A detachment of magnificent life-guards, led by a bugler, descended Avenue de Neuilly. The white flag, faintly pink in the sunset, fluttered above the dome of the Tuileries. Place de la Concorde, which had become once more Place Louis XV, was teeming with happy pedestrians. Many wore the silver fleur-de-lys on the moire ribbon that in 1817 had not yet entirely disappeared from buttonholes. Here and there, among applauding passers-by who gathered around them, little girls danced in a ring to a then well known Bourbon rhyme destined to spell the end of the Hundred Days, which had as its refrain, 'Give us back our *père de Gand**, Give us back our *père*.'

Scattered groups of suburban folk, dressed in their Sunday best, sometimes even wearing the fleur-de-lys like city-dwellers, played the ring game and went round on the wooden carousel horses in the spacious Carré Marigny. Others drank. A few – printers' apprentices – wore paper caps. They could be heard laughing. Everything was radiant. It was a time of undeniable peace and the utmost royalist security. It was the period when a special private report from Prefect of Police Anglès to the king about the suburbs of Paris concluded with these lines:

'All things considered, sire, there is nothing to be feared from these people. They are as easy-going and indolent as cats. The populace is restless in the provinces, not in Paris. All these men are small fry. It would take two of them, one standing on the other, sire, to match one of your grenadiers. There is nothing to be feared from the capital's populace. It is remarkable that the average height of this population has fallen in the last fifty years. And the people of Paris's suburbs are smaller than before the Revolution. They are not dangerous. In short, they are harmless riff-raff.'

Police prefects do not believe a cat can possibly turn into a lion. Yet it can, and that is the miracle of the Paris populace. Moreover, the cat so despised by Comte Anglès was held in esteem by the republics of antiquity. It embodied freedom, in their eyes; and as though to serve as a pendant to the Wingless Minerva of Piraeus, there stood on the public square in Corinth the bronze colossus of a cat. The naive police of the Restoration took too 'favourable' a view of the people of Paris. They are not such 'harmless riff-raff' as is thought. The Parisian is to the Frenchman what the Athenian was to the Greek: no one sleeps more soundly than he, no one is more downright frivolous and lazy, no one more apparently forgetful. Yet in this he is not to be trusted. He is prone to indolence of every sort, but when there is glory at stake he is a wonder, capable of all kinds of fury. Give him a pike, he will deliver the tenth of August. Give him a gun, you will have Austerlitz. He is Napoleon's mainstay and Dan-

---

* During the Hundred Days Louis XVIII fled to Ghent ('Gand' in French). The children's rhyme contains a playful pun – *notre père de Gand* ('our father in Ghent') sounds the same as *notre paire de gants* ('our pair of gloves').

ton's powerbase. Is his country at stake? He enlists. Is liberty at stake? He rips up the cobblestones. Beware! His hair bristles with epic rage, his shirt hangs about him like the chlamys. Watch out! He will make Caudine Forks of any Rue Greneta. If the hour strikes, this working-class Parisian will grow in stature. This little man will rise up and his gaze will be terrible and his breath will become a hurricane, and from that poor puny chest will issue wind enough to reshape the contours of the Alps. It is thanks to the working-class Parisian that the Revolution, taken to the army, conquers Europe. He sings. That is his pleasure. Give him a song to match his nature, and you will see! As long as he has only the 'Carmagnole' to sing, all he does is overthrow Louis XVI. Have him sing the 'Marseillaise', and he will free the world.

With this note written in the margin of Anglès's report, we return to our four couples. The meal, as we said, was drawing to a close.

VI
Chapter in which Lovers Adore

Table talk, lovers' talk – both are equally elusive. Lovers' talk is castle-building, table talk is pipe-dreaming.

Fameuil and Dahlia were humming, Tholomyès drinking, Zéphine laughing, Fantine smiling. Listolier was blowing a wooden trumpet he had bought at St-Cloud. Favourite gazed tenderly at Blachevelle and said, 'Blachevelle, I adore you.'

This prompted Blachevelle to ask, 'What would you do, Favourite, if I stopped loving you?'

'What would I do!' cried Favourite. 'Oh, don't say that even as a joke! If you stopped loving me, I'd come after you, I'd scratch and claw you, I'd throw water over you, I'd have you arrested.'

Blachevelle smiled with the voluptuous self-conceit of a man whose vanity is flattered.

Favourite went on, 'Yes, I'd send the police after you! Oh, I'd make no end of a fuss! You scoundrel!'

Blachevelle threw himself back in his chair in ecstasy and proudly closed his eyes.

As she ate, Dahlia said quietly to Favourite amid the uproar, 'So you really worship your Blachevelle, do you?'

'I detest him,' replied Favourite in a similar undertone, picking up her fork again. 'He's stingy. It's the lad who lives opposite me I love. He's very well mannered, that young man – you know the one? You can see he's got the makings of an actor. I love actors. As soon as he comes home, his mother says, "Oh Lord! That's the end of my peace and quiet! Now he's going to start shouting. My dear boy, you drive me crazy!" Because he goes right up to the top of the house, climbs up to some rat-ridden attic, some dark poky corner, and then sings and recites – don't ask me what – and you can hear him all the way downstairs! He earns twenty sous a day writing pettifogging documents for some lawyer. He's the son of a former choirmaster at St-Jacques-du-Haut-Pas. Oh, he's a real gentleman! He adores me so much that one day when he saw me making pancake batter he said to me, "Mam'selle, make your gloves into fritters and I'll eat them." Only an artist would say something like that. Oh, he's such a gentleman. I'm falling madly in love with that boy. All the same, I tell Blachevelle I adore him. What a liar I am! Eh? What a liar!'

Favourite paused, then went on, 'You see, Dahlia, I feel miserable. It's done nothing but rain all summer, the wind's always blowing, it gets on my nerves, Blachevelle's very tight-fisted, there are hardly any peas in the market, you don't know what to eat. I'm down in the dumps, as the English say, butter's so expensive, and look, here we are eating in a room with a bed in it. It's disgusting! It makes me fed up with life.'

VII
Tholomyès's Wisdom

In the meantime, a few of them sang while the others engaged in rowdy conversation, all speaking at once. In the end it was just noise. Tholomyès intervened.

'Let's not speak too quickly or without reflecting!' he exclaimed. 'Let's think first, if we want to be brilliant. Too much spontaneity simply empties the mind. Spilled beer gathers no froth. Slow down, gentlemen. Let's bring some dignity to the banquet. Let's eat thoughtfully, feast slowly. Let's not be in any hurry. Consider the springtime. If it arrives too soon it's blasted, that's to say, frostbitten. Overeagerness spells the ruin of peach and apricot trees. Overeagerness kills the graciousness and pleasure of a good dinner party. "No overeagerness, gentlemen!" Grimod de la Reynière agrees with Talleyrand on that.'

A murmur of rebellion rumbled within the group.

'Leave us alone, Tholomyès,' said Blachevelle.

'Down with the tyrant!' said Fameuil.

'Bombarda, Bombance and Bamboche!'* cried Listolier.

'A Sunday's a Sunday,' Fameuil declared.

'We're sober,' added Listolier.

'Tholomyès,' remarked Blachevelle, 'observe my calm.'

'You're the marquis of that estate,' retorted Tholomyès.

This feeble play on words – the Marquis de Montcalm† was a renowned royalist – had the same effect as a stone thrown into a pond. All the frogs fell silent.

'Friends!' cried Tholomyès in the voice of a man reasserting his authority. 'Pull yourselves together. This unexpected pun shouldn't be greeted with too much amazement. Not everything that comes out of the blue is necessarily worthy of admiration and respect. Puns are the droppings of the mind on the wing. The joke lands wherever it falls, and after excreting a joke the mind soars. A white splodge splattered on a rock does not prevent the condor from scaling the heights. Far be it from me to belittle the pun! I have a due respect for its merits, nothing more. The most noble, the most sublime, the most delightful of humankind, and perhaps other than humankind, have played on words. Jesus Christ made a pun about St Peter, Moses about Isaac, Aeschylus about Polynices, Cleopatra about Octavian. And note that Cleopatra's pun preceded the battle of Actium and without it no one would remember the city of Toryne, a name that sounds like a Greek word meaning ladle. That said, I go back to my exhortation. I repeat, brothers, no overeagerness, no hurly-burly, no excess, even in witticisms, jollifications, high spirits, or quips. Listen to me – I have Amphiaraus' prudence and Caesar's baldness. There must be a limit, even to rebuses. *Est modus in rebus.*‡ There must be a limit, even to meals. You're fond of apple turnovers, ladies. Don't overindulge your fondness. Even in the matter of turnovers, good sense and artfulness are required. Gluttony punishes the glutton, *Gula punit gulax.* The good Lord has given indigestion the task of teaching our stomachs a lesson. And remember this: every one of our passions, even love, has a stomach that mustn't be overfed. In all things the word *finis* must be written in good time. We must keep

---

* This is virtual nonsense, words with a loose lexical connection chosen for their similar sound. Bombarda is the name of the restaurant. *Bombance* and *bamboche* are colloquial words for a feast, or blowout.

† The ultra-royalist marquis Décadon de Montcalm, pronounced *mon calme*, 'my calm' (1775–1857).

‡ 'Moderation in all things', Horace, *Satires* I:1, line 106. Tholomyès plays on 'in [all] things' and the Latin word *rebus*, meaning 'puzzle'.

ourselves in check, and when it becomes a matter of urgency draw the bolt on our appetite, lock up our cravings and put ourselves behind bars. The wise man is he who knows how to put himself under arrest at any given moment. Trust me a little. Just because I've studied a bit of law, so my exam results say, and because I know the difference between a mooted case and a *sub judice* case, and because I've defended a thesis in Latin on the way torture was administered in Rome during the period when Munatius Demens was the Parricide's magistrate who investigated murder, and because, it would seem, I'm going to qualify as a doctor, it doesn't necessarily follow that I'm an idiot. I advise you to observe moderation in your desires. As sure as my name is Félix Tholomyès, what I say is right. Happy the man who, when the time comes, shows a hero's resolve and abdicates like Sulla, or Origen.'

Favourite listened with close attention. 'Félix,' she said, 'what a pretty word! I love that name. It's Latin. It means the same as Prosper.'

Tholomyès went on. '*Quirites**, gentlemen, *caballeros*†, my friends. Do you wish to feel no itch, to spare yourself the nuptial bed and defy love? Nothing simpler. Here's the recipe: lemonade, strenuous exercise, hard labour. Tire yourself out, haul boulders, don't sleep, stay awake, sate yourself with gassy drinks and lotus tea, savour emulsions of poppyseed and agnus castus, with the added spice of a strict diet, starve yourself, and combine this with cold baths, girdles of herbs, the application of a lead plaque, lotions made with Goulard's extract and poultices made with vinegar and water.'

'I'd rather have a woman,' said Listolier.

'Beware of women!' Tholomyès responded. 'Woe to the man who surrenders himself to the fickle heart of a woman! A woman is scheming and perfidious. She hates the serpent out of professional jealousy. The serpent is the shop across the way.'

'Tholomyès!' cried Blachevelle. 'You're drunk!'

'Of course I am!' said Tholomyès.

'Be cheerful then,' said Blachevelle.

'Agreed,' replied Tholomyès.

And refilling his glass, he rose to his feet. 'Glory be to wine! *Nunc te, Bacche, canam!*‡ Forgive me, ladies, that's Spanish. And the proof, señoras, is this: such being the people, such is the cask. The *arroba* of Castile contains sixteen litres, the *cántaro* of Alicante, twelve, the

---

* Latin, denoting 'Roman citizens'.
† Spanish for 'gentlemen'.
‡ 'Now, Bacchus, will I sing of you!', Virgil, *Georgics*, bk II, line 2. This of course is not Spanish, but Latin.

almude of the Canaries, twenty-five, the *cuartin* of the Balearic Isles, twenty-six, Tsar Peter's barrel, thirty. Long live that great tsar and long live his barrel, which was greater still! Ladies, a word of friendly advice: take the man sitting on the wrong side of you for your lover, if you so please. It's in the nature of love to err. Romance isn't meant to make life a brutalizing misery for itself, like an English housemaid with calluses on her knees from scrubbing floors. Sweet romance isn't meant for that – it gladly roves! It has been said that to err is human; I say, to err is to be amorous. Ladies, I adore you all.

'O Zéphine, O Joséphine, with your more than unconventional prettiness you'd be attractive if you weren't crumpled. You look like a pretty face that someone has sat on by mistake.

'As for Favourite, O nymphs and muses! Blachevelle was stepping over the gutter in Rue Guérin-Boisseau one day when he saw a beautiful girl in smooth white stockings, showing off her legs. This prelude was to his liking, and Blachevelle fell in love. The girl he loved was Favourite. O Favourite, you have Ionian lips. There was a Greek painter called Euphorion, nicknamed "the painter of lips". That Greek alone would have been worthy to paint your mouth. Listen, before you there was no creature worthy of that name. You were made to win the apple, like Venus, or to eat it, like Eve. Beauty begins with you. I've just mentioned Eve. It was you that created her. You deserve the patent for the invention of the beautiful woman. O Favourite, I'll now stop addressing you in familiar terms because I'm switching from poetry to prose.* You spoke of my name a little while ago. I was touched. But whoever we may be, let us distrust names. They can be misleading. My name's Félix, but I'm not happy. Words are liars. Let's not blindly accept the suggestions they give us. It would be a mistake to write to Liège for corks and to Pau for leather gloves.†

'Miss Dahlia, in your place I'd call myself Rosa. A flower should smell sweet and a woman should have some wit.

'I say nothing of Fantine. She's a star-gazer, a dreamy, pensive, sensitive soul. She's a phantom in the form of a nymph, with the modesty of a nun, astray in the life of the Parisian grisette but taking refuge in her illusions, singing and praying and gazing into the blue without really knowing what she's seeing or what she's doing, and who, with eyes turned heavenwards, wanders about in a garden where there are more birds than actually exist. O Fantine, let me tell you this: I, Tholomyès,

---

* In this paean to Favourite, Tholomyès has been using the *tu* form.

† Cork (*liège*) does not come from Liège in Belgium, and leather skin (*peau*) does not come from Pau (pronounced identically) in south-west France.

am an illusion. But she doesn't even hear me, this fair maid of fancy! Besides, everything about her is freshness, softness, youth, sweet morning light. O Fantine, a girl who deserves to be called marguerite or pearl*, you're a woman of the most lustrous beauty.

'Ladies, a second piece of advice: do not marry. Marriage is a form of grafting. It can take well or badly. Avoid that risk. But why bother telling you this? I'm wasting my breath. Girls are incurable when it comes to marriage. And whatever we sensible chaps may say won't prevent the waistcoat-makers and shoe-stitchers from dreaming of husbands with diamonds galore. Well, that's as may be, but remember this, my dears: you eat too much sugar. You have but one fault, O women, and that's nibbling sugar. O rodent sex, your pretty little white teeth adore sugar. Now, listen carefully, sugar is a salt. All salts cause dehydration. Sugar is the most dehydrating of all salts. It draws the blood fluids out of the veins. Hence, coagulation, then solidification of the blood. Hence, tubercles in the lungs. Hence, death. That's why diabetes is little short of consumption. So don't crunch sugar and you'll live!

'I now turn to the men. Gentlemen, make conquests. Steal your darlings from each other without remorse. Change partners. There are no friends in matters of love. Wherever there's a pretty woman there's open hostility. No quarter given, all-out war! A pretty woman is a *casus belli*. A pretty woman is flagrant provocation. All the invasions of history have been brought about by petticoats. Woman is man's entitlement. Romulus carried off the Sabines, William carried off the Saxons' womenfolk, Caesar carried off the Romans'. The man who isn't loved hovers like a vulture over other men's mistresses. And as for myself, to all those poor unfortunates who are widowers I give you Bonaparte's sublime address to the army of Italy: "Soldiers, you have nothing; the enemy has it all." '

Tholomyès paused.

'Catch your breath, Tholomyès,' said Blachevelle.

At that point Blachevelle, accompanied by Listolier and Fameuil, launched into one of those art-student songs, sung to a plaintive tune, composed of the first words that spring to mind, extravagantly rhymed or not at all, as devoid of meaning as the swaying of a tree or the sound of the wind; words born out of pipe smoke, and dispersing with it as it clears. This is the verse with which the group responded to Tholomyès's tirade:

* An archaic meaning of *marguerite* is 'pearl'.

The simple Simons paid a fee
To an intermediary
For Sire Clermont-Tonnerre
To be made abbot on St John's Day.
But abbot he could never be
For no anointed monk was he;
So their intermediary
Resentfully returned their fee.

This was no way to dampen Tholomyès's exuberances. He drained his glass, refilled it and resumed.

'Down with wisdom! Forget everything I said. Let's be neither prudish nor prudent, nor pompous asses. I propose a toast to merriment. Let's be merry. Let's complete our law studies with food and folly! Indigestion and digest. Let Justinian be lord of Misrule and Revelry be his mistress! Joy in the lower depths! Live, O creation! The world is a great diamond. I'm happy. The birds are amazing. What jollity everywhere! The nightingale is an Elleviou who sings gratis. Summer, I salute you! O Luxembourg! O Georgics of Rue Madame and Allée de l'Observatoire! O romantic soldier boys! O all those lovely nursemaids who have nothing better to think of while minding children than having children of their own! The pampas of America would attract me, had I not the arcades around the Odéon. My soul soars over virgin forests and savannahs. Everything is beautiful. Flies are buzzing in the sunbeams. The sun has with a sneeze produced the hummingbird. Kiss me, Fantine!'

He got the wrong girl, and kissed Favourite.

VIII
Death of a Horse

'The food's better at Edon than at Bombarda,' exclaimed Zéphine.

'I prefer Bombarda to Edon,' declared Blachevelle. 'It's more luxurious. More oriental. Look at the room downstairs. There are mirrors on the walls.'

'I prefer ices on my plate,'* said Favourite.

Blachevelle was insistent. 'Look at the knives. Bombarda's have silver handles, the ones at Edon are bone. Well, silver's more valuable than bone.'

'Except for those who have a silver chin,' observed Tholomyès.

* The word for 'mirror' and 'ice' is the same in French, *glace*.

At that moment he was looking at the dome of Les Invalides, visible from Bombarda's windows.

There was a pause.

'Tholomyès,' exclaimed Fameuil, 'Listolier and I were having a discussion just now.'

'A discussion's good,' replied Tholomyès, 'a quarrel's better.'

'We were having a philosophical argument.'

'Well?'

'Which do you prefer, Descartes or Spinoza?'

'Désaugiers,' said Tholomyès. Having delivered this verdict, he drank and went on: 'I consent to live. It's not all over yet for this earth, since we can still rave. For this I give thanks to the immortal gods. We lie but we laugh. We affirm but we doubt. The unexpected springs from the syllogism. That's wonderful. There are still human beings on earth capable of gleefully opening and closing the jack-in-the-box of paradox. What you're thoughtlessly consuming, ladies, is Madeira wine, I'll have you know, from the Coural das Freiras vineyard, which is eighteen hundred feet above sea level. Consider what you're drinking! Eighteen hundred feet! And Monsieur Bombarda, the magnificent proprietor of this restaurant, gives you those eighteen hundred for four francs and fifty centimes.'

Fameuil again broke in. 'Tholomyès, your opinions inspire confidence. Who's your favourite author?'

'Ber . . .'

'. . . quin?'

'No . . . choux.'

And Tholomyès went on. 'All honour to Bombarda! If he could procure me an oriental dancing-girl he would be the equal of Munophis of Elephanta, and of Thygelion of Chaeronea if he could bring me a Greek courtesan. For, O mesdames, there were Bombardas in Greece and Egypt. Apuleius tells us so. Alas! It's always the same, there's nothing new. Nothing we haven't already seen in the Creator's creation! *Nil sub sole novum*, says Solomon.* *Amor omnibus idem*, says Virgil.† And Carabine joins Carabin‡ on the river boat to St-Cloud, just as Aspasia joined Pericles with the fleet at Samos. One

---

* Ecclesiastes 1:9, 'There is no new thing under the sun.' Traditionally attributed to Solomon.

† 'Love is the same for all', Virgil, *Georgics*, bk III, line 244.

‡ The word *carabin* (originally, 'a mounted soldier') came to be a familiar term for a medical student, and a *carabine* ('cavalry rifle'), as used here, would be the medical student's lady-friend.

last word. Do you know who Aspasia was, ladies? Although she lived at a time when women did not yet have a soul, she was a moving spirit. A spirit of a rosy and crimson hue, fierier than fire, fresher than the dawn. Aspasia was a creature in whom the two extremes of womanhood met; the harlot-goddess. Socrates combined with Manon Lescaut. Aspasia was created in case Prometheus needed a whore.'

Now in full flight, Tholomyès would have found it difficult to stop had not a horse dropped dead on the embankment at that very moment. Shocked, cart and speaker were pulled up short. It was a mare from the Beauce region, old and thin and fit for the knacker's yard, pulling a very heavy cart. Just in front of Bombarda's the defeated, worn-out beast refused to go any further. The incident attracted a crowd. Cursing and indignant, the carter hardly had time to utter with appropriate energy the fateful words 'Damn you!', backed up with a ruthless lash of the whip, than the nag collapsed, never to rise again. At the outcry from the passers-by Tholomyès's cheerful audience looked round, and he took the opportunity to end his homily with this doleful verse:

> It belonged to a world where coaches and carriages
> Share the same fate;
> And being a nag, it lived as nags do,
> But the space of a 'damn you'!*

'Poor horse!' sighed Fantine.

And Dahlia exclaimed, 'There goes Fantine feeling sorry for horses now! How can anyone be so stupid!'

Folding her arms and tossing her head, Favourite at that moment gave Tholomyès a determined look and said, 'Now then, what about this surprise?'

'Well may you ask. The moment has arrived,' replied Tholomyès. 'Gentlemen, it's now time to surprise these ladies. Ladies, give us a moment.'

'It begins with a kiss,' said Blachevelle.

'On the forehead,' added Tholomyès.

Each solemnly planted a kiss on his mistress's forehead. Then,

---

* Tholomyès is parodying four lines of verse by Malherbe, from his poem 'Consolation à Monsieur du Périer': 'She belonged to a world / Where the loveliest things meet the worst fate. / And being a rose, she lived as roses do, / But the space of a morning.'

placing a finger to their lips, all four headed for the door, one after the other.

Favourite clapped her hands as they left. 'This is already good fun,' she said.

'Don't be gone too long,' murmured Fantine. 'We'll be waiting for you.'

IX
A Merry End to Mirth

Left by themselves, the young girls, two at each window, rested their elbows on the window-sills, chatting, leaning out and talking from one casement to the other.

They saw the young men emerge arm in arm from the Bombarda tavern. Their lovers turned round, waved to them, laughing, and disappeared into the dusty Sunday throng that invades the Champs-Élysées every week.

'Don't be gone long!' cried Fantine.

'What are they going to bring us?' said Zéphine.

'Something pretty, for sure,' said Dahlia.

'Something gold for me,' said Favourite.

They were soon distracted by the activity on the riverside, which they could discern through the branches of the tall trees and which kept them very entertained. It was the time of day when the mail-coaches and stage-coaches set off. Nearly all the mail-coaches en route for the south and west passed along the Champs-Élysées. Most of them followed the embankment and went through the Passy gate. Every minute some huge carriage, painted yellow and black, heavily loaded, noisily harnessed, its shape distorted with trunks, tarpaulins and cases, filled with passengers who immediately disappeared from sight, came hurtling through the crowd in apparent fury, pulverizing the roadway, turning all the cobbles into flint-stones, sending sparks flying, for all the world like a blacksmith's forge, with dust for smoke. This commotion delighted the young women.

Favourite exclaimed, 'What a din! It sounds like a pile of chains flying off.'

Now one of these vehicles, which was not very clearly visible through the thick foliage of the elm trees, happened to stop for a moment, then set off again at a gallop. This surprised Fantine.

'That's odd!' she said. 'I thought the stage-coach never stopped.'

Favourite shrugged. 'She's amazing, this Fantine. A curiosity worth coming to see in her own right. She marvels at the simplest things.

Suppose I'm a traveller. I say to the stage-coach, "I'm going on ahead. You can pick me up on the embankment as you come by." The stage-coach comes by, sees me, stops and picks me up. It happens every day. You know nothing of life, my dear.'

A certain amount of time went by in this way. All at once Favourite seemed to wake up.

'Well now,' said she, 'what about that surprise?'

'Yes, you're right,' said Dahlia, 'where's the famous surprise?'

'They're taking a very long time!' said Fantine.

As Fantine concluded this wistful remark, the waiter who had served their meal came in. He held in his hand something that looked like a letter.

'What's that?' asked Favourite.

The waiter replied, 'It's a note those gentlemen left for you ladies.'

'Why didn't you bring it straight away?'

'Because,' said the waiter, 'the gentlemen told me not to deliver it to you ladies before an hour had gone by.'

Favourite snatched the piece of paper from the waiter's hand. It was indeed a letter.

'Strange!' she said. 'There's no address. But look what's written on it: "THIS IS THE SURPRISE."'

She hurriedly unsealed the letter, opened it and read (she could read):

O loving mistresses!

We would have you know that we have parents. Parents are not something you are very familiar with. In the civil code for respectable children, they are called fathers and mothers. Now, these parents are complaining, these old folk are appealing to us, these good men and women are calling us prodigal sons, they want us to come home, and are offering to kill calves for us. Being dutiful, we are obeying them. By the time you read this, five spirited horses will be taking us back to our papas and mamas. We are decamping, as Bossuet puts it.* We are leaving. We have left. We are fleeing in the arms of Laffitte and on the wings of Caillard. The Toulouse stage-coach wrests us from the abyss, and the abyss is you, O our beautiful darlings! We are returning to order, to duty, to society, at a brisk pace, at the speed of eight miles an hour. It is important for the country that like everyone else we should be prefects, family men, rural police officers and state councillors. Respect us. We are sacrificing ourselves. Lament

* The expression used here, 'Nous fichons le camp', is informal and is facetiously ascribed to the great clerical orator Jacques-Bénigne Bossuet (1627–1704).

133

us briefly and replace us rapidly. If this letter distresses you, tear it to pieces. Farewell.

For nearly two years we have made you happy. Do not hold it against us.

> Signed: Blachevelle.
> Fameuil.
> Listolier.
> Félix Tholomyès.

> P.S. The meal is paid for.

The four young women looked at each other.

Favourite was the first to break the silence. 'Well, anyway,' she exclaimed, 'it's a good joke!'

'It's very funny,' said Zéphine.

'It must have been Blachevelle who thought of it,' said Favourite. 'I love him for it. Absence makes the heart grow fonder. That's life.'

'No,' said Dahlia, 'it's one of Tholomyès's ideas. It's just like him.'

'In that case,' retorted Favourite, 'down with Blachevelle and long live Tholomyès!'

'Long live Tholomyès!' cried Dahlia and Zéphine. And they burst out laughing.

Fantine laughed with them.

An hour later, back in her room, she wept. He was, as we said, her first love – she had given herself to this Tholomyès as to a husband. And the poor girl had a child.

BOOK FOUR
ENTRUSTING SOMETIMES MEANS GIVING AWAY

I
One Mother Meets Another

There was at Montfermeil near Paris during the first quarter of this century an inn of sorts, which no longer exists. This place was run by people called Thénardier, husband and wife. It was located in Ruelle du Boulanger. Above the door was a board nailed flat against the wall. On this board was painted something that looked like a man carrying on his back another man who wore the big gilt epaulettes of a general, with large silver stars on them. Red splotches represented blood. The rest of the picture was all smoke and probably depicted a battle. Underneath were written these words: 'THE SERGEANT OF WATERLOO'.

Nothing is more commonplace than a wagon or cart at the door of an inn. Nevertheless, the vehicle, or to be more accurate the segment of a vehicle, that one evening in the spring of 1818 blocked the street in front of the Sergeant of Waterloo by its massive presence would surely have attracted the attention of any painter who happened to be passing that way.

It was the front section of one of those trailers commonly used in woodland regions, and which serve to transport timber beams and tree trunks. This front section consisted of a massive swivelling iron axle, fitted with a heavy shaft, supported on two huge wheels. The whole thing was bulky, imposing and misshapen. It looked like the mounting of a gigantic cannon. Ruts had left on the wheels, rims, hub, axle and shaft a layer of mud, a hideous jaundiced coating quite similar to that which is apt to be used for the embellishment of our cathedrals. The wood was hidden under the mud and the iron under the rust. Draped under the axle was a huge chain worthy of a fettered Goliath. This chain conjured up not the wooden beams it was meant to haul but the mastodons and mammoths it might have harnessed. There was something suggestive of the forced-labour camp about it, but a forced-labour camp on a Herculean and superhuman scale; it looked like the loosed chain of some monster. Homer would have tethered Polyphemus with it, and Shakespeare, Caliban.

Why was that trailer front section standing there in the street? First, to block the street. Then, also, to rust away completely. There is a host of institutions in the old social order that are to be found similarly left in the way, out in the open, and which have no other reason for being there.

The centre of the chain hung quite close to the ground beneath the axle, and on that particular evening, sitting coupled in the curve of it, as on the rope of a swing, were two little girls exquisitely entwined, one about two and a half years old, the other eighteen months, the younger in the arms of the elder. A cleverly knotted neckerchief prevented them from falling off. A mother had seen this dreadful chain and said, 'Now, there's something for my children to play on.'

The two children, charmingly dressed moreover, and with some care, were radiant. They looked like two roses on a scrap heap. Their eyes were glorious, their fresh cheeks glowing with happiness. One had chestnut hair, the other, brown. Their innocent faces were two pictures of wonder and delight. Scents wafting from a nearby flowering shrub seemed to passers-by to emanate from them. The eighteen-month-old displayed her sweet bare little tummy with that chaste immodesty of infancy. Above and around these two delicate creatures, basking in happiness and infused with light, the gigantic trailer section, black with rust, almost fearsome, a tangled snarl of curves and sharp angles, looked like the rounded entrance to a cave. A few paces away, squatting on the doorstep of the inn, the mother, not in fact a very prepossessing woman though an affecting sight at that moment, was swinging the two children by means of a long rope, watching over them for fear of any accident with that animal-like and sublime expression typical of motherhood. With every movement back and forth the hideous links emitted a strident noise that sounded like a screech of anger. The little girls were ecstatic. The setting sun commingled with this joy, and there was nothing to match the charm of this capriccio of chance that had made a cherubim's swing of a Titan's chain.

As she swung her two little ones, the mother hummed in a discordant voice a then well known ballad: 'A warrior so bold and a virgin so bright . . .'

Her song and the contemplation of her daughters prevented her from hearing and seeing what was going on in the street.

In the meantime, someone had approached her as she began the first couplet of the ballad, and suddenly she heard a voice saying very close to her ear, 'You have two lovely children there, madame.'

'. . . Alonzo the brave was the name of the knight, the maid's was the fair Imogine,' responded the mother, continuing with her ballad. Then she looked round.

A woman stood before her a few steps away. This woman too had a child, which she carried in her arms.

She was also carrying quite a big travelling-bag that looked very heavy.

This woman's child was one of the most divine creatures anyone might hope to see. It was a little girl aged two or three. She could have vied with the other two youngsters in the prettiness of her clothing. She wore a frilled cap of fine linen, with ribbons on her sleeved top and Valenciennes lace on her bonnet. Her rucked-up skirt revealed her firm, white, chubby thigh. She was wonderfully pink and healthy. You felt like biting into the lovely little darling's apple cheeks. Nothing could be said about her eyes except that they must be very big, and they had magnificent eyelashes. She was asleep.

She was sleeping that totally trustful sleep of children of that age. Mothers' arms are created out of tenderness, children sleep deeply in them.

As for the mother, she was a poor and sorry sight. She was dressed like a seamstress reverting to peasant again. She was young. Was she beautiful? Maybe, but the way she was dressed it was hard to tell. Her hair looked very thick but was austerely hidden under an ugly, thick-woven, close-fitting coif tied under the chin, with one blonde lock escaping. Laughter shows off beautiful teeth if you have them, but she did not laugh. Her eyes looked as if they had not been dry for a very long time. She was pale. She seemed very weary and a little unwell. She gazed at her daughter sleeping in her arms with that distinctive look of a mother who has nursed her child. A large blue handkerchief, such as war veterans use for blowing their noses, folded into a fichu, unflatteringly concealed her figure. She had weathered hands all covered with freckles, a forefinger hardened and roughened by the needle, a cloak of coarse brown woollen stuff, a calico gown and heavy shoes. It was Fantine.

It was Fantine. Not easily recognizable. Nevertheless, on close examination she still retained her beauty. A dejected line that looked like the beginnings of irony creased her right cheek. As for her clothes, that ethereal outfit of muslin and ribbons, seemingly fashioned of mirth, frivolity and music, all tinkling bells and the scent of lilac, had vanished like those beautiful glittering frosts mistaken for diamonds in the sunshine; they melt away and leave the branch completely black.

Ten months had elapsed since the 'great lark'.

What had happened in those ten months? We can guess.

After abandonment came hardship. Fantine had immediately lost contact with Favourite, Zéphine and Dahlia. The bond, once broken on the men's side, unravelled between the women. They would have been greatly astonished a fortnight later had anyone said they were friends. There was no reason to be any more. Fantine was left on her own. With the father of her child gone – alas! such partings are irrevocable – she found herself totally isolated, minus the habit of work and plus the taste for pleasure. Led by her relationship with Tholomyès to disdain the modest trade she knew, she had neglected any openings. They were now closed to her. Nothing to fall back on. Fantine could hardly read and could not write. She had been taught as a child only to sign her name. She got a public letter-writer to write to Tholomyès, a first letter, then a second, then a third. Tholomyès had not replied to any of them. One day Fantine heard some gossiping women say, while looking at her daughter, 'Does anyone take these children seriously! Everyone shrugs their shoulders at such children!' Then she thought of Tholomyès who shrugged off his child and did not take this innocent creature seriously. And her feelings darkened towards that man. But what was she to do? She was at a loss to know who to turn to now. She had done wrong but she was by nature, let us remember, fundamentally modest and virtuous. She vaguely sensed she was on the brink of falling into destitution and sliding towards the very worst. Courage was needed. Courage she had, and she steeled herself. It occurred to her to return to her home town of Montreuil-sur-Mer. There might be someone there who knew her and would give her work. Yes, but she would have to conceal her wrong-doing. And in a confused way she foresaw the need for a separation even more painful than the first. It wrung her heart, but she made her decision. Fantine, as we shall see, had the fierce bravery of life itself.

Valiantly, she had already given up all finery, dressing herself in calico, and had put all her silks, all her trimmings, ribbons and lace, on her daughter, her sole remaining vanity, and a saintly one at that. She sold everything she had, which yielded two hundred francs. Having paid off her modest debts, she had only about eighty francs remaining. At the age of twenty-two, on a beautiful spring morning, she left Paris carrying her child on her back. Anyone seeing the two of them pass by would have felt pity for them. This woman had no one else in the world but her child, and the child no one else in the world but this woman. Fantine had nursed her child. This strained her chest and she was coughing a little.

We shall have no further occasion to speak of Monsieur Félix

Tholomyès. All we wish to say is that twenty years later, under King Louis-Philippe, he was a well established provincial lawyer, wealthy and influential, a sound voter and a very severe magistrate; still a man of pleasure.

Having taken a ride now and then – at roughly one or two sous per mile, with what was then known as the Petites Voitures coach company serving the outlying areas of Paris – to give herself a rest, Fantine found herself towards the middle of the day at Montfermeil, in Ruelle du Boulanger.

As she passed the Thénardier inn the two little girls delighting in their monster swing had, as it were, dazzled her, and she stopped in front of that vision of joy.

There are such things as spells. These two little girls acted as a spell on this mother.

She observed them, overcome with emotion. Paradise is heralded by the presence of angels. She thought she could see above this inn the mysterious *here* of providence. These two little ones were so obviously happy! She gazed at them, she marvelled at them, with such feeling that as their mother drew breath between two lines of her song she could not help saying to her those few words you have just read: 'You have two lovely children there, madame.'

The most ferocious of creatures is disarmed by the petting of its young.

The mother looked up and thanked her, and invited the wayfarer to sit on the bench by the door, she herself being on the doorstep. The two women chatted together.

'My name's Madame Thénardier,' said the mother of the two little girls. 'We're the keepers of this inn.'

Then, continuing with the same ballad, she sang in an undertone: '. . . tomorrow I go / To fight in a far distant land . . .'

This Madame Thénardier was a brawny and angular sandy-haired woman, the archetypal soldier's wife in all her charmlessness. And, bizarrely, with an introspective air that she owed to her penchant for romances. She was simpering yet mannish. Old-fashioned love stories that have rubbed off on the imaginations of canteen cooks have that effect. She was still young, barely thirty. Being very tall and built like a walking colossus such as you might expect to find in a fairground, this woman, who was squatting down, had she stood upright might perhaps have scared the traveller from the outset, undermined her trustfulness and forestalled what we have to relate. Someone sitting instead of standing – destinies hang on this.

The traveller told her story with some slight alteration.

That she was a seamstress. That her husband was dead. That there was no work for her in Paris and she was going to look for some elsewhere, back home where she came from. That she had left Paris that morning on foot. That, as she was carrying her child and felt tired, when the Villemomble coach had come by, she had taken it. That from Villemomble to Montfermeil she had walked. That her little one had walked a bit of the way but not much, being so young. And that she had to pick her up and carry her, and the precious darling had fallen asleep.

Whereupon she gave her daughter a fervent kiss that woke her. The child opened her eyes, big blue eyes like her mother's, and looked at – what? Nothing. Everything. With that serious and sometimes stern expression of young children, which is a mystery of their luminous innocence in the face of our twilight virtues. It is as if they feel like angels and know us to be men. Then the child began to laugh, and although her mother held her she slipped to the ground with the untameable energy of a young creature that wants to run free. All of a sudden she caught sight of the other two on their swing, came to a standstill and stuck out her tongue, a sign of awe.

Madame Thénardier released her daughters, helped them down from the swing, and said, 'You three play together.'

At that age children are quick to socialize and after a minute the little Thénardiers were playing with the newcomer, digging holes in the ground together with great delight.

This newcomer was very cheerful. You can tell a mother's goodness from the cheerfulness of her toddler. She had found a stick that served her as a spade and she was energetically digging a hole big enough for a fly. What the grave-digger does becomes amusing when done by a child.

The two women went on chatting.

'What's your little one's name?'

'Cosette.'

For Cosette, read Euphrasie. The child's name was Euphrasie. But with that endearing and charming instinct that mothers and the populace have, by which Josefa is turned into Pepita and Françoise into Sillette, Euphrasie became Cosette to her mother. This is the kind of derivation that confuses and confounds all the learning of etymologists. We know of one grandmother who managed to turn Théodore into 'Gnon'.

'How old is she?'

'She's going on three.'

'The same as my eldest.'

In the meantime the three little girls were clustered in an attitude of deep anxiety and rapture. Something had happened. A big worm had emerged from the ground. And they were scared and entranced.

With their radiant foreheads touching, it was as if their three heads were surrounded by a single halo.

'Children make friends in no time!' exclaimed Madame Thénardier. 'Seeing them together like that, you'd swear they were three sisters!'

This remark was the spur the other mother had probably been waiting for. She seized the Thénardier woman's hand, looked at her intently, and said, 'Will you look after my child for me?'

The Thénardier woman gave one of those starts of surprise that are neither assent nor refusal.

Cosette's mother went on, 'You see, I can't take my daughter with me. Working won't allow it. You can't get a job with a child. They're so ridiculous in that part of the world. It was the good Lord that guided me to your inn. When I saw your little ones looking so pretty and so clean and so happy, my heart turned over. I said to myself: Here's a good mother. For sure, they'll be like three sisters. And then it won't be long before I return. Will you look after my child for me?'

'We'd have to see,' replied the Thénardier woman.

'I'd pay six francs a month.'

At this point a man's voice called out from inside the inn, 'Not for less than seven francs. And six months paid in advance.'

'Six sevens, forty-two,' said the Thénardier woman.

'I'll pay it,' said the mother.

'And fifteen francs extra for initial expenses,' the man's voice added.

'Fifty-seven francs total,' said Madame Thénardier. And throughout these calculations she hummed vaguely: '. . . tomorrow I go / To fight in a far distant land . . .'

'I'll pay it,' said the mother. 'I have eighty francs. I'll have enough left over to get home. If I walk. I'll earn some money there, and as soon as I have a little I'll come back to fetch my little angel.'

The man's voice spoke again, 'The child has clothes?'

'That's my husband,' said the Thénardier woman.

'Certainly she has clothes, poor precious darling. Of course I realized it was your husband. And lovely clothes too! A real extravagance. A dozen of everything. And silk gowns like a lady. They're all here in my bag.'

'You'll give those to us,' said the man's voice.

'I should think so too,' said the mother. 'It would be a very odd thing indeed if I were to leave my daughter without a stitch!'

141

The master's face appeared.

'That's fine,' he said.

The deal was concluded. The mother spent the night at the inn, handed over the money and left her child, refastened her travelling-bag, now lightened with the child's things taken out, and set out the following morning, intending to return soon. Such departures are easily arranged, but they are harrowing!

A neighbour of the Thénardiers met the mother as she was walking away, and came back saying, 'I've just seen a woman crying in the street, it was heart-rending.'

When Cosette's mother had gone the man said to the woman, 'That'll pay off my debt for a hundred and ten francs that falls due tomorrow. I was fifty francs short. You know, I'd have had the bailiff on to me with a warrant? That was a clever mouse-trap you laid there with your babes.'

'Without realizing it,' said the woman.

II
First Sketch of Two Shady Characters

It was a very poor mouse that had been caught, but the cat is happy even with a scraggy mouse.

Who were these Thénardiers?

Let us say a few words about them right now. We will complete the sketch later.

These individuals belonged to that bastard class between the so-called middle class and the so-called lower class, which is made up of crass people who have come up in the world and clever people who have gone down, and combines some of the faults of the latter with nearly all the vices of the former without having the generous impulse of the working man or the law-abiding decency of the solid citizen.

They were of that stunted nature that easily turns monstrous if some dark passion is by chance kindled in them. There was in the woman the essence of a bully and in the man the makings of a scoundrel. Both were most highly susceptible to the sort of hideous progress that occurs in the development of evil. There are souls like lobsters, continually retreating into the shadows, retrogressing rather than advancing through life, using experience to add to their monstrosity, becoming ever more wicked and ever more imbued with an intensifying foulness. This man and this woman were such souls.

Thénardier in particular gave the physiognomist pause. You have only to look at some men to distrust them. You sense a shadiness in their lives, at both ends. Behind them is a restlessness, taken forward with menace. They have something of the unknown in them. You can no more answer for what they have done than for what they will do. The darkness they have in their eyes betrays them. You have only to hear them say one word, or see them make one gesture, to glimpse sinister secrets in their past and sinister mysteries in their future.

If he was to be believed, this fellow Thénardier had been a soldier, a sergeant, he said. He had probably taken part in the campaign of 1815, and had even acquitted himself quite bravely, it would seem. We shall see later what the truth of this was. His inn sign was an allusion to one of his feats of arms. He had painted it himself, for he knew how to do a little of everything, badly.

It was the age when the classic period novel – that having once been *Clélie* was now a mere *Lodoïska*, still high-minded but increasingly vulgar, reduced from Mademoiselle de Scudéry to Madame Barthélémy-Hadot, and from Madame de Lafayette to Madame Bournon-Malarme – inflamed the lovesick souls of Paris's doorkeepers and even wreaked a little havoc in the suburbs. Madame Thénardier was just intelligent enough to read books of this kind. They were her staple diet. She steeped in them what brain she possessed. This had given her, when she was very young and even a little later, a kind of pensiveness in the company of her husband, a rascal of a certain knowingness, a literate ruffian but no grammarian, at once coarse and shrewd, but as regards sentiment a reader of Pigault-Lebrun; and as for 'anything to do with sex', as his own turn of phrase would have it, an absolute thoroughgoing lout. His wife was twelve or fifteen years younger than he was. Later, when her Romantically cascading hair began to turn grey, when out of Pamela emerged Megaera, the Thénardier woman was just a nasty fat woman with a taste for silly novels. Now, nonsense cannot be read with impunity. The result was that her elder daughter's name was Éponine. As for the younger, the poor little thing was very nearly named Gulnare. She owed it to who knows what happy distraction afforded by one of Ducray-Duminil's novels only to be called Azelma.

By the way, the fact is that not everything about that curious era we are alluding to here, which might be called one of first-name anarchy, is absurd and superficial. Alongside this Romantic element we have just referred to there is the social factor. It is not uncommon nowadays for the young cowherd to be called Arthur, Alfred or Alphonse, and for the vicomte – if there are any vicomtes left – to be called Thomas, Pierre or Jacques. This displacement whereby the 'distinguished' name is given to the common man and the rustic name to the aristocrat is nothing other than the stirrings of egalitarianism. The irresistible penetration of the new spirit is in this as in everything else. Behind this apparent discrepancy there is something great and profound: the French Revolution.

III
The Lark

Just being wicked is not enough to prosper. Business was bad at the inn.

Thanks to the traveller's fifty-seven francs, Thénardier managed to avoid a protest for non-payment and to honour what he had put his signature to. The following month they were again in need of money. The woman took Cosette's clothes to Paris and pawned them for sixty francs. Once that sum was spent, the Thénardiers came to regard the little girl as no more than a child they had taken in out of charity, and treated her accordingly. As she no longer had any clothes of her own they dressed her in the little Thénardier girls' cast-off petticoats and chemises, that is to say, in rags. They fed her on everyone's scraps – a little better than the dog, a little worse than the cat. In fact the cat and the dog were her habitual dining companions. Cosette ate with them under the table, from a wooden bowl like theirs.

Her mother, who had settled in Montreuil-sur-Mer, as we shall see, wrote a letter every month, or to be more accurate had someone else write, asking for news of her child. The Thénardiers invariably replied, 'Cosette is thriving.'

At the end of the first six months the mother sent seven francs for the seventh month, and continued sending her payments quite punctually month by month. Before the year was over Thénardier said, 'A fine favour she's doing us! How does she expect us to manage on her seven francs?' And he wrote demanding twelve francs. Led by them to believe that her child was happy 'and doing well', the mother submitted to the demand and sent the twelve francs.

Certain natures are incapable of loving on the one hand without hating on the other. Madame Thénardier loved her two daughters passionately, which meant she hated the outsider.

It is sad to think that a mother's love can have ugly aspects to it. No matter how little space Cosette took up in her home, she felt it was space taken from her own children and that this little girl reduced the air her daughters breathed. This woman, like many women of her kind, had a certain quantity of endearments and a certain quantity of blows and harsh words to dispense each day. For all that they were idolized, her daughters would have undoubtedly got the lot if she had not had Cosette there. But the outsider did them the service of diverting the blows on to herself. For her daughters, she had only endearments. Cosette could not make a single move that did not bring down on her a hailstorm of violent and undeserved punishments. Sweet defenceless creature, to whom this world and God must have been a complete mystery, incessantly punished, scolded, ill-used and beaten, seeing beside her two little creatures just like her who lived within the glow of a kindly light!

Madame Thénardier was cruel to Cosette. Éponine and Azelma were cruel. Children at that age are simply copies of their mother. They come in a smaller size, that is all.

A year went by, then another.

It was said in the village, 'Those Thénardiers are good people. They're not rich and yet they're bringing up a poor abandoned child they were left with!'

It was thought Cosette had been forgotten by her mother.

Meanwhile, having learned by who knows what obscure channels that the child was probably illegitimate and that the mother could not acknowledge her as her own, Thénardier demanded fifteen francs a month, saying 'the creature' was growing up and '*eating*', and threatening to turn her out. 'She'd better not give me any trouble!' he shouted. 'I'll send her brat back to her and her little secrets will blow up in her face. I must have more.'

The mother paid the fifteen francs.

As the child grew, year by year, so did her wretchedness.

As long as Cosette was very small, she was the two other children's scapegoat. As soon as she got a little bigger, that is to say, before she was even five, she became the household servant.

Five years old, the reader will say, that is incredible. Alas! it is true. Social suffering begins at all ages. Have we not recently seen the trial of a certain Dumollard by name, an orphan turned bandit, who from the age of five, official documents state, being all alone in the world, 'worked for his living and stole'?

Cosette was made to run errands, sweep the rooms, the courtyard and the street, wash the dishes, even to carry heavy loads. The Thénardiers considered themselves all the more entitled to behave in this way since the mother, who was still at Montreuil-sur-Mer, began to fall behind with her payments. She was some months in arrears.

If this mother had returned to Montfermeil at the end of those three years, she would not have recognized her child. So pretty and fresh when she first came to that house, Cosette was now thin and pale. She had an indefinably anxious look. 'Sly,' said the Thénardiers.

Injustice had made her resentful and misery had made her ugly. All that was left of her prettiness were those lovely eyes that were pitiful to behold because, huge as they were, the sadness that was visible in them appeared so much the greater.

It was a heart-breaking thing to see in winter, this poor child, not yet six years old, shivering in her tattered old rags of coarse cloth, sweeping the street before daylight with an enormous broom in her tiny red hands and a teardrop in those big eyes.

Locally, they called her Alouette*. The common people, who like figurative images, had chosen to give this name to this tiny creature, no bigger than a bird, trembling, frightened and shivering, the first one awake every morning, in the house and in the village, always out on the street or in the fields before daybreak.

Only, poor Alouette never sang.

* 'L'alouette' is the morning bird 'the lark'.

BOOK FIVE
THE DESCENT

I
Story of an Advance in the Manufacture of Black Glass Jewellery

What had become of that mother in the meantime, who according to the people of Montfermeil appeared to have abandoned her child? Where was she? What was she doing?

After leaving her little Cosette with the Thénardiers she had continued on her way and arrived at Montreuil-sur-Mer.

This, remember, was in 1818.

Fantine had left her provincial home some ten years earlier. Montreuil-sur-Mer had changed. While Fantine's fortunes were slowly declining, her native town had prospered.

About two years previously there had been one of those industrial developments that have a great impact on small places.

This detail is significant and one we think worth while expanding on – we would almost say, emphasizing.

From time immemorial Montreuil-sur-Mer's specialized industry had been the imitation of English jet jewellery and of the black glass jewellery of Germany. This industry had always languished because of the high price of the raw materials, which affected the workers' pay. When Fantine returned to Montreuil-sur-Mer an amazing transformation had taken place in this production of 'black ware'. Towards the end of 1815 a man, a stranger, had come and set up business in the town, and had the idea of substituting shellac for resin in the manufacturing process and, for bracelets in particular, using metal clasp links that were simply pinched together instead of soldered. This very small change had been a revolution.

This very small change had in fact dramatically reduced the cost of the raw materials, which made it possible firstly for the labour costs to rise to the benefit of the local community, secondly to improve the workmanship, an advantage for the consumer, and thirdly to sell more cheaply while at the same time trebling profits, by which the manufacturer gained.

So three positive results from one idea.

In less than three years the inventor of this process had become rich, which is good, and made everyone around him rich, which is better. He came from outside the *département*. Nothing at all was known about his background, very little about his early career.

The story was that he had come to the town with very little money, a few hundred francs at most.

It was from this limited capital, used to implement an ingenious idea and systematically and thoughtfully husbanded, that he had built up his fortune and the fortunes of the whole community.

When he first arrived in Montreuil-sur-Mer the clothes he wore, his bearing and his language were no more than those of a labourer.

Apparently on the very day he made his obscure entry into the small town of Montreuil-sur-Mer, at nightfall one December evening, with his knapsack on his back and a hawthorn staff in his hand, a serious fire had just broken out in the town hall. This man had rushed into the blaze and at the risk of his own life saved two children, who turned out to belong to the captain of the gendarmerie. As a result no one had thought to ask him for his passport. Since then his name had come to be common knowledge. He was called Père Madeleine.

II
Madeleine

He was a man of about fifty who looked as if he had something on his mind, and was kind-hearted. That was all that could be said about him.

Thanks to the rapid development of the industry he had so admirably restructured, Montreuil-sur-Mer became an important centre of commerce. Spain, which buys a great deal of black jet, placed huge orders there every year. Montreuil-sur-Mer almost rivalled London and Berlin in this trade. Père Madeleine's profits were such that by the second year he was able to build a large factory in which there were two huge workrooms, one for men and the other for women. Anyone who was hungry could go there and be sure of finding work and being fed. Père Madeleine expected willingness of the men, respectability of the women, and honesty of everybody. He had divided the workrooms to keep the two sexes apart and so that the girls and the women might remain virtuous. On this point he was adamant. It was the only thing about which he was in any way intolerant. He was all the more justified in this strictness because, Montreuil-sur-Mer being a garrison town, opportunities for depravity were rife. In any event, his coming had been a boon and his presence was a godsend. Before Père Madeleine's arrival the whole place was languishing. Now everything there was sustained by the wholesomeness of the working life. A strong circulation is entirely beneficial and reaches everywhere. Unemployment and poverty were unknown. There was no pocket so obscure that it had not a little money in it, no home so poor that it had not a little gladness in it.

Père Madeleine would employ anyone. He insisted on one thing only: Be an honest man! Be an honest woman!

As we have said, out of this activity of which he was the prime mover and linchpin, Père Madeleine made his fortune. But rather curiously in a simple man of business, this was not apparently his chief concern. He seemed to give a great deal of thought to others and little to himself. In 1820 he was known to have a sum of six hundred and thirty thousand francs to his name invested with Laffitte. But before setting aside these six hundred and thirty thousand francs he had spent more than a million on the town and its poor.

The hospital was ill-funded. He financed ten beds there. Montreuil-sur-Mer is divided into the upper town and the lower town. The lower town, where he lived, had but one school, a miserable hovel that was falling into ruin. He built two, one for the girls, the other for the boys. Out of his own pocket he paid the two schoolteachers an additional allowance, doubling their meagre official salary, and one day he said to someone who wondered at this, 'The state's two most important servants are the woman at whose breast the child is nurtured and the schoolmaster.' He created at his own expense a nursery, something almost unknown in France at that time, and a welfare fund for old and infirm workers. His factory being a central point, a new neighbourhood with a great many poor families rapidly sprang up around it. He set up a free pharmacy here.

In the early days, watching him start out, charitable souls said, 'He's a self-seeker who wants to become rich.' When they saw him enriching the community before he enriched himself, the same charitable souls said, 'He's an ambitious fellow.' This seemed all the more probable as the man was religious, and even to some extent religiously observant, something very favourably looked on at that time. He regularly attended low mass every Sunday. Before long the local deputy, who suspected rivals everywhere, began to fret about this religion. The deputy, who had been a member of the Legislative Corps under the Empire, shared the religious views of an Oratorian father known by the name of Fouché, Duc d'Otrante, whose creature and friend he had been. Behind closed doors he quietly made fun of God. But when he saw the wealthy manufacturer Madeleine going to low mass at seven o'clock, he detected in him a likely candidate and resolved to outdo him. He took a Jesuit confessor and attended high mass and vespers. At that time ambition was literally a steeplechase. The poor as well as the good Lord profited by his dread, for the honourable deputy also funded two beds in the hospital, which made a total of twelve.

Nevertheless, in 1819 the rumour went around town one morning that as a result of representations made by the prefect, and in consideration of his services to the town, Père Madeleine was to be appointed mayor of Montreuil-sur-Mer by the king. Those who had declared the newcomer to be 'an ambitious fellow' seized with delight on this opportunity that everybody longs for to exclaim, 'There! What did we tell you!' The whole of Montreuil-sur-Mer was in ferment. The rumour was well founded. Several days later the appointment appeared in *Le Moniteur*. The next day Père Madeleine declined the appointment.

In this same year of 1819 the products of the new process invented by Madeleine featured in the industrial exhibition. On the recommendation of the jury the king named the inventor a knight of the Legion of Honour. Fresh rumblings in the small town. Well then! It was the cross he wanted! Père Madeleine refused the cross.

No doubt about it, the man was an enigma. The charitable souls defended themselves by saying, 'After all, he's some sort of adventurer.'

We have seen that the community owed him a great deal, the poor owed him everything. He was so useful, it was inevitable that he should eventually be honoured, and he was so kind-hearted it was inevitable that he should eventually be loved. His workers in particular adored him, and he bore this adoration with a sort of melancholy gravity. When his wealth was established, 'society people' greeted him, and in town he was called Monsieur Madeleine. His workers and the children continued to call him Père Madeleine, and this was the thing best able to make him smile. As his stock rose, he was showered with invitations. 'Society' clamoured for him. The prim little drawing rooms of Montreuil-sur-Mer, at first closed of course to the artisan, were opened wide to the millionaire. Countless overtures were made to him. He declined them all.

This time, again, the charitable souls were quite unabashed. 'He's an ignorant man of little education. God knows what his background is. He wouldn't know how to behave in society. There's no proof at all that he can read.'

When he was seen making money they said, 'He's a tradesman.' When he was seen distributing his money they said, 'He's an ambitious fellow.' When he was seen rejecting honours they said, 'He's an adventurer.' When he was seen rejecting society they said, 'He's a crass ignoramus.'

In 1820, five years after his arrival in Montreuil-sur-Mer, the services he had rendered to the community were so outstanding, the will of the entire region so unanimous, that the king again appointed him mayor of the town. Again he declined. But the prefect would not accept his refusal, all the dignitaries came to entreat him, the people in the street implored him. So intense was their insistence that in the end he accepted. It was noted that what seemed especially to make up his mind was the almost angry rebuke of an old woman, one of the common people, who called out to him crossly from her doorstep: 'A good mayor can be useful. Why shrink from doing good?'

This was the third phase of his ascent. Père Madeleine had become Monsieur Madeleine. Monsieur Madeleine became monsieur le maire.

III
Sums Deposited with Laffitte

Nevertheless, he remained as unassuming as he was on the first day. He had grey hair, a serious gaze, the weathered complexion of a labourer, the pensive face of a philosopher. He usually wore a broad-brimmed hat and a long frock-coat of coarse cloth buttoned to the chin. He fulfilled his duties as mayor, but aside from that he lived a solitary life. He spoke to few people. He would sidestep social pleasantries, pay his respects in passing and quickly slip away; smile by way of apology for not chatting, give by way of apology for not smiling. Women said of him, 'What a kindly old bear!' His pleasure was to go walking in the countryside.

He always took his meals alone, with a book open in front of him that he would be reading. He had a small but well selected library. He loved books. Books are cold and dependable friends. With wealth came leisure, which he seemed increasingly to take advantage of to cultivate his mind. It was observed that since he had been in Montreuil-sur-Mer his language had year by year grown more refined, more carefully chosen, gentler. He liked to carry a shotgun with him on his walks but he rarely made use of it. Whenever he happened to do so, his shooting was fearsomely accurate. He never killed a harmless animal. He never shot a small bird.

Although he was not a young man any more, stories were told of his remarkable strength. He would lend a hand to anyone in need of it, lift a horse, push a wheel stuck in the mud, or stop a runaway bull by the horns. His pockets were always full of money when he went out, and empty when he came home. Whenever he passed through a village, ragged urchins ran gleefully after him and surrounded him like a swarm of gnats.

People thought they could tell he must have once lived a country life since he knew all sorts of useful secrets, which he passed on to the peasants. He taught them how to destroy corn moth by spraying the granary and dousing cracks in the floorboards with a solution of common salt, and how to ward off weevils by hanging flowering orviot everywhere, on the walls and in the rafters, in the barns and inside the houses.

He had 'recipes' for ridding a field of yellow vetchling, corncockle, vetch, cow wheat, meadow foxtail, all the parasitic weeds that choke the wheat crop. He would protect a rabbit hutch against rats just by the smell of a small guinea-pig he put inside it.

One day he saw some local country folk very busy pulling up nettles. He looked at their pile of uprooted and already dried-out plants and said, 'That's all dead. Yet it would be a good thing if you knew how to make use of it. When the nettle's young the leaf makes an excellent vegetable. When it ages it has filaments and fibres like hemp and flax. Cloth made from nettles is as good as linen cloth. Chopped up, nettles are good for poultry. Pounded, they're good for horned livestock. The seed of the nettle mixed with fodder gives a shine to animals' coats. The root mixed with salt produces a beautiful yellow colour. Also, it makes an excellent hay that can be harvested twice. And what does the nettle need? A little soil, no tending, no cultivation. Only, the seeds fall as they ripen and they're difficult to harvest. That's all. With even the minimum of care, the nettle would be useful. Neglected, it becomes a nuisance. So we kill it. How like the nettle are so many men!' He added after a pause, 'My friends, remember this: there are no such things as bad plants or bad men. There are only bad farmers.'

Children also loved him because he could make delightful little toys out of straw and coconuts.

Whenever he saw the church door draped in black he would go in. He sought out funerals as others seek out christenings. Widowhood and the grief of others attracted him because of his great kindness. He would mingle with friends in mourning, families dressed in black, priests murmuring round a coffin. He seemed to take readily as subject for his thoughts those funeral chantings filled with the vision of another world. With his eyes turned heavenward, with a kind of yearning towards all the mysteries of infinity, he listened to those sad voices singing at the edge of death's dark abyss.

He performed a host of good deeds in the same way that others do bad: by stealth. He would slip into houses surreptitiously in the evening, and furtively climb the stairs. Some poor devil coming home to his attic would find that during his absence his door had been opened, sometimes even forced. The poor man would cry out: 'Some burglar has got in!' He would go inside and the first thing he would see was a gold coin left lying on a piece of furniture. The 'burglar' who had got in was Père Madeleine.

He was affable, and sad. The common people said, 'There's a rich man who doesn't give himself airs. There's a fortunate man who doesn't look happy.'

Some people held the view that he was a mysterious character and said that no one ever went into his bedroom, which was a veritable anchorite's cell, furnished with winged hour-glasses and ornamented with skulls and cross-bones! There was so much talk of this that some sly, sophisticated young women of Montreuil-sur-Mer came to him one day and asked, 'Monsieur le maire, do show us your room. It's said to be a grotto.' He smiled, and showed them into his 'grotto' there and then. They got their just deserts for their curiosity. It was a very ordinary room with rather ugly mahogany furniture like all furniture of that kind, and papered with inexpensive wallpaper. They could see nothing remarkable about it except two candlesticks of an old-fashioned design that stood on the mantelpiece and appeared to be of silver, 'from the way they were treasured'. A thoroughly small-town witticism.

It continued to be said, regardless, that no one was ever let into this room and that it was a hermit's cave, a mysterious retreat, a cubby-hole, a tomb.

It was also whispered that he had 'immense' sums deposited with Laffitte on the specific condition that the money was always immediately available to him; which meant, it was added, that Monsieur Madeleine could turn up at Laffitte's one morning, and in ten minutes sign a receipt and carry off his two or three million. In reality, these 'two or three million', as we have said, amounted to no more than six hundred and thirty or forty thousand francs.

IV
Monsieur Madeleine in Mourning

At the beginning of 1821 the newspapers announced the death of Monsieur Myriel, bishop of Digne, better known as 'Monseigneur Bienvenu', who had passed away in the odour of sanctity at the age of eighty-two.

To add here a detail that the papers omitted, when the bishop of Digne died he had for many years been blind, and contentedly blind, having his sister with him.

Incidentally, let us say that on this earth where nothing is perfect, to be blind and to be loved is in fact one of the most strangely exquisite forms of happiness. To have continually at your side a wife, a daughter, a sister, a delightful human being who is there because you need her and because she cannot do without you, to know you are indispensable to a person who is necessary to you, to be able constantly to measure her affection by how much of her presence she grants you and to say to yourself, 'Since she devotes all of her time to me, I must have all of her love'; to see the mind though you cannot see the face, to be able to count on the loyalty of one person when the world is eclipsed; to perceive in the rustle of a gown the fluttering of wings, to hear her to-ing and fro-ing, going out, coming home, talking, singing, and to think that you are at the centre of these footsteps, of this talking and singing; to demonstrate at every moment your own magnetic power, to feel all the more powerful the more infirm you are, to become in the darkness and by means of the darkness the star round which this angel gravitates – few joys equal this. The supreme happiness of life is the conviction that you are loved, loved for yourself, better still, loved despite yourself. This conviction the blind man has. In his plight, to be assisted is to be cherished. Does he lack anything? No. There is no loss of light in having love. And what love! A love that is all goodness. There is no blindness where there is certainty. Soul gropes for soul, and finds it. And the soul found and tested is a woman. A hand supports you, it is hers. Lips brush your forehead, they are her lips. You hear someone breathing right beside you, it is she. To have all of her, from her devotion to her pity, never to be left alone, to have that sweet frailty helping you, to lean on that sturdy reed, to touch providence with your hands and to be able to take it in your arms. God made tangible – what rapture! The heart, that obscure celestial flower, comes into mysterious bloom. You would not exchange this darkness for any brightness! The angel soul is there, ever there. If she goes away, it is only to return again. She vanishes like a dream and reappears as reality. You feel a warmth approaching, here she is. Your serenity, cheerfulness and bliss are abounding, you are a radiance in the dark. And so much care and consideration. Little things that count enormously in that void. The most ineffable tones of the female voice devoted to soothing you and making up for the vanished universe. You are spiritually cherished. You see nothing, but you feel adored. It is a dark paradise.

It was from this paradise that Monseigneur Bienvenu had passed on to the next.

The announcement of his death was reported by Montreuil-sur-Mer's local newspaper. The following day Monsieur Madeleine appeared dressed entirely in black with a mourning band on his hat.

These mourning clothes were noticed in town and set tongues wagging. It seemed to throw a light on Monsieur Madeleine's origins. The conclusion was drawn that he had some relationship with the venerable bishop. 'He's wearing mourning for the bishop of Digne,' was the word in the drawing rooms. This greatly enhanced Monsieur Madeleine's standing and immediately gained him a certain respect among Montreuil-sur-Mer's nobility. The local miniature Faubourg St-Germain decided to end their exclusion of Monsieur Madeleine, assumed to be related to a bishop. Monsieur Madeleine was alerted to the advancement he had obtained by more bows of respect from the older women and more smiles from the younger ones. One evening, curious by right of seniority, a doyenne of that small, grand world ventured to ask him, 'Monsieur le maire is doubtless a cousin of the late bishop of Digne?'

'No, madame,' he said.

'But you're wearing mourning for him,' the dowager persisted.

He replied, 'That's because in my youth I was a servant in his family.'

It was also noted that every time a young Savoyard, roaming around the area looking for chimneys to sweep, came into town monsieur le maire would send for him, ask him his name and give him money. The little Savoyards told each other about this and a great many of them came by.

V

Vague Glimmerings on the Horizon

Little by little over the course of time, all opposition to him fell away. By virtue of a sort of law to which those who better themselves are always subject, there had at first been slanders and calumnies against Monsieur Madeleine, then there were just malicious comments, then just rude remarks, then that was the end of it. Respect for him was total, unanimous and cordial, and there came a time around 1821 when the words 'monsieur le maire' were uttered at Montreuil-sur-Mer with almost the same expression as the words 'Monseigneur l'évêque' had been uttered at Digne in 1815. People came from twenty-five miles around to consult Monsieur Madeleine. He ended disagreements, prevented lawsuits, reconciled enemies. Everyone recognized his authority as judge. It was as if he were animated by the book of natural law. It was like a contagion of respect that over six or seven years was passed on from one to another and infected the whole area.

One man alone in the town and its surroundings totally escaped this contagion, and no matter what Père Madeleine did, he remained resistant, as if some sort of incorruptible and imperturbable instinct kept him alert and uneasy. It would seem to be the case that there exists in certain men a real animal instinct – like all instincts pure and true to itself, one that creates antipathies and sympathies, that inevitably separates one type of person from another, that does not waver, is never perplexed, never silenced and never failing, an instinct clear in its obscurity, infallible, compelling, intractable to all counsel of the intellect and all powers of reasoning against it; an instinct that, however destinies may be shaped, secretly warns the dog-man of the presence of the cat-man and the fox-man of the presence of the lion-man.

Often when Monsieur Madeleine went by in the street, peaceable, loving, with the blessings of everyone around him, a tall man dressed in an iron-grey frock-coat, armed with a stout walking-stick and wearing his hat pulled down, would swing round behind him and follow him with his eyes until he was out of sight, folding his arms, slowly shaking his head and pursing his upper and lower lips towards his nose, a sort of meaningful grimace that might be translated as 'Now who on earth is that man? I'm sure I've seen him somewhere before . . . Anyhow, I'm not in the least taken in by him.'

This person whose gravity was almost menacing was one of those men who even when only fleetingly glimpsed arrest the viewer's attention.

His name was Javert, and he was with the police.

At Montreuil-sur-Mer he had the invidious but useful job of inspector. He had not witnessed Madeleine's career from the outset. Javert owed the position he held to the protection of Monsieur Chabouillet, secretary to the minister of state Comte Anglès, then prefect of police in Paris. When Javert arrived at Montreuil-sur-Mer the great manufacturer's fortune was already made, and Père Madeleine had become Monsieur Madeleine.

Certain police officers have a distinctive physiognomy, one in which an air of baseness is combined with an air of authority. Javert had this physiognomy without the baseness.

It is our firm belief that if souls were visible to the eye we should clearly see that strange thing whereby every single member of the human species corresponds to some species of the animal world. And we would easily be able to recognize that truth barely apprehended by the philosopher, which is that, from the oyster to the eagle, from the pig to the tiger, all animals are to be found in mankind, and each one of them is to be found in some man. Sometimes even several at a time.

Animals are nothing other than the physical representation of our virtues and vices, wandering about before our eyes, the visible spectres of our souls. God lets us see them so as to make us think. However, since animals are mere shadows, God has made them capable only of being trained, not educated. What good would it serve? By contrast, our souls being realities and having a purpose of their own, God has given them intelligence, that is to say the capability to be educated. A good social education can always elicit from any soul whatsoever the usefulness it contains.

This of course is said from the limited viewpoint of visible earthly life, without prejudice to the profound question of the prior and ulterior personality of living beings other than man. The visible self in no way authorizes the philosopher to deny the hidden self. With this reservation, let us continue.

Now, if the reader will grant for a moment that there is in every man one of the animal species in creation, it will be easy for us to say which of them resided in police officer Javert.

The peasants of Asturias are convinced that in every she-wolf's litter there is one dog, which is killed by the mother because otherwise as it grew up it would eat the rest of her young.

Give this son-of-a-wolf dog a human face, and you have Javert.

Javert was born in prison of a fortune-teller whose husband was a convicted felon. As he grew up, he believed he was on the outside of society and had no hope of ever being let in. He observed that society unforgivingly kept out two classes of men, those who attack it and those who guard it. He had the choice between these two classes only. At the same time he was conscious of some underlying inflexibility, steadiness and probity within him, compounded by an inexpressible hatred for that gypsy race to which he belonged. He joined the police.

He made his mark. By the age of forty he was an inspector.

As a young man he worked with the chain gangs in the south.

Before going any further, let us be clear about the term 'human face' that we have just applied to Javert.

Javert's human face consisted of a flat nose with two deep nostrils and enormous whiskers growing up his cheeks towards them. The first time you saw those two forests and those two cavernous holes, you felt unnerved. When Javert laughed, which was rare and dreadful, his thin lips parted and revealed not only his teeth but his gums, and a ferocious, flattened crease formed round his nose as on the muzzle of a wild beast. Javert in serious mood was a mastiff. When he laughed he was a tiger. Besides which, a low brow, a full jaw, his hair concealing his forehead and falling over his eyebrows, between his eyes a permanent central furrow like a blaze of anger, an impenetrable gaze, a tight-lipped and fearsome mouth, a fierce air of command.

This man was made up of two very simple sentiments, and within reason very good ones, which he rendered almost bad by taking them to extremes: respect for authority and hatred of rebellion. And in his eyes theft, murder, any crime, was simply a form of rebellion. He looked on any state official, from the prime minister to the rural policeman, with a deep-seated blind faith. On anyone who had once crossed the legal threshold of wrong-doing he heaped scorn, loathing and disgust. He was uncompromising, and he allowed of no exceptions. On the one hand he said, 'The state official is incapable of making a mistake. The magistrate is never wrong.' On the other he said, 'These people are lost beyond redemption. Nothing good can come of them.' He fully shared the view held by those extremists who attribute to human law some extraordinary power of creating or, if you will, of recognizing outcasts, and who place a Styx at the bottom of society. A melancholy dreamer, he was stoical, serious, austere; and like fanatics, humble and haughty. He was gimlet-eyed, his gaze cold and piercing. His whole life was contained in these two words: watchfulness, vigilance. He had introduced a straight line into what is most tortuous in the world. Conscientious in his usefulness, he made a religion of his duties, and he was a spy as other men are priests. Woe betide the man who fell into his hands! He would have arrested his father for escaping from prison and denounced his mother for contravening the terms of her release from gaol. And he would have done so with that kind of inward satisfaction conferred by virtuousness. To accompany this, a life of privation, isolation, abnegation, chastity, never a moment's recreation. This was implacable duty, an understanding of the police like the Spartans' understanding of Sparta, pitiless surveillance, ferocious honesty, a sleuth of marble-like coldness, Brutus in Vidocq.

Javert's entire person was an expression of the man who spies and keeps out of sight. Joseph de Maistre's mystical school of thought, which at that time was spicing up with high-flown cosmogony what were called the 'ultra' newspapers, would surely have said that Javert was a symbol. You could not see his forehead, which disappeared under his hat. You could not see his eyes that lurked beneath his eyebrows. You could not see his chin that sank into his cravat. You could not see his hands that vanished up his sleeves. You could not see his cane that he carried under his coat. But when the occasion arose, suddenly emerging from all this shadow as from an ambush, you could see a narrow angular forehead, a baleful glance, a threatening chin, huge hands and a monstrous truncheon.

Even though he hated books, in his moments of leisure, which were few and far between, he read, with the result that he was not completely uneducated. This was made evident in a certain pomposity in his manner of speaking.

As we have said, he had no vices. When he was pleased with himself, he allowed himself a pinch of snuff. This was his link with humanity.

It will not be hard to understand that Javert was the terror of that whole class referred to in the annual report of the Ministry of Justice under the heading: Vagrants. At the mention of Javert's name they would make themselves scarce. An appearance by Javert himself would petrify them.

Such was this formidable man.

Javert was like an eye constantly fixed on Monsieur Madeleine. An eye full of suspicion and conjecture. Monsieur Madeleine eventually noticed, but it appeared that this was of no interest to him. He did not even question Javert. He neither sought him out nor avoided him. And he bore that intrusive and almost oppressive gaze without appearing to pay any attention to it. He treated Javert the same way he treated everybody, with unassuming kindness.

From a few words Javert let drop, it was clear that with that curiosity bred in the bone, in which instinct plays as great a part as willpower, he had secretly investigated all previous traces Père Madeleine might have left elsewhere. He seemed to know, and sometimes he said cryptically, that someone had made certain inquiries in a certain place about a certain family that had disappeared. Talking to himself, he once happened to remark, 'I think I've got him!' Then he remained preoccupied for three days without uttering a word. It seemed the lead he thought he had, had come to nothing.

In any case – and this is the necessary corrective to any oversimplification that certain words might have implied – there can be nothing truly infallible about any human being and it is precisely in the nature of instinct that it can become confused, thrown off the scent and led astray. Otherwise, instinct would be superior to intelligence and beasts would turn out to have a better understanding than man.

Javert was evidently somewhat disconcerted by Monsieur Madeleine's complete naturalness and calm.

One day, however, his strange manner seemed to make an impression on Monsieur Madeleine. This was the occasion.

VI
Père Fauchelevent

One morning Monsieur Madeleine was walking along an unpaved side street in Montreuil-sur-Mer. He heard a noise and saw a group of people some way off. He approached them. An old man called Père Fauchelevent had just fallen under his cart when his horse had pitched to the ground.

This Fauchelevent was one of the few enemies Monsieur Madeleine still had at that time. When Madeleine first came to the town Fauchelevent, a former copyist, of peasant stock and almost literate, had a business that was beginning to go badly. Fauchelevent had seen this ordinary labourer grow rich, while he, a skilled tradesman, was being ruined. This had filled him with jealousy and he had done all he could on every occasion to discredit Madeleine. Then came bankruptcy, and the old man, left with nothing but a horse and cart, with no family and no children, had turned carter to earn a living.

The horse had two broken haunches and could not get up again. The old man was trapped between the wheels. So calamitous was the collapse of the vehicle that the whole weight of it was resting on his chest. The cart was quite heavily laden. Père Fauchelevent was wheezing pitifully. People had tried to pull him out, but to no avail. One reckless move, one clumsy intervention, one inadvertent jolt might finish him off. It was impossible to free him other than by lifting the cart off him. Javert, who had turned up just as the accident occurred, sent for a jack.

Monsieur Madeleine arrived. People stood aside respectfully.

'Help!' cried old Fauchelevent. 'What kindly lad will save this old man?'

Monsieur Madeleine turned to those gathered round. 'Has anyone got a jack?'

'Someone's gone to fetch one,' replied a peasant.

'How long will that take?'

'They've gone to the nearest place where there's a farrier, which is Flachot, but all the same it'll take a good quarter of an hour.'

'A quarter of an hour!' exclaimed Madeleine.

It had rained the day before, the ground was wet. With every moment the cart was settling deeper into the ground and compressing the old carter's chest more and more. It was obvious that within five minutes his ribs would be broken.

'We can't wait a quarter of an hour,' said Madeleine to the peasants, who were staring at him.

'We'll have to!'

'But it'll be too late by then! Can't you see the cart is sinking?'

'It can't be helped!'

'Listen,' said Madeleine, 'there's still room enough under the cart to allow a man to crawl under it and lift it on his back – for just half a minute – and the poor man can be pulled out. Is there anyone here who has the strength and the courage? For five gold louis!'

No one in the group moved.

'Ten louis,' said Madeleine.

Those present lowered their eyes. One of them muttered, 'A man would need to be devilish strong. And then he runs the risk of getting crushed!'

'Come on,' said Madeleine. 'Twenty louis.'

The same silence.

'It's not willingness they lack,' said a voice.

Monsieur Madeleine turned round and recognized Javert, whom he had not noticed on his arrival.

Javert went on, 'It's strength. It would take an extraordinary man to do such a thing as lift a cart like that on his back.'

Then, staring intently at Monsieur Madeleine, he went on, dwelling on every word he uttered, 'Monsieur Madeleine, I've never known but one man capable of doing what you ask.'

Madeleine flinched.

Javert added with an air of indifference but without taking his eyes off Madeleine, 'He was a convict.'

'Ah!' said Madeleine.

'Serving a penal sentence at Toulon.'

Madeleine turned pale.

Meanwhile, the cart continued to sink slowly. Père Fauchelevent wheezed and shrieked, 'I can't breathe! It's breaking my ribs! A jack! Something! Ah!'

Madeleine looked round. 'Is there no one, then, who wants to earn twenty louis and save the life of this poor old man?'

None of those present stirred.

Javert spoke again. 'I've never known more than one man who could substitute for a jack. It was that convict.'

'Ah! It's crushing me!' cried the old man.

Madeleine looked up, met Javert's hawk eye still fixed on him, gazed at the motionless peasants and smiled sadly. Then without a word he fell on his knees, and before the crowd had time even to utter a cry he was underneath the cart.

There was a dreadful moment of expectation and silence.

They saw Madeleine, almost flat on his stomach under that tremendous weight, make two vain efforts to draw his elbows closer to his knees. They shouted to him, 'Père Madeleine, come out from under there!' Old Fauchelevent himself said to him, 'Monsieur Madeleine! Get out! Don't you see, it can't be helped, I'm going to die! Just leave me! You're going to get crushed as well!'

Madeleine did not reply.

The spectators gasped. The wheels had continued to sink, and already it had become almost impossible for Madeleine to get out from under the vehicle.

Suddenly the enormous mass was seen to quiver, the cart rose slowly, the wheels half emerged from the ruts. They heard a choked voice crying, 'Quick! Help!' It was Madeleine, who had just made one last effort.

They rushed forward. The self-sacrifice of a single man had given strength and courage to all. The cart was lifted by twenty men. Old Fauchelevent was saved.

Madeleine stood up. He was pale though dripping with sweat. His clothes were torn and covered with mud. Everyone was tearful. The old man kissed his knees and called him the good Lord. He himself had on his face an indescribable expression of blissful and heavenly suffering, and he fixed his calm gaze on Javert, who was still staring at him.

VII
Fauchelevent Becomes a Gardener in Paris

Fauchelevent had dislocated his kneecap in falling. Père Madeleine had him conveyed to an infirmary that he had established for his workers in the factory building itself, and which was staffed by two Sisters of Charity. The next morning the old man found a thousand-franc banknote on his bedside table with this note in Père Madeleine's handwriting: 'For the purchase of your horse and cart.' The cart was a wreck and the horse was dead. Fauchelevent recovered, but his knee remained stiff. On the recommendation of the Sisters of Charity and of his parish priest, Monsieur Madeleine got the old boy a position as gardener at a convent in Rue St-Antoine in Paris.

Some time afterwards, Monsieur Madeleine was appointed mayor. The first time Javert saw Monsieur Madeleine wearing the sash that gave him full authority over the town, he felt a shudder of the kind a watch-dog might feel on smelling a wolf in his master's clothes. From then on he avoided him as much as he could. When his duties made it absolutely necessary and he had no alternative but to be with monsieur le maire, he addressed him with profound respect.

Besides the visible signs we have mentioned of this prosperity created at Montreuil-sur-Mer by Père Madeleine, there was another indicator nonetheless significant for not being visible. Always a sure sign, this. When the population is hard-pressed, when there is a shortage of work, when business is disastrous, the taxpayer, being short of money, is reluctant to pay taxes, delays as much as possible and then exceeds the respite granted, and the state spends a great deal of money on the costs of enforcement and collection. When there is plenty of work, when the country is happy and wealthy, taxes are paid willingly at little cost to the state. It may be said this is one infallible gauge of public wealth and poverty: the cost of collecting taxes. In seven years the cost of collecting taxes had dropped by seventy-five per cent in the *arrondissement** of Montreuil-sur-Mer, which led to this *arrondissement* being frequently cited above all others by Monsieur de Villèle, then minister of finance.

These were the local circumstances when Fantine returned. No one remembered her. Fortunately, the door of Monsieur Madeleine's factory was like a friendly face. She applied there and was taken on in the women's workshop. The work being entirely new to Fantine, she could not be very adept at it. So she made very little money for her day's work, but still it was enough. The problem was solved. She was earning her living.

VIII
Madame Victurnien Spends Thirty-five Francs for the Sake of Morality

When Fantine saw that she was making her living she enjoyed a moment of happiness. To live honestly by the work she did – what a blessing! She

* An administrative subdivision of a *département*.

truly regained a liking for work. She bought a looking-glass and took pleasure in seeing in it her youth, her beautiful hair, her fine teeth. She forgot many things. She thought only of Cosette and the possibilities of the future, and was almost happy. She rented a small room and furnished it on credit against her future earnings – a vestige of her improvident ways.

Not being able to say she was married, she had been very careful, as we have already indicated, not to talk about her little girl.

In these early days, as we have seen, she paid the Thénardiers promptly. As all she could do was sign her name she was obliged to write to them using a public letter-writer.

She wrote often. This was noticed. There started to be mutterings in the women's workroom that Fantine 'wrote letters' and that 'she put on airs and graces'.

There is nothing like those for whom it is none of their business, for spying on other people's actions. Why is it that gentleman only ever comes at dusk? Why does Monsieur So-and-so never hang his key on the hook on Thursdays? Why does he always go down the back streets? Why does madame always get out of her cab before she reaches the house? Why does she send out for a pad of writing-paper when she has 'a whole writing-case full of it'? et cetera, et cetera. There are people who to find out the answer to these mysteries, which in any case are absolutely no concern of theirs, spend more money, waste more time, take more trouble than it would take to do ten good deeds. And all this for nothing, just for the pleasure of it, with no other reward for their curiosity except curiosity. They will follow this man or that woman for days on end, keeping watch for hours on street corners, in gateways, at night, in the cold and rain. They will grease the palms of errand boys, get cab drivers and lackeys drunk, bribe a chambermaid, offer inducements to a doorkeeper. Why? For no reason. Sheer desperation to see, to know, and to find out. Sheer compulsion to gossip. And often, to the great joy of those who have 'uncovered all', with nothing to be gained by it, out of sheer instinct, these secrets once found out and these mysteries made public, these enigmas exposed to the light of day lead to catastrophes, duels, bankruptcies, ruined families, devastated lives. A sorry state of affairs.

Certain individuals are malicious solely because of their need to talk. Their conversation, drawing-room chatter, boudoir gossip, is like those chimneys that burn wood fast. They need a great deal of fuel, and their fuel is their fellow human being.

So Fantine was watched.

Besides which, more than one woman was jealous of her golden hair and her white teeth.

It was noted that in the workroom, among the others, she often turned aside to wipe away a tear. These were the moments when she was thinking of her child, perhaps also of the man she had loved.

Severing unhappy ties with the past is a painful and arduous process.

It was noted that she wrote at least twice a month, always to the same address, and that she paid for the postage. A way was found to obtain the address: Monsieur, Monsieur Thénardier, Innkeeper, at Montfermeil. The public letter-writer, an old fellow who could not fill his stomach with red wine without emptying his bag of secrets, was encouraged to blab in the tavern. In short, it came to be known that Fantine had a child. 'She must have been some kind of prostitute.' There was one old busybody who made the trip to Montfermeil, talked to the Thénardiers, and said on her return, 'For my thirty-five francs I've got to the bottom of it. I've seen the child.'

The busybody who did this was a gorgon named Madame Victurnien, guardian and doorkeeper of everyone's virtue. Madame Victurnien was fifty-six and her mask of ugliness was overlaid with the mask of old age. Quavering voice, crotchety mind. Hard to believe, this old woman had once been young. In her youth, when '93 was in full spate, she married a monk who fled the cloister wearing the Revolutionary's red cap, switching from the Bernardines to the Jacobins. She was unfeeling, unpleasant, unapproachable, peevish, prickly, almost poisonous; and now widowed, still harbouring the memory of the monk who had thoroughly subdued her and bent her to his will. She was a nettle that you could see had been crushed by the cassock.* With the Restoration she became devout, and so zealously that the priests forgave her her monk. She had a small property that she made a great fuss about bequeathing to a religious community. She was very highly regarded at the episcopal palace of Arras. So this Madame Victurnien went to Montfermeil and returned saying, 'I've seen the child.'

All this took time. Fantine had been at the factory for over a year when one morning the workshop supervisor gave her fifty francs on behalf of monsieur le maire, telling her she no longer had a job at the workshop and urging her on behalf of monsieur le maire to leave town.

It was the very same month that the Thénardiers, having asked for twelve francs instead of six, had just demanded fifteen francs instead of twelve.

* An allusion to the expression *jeter le froc aux orties*, literally 'to throw the cassock into the nettles', i.e. to give up the monastic life.

Fantine was devastated. She could not leave town, she owed money for her rent and her furniture. Fifty francs was not enough to pay off this debt. She stammered out a few pleading words. The supervisor made clear to her she must leave the workshop immediately. Besides, Fantine was not an especially good worker. Overcome with shame even more than despair, she left the workshop and returned to her room. So her offence was now known to all!

She felt she had not the strength left to say another word. She was advised to go and see monsieur le maire. She did not dare. Monsieur le maire gave her fifty francs because he was kind and sacked her because he was just. She submitted to that judgement.

IX

Success for Madame Victurnien

So the monk's widow was good for something. But Monsieur Madeleine knew nothing of all this. It was one of those combinations of circumstances that life is full of. As a rule Monsieur Madeleine almost never went into the women's workshop. He had placed in charge of this workshop an elderly spinster provided by the parish priest, and he had full confidence in this supervisor, a truly respectable person, firm, fair-minded, full of the charity that consists in donating but not so much of the charity that consists in understanding and forgiving. Monsieur Madeleine left everything to her. The best of men are often obliged to delegate their authority. It was invested with this full power and in the conviction she was doing the right thing that the supervisor tried, judged, condemned and executed Fantine.

As for the fifty francs, she donated them out of a fund Monsieur Madeleine had entrusted to her for the benefit and assistance of the working women, and for which she did not have to account.

Fantine sought work locally as a servant. She went from house to house. No one would have her. She could not leave town. The second-hand dealer to whom she was in debt for her furniture, such as it was, said to her, 'If you leave, I'll have you arrested as a thief.' The landlord to whom she owed rent said to her, 'You're young and pretty, you can pay.' She divided the fifty francs between the landlord and the furniture dealer, returned to the latter three-quarters of his goods, kept only the bare minimum, and found herself with no work, with no place in society, left with only her bed, and still owing about fifty francs.

She began to make plain shirts for the soldiers of the garrison and earned twelve sous a day. Her daughter cost her ten. It was at this point that she began to fall behind with her payments to the Thénardiers.

However, an old woman who lighted her candle for her when she came home at night taught her the art of living in poverty. Beyond living on little, there is living on nothing. They are two rooms. The first is dark, the second is pitch-black.

Fantine learned how to go without any fire at all in winter, how to give up a bird that eats a quarter of a sou's worth of millet every two days, how to make a coverlet of your underskirt and an underskirt of your coverlet, how to save your candle by taking your meals by the light from the window opposite. We do not know how much some poor creatures who have grown old in honest destitution can get out of one sou. It eventually becomes a talent. Fantine acquired this sublime talent, and again took heart a little.

At this period she said to a neighbour, 'Puh! I tell myself, with only five hours' sleep and working all the rest of the time at my sewing, I'll always be able to earn just about enough to live on. And anyway, when you're sad you eat less. Oh well, some hardship, some worries, a little bread on the one hand and heartache on the other, all that will keep me going.'

In this predicament it would have been a peculiar joy to have her little girl with her. She thought of fetching her. But *what*? Make her share this hardship! And besides, she owed money to the Thénardiers! How was she to settle her debt? And the journey! How was she to pay for that?

The old woman who had given her what might be called lessons in a life of poverty was a saintly spinster called Marguerite, a woman of true devoutness, poor, and charitable towards the poor and even towards the rich, able to write just well enough to sign her name 'Margeritte', and believing in God, which is true knowledge.

There are many of these saints here below. Some day they will have their place on high. This life has a tomorrow.

At first Fantine felt so ashamed, she dared not go out.

When she was in the street, she sensed that people turned round behind her and pointed. Everyone stared at her and no one greeted her. The cold, bitter scorn of passers-by penetrated her, body and soul, like a north wind.

In small towns an unmarried mother might as well be exposed naked to everyone's taunts and prying. At least in Paris no one knows you, and this obscurity clothes you. Oh! how she must have yearned to come to Paris! Impossible!

She had to get used to disrepute just as she had to get used to penury. Gradually she resigned herself to it. After two or three months she shook off her shame and began to go about as though nothing bothered her. 'It's all the same to me,' she would say.

She came and went with head held high and a bitter smile, and felt she was becoming brazen.

From her window Madame Victurnien sometimes saw her passing, observed the plight of 'that creature' who 'thanks to her' had been 'put in her rightful place', and congratulated herself. The wicked have a cruel happiness.

Fantine was exhausted by overwork, and the little dry cough she had, worsened. She sometimes said to her neighbour Marguerite, 'Just feel how hot my hands are!'

Still, when in the morning with an old broken comb she combed her beautiful hair, like cascades of floss-silk, she took a moment's pleasure in her appearance.

X
The Consequences of Her Success

Fantine had been sacked towards the end of winter. Then it was summer, but winter came again. Short days, less work. Winter: no warmth, no light, no middle of the day, evening following on morning, fog, twilight, the window grey, the light so bad you cannot see. The sky is a basement window, the whole day a cellar. The sun looks like a pauper. What a dreadful time of year! Winter turns to stone both the rain from heaven and the heart of man. Her creditors harried her.

Fantine earned too little. Her debts had grown. Not getting their money, the Thénardiers were constantly writing her letters whose contents upset her terribly, and the cost of their delivery was ruining her. One day they wrote saying that her little Cosette was going stark-naked in that cold weather, that she needed a woollen skirt, and the least her mother could do was to send ten francs for it. She received the letter and crumpled it in her hands all day long. That evening she went into a barber's shop at the corner of the street and pulled out her hair pin. Her lovely golden hair fell to below her waist.

'What beautiful hair!' exclaimed the barber.

'How much will you give me for it?' she said.

'Ten francs.'

'Cut it off.'

She bought a knitted skirt and sent it to the Thénardiers.

This skirt infuriated the Thénardiers. It was the money they wanted. They gave the skirt to Éponine. Poor Alouette continued to shiver.

Fantine thought, 'My child's not cold now. I've clothed her with my hair.' She wore little round caps that concealed her shorn head, and she still looked pretty in them.

A sinister process was at work in Fantine's heart. When she saw she could no longer dress her hair she began to feel hatred for everything around her. She had long shared everyone's reverence for Père Madeleine. Yet by telling herself over and over again that it was he who had sacked her, that he was the cause of her unhappiness, she came to hate him too, him especially. If she passed by the factory at times when the workers were at the gate, she put on a show of laughing and singing.

An old woman working there, who once saw her laughing and singing like that, said, 'There's a girl who'll come to a bad end.'

She took a lover, just anybody, a man she did not love, out of bravado, with rage in her heart. He was a scoundrel, some sort of beggar musician, a lazy tramp, who beat her and left her as she had taken him, in disgust.

She adored her child.

The further she fell and the darker everything around her became, the more brightly shone that sweet little angel deep in her soul. She said, 'When I'm rich, I'll have my Cosette with me.' And she laughed. She could not get rid of her cough and she had sweats down her back.

One day she received from the Thénardiers a letter that read as follows: 'Cosette is ill with a local sickness. A miliary fever, they call it. She needs expensive drugs. This is ruining us and we cannot pay out any more. If you do not send us forty francs before the week is out, the little one will die.'

She burst out laughing and said to her old neighbour, 'Oh! Very funny! Forty francs! Is that all? That's two napoleons! Where do they expect me to find them? Are they stupid, these peasants?'

Yet she went out on to the staircase and reread the letter by a skylight. Then she carried on down the stairs and went out, running and skipping, still laughing.

Somebody who met her said, 'What have you got to be so cheerful about?'

She replied, 'There are some people in the country who have just written me a very silly letter. They want forty francs from me. That's peasants for you!'

As she crossed the square she saw a number of people gathered round a bizarre-shaped carriage with a man dressed in red standing on top of it, holding forth. He was a travelling mountebank dentist who was offering the public full sets of dentures, opiates, powders and elixirs.

Fantine mingled with the crowd and began to laugh like everyone else at this harangue, which included slang for the riff-raff and scientific jargon for respectable folk. The tooth-puller saw this pretty girl laughing and suddenly cried out, 'You, the girl there laughing, you have pretty teeth! If you want to sell me your two gnashers I'll give you a gold napoleon for each of them.'

'What are my gnashers?' asked Fantine.

'Your gnashers', replied the dental professor, 'are your front teeth, the two top ones.'

'How horrible!' exclaimed Fantine.

'Two napoleons!' mumbled a toothless old crone standing there. 'Well, there's a lucky girl!'

Fantine fled and blocked her ears so as not to hear the hoarse voice of the man shouting after her, 'Think about it, pretty girl! Two napoleons can come in handy! If you fancy it, come to the Tillac d'Argent inn this evening, you'll find me there.'

Fantine returned home. She was furious and recounted the incident to her good neighbour Marguerite. 'Can you imagine? My God, what a dreadful man! How can such people be allowed to go about the place! Pull out my two front teeth! Why, I'd look horrible! Hair grows again, but teeth! Uh! The man's a monster! I'd rather throw myself head first into the street from the fifth floor! He told me he'd be at the Tillac d'Argent this evening.'

'And what did he offer?' asked Marguerite.

'Two napoleons.'

'That's forty francs.'

'Yes,' said Fantine, 'that's forty francs.'

She remained pensive and took up her sewing. After a quarter of an hour she left her sewing and went out on to the staircase to reread the Thénardiers' letter.

Coming back into the room she said to Marguerite, who was working with her, 'What is this miliary fever? Do you know?'

'Yes,' replied the old maid, 'it's a sickness.'

'So it calls for a lot of drugs?'

'Oh! an awful lot of drugs.'

'How do you get it?'

'It is a sickness that just comes over you.'

'So it attacks children?'

'Especially children.'

'Do people die of it?'

'Very easily,' said Marguerite.

Fantine went out on to the staircase again to reread her letter.

That evening she came downstairs and was seen heading in the direction of Rue de Paris, where the inns are.

The next morning when Marguerite went into Fantine's room before daylight, for they always worked together and so lit just one candle between the two of them, she found Fantine sitting on her bed, looking pale, cold as ice. She had not laid her head on the pillow. Her bonnet had dropped into her lap. Her candle had been burning all night and was almost entirely consumed.

Marguerite stopped in the doorway, paralysed by this enormous disarray, and cried, 'Lord! the candle's burned right down! Something's happened.'

Then she looked at Fantine, who turned her shorn head towards her.

Fantine had aged ten years since the day before.

'Dear Jesus!' said Marguerite. 'What's wrong with you, Fantine?'

'Nothing's wrong,' replied Fantine. 'Quite the contrary. My child won't die of that awful sickness for want of help. I'm pleased.'

So saying, she showed the old maid two napoleons glinting on the table.

'Good Lord!' cried Marguerite. 'Why, that's a fortune! Where did you get those gold louis?'

'Got them, I did!' replied Fantine.

At the same time she smiled. The candle lit her face. It was a bloody smile. Red-tinged saliva stained the corners of her mouth and there was a black hole between her lips.

The two teeth had been pulled out. She sent the forty francs to Montfermeil. It was actually a ruse on the part of the Thénardiers to get money out of her. Cosette was not ill.

Fantine threw her mirror out of the window. She had long since left her small cell on the second floor for a garret with a latch door under the roof, one of those attic spaces with the ceiling sloping down to the floor that you keep banging your head against. The poor can no more reach the end of their room than the end of their life without having to stoop lower and lower.

Her bed was gone. All she had left was a rag she called her coverlet, a mattress on the floor and a broken-down chair. Now standing withered in a corner, forgotten, was a little rosebush she had. In the other corner was a butter-cooler to hold water, which froze in winter, rings of ice leaving long-lasting marks indicating the different water levels.

She had lost her shame, she now lost her vanity. Sign of ultimate despair. She went out wearing dirty bonnets. Whether for want of time or out of indifference, she no longer mended her clothes. As the heels wore out she pulled her stockings down into her shoes. This was evident from the vertical wrinkles. She patched her bodice, which was old and worn, with scraps of calico that tore at the slightest movement. The people she owed money to 'made scenes' and gave her no peace. She found them in the street, she found them again on her staircase. She spent nights weeping and thinking. Her eyes were very bright, and she felt a constant pain in her shoulder, near the top of her left shoulder blade. She coughed a great deal. She hated Père Madeleine intensely, but did not complain. She sewed seventeen hours a day. But a prison-labour contractor, who made the prisoners work for less, brought prices down all of a sudden, which reduced the daily earnings of ordinary working women to nine sous. Seventeen hours of toil and nine sous a day! Her creditors were more pitiless than ever. The second-hand dealer, who had taken back nearly all his furniture, kept on at her, 'When will you pay me, you hussy?'* In God's name, what did they want of her! She felt hunted, and something of the wild beast developed in her. About the same time Thénardier wrote to her saying that, really, he had been far too good about waiting and he must have a hundred francs immediately. Otherwise, he would turn little Cosette, just convalescing from her serious illness, out of the house, into the cold and on to the street, and she'd have to look after herself as best she could. And that she would die, if that's what her mother wanted. 'A hundred francs,' thought Fantine. 'But where's there a job that will pay a hundred sous a day?'

'Well,' she said, 'let's get on with it and sell the rest.'

The poor girl became registered as a common prostitute.

XI
Christus Nos Liberavit†

What is this story of Fantine about? It is about society buying a slave.

From whom? From wretchedness.

From hunger, cold, isolation, neglect, destitution. A hard bargain. A soul for a morsel of bread. Society accepts what wretchedness offers.

The sacred law of Jesus Christ governs our civilization but does not

---

* From now on, Fantine is addressed by all and sundry as 'tu'.
† St Paul's Epistle to the Galatians 5:1: 'Christ hath made us free.'

yet pervade it. It is said that slavery has disappeared from European civilization. This is false. It still exists, but only women suffer this oppression now, and its name is prostitution.

It oppresses women, that is to say feminine charm, weakness, beauty, motherhood. This is not one of the least of man's reasons to be ashamed.

At the point we have now reached in this painful tragedy, there is nothing left of the Fantine she once was. Sinking into the mire, she has hardened into stone. Anyone who touches her feels cold. She passes by, enduring you, ignoring you. She is the stern figure of disgrace. Life and the social order have said all they have to say to her. Everything that will happen to her has happened. She has been through everything, borne everything, sustained everything, suffered everything, lost everything, mourned everything. She is resigned with a resignation that resembles indifference as death resembles sleep. There is nothing more she shrinks from, nothing more she fears. Let the whole rain-cloud come down on her and the entire ocean sweep over her! What does she care? She is a saturated sponge.

This at least is what she believes, but it is a mistake to imagine that fate has no more in store and that there is a limit to everything.

Alas! What are all these lives, driven on in such confusion? Where are they going? Why are they like this?

He who knows this sees the full extent of the darkness.

There is none but he. His name is God.

XII
Monsieur Bamatabois's Idleness

There is in all small towns, and there was in Montreuil-sur-Mer in particular, a class of young men who nibble on an income of fifteen hundred francs much as others like them gobble up two hundred thousand francs a year in Paris. These are creatures of the great neuter species: geldings, parasites, nonentities, who have a little land, a little foolishness and a little wit, who would be boors in a salon and think themselves gentlemen in the tavern. Who say, 'My fields, my peasants, my woods.' Who boo actresses at the theatre to prove they are men of taste, and quarrel with officers of the garrison to prove they are men of war. Who hunt, smoke, yawn, drink, smell of tobacco, play billiards, stare at the travellers that arrive by stage-coach, live at the café, dine at the inn, have a dog that eats the bones under the table and a mistress who puts the dishes on the table. Who count every sou, take fashion to extremes, admire tragedy, despise women, wear out their old boots, copy London from Paris and Paris from Pont-à-Mousson, become gaga old men, never work, serve no purpose and do no great harm.

Monsieur Félix Tholomyès, had he remained in the country and never seen Paris, would have been one of these men.

If they were richer you would say: they are dandies. If they were poorer you would say: they are good-for-nothings. They are simply idlers. Among these idlers are the boring, the bored, the daydreamers and a few wags.

In those days a dandy consisted of a big collar, a big cravat, a watch with watch charms attached to it, three waistcoats of different colours worn one on top of the other with the red and the blue underneath, a short-waisted olive swallow-tail coat with a double row of close-set silver buttons running up to the shoulder, trousers of a lighter shade of olive decorated on the two seams with rows of piping, the number of rows varying but always uneven, ranging between one and eleven, a limit that was never exceeded. Add to this, ankle-boots with little metal heel-plates, a narrow-brimmed top hat, hair worn in a quiff, an enormous cane, and conversation spiced with Potier's puns. On top of all that, spurs and a moustache. At that time a moustache signified respectability, and spurs, one who got about on foot.

The provincial dandy wore the longest of spurs and the bushiest of moustaches.

It was the period when the republics of South America were fighting against the king of Spain, Bolívar against Morillo. Narrow-brimmed hats were royalist and called 'morillos'. Liberals wore hats with wide brims, called 'bolivars'.

Now, eight or ten months after what has been recounted in the preceding pages, sometime about the beginning of January 1823, on an evening when snow had fallen, one of these dandies, one of these idlers – a 'right-minded' fellow, for he wore a morillo, as well as being warmly wrapped in one of those big cloaks that in cold weather completed the fashionable outfit – was having fun tormenting a creature who was loitering in front of the window of the officers' café in a dance dress, with her neck and shoulders bare and with flowers on her head. This dandy was smoking, for that was very much the fashion.

Each time this woman passed in front of him he directed at her, along with a puff from his cigar, some insult he considered witty and amusing, such as 'How ugly you are!' 'Spare me the sight of you!' 'You've no teeth!' et cetera, et cetera. This gentleman's name was Monsieur Bamatabois. The woman, a sorry-looking dolled-up spectre, walking back and forth in the snow, did not respond, did not even glance at him, and in silence, with sombre regularity, carried on regardless with her perambulations which every five minutes brought her back to this taunting, like the soldier condemned to a flogging who keeps regaining consciousness. Making so little impression on her no doubt piqued the idler, and taking advantage of a moment when her back was turned he crept up behind her and, stifling his laughter, bent down, picked up a handful of snow from the pavement, and suddenly thrust it down her back between her bare shoulders. The trollop howled, turned, leapt like a panther and hurled herself at the man, sinking her fingernails into his face with the most dreadful oaths that could possibly spill out of the barrack-room into the gutter. These foul words, disgorged in a voice thickened by alcohol, issued hideously from a mouth in which, sure enough, the two front teeth were missing. It was Fantine.

At the rumpus this created, the officers flocked out of the café, passers-by gathered, and a big circle, laughing, hooting and clapping, formed round this frenzied whirl consisting of two creatures that it was difficult to recognize as a man and a woman: the man trying to defend himself, his hat on the ground; the woman kicking and punching, bareheaded, screaming, toothless and shorn, livid with anger, horrible.

Suddenly a tall man burst through the crowd, grabbed the woman by her muddied satin bodice and said to her, 'Follow me!'

The woman looked up. Her furious voice suddenly died away. Her eyes were dull, from livid she turned ashen, and she trembled, terror-stricken. She had recognized Javert.

The dandy took advantage of this turn of events to make his escape.

XIII
Resolving Some Questions of Municipal Policing

Javert moved the bystanders aside, broke up the circle and strode off towards the police station, which is on the far side of the square, dragging the poor wretch after him. With no will of her own, she offered no resistance. Neither he nor she said a word. Beside themselves with joy, the crowd of spectators followed after them, jeering. Utter wretchedness prompting obscenities.

On arriving at the police station, a low-ceilinged room heated by a stove with an armed guard and a barred glazed door opening on to the street, Javert opened the door, entered with Fantine, and shut the door behind him to the great disappointment of the curious onlookers, who stood on tip-toe and craned their necks in front of the dingy window of the station house, trying to see. Curiosity is a form of gluttony. To see is to devour.

Inside, Fantine went and collapsed in a corner, still and silent, cowering there like a frightened dog.

The sergeant of the guard brought a lighted candle to the table. Javert sat down, drew a sheet of official paper from his pocket, and began to write.

Under our laws women of this social category are placed entirely in the hands of the police. The latter do with them what they please, punish them as they see fit and confiscate at will those two sad things the women call their trade and their freedom. Javert was impassive. His solemn face betrayed no emotion. Yet he was seriously and deeply preoccupied. It was one of those moments when he was exercising his formidable discretionary powers, with no one to answer to but with all the scruples of an exacting conscience. At that moment, he felt, the policeman's stool he sat on was a judge's bench. He was sitting in judgement. He was sitting in judgement, and he was passing sentence. He summoned up every conceivable thought he might have about the great thing he was doing. The more he considered this woman's deed, the more outraged he felt. It was evident he had just witnessed a crime being committed. He had just seen society, represented by an enfranchised property owner, insulted and attacked out there in the street by a creature totally beyond the pale. A prostitute had assaulted a respectable citizen. He, Javert, had seen this. He wrote in silence.

When he had finished he signed the paper, folded it, and said to the sergeant of the guard as he handed it to him, 'Take three men and conduct this whore to the cells.' Then turning to Fantine, 'You've got six months.'

The poor creature gave a start.

'Six months! Six months in prison!' she cried. 'Six months earning seven sous a day! But what will become of Cosette? My daughter! My daughter! But I still owe the Thénardiers more than a hundred francs – do you know that, monsieur l'inspecteur?'

She dragged herself across the floor that was wet from the muddy boots of all those men, without getting to her feet, with her hands joined, taking great strides on her knees.

'Monsieur Javert,' she said, 'I beg you for mercy. I assure you I'm not to blame. If you'd seen how it started, you'd have seen that. I swear by the good Lord I'm not to blame! It was that gentleman, someone I don't know, who put snow down my back. Do people have the right to put snow down our backs when we're just walking past quietly doing no one any harm? It gave me a turn. I'm not very well, you see. And he'd already been having a go at me for a while. "You're ugly! You've no teeth!" I know full well I haven't got my teeth any more. I didn't do anything. I thought, he's a gentleman having his fun. I behaved myself, I didn't speak to him. It was at that moment he put the snow down my back. Monsieur Javert, my dear monsieur l'inspecteur! Isn't there someone who might have seen it and could tell you this is the absolute truth? Perhaps I was wrong to get angry. You know, in that first instant you're not in control of yourself. You overreact. And then having something cold put down your back just when you are not expecting it! I was wrong to ruin the gentleman's hat. Why did he go away? I'd beg his forgiveness. Oh, God! I wouldn't mind at all begging his forgiveness. Spare me today, for this once, Monsieur Javert. Listen, this is something you don't know – in prison you can only earn seven sous a day, it's not the government's fault but you earn seven sous and, can you imagine, I have to pay a hundred francs or my little girl will be sent back to me. Oh, my God! I can't have her with me. It's so sordid, what I do! Oh, my Cosette, my little angel of the dear Blessed Virgin, what will become of her, poor darling? I'll tell you, it's the Thénardiers, they're innkeepers, peasants, there's no reasoning with them. They must be paid. Don't put me in prison! You see, it would mean a little girl being abandoned on the high road to fend for herself, in the depths of winter, that's the thing you must have pity on, my dear Monsieur Javert. If she were older she'd earn her living but they can't at that age. I'm not a wicked woman at heart. It's not indolence and greed that have made me like this. I drink spirits out of misery. I don't like it but it's deadening. In happier times you'd only have had to look in my closets to see I wasn't a wanton hussy. I had decent underclothes, lots of decent underclothes. Have pity on me, Monsieur Javert!'

She went on like this, utterly dashed, shaken with sobs, blinded with tears, her shoulders and neck bare, wringing her hands, coughing with a short dry cough and mumbling quietly in a voice of anguish. Great grief is a terrible divine illumination that transfigures the wretched. At that point Fantine had become beautiful again. At certain moments she paused and tenderly kissed the hem of the policeman's coat. She would have softened a heart of granite, but the heart of a man without feeling cannot be softened.

'Right!' said Javert. 'I've listened to you. Have you nothing more to say? Now get moving! You've got your six months! The Eternal Father himself wouldn't be able to do anything about it.'

At those solemn words – 'The Eternal Father himself wouldn't be able to do anything about it' – she understood that her fate had been decided. She collapsed in a heap, murmuring, 'Mercy!'

Javert turned his back on her.

The soldiers grabbed her by the arms.

A few moments earlier a man had entered, unobserved. He shut the door, leaned his back against it, and listened to Fantine's despairing entreaties.

Just as the soldiers laid hands on the poor wretch, who would not get up, he took a step forward, emerged from the shadows and said, 'One moment, please.'

Javert looked up and recognized Monsieur Madeleine. He removed his hat, and bowing with a kind of aggrieved awkwardness, he said, 'Excuse me, monsieur le maire—'

Those words, 'monsieur le maire', had a curious effect on Fantine. She stood up all at once like a spectre rising from the earth, thrust aside the soldiers with both arms, walked straight up to Monsieur Madeleine before anyone could prevent her, and staring at him wildly she cried, 'Ah! so you're monsieur le maire!'

Then she burst out laughing and spat in his face.

Monsieur Madeleine wiped his face and said, 'Inspector Javert, set this woman free.'

Javert felt he was about to go mad. At that moment he underwent in rapid succession and almost all at once the most violent emotions he had ever experienced in his life. To see a common prostitute spit in the face of a mayor – this was something so monstrous that in his most dreadful imaginings he would have regarded it as sacrilege to believe it were possible. On the other hand, obscurely, at the back of his mind, he made a hideous comparison between what this woman was and what this mayor might be, and then he had an inkling of something very simple about this extraordinary attack that appalled him. But when he saw this mayor, this magistrate, calmly wipe his face and say, 'Set this woman free', he was stunned, thoughts and words failed him equally. His capacity for astonishment was exceeded. He remained speechless.

These words had an impact on Fantine no less strange. She raised her bare arm and clung to the damper of the stove like a person reeling. Meanwhile, she looked all around her and began to speak in a low voice as though talking to herself.

'Set free! I'm to be let go! I'm not to be put in prison for six months! Who said that? It's impossible anyone could have said that. I misheard. It can't have been this monster of a mayor! Was it you, my dear Monsieur Javert, who said I was to be set free? Oh, listen, I'll tell you, and you'll let me go. This monster, this old villain of a mayor, he's the one responsible for everything. Just imagine, Monsieur Javert, he sacked me! Because of a bunch of shrews gossiping in the workroom. Isn't that a dreadful thing to do! To sack a poor girl who's doing her job honestly! Then I couldn't earn enough and that's when everything went wrong. For a start, there's one thing these gentlemen of the police certainly ought to do to make things better, that's to stop prison contractors cheating poor people. Listen, I'll explain it to you: you're earning twelve sous making shirts, it drops to nine sous, you can't make a living any more. Then you have to do the best you can. I had my little Cosette, I was forced to become a bad woman. You can see now, it's that wretched mayor who did all the harm. Afterwards I stamped on that gentleman's hat in front of the officers' café. But with that snow he completely spoiled my dress. Women like me have only one silk dress for the evenings. You see, truly, Monsieur Javert, I've never deliberately done anything wrong, and I see women everywhere, far more wicked than I am, who are much better off. Oh, Monsieur Javert, it was you that gave orders I was to be set free, wasn't it? Make inquiries, speak to my landlord, I'm up to date with my rent now, people will tell you, I pay my way. Oh God! I'm sorry, without minding what I was doing I've moved the damper on the stove, and now it's smoking.'

Monsieur Madeleine listened to her intently. While she was speaking he fumbled in his waistcoat, drew out his purse and opened it. It was empty. He put it back in his pocket. He said to Fantine, 'How much did you say you owed?'

Fantine, who had been looking at no one else but Javert, turned to him. 'I wasn't speaking to you!'

Then addressing the soldiers, 'Now, you there, did you see how I spat in his face? Ah! you villainous old mayor, you're here to frighten me but I'm not afraid of you. I'm afraid of Monsieur Javert. I'm afraid of my dear Monsieur Javert!'

As she said this she turned back to the inspector. 'You see, at the same time, monsieur l'inspecteur, you have to be fair. I realize that you are fair, monsieur l'inspecteur. Indeed, it's quite simple: a man putting snow down a woman's back for fun, that made the officers laugh, they have to amuse themselves somehow, and that's what women like me are here for, of course! And then you come along, you've no choice but to restore order, you take away the woman who's to blame, but on reflection, seeing as you're kind-hearted, you say I'm to be set free. It's for the sake of the little one, because, spending six months in prison, that would mean I couldn't support my child. Only, don't do it again, you hussy! Oh! I won't do it again, Monsieur Javert! Whatever anyone does to me now, I won't react in any way. But you see, today I yelled because it hurt, I wasn't at all expecting that snow from the gentleman, and besides, as I told you, I'm not well, I cough, I have what feels like a lump in my stomach, which hurts, and the doctor tells me, "Take care of yourself." Here, feel, give me your hand, don't be afraid, it's here.'

She was no longer weeping, her voice was caressing. She placed Javert's huge hand on her delicate white chest and gazed at him, smiling.

Briskly, she tidied the disarray of her clothes, smoothed down the folds of her skirt that in dragging herself along had ridden almost up to her knee, and walked towards the door, saying to the soldiers in a subdued voice and with a friendly nod, 'Monsieur l'inspecteur said I was to be released, lads, I'll be on my way.'

She laid her hand on the door latch. One more step and she was in the street.

Up to that moment Javert had stood stock still, staring at the ground, out of place in the midst of this scene like some statue left in the way, waiting to be put somewhere.

The sound of the latch roused him. He raised his head with an expression of supreme authority, an expression that is always the more frightening the lower the level at which power is invested, ferocious in the wild beast, atrocious in the man of no account.

'Sergeant!' he cried. 'Can't you see that minx is walking out of here! Who told you to let her go?'

'I did,' said Madeleine.

At the sound of Javert's voice Fantine trembled and let go of the latch like a thief dropping the stolen article. At the sound of Madeleine's voice she turned round, and from that moment on, without her uttering a word, without her so much as daring to breathe freely, her eyes travelled back and forth, from Madeleine to Javert and from Javert to Madeleine, depending on which of them was speaking.

It was obvious that Javert must have been 'thrown out of kilter', as they say, to allow himself to address the sergeant the way he did after the mayor's request that Fantine should be set free. Could he have forgotten monsieur le maire's presence? Had he in the end convinced himself it was impossible that any 'authority' could have given such an order, and that surely monsieur le maire must have said one thing instead of another without meaning to? Or in view of the outrages he had witnessed over the past two hours, did he tell himself it was necessary to act with the utmost resolve, that the humble must assume greatness, the sleuth must turn himself into a judge, the police agent must become the agent of justice, and that in this exceptional extremity he, Javert, was the personification of law, order, morality, government, the whole of society?

In any case, when Monsieur Madeleine uttered the words we have just heard, 'I did', Police Inspector Javert, pale, cold, with blue lips and a look of despair, his whole body quivering almost imperceptibly, was seen to turn to the mayor and – what was incredible – say to him with downcast eyes but in a firm voice, 'Monsieur le maire, that cannot be.'

'Why not?' said Monsieur Madeleine.

'This wretch has insulted a gentleman.'

'Inspector Javert,' replied the mayor in a calm and conciliatory tone, 'listen. You're an honest man, and I've no objection to explaining myself to you. This is the truth of the matter: I was passing through the square as you were taking this woman away, there were still some stragglers, I made inquiries, I got the whole story. The gentleman was to blame and by rights it was he who should have been arrested by the police.'

Javert retorted, 'This wretch has just insulted monsieur le maire.'

'That's my concern,' said Monsieur Madeleine. 'The insult to me is mine, you know. I can do what I like about it.'

'I beg monsieur le maire's pardon. The insult is not to him but to the rule of law.'

'Inspector Javert,' replied Monsieur Madeleine, 'the highest law is conscience. I heard this woman. I know what I'm doing.'

'And I don't understand what I'm seeing, monsieur le maire.'

'Then be satisfied with obeying.'

'I'm obeying my duty. My duty demands that this woman serve six months in prison.'

Monsieur Madeleine replied quietly, 'Listen carefully to what I say. She will not serve a single day.'

At this peremptory statement Javert dared to gaze intently at the mayor and to say, but in a still profoundly respectful tone of voice, 'I deeply regret opposing monsieur le maire, this is the first time in my life, but he will be so good as to allow me to point out that I am acting within the scope of my authority. Since monsieur le maire so wishes, I restrict myself to the incident involving the gentleman. I was there. This woman hurled herself at Monsieur Bamatabois, who is the enfranchised owner of that handsome three-storey freestone house with a balcony that stands on the corner of the parade. After all, there are some undeniable facts in this world! In any case, monsieur le maire, this is a matter of policing the streets, which is my concern, and I am detaining this woman Fantine.'

Then Monsieur Madeleine folded his arms and said in a stern voice that no one in the town had heard up till now, 'The matter to which you refer is a municipal police matter, of which according to the terms of Articles 9, 15 and 66 of the Criminal Procedures Code I am the judge. I order this woman to be set free.'

Javert was determined to make one last effort. 'But monsieur le maire—'

'I would remind you, monsieur, of Article 81 of the law passed on the thirteenth of December 1799, regarding arbitrary detention.'

'Monsieur le maire, allow—'

'Not another word.'

'But—'

'Go,' said Monsieur Madeleine.

Javert took the blow like a Russian soldier, upright, facing it and full in the chest. He gave the deepest of bows to monsieur le maire and left.

Fantine moved away from the door and stared in amazement as he passed in front of her.

However, she too was thrown into a strange confusion. She had just seen herself in some way fought over by two opposing powers. Before her very eyes she had seen the battle between two men holding in their hands her freedom, her life, her soul, her child. One of these men was dragging her towards darkness, the other leading her back to the light. In this conflict, seen magnified by terror, these two men appeared to her as two giants. One spoke like her demon, the other like her good angel. The angel had conquered the demon, and what made her shudder from head to foot was that this angel, this liberator, was precisely the man she abhorred, that same mayor she had so long regarded as the author of all her woes, that Madeleine! And at the very moment when she had just insulted him in a hideous manner, he saved her! Had she, then, been mistaken? Must she, then, have a complete change of heart? She did not know. She trembled. She listened in bewilderment, she watched in dismay, and at every word that Monsieur Madeleine said she felt the dissolution and dispersal inside her of the frightful shades of hatred, and the birth in her heart of something beyond expression, an indefinable warmth that was joy, trust, love.

When Javert had gone Monsieur Madeleine turned to her and said in a deliberate voice, having difficulty speaking, like a serious-minded person who does not want to give way to tears, 'I heard you.* I knew nothing of what you said. I believe it's true, and I feel that it's true. I didn't even know you'd left my factory. Why didn't you come to me? But listen, I'll pay your debts, I'll send for your child, or you shall go

* Fantine is now addressed as 'vous'.

182

to her. You shall live here, in Paris, wherever you like. I'll take care of you and your child. If you want, you shan't work again. I'll give you all the money you need. In regaining your happiness you'll regain respectability. And listen, let me tell you right now: if everything is as you say, and I don't doubt it, you've never ceased to be virtuous and holy in the sight of God. Oh, poor woman!'

This was more than Fantine could bear. To have Cosette! To leave behind this life of degradation. To live free, rich, happy and respectable. With Cosette! To see the sudden unfolding in the midst of her misery of all this paradise come true. She stared as though stupefied at this man who was talking to her, and she could only give vent to two or three sobs, 'Oh! Oh! Oh!' Her legs buckled. She knelt before Monsieur Madeleine and before he could prevent her he felt her take his hand and press her lips to it.

Then she fainted.

BOOK SIX
JAVERT

I
An Initial Rest

Monsieur Madeleine had Fantine taken to the infirmary he had in his own factory. He entrusted her to the care of the sisters, who put her to bed. She had developed a burning fever. She spent part of the night delirious and talking out loud. However, she eventually fell asleep.

Towards noon the next day Fantine woke up, heard someone breathing very close to her bed, drew aside the curtain and saw Monsieur Madeleine standing there, looking at something above her head. His gaze was full of pity and anguish, and imploring. She followed it and saw that it was directed at a crucifix hanging on the wall.

Monsieur Madeleine was now transfigured in Fantine's eyes. To her, he appeared enveloped in light. He was absorbed in some kind of prayer. She observed him for a long time without daring to interrupt. At last she said timidly, 'What are you doing here?'

Monsieur Madeleine had been standing there for an hour. He was waiting for Fantine to wake up. He took her hand, felt her pulse and replied, 'How are you feeling?'

'Fine,' she replied, 'I slept, I think I'm better. It's probably nothing.'

He went on, responding to the question she had originally put to him as though he had only just heard it. 'I was praying to the martyr up above.'

And mentally he added, 'For this martyred woman here below.'

Monsieur Madeleine had spent the night and that morning making inquiries. He was now fully informed. Fantine's story was known to him in all its heart-breaking detail. He continued, 'Poor mother, you've suffered a great deal. Oh! don't be sorry, now you have a dowry, the dowry of the chosen. Such is the way that men create angels. It's not their fault. They don't know how to go about it any differently. You see, the hell that is behind you now is the first form of heaven. You had to start there.'

He sighed deeply. But she smiled on him with that sublime smile with two teeth missing.

That same night Javert wrote a letter. The next morning he took it himself to Montreuil-sur-Mer's post office. It was to go to Paris and was addressed to Monsieur Chabouillet, secretary to the prefect of police. As word had spread about the incident at the police station, the post-mistress and a few other people who saw the letter before it went off, and who recognized Javert's handwriting from the address, thought it was his resignation he was sending in.

Monsieur Madeleine lost no time in writing to the Thénardiers. Fantine owed them one hundred and twenty francs. He sent them three hundred francs, telling them to pay themselves out of that sum and to bring the child immediately to Montreuil-sur-Mer where her sick mother was anxious to see her.

Thénardier was dazzled by this. 'I'll be damned!' he said to his wife. 'We're not giving up that child. This little songbird's going to turn into a milch cow. I can imagine what's happened. Some fool's taken a fancy to the mother.'

He sent back a very neatly drawn up account for five hundred-odd francs. In this account were two indisputable bills amounting to over three hundred francs, one from a doctor, the other from a pharmacist, who had attended and treated Éponine and Azelma through two long illnesses. Cosette, as we have already said, had not been ill. It was a matter of the mere substitution of names. At the bottom of the account Thénardier wrote, 'Received on account, three hundred francs'.

Monsieur Madeleine immediately sent another three hundred francs and wrote, 'Hurry. Bring Cosette.'

'By heaven!' said Thénardier. 'We're not giving up that child.'

In the meantime, Fantine was getting no better. She was still in the infirmary.

The sisters had at first only reluctantly accepted and nursed 'that woman'. Those who have seen the bas-reliefs at Reims will recall the protruding lower lips of the wise virgins at the sight of the foolish virgins. That ancient scorn of the vestal virgins for the ambubaiae* is one of the most deep-rooted instincts of feminine self-regard. The sisters felt it with the added intensity of religion. But within a few days Fantine had disarmed them. She said all kinds of meek and humble things, and the mother in her softened their hearts. One day the sisters heard her say in her feverishness, 'I've been a sinner but when I have my child beside me it will mean that God has forgiven me. While I was leading a bad life I wouldn't have wanted to have my Cosette with me. I wouldn't have been able to bear her sad staring eyes. Yet it was for her sake I was leading a bad life, and that's why God forgives me. I shall feel the good Lord's blessing when Cosette is here. I shall look on

* Syrian flute-girls.

her, it will do me good to see that innocent creature. She knows nothing at all. You see, sisters, she's an angel. At that age they've not yet lost their wings.'

Monsieur Madeleine went to see her twice a day and she asked him every time, 'Will I be seeing my Cosette soon?'

He answered, 'Tomorrow, perhaps. I'm expecting her to arrive at any moment.'

And the mother's pale face grew radiant. 'Oh!' she said. 'How happy I'm going to be!'

As we have mentioned, she was getting no better. On the contrary, her condition seemed to worsen week by week. That handful of snow between the shoulder blades on her bare skin had caused a sudden suppression of perspiration, as a result of which the illness for which she had been sickening for many years finally declared itself with a vengeance. At that time, people were beginning to follow Laennec's admirable lead in the study and treatment of chest ailments. The doctor sounded Fantine's chest and shook his head.

Monsieur Madeleine said to the doctor, 'Well?'

'Does she not have a child she wants to see?' said the doctor.

'Yes.'

'Well, lose no time in getting the child here!'

Monsieur Madeleine shuddered.

Fantine asked, 'What did the doctor say?'

Monsieur Madeleine forced a smile. 'He said to get your child to come very quickly. And that will restore your health.'

'Oh!' she responded. 'He's right! But what do those Thénardiers mean by keeping my Cosette from me! Oh! she's coming. At last I see happiness almost within reach!'

Thénardier, however, was 'not giving up that child', and gave countless bogus excuses. Cosette was not quite well enough to travel in winter. And then there were some small pressing debts outstanding for which he was gathering together the bills from local creditors, et cetera.

'I'll send someone to fetch Cosette!' said Père Madeleine. 'If necessary, I'll go myself.'

He wrote the following letter at Fantine's dictation and got her to sign it:

Monsieur Thénardier,

You are to hand Cosette over to this person.

You will be paid whatever small amounts are owing.

Yours respectfully,

Fantine.

In the meantime a serious incident occurred. Though we shape to the best of our ability the mysterious block of which our life is made, the black vein of destiny is ever reappearing.

II
How Jean *May Become* Champ

Monsieur Madeleine was in his office one morning, dealing in advance – should he decide to make the journey to Montfermeil – with some urgent municipal business, when he was informed that Police Inspector Javert wished to speak to him. At the mention of this name Monsieur Madeleine could not help forming a disagreeable impression. Javert had avoided him more than ever since the unexpected turn of events at the police station, and Monsieur Madeleine had not seen him since.

'Send him in,' he said.

Javert entered.

Monsieur Madeleine remained seated by the fire, pen in hand, his eyes on a file he was leafing through and annotating, which contained reports of offences against highway regulations. He did not bother to acknowledge Javert. He could not help thinking of poor Fantine and it suited him to be frosty.

Javert bowed respectfully to monsieur le maire, who had his back turned to him. Monsieur le maire did not look at him and went on annotating his file.

Javert took two or three steps into the study, and stood there without breaking the silence.

A physiognomist who might have been familiar with Javert's character, and who might have been studying for a long time this savage in the service of civilization, this bizarre combination of the Roman, the Spartan, the monk and the corporal, this spy who was incapable of a lie, this untarnished sleuth, a physiognomist who might have known of his secret and long-standing aversion to Monsieur Madeleine, his conflict with the mayor on the subject of Fantine, and who might have observed Javert at that moment, would have said to himself, 'What has happened?' It was obvious to anyone acquainted with that scrupulous, clear, genuine, upright, austere, fierce conscience that Javert had been through some great inner cataclysm. Javert had nothing in his soul that would not also have shown on his face. He was, in the way of violent people, given to abrupt changes of feeling. His physiognomy had never been more peculiar or more unexpected. On entering he bowed to Monsieur Madeleine with no resentment, anger or mistrust in his gaze. He halted a few paces behind the mayor's armchair, and there he stood, in an almost chastened attitude, with the cold, naive boorishness of a man who has never been agreeable and has always been patient. Until it should please monsieur le maire to turn round, he waited in total silence, in total immobility, in genuine humility and tranquil resignation, calm, serious, with hat in hand, eyes downcast, and an expression that was something between that of a soldier in the presence of his officer and a criminal in the presence of his judge. All the sentiments and all the memories that it might have been supposed he harboured had disappeared. There was nothing now but a mournful sadness on that face as impenetrable and simple as granite. His whole person emanated abjection and determination, and some suggestion of brave defeat.

At last monsieur le maire laid down his pen and half turned round. 'Well! What is it? What have you to say, Javert?'

Javert remained silent for a moment as though collecting his thoughts, then spoke up with a sort of sad solemnity that did not, however, preclude simplicity. 'What I have to say, monsieur le maire, is that an unpardonable offence has been committed.'

'What offence?'

'A subordinate police officer has in the gravest manner shown lack of respect towards a magistrate. I've come to inform you of this fact as it is my duty to do so.'

'Who is this police officer?' asked Monsieur Madeleine.

'It is I,' said Javert.

'You?'

'I.'

'And which magistrate would have reason to complain of the officer?'

'You, monsieur le maire.'

Monsieur Madeleine straightened up in his armchair.

Looking stern, his eyes still lowered, Javert went on, 'Monsieur le maire, I've come to ask if you would be so good as to start proceedings to have me dismissed from the police.'

In his astonishment Monsieur Madeleine opened his mouth.

Javert interrupted him. 'You'll say I could have handed in my resignation, but that's not adequate. Resigning is honourable. I've done wrong, I should be punished. I must be sacked.'

And after a pause he added, 'Monsieur le maire, you were unjustly hard on me the other day. Be justly hard today.'

'But why?' exclaimed Monsieur Madeleine. 'What is this gibberish? What's the meaning of it? What offence have you committed against me? What have you done to me? In what way have you wronged me? You accuse yourself, you want to be replaced—'

'Sacked,' said Javert.

'Sacked, then. That's all very well. I don't understand.'

'You will, monsieur le maire.' Javert gave the deepest of sighs and resumed, still coldly and sadly. 'Monsieur le maire, six weeks ago, after that row about that woman, I was furious and I denounced you.'

'Denounced me!'

'To police headquarters in Paris.'

Monsieur Madeleine, who was not much more frequently given to laughter than Javert, began to laugh. 'As a mayor who had encroached on police authority?'

'As an ex-convict.'

The mayor paled.

Javert, who had not looked up, went on. 'I believed it. I had my suspicions for a long time. Don't ask me why! Absurdities! A resemblance, some inquiries made at Faverolles on your behalf, your physical strength, the incident with old Fauchelevent, your shooting skills, your leg being a little lame – I don't know, all sorts of ridiculous things. But the fact is I took you for a certain Jean Valjean.'

'A certain – what did you say the name was?'

'Jean Valjean. He was a convict I saw twenty years ago when I was assistant warder of the chain gangs at Toulon. After his release this Jean Valjean apparently robbed a bishop, then committed armed robbery on a public highway against a young Savoyard. He's been lying low for the past eight years, no one knows how, and he was a wanted man . . . I had a notion . . . Anyway, that's what I did! It was anger that decided me: I denounced you to police headquarters!'

Monsieur Madeleine, who had picked up the file again a few moments earlier, spoke with an air of perfect indifference. 'And what was their response?'

'That I was mad.'

'Well?'

'Well, they were right.'

'It's a good thing you admit it.'

'I'm bound to, since the real Jean Valjean has been found.'

The sheet of paper Monsieur Madeleine was holding slipped from his hand. He looked up, stared intently at Javert, and said in an indescribable tone of voice, 'Ah!'

Javert continued. 'It's like this, monsieur le maire. It seems there was in these parts, over towards Ailly-le-Haut-Clocher, some old fellow who went by the name of Père Champmathieu. A pitiful wretch. No one took any notice of him. People like that – who knows how they keep themselves alive. Recently, last autumn, Père Champmathieu was arrested for the theft of some cider apples from – well, never mind that! There was a theft, a wall scaled, branches of a tree broken. My Champmathieu was arrested. He still had the apple branch in his hand. The rascal gets put inside. So far, what we're dealing with is not much more than a minor offence. But now providence intervenes. The gaol being in a poor state of repair, the examining magistrate considers it appropriate to have Champmathieu transferred to Arras, where the *département*'s central prison is. In this prison at Arras there's an ex-convict named Brevet, why he's being held there I don't know, and because of his good behaviour he has been put in charge of the dormitory. Monsieur le maire, Champmathieu no sooner turns up than Brevet exclaims, "Hey! I know that man! He's a *fagot**! Look at me, man! You're Jean Valjean!" "Jean Valjean? Who's Jean Valjean?" Champmathieu pretends to be surprised. "Don't play the *sinvre*†," says Brevet. "You're Jean Valjean! You were in the prison hulks at Toulon. Twenty years ago it was. We were there together."

'Champmathieu denies it. Of course he does! Further inquiries are made. The case is thoroughly investigated. These are the findings: some thirty years ago this Champmathieu was a tree-pruner in various localities, Faverolles among others. Then all trace of him is lost. A long time afterwards he's seen again in the Auvergne, then in Paris where he is said to have been a cartwright and to have had a daughter who was a laundress. But there's no proof of that. Now, before serving time with the chain gang for aggravated theft, what was Jean Valjean? A pruner of trees. Where? At Faverolles. Another fact. This Valjean's Christian name was Jean and his mother's maiden name was Mathieu. What could be more reasonable than to imagine that when he left prison he took his mother's name in order to conceal his identity and called himself Jean Mathieu? He goes to the Auvergne. The local pronunciation turns "Jean" into "Chan", he's called Chan Mathieu. Our man offers no objection and there he is, transformed into Champmathieu. You follow me, don't you? Inquiries are made at Faverolles. Jean Valjean's family's no longer there. It's not known where they've gone. You know, in that class of society, families are often disappearing like that. Look for them, and you find there's noth-

---

* Hugo's footnote: 'Ex-convict'.
† Hugo's footnote: 'The innocent'.

ing left of them. People like that, if they're not dirt, they're dust. And then, seeing as it's thirty years since this whole story began there's no one at Faverolles any more who knew Jean Valjean. Inquiries are made at Toulon. Apart from Brevet, there are only two convicts remaining who've seen Jean Valjean. They're Cochepaille and Chenild-ieu, serving life sentences. They're hauled out of the prison hulks and brought to Arras. They're brought face to face with the so-called Champmathieu. They don't hesitate. For them, just as for Brevet, he's Jean Valjean. The same age – he's fifty-four – same height, same manner, in short the same man, it's him. It was precisely at this point that I sent my denunciation to Paris police headquarters. I'm told I'm out of my mind, that Jean Valjean's at Arras in the hands of the judiciary. You can imagine my surprise, when there was I thinking I had that same Jean Valjean here. I write to the examining judge. He sends for me, Champmathieu is brought before me—'

'And?' Monsieur Madeleine interposed.

Javert replied with his sad and incorruptible face, 'Monsieur le maire, the truth's the truth. I'm sorry but that man is Jean Valjean. I too recognized him.'

Monsieur Madeleine said in a very low voice, 'You're sure?'

Javert began to laugh with that mournful laugh let out by deep conviction. 'Oh! Absolutely!'

He remained thoughtful for a moment, absent-mindedly taking pinches of sawdust, used for blotting ink, from the wooden bowl on the table, and added, 'And indeed, now that I've seen the real Jean Valjean, I don't understand how I could have thought otherwise. I beg your pardon, monsieur le maire.'

As he addressed these grave words of entreaty to the man who six weeks earlier had publicly humiliated him at the police station and told him 'Go!', this proud man Javert was unwittingly full of simplicity and dignity.

Monsieur Madeleine's only reply to his entreaty was to ask this abrupt question: 'And what does this man say?'

'Ah, well, monsieur le maire, he's in serious trouble. If he is Jean Valjean, he's guilty of re-offending. Climbing a wall, breaking a branch, pilfering apples, for a child, is an act of mischief. For a man, it's a misdemeanour. For an ex-convict it's a crime. Trespass and robbery, that's what we're talking about. It's no longer a minor offence, it's a matter for the court of assizes. It's no longer a few days in prison, it's penal servitude for life. And then there's the matter of the young Savoyard, who I very much hope will turn up again. Hang it! There's good reason to put up a fight, isn't there? Yes, for anyone but Jean Valjean. But Jean Valjean's a cunning one. It's there again that I recognize him. Any other man would have started to feel the heat. He'd kick up a fuss, he'd shout. The kettle sings on the fire. He wouldn't want to be Jean Valjean, et cetera. But this fellow appears not to understand. He says, "I'm Champmathieu, that's all I've got to say!" He looks bewildered, he pretends to be a simpleton, that's far better. Oh, he's a crafty rogue! But it makes no difference, the evidence is there. He's been recognized by four people. The old villain will be found guilty. It's been referred to the assizes at Arras. I'm going there to testify. I've been served a summons.'

Monsieur Madeleine had gone back to his desk, picked up his file again, and was calmly leafing through it, reading and writing by turns like a busy man. He turned to Javert.

'That's enough, Javert. All these details are in fact of very little interest to me. We're wasting time and we have urgent matters to deal with. Javert, you're to go at once to the house of Madame Buseaupied, who sells herbs down on the corner of Rue St-Saulve. Tell her to lodge an official complaint against the carter Pierre Chesnelong. The man's a ruffian who almost ran over this woman and her child. He must be punished. You will then go to Monsieur Charcellay, Rue Montre-de-Champigny. He's made a complaint about a gutter on the house next door that is pouring rainwater on to his premises and undermining the foundations of his house. After that, check on reported violations of police regulations in Rue Guibourg at the widow Doris's place and in Rue du Garraud-Blanc at Madame Renée Le Bossé's, and take down particulars. But I'm giving you a great deal of work there. Aren't you going to be away? Didn't you say you were going to Arras for that trial in a week or so?'

'Sooner than that, monsieur le maire.'

'What day would that be?'

'Why, I thought I told monsieur le maire the case was to be tried tomorrow and that I'm taking the coach tonight.'

Monsieur Madeleine gave a slight start. 'And how long will the case go on for?'

'One day at the most. The judgement will be delivered no later than tomorrow evening. But I shan't wait for the judgement, which is bound to be a guilty verdict. As soon as I've testified I'll be coming back here.'

'Very well,' said Monsieur Madeleine. And he dismissed Javert with a wave of his hand.

Javert did not go away. 'Excuse me, monsieur le maire,' he said.

'What is it now?' asked Monsieur Madeleine.

'Monsieur le maire, there's still one thing I must remind you of.'

'What's that?'

'I must be relieved of my duties.'

Monsieur Madeleine rose. 'Javert, you're a man of honour and I respect you. You exaggerate your misconduct. Besides, this is another offence relating to me. Javert, you deserve to rise, not fall. I intend to keep you in your post.'

Looking at Monsieur Madeleine with that unenlightened but pure and inflexible conscience seemingly visible in the depths of his candid gaze, Javert said to him in a calm voice, 'Monsieur le maire, I cannot agree to that.'

'I repeat,' replied Monsieur Madeleine, 'I'm the one affected by this, it's for me to decide.'

But Javert single-mindedly kept on. 'As for exaggerating, I don't exaggerate at all. This is my reasoning: I suspected you unjustly. In itself, that's nothing. It's within our rights for the likes of us to be suspicious, although to suspect your betters is to overstep the mark. But with no proof, in a fit of rage, with the aim of gaining revenge, I denounced you as a convict – you, a respectable man, a mayor, a magistrate! This is serious. Very serious. I insulted the authority invested in your person, I, an agent of that authority! If one of my subordinates had done what I did, I'd have declared him unworthy of his job and sacked him. Well then?

'Listen, monsieur le maire, one word more. I've often been harsh in my life. With others. It was just. I did the right thing. Now, if I were not harsh on myself, everything I did that was once just would become unjust. Should I spare myself more than others? No! What? I'd only be capable of disciplining others and not myself! But that would make me despicable! And those who say "that skunk Javert" would be right. Monsieur le maire, I've no wish for you to treat me kindly. I found your kindness galling enough when it was extended to others. I want none of it for myself. The kindness that consists in favouring a common prostitute over a gentleman, a policeman over the mayor, the man of low estate over the man of high estate, is what I call pernicious kindness. It's kindness like that that creates disorder in society. Good Lord! It's very easy to be kind, the difficult thing is to be just. Believe me, if you'd been what I thought you were, I certainly wouldn't have been kind to you! You can be sure of that! Monsieur le maire, I must treat myself the same way I would treat anyone else. When I pursued criminals, when I dealt harshly with offenders, I often said to myself, "If ever you stumble, if ever I catch you doing wrong, you know what's coming to you!" I stumbled, I've caught myself doing wrong, too bad! So let's get on with it – dismissed, demoted, sacked! That's fine. I'm able-bodied, I'll work on the land, I don't mind. Monsieur le maire, an example needs to be made for the good of the police force. I simply ask for Inspector Javert's dismissal.'

All this was delivered in a humble, proud, hopeless and earnest tone of voice, which lent some sort of bizarre grandeur to this strange honest man.

'We'll see,' said Monsieur Madeleine. And he held out his hand.

Javert recoiled and said grimly, 'Forgive me, monsieur le maire, but that cannot be allowed. A mayor does not offer his hand to a nark.' He muttered, 'A nark, yes. Seeing as I've played false with the police, I've become no more than a nark.' Then he bowed deeply and made for the door.

There he turned and with his eyes still lowered he said, 'Monsieur le maire, I shall continue to serve in office until I'm replaced.'

He made his exit. Monsieur Madeleine was left listening thoughtfully to that firm and confident footstep receding down the corridor.

BOOK SEVEN
THE CHAMPMATHIEU AFFAIR

I
Soeur Simplice

Not all the incidents that are to be read about here were generally known in Montreuil-sur-Mer, but the little that did come to public knowledge left such a lasting memory in that town that it would constitute a serious lacuna in this book if we did not relate them in the smallest detail.

Among these details the reader will encounter two or three improbable circumstances that we preserve out of respect for the truth.

On the afternoon following Javert's visit, Monsieur Madeleine went as usual to visit Fantine.

Before going in to see Fantine he asked for Soeur Simplice. The two nuns who ran the infirmary, Lazarists like all Sisters of Charity, bore the names of Soeur Perpétue and Soeur Simplice.

Soeur Perpétue was an ordinary countrywoman, a Sister of Charity in a rough-and-ready way, who had entered the service of God as others go into domestic service. She was a nun as other women are cooks. This type is not unusual. The monastic orders gladly accept this heavy peasant clay, easily moulded into a Capuchin or Ursuline. These rustics are used for piety's heavy work. The transition from cowherd to Carmelite is nothing if not smooth. The one becomes the other without great exertion. The substratum of ignorance shared by the village and the cloister is ready-prepared ground, immediately placing the peasant on an equal footing with the monk. A little extra fullness in the smock, and you have the habit. Soeur Perpétue was a stout nun from Les Marines near Pontoise, patois-speaking, prayer-reciting, grumbling, sugaring the invalids' tea according to their sanctimoniousness or their hypocrisy, chivvying the sick, gruff with the dying, almost throwing God in their faces, pelting their mortal agony with angry prayers, bluff, well-meaning and ruddy-faced.

Soeur Simplice was the clear white of candlewax. Compared with Soeur Perpétue, she was the taper beside the tallow candle. Vincent de Paul has with divine inspiration defined the figure of the Sister of

Charity in these marvellous words, combining so much freedom with so much servitude: 'They shall have no convent but the homes of the sick, no cell but a rented room, no chapel but the parish church, no cloister but the streets of the town or the hospital ward, no enclosure but obedience, no grille but the fear of God, no veil but modesty.' Soeur Simplice was the living embodiment of this ideal. No one could have said what age Soeur Simplice was: she had never been young and she seemed destined never to grow old. She was a calm, austere, well-bred, cold person – we dare not say a woman – who had never lied. She was so gentle she seemed fragile, though actually more solid than granite. The needy she touched with lovely, slender, delicate fingers. There was, as it were, silence in her speech. She said no more than was strictly necessary, and the sound of her voice would have both favourably impressed a confessional and enchanted a drawing room. This fineness was content to wear the serge gown, finding in the feel of its roughness a continual reminder of heaven and of God. Let us stress one detail. Never to have lied, never, for whatever reason, even a disinterested reason, to have said a single thing that was not the truth, the sacred truth, was Soeur Simplice's distinctive characteristic. It was the hallmark of her virtue. She was almost famous in the order for this imperturbable truthfulness. Abbé Sicard speaks of Soeur Simplice in a letter to the deaf-mute Massieu. However sincere, frank and honest we may be, all of us have at least the flaw of the little white lie in our candour. Not she. A little lie, a white lie – does such a thing exist? To lie is an absolute evil. It is not possible to lie a little. The liar tells an indivisible falsehood. Lying is the very face of the devil. Satan has two names, he is called Satan and he is called Falsehood. That is what she thought. And she put into practice what she thought. The result was the clear white we have mentioned – a whiteness that bathed in its radiance even her lips and eyes. Her smile was clear, her gaze was clear. There was not one cobweb, not a speck of dust, on the clear glass of that conscience. When she joined the order of St Vincent de Paul she had specially chosen to take the name of Simplice.

Simplice of Sicily, as we know, is the saint who preferred to have both breasts ripped off rather than say she was born at Segesta when she was actually born at Syracuse, a lie that would have saved her. She was the appropriate patron of this soul.

On entering the order Soeur Simplice had two shortcomings that she gradually corrected: she had a sweet tooth and she liked to receive letters. The only thing she ever read was a book of prayers set in large type, in Latin. She did not understand Latin but she understood the book.

This pious woman had grown fond of Fantine, probably detecting the latent virtue in her, and she had devoted herself almost exclusively to her care. Monsieur Madeleine took Soeur Simplice aside and asked her to look after Fantine in a peculiar tone of voice the nun later recalled. When he left the nun he went to Fantine.

Fantine awaited Monsieur Madeleine's appearance every day as one awaiting a ray of warmth and happiness. She said to the sisters, 'I'm alive only when monsieur le maire is here.'

She was very feverish that day. As soon as she saw Monsieur Madeleine she asked him, 'And Cosette?'

He replied with a smile, 'Soon.'

Monsieur Madeleine was the same as ever with Fantine. Only, to Fantine's great delight, he remained an hour instead of half an hour. He kept telling everyone the sick woman should want for nothing. There was a moment, it was observed, when his face became very sombre. But this was explained when it was learned that the doctor had leaned towards him and said in his ear, 'She's fading fast.'

Then he returned to the town hall and the clerk saw him closely studying a road map of France that hung in his study. He pencilled a few figures on a piece of paper.

II
Maître Scaufflaire's Shrewdness

He went from the town hall to the edge of town, to a Belgian from Flanders named Maître Scaufflaer, Gallicized as Scaufflaire, who rented out horses and offered 'gigs for hire'.

To reach Scaufflaire's place, the shortest route to take was down a quiet street in which the house of Monsieur Madeleine's parish priest was located. This parish priest was, so people said, an honourable, respectable and sensible man. When Monsieur Madeleine reached the priest's house there was only one passer-by in the street, and this person noticed the following: having walked past the priest's house Monsieur Madeleine stopped, stood still, then turned and retraced his steps to the door of the house, which was a modest entrance with an iron knocker. He briskly laid his hand on the knocker and lifted it. Then he stopped again and remained suspended in the act, as if thinking, and after a few seconds, instead of allowing the knocker to fall with a clatter, he quietly replaced it and continued on his way with a degree of haste he had not shown before.

Monsieur Madeleine found Maître Scaufflaire at his premises, busy mending a harness.

'Maître Scaufflaire, have you a good horse?' he asked.

'Monsieur le maire,' said the Fleming, 'all my horses are good. What do you mean by a good horse?'

'I mean a horse capable of doing fifty miles in a day.'

'By God!' said the Fleming. 'Fifty miles!'

'Yes.'

'Harnessed to a gig?'

'Yes.'

'And how much rest will it have after making that journey?'

'It must be able to set off again the next day if necessary.'

'To make the return journey?'

'Yes.'

'By God! By God! And it's fifty miles?'

Monsieur Madeleine drew from his pocket the paper on which he had pencilled some figures. He showed it to the Fleming. The figures were 12½, 15, 21.

'You see,' he said. 'Total, forty-eight and a half – we might as well say fifty.'

'Monsieur le maire,' said the Fleming, 'I have just what you need. My little white horse. You may have seen it go by occasionally. It's a small beast of Lower Boulonnais stock. Full of mettle. They tried to make a saddle-horse out of it at first. Bah! It bucked, it unseated everyone. It was thought to be vicious and no one knew what to do with it. I bought it. I put it to drawing a gig. Monsieur, that's what it wanted. It's as meek as a young girl, it goes like the wind. Ah, it's certainly not to be mounted. It has no intention of being a saddle-horse. Each to his own ambition. A carriage horse? Yes. A mount? No. We must assume that's what it said to itself.'

'And it will stay the course?'

'Your fifty miles. At a smart pace all the way, and in less than eight hours. But there are conditions.'

'State them.'

'In the first place, you're to give it an hour's breather halfway. It's to be fed, and someone will be there while it's feeding to prevent the stable-boy at the inn from stealing the oats, for I've noticed that at inns the oats are more often drunk by the stable-boys than eaten by the horses.'

'Someone will be there.'

'In the second place – is the gig for monsieur le maire?'

'Yes.'

'Does monsieur le maire know how to drive?'

'Yes.'

'Well, monsieur le maire will travel alone and without baggage so as not to put too much strain on the horse.'

'Agreed.'

'But as monsieur le maire will have no one with him, he'll have to take it on himself to see that the oats aren't stolen.'

'You have my word.'

'I'll need thirty francs a day. With rest days also paid for. Not a quarter of a sou less, and the beast's feed at monsieur le maire's expense.'

Monsieur Madeleine drew three napoleons from his purse and laid them on the table.

'That's two days in advance.'

'Fourthly, a cabriolet would be too heavy for a journey like this and would tire the horse. Monsieur le maire must agree to travel in a little tilbury I have.'

'I agree.'

'It's light but uncovered.'

'I don't mind that.'

'Has monsieur le maire taken into consideration that it's winter?'

Monsieur Madeleine did not reply.

The Fleming went on, 'That it's very cold?'

Monsieur Madeleine remained silent.

Maître Scaufflaire continued, 'That it may rain?'

Monsieur Madeleine raised his head and said, 'The tilbury and the horse are to be outside my door at half-past four tomorrow morning.'

'Very well, monsieur le maire,' replied Scaufflaire. Then, scratching with his thumbnail at a stain in the wood of the table, he added in that casual manner the Flemings are so adept at combining with their shrewdness, 'But it's just now occurred to me, monsieur le maire hasn't told me where he's going. Where is monsieur le maire going?'

He had been thinking of nothing else since the beginning of the conversation, but he did not know why he had not dared put this question.

'Has your horse got strong forelegs?' said Monsieur Madeleine.

'Yes, monsieur le maire. Best hold him in a little, on the downhill. Are there many downhill stretches between here and where you are going?'

'Don't forget to be outside my door tomorrow morning at half-past four precisely,' replied Monsieur Madeleine. And he departed.

The Fleming was left 'completely baffled', as he himself said some time afterwards.

The mayor had been gone two or three minutes when the door opened again. It was monsieur le maire.

He still had the same impassive and preoccupied air.

'Monsieur Scaufflaire,' he said, 'how much would you say the horse that you'll be hiring out to me is worth, on top of the tilbury?'

'In front of the tilbury, monsieur le maire,' said the Fleming, with a guffaw.

'If you say so. Well?'

'Does monsieur le maire want to buy them from me?'

'No, but I want to indemnify you should anything happen to them. You can pay back the money on my return. How much do you think your horse and gig are worth?'

'Five hundred francs, monsieur le maire.'

'Here you are.'

Monsieur Madeleine laid a banknote on the table, then left, and this time he did not return.

Maître Scaufflaire bitterly regretted not having said a thousand francs. As it was, the horse and tilbury together were worth only three hundred.

The Fleming called his wife and told her what had happened. Where the devil could monsieur le maire be going? They debated the matter.

'He's going to Paris,' said the wife.

'I don't think so,' said the husband.

Monsieur Madeleine had left behind on the mantelpiece the piece of paper with the figures he had written on it. The Fleming picked it up and studied it.

'Twelve and a half, fifteen, twenty-one? They must be the distances between staging posts.' He turned to his wife. 'I've worked it out.'

'How?'

'It's twelve and a half miles from here to Hesdin, fifteen from Hesdin to St-Pol, twenty-one from St-Pol to Arras. He is going to Arras.'

Meanwhile, Monsieur Madeleine had returned home.

Coming back from Maître Scaufflaire's he had taken the long way round, as if the priest's front door had been a temptation to him and he wanted to avoid it. He went up to his room and remained closeted there, which was in no way out of the ordinary as he liked to go to bed early. Yet the caretaker of the factory, who was also Monsieur Madeleine's only servant, noticed that his light went out at half-past eight, and she mentioned it to the cashier as he came in, adding, 'Is monsieur le maire ill? I thought he looked a little strange.'

The cashier occupied a room directly below Monsieur Madeleine's room. He paid no attention to what the caretaker said, went to bed and fell asleep. Towards midnight he suddenly woke up. In his sleep he had heard a noise above his head. He listened. It was footsteps going back and forth, as if someone were walking about in the room above him. He listened more closely and recognized Monsieur Madeleine's footstep. This struck him as odd. Usually there was no noise from Monsieur Madeleine's room until he got up in the morning. A moment later the cashier heard something that sounded like a wardrobe being opened then shut again. Then a piece of furniture was moved. There was a pause, and the pacing resumed. The cashier sat up in bed, fully awakened, stared, and through the window-panes he saw on the wall opposite the reddish reflection of a lighted window. From the direction of the rays of light, it must have been the window of Monsieur Madeleine's room. The reflection flickered as if it came from a lighted fire rather than a candle. There was no shadow cast by the frames of the window-panes, which meant the window was wide open. In such cold weather the open window was surprising. The cashier went back to sleep. An hour or two later he woke again. The same slow and regular footstep was still pacing back and forth overhead.

The reflection was still visible on the wall but now it was pale and steady, like the reflection of a lamp or a candle. The window was still open.

This is what was going on in Monsieur Madeleine's room.

III
A Storm in the Mind

The reader has no doubt guessed that Monsieur Madeleine is none other than Jean Valjean.

We have already gazed into the depths of that conscience. The moment has come to take another look. We do so not without emotion and trepidation. There is nothing more terrifying than a contemplation of this kind. The mind's eye can nowhere find more brilliant splendour and more tenebrous gloom than in man. It cannot set its gaze on anything more fearsome, more complicated, more mysterious and infinite. There is a spectacle greater than the sea: that is the sky. There is a spectacle greater than the sky: that is the inner soul.

To create a poem about the human conscience, were it only with regard to a single man, only to the least of men, would be to amalgamate all epics in one superior and definitive epic. Conscience is a confusion of chimeras, of desires and temptations, the furnace of dreams, the retreat of thoughts that shame us. It is a pandemonium of sophisms, it is the battleground of the passions. Probe, at certain moments, the ghastly pale face of a human being immersed in thought, and look behind it, look into that soul, look into that obscurity. There, beneath the outward silence, are battling giants, as in Homer, tumultuous dragons and hydras and phantom hosts, as in Milton, visionary vortices, as in Dante. What a solemn thing is this infinity that every man bears within him and against which he measures with despair the wishes of his brain and the actions of his life!

One day Alighieri came to a sinister-looking door at which he hesitated. Here is another before us, on whose threshold we hesitate. Yet let us enter.

We have very little to add to what the reader already knows of the fate that befell Jean Valjean after his encounter with Petit-Gervais. From that moment on he was, as we have seen, a totally different man. What the bishop wanted to achieve in him, he fulfilled. It was more than a transformation, it was a transfiguration.

He managed to disappear, sold the bishop's silver, keeping only the candlesticks as a memento, sneaked from town to town, crossed France, came to Montreuil-sur-Mer, had the idea that we have mentioned, accomplished what we have related, succeeded in making himself elusive and inaccessible; and now, having settled at Montreuil-sur-Mer, happy in the awareness that his conscience was saddened by his past and that the first half of his life was belied by the latter half, he lived peacefully, heartened and hopeful, left with only two intentions: to conceal his name and to sanctify his life, to escape men and to return to God.

These two intentions were so closely associated in his mind that they formed but one. Both were equally preoccupying and imperative, and ruled his slightest actions. In general, they worked in accord to govern the conduct of his life. They disposed him to be retiring, they made him kindly and simple, they counselled the same things. Sometimes, however, they conflicted with each other. In that case, let us remember, the man the entire population of Montreuil-sur-Mer called Monsieur Madeleine did not hesitate to sacrifice the former to the latter, his safety to his virtue. So, contrary to all caution and all prudence, he kept the bishop's candlesticks, wore mourning for him, summoned and questioned all the little Savoyards who came along, made inquiries about families at Faverolles and saved old Fauchelevent's life, notwithstanding Javert's disquieting insinuations. As we have already observed, it seemed that, following the example of all those who have been wise, saintly and just, he thought his first duty was not to himself.

However, it must be said, nothing like this had ever arisen before. Never had the two precepts that governed the unfortunate man whose tribulations we are recounting come into such serious contention. He was vaguely but profoundly aware of this from the very first words that Javert uttered on entering his office. The moment that name which he had buried beneath such deep layers was so strangely mentioned, he was seized with amazement and as though befuddled by the sinister whimsicality of his destiny, and amid his amazement he felt the tremor that precedes great upheavals. He bent like an oak at the approach of a storm, like a soldier at an oncoming assault. He sensed shadows filled with thunder and lightning gathering overhead. As he listened to Javert his first thought was to go running off and denounce himself, to drag that Champmathieu out of prison and take his place. This was as painful and agonizing as an incision in living flesh. Then it passed, and he said to himself, 'Come, now! Come, now!' He repressed this first generous instinct and recoiled before heroism.

It would doubtless have been noble, after the bishop's saintly words, after so many years of repentance and abnegation, in the middle of a penance so admirably begun, if this man even though facing so terrible a predicament had not wavered for an instant but had continued to walk steadily towards that yawning precipice at the bottom of which lay heaven. It would have been noble, but it did not happen like that. After all, we have to give account of what was happening in that soul, and we can only report what that was. What got the better of him at first was the instinct of self-preservation. He hastily rallied his thoughts, stifled his emotions, took heed of the presence of that great peril Javert, with the firmness of terror deferred any decision, mindlessly got on with whatever he had to attend to, and resumed his calm as a warrior picks up his shield.

For the rest of the day he was in this state of tumult within, of profound tranquillity without. He did not take what might be called 'self-preserving measures'. Everything was still confused and warring in his brain. So great was the confusion he could distinguish no clear idea of any form, and he had nothing to say for himself except that he had just suffered a great blow. He turned up as usual to see Fantine in her sickbed and prolonged his visit out of an instinct of kindness, telling himself this is what he must do, urging the sisters to look after her in the event that he should have to absent himself. He had a vague feeling he might be obliged to go to Arras, and without having in the least made up his mind about this trip he told himself that since he was entirely above suspicion there could be no harm in being present to see what happened, and he hired the tilbury from Scaufflaire in order to be prepared for all eventualities.

He dined with a fair appetite.

Back in his room, he fell to thinking.

He considered the situation and found it extraordinary, so extraordinary that, prompted by some impulse of almost inexplicable anxiety, in the midst of his introspection he rose from his chair and bolted the door. He was afraid something else might come in. He barricaded himself against any possibility.

A moment later, he extinguished his light. It made him uneasy.

He had the feeling that someone could see him.

Someone? Who?

Alas! What he wanted to shut out had already entered. What he wanted to strike blind was staring at him. His conscience.

His conscience, that is to say, God.

Nevertheless, at first he deluded himself. He had a sense of security and of solitude. Having bolted the door, he felt impregnable. Having blown out the candle, he felt invisible. Then he took hold of himself. He set his elbows on the table, rested his head on his hand, and began to ponder in the dark.

'Where do I stand? Am I not dreaming? What was I told? Is it really true that I saw Javert and he said those things to me? Who can this Champmathieu be? So he looks like me? Is that possible? When I think that yesterday I had such peace of mind and was so far from suspecting any of this! What was I doing this time yesterday? What's to be made of this incident? How will it be resolved? What am I to do?'

Such was the turmoil he was in. His brain had lost the power to retain its thoughts. They washed through it like waves, and he clutched his brow in both hands to arrest them.

Out of this tumult that undermined his willpower and his reason, and from which he tried to extract some clarity and resolution, nothing emerged but anguish.

His head was boiling. He went to the window and threw it wide open. There were no stars in the sky. He came back and sat down at the table.

So the first hour went by.

Gradually, however, in his reflections vague features began to take shape and gain definition, and he was able to envisage with the precision of reality not the whole situation but some of the details.

He began by recognizing that, extraordinary and momentous as this situation was, he had complete control over it.

This only increased his amazement.

Irrespective of the austere religious purpose his actions were intended to serve, everything he had done up until that day was nothing but a hole he had been digging in which to bury his name. What he had always feared most, during his hours of introspection, during his sleepless nights, was ever to hear that name pronounced. He told himself that if he did, it would spell the end of everything for him. That the day that name resurfaced it would cause his new life to vanish, and even perhaps – who knows? – the new soul within him. He shuddered at the very thought that this was possible. Certainly, if anyone had told him during those moments that the time would come when that name would ring in his ears, when the hideous words 'Jean Valjean' would suddenly emerge from the darkness and loom before him, when that formidable light destined to dissipate the mystery in which he had shrouded himself would suddenly shine on him, and this name would not threaten him, this light would create only denser obscurity, this rent veil would increase the mystery, this earthquake would consolidate his edifice, this extraordinary incident would have no other result, if it was what he wanted, than to make his existence at once more transparent and more impenetrable, and out of his confrontation with the ghost of Jean Valjean the good and worthy gentleman Monsieur Madeleine would emerge more honoured, more at peace and more respected than ever – if anyone had told him this he would have shaken his head and regarded those words as insane. Well, all this was precisely what had just come to pass. This whole accumulation of impossibilities was a fact, and God had allowed these mad things to become realities!

His ruminations continued to gain clarity. He came to understand his position more and more.

He felt as if he had just woken from some sort of dream and had found himself sliding down a slope in the middle of the night, standing, shivering, backing away in vain, on the very brink of an abyss. He distinctly perceived in the gloom a man he did not know, a stranger that destiny mistook for him and was pushing into the chasm in his place. In order for the chasm to close up again someone had to fall in, he or that other man.

He had only to let events take their course.

All became clear, and he admitted this to himself: that his place in the prison hulks was empty, that whatever he did it was still waiting for him, that robbing Petit-Gervais led him back to it, that this vacant place awaited him and would keep drawing him back to it until he returned, that this was inevitable. And then he said to himself that now he had a substitute, that apparently someone by the name of Champmathieu had that misfortune, and that as far as he himself was concerned, being present in the prison hulks in the person of Champmathieu and being present in society under the name of Monsieur Madeleine, he had nothing more to fear provided he did not prevent his fellow men from sealing Champmathieu's life with the stone of infamy which, like the stone of the sepulchre, once put in place is never to be removed.

All this was so tumultuous and so strange that there suddenly came over him that sort of indescribable impulse no man experiences more than two or three times in his life, a convulsion of the conscience, as it were, that stirs up all the heart's uncertainty, a combination of irony, joy and despair that might be called a burst of inward laughter.

He quickly relit his candle.

'Well,' he said to himself. 'What am I afraid of? Why should I be thinking like this? I'm safe now. It's all over. I had only one door still standing ajar through which my past might come bursting into my life. That door is now walled up. For ever! This Javert who has been worrying me for so long, this terrible instinct that seemed to have found me out – which had indeed found me out, by God, and followed me everywhere – this dreadful hunting-dog that was always pointing me is now on a different track, nosing around elsewhere, completely thrown off the scent! Now he's satisfied, he'll leave me alone. He has his Jean Valjean. In fact, who knows, he'll probably want to leave town! And all this has happened without me. I've had nothing to do with it! Well now, where's the misfortune in that? On my word of honour, anyone who saw me would think some catastrophe had befallen me! After all, if there's anyone harmed by it, it's not my fault at all. Providence alone is responsible. Apparently that's what it wants. Do I have any right to upset its arrangements? What is it I want now? Why should I start to meddle? It's none of my business. What! I'm not satisfied? What more do I want? The goal I've aspired to for so many years, what I dream of at night, the object of my prayers to heaven, security, is now within my reach. It's God's will. I can do nothing against the will of God. And why is it God's will? So that I may continue what I've begun, that I may do good, that I may one day be a great and inspiring example, that it may be said there was at last a little happiness attached to the penance I've endured and the virtue I've returned to. I really don't understand why I was afraid a little while ago to call on that good priest and tell him everything as

I would to a confessor, and ask his advice; that's obviously what he would have told me. It's settled, we'll leave well alone and not interfere with the ways of the good Lord!'

So he talked to himself in the depths of his own conscience, looking into what might be called his own abyss. He rose from his chair and began to pace the room.

'Now then,' he said, 'let's not think about it any more. The decision's made!'

But he felt no joy. On the contrary.

The mind is no more to be prevented from returning to an idea than the sea from returning to the shore. For the sailor, this is called the tide. For the guilty man, it is called remorse. God stirs the soul as he causes the ocean to swell.

After a few moments he could not help but resume the grim dialogue in which it was he who spoke and he who listened, saying what he wanted to leave unsaid, and listening to what he did not want to hear, yielding to that mysterious power that said to him, 'Think!' as it had said to another condemned man two thousand years earlier, 'Onward!'

Before going any further, and so as to be fully understood, let us make one observation that needs underlining.

It is certain that people talk to themselves. There is no being capable of thought who has no experience of this. It might even be said that the word is a mystery never more magnificent than when it passes inwardly from a man's mind to his conscience and returns from his conscience to his mind. It is in this sense only that the words often employed in this chapter – 'he said', 'he exclaimed' – are to be understood. We tell ourselves, talk to ourselves, exclaim to ourselves, while the outward silence remains unbroken. There is a great hubbub. Everything inside us talks except our mouths. The realities of the soul, though not visible and not palpable, are nonetheless realities.

So he asked himself where he stood. He questioned himself about that 'decision made'. He admitted to himself that everything he had just settled in his mind was monstrous, that 'leaving well alone and not interfering with the ways of the good Lord' was simply horrible. To allow this mistake to be made by fate and by men, not to prevent it, to be a party to it through his silence – to do nothing, in short – was to do everything! It was the ultimate hypocritical infamy! It was a vile, cowardly, sly, abject, hideous crime!

For the first time in eight years this poor man had just experienced the bitter taste of a wicked deed.

He spat it out in disgust.

He continued to question himself. He sternly asked himself what he had meant by this: 'I've reached my goal!' He told himself that his life indeed had a goal. But what goal? To conceal his name? To deceive the police? Was it for so petty a thing he had done all that he had done? Did he not have another goal, the one true noble goal? To save not his physical being but his soul? To become once more honest and good? To be righteous? Was it not *that* above all, that alone, he had always wanted and the bishop had demanded of him? Shut the door on his past? But, dear God, he wasn't shutting it, he was reopening it by doing something despicable! He was becoming a thief again, and the most abominable of thieves! He was robbing another man of his existence, his life, his peace, his place in the sun. He was becoming an assassin. He was killing a poor wretch, morally killing him. He was inflicting on him that frightful living death, that death beneath the open skies which is called penal servitude. On the contrary, to give himself up, to save that man, the victim of such a dire misapprehension, to resume his own name, out of a sense of duty to become the convict Jean Valjean again, that was truly to achieve his resurrection and to seal off for ever the hell he had left behind! Apparently to fall back into it was actually to escape it. This is what he must do! He had done nothing if he did not do this. His whole life was pointless, his whole penance wasted, and there was nothing else to say but 'What's the good of it?' He felt that the bishop was there, that the bishop was all the more present for being dead, that the bishop was gazing steadily at him, that from now on Mayor Madeleine with all his virtues would be abhorrent to him, and the convict Jean Valjean would be pure and admirable in his sight. That men saw his mask, but the bishop saw his face. That men saw his life, but the bishop saw his conscience.

So he must go to Arras, rescue the false Jean Valjean and denounce the real one. Alas! that was the greatest of sacrifices, the most poignant of victories, the last step to be taken. But it must be done. A grievous fate! He would acquire saintliness in the eyes of God only if he regained infamy in the eyes of men.

'Well,' he said, 'let's take this course! Let's do our duty! Let's save this man.'

He uttered these words aloud without noticing that he was actually voicing them. He took his books, checked them, and put them in order. He threw on the fire a bundle of credit notes for monies owed to him by some small shopkeepers in financial difficulties. He wrote a letter, which he sealed, and had there been anyone in his room at the time, that individual might have read on the envelope: 'To Monsieur Laffitte, Banker, Rue d'Artois, Paris'.

He drew from a writing-desk a wallet containing several banknotes and the passport he had used that same year to vote in the elections. Anyone who had seen him while he was doing these various things that involved such serious contemplation would have had no suspicion of what was going on inside him. Only, occasionally his lips moved. At other times he looked up and stared at some point or other on the wall as if there were in precisely that place something he wished to elucidate or query.

When the letter to Monsieur Laffitte was completed he put it in his pocket together with the wallet, and began pacing again.

There was no deviation in his thinking. He continued to see his duty clearly written in luminous characters that blazed before his eyes wherever he directed his gaze: 'Go! Give your name! Denounce yourself!'

Similarly, he saw, as if they moved before him in visible form, the two notions that had till now been the twofold rule of his life: to hide his name, to sanctify his soul. For the first time they appeared absolutely distinct to him and he saw the difference between them. He recognized that one of these notions was inevitably good while the other could turn bad. That one was self-sacrifice and the other individualism. That one said 'my neighbour', and the other said 'myself'. That one originated from light and the other from darkness.

They fought against each other. He saw them fight. As he continued to ponder, they had grown bigger in his mind's eye. They were now of colossal stature. And it seemed to him that he could see within himself, in that infinity we mentioned earlier, among shadows and glimmerings of light, a goddess and a giant in combat.

He was filled with terror, but it looked to him as if the good intention was triumphing. He felt he had come to the next decisive moment for his conscience and his destiny. That the bishop had marked the first phase of his new life and that Champmathieu marked the second. After the great crisis, the great test.

But the fever that had subsided for a while gradually returned. A thousand thoughts ran through his mind but they continued to strengthen him in his resolve.

At one moment he said to himself, perhaps he was overreacting. After all, this Champmathieu was no saint. He had actually stolen. He responded inwardly: Very well, if this man has stolen a few apples, that's a month in prison. There's a great difference between that and the chain gang. And even then, who knows? Did he steal? Has it been proven? The name of Jean Valjean damns him and seems to make proof dispensable. Don't crown prosecutors always behave like that? He's believed to be a thief because he's known to be a convict.

A moment later the idea struck him that when he denounced himself the heroism of his deed, and his honest life for the last seven years, and what he had done for the area, might perhaps be taken into consideration, and he would be pardoned.

But this notion faded very quickly, and he smiled bitterly, reflecting that the theft of forty sous from Petit-Gervais made him guilty of re-offending, that this incident would surely be raised again, and under the terms laid down by the law would make him liable to penal servitude for life.

He turned his back on any illusion, detached himself more and more from this world, and sought consolation and strength elsewhere. He told himself he must do his duty. That maybe he would be no worse off after doing his duty than after shirking it. That if he *didn't interfere*, if he stayed in Montreuil-sur-Mer, his prestige, his good name, his good works, the respect and veneration in which he was held, his charity, his wealth, his popularity, his virtue, would be dependent on a crime. And how could his pleasure in all these blessed things not be tainted by their association with this hideous thing? Whereas if he made his sacrifice it would bring to the prison hulks, to the pillory post, to the iron collar, to the green cap, to the unceasing toil and the pitiless shame, a touch of the sublime.

Finally he told himself it could not be helped, such was his destiny, he had no authority to upset the arrangements made on high, that in any case there was a choice to be made: outward virtue and inward loathing, or inward saintliness and outward ignominy.

Though his courage did not falter, brooding over such dismal thoughts tired him. In spite of himself he began to think of other things, unimportant things.

The veins in his temples throbbed violently. He went on pacing to and fro. Midnight struck, first at the parish church, then at the town hall. He counted the twelve strokes of the two clocks and compared the sounds of the two bells. He was reminded that a few days previously he had seen an old clock for sale, at a scrap merchant's, on which was written the name 'Antoine-Albin de Romainville'.

He felt cold. He lit a small fire. It did not occur to him to close the window. In the meantime he had relapsed into his stupor. He had to make quite an effort to remember what he had been thinking about before midnight struck. Finally it came back to him.

'Ah! yes,' he said to himself, 'I'd made up my mind to denounce myself.'

And then all at once he thought of Fantine.

'Wait!' said he. 'What about that poor woman?'

Now a new feverishness erupted.

Fantine, suddenly coming to mind, was like an unexpected ray of light. It seemed to him that everything around him looked different. He exclaimed, 'But I've only considered myself till now! Whether I should remain silent or denounce myself, hide myself or save my soul, be a contemptible and respected magistrate or a vile and venerable convict. It's just me, me, me, all the time! But, good God, either way it's egotism! Different forms of egotism, but egotism all the same. Suppose I gave some thought to others? The supreme godliness is to think of others. Now, let's consider the matter. If I'm removed, excluded, forgotten, what will happen as a result? Suppose I denounce myself. I'm arrested, this Champmathieu is released, I'm sent back to the prison hulks, that's fine. And what then? What happens here? Ah! here, we have a community, a town, factories, an industry, workers, men and women, aged grandfathers, children, poor folk! I've created all this, I sustain all this. Wherever there's a smoking chimney, it is I who have put the log on the fire and the meat in the pot. I've created wealth, commerce, credit. Before me there was nothing. I've improved, revitalized, regenerated, invigorated, stimulated, enriched the whole countryside. With me gone, the moving spirit's gone. Remove myself, and everything dies. And this woman who's suffered so much, whose merits in her downfall are so great, and I the unwitting cause of all her misery! And the child I meant to go and fetch, as I promised her mother. Don't I owe this woman something too, in reparation for the harm I've done her? If I disappear, what will happen? The mother dies. The child's left to fend for itself. That's what happens if I denounce myself.

'What if I don't denounce myself? Well, suppose I don't?'

After putting this question to himself, he paused. He had, as it were, a moment's hesitation and trepidation. But this moment did not last long and he responded calmly: 'Well, this man will join the chain gang, that's true, but he's stolen, damn it! It's no use saying he hasn't, because he has! Meanwhile I stay here and carry on. In ten years I'll have made ten million, I redirect it into the community, I keep nothing for myself, what is it to me? I'm not doing it for myself. General prosperity continues to increase, industries start up and develop, factories and shops multiply, families, dozens of families, hundreds of families, are happy. The region's population grows, villages spring up where before there were only farms, farms spring up where there was nothing. Poverty disappears and, along with poverty, debauchery, prostitution, theft, murder, all vices, all crimes! And this poor mother raises her child! And a whole community becomes wealthy and respectable! Honestly! I was out of my mind! I was being absurd! Why on earth was I talking about denouncing myself? Really, I must be careful, and not do anything hasty. What! Because I wanted to play the brave, noble-hearted soul – after all, that's so melodramatic! – because I was just thinking of myself, and no one else. In order to save from punishment – a little excessive, maybe, but basically justified – some unknown person, a thief, an obvious good-for-nothing, a whole region must perish! A poor woman must die in hospital! A poor little girl must die in the street! Like dogs! But this is appalling! And without the mother even seeing her child again! And the child almost not having known her mother. And all for the sake of that apple-thieving old rogue who surely deserves to be sentenced to hard labour for something else, if not for that. Fine scruples that save a criminal and sacrifice the innocent; that save an old vagrant – with only a few more years to live, after all, who will hardly be any worse off in the prison hulks than in his own hovel – and sacrifice a whole population, mothers, wives, children. Poor little Cosette who has no one in the world but me and is no doubt blue with cold right now in those Thénardiers' doss-house. There's another bad lot! And I'd be prepared to neglect my responsibilities to all these poor creatures! And I'd go off and denounce myself! And I'd do something so downright stupid! Let's assume the worst: suppose there is some wickedness on my part in all this and my conscience one day reproaches me for it. Resigning myself, for the sake of others, to those reproaches weighing only against me and to this wicked deed that imperils no one else's soul but mine – that's self-sacrifice, that's virtue.'

He rose and started pacing again. This time he thought he was satisfied.

Diamonds are found only in the darkness of the earth. Truths are found only in the depths of the mind. It seemed to him that having descended into those depths, having long groped in the pitch-black of that darkness, he had at last found one of those diamonds, one of those truths, and he now held it in his hand. And he was dazzled by the sight of it.

'Yes,' he thought, 'that's the answer. I'm doing the right thing. I have the solution. In the end some decision has to be reached. I've made up my mind. Leave well alone. No more shilly-shallying, no more backsliding. This is in everybody's interests, not mine. I am

Madeleine, Madeleine I remain. Whoever Jean Valjean is, let him perish! He's not myself any more. I don't know that man, he's nothing to do with me now. If there happens to be someone called Jean Valjean at this moment, that's his lookout! It's not my concern. It's a fateful name hovering about in the dark. If it stops and swoops down on someone, that's just too bad!'

He looked at himself in the little mirror on his mantelpiece, and said, 'Well! It's a relief to have come to a decision. I feel much better now.'

He took another few steps, then stopped in his tracks.

'Come now!' he said. 'There must be no faint-heartedness over any of the consequences of this decision. There are still links connecting me with that Jean Valjean. They must be destroyed. There are objects here in this very room that would betray me, things that cannot speak that would testify against me. Well then, all these things must disappear.'

He fumbled in his pocket, drew out his purse, opened it, and took out a small key. He inserted this key into a keyhole that could hardly be seen, camouflaged as it was in the darkest hues of the patterned wallpaper. A hiding-place opened, a kind of false cupboard constructed in the angle between the wall and the chimney-breast. There was nothing but a few bits of rubbish in this hiding-place, a blue overall, an old pair of trousers, an old knapsack, and a big hawthorn stick ferruled at both ends. Those who had seen Jean Valjean when he passed through Digne in October 1815 would easily have recognized all the elements of this miserable outfit.

He had kept them as he had kept the silver candlesticks, to remind himself always of where he had started from. Only, he concealed these things that came from the prison hulks and displayed the candlesticks that came from the bishop.

He cast a furtive glance towards the door as if he feared it would open, despite being bolted. Then, without even glancing at these things that he had kept so religiously and at such great peril all these years, with a sudden brisk movement he swept them up in a single armful and threw the whole lot, rags, stick and knapsack, on to the fire.

He closed the secret cupboard, and taking extra precautions, no longer necessary since it was now empty, he concealed the door behind a piece of heavy furniture that he pushed in front of it.

After a few seconds the room and the opposite wall were lit up with a fierce red wavering glow. Everything was ablaze. The hawthorn stick crackled and threw sparks reaching the middle of the room.

As the knapsack burned away, along with the hideous rags it contained, something shiny was left lying in the ashes. Anyone who took a closer look would easily have recognized it as a silver coin. No doubt the forty-sou piece stolen from the little chimney-sweep.

He did not look at the fire, but kept steadily pacing back and forth. All at once his eyes fell on the two silver candlesticks dimly gleaming on the mantelpiece in the reflected glow.

'Now wait!' he thought. 'There is still everything of Jean Valjean in those. They too must be destroyed.'

He seized the two candlesticks. There was enough of a blaze to be able to quickly distort them and make some sort of unrecognizable metal bar out of them.

He bent over the hearth and warmed himself for a moment. It gave him a real sense of well-being. 'How good to be warm!' he said.

He stirred the embers with one of the two candlesticks. A minute later and they would have been in the fire.

At that moment he thought he heard a voice cry out within him: 'Jean Valjean! Jean Valjean!'

His hair stood on end. He became like a man listening to something terrifying.

'Yes, go on, do it!' said the voice. 'Finish what you're about! Destroy those candlesticks! Obliterate that memory! Forget the bishop! Forget everything! Ruin that Champmathieu! Go on! That's fine! Congratulate yourself! And so it's settled, resolved, decided: there's a man, an old man, who doesn't know what lies in store for him, who's done nothing wrong perhaps, an innocent man, to whom your name has brought total disaster, who's burdened with your name as with a crime, who's going to be mistaken for you, who's going to be convicted, who will end his days in abject horror. That's fine! You yourself, be an honest man. Continue as monsieur le maire. Continue to be respectable and respected. Enrich the town. Feed the poor. Give orphans an upbringing. Live happy, virtuous and admired. And in the meantime, while you're here enjoying happiness and light, there'll be someone wearing your red jacket, bearing your name in ignominy and dragging your chain in prison. Yes, that's a fine arrangement. Ah, you wretch!'

Sweat trickled from his brow. He stared wild-eyed at the candlesticks. But that which spoke within him had not finished. The voice went on: 'Jean Valjean, there will be many voices around you that will make a great deal of noise, that will talk very loudly and bless you, and only one voice that no one will hear, a voice that will curse you in the shadows. Well, listen, vile impostor! All those blessings will fall back to earth again before reaching heaven, and only the curse will rise up to God.'

This voice, very faint at first and coming from the darkest depths of his conscience, had gradually become loud and formidable, and he now heard it in his ear. It seemed to him it had escaped from inside him and now spoke from without. He thought he heard those last words so distinctly that he looked around the room with a kind of terror.

'Is there anyone here?' he asked out loud, and utterly distraught.

Then, with a laugh like the laugh of an idiot, he said, 'How stupid of me! There can't be anybody!'

There was somebody, but the somebody who was there was not one of those the human eye is capable of seeing.

He put the candlesticks back on the mantelpiece.

Then he resumed that monotonous and gloomy pacing that disturbed the dreams of the sleeping man below and woke him with a start.

This pacing calmed and at the same time agitated him. It seems that sometimes, at the most critical moments, we move about so as to seek the advice of everything we may encounter in bestirring ourselves. After a few moments he no longer knew what to do.

He now recoiled with equal horror before the two decisions he had come to in turn. Both ideas that suggested themselves seemed no less deplorable one than the other. What a quirk of fate! What a freak of chance that Champmathieu should have been mistaken for him. To be ruined by precisely the means providence seemed at first to have employed to safeguard him!

There was a moment when he considered the future. Good God! Denounce himself! Give himself up! He envisaged with immense despair everything he would have to leave behind, everything he would have to return to. He would have to say goodbye to this life, a life so good, so pure, so radiant, to this respect from everyone, to honour, to freedom. Never again would he go walking in the countryside, never again hear the birds sing in the month of May, never again give money to the little children. He would never again experience the sweetness of meeting those gazes filled with gratitude and love. He would leave this house he had built, this room, this dear room! Everything seemed delightful to him at that moment. Never again would he read these books, never again would he write at this dear pinewood table. His old caretaker, the only servant he had, would never again bring him his coffee in the morning. Good God! Instead of this, the convict gang, the iron collar, the red jacket, the chain round his ankle, exhaustion, the cell, the camp bed, all those familiar horrors! At his age, having been what he was now! If he were still young, at least! But to be old, and to be shown no respect by anyone, to be searched by the warder, beaten by the galley-sergeant, to wear hobnailed shoes on his bare feet and allow the shackles on his leg to be checked morning and night by the guard on patrol with his hammer, to endure the curiosity of strangers who would be told: 'That one there is the famous Jean Valjean, who was mayor of Montreuil-sur-Mer!' And in the evening, dripping with sweat, overwhelmed with weariness, the green cap pulled down over his eyes, to climb the ladder on to the prison hulks, in pairs, under the sergeant's whip. Oh, what misery! Can destiny, then, be as vicious as an intelligent being and become as monstrous as the human heart?

And whatever he did, he kept coming back to this agonizing dilemma that underlay his reflections: Remain in paradise and become a demon! Return to hell and become an angel!

What should he do? God Almighty! What should he do?

The turmoil he had with so much difficulty put behind him once more raged within him. His thoughts started to become confused again. They took on that somehow bewildered and mechanical aspect typical of despair. The name of Romainville kept coming back into his mind with two lines of a song that he had once heard. He remembered that Romainville was a little forest close to Paris where young lovers went to gather lilacs in the month of April.

He reeled outwardly as well as inwardly. He tottered like a small child left to walk on its own.

At certain moments, struggling against weariness, he strove to retake command of his intellect. He tried to confront once and for all the problem over which he had, as it were, collapsed with exhaustion. Should he denounce himself? Should he remain silent? He could see nothing with any clarity. The vague aspects of all the lines of reasoning sketched out by his ruminations flickered and went up in smoke one after the other. Yet he felt that whatever he decided, some part of him was bound to die, and there was no possibility of avoiding this. That either way he was entering a tomb. That he was in the throes of death, the death of his happiness or the death of his virtue.

Alas! all his indecision had got the better of him again. He was no further advanced than to begin with.

Thus did this poor soul struggle in its anguish. Eighteen hundred years before this ill-fated man, the mysterious being in whom are concentrated all the saintliness and all the sufferings of humanity had also refused for a long time the terrible chalice, streaming with darkness and brimming with shadows, that appeared to him in the star-filled depths while the olive trees shook in the fierce blast of the infinite.

IV
Forms That Suffering Takes in Sleep

Three o'clock in the morning had just struck and he had been pacing like this for five hours, almost without interruption, when he dropped on to his chair.

There he fell asleep and had a dream.

This dream, like most dreams, related to the situation only in that there was something vaguely sinister and disturbing about it, but it made an impression on him. So struck was he by this nightmare that he later wrote it down. It is one of the papers written in his own hand that he has left. Here we think we ought to transcribe this thing word for word.

Whatever the dream, the story of this night would be incomplete if we were to omit it. It is the grim experience of a sick soul.

Here it is. We find this line written on the envelope: 'The dream I had that night'.

I was in the countryside. Bleak open countryside where there was no grass growing. It did not seem to me to be either light or dark.

I was walking with my brother, the brother of my childhood years, the brother that, I have to say, I never think about and I can scarcely remember now.

We were chatting, and we encountered some passers-by. We were talking about a neighbour we had in the past who always worked with her window on to the street open all the time that she lived there. Even as we chatted we felt cold because of that open window.

There were no trees in the countryside.

We saw a man who passed close by. He was stark-naked, ashen-hued, mounted on an earthen-hued horse. The man had no hair. We could see his skull and the veins on his skull. In his hand he held a switch as pliant as a vine shoot and as heavy as iron. This horseman passed by and said nothing to us.

My brother said to me, 'Let's take the sunken road.'

There was a sunken road where not a bush or a patch of moss was to be seen. Everything was earth-coloured, even the sky. After a few paces there was now no reply when I spoke. I realized my brother was not with me any more.

I entered a village that I saw. I thought it must be Romainville (why Romainville?)*.

The first street I entered was deserted. I turned into a second street. Round the corner where the two streets met, there was a man standing against the wall. I said to this man, 'What village is this? Where am I?' The man did not reply. I saw a house with the door open, I went inside.

The first room was deserted. I went into the second. Behind the door of this room, a man was standing against the wall. I asked this man, 'Whose house is this? Where am I?' The man did not reply. The house had a garden.

I left the house and went into the garden. The garden was deserted. Behind the first tree I found a man standing there. I said to this man, 'What is this garden? Where am I?' The man did not reply.

I wandered through the village and realized it was a town. All the streets were deserted, all the doors were open. Not a living soul walked in the streets, moved about the rooms or strolled in the gardens. But behind every corner, behind every door, behind every tree, stood a man who did not speak. There was never more than one of them to be seen at any one time. These men watched me go by.

I left the town and began to walk through the fields.

After some time I turned round and saw a large crowd coming after me. I recognized all the men I had seen in the town. They had strange expressions. They did not seem to be hurrying and yet they walked faster than I did. They made no sound as they walked. Within an instant this crowd caught up with me and surrounded me. The faces of these men were earth-coloured.

Then the first one I had seen and questioned on entering the town said to me, 'Where are you going! Don't you know that you've long been dead?'

I opened my mouth to reply, and I saw there was no one around.

He woke up. He felt frozen. A cold wind like the morning wind made the casements that had been left open swing on their hinges. The fire had gone out. The candle was almost burned right down. It was still pitch-black.

He rose and went to the window. There were still no stars in the sky.

The yard of the house and the street could be seen from the window.

* Hugo's footnote: This parenthesis is in Jean Valjean's hand.

A sharp, harsh sound, a sudden clattering on the ground, made him look down.

He saw below him two red stars whose rays bizarrely lengthened and shortened in the darkness.

His mind still half submerged in the fog of dreams, 'Look at that!' he thought. 'There are none in the sky. They're on earth now.'

However, this fog cleared, a second sound like the first wakened him completely. He looked again and realized the two stars were carriage lanterns. By the light they cast he was able to make out the shape of that carriage. It was a tilbury harnessed to a small white horse. The noise he heard was that of the horse's hoofs striking the paving.

'What's that carriage doing here?' he said to himself. 'Now who would be arriving so early in the morning?'

At that moment there was a tap at the door of his room.

He shuddered from head to foot and cried out in a terrible voice, 'Who is it?'

Someone replied, 'Monsieur le maire, it's me.'

He recognized the voice of the old woman, his doorkeeper. 'Well,' he replied, 'what is it?'

'Monsieur le maire, it'll soon be five o'clock in the morning.'

'What's that to me?'

'It's the gig, monsieur le maire.'

'What gig?'

'The tilbury.'

'What tilbury?'

'Did monsieur le maire not order a tilbury?'

'No,' he said.

'The coachman says he's come for monsieur le maire.'

'What coachman?'

'Monsieur Scaufflaire's coachman.'

'Monsieur Scaufflaire?'

This name made him start, as if a streak of lightning had flashed in front of him.

'Ah! yes,' he said. 'Monsieur Scaufflaire!'

If the old woman could have seen him at that moment she would have been terror-stricken.

There was quite a long silence. He stared stupidly at the candle flame, then from round the wick he took some of the molten wax, which he rolled between his fingers. The old woman was waiting.

Yet she ventured to raise her voice once more: 'Monsieur le maire, what am I to reply?'

'Tell him, very well, I'm coming.'

V
Spokes in the Wheels

The post service from Arras to Montreuil-sur-Mer was still operated at that time by small mail-coaches dating back to the Empire. These coaches were two-wheeled cabriolets, upholstered on the inside in buff leather, with spring suspension and only two seats, one for the postman, the other for a passenger. The wheels were mounted on those aggressive protruding axle arms that keep other vehicles at bay and are still to be seen on the roads in Germany. The dispatch box, a huge oblong coffer, was positioned at the back of the cabriolet and formed an integral part of it. This coffer was painted black and the cabriolet yellow.

These vehicles, unlike anything today, had something of a distorted, hunchbacked look about them, and when seen going by in the distance, climbing some road to the horizon, they resembled those insects, called termites, I believe, with a small thorax and a large abdomen trailing behind. Moreover, they went very fast. The mail-coach that set out from Arras every night at one o'clock, after the Paris mail had been through, arrived at Montreuil-sur-Mer a little before five in the morning.

That night, just as it was entering the town, the coach going down to Montreuil-sur-Mer on the Hesdin road collided at a street corner with a little tilbury drawn by a white horse coming from the opposite direction, which had just one person in it, a man wrapped in a cloak. The wheel of the tilbury took quite a severe knock. The postman cried out to this man to stop, but the traveller did not listen and continued on his way at a fast trot.

'There's a man in a devilish hurry!' said the postman.

The man in such a hurry was the one we have just seen floundering in paroxysms and surely deserving of pity. Where was he going? He could not have said. Why was he hurrying? He did not know. He headed on blindly. Where to? Arras, no doubt. But maybe he was also heading elsewhere. Now and then he felt this, and shuddered.

He plunged into that darkness as into an abyss. Something drove him, something drew him. What was going on inside him none could say, all will understand. What man has not at least once in his life entered that dark cavern of the unknown?

Besides, he had resolved on nothing, decided on nothing, settled on nothing, done nothing. None of the edicts of his conscience had been definitive. He was more than ever in the same predicament as in the very first instance.

Why was he going to Arras?

He kept repeating what he had already said to himself when he hired Scaufflaire's cabriolet: that whatever the outcome might be, there was no harm in seeing for himself and reaching his own judgement about things. In fact this was prudent, he needed to know what happened. It was impossible to make a decision without having watched and observed. From a distance, you got everything out of proportion. After all, once he had seen this Champmathieu, his conscience would probably be greatly relieved to let such an insignificant wretch take his place in the prison hulks. True, Javert would be there, and those fellows Brevet, Chenildieu and Cochepaille, former convicts who had known him. But they certainly would not recognize him. Bah! the very idea! And Javert wouldn't even dream of it. All conjectures and assumptions were focused on this Champmathieu, and nothing is so stubborn as assumptions and conjectures. So there was no danger.

It was certainly a dark moment, but he would come through it. After all, his fate, however bad it might be, was in his own hands. He was master of it. He clung to this idea.

Deep down, to be quite frank, he would have preferred not to go to Arras.

Nevertheless, that was where he was going.

Letting his thoughts run on, he whipped his horse, which kept up that good, steady, even pace to cover six and a half miles an hour. As the tilbury advanced, he felt something inside him receding.

At daybreak he was in open countryside. The town of Montreuil-sur-Mer lay some distance behind him. He beheld the whitening horizon. Unseeing, he beheld all the frigid features of a winter's dawn pass before his eyes. The morning has its spectres, as well as the evening. He did not see them, but without his being aware of it and by a kind of almost physical penetration, these black silhouettes of trees and hills added something vaguely gloomy and ominous to his tumultuous state of mind.

Every time he passed one of those isolated houses bordering the road, he said to himself, 'And yet there are people asleep in that house!'

The trotting of the horse, the bells on the harness, the wheels on the paving, produced a subdued and monotonous sound. Such things are delightful when you are happy, and mournful when you are sad.

It was broad daylight when he arrived at Hesdin. He stopped in front of an inn to give the horse a breather and feed it some oats.

As Scaufflaire had said, the horse was of that small Boulonnais breed, which is too heavy in the head, too big in the belly and too short in the neck and shoulders, but with a full chest, a broad rump, lean slender legs and a firm foot: an ugly but robust and healthy breed. This excellent beast had covered twelve and a half miles in two hours and had not a drop of sweat on its rump.

He had not descended from the tilbury. The stable-hand who brought the oats suddenly bent down and examined the left wheel.

'Are you going far like that?' said this man.

Almost without emerging from his introspection, he replied, 'Why?'

'Have you come far?' the man went on.

'Twelve and a half miles.'

'Ah!'

'Why do you say "Ah"?'

The stable-lad bent down once more, remained silent for a moment, staring at the wheel, then straightened up and said, 'Because that's a wheel that, like as not, has just done twelve and a half miles but isn't going to do another half-mile, for sure.'

He jumped down from the tilbury. 'What are you saying, my friend?'

'I'm saying it's a miracle that you've come twelve and a half miles without overturning, you and your horse, in some ditch on the highway. Look!'

The wheel was indeed seriously damaged. The collision with the mail-coach had split two spokes and gouged the hub so that the axle nut was no longer holding.

'My friend,' he said to the groom, 'is there a wheelwright in this place?'

'Certainly, monsieur.'

'Be so good as to go and fetch him.'

'He's right here. Hey! Maître Bourgaillard!'

Maître Bourgaillard, the wheelwright, was standing on his doorstep. He came and examined the wheel, and made a face like a surgeon who thinks a limb is broken.

'Can you repair this wheel immediately?'

'Yes, monsieur.'

'When will I be able to set off again?'

'Tomorrow.'

'Tomorrow!'

'It'll take a full day's work. Is monsieur in a hurry?'

'A very great hurry. I must be on my way in no more than an hour.'

'Impossible, monsieur.'

'I'll pay anything you like.'

'Impossible.'

'Well, in two hours, then.'

'Today's impossible. Two spokes and a hub need to be remade. Monsieur will not be able to set off again before tomorrow.'

'What I have to do can't wait till tomorrow. What if you were to replace this wheel instead of repairing it?'

'What do you mean?'

'You're a wheelwright?'

'Certainly, monsieur.'

'Haven't you got a wheel you could sell me? Then I could set off again at once.'

'A spare wheel?'

'Yes.'

'I haven't got a ready-made wheel to fit your gig. Wheels go in matching pairs. Wheels aren't paired at random.'

'In that case, sell me a pair of wheels.'

'All wheels don't fit all axles, monsieur.'

'Try, at least.'

'It's no good, monsieur. I've nothing but cartwheels to sell. This is just a small place.'

'Would you have a gig to hire out to me?'

The wheelwright had realized at first glance that the tilbury was a hired vehicle. He shrugged.

'A fine way you have of treating the gigs you hire! Even if I had one I wouldn't hire it out to you!'

'Well, one to sell, then.'

'No, I haven't.'

'What! Not even a trap? I'm not particular, as you see.'

'This is just a small place. I've got an old calash in the shed there,' added the wheelwright, 'which belongs to a gentleman in town who's given it to me to look after and only uses it once in a blue moon. I'd happily hire that out to you, what do I care? But the gentleman mustn't see it go by. And besides, it's a calash, it would need two horses.'

'I'll take post-horses.'

'Where is monsieur going?'

'To Arras.'

'And monsieur wants to get there today?'

'Yes, I tell you.'

'With post-horses?'

'Why not?'

'Is it all the same to monsieur if he arrives at four o'clock in the morning?'

'Certainly not.'

'Well, you see, one thing that needs to be said, with post-horses – has monsieur got his passport with him?'

'Yes.'

'Well, with post-horses, monsieur won't get to Arras before tomorrow. We're on a cross-route. The relay stations are badly supplied, the horses are in the fields. It's the start of the ploughing season, strong draught animals are needed, and horses are taken from all quarters, from the post like everywhere else. Monsieur will be waiting at least three or four hours at every relay. And then you'll be going at walking pace. There are a lot of hills to climb.'

'Very well, I'll go on horseback. Unhitch the gig. Someone in the locality will surely sell me a saddle.'

'No doubt. But does this horse accept the saddle?'

'That's true, you've reminded me. No, it doesn't.'

'Well then—'

'But surely I'll find a horse to hire in the village?'

'A horse to go all the way to Arras without a break?'

'Yes.'

'You'd need a horse of a kind we haven't got in these parts. In any case you'd have to buy it because no one knows you. But you won't find one – not for sale or for hire, not for five hundred francs or a thousand.'

'What's to be done?'

'Look, the best and most sensible thing is for me to repair the wheel and for you to delay your journey until tomorrow.'

'Tomorrow will be too late.'

'Dear me!'

'What about the mail-coach that goes to Arras? When does that come by?'

'Tonight. Both mail-coaches do the run at night, the one going there as well as the one coming back.'

'So it will take you a day to mend this wheel?'

'And a good long day at that.'

'With two men working on it?'

'With ten men working on it!'

'What about binding the spokes with twine?'

'The spokes, yes, the hub, no. And anyway, the rim's in a bad state, too.'

'Is there anyone in town who hires out carriages?'

'No.'

'Is there another wheelwright?'

The stable-hand and the wheelwright responded simultaneously by shaking their heads. 'No.'

He felt an immense joy.

It was obvious that providence was intervening. It was providence that had broken the wheel of the tilbury and was preventing him from continuing his journey. He had not given in at the first challenge, as it were. He had made every possible effort to continue his journey. He had honestly and scrupulously exhausted every alternative. He had not balked at winter weather, tiredness or expense. He had nothing with which to reproach himself. If he went no further, he could not be blamed any more. It was not his fault, it was the doing not of his conscience but of providence.

He breathed again. He breathed freely and deeply for the first time since Javert's visit. He felt as if he had just been released from the iron grip that had squeezed his heart for the past twenty hours.

It seemed to him that God was now on his side and was coming out in his favour.

He told himself that he had done everything within his power, and all he could do now was to go home quietly.

If his conversation with the wheelwright had taken place in a room inside the inn there would have been no witnesses, no one would have heard him, things would have gone no further, and we probably would not have had to relate any of the events of which you are going to read. But this conversation had taken place in the street. Any discussion in the street inevitably attracts a circle of onlookers. There are always people only too willing to be spectators. While he was questioning the wheelwright, some passers-by had stopped and gathered round them. After listening for a few minutes, a young lad no one had noticed broke away from the group and ran off.

Just as the traveller was deciding to turn back, after the inward deliberations we have described above, this child returned. He was accompanied by an old woman.

'Monsieur,' said the woman, 'my boy tells me you wish to hire a gig.'

These simple words uttered by an old woman led by a child made the sweat trickle down his back. He fancied he saw the hand that had released him reappear in the shadows behind him, ready to recapture him.

He replied, 'Yes, my good woman, I'm trying to find a gig for hire.' And he hastened to add, 'But there's none to be had here.'

'Yes, there is,' said the old woman.

'Where from then?' said the wheelwright.

'From me,' replied the old woman.

He shuddered. The fateful hand had seized hold of him again.

The old woman did indeed have a kind of wicker carriole. Dismayed that the traveller should escape them, the wheelwright and the stable-hand spoke out: it was a frightful rattletrap, it was unsprung, resting directly on the axle – admittedly the seats were suspended inside with leather thongs – it let the rain in, the wheels were rusted and corroded with damp, it would not go much further than the tilbury, a real boneshaker! This gentleman would be very unwise to go anywhere in it, et cetera.

All this was true, but this rattletrap, this boneshaker, this thing whatever it was, had two wheels and was mobile, and could go to Arras.

He paid the price asked, left the tilbury with the wheelwright to be repaired so he could pick it up on his return, had the white horse harnessed to the cart, climbed in, and resumed the journey on which he had set out that morning.

As the cart moved off, he confessed to himself that he had felt a certain joy a moment earlier at the thought that he would not be going where he was going. He considered this joy with a sort of anger, and found it absurd. Why feel joyful at turning back? After all, he was making this journey of his own free will. No one was forcing him to make it. And certainly nothing would happen that was not something he wanted.

As he left Hesdin he heard a voice shouting, 'Stop! Stop!' He stopped the cart with a jerk, which had a vague feverishness and convulsiveness about it, resembling hope.

It was the old woman's little boy. 'Monsieur,' said the lad, 'it was I who found you the cart.'

'Well?'

'You've not given me anything.'

He who gave to all, and so readily, found this claim unreasonable, almost outrageous.

'Ah! you, young man,' said he, 'you shall have nothing.'

He whipped the horse and set off at a fast trot.

He had lost a lot of time at Hesdin. He wanted to make it up. The little horse was plucky and pulled as well as two, but it was the month of February, it had been raining, the roads were bad. And besides, it was no longer the tilbury. The cart was solid and very heavy. And what is more, there were numerous climbs.

It took him nearly four hours to get from Hesdin to St-Pol. Four hours to cover twelve and a half miles*.

* In the French text, 'cinq lieues', although it has previously been indicated that this stage of the journey would be 'six lieues', (p. 200), which is fifteen miles.

At St-Pol, he had the horse unharnessed and taken to the stable at the first inn he came to. As he had promised Scaufflaire, he stood by the fodder rack while the horse was feeding. The thoughts on his mind were gloomy and confused.

The innkeeper's wife came into the stable.

'Does monsieur not want to eat?'

'Ah, indeed I do,' he said, 'in fact I've got a hearty appetite.'

He followed this woman, who had a bright and cheerful face. She led him to a low-ceilinged room where there were tables with oilcloth coverings for tablecloths.

'Be quick!' he said. 'I must be on my way. I'm in a hurry.'

A plump Flemish serving-girl swiftly laid him a place. He watched the girl with a sense of well-being.

'That's what was wrong with me,' he thought. 'I hadn't eaten.'

His food came. He fell on the bread, took a bite, and then slowly put it back on the table and did not touch it again.

A carter was eating at another table. He said to this man, 'Why is their bread so bitter here?'

The carter was German and did not understand.

He returned to the horse in the stable.

An hour later he had left St-Pol and was heading for Tinques, which is only twelve and a half miles from Arras.

What did he do during this journey? What did he think about? As in the morning, he watched the trees, the thatched roofs, the tilled fields going by, and the disappearing landscape, displaced at every bend in the road. This is contemplation of a kind that is sometimes sufficient for the soul and almost relieves it of thought. What could be more melancholy and profound than seeing a thousand objects for the first and last time? To travel is to be born and die at every instant. Perhaps in the haziest region of his mind he drew parallels between these shifting horizons and human existence. All things in life are perpetually fleeing before you. Brightness and dark intermingle: after radiance, an eclipse. You watch, you hurry, you reach out to seize what is passing. Every event is a bend in the road. And all of a sudden you are old. You feel a kind of jolt, all is darkness, you make out a dim doorway, the lugubrious horse of life that was drawing you comes to a halt, and you see a muffled stranger in the shadows unharness it.

Twilight was falling when some children coming out of school saw this traveller drive in to Tinques. It is true the days were still short at that time of year. He did not stop in Tinques. As he came out of the village a road-mender laying stones on the road looked up and said, 'That's a very tired horse.'

Indeed, the poor beast was going at no more than a walking pace.

'Is it Arras you're going to?' added the road-mender.

'Yes.'

'You won't make very good time at that rate.'

He stopped the horse and asked the road-mender, 'How much further is it from here to Arras?'

'Near enough a good seventeen miles.'

'How so? In the post book it's marked as only thirteen.'

'Ah!' replied the road-mender. 'Don't you know the road's under repair? You'll find it blocked a quarter of an hour from here. Impossible to go any further.'

'Really?'

'Take the turning on the left, which goes to Carency, cross the river, and when you get to Camblin, turn right. That's the Mont-St-Éloy road to Arras.'

'But it's getting dark, I'll lose my way.'

'You don't come from these parts?'

'No.'

'And what's more, it's all cross-country. Listen, monsieur,' the road-mender went on, 'do you want my advice? Your horse is tired. Go back to Tinques. You'll find a good inn there. Stay the night. Go to Arras tomorrow.'

'I must be there this evening.'

'That's different. Then go to the inn in any case and hire a trace horse there. The tracer will guide you cross-country.'

He followed the road-mender's advice, went back, and half an hour later drove past the same spot but this time at a fast trot with a good trace horse. The horse-handler, who called himself a postilion, sat on the cart shaft.

All the same, he felt he was running out of time. It was completely dark now.

They turned into the country lane. The roadway became terrible. The cart lurched from one rut to another. He said to the postilion, 'Keep going at a trot, and I'll double your tip.'

A jolt, and the swingle-bar broke.

'Monsieur, that's the swingle-bar broken,' said the postilion. 'I don't know how to harness my horse now. This road's very bad at night. If you'd only go back and sleep at Tinques, we could be in Arras early tomorrow morning.'

He replied, 'Have you a piece of string and a knife?'

'Yes, monsieur.'

He cut a branch from a tree and made a swingle-bar out of it.

This was another twenty minutes' delay, but they set off again at a gallop.

The plain was shadowy. Dark low-lying patches of fog crept up the hills and broke away from them like smoke. There were pale glimmerings in the clouds. A strong wind blowing in from the sea made a noise in the sky all around like furniture being moved. Everything glimpsed was caught in an attitude of terror. What a multitude of things shudder in these vast exhalations of the night!

The cold penetrated him. He had eaten nothing since the night before. He vaguely recalled his other night-time wayfaring on the great plain outside Digne. That was eight years ago, and it seemed like only yesterday.

The hour struck in some distant bell-tower. He asked the boy, 'What time is it?'

'Seven o'clock, monsieur. We'll be at Arras by eight. We've only another seven and a half miles to go.'

At that moment it occurred to him for the first time – he found it odd that it had not occurred to him sooner – that all the trouble he was taking might well prove useless. He did not even know what time the trial was. He should at least have enquired about that. It was absurd to keep pressing on like this without knowing whether it would serve any purpose. Then he made a few rough calculations in his head. Usually the sittings of the court of assizes began at nine o'clock in the morning. It could not take too long, this case: the theft of the apples, that would be very brief, then it would just be a question of identification, four or five statements, not much for the lawyers to say. He was going to arrive after it was all over.

The postilion whipped the horses. They had crossed the river and left Mont-St-Éloy behind them.

It was getting darker and darker.

VI

Soeur Simplice Is Put to the Test

Meanwhile, at that very moment, Fantine was full of joy.

She had had a very bad night. Terrible coughing, her fever worse than ever; she had had nightmares. In the morning when the doctor came, she was delirious. He looked alarmed and asked to be informed as soon as Monsieur Madeleine arrived.

All morning she was dejected, said little, plucked at her sheets, murmuring in a low voice what sounded like calculations of distances. Her eyes were sunken and staring. They seemed almost lifeless, then now and again they lit up and shone like stars. Seemingly, at the approach of a certain dark hour the light of heaven fills those whom the earth's light is deserting.

Every time Soeur Simplice asked her how she felt, she invariably replied, 'Fine. I'd like to see Monsieur Madeleine.'

A few months earlier, when Fantine had just lost the last of her modesty, the last of her shame, the last of her joy, she was the mere shadow of herself. Now she was the ghost of herself. Physical malady had completed the work of moral malady. This creature of twenty-five had a lined brow, wasted cheeks, pinched nostrils, loose teeth, a leaden complexion, a scraggy neck, prominent shoulder blades, weak limbs, a sallow complexion, and her blonde hair now grew sprinkled with grey. Alas! how illness contrives to imitate old age!

At midday the doctor returned, issued some instructions, enquired whether monsieur le maire had turned up at the infirmary, and shook his head.

Monsieur Madeleine usually came to see the patient at three o'clock. As promptness was a kindness, he was prompt.

At about half-past two Fantine began to fret. In the space of twenty minutes she asked the nun more than ten times, 'What time is it, sister?'

Three o'clock struck. At the third stroke Fantine sat bolt upright – she who as a rule could barely move in her bed – and in a convulsive gesture joined together her two bony yellow hands, and the nun heard emerging from her chest one of those deep sighs that seem to throw off the weight of despondency. Then Fantine turned and gazed at the door.

No one came in. The door did not open.

She remained like this for a quarter of an hour, her eyes riveted on the door, motionless and as if holding her breath. The nun dared not speak to her. The clock struck a quarter-past three. Fantine sank back on her pillow.

She said nothing and began to pluck at her sheet again.

Half an hour passed, then an hour. No one came. Every time the clock struck, Fantine sat up and looked towards the door, then fell back again.

It was clear what she was thinking but she mentioned no name, made no complaint, voiced no criticism. But she coughed mournfully. It seemed as though something dark was descending on her. She was ghastly pale and her lips were blue. Occasionally she smiled.

Five o'clock struck. Then the nun heard her say very quietly and softly, 'But it's wrong of him not to come today, since I'll be gone tomorrow.'

Soeur Simplice herself was surprised at Monsieur Madeleine's delay.

In the meantime, Fantine was staring up at the canopy above her bed. She seemed to be trying to recall something. All at once she began to sing in a voice as faint as a whisper. The nun listened. This is what Fantine was singing:

> We shall buy such pretty things
> As we stroll down the avenues,
> Roses are red, cornflowers are blue,
> Cornflowers are blue, my heart is true.
>
> Yesterday the Virgin Mary by my stove
> In her embroidered mantle stood.
> You one day prayed for a child to love,
> I have it hidden beneath my veil, she said.
> Run to town and fetch some cloth,
> Buy some thread, and buy a thimble.
>
> We shall buy such pretty things
> As we stroll down the avenues.
>
> Dear Blessed Virgin, beside my stove
> I've placed a beribboned cradle.
> Though God were to give me his loveliest star
> The child you have given me is better by far.
> What's to be done with this cloth, ma'am?
> Use it to dress my new-born babe.
>
> Roses are red, cornflowers are blue,
> Cornflowers are blue, my heart is true.
>
> Wash this cloth. Where? In the stream.
> Do not spoil it, keep it clean,
> And make a pretty skirt and vest of it.
> With flowers all over I'll embroider it.
> The child's no more. What now, ma'am?
> Use it for my winding sheet.
>
> We shall buy such pretty things
> As we stroll down the avenues,
> Roses are red, cornflowers are blue,
> Cornflowers are blue, my heart is true.

This song was an old lullaby with which she once used to sing her little Cosette to sleep, and it had not come to mind in all the five years she had been parted from her child. She sang it in so sad a voice and to so sweet a tune it was enough to make even a nun cry. Inured to austerity, the sister felt a tear welling in her eye.

The clock struck six. Fantine seemed not to hear. She seemed no longer to be paying attention to anything around her.

Soeur Simplice sent a ward maid to enquire of the factory door-keeper whether the mayor had returned, and if he would not be coming up to the infirmary soon. The girl was back within a few minutes.

Fantine was still lying motionless, and seemed absorbed in her own thoughts.

The ward maid very quietly told Soeur Simplice that monsieur le maire had left before six that morning in a little tilbury harnessed to a white horse, in this cold weather, that he had gone alone without even a driver, that no one knew what road he had taken – some people said they had seen him take the turning for the road to Arras, and others insisted they had passed him on the road to Paris. That when he left he had been very mild-mannered as usual, and he had merely told the doorkeeper not to expect him back tonight.

While the two women stood whispering with their backs turned to Fantine's bed, the nun questioning, the maid surmising, Fantine, with the feverish animation of certain organic diseases that combines good health's freedom of movement with the frightful emaciation of death, had got into a kneeling position on her bed, her two clenched fists resting on the bolster; and with her head poking through the opening in the curtains, she listened.

She cried out suddenly, 'You're talking about Monsieur Madeleine! Why are you whispering? What's he doing? Why doesn't he come?'

Her voice was so abrupt and harsh, the two women thought it was a man's voice they heard. They turned round in alarm.

'Go on, answer me!' cried Fantine.

The maid stammered, 'The doorkeeper told me he couldn't come today.'

'My child,' said the nun, 'calm yourself, lie down.'

Without changing her position, Fantine continued to speak loudly and in a tone of voice at once imperious and heart-rending, 'He can't come? Why not? You know the reason. You're whispering about it to each other. I want to be told.'

The maid quickly said in the nun's ear, 'Tell her he's busy with the city council.'

Soeur Simplice flushed a little. What the maid suggested was a lie. On the other hand, it seemed clear to her that telling this sick woman the truth would surely be a terrible blow to her, and this was of serious consequence in Fantine's present state. That flush did not last long. With her calm, sad gaze the sister looked up at Fantine and said, 'Monsieur le maire has gone.'

Fantine straightened up and sat back on her heels. Her eyes sparkled. Sublime joy illuminated that tragic face.

'Gone!' she cried. 'He's gone to fetch Cosette.'

Then she raised her arms to heaven and her whole face became indescribable. Her lips moved: she was praying under her breath.

When she had finished her prayer she said, 'I'll lie down now, sister, I'll do whatever I'm asked to. I behaved badly just now, I'm sorry I shouted like that, it's very wrong to shout, I know full well, my dear sister, but you see, I am very happy. The good Lord is kind, Monsieur Madeleine is kind. Just think! He's gone to Montfermeil to fetch my little Cosette.'

She lay down again, helped the nun to arrange the pillow, and kissed the little silver cross that she wore round her neck and that Soeur Simplice had given her.

'My child,' said the nun, 'try to rest now, and don't talk any more.'

Fantine took the nun's hand in her own clammy hands, and it pained the nun to feel this sweat on her.

'He set out this morning for Paris. Actually he doesn't even need to go through Paris. Montfermeil lies a little to the left on the way here. Do you remember how he said to me yesterday, when I was talking to him about Cosette, "Soon, soon"? He wants it to be a surprise for me. You know, he made me sign a letter to get her back from the Thénardiers. They won't have any objection, will they? They'll give her back. Since they've been paid. The authorities wouldn't allow anyone to keep a child, once they've been paid off. Don't shush me, sister! I'm extremely happy. I feel very well, I'm not at all in pain now, I'm going to see Cosette again, I even feel quite hungry. It's nearly five years since I last saw her. You can't imagine, sister, how much they mean to you, children! And then she'll be so pretty, you'll see! I tell you, she has such lovely little pink fingers! For a start she'll have very beautiful hands. At the age of one she had tiny hands. Like that! She must be tall now. Seven years old, if you please. She's a young lady. I call her Cosette, but her name's Euphrasie. You know, this morning I was looking at the dust on the chimneypiece and I just had this wonderful feeling I'd be seeing Cosette again soon. God! what a mistake to go years without seeing your children! We really ought to bear in mind that life's not eternal! Oh, how kind of monsieur le maire to have gone! It's true, it's very cold! Had he his cloak, at least? He'll be here tomorrow, won't he? Tomorrow will be a day of celebration. Tomorrow morning, sister, you must remind me to put on my little cap with the lace trim. It's a village, Montfermeil. I made that journey on foot once. It was a very long way for me. But the coaches go very quickly! He'll be here tomorrow with Cosette. How far is it from here to Montfermeil?'

The sister, who had no idea of distances, replied, 'Oh, I should think he might be here by tomorrow.'

'Tomorrow! Tomorrow!' said Fantine. 'I'll see Cosette tomorrow! You see, sister, the dear Lord's dear sister, I'm not ill any more. I'm so excited. I could dance if anyone wanted.'

Whoever had seen her a quarter of an hour earlier would have been at a complete loss to understand. She was now looking quite rosy, she spoke in a bright and natural voice, her face was one big smile. Now and then she laughed, murmuring quietly to herself. Maternal joy is almost childlike joy.

'Well,' said the nun, 'now you're happy, do as I say, and no more talking.'

Fantine laid her head on the pillow and said in a subdued voice, 'Yes, lie down again, be good since you're going to be with your child again. Soeur Simplice is right. Everyone here is right.'

And then without stirring, without moving her head, she began to look all around her with eyes wide open and an expression of delight, and said not another word.

The nun closed the curtains around her, hoping she would doze off.

Between seven and eight o'clock the doctor came. Not hearing a sound, and thinking Fantine was asleep, he came in quietly and went over to her bed on tip-toe. He parted the curtains, and by the glow of the night-light he saw Fantine's big, calm eyes staring at him.

She said, 'Monsieur, she will be allowed to sleep beside me in a little bed, won't she?'

The doctor thought she was raving.

She added, 'Well, look, there's just enough room.'

The doctor took Soeur Simplice aside, and she explained the situation: that Monsieur Madeleine was away for a day or two, and without knowing for sure they thought they should not disabuse the patient, who believed monsieur le maire had gone to Montfermeil. After all, it was possible she had guessed correctly. The doctor agreed.

He returned to Fantine's bedside.

She continued, 'You see, when she wakes up in the morning, I'll say good morning to the poor little pet, and when I can't sleep at night, I'll hear her sleeping. It'll do me good, the lovely sweet sound of her breathing.'

'Give me your hand,' said the doctor.

She held out her arm and exclaimed, laughing, 'Ah, now, of course, it's true, you don't know. The thing is, I'm cured! Cosette will be here tomorrow.'

The doctor was surprised. She was better. She was breathing more easily. Her pulse was stronger. Some kind of unexpected vitality all of sudden reanimated this poor exhausted creature.

'Doctor,' she went on, 'did sister tell you that monsieur le maire has gone to fetch the little mite?'

The doctor advised silence and the avoidance of any emotional distress. He prescribed an infusion of cinchona and a calmative draught in the event of a recurrence of fever during the night.

As he was leaving he said to the nun, 'She's doing better. If by some good fortune the mayor were to turn up tomorrow with the child, who knows? There are some truly astonishing recoveries, great joys have been known to arrest illnesses. Of course I know this is an organic disease and far advanced, but it's all such a mystery! We may yet save her.'

VII
The Traveller on Arrival Makes Sure of Being Able to Leave

It was nearly eight o'clock in the evening when the cart we left en route entered the gateway of the Hôtel de la Poste in Arras. The man we have been following till now climbed down, responded in a distracted way to the eagerness of the staff at the inn to be helpful, sent back the extra horse, and personally led the little white horse to the stable. Then he pushed open the door of a billiard room on the ground floor, sat down, and rested his elbows on the table. It had taken him fourteen hours to make this journey that he had expected to complete in six. He did not blame himself, it was not his fault, but in his heart of hearts he was not sorry.

The landlady of the hotel came in.

'Is monsieur staying the night? Will monsieur be having supper?'

He shook his head.

'The groom says monsieur's horse is very tired!'

At this point he broke his silence. 'Will the horse not be able to set off again tomorrow morning?'

235

'Oh, monsieur, that horse needs at least two days' rest!'

He asked, 'Isn't this the post house?'

'Yes, monsieur.'

The landlady took him to the office. He showed his passport and enquired whether it was possible to return that same night to Montreuil-sur-Mer by the mail-coach. It so happened that the seat beside the postman was free. He booked it and paid for it.

'Monsieur,' said the clerk, 'be here without fail, ready to leave punctually at one o'clock in the morning.'

This done, he left the hotel and began to walk through the town.

He was not familiar with Arras, the streets were dark and he did not know where he was going. Yet he seemed determined not to ask directions of any passer-by. He crossed the little River Crinchon and found himself in a labyrinth of narrow lanes, where he lost his way.

A townsman was walking along with a lantern. After some hesitation he made up his mind to speak to this man, not without having first looked ahead and behind, as though afraid someone might hear the question he was about to ask.

'Monsieur,' he said, 'where are the law courts, if you please?'

'You're a stranger to the town, monsieur?' replied the gentleman, who was quite elderly. 'Well, follow me. I'm actually going in the direction of the law courts, that's to say in the direction of the prefectural building. Because the law courts are under repair at the moment, and in the meantime trials are being held at the Prefecture.'

'Is it there the assizes are held?' he asked.

'Indeed, monsieur. You see, where the Prefecture is today was the bishop's palace before the Revolution. Monsieur de Conzié, who was bishop in '82, had a great hall built there. It's in that great hall that the court sits.'

The man said to him as they walked along, 'If it's a trial that monsieur wants to watch, it's rather late. Usually the sittings end at six o'clock.'

However, when they came to the main square the man pointed out to him four long lighted windows in the façade of a huge dark building.

'Upon my word, monsieur, you're not too late, you're in luck. Do you see those four windows? That's the court of assizes. It's lit up. So it's not over. The case must have dragged on and they're having an evening hearing. Have you an interest in this case? Is it a criminal trial? Are you a witness?'

He replied, 'I haven't come for any trial, I just need to speak to a lawyer.'

'That's different,' said the man. 'Look, monsieur, that's the door there. Where the sentry's standing. You just have to go up the main staircase.'

He followed the man's directions and a few minutes later he was in a crowded hall where groups of people, along with robed lawyers, were whispering together here and there.

It is always intimidating to see these congregations of men clad in black, murmuring among themselves in low voices outside the chambers of justice. Rarely do charity or pity result from all this talk. What result more often than not are convictions decided in advance. To the passing and fanciful observer all these groups are like so many forbidding hives where buzzing spirits, of some sort or other, co-operate in the construction of all manner of sinister edifices.

This spacious hall, illuminated by a single lamp, was formerly an antechamber of the episcopal palace and now served as the waiting hall. A double-panelled door, presently closed, separated it from the main hall in which the court was sitting.

It was so ill-lit he was not afraid to address the first lawyer he encountered.

'Monsieur, what stage are they at?' he asked.

'It's over,' said the lawyer.

'Over!'

This word was repeated in such a tone of voice that the lawyer turned round.

'Forgive me, monsieur, are you perhaps a relative?'

'No. I don't know anyone here. Has sentence been passed?'

'Indeed. It was almost inevitable.'

'Penal servitude?'

'For life.'

He continued in a voice so weak it was barely audible, 'Identification was made then?'

'What identification?' replied the lawyer. 'There was no identification to be made. The case was straightforward. The woman killed her child, infanticide was proven, the jury ruled out premeditation, she was sentenced to life imprisonment.'

'Then it's a woman?' he said.

'But of course. The woman from Limoges. What is it you're talking about, then?'

'Nothing. But if it's all over, why would the hall still be lit up?'

'For the other case that began about two hours ago.'

'What other case?'

'Oh, that one's also straightforward. Some sort of ruffian, a

237

re-offender, a convicted felon, up for stealing. I don't remember quite what his name is. Now there's someone who looks like a villain! Just for having a face like that, I'd clap him in chains.'

'Monsieur, is there any chance of getting into the court room?' he said.

'I really don't think so. It's very crowded. However, the hearing's been adjourned. There were some people who came out. When the hearing resumes you could try.'

'Where's the entrance?'

'That big door over there.'

The lawyer left him. Within a few moments he had experienced every possible emotion, almost simultaneously, almost conflated. This indifferent bystander's words had pierced his heart like icicles one moment, like jets of flame the next. When he saw that nothing was over, he breathed again. But he could not have said whether it was satisfaction or pain that he felt.

He went and stood close to several groups and listened to what was being said. With a very full court roll, the presiding judge had selected for that same day two simple, straightforward cases. They had begun with the infanticide and now they were dealing with the ex-convict, the re-offender, the 'old lag'. This man had stolen some apples, though apparently this had not been proved conclusively. What had been proved was that he had already served a penal sentence at Toulon. This was what made things look bad for him. The questioning of the defendant was now ended and the witnesses had testified, but still to come was the defence counsel and public prosecutor's summing-up. It was unlikely to be over before midnight. The man would probably be found guilty. The public prosecutor was very able and did not fail to secure convictions. He was a witty fellow, who wrote verse.

An usher stood by the door leading into the assize court.

He enquired of this usher, 'Monsieur, is the door going to open soon?'

'It isn't going to open,' said the usher.

'What do you mean? Won't it open when the hearing resumes? Isn't the hearing adjourned?'

'The hearing has just resumed,' replied the usher, 'but the door's not going to open again.'

'Why not?'

'Because the court room is full.'

'What! There isn't a single seat left?'

'Not one. The door's closed. No one else can go in.'

'Of course,' the usher added after a pause, 'there are still two or

238

three places behind monsieur le président, but monsieur le président only lets public officials sit there.'

Having said this, the usher turned his back on him.

He walked away with his head bowed, crossed the antechamber, and slowly descended the staircase as though hesitating at every step. He was probably debating with himself. The violent conflict that had been raging inside him since the day before was not yet over, and at every moment he went through some new crisis. When he got to the landing halfway down the stairs he leaned back against the banister and crossed his arms. All of a sudden he opened his frock-coat, found his wallet, took out a pencil, tore out a sheet of paper, and on that sheet of paper, by the lamp-light, scribbled down this line: 'Monsieur Madeleine, mayor of Montreuil-sur-Mer'. Then he strode back upstairs, forced his way through the crowd, walked straight up to the usher, handed him the note, and said with authority, 'Take this to monsieur le président.'

The usher took the note, glanced at it, and obeyed.

VIII
Privileged Access

Though he was entirely unaware of it, the mayor of Montreuil-sur-Mer enjoyed a kind of celebrity. After seven years in which the reputation of his goodness filled the whole of Lower Boulonnais, it had eventually crossed the boundaries of a small community and spread into two or three neighbouring *départements*. Aside from the considerable service he had rendered the chief town of Montreuil-sur-Mer itself by reviving the black-glass industry, there was not one out of the one hundred and forty-one local municipalities in the *arrondissement* that did not owe some benefit to him. He had even succeeded in helping to foster where necessary the industries of other *arrondissements*. So it was that he had at one time or another supported with his credit and his funding the Boulogne tulle factory, Frévent's mechanized linen mill, and the hydraulically powered looms at Boubers-sur-Canche. Monsieur Madeleine was a name everywhere mentioned with great esteem. Arras and Douai envied the fortunate little town of Montreuil-sur-Mer its mayor.

Douai's Royal Court judge, who was presiding over this session of the assizes at Arras, was no less familiar than anyone else with this name that was so profoundly and universally respected. When the usher, discreetly opening the door that connected the council chamber with the court room, bowed behind the judge's chair and handed him the piece of paper on which was written the line we have just read, adding, 'This gentleman wishes to attend the hearing', the judge gave a deferential start, snatched up a pen, wrote a few words on the bottom of the piece of paper and returned it to the usher, saying, 'Show him in.'

The poor man whose history we are relating had remained at the door of the hall in exactly the same place and in exactly the same stance as the usher had left him. In the midst of his musings he heard someone say to him, 'Would monsieur kindly do me the honour of following me?' It was this same usher who had turned his back on him only a moment earlier and who was now bowing and scraping before him. At the same time, the usher handed him the piece of paper. He unfolded it and, happening to be near the lamp, he was able to read it.

'The Presiding Judge of the Court of Assizes presents his respects to Monsieur Madeleine.'

He crushed the paper in his hand as if these words might have had for him a strange and bitter aftertaste.

He followed the usher.

A few minutes later he found himself alone in an austere-looking panelled room, lit by two candles set on a green baize table. He could still hear the last words spoken by the usher who had just left him: 'Monsieur, you are now in the council chamber. You have only to turn the brass handle of that door and you'll find yourself in the court room behind monsieur le président's chair.' These words mingled in his thoughts with a vague memory of narrow corridors and dark staircases that he had just passed through.

The usher had left him on his own. The final moment had come. He tried to gather his thoughts, but without succeeding. It is especially at those times when they most need to be attached to the painful realities of life that the threads of thought all break in the mind. He was in the very place where the judges deliberate and reach a verdict. With a dazed tranquillity he surveyed this quiet and forbidding room where so many lives had been destroyed, where his name was soon to reverberate, and through which his fate was now taking him. He stared at the wall, then stared at himself, wondering at this chamber and wondering at his being here.

He had eaten nothing for more than twenty-four hours, he was exhausted by the jolting of the cart, but he did not feel it. It seemed to him that he did not feel anything.

He approached a black frame that hung on the wall and contained, under glass, an old autograph letter of Jean-Nicolas Pache, minister and mayor of Paris, dated, no doubt mistakenly, 9 June year II, in which Pache sent the Commune the list of ministers and deputies under house arrest. Anyone who might have seen him and observed him at that moment would probably have imagined that he found this letter very intriguing, for he did not take his eyes off it, and read it two or three times. He read it unknowingly, without paying any attention to it. He was thinking of Fantine and Cosette.

While musing, he turned round, and his eyes fell on the brass handle of the door that separated him from the assizes court room. He had almost forgotten about this door. His gaze, at first calm, settled on it, remained fastened on that brass handle, then became scared and intent, and little by little was stamped with terror.

Beads of sweat seeped through his hair and trickled down his temples. At a certain moment, with a kind of authority mixed with rebellion, he made that indescribable gesture that expresses its meaning very well: 'Damn it! Who's forcing me to do this?' Then he wheeled round, saw before him the door he had come in by, went over to it, opened it, and walked out. He was no longer in that chamber, he was outside in a corridor, a long narrow corridor, intersected with steps and passageways, turning this way and that, lighted here and there by lamps similar to the night-lights of the sick: the corridor that had brought him here. He inhaled, he listened: not a sound behind him, not a sound ahead of him. Then he fled as if he were being chased.

When he had turned several corners along this corridor he listened again. There was still the same silence and the same gloom around him. He was breathless. He was reeling. He leaned against the wall. The stone was cold. His sweat was icy on his brow. He drew himself up with a shiver.

Then, standing there alone in the darkness, trembling with cold, and something else as well perhaps, he pondered.

He had been pondering the whole night. He had been pondering the whole day. All he could hear within him now was a voice that said, 'Alas!'

A quarter of an hour went by like this. Finally he bowed his head, sighed with anguish, let his arms drop, and retraced his steps. He walked slowly and as though crushed. It was as if someone had caught up with him as he fled and was bringing him back.

He re-entered the chamber. The first thing he saw was the door knob. That round knob of polished brass shone for him like some terrible star. He stared at it as a lamb would stare into the eyes of a tiger. He could not tear his gaze away from it.

From time to time he took a step forward and moved closer to the door.

Had he listened, he might have heard the sound, a kind of vague murmur, that came from the next room. But he did not listen and he did not hear.

Without knowing how, he suddenly found himself at the door. He grabbed the knob convulsively. The door opened.

He was inside the court room.

IX
Where Convictions Take Shape

He took a step forward, unconsciously closed the door behind him, and stood there, taking stock of what he saw.

It was quite a spacious and dimly lit interior, now full of uproar, now full of silence, where all the ritual of a criminal trial was played out with shabby and dismal gravity in the midst of the crowd.

At one end of the room, the one where he was standing, listless-looking magistrates in threadbare robes, biting their fingernails or closing their eyes; at the other end, a ragged throng; lawyers striking all sorts of attitudes, soldiers with stern but honest faces, old stained wood-panelling, a dirty ceiling, tables covered with serge more yellowed than green, finger-blackened doors; on nails driven into the panelling, tap-room lamps giving off more smoke than light; on the tables, candles in brass candlesticks. Gloom, ugliness, dreariness. And all this created an austere and imposing impression, for there was a sense here of that great human thing called the law and of that great divine thing called justice.

No one in this crowd paid any attention to him. All eyes were focused on a single object, a wooden bench set against a small door in the wall to the left of the presiding judge. On this bench, illuminated by several candles, was a man sitting between two gendarmes.

This man was the man. He did not look for him. He saw him. His eyes went to him naturally as if they knew in advance where that figure was.

He thought he saw himself, aged, with not exactly the same features, to be sure, but identical in attitude and appearance, with that bristling hair, those wary brown eyes, that smock, just as he was the day he arrived at Digne, full of hatred and concealing in his heart that hideous hoard of dreadful thoughts he had spent nineteen years accumulating in the chain gang.

He said to himself with a shudder, 'God! Will I become like that again?'

This creature looked at least sixty. There was something coarse, stupid and bewildered about him.

Hearing the door open, people had moved aside to make room for him, the judge had looked round, and realizing that the individual who had just entered was the mayor of Montreuil-sur-Mer he had acknowledged him. The public prosecutor, who had seen Monsieur Madeleine at Montreuil-sur-Mer where he had been called more than once to act in his official capacity, recognized him and acknowledged him also. He barely noticed. He was in the grip of a kind of hallucination. He kept looking.

Magistrates, a clerk, gendarmes, a crowd of cruelly curious faces, he had seen this once already, in days gone by, twenty-seven years ago. These ominous things he was re-experiencing – they were here, they were astir, they existed. This was no longer an effort of memory, no mental illusion, these were real gendarmes and real magistrates, a real crowd and real men of flesh and blood. The worst had happened: he saw around him the monstrous aspects of his past, reappearing, reviving, with all the fearsomeness of reality.

All this yawned before him. He was horrified, he closed his eyes, and cried out in the deepest recesses of his soul: Never!

And by a tragic twist of fate that made all his thoughts quake and almost drove him mad, it was another incarnation of himself who sat there! The man being tried, everybody called Jean Valjean.

He had before his eyes an extraordinary vision, a kind of re-enactment of the most horrible moment of his life, played by his ghost.

It was all there: the same trappings, the same late hour, almost the same faces of magistrates, soldiers and spectators. Only, above the judge's head there was a crucifix, something that was missing from the courts at the time of his conviction. When he was tried, God was absent.

There was a chair behind him. He dropped into it, terrified at the thought that he could be seen. When he was seated he took advantage of a stack of files that lay on the magistrates' desk to conceal his face from the whole room. He could now see without being seen. Little by little he recovered. He fully regained his sense of reality. He reached that stage of composure where it is possible to listen.

Monsieur Bamatabois was one of the jurors.

He looked for Javert but did not see him. The witness bench was hidden from him by the clerk's table. And besides, as we have just said, the room was dimly lit.

When he had come in, the defendant's lawyer was just finishing his speech. Everyone's attention was as taut as could be; the trial had been going on for three hours. For three hours this crowd had been watching a man, a nobody, a miserable specimen of humanity, either extremely stupid or extremely crafty, gradually sag beneath the burden of a terrible likeness. This man, as we already know, was a vagrant who had been found in a field carrying away a branch laden with ripe apples, broken off an apple tree in a nearby orchard, called the Pierron orchard. Who was this man? An investigation had been conducted. Witnesses had just been heard, they were unanimous, some light had emerged from all the proceedings. The prosecution said, 'We have here not only a fruit thief, a petty pilferer, we have here a ruffian, a re-offender in breach of the terms of his release, an ex-convict, a most dangerous villain, a criminal named Jean Valjean, long sought by the law, and who eight years ago on leaving the prison hulks at Toulon committed highway robbery with threat of violence on the person of a Savoyard child named Petit-Gervais, a felony under Article 383 of the Penal Code, for which we reserve the right to try him subsequently when his identity has been legally established. He has now committed another theft. We're dealing here with a repeat offender. Convict him for the recent offence. He will be tried for the previous offence later.'

In the face of this charge, in the face of the unanimity of the witnesses, the accused seemed mostly surprised. He made signs and gestures of negation, or else he stared up at the ceiling. Words did not come easily to him, his replies were confused, but his whole person, from head to foot, expressed denial. He was like an idiot in the presence of all these intellects lined up around him ready to do battle, and like a stranger in the midst of this society that detained him. Yet there was for him the most ominous future at stake, one that every moment became increasingly likely, and the entire audience regarded with greater apprehension than he himself this ruinous sentence looming closer and closer. There was even a possibility of not just penal servitude, but a death sentence, to be envisaged if this identity were to be established and the Petit-Gervais incident were subsequently to lead to a conviction. What manner of man was this? What was the nature of his unconcern? Was it imbecility or craftiness? Did he understand too well or did he not understand at all? Questions that divided the crowd and seemed to set the jury at odds. There was in this trial elements of both the terrifying and the intriguing: the drama was not only dark, it was obscure.

The defence lawyer had argued his case quite well in that provincial language that has long constituted the eloquence of the bar, and which was formerly used by all lawyers, in Paris as well as at Romorantin or at Montbrison. Now become antiquated, it is today hardly spoken at all any more except by barristers in court, being suited to them by its solemn ring and majestic style. A language in which a husband is called 'a spouse', and a wife 'a consort'; Paris, 'the centre of art and civilization'; the king, 'the monarch'; Monseigneur the bishop, 'a saintly pontiff'; the public prosecutor, 'the eloquent voice of the prosecution'; the summing-up, 'the arguments we have just heard'; the age of Louis XIV, 'the great age'; a theatre, 'the temple of Melpomene'; the ruling family, 'the august dynasty of our royal sovereigns'; a concert, 'a display of musicianship'; monsieur le général, commanding officer of the *département*, 'the illustrious warrior who . . .'; seminary students, 'these young Levites'; errors imputed to newspapers, 'the deceit that distils its poison in the columns of these organs', et cetera. So the lawyer had begun by expounding on the apple theft – no easy task, in grandiose style – but Bénigne Bossuet himself was obliged in the middle of a funeral oration to allude to a chicken, and he acquitted himself magnificently. The lawyer had established the fact that the apple theft was not actually proven.

His client, whom he persisted in his capacity as defence counsel in calling Champmathieu, had not been seen, by anyone, climbing the wall or breaking off the branch. He had been apprehended in possession of that branch (which the lawyer more readily called a 'bough'), but he said he had found it on the ground and picked it up. Where was the proof to the contrary? This branch had undoubtedly been broken off and stolen after the wall had been climbed, then thrown down by the frightened thief. Undoubtedly there was a thief. But what proved that Champmathieu was that thief? One thing only: the fact that he was a convicted felon. The lawyer did not deny that, unfortunately, this fact seemed to be well established: the accused had been resident at Faverolles; the accused had been a tree-pruner there; the name of Champmathieu might well have been Jean Mathieu in origin. All this was true. After all, four witnesses without hesitation positively identified Champmathieu as the convicted felon Jean Valjean. To counter these arguments, these testimonies, the lawyer could offer only his client's denial, a self-interested denial. But supposing he was the convicted felon Jean Valjean, did that prove he was the apple thief? That was a presumption at most, not a proof. True – and 'in good faith' the defence counsel had to admit it – the prisoner had adopted 'a poor line of defence'. He persisted in denying everything, the theft and the fact that he was a convicted felon. An admission on this last point would surely have been better, and would have gained him the leniency of the bench. This was what his lawyer had advised him but the accused had obstinately refused, thinking no doubt to save everything by admitting nothing. This was wrong. But should not the paucity of his intelligence be taken into consideration? The man was obviously stupid. Interminable misery in prison, interminable hardship out of prison, had addled his wits, et cetera. He defended himself badly. Was that any reason to convict him? As for the Petit-Gervais incident, the lawyer had no need to address that. It was not relevant to this case. The lawyer concluded by entreating the court and the jury – if it seemed to them Jean Valjean's identity had been proven – to apply the legal penalties pertaining to a breach of parole and not the appalling punishment imposed on the convicted felon who re-offends.

The public prosecutor responded to the defence counsel. He was fierce and florid, as public prosecutors usually are.

He congratulated the defence counsel on his 'fairness', and skilfully exploited this fairness. With every concession made by his lawyer, he struck a blow against the defendant. The lawyer seemed to admit the defendant was Jean Valjean. He took cognizance of the fact. So this man was Jean Valjean. The point had been conceded to the prosecution and could no longer be disputed. Here, in an adroit use of a rhetorical device, in tracing back the sources and causes of crime the public prosecutor thundered against the immorality of the then budding Romantic school, referring to it as 'the satanic school', a term used by the critics of *L'Oriflamme* and *La Quotidienne*; not wholly unreasonably, he attributed to the influence of this perverse literature the crime of Champmathieu, or to be more accurate, of Jean Valjean. Having exhausted these reflections, he moved on to Jean Valjean himself. Who was this Jean Valjean? Description of Jean Valjean: a spewed-up monster, and so on. The model for descriptions of this sort is contained in Théramène's speech, which is of no use to tragedy but every day renders great service to judicial eloquence. The court and the jury 'shuddered'. His description concluded, the public prosecutor went on with an oratorial flourish calculated to excite the utmost enthusiasm in next morning's *Journal de la Préfecture*:

'And it is such a man – a vagrant, a beggar, with no means of existence . . . inured by a life of crime and little reformed by his sentence of penal servitude, as proved by the offence committed against Petit-Gervais . . . caught red-handed on the public highway, committing theft, a few paces from a scaled wall, still clutching the stolen object – it is such a man who denies the obvious crime, the theft, the climbing of the wall, denies everything, denies even his own name, denies his identity! In addition to countless other proofs that we shall not hark back to, four witnesses recognize him – Javert, the upright inspector of police

Javert, and three of his former companions in ignominy, the convicts Brevet, Chenildieu and Cochepaille. How does he counter this damning unanimity? With denial. What a hardened criminal! You will deal justly, gentlemen of the jury . . .'

While the public prosecutor spoke, the accused listened open-mouthed with a kind of amazement in which there was a considerable element of admiration. He was obviously surprised that a man should be capable of talking like this. From time to time, at the most vigorous moments of the prosecutor's indictment, at those moments when eloquence, unable to contain itself, spills over in a flood of withering epithets and invests the accused like a storm, he slowly moved his head from left to right and from right to left, a sad and silent form of protest with which he had contented himself since the start of the proceedings.

Two or three times the spectators seated nearest to him heard him say to himself, 'This is what comes of not having asked Monsieur Baloup.' The public prosecutor directed the attention of the jury to this vacant attitude, which was obviously calculated and an indication not of imbecility but of guile, cunning, the habit of eluding justice, and revealing in all its clarity the 'profound perversity' of this man. He concluded by reserving the right to press charges relating to the Petit-Gervais incident and demanding a harsh sentence.

This was, for the time being, remember, penal servitude for life.

The defence counsel rose, began by complimenting 'monsieur l'avocat-général' on his 'admirable speech', then responded as best he could, but he was weakening. The ground was evidently being cut from under him.

X

Systematic Denials

It was time to bring the proceedings to a close. The presiding judge asked the defendant to rise and put the customary question to him, 'Have you anything to add to your defence?'

Standing there, twisting a hideous cap that he had in his hands, the man apparently did not hear. The judge repeated the question.

This time the man heard. He seemed to understand, he stirred like someone waking up, looked round, stared at the public, the gendarmes, his lawyer, the jury, the court, placed his huge fist on the edge of the wood panelling in front of his bench, looked round again, and fixing his eyes on the public prosecutor all of a sudden he began to speak. It was like an eruption. From the way in which the words burst from his mouth – incoherent, impetuous, jumbled, pell-mell – it sounded as though they were all rushing to get out at the same time.

He said, 'I have this to say. That I was a cartwright in Paris, in fact it was with Monsieur Baloup. It's a hard occupation. As a cartwright you're always working in the open air, in courtyards – under open sheds, with good masters – never in closed workshops, because you need space, you see. In winter you get so cold you slap your arms to get warmed up. But the masters are against that, they say it's time-wasting. It's punishing handling iron when there's ice between the paving-stones. It wears a man down fast. You get old very young in that trade. At forty years old a man's finished. I was fifty-three, I found it really hard. And then, workmen, they're so cruel! When a fellow isn't young any more they're always calling him an old fool, an old idiot! I was earning no more than thirty sous a day, the masters took advantage of my age, they paid me as little as they could. Besides that, I had my daughter working as a washerwoman at the river. She earned a bit as well. With the two of us, we managed. It was hard for her too. Up to her waist in a tub all day long, in the rain, and the snow, with the wind cutting into your face when it's freezing, it makes no difference, the washing still has to be done. There are people who haven't much linen and need to have it back. If you didn't do the washing you'd lose customers. The planks are badly joined and you get drops of water falling all over you. Your skirts and petticoats are all wet, you get soaked right through. She also worked at the Enfants-Rouges laundry-house where the water comes out of taps. You're not standing in the tub there. You do your washing at the tap in front of you and rinse in the basin behind you. As it's closed in, you're not so cold. But there's the steam from the hot water that's terrible and ruins your eyes. She used to get home at seven in the evening and went to bed very soon after, she was so tired. Her husband used to beat her. She died. We've not been very lucky. She was a good girl, didn't go out dancing, very steady. I remember one Mardi Gras when she went to bed at eight o'clock. There. I'm telling the truth. Ask anybody. Oh, of course, you may well ask! How stupid of me! Paris is an abyss. Who's ever heard of Père Champmathieu? But I tell you, there's Monsieur Baloup. Go and look up Monsieur Baloup. I don't know what more you want of me.'

The man fell silent and just stood there. He had said all this in a loud, rapid, raw, harsh, hoarse voice with a kind of cross and primitive ingenuousness. Once, he broke off to greet someone in the crowd. The statements, such as they were, that he seemed to toss out at random erupted from him like hiccups, and to each of them he added the gesture of a woodcutter splitting wood. When he had finished, the audience burst out laughing. He stared at the public, and seeing everyone laughing and not understanding why, he began to laugh himself.

It was sinister.

The presiding judge, a scrupulous and well-meaning man, raised his voice. He reminded 'members of the jury' that 'the gentleman by the name of Baloup', the former master-wheelwright the accused claimed to have worked for, had been cited to no purpose. He had gone bankrupt and was not to be found.

Then, turning to the accused, he urged him to listen to what he was about to say, adding, 'You are in a situation in which you need to think carefully. The most serious allegations are hanging over you and could entail consequences of the utmost gravity. Prisoner at the bar, for one last time, in your own interest I call on you to explain yourself clearly on two points. First, did you climb over the wall of the Pierron orchard, break off the branch and steal the apples, that is to say, commit the crime of theft aggravated by trepass, yes or no? Second, are you the freed convicted felon Jean Valjean, yes or no?'

The accused shook his head with a capable air, like a man who has well understood and knows what he is going to reply. He opened his mouth, turned to the presiding judge, and said, 'First of all—'

Then he stared at his cap, stared at the ceiling and remained silent.

'Prisoner at the bar,' said the public prosecutor in a stern voice, 'beware. You do not reply to anything you are asked. Your confusion condemns you. It is obvious that your name is not Champmathieu, that you are the convicted felon Jean Valjean originally hiding under the name of Jean Mathieu, which was his mother's name, that you went to the Auvergne, that you were born at Faverolles where you were a tree-pruner. It is obvious that you have trespassed and stolen ripe apples from the Pierron orchard. The gentlemen of the jury will reach the same conclusion.'

The accused had eventually sat down again. He leapt up when the public prosecutor had finished, and shouted, 'You're very wicked, you are! This is what I wanted to say. It didn't come to me at first. I haven't stolen anything. I'm a man that doesn't eat every day. I was coming from Ailly. I was walking across country after a downpour that had made the whole countryside yellow, even the ponds had flooded, and there were just little blades of grass sticking out of the grit by the roadside. I found a broken branch lying on the ground, with apples on it, I picked up the branch without knowing it would get me into trouble. It's three months now I've been in prison and getting pushed around. More than that, I can't say. People speak out against me, they tell me, "Answer!" The gendarme, who's a decent lad, nudges my elbow and whispers to me, "Go on, answer!" I'm no good with words, I didn't go to school, I'm a poor man. That's where people are making a mistake, in not understanding that. I didn't steal, I picked up things that were lying on the ground. You say, Jean Valjean, Jean Mathieu! I don't know these people. They're country folk. I worked for Monsieur Baloup, Boulevard de l'Hôpital. My name is Champmathieu. It's very clever of you to tell me where I was born. I don't know myself. It's not everybody has a house to live in when they come into the world. That would be too easy. I think my father and mother were travelling people. I don't actually know. When I was a child I was called Lad, now I'm called Old Man. Those are my Christian names. Make of that what you will. I was in the Auvergne, I was at Faverolles, by God. Well? Can't a man have been in the Auvergne and at Faverolles without having been in a chain gang? I tell you, I didn't steal, and I'm Père Champmathieu. I worked for Monsieur Baloup, that was my fixed abode. I'm beginning to get tired of this nonsense of yours! Why are other people hounding me like this?'

The public prosecutor had remained standing. He addressed the presiding judge: 'Monsieur le président, in view of the confused but extremely crafty denials of the accused, who would like to pass himself off as an idiot but will not succeed in so doing, we give him warning of this – if it please you and if it please the court, we request that the convicts Brevet, Cochepaille and Chenildieu, and Police Inspector Javert, be recalled and questioned one last time with regard to their identification of the prisoner as the convicted felon Jean Valjean.'

The judge said, 'I draw monsieur l'avocat général's attention to the fact that Police Inspector Javert, recalled by his duties to the chief town of a neighbouring *arrondissement*, left the court room, indeed left town, as soon as he had made his statement. We gave him permission to do so with the consent of both monsieur l'avocat général and the defence counsel.'

'Quite so, monsieur le président,' replied the public prosecutor. 'In the absence of Monsieur Javert, I believe it to be incumbent on me to remind the gentlemen of the jury of what he said in this very place a few hours ago. Javert is a respected man who by his unrelenting and rigorous integrity does credit to lesser but important duties. His statement was made in these terms: "I have no need even of any of the moral arguments and material evidence that contradict the denials of the accused. I recognize him full well. This man's name is not Champmathieu. He is a very wicked and very dangerous ex-convict named

Jean Valjean. He was released at the end of his sentence only with extreme misgivings. He served nineteen years of hard labour for aggravated theft. He attempted to escape five or six times. Besides the Petit-Gervais robbery and the Pierron theft, I also suspect him of a theft committed at the home of His Grace the late bishop of Digne. I often saw him during the time I was assistant warder of the chain gangs at Toulon. I repeat, I recognize him full well." '

This very emphatic statement appeared to make a strong impression on the public and on the jury. The public prosecutor concluded by insisting that despite the absence of Javert the three witnesses Brevet, Chenildieu and Cochepaille should be heard again and formally questioned.

The judge conveyed an order to an usher, and a moment later the door to the witnesses' room opened. Accompanied by a gendarme ready to lend armed assistance, the usher led in the convict Brevet. The court was on tenterhooks, and all hearts were beating as one.

The ex-convict Brevet wore the black and grey jacket of the *maison centrale* prisons*. Brevet was a person of some sixty years of age, who had a kind of businessman's face and the air of a crook. The two sometimes go together. In the prison where his fresh misdeeds had brought him, he had become something in the nature of a turn-key. He was a man of whom his superiors said, 'He tries to make himself useful.' The chaplains testified favourably as to his religious observances. It must not be forgotten, this was happening during the Restoration.

'Brevet,' said the presiding judge, 'as a convicted felon, you have lost your civil rights and you cannot take the oath.'

Brevet lowered his gaze.

'Nevertheless,' the judge went on, 'if divine mercy be so willing, even in the man whom the law has stripped of his civil rights there may remain a sense of honour and of justice. It is to this sense that I appeal at this critical hour. If it still exists in you, and I hope it does, reflect before you answer. Consider on the one hand this man: a word from you may ruin him; on the other hand, justice: a word from you may enlighten it. This is a solemn moment, and there is still time to retract if you think you were mistaken. Prisoner at the bar, rise. Brevet, take a good look at the accused, summon up your memories and tell us in all good faith if you persist in recognizing this man as your former fellow convict, Jean Valjean.'

---

* Detention centres for long-term prisoners not condemned to penal servitude.

Brevet looked at the accused, then turned to the court.

'Yes, monsieur le président. It was I who first recognized him, and I do persist. That man is Jean Valjean. Who came to Toulon in 1796 and left in 1815. I left a year later. He has the air of a dolt now, so it must be age that has dulled him. He was cunning in prison. I recognize him without the shadow of a doubt.'

'Go and sit down,' said the judge. 'Prisoner at the bar, remain standing.'

A convict serving a life sentence of hard labour, as indicated by his red tunic and green cap, Chenildieu was brought in. He was serving his sentence in the prison hulks at Toulon, from where he had been plucked for this trial. He was a small man of about fifty, alert, wrinkled, puny, yellow, brazen, excitable, who had a kind of sickly feebleness in his every limb and about his whole person, and an immense forcefulness in his gaze. His companions in the prison hulks had nicknamed him 'Je-nie-Dieu'*.

The judge said to him more or less what he had said to Brevet. At the point when he reminded him that his criminal status deprived him of the right to take an oath, Chenildieu looked up and stared directly at the crowd. The judge invited him to think carefully, and asked him as he had asked Brevet if he persisted in recognizing the prisoner.

Chenildieu burst out laughing.

'By God! Do I recognize him! We were chained together for five years. Afraid of what's coming to you, old boy?'

'Go and sit down,' said the judge.

The usher brought in Cochepaille. This other lifer, who like Chenildieu came from the prison hulks and was dressed in red, was a peasant from Lourdes, a bear-man of the Pyrenees. He had guarded flocks in the mountains, and from being a shepherd he had slipped into brigandage. Cochepaille was no less primitive and seemed even more stupid than the accused. He was one of those unfortunate men that nature rough-casts as wild beasts and society finishes off as convicted felons.

The presiding judge tried to inspire him with some solemn and stirring words, and asked him as he had asked the other two if he persisted in recognizing unhesitatingly and unequivocally the man standing before him.

'That is Jean Valjean,' said Cochepaille. 'Indeed, he was called Jean-le-Cric because he was so strong.'

* 'I deny God'. In French this sounds very similar to his name, Chenildieu.

Each of these statements from these three men, evidently sincere and made in good faith, had raised in the audience a murmur that boded ill for the accused, a murmur that grew louder and lasted longer each time a fresh declaration was added to the previous one. The accused, meanwhile, had listened to them with that amazement on his face that according to the prosecution was his main method of defence. At the first declaration, the gendarmes next to him had heard him mutter under his breath, 'Well, he's a fine one!' After the second, he said a little louder with an almost satisfied air, 'Right!' At the third, he cried, 'Terrific!'

The presiding judge addressed him. 'Prisoner at the bar, you have heard these men. What have you to say?'

He replied, 'I say: Terrific!'

A clamour broke out in the public gallery and almost spread to the jury. It was obvious the man was doomed.

'Ushers,' said the judge, 'call for silence. I am going to close the proceedings.'

At that moment there was a stir very close to the judge. A voice was heard to cry out, 'Brevet! Chenildieu! Cochepaille! Look over here!'

All who heard that voice felt chilled, so mournful and terrible was it. All eyes turned to the place it came from. A man who had been among the privileged spectators seated behind the bench had just got to his feet, pushed open the breast-high door that separated the bench from the floor of the court, and was standing in the middle of the chamber.

The judge, the public prosecutor, Monsieur Bamatabois, two dozen people recognized him and cried out in unison, 'Monsieur Madeleine!'

XI
Champmathieu Is Ever More Amazed

He it was indeed. The clerk's lamp lit his face. He held his hat in his hand, there was no disarray in his clothing, his frock-coat was carefully buttoned. He was very pale and slightly trembling. His hair, still grey when he arrived in Arras, was now completely white. It had turned white during the hour he had been there.

All heads were raised. The sensation caused was indescribable. There was a momentary uncertainty in the court. The voice had been so harrowing. The man who stood there appeared so calm that at first people did not understand. They wondered who had cried out. They could not believe it was this unruffled man who had uttered that ghastly cry.

This uncertainty lasted only a few seconds. Even before the judge and the public prosecutor could utter a word, before the ushers and the gendarmes could make a move, the man whom all at that moment still called Monsieur Madeleine stepped towards the witnesses Cochepaille, Brevet and Chenildieu.

'You don't recognize me?' he said.

All three remained dumbfounded and indicated by a shake of the head that they did not know him. Feeling intimidated, Cochepaille gave a military salute.

Monsieur Madeleine turned to the jury and the court, and said in a quiet voice, 'Gentlemen of the jury, let the defendant go free! Monsieur le président, have me arrested. That is not the man you seek. I am. I am Jean Valjean.'

Not a soul breathed. After the initial hubbub of amazement a sepulchral silence followed. In the court room there was a feeling of that kind of religious terror that grips the masses when something of great magnitude occurs.

Meanwhile, the face of the judge filled with sympathy and sadness. He had exchanged a rapid nod with the public prosecutor and a few words in a low voice with the legal counsellors. He turned to the public and asked in a tone that was understood by all, 'Is there a doctor present?'

The public prosecutor then spoke. 'Gentlemen of the jury, strange and unexpected as it is, the incident that disrupts this hearing only inspires us, as it does you, with a sentiment we need not put into words. You are all familiar, by reputation at least, with the honourable Monsieur Madeleine, mayor of Montreuil-sur-Mer. If there is a doctor in the court room, we join monsieur le président in asking him to be good enough to attend to Monsieur Madeleine and take him home.'

Monsieur Madeleine did not allow the public prosecutor to finish. He interrupted him in a tone full of indulgence and authority. These are the words he used, exactly as they were written down immediately after the trial by one of the witnesses of this scene, and as they now ring in the ears of those who heard them nearly forty years ago today:

'Thank you, monsieur l'avocat général, but I am not mad. You shall see. You were on the point of committing a grave mistake. Release that man. I'm doing what I have to. I am that wretched felon. I'm the only one here who understands the situation clearly, and I'm telling you the truth. What I'm doing at this moment God is watching from above, and that's enough. You can take me into custody, here I am. Yet I did the best I could. I hid behind an assumed name. I became rich. I became mayor. I wanted to return among honest folk. It seems that cannot be.

Anyway, there are many things I can't express, I'm not going to tell the story of my life, one day it will become known. I robbed Monseigneur l'évêque, that's true; I robbed Petit-Gervais, that's true. What you were told was right, Jean Valjean is a very wicked wretch. It may not have been entirely his fault. Listen, messieurs les juges, a man who has sunk as low as I is in no position to chide providence or to give advice to society, but you see, the infamy from which I tried to escape is a harmful thing. Harsh prisons make hardened criminals. Reflect on that, if you will. Before I was in the prison hulks I was a poor peasant and not very bright, something of a dolt. The prison hulks changed me. I was stupid, I became wicked. I was a blockhead, I became a firebrand. Later on, kindness and goodness saved me, as harshness had been the ruin of me. But, forgive me, you can't understand what I'm saying. You'll find at my house among the ashes in the fireplace the forty-sou coin I stole from Petit-Gervais seven years ago. I've nothing more to add. Arrest me. My God! Monsieur l'avocat général shakes his head. Monsieur Madeleine has taken leave of his senses, you say! You don't believe me! Now that's distressing. Don't convict this man, at least! What! These men don't recognize me! I wish Javert were here. He would certainly recognize me.'

Nothing could convey what sombre and kindly melancholy marked the tone of voice that accompanied these words.

He turned to the three convicts and said, 'Well, I recognize you. Brevet! Do you remember—'

He paused, hesitated for a moment, and said, 'Do you* remember those chequered knitted braces you had in the prison hulks?'

Brevet gave, as it were, a start of surprise, and looked him up and down in a fearful manner.

He went on: 'Chenildieu, who gave yourself the nickname "Je-nie-Dieu", the whole of your right shoulder is badly burned because one day you lay with your shoulder on a chafing-dish full of hot coals in order to efface the three letters TFP†, which for all that are still visible. Answer, is this true?'

'It is true,' said Chenildieu.

---

* Having started to address Brevet as 'vous', Monsieur Madeleine pauses, then continues to address the convicts individually as 'tu', underlining his close association with them.
† A practice abolished in 1792 but reinstated under Article 20 of the Penal Code of 1810, convicted criminals condemned to penal servitude were to be branded on the right shoulder with the letter T (for *travaux forcés*) for a limited sentence and TP for a life sentence (*à perpétuité*), and the letter F was to be added in cases where counterfeiting or forgery (*le faux*) was involved.

He turned to Cochepaille. 'Cochepaille, near the crook of your left arm you have a date in blue letters burned into your flesh with gunpowder. That date is the day the emperor landed at Cannes, the first of March 1815. Pull up your sleeve!'

Cochepaille pulled up his sleeve, all eyes around him focused on his bare arm. A gendarme held a lamp to it. There was the date.

The poor man turned to the spectators and the judges with a smile that when they think of it still grieves those who saw it. It was the smile of triumph, it was also the smile of despair.

'You can see now,' he said, 'that I am Jean Valjean.'

In that court room there were no longer judges, prosecutors or gendarmes. There were only riveted gazes and aching hearts. No one was mindful any longer of the role that each might have to play. The public prosecutor forgot he was there to seek a conviction, the presiding judge that he was there to preside, the defence counsel that he was there to defend. Remarkably, no question was asked, no authority intervened. It is in the nature of sublime spectacles that they capture all souls and turn all witnesses into spectators. Probably no one could have explained what he felt. Probably no one said to himself that he saw a great light shining there. Inwardly all felt dazzled.

It was obvious they had Jean Valjean before their eyes. It was radiantly clear. The appearance of this man was enough to bring abounding light to this affair that but a moment earlier had been so obscure. Without any further explanation being necessary, as if by a kind of electric exposure, this whole crowd understood immediately and at a single glance the simple and magnificent story of a man who was giving himself up so that another man might not be condemned in his place. The details, the waverings, the small resistances there might have been, disappeared in that immense luminous fact.

A fleeting impression, but overwhelming at the time.

'I don't want to disturb the hearing any further,' said Jean Valjean. 'I'm going, since no one's arresting me. I have several things to do. The public prosecutor knows who I am, he knows where I'm going, he can have me arrested when he pleases.'

He made his way towards the door. Not a voice was raised, not an arm extended to prevent him. Everyone stood aside. There was at that moment something divine about him, something that causes multitudes to fall back and make way for one man. He walked through the crowd slowly. It was never known who opened the door but it is certain the door was open when he reached it.

At the door he turned and said, 'Monsieur l'avocat général, I remain at your disposal.'

Then he addressed the assembly. 'All of you here, you all think I am to be pitied, don't you? My God! When I think of what I was about to do, I think I'm to be envied. All the same, I would rather that none of this had happened.'

He went out, and the door closed behind him as it had been opened, for those who do certain majestic things are always sure of being served by someone in the crowd.

Less than an hour later the jury's verdict cleared the man named Champmathieu of all charges. And Champmathieu, immediately released, went away astounded, thinking all men were crazy and understanding nothing of what he had seen.

BOOK EIGHT
AFTER-EFFECT

I

The Mirror in Which Monsieur Madeleine Sees His Hair

It was beginning to grow light. Fantine had had a feverish and sleepless night, and one full of happy visions. At dawn she fell asleep. Soeur Simplice, who had sat up with her, took advantage of this sleep to go and prepare another dose of cinchona. The worthy nun had been in the infirmary's laboratory a few moments, bent over her drugs and phials and peering closely because of the indistinctness the dawning light imparts to objects. Suddenly she looked round and gave a little cry. Monsieur Madeleine stood before her. He had just entered silently.

'It's you, monsieur le maire!' she exclaimed.

He responded quietly, 'How is that poor woman?'

'Not so bad right now. But we have been very worried, believe me!'

She explained to him what had happened, that Fantine had been very poorly the day before, and that she was better now because she thought that monsieur le maire had gone to Montfermeil to fetch her child. The nun dared not question monsieur le maire, but from the way he looked she could see quite clearly that was not where he had come from.

'That's just as good,' he said. 'You were quite right not to disillusion her.'

'Yes,' replied the nun, 'but now, monsieur le maire, she's going to see you and she won't see her child. What shall we tell her?'

He remained pensive for a moment. 'God will inspire us,' he said.

'We wouldn't be able to lie, though,' the nun murmured quietly.

It had grown fully light in the room. And the light fell on Monsieur Madeleine's face, opposite her. The nun happened to look up.

'My goodness, monsieur!' she exclaimed. 'Whatever has happened to you? Your hair's completely white!'

'White!' he said.

Soeur Simplice had no looking-glass. She rummaged in a box and pulled out the little mirror the infirmary doctor used to check that a patient was dead and no longer breathing. Monsieur Madeleine took the mirror, looked at his hair, and said, 'Well now!'

He uttered this with indifference and as though he were thinking of something else.

The nun felt chilled by something unknown that she vaguely sensed in all this.

'Can I see her?' he asked.

'Will monsieur le maire not have her child fetched?' said the nun, hardly daring to hazard a question.

'Of course, but it will take two or three days at least.'

'If she were not to see monsieur le maire between now and then,' the nun went on timidly, 'she wouldn't know that monsieur le maire had returned, it would be easy to urge her to have patience, and when the child arrived she would naturally think monsieur le maire came with the child. We wouldn't have to tell any lies.'

Monsieur Madeleine seemed to reflect for a few moments, then with his calm gravity he said, 'No, sister, I must see her. I may not have much time.'

The nun seemed not to notice the words 'may not', which gave an obscure and peculiar connotation to monsieur le maire's words. Lowering her gaze and her voice respectfully, she replied, 'In that case, she's resting, but monsieur le maire may enter.'

He made some comment about a door that did not close properly, whose noise might wake the patient, then entered Fantine's room, went over to the bed and drew the curtains aside. She was asleep. Her breath issued from her chest with that tragic sound characteristic of these illnesses, one that breaks poor mothers' hearts when they sit up at night with their doomed and sleeping child. But this laboured breathing hardly disturbed a kind of ineffable serenity that suffused her face, transfiguring her in her sleep. Her wanness had become a whiteness, her cheeks were crimson. Her long fair eyelashes, sole remnant of the beauty of her virginal youth, fluttered though remaining lowered and closed. Her whole being trembled with some suggested unfolding of wings about to spread and carry her away, wings whose quivering could be sensed though not seen. Seeing her like this, no one would ever have believed this was a sick person at death's door. She looked more like something about to fly away than to die.

The branch thrills when a hand approaches it to pick a flower, and seems at once to draw back and to offer itself. The human body has something of this thrill at that moment when the mysterious fingers of Death are about to pluck the soul.

Monsieur Madeleine remained for some time motionless beside that bed, gazing in turn at the sick woman and at the crucifix as he had done two months earlier, the day he came to see her for the first time in this hospital. They were both still there in the same attitudes – she sleeping, he praying. Only now, after those two months had passed, her hair was grey and his was white.

The nun had not entered the room with him. He stood beside the bed with his finger to his lips as though there were someone in the room to hush.

She opened her eyes, saw him, and said calmly with a smile, 'And Cosette?'

II
Fantine Happy

She gave no start of surprise or expression of joy. She was joy itself. That simple question 'And Cosette?' was put with such profound faith, such certainty, such a complete absence of anxiety and doubt, he was left speechless.

She went on, 'I knew you were here. I was asleep but I was watching you. I've been watching you for a long time. My eyes have been following you all night. You were in a halo of light and you had all kinds of heavenly figures around you.'

He looked up at the crucifix.

'But tell me now,' she said, 'where's Cosette? Why didn't you put her on my bed to be there when I woke up?'

Responding instinctively, he gave some reply he was never afterwards able to recall. Fortunately, having been told of his arrival, the doctor had turned up. He came to Monsieur Madeleine's aid.

'My child,' said the doctor, 'calm yourself. Your child is here.'

Fantine's eyes lit up, brightening her whole face. She clasped her hands with an expression containing at once all the most violent and most tender feelings of which entreaty is capable.

'Oh!' she exclaimed, 'bring me my little baby!'

A mother's pathetic delusion! For her Cosette was still a babe-in-arms.

'Not yet,' said the doctor, 'not right now. You still have a lingering fever. Seeing your child would excite you and be bad for you. You must get better first.'

She interrupted him vehemently, 'But I am better! I tell you I am better! Is he a fool, this doctor? Honestly! I want to see my child!'

'You see how worked up you're getting,' said the doctor. 'So long as you're like this I won't allow you to have your child. It isn't enough to see her, you have to live for her. When you behave sensibly I'll bring her to you myself.'

The poor mother bowed her head. 'I'm sorry, doctor, I'm truly sorry. In the past I would never have spoken the way I did just now. I've suffered so many setbacks I don't know what I'm saying sometimes. I understand, you're afraid of it being too much for me. I'll wait as long as you like but I swear to you it wouldn't have done me any harm to see my daughter. I can see her, I've not taken my eyes off her since yesterday evening. You know, if she were brought to me now I'd just talk to her quietly. That's all. Isn't it perfectly natural I should want to see my child that someone's gone specially to fetch from Montfermeil? I'm not angry. I know I'm going to be happy. All through the night I saw these white things and people smiling at me. The doctor will bring my Cosette to me when he wants to. I haven't any fever because I'm better now. I feel sure there's nothing at all the matter with me any more, but just to please these good women I'm going to behave as if I were ill and lie still. Once they see I'm quite calm, they'll say, "She must be allowed to have her child."'

Monsieur Madeleine sat on a chair beside the bed. She turned to him, visibly striving to appear calm and 'well behaved', as she put it, in that state of weakness resembling infancy to which she was reduced by illness, so that, seeing she was so quiet, there would be no objection to having Cosette brought to her. However, even as she held herself in check, she could not help asking Monsieur Madeleine countless questions.

'Did you have a good journey, monsieur le maire? Oh, how kind of you to go and fetch her for me! Just tell me how she is. Was the travelling not too much for her? Oh dear! she won't recognize me. After all this time she'll have forgotten me, poor little mite! Children don't remember. They're like birds. They see one thing today and another thing tomorrow, and they don't remember anything. Did she have some clean clothes at least? Did those Thénardiers look after her properly? How did they feed her? Oh, if you only knew how much I've suffered wondering about all these things during the bad times I've had. That's in the past now! I'm overjoyed! Oh, how I should like to see her! Monsieur le maire, did you find her pretty? Isn't she beautiful, my daughter? You must have been very cold in that coach! Couldn't she be brought to me just for a moment? They could take her away straight after. You tell them! Being the mayor, you could if you wanted to!'

He took her hand. 'Cosette is beautiful,' he said, 'Cosette is in good health. You'll see her soon. But calm down. You're getting too excited, and besides you're not keeping your arms covered and that's making you cough.'

Indeed, fits of coughing interrupted Fantine at almost every word.

Fantine did not grumble, she was afraid of having jeopardized with a few over-impassioned complaints the trust she wanted to inspire, and she started prattling.

'Montfermeil's quite pretty, isn't it? People go there on outings in the summer. Do those Thénardiers do good business? Not many people pass through their part of the world. It's a bit run-down, that inn of theirs.'

Monsieur Madeleine was still holding her hand and observing her with anxiety. It was evident he had come to tell her things he was now in two minds about mentioning. His visit over, the doctor had left. Soeur Simplice remained alone with them.

But in the midst of this pause Fantine exclaimed, 'I can hear her! My God, I can hear her!'

She stretched out her arm to stop them talking, held her breath, and began to listen, enraptured.

There was a child playing in the yard, the child of the doorkeeper or one of the women workers. It was one of those coincidences you keep coming across that seem to form part of the mysterious staging of woeful events. The child, a little girl, was running to and fro to keep warm, laughing, singing at the top of her voice. Children's games get mixed up with everything else, more's the pity! It was this little girl that Fantine heard singing.

'Oh!' she said. 'It's my Cosette! I recognize her voice.'

Then the child was off again, and her voice died away.

Fantine listened for a while longer, then her face clouded over, and Monsieur Madeleine heard her say quietly, 'How cruel that doctor is not to let me see my daughter! He has a nasty face, that man.'

But the underlying gladness of her thoughts came to the surface again. With her head resting on the pillow, she continued to talk to herself.

'How happy we're going to be! For a start, we'll have a little garden. Monsieur Madeleine promised me. My daughter will play in the garden. She must have learned her letters by now. I'll teach her to spell. She'll run through the grass chasing butterflies. I'll watch her. Then she'll make her first communion. Now let's see, when will she make her first communion?'

She began to count on her fingers. 'One, two, three, four . . . she's seven years old. In five years' time. She'll have a white veil and lace stockings. She'll look like a little lady. Oh my dear sister, you don't know how foolish I am, I was just thinking of my daughter's first communion!' And she started laughing.

He had let go of Fantine's hand. He listened to these words as if listening to the wind blowing, with his eyes on the ground, his mind deep in fathomless thoughts. All at once she stopped talking and this automatically made him raise his head. Fantine now looked ghastly.

She did not speak, she did not breathe. She was half sitting up. Her thin shoulder emerged from her nightdress. Her face, radiant the moment before, was deathly pale, and with eyes widened in terror she seemed to be staring at something appalling in front of her on the other side of the room.

'My God!' he exclaimed. 'Fantine, what's wrong?'

She did not reply. She did not take her eyes off whatever it was she thought she saw. She touched his arm with one hand and with the other pointed behind him.

He turned and saw Javert.

III
Javert Satisfied

This is what had happened.

Half-past midnight had just struck when Monsieur Madeleine left the court of assizes in Arras. He returned to his inn just in time to set out again by the mail-coach, in which it will be remembered he had reserved his seat. A little before six in the morning he had arrived at Montreuil-sur-Mer, and his first concern had been to drop his letter to Monsieur Laffitte in the post, then go to the infirmary and see Fantine.

However, he had hardly left the court room when the public prosecutor, recovering from his initial shock, had taken the floor to deplore the honourable mayor of Montreuil-sur-Mer's act of insanity, to declare that his own convictions were in no way altered by this bizarre incident that would later be elucidated, and to demand in the meantime the conviction of this Champmathieu, clearly the real Jean Valjean. The public prosecutor's persistence was obviously at odds with everyone else's feeling, that of the public, the court and the jury. The defence counsel had little difficulty in refuting this argument and establishing that the revelations made by Monsieur Madeleine, that is to say, by the real Jean Valjean, put a completely different complexion on the case, and all that the jury now had standing before them was an innocent man. The lawyer had drawn from this a few sententious and unfortunately not unfamiliar conclusions regarding judicial errors, and suchlike. The presiding judge in his summing up had aligned himself with the defence counsel, and within a few minutes the jury had cleared Champmathieu of any wrong-doing.

Nevertheless, the public prosecutor had to have a Jean Valjean, and not having Champmathieu any more, he took Madeleine.

Immediately after Champmathieu had been released, the public prosecutor closeted himself with the presiding judge. They conferred 'as to the necessity of the taking into custody of the person of monsieur le maire of Montreuil-sur-Mer'. This phrase, in which there were a great many 'of's, was monsieur l'avocat général's, penned entirely by the public prosecutor in his report to the public prosecutor-in-chief. His initial sympathy having dissipated, the presiding judge raised few objections. After all, justice must take its course. And then, all things considered, although the judge was a decent and fairly intelligent man, he was at the same time a strong and almost ardent royalist and had been shocked to hear the mayor of Montreuil-sur-Mer refer to 'the emperor' and not 'Bonaparte' when speaking of the landing at Cannes.

The arrest warrant was accordingly issued. The public prosecutor sent it by special messenger, riding as fast as he could go, to Montreuil-sur-Mer, instructing Police Inspector Javert to implement it.

As we know, Javert had returned to Montreuil-sur-Mer immediately after having made his statement.

Javert was just getting up when the messenger delivered the arrest warrant and summons. The messenger was also a very capable policeman, who succinctly informed Javert of what had taken place at Arras. The arrest warrant, signed by the public prosecutor, was worded as follows: 'Inspector Javert will arrest Sieur Madeleine, mayor of Montreuil-sur-Mer, who in this day's court hearing was identified as the convicted felon freed on parole, Jean Valjean.'

Anyone who did not know Javert and had seen him as he came through the entrance hall to the infirmary could have had no idea of what was going on and would have thought he was just his usual self. He was cold, calm, serious, his grey hair perfectly smooth over his temples, and he had just climbed the stairs with his usual deliberation. Anyone who knew him well and observed him closely would have quaked. Instead of being at the nape of his neck, the buckle on his leather collar was below his left ear. This betrayed unprecedented agitation.

Javert was a consistent character, allowing no flaw in the execution of his duty or in his uniform, rigorous with villains, uncompromising with his coat buttons. For him to have buckled his collar awry there must have been one of those emotional upheavals inside him that might be called inner earthquakes.

He had come without any fuss, had requisitioned from the nearby guard-house a corporal and four soldiers, left the soldiers in the court-yard, and asked the unsuspecting doorkeeper, accustomed as she was to seeing armed men ask for the mayor, to be directed to Fantine's room.

When he came to Fantine's room Javert turned the handle, pushed the door open as softly as a sick-nurse or a police spy, and entered.

Strictly speaking, he did not enter. He stood in the half-open doorway, his hat on his head and his left hand inside his coat that was buttoned up to the chin. In the crook of his arm could be seen the metal knob of his enormous cane, which disappeared behind him.

So he remained for almost a minute without anyone noticing his presence. All at once Fantine looked up, saw him, and made Monsieur Madeleine turn round.

The instant Madeleine's eyes met Javert's, Javert, without moving, without stirring, without stepping closer, became atrocious. No human sentiment can be quite as appalling as joy.

It was the face of a demon on retrieving one of his damned.

The certainty that at last he had Jean Valjean in his grasp revealed in his countenance everything that was in his soul. The stirred depths rose to the surface. The humiliation of having lost the trail for a while and having been briefly mistaken about that Champmathieu was blotted out by his pride in having so shrewdly suspected in the first place, and in having had for so long the right instinct. Javert's contentment was blatant in his lordly attitude. Warped triumph illuminated that narrow brow. It was a display of the full horror that a satisfied face can present.

Javert was in seventh heaven at that moment. Without being distinctly aware of it, yet with a vague intuition of his indispensability and his success, he, Javert, personified justice, light and truth in their heavenly capacity for crushing evil. Behind and around him, reaching to infinite depths, he had authority, reason, a definitive verdict, legal integrity, the vindication of public morality, every star in his favour. He was protecting order, delivering the law's thunderbolt, avenging society; he was the enforcer of the absolute. He rode on a cloud of glory. There was in his victory a trace of defiance and challenge. Standing proud and resplendent, he paraded in the azure heavens the superhuman bestiality of a ferocious archangel. The terrible shadow of the deed he was doing revealed the dim gleam of society's sword in his clenched fist. Rejoicing and indignant, under his heel he crushed crime, vice, rebellion, damnation, hell. He blazed, he exterminated, he smiled, and there was an incontestable grandeur in this monstrous St Michael.

There was nothing ignoble about Javert in his frightfulness.

Probity, sincerity, forthrightness, conviction, the concept of duty, are things that may grow hideous when misguided but, even hideous, remain grand. Intrinsic to the human conscience, their majesty persists even in horror. They are virtues that have one vice: delusion. The ruthless and true joy of a fanatic in perpetrating atrocity retains a certain bleakly venerable radiance. Unaware of it himself, Javert in his fearsome gladness, like every benighted individual who triumphs, was to be pitied. There was nothing so poignant and terrible as this face, displaying what might be called all the evil of goodness.

IV
Authority Reasserts Its Rights

Fantine had not seen Javert since the day the mayor had rescued her from this man. Though nothing made sense to her sick brain, she had no doubt he had come back for her. She could not bear that terrible face, she felt she was dying, she hid her face in both hands and cried in anguish, 'Monsieur Madeleine, save me!'

Jean Valjean – from now on we shall not refer to him otherwise – had stood up. He said to Fantine in his gentlest and calmest voice, 'Don't worry. It's not you that he's come for.'

Then he turned to Javert and said, 'I know what you want.'

Javert replied, 'Let's get a move on!'

There was in the modulation of the voice that accompanied these words something indescribably fierce and frenzied. Javert did not say, 'Let's get a move on!' He said, 'Lessghehmwuhahn!' No spelling can do justice to the way in which it was uttered: it was no longer human speech, it was an animal roar.

He did not behave as usual, he did not explain the situation, he did not produce any arrest warrant. In his eyes Jean Valjean was a kind of mysterious and elusive combatant, a sinister opponent with whom he had been wrestling for the past five years without ever being able to fell him. This arrest was not a beginning, but an end. He merely said, 'Let's get a move on!'

He remained exactly where he was as he said this. He cast a glance at Jean Valjean, that violently compelling glance, like a grappling-hook, by which he was accustomed to draw scoundrels to him. It was this glance by which Fantine had felt pierced to the core two months earlier.

At Javert's cry Fantine opened her eyes again. But monsieur le maire was here. What could she possibly have to fear? Javert stepped into the middle of the room and shouted, 'Now get moving!'

The poor woman looked around. There was no one other than the nun and the mayor. Who could be the object of this contemptuous familiarity? Only herself. She shuddered.

Then she saw something unbelievable, so unbelievable that nothing to equal it had appeared to her even in the darkest of her feverish fits of delirium. She saw the police detective Javert seize monsieur le maire by the collar. She saw monsieur le maire bow his head. To her, it was as if the world had been turned upside-down.

Javert had indeed grabbed Jean Valjean by the collar.

'Monsieur le maire!' shrieked Fantine.

Javert burst into laughter, that frightful laughter with all his teeth bared. 'There's no monsieur le maire here any more!'

Jean Valjean made no attempt to remove the hand on his coat collar. He said, 'Javert—'

Javert cut him short. 'Call me monsieur l'inspecteur.'

'Monsieur,' said Jean Valjean, 'I should like to have a word with you in private.'

'Out loud! Speak out loud!' replied Javert. 'Anyone who has anything to say to me speaks out loud.'

Jean Valjean continued, keeping his voice low. 'It's a favour I have to ask of you—'

'Speak out loud, I tell you!'

'But it's something only you should hear.'

'What do I care? I'm not listening.'

Jean Valjean turned to him and said rapidly in a very low voice, 'Grant me three days' grace! Three days in which to go and fetch this poor woman's child. I'll pay whatever's necessary. You can accompany me if you wish.'

'You're joking!' cried Javert. 'Honestly! I didn't take you for a fool! You're asking me to let you go away for three days! You say it's to go and fetch this whore's child! Hah-hah! That's good! That's really good!'

Fantine trembled.

'My child!' she cried. 'Fetch my child! She's not here, then! Sister, answer me, where's Cosette? I want my child! Monsieur Madeleine! Monsieur le maire!'

Javert stamped his foot. 'Now the other one! Shut up, you hussy! The degeneracy of this place, where convicted felons are magistrates and prostitutes are treated like duchesses! But all that's going to change. And high time too!'

He gazed intently at Fantine, and once again grabbing hold of Jean Valjean's cravat, shirt and collar he added, 'I tell you there's no

Monsieur Madeleine and no monsieur le maire. There's a thief, a ruffian, a convicted felon named Jean Valjean! And I have him here! That's what there is!'

Fantine sat bolt upright, her arms stiff and both hands supporting her. She stared at Jean Valjean, she stared at Javert, she stared at the nun. She opened her mouth as though to speak. A rattle issued from deep in her throat, her teeth chattered, she stretched out her arms in anguish, opening her hands convulsively and groping about her like someone drowning. Then she suddenly fell back on her pillow. Her head struck the bed frame and dropped forward on to her chest, her mouth gaping, her eyes open and dull.

She was dead.

Jean Valjean laid his own hand on Javert's restraining hand and prised it open as he would have prised open the hand of a baby. Then he said to Javert, 'You killed that woman.'

'Enough!' shouted Javert in a fury. 'I'm not here to argue with you. We haven't time for all this. The guard's downstairs. Now move, or I'll have you in thumb-cuffs!'

In a corner of the room there was an old iron bed in quite a poor state that served the nuns as a camp-bed when they were keeping vigil. Jean Valjean went over to this bed, in a split second dismantled the already very dilapidated bedstead, no obstacle to muscles like his, seized the main strut in his clenched fist, and eyed Javert. Javert retreated towards the door.

With the iron strut in his hand Jean Valjean walked slowly over to Fantine's bed. When he reached it he turned and said to Javert in a barely audible voice, 'I advise you not to disturb me just now.'

One thing is certain: Javert was trembling.

He thought of going to summon the guard, but Jean Valjean might take advantage of that one moment to escape. So he stayed, grasped his cane by the thinner end, and backed up against the door frame without taking his eyes off Jean Valjean.

Jean Valjean rested his elbow on the knob of the bedstead and his forehead on his hand, and fell to gazing at Fantine, lying there motion-less. So he remained, absorbed, silent, and obviously no longer thinking of anything to do with this life. There was nothing but inex-pressible pity now on his face and in his attitude. After a few moments of this meditating he bent down and spoke to Fantine in a whisper.

What did he say to her? What could this man, social outcast that he was, possibly have to say to that woman who was dead? What were those words? Not a living soul heard them. Did the dead woman hear them? There are some touching illusions that may perhaps be sublime realities. What is beyond doubt is that Soeur Simplice, sole witness to what happened, often said that at the moment Jean Valjean whispered in Fantine's ear she distinctly saw an ineffable smile appear on those pale lips and in those vacant eyes filled with the terror of death.

Jean Valjean took Fantine's head in both hands and settled it straight on the pillow as a mother might have done to her child. He retied the fastening of her nightdress, and tidied her hair under her cap. Having done that, he closed her eyes.

Fantine's face seemed strangely illuminated at that moment. Death is the entrance to the supreme light.

Fantine's hand was hanging out of the bed. Jean Valjean knelt down before that hand, gently raised it, and kissed it.

Then he stood up again and turned to Javert. 'Now, I'm at your disposal,' he said.

V
A Suitable Grave

Javert put Jean Valjean in the town gaol.

The arrest of Monsieur Madeleine caused a sensation, or rather, had an extraordinary impact on Montreuil-sur-Mer. Sadly, we cannot ignore the fact that at that simple statement 'He was a convicted felon', almost everyone deserted him. In less than two hours all the good he had done was forgotten, and he was nothing but 'a convicted felon'. It is true to say that the details of what had happened at Arras were not yet known. Conversations like the following were to be heard all day long in every part of town:

'You don't *know*? He was a freed convict!' 'Who?' 'The mayor.' 'No! Monsieur Madeleine?' 'Yes.' 'Really?' 'Madeleine wasn't his real name, he has some frightful name, Béjean, Bojean, Boujean.' 'Oh my God!' 'He's been arrested.' 'Arrested!' 'In prison, in the town gaol, waiting to be transferred.' 'Transferred! He's going to be transferred! Where are they transferring him?' 'He's going to face trial for a high-way robbery he committed some time ago.' 'Well! I suspected as much. That man was too good, too perfect, too sanctimonious. He refused the Legion of Honour. He gave money to every little gutter-snipe he came across. I always thought there was some unsavoury story at the bottom of it all.'

The 'best circles', especially, were very much of this opinion. One old lady, a subscriber to *Le Drapeau Blanc*, made the following unfathomably deep remark: 'I'm not sorry. That will teach the Buona-partists!'

So it was that the ghost who had called himself Monsieur Madeleine vanished from Montreuil-sur-Mer. Only three or four individuals in the whole town remained faithful to his memory. The old doorkeeper who had worked for him was one of them.

The evening of that same day this worthy old woman was sitting in her lodge, still thoroughly shocked, and sadly pondering the matter. The factory had been closed all day, the main entrance was locked, the street was deserted. There was no one in the house but the two nuns, Soeur Perpétue and Soeur Simplice, who were keeping vigil over Fantine's body.

Towards the time Monsieur Madeleine usually came home, the honest doorkeeper automatically got up, took out of a drawer the key to Monsieur Madeleine's room and picked up the candle-holder he used every evening to go up to his quarters, then she hung the key on the nail from where he would take it, and placed the candle-holder near by, as if she was expecting him. Then she sat down in her chair again, and returned to her thoughts. The poor kind-hearted old woman had done all this without being conscious of it.

It was not until more than two hours later that she emerged from her musings and exclaimed, 'Oh goodness me! My sweet Lord Jesus! And there was I hanging his key on the nail!'

At that moment the small window in her lodge opened, a hand passed through the opening, took the key and the candle-holder, and lit the candle from the burning rush-light. The doorkeeper looked up and was left open-mouthed with a cry in her throat that she stifled. She knew that hand, that arm, the sleeve of that coat.

It was Monsieur Madeleine.

It was several seconds before she could speak, stunned as she was, as she said herself when later recounting her adventure.

'My God, monsieur le maire!' she cried at last. 'I thought you were—'

She broke off. The end of her sentence would have been disrespectful to the beginning of it. Jean Valjean was still monsieur le maire to her.

He completed the thought that was in her mind.

'In prison,' he said. 'I was. I broke a bar in one of the windows. I jumped down from a rooftop, and here I am. I'm going up to my room. Go and fetch Soeur Simplice for me. She's probably with that poor woman.'

The old woman rushed to obey.

He gave her no other instructions. He was quite sure she would protect him better than he would protect himself.

No one ever found out how he managed to get into the courtyard without the main gate being opened. He had, and always carried with him, a pass-key that opened a little side door. But he must have been searched and his pass-key taken from him. This point was never explained.

He climbed the staircase that led to his room. When he got to the top, he left his candle on the stairs, opened his door almost without a sound, and, feeling his way, went over and closed his window and the shutter, then returned for the candle and came back into the room.

It was a necessary precaution. Remember, his window could be seen from the street.

He glanced around, at his table, his chair, his bed which had not been slept in for three days. There was no trace of the disorder of the night before last. The doorkeeper had tidied his room. She had, moreover, picked out of the ashes and placed neatly on the table the two ferrules of his staff and the forty-sou piece blackened by the fire.

He took a sheet of paper on which he wrote: 'These are the two ferrules of my staff and the forty-sou piece stolen from Petit-Gervais that I mentioned at the court of assizes.' And he laid on this piece of paper the coin and the two bits of metal so that this would be the first thing anyone would see on entering the room. He pulled out of a cupboard one of his old shirts, which he tore up. This gave him some pieces of cloth in which he wrapped the two silver candlesticks. Moreover, he was neither hurried nor agitated, and as he wrapped up the bishop's candlesticks he bit into a piece of black bread. It was probably the prison bread he had brought with him when escaping.

This was indicated by the crumbs found on the bedroom floor when the legal authorities later searched the premises.

There were two little taps at the door.

'Come in,' he said.

It was Soeur Simplice.

She was pale, her eyes were red, the rush-light she was holding shook in her hand. It is a characteristic of the vicissitudes of fate that, no matter how cool and collected we may be, they wrest from our entrails our human nature and force it to reappear on the surface. In the emotional turmoil of that day the nun had become a woman once more. She had been weeping and she was trembling.

Jean Valjean had just finished writing a few lines on a piece of paper which he held out to the nun, saying, 'Sister, will you give this to monsieur le curé?'

The piece of paper was not folded over. She glanced at it.

'You may read it,' he said.

She read the following: 'I ask monsieur le curé to look after everything I am leaving here, from which he will kindly deduct the expenses of my trial and the burial of the woman who died yesterday. The rest is for the poor.'

The sister tried to speak, but could scarcely stammer out a few inarticulate sounds. However, she did manage to say, 'Does monsieur le maire not want to see that poor unfortunate woman one last time?'

'No,' he said, 'they'll be coming after me, I'd only have to be arrested in her room, and that would disturb her peace.'

He had hardly finished when there was a great commotion on the staircase. They heard a thundering of footsteps coming up and the old doorkeeper saying in her loudest and most piercing voice, 'My good monsieur, I swear to God, no one's entered this house all day and all evening, and I haven't once left the door unattended.'

A man responded, 'Yet there's a light in that room.'

They recognized Javert's voice.

The room was so arranged that when the door opened it screened the right-hand corner. Jean Valjean blew out the candle and went and stood in this corner. Soeur Simplice fell to her knees by the table.

The door opened. Javert entered.

The whisperings of several men and the protests of the doorkeeper could be heard coming from the corridor. The nun did not raise her eyes. She was praying.

The rush-light was on the mantelpiece and gave only very little light.

Javert saw the nun and stopped, taken aback.

Remember, Javert's very essence, his natural element, the medium in which he could breathe, was veneration for all authority. He was uncompromising and would allow no objections or reservations. For him, of course, ecclesiastical authority was the highest of all. On this issue as on all others he was zealous, superficial and punctilious. In his eyes a priest was an unerring spirit; a nun, a creature incapable of sin. They were souls walled off from this world with only one connecting door that never opened except to let the truth come out.

On seeing the nun his first instinct was to withdraw.

However, there was another duty that also bound him, an overriding duty that drove him in the opposite direction. His second instinct was to stay and venture at least one question.

This was Soeur Simplice, who never in her life had lied. Javert knew this and specially venerated her because of it.

'Sister,' he said, 'are you alone in this room?'

There was a dreadful moment in which the poor doorkeeper felt faint. The nun looked up and replied, 'Yes.'

272

'Then,' Javert went on, 'forgive me for pressing you, it's my duty to do so – you haven't seen a certain individual, a man, this evening? He has escaped. We're looking for him – this man by the name of Jean Valjean, you've not seen him?'

The nun replied, 'No.'

She lied. She lied twice in succession, without hesitation, with the swiftness of self-sacrifice.

'Pardon me,' said Javert, and retired with a deep bow.

O sainted woman! You've been gone from this world for many years. You have rejoined your virgin sisters and angel brothers in the light. May this untruthfulness be counted in your favour in paradise!

The nun's affirmation was for Javert something so conclusive that he did not even notice the peculiarity of that candle, which had only just been blown out and was still smoking on the table.

An hour later a man was walking through the mist and the trees, hurrying away from Montreuil-sur-Mer in the direction of Paris. That man was Jean Valjean. It has been established through the testimony of two or three carters who met him that he was carrying a bundle and was dressed in a smock. Where had he obtained that smock? It was never found out. But an old workman had died in the factory's infirmary a few days before, leaving only his smock. Perhaps it was that one.

One last word about Fantine.

We all have a mother: the earth. Fantine was returned to that mother.

The parish priest thought he was doing the right thing, and perhaps he was, in preserving for the poor as much money as possible from what Jean Valjean had left. After all, who were these people? A convicted felon and a common prostitute. That is why he kept Fantine's burial simple, and reduced it to that bare minimum called a pauper's grave.

So Fantine was buried in that free corner of the cemetery that belongs to everybody and to nobody, in which the poor are doomed to disappear. Fortunately, God knows where to find the soul. Fantine was laid in darkness among the bones of anonymous others. She suffered the promiscuous fate of ashes. She was thrown into the common grave. Her last resting-place was like her bed.

PART TWO

COSETTE

BOOK ONE
WATERLOO

I
On the Way from Nivelles

Last year (1861), one beautiful May morning, a traveller, the person telling this story, was coming from Nivelles on his way to La Hulpe. He was on foot. He was following a broad paved road undulating between two rows of trees over rolling hills that carry the road up and down again, creating the effect of enormous waves. He had passed Lillois and Bois-Seigneur-Isaac. He could see to the west the slate-roofed bell-tower of Braine-l'Alleud, which has the shape of an upturned vase. He had just left behind him a wood that stood on higher ground and, at the corner of a crossroads, by the side of a kind of decrepit gallows bearing the inscription 'Former toll-gate no. 4', a tavern with this sign on the front of it: 'Aux Quatre Vents. Échabeau, privately owned café'.

Some five hundred yards beyond this tavern he came to the bottom of a little valley, where water flows in a vaulted drain built into the road embankment. The sparse but very green cluster of trees that fills the valley on one side of the road disperses in the meadows on the other side, and trails off gracefully and as though in disarray in the direction of Braine-l'Alleud.

On the right, by the roadside, was an inn, with a four-wheeled cart in front of the door, a large bundle of hop-poles, a plough, a heap of dried brushwood by a quickset hedge, lime smoking in a square pit, a ladder lying beside an old shed with straw partitioning. A young girl was hoeing in a field where a big yellow poster, probably for a travelling show at some village fair, fluttered in the wind. At the corner of the inn, beside a pond on which sailed a flotilla of ducks, an ill-paved path plunged into the undergrowth. This wayfarer took that path.

Some one hundred yards along it, after skirting a fifteenth-century wall capped with pitched coping of crenellated brick, he found himself in the presence of a big stone gateway with a lintel in the sober style of Louis XIV, flanked by two flat medallions. An austere façade rose above this gateway. A wall perpendicular to the façade came almost up to the gateway at an abrupt right-angle just to one side of it. In the grass in front of the gateway lay three harrows with all the May flowers growing haphazardly among them. The gateway was closed. The gates themselves were two dilapidated panels bearing a rusty old knocker.

The sunshine was delightful. There was that gentle rustling of the branches in Maytime that seems to come even more from nests than from the wind. A bonny little bird, probably in love, was singing its heart out in a big tree.

The traveller bent down to examine a rather large circular hollow that looked like the indentation made by some spherical object in the stone at the foot of the left-hand gatepost. At that moment the gates opened and a peasant woman came out.

She saw the traveller and realized what he was looking at.

'It was a French cannon-ball that did that,' she said to him. And she added, 'What you see higher up there, in the gate, close to a nail, is the hole made by a big biscayen bullet. The bullet didn't go right through the wood.'

'What's the name of this place?' asked the traveller.

'Hougomont,' said the peasant woman.

The traveller stood up. He took a few steps and went to look beyond the hedges. He saw on the horizon through the trees a kind of hillock, and on this hillock something that from a distance looked like a lion.

He was on the battlefield of Waterloo.

II
Hougomont

Hougomont was a fateful place, the initial obstruction, the first resistance encountered at Waterloo by that great tree-feller of Europe whose name was Napoleon: the first knot under the fall of his axe.

It was a manor house then, it is just a farm now. Hougomont, for the antiquarian, is 'Hugomons'. This manor was built by Hugo, Sire de Somerel, he who endowed the sixth chaplaincy of Villers Abbey.

The traveller pushed open the gate, brushed past an old calash under the porch, and entered the courtyard.

The first thing that struck him in this inner courtyard was a sixteenth-century doorway pretending to be an arch, everything else having collapsed around it. A monumental appearance is often born of ruin. In a wall near the arch is another arched doorway, dating from Henri IV, through which the trees of an orchard can be seen. Beside this door is a manure pit, some pickaxes, shovels, a few hand-carts, an old well with its flagstone and iron winch, a skittish colt, a strutting turkey, a chapel with a small bell-tower, a pear tree in blossom espaliered against the chapel wall: this is the courtyard that it was Napoleon's ambition to capture. Had he been able to take it, this patch of ground might perhaps have given him the world. Chickens scatter the dust with their beaks. A growl is heard: it is, in lieu of the English, a huge dog baring its teeth.

The English were admirable here. Cooke's four companies of Guards held out for seven hours against the onslaught of an army.

Viewed on a planimetric map, Hougomont, its buildings and enclosures included, forms a kind of irregular rectangle with one corner indented. It is at this corner that the southern gate stands, guarded by the wall that comes at it from point-blank range. Hougomont has two gates: the south gate, leading to the manor house, and the north gate, leading to the farm. Napoleon dispatched his brother Jerome against Hougomont; divisions led by Guilleminot, Foy and Bachelu assaulted it, nearly the whole of Reille's corps was deployed against it and came to grief here; Kellermann's cannon-balls were exhausted on this heroic section of wall. Only a few of Bauduin's brigade succeeded in storming Hougomont to the north, and Soye's brigade could only make a breach to the south, without taking it.

Farm buildings border the courtyard to the south. A piece of the north gate, hacked off by the French, hangs on the wall. It consists of four planks nailed to two cross-beams, on which the scars of the attack are discernible.

The north gate, which the French broke through and which has been patched up to replace the panel hanging on the wall, stands half open at the far end of the yard. It is actually cut into a wall, stone-built below with brick on top, that encloses the courtyard on the north side. It is a simple cart entrance of the kind to be found on all tenant farms, huge double doors made of rough planks: beyond lie the meadows. The fight for this gate was furious. Long afterwards all kinds of bloody hand-prints were visible on the gateposts. It was here that Bauduin was killed.

The tumult of battle is still in this courtyard; the horror is visible; the confusion of the fighting is frozen here; it lives on, the dying continues; it was yesterday. Walls agonize, stones fall, breaches yell; holes are wounds; the leaning and quivering trees look as if they are straining to run away.

This courtyard was more built up in 1815 than it is today. Buildings that have since been pulled down then formed salients and corners and right-angles.

The English barricaded themselves here. The French got in but could not hold their position. Beside the chapel, one wing of the house, all that is left of Hougomont manor, stands in ruins, gutted, you might say. The manor served as a keep, the chapel served as a blockhouse. There was mutual extermination here. Shot at from all sides, from behind the walls, from up in the granaries, from down in the cellars, through every casement, every basement window, every chink between the stones, the French brought bundles of wood and set fire to walls and men. Bullets were answered with flames.

In the ruined wing the demolished rooms of a brick building are discernible through windows fitted with iron bars. The English Guards were positioned in these rooms. The spiral staircase, cleft from the ground floor to the roof, looks like the inside of a broken seashell. The staircase connects two floors. Besieged on the staircase and massed on the higher steps, the English had removed the lower steps. Those are the large slabs of blue stone heaped in the nettles. About a dozen steps are still attached to the wall; on the first is etched the image of a trident. These inaccessible steps remain firmly in place. All the rest resembles a toothless jaw. There are two old trees here: one is dead, the other has a foot wound and comes into leaf again in April. Since 1815 it has started growing across the staircase.

The two sides massacred each other in the chapel. The interior, now quiet again, is strange. Mass has not been said in it since the carnage. Yet the altar is still here, a crudely fashioned wooden altar backed up against rough-hewn stone. Four whitewashed walls, a door opposite the altar, two small arched windows, a large wooden crucifix on the door, above the crucifix a square transom window blocked up with a truss of hay, on the ground in one corner an old broken window-frame – such is the chapel. Fixed in place by the altar is a fifteenth-century wooden statue of St Anne; the Baby Jesus's head was blown off by a biscayen bullet. The French, who held the chapel for a while and were then driven out, set fire to it. Flames filled this coop, it was a furnace. The door burned, the floor burned, the wooden Christ did not burn. The fire consumed his feet – all you can see now are the blackened stumps – then stopped. A miracle, the local people call it. Decapitated, the Baby Jesus was not as lucky as Christ.

The walls are covered with inscriptions. Near Christ's feet this name can be read: 'Henquinez'. Then these others: 'Conde de Rio Maior', 'Marques y Marquesa de Almagro (Habana)'. There are French names with exclamation marks, signs of anger. The wall was whitewashed again in 1849. Nations used to insult each other on it.

It was at the door to this chapel that a body was found holding an axe in its hand. That was the body of Sous-Lieutenant Legros.

You come out of the chapel and on the right you see a well. There are two in this courtyard. You ask, Why does this one have no bucket and pulley? The reason is, water is no longer drawn here. Why is water no longer drawn here? Because it is full of skeletons.

The last person who drew water from this well was named Guillaume van Kylsom. He was a peasant who lived at Hougomont and worked as the gardener there. On the eighteenth of June 1815, his family fled and went into hiding in the woods.

The forest surrounding Villers Abbey sheltered all those poor scattered people for several days and nights. Even today certain recognizable traces, such as charred old tree trunks, mark the location of those wretched quaking campsites deep in the thickets.

Guillaume van Kylsom remained at Hougomont 'to guard the manor', and hid in the cellar. The English discovered him there. He was dragged out of his hiding-place, and whacking him with the flat of their swords the soldiers forced this terrified man to serve them. They were thirsty. This Guillaume brought them water. It was from this well that he drew it. Many drank their last draught here. This well, where so many of the dead drank, was itself to die.

After the battle there was a rush to do one thing: bury the corpses. Death has its own way of harrying victory, and brings pestilence in the wake of glory. Typhus is a concomitant of triumph. This well was deep. It was turned into a tomb. Three hundred dead were thrown into it. Perhaps too hastily. Were all of them dead? Legend says not. It seems that on the night after the burial, feeble voices were heard calling from the well.

This well stands alone in the middle of the courtyard. Three walls, half stone, half brick, like the panels of a folding screen set up like a square turret, surround it on three sides. The fourth side is open. It is from here that water was drawn. The wall opposite has a kind of misshapen bull's-eye window in it, possibly a shell hole. This turret had a roof of which only the beams remain. The iron bracing on the right-hand wall is cross-shaped. Lean over, and the eye plumbs the depths of a deep brick shaft filled with a gathering of shadows. All around the well the foot of the walls disappears into the nettles.

This well does not have in front of it that large blue flagstone that serves as an apron to all wells in Belgium. The blue flagstone has here been replaced by a plank, with five or six gnarled and knotted wooden logs that look like huge bones resting on it. It no longer has a bucket, chain or pulley, but it still has the stone basin that served to catch the spillage. Rainwater collects here, and from time to time a bird from the neighbouring forests comes to drink from it and flies away again.

One house in this ruin, the farmhouse, is still inhabited. The door opens on to the courtyard. Set askew on this door, beside a pretty Gothic lock-plate, is an iron trefoil door handle. When the Hanoverian Lieutenant Wilda seized this handle to take refuge in the farm, a French sapper chopped off his hand with an axe.

The old gardener van Kylsom, now long dead, was the grandfather of the family now living in the house. A grey-haired woman tells you, 'I was there. I was three years old. My older sister was frightened, and wept. They took us into the woods. I was in my mother's arms. We pressed our ears to the ground to listen. I imitated the cannon, going boom, boom!'

As mentioned above, a door on the left leads from the courtyard into the orchard.

The orchard is dreadful.

It is in three sections, you might almost say, three acts. The first section is a garden, the second the orchard itself, the third is a wood. These three sections all lie within the same enclosure: on the entrance side, the manor and farm buildings, on the left, a hedge, on the right, a wall, at the far end, a wall. The wall on the right is brick, the far wall stone. You come into the garden first. It is on a lower level, planted with currant bushes, choked with wild vegetation and closed off by a dressed-stone-faced terrace with double-bellied balusters. It was a seigneurial garden in that early French style that predated Le Nôtre. All ruin and brambles today. The pilasters are topped with orbs that look like stone cannon-balls. The number of balusters still standing on their pedestals is forty-three. The others are lying in the grass. Almost all of them bear marks of rifle-fire. One fragmented baluster stands on its stem like a broken leg.

It was in this garden, below the orchard, that six skirmishers of the French 1st Light Infantry, having got in and not being able to get out again, trapped and run to earth like bears in a pit, took on two Hanoverian companies, one of which was armed with carbines. The Hanoverians lined up along the balustrade and fired from above. Countering from below, six against two hundred, those undaunted skirmishers with only the currant bushes for cover took a quarter of an hour to die.

You climb a few steps and pass from the garden into the orchard proper. There, within those few square yards, fifteen hundred men fell in less than an hour. The wall looks ready for renewed fighting. The thirty-eight loopholes, pierced by the English at irregular heights, are there still. In front of the sixteenth lie two granite tombs of English dead. There are loopholes only in the south wall – the main attack came from that direction. This wall is concealed on the outside by a tall quickset hedge. The French arrived thinking they had only the hedge to tackle, got through it and met with this wall, both an obstacle and an ambush, with the English Guards behind it, all thirty-eight loopholes firing at once, a hail of grapeshot and bullets. And here Soye's brigade were dashed to pieces. So began Waterloo.

Nevertheless, the orchard was taken. As they had no ladders, the French clawed their way over it. There was hand-to-hand fighting under the trees. All this grass was soaked with blood. A Nassau battalion, seven hundred strong, was obliterated here. The outside of the wall, targeted by Kellermann's two batteries, is pitted with grapeshot.

This orchard is as susceptible to the month of May as any other. It has its buttercups and daisies, the grass here is high, cart-horses graze, horse-hair ropes with washing hung out to dry on them are suspended between the trees, forcing passers-by to duck, and walking over this untended ground your foot sinks into mole-holes. You notice an uprooted tree bole coming into leaf lying in the middle of the grass. Major Blackman rested against it as he died. Under a big tree close by fell the German general Duplat, descended from a French family that fled abroad when the Edict of Nantes was revoked. Just beside it leans an ailing old apple tree, dressed with a bandage of straw and clayey loam. Nearly all the apple trees are decrepit with age. There is not one that does not have its bullet or biscayen ball. The skeletons of dead trees abound in this orchard. Crows fly in their branches, and at the far end is a wood full of violets.

Bauduin killed, Foy wounded, fire, massacre, carnage, a stream of English blood, French blood, German blood, mingled in fury; a well crammed with corpses, the Nassau regiment and the Brunswick regiment destroyed, Duplat killed, Blackman killed, the English Guards slaughtered, twenty French battalions out of the forty in Reille's corps decimated; three thousand men in that single farmstead at Hougomont cut down, slashed to pieces, butchered, shot, burned. And all this so that today a peasant can say to the traveller: 'Monsieur, give me three francs – if you like, I'll explain to you what happened at Waterloo!'

III
The Eighteenth of June 1815

Let us go back now – it is one of the narrator's privileges – and return to the year 1815, in fact shortly before the period when the story related in the first part of this book begins.

If it had not rained during the night of the seventeenth to the eighteenth of June 1815, the future of Europe would have been very different. A few drops of water more or less decided Napoleon's fate. For Waterloo to be the end of Austerlitz, providence needed only a little rain, and an unseasonal cloud in the sky was enough to bring a world to ruin.

The battle of Waterloo could not begin – and this gave Blücher time to get there – until half-past eleven. Why? Because the ground was wet. This meant waiting until it became a little firmer so that the artillery could be deployed.

Napoleon was an artillery officer, and that left its mark on him. This remarkable leader was at heart the man who in his report on Aboukir to the Directory said: 'One of our cannon-balls killed six men.' All his battle plans are designed for artillery fire. Concentrating the artillery on a given point – that was his key to victory. He treated the enemy general's strategy like a citadel and battered it to create a breach. He pounded the weak point with grapeshot. He fought battles and won them with the cannon. He had a genius for firepower. To break squares, pulverize regiments, rout lines, crush and disperse mass formations, for him everything lay in this, to strike and strike and keep on striking, and he entrusted this task to the cannon-ball. An awesome method and, combined with genius, one that made invincible for fifteen years this forbidding exponent of a pugilist's war.

On the eighteenth of June 1815, he expected all the more of his artillery because he had the greater strength of numbers. Wellington had only one hundred and fifty-nine guns, Napoleon had two hundred and forty.

Suppose the ground had been dry, with the artillery able to move freely, the action would have begun at six o'clock in the morning. The battle would have been won and over by two o'clock, three hours before the fateful Prussian intervention.

How much blame lies with Napoleon for the loss of this battle? Is the shipwreck attributable to the helmsman?

Was Napoleon's obvious physical decline further complicated at that time by a certain diminishing of his inner capabilities? Had the twenty years of war taken their toll on the sword as well as on the scabbard, the spirit as well as the body? Was the veteran intrusively making himself felt in the leader? In a word, was this genius, as many eminent historians have thought, now failing? Was he frenetically trying to hide from himself his debilitation? Was he beginning to falter, confounded by the winds of chance? Was he becoming oblivious to danger – a matter of serious consequence in a general? In this category of men of great physical capability, who might be called giants of action, is there an age when their genius develops myopia? Old age has no effect on intellectual geniuses. For the Dantes and Michelangelos, to grow old is to grow in stature. For the Hannibals and Bonapartes, is it to shrink? Had Napoleon lost his sense for victory? Was he now unable to recognize the reef, to suspect the pitfall, to discern the crumbling edge of the abyss? Had he no instinct for catastrophes? Was he, who in the past knew all the roads to triumph and who from the lofty heights of his chariot of lightning with a sovereign finger would point the way, now in dire confusion riding his thunderous harnessed legions to destruction? Was he seized at the age of forty-six with a supreme madness? Was this titanic charioteer of destiny no more than a colossal daredevil?

We think not.

His battle plan was, it is universally acknowledged, a masterpiece. To target the centre of the Allied line, open a gap and cut the enemy in two, drive the British half back on Hal and the Prussian half back on Tongres, separate Wellington and Blücher, carry Mont-St-Jean, capture Brussels, drive the German into the Rhine and the Englishman into the sea. For Napoleon, all of this was in this battle. What came next remained to be seen.

It goes without saying, we have no intention of writing the history of Waterloo in these pages. One of the formative scenes of the story we are telling is connected with this battle but the history of Waterloo is not our theme. In any case that history has already been written, and authoritatively so, from one point of view by Napoleon, and from the other point of view by a whole host of historians.* For our own part, we leave the historians to their task. We are but a remote witness, a passer-by on the plain, one seeking to learn from that soil composted with human flesh, perhaps mistaking appearances for realities. We have no right to challenge in the name of science a set of circumstances in which there is surely something of the mirage. We have neither the military experience nor the strategic expertise to validate some theoretical construction. In our view, the two leaders at Waterloo are ruled by a concatenation of accidents. And where that mysterious culprit destiny is involved, we share the verdict of that naive judge, the people.

* Hugo's footnote: Walter Scott, Lamartine, Vaulabelle, Charras, Quinet, Thiers.

IV
A

Those who wish to visualize clearly the battle of Waterloo have only to lay on the ground in their mind's eye a capital A. The left leg of the A is the road to Nivelles, the right leg the road to Genappe, the bar across the A is the sunken road from Ohain to Braine-l'Alleud. The apex of the A is Mont-St-Jean, where Wellington is. The left foot is Hougomont, where Reille is, with Jerome Bonaparte. The right foot is La Belle-Alliance, where Napoleon is. Just above the point where the bar across the A meets and intersects with the right leg is La Haie-Sainte. In the middle of the bar is exactly where the last word of the battle was spoken. It was here that the lion was placed, the unintentional symbol of the supreme heroism of the Imperial Guard.

The triangle contained in the upper part of the A, between the two legs and the bar, is the plateau of Mont-St-Jean. The entire battle consisted of the fight for this plateau.

The flanks of the two armies extend to the right and left of the two roads to Genappe and Nivelles, with d'Erlon facing Picton, and Reille facing Hill.

Behind the tip of the A, behind the plateau of Mont-St-Jean, is the forest of Soignes.

As for the plain itself, picture a vast undulating expanse. Each fold in the ground is higher than the next, and all the undulations rise towards Mont-St-Jean, and end there at the forest.

Two enemy forces on a battlefield are two wrestlers. They grapple with each other. Both seek to bring down the other. They clutch at anything: a bush lends support; a corner of a wall offers protection; for want of a shack to lean back on, a regiment gives ground; a depression in the plain, a break in the landscape, a side path in the right place, a grove, a gully, can stay the heel of that colossus called an army and prevent its retreat. He who quits the field is beaten. Hence the responsible leader's need to scrutinize the least clump of trees and investigate the slightest irregularity of terrain.

The two generals had carefully studied the Mont-St-Jean plain, now called the plain of Waterloo. With far-sighted shrewdness Wellington had already examined it the year before as the possible site of a major engagement. On this terrain and for this duel, on the eighteenth of June, Wellington occupied the better position, Napoleon the worse. The English army being on higher ground, the French army below.

It is almost superfluous to sketch here Napoleon's appearance, on horseback, with his field-glasses in his hand, on the heights of Rossomme, at dawn on the eighteenth of June 1815. There is no need, everyone has seen him. That calm profile under the small Brienne Academy hat, that green uniform, the white revers hiding his plaque, the grey coat hiding his epaulettes, the corner of red sash under his waistcoat, the leather breeches, the white horse with its saddle-cloth of purple velvet bearing in the corners crowned Ns and eagles, the riding-boots over silk stockings, the silver spurs, the Marengo sword – the complete figure of this last of the Caesars stands in the mind's eye, acclaimed by some, severely judged by others.

This figure was for a long time all brightness. This was owing to a kind of obfuscation that emanates from most legendary heroes and that always obscures the truth for a longer or shorter while. But history and the light of day prevail.

This clarity, history, is unforgiving. What is strange and divine about it is that, though it brings light, and precisely because it brings light, it often casts a shadow in places where brightness used to be seen. It creates two different phantoms of the same man, and the one attacks the other and exposes him for what he is, and the shadows of the despot contend with the brilliancy of the leader. This gives a truer measure for the people's final assessment. Babylon plundered diminishes Alexander, Rome enchained diminishes Caesar, Jerusalem slain diminishes Titus. Tyranny follows the tyrant. It is a tragedy for a man to leave behind him darkness in his own image.

V
The Quid Obscurum* *of Battles*

Everyone is familiar with the first phase of this battle; a confused, uncertain start, hesitant, ominous for both armies but more so for the English than for the French.

It had rained all night. The ground was rutted by the downpour. Here and there water had gathered in depressions on the plain as if in bowls. In certain places the supply and munitions carts were mired up to their axles, the girth straps on the harnessings dripped with liquid mud. If the wheat and rye trampled down by this vast throng on the

---

* A phrase meaning 'that which is obscure', which Hugo took from Hippocrates, the Greek physician of the fifth century BC, who used it in reference to the diagnosis of disease.

move had not filled in the ruts and laid a bedding beneath the wheels, all movement would have been impossible, particularly in the vales around Papelotte.

The whole thing got off to a late start. Napoleon, as we have already explained, was in the habit of holding all the artillery in his hand like a pistol, aiming it now at one point of the battlefield, now at another, and he preferred to wait until the horse batteries could manoeuvre and gallop freely. For this, the sun needed to come out and dry the soil. But the sun did not come out. This was no repetition of the Austerlitz experience. When the first cannon was fired the English general Colville looked at his watch and noted that it was eleven thirty-five.

The action began with a furious attack, more furious perhaps than the emperor would have wished, by the French flank on Hougomont. At the same time Napoleon attacked the centre by hurling Quiot's brigade at La Haie-Sainte, and Ney pushed the French right flank forward against the English left flank, which was anchored on Papelotte.

The attack on Hougomont was something of a feint. The plan was to lure Wellington, to draw him to the left. This plan might have succeeded had the four companies of English Guards and the brave Belgians of Perponcher's division not stoutly defended the position, and Wellington, instead of massing his troops there, was able to send no more than an additional four companies of Guards and one Brunswick battalion as sole reinforcements.

The attack on Papelotte by the French right flank was completely genuine. Overwhelm the English left flank, cut off the road to Brussels, bar the way against any Prussians who might turn up, storm Mont-St-Jean, drive Wellington back on Hougomont, then Braine-l'Alleud, then Hal, nothing could be more clear-cut. Apart from a few hitches, this attack succeeded. Papelotte was taken. La Haie-Sainte was stormed.

One noteworthy detail. There were in the English infantry, particularly in Kempt's brigade, a great many raw recruits. In the face of our redoubtable infantry these young soldiers were valiant. Their inexperience proved dauntless, in particular they provided excellent service as sharpshooters: as sharpshooter, left somewhat to himself, the soldier becomes, so to speak, his own general. These recruits displayed something of the French ingenuity and fury. This novice infantry had spirit. It was not to Wellington's liking.

After the taking of La Haie-Sainte, the battle fluctuated.

There is in the course of this day an obscure period, between noon and four o'clock. The midpoint of this battle is almost a blur and shares the murkiness of the fray. A semi-darkness sets in. Discernible in this fog are vast movements to and fro, a dizzying mirage, contemporary accoutrements of war almost unknown today – busbies and busby bags, flying sabretaches, cross-belts, grenade pouches, hussars' dolmans, red boots with countless creases in them, heavy shakos trimmed with braid of gold or silver; the almost black infantry of Brunswick intermingled with the scarlet infantry of England, the English soldiers with thick white padded rolls round the armholes for epaulettes, the Hanoverian light horse with their oblong leather helmets with strips of brass and tails of red horse-hair, the Scotsmen with their bare knees and tartan kilts, the tall white gaiters of our grenadiers, belonging to paintings not to strategic lines, what Salvator Rosa needs, not what Gribeauval needs.

There is always a certain amount of turmoil that enters into a battle. *Quid obscurum, quid divinum.** Every historian tends to see what he wants to see in this muddle. Whatever the generals' scheme might be, the clash of armed multitudes has incalculable repercussions. In action, the two plans of the two leaders impinge on each other and are distorted by each other. A certain part of the battlefield will devour more combatants than another, in the same way as more or less pervious soils will more or less quickly soak up water thrown on them. This means having to pour in more soldiers than you would have wanted to. An unforeseen drain on resources. Ribbon-like, the battle line wavers and winds, streams of blood follow illogical courses, the battlefronts are in constant flux, the regiments coming up or falling back forming promontories or inlets. All these reefs are continually moving in front of each other. Where the infantry was, the artillery arrives, where the artillery was, the cavalry rides up. Battalions are insubstantial vapours. There was something there – look for it, and it is gone. Clear patches shift, dark troughs advance and retreat, a kind of sepulchral wind drives on, forces back, swells, and disperses these tragic multitudes. What is a conflict? Oscillation. The fixity of a mathematical plan expresses a minute, not a day. To depict a battle, one of those powerful painters with a sense of chaos in their brush-stroke is needed. Rembrandt is better than van der Meulen. Accurate at noon, at three o'clock van der Meulen lies. Geometry is misleading. The hurricane alone is truthful. That is what gives Folard the right to contradict Polybius. Let us add, there is always a certain moment when the battle degenerates into fighting, loses cohesion and breaks up into

---

* 'That which is obscure' is also, for Hippocrates, 'that which is divine': *quid divinum.*

countless individual incidents that, to borrow the expression of Napoleon himself, 'belong rather to the biography of regiments than to the history of the army'. In this circumstance the historian obviously has the right to summarize. He can only capture the main outlines of the conflict, and it is not given to any one narrator, however conscientious he may be, to determine absolutely the shape of that dreadful cloud that we call a battle.

This, which is true of all great armed clashes, is particularly relevant to Waterloo.

Nevertheless, at a certain moment in the afternoon the battle became clear.

VI

Four o'Clock in the Afternoon

Around four o'clock the situation for the English army was serious. The Prince of Orange commanded the centre, Hill the right wing, Picton the left. Fervent and intrepid, the Prince of Orange shouted to the Dutch-Belgians, 'Nassau! Brunswick! Never retreat!' Weakened, Hill had rallied to Wellington. Picton was dead. At the very moment the British captured from the French the colours of the 105th Line Infantry, the French killed General Picton with a bullet through the head. For Wellington, the battle had two key positions, Hougomont and La Haie-Sainte. Hougomont still held out but was in flames; La Haie-Sainte was taken. Of the German battalion defending it, only forty-two men survived. All but five officers were dead or captured. Three thousand combatants had been massacred in that barnyard. A sergeant of the English Guards, the foremost boxer in England, reputed by his companions to be invulnerable, was killed there by a little French drummer-boy. Baring was dislodged, Alten sabred. Several flags had been lost, one from Alten's division and one from the Lüneburg battalion that was being carried by a prince of the Deux-Ponts family. The Scots Greys were no more; Ponsonby's heavy dragoons had been hacked to pieces. That valiant cavalry were overwhelmed by Bro's lancers and Travers's cuirassiers; of twelve hundred horses six hundred were left; of three lieutenant-colonels two had been brought down, Hamilton wounded, Mater slain. Ponsonby had fallen, stuck through with a lance seven times. Gordon was dead. Marsh was dead. Two divisions, the fifth and the sixth, were destroyed.

Hougomont breached, La Haie-Sainte taken, there now existed but one focal point, the centre. That point still held firm. Wellington reinforced it. He summoned Hill, who was at Merbe-Braine, he summoned Chassé, who was at Braine-l'Alleud.

The centre of the English army, curved slightly inwards, very dense and very compact, was strongly positioned. It occupied the plateau of Mont-St-Jean, with the village behind and the slope, at that time quite steep, in front of it. It was protected from the rear by the solid stone house, which in those days belonged to the Nivelles estate and marks where the roads intersect, a sixteenth-century pile so sturdy that cannon-balls rebounded off it without breaching it. All over the plateau the English had here and there hewn the hedges, cut embrasures in the hawthorn trees, placed the barrel of a cannon between two branches, crenellated bushes. Their artillery lay in ambush beneath the scrub. This Punic labour, undeniably sanctioned by war that permits ruse, was so well executed that Haxo, sent by the emperor at nine o'clock in the morning to reconnoitre enemy batteries, saw nothing and returned to tell Napoleon that there was no obstacle except for the two barricades blocking the roads to Nivelles and Genappe. It was just that time of year when the cereal crops are high. On the edge of the plateau a battalion of Kempt's brigade, the 95th, lay in the rye, armed with carbines.

Thus protected and buttressed, the centre of the Anglo-Dutch army was well positioned.

The risk in this position was the forest of Soignes, then bordering the battlefield, with the Groenendael and Boitsfort lakes cutting across it. An army could not draw back into it without dispersing. Regiments would have disbanded immediately. The artillery would have come to grief in the boggy ground. In the opinion of a number of experts, disputed by others, any retreat here would have been a rout.

Wellington added to this centre one of Chassé's brigades, brought in from the right wing, and one of Vincke's brigades, brought in from the left, plus Clinton's division. To his English troops, Halkett's regiments, Mitchell's brigades, Maitland's Guards, he gave as bulwarks and reinforcements the Brunswick infantry, Nassau's contingent, Kielmansegge's Hanoverians and Ompteda's Germans. This gave him twenty-six battalions. 'The right wing,' as Charras says, 'was brought in behind the centre.' On the spot where now stands what is called 'the Museum of Waterloo' an enormous battery was screened behind sacks of earth. And in a dip in the terrain Wellington had Somerset's Dragoon Guards, some fourteen hundred horse. It was the other half of that English cavalry, so justly renowned. With Ponsonby destroyed, there remained Somerset.

The battery position, which would have been almost a redoubt if completed, was ranged behind a very low garden wall, hastily reinforced with sandbags and a big earth embankment. These defence works were unfinished; there was no time to stockade them.

Anxious but impassive, Wellington was mounted on horseback and remained so the whole day, in the same position, a little to the fore of the old Mont-St-Jean windmill, which still exists, under an elm tree since bought for two hundred francs by an enthusiastic vandal of an Englishman who cut it down and carried it away. Here, Wellington was coldly heroic. Bullets rained down. His aide-de-camp, Gordon, had just fallen at his side. Pointing to an exploding shell, Lord Hill said to him, 'My lord, what are your instructions, and what orders do you leave us, if you are killed?' 'To do as I do,' replied Wellington. To Clinton he said laconically, 'Hold this place to the last man.' The day was obviously turning out badly. Wellington exhorted his old companions of Talavera, Vitoria and Salamanca. 'Boys, are we to give ground? Think of old England!'

Around four o'clock the English line fell back. All of a sudden only artillery and sharpshooters were to be seen on the ridge of the plateau, the rest disappeared. Repulsed by French shells and bullets, the regiments retired to where the track leading to Mont-St-Jean farm still passes today, there was a withdrawal, the English battlefront disappeared, Wellington dropped back. 'They're starting to retreat!' cried Napoleon.

VII
Napoleon in Good Humour

Though ill and uncomfortable on horseback because of a painful indisposition, the emperor had never been in such good humour as on that day. Ever since morning his had been a smiling inscrutability. On the eighteenth of June that deep, marmoreally masked soul beamed blindly. The man who had been grim at Austerlitz was cheerful at Waterloo. Those with the greatest destinies to fulfil often make these mistakes. Our joys are illusory. The supreme smile belongs to God.

'*Ridet Caesar, Pompeius flebit*,'* said the soldiers of the Fulminata legion. Pompey was not to weep this time, but Caesar certainly laughed.

---

* 'Caesar laughs, Pompey will weep.' Pompey was defeated by Caesar in 48 BC at the battle of Pharsalus, in which Caesar's 12th Legion, the Fulminata, took part.

Even the night before, at one o'clock, riding out with Bertrand in rain and storm to reconnoitre the hills around Rossomme, he was satisfied to see the long line of English camp fires illuminating the horizon all the way from Frischemont to Braine-l'Alleud, and felt that destiny, summoned to meet him on this field at Waterloo, was keeping its appointment. He had halted his horse and remained for some time motionless, gazing at the lightning, listening to the thunder, and this fatalist was heard to blurt out in the darkness these mysterious words, 'We are in accord.' Napoleon was mistaken. They were no longer in accord.

Not one moment's sleep had he snatched. For him every second of that night had been marked by joy. He went all along the picket line, stopping here and there to speak to the sentries. At half-past two, close to Hougomont wood, he heard the tread of a column on the march. For a moment he thought it was Wellington retreating. He said to Bertrand, 'It's the English rear-guard starting to decamp. I shall take prisoner the six thousand Englishmen who have just arrived at Ostend.' He talked expansively. He had regained the zest of that first of March landing when he showed off to the grand-marshal the enthusiastic peasant in the Juan Gulf, crying, 'You see, Bertrand, reinforcements already!' On the night of the seventeenth to the eighteenth of June he railed against Wellington. 'That poor Englishman needs to be taught a lesson,' said Napoleon. The rain intensified. Thunder rolled as the emperor spoke.

At half-past three in the morning he lost one illusion: officers sent out on reconnaissance told him the enemy was not engaged in any movement. Nothing stirred. Not one camp fire had gone out. The English army was sleeping. The silence on earth was profound. The only sound was in the heavens. At four o'clock a peasant was brought to him by the scouts. This peasant had served as guide to a brigade of English cavalry, probably Vivian's brigade, on its way to take up position in the village of Ohain on the far left. At five o'clock two Belgian deserters informed him they had just left their regiment and the English army was waiting to do battle. 'So much the better!' exclaimed Napoleon. 'I'd rather trounce them than drive them back.'

In the morning he dismounted in the mud on the slope at the corner of the Plancenoit road and had a kitchen table and a straw-bottomed chair brought to him from Rossomme farm, sat down with a truss of hay for a carpet and spread out on the table his map of the battlefield, saying to Soult, 'A pretty chequerboard!'

After the rains during the night the supply convoys, mired in the rutted roads, failed to arrive in the morning. The French soldier had not slept, was wet and hungry. This did not prevent Napoleon from declaring cheerfully to Ney, 'The chances are ninety per cent in our favour.' At eight o'clock the emperor's breakfast was brought to him. He had invited a number of generals. During breakfast it was said that Wellington had been at a ball held in Brussels by the Duchess of Richmond the night before last, and Soult, the tough man of war with the face of an archbishop, said, 'The ball's today.' The emperor had bantered with Ney, who said, 'Wellington won't be so foolish as to wait for Your Majesty.' This was in any case his usual way. 'He joked readily,' says Fleury de Chaboulon. 'He was essentially playful by nature,' says Gourgaud. 'He was full of quips, more droll than witty,' says Benjamin Constant. It is worth insisting on this giant's light-heartedness. It was he who called his grenadiers 'the grousers'; he pinched their ears; he pulled their moustaches. 'The emperor did nothing but play pranks on us,' one of them commented. On the twenty-seventh of February during the clandestine crossing from the island of Elba to France, the French brig-of-war *Le Zéphyr* met on the open sea the brig *L'Inconstant* on which Napoleon was hiding, and asked *L'Inconstant* for news of Napoleon. Still wearing in his hat the white and purple cockade with a bee motif that he had adopted on the isle of Elba, the emperor laughingly seized the loud-hailer, and answered for himself, 'The emperor is in fine fettle.' A man who laughs like that is on familiar terms with history in the making. Napoleon had several of these bouts of laughter during his breakfast at Waterloo. After the meal he ruminated for some quarter of an hour, then two generals sat on the truss of straw, pen in hand and sheet of paper on their knees, and the emperor dictated to them the order of battle.

At nine o'clock when the French army deployed – five columns moving forward in staggered formation, the divisions in two lines and the artillery between the brigades, with music leading the march into battle and setting the pace with drum rolls and trumpet blasts, a mighty, vast, joyous sea of helmets, sabres and bayonets along the skyline – the emperor was stirred and twice exclaimed, 'Magnificent! Magnificent!'

Between nine o'clock and half-past ten the entire army, incredible as it may seem, took up position. They were drawn up in six lines, creating 'the figure of six Vs', to quote the emperor. A few moments after the formation of the battlefront, amid that profound silence before the storm that precedes engagements, the emperor saw the three batteries of twelve-pounders, detached on his orders from the three corps of d'Erlon, Reille and Lobau, go rolling by, destined to begin the action by pounding Mont-St-Jean where the Nivelles and Genappe roads intersect; and tapping Haxo on the shoulder, he said to him, 'There go twenty-four beauties, general.'

Confident of the outcome, he had encouraged with a smile, as they passed before him, the 1st Corps company of sappers, detailed by him to barricade Mont-St-Jean as soon as the village was taken. All this serenity only gave way to an expression of superior pity: seeing on his left, at a spot where a large tomb now stands, those admirable Scots Greys massing with their superb horses, he said, 'What a shame!'

Then he mounted his own horse, rode up in front of Rossomme, and chose for his observation post a narrow grassy ridge to the right of the Genappe–Brussels road, his second position during the battle. The third position, taken up at seven o'clock in the evening, between La Belle-Alliance and La Haie-Sainte, was a dangerous one. It was on quite a high hillock, which still exists, and behind which the Guard was massed in a dip in the plain. Around this hillock, cannon-balls ricocheted off the paved road right up to Napoleon. As at Brienne, he had bullets and grapeshot whistling over his head. From almost the very spot where his horse's hoofs had been, pitted cannon-balls, old sabre blades and shapeless projectiles consumed with rust have been retrieved. *Scabra rubigine.** A few years ago a sixty-pound bombshell was unearthed, still charged with explosive, with its fuse broken off flush with the shell's surface. It was in this last position that the emperor said to his guide Lacoste, a resentful and terrified peasant strapped to a hussar's saddle who kept wheeling round at every discharge of canister-shot and trying to hide behind him, 'Idiot! this is disgraceful, you're going to get yourself killed, shot in the back.' Digging into the sand on the friable slopes of this hillock, the author of these lines has himself found the disintegrating remains of the neck of a bomb after forty-six years' corrosion, and old fragments of iron that snapped like elder-twigs between his fingers.

As everyone knows, the undulations of the variously sloping plains where the engagement between Napoleon and Wellington took place are no longer what they were on the eighteenth of June 1815. By taking

---

* 'Flaky with rust', an allusion to Virgil's *Georgics*, bk I, lines 493–7: vestiges of the battle of Philippi – fought in 42 BC between Caesar's assassins Brutus and Cassius, and Caesar's avengers Mark Antony and Octavian – are ploughed up by a peasant working the land.

from this mournful field what was used to raise a monument to it its true relief has been obliterated, and history, baffled, no longer recognizes the place. For the sake of glorifying it, it has been disfigured. On seeing Waterloo again two years later, Wellington exclaimed, 'My battlefield has been altered!' Where the great pyramid of earth surmounted by the lion is today, there was a ridge that fell away at a negotiable gradient towards the Nivelles road, but on the other side, towards the Genappe road, was virtually an escarpment. The height of this escarpment can still be measured by the height of the two great burial sites that rise up on either side of the Genappe–Brussels road: one on the left, the English grave, and one on the right, the German grave. There is no French grave. For France, the whole of this plain is a burial place. Thanks to the thousands upon thousands of cartloads of earth employed for the mound, one hundred and fifty feet in height and half a mile in circumference, the approach to the Mont-St-Jean plateau is now a gentle rise. On the day of the battle it was a steep and difficult climb, especially on the side of La Haie-Sainte. So sharply did the ground rise there that the English cannon could not see below them the farm at the bottom of the vale, on which the fighting centred. On the eighteenth of June 1815 the rains had made this steepness even more abrupt, mud complicated the ascent, and not only was it a climb but the climbers were floundering in the mire. Along the crest of the plateau ran a kind of trench that a distant observer could not have suspected.

What was this trench? Let us explain. Braine-l'Alleud is a Belgian village, Ohain is another. These villages, both of them concealed in the folds of the landscape, are connected by a lane about four miles long that crosses a rolling plain, often running into hills and cutting through them like a furrow, which means that at certain points this route is a gully. In 1815, as today, this lane ran across the ridge of the Mont-St-Jean plateau between the two paved roads to Genappe and Nivelles. Only, today it is flush with the plain. Then, it was a sunken road. Its two embankments have been removed to build the monument hill. Along most of its route this lane was, and still is, a trench; a trench sometimes a dozen feet deep, and whose too precipitous banks would collapse in places, particularly in winter, under heavy downpours. There were accidents. The road was so narrow at the Braine-l'Alleud end that a passer-by was crushed by a cart there, as attested by a stone cross standing near the graveyard, which gives the name of the dead man, 'Monsieur Bernard Debrye, merchant at Brussels', and the date of the accident, 'February

1637'.* It ran so deep across the Mont-St-Jean plateau that a peasant, Mathieu Nicaise, was buried under a landslip in 1783, as attested by another stone cross, the top of which disappeared in the clearances but whose overturned pedestal can still be seen today on the grassy slope on the left-hand side of the road between La Haie-Sainte and Mont-St-Jean farm.

On a day of battle this sunken road of which there was no warning, running along the edge of the Mont-St-Jean ridge – a ditch at the top of the escarpment, a hidden rut in the ground – was invisible, that is to say, dire.

VIII
The Emperor Asks His Guide Lacoste a Question

So on the morning of Waterloo, Napoleon was feeling pleased.

He had reason to be. The battle plan he had devised, as we have established, was indeed admirable.

Once the battle had started, the very different turn that events had taken – the resistance of Hougomont, the tenacity of La Haie-Sainte, Bauduin killed, Foy put out of action, the unexpected wall against which Soye's brigade had dashed itself, Guilleminot's fatal blunder in having neither shot nor gunpowder pouches, the batteries floundering in the mud, the fifteen unescorted guns toppled by Uxbridge into a sunken road, the limited effect of the bombs falling on the English lines – embedding themselves in the rain-sodden ground and only succeeding in producing volcanoes of mud so that grapeshot turned into a splattering; the futility of Piré's show of force on Braine-l'Alleud – all that cavalry, fifteen squadrons, more or less wiped out; the English right wing ineffectually harassed, the left wing ineffectually breached; Ney's strange misunderstanding in massing, instead of deploying in echelon formation, the four divisions of the 1st Corps, ranks twenty-seven deep with fronts of two hundred men thus exposed to artillery fire, the terrifying inroads into these masses made by cannon-balls, the attack columns divided, the broadside battery suddenly revealed on their flank; Bourgeois, Donzelot and Durutte placed in jeopardy, Quiot repulsed; that Herculean graduate of the Polytechnic School Lieutenant Vieux wounded while hacking with an axe at the gate of

* Hugo's footnote: This is the inscription: DOM / CY. A ÉTÉ ÉCRASÉ / PAR MALHEUR / SOUS UN CHARIOT / MONSIEUR BERNARD / DE BRYE MARCHAND / A BRUXELLE LE (illegible) / FEBVRIER 1637.

La Haie-Sainte under plunging fire from the English barricade across the sharp bend in the Genappe–Brussels road; Marcognet's division trapped between infantry and cavalry, shot down in the rye at point-blank range by Best and Pack and put to the sword by Ponsonby; the Prince of Saxe-Weimar, whose seven-gun battery had been spiked, holding and retaining Frischemont and Smohain despite Comte d'Erlon; the 105th's colours captured, the 45th's colours captured, that Prussian black hussar arrested by the scouts of a flying column of three hundred light cavalry reconnoitring between Wavre and Plancenoit, the disquieting things this prisoner had said, Grouchy's delay, the fifteen hundred men killed in less than an hour in the orchard at Hougomont, the eighteen hundred men mown down in even less time round La Haie-Sainte – all these ominous incidents, passing before Napoleon like the clouds of battle, had barely troubled his gaze and cast no shadow on the certitude in that imperial face. Napoleon was used to looking at war steadily. He never counted the cost in the heart-rending detail of its individual numbers. Numbers mattered little to him, provided they gave this total: victory. It did not alarm him that things should not go according to plan in the early stages; believing as he did that he was master and owner of the outcome, he could wait, assuming that he was beyond question, and he treated destiny as his equal. He seemed to say to fate: You would not dare.

Half light, half shadow, Napoleon felt protected in acting for the good and tolerated in doing wrong. He had in his favour, or thought he had, a connivance, one might almost say, a complicity of events, equivalent to antiquity's invulnerability.

Yet anyone with Beresina, Leipzig and Fontainebleau behind him might well have been wary of Waterloo. A mysterious scowl is growing visible in the far reaches of the sky.

The moment when Wellington fell back, Napoleon felt a thrill. He suddenly saw the Mont-St-Jean plateau emptying and the English front disappearing. Their army was rallying, but not in view. The emperor half rose in his stirrups. The gleam of victory flashed in his eyes.

Wellington cornered in the forest of Soignes, and destroyed – this was the ultimate overthrow of England by France. It was Crécy, Poitiers, Malplaquet and Ramillies avenged. The man of Marengo was cancelling out Agincourt.

Reflecting on this tremendous change of fortune, the emperor then swept his field-glasses one last time over every part of the battlefield. His Guard, standing at attention behind him, gazed up at him with a kind of veneration. He was turning things over in his mind. He examined the slopes, noted the inclines, scrutinized the clumps of trees, the patch of rye, the path. He seemed to be counting every bush. He gazed with some intentness at the two English barricades blocking the roads, two huge ramparts of felled trees: one on the Genappe road above La Haie-Sainte, armed with two cannons – of the entire English artillery these alone could see the floor of the battlefield; and one on the Nivelles road where the Dutch bayonets of Chassé's brigade glinted. He noticed near this barricade the old white-painted chapel of St Nicolas that stands at the corner of the road that cuts across towards Braine-l'Alleud. He leaned over and spoke in an undertone to his guide Lacoste. The guide gave a negative, probably perfidious, shake of the head.

The emperor straightened up again and pondered.

Wellington had withdrawn. It only remained to complete this withdrawal by extirpation.

Turning round abruptly, Napoleon dispatched a courier to ride to Paris at full gallop with the news that the battle was won.

Napoleon was one of those geniuses from which lightning strikes.

He had just found his thunderbolt.

He gave the order to Milhaud's cuirassiers to take the Mont-St-Jean plateau.

IX
The Unexpected

They numbered three thousand five hundred. They formed a front over half a mile long. They were giant men on colossal horses. They were twenty-six squadrons and they had behind them for support Lefebvre-Desnouettes's division, the one hundred and six elite gendarmes, the light cavalry of the Guard, eleven hundred and ninety-seven men, and the lancers of the Guard, eight hundred and eighty lances. They wore helmets without plumes and cuirasses of wrought steel, with horse-pistols in their saddle holsters and the long sabre-sword. That morning the whole army had admired them when at nine o'clock, with trumpets sounding and all the bands playing 'Veillons au salut de l'empire', they had come in a dense column, one of their batteries on one flank, the other at their centre; and deploying in two ranks, between the Genappe road and Frischemont, had taken up their battle position in that strong second line so astutely drawn up by Napoleon which, with Kellermann's cuirassiers on its far left and Milhaud's cuirassiers on the far right, had, so to speak, two wings of steel.

Aide-de-camp Bernard brought them the emperor's order. Ney

drew his sword and placed himself at their head. The enormous squadrons set off.

It was a magnificent spectacle.

All this cavalry with sabres raised, standards flying and trumpets sounding, in column by division formation, moving simultaneously as one, with the precision of a bronze battering-ram opening a breach, descended the hill of La Belle-Alliance, plunged into the fearsome depths where so many had already fallen, disappeared in the smoke, then emerging from that obscurity reappeared on the other side of the vale, still massed in close array, riding at full trot through a hail of grapeshot bursting over them, up the dreadful mud slope of the Mont-St-Jean plateau. Up they rode, solemn, menacing, imperturbable. In the intervals of musket and artillery fire could be heard that great thundering of hoofs. As there were two divisions, there were two columns, with Wathier's division on the right and Delort's on the left. From a distance they looked like two huge adders of steel streaking towards the crest of the plateau. This thing moved through the battle like something supernatural.

Nothing like it had been seen since the heavy cavalry's capture of the great redoubt at Borodino. Murat was not here, but Ney was again present. This mass seemed to have turned into a monster and to have but a single soul. Glimpsed through the occasional rift in a vast fog of smoke, each squadron rippled and bulged like a polyp ring. A jumble of helmets, cries, sabres, a turbulent bounding of horses' rumps amid cannon and fanfare – a terrible, disciplined tumult; the cuirasses on top of this like scales on the hydra.

This seems a chronicle of another age. Something similar to this vision appeared no doubt in the old Orphic epics telling of centaurs, those ancient hybrids, those giant creatures with human faces and equine breasts who scaled Olympus at a gallop, horrible, invulnerable, sublime: gods and beasts.

By a bizarre numerical coincidence, twenty-six battalions were to meet these twenty-six squadrons. Calm, silent, motionless, behind the crest of the plateau, in the shadow of their concealed battery, in thirteen square formations, two battalions to a square, arranged in two lines, seven in the first, six in the second, with rifle butts to their shoulders, aiming at what was about to appear, the English infantry lay in wait. They could not see the cuirassiers and the cuirassiers could not see them. They listened to this rising tide of men. They heard the swelling sound of the three thousand horse, the alternate and symmetric beat of their cantering hoofs, the rattle of the cuirasses, the clinking of the sabres and a kind of mighty fierce breathing. There was a terrible silence, then suddenly a long row of raised arms brandishing sabres appeared over the ridge, and helmets and trumpets and standards, and three thousand grey-mustachioed heads shouting, 'Long live the emperor!' All this cavalry surged on to the plateau, and it was like the arrival of an earthquake.

All at once tragedy struck: on the English left, our right, the head of the column of cuirassiers reared up with a frightful clamour. Just when they reached the top of the ridge, riding furiously, totally bent on destruction in their headlong charge on the squares and the cannon, the cuirassiers had noticed a trench, a death trap, lying between them and the English. It was the sunken road to Ohain.

This was a moment of horror. There, directly under the horses' hoofs, twelve feet deep between the double embankment, yawned the unexpected ravine. The second line drove the first into it, and the third drove the second. The horses reared then lunged backwards, landed on their rumps, slid with all four legs in the air, unseating and flattening their riders; unable to reverse, the whole column solely a projectile, the impetus gathered to trample the English now trampling the French. The inexorable ravine could only capitulate when filled. Riders and horses rolled pell-mell into the pit, crushing each other, together forming but one flesh, and when this trench was filled with living men they were trodden underfoot and the rest were able to pass. Almost a third of Dubois's brigade fell into that abyss.

This is when the battle started to be lost.

One local tradition, obviously exaggerating, says two thousand horses and fifteen hundred men were entombed in the Ohain sunken road. This figure probably includes all the other dead bodies thrown into this pit the day after the battle.

Let us note in passing that it was this Dubois brigade, now meeting with such disaster, that in another charge an hour earlier had captured the standard of the Lüneburg battalion.

Before ordering this charge by Milhaud's cuirassiers, Napoleon had scanned the terrain but had not been able to see the sunken road, which did not show up even as a line in the surface of the plateau. Alerted nevertheless and made wary by the little white chapel that stands on the corner where it meets the Nivelles road, he had probably asked the guide Lacoste whether there might be some obstacle. The guide had answered no. It might almost be said, that shake of a peasant's head was Napoleon's undoing.

Yet other disasters were destined to occur. Was it possible Napoleon might have won that battle? We say no. Why? Because of Wellington? Because of Blücher? No. Because of God. Bonaparte victorious at Waterloo was no longer in the rubric of the nineteenth century. Another chapter of history was now in the making in which Napoleon no longer had any place. Events had long ago indicated their lack of goodwill. It was time for this immense man to fall.

The inordinate weight of this man was disturbing the balance of human destiny. This individual alone counted for more than the rest of the world put together. These excessive quantities of human vitality concentrated in a single person – the world going to one man's head – would be fatal to civilization if it were to continue. The moment had come for the incorruptible supremacy of natural justice to intervene. The principles and elements on which depend the normal gravitations within both the moral order and that of the physical world were probably protesting. The stench of spilled blood, cemeteries filled to overflowing, weeping mothers – these make an unanswerable case. When the earth is glutted, mysterious groanings that emerge from the shadows are heard in the unfathomable abyss.

Napoleon had been denounced in the realms of the infinite and his downfall had been decided. He was an inconvenience to God.

Waterloo is no battle. It is a change of front in the universe.

X
The Mont-St-Jean Plateau

The battery revealed itself at the same time as the ravine.

Sixty cannons and the thirteen squares fired at the cuirassiers at close range. The intrepid General Delort gave the English battery the military salute.

All the English flying artillery had galloped back inside the squares. The cuirassiers did not even pause. The sunken road disaster had taken its toll but had not daunted them. They were men whose courage increases as their numbers diminish.

Wathier's column alone had suffered in the disaster. Delort's column, which Ney had ordered to veer to the left, as though sensing the pitfall, arrived intact.

The cuirassiers hurled themselves on the English squares. Riding flat out, no reining back, sabres clamped between teeth, pistols in hand, such was the attack. There are moments in battle when the soul so hardens the man, the soldier changes into a statue, when all this flesh turns to granite. The English battalions under furious assault stood fast. So what followed was terrifying.

The English squares were attacked on all sides simultaneously. A frenzied whirl enveloped them. The infantry remained coldly impassive. The first rank, kneeling, met the cuirassiers with their bayonets, the second rank fired on them. Behind the second rank the gunners charged their cannons, the front of the square opened up allowing a blast of grapeshot through, then closed again. The cuirassiers replied by pressing on. Their huge horses reared, took the ranks in their stride, leapt over the bayonets and came down, gigantic as they were, in the middle of these four living walls. The cannon-balls ripped through the cuirassiers, the cuirassiers made breaches in the squares. Rows of men disappeared, crushed under the horses. Bayonets were plunged into the bellies of these centaurs. Hence the hideous wounds of a kind perhaps not seen elsewhere. This frenzied cavalry having taken its toll on them, the squares closed up with no failure of nerve. With inexhaustible supplies of grapeshot, they created explosions in their assailants' midst. The face of this battle was monstrous. These squares were no longer battalions, they were craters. These cuirassiers were no longer cavalry, they were a storm. Each square was a volcano attacked by a cloud. Lava strove against thunderbolts.

From the very first of these onslaughts, the square on the extreme right, the most exposed of all, being out on a limb, was almost annihilated. It was formed of the 75th Regiment of Highlanders. As the killing went on around him, the bagpiper in the middle, with his eyes downcast in profound heedlessness, his melancholy gaze filled with the reflection of forests and lakes, sat on a drum with the bag under his arm, playing the Highland airs. These Scotsmen died thinking of Ben Lothian, as the Greeks died remembering Argos. The sword of a cuirassier, lopping off the bag and the arm that held it, put an end to the song by killing the singer.

Relatively few in number, and reduced by the trench catastrophe, the cuirassiers were up against almost the entire English army here, but they excelled themselves, each man the equal of ten. Meanwhile, some Hanoverian battalions gave ground. Wellington saw this and his thoughts turned to his cavalry. Had Napoleon's thoughts at that same moment turned to his infantry, he would have won the battle. This oversight was his great fatal mistake.

All of a sudden the cuirassiers, who had been the assailants, found themselves assailed. The English cavalry was at their back. Before them, the squares, behind them, Somerset, that is to say fourteen hundred Dragoon Guards. Somerset had Dornberg with the German light horse on his right, and on his left Trip with the Belgian carabineers. Attacked on their flank and head-on, before and behind, by infantry and cavalry, the cuirassiers had to defend themselves on all sides. What did they care? They were a whirlwind. Their valour was beyond words.

Furthermore, they had the battery still thundering away behind them. It must have been so, for these men to have been wounded in the back. One of their cuirasses, holed by a biscayen ball in the left shoulder plate, is in the collection of the so-called Waterloo Museum. For such Frenchmen, no less than such Englishmen were required.

It was no longer a fray, it was a darkness, a fury, a vertiginous rage of souls and spirits, a hurricane of flashing swords. In an instant the fourteen hundred Dragoon Guards were no more than eight hundred. Fuller, their lieutenant-colonel, was killed. Ney brought up Lefebvre-Desnouettes's lancers and light horse. The Mont-St-Jean plateau was captured, recaptured, captured again. The cuirassiers relinquished the cavalry and returned to the infantry, or rather that whole tremendous throng was engaged in close combat, none letting go of the other. The squares still held firm. There were twelve assaults. Ney had four horses killed under him. Half the cuirassiers remained on the plateau. This fighting went on for two hours.

The English army was deeply shaken by it. There is no doubt that had they not been weakened in their first assault by the disaster at the sunken road the cuirassiers would have overwhelmed the centre and decided the victory. This extraordinary cavalry struck terror in Clinton, who had lived through Talavera and Badajoz. Three-quarters vanquished, Wellington expressed a hero's admiration. 'Splendid!'* he said under his breath.

The cuirassiers destroyed seven of the thirteen squares, seized or spiked sixty guns and captured from the English regiments six flags, which three cuirassiers and three light cavalry of the Guard brought to the emperor in front of the farm at La Belle-Alliance.

Wellington's situation had worsened. This strange battle was like a ferocious duel between two wounded men who, while still fighting and holding out against each other, are both bleeding to death. Which of the two will be the first to fall?

The struggle for the plateau continued.

How far did the cuirassiers get? No one could rightly say. What is certain is that on the day after the battle a cuirassier and his horse were found dead in a weighbridge structure at Mont-St-Jean, at the very point where the four roads from Nivelles, Genappe, La Hulpe and Brussels meet and intersect. This horseman had passed right through the English lines. One of the men who found the body still

* In the French text, 'Sublime!', which Hugo footnotes: Splendid! *mot textuel* [meaning, 'the word he actually said'].

lives at Mont-St-Jean. His name is Dehaze. He was eighteen years old at the time.

Wellington felt the scales tipping against him. The crisis was approaching.

The cuirassiers had not succeeded, in the sense that there had been no breakthrough in the centre. With everyone holding the plateau, no one held it, and in short it remained for the most part with the English. Wellington had the village and the flat ground above, Ney had only the ridge and the slope. On both sides they seemed rooted in that lugubrious soil.

But the English were sinking – beyond recovery, it seemed. The haemorrhaging of this army was horrible. Kempt on the left wing demanded reinforcements. 'There are none,' replied Wellington, 'let him fight to the death!' By a singular coincidence which reflects the exhaustion of both armies, almost at that same moment Ney asked Napoleon for additional infantry and Napoleon exclaimed, 'Infantry! Where does he expect me to find any? Does he expect me to create infantry?'

Nevertheless, the English army was the more stricken of the two. The furious charges of those great squadrons with their metal cuirasses and steely breasts had pounded the infantry. A few men around a flag marked where a regiment had been posted, many a battalion was now commanded by a mere captain or lieutenant. Alten's division, which had already suffered so badly at La Haie-Sainte, was almost destroyed. The intrepid Belgians of van Kluze's brigade lay strewn on the rye fields along the Nivelles road. Almost nothing was left of those Dutch grenadiers who in 1811 fought alongside us in Spain against Wellington and in 1815 joined the English side to fight against Napoleon. The number of officers lost was considerable. Lord Uxbridge, who buried his leg the following day, had a shattered knee. While on the French side, in that assault by the cuirassiers, Delort, Lhéritier, Colbert, Donop, Travers and Blancard were put out of action, on the English side Alten was wounded, Barnes was wounded, Delancey was killed, van Merlen killed, Ompteda killed, the whole of Wellington's general staff decimated, and England had the worst of it in that bloody deadlock. The 2nd Regiment of Foot Guards had lost five lieutenant-colonels, four captains and three ensigns; the 1st Battalion of the 30th Infantry had lost twenty-four officers and one hundred and twelve soldiers; the 79th Highlanders had lost twenty-four officers wounded, eighteen officers dead, four hundred and fifty soldiers killed. The entire regiment of the Hanoverian Cumberland Hussars, commanded by Colonel Hake, who was later to be court-martialled and cashiered, had turned tail at the sight of the fighting and fled into the forest of Soignes, sowing panic all the way to Brussels. Transport vehicles, munitions trucks, baggage wagons, carts full of wounded casualties, seeing the French gaining ground and approaching the forest, made a dash for it. The Dutch who had been attacked by the French cavalry fuelled the alarm. From Vert-Coucou to Groenendael, over a distance of nearly five miles in the direction of Brussels, according to the testimony of eyewitnesses still alive today, the roads were choked with those fleeing. This panic was such that it spread to the Prince de Condé at Mechlin and to Louis XVIII at Ghent. Apart from the weak reserve force positioned behind the field hospital set up at Mont-St-Jean farm, and Vivian and Vandeleur's brigades that flanked the left wing, Wellington had no more cavalry. A number of batteries lay dismounted. These facts are acknowledged by Siborne. And Pringle, exaggerating the disaster, goes so far as to say that the Anglo-Dutch army was reduced to thirty-four thousand men. The Iron Duke remained calm, but his lips had paled. The Austrian commissioner Vincent and the Spanish commissioner Álava, present at the battle on the English general staff, thought the duke was defeated. At five o'clock Wellington drew out his watch and was heard to murmur these grim words, 'Night or Blücher!'

It was at about that moment that a distant line of bayonets glinted on the high ground above Frischemont.

That was the turning point in this huge drama.

XI
A Bad Guide for Napoleon,
a Good Guide for Bülow

Napoleon's bitter disappointment is common knowledge, the hoped-for Grouchy turning out to be Blücher. Death instead of life.

Fate takes these turns. You were expecting to rule the world; St Helena comes into view.

If the shepherd boy who served as guide to Blücher's second-in-command Bülow had advised him to exit the forest above Frischemont instead of below Plancenoit, the shape of the nineteenth century might have been different. Napoleon would have won the battle of Waterloo. By any other route than the one below Plancenoit, the Prussian army would have come to a gully their artillery could not have negotiated, and Bülow would not have arrived.

Now, we have it from the Prussian general Muffling that an hour's delay and Blücher would have found Wellington no longer holding his own: 'The battle was lost.'

Clearly, Bülow arrived just in time. He had, after all, been greatly delayed. He had bivouacked at Dion-le-Mont and set out at first light. But the roads were impassable and his divisions had become mired. The ruts came up to the cannons' wheel hubs. Furthermore, he had to cross the Dyle over the narrow bridge at Wavre. The street leading to the bridge had been set on fire by the French, so the ammunition supplies and artillery vehicles, unable to pass between two rows of burning houses, had to wait until the fire was extinguished. It was midday before Bülow's vanguard even reached Chapelle-St-Lambert.

Had the action begun two hours earlier, it would have been over by four o'clock, and Blücher would have turned up at the battle won by Napoleon. Such are these immense quirks of fate, commensurate with an infinite we cannot comprehend.

As early as midday the emperor with his telescope had been the first to notice on the far horizon something that arrested his attention. He said, 'I see a cloud over there that looks like troops to me.' Then he asked the Duc de Dalmatie, 'Soult, what do you see over towards Chapelle-St-Lambert?' Training his field-glass, the marshal answered, 'Four or five thousand men, sire. Obviously Grouchy.' Yet whatever it was remained motionless in the haze. All the general staff's field-glasses studied 'the cloud' pointed out by the emperor. Some said, 'They're columns resting.' Most said, 'They're trees.' The truth is, the cloud did not move. The emperor sent Domon's division of light cavalry as a reconnaissance detachment to investigate.

Indeed, Bülow had not moved. His vanguard was very weak and could do nothing. He was having to wait for the main body of the army, and he had been ordered to assemble his forces before entering the fray. But at five o'clock, seeing Wellington imperilled, with these remarkable words Blücher ordered Bülow to attack: 'We must give the English army some air.'

Shortly afterwards, the divisions of Losthin, Hiller, Hake and Ryssel deployed in front of Lobau's corps, Prince William of Prussia's cavalry emerged from the Bois de Paris, Plancenoit was in flames, and Prussian cannon-balls began to rain even on the ranks of the reserve guard behind Napoleon.

XII
The Guard

We know the rest: the intervention of a third army, the battle reconfigured, the thundering of eighty-six guns firing simultaneously, Pirch I turning up along with Bülow, Zieten's cavalry led by Blücher himself, the French driven back, Marcognet swept from the Ohain plateau, Durutte dislodged from Papelotte, Donzelot and Quiot falling back, Lobau caught obliquely, a fresh battle unleashed on our shattered regiments as dusk fell; the whole English line resuming the offensive and pressing forward, the gigantic breach opened up in the French army, English grapeshot and Prussian grapeshot assisting each other; the slaughter; disaster on the front line, disaster on the flanks; the Guard entering the fray amid this dreadful destruction.

Sensing they were about to die they shouted, 'Long live the emperor!' There is nothing more stirring in history than the roar of these acclamations in the throes of death.

The sky had been overcast all day. Suddenly, at that very moment – it was eight o'clock in the evening – the clouds on the horizon parted, letting the great sinister glow of the setting sun filter through the elms on the Nivelles road. At Austerlitz they had seen the sun rise.

For this final act, every battalion of the Guard was commanded by a general. Friant, Michel, Roguet, Harlet, Mallet, Poret de Morvan were there. When, through the fog of this battle, the Grenadier Guards' tall hats with their large eagle plates appeared, identical, aligned, steady, splendid, the enemy felt a respect for France. It was like seeing twenty Victories entering on the field of battle with their wings spread, and those who were the victors, believing themselves to be vanquished, fell back. But Wellington shouted, 'Up, Guards, and at 'em!' The red regiment of English Guards lying behind the hedges sprang up, a hail of grapeshot riddled the tricolour flag fluttering round our eagles, all charged at each other, and the final carnage began. The Imperial Guard sensed in the dusk the army falling back around it, and the immense panic of a rout; it heard the desperate 'Every man for himself!' that had replaced 'Long live the emperor!' And while those behind fled, they continued to advance, with more and more of them stricken and dying with every step they took. There were no falterers, no faint-hearts. The soldier in that troop was as much a hero as the general. Not a man among them shirked that suicide.

Frenzied, with all the noble grandeur of death accepted, Ney put himself in the way of every onslaught in that bloodbath. That is where he had his fifth horse killed under him. Sweating, with fire in his eyes, foam on his lips, his uniform unbuttoned, one of his epaulettes cut in half by a sabre stroke from a horseguard, his great-eagle plate dented by a bullet, bleeding, muddied, magnificent, a broken sword in his hand, he said, 'Come and see how a marshal of France dies on the battlefield!' But to no avail. He did not die. He was distraught and incensed. To Drouet d'Erlon he threw down this challenge, 'Are you not going to get yourself killed?' In the midst of all that artillery that was destroying a handful of men, he cried, 'Is there nothing, then, for me! Oh! I wish all these English shells would strike me in the belly!' Ill-fated man, you were saved for French bullets!

XIII
The Catastrophe

The rout behind the Guard was grim.

The army suddenly collapsed on all sides at once, at Hougomont, La Haie-Sainte, Papelotte, Plancenoit. The cry of 'Treachery!' was followed by the cry of 'Every man for himself!' An army on the run is a thaw setting in. Everything gives way, splits, cracks, wobbles, overturns, falls, jostles, hurries, hurtles on. Extraordinary disintegration. Ney borrows a horse, leaps on it, and without a cravat, hatless and swordless, stands astride the Brussels road, stopping both English and French. He tries to detain the army, he calls it back, he insults it, he grasps at the absconders. He is overwhelmed. The soldiers flee from him, shouting 'Long live Marshal Ney!' Two of Durutte's regiments go back and forth, bewildered, as though tossed between the uhlans' sabres and the fusillades of Kempt, Best, Pack and Rylandt's brigades. The worst of frays is a rout. Friends kill each other so as to make their escape. Squadrons and battalions dash against each other and disperse, a vast battle spume. Lobau at one end and Reille at the other are caught up in the surge. In vain does Napoleon form defence lines with what he has left of the Guard. In vain does he expend in a final effort the squadrons serving as his personal escort. Quiot retreats before Vivian, Kellermann before Vandeleur, Lobau before Bülow, Morand before Pirch, Domon and Subervie before Prince William of Prussia. Guyot, who led the emperor's squadrons in their charge, falls under the feet of the English dragoons. Napoleon gallops along the line of fugitives, harangues, urges, threatens, entreats them. All those mouths that had shouted that morning 'Long live the emperor!' remain agape. They hardly recognize him. The Prussian cavalry, newly arrived, comes in hot pursuit, swoops, sabres, slashes, hacks, kills, exterminates. The draught animals bolt, the cannons flee. The soldiers of the artillery-train unhitch the ammunition wagons and use the horses to escape. Overturned wagons with their wheels in the air block the road and cause havoc. Men crush and trample one another, walk over the living and the dead. Arms flail. A dizzying multitude fills the roads, paths, bridges, plains, hills, valleys, woods, choked by this invasion of forty thousand men. Cries, desperation, knapsacks and guns tossed into the rye, swords used to slash a way through, no comrades now, no officers, no generals, indescribable terror. Zieten cutting France down at his leisure. The lions turned into hunted deer. Such was this flight.

At Genappe there was an attempt to turn and make a stand, to check the rout. Lobau rallied three hundred men. The entrance to the village was barricaded, but at the first volley of Prussian artillery fire all fled again and Lobau was taken. That volley of fire can be seen today imprinted on the gable of an old brick farm building on the right-hand side of the road a few minutes before the entrance to Genappe. The Prussians fell on Genappe, no doubt infuriated at having so little proved themselves victors. Their pursuit was monstrous. Blücher gave the orders for slaughter. Roguet had set a macabre example by threatening with death any French grenadier who brought him a Prussian prisoner. Blücher outdid Roguet. Cornered in the doorway of an inn at Genappe, the general of the Young Guard, Duhesme, surrendered his sword to a death's-head hussar who took the sword and slew his prisoner. Victory ended with the assassination of the vanquished. Let us punish, since history is ours: old Blücher brought dishonour on himself. This ferocity was the culmination of the disaster. The desperate rout continued, through Genappe, Quatre-Bras, Gosselies, Frasnes, Charleroi, Thuin, and only stopped at the frontier. Alas! And who was it that fled in this way? The Grand Army.

This madness, this terror, this collapse into ruin of the greatest bravery that has ever amazed history – was this without cause? No. The shadow of an enormous right hand falls on Waterloo. It was the day of destiny. The power that exceeds man shaped that day. Hence the terrified furrow on those brows. Hence all those noble souls surrendering their swords. Those who had conquered Europe were completely cast down, having nothing more to say or do, sensing a terrible presence in that shadow. *Hoc erat in fatis.** On that day the prospects of the human race changed. Waterloo is the pivot of the nineteenth century. The demise of the great man was essential to the advent of the great century. Someone who is not to be challenged took care of it. The heroes' panic is understandable. The battle of Waterloo was not just a matter of cloud – it was a matter of meteorology. God intervened.

At nightfall in a meadow near Genappe, Bernard and Bertrand

---

* 'This was fated', an allusion to lines 481–2 from Ovid's *Fasti*: 'Sic erat in fatis, nec te tua culpa fugavit, / sed deus: offenso pulsus es urbe deo' ('It was fated so: it is no fault of yours that exiled you / But god; you are expelled from the city by an offended god').

stopped a man, grabbing hold of him by the skirt of his coat. Distraught, bemused, this desperado caught up in the rout and carried along this far had just dismounted, tucked the reins of his horse under his arm and, wild-eyed, was making his way back, alone, to Waterloo. It was Napoleon, still trying to keep going, immense somnambulist of this shattered dream.

XIV
The Last Square

Several squares of the Guard, steadfast in this tide of disorderly retreat, like rocks in flowing water, held out until nightfall. With darkness descending and death too, resolute, they awaited that twofold obscurity and allowed it to close in on them. Isolated from the others and cut off from the army now scattered in every direction, each regiment died alone. To make this final stand they had taken up position, some on the Rossomme heights, others on the Mont-St-Jean plain. There, abandoned, vanquished, awesome, these grim squares died magnificently. Ulm, Wagram, Jena, Friedland, died with them.

At twilight, around nine o'clock in the evening, below the Mont-St-Jean plateau, there was one left. In that fateful valley, at the foot of the slope the cuirassiers had climbed and that was now thronged with the massed English, under the converging fire of the victorious enemy's artillery, under an appalling density of missiles, this square fought on. It was commanded by an unknown officer named Cambronne. At each discharge the square diminished, and countered. It replied to grapeshot with gunfire, its four walls continually contracting. Far away, fugitives pausing breathless for a moment listened in the shadows to that dismal diminishing thunder.

When this legion was no more than a handful, when their flag was no more than a tatter; when, having used up all their bullets, their guns were no more than truncheons; when the heap of corpses was larger than the group left alive, there was among the victors a sort of sacred terror around these noblest of dying men, and the English artillery, pausing for breath, fell silent. It was a respite of sorts. These combatants had what seemed like spectres milling around them, silhouettes of men on horseback, the dark profiles of cannons, the white sky glimpsed through wheels and gun-carriages. The colossal death's-head that heroes always glimpse through the smoke in the thick of battle advanced on them, and watched. Through the shades of dusk they could hear the artillery guns being loaded. The lighted linstocks formed a circle round them, like tigers' eyes in the dark. All the gunners of the English batteries approached their cannons, and then, holding the moment of death suspended above these men, an English general, Colville according to some, Maitland according to others, his emotions stirred, shouted to them, 'Brave Frenchmen, surrender!' Cambronne replied, '*Merde!*'

XV
Cambronne

The French reader wishing to be respected, what may be the finest word a Frenchman has ever uttered cannot be repeated to him. It is forbidden to dump on history an instance of the sublime.

At our own risk and peril, we infringe this ban.

So among those giants there was one Titan: Cambronne.

To say that word, and then die. What could be nobler? For having the will to do so is to die, and it was not this man's fault if, fired on by cannons, he survived.

The man who won the battle of Waterloo was not Napoleon routed, it was not Wellington buckling at four o'clock, in despair at five, it was not Blücher, who did not fight. The man who won the battle of Waterloo was Cambronne.

To hurl such a verbal thunderbolt at the bombshells that are killing you is to be victorious!

To have this response to the catastrophe, to say this to destiny, to provide this base for the future lion, to deliver this retort to the night rain, to Hougomont's treacherous wall, to Ohain's sunken road, to Grouchy's delay, to Blücher's arrival, to be sarcastic in the grave, to contrive to remain standing even after you have fallen, to send the European coalition packing in two syllables, to offer to kings those latrines already familiar to the Caesars, to make the basest of words the most elevated by combining it with the glory of France, to have the nerve to bring Waterloo to a close with Mardi Gras, to complement Leonidas with Rabelais, to sum up this victory in a last word that cannot be spoken, to lose on the battlefield and carry off the prize of history, after this carnage to have the last laugh – this is tremendous.

It is thumbing your nose at disaster! It reaches the heights of Aeschylean grandeur!

Cambronne's word is like a rupture. It is the rupturing of a breast with disdain. It is an explosion caused by excess of anguish. Who was victorious? Was it Wellington? No! Without Blücher he was lost. Was it Blücher? No! What Wellington had not begun, Blücher could not have finished. This Cambronne, this eleventh-hour extra, this unknown soldier, this infinitely small player in the war, senses there is an untruth here, more intensely distressing, an untruth in a catastrophe, and while he is bursting with rage he is offered this paltry thing, his life! How could he not react?

There they are, all the kings of Europe, the satisfied generals, the thundering Jupiters, they number a hundred thousand victorious soldiers, and behind the hundred thousand a million; their cannons with their fuses lit stand gaping, they have the Imperial Guard and the Grand Army under their heel, they have just crushed Napoleon, and there is no one left but Cambronne. There is no one left to protest but this worm. He will protest. So he searches for a word as a man searches for a sword. A spume rises within him, and this spume is the word. In the face of this extraordinary and undistinguished victory, in face of this victory with none victorious, this despairing man draws himself up. He suffers the enormity of it but he can see its emptiness. And he more than spits on it. And overwhelmed by numbers, by superior force and circumstance, he finds in his soul an expression: excrement! We repeat it. To say that, to do that, to light on that, is to be the victor!

At that fateful moment the spirit of the great days of the past entered that unknown man. Cambronne alights on the word for Waterloo as Rouget de l'Isle alights on the 'Marseillaise', visited by inspiration from on high. An emanation of the divine whirlwind is released and these men are imbued with it, and they quiver, and one of them sings the supreme song, and the other utters the terrible cry. This word of titanic disdain Cambronne hurls not only at Europe in the name of the Empire – that would be of little consequence – he hurls it at the past in the name of the Revolution. It is heard, and the giants' spirit of old is recognized in Cambronne. It could be Danton speaking, or Kléber roaring!

At that word from Cambronne, the English voice responded, 'Fire!' The batteries blazed, the hill trembled, from every cannon issued a last dreadful belch of grapeshot; the immense smoke billowed, a dim whiteness under the moonrise, and when the smoke cleared, there was nothing left. That formidable remnant had been annihilated. The Guard was dead. The four walls of the living redoubt lay on the ground, only the merest quiver detectable here and there among those bodies. And so it was that the French legions, greater than the Roman legions, expired on Mont-St-Jean, on the rain- and blood-soaked earth in the mournful ryefields, on the spot where Joseph, who drives the Nivelles mail-coach, now passes, at four o'clock in the morning, whistling and cheerfully lashing his horse.

XVI

Quot Libras in Duce?*

The battle of Waterloo is an enigma. It is as obscure to those who won it as it is to those who lost it. For Napoleon it was panic.† Blücher sees only gunfire. Wellington cannot make sense of it. Look at the reports. The accounts are confused, the commentaries muddled. Some mumble, others stammer. Jomini divides the battle of Waterloo into four phases. Muffling breaks it down into three acts. Although on a few points our opinion differs, Charras alone captured in his fine survey the distinctive features of this catastrophe of human genius grappling with divine chance. All the other historians are to some extent blinded, and their blindness leaves them groping in the dark. A blinding day indeed, with the collapse of the military monarchy, which to the great amazement of kings brought down all kingdoms with it, the downfall of might, the routing of war.

In this event, which bears the stamp of transcendent necessity, the role of men counts for nothing.

To take Waterloo away from Wellington and Blücher, is that to deprive England and Germany of anything? No. Neither illustrious England nor majestic Germany is called into question by the problem of Waterloo. Thank heavens, nations are great regardless of the grim fortunes of war. Neither England, nor Germany, nor France is defined by the scabbard. During a period when Waterloo is no more than a clatter of sabres, over and beyond Blücher Germany has Goethe; over and beyond Wellington England has Byron. A great intellectual dawn distinguishes our century, and in this advent of light England and Germany have their own magnificent radiance. They have majesty because they think. The advancement they bring to civilization is intrinsic to them. It derives from themselves and not from an accident. Their greater power and influence in the nineteenth century are not founded on Waterloo. It is only barbarous peoples that suddenly flourish after a victory, such being the fleeting vanity of torrents

---

* From Juvenal's Satire X, lines 147–8: 'Expende Hannibalem: quot libras in duce summo invenies?' (literally, 'Weigh Hannibal: how many pounds in the greatest of leaders do you find?') – or, as Byron put it in his 'Ode to Napoleon Buonaparte', written on Napoleon's abdication in 1814: 'Weigh'd in the balance, hero dust / Is vile as vulgar clay.'

† Hugo's footnote: 'A battle over, a day ended, mistakes mended, greater successes assured for the morrow, all was lost through a moment of terrified panic' (Napoleon, *Dictées de Ste-Hélène*).

swollen by a storm. Civilized peoples, especially in our own times, neither rise nor fall by the good or bad fortune of a leader. Their specific weight within the human race results from something more than a conflict. Their honour, thank God, their dignity, their understanding, their genius, are not numbers that those gamblers the heroes and conquerors can throw into the lottery of battle. Often a battle lost is progress gained. Less glory, more freedom. The drum falls silent, reason speaks. It is the game of loser wins. So let us discuss Waterloo dispassionately from both sides. Let us render to chance what is due to chance, and to God what is due to God. What is Waterloo? A victory? No. A lottery. A lottery won by Europe at France's expense. It was not really worth putting a lion there.

Besides, Waterloo is the strangest encounter in history. Napoleon and Wellington. They are not enemies, they are opposites. Never did God, who delights in antithesis, set up a more striking contrast, a more extraordinary comparison. On the one hand, precision, foresight, analysis, prudence, retreat secured, reserves husbanded, a steady nerve, imperturbable method, strategy that makes the most of the terrain, tactics that balance battalions, carnage by the rule book, war regulated by the clock, nothing willingly left to chance, the old classic courage, absolute correctness. On the other hand, intuition, guesswork, military unorthodoxy, supernatural instinct, a fiery glance, something indefinable that has the eye of an eagle and strikes like a thunderbolt, extraordinary artfulness exercised with disdainful impetuosity, all the mysteries of a deep soul, an alliance with destiny, with river, plain, forest, hill summonsed and to some extent forced to obey, the despot extending his tyranny over the battlefield, trust in the stars combined with strategic skill, enhancing it, but in an unsettling way. Wellington was the Barrême of warfare, Napoleon was its Michelangelo. And this time genius was defeated by calculation.

On both sides an arrival was expected. It was the accurate calculator who succeeded. Napoleon expected Grouchy; he did not come. Wellington expected Blücher; he came.

Wellington is classic warfare taking its revenge. Bonaparte had encountered it in Italy at the dawn of his career and magnificently defeated it. The old owl had fled before the young vulture. Time-honoured tactics had been not only routed, but outraged. Who was this twenty-six-year-old Corsican? What was the meaning of this glorious ignoramus who, with everything against him, nothing in his favour, without supplies, without munitions, without cannons, without shoes, almost without an army, with a handful of men against masses, kept hurling himself against a united Europe and preposterously winning impossible victories? Where did this devastating madman come from, who almost without pausing for breath, and playing the same hand in terms of the forces at his disposal, smashed the emperor of Germany's five armies, one after the other, toppling Beaulieu after Alvinzi, Wurmser after Beaulieu, Melas after Wurmser, Mack after Melas? Who was this newcomer-to-war with the audacity of a luminary? The orthodox military establishment anathematized him even as they gave ground to him. Hence the implacable rancour of the old imperialism against the new, of the regular sabre against the flaming sword, and of chessboard thinking against genius. On the eighteenth of June 1815 that rancour had the last word, and under Lodi, Montebello, Montenotte, Mantua, Arcola, it wrote: Waterloo. Triumph of the undistinguished, pleasing to the majority. Destiny allowed this irony. When his sun was setting, Napoleon was confronted with a young Wurmser.

After all, you have only to give Wellington white hair, and you have Wurmser.

Waterloo is a first-rate battle won by a second-rate commander.

What must be admired in the battle of Waterloo is England, English steadfastness, English resolution, English blood. With all due respect, what was superb about England in this instance was England herself. It was not her captain, it was her army.

Peculiarly ungrateful, Wellington declares in a letter to Lord Bathurst that his army, the army that fought on the eighteenth of June 1815, was an 'infamous army'. What does that grievous jumble of human remains buried in the fields of Waterloo think of that?

England has been too modest in relation to Wellington. To make Wellington so great is to belittle England. Wellington is just a hero like any other. Those Scots Greys, those Horse Guards, those regiments of Maitland and Mitchell, that infantry of Pack and Kempt, that cavalry of Ponsonby and Somerset, those Highlanders playing their bagpipes under artillery fire, those battalions under Rylandt, those raw recruits who hardly knew how to handle a musket holding their own against the veteran troops of Essling and Rivoli, that is what is great. Wellington was tenacious, that was his virtue, and we do not begrudge him that, but the least of his footsoldiers and cavalry were just as staunch as he. The iron soldier is quite as good as the Iron Duke. As far as we are concerned, all our praise goes to the English soldier, the English army, the English people. If trophy there be, it is to England the trophy is due. The Waterloo memorial would be more legitimate if, instead of the figure of one man, the column raised to the skies the statue of a people.

But this great England will be annoyed by what we say. After her own 1688 and our 1789 she still cherishes the feudal illusion. She believes in heredity and hierarchy. This people that none surpasses in power and glory respects itself as a nation, not as the people. And as the people it willingly submits to authority and takes a lord for its leader. It lets the English workman be scorned, it lets the English soldier be flogged. Remember, at the battle of Inkerman, a sergeant who apparently saved the army could not be mentioned by Lord Raglan, as the English military hierarchy did not allow any hero below officer rank to be mentioned in a report.

What we admire above all in a conjuncture such as that of Waterloo is the amazing ingenuity of chance. Night rain, the Hougomont wall, Ohain's sunken road, Grouchy deaf to the cannon, Napoleon deceived by his guide, Bülow reliably informed by his – the entire disaster is wonderfully orchestrated.

Let us be honest, all things considered, what happened at Waterloo was more of a massacre than a battle.

Of all pitched battles Waterloo is the one with the smallest front in relation to the number of combatants. Napoleon, three thousand three hundred yards; Wellington, two thousand two hundred yards; seventy-two thousand combatants on each side. It was from this density that the carnage resulted.

The following calculation has been made and this ratio established for lives lost: at Austerlitz, French, fourteen per cent; Russians, thirty per cent; Austrians, forty-four per cent. At Wagram, French, thirteen per cent; Austrians, fourteen. At Borodino, French, thirty-seven per cent; Russians, forty-four. At Bautzen, French, thirteen per cent; Russians and Prussians, fourteen. At Waterloo, French, fifty-six per cent; Allies, thirty-one. Total for Waterloo, forty-one per cent. One hundred and forty-four thousand combatants; sixty thousand dead.

The field of Waterloo today has a peacefulness that belongs to the earth, man's impassive pedestal, and it looks like every other plain.

Yet at night a kind of visionary mist arises from it, and if some traveller wanders there, if he looks, if he listens, if he dreams like Virgil before the fateful plains of Philippi, the haunting catastrophe grips him. That ghastly eighteenth of June comes to life again. The spurious monument hill disappears, that undistinguished lion vanishes, the battlefield regains its reality. Lines of infantry ripple over the plain, galloping charges sweep across the horizon. The terror-stricken dreamer sees the flash of sabres, the glint of bayonets, the flare of bombshells, the monstrous exchange of thunderous fire. He hears, like a dying rasp from deep in the grave, the indistinct clamour of the phantom battle. Those shadows are grenadiers, those glistenings are cuirassiers. This skeleton is Napoleon, that skeleton is Wellington. All this is no more, and still they clash and the fighting goes on. And the gullies turn red, and the trees tremble, and there is fury even in the clouds. And all those untamed heights – Hougomont, Mont-St-Jean, Frischemont, Papelotte, Plancenoit – appear in the gloom indistinctly crowned with tumults of spectres slaughtering each other.

XVII
Should Waterloo Be Regarded as a Good Thing?

There is a very respectable liberal school of thought that does not abhor Waterloo. We are not of that school. For us, only to its astoundment is Waterloo a day of liberty. That such an eagle should emerge from such an egg is most certainly unexpected.

Looked at from the point of view of its immediate aftermath, Waterloo is meant to be a counter-revolutionary victory. It is Europe against France. It is Petersburg, Berlin and Vienna against Paris. It is the status quo against any initiative. It is the fourteenth of July 1789 attacked through the twentieth of March 1815. It is the monarchies taking action against the indomitable French mob. Finally to suppress that vast populace, in eruption now for twenty-six years, this was the dream. The Brunswicks, Nassaus, Romanoffs, Hohenzollerns, Habsburgs showing solidarity with the Bourbons. Divine right rides on the back of Waterloo. It is true that, the Empire having been despotic, by a natural reaction in the order of things royalty was bound to be liberal, and grudgingly, to the great regret of the victors, a constitutional order emerged from Waterloo. The fact is, revolution cannot be truly quelled and, being providential and absolutely inevitable, it keeps recurring: before Waterloo, with Bonaparte bringing down the old dynasties, after Waterloo, with Louis XVIII granting and submitting to the Charter. Bonaparte puts a coachman on the throne of Naples and a sergeant on the throne of Sweden, using inequality to demonstrate equality. Louis XVIII at St-Ouen countersigns the Declaration of the Rights of Man. If you want to understand what revolution is, call it Progress. And if you want to understand what progress is, call it Tomorrow. Tomorrow comes into effect irresistibly, and does so even today. It always achieves its end by strange means. It employs Wellington to turn Foy, a mere soldier, into an orator. Foy falls at Hougomont and rises as a politician. This is how progress operates. No such thing as a bad tool for this workman. Not to be deterred, he adapts to his divine task the man who bestrode the Alps and Père

Élysée's good old doddering invalid. He makes use of the gout-sufferer as well as the conqueror; of the conqueror abroad, the gout-sufferer at home. By cutting short the extirpation by the sword of the European monarchies, the effect of Waterloo was none other than to perpetuate the revolutionary enterprise in a different way. The swordsmen have finished, it is the turn of the thinkers. The century that Waterloo tried to halt walked right over it and continued on its way. That inauspicious victory was vanquished by liberty.

In short, and indisputably, what triumphed at Waterloo, what smiled on Wellington, what brought him the baton of every marshal of Europe, including, it is said, the baton of a marshal of France, what gladly trundled the barrowloads of earth full of human remains to raise the lion mound, what triumphantly inscribed on that pedestal the date '18 June 1815', what spurred Blücher in hacking the routed army to pieces, what loomed over France from the heights of the Mont-St-Jean plateau, as if over its prey, was the counter-revolution. It was the counter-revolution that murmured the infamous word 'dismemberment'. Once it got to Paris, it saw the volcano at close hand, it felt the volcanic ash burning its feet, and it had second thoughts. It reverted to stammering about a charter.

Let us not see Waterloo for anything other than what it was. Not intentionally liberal. The counter-revolution was inadvertently liberal just as, by a corresponding phenomenon, Napoleon was inadvertently revolutionary. On the eighteenth of June 1815, the mounted Robespierre was unseated.

XVIII
Another Outbreak of Divine Right

The end of dictatorship. A whole European system collapsed.

The Empire sank into a gloom resembling that of the dying Roman world. Once again people looked into the abyss as in the days of the barbarians. Only, the barbarism of 1815, which must be called by its own name, 'counter-revolution', was short-winded, soon ran out of breath and came to a standstill. Admittedly, tears were shed for the Empire, and heroes' eyes shed them. If glory lies in the sword made sceptre, the Empire was glory itself. It cast over the earth all the light of which tyranny is capable: a sombre light. Let us go further: an obscure light. Compared with true daylight it is darkness. The dispelling of this darkness created the effect of an eclipse.

Louis XVIII returned to Paris. The ring dances of July the eighth blotted out the revels of March the twentieth. The Corsican became the antithesis of the Béarnais. The flag on the dome of the Tuileries was white. Exile came to the throne. The pine table from Hartwell took its place in front of Louis XIV's fleur-de-lys covered armchair. Bouvines and Fontenoy were spoken of as if they had happened only yesterday, and Austerlitz had become old news. Church and monarchy fraternized majestically. One of the most undisputed symbols of nineteenth-century society's salvation was taken up throughout France and throughout the continent: Europe adopted the white cockade. Trestaillon was celebrated. The device *non pluribus impar** reappeared in the stone rays representing a sun on the front of the barracks on the Quai d'Orsay. Where there had been an Imperial Guard was now the royal household guard. All heaped with unfitting victories and out of place amid these new developments, a little ashamed perhaps of Marengo and Arcola, the Arc du Carrousel made the best of it with a statue of the Duc d'Angoulême. A ghastly common grave in 1793, the Madeleine Cemetery, with the bones of Louis XVI and Marie-Antoinette lying in that dust, was now covered with jasper and marble. In the moat of Vincennes a tombstone sprang up, recalling the fact that the Duc d'Enghien had perished in the same month that Napoleon was crowned. Pope Pius VII, who solemnized that coronation very soon after that death, placidly blessed the downfall just as he had blessed the elevation. There was at Schönbrunn a little ghost, aged four, whom it was seditious to call the king of Rome. And these things happened, and these kings regained their thrones, and the master of Europe was put in a cage, and the old regime became the new regime, and all the earth's light and all the earth's shadow changed places, because one afternoon on a certain summer's day a shepherd said to a Prussian in the forest: Go this way, not that!

This 1815 was a kind of gloomy April. Old, insalubrious and poisonous realities took on a new appearance. Untruth espoused 1789, divine right masked itself with a charter, fictions became constitutional; with Article 14 in their hearts, prejudices, superstitions and reservations took on a veneer of liberalism. Snakes changing their skin.

Man had been both magnified and diminished by Napoleon. During that reign of glorious physical achievement, the ideal had been given the strange name of ideology. A grave imprudence in a great

* 'Not unequal to many'. This motto was adopted, in a challenge to Habsburg hegemony, by the Sun King, Louis XIV; meaning, 'not unequal [to being a sun] to many [people/peoples]'.

man, to deride the future. The populace, however, that cannon fodder so fond of the cannon loader, kept looking to him. Where is he? What is he doing? 'Napoleon's dead,' said a passer-by to a veteran of Marengo and Waterloo. 'Napoleon dead!' cried the soldier. 'That's how well you know him.' The popular imagination threw down a challenge to this defeated man. After Waterloo there was dinginess at the heart of Europe. Napoleon's demise left a great emptiness that long remained unfilled.

Kings stepped into this void. Old Europe took the opportunity to reform. There was a Holy Alliance. Belle-Alliance!* the fateful field of Waterloo had said in anticipation.

Confronted with the presence of that old Europe recast, the features of a new France took shape. Disparaged by the emperor, the future made its entry. On its brow was that star, liberty. The ardent eyes of young generations turned to it. Strangely, people were inspired both by that future, liberty, and by that past, Napoleon. Defeat increased the stature of the vanquished. Bonaparte overthrown seemed greater than Napoleon standing. Those who had triumphed were scared. England had him guarded by Hudson Lowe, and France had him watched by Montchenu. His folded arms became the disquiet of monarchs. Alexander called him 'my insomnia'. This fear stemmed from how much of the revolutionary there was in him. Which is what explains and excuses Bonapartist liberalism. This spectre caused the old world to tremble. Kings reigned uneasily with the rock of St Helena on the horizon.

While Napoleon was dying at Longwood, the sixty thousand men who had fallen in battle at Waterloo quietly rotted, and something of their peacefulness spread throughout the world. And out of this the Congress of Vienna made the treaties of 1815, and Europe called this the Restoration.

That is what Waterloo is.

But what does it matter to the infinite? All this storm, all this cloud, this war, then this peace, all this shadow did not for an instant dim the gleam of that immense eye in which an aphid hopping from one blade of grass to another is equal to the eagle flying from belfry to belfry between the towers of Notre-Dame.

---

* The name of the farm that was one of the landmarks at Waterloo is cited here as an ironic comment – 'A fine alliance!'

The Battlefield at Night

Let us return, as we must for this book, to that fateful battlefield.

On the eighteenth of June there was a full moon. This brightness favoured Blücher's ferocious pursuit, betrayed the fugitives' traces, delivered up that hapless mass to the frenzied Prussian cavalry and contributed to the massacre. Sometimes catastrophes occur with the tragic collusion of the night.

After the last cannon-shot had been fired, the plain of Mont-St-Jean was left deserted.

The English occupied the French encampment, such is the way victory usually asserts itself: by sleeping in the bed of the vanquished. They bivouacked beyond Rossomme. The Prussians, unleashed on the routed army, pushed forward. Wellington went to the village of Waterloo to write his report to Lord Bathurst.

If ever *sic vos non vobis** was applicable, it is definitely to this village of Waterloo. Waterloo did nothing and remained over a mile away from the action. Mont-St-Jean was shelled, Hougomont was set ablaze, Papelotte was set ablaze, Plancenoit was set ablaze, La Haie-Sainte was stormed, La Belle-Alliance witnessed the embrace of the two victors. These names are scarcely known and Waterloo, which made no contribution to the battle, gets all the credit.

We are not one of war's sycophants. When the opportunity arises, we tell the truth about it. War has a terrible beauty of which we have made no secret. We can all agree it also has some uglinesses. One of the most surprising is the summary stripping of the dead after victory. The day after a battle always dawns on naked bodies.

Who does this? Who defiles triumph in this way? What hideous furtive hand is it that steals into victory's pocket? Who are these sneak thieves that ply their trade in the wake of glory? Some philosophers, Voltaire among them, maintain they are precisely those who won that glory. It is the same men, they say, there are no others who step in; those left standing pillage those lying on the ground. The hero of the

---

* 'So not for yourselves do you . . .' Words written out four times by Virgil, as a challenge to a poet who had claimed credit for some of his verse but was unable to complete these four lines, as Virgil then went on to do: 'I wrote these lines, another has gained the praise. / So not for yourselves do you draw the plough, oxen; / So not for yourselves do you make honey, bees; / So not for yourselves do you bear fleeces, sheep; / So not for yourselves do you build nests, birds.'

day is the vampire of the night. After all, a man surely has the right to a bit of thieving from a corpse when he is the author of its death. This is not what we believe. It seems impossible to us that winning the laurels and stealing the shoes from a dead man could be done by the same hand.

What is certain is that, as a rule, after the victors come the thieves. But let us not blame the soldier, especially not the contemporary soldier.

Every army has a tail-end and that is where the blame must lie. Hybrid creatures, half brigand half servant, every type of flying rat that this twilight, known as war, engenders – non-combatant wearers of uniform, fake invalids, intimidating cripples, unlicensed victuallers, sometimes with their wives, riding in little carts and stealing what they then sell on, beggars offering themselves as guides to officers, hangers-on, marauders. In days gone by (we are not speaking of the present), armies on the march had all this trailing after them, so much so that in military jargon they were called 'camp followers'. No army, no nation was responsible for these creatures. They spoke Italian and followed the Germans, they spoke French and followed the English. It was by one of these wretched camp followers, a French-speaking Spaniard, that the Marquis de Fervacques, taken in by his Picardy gabble and mistaking him for one of our own, during the night following the victory of Ceresole was treacherously slain and robbed on the very battlefield itself. The looter was born of looting. That ghastly maxim, 'Live off the enemy', produced this plague, which only strict discipline could cure. Some reputations are misleading; it is not always known why certain generals, indeed great generals, have been so popular. Turenne was adored by his soldiers because he tolerated looting. Making allowances for wrong-doing is an element of goodness. Turenne was so good that he allowed the Palatinate to be put to fire and sword. The marauders to be seen in the wake of an army were more or less numerous depending on whether the man in charge was more or less of a disciplinarian. Hoche and Marceau had no camp followers, Wellington had few, and we gladly give him credit for this.

Nevertheless, on the night of the eighteenth to the nineteenth of June, the dead were stripped. Wellington was uncompromising: he gave the order that anyone caught looting was to be shot. But looting is hard to stamp out. Looters stole in one corner of the battlefield while they were being shot in another.

The effect of the moonlight on this plain was lurid.

Around midnight a man was prowling, or rather lurking, over by the Ohain sunken road. He was to all appearances one of those specimens we have just described, neither English nor French, neither peasant nor soldier, not so much a man as a ghoul, drawn by the smell of the dead and, victory to him meaning theft, coming to pillage Waterloo. He wore a loose overgarment that was a bit like a great-coat. He was jittery and bold, he went forward and looked behind. Who was this man? Night probably knew more about him than day. He had no bag but evidently some capacious pockets under his coat. From time to time he halted, scanned the plain around him as though to check whether he was being watched, abruptly bent down, fiddled on the ground with something still and silent, then rose and slipped away. His stealth, his behaviour, his hurried and mysterious movements made him look like those twilight spectres that haunt ruins, and in old Norman legends are called 'les Alleurs'.

Certain nocturnal wading birds appear as such silhouettes in the marshes.

Any searching gaze that probed all that mist would have noticed, standing some distance away as if hidden behind the farm building on the Nivelles high road, at the corner of the road from Mont-St-Jean to Braine-l'Alleud, a little victualler's wagon of some sort with a tar-coated wicker hood, harnessed to a half-starved nag grazing on nettles through its bit, and in this wagon some woman sitting on top of various boxes and bundles. Maybe there was a connection between this wagon and this prowler.

The darkness was serene. Not a cloud in the sky above. So what, if the earth is red – the moon stays white. Such is the indifference of the heavens. In the meadows, branches of trees broken by shelling but not brought down, with their bark still holding, swayed gently in the night breeze. A breath of air, almost a sigh, stirred the scrub. There were quiverings in the grass, like souls departing.

The coming and going of patrols and of officers doing their rounds in the English camp could be heard indistinctly in the distance.

Hougomont and La Haie-Sainte continued to burn, raising two great blazes, to east and west, joined together by the line of English camp fires strung out over the hills on the horizon in a vast semicircle, like an unfastened necklace of rubies with two carbuncles at either end.

We have told of the disaster at the Ohain cutting. The heart is appalled at the thought of what a death that must have been for so many gallant men.

If there is one thing that is horrifying, if there exists a reality that is worse than any dream, it is this: to live, to see the sun, to be in the prime of manhood, to have health and happiness, to laugh bravely, to rush towards the glory that lies ahead of you, to feel in your breast breathing lungs, a beating heart, a reasoning will, to speak, think, hope, love, to have a mother, to have a wife, to have children, to have light, and all at once, in the time it takes to cry out, in less than a minute, to plunge into an abyss, to fall, tumble, crush, be crushed, to see ears of wheat, flowers, leaves, branches, not to be able to catch hold of anything, to feel your sword is useless, with men beneath you, horses on top of you, to struggle in vain, your bones broken by a kick in the dark, to feel a heel burst your eyeballs, to bite frantically on horseshoes, to suffocate, yell, writhe, to be buried, and to say to yourself, 'A moment ago I was alive!'

Where there had been the agonized moans of that dreadful calamity, all was silence now. The hollow of the sunken road was filled with horses and riders inextricably piled on top of each other. A terrible jumble. There was no embankment any more. The corpses had levelled the road with the plain, and came right up to the brim like a well filled bushel of barley. A heap of dead bodies on top, a river of blood below, such was this road on the evening of the eighteenth of June 1815. The blood ran all the way to the Nivelles high road and there formed a large pool in front of the felled trees that barred the way at a spot that is pointed out even today. It was, remember, on the opposite side, towards the Genappe road, that the cuirassiers came to grief. The pile of corpses varied in density according to how deep the sunken road was. Towards the middle, where it was flush with the plain, and where Delort's division had passed, the layer of corpses thinned out.

The night prowler, whom we have just brought to the reader's attention, made his way over there. He ferreted about in that vast tomb. He kept looking. He was carrying out who knows what hideous inspection of the dead. There was blood underfoot where he walked.

All of a sudden he stopped.

A few paces in front of him in the sunken road, just where the pile of dead bodies ended, sticking out from underneath that heap of men and horses was an open hand caught in the moonlight.

That hand had on its finger something that gleamed, and that something was a gold ring.

The man bent down, remained crouching for a moment, and when he stood up again there was no longer a ring on that hand.

He did not exactly stand up. He remained in a feral and fearful attitude, with his back to the pile of dead, scanning the horizon, kneeling, with the whole weight of his upper body borne on his two index fingers resting on the ground, his head peering over the edge of the sunken road. The jackal's four paws are suited to certain actions.

Then making a decision, he straightened up.

At that moment he gave a start. He felt someone holding on to him from behind.

He turned. It was the open hand, which had closed and grabbed the skirt of his coat.

An honest man would have been frightened. This one began to laugh.

'Well,' he said, 'it's only the corpse. I prefer a ghost to a gendarme.'

But the hand weakened and released him. Exertion is quickly spent in the grave.

'Now then,' said the prowler, 'is this corpse alive? Let's see.'

He bent down again, fumbled in the heap, pushed aside whatever was causing an obstruction, seized the hand, gripped the arm, freed the head, pulled out the body, and a few moments later he was dragging into the shadow of the sunken road a lifeless, or at least unconscious, man. He was a cuirassier, an officer, and indeed a fairly high-ranking officer; a large gold epaulette showed under his breast-plate. This officer had lost his helmet. A vicious sabre cut had slashed his face, so that all you could see was blood. That apart, he did not appear to have any broken limbs, and by a stroke of good luck, if that term may be used in this context, the dead had formed a buttress over him in such a way as to save him from being crushed. His eyes were closed.

On his breast-plate he wore the Legion of Honour silver cross.

The prowler tore off this cross, which disappeared into one of those deep pouches under his coat.

After which he patted the officer's fob-pocket, felt a watch there, and took it. Then he searched his waistcoat, found a purse and pocketed it.

When he reached this stage in delivering aid to this dying man, the officer opened his eyes.

'Thanks,' he said feebly.

The roughness of the way he had been manhandled, the night freshness, the air he could now breathe freely, had brought him out of his insensibility.

The prowler did not reply. He raised his head. The tread of feet on the plain could be heard – probably some patrol approaching.

The officer murmured, for there was still the anguish of death in his voice, 'Who won the battle?'

'The English,' answered the prowler.

The officer spoke again. 'Look in my pockets. You'll find a watch and a purse. Take them.'

That had already been done.

The prowler went through the motions of doing as he was asked, and said, 'There's nothing there.'

'I've been robbed,' said the officer. 'I'm sorry. They would have been yours.'

The patrol's footfalls became increasingly distinct.

'There's someone coming,' said the prowler with a start, like a man about to be off.

Raising his arm with difficulty, the officer detained him. 'You've saved my life. Who are you?'

The prowler spoke quickly and in a low voice. 'Like you, I was with the French army. I must leave you. If they were to catch me I'd be shot. I've saved your life. Now fend for yourself.'

'What's your rank?'

'Sergeant.'

'What's your name?'

'Thénardier.'

'I shan't forget that name,' said the officer. 'And you remember mine. My name is Pontmercy.'

BOOK TWO
THE SHIP *ORION*

I
Number 24601 Becomes Number 9430

Jean Valjean had been recaptured.

It will be appreciated if we do not dwell on the painful details. We will confine ourselves to reproducing two items published by contemporary newspapers a few months after the surprising events that had taken place at Montreuil-sur-Mer.

These articles are rather perfunctory. Remember, at that time there was no *Gazette des Tribunaux*.

The first is taken from *Le Drapeau Blanc*. It is dated the twenty-fifth of July 1823:

An *arrondissement* in the Pas de Calais has just been the scene of no ordinary event. A man from outside the *département*, named Monsieur Madeleine, had over the past few years, thanks to some new processes, rebuilt a local industry of long standing, the manufacture of jet and black glass trinkets. He had made his fortune by it and, admittedly, that of the *arrondissement*. In recognition of his services he had been appointed mayor. The police have discovered that this Monsieur Madeleine was none other than an ex-convict in breach of parole, imprisoned for theft in 1796, and named Jean Valjean. Jean Valjean has been sent back to prison. It appears that before his arrest he had succeeded in withdrawing from Monsieur Laffitte's bank a sum amounting to more than half a million, which he had deposited there and moreover earned perfectly legitimately, it is said, through his business activities. Since his return to the prison hulks at Toulon it has not been possible to find out where Jean Valjean has concealed this money.

The second article, a little more detailed, is taken from the *Journal de Paris* of the same date:

A freed convict named Jean Valjean has just appeared before the Var court of assizes in circumstances bound to attract attention. This villain had managed to elude police vigilance. He had changed his name and succeeded in getting himself appointed mayor of one of our small northern towns. He had established in this town a rather considerable business. He has finally been unmasked and arrested, thanks to the indefatigable zeal of the public prosecutor's office. He had for a mistress a common prostitute who died of a seizure at the time of his arrest. This wretch, who is endowed with Herculean strength, contrived to escape, but three or four days after his escape the police recaptured him, right here in Paris, just as he was getting into one of those small carriages that ply the route between the capital and the village of Montfermeil (Seine-et-Oise). He is said to have profited by this interval of three or four days' liberty to regain possession of a considerable sum that had been deposited by him with one of our leading bankers. This sum has been estimated at six or seven hundred thousand francs. According to the charges that have been brought against him, he has hidden it in some place known only to himself and it has proved impossible to seize it. However that may be, the said Jean Valjean has just been brought before the assizes of the *département* of the Var, accused of armed highway robbery, committed about eight years ago on the person of one of those honest children who, as the patriarch of Ferney has said in those immortal lines:

> . . . arrive from Savoy every year,
> And by whose hand are nimbly cleared
> Those long flues clogged with soot.

This brigand refused to defend himself. It was proved by the skilful and eloquent representative of the public prosecutor that there had been a conspiracy to rob, and that Jean Valjean belonged to a gang of thieves in the south of the country. Found guilty, Jean Valjean was given a death sentence. The criminal refused to lodge an appeal. The king, in his inexhaustible clemency, has been so good as to commute his sentence to penal servitude for life. Jean Valjean was immediately taken to the prison hulks at Toulon.

It will not be forgotten that Jean Valjean was a regular church-goer at Montreuil-sur-Mer. Some papers, among others *Le Constitutionnel*, represented this commutation as a triumph of the clerical party.

Jean Valjean's prisoner number changed. He was now 9430.

Anyway, let it be said once and for all, when Monsieur Madeleine went, the prosperity of Montreuil-sur-Mer went with him. Everything he had foreseen during his night of feverishness and indecision came true. With him gone, the moving spirit was indeed gone. After his downfall there was at Montreuil-sur-Mer that self-interested parcelling-out of the spoils of the once great, that fatal carving-up of flourishing enterprises that takes place in obscurity every day among humankind, and which history has noted only once because it occurred after the death of Alexander. Lieutenants crowned themselves king. Foremen acted as factory-owners. Envious rivalries sprang up. Monsieur Madeleine's vast workshops were closed down. The buildings fell into ruin. The workmen went their separate ways, some of them left the area, others left the trade. From then on, everything was done on a small scale instead of being done on a large scale, for money instead of the general good. The centre now gone, competition rife, and everywhere rapacious greed. Monsieur Madeleine had it all under control, and he gave direction. With his removal, it was every man for himself. The spirit of organization gave way to the spirit of conflict. Cordiality gave way to bitterness. The founder's benevolence towards all gave way to hatred of one another. The threads Monsieur Madeleine had woven together became tangled and broke. Manufacturing processes were compromised, the quality of the products deteriorated, trust was destroyed, markets shrank, orders fell, wages dropped, workshops stood idle, bankruptcy followed. And then the poor were left with nothing. It all disappeared.

The state itself noticed that someone had been put out of business somewhere. Less than four years after the court of assizes' ruling whereby Monsieur Madeleine was identified as Jean Valjean to the benefit of the prison hulks, the cost of collecting taxes had doubled in the *arrondissement* of Montreuil-sur-Mer, and Monsieur de Villèle pointed this out in an address to parliament in February 1827.

II
In Which Are to Be Read Two Lines of Verse Perhaps by the Devil

Before going any further, it is appropriate at this point to relate in some detail a singular incident that took place at Montfermeil at about the same time, and which may be not unconnected with certain conjectures made by the public prosecutor.

There is at Montfermeil a very ancient local superstition, all the more curious and all the more precious because a popular superstition anywhere near Paris is like an aloe in Siberia. We are among those who have respect for anything in the way of a rare plant. This, then, is the superstition of Montfermeil: people believe that the devil has from time immemorial chosen to hide his treasures in the forest. The womenfolk say it is not uncommon at nightfall in out-of-the-way parts of the forest to encounter a black man, looking like a carter or a wood-cutter, wearing wooden clogs, dressed in trousers and a coarse smock, and recognizable by the fact that instead of a cap or hat he has two huge horns on his head. Sure enough, this must make him recognizable. The man is usually busy digging a hole. There are three ways of dealing with such an encounter. The first is to approach the man and speak to him. Then you realize that the man is just a peasant, that he looks black because it is dusk, that he is not digging a hole at all but cutting grass for his cows, and what you mistook for horns is nothing but a pitchfork he is carrying on his back, the prongs of which, thanks to the twilight distortion of perspective, appeared to be sprouting out of his head. You go home and die within the week. The second method is to watch him, wait until he has dug his hole, filled it in and gone away, then to run over very quickly to where he was digging, open up the hole again and take the 'treasure' which the black man has inevitably left there. In this case you die within the month. Finally, the third method is not to speak to the black man, not to look at him, and to run away as fast as your legs can carry you. You die within the year.

As all three methods have their drawbacks, the second, which at least offers some advantages – among others, that of owning a treasure, if only for a month – is the one most generally adopted. So, always tempted to try their luck, bold men have quite frequently, we are assured, opened up the holes dug by the black man and tried to rob the devil. Apparently it is a poor deal – at least if tradition is anything to go by, and in particular the two enigmatic lines on the subject, in barbarous Latin, left by a wicked Norman monk named Tryphon, who was a bit of a sorcerer. This Tryphon is buried at the abbey of St-Georges de Bocherville, near Rouen, and toads breed on his grave.

So tremendous exertions are made, usually these holes are very deep, a man sweats, digs, toils all night (for this is done at night), he gets his shirt soaked, he burns out his rush-light, he damages his pick, and when at last he reaches the bottom of the hole, when he lays his hand on the 'treasure', what does he find? What is this devil's treasure? A sou, occasionally a silver coin, a stone, a skeleton, a bleeding corpse, sometimes a ghost folded in four like a sheet of paper in a wallet, sometimes nothing. Which is what Tryphon's lines of verse seem to warn meddlesome snoopers:

> *Fodit, et in fossa thesauros condit opaca,*
> *As, nummos, lapides, cadaver, simulacra, nihilque.**

---

* 'He digs, and in the dark hole buries treasure, / a sou, coins, stones, a corpse, phantoms and nothing.'

These days, apparently, people sometimes also find a powder flask with bullets, sometimes an old pack of greasy, singed playing-cards that has obviously been used by devils. Tryphon does not record these two finds, since Tryphon lived in the twelfth century and the devil does not seem to have had the wit to invent gunpowder before Roger Bacon, or playing-cards before Charles VI.

What is more, if you play with these cards, you are sure to lose everything you possess, and as for the powder in the flask, it has the property of causing your gun to blow up in your face.

Now, very shortly after the period when it seemed to the public prosecutor that, while on the loose for several days, the freed convict Jean Valjean had been prowling around Montfermeil, in that very same village people noticed that an old road-mender named Boulatruelle was 'behaving oddly' in the forest. Locally, it was generally taken for a fact that this Boulatruelle was an ex-convict. He was subject to some sort of police surveillance, and as he could not find a job anywhere else the authorities employed him for a pittance as a road-mender on the Gagny to Lagny byway.

This fellow Boulatruelle was a man regarded with distrust by the local people, too respectful, too humble, quick to doff his cap to everyone, trembling and smiling in the presence of gendarmes, probably connected with robber bands, they said, suspected of lying in ambush on the edge of the woods at nightfall. The only thing in his favour was that he was a drunkard.

This is what was thought to have been observed:

Of late, Boulatruelle had taken to leaving his job of stone-laying and road maintenance very early and going off into the forest with his pickaxe. People encountered him towards the close of day in the most deserted clearings, in the wildest thickets, looking as if he was searching for something, sometimes digging holes. The women who passed by at first mistook him for Beelzebub, then they would recognize Boulatruelle and were scarcely more reassured. These encounters seemed to vex Boulatruelle deeply. It was obvious that he was trying to keep out of sight, and there was some mystery in what he was doing.

It was said in the village, 'Clearly the devil has made some sort of appearance. Boulatruelle saw him, and he's now searching. He has actually got it in him to steal Lucifer's hoard.' Voltairians added, 'Will it be Boulatruelle that gets the better of the devil, or the devil that gets the better of Boulatruelle?' Old women made a great many signs of the cross.

Meanwhile Boulatruelle's antics in the forest ceased, and he went back to his usual road-mending. The talk turned to something else.

Nevertheless, a few individuals remained curious, thinking that what was involved here was probably not the fabulous legendary treasures but some stroke of good luck, more serious and more tangible than the devil's banknotes, of which the road-mender had no doubt half discovered the secret. The most 'intrigued' were the schoolmaster and the innkeeper Thénardier, who was friendly with everybody and not above striking up a relationship with Boulatruelle.

'He's been in the prison hulks?' said Thénardier. 'Well, by God, who's to say who's there now or will be in the future?'

One evening the schoolmaster declared that in the old days the law would have investigated what Boulatruelle was up to in the forest, and he would have been made to talk, and put to torture if necessary, and that Boulatruelle would not have held out against the water test, for instance.

'Let's put him to the wine test,' said Thénardier.

They did their utmost to get the old road-mender drunk. Boulatruelle drank an enormous amount and said very little. He combined with admirable skill and in masterly proportion a guzzler's thirst with the discretion of a judge. Nonetheless, by dint of making repeated attempts, and piecing together and milking the few obscure words he did let slip, this is what Thénardier and the schoolmaster thought they deduced:

One morning at daybreak, when Boulatruelle was on his way to work, somewhere in the woods he had been surprised to see a shovel and pick under a bush, 'almost as if they'd been hidden'. However, he supposed they were probably the shovel and pick of Père Six-Fours the water-carrier, and thought no more about it. But on the evening of the same day, he had seen – though he himself could not be seen, being hidden behind a large tree – 'a certain individual who wasn't at all from these parts, and that he, Boulatruelle, knew very well' (translation by Thénardier: 'a fellow inmate of the prison hulks'), heading away from the road into the densest part of the forest. Boulatruelle stubbornly refused to reveal his name. This individual was carrying a package, something square, like a large box or a small chest. Surprisingly, to Boulatruelle. Yet not until seven or eight minutes had passed did the idea of following 'this certain individual' occur to him. But it was too late. The individual was already in the thick of the forest, darkness had fallen, and Boulatruelle had not been able to catch up with him. So he decided to keep watch on the edge of the woods. 'There was moonlight.' Two or three hours later Boulatruelle saw his man emerge from the woods, carrying not the little coffer any more but a shovel and pick. Boulatruelle let the individual go past, and did not dream of accosting him because he said to himself the other fellow was three times stronger than he was and armed with a pick and would probably bash him over the head when he recognized him and realized that he himself had been recognized. Touching demonstrations of feeling on the part of two old comrades encountering each other again. But the shovel and pick had been a ray of light to Boulatruelle. He hurried to the bush he had noticed that morning, and found that neither shovel nor pick was there any more. From this he concluded that having gone into the forest, his man had dug a hole with his pick, buried the chest, and filled in the hole with his shovel. Now, the chest was too small to contain a body, so it contained money. Hence the searching. Boulatruelle had explored, scoured, combed the whole forest, and had dug wherever he thought the earth had been recently disturbed. In vain.

He had 'turned up' nothing. No one in Montfermeil thought any more about it. There were only a few old crones who said, 'You may depend on it, the Gagny road-mender didn't do all that spadework for nothing. The devil came, for sure.'

III
The Ankle-chain Must Have Been Worked on Previously, to Break at a Single Hammer Blow

Towards the end of October of that same year of 1823 the inhabitants of Toulon saw the return to their port, for the repair of some damage after heavy weather, of the ship *Orion*, later used at Brest as a training-ship, and at that time part of the Mediterranean fleet.

Crippled as it was, for the seas had been rough with it, this vessel created an impression as it came into harbour. It flew some flag or other that earned it a statutory eleven-gun salute, which was returned shot for shot. Total: twenty-two. It has been calculated that in salvoes, royal and military honours, exchanges of courtesy volleys, ceremonial signals, harbour and citadel formalities, sunrise and sunset salutes every day by all forts and all ships of war, port openings and closings et cetera, the civilized world was discharging around the globe every twenty-four hours one hundred and fifty thousand unnecessary cannon shots. At six francs per cannon shot, that comes to nine hundred thousand francs a day, three hundred million a year, that go up in smoke. This is just one small detail. Meanwhile the poor are dying of hunger.

The year 1823 was what the Restoration called 'the time of the Spanish war'.

A single event of great incident, this war had many peculiarities. A big family affair for the Bourbon dynasty, the French branch aiding and protecting the Madrid branch, that is to say, exercising its seniority; an apparent return to our national traditions complicated by subjection to constraints imposed by the governments of the north; Monsieur le Duc d'Angoulême, dubbed 'the hero of Andújar' by the liberal press, striking a triumphant pose somewhat at odds with his peaceable manner, curbing the old and very real terrorism of the Holy Office in its dealings with the imaginary terrorism of the liberals; the sans-culottes revived, to the great horror of dowagers, under the name of *descamisados*; monarchism impeding progress portrayed as anarchy; the theories of '89 suddenly sapped of strength; a European stop put to the French idea spreading around the world; in that crusade of kings against peoples, the Prince of Carignano, later Charles Albert, enrolling as a volunteer with the red worsted epaulettes of a grenadier, alongside the generalissimo son of France; soldiers of the Empire going to war again, but after eight years' rest, aged, saddened and under the white cockade; the tricolour flag waved abroad by a handful of heroic Frenchmen, just as thirty years earlier the white standard was waved at Koblenz; monks mingling with our troops; the spirit of liberty and change made to see reason by bayonets; principles battered by cannon fire; France undoing by force of arms what she had achieved by force of intellect; in addition to this, enemy leaders bribed, soldiers irresolute, towns besieged by millions; no military risks and yet the possibility of explosions, as with all undermining in the event of discovery and penetration; little bloodshed, little honour won, shameful for some, glorious for none – such was this war waged by princes descended from Louis XIV and conducted by generals who had made their careers under Napoleon. Its sad fate was to be a revival of neither great war nor great politics.

There were a few genuine feats of arms. The capture of Trocadero, among others, was a fine military action; but overall, we repeat, the trumpets of this war produce a cracked sound, the whole enterprise was dubious, history endorses France in finding it hard to accept this spurious triumph. It seemed clear that certain Spanish officers whose duty was to resist yielded too easily. The victory gave rise to a suggestion of corruption. It appeared that generals rather than battles had been won, and the conquering soldier came home humbled. A belittling war indeed, in which the words 'Bank of France' could be read in the folds of the flag.

Soldiers of the 1808 war, on whom Saragossa had fallen mightily, frowned in 1823 at the easy opening-up of citadels and began to regret

Palafox. France's temperament is such that it would far rather have to face Rostopchin than Ballesteros.

From a yet more serious point of view, and one that ought also to be emphasized, this war that offended the military spirit in France incensed the democratic spirit. It was an enterprise of subjugation. In this campaign the object of the French soldier, son of democracy, was the conquest of a yoke for others. Hideous inconsistency. France is meant to stir the soul of nations, not to stifle it. Since 1792 all revolutions in Europe have been the French Revolution: liberty radiates from France. It is a solar phenomenon. None but the blind can fail to see it! Bonaparte said so.

The war of 1823, an outrage against the brave Spanish people, was at the same time, therefore, an outrage against the French Revolution. It was France that committed this monstrous offence – by violence, for aside from wars of liberation everything armies do is done by violence. The term 'unquestioning obedience' indicates this. An army is a strangely contrived masterpiece by which force results from an enormous amount of powerlessness. This is the explanation of war, waged by humanity against humanity despite humanity.

As for the Bourbons, the war of 1823 was disastrous for them. They regarded it as a success. They did not see the danger that lies in suppressing an idea by decree. They were so mistaken in their naivety that they introduced into their institution as an element of strength the great undermining weakness of a crime. The spirit of machination entered their government. The seed of 1830 was sown in 1823. In their decision-making the Spanish campaign became an argument for the use of force and for divine-right initiatives. Having re-established *el rey neto** in Spain, France could surely re-establish the absolute monarch at home. They fell into the dreadful error of mistaking the obedience of the soldier for the consent of the nation. That kind of misplaced confidence leads to the loss of thrones. Fall asleep at your peril in the shade of a manchineel tree, or in the shadow of an army.

But to return to the ship *Orion*:

While the army conducted its operations under the command of the prince-generalissimo, a fleet cruised in the Mediterranean. We have just mentioned that the *Orion* was in this fleet and that events at sea had brought it back to port at Toulon.

There is something about the presence of a warship in a port that fascinates and draws the crowd. It is because it has grandeur, and the crowd loves grandeur.

---

* Spanish: 'the absolute king'.

A ship of the line is one of the most magnificent conjunctions of the genius of man and the power of nature.

A ship of the line combines both the heaviest and lightest of components because it operates at one and the same time with the three forms of matter, solid, liquid and gas, and must contend with all three. It has eleven iron claws to grab the granite sea-bed, and to catch the wind in the clouds it has more wings and feelers than any flying insect. Its breath is expelled from its one hundred and twenty cannons as from enormous bugles, and proudly answers thunder. The ocean tries to lead it astray in the frightening sameness of its waves, but the vessel has a soul, its compass, that guides it and always indicates north. On dark nights its lanterns act as substitutes for the stars. So against the wind, it has rope and canvas; against water, timber; against rock, iron, brass and lead; against darkness, light; against immensity, a needle.

If you wish to get some idea of all these gigantic proportions that together constitute the ship of the line, you have only to go into one of the six-storey building-sheds in the port of Brest or Toulon. There, under a bell jar, as it were, are the vessels under construction. This colossal beam is a yard, that great column of wood lying on the ground, stretching as far as the eye can see, is the mainmast. Measured from its root in the hold to its top in the clouds, it is three hundred and sixty feet long, and three feet in diameter at the base. The English mainmast rises to a height of two hundred and seventeen feet above the water line. Our ancestors' navy used ropes, ours uses chains. The ordinary pile of chains for a one-hundred-gun ship is four feet high, twenty feet wide and eight feet deep. And how much timber is needed to build this vessel? One hundred and ten thousand cubic feet. It is a floating forest.

And furthermore, it should be noted, we are talking only about the naval vessel of forty years ago here, the simple sailing-ship. Steam, then in its infancy, has since added new miracles to that wonder called the warship. At the present time, for example, the hybrid vessel with a screw propeller is an astonishing machine, driven by a spread of over three thousand five hundred square yards of canvas and a two thousand five hundred horse-power steam engine.

Leaving aside these new marvels, the old-fashioned vessel of Christopher Columbus and de Ruyter is one of man's great masterpieces. It is as limitless in power as is the infinite in breezes, it gathers the wind in its sails, it is unerring in the immense diffusiveness of the waves; afloat it rules.

Yet there comes a time when the gale snaps this sixty-foot yard like a twig, when the wind bends this four-hundred-foot mast like a reed, when this anchor, weighing ten thousand pounds, swings about in the trough of the wave like a fisherman's hook in the jaws of a pike, when those monstrous cannons utter plaintive and futile roars that the hurricane carries away into the darkness and into the void, when all that might and all that majesty are engulfed in a superior might and majesty.

Whenever immense force is deployed and ends up as immense weakness, men's imaginations are stirred. Hence the curious observers in seaports who, without quite understanding why, come flocking round these marvellous machines of war and navigation.

So every day from morning till evening, the quays, pierheads and jetties of Toulon harbour were crowded with a multitude of idlers and gawpers, *badauds* as they say in Paris, making it their business to view the *Orion*.

The *Orion* was a ship that had been in poor shape for a long time. On her previous sailings, thick layers of barnacles had collected on the hull, so much so that her speed was reduced by half. She had gone into dry dock the year before to have these barnacles scraped off, then she put out to sea again. But this scraping had weakened the bolting on the hull. When the ship reached the Balearic Isles the strained planking opened up and, as the hull was not lined with sheet metal in those days, the vessel had shipped water. A violent equinoctial gale had sprung up and staved in the ship's head and broken through a porthole on the port side, and damaged the foresail chain-wales. After sustaining these injuries the *Orion* had returned to Toulon.

She was anchored near the Arsenal. She was in commission and under repair. The hull was not damaged on the starboard side, but in the usual way a few planks had been prised open here and there to let air into the hold.

One morning, the crowd watching her witnessed an accident.

The crew were busy bending sails. The yardman responsible for fastening the earings on the main-topgallant on the starboard side lost his balance. He was seen to wobble. The multitude thronging the Arsenal quay gave a cry. Plunging head first, the man went over the yard, his hands stretched out towards the abyss. He grabbed at the footrope in passing, first with one hand, then the other, and there he was left dangling. The sea lay dizzyingly far below him. The impact of his fall set the footrope swinging violently. The man swayed back and forth on that rope like a stone in a sling.

To go to his aid was to take a terrifying risk. Not one of the sailors, all fishermen from along the coast recently levied for service, dared venture it. Meanwhile, the poor yardman was tiring. The anguish on his face could not be seen but his exhaustion showed in every limb. His arms were horribly stretched by his own weight. Every effort he made to hoist himself up served only to make the footrope swing more wildly. He did not shout, for fear of wasting his strength. With no expectation of rescue, the moment when he should let go of the rope was inevitable, and all heads turned aside every now and then so as not to see him fall. There are moments when a piece of rope, a pole, the branch of a tree, represents life itself, and it is a terrible thing to see a human being separate from it and drop like a ripe fruit.

All of a sudden came the glimpse of a man climbing up the rigging with the agility of a tiger-cat. This man was dressed in red, he was a convict. He wore a green cap, he was a lifer. When he reached the top a gust of wind carried his cap away and revealed him to be completely white-haired. This was not a young man.

Indeed, a convict working on board with a forced-labour gang from the prison hulks had rushed up to the officer of the watch in the very first instant, and amid the crew's consternation and hesitation, while all the sailors trembled and backed away he had asked the officer's permission to risk his life to save the yardman. At a nod from the officer, with one blow of a hammer he had broken the chain riveted to the shackle round his ankle, then grabbed a rope, and leapt up into the shrouds. No one noticed at the time how easily that chain was broken. It was only later that people remembered.

In an instant he was on the yard. He paused for a few seconds and seemed to be eyeing it up. Those seconds during which the yardman swung in the breeze, hanging by a thread, seemed like centuries to those watching. At last the convict looked up to heaven and took a step forward. The crowd breathed again. They saw him run along the yard. When he reached the yardarm he fastened to it one end of the rope he had brought with him, and let the other hang down; then he began to lower himself down this rope, hand over hand, and now the tension was indescribable: instead of one man suspended over the abyss, there were two.

It looked like a spider coming to catch a fly, only in this case the spider brought life, not death. Ten thousand pairs of eyes were fixed on those two. Not a cry, not a word, the same contraction furrowed every brow. Every mouth held its breath as if afraid to add in the slightest to the breeze that shook those two poor wretches.

Meanwhile, the convict managed to lower himself to within reach of the sailor. Just in time: another minute, and the exhausted and despairing man would have dropped into the abyss. The convict securely lashed round him the rope to which he clung with one hand, as he worked with the other. At last they saw him climb back on to the yard and haul the sailor up after him. He held him there for a moment to let him regain strength, then picked him up and carried him, walking along the yard to the mast cap and from there down into the mast top, where he left him in the hands of his shipmates.

At that moment the crowd applauded: there were old chain-gang warders who wept, and women embraced each other on the quayside, and all voices were heard to cry with a kind of surge of compassion, 'The selflessness of that man!'

He, meanwhile, immediately set about climbing down to rejoin his fellow convict-labourers. To hasten his descent he slid down the rigging, and started running along one of the lower yards. All eyes followed him. At a certain moment everyone was stricken with fear. Whether it was that he was exhausted or overcome with dizziness, he seemed to falter and teeter. All at once the crowd gave a great cry: the convict had just fallen into the sea.

It was a perilous drop. The frigate *Algésiras* was moored alongside the *Orion*, and the poor convict had fallen between the two ships. There was reason to fear he might be trapped under one or the other. Four men quickly leapt into a boat. The crowd cheered them on, again every soul was filled with anxiety. The man had not risen to the surface. He had vanished into the sea without causing a ripple, as though he had fallen into a vat of oil. They searched, they dived. It was to no avail. The search continued until nightfall. They did not even find the body.

The following day the Toulon newspaper published these few lines:

17 November, 1823. Yesterday a convict with a forced-labour gang on board the *Orion*, on his way back after going to the rescue of a sailor, fell into the sea and was drowned. His body could not be found. It is assumed it must have become trapped under the pilings at the Arsenal point: this man was registered as prisoner number 9430, and his name was Jean Valjean.

BOOK THREE
A DEATHBED PROMISE
IS HONOURED

The Problem of Water at Montfermeil

Montfermeil is situated between Livry and Chelles on the southern edge of that high plateau separating the Ourcq from the Marne. Today it is a fairly large market-town, graced throughout the year by stuccoed villas and on Sundays by prosperous gentry. In 1823 there were neither so many white houses nor so many satisfied gentry at Montfermeil. It was just a village in the woods. You certainly came across a few country houses dating from the last century, recognizable by their air of grandeur, their wrought-iron balconies, and those long windows with little panes of glass that reflect all kinds of different shades of green on the white of the closed shutters. But Montfermeil was nonetheless a village. Retired drapers and professional holidaymakers had not yet discovered it. It was a peaceful and charming place that was not on the way to anywhere. There, at little expense, people lived that peasant life of great bounty and ease. Only water was scarce, on account of the height of the plateau.

You had to go quite far to fetch it. The Gagny side of the village drew its water from the magnificent ponds they have in the woods over there. The only drinking-water to be found at the other end of the village, round by the church, on the Chelles side, came from a little spring halfway down the hill, close to the Chelles road, about a quarter of an hour from Montfermeil.

So this fetching of water was quite a heavy chore for every household. The large houses, the aristocracy, which included the Thénardier inn, paid a quarter-sou per bucketful to a fellow who made his living in this way, and who earned about eight sous a day from this business of supplying Montfermeil with water. But this fellow worked only until seven o'clock in the evening in summer and five o'clock in winter, and once darkness had fallen, and the ground-floor shutters were closed, anyone who had no water to drink went to fetch it or went without.

Now this was the terror of that poor creature the reader may not

341

have forgotten, little Cosette. Remember, Cosette was useful to the Thénardiers in two ways: they got the mother to pay them, and the child to wait on them. So when her mother stopped paying altogether – the reader learned why in preceding chapters – the Thénardiers kept Cosette. They treated her as a servant. As such, she it was who ran to fetch water when it was needed. And quite terrified at the idea of going to the spring at night, the child made sure there was never a lack of water in the house.

Christmas of the year 1823 was particularly jolly at Montfermeil. The onset of winter had been mild. There had been no snow or frost yet. Some street entertainers from Paris had obtained permission from the mayor to put up their booths in the village's main street, and by the same licence a group of itinerant merchants had erected their stalls on the church square and even as far down as Ruelle du Boulanger where, the reader may remember, the Thénardier inn was located. As a result the inns and taverns were full, and that quiet little village acquired a rowdy and cheerful liveliness. We should even mention, for the sake of historical accuracy, that among the curiosities displayed in the square was a menagerie in which some dreadful touts, dressed in tatters and from who knows where, exhibited to the peasants of Montfermeil in 1823 one of those terrifying vultures from Brazil that our Royal Museum did not possess until 1845, and which have a tri-colour cockade for an eye. Naturalists, I believe, call this bird *Caracara polyborus*. It belongs to the order Accipitres and to the family of vultures. A few good old Bonapartist soldiers in retirement in the village went religiously along to see this creature. The mountebanks said the tricolour cockade was a unique phenomenon created by the good Lord especially for their menagerie.

That Christmas evening several men, carters and pedlars, were seated at a table around four or five candles, drinking in the low-ceilinged room of the Thénardier inn. This room was like all tavern rooms: tables, pewter jugs, bottles, drinkers, smokers; dimly lit, very noisy. However, the date was signalled as that of the year 1823 by two objects on the table that were then fashionable among the bourgeois class, namely a kaleido-scope and a moiré-métallique lamp. Thénardier's wife was attending to the supper, which was roasting in front of a good blazing fire. Her husband was drinking with his customers and talking politics.

As well as the political conversations, which were mainly on the subject of the Spanish war and Monsieur le Duc d'Angoulême, audible amid the hubbub were comments on matters of entirely local concern, such as the following:

'Round Nanterre and Suresnes they produced a lot of wine this year. Where they were expecting ten barrels they ended up with twelve. There was a lot of juice got out of the pressing.'

'But the grapes can't have been ripe?'

'In those parts the grapes mustn't be harvested ripe. If they're harvested ripe the wine turns oily by spring.'

'Then the wine's very light?'

'Those wines are even lighter than the ones from round here. The harvesting has to be done early.' Et cetera.

Or a miller was shouting, 'Are we responsible for what's in the sacks? We find countless small seeds in them that we can't afford to spend time picking out and that just have to be left to go through the mill. There's darnel, yellow vetchling, corncockle, vetch, hempseed, couch grass, meadow fox-tail and a host of other tares, not to mention the quantity of grit in certain types of grain, particularly Breton grain. I don't like milling Breton wheat any more than pit sawyers like to saw beams with nails in them. Imagine all the unwholesome dust that adds to the yield. And then people complain about the flour. They shouldn't. The flour's no fault of ours.'

In a space between two windows a reaper, sat at the same table as a landowner negotiating a price for some work to be done on a meadow in the spring, was saying, 'There's no harm in the grass being wet. It cuts better. Dew helps, monsieur. In any case grass like that, your grass, it's still young and very hard to cut. Being as it's so tender, you see, it flattens before the blade.' Et cetera.

Cosette was in her usual place, seated on the crossbar of the kitchen table near the chimney. She was in rags, with her bare feet in wooden clogs, and she was knitting by the firelight some woollen stockings for the little Thénardier girls. A kitten was playing under the chairs. The clear voices of two children could be heard laughing and chattering in a neighbouring room: Éponine and Azelma.

In the chimney corner a leather strap hung from a nail.

Intermittently the cries of a very young child somewhere in the house pierced the tavern din. It was a little boy Thénardier's wife had given birth to one winter – 'without knowing why,' she said, 'as a result of the cold' – and who was a little over three years old. The mother had nursed him but she did not love him. When the little mite's desperate wailing became too hard to ignore, Thénardier would say, 'Your son's squalling, go and see what he wants.' 'Bah!' the mother would reply, 'I can't be bothered with him.' And the neglected infant would carry on crying in the dark.

Two Finished Portraits

So far in this book the Thénardiers have been seen only in profile. The time has come to circle around this couple and consider them from every angle.

Thénardier had just turned fifty. Madame Thénardier was close to forty, which is fifty for a woman, so husband and wife were of equivalent age.

Our readers may have retained, from her very first appearance, some memory of this Thénardier woman, tall, blonde, ruddy, greasy, brawny, robust, huge and agile. She was, as we have said, akin to that race of feral giant-women at fairs who strut about with paving-stones suspended from their hair. She did everything in the house, the bed-making, the cleaning, the washing, the cooking, the this, the that and the other. Her only domestic help was Cosette: a mouse in the service of an elephant. Everything trembled at the sound of her voice, window-panes, furniture and people. Her broad face was as covered with freckles as a skimming ladle is riddled with holes. She had something of a beard. She was the archetypal market porter dressed up as a girl. She swore magnificently. She boasted of being able to crack a walnut with a single blow of her fist. Were it not for the romances she had read, which at times caused the mincing maid beneath the ogress to make a bizarre reappearance, it would never have occurred to anyone to say of her, 'That's a woman.' This Thénardier woman was like the product of grafting a young little miss on a fishwife. If you heard her speak, you would say, 'That's a martinet.' If you watched her drink, you would say, 'That's an old soak.' If you saw the way she treated Cosette, you would say, 'That's a vicious brute.' In repose, a tooth stuck out of her mouth.

A small, thin, pale, angular, bony, puny man, Thénardier looked poorly and was in the best of health – this is where his cunning began. To be on the safe side he smiled habitually, and was more or less polite to everybody, even the beggar to whom he refused a quarter-sou. He had the eyes of a ferret and the appearance of a man of letters. He greatly resembled portraits of Abbé Delille. He indulged his own vanity by drinking with carters. No one had ever managed to get him drunk. He smoked a large pipe. He wore a smock and under his smock an old black coat. He had pretensions in the way of literature and materialism. There were certain names he often mentioned to support whatever he was saying: Voltaire, Raynal, Parny, and oddly enough St Augustine. He claimed to have 'a system'. All in all, a great swindler. A crook philosopher – a *filousophe**. This is a distinct category that does exist. Remember, he claimed to have served in the army. He would relate with some relish how at Waterloo, as a sergeant in the 6th or the 9th Light something or other, under a hail of fire, alone against a squadron of death's-head hussars, he had protected with his body and saved 'a dangerously wounded general'. Hence the gaudy sign on his wall and the name by which his inn was known locally, 'the Sergeant of Waterloo tavern'. He was liberal, classicist and Bonapartist. He had contributed to the Champ d'Asile fund. In the village the story was that he had studied for the priesthood.

We believe he had merely studied in Holland to be an innkeeper. This fraudster of a mongrel order was most likely a Fleming from Lille when in Flanders, a Frenchman in Paris, a Belgian in Brussels, conveniently astride two frontiers. His valour at Waterloo we are already familiar with. As we can see, he exaggerated a little. The shifting, the devious, the accidental, was his natural element. A slippery conscience leads to an unsettled life, and probably at that tumultuous time around the eighteenth of June 1815 Thénardier belonged to that breed of marauding purveyors we have already mentioned, roaming about, selling to some, stealing from others, and travelling as a family man with wife and children, in some rickety cart in the wake of troops on the march, with an instinct for always attaching themselves to the victorious army. With this campaign behind him and having, as he said, 'the wherewithal', he had come to Montfermeil and opened an inn.

The wherewithal, consisting of purses and watches, gold rings and silver crosses gathered at harvest time from furrows sown with corpses, did not amount to a large sum, and had not carried this victualler turned innkeeper very far.

Thénardier had that suggestion of straightness in his gestures that when accompanied by an oath conjures up the barracks, and by a sign of the cross, the seminary. He was a fine talker. He did nothing to discourage the belief that he was a man of learning. Nevertheless, the schoolmaster noticed that he 'took some liberties' in his use of language.† He wrote out travellers' bills with an air of superiority, but keen eyes sometimes spotted spelling mistakes. Thénardier was cunning, greedy, idle and crafty. He was not above philandering with his servants, which meant his wife no longer kept any. This giantess was

---

* Hugo creates his own word for this hybrid, *un filousophe* being a combination of *philosophe* ('philosopher') and *filou* ('swindler').

† Thénardier makes pronounciation errors, 'des cuirs', typical of someone with social or intellectual pretensions.

jealous. She thought this thin sallow little man must be the object of universal desire.

Above all an astute and level-headed man, Thénardier was a restrained sort of villain. This is the worst type; hypocrisy is involved.

It was not that Thénardier was not on occasion capable of at least as much anger as his wife, but this was very rare. And since he bore a grudge against the entire human race, since he had a deep furnace of hatred burning within him, since he was one of those people who are perpetually avenging themselves, who blame any passing scapegoat for everything that has gone wrong for them and who are always ready, as if justifiably aggrieved, to foist on anybody but themselves responsibility for the sum total of deceptions, bankruptcies and calamities in their lives, with all this leaven fermenting inside him, frothing in his mouth and bubbling in his eyes, on such occasions he was terrible. Woe betide the person who came in the way of his fury then!

In addition to his other qualities Thénardier was keen and discerning, silent or talkative as appropriate, and always with supreme intelligence. He had something of a sailor's gaze, accustomed as they are to screwing up their eyes when looking through their telescopes. Thénardier was a statesman*.

At the sight of Madame Thénardier every newcomer to the inn would say, 'That's the master of the household.' Wrong. She was not even the mistress. It was the husband who was both master and mistress. She was the agent, he was the author. He controlled everything by a kind of invisible and constant magnetic power. Just a word from him, sometimes a sign, was enough. The mammoth obeyed. Though she was not fully aware of it, in the eyes of his wife Thénardier was a special and sovereign kind of being. She had the virtues of her own nature. If she were ever in disagreement over any detail with 'Monsieur Thénardier', an unthinkable eventuality in any case, never would she have contradicted her husband in public about anything. She would never have committed 'in front of strangers', as women so often do, the offence of what in parliamentary language is called 'exposing the crown'. Although the harmony between them resulted only in evil, there was spiritual communion in Madame Thénardier's submission to her husband. That rowdy mountain of flesh was directed by the little finger of that weedy despot. Seen in its dwarfish

---

* Hugo uses the term *homme d'État*, of which he wrote: 'A great thinker does not become a great statesman without absorbing into his spirit a larger or smaller dose of the mediocrity of men and matters. In the language of our times that means becoming practical.' From *Choses vues* (1887–1900).

and freakish mode, this was that great universal phenomenon: matter's adoration of mind. For some ugliness derives its reason for being from the very depths of eternal beauty. There was something of the unknown about Thénardier. Hence the absolute domination of that woman by that man. At certain moments she saw him as a beacon of light, at others she felt his menace.

This woman was a formidable creature who loved only her children and feared only her husband. She was a mother because she was a mammal. In fact her maternal instinct was confined to her daughters and, as we shall see, did not extend to boys. As for him, that man had only one thing in mind: to enrich himself.

He was not succeeding in this. This great talent lacked a worthy stage. Thénardier was on his way to ruin in Montfermeil, if ruin is possible with nothing. In Switzerland or the Pyrenees this have-not would have become a millionaire. But the innkeeper must graze wherever fate has tethered him.

Of course, the word 'innkeeper' is used here in a restricted sense and does not apply to a whole generic class.

In that same year of 1823 Thénardier owed some fifteen hundred francs to pressing creditors, which was a worry to him.

Whatever fate's relentless injustice towards him, Thénardier was one of those men who best understand, with the utmost insight and in the most modern way, what among barbarous peoples is a virtue and among civilized peoples a commodity: hospitality. He was also an excellent poacher and admired as a good shot. He had a certain cold, quiet laugh that was particularly dangerous.

His theories as a landlord sometimes erupted from him in illuminating outbursts. He had professional aphorisms that he implanted in his wife's mind. 'The duty of the innkeeper,' he told her one day in a fierce, low voice, 'is to sell to anybody that comes along some hot grub, somewhere to rest, light, warmth, dirty sheets, good cheer, bed lice and a smile, to stop passers-by, to empty small purses and within reason to lighten fat ones, to accommodate travelling families with consideration, to leech the man, fleece the woman, pluck the child, to charge for the open window, the closed window, the chimney corner, the armchair, the chair, the high stool, the wooden stool, the feather bed, the mattress and the truss of straw, to know how much the mirror is worn out by being obscured and set a price on it, and by every devilish means to make the traveller pay for everything, even the flies his dog eats!'

This man and this woman were guile wedded to rage, a hideous and terrible coupling.

While Thénardier pondered and plotted, his wife gave no thought to absent creditors, had no care of yesterday or tomorrow, and lived in a state of fury, entirely in the present moment.

Such were these two beings. Cosette was trapped between them, enduring their twofold assault on her, like a creature who is at the same time being crushed in a mill and pulled to pieces with pincers. The man and the woman each had a different method. Cosette was beaten black and blue – this was the woman's doing. She went barefoot in winter – this was the man's.

Cosette was up and down the stairs, washing, sweeping, scrubbing, dusting, hurrying, slaving, panting, lifting heavy objects; tiny as she was, she was doing all the hard work. No pity whatsoever: a vicious mistress, a malicious master. The Thénardier inn was like a spider's web in which Cosette was caught, trembling with fear. This sinister household represented a paradigm of oppression. It was a bit like the fly being the servant of spiders.

Unprotesting, the poor child said nothing.

When they find themselves in such a situation from the very start, so weak and so defenceless among mankind, what goes on inside those souls who have only just left God?

III
Men Must Have Wine and Horses Must Have Water

Another four travellers had turned up.

Cosette was sadly pensive. For although she was only eight years old she had already suffered so much that when lost in thought she looked like a gloomy old woman.

She had a bruised eyelid from being hit by Thénardier's wife, which prompted the woman to remark from time to time, 'How ugly she is with that black eye!'

So Cosette was thinking that it was dark, very dark, that the pitchers and carafes in the rooms of the unforeseen guests had unexpectedly to be filled, and now there was no water left in the cistern.

What slightly reassured her was that not much water was drunk in the Thénardier establishment. There was no lack of thirsty people, but theirs was the kind of thirst that reaches more readily for the jug of wine than for the jug of water. Anyone asking for a glass of water would have seemed uncivilized to all those men with their glasses of wine. But there came a moment when the child trembled. The Thénardier woman lifted the lid of a stewing-pot bubbling on the stove, then took a glass and suddenly approached the cistern. She turned the tap. The child had raised her head and was following her every movement. A thin trickle of water flowed from the tap and half filled the glass.

'Look at that,' said she, 'there's no more water!'

She remained silent for a moment. The child did not breathe.

'Bah!' said the Thénardier woman, examining the half-filled glass, 'this will be enough.'

Cosette returned to her task but for more than fifteen minutes she felt her heart fluttering in her chest like a big snowflake. So she counted the minutes that passed and wished it was already the next morning.

Now and then one of the drinkers would look out into the street and exclaim, 'It's pitch black!' Or, 'You'd need to be a cat to walk the streets without a lantern at this hour!' And Cosette quailed.

All of a sudden one of the pedlars staying at the inn came in and said in a harsh voice, 'My horse hasn't been watered.'

'Yes, it has,' said the Thénardier woman.

'I tell you, ma'am, it hasn't,' retorted the pedlar.

Cosette emerged from under the table.

'Oh, it has, monsieur!' she said. 'The horse drank, it drank from the bucket, a whole bucketful, I was the one that took it the water, and I spoke to it.'

This was not true. Cosette was lying.

'She's no bigger than your hand, that one, but she tells monumental lies,' exclaimed the pedlar. 'I tell you, it hasn't been watered, you cheeky little brat! It has a way of blowing when it hasn't been watered that I well recognize.'

Cosette persisted and added in a voice hoarse with anguish and hardly audible, 'It drank its fill, it did.'

'Now this isn't getting us anywhere,' said the pedlar angrily. 'I want my horse watered, and let that be the end of it!'

Cosette crept under the table again.

'Well, that's right,' said the Thénardier woman, 'if that beast hasn't been given water, it must be given some.'

Then, glancing about her, 'Now, where's she got to?'

She bent down and saw Cosette cowering at the other end of the table, almost under the drinkers' feet.

'Will you come out of there?' shouted the Thénardier woman.

Cosette crawled out of the hole, as it were, in which she had been hiding.

'Mademoiselle Dog, for want of a better name,' said the woman, 'go and water that horse.'

'But madame,' said Cosette feebly, 'there's no water.'

The Thénardier woman threw the street door wide open, 'Well then, go and fetch some!'

Cosette's head dropped, and she went to pick up an empty bucket in the chimney corner. This bucket was bigger than she was, and the child could have sat inside it and been comfortable there.

The Thénardier woman returned to her stove and with a wooden spoon tasted what was in the stewing-pot, grumbling the while, 'There's water at the spring. You needn't be a genius to know that. I think I should have browned the onions.'

Then she rummaged in a drawer containing some small coins, pepper and shallots.

'Now, Mam'zelle Ugly Toad,' she added, 'on your way back you can pick up a large loaf from the baker's. There's a fifteen-sou piece.'

Cosette had a little side pocket in her pinafore. She took the coin without a word and put it in that pocket.

Then she stood there motionless, with the bucket in her hand, the door open in front of her. She seemed to be waiting for someone to come to her rescue.

'Go on, then!' shouted the Thénardier woman.

Cosette went out. The door closed behind her.

IV
A Doll Makes Its Appearance

The row of open-air stalls that started at the church extended, the reader will remember, as far as the Thénardier inn. Because the gentry would soon be passing by on their way to midnight mass these stalls were all lit up with candles burning in paper cones, which produced 'a magical effect', as Montfermeil's schoolmaster, at that moment seated at one of the Thénardiers' tables, observed. However, there was not a single star to be seen in the sky.

The last of these stalls, set up exactly opposite the Thénardiers' doorway, was a fancy goods stall, all glittering with tinsel, glass trinkets and wonderful things made of tin. In pride of place, right in front, on a white cloth, the stallholder had placed a huge doll nearly two feet high, wearing a pink crêpe dress, with a gold tiara on its head, and real hair and enamel eyes. All day long this marvel had been on display to the wonderment of passers-by under ten years old, and no mother in Montfermeil found rich enough or extravagant enough to give it to her child. Éponine and Azelma had spent hours gazing at it, and furtively, it is true, even Cosette had dared to look at it.

For all her great despondency and distress, as Cosette stepped out, bucket in hand, she could not help looking up at that amazing doll, 'the lady', as she called it. The poor child stood there paralysed. She had not yet seen the doll from so close up. The entire stall seemed a palace to her: this doll was not a doll, it was a vision. It was joy, splendour, wealth, happiness that appeared in a kind of fabulous radiance to this wretched little creature so deeply submerged in cold and dreary poverty. With the sad and naive wisdom of childhood Cosette measured the abyss that separated her from that doll. She said to herself that you would have to be a queen or a princess at least to have something like that belong to you. She considered that lovely pink dress, that lovely sleek hair, and she thought, 'How happy that doll must be!' She could not take her eyes off that fantastic stall. The more she looked, the more dazzled she was. She thought she was seeing paradise. There were other dolls behind the big one that looked like fairies and spirits to her. The trader pacing to and fro at the back of his stall seemed to her a little like the Eternal Father.

In her adoration she forgot everything, even the errand she had been sent on. All at once the Thénardier woman's harsh voice jolted her back to reality. 'What! Not on your way yet, you witless girl! Just you wait! I'll be right with you! What's she doing here, I ask you! Little monster, she is!'

Thénardier's wife had glanced out into the street and caught sight of the spellbound Cosette.

Cosette fled with her pail, moving as fast as she could.

V
The Little Girl All Alone

As the Thénardier inn was in that part of the village near the church, it was at the spring in the forest, over towards Chelles, that Cosette had to go to draw water.

She did not look at any other tradesman's stall. So long as she was in Ruelle du Boulanger and in the vicinity of the church, the illuminated stalls lit the road, but soon the last glimmer of light from the last stall vanished from sight. The poor child found herself in the dark. She ploughed on. But with fear mounting in her, she rattled the handle of her bucket as much as she could as she walked along. This made a noise that kept her company.

The further she went, the darker it became. There was no one else out on the streets. However, she did come across one woman, who seeing her pass by turned round and stood there muttering to herself,

'Now where on earth can that child be going? Is it a werewolf child?' Then the woman recognized Cosette. 'Oh,' said she, 'it's Alouette!'

Cosette thus made her way through the labyrinth of tortuous and deserted streets in which the village of Montfermeil on the Chelles side ends. As long as she had houses or even just walls on either side of the road, she kept going fairly confidently. From time to time she saw the glow of a candle through the chink in a shutter. That was light and life, there were people there, which reassured her. But as she went on her pace slowed as if automatically. When she had passed the corner of the last house Cosette stopped. It had been hard to go beyond the last stall. It became impossible to go beyond the last house. She put down her bucket, thrust her hand into her hair and began slowly to scratch her head, a gesture characteristic of children who are terrified and do not know what to do. This was no longer Montfermeil. It was open countryside. Before her lay the dark and deserted emptiness. She gazed in despair into this blackness where there was no one now, where there were beasts, maybe ghosts. She looked hard and heard the beasts moving in the grass and she distinctly saw the ghosts stirring in the trees. Then she picked up her bucket again. Fear made her daring. 'Puh!' she said. 'I'll tell her there was no water left!'

And she resolutely retraced her steps into Montfermeil.

She had hardly gone a hundred paces when she stopped again and went back to scratching her head. Now it was the Thénardier woman who loomed before her, looking hideous, with that hyena's mouth and anger blazing in her eyes. The child looked ahead, then behind her, with a pitiful gaze. What was she to do? What would become of her? Where was she to go? Ahead was the spectre of the Thénardier woman, behind her all the shades of the night and the spectres of the forest. It was from the Thénardier woman that she retreated. She set off towards the spring again and started to run. She ran out of the village, she ran into the forest, not looking at anything now, not listening to anything. She did not stop running until she was out of breath, but still she went on walking. She kept on going, panic-stricken.

As she ran she felt close to tears.

The nocturnal rustling of the forest completely enveloped her. Her mind was a blank, she could see nothing. The immensity of night confronted this tiny creature. On the one hand utter darkness, on the other an atom.

It was only seven or eight minutes' walk from the edge of the woods to the spring. Cosette knew the way, having walked it many times in daylight. Strange to say, she did not get lost. A vestigial instinct somehow guided her. Yet she glanced to neither left nor right for fear of seeing things in the branches and in the undergrowth. And so she reached the spring.

It was a small natural basin, hollowed out by the water in clayey soil, about two feet deep, surrounded by moss and by those tall frilly grasses called 'Henri IV ruffs', and paved with a few large stones. A quietly murmuring stream flowed from it.

Cosette did not stop to catch her breath. It was very dark, but she was used to coming to this spring. With her left hand she groped in the darkness for a young oak leaning over the spring that usually served her as something to hold on to, found one of its branches, and hanging from it bent down and plunged the bucket into the water. So violent was her state of turmoil that her strength was three times normal. As she bent over like this she did not notice the pocket of her pinafore empty into the spring. The fifteen-sou piece fell into the water. Cosette neither saw nor heard it fall. She pulled out the bucket, almost full, and set it down on the grass.

Having done so, she realized she was drained by exhaustion. She would have liked to start back at once but it had been such an effort to fill the bucket she could not go one step further. She just had to sit down. She dropped to the grass and remained crouching there. She shut her eyes, then opened them again, without knowing why but unable to do otherwise.

The unsettled water in the bucket beside her formed circular ripples that looked like snakes of blazing white.

The sky overhead was overcast with enormous black clouds, like palls of smoke. The tragic mask of darkness seemed in some indeterminate way to bend over this child.

Jupiter was setting in the heavens.

The child gazed wild-eyed at this huge star that was unfamiliar to her and terrified her. The planet at that moment was actually very close to the horizon and passing through a thick layer of mist that gave it a horrible ruddiness. The gruesomely crimson-tinged mist magnified the star. It was like a luminous wound.

A cold wind blew off the plain. The forest was gloomy, with no rustling of leaves, none of those vague bright glimmers of summer. Great boughs were horribly upraised. Stunted, gnarled bushes whistled in the clearings. Tall grasses were like a wriggling mass of eels beneath the icy blast. Brambles writhed with what looked like long arms equipped with claws attempting to catch prey. Scraps of dried heather flew past, chased by the wind, seeming to flee in terror before something coming. Forbidding expanses stretched away on all sides.

Darkness is harrowing. Man needs light. Anyone plunging into the opposite of daylight feels the heart contract. When the eye sees darkness the mind is perturbed. In obscurity, in darkness, in murky impenetrability, there is anxiety even for the mightiest. No one walks alone in the forest at night without trembling. Shadows and trees, two dreadful densities. A fanciful reality appears in blurry depths. The inconceivable takes shape with spectral clarity a few paces before you. You see floating, either in space or in your own mind, something indefinably vague and elusive, like the dreams of sleeping flowers. There are menacing shapes on the horizon. You inhale the emanations of the great black void. You are afraid to look behind you and at the same time you want to. Pits of darkness, things that have grown frenzied, silent silhouettes that dissipate when you approach, dimly perceived tangles, agitated clusters, murky puddles, the dismal reflected in the gloomy, the sepulchral immensity of silence, possible alien beings, mysteriously bending branches, terrifying tree trunks, long hanks of rustling plants – against all this you are defenceless. None so bold that does not quail and feel the closeness of anguish. You experience something ghastly as if your soul were blending with the darkness. This impregnation with shadows is unutterably sinister for a child.

Forests are apocalyptic, and the beating of a tiny soul's wings creates a sound of agony beneath their monstrous vault.

Without understanding what she was experiencing Cosette felt captured by that black enormity of nature. It was not just terror that overcame her now, it was something even more terrifying than terror. She shuddered. There are no words to express the strangeness of that shudder, which chilled her to her heart's core. She had grown wild-eyed. She almost had the feeling she might not be able to resist coming back again at the same time the next day.

Then by a kind of instinct, to escape from this peculiar state of being, which she did not understand but which scared her, she began to count aloud, one, two, three, four, and so on up to ten, and when she had finished she started from the beginning again. This gave back to her a true perception of the things around her. She felt the coldness of her hands, which she had got wet while drawing water. She stood up. Her fear had returned, a natural and unconquerable fear. She had but one thought now, to flee. As fast as her legs could carry her, through the woods, through open countryside, back to the houses, the windows, the lighted candles. Her glance fell upon the bucket that stood in front of her. Such was the dread the Thénardier woman inspired in her, she dared not flee without the pail of water. She seized the handle with both hands. She could hardly lift the bucket.

She went a dozen paces like this but the bucket was full, it was heavy, she was forced to put it down again. She caught her breath for a moment, then once more lifted the handle and set off again, going a little further this time. But she had to stop again. After a few seconds' rest she went on. She walked stooping forward, her head bowed, like an old woman. The weight of the bucket strained and stiffened her thin arms. The iron handle numbed and chilled her little wet hands even more. She was forced to stop every now and then, and each time she stopped the cold water that splashed from the pail fell on her bare legs. This was happening in the depths of a forest, at night, in winter, far from all human eyes. She was an eight-year-old child. At that moment there was no one but God watching this sorry sight.

And doubtless her mother, alas! For there are things that make women lying dead in their graves open their eyes.

She panted with a sort of painful rasp. Sobs choked her throat but she dared not weep, so afraid was she of the Thénardier woman, even at a distance. She had acquired the habit of always imagining the Thénardier woman was right there.

However, she could not cover much ground like this and she went very slowly. Despite shortening the length of her stops and walking as far as she could between them, she thought apprehensively that at this rate it would take her more than an hour to get back to Montfermeil, and the Thénardier woman would beat her. This apprehensiveness mingled with her terror at being alone in the woods at night. She was utterly exhausted and not yet out of the forest. When she reached an old chestnut tree that she recognized she made a final stop, longer than the other breaks she had taken, so as to be well rested, then she gathered all her strength, picked up her bucket, and pluckily set off again. Yet the poor little creature could not help crying out in desperation, 'O my God! my God!'

At that moment, she suddenly felt her bucket no longer weighed anything. A hand, which looked enormous to her, had just seized the handle and vigorously lifted it. She looked up. Towering above her, a huge black figure was walking beside her in the dark. It was a man who had caught up with her and she had not heard him coming. Without a word this man had taken the handle of the bucket she was carrying.

There is an instinct for every encounter in life. The child was unafraid.

VI

Which May Prove Boulatruelle's Intelligence

In the afternoon of that same Christmas Eve 1823 a man walked for quite a long time along the most deserted part of Boulevard de l'Hôpital in Paris. This man looked like someone in search of lodgings, and he seemed to have a preference for stopping at the most modest houses in this run-down area on the fringes of the outlying St-Marceau district.

We shall see later that the man did actually rent a room in this remote neighbourhood.

In the clothes he wore, as in his entire person, this man was the embodiment of the type that might be called the gentleman beggar, combining extreme poverty with extreme cleanliness. This is quite a rare mixture that inspires intelligent hearts with that dual respect felt for the person who is very poor and the person who is very respectable. He wore an extremely old and well brushed round hat, a threadbare frock-coat of a coarse cloth of yellow ochre, a colour not at all out of the ordinary at that time, a generous waistcoat with pockets cut in the old-fashioned style, black breeches faded grey at the knees, stockings of black worsted and sturdy shoes with copper buckles. He looked like a former tutor to a good family, an émigré who had now returned. From his completely white hair, his wrinkled brow, his pale lips, from his whole face that denoted dejection and weariness of life, you would have assumed he was well over sixty. From his firm albeit slow step, from the remarkable vigour that stamped his every movement, you would have reckoned he was scarcely fifty. The wrinkles on his brow inspired confidence and would have predisposed in his favour anyone who observed him closely. His lips were contracted in a strange twist of what looked like severity but was actually humility. There was in the depth of his gaze some indefinably melancholic serenity. In his left hand he carried a little bundle tied up in a handkerchief. With his right hand he leaned on some sort of staff cut from a hedgerow. This staff had been trimmed with a degree of care, and did not look too rough. The best had been made of the knots in it, and a coral-like knob had been fashioned out of red wax: it was a cudgel and it looked like a cane.

There are few passers-by on that boulevard, particularly in winter. The man seemed to avoid them rather than seek them out, yet without making too much of it.

At that time King Louis XVIII went nearly every day to Choisy-le-Roi. It was one of his favourite excursions. Around two o'clock, almost invariably, the royal carriage and cavalcade came racing headlong down Boulevard de l'Hôpital.

This served as a substitute for a watch or clock to the local beggar-women, who said, 'It's two o'clock, there he goes on his way back to the Tuileries.'

And some came running, and others lined up, for there is always a noisy crowd when a king goes by. Besides, the appearance and disappearance of Louis XVIII created a certain impression on the streets of Paris. It was swift but majestic. This impotent king liked to ride at full gallop. Unable to walk, he wanted to go fast: this cripple would gladly have had himself drawn by lightning. Peaceable and severe, he went about surrounded by drawn sabres. His massive coach, all gilt with large emblems of lilies painted on the panels, would thunder by. There was hardly time to catch a glimpse of it. You would see in the rear right-hand corner against white satin upholstered cushions an impassive broad scarlet face, a freshly powdered forehead with a *oiseau royal* hairstyle*; a proud, stern, shrewd eye, a scholar's smile, two big epaulettes with bullion fringes on a civilian coat, the Golden Fleece, the cross of St Louis, the cross of the Legion of Honour, the Holy Spirit silver plaque, a large belly and a wide blue sash: it was the king. Outside of Paris he kept his white-plumed hat on his knees wrapped in their long English gaiters. When he came back into the city he put his hat on his head, waving rarely. He stared coldly at the people, who responded likewise. When he appeared for the first time in the St-Marceau district, his entire success resided in the remark one local inhabitant made to his companion, 'That bigwig there's the government.'

So the king going by, always at the same time, with this unfailing regularity, was the main event of the day on Boulevard de l'Hôpital.

The pedestrian in the yellow frock-coat was obviously not from this area, and probably not from Paris, for he was unaware of this fact. When at two o'clock the royal carriage, surrounded by a squad-ron of lifeguards all silver-braided, appeared in the boulevard, having driven round La Salpêtrière, he seemed surprised and almost alarmed. There was no one but him on the side avenue. He hastily stepped back behind a corner in the perimeter wall, though this did not prevent Monsieur le Duc d'Havré from noticing him. As captain of the guard on duty that day, Monsieur le Duc d'Havré was seated in the carriage opposite the king. He said to His Majesty, 'There's a rather villainous-looking man.' Some policemen who were clearing

---

* Powdered, possibly styled into two 'wings'.

the way for the king also noticed him, and one of them received the order to follow him. But the man dived down the deserted little streets of that neighbourhood, and as the light was beginning to fade the policeman lost track of him, as stated in a report addressed that same evening to Monsieur le Comte Anglès, minister of state and prefect of police.

When the man in the yellow frock-coat had given the policeman the slip, he quickened his pace, not without having looked round many times to reassure himself he was not being followed. At a quarter-past four, that is to say after dark, he passed in front of the Porte St-Martin theatre where *The Two Convicts* was playing that day. He was struck by the poster, illuminated by the streetlights outside the theatre, for although he was walking fast he stopped to read it. A moment later he was in Cul-de-Sac de La Planchette and entered the Plat d'Étain inn, where the office for the coach to Lagny used to be. This coach left at half-past four. The horses were harnessed and, summoned by the coachman, the travellers were hastily clambering up the steep iron steps of the carriage.

The man asked, 'Are there any seats left?'

'Only one, beside me on the box,' said the coachman.

'I'll take it.'

'Climb up.'

Nevertheless, before setting out, the coachman cast a glance at the traveller's shabby attire, the small size of his bundle, and made him pay his fare.

'Are you going as far as Lagny?' asked the coachman.

'Yes,' said the man.

The traveller paid the fare to Lagny.

They set off. When they had passed the toll-gate the coachman tried to start a conversation but the traveller replied only in monosyllables. The coachman resorted to whistling and swearing at his horses.

The coachman wrapped himself up in his cloak. It was cold. The man appeared to pay no heed to this. Thus they passed through Gournay and Neuilly-sur-Marne.

Towards six o'clock in the evening they reached Chelles. The coachman stopped to rest his horses in front of the carters' inn housed in the old outbuildings of the royal abbey.

'I'm getting off here,' said the man.

He took his bundle and his staff and jumped down from the vehicle. A moment later he had disappeared. He did not go into the inn.

When a few minutes later the coach started off again for Lagny it did not pass him on Chelles's main street.

The coachman turned to the travellers inside the coach. 'That one there,' he said, 'is a man who's not from these parts, for I don't know him. He looks as if he's hard up yet he's not careful with money. He pays the fare to Lagny and only goes as far as Chelles. It's dark, all the houses are closed up, he doesn't go to the inn, and there's no sign of him. The ground must have opened up and swallowed him.'

The man had not been swallowed up into the ground but had hurried down Chelles's main street in the dark, then like someone who was familiar with the area and had already been here before, he turned left before the church, down the lane leading to Montfermeil.

He made his way rapidly along this lane. Where the old tree-lined road from Gagny to Lagny cuts across it, he heard people coming. He hastily hid in a ditch and waited there until the passers-by were gone. Actually, this precaution was almost unnecessary, for as we have already said, it was a very dark December night. There were scarcely more than two or three stars to be seen in the sky.

It is at this point that the hill starts to rise. The man did not go back on to the Montfermeil road. He struck across the fields to the right and went striding towards the forest.

Once in the forest he slackened his pace, and began to look carefully at all the trees, making his way step by step as though seeking and following some mysterious route known only to himself. There came a moment when he appeared to be lost, and stopped in indecision. Proceeding tentatively all the time, at last he came to a clearing where there was a pile of large whitish stones. He moved quickly towards these stones, and studied them closely in the night mist as though inspecting them. A few paces away from the pile of stones was a large tree, covered with those growths that are the warts of vegetation. He went up to this tree and ran his hand over the bark of the trunk, as if trying to recognize and count all the warts.

Opposite this tree, which was an ash, was a chestnut tree, which had been barked and to which a band of zinc had been nailed by way of a dressing for the wound. He raised himself on tip-toe and touched this band of zinc.

Then he stamped on the ground for a while in the space that lay between the tree and the stones, like someone checking that the soil has not recently been disturbed.

This done, he took his bearings, then carried on walking through the forest.

It was this man who had just encountered Cosette.

As he walked through the woods towards Montfermeil he noticed that tiny figure, groaning as it went, setting down its burden, then picking it up again and resuming its progress. He came nearer and saw it was a very small child carrying an enormous bucket of water. Then he went up to the child and silently took the handle of the bucket.

VII

Cosette at the Stranger's Side in the Dark

Cosette, as we have said, was not afraid. The man spoke to her. He spoke in a deep, almost quiet voice.

'My child, what you're carrying there is very heavy for you.'

Cosette looked up and replied, 'Yes, monsieur.'

'Give it to me,' said the man. 'I'll carry it for you.'

Cosette let go of the bucket. The man started walking alongside her.

'It really is very heavy,' he muttered. Then he added, 'How old are you, little one?'

'Eight, monsieur.'

'And have you come far like this?'

'From the spring in the forest.'

'Have you got far to go?'

'A good quarter of an hour's walk from here.'

The man remained silent for a moment, then said abruptly, 'So you've no mother?'

'I don't know,' replied the child.

Before the man had time to respond she added, 'I don't think so. Other people do. But I don't.'

And after a pause she went on, 'I think I never had one.'

The man stopped, put down the bucket, bent over and placed both hands on the child's shoulders, straining to look at her and to see her face in the dark. Cosette's thin, pinched features appeared as a vague blur in the sky's wan light.

'What's your name?' said the man.

'Cosette.'

It was as though the man had received an electric shock. He took another look at her, then removed his hands from Cosette's shoulders, picked up the bucket and set off again.

After a moment he asked, 'Where do you live, little one?'

'At Montfermeil, if you know where that is.'

'Is that where we're going?'

'Yes, monsieur.'

There was another pause, then he spoke again. 'So who was it that sent you out at this hour to fetch water from the forest?'

'It was Madame Thénardier.'

The man went on, striving to keep any trace of emotion out of his voice, but there was nevertheless a noticeable tremor in it, 'What does your Madame Thénardier do?'

'She's my mistress,' said the child. 'She keeps the inn.'

'The inn?' said the man. 'Well, I'm going to stay there tonight. Show me the way.'

'That's where we're going,' said the child.

The man walked quite fast. Cosette had no trouble keeping up with him. She no longer felt any tiredness. From time to time she looked up at the man with a kind of ineffable tranquillity and trust. She had never been taught to turn to providence or to pray. Yet she felt within her something that resembled hope and joy, something that climbed heavenwards.

Several minutes elapsed. The man resumed, 'Is there no servant in Madame Thénardier's house?'

'No, monsieur.'

'You're by yourself?'

'Yes, monsieur.'

Another pause ensued. Cosette raised her voice. 'That's to say, there are two little girls.'

'What little girls?'

'Ponine and Zelma.'

This was how the child shortened those Romantic names close to the Thénardier woman's heart.

'Who are Ponine and Zelma?'

'They're Madame Thénardier's young misses. That's to say, her daughters.'

'And what do they do?'

'Oh!' said the child. 'They have beautiful dolls, things that have gold in them, all kinds of things. They play, they have fun.'

'All day long?'

'Yes, monsieur.'

'And you?'

'I work.'

'All day long?'

The child looked up with those big eyes of hers that had a tear in them you could not see because of the dark, and replied softly, 'Yes, monsieur.'

After an interval of silence she went on, 'Sometimes, when I've finished working, and they don't mind, I can play too.'

'And how do you play?'

'As best I can. I'm left to myself. But I haven't many toys. Ponine and Zelma won't let me play with their dolls. I've only a little lead sword that's no bigger than that.'

The child held up her little finger.

'And it doesn't cut?'

'Yes, it does, monsieur,' said the child. 'It cuts salad and the heads off flies.'

They reached the village. Cosette led the stranger through the streets. They passed in front of the bakery but Cosette did not think of the bread that she was supposed to bring back. The man had stopped asking her questions and now kept a sombre silence. When they had left the church behind them, seeing all the open-air stalls the man asked Cosette, 'So is this the market?'

'No, monsieur, it's Christmas.'

As they approached the inn Cosette timidly touched his arm. 'Monsieur?'

'What, my child?'

'We're very close to the house.'

'Well?'

'Will you let me take my bucket now?'

'Why?'

'The thing is, if Madame sees that someone has carried it for me, she'll beat me.'

The man handed her the bucket. A moment later they were at the door of the inn.

VIII

The Vexation of Playing Host to a Poor Man Who May Be Rich

Cosette could not help casting a sidelong glance at the big doll still on display at the fancy goods stall. Then she knocked. The door opened. The Thénardier woman appeared holding a candle.

'Ah! so it's you, you little beggar! Thank heavens, it's taken you long enough! The minx! She must have been dawdling!'

'Madame,' said Cosette trembling all over, 'here's a gentleman who's come to stay.'

The Thénardier woman very quickly replaced her churlish scowl

362

with her amiable grimace, a change of expression characteristic of innkeepers, and avidly peered at the newcomer.

'Is this the gentleman?' she said.

'Yes, madame,' replied the man, raising his hand to his hat.

Wealthy travellers are not so polite. This gesture and an inspection of the stranger's clothing and baggage, which the Thénardier woman assessed at a glance, caused the amiable grimace to vanish and the churlish scowl to reappear. She responded drily, 'Come in, old man.'

The 'old man' entered. The Thénardier woman cast a second glance at him, taking particular note of his frock-coat, which was completely threadbare, and his hat, which was a little battered, and with a toss of her head, a wrinkling of her nose and a screwing-up of her eyes consulted her husband, who was still drinking with the carters.

The husband replied with that imperceptible motion of the fore-finger which together with a pursing of the lips signifies in such cases: flat broke.

At which point the Thénardier woman exclaimed, 'Now see here, my good fellow, I'm very sorry, but I've no room left.'

'Put me where you like,' said the man, 'in the attic, in the stable. I'll pay the price of a room.'

'Forty sous.'

'Forty sous. Agreed.'

'Very well!'

'Forty sous!' a carter muttered to the Thénardier woman. 'But it's only twenty!'

'For him, it's forty sous,' the Thénardier woman replied in the same undertone. 'I don't give lodgings to paupers for less.'

'That's true,' her husband added softly, 'it lowers the tone of a place to have people like that staying in it.'

In the meantime, having left his bundle and staff on a bench, the man had sat down at a table on which Cosette had been eager to place a bottle of wine and a glass. The pedlar who had asked for the bucket of water had gone to take it out to his horse himself. Cosette had resumed her place under the kitchen table with her knitting.

The man, who barely moistened his lips with the glass of wine he poured for himself, observed the child with peculiar attention.

Cosette was ugly. Had she been happy, she might have been pretty. We have already given a quick sketch of that forlorn little figure. Cosette was thin and pale. She was nearly eight years old, she hardly looked six. Her huge eyes, sunk in a kind of deep shadow, were almost dull with weeping. The corners of her mouth had that downward turn of habitual anguish to be observed in the condemned and the incurably sick. As her mother had suspected, her hands were 'covered with chilblains'. The light cast on her by the fire at that moment brought out the angularity of her bones and made obvious her frightful thinness. As she was always shivering she had acquired the habit of pressing her knees together. She wore no more than a rag of clothing that would have been pitiful in summer and was horrifying in winter. All she had on was tattered cotton, not a scrap of wool. Her skin showed through here and there, marked black and blue all over, indicating where the Thénardier woman had hit her. Her naked legs were red and skinny. The prominence of her collarbones made you want to weep. This child's whole person, her behaviour, the way she moved, the sound of her voice, her pauses between one word and the next, the expression in her eyes, her silence, her slightest gesture, expressed and conveyed one idea only: fear.

Fear was written all over her. She was, so to speak, steeped in it. Fear drew her elbows in close to her hips, kept her feet tucked under her skirt, made her take up as little space as possible, allowed her to breathe only the bare minimum, and had become what might be called her habit of body, with no possibility of change except to intensify. Deep in her eyes was a kernel of stupefied terror.

This fear was such that when she got back, wet through though she was, Cosette dared not go and dry herself in front of the fire, and silently applied herself to her task again.

The expression in the eyes of this eight-year-old child was usually so dejected and sometimes so tragic that at certain moments she seemed to be turning into an idiot or a demon.

Never, as we have said, had she known what it means to pray. Never had she set foot in a church. 'Have I got time for that?' said the Thénardier woman.

The man in the yellow frock-coat did not take his eyes off Cosette.

'Now that I think of it, what about that bread?'

Responding as she always did whenever the Thénardier woman raised her voice, Cosette very quickly came out from under the table.

She had completely forgotten about the bread. She resorted to the tactic adopted by children in constant fear. She lied.

'Madame, the bakery was shut.'

'You should have knocked.'

'I did knock, madame.'

'Well?'

'The baker didn't open the door.'

'I'll find out tomorrow whether that's true,' said the Thénardier woman. 'And if you're lying, there'll be the devil to pay. In the meantime, give me back the fifteen sous.'

Cosette stuck her hand into the pocket of her pinafore and turned sickly pale. The fifteen-sou coin was not there any more.

'Come on,' said the Thénardier woman, 'you heard me!'

Cosette turned her pocket inside out, there was nothing in it. What could have become of that money? The poor little creature was completely dumbfounded. She was petrified.

'That fifteen-sou coin,' scolded the Thénardier woman, 'did you lose it? Or are you trying to steal it from me?'

At the same time she reached out for the strap hanging by the fireplace. This ominous gesture gave Cosette the strength to cry, 'Spare me! Madame! Madame! I won't do it again!'

The Thénardier woman unhooked the strap.

Meanwhile the man in the yellow frock-coat had been fumbling in his waistcoat pocket without anyone noticing. In fact the other travellers were drinking or playing cards and paying no attention to anything else.

Cosette cringed in the corner of the fireplace, trying to keep her poor half-naked limbs tucked in and covered up. The Thénardier woman raised her arm.

'Excuse me, madame,' said the man, 'but I saw something fall out of the little one's apron pocket just now and roll away. Perhaps that was it.' At the same time he bent down and seemed to search on the floor for a moment.

'Just as I thought. Here it is,' he said, straightening up. And he held out a silver coin to the Thénardier woman.

'Yes, that's it,' said she.

No, it was not, for it was a twenty-sou coin, but this was to the Thénardier woman's advantage. She put the coin in her pocket and merely scowled fiercely at the child, saying, 'All the same, just you mind it doesn't happen again!'

Cosette returned to what the Thénardier woman called 'her kennel', and her big eyes, riveted on the wayfaring stranger, began to take on an expression they had never had before. It was as yet only naive amazement but tinged with a kind of stunned trustfulness.

'By the way, do you want supper?' the Thénardier woman asked the traveller.

He did not reply. He appeared to be deep in thought.

'What on earth is anyone to make of that man?' she muttered. 'He's some frightful pauper. One that can't afford to pay for supper.

Will he even pay for his lodging? Anyway, it's just as well he didn't take it into his head to steal the money that was on the floor.'

Meanwhile, a door had opened and Éponine and Azelma had come in.

They really were two pretty little girls, more like gentry than peasants, extremely charming, one with very glossy brown hair, the other with long black braids hanging down her back, both lively, clean, plump, fresh and healthy, a pleasure to behold. They were warmly clothed but with so much of a mother's special care that the heaviness of the materials did not detract from the daintiness of the outfit. Winter was catered for without the loss of spring. These two little girls emanated light. Moreover, they behaved like royalty. There was sovereignty in their dress, in their mirth, in the noise they made.

When they came in the Thénardier woman said to them in a grumbling tone of voice that was yet full of adoration, 'Ah! there you are!'

Then pulling them on to her lap one after the other, smoothing their hair, retying their ribbons, and then letting them go, giving them a shake in that gentle way mothers do, she exclaimed, 'Don't they look a fright!'

They went and sat by the fireside. They had a doll, which they turned round and round on their knees, merrily prattling away. From time to time Cosette looked up from her knitting and dolefully watched them play.

Éponine and Azelma did not look at Cosette. For them she was like the dog. These three little girls' ages did not add up to twenty-four years between them but they already represented the whole of human society: envy on the one hand, scorn on the other.

The Thénardier sisters' doll was very shabby, very old, and very much the worse for wear but seemed nonetheless wonderful to Cosette, who had never had a doll in her life, *a real doll*, to use an expression that all children will understand.

Suddenly the Thénardier woman, who was constantly moving about the room, going to and fro, noticed that Cosette was distracted and that instead of working she was watching the little ones play.

'Ah! I've caught you!' she cried. 'So that's how you work! I'll make you work with a feel of the strap.'

Without rising from his chair the stranger turned to the Thénardier woman. 'Madame,' he said, smiling with an almost apprehensive look, 'go on, let her play!'

From any traveller who had eaten a slice of mutton and drunk a couple of bottles of wine with his supper, and did not look like 'some frightful pauper', such a wish would have been a command. But that a man wearing a hat like that should take the liberty of making any request, and that a man wearing a coat like that should take the liberty of expressing his will, was something that Madame Thénardier did not think she had to tolerate.

She retorted sourly, 'Since she eats she has to work. I don't feed her to do nothing.'

'Well, what is it she's making?' said the stranger in that gentle voice so strangely at odds with his beggarly clothes and stevedore's shoulders.

The Thénardier woman condescended to reply, 'Stockings, if you please. Stockings for my little girls, who have none to speak of and who'll soon be going around barefoot.'

The man looked at Cosette's poor little red feet and went on, 'When will she have finished that pair of stockings?'

'The lazybones! She has at least three or four full days' work still!'

'And how much might that pair of stockings be worth when she's finished them?'

The Thénardier woman threw him a contemptuous glance. 'At least thirty sous.'

'Would you sell them for five francs?' said the man.

'Good God!' a carter listening to this exclaimed with a guffaw. 'Five francs! I should damn well think so! Five francs!'

Thénardier thought he ought to put in a word.

'Yes, monsieur, if that's your pleasure, we'll sell you that pair of stockings for five francs. We can't refuse travellers anything.'

'You'd have to pay right away,' said the Thénardier woman in her curt and peremptory fashion.

'I'm buying that pair of stockings,' replied the man, 'and', he added, drawing from his pocket a five-franc coin that he laid on the table, 'there's the payment for them.'

Then he turned to Cosette. 'Now your work belongs to me. Play, my child.'

The carter was so impressed by the five-franc coin that he left his glass where it was and rushed over.

'It's true, would you believe it!' he cried, examining it. 'It's a hind coachwheel*all right! And not counterfeit!'

Thénardier came up and silently put the coin in his pocket.

---

* Eighteenth-century English slang for a crown or five-shilling piece, used in French (*roue de derrière*) for a five-franc coin; a fore coachwheel was half a crown.

There was nothing the Thénardier woman could say. She chewed her lips and her face took on an expression of hatred.

Meanwhile, Cosette trembled. 'Is it true, madame?' she dared to ask. 'May I play?'

'Play!' said the Thénardier woman in a terrible voice.

'Thank you, madame,' said Cosette. And while with her voice she thanked the Thénardier woman, with all her little soul she thanked the traveller.

Thénardier went back to his drinking.

His wife whispered in his ear, 'Who the devil can this yellow man be?'

'I've seen millionaires who had frock-coats like that,' Thénardier replied in a lordly manner.

Cosette had put aside her knitting but had not left her place. Cosette always moved as little as possible. From a box behind her she had taken some old rags and her little lead sword.

Éponine and Azelma paid no attention to what was going on. They had just carried out a very important operation: they had got hold of the cat. They had thrown the doll on the floor, and despite its miaowings and contortions, Éponine, who was the elder, was swaddling the kitten with a heap of old red and blue dressing-up clothes. While performing this serious and difficult task she was talking to her sister in that sweet and adorable way children have, which like the splendour of a butterfly's wings loses its magic when you try to pin it down.

'You see, sister, this doll's more fun than the other one. It moves, it cries, it's warm. Look, sister, let's play with it. Pretend this is my little girl. That I'm a lady. That I come to see you and you look at her. That little by little, you notice her whiskers and you're surprised. And then you see her ears, and then you see her tail, and you're amazed. And you say to me, "Good gracious!" And I say, "Yes, madame, this little girl of mine is like that. That's the way little girls are nowadays."'

Azelma listened in wonder to Éponine.

In the meantime the drinkers had started singing an obscene song that made them laugh fit to shake the rafters. Thénardier encouraged them and joined in.

Just as birds use anything to build a nest, so do children make a doll out of anything. While Éponine and Azelma swaddled the cat, Cosette swaddled her sword. When she had done that, she laid it in her arms and softly sang lullabies to it.

Playing with dolls is one of the most urgent needs and at the same time one of the most charming instincts that little girls have. Nursing, dressing, adorning, putting clothes on, taking them off, putting them on again, teaching, scolding a little, cradling, dandling, lulling to sleep, imagining that something is someone – a woman's entire future lies in this. While dreaming and chattering, making little trousseaux and layettes, sewing little dresses, blouses and vests, the baby girl grows into a little girl, the little girl into a big girl, the big girl into a woman. The first child follows on from the last doll.

A little girl without a doll is almost as unhappy and quite as inconceivable as a woman without a child.

So Cosette had made herself a doll out of the sword.

The Thénardier woman went over to the 'yellow man'. 'My husband's right,' she thought. 'He could be Monsieur Laffitte. There are some very weird rich folk!'

She came and leaned on his table. 'Monsieur . . .' she said.

At this word 'monsieur' the man turned round. Up until then the Thénardier woman had addressed him only as 'old fellow' or 'old man'.

'You see, monsieur,' she went on, adopting a sickly-sweet expression that was even more unpleasant to look at than her ferocious one, 'I'm all for the child playing, I'm not against it, but just this once, because you're generous. You see, she has nothing. She has to work.'

'Then she's not yours, this child?' asked the man.

'Good God! No, monsieur! She's a little pauper we've just taken in out of charity. Some sort of idiot child. She must have water on the brain. She has a large head, as you can see. We do what we can for her, after all we're not rich. Though we keep writing to where she comes from, we've not had any reply for the last six months. Her mother must be dead.'

'Ah!' said the man, and returned to his reflections.

'She was no better than she should be, that mother of hers,' added the Thénardier woman. 'She abandoned her child.'

As though some instinct had alerted her that she was being talked about, Cosette did not take her eyes off the Thénardier woman throughout this entire conversation. She listened vaguely. She heard the odd few words.

Meanwhile, the boozers, all of them three-quarters drunk, were repeating their scurrilous refrain with redoubled merriment. It was a highly ribald song involving the Virgin and the infant Jesus. The Thénardier woman went over to join in the hearty laughter. From under the table Cosette gazed into the fire, which was reflected in her staring eyes. She began rocking in her arms again the swaddled bundle she had made, and as she rocked it she sang in a low voice, 'My mother's dead! My mother's dead! My mother's dead!'

Pressed again by the hostess, the yellow man, 'the millionaire', at last consented to have some supper.

'What does monsieur want?'

'Bread and cheese,' said the man.

'He's surely a beggar,' thought the Thénardier woman.

The drunks were still singing their song and the child under the table was singing hers.

All at once Cosette broke off. She had just turned round and caught sight of the little Thénardier girls' doll, which they had abandoned for the cat and left on the floor a few feet from the kitchen table.

So she dropped the swaddled sword that only half satisfied her and then let her eyes wander slowly around the room. The Thénardier woman was talking quietly to her husband and counting some money, Ponine and Zelma were playing with the cat, the travellers were eating or drinking or singing, there was no one looking at her. She had not a moment to lose. She crept out from under the table on her hands and knees, made sure once more that she was not being watched, then swiftly slithered over to the doll and grabbed it. A moment later she was back in her place, sitting still, but turned in such a way as to keep in shadow the doll she held in her arms. The joy of playing with a doll was so rare for her that it had all the intensity of a real thrill.

No one had seen her, except the traveller, who was slowly eating his frugal meal.

This joy lasted for almost a quarter of an hour.

But careful though she was, Cosette did not notice one of the doll's feet was sticking out and that it was very brightly lit by the fire in the hearth. That pink foot shining in the shadows suddenly caught Azelma's eye, and she said to Éponine, 'Look, sister!'

The two little girls left off what they were doing, flabbergasted. Cosette had dared to take the doll! Éponine stood up, and without letting go of the cat went over to her mother and began to tug at her skirt.

'Leave me alone!' said her mother. 'What do you want?'

'Mother,' said the child, 'look!'

And she pointed to Cosette. Completely transported in her possession of the doll, Cosette was blind and deaf to everything else.

The Thénardier woman's face took on that peculiar expression which consists of a terrible fury concerning life's trivialities, and which has led to such women being called harpies. This time wounded pride incensed her even more. Cosette had overstepped all boundaries. Cosette had violated the doll belonging to these 'little misses'. The look on a czarina's face, seeing a muzhik trying on her imperial son's broad blue sash, would have been no different.

She shouted in a voice husky with indignation, 'Cosette!'

Cosette started as if the earth had trembled beneath her. She turned round.

'Cosette!' repeated the Thénardier woman.

Cosette took the doll and laid it gently on the floor with a kind of reverence mixed with despair. Then without taking her eyes off it, she clasped her hands and wrung them, which is a dreadful thing to say of a child that age. Then – what none of her emotions that day had managed to achieve, neither her flight through the forest, nor the weight of the bucket of water, nor the loss of the money, nor the sight of the strap, nor even the ominous words she had heard Madame Thénardier utter – she wept. She burst into sobs.

Meanwhile the traveller had risen to his feet.

'What's the matter?' he said to the Thénardier woman.

'Don't you see?' said the woman, pointing to the *corpus delicti* that lay at Cosette's feet.

'Well, what is it?' said the man.

'That guttersnipe', replied the Thénardier woman, 'has dared to touch the children's doll!'

'All this fuss just for that!' said the man. 'Well, what if she did play with the doll?'

'She touched it with her dirty hands!' the Thénardier woman went on. 'With her horrible dirty hands.'

At this, Cosette sobbed all the more.

'Will you stop that noise!' shouted the Thénardier woman.

The man walked straight over to the street door, opened it, and went out.

As soon as he was gone the Thénardier woman took advantage of his absence to give Cosette a hefty kick under the table, which made the child cry out loud.

The door opened again and the man reappeared, carrying with both hands the fabulous doll that has already been mentioned, which had held all the youngsters in the village in thrall since morning, and he stood it in front of Cosette, saying, 'Here, this is for you.'

We can only assume that in the time he had been there, which was an hour or more, he had been dimly aware of the fancy goods stall so splendidly illuminated with lanterns and candles that its brightness could be seen through the window of the tavern.

Cosette looked up. She had seen the man approach her with that doll as if it might have been the sun approaching. She heard those incredible words, 'This is for you.' She stared at him. She stared at the doll. Then she slowly retreated, and went and hid under the far end of the table in the corner by the wall.

She was not crying any more, she was not wailing, she looked as if she dared not breathe.

The Thénardier woman, Éponine and Azelma might have been statues. Even the drinkers were held in suspense. There was a solemn silence throughout the tavern.

Paralysed and speechless, the Thénardier woman returned to her speculations. 'Who the hell is this old man? Is he a pauper? Is he a millionaire? He may be both, in other words a thief.'

On her husband's face appeared that particular expression that marks the human countenance whenever overriding instinct appears there in all its bestial strength. The innkeeper stared at the doll and the traveller in turn. He seemed to be getting the scent of the man as he might have got the scent of a bag of money. This lasted no more than a fleeting moment.

He went over to his wife and said to her quietly, 'That thing costs at least thirty francs. No fooling about. Grovel to the man!'

The crass and the guileless have this in common: the transitional mode is not in their nature.

'Well, Cosette,' said the Thénardier woman in a voice that strove to be sweet and consisted entirely of the bitter honey of vicious women, 'aren't you going to take your doll?'

Cosette ventured out of her hiding-place.

'My little Cosette,' said the Thénardier woman caressingly, 'monsieur has given you a doll. Take it, it's yours.'

Cosette gazed at the marvellous doll with a kind of terror. Her face was still streaked with tears but her eyes began to fill like the sky at daybreak with strange glimmerings of joy. What she was going through at that moment was a bit like what she would have felt if she had suddenly been told, 'Little one, you're the queen of France.'

She had the feeling that if she touched that doll it would release a thunderbolt. Which was true up to a certain point, for she said to herself that the Thénardier woman would scold and beat her. Yet the attraction was too strong to resist. In the end she moved closer, and turning to the Thénardier woman she murmured timorously, 'May I, madame?'

No words can convey that look she had, at once hopeless, terrified and ecstatic.

'Heavens!' cried the Thénardier woman. 'It's yours. Since monsieur's giving it to you.'

'Really, monsieur?' said Cosette. 'Is she really and truly mine, the lady?'

The stranger's eyes appeared to be full of tears. He looked as if his emotion was at that pitch of intensity when you say nothing so as not to weep. He nodded, and placed 'the lady's' hand in Cosette's tiny hand.

Cosette snatched her hand back as if the 'lady's' had burned it, and began to stare at the floor. We are obliged to add that at that moment she was sticking her tongue out in the most exaggerated way. All of a sudden she turned and seized the doll with a passion.

'I'll call her Catherine,' she said.

It was a bizarre moment when Cosette's rags encountered and embraced the doll's ribbons and pretty pink muslins.

'Madame,' she said, 'may I put her on a chair?'

'Yes, my child,' replied the Thénardier woman.

It was now Éponine and Azelma who gazed at Cosette with envy. Cosette placed Catherine on a chair, then sat there motionless on the floor in front of her without saying a word, in an attitude of contemplation.

'Play, Cosette,' said the stranger.

'Oh, I'm playing!' replied the child.

This stranger, this unknown individual who seemed to be a visitation to Cosette made by providence, was at that moment the most hated thing in the world to the Thénardier woman. However, she had to control herself. And no matter how much in her effort to imitate her husband in all his actions she had made a habit of dissimulation, this was more of a strain on her emotions than she could bear. She lost no time in sending her daughters to bed, then asked the yellow man's 'permission' to send Cosette to bed too. 'It's been a very tiring day for her,' she added in a motherly way. Cosette went off, carrying Catherine in her arms.

Now and again the Thénardier woman went to the other end of the room where her husband was, 'to make her feel better', she said. She exchanged a few words with her husband that were all the more furious because she dared not voice them out loud.

'Old fool! What's he up to? Coming here and upsetting us! Wanting that little monster to play! Giving her dolls! Giving forty-franc dolls to a little bitch I'd gladly exchange for forty sous! It wouldn't take much for him to be calling her Your Majesty as if she were the Duchesse de Berry! Does that make any sense? Is he out of his mind, this mysterious old gaffer?'

'Why? It's quite simple,' replied Thénardier. 'If that's his pleasure! It's your pleasure to have the little one work, it's his pleasure to have her play. He's entitled to it. A traveller can do what he likes when he pays for it. If this old boy's a philanthropist, what's that to you? If he is a fool, it's no concern of yours. Why interfere, so long as he has money?'

A master's way of talking and an innkeeper's line of reasoning, neither of which brooked any challenge.

The man had rested his elbows on the table and appeared lost in thought again. All the other travellers, pedlars and carters, had moved a little way off and were no longer singing. They observed him from a distance with a kind of respectful awe. This individual who was so poorly dressed, who so readily drew hind coachwheels from his pocket and lavished huge dolls on little urchins in wooden clogs, was certainly a magnificent and intimidating fellow.

Several hours went by. Midnight mass was over, the late-night festivities had ended, the drinkers had left, the bar was closed, the room was deserted, the fire had died down, the stranger was still in the same place and in the same position. From time to time he changed the elbow he was leaning on from one to the other. That was all. But he had said not a word since Cosette had been gone.

Only the Thénardiers, out of a sense of obligation and out of curiosity, had remained in the room.

'Is he going to spend the night like that?' grumbled the Thénardier woman.

When two o'clock in the morning struck she admitted defeat and said to her husband, 'I'm going to bed. You do as you like.'

Her husband sat at a table in the corner, lit a candle and settled down to read *Le Courrier Français*.

A good hour went by in this way. The worthy innkeeper had read *Le Courrier Français* at least three times, from the date of issue to the printer's name. The stranger did not stir.

Thénardier fidgeted, coughed, spat, blew his nose, made his chair creak. No movement at all from the man. 'Is he asleep?' Thénardier wondered. The man was not asleep, but nothing could rouse him. At last Thénardier took off his cap, quietly went over and ventured to say, 'Is monsieur not going to retire?'

'Not going to go to bed' would have seemed too graceless and familiar. 'To retire' suggested luxury and sounded respectful. These words have the mysterious and admirable peculiarity of inflating the bill the next day. A room where you 'go to bed' costs twenty sous. A room to which you 'retire' costs twenty francs.

'Of course,' said the stranger, 'you're right. Where's your stable?'

'Monsieur,' said Thénardier with a smile, 'I'll show you the way, monsieur.'

He took the candle, the man took his bundle and staff, and Thénardier led him to a room on the first floor that was of rare splendour, fully furnished in mahogany, with a boat bed and red calico curtains.

'What's this?' said the traveller.

'It's our own bridal chamber,' said the innkeeper. 'My wife and I use another room. No one comes in here more than three or four times a year.'

'I'd have just as soon stayed in the stable,' said the man curtly.

Thénardier pretended not to hear this somewhat disobliging remark.

He lit two brand-new wax candles that stood on the mantelpiece. There was quite a good fire burning in the hearth. Under a glass dome on the mantelpiece was a woman's head-dress made of silver wire and orange blossom.

'And what's this?' said the stranger.

'That, monsieur,' said Thénardier, 'is my wife's bridal head-dress.'

The traveller observed the object with a look that seemed to say, 'So there was actually a time when that monster was a virgin?'

Thénardier was lying, however. When he took a lease on this place in order to set up an inn, he found the room already furnished like this, and he bought the furniture and the orange blossom second-hand, thinking they would lend 'his spouse' a suggestion of former elegance, and consequently his establishment would gain what the English call respectability.

When the traveller turned round the landlord had disappeared. Thénardier had discreetly slipped away without daring to wish him goodnight, not wanting to treat with disrespectful cordiality a man he intended to fleece royally the next morning.

The innkeeper went to his room. His wife was in bed but she was not asleep. When she heard her husband's footstep she turned over and said, 'You know, I'm turning Cosette out of the house tomorrow.'

Thénardier replied coldly, 'You do take on so!'

They exchanged no other words and a few moments later their candle was extinguished.

As for the traveller, he laid aside in a corner his staff and his bundle. After the landlord had gone he sat in an armchair and remained thoughtful for some time. Then he took off his shoes, picked up one of the two candles, blew out the other, opened the door and went out of the room, looking around as if in search of something. He went down a corridor and reached the staircase. There he heard a very faint sound, like the breathing of a child. He followed this sound and came to a sort of triangular alcove built under the staircase, or rather formed by the staircase itself. This alcove was nothing more than the space underneath the stairs. There, among all sorts of old baskets and old broken pottery, in the dust and the cobwebs, was a bed. If bed it can be called: a pallet so full of holes it let the straw show through, and a coverlet so full of holes it let the pallet show through. No sheets. It lay on the tiled floor. Cosette was asleep in this bed.

The man moved closer and observed her. Cosette was fast asleep. She was fully dressed. In winter she did not get undressed, so as to be less cold. She held the doll close to her, its big staring eyes gleaming in the dark. From time to time she gave a deep sigh as if she were going to wake up, and she hugged the doll in her arms almost convulsively. At the side of her bed was only one of her wooden clogs.

An open door close to Cosette's cubby-hole revealed a rather large, dark room. The stranger stepped inside. Through a glass-panelled door at the far end could be seen two small, very white twin beds. They belonged to Éponine and Azelma. Behind these beds, half out of sight, was an uncurtained wicker cradle in which slept the little boy who had been crying all evening.

The stranger assumed this room connected with that of the Thénardier couple. He was about to withdraw when his gaze fell on the fireplace, one of those vast fireplaces that inns have, where there is always such a small fire – when there is any fire at all – and the sight of which makes you feel so cold. There was no fire in this one, not even any embers. Yet there was something that attracted the traveller's attention. There were two dainty little children's shoes of different sizes. The traveller recalled that charming and age-old custom among children of leaving their shoes in the fireplace on Christmas night to await there in the darkness some gleaming gift from their good fairy. Éponine and Azelma had taken good care not to forget, and each of them had placed one of her shoes on the hearth.

The traveller bent down.

The fairy, that is to say their mother, had already paid her visit, and a bright new ten-sou coin could be seen shining inside each shoe.

The man straightened up and was about to go away when he caught sight of another object, tucked away far back in the darkest corner of the hearth. He peered at it and recognized a wooden clog, a hideous wooden clog of the roughest kind, half split and all covered with ashes and dried mud. It was Cosette's clog. With that touching trust of children that may always be betrayed without ever being discouraged, Cosette too had put her clog in the fireplace.

A sublime and sweet thing is hope in a child who has never known anything but despair.

There was nothing in this wooden shoe. The stranger fumbled in his waistcoat, bent down and put inside Cosette's shoe a gold louis.

Then he stole back to his room.

IX
Thénardier Up to His Tricks

The next morning at least two hours before daybreak Thénardier was seated beside a candle in the tavern room downstairs, pen in hand, making out the bill for the yellow-frock-coated traveller.

Hunched over him, his wife stood and watched. They exchanged not a single word. There was deep thought on the one hand, and on the other the devout admiration of one who was witnessing the birth and development of a wonder of the human mind. Some noise could be heard in the house. It was Alouette sweeping the stairs.

After a good quarter of an hour and a bit of crossing out, Thénardier produced this masterpiece:

BILL FOR THE GENTLEMAN IN No. 1

Supper	3 francs
Room	10
Candle	5
Fire	4
Service	1
TOTAL	23 francs.

Service was written 'servise'.

'Twenty-three francs!' cried the woman with an enthusiasm mixed with some misgiving.

Like all great artists, Thénardier was dissatisfied. 'Bah!' he exclaimed. Such was Castlereagh's feeling at the Congress of Vienna when drawing up the bill that France would have to pay.

'Monsieur Thénardier, you're right, it's no more than what he owes,' murmured the woman, thinking of the doll that had been given to Cosette in front of her daughters. 'It's correct but it's too much. He won't pay it.'

Thénardier gave his cold laugh and said, 'He'll pay.'

That laugh was the ultimate expression of certainty and authority.

Whatever was spoken like that must be so. The woman did not argue. She began putting the tables in order. Her husband paced the room.

A moment later he added, 'I've a debt of fifteen hundred francs to pay!'

He went and sat by the fire, musing, his feet on the warm embers.

'Now, you won't forget, I'm throwing Cosette out of the house today?' said the woman. 'That monster! She's torturing me with that doll of hers! I'd rather marry Louis XVIII than keep her in the house another day!'

Thénardier lit his pipe and replied between two puffs, 'You give the man that bill.'

Then he went out. He was no sooner out of the room than the traveller entered.

Thénardier instantly reappeared behind him and remained motionless in the half-open doorway, visible only to his wife.

The yellow man carried his staff and his bundle in his hand.

'Up so early?' said the Thénardier woman. 'Monsieur is leaving us already?'

As she said this she kept turning the bill in her hands with an air of diffidence, running the folds between her fingernails. Her hard face revealed an untypical shade of emotion: apprehension and embarrassment.

Presenting such a bill to a man whose appearance was so thoroughly that of 'a pauper' was not, she felt, an easy thing to do.

The traveller seemed preoccupied and absent-minded. He replied, 'Yes, madame, I'll be on my way.'

'So monsieur had no business to attend to in Montfermeil?'

'No. I'm passing through. That's all. Madame,' he added, 'what do I owe?'

Without replying the Thénardier woman handed him the folded bill.

The man unfolded the sheet of paper and glanced at it but his mind was clearly elsewhere.

'Madame,' he said, 'do you do a good trade here in Montfermeil?'

'So so, monsieur,' replied the Thénardier woman, amazed not to witness some outburst.

She went on in a plaintive and querulous tone, 'Oh, monsieur, times are so hard! And then, we've so few gentry in these parts! It's just humble folk, you see. If it weren't for the occasional rich and generous traveller like yourself, monsieur! We've so many expenses. I tell you, that child costs us the earth.'

'What child?'

'Why, you know, the child! Cosette! Alouette, as they call her in the village!'

'Ah!' said the man.

She went on: 'They're stupid with their nicknames, these peasants! She looks more like a bat than a lark. You see, monsieur, we don't ask for charity but nor can we afford it. We earn nothing and we've a lot to pay out. The licence, taxes, duty on the door and windows, sur-taxes! Monsieur knows the government claims a huge amount of money. And besides, I have my own daughters. I don't need to raise other people's children.'

In a voice that he strove to keep emotionless but in which there was a tremor, the man said, 'What if she were to be taken off your hands?'

'Who? Cosette?'

'Yes.'

The woman's fierce, ruddy face lit up in hideous smiles.

'Ah monsieur, my dear monsieur, you can have her, keep her, take her away, remove her, sugar her, truffle her, drink her, eat her, and may the Holy Virgin and all the saints in paradise bless you!'

'Agreed.'

'Really! You'll take her away?'

'I'll take her away.'

'Right now?'

'Right now. Call the child.'

'Cosette!' yelled the Thénardier woman.

'In the meantime,' the man went on, 'I still have the bill to pay. How much is it?'

He glanced at the bill and could not help being startled.

'Twenty-three francs!'

He looked at the landlady and repeated, 'Twenty-three francs?'

There was, in the pronunciation of these words thus repeated, a change of tone that marks the distinction between an exclamation mark and a question mark.

The Thénardier woman had had time to prepare herself for his reaction. She replied with assurance, 'Quite right, monsieur, it's twenty-three francs.'

The stranger laid five five-franc coins on the table. 'Go and get the child,' he said.

At that moment Thénardier walked into the middle of the room and said, 'Monsieur owes twenty-six sous.'

'Twenty-six sous!' cried his wife.

'Twenty sous for the room,' said Thénardier coldly, 'and six sous

379

for his supper. As for the child, I need to have a little chat with monsieur about that. Leave us, wife.'

The Thénardier woman had one of those blinding experiences brought about by the unexpected revelation of a brilliant talent. She sensed that a great actor was coming on to the stage, and without a word of objection, off she went.

As soon as they were alone Thénardier offered the traveller a chair. The traveller sat down. Thénardier remained standing and his face assumed a peculiar expression of good-natured simplicity and straightforwardness.

'Now, I tell you something, monsieur,' he said. 'The fact is, I adore that child.'

The stranger stared intently at him. 'What child?'

Thénardier continued, 'It's strange how attached you get! What's all that money for? Keep your hundred-sou coins. I adore the child.'

'Who are you talking about?' asked the stranger.

'Our little Cosette, of course! Don't you want to take her away from us? Well, to be frank, as sure as you're an honest man, I can't agree to it. I'd miss that child. I've known her since she was just a baby. It's true she costs us money, it's true she has her faults, it's true we're not rich, it's true I've paid out over four hundred francs for drugs just for one of her illnesses! But a man must do something for the good Lord. She has no father or mother, I raised her. I'm happy to share my bread with her. I actually care for that child. You understand, there's a fondness that develops. I'm soft-hearted, I am. For me, reason doesn't come into it. I love that little girl. My wife's quick-tempered but she loves her too. You see, she's like a child of our own. I need her in the house, chattering away.'

The stranger continued to stare at him intently.

He went on, 'Forgive me, monsieur, I'm sorry, but you don't give your child away to a passer-by just like that. Am I not right? Other than that, I can't say, you're rich, you seem a very decent man – if it were for her own good? But we'd need to know. You understand? Supposing I were to let her go, and deny myself, I'd want to know where she was going, I wouldn't want to lose sight of her, I'd want to know who she was living with so I could go and see her now and then, so that she'd know her dear old foster-father was there, keeping an eye out for her. After all, some things are just not possible. I don't even know your name. If you were to take her away, I'd say, "And Alouette? Where's she gone?" I'd need to see some basic document at least, some sort of a passport, you know!'

Without ceasing to stare at him with that gaze that penetrates, as it were, the depths of conscience, the stranger replied in a firm and deliberate voice, 'Monsieur Thénardier, you do not need a passport to travel twelve and a half miles out of Paris. If I take Cosette away I shall take her away, that's all. You will not know my name, you will not know where I live, you will not know where she is, and my intention is that she will not see you again for the rest of her life. I break the cord she has around her ankle, and she goes. Does that suit you? Yes or no?'

Just as demons and genies recognize from certain signs the presence of a superior god, Thénardier realized he was dealing with someone very powerful. It was like an intuition. He realized this with his sharp, shrewd quickness. The day before, while drinking with the carters and smoking and singing dirty songs, he had spent the evening observing the stranger, watching him like a cat and studying him like a mathematician. He had watched him on his own account, for the pleasure of it and by instinct, and spied on him as if he had been paid to do so. Not a gesture, not a movement made by the man in the yellow coat escaped him. Even before the stranger had so clearly expressed his interest in Cosette, Thénardier had guessed it. He had noticed the way the old man's intense gaze kept returning to the child. Why this interest? Who was this man? Why, with so much money in his purse, so poorly dressed? Questions that he put to himself without being able to answer them, questions that vexed him. He had been thinking about it all night long. This could not be Cosette's father. Was it her grandfather? Then why not make himself known at once? When you have a right, you assert it. This man evidently had no right over Cosette. Then who was he? Thénardier was lost in speculation. He envisaged everything and saw nothing. Anyway, when he started this conversation with the man, feeling sure there was some secret in all this, sure that the man was interested in remaining in obscurity, he felt strong. At the stranger's clear and firm response – when he saw that this mysterious individual was so uncomplicatedly mysterious – he felt weak. He was not expecting anything like this. It routed his conjectures. He rallied his thoughts. He weighed all this up in a second. Thénardier was one of those men who take in a situation at a glance. He decided it was time to proceed quickly and directly. He did as great leaders do at that decisive moment they alone have the ability to recognize. He showed his hand.

'Monsieur,' he said, 'I need fifteen hundred francs.'

The stranger took from his side pocket an old black leather wallet, opened it and drew out three banknotes, which he laid on the table.

Then he pressed his large thumb on these banknotes and said to the innkeeper, 'Send for Cosette.'

What was Cosette doing while this was going on?

When she woke up Cosette went rushing to her clog. She found the gold coin inside it. It was not a napoleon, it was one of those freshly minted twenty-franc Restoration coins with the little Prussian pig-tail replacing the laurel crown on the effigy they bore. Cosette was dazzled. Her change of fortune was beginning to go to her head. She did not know what a gold coin was, she had never seen one before, she very quickly hid it in her pocket as if she had stolen it. Yet she sensed it really was hers, she guessed where this gift had come from, but she felt a kind of joy that was full of fear. She was pleased. More than anything else she was amazed. These things that were so magnificent and so pretty did not seem real to her. The doll frightened her, the gold coin frightened her. She quailed slightly at these splendours. The stranger alone did not frighten her. On the contrary, he reassured her. Since the day before, through her wonder, during her sleep, in her little childish mind she had been thinking about this man, who looked old and poor and so sad, and who was so rich and so kind. Since she had met this man in the forest everything seemed to have changed for her. Less fortunate than any swallow in the sky, Cosette had never known what it was to find refuge at her mother's side and be taken under her wing. For the last five years, that is to say as far back as she could remember, the poor child had shivered and trembled. She had always been exposed completely naked to the bitter, chill wind of adversity; now she felt clothed. Before, she was cold in her soul, now she was warm. Cosette was no longer afraid of the Thénardier woman. She was no longer alone. There was someone there.

She was very soon busy with the housework she had to do every morning. That louis, which she kept with her, in the very same apron pocket that the fifteen-sou coin had fallen out of the night before, was a source of distraction. She dared not touch it but she spent five minutes at a time contemplating it, with her tongue stuck out, it has to be said. While sweeping the stairs she would stop and stand there motionless, forgetful of her broom and of the entire universe, gazing at that shining star at the bottom of her pocket.

It was during one of these spells of contemplation that the Thénardier woman came upon her.

She had gone to fetch her at her husband's command. Unbelievably, she did not slap her nor did she say anything abusive. 'Cosette,' she said almost sweetly, 'come at once.'

A moment later Cosette entered the room downstairs.

The stranger picked up the bundle he had brought with him and untied it. This bundle contained a little woollen dress, a pinafore, a sleeved fustian vest, a shawl, a petticoat, woollen stockings, shoes, a complete outfit for an eight-year-old girl. Everything was black.

'My child,' said the man, 'take these and go and put them on, as quickly as you can.'

Daylight was breaking when those of Montfermeil's inhabitants who were beginning to open their doors saw an old man in shabby clothes walk past on the Paris road, holding by the hand a little girl, in full mourning, who was carrying a big pink doll in her arms. They were heading towards Livry. These were our man and Cosette.

No one knew the man. As Cosette was no longer in rags many did not recognize her.

Cosette was going away. With whom? She did not know. Where? She could not tell. All she understood was that she was leaving behind her the Thénardier inn. No one thought of saying goodbye to her, nor did she think of saying goodbye to anyone. She was escaping from that hated and hateful house.

Poor meek creature whose heart until that moment had never been other than constricted!

Cosette walked along gravely, her big eyes wide open, gazing at the sky. She had put her louis in the pocket of her new pinafore. From time to time she leaned over to take a peek at it, then she looked at the man. She felt something that was almost as if she was with the good Lord.

X
Who Seeks to Gain May End Up Worse Off

As usual the Thénardier woman had left everything to her husband. She had great expectations. Once the man and Cosette were gone, Thénardier let a full quarter of an hour go by, then he took her aside and showed her the fifteen hundred francs.

'Is that all?' she said.

It was the first time since they had been living together as husband and wife that she had dared to criticize something the master had done. It had an effect.

'In the circumstances, you're right,' he said, 'I'm a fool. Give me my hat.'

He folded the three banknotes, stuffed them into his pocket and went rushing out, but he went the wrong way and first turned right. Some neighbours he consulted put him back on the right track, Alouette and the man had been seen going towards Livry. He followed in this direction, taking great strides and talking to himself.

'The man's obviously a fortune dressed up in yellow, and I'm an ass. First he hands over twenty sous, then five francs, then fifty francs, then fifteen hundred francs, just as easily every time. He'd have handed over fifteen thousand francs. But I'll catch up with him.'

And then that bundle of clothes he had all ready for the child, that was odd. There were many mysteries behind that. You do not let go of mysteries once you've got hold of them. The secrets of the wealthy are sponges full of gold. You need to know how to squeeze them. All these thoughts whirled about inside his brain. 'I'm an ass,' he said.

When you leave Montfermeil and come to the bend in the road that goes to Livry, you can see it stretching out before you far across the plain. Once he got there, he reckoned the old man and the child ought to be within sight. He looked as far as his eye could reach, and saw nothing. He made further enquiries. However, this was time lost. Some passers-by told him the man and child he was looking for had been heading for the woods over towards Gagny. He hurried off in that direction.

They were ahead of him, but a child walks slowly and he was going fast. And besides, it was very familiar countryside to him.

Suddenly he stopped and slapped his forehead like a man who has forgotten something vital and who is all set to retrace his steps.

'I should have brought my gun,' said he to himself.

Thénardier was one of those dual natures that sometimes pass through our midst without our knowledge, and disappear leaving us none the wiser because fate has revealed only one side of them. It falls to many men to live half submerged like this. In a quiet and peaceful situation Thénardier had everything it takes to live as – we do not say 'to be' – what by general agreement is called an honest tradesman, a solid citizen. At the same time, given certain circumstances, certain disturbances bringing his underlying nature to the surface, he had everything it takes to be a villain. He was a shopkeeper with an element of the monster in him. In some corner of that doss-house where Thénardier lived, Satan must have crouched in wonderment at times at this hideous masterpiece.

After a moment's hesitation, 'Bah!' he thought, 'they'll have time to get away.'

And he pressed on, advancing rapidly, and almost confidently, with the wiliness of a fox scenting a covey of partridges.

Sure enough, when he had passed the ponds and cut across the large clearing to the right of Avenue de Bellevue, as he reached that grassy walk that goes almost all the way round the hill, overlying Chelles Abbey's ancient underground aqueduct, he saw over the top of a bush the hat on which he had already built many conjectures. It was the man's hat. The bush was low. Thénardier realized that the man and Cosette were sitting there. You could not see the child because she was so small, but the doll's head was visible.

Thénardier was not mistaken. The man had sat down to let Cosette have a little rest. The innkeeper walked round the bush and suddenly appeared before those he was seeking.

'Forgive me, monsieur,' he said, quite out of breath, 'I'm sorry, but here are your fifteen hundred francs.' So saying, he held out to the stranger the three banknotes.

The man looked up. 'What's the meaning of this?'

Thénardier replied respectfully, 'It means, monsieur, I'm taking Cosette back.'

Cosette shuddered and huddled up close to the old man.

Looking Thénardier straight in the eye and separately articulating every syllable, he replied, 'You are ta-king Co-sette back?'

'Yes, monsieur, I am. I'll tell you why. I've been thinking. The thing is, I've no right to give her away to you. You see, I'm an honest man. The little girl doesn't belong to me, she belongs to her mother. It was her mother who left me in charge of her, I can only hand her back to her mother. You'll say to me, "But the mother's dead." Very well. In that case I can hand the child over only to a person who brings me a document, signed by her mother, saying that I'm to hand the child over to that person. That's clear.'

Without replying, the man fumbled in his pocket and Thénardier saw the wallet with the banknotes in it reappear.

The innkeeper felt a thrill of joy. 'Good!' he thought. 'Hold steady. He's going to bribe me!'

Before opening the wallet the traveller glanced around. The place was absolutely deserted. There was not another soul in the woods or in the valley. The man opened his wallet and took out, not the handful of banknotes Thénardier was expecting, but just a small piece of paper which he unfolded and presented, opened out, to the innkeeper, saying, 'You're right. Read that!'

Thénardier took the piece of paper and read the following:

Montreuil-sur-Mer, 25th March 1823

Monsieur Thénardier,

You will hand over Cosette to this person. You will be paid whatever is owing.

Respectfully yours,

Fantine

'You recognize that signature?' said the man.

It was Fantine's signature. Thénardier recognized it.

There was no arguing with this. He felt two violent disappointments: the disappointment of not getting the bribe he had been expecting, and the disappointment of being defeated.

The man added, 'You may keep that piece of paper as your receipt.'

Thénardier made a tactical retreat.

'This signature's quite well forged,' he grumbled under his breath. 'Still, if you say so!'

Then he tried his luck with a desperate bid. 'Monsieur,' he said, 'that's fair enough. Seeing as you're the person. But you have to pay me "whatever is owing". I'm owed a great deal.'

The man got up, and flicking the dust from his threadbare sleeve he said, 'Monsieur Thénardier, in January the mother reckoned she owed you one hundred and twenty francs. In February you sent her a bill for five hundred francs. You received three hundred francs at the end of February, and three hundred francs at the beginning of March. It has been nine months since then, at the agreed price of fifteen francs a month, which comes to one hundred and thirty-five francs. You received an extra one hundred francs. Leaving thirty-five still owing to you. I've just given you fifteen hundred francs.'

Thénardier experienced what a wolf experiences at that moment when he feels himself bitten and caught in the steel jaws of the trap. 'Who is this devil of a man?' he thought.

He did what the wolf does. He shook himself. Audacity had already stood him in good stead once. 'Monsieur-whose-name-I-don't-know,' he said resolutely, and this time casting aside all forms of respect, 'either you give me three thousand francs or I take back Cosette.'

The stranger said calmly, 'Come along, Cosette.'

He took hold of Cosette with his left hand and with his right he picked up his staff that was lying on the ground. Thénardier noted the extraordinary heaviness of the stick and the loneliness of the spot.

The man plunged into the forest with the child, leaving the innkeeper standing there, dumbfounded. As they walked away Thénardier considered those slightly stooped broad shoulders and huge fists. Then his eyes, turning back to himself, saw his own scrawny arms and thin hands.

'I must be really stupid not to have brought my gun,' he said to himself, 'seeing as I was going hunting!'

However, the innkeeper did not give up. 'I want to know where he's going,' he said. And he started following them at a distance. He was left in possession of two things: a barb – the scrap of paper signed 'Fantine'; and a consolation – the fifteen hundred francs.

The man led Cosette in the direction of Livry and Bondy. He walked slowly with his head bowed, looking sad and pensive. Winter had thinned out the forest so that, while remaining quite far behind, Thénardier did not lose sight of them. The man turned round from time to time to see if anyone was following. All at once he caught sight of Thénardier. Together with Cosette he darted into a thicket where both were able to disappear from sight.

'Damn it!' said Thénardier. And he quickened his pace.

The density of the undergrowth forced him to close in on them. When the man reached the very densest part of the thicket he turned round. Try as he might to hide in the branches, Thénardier could not help being seen. The man cast a troubled glance at him, then shook his head and continued on his way. The innkeeper resumed his pursuit. They went on like this for two or three hundred paces. All of a sudden the man turned round again. He saw the innkeeper. This time he stared at him in such a sinister way that Thénardier decided it was 'no use' going any further. Thénardier retraced his steps.

XI
Number 9430 Reappears and Cosette Wins the Lottery

Jean Valjean was not dead.

When he fell into the sea, or rather threw himself into it, he was, as we have seen, unshackled. He swam under the water to a ship riding at anchor with a boat moored to it. He contrived to hide in this boat until nightfall. After dark he took the plunge again and swam for it, and came ashore not far from Cap Brun. There, as he was not without money, he was able to buy some clothes. A country café close to Balaguier was at that time the outfitters for escaped convicts, a lucrative line of business. Then, like all those sorry fugitives who try to outwit the vigilance of the law and evade their social doom, Jean Valjean followed an obscure and complicated itinerary. He found initial refuge at Pradeaux, near Beausset. Then he headed for Grand-Villard near Briançon in the Hautes-Alpes. A groping and harassed flight through a moles' maze of secret tunnels. Later, some trace was found of his having been in the Civrieux area of Ain, in the Pyrenees, at Accons in the locality of La-Grange-de-Doumecq, near the hamlet of Chavailles, and in the Périgueux area, at Les Brunies, canton of La Chapelle-Gonaguet. He got to Paris. We have just seen him at Montfermeil.

His first concern on arriving in Paris had been to buy mourning clothes for a little girl of about seven or eight, then to find lodgings. Having done that, he went off to Montfermeil.

The reader will recall that he had already, during his earlier escape, made a mysterious trip here, or somewhere in the vicinity, of which the law had some inkling. Now he was believed to be dead, and this intensified the obscurity that had developed around him. In Paris he happened to come across one of the newspapers that reported the event. He felt reassured and almost at peace, as if he really had died.

On the evening of the same day that he rescued Cosette from the Thénardiers' clutches, Jean Valjean returned to Paris. He returned at nightfall with the child, by way of the Monceaux toll-gate. There, he climbed into a cab that took him to Esplanade de l'Observatoire, where he descended, paid the coachman, took Cosette by the hand, and together in the darkness of night, through the deserted streets around Lourcine and La Glacière, they made their way towards Boulevard de l'Hôpital.

For Cosette it had been a strange day full of excitement. They had sat behind hedges to eat bread and cheese bought from out-of-the-way taverns, they had changed coaches frequently, they had gone some parts of the way on foot. She was uncomplaining but she was tired, and Jean Valjean became aware of this from her pulling on his hand more as they walked along. He lifted her on to his back. Without letting go of Catherine, Cosette laid her head on Jean Valjean's shoulder and fell asleep.

BOOK FOUR
THE GORBEAU TENEMENT

I
Maître Gorbeau

Forty years ago the solitary wayfarer who ventured into the God-forsaken wastes of La Salpêtrière and followed the boulevard to the Italie toll-gate came to places where Paris might be said to peter out. It was not solitary, there were passers-by. It was not countryside, there were houses and streets. It was not a town, the streets were rutted like the open roads and grass grew over them. It was not a village, the houses were too tall. What was it, then? It was an inhabited place where there was nobody, it was a deserted place where there was somebody. This was one of the city's boulevards, one of the streets of Paris, a greater wilderness at night than any forest, bleaker by day than any cemetery.

It was the old Marché-aux-Chevaux neighbourhood.

If he were bold enough to step outside the four decrepit walls of this Marché-aux-Chevaux, if he actually agreed to venture beyond Rue du Petit-Banquier, having left behind on his right a cottage garden protected by high walls, then a wasteground where tanning mills rose like gigantic beavers' lodges, then an enclosure full of timber with piles of logs, sawdust and shavings, with a big dog barking on top of them; then a long, low wall in total ruin, overgrown with moss that became dense with flowers in spring, and in it a small black door in mourning; then, where most desolate, a hideous and decrepit building on which could be read in large letters 'POST NO BILLS', this audacious wayfarer would come to the corner of Rue des Vignes-St-Marcel, latitudes that are little known. There, close to an industrial building and between two garden walls, you would have seen in those days a run-down tenement that at first glance seemed as small as a thatched cottage and was actually as large as a cathedral. It stood sideways, gable-end on to the public road, hence its apparent smallness. Nearly the whole of the house was concealed. All that could be seen were the door and one window.

This run-down tenement was only two storeys high.

The first detail to strike the observer was that this door could never have been anything but the door of a hovel, whereas if the window had been set in dressed stone instead of rubble-stone it might have been the casement of a fine mansion.

The door was nothing more than a collection of worm-eaten planks roughly joined together with battens that looked like rough-hewn logs. It opened directly on to a steep staircase of muddy, chalky, dusty high steps, the same width as the door, and which could be seen from the street rising straight up like a ladder between two walls and disappearing into the gloom. The top of the crude opening in which this door was set was covered with a thin panel, in the centre of which a triangular hole had been sawn, as both fanlight and ventilator when the door was shut. On the door itself a brush dipped in ink had in a couple of strokes traced the figure 52, and above the panel the same brush had daubed the number 50, thereby creating uncertainty. Where are we? Above the door said number 50. The door below replied, no, number 52. Some indeterminate dust-coloured rags hung like curtains over the triangular opening.

The window was large, set reasonably high, fitted with large panes of glass and louvred shutters. Only, these large panes had suffered various injuries, at once concealed and betrayed by clever paper bandaging, and the louvred shutters, which were ramshackle and falling apart, were more a threat to passers-by than any protection for the occupants. Horizontal slats were missing here and there and had simply been replaced with boards nailed on flat, so that what had started out as a louvred shutter ended up as a solid one.

This squalid-looking door and this respectable-looking, albeit dilapidated, window, seen as part of the same house, created the effect of two mismatched beggars, going about together and walking side by side, but of two different complexions beneath the same rags, the one having always been a vagrant and the other having once been a gentleman.

The main body of the building to which this staircase led was very spacious, like a barn that had been converted into a dwelling. The body's intestinal tract was a long corridor that had, opening on to it to left and right, compartments, as it were, of various dimensions that were just about habitable and more like booths than cells. These rooms looked out over surrounding wasteland. The whole place was gloomy, grim, drab, dismal, sepulchral, with cold shafts of light or chill winds cutting through it, depending on whether the cracks were in the roof or the door. An interesting and picturesque feature of this type of abode is the enormous size of the spiders.

To the left of the front door on the street, at the height of the average man, a small walled-up window formed a square niche full of stones thrown into it by children passing by.

A part of this building has recently been demolished. From what remains of it today, you can still get an impression of what it was like before. The building as a whole is no more than a hundred years old. A hundred years is young for a church and old for a house. It is as though a man's house is, like himself, short-lived, and God's house shares his eternity.

The postmen called this tenement number 50–52, but it was known in the neighbourhood as 'Gorbeau's house'. Let us explain where this name came from.

Collectors of trivial information who compile herbariums of anecdotes and retain elusive dates in their memories by sticking them with a pin, know that during the last century, around 1770, there were in Paris two lawyers at the Châtelet, one named Corbeau, the other Renard. Two names anticipated by La Fontaine. This was too good an opportunity for the legal fraternity not to make the most of it. A parody in somewhat lame verse immediately circulated in the corridors of the law courts:

> Maître Corbeau, perched high on a brief,
> Held a notice of seizure in his beak,
> Maître Renard of its smell caught a whiff,
> And these words more or less did he speak:
> Ah, good day to you! . . .*

Embarrassed by these taunts, and their dignity undermined by the bursts of laughter that followed in their wake, these two honest practitioners resolved to rid themselves of their names and decided to appeal to the king. Their petition was presented to Louis XV on the same day that the papal nuncio on the one hand and Cardinal de la Roche-Aymon on the other, both piously kneeling in his majesty's presence, each put a slipper on one of Madame du Barry's two bare feet as she got out of bed. The king, who had been laughing, continued to laugh, cheerfully moving on from the two bishops to the two lawyers, and absolved these two chicaners of their names, or near

---

* La Fontaine's 'Le Corbeau et le Renard' ('The Crow and the Fox'; bk 1, fable 2), in which the fox is drawn by the smell of the cheese the crow holds in its beak, gives rise to the parody (*maître* being a term of respect by which lawyers, professors and the like are addressed).

enough. Permission was given by the king for Maître Corbeau to add a stroke to his initial letter and to call himself Gorbeau. Maître Renard was less fortunate, obtaining leave only to place a P in front of his R and to call himself Prenard, so that the second name was hardly any less truthful than the first.*

Now, according to local tradition this Maître Gorbeau had once owned the building numbered 50–52 Boulevard de l'Hôpital. He was even responsible for the grandiose window. Which was how this tenement came by the name of 'Gorbeau's house'.

In front of number 50–52, among more recent plantings on the boulevard, stood a giant elm, more than half dead. Almost directly opposite was the beginning of Rue de la Barrière des Gobelins, a street at that time without any houses on it, unpaved, lined with trees of stunted growth, and grassy or muddy according to the season. It actually led right up to Paris's perimeter wall. Blasts of a sulphuric-acid smell emanated from the roofs of a neighbouring factory.

The toll-gate was very close by. In 1823 the perimeter wall was still in existence.

The toll-gate itself brought macabre figures to mind. This was the road to Bicêtre. It was by this road that under the Empire and the Restoration those sentenced to death came back into Paris on the day of their execution. It was here that around 1829 that mysterious murder, the so-called Fontainebleau toll-gate murder, was committed, whose perpetrators the law was unable to identify, a murky matter that has never been elucidated, a dreadful enigma that has never been solved. Take another few steps and you will come to that fateful Rue Croulebarbe where, as in a melodrama, Ulbach stabbed the goat-girl of Ivry to the sound of thunder. A few paces further will bring you to the St-Jacques toll-gate and those ghastly pollarded elm trees, that philanthropists' expedient for hiding the scaffold – at this shabby and shameful Place de Grève – from a shopkeeping and bourgeois society that shrank from the death penalty, daring neither to abolish it with magnanimity nor to uphold it with authority.

Leaving aside this Place St-Jacques, which was almost foredoomed and has always been horrible, probably the bleakest spot on all that bleak boulevard thirty-seven years ago was the place, so unattractive even today, where the tenement, number 50–52, was to be found.

Bourgeois houses only first began to appear here twenty-five years later. It was a forbidding landscape. In addition to the macabre

---

* Both *Renard*, meaning 'fox', and *Prenard*, suggestive of someone grasping (from *prendre*, 'to take'), being true to the nature of the lawyer.

thoughts that assailed you here, you were aware of being between La Salpêtrière, within sight of the dome, and Bicêtre, within striking distance of the toll-gate – in other words, between the madness of women and the madness of men. As far as the eye could reach, all you could see were abattoirs, the perimeter wall and the frontage of the occasional factory building, looking like barracks or monasteries. Shacks and rubble everywhere, old walls as black as shrouds, new walls as white as winding-sheets. Everywhere parallel rows of trees, straight-edged buildings, drab constructions, long cold lines, and the grim dreariness of right-angles. No unevenness of terrain, no architectural quirk, no irregularity. It was a frigid, featureless, hideous whole. Nothing oppresses the heart like symmetry. This is because symmetry is boredom, and boredom is the very foundation of grief. Despair yawns. It is possible to imagine something more terrible than a hell of suffering, and that is a hell of boredom. If such a hell existed, this bit of Boulevard de l'Hôpital might have been the approach to it.

Nevertheless, at nightfall – when the light fails, especially in winter, and the cold evening wind rips from the elm trees their last russet leaves, when the darkness is deep and starless, or the moon and the wind create holes in the clouds – this boulevard suddenly became frightening. The straight lines sank into the shadows and disappeared like sliced-off sections of the infinite. The passer-by could not help thinking of the countless traditional associations this place had with the gibbet. There was something terrible about the loneliness of this spot where so many crimes had been committed. You thought you sensed pitfalls in this obscurity. Every blurred form in the dark seemed suspect, and the long sunken plots between the trees looked like graves. By day it was ugly. In the evening it was gloomy. By night it was sinister.

In summer, at twilight, you saw here and there a few old women seated at the foot of the elm trees on benches mildewed with rain. These old dears were given to begging.

However, this neighbourhood, which looked neglected rather than antiquated, was already then beginning to change. Even at that time anyone who wanted to see it had to hurry. Every day some detail of this environment was being lost. The Paris–Orléans railway terminus is now located here, as it has been for the last twenty years, and is having an impact on the old *faubourg* close by. Wherever a railway station is sited on the outskirts of a capital, it spells the death of a suburb and the birth of a town. It seems that around these great centres for the movement of people, at the rumbling of these powerful machines, at the puffing of these monstrous horses of civilization that devour coal and vomit fire, the gravid earth trembles and opens up to swallow the human dwelling-places of the past and allow fresh ones to emerge. The old houses come down, new houses go up.

Since the Paris–Orléans railway station invaded the Salpêtrière area, the ancient narrow streets close to Fossés-St-Victor and the Jardin des Plantes have been shaken by those streams of coaches, carriages and omnibuses, violently passing through three or four times a day, that over a period time thrust aside the houses to right and left. For there are things that, peculiar as they sound, are undeniable facts, and just as it is true to say that in large cities the sun makes the south-facing façades of houses grow verdant, it is certain that the frequent passage of vehicles widens streets. Symptoms of a new life are obvious. In the most uncharted corners of this old parochial neighbourhood, paving appears; the pavements begin their creeping progress even where there are as yet no pedestrians. One memorable morning in July 1845 steaming black pots of bitumen were suddenly to be seen. On that day it might be said that civilization reached Rue de Lourcine and Paris entered the outlying district of St-Marceau.

II
A Nest for Two Birds of a Different Feather*

It was in front of this Gorbeau tenement that Jean Valjean came to a halt. Like birds of the wild, he had chosen the most deserted spot in which to build his nest.

He fumbled in his waistcoat, pulled out a kind of a pass-key, opened the door and went inside, carefully closed the door behind him and climbed the stairs, still carrying Cosette. At the top of the staircase he drew from his pocket another key, with which he opened another door. The room he entered, immediately shutting the door behind him, was a fairly spacious sort of garret, furnished with a mattress laid on the floor, a table and several chairs. There was a lighted stove in one corner – you could see the embers glowing. The street lamp on the boulevard dimly lit this humble interior. At the far end

---

* In French, 'Nid pour Hibou et Fauvette', meaning literally 'Nest for owl and warbler'. The word *hibou* ('owl') also means metaphorically a reclusive person, as in English one might say 'a lone wolf'. An old deserted house may be referred to as *un nid d'hiboux*, 'an owls' nest'. *Fauvette*, a delicate little songbird, is an apt description of Cosette, also carrying suggestions of not being part of human society, *fauve* meaning wild.

was a small cubicle with a folding bed in it. Jean Valjean carried the child to this bed and laid her on it without waking her.

He struck the flint and lit a candle. All this had been set out on the table beforehand. And as on the previous evening he began to study Cosette's face with a wholly enraptured gaze in which the expression of kindness and tenderness mounted almost to bewilderment. With that calm trustfulness that is a characteristic only of the utmost strength and the utmost weakness, the little girl had fallen asleep not knowing who she was with, and went on sleeping not knowing where she was.

Jean Valjean bent down and kissed the child's hand. Nine months earlier he had kissed the mother's hand, she too having just fallen asleep. The same sorrowful, religious, overwhelming feeling filled his heart. He knelt at Cosette's bedside.

Even after it was fully light the child slept on. A pale ray of the December sun shone through the garret window and cast long gossamer threads of light and shadow on the ceiling. Suddenly a heavily laden quarryman's cart, passing by on the boulevard, shook the place like a roll of thunder and made it vibrate from top to bottom.

'Yes, madame!' cried Cosette, who woke with a start. 'Coming! Coming!'

And she sprang out of bed, her eyelids still half closed with the heaviness of sleep, reaching her arm out towards the corner of the room.

'Oh dear God!' she said. 'My broom!'

She opened her eyes fully and saw Jean Valjean's smiling face.

'Ah! So it's true!' said the child. 'Good morning, monsieur.'

Being themselves joy and happiness by nature, children immediately welcome joy and happiness with familiarity.

Cosette caught sight of Catherine at the foot of her bed and seized on her, and she asked Jean Valjean countless questions as she played: where she was, whether it was a big place, Paris, whether Madame Thénardier was very far away, whether she wouldn't reappear, et cetera, et cetera. All of a sudden she exclaimed, 'This is such a nice place!'

It was a dreadful hovel, but she had a sense of freedom.

'Do I have to sweep?' she said finally.

'You play,' said Jean Valjean.

And so the day passed. Without trying to understand what was beyond her comprehension, Cosette was unutterably happy with her doll and this kind man.

III
Happiness in Shared Misfortune

The next morning at daybreak Jean Valjean was again at Cosette's bedside. He waited there, motionless, and he watched her wake up.

Something new was entering his soul.

Jean Valjean had never loved anything. For twenty-five years he had been alone in the world. He had never been father, lover, husband, or friend. In prison he was ill-natured, sullen, celibate, ignorant and unsociable. That old criminal's heart was full of virginal innocence. His sister and his sister's children had left him with only a dim and distant memory that had eventually faded almost completely. He had made every effort to find them, and unable to find them he had forgotten them. Such is human nature. Other feelings of tenderness in his youth, if he ever had any, had been lost in oblivion.

When he saw Cosette, when he took charge of her, carried her away and rescued her, he felt stirred to the roots of his being. Whatever passion and affection there was within him came to life and was eagerly projected on to that child. He approached the bed where she slept and trembled with joy. He felt pangs like those of a mother in childbirth and he did not understand what was happening to him. For it is a thoroughly obscure and delightful thing, that great and extraordinary stirring in a heart that starts to love.

Poor old heart coming to this quite fresh!

Only, as he was fifty-five and Cosette was eight, all the love he might have felt throughout his life blended in a kind of ineffable light.

This was the second vision of whiteness he had experienced. The bishop had brought the dawn of virtue to his horizon. Cosette brought the dawn of love.

These first days were days of wonder.

Cosette too, poor little creature, was unconsciously becoming a different person! She was so young when her mother left her, she could not remember her any more. Like all children, resembling the tendrils of the vine that cling to everything, she had tried to love. It had done her no good. Everyone had rejected her, the Thénardiers, their children, other children. She had loved the dog, which died. After that there was nothing, no one, willing to take any interest in her. Sad to say, and this is something we have already suggested, at eight years of age she was cold-hearted. It was not her fault. It was not that she lacked the capacity to love, but alas! the possibility of doing so! Thus, from the very first day, all her thoughts and feelings turned to loving this kind man. She experienced what she had never experienced before, a sense of fulfilment.

He did not even give her the impression of being old or poor any more. She found Jean Valjean a fine-looking man, just as she found that hovel lovely.

These are the effects of a bright new day, of childhood, youth, joy. The novelty of the earth and of life has something to do with it. Nothing is so charming as the enhancing reflection of happiness on a garret. We all have in our past our own delightful garret.

Nature, a gap of fifty years, had placed a deep divide between Jean Valjean and Cosette. Destiny made good this divide. With its irresistible power, destiny suddenly united and plighted to each other these two uprooted lives, differing in age, alike in their distress. One, in fact, complemented the other. Cosette's instinct sought a father as Jean Valjean's instinct sought a child. To meet was to find each other. In that mysterious moment when their two hands touched, they were conjoined. Each recognizing the other on sight as the answer to their need, these two souls fell into close embrace.

With walls of entombment separating them from all else, it might be said that, taking the words in their broadest and most absolute sense, Jean Valjean was the Bereft Parent and Cosette was the Orphaned Child. In this situation Jean Valjean became in some heavenly way Cosette's father. And in truth, the mysterious impression made on Cosette in the depths of the forest of Chelles, by Jean Valjean's hand taking hold of hers in the dark, was not an illusion but a reality. The appearance of this man in this child's life was the advent of God.

Anyway, Jean Valjean had chosen his refuge well. Here, it would seem, he was perfectly safe.

The room with a cubicle that he occupied with Cosette was the one whose window looked out on the boulevard. Being the only window in the house that did so, no neighbour's gaze was to be feared from either side or from across the way.

The ground floor of number 50–52, a kind of ramshackle shed, served as a storehouse for market-gardeners, and had no access to the floor above. It was separated by floorboarding that had no trap-door in it, nor any staircase, and was, as it were, the tenement's diaphragm. The first floor contained, as we have said, numerous rooms and several garrets, only one of which was occupied, by an old woman who did the housekeeping for Jean Valjean. All the rest was uninhabited.

It was this old woman, grandly styled the 'principal tenant' and in reality having the job of doorkeeper, who had rented these lodgings to him on Christmas Eve. He had given her to understand that he was a gentleman of means ruined by Spanish bonds, who was going to come and live there with his granddaughter. He paid her six months in advance and got the old woman to furnish the room and the cubicle as we have seen. It was this old woman who had lit the stove, and had everything made ready for them, on the evening of their arrival.

The weeks went by. These two individuals led a happy life in that wretched hovel. From first light Cosette laughed, chattered and sang. Like birds, children have their morning song.

It sometimes happened that Jean Valjean would take her little red hand, chapped with chilblains, and kiss it. Used to being beaten, the poor child did not understand the meaning of this and would go away completely abashed.

At times she became serious and contemplated her little black dress. Cosette was no longer in rags, she was in mourning. Leaving destitution behind, she was making her start in life.

Jean Valjean set about teaching her to read. Sometimes, as he made the child spell out her words, he reflected that it was with the idea of doing evil that he had learned to read in the prison hulks. This idea had turned into teaching a child to read. Then the old convict smiled an angelic pensive smile.

He sensed in this a higher design, the will of someone other than man, and he became lost in reverie. Virtuous thoughts are as deep as evil ones.

To teach Cosette to read, and to let her play, this was more or less Jean Valjean's whole life. And then he would talk to her about her mother, and get her to pray.

She called him 'father' and knew him by no other name.

He spent hours watching her dress and undress her doll, and listening to her prattle. Life seemed full of interest to him now, men seemed good and just. In his mind he no longer held anything against anybody. He saw no reason why he should not live to be a very old man, now that this child loved him. He saw a whole future for himself illuminated by Cosette as by a comforting light. The best of us are not exempt from a selfish way of thinking. At times he imagined with a kind of gladness that she would be ugly.

This is only a personal opinion but, to speak our mind in full, at the stage Jean Valjean had reached when he began to love Cosette we have yet to be convinced he did not need this encouragement to persevere in his efforts to lead a good life. He had just seen the wickedness of men and social hardship in a new perspective, a limited perspective that inevitably revealed only one side of the truth, the fate of women represented by Fantine, and public authority personified by Javert. He had been sent back to prison, this time for good behaviour. Fresh resentments had brewed within him. Disgust and weariness overcame him once more. Even the memory of the bishop suffered what might have been a temporary eclipse, possibly to appear bright and triumphant again later, but undoubtedly that sacred memory was fading. Who knows whether Jean Valjean was on the verge of losing heart and relapsing? He loved, and he became strong again. Alas! he was hardly any less unsteady on his feet than was Cosette. He protected her and she bolstered him. Thanks to him, she could make her way in life. Thanks to her, he could continue on the path of virtue. He was the child's support, and the child was his stay. Oh, unfathomable and divine mystery of destiny's counterbalances!

IV
The Remarks of the Principal Tenant

Jean Valjean took the precaution of never going out by day. Every evening at twilight he went for a stroll for an hour or two, sometimes alone, often with Cosette, seeking out the loneliest of the boulevard's parallel side lanes or entering churches at nightfall. He often chose to go to St-Médard, the nearest church. When he did not take Cosette with him she remained with the old woman. But it was the child's delight to go out with the old man. She preferred an hour with him to her enchanting private conversations with Catherine. On their walks he held her by the hand and said kindly things to her.

Cosette turned out to be very lively.

The old woman did the cooking and cleaning and went shopping.

They lived frugally, never without a little fire, but in the manner of people of very limited means. Jean Valjean made no change to the way the room was furnished on the first day, only he had the glass door to Cosette's cubicle replaced with a solid one.

He still wore his yellow frock-coat, black breeches and old hat. In the street he was taken for a pauper. Occasionally some kind-hearted woman would turn back and give him a sou. Jean Valjean always accepted the sou with a deep bow. It also happened occasionally that he would come across some poor wretch soliciting charity. Then he would look around to make sure no one could see him, furtively approach the hapless creature, put a coin in his hand, often a silver coin, and rapidly walk away. This had its disadvantages. He began to be known in the neighbourhood as 'the beggar who gives alms to the poor'.

The principal tenant, a sour-tempered old woman, consumed with that close interest that the envious take in their fellow men, observed Jean Valjean a great deal without his being aware of it. She was slightly deaf, which made her talkative. From her past she retained two teeth, one top tooth and one bottom tooth, that she kept clacking against each other. She had questioned Cosette, who, knowing nothing, had been able to tell her nothing except that she came from Montfermeil. One morning this watchful eye saw Jean Valjean going into one of the tenement's uninhabited rooms with what seemed to the old crone a strange look about him. She followed him like a stealthy old cat and was able to observe him, without being seen, through a chink in the closed door. For greater security, no doubt, Jean Valjean had his back to this door. The old woman saw him fumble in his pocket and take out of it a little case, some scissors and thread. Then he began to unstitch the lining of one of his coat-tails, and out of the opening he brought a yellowish piece of paper that he unfolded. The old woman realized with alarm that it was a one-thousand-franc banknote. It was the second or third she had seen in all her life. She fled in great fright.

A moment later Jean Valjean accosted her and asked her to go and change this one-thousand-franc note for him, adding that it was his six-monthly revenue payment he had received the day before.

'Where?' thought the old woman. 'He did not go out until six in the evening and the government bank certainly isn't open at that time.'

The old woman went to get the note changed and formed her own conjectures. That one-thousand-franc note, much talked about and multiplied, produced a host of terrified conversations among the old biddies of Rue des Vignes-St-Marcel.

Some days later Jean Valjean happened to be in the corridor sawing wood in his shirt-sleeves. The old woman was in the room, cleaning up. She was alone, while Cosette was busy watching the wood being sawn. The old woman saw the coat hanging on a nail and examined it: the lining had been sewn up again. The old woman patted it carefully and thought she could feel some thickness of paper in the coat-tails and round the armholes. More one-thousand-franc banknotes, no doubt!

She also noticed there were all sorts of things in the pockets, not only the needles, scissors and thread she had seen but a big wallet, a very large knife and, what seemed suspicious, several wigs of various colours. Each pocket of this frock-coat seemed to be a kind of first-aid kit for unexpected emergencies.

So the inhabitants of the tenement arrived at the last days of winter.

V
A Five-franc Piece Falling on the Floor Makes a Noise

Near St-Médard's church there was a poor man who used to squat on the kerbstone of a boarded-up public well, to whom Jean Valjean was often charitable. He never went by this man without giving him a few sous. Sometimes he spoke to him. Those who envied this beggar said he was 'with the police'. He was an old verger of seventy-five, who was constantly mumbling his prayers.

One evening as Jean Valjean was passing by, without Cosette, he saw the beggar in his usual place, under the street lamp that had just been lit. The man appeared, as ever, to be praying and was all bent over. Jean Valjean went up to him and put in his hand his customary donation. The beggar suddenly looked up, stared intently at Jean Valjean, then quickly bowed his head. This movement was like a flash of lightning. Jean Valjean gave a shudder. He thought he had just caught a glimpse by the light of the street lamp not of the old verger's placidly beatific face but of a face terrifying and familiar. It made the same impression on him as suddenly coming face to face in the dark with a tiger. He shrank back, scared stiff, not daring to breathe, speak, stay or flee, staring at the beggar who had lowered his rag-covered head and seemed unaware he was still there. At that strange moment an instinct, possibly the mysterious instinct of self-preservation, kept Jean Valjean from uttering a word. The beggar was of the same stature, dressed in the same rags, and looked the same as he looked every day. 'Bah!' said Jean Valjean, 'I'm mad! I'm dreaming! Impossible!' And he went home feeling deeply disturbed.

He hardly dared admit even to himself that the face he thought he had seen was Javert's.

Pondering about it that night, he regretted not having questioned the man so as to force him to look up again.

The next day at dusk he went back. The beggar was at his post. 'Good day, old man,' Jean Valjean said resolutely, handing him a sou. The beggar looked up and replied in a plaintive voice, 'Thank you, monsieur.' There was no mistaking the old verger.

Jean Valjean felt completely reassured. He began to laugh.

'How the devil could I have seen Javert there?' he thought. 'Is my eyesight failing me now?'

He thought no more about it.

A few days later, it might have been eight in the evening, he was in his room, making Cosette read aloud, when he heard the front door open, then shut again. This struck him as odd. The old woman, who was the only inhabitant of the house apart from him, always went to bed at nightfall so as not to use up her candles. Jean Valjean signalled to Cosette to be quiet. He heard someone coming upstairs. It was just possible it could be the old woman, who might have felt unwell and gone out to the pharmacy. Jean Valjean listened. It was a heavy footfall and sounded like a man's, but the old woman wore stout shoes and there is nothing so like a man's footfall as that of an old woman. All the same, Jean Valjean blew out his candle.

He had sent Cosette to bed, saying to her in a whisper, 'Get into bed very quietly.' And as he kissed her forehead the footsteps came to a halt. Jean Valjean remained silent, motionless, with his back to the door, sitting on the chair from which he had not stirred, holding his breath in the dark. Having heard nothing after quite a long while, not making a sound he turned round, and as he looked up at the door to his room he saw a light through the keyhole. This light created the effect of a sinister star in the blackness of the door and the wall. There was obviously someone there, holding a candle, listening.

Several minutes went by and the light went away. But he heard no sound of footsteps, which seemed to indicate that whoever had been listening at the door had removed their shoes.

Jean Valjean fell on his bed fully dressed and could not sleep a wink all night.

At daybreak just as he was dozing off through tiredness, he was woken by the creak of a door opening into some garret room at the end of the corridor, then he heard that same footstep, belonging to a man, that had climbed the staircase the night before. The footsteps were approaching. He leapt out of bed and put his eye to the keyhole, which was quite big, hoping to see, as the person went by, whoever it was that had entered the tenement by night and had been listening at his door. It was indeed a man who went past Jean Valjean's room, this time without stopping. The corridor was still too dark for his face to be distinguishable but when the man reached the staircase a ray of light from outside picked him out in silhouette, and Jean Valjean had a full view of him from behind. The man was tall, wearing a long frock-coat, with a truncheon under his arm. He had Javert's solid build.

Jean Valjean might have attempted to catch another glimpse of him from his window on the boulevard, but he would have had to open the window. He dared not.

It was obvious this man had got in with a key, as though he lived here. Who had given him that key? What did this mean?

When the old woman came to clean the room at seven o'clock in the morning, Jean Valjean gave her a searching look but did not question her. The old woman was no different from usual.

As she swept she said, 'Monsieur may have heard someone come in last night?'

At her age, and on that boulevard, eight o'clock in the evening was the dead of night.

'Now you mention it, that's true,' he replied in the most natural tone of voice. 'Who was it?'

'A new lodger,' said the old woman, 'who's come to stay in the house.'

'And what's his name?'

'I'm not quite sure, Dumont or Daumont. A name something like that.'

'And who is this Monsieur Dumont?'

The old woman looked at him with her little ferrety eyes and replied, 'A man of means, like yourself.'

Perhaps she did not intend anything by this. Jean Valjean thought there was something to be gleaned from it. When the old woman was gone he made a roll of some one hundred francs that he had in a cupboard and put it in his pocket. Despite all the precautions he took during this operation so that no clink of money should be heard, one five-franc coin escaped from his hands and rolled noisily across the floor.

At dusk he went downstairs and took a good look along the boulevard in every direction. He saw no one. The boulevard looked totally deserted. True, a person could be hiding behind the trees.

He went back upstairs.

'Come along,' he said to Cosette.

He took her by the hand and they both went out.

BOOK FIVE
SILENT STALKERS IN THE DARK

I
A Zigzag Strategy

Here, something needs to be said regarding the pages you are about to read, as well as others that you will come to later.

Reluctantly obliged to speak of himself, the author of this book has not been in Paris for many years now. Since he left it, Paris has been transformed. A new city has grown up that is, as it were, unknown to him. Needless to say, he loves Paris. Paris is his spiritual home. As a result of demolitions and rebuildings the Paris of his youth, the Paris he religiously took away with him in his memory, is now a Paris of the past. Let him speak of that Paris as though it still existed. It is possible that where the author is going to take his readers, telling them, 'In this street stands this house', neither the street nor the house is there any more. Readers can check, if they care to take the trouble. For his own part, the author is not familiar with the new Paris and he writes with the old Paris before his eyes, treasuring that illusion. It is a comfort to him to fancy that something still remains of what he used to see when he was in his native city, and that not everything has vanished. While you come and go in the place where you were born, you imagine that those streets are a matter of indifference to you, those windows, roofs, doors mean nothing to you, those walls are strangers to you, those trees are just any old trees, those houses you never enter are of no good to you, those cobbles you walk on are but stones. Later, when you are no longer there, you realize that you cherish those streets, you miss those roofs, windows, doors, you need those walls; that those trees are favourites of yours, those houses never entered you entered every day, and that you have left behind on those cobbles something of your blood and your guts and your heart. All those places you do not see any more, that you may never see again and that you have kept a picture of in your mind, take on a melancholy charm; they come back to you with the mournfulness of an apparition, make the holy land visible to you, and are, so to speak, the very embodiment of France. And you love them and you conjure them up as they are, as they were, and you persist in this, and you will make no change to them: for the face of your homeland is as dear to you as the face of your mother.

Allow us, then, to speak of the past in the present tense. That said, we would ask the reader to bear it in mind, and we shall continue.

Jean Valjean had immediately turned off the boulevard and plunged into the narrower streets, striking off in a different direction as often as he could, sometimes abruptly retracing his steps to make sure he was not being followed.

This behaviour is typical of the hunted stag. Over terrain on which tracks may be left, such behaviour has the advantage, among others, of confusing huntsmen and dogs by overlaying the trail with a back-scent. In hunting this is called a 'false return to cover'.

There was a full moon that night. Jean Valjean was not sorry for this. Still very low on the horizon, the moon divided the streets into great blocks of light and shadow. Jean Valjean could steal past the houses on the dark side with the light side in view. Perhaps he gave too little consideration to what the dark side hid from him. Yet in all the deserted side streets around Rue de Poliveau he felt certain no one was following him.

Cosette kept on walking without asking any questions. The trials and tribulations of the first six years of her life had brought something passive to her nature. Moreover, and this is an observation we shall have more than one occasion to return to, without being much aware of it she had grown used to the old man's peculiarities and the eccentricities of fate. And anyway, being with him, she felt safe.

Jean Valjean no more knew where he was going than Cosette did. He trusted in God as she trusted in him. He too felt as if he were holding the hand of someone bigger than him. He thought he sensed some invisible being leading him. Otherwise, he had no firm idea, no plan, no project. He was not even absolutely sure it was Javert, and then it might have been Javert without Javert knowing he was Jean Valjean. Was he not disguised? Was he not thought to be dead? Yet for some days now, peculiar things had been happening. That was enough for him. He was determined not to return to the Gorbeau house. Like the wild animal chased from its lair he was seeking a place to hide until he found a place where he could settle.

Jean Valjean traced various labyrinthine routes in the Mouffetard district, which was already sleeping, as though the rule of the Middle Ages still applied and the curfew was still enforced. He linked in various ways, with devious cunning, Rue Censier and Rue Copeau, Rue du Battoir-St-Victor and Rue du Puits-l'Ermite. There are lodging houses around here but he did not even enter them, finding nothing that suited him. Then again, he had no doubt that if by chance anyone had been looking for him they would have lost track of him.

As eleven o'clock struck at St-Étienne-du-Mont he was walking along Rue de Pontoise in front of the police station, which is at number fourteen. A few seconds later that instinct we mentioned above made him turn round. At that moment, thanks to the police station lantern, which betrayed them, he distinctly saw three men, who were following him quite closely, pass under that lantern one after the other on the dark side of the street. One of those three men entered the passage to the superintendent's house. He definitely did not like the look of the one leading the way.

'Come along, child,' he said to Cosette. And he wasted no time in leaving Rue de Pontoise.

He circled around, avoiding Passage des Patriarches, which was closed at that time of night, hurried along Rue de l'Épée-de-Bois and Rue de l'Arbalète, and plunged into Rue des Postes.

There is a crossroads, where the Collège Rollin stands today, with Rue Neuve-Ste-Geneviève branching off it. (It goes without saying, Rue Neuve-Ste-Geneviève is an old street, and decades go by with no mail-coach ever going down Rue des Postes. This Rue des Postes was inhabited by potters in the thirteenth century and its real name is Rue des Pots.)*

The moon cast a bright light on this intersection. Jean Valjean hid in a doorway, reckoning that if those men were still following him he could not fail to get a very good look at them when they crossed this illuminated expanse.

Sure enough, not three minutes had gone by before the men appeared. There were four of them now, all of them tall, dressed in long brown frock-coats, with round hats, and big truncheons in their hands. They were no less alarming for their tall stature and huge fists than for the sinister way they skulked in the shadows. They looked like four spectres disguised as respectable citizens.

They stopped in the middle of the crossroads and gathered in a group, like people conferring with each other. They seemed undecided. The one who appeared to be leading them turned round and pointed vigorously with his right hand in the direction Jean Valjean had taken. One of the others seemed to be pointing with some degree of stubbornness in the opposite direction. Just as the first man turned round, the moonlight caught him full in the face. Jean Valjean recognized Javert, with absolute certainty.

* The point is that the names of the streets Neuve[New]-Ste-Geneviève and des Postes (Mail Service) are misleading.

Luckily the Pont d'Austerlitz Takes Vehicles

For Jean Valjean, the uncertainty was over. Fortunately it continued for those men. He took advantage of their indecision. It was time lost for them, gained for him. He slipped out of the doorway where he had been hiding, and hurried on down Rue des Postes towards the area around the Jardin des Plantes. Cosette was beginning to tire. He took her in his arms and carried her. There was not a soul about and the street lamps had not been lit because of the moon.

He quickened his pace.

In a few strides he had reached the Goblet pottery works on the front of which, clearly legible in the moonlight, was the old inscription:

> These are the factory premises of Goblet Son.
> Makers of pots and vases of various types,
> Of jugs and pitchers, bricks and tiles and pipes.
> Come buy – we sell our wares gladly to anyone.

He left behind him Rue de la Clef, then the St-Victor fountain, skirted the Jardin des Plantes by the streets on the lower side and came to the embankment. There he turned round. The embankment was deserted. The streets were deserted. There was no one behind him. He breathed freely again.

He arrived at the Pont d'Austerlitz.

A toll was still collected on it at that time.

He went up to the toll collector's office and handed over a sou.

'It's two sous,' said the veteran soldier manning the bridge. 'You're carrying a child who can walk. You pay for two.'

He paid up, annoyed that his use of the bridge had given rise to comment. All flight should go unnoticed.

A heavy cart was crossing the Seine at the same time, going over to the right bank as he was. This was useful. He was able to cross the bridge in the shadow of this cart.

Towards the middle of the bridge Cosette, whose feet had gone numb, wanted to walk. He put her down and took her by the hand again.

Having crossed the bridge, he noticed some building sites ahead of him, a little to the right. He walked towards them. Getting there meant having to venture across quite a large exposed and brightly lit expanse. He did not hesitate. Those in pursuit had obviously lost track of him, and Jean Valjean believed himself to be out of danger. Hunted, yes. Followed, no.

A little street, Rue du Chemin-Vert-St-Antoine, ran between two walled builders' yards. This street was dark and narrow, and seemed specially designed for him. Before entering it, he looked back.

From where he stood he could see the whole length of the Pont d'Austerlitz.

Four shadowy figures had just started to cross the bridge.

These figures had their backs to the Jardin des Plantes and were heading towards the right bank.

These four shadowy figures were those four men.

Jean Valjean gave a shudder like that of the resighted quarry.

He had one remaining hope: that the men might not yet have been on the bridge, and might not have seen him, as he crossed the large, brightly lit square, holding Cosette by the hand.

In that case, by disappearing up the little street ahead him, if he could reach the builders' yards, the marshes, the market-gardens, the undeveloped land, he might escape. It seemed to him they could trust themselves to that silent little street. He started along it.

III
Consult the 1727 Map of Paris

Three hundred paces further on he arrived at a point where the street forked. It divided into two streets, one bearing to the left, the other to the right. Jean Valjean had before him what looked like the two arms of a Y. Which one to choose?

He did not hesitate, and took the right-hand one.

Why?

Because the left-hand fork went towards the built-up part of this outlying district, in other words an inhabited area, and the one on the right led to open countryside, in other words, an uninhabited area.

However, they were not walking very fast any more. Cosette's pace was slowing down Jean Valjean's.

He picked her up and carried her again. Cosette laid her head on the old man's shoulder and did not say a word.

He turned round to look from time to time. He took care always to keep on the dark side of the street. The street ran straight behind him. The first two or three times he turned round he saw nothing, there was deep silence, and he continued on his way somewhat reassured. Then at a certain moment, having turned round, he thought he saw –

away in the darkness, in that part of the street he had just passed through – something moving.

He did not so much walk as race ahead, hoping to find some side street and escape that way, covering up his tracks once more.

He came to a wall.

This wall did not make going any further impossible, though. It was a wall running along a lane that cut across the end of the street he was in.

Here again, he had to make a decision: to go left or right.

He looked to the right. The lane extended only a short distance between buildings that were either sheds or storehouses, then came to a dead end. The bottom of this blind alley was clearly visible: a high blank wall.

He looked to the left. The lane on that side was open-ended and about two hundred paces away fed into a main thoroughfare. It was in that direction that safety lay.

Just as Jean Valjean was thinking of turning left, to try and reach that main street, he could see at the end of the lane, on the corner where it met the street, some sort of motionless black statue.

It was a person, a man, who had obviously just been posted there and was waiting to stop anyone getting through.

Jean Valjean shrank back.

Where Jean Valjean was, between Faubourg St-Antoine and La Râpée, is one of those parts of Paris that recent building works have completely transformed, for worse according to some, for better according to others. The market-gardens, depots and old shacks are gone. Today there are brand-new broad avenues, amphitheatres, circuses, race courses, railway stations, and the Mazas prison – progress, as we see, comes with its corrective.

Half a century ago in everyday popular parlance, which is thoroughly steeped in tradition and persists in calling the Institut the 'Quatre-Nations' and the Opéra-Comique the 'Feydeau', the precise spot Jean Valjean had come to was called 'Petit-Picpus'. Porte St-Jacques, Porte Paris, Barrière des Sergents, Porcherons, Galiote, Célestins, Capucins, Mail, Bourbe, Arbre de Cracovie, Petite-Pologne, Petit-Picpus – these are names of the old Paris surviving into the new. The memory of the common people lingers on in these relics of the past.

Petit-Picpus, which in fact scarcely existed and was never more than a roughly defined area, had the almost monastic appearance of a Spanish town. The roads were rarely paved, the streets not much built up. Apart from the two or three streets we are going to talk about, it was all blank walls and desolation. Not one shop, not one vehicle, only the occasional lighted candle here and there at the windows, and all light extinguished after ten o'clock. Gardens, convents, yards, allotments, the odd low-built house, and solid walls as high as the houses.

Such was this neighbourhood in the last century. The Revolution had already firmly turned its back on it. The Republican municipal administration demolished, cut through and made holes in it. Rubble dumps were established there. Thirty years ago this neighbourhood was vanishing, erased by new buildings. Now it has been completely obliterated. Petit-Picpus, of which no present map has retained any trace, is quite clearly marked on the 1727 map published in Paris by Denis Thierry of Rue St-Jacques opposite Rue du Plâtre, and in Lyon by Jean Girin of Rue Mercière at the sign of Prudence. As mentioned above, Petit-Picpus had a Y-shaped configuration of streets, formed by Rue du Chemin-Vert-St-Antoine, which divides in two, the left-hand fork taking the name Petite-Rue-Picpus, and the right-hand fork, Rue Polonceau. The two arms of the Y were connected by a bar, as it were, across the top of them. This bar was called Rue Droit-Mur. Rue Polonceau ended here. Rue Petit-Picpus continued beyond it, leading up towards Marché Lenoir. When anyone coming from the Seine reached the end of Rue Polonceau, they had Rue Droit-Mur at a sharp right-angle on their left, in front of them the wall that ran along that street, and to the right a truncated extension of Rue Droit-Mur that came to a dead end, called Cul-de-Sac Genrot.

This is where Jean Valjean was standing.

As we have just said, on catching sight of that dark figure standing guard at the corner of Rue Droit-Mur and Petite-Rue-Picpus, he shrank back. No doubt about it. That phantom was lying in wait for him.

What was he to do?

It was too late to go back. What he had seen a moment ago, moving in the shadows some distance behind him, was undoubtedly Javert and his squad. Javert was probably already at the top of the street that Jean Valjean was standing at the end of. All the signs were that Javert was familiar with this little maze and had taken the precaution of sending one of his men to guard the exit. These conjectures, seemingly so close to the truth, immediately whirled through Jean Valjean's anguished brain like a handful of dust caught up by an unexpected gust of wind. He considered Cul-de-Sac Genrot. That way: blocked. He considered Petite-Rue-Picpus. That way: guarded. He saw a dark figure standing out, black, against the white pavement bathed in moonlight. To go on was to run into that man. To go back was to run straight into Javert. Jean Valjean felt caught in a slowly tightening net. He looked up to heaven in despair.

IV
Fumbling for a Way Out

In order to understand what follows, the reader needs to have an accurate picture of that Droit-Mur lane, and in particular of the corner you passed on your left as you emerged from Rue Polonceau to enter Rue Droit-Mur. The lane was bordered almost all the way along the right-hand side, down to Petite-Rue-Picpus, by shabby-looking houses, and on the left-hand side by a single grimly structured building, composed of several blocks that became gradually higher by one or two storeys as they approached Petite-Rue-Picpus. So that this building, which was very high at the Petite-Rue-Picpus end, was quite low at the Rue Polonceau end. There, on the corner we have mentioned, it came down so low it had only an outside wall. This wall did not come right out to the corner of the street. It was set well back, with the corner cut off at an angle, making that vertical face invisible to any two observers that there might have been, one in Rue Polonceau and the other in Rue Droit-Mur.

The wall extended on either side of the cut-off corner, along Rue Polonceau to a house bearing the number 49, and for a much shorter distance along Rue Droit-Mur to that gloomy building we have already mentioned, meeting its gable end and thus forming another recessed corner on that street. This gable end had a bleak appearance. It presented only one window, or rather two zinc-faced shutters kept permanently closed.

This detailed layout that we are giving here is a meticulously accurate one, and will surely awaken a very distinct memory in the minds of former residents of the neighbourhood.

The vertical face of the cut-off corner was entirely filled by something that looked like an enormous ramshackle gate. It was a huge structure of vertical planks, crudely put together, the top ones wider than the bottom ones, held together with long horizontal strips of iron. Alongside it was a carriage gate of normal size, which had obviously not been there more than about fifty years.

The boughs of a linden tree could be seen above this frontage, and the wall on the Rue Polonceau side was covered with ivy.

In imminent danger as Jean Valjean was, this gloomy building had a desolate and uninhabited look about it that appealed to him. His gaze rapidly scanned it. He told himself, if he could manage to get inside there he might be saved. First an idea came to him, then hope.

In the central part of the front of this building on Rue Droit-Mur there were old lead rainwater heads at every window on the various floors. The multiple branches of piping that led from one central pipe to all these little rainwater collectors sketched out a kind of tree on the façade. These ramifications of pipes with their many elbow joints bore a resemblance to those leafless old vine stocks twisting over the front of ancient farmhouses.

This bizarre espalier with its branches of lead and iron was the first thing that caught Jean Valjean's eye. He sat Cosette with her back against a bollard, telling her to keep quiet, and ran to the spot where the pipe came down to the pavement. Perhaps there was some way of climbing it and entering the house. But the pipe was in a sorry state and unserviceable and barely secured to the wall. Moreover, all the windows of this silent building had thick iron bars over them, even the attic windows in the roof.

And besides, this façade was in full moonlight, and the man watching from the end of the street would have seen Jean Valjean climbing it. And then what was to be done with Cosette? How was she to be hauled to the top of a three-storey house?

He gave up all idea of climbing the drainpipe, and crept along the wall back to Rue Polonceau.

When he reached the cut-off corner where he had left Cosette, he noticed no one could see him there. As we have just explained, he was invisible to all eyes, whichever direction they came from. And he was in shadow. Moreover, there were two gates. Perhaps they could be forced. The wall above which he could see the linden tree and the ivy obviously gave on to a garden where, leafless though the trees still were, he could at least hide and spend the rest of the night.

Time was passing. He had to act quickly.

He tried the carriage entrance, feeling over it with his hands, and realized at once it was boarded up on both sides.

He approached the other big gate more hopefully. It was terribly rickety, made less solid by its very size, the planks were rotten, the iron strips – there were only three – were rusted. It seemed as if it might be possible to get through this rickety barrier.

On examining it he saw that this gate was not a gate. It had neither hinges nor hinge pins, no lock, no opening in the middle. The iron bands went all the way across it in an unbroken line. Through the chinks between the planks he made out crudely cemented stone and rubble that passers-by could still see there ten years ago. He was forced to acknowledge with dismay that what seemed to be a gate was simply the wooden panelling on a building standing behind it.

It was easy to tear off a plank, but you came up against a wall.

V
Something Gas Lighting Would Make Impossible

At that moment a measured tramping sound began to make itself heard from some distance away. Jean Valjean risked taking a peek round the corner of the street. Seven or eight soldiers in a body had just entered Rue Polonceau. He saw the gleam of their bayonets. They were coming towards him.

These soldiers, led by a tall figure he identified as Javert, advanced slowly and cautiously. They halted frequently. It was plain they were searching every recess in the walls and every doorway and alleyway.

This was – and it was impossible to be mistaken in this conjecture – some patrol Javert had encountered and requisitioned. Javert's two henchmen were marching in their ranks.

At the pace they were moving and with the stops they were making, it would take them about a quarter of an hour to reach Jean Valjean's position. It was a frightful predicament. A few minutes separated Jean Valjean from the appalling abyss that was opening up before him, for the third time. And penal servitude now meant not just penal servitude but Cosette lost to him for ever, in other words, a living death.

There was only one possibility left.

It was a characteristic of Jean Valjean that he might have been said to carry two bags: in one he kept his saintly thoughts, in the other the formidable talents of a convict. He dug into one or the other, depending on circumstances.

Among other resources, thanks to his numerous escapes from the prison hulks at Toulon, he was, the reader will remember, a past master in that incredible art of climbing the inside corner of a wall, as much as six storeys high if necessary, without a ladder, without irons, by sheer muscular force, using neck, shoulders, hips and knees for support, scarcely relying at all on the odd irregularity in the stones' surface, an art that has rendered so awesome and so famous that corner of the courtyard in the Conciergerie of Paris by which some twenty years ago the convicted criminal Battemolle, facing execution, made his escape.

Jean Valjean sized up the wall above which he could see the linden tree. It was about eighteen feet high. The corner where it met the gable end of the large building was filled at ground level with a triangular pile of rubble, probably intended to save this too suitable corner from being used as a public convenience by passers-by. This preventive filling-up of corners is commonplace in Paris.

This pile was about five feet high. From the top of the pile the distance to be climbed to reach the top of the wall was no more than fourteen feet. The wall was capped with a flat stone coping.

The problem was Cosette. She could not climb a wall. Abandon her? Jean Valjean had no intention of doing so. It was impossible to carry her. A man needs all his strength to succeed in these extraordinary ascents. Any additional burden would interfere with his centre of gravity and make him fall.

He needed a rope. Jean Valjean had not got one. Where was he to find a rope at midnight in Rue Polonceau? Certainly at that moment Jean Valjean, if he had had one, would have given his kingdom for a rope.

All dire situations are electrifying, sometimes blindingly so, sometimes to illuminating effect. Jean Valjean's despairing gaze fell on the lamp post in Cul-de-Sac Genrot.

At that time there were no gas-lights on the streets of Paris. Street lanterns, placed at regular intervals, were lit at nightfall. They were raised and lowered by means of a rope running from one side of the street to the other which fed through the groove in a supporting bracket. The winch on which this rope was wound was locked in a little iron box underneath the lantern, to which the lamp-lighter had the key, and the rope itself was protected to a certain height by metal casing.

With the energy of a man whose life is at stake, Jean Valjean dashed across the street, entered the blind alley, picked the lock of the little box with the point of his knife, and a moment later was back with Cosette. He had a rope. They are fast workers, these desperately resourceful people contending with fate.

We have already explained that the street lamps had not been lit that night. So the lantern in Cul-de-Sac Genrot was of course dark like all the others and you could go by without even noticing it was no longer where it should have been.

Nevertheless, the time, the place, the darkness, Jean Valjean's concern, his peculiar behaviour, his comings and goings, had all begun to alarm Cosette. Any other child would have long since been complaining. She merely tugged at Jean Valjean by the skirt of his coat. They could hear ever more distinctly the sound of the patrol approaching.

'Father,' she whispered, 'I'm scared. Who is it that's coming this way?'

'Hush!' replied the poor man. 'It's Madame Thénardier.'

Cosette shuddered.

He added, 'Keep quiet. Leave it to me. If you call out, if you cry, that Thénardier woman's ready to pounce. She's come to take you back.'

Then, unhurriedly but without a wasted move, with quick and resolute precision – all the more remarkable at such a moment, when the patrol and Javert might appear at any instant – he untied his scarf, passed it round Cosette's body, under her armpits, making sure it could not hurt the child, fastened the scarf to one end of the rope by means of that knot seafarers call a swallow knot*, took the other end of the rope between his teeth, pulled off his shoes and stockings, which he threw over the wall, climbed up the pile of masonry, and began to raise himself in the angle between the wall and the gable end as surely and as steadily as if he had ladder rungs under his feet and elbows. Half a minute had not gone by before he was kneeling on the wall.

Cosette stared at him in amazement, not uttering a word. Jean Valjean's warning and the Thénardier woman's name had petrified her.

All of a sudden she heard Jean Valjean calling down to her, though still in a very quiet voice, 'Come and stand with your back to the wall.'

She obeyed.

'Don't say a word and don't be afraid,' said Jean Valjean.

And she felt herself being lifted from the ground. Before she knew it, she was on the top of the wall.

Jean Valjean picked her up, put her on his back, held her two little hands in his left hand, lay flat on his stomach and crawled along the top of the wall to where it cut across the corner. As he had surmised, there was some sort of outhouse with a roof, quite gently pitched, sloping down from the top of the wooden fence to very close to the ground, almost touching the linden tree. Just as well, because the wall was much higher on the inside than on the street side. Though Jean Valjean could see the ground, it seemed a very long way down.

He had just reached the sloping roof and was still on top of the

---

* In French, 'noeud d'hirondelle'. Although it would not be tied in quite the way described, is it possible that Hugo is thinking here of the so-called lark's-head knot (*noeud d'alouette*)?

wall when a great hullaballoo announced the arrival of the patrol. Javert's voice could be heard roaring out, 'Search the blind alley! Rue Droit-Mur is guarded! Petite-Rue-Picpus as well. I guarantee he's in the blind alley.'

The soldiers rushed into Cul-de-Sac Genrot.

Jean Valjean slid down the roof, holding Cosette, reached the linden tree and jumped to the ground. Either through terror or bravery Cosette had not uttered a sound. Her hands were a little grazed.

VI

The Beginning of a Mystery

Jean Valjean found himself in an extremely large and unusual-looking sort of garden, one of those melancholy gardens that seem designed to be viewed in winter and at night. This garden was rectangular in shape, with an avenue of tall poplars at the far end, some quite old trees in the corners, and an exposed space in the middle where you could make out one very big tree on its own, then several gnarled fruit trees bristling like bushes, some vegetable patches, a melon bed with its bell jars glinting in the moonlight, and an old drainage well. There were stone benches here and there, apparently black with moss. The paths were edged with little dark shrubs and were very straight. They were half overgrown with grass, and green mildew covered the rest.

Jean Valjean had next to him the outbuilding with the roof he had used to climb down, a stack of firewood, and behind the firewood, right up against the wall, a stone statue, its disfigured face now no more than a featureless mask dimly visible in the darkness.

The outbuilding was a kind of ruin in which some derelict rooms were discernible, one of which was very cluttered and seemed to be used as a garden shed.

The large building on Rue Droit-Mur that also faced on to Petite-Rue-Picpus had two façades overlooking this garden, at right-angles to each other. These interior façades were even more grim than the ones on the outside. All the windows were grated. Not a gleam of light was to be seen at any one of them. The top floors had hooded windows like those of prisons. One of these façades threw the other into its shadow, which fell over the garden like an immense black pall.

There was no other house to be seen. The bottom of the garden was lost in mist and darkness. Yet, beyond, you could vaguely make out some intersecting walls, as if there were other gardens there, and the low roofs of Rue Polonceau.

It was impossible to imagine anything more neglected and lonely

416

than this garden. There was no one in it, which was only natural given what time it was, but the place did not seem to be designed for anyone to walk in, even in broad daylight.

Jean Valjean's first concern had been to find his shoes and put them back on, then to get inside the outhouse with Cosette. No one on the run ever feels well enough hidden. Still thinking of Madame Thénardier, the child shared his instinct to be as inconspicuous as possible.

Cosette shivered, and huddled close to him. They could hear the racket made by the patrol searching the blind alley and the street, their gun butts striking the stones, Javert calling to the lookouts he had posted, and his cursing mixed with words that were indistinguishable.

After a quarter of an hour it sounded as if this rumbling storm, as it were, was beginning to move away. Jean Valjean held his breath.

He had gently placed his hand over Cosette's mouth.

Actually, the loneliness of the place they were in was so strangely peaceful that the frightful din raging so furiously and so close at hand did not disturb it in the slightest. The walls might have been built of those deaf stones mentioned in the Scriptures.

Suddenly out of this profound peacefulness rose a new sound, a sound as celestial, divine, ineffable, ravishing as the other was horrible. It was a hymn that issued from the shadows, a dazzling radiance of prayer and harmony, in the dark and frightening silence of the night. Women's voices, but voices simultaneously combining the pure strains of virgins and the innocent strains of children, like voices that are not of this earth, that sound like those the newborn can still hear, and the dying already hear. The singing came from the bleak edifice overlooking the garden. As the devils' pandemonium receded, it might have been a choir of angels approaching in the darkness.

Cosette and Jean Valjean fell on their knees.

They did not know what it was, they did not know where they were, but both man and child, penitent and innocent, felt they must kneel.

The strange thing about these voices was that the building seemed nonetheless deserted. It was like a transcendental song in an uninhabited abode. While these voices sang, Jean Valjean's mind was empty of thought. It was no longer the darkness he saw, it was blue skies. He seemed to feel the spreading of those wings we all have within us.

The singing stopped. It might have lasted a long time. Jean Valjean could not have said. Hours of ecstasy are never more than momentary.

All had fallen silent. Not another sound in the street, not another sound in the garden. The menacing, the comforting, all had died away. The breeze ruffled a few dry weeds on top of the wall, creating a quietly mournful sound.

VII
The Mystery Continues

The cold night wind had risen, which suggested it must be between one and two o'clock in the morning. Poor Cosette said nothing. As she had sat down on the ground beside him and rested her head against him, Jean Valjean thought she had fallen asleep. He bent down to look at her. Cosette's eyes were wide open and she had a pensive expression that Jean Valjean found heart-rending. She was still shivering.

'Are you sleepy?' said Jean Valjean.

'I'm very cold,' she replied.

A moment later she said, 'Is she still there?'

'Who?' said Jean Valjean.

'Madame Thénardier.'

Jean Valjean had already forgotten how he had contrived to keep Cosette quiet.

'Ah!' he said. 'She's gone. Nothing to be frightened of any more.'

The child sighed as though a load had been lifted off her chest.

The ground was damp, the outhouse exposed on every side, the wind freshening every moment. The old man took off his coat and wrapped it around Cosette.

'Are you less cold now?' he said.

'Oh, yes, father.'

'Now wait here for a moment. I'll be back straight away.'

He left the tumbledown shelter and began to skirt the large building, seeking some better refuge. He came across doors, but they were locked. There were bars on all the ground-floor windows.

He had just gone round the inside corner of the building when he noticed he was coming to some arched windows, and he saw a light shining from them. He stood on tip-toe and peeped through one of these windows. They all gave on to quite a vast interior, paved with large flagstones, divided up by arches and pillars, where nothing but a little glimmer of light and great shadows were to be seen. The glimmer came from a night lamp burning in one corner. This hall was deserted, and nothing stirred in it. Yet, straining his eyes, he thought he could see something on the ground that seemed to be covered with a shroud and looked like a human figure. It lay flat on the stone, face down, its arms extended on either side, in the stillness of death. This sinister figure appeared to have a rope round its neck, like some sort of snake trailing across the floor.

The entire hall was steeped in that mistiness of dimly lit places that adds to their horror.

Jean Valjean often said afterwards that although he had encountered many macabre sights in his life he had never seen anything more chilling and terrible than this mysterious figure, fulfilling who can say what unknown mystery in that dismal place and thus glimpsed in the gloom. It was harrowing to suppose that what lay there might be dead, and more harrowing still to think it might be alive.

He had the courage to press his forehead to the glass, watching to see if this thing would stir. Though he remained there for what seemed to him a very long time, the outstretched figure made no movement. Suddenly he was overcome with inexpressible terror, and he fled. He began to run towards the outhouse, not daring to look behind him. He had the feeling that if he turned round he would see that figure come striding after him, waving its arms.

He reached the ruined building panting for breath. His knees felt weak, the sweat trickled down his back.

Where was he? Who could ever have imagined anything of this kind in the middle of Paris! What was this strange sepulchral house? A building full of nocturnal mysteries, summoning souls in the darkness with the voices of angels, and when they came, springing on them that dreadful vision, promising to open the radiant gates of heaven and then opening the horrific entrance to the tomb! And this was a real building, a house that had its own number on the street! It was no dream! He had to touch the stones to convince himself of it.

The cold, the anxiety, the worry, the excitement of that evening made him genuinely feverish, and all these thoughts jostled in his brain.

He came back to Cosette. She was sleeping.

VIII
The Mystery Deepens

The child had laid her head on a stone and fallen asleep.

He sat down beside her and began to contemplate her. Little by little, as he gazed at her, he grew calm and regained control of his freedom of mind.

He clearly perceived this truth, the bedrock of his life from now on, that so long as she was there, so long as he had her by him, he would have no need of anything but for her sake, nor fear of anything except on her account. He was not even aware of being very cold, having taken off his coat to cover her with it.

But through the reverie into which he had fallen he had for a while been able to hear a curious sound. It was like a little bell being shaken. The sound came from the garden. Distinctly, albeit faintly, audible, it was reminiscent of the hesitant little tunes produced by cow bells in the pastures at night. This sound made Valjean turn round. He looked, and saw there was someone in the garden.

What appeared to be a man was walking among the bell jars in the melon bed, standing up, bending down, stopping, with regular movements, as if he were dragging something or spreading it out on the ground. This person seemed to be limping.

Jean Valjean shuddered with that continual tremor of the wretched. Everything is hostile and suspect to them. They distrust the daylight because, with the help of it, they can be seen, and the dark because, with the help of it, they can be taken by surprise. A little while ago he had been quaking because the garden was deserted, now he was quaking because there was someone there.

Fanciful terrors gave way to real ones. He said to himself that Javert and the spies might not have gone, that they had probably left people on the watch, that if this man found him in his garden he would cry for help and hand him over as a thief. He took the sleeping Cosette gently in his arms and carried her behind a heap of old disused furniture in the remotest corner of the outhouse. Cosette did not stir.

From there he observed the movements of the person in the melon bed. The strange thing was that the sound of the bell followed all of this man's movements. When the man came nearer, the sound came nearer. When the man moved away, the sound moved away. If he made any hurried gesture, a tremolo accompanied it. When he stopped, the sound ceased. It seemed obvious that the bell was attached to this man. But then what could be the meaning of it? Who was this man with a little bell hanging from him like a ram or an ox? As he asked himself all these questions, he touched Cosette's hands. They were freezing-cold.

'Oh my God!' he said.

He called to her in a low voice, 'Cosette!' She did not open her eyes.

He shook her vigorously. She did not wake.

'What if she were dead!' he said to himself. And he stood up, trembling from head to toe.

A jumble of the most frightful thoughts passed through his mind. There are moments when horrible assumptions assail us like a pack of

Furies, and violently storm our brains' defences. When those we love are at stake, our prudence imagines all sorts of madness. He remembered that sleeping in the open air on a cold night can be fatal.

Pallid, Cosette had sunk back down on the ground and lay at his feet, not moving. He listened for her breath. She was breathing, but her breathing seemed to him weak and about to fade away.

How was he to warm her? How was he to rouse her? Everything but this was wiped from his mind. He rushed from the outhouse in panic. It was absolutely essential that Cosette be in bed in front of a fire within fifteen minutes.

IX
The Man with the Bell

He walked straight up to the man he saw in the garden. He put his hand on the roll of silver coins in the pocket of his waistcoat.

The man had his head bent down and did not see Jean Valjean coming. In a few strides Jean Valjean was beside him. Jean Valjean accosted him with the cry, 'One hundred francs!'

The man gave a start and looked up.

'A hundred francs are yours,' Jean Valjean went on, 'if you'll give me shelter for the night.'

The moon shone full on Jean Valjean's frantic face.

'Oh! It's you, Père Madeleine!' said the man.

That name, spoken in these circumstances at this late hour in this unknown spot by this strange man, made Jean Valjean recoil.

He had expected anything but that. The person speaking to him was a stooped, lame old man, dressed almost like a peasant, who wore on his left knee a leather knee-pad with quite a large bell hanging from it. His face, which was in shadow, could not be seen clearly.

But this fellow had removed his cap and was all atremble, crying, 'Oh, my God! What are you doing here, Père Madeleine? How in the name of Jesus did you get in? You must have fallen from heaven! Not that it's impossible – if ever you do fall, that's where you'll fall from. And what a state you're in! You've no scarf, you've no hat, you've no coat! Do you realize, you'd have frightened anyone who didn't know you. No coat! Good Lord! Are the saints going mad these days? But how on earth did you get in here?'

The words came tumbling out. The old man spoke with a rustic volubility that gave no cause for concern. All this was said with a mixture of bewilderment and simple kindliness.

'Who are you? And what is this house?' asked Jean Valjean.

'Ah! Glory be, that's a good one!' exclaimed the old man. 'I'm the person you placed here, and this house is the one where you placed me. What, don't you recognize me?'

'No,' said Jean Valjean. 'And how was it you came to know me?'

'You saved my life,' said the man.

He turned, a moonbeam caught his face in profile, and Jean Valjean recognized old Fauchelevent.

'Ah!' said Jean Valjean. 'So it's you! Yes, I recognize you.'

'I should think so too,' said the old man in a reproachful tone.

'And what are you doing here?' said Jean Valjean.

'Why, covering my melons, of course!'

When Jean Valjean accosted him, old Fauchelevent had in fact been holding in his hand the end of a straw mat that he was busy laying over the melon bed. He had already laid down a number of them during the hour or so he had been in the garden. It was this operation that had caused him to make the peculiar movements observed from the outhouse by Jean Valjean.

He went on, 'I said to myself: The moon's bright, there'll be a frost. Maybe I should get my melons into their winter coats? And goodness knows,' he added, looking at Jean Valjean with a chuckle, 'you surely should have done the same for yourself! But how do you come to be here?'

Aware that he was known to this man, at least by the name of Madeleine, Jean Valjean now proceeded with the utmost caution. He kept asking questions. Strange to say, their roles seemed to be reversed. It was he, the intruder, who was asking the questions.

'And what's this bell you're wearing on your knee?'

'This?' replied Fauchelevent. 'It's so I can be kept clear of.'

'What do you mean! So you can be kept clear of?'

Old Fauchelevent winked, with an expression beyond words. 'I tell you, there are only women in this house, many young girls. It seems I'd be dangerous for them to meet. The bell warns them. When I come along, they go away.'

'What is this house?'

'Come now, you know well enough.'

'No, I don't.'

'But you got me the job here as gardener!'

'Tell me as if I knew nothing about it.'

'Well then, this is the Petit-Picpus convent.'

Memories started coming back to Jean Valjean. Chance, that is to say, providence, had cast him into that very convent in the St-Antoine neighbourhood where old Fauchelevent, crippled by his overturned cart, had been taken in, on his recommendation, two years ago now. He repeated, as if talking to himself, 'The Petit-Picpus convent.'

'Now then,' said Fauchelevent, 'more to the point, how the devil did you get in here, Père Madeleine? For all that you're a saint, you're a man, and no men are allowed into this place.'

'You're here.'

'I'm the only one.'

'All the same,' said Jean Valjean, 'I must stay here.'

'My God!' cried Fauchelevent.

Jean Valjean drew closer to the old man and said to him in a grave voice, 'Père Fauchelevent, I saved your life.'

'I was the first to remember it,' replied Fauchelevent.

'Well, today you can do for me what I once did for you.'

Fauchelevent took in his old, wrinkled and trembling hands Jean Valjean's two sturdy hands and for several minutes seemed unable to speak. Finally he exclaimed, 'Oh! that would be a blessing from the good Lord if I could pay you back a little! I, save your life! Monsieur le maire, this old man is at your service!'

A wonderful joy had in some way transfigured the old man. His face seemed to radiate light.

'What do you want me to do?' he said.

'I shall explain. Have you got a room?'

'I have an isolated hut, over there, behind the ruins of the old convent, in a corner out of sight. It has three rooms.'

The hut was actually so well hidden behind the ruins, and so well positioned so as not to be visible, that Jean Valjean had not noticed it.

'Good,' said Jean Valjean. 'Now there are two things I ask of you.'

'What are they, monsieur le maire?'

'Firstly, not to tell anyone what you know about me. Secondly, not to ask for any more explanations.'

'Whatever you say. I know you couldn't do anything that wasn't honourable and you've always been a man of God. And besides, it was you who placed me here. That's your own business. I'm at your service.'

'That's settled. Now, come with me. We'll go and fetch the child.'

'Ah!' said Fauchelevent. 'There's a child!'

He said not another word and followed Jean Valjean like a dog following its master.

Less than half an hour later, Cosette, her rosy colouring restored by the warmth of a good fire, was asleep in the old gardener's bed. Jean Valjean had put his scarf and coat back on. The hat he had tossed over the wall had been found and retrieved. While Jean Valjean was putting on his frock-coat, Fauchelevent had removed his knee-pad with the bell on it, which was now hanging on the wall from a nail beside a gardener's pannier. The two men were warming themselves, seated at a table where Fauchelevent had placed a piece of cheese, some brown bread, a bottle of wine and two glasses, and laying his hand on Jean Valjean's knee the old man was saying to him, 'Ah! Père Madeleine! You didn't recognize me straight away. You save people's lives, and then you forget them! Oh, that's bad! They remember you! Heartless, that's what you are!'

X
How Javert Came to Find the Bird Had Flown

The events of which we have just seen the reverse side, as it were, unfolded in the most straightforward manner.

When, on the day that Javert arrested him at Fantine's deathbed, Jean Valjean escaped from Montreuil-sur-Mer's town gaol, the police assumed the escaped convict must have made his way to Paris. Paris is a maelstrom in which all is lost, and all disappears inside this earthly vortex as it does in the vortex of the seas. No forest hides a man as effectively as this throng. All manner of fugitives know this. They go to Paris to be swallowed up. There is salvation in being swallowed up. The police know this too, and it is in Paris they go looking for what they have lost elsewhere. That is where they went looking for the former mayor of Montreuil-sur-Mer. Javert was summoned to Paris to assist in the search. And indeed Javert contributed considerably to the recapture of Jean Valjean. Javert's zeal and intelligence in that instance were noted by Monsieur Chabouillet, secretary of the Prefecture under Comte Anglès. Monsieur Chabouillet, who was in any case already a patron of Javert, arranged for the inspector of Montreuil-sur-Mer to be transferred to the Paris police. There, Javert in various ways made himself useful, and let us say, unexpected as the word may seem with regard to such services, honourably so.

He had stopped thinking about Jean Valjean – for dogs that hunt all the time, today's fox drives yesterday's fox out of mind – when in December 1823 he read a newspaper. Javert never read newspapers, but being a monarchist he wanted to know the details of the 'prince-generalissimo's' triumphal entry into Bayonne. Just as he was finishing the article that interested him a name at the bottom of a page, the name of Jean Valjean, caught his attention. The paper announced that the convict Jean Valjean was dead and reported the fact in such categorical terms that Javert did not doubt it. All he said was, 'There's no escape from that place!' Then he threw aside the paper and thought no more about it.

Some time afterwards a report was sent to the Paris police head-quarters by the Seine-et-Oise Prefecture, concerning the abduction of a child, said to have taken place under unusual circumstances in the commune of Montfermeil. The report said a little girl of seven or eight years of age, placed by her mother in the care of a local innkeeper, had been stolen by a stranger. This child answered to the name of Cosette and was the daughter of a prostitute named Fantine, who had died in hospital, it was not known when or where. This report came to Javert's notice and set him pondering.

The name of Fantine was well known to him. He remembered that Jean Valjean had made him burst out laughing by asking for three days' grace in order to go and fetch that creature's child. He recalled that Jean Valjean had been arrested in Paris as he was getting into the coach for Montfermeil. Some indications even then had led to specu-lation that it was the second time he was taking that coach, and that he had already made a previous trip the day before to somewhere on the outskirts of that village, for he had not been seen in the village itself. Why was he going to that place, Montfermeil? No one could work it out. Javert now understood. Fantine's daughter was there. Jean Valjean was going to fetch her. Well, this child had just been stolen by a stranger! Who could that stranger be? Could it be Jean Valjean? But Jean Valjean was dead. Without saying anything to any-body, Javert took the coach from the Plat-d'Étain at Cul-de-Sac de la Planchette and travelled to Montfermeil.

He expected to find great illumination. What he found was great obscurity.

For the first few days, the smarting Thénardiers had a lot to say for themselves. The disappearance of Alouette had created a sensation in the village. There were immediately several versions of the story that had ended up as a child theft. Hence the police report. But after his initial fury Thénardier, with that wonderful instinct of his, very quickly realized that it never pays to involve the crown prosecutor and that the first result of his complaints about Cosette's 'abduction' would be to bring the glinting eye of justice to bear on himself and on many shady affairs he was involved in. The last thing owls want is to have a light shone on them. In the first place, how would he explain the fifteen hundred francs he had received? In a complete turnaround he stopped his wife talking, and feigned astonishment at any mention of the 'stolen child'. He was at a loss to understand any such talk. No doubt in the heat of the moment he had complained of having that little darling 'taken away from him' so quickly. Out of affection he would have liked to keep her another two or three days, but it was her 'grandfather' who had come to fetch her, quite naturally enough. He had added the grandfather for good measure. It was this story that Javert heard when he turned up at Montfermeil. The grandfather eliminated Jean Valjean.

Nevertheless, Javert did ask a few questions by way of checking Thénardier's story. Who was this grandfather and what was his name? Thénardier replied straightforwardly, 'He's a wealthy farmer. I saw his passport. I think his name was Monsieur Guillaume Lambert.'

Lambert is a good honest name and extremely reassuring. Javert returned to Paris.

'Jean Valjean is dead, for sure,' he said, 'and I'm a fool.'

Again he was beginning to forget this whole story when in March 1824 he heard about some odd character living in the parish of St-Médard who had been nicknamed 'the beggar who gives alms to the poor'. This individual was, it was said, a man of means, no one quite knew what his name was, and he lived alone with a little girl of eight who herself knew nothing except that she came from Montfermeil. Montfermeil! That name kept turning up, and it made Javert prick up his ears. Acting as a police informer, an old beggar and former verger, to whom this person gave money, provided a few more details. This man of means was a very unsociable person – only ever went out in the evening, spoke to no one, just occasionally to the poor, and never let anyone get near him. He wore a horrible old yellow frock-coat that was worth several million, being completely padded with banknotes. This definitely piqued Javert's curiosity. In order to get a really close look at this unlikely man of means without scaring him off, he borrowed the verger's garb for a day, and the patch on which the old police informer sat huddled every evening, muttering prayers and spying through his prayerfulness.

'The suspect individual' did indeed come up to Javert in this disguise, and gave him money. At that moment Javert looked up, and the shock that Jean Valjean had, thinking he recognized Javert, Javert also had, thinking he recognized Valjean.

However, the darkness might have deceived him. Jean Valjean's death was official. Javert still had doubts, serious doubts; and when in doubt, Javert, a scrupulous man, never collared anybody.

He followed his man to the Gorbeau tenement and got 'the old biddy' talking, which was not difficult. The old biddy confirmed the information regarding the coat lined with millions, and related the episode of the thousand-franc note. She saw it! She had it in her hands! Javert rented a room. That same evening he moved in. He came and listened at the mysterious lodger's door, hoping to hear the sound of his voice, but Jean Valjean saw his candlelight through the keyhole and thwarted the spy by remaining silent.

The next day Jean Valjean decamped. But the sound of the five-franc piece that he dropped was noted by the old woman, who, hearing the jingle of money, thought he was going to move out and wasted no time in alerting Javert. At nightfall, when Jean Valjean emerged, Javert was waiting for him with two men behind the trees on the boulevard.

Javert had asked police headquarters for support but had not disclosed the name of the individual he hoped to seize. That was his secret, and he kept it for three reasons. First, because the slightest indiscretion might put Jean Valjean on his guard. Also, because capturing an escaped old lag believed to be dead, a convicted criminal classified once and for all in the legal records as 'a felon of the most dangerous kind', was a sensational coup that the Paris police veterans would certainly not leave to a newcomer like Javert, and he was afraid of being robbed of his hardened offender. Lastly, because Javert, being an artist, had a taste for the unexpected. He hated those much heralded successes that have the shine taken off them by being talked of long in advance. He preferred to prepare his masterstrokes in the dark and then suddenly reveal them.

Javert followed Jean Valjean from tree to tree, then from street corner to street corner, did not lose sight of him for a single moment. Even when Jean Valjean felt safest, Javert's eye was on him.

Why did Javert not arrest Jean Valjean? Because he was still doubtful.

It must be remembered that at that time things were not exactly comfortable for the police. The free press was making things difficult for them. Several arbitrary arrests, denounced by the newspapers, had caused a stir even in parliament and had made the police authorities apprehensive. Violating the freedom of the individual was a serious matter. Policemen were afraid of making a mistake. The chief of police made them take the blame for it. A mistake meant getting the sack. Imagine the effect this brief paragraph, reproduced in twenty newspapers, would have had in Paris: 'Yesterday a white-haired old grandfather and respectable man of means while out for a walk with

427

his eight-year-old granddaughter was arrested as an escaped convict and taken to the central police station'!

And anyway, it is worth repeating, Javert had scruples of his own. The exhortations of his conscience reinforced the exhortations of the police chief. He was genuinely in doubt.

And Jean Valjean was walking with his back to him, in darkness.

Sorrow, worry, anxiety, despondency, this new setback of having to flee by night and blindly seek a safe shelter in Paris for Cosette and himself, the need to adjust his pace to that of the child, all this, without his even being aware of it, had altered Jean Valjean's gait and placed such a stamp of old age on his usual bearing that even the police, embodied by Javert, might be misled, and indeed he was. The impossibility of getting very close, the way he was dressed as an elderly émigré tutor, Thénardier's statement that made him a grandfather, and the belief that he had died in prison, added further to the growing uncertainties in Javert's mind.

At one moment he considered asking him bluntly for his papers. But if this man was not Jean Valjean, and if he was not a respectable old gentleman of independent means, he was probably some bruiser who was deeply and cleverly involved in the Parisian criminal underworld, some dangerous gang leader giving money to the poor to conceal his other talents – an old trick, that one. He would have trusted henchmen, accomplices, bolt-holes where he was no doubt going to take refuge. All these detours he was making seemed to indicate he was no ordinary customer. To arrest him too hastily would be 'to kill the goose that lays the golden egg'. What was the harm in waiting? Javert was very confident the man could not escape. So he carried on, somewhat perplexed, asking himself countless questions about this mysterious character.

It was only quite late, in Rue de Pontoise, that, thanks to the bright light spilling out from a bar, he definitely recognized Jean Valjean.

There are in this world two creatures that quiver intensely: the mother who finds her lost child and the tiger that comes on its prey. Javert had that intense quivering.

As soon as he had positively identified the fearsome convicted criminal Jean Valjean, he realized there were only three of them and asked for reinforcements at the police station on Rue de Pontoise.

Before you grasp a thorny stick, you put on gloves.

This delay, and stopping at Carrefour Rollin to confer with his men, almost made him lose the trail. However, he very soon worked out that Jean Valjean would want to put the river between himself and his pursuers. Like a bloodhound setting its nose to the ground to keep on the right track, he bowed his head and reflected. With his powerful sureness of instinct Javert made straight for the Pont d'Austerlitz. A word with the toll collector told him all he needed to know.

'Have you seen a man with a little girl?'

'I made him pay two sous,' replied the toll collector.

Javert reached the bridge in time to see Jean Valjean on the other side of the water walking across the moonlit open space holding Cosette by the hand. He saw him enter Rue du Chemin-Vert-St-Antoine. He pictured Cul-de-Sac Genrot laid out there like a trap, and the only way out of Rue Droit-Mur into Petite-Rue-Picpus. He 'organized a drive', as huntsmen say. He quickly sent one of his agents by a roundabout route to guard that exit. When an army patrol came by, on its way back to the Arsenal, he requisitioned it to go with him. In such circumstances soldiers are an asset. Moreover, the rule is, to get the better of a wild boar you need the expertise of a huntsman and plenty of dogs. Having made these arrangements, and aware that Jean Valjean was trapped between the Genrot blind alley on his right, Javert's man on his left, and Javert himself behind, he took a pinch of snuff.

Then he began to have fun. He experienced a moment of fiendish delight, letting his man go on ahead, knowing he had him in his grasp but wanting to delay to the utmost the moment of arrest, taking pleasure in being aware that the man was caught; and seeing him free, gloating over him with that relish the spider takes in the flitting of the fly and the cat takes in the scurrying of the mouse. Claws and talons enjoy a monstrous thrill: that is, the unseen movements of the creature imprisoned in their grip. How delicious is this snuffing-out!

Javert was in ecstasy. His net was firmly staked. He was sure of success. All he had to do now was tighten his grip.

With the back-up he had, the very idea of resistance was absurd, no matter how energetic, strong and desperate Jean Valjean might be.

Javert advanced slowly, delving into every nook on his way down the street, as into the pockets of a thief.

When he reached the centre of his web he found the fly was gone.

You can imagine his fury.

He questioned his lookout at the corner of Droit-Mur and Picpus. This agent had remained stolidly at his post and had not seen the man go by.

It sometimes happens that a stag finds escape cover, in other words gets away, even with the pack at his heels, and then the oldest huntsmen are lost for words. Duvivier, Ligniville and Desprez are dumbfounded. In a reversal of this kind Artonge exclaimed, 'That's not a stag – it's a sorcerer!' Javert might easily have given vent to the same cry.

For a moment there was an element of despair and rage in his disappointment.

Certainly, Napoleon made mistakes during the war in Russia, Alexander made mistakes during the war in India; Caesar during the war in Africa, Cyrus during the war in Scythia; and Javert made mistakes in this campaign against Jean Valjean. He was perhaps wrong to hesitate in recognizing the ex-convict. That first glance should have been enough. He was wrong not just simply to arrest him at the tenement. He was wrong not to detain him when he positively identified him in Rue de Pontoise. He was wrong to confer with his aides in Carrefour Rollin in full moonlight. Certainly expert advice is useful, and it is a good thing to know which dogs can be relied on, and to look to them. But the huntsman cannot afford to take too many precautions when hunting nervous animals like the fox and the convict. Too anxious to set a pack of bloodhounds on the trail, Javert alerted the beast by letting it get wind of them and caused it to bolt. Most of all, when he picked up the scent again on the Pont d'Austerlitz he was wrong to play that dreadful and childish game of teasing, keeping such a man on the end of a line. He overestimated himself by thinking he could play cat-and-mouse with a lion. At the same time he underestimated himself by deeming it necessary to recruit back-up. A fatal precaution, a waste of precious time! Javert made all these mistakes, yet was one of the cleverest and most competent spies that ever existed. He was in the full sense of the term what in hunting is called a 'steady hound'. But which of us is perfect?

Great strategists have their weaknesses.

The greatest follies, like the stoutest ropes, are often composed of a multitude of strands. Take the cable thread by thread, take separately each petty determining motive, and you can snap them one by one and say, 'There's no more to it than that!' Braid them and twist them together, and what you have is momentous: Attila wavering between Marcian in the east and Valentinian in the west, Hannibal lingering at Capua, Danton going to sleep at Arcis-sur-Aube.

In any case, even when he saw that Jean Valjean had escaped him Javert did not lose his head. Sure that the ex-convict who had violated the conditions of his release could not be very far away, he posted lookouts, set up traps and ambushes, and combed the neighbourhood all night long. The first thing he saw was the damage to the street lamp whose rope had been cut. A precious clue that led him astray, however, by directing all his searches around Cul-de-Sac Genrot.

There were in this blind alley fairly low walls enclosing gardens whose boundaries bordered on vast tracts of wasteland. Evidently Jean Valjean must have fled in that direction. The fact is, had he gone a little further down Cul-de-Sac Genrot, he might well have done so, and that would have been his undoing. Javert scoured these gardens and this wasteland as if he might have been searching for a needle.

At daybreak he left two sharp-witted men to keep watch, and returned to the Prefecture, ashamed, like a nark bested by a thief.*

---

* There is an allusion here to La Fontaine's 'Le Renard et la Cigogne' ('The Fox and the Stork'; bk 1, fable 18), in which the fox is outwitted by the stork: 'He had to return home with an empty stomach, / Ashamed, like a Fox bested by a Hen.'

BOOK SIX
PETIT-PICPUS

I
Number 62 Petite-Rue-Picpus

Half a century ago nothing more resembled an ordinary carriage gate than the carriage gate of number 62 Petite-Rue-Picpus. This entrance, usually standing ajar in the most inviting manner, revealed two things with nothing very dismal about them: a courtyard surrounded by vine-covered walls and an idling porter's face. Above the far wall you could see some tall trees. When a ray of sunshine brightened up the court-yard, when a glass of wine brightened up the porter, it was difficult to pass number 62 Petite-Rue-Picpus without taking away a cheerful impression of it. Yet it was a sombre place that you had glimpsed.

Behind the smiling doorway the house prayed and wept.

If you succeeded in getting past the porter, which was not at all easy – indeed, for nearly everybody it was almost impossible, for there was an open sesame you had to know – if, having got past the porter, you entered a little vestibule on the right with a staircase squeezed in between two walls and so narrow that only one person could use it at a time, if you did not allow yourself to be scared off by the canary-yellow distemper with a chocolate-brown dado on the staircase walls, if you ventured to climb the staircase, you went past a first landing, then a second, and you came to a corridor on the first floor where the yellow distemper and the chocolate-brown dado pursued you with placid relentlessness. Staircase and corridor were lighted by two hand-some windows. The corridor turned sharply and became gloomy. If you rounded this corner you came to a door a few paces further on that was all the more mysterious for not being locked. Push it open and you found yourself in a little room about six feet square, with a tiled floor, well scrubbed, clean, cold, the walls papered with green-flowered nankin at fifteen sous a roll. A dull white light entered from a large small-paned window on the left that took up the whole width of the room. You looked, but saw no one. You listened, but heard neither a footstep nor the murmur of a human voice. The walls were bare, the room unfurnished, not so much as a chair.

You looked again, and you saw on the wall opposite the door a hatch, about a foot square, filled with a grid of knobbly, solid, black iron bars forming squares – I almost said a mesh – with a diagonal of less than an inch and a half. The little green flowers on the nankin wallpaper came up to those iron bars in a calm, orderly fashion without being frightened or thrown into confusion by this grim contact. Even supposing that some human being were so wonderfully thin as to try to enter or exit through the square hatch, this grille would have prevented it. It kept out the body but not the eyes; that is to say, the mind. Apparently this had been thought of, for it was backed by a sheet of tin set a little further behind in the wall and pierced with a thousand holes more microscopic than the holes in a sieve. At the bottom of this plaque an opening had been made exactly like the mouth of a letter-box. To the right of the grilled hatch hung a wire attached to a bell mechanism.

If this wire was pulled a little bell tinkled and you heard a voice very close to you that made you start.

'Who's there?' the voice would ask.

It was a woman's voice, a subdued voice, so subdued it sounded mournful.

Here again there was a magic word you had to know. If you did not know it, the voice would say nothing and the wall would fall silent again as if the affrighted darkness of the tomb had been on the other side of it.

If you knew the password the voice went on, 'Enter the door on your right.'

You then noticed to your right, opposite the window, a glazed door painted grey with a fanlight above it. You lifted the latch, you went through the door, and you had exactly the same impression as when you go into a grilled box at the theatre before the grille is taken down and lighting is introduced. You were indeed in a kind of theatre box, dimly lit by the muted light from the glazed door, confined, furnished with two old chairs and a much frayed straw mat, and just like a real box with its elbow-high frontage and a black wooden shelf on top. This box was grilled, only not with a gilded wooden grille like the one at the Opéra, but a monstrous lattice of iron bars, hideously close-knit and fixed in the wall with enormous fittings that looked like clenched fists.

After the first few minutes, when your eyes began to adjust to this cellar-like gloom, they tried to see through the grating but travelled no further than six inches beyond it. There they encountered a barrier of black shutters, fortified with wooden cross-supports painted a gingerbread-yellow. These were folding shutters divided into long narrow slats and they screened the entire width of the grating. They were always closed.

After a few moments you heard a voice address you from behind these shutters that said, 'I am here. What is it you want?'

It was a cherished voice, sometimes an adored voice. No one could be seen. Only the faintest breath could be heard. It was like a ghost speaking to you through the walls of the tomb.

Very rarely, if you happened to meet certain specified conditions, the narrow slat of one of the shutters opened in front of you, and the ghost became an apparition. Behind the grating, behind the shutter, you glimpsed, in as much as the grating allowed you to, a head with only the mouth and chin visible. The rest was covered with a black veil. A black wimple could be discerned and a barely distinguishable figure covered in a black shroud. This person spoke to you but did not look at you, and never smiled at you.

It was contrived, with the light coming from behind you, so that you saw her as white and she saw you as black. This light was symbolic.

All the same, you peered eagerly, through the gap that had opened up, into that place that was closed against all eyes. A deep obscurity surrounded the figure dressed in mourning. Your eyes probed the obscurity and tried to make out what was around the apparition. After a very short time you realized you could see nothing. What you saw was darkness, emptiness, shadows, a wintry mist combined with the atmosphere of the grave, a kind of terrifying peacefulness, a silence in which nothing was detectable, not even sighs, a gloom in which nothing was distinguishable, not even phantoms.

What you saw was the interior of a cloister.

It was the interior of that austere and gloomy house called the Convent of the Bernardines of Perpetual Adoration. The box you were in was the parlour. That voice, the first that spoke to you, was the voice of the extern nun who always sat, still and silent, on the other side of the wall by the square hatch, protected as with a double visor by the iron grating and the multi-perforated screen.

The obscurity in which the grilled box was steeped resulted from the parlour having a window on one side, that of the outside world, and not on the other, that of the convent. Profane eyes were not meant to see anything of that sacred place.

Yet there was something beyond that gloom. There was a light. There was life in that death. Although this was the most closed of all convents, we are going to try to enter it, and take the reader inside, and with all due respect say things that storytellers have never seen and therefore never spoken of.

II
The Observance of Martin Verga

This convent, which in 1824 had already existed for many a long year in Petite-Rue-Picpus, was a community of Bernardine nuns of the observance of Martin Verga.

Consequently these Bernardine nuns were attached not to Clairvaux like the Bernardine monks but to Cîteaux like the Benedictines. In other words, they were subject to the authority not of St Bernard but of St Benedict.

Anyone with even a slight familiarity with old folios knows that Martin Verga founded in 1425 a congregation of Bernardine-Benedictines, with Salamanca its main foundation and Alcalá a dependency. This congregation developed branches in all the Catholic countries of Europe.

There is nothing unusual in the Latin Church about such graftings of one order on to another. To take just the order of St Benedict here in question, without counting the observance of Martin Verga there are attached to this order four congregations, two in Italy, Monte Cassino and St Justina of Padua, two in France, Cluny and St Maur, and nine orders, Vallombrosa, Grandmont, the Celestines, Camaldolese, Carthusians, Humiliants, Olivetans, Silvestrines, and lastly Cîteaux. For Cîteaux itself, the root-stock for other orders, is only an offshoot for St Benedict. Cîteaux dates back to St Robert, Abbé de Molesme in the diocese of Langres in 1098. However, it was in 529 that the devil, who had retired to the wilderness of Subiaco (he was old – had he become a hermit?*), was chased out of the ancient temple of Apollo, where he dwelt, by St Benedict, then aged seventeen.

After the rule of the Carmelite nuns, who go barefoot, wear a piece of willow on their breasts and never sit down, the harshest rule is that of the Bernardine-Benedictines of Martin Verga. They are dressed in black with a wimple that, as expressly stipulated by St Benedict, comes right up to the chin. A wide-sleeved serge robe, a large woollen veil, the wimple up to the chin cut square across the breast with the head-band right down to their eyes – this is their habit. Everything is black except the head-band, which is white. The novices

---

* There is a French proverb: 'Quand le diable devient vieux, il se fait ermite' ('When the devil grows old, he becomes a hermit'). In other words, a misspent youth is often followed by a pious old age.

wear the same habit, all in white. The professed nuns also have a rosary at their side.

The Bernardine-Benedictines of Martin Verga practise Perpetual Adoration like those Benedictine nuns called the Sisters of the Blessed Sacrament, who at the beginning of this century had two houses in Paris, one in the Temple district, the other in Rue Neuve-Ste-Geneviève. However, the Bernardine-Benedictines of Petit-Picpus whom we are talking about were a totally different order from the Sisters of the Blessed Sacrament cloistered in Rue Neuve-Ste-Geneviève and at the Temple. There were numerous differences in their rule; there were also differences in their dress. The Bernardine-Benedictines of Petit-Picpus wore the black wimple, while the Benedictines of the Blessed Sacrament and of Rue Neuve-Ste-Geneviève wore the white one and also had on their breasts an image of the Blessed Sacrament, about three inches high, of gilded silver or gilded copper. The nuns of Petit-Picpus did not wear this image. Though Perpetual Adoration is common to both the Petit-Picpus community and the Temple community, the two orders are otherwise quite distinct. Only in that practice is there any resemblance between the Sisters of the Blessed Sacrament and the Bernardines of Martin Verga, just as there was a similarity – in their study and glorification of all the mysteries relating to the infancy, life and death of Jesus Christ and the Virgin – between another two very different and sometimes mutually hostile orders: the Oratory in Italy, established at Florence by Filippo de' Neri, and the French Oratory, established by Pierre de Bérulle. The French Oratory claimed supremacy, Filippo de' Neri being only a saint and Bérulle being a cardinal.

Let us return to the austere Spanish rule of Martin Verga. The Bernardine-Benedictines of this obedience abstain from meat all year round, fast in Lent and on many other days of special significance to them, rise from their first sleep to read their breviary and sing matins from one o'clock until three o'clock in the morning, sleep on straw and between serge sheets in all seasons, do not take baths, never light a fire, scourge themselves every Friday, observe the rule of silence, speak to each other only during recreation periods, which are very brief; and for six months wear homespun woollen chemises, from the fourteenth of September, feast of the Exaltation of the Holy Cross, until Easter. These six months are a mitigation; the rule says all year round, but this homespun woollen chemise, intolerable in the heat of summer, would cause fevers and nervous spasms. Its usage had to be restricted. Even with this relaxation, when the nuns don the chemise on the fourteenth of September they suffer three or four days of fever.

Obedience, poverty, chastity and stability – these are their vows, made more onerous by the extreme harshness of their rule.

The prioress is elected for three years by the senior nuns, who are called 'vocal mothers' because they vote in the chapter. A prioress can only be re-elected twice, which limits the longest possible reign of a prioress to nine years.

They never see the officiating priest, who is always hidden from them by a serge curtain seven feet high. During the sermon, when the preacher is in the chapel, they lower their veils over their faces. They must always speak very quietly, walk with their eyes downcast and their heads bowed. One man only is allowed to enter the convent: the archbishop of the diocese.

Actually there is one other, the gardener. But he is always an old man, and so that he should be perpetually isolated in the garden and the nuns be given warning so as to avoid him, a small bell is attached to his knee.

Their obedience to the prioress is an absolute and unquestioning obedience. It is canonical subjection in all its self-abnegation: as if to the voice of Christ, *ut voci Christi*, at a gesture, at the first indication, *ad nutum, ad primum signum*, immediately, with joy, with steadfastness, with a certain blind obedience, *prompte, hilariter, perseveranter et caeca quadam obedientia*, like the file in the hands of the workman, *quasi limam in manibus fabri*, unable to read or to write anything whatsoever without express permission, *legere vel scribere non addiscerit sine expressa superioris licentia*.

Each one in turn makes what they call 'reparation'. Reparation is prayer for all the sins, all the lapses, all the transgressions, all the profanations, all the iniquities, all the crimes committed on earth. For twelve consecutive hours, from four o'clock in the evening till four o'clock in the morning, or from four o'clock in the morning until four o'clock in the evening, the sister who is making reparation remains kneeling on the stone floor in front of the Blessed Sacrament, her hands joined, a rope around her neck. When her tiredness grows unendurable, she prostrates herself, lying flat on the ground, face down, with her arms outstretched, in the shape of a cross. This is her only relief. In this attitude she prays for all who are guilty in the universe. There is a greatness in this that attains the sublime.

As this act is performed in front of a post with a candle burning on the top of it, it is referred to equally as 'making reparation' or 'being at the post'. Out of humility, the nuns even prefer the latter expression, which contains an idea of torture and abasement.

Making reparation is an undertaking in which the soul is wholly absorbed. The sister at the post would not look round, were a thunderbolt to strike behind her.

Moreover, there is always a nun kneeling before the Blessed Sacrament. This vigil lasts an hour. They relieve each other like soldiers on sentry duty. This is Perpetual Adoration.

The prioresses and the mothers almost always have names marked by particular solemnity, recalling not the saints and martyrs but moments in the life of Jesus Christ: such as Mère Nativité, Mère Conception, Mère Présentation, Mère Passion. However, saints' names are not forbidden.

When you see them, you never see anything but their mouths. They all have yellow teeth. No toothbrush has ever entered that convent. Brushing your teeth is the top rung of a ladder at the bottom of which is perdition of the soul.

They never say 'my'. They have nothing of their own and must not feel any attachment to anything. They refer to everything as 'our', so our veil, our chaplet; if they were speaking of their chemises they would say 'our chemise'. Sometimes they do become attached to some little object, a book of hours, a relic, a holy medal. As soon as they realize they are beginning to value this object, they must give it up. They recall the words of St Theresa when a great lady who was about to enter her order said, 'Allow me, mother, to send for a Holy Bible to which I'm greatly attached.' 'Ah, you're attached to something! In that case, don't join our community!'

No one, whosoever she may be, is allowed to shut herself away, or to have a place of her own, a room. They live in open cells. When they encounter each other, one says, 'Praised and adored be the Most Blessed Sacrament of the altar!' The other responds, 'For ever and ever.' The same ritual when one taps at another's door. Hardly has the door been touched when a soft voice on the other side is heard saying quickly, 'For ever and ever!' Like all practices, this becomes mechanical by force of habit, and one sometimes says 'For ever and ever' before the other has had time to say 'Praised and adored be the Most Blessed Sacrament of the altar', which is quite a mouthful.

Among the Sisters of the Visitation, the one who enters says 'Ave Maria', and the one whose cell is entered says 'Gratia plena'. This is their greeting, which is indeed 'full of grace'.

At each hour of the day the convent's church bell strikes an extra three times. At this signal, prioress, vocal mothers, professed nuns, lay sisters, novices, postulants, interrupt what they are saying, what they are doing or what they are thinking, and all say in unison, if it is five o'clock, for instance, 'At five o'clock and at every hour, praised and adored be the Most Blessed Sacrament of the altar!' If it is eight o'clock, 'At eight o'clock and at every hour', and so on, according to whatever time it is.

This practice, which is intended to train the mind and to keep bringing it back to God, exists in many communities. Only the formula varies. So at the Infant Jesus convent they say, 'At this hour and at every hour may the love of Jesus burn in my heart!'

The Bernardine-Benedictines of Martin Verga, cloistered in Petit-Picpus fifty years ago, intone the offices in a low-pitched simple plain-chant, and always at full volume throughout the office. Wherever in the missal there is an asterisk they pause and say under their breath, 'Jesus – Mary – Joseph'. For the office of the dead they adopt a tone so deep that women's voices are hardly capable of descending so low. The effect this creates is thrilling and tragic.

The nuns of Petit-Picpus had had a crypt made under their high altar in which to bury members of their community. 'The government', as they would say, does not allow this crypt to house coffins. So they left the convent when they died. This grieved and dismayed them as a violation of their vows.

They did manage to get permission to be buried at a special time and in a special corner of the old Vaugirard Cemetery, which was on land that had formerly belonged to their community. A poor consolation.

On Thursdays the nuns attend high mass, vespers and all the offices, as on Sunday. They scrupulously observe as well all the minor feast days, practically unknown to secular people, of which the Church used to have so many in France, and still does in Spain and Italy. Their vigils in chapel are interminable. As for the number and duration of their prayers, we can give no better an idea of them than to quote the ingenuous remark of one of the sisters: 'The prayers of the postulants are fearsome, the prayers of the novices even worse, and the prayers of the professed nuns worse still.'

The chapter assembles once a week: the prioress presides, the vocal mothers are present. Each sister in turn comes and kneels on the stone floor and confesses aloud, in the presence of all, the transgressions and sins she has committed during the week. The vocal mothers confer after each confession and impose the penance for all to hear.

Apart from the confession made aloud, for which all transgressions of any seriousness are reserved, they have for their venial offences what they call 'the admission of guilt'. To make an admission of guilt means to lie prostrate in front of the prioress until the latter, who is only ever addressed as 'notre mère', notifies the culprit by a little tap on the wood of her stall that she may rise. The admission of guilt is made for the most trifling thing. A broken glass, a torn veil, unintentionally arriving a few seconds late for an office, a false note sung in church, et cetera, is all it takes, and an admission of guilt is made. The admission of guilt is entirely spontaneous. It is the culprit herself who is her own judge and inflicts it on herself. On feast days and Sundays there are four mother precentors who chant the offices before a large four-sided lectern. One day one of the mother precentors intoned a psalm that began with 'Ecce', and instead of 'Ecce' she voiced aloud these three notes: doh te soh. For this inattentiveness she made an admission of guilt that lasted the entire service. What made her offence an enormity was that the chapter had laughed.

When a nun, even the prioress herself, is summoned to the parlour, she lowers her veil so that, remember, only her mouth is visible.

The prioress alone may communicate with strangers. The others may see only their immediate family, and that very rarely. If by chance any outside person applies to see a nun they have known or loved in the outside world, extensive negotiations are required. If it is a woman, permission may sometimes be granted. The nun comes and the visitor speaks to her through the shutters, which are opened only for a mother or a sister. It goes without saying that permission is always refused to men.

Such is the Rule of St Benedict under Martin Verga's strict observance.

These nuns are not cheerful, rosy and fresh-faced as the daughters of other orders often are. They are pale and solemn. Between 1825 and 1830 three of them went mad.

III
Austerities

The women are postulants for two years at least, often four, then four years as novices. It is rare that their final vows can be taken under the age of twenty-three or twenty-four. The Bernardine-Benedictines of Martin Verga do not accept widows in their order.

In their cells they subject themselves to many secret mortifications, of which they must never speak.

On the day that a novice makes her profession she is beautifully arrayed, her hair is brushed to a shine and curled and dressed with white roses. Then she prostrates herself. A great black veil is thrown over her, and the office for the dead is sung. Then the nuns divide into two columns, one passes close by her, saying sorrowfully, 'Our sister is dead', and the other responds in a ringing voice, 'Alive in Jesus Christ!'

At the time when this story takes place, a boarding-school was attached to the convent. A boarding-school for young girls of noble and mostly wealthy families, notable among whom were Mademoiselle de Sainte-Aulaire and Mademoiselle de Bélissen, and an English girl bearing the illustrious Catholic name of Talbot. These young girls, raised in isolation by these nuns, grew up with a horror of the world and of the age. One of them said to us one day, 'The sight of street paving made me shudder from head to foot.' They were dressed in blue with white bonnets and a Holy Spirit cross of gilded silver or gilded copper pinned to their breasts. On certain major feast days, particularly St Martha's Day, as a great favour and supreme delight they were allowed to dress as nuns and to perform the offices and observances of St Benedict for a whole day. In earlier days the nuns would lend them their black robes. This seemed profane, and the prioress forbade it. Only the novices were allowed to make this loan. It is remarkable that these activities, no doubt tolerated and encouraged in the convent in a secret spirit of proselytism and in order to give these children a foretaste of the blessed habit, were a real delight and a genuine pleasure for the boarders. They quite simply enjoyed themselves. 'It was something new, it made a change for them.' Innocent, childish reasons that do not actually succeed in making us worldlings comprehend the joy of holding in your hand a holy-water sprinkler and standing for hours on end singing in groups of four at a lectern.

Austerities aside, the pupils abided by all the rituals of the convent. There was a certain young woman who went out into the world and after several years of marriage had not yet managed to shed the habit of saying instantly every time anyone knocked at her door, 'For ever and ever'! Like the nuns, the pupils saw only their relatives in the parlour. Not even their mothers were granted permission to kiss them. This is how strictly that rule was enforced: One day a young girl received a visit from her mother, accompanied by a little sister, aged three. The young girl wept, for she very much wanted to embrace her sister. Impossible. She begged that at least the child might be allowed to put her little hand through the bars so that she could kiss it. This was refused, almost with a sense of moral outrage.

IV
Gladness

These young girls have nonetheless filled this grim house with charming memories.

At certain times childhood lit up this cloister. The bell for recreation rang. A door swung on its hinges. The birds said, 'Good! Here come the children!' An irruption of youth burst into that garden with a cross-shape marked out on it like a shroud. Radiant faces, clear brows, innocent eyes full of cheerful brightness, all sorts of budding charms darted among these shadows. Breaking out abruptly, after the chanting, the ringing of bells, the chiming, the tolling, the offices, was this sound of little girls, sweeter than the sound of bees. The hive of joy opened, and each one brought her honey to it. They played, they called out to each other, they clustered in groups, they ran about. Pretty little white teeth chattered in corners. Veils superintended the laughter from afar, shadows oversaw the rays of sunshine, but they did not mind. They shone brightly and they laughed. Those four gloomy walls had their moment of bedazzlement. Faintly illuminated by the reflection of so much joy, they watched this delightful swarming flurry. It was like a shower of rose petals amid all this mournfulness. The young girls frolicked under the gaze of the nuns. The watchful eye of sinlessness does not bother innocence. Thanks to these children, among so many austere hours there was an hour of artless simplicity. The little ones skipped, the older ones danced. In this cloister, play was combined with the heavenly. Nothing was so enchanting and awesome as all these pure and radiant souls. Homer would have come here to laugh with Perrault, and there was in this dark garden such youth, well-being, noise, cries, giddiness, pleasure and happiness as to cheer all their female forebears, whether of epic or fairy-tale, the high-born and the humble, from Hecuba to Little Red Riding Hood's grandmother.

In that house, more than anywhere else perhaps, were heard some of those childish sayings that are always so charming and give rise to amusement that is deeply thought-provoking. It was within those four grim walls that a child of five exclaimed one day: 'Mother! One of the big girls has just told me I only have to be here another nine years and ten months. What a blessing!'

It was here, too, that this memorable dialogue took place:

A vocal mother: 'Why are you crying, my child?'

The child (aged six): 'I told Alix I knew my French history. She says I don't know it, but I do.'

Alix (the older girl, aged nine): 'No, she doesn't.'

The mother: 'Explain yourself, my child.'

Alix: 'She told me to open the book at random and to ask her any question in the book and she'd answer it.'

'Well?'

'She didn't answer it.'

'Come now, what did you ask her?'

'I opened the book at random, just as she said, and I asked her the first question I came across.'

'And what question was that?'

'It was "What happened next?"'

Here it was that this profound remark was made about a rather greedy parakeet that belonged to a resident noblewoman: 'Isn't that clever? It eats the jam and butter off the top of its slice of bread, just like a person!'

Here, on one of the flagstones of this cloister, was where this confession was found, written out beforehand, so that she would not forget it, by a seven-year-old sinner:

> Father, I confess to being guilty of avarice.
> Father, I confess to being guilty of adultery.
> Father, I confess to being guilty of having raised my eyes and looked at gentlemen.

And it was on one of the grassy banks in this garden that blue-eyed four- to five-year-olds listened to this tale from the pink lips of an inventive six-year-old: 'There were three little cockerels who came from a place where there were plenty of flowers. They picked the flowers and put them in their pockets. After that they picked the leaves and put them in their toys. There was a wolf near by and there were lots of woods. And the wolf was in the woods. And he ate the little cockerels.'

Then there was this poem:

> Somebody used a truncheon.
> It was Punch who hit the cat with it.
> It didn't do the cat any good, it hurt.
> So a lady put Punch in prison.

Here, an abandoned child, a little foundling the convent was raising out of charity, uttered these sweet, heart-rending words. She heard the others talking about their mothers and she murmured in her corner, 'Well, my mother wasn't there when I was born!'

There was a stout extern nun, always to be seen hurrying along the corridors with her bunch of keys, whose name was Soeur Agathe. The 'big girls' – older than ten – called her Agathocles*.

The refectory, a large rectangular room with no other light coming into it except from a covered arcade at garden level, was dark and damp and, as children say, full of creepy-crawlies. All the neighbouring areas supplied their own contingents of insects. For each of its four corners the girls had a special, suggestive name. There was Spiders' Corner, Caterpillars' Corner, Woodlice's Corner and Crickets' Corner. Crickets' Corner was near the kitchen and was highly rated. It was less cold there than elsewhere. From the refectory the names had transferred to the boarding-school and served to distinguish four nations, as in the old Collège Mazarin. Each pupil belonged to one of these four nations, depending on the corner of the refectory in which she sat at mealtimes. One day the arch-bishop, on a pastoral visit, saw a pretty little girl, all rosy-complexioned with lovely blonde hair, enter the classroom while he was there. He asked another pupil, a charming fresh-cheeked brunette near by:

'What little girl is that?'

'She's a spider, Monseigneur.'

'Oh! And that one over there?'

'She's a cricket.'

'And that one?'

'She's a caterpillar.'

'Really! And you?'

'I'm a woodlouse, Monseigneur.'

Every house of this kind has its own idiosyncrasies. At the beginning of this century Écouen was one of those elegant and imposing places where young girls spend their childhood in almost majestic seclusion. At Écouen, depending on the girls' places in the procession of the Blessed Sacrament, a distinction was made between 'virgins' and flower-bearers. There were also 'canopies', carrying the cords of the canopy, and 'censers', censing the Blessed Sacrament. The flowers rightfully fell to the flower-bearers. Four 'virgins' led the procession. On the morning of that great day it was not unusual to hear the question being asked in the dormitory, 'Who's a virgin?'

Madame Campan used to quote a 'junior', aged seven, talking to a 'senior', aged sixteen, who was leading the procession while she, the junior, followed behind: 'You're a virgin but I'm not.'

---

* The ancient Greek name as in, for instance, Agathocles of Syracuse, in French is Agathoclès, pronounced *Agathe-aux-clés*, meaning 'Agatha with the keys'.

V
Diversions

Above the door of the refectory was inscribed in large black letters this prayer, called the White Paternoster, which had the power to send people straight to paradise:

Little white Paternoster that God made, that God said, that God placed in paradise. When I went to bed at night I found three angels lying there, one at the foot and two at the head, and between them the Blessed Virgin Mary, who told me to lie there, to have no fear. God is my father, the Blessed Virgin is my mother, the three apostles are my brothers, the three virgins are my sisters. The shirt that God was born in wraps my body. St Margaret's cross is drawn on my breast. Our Lady went walking through the meadows, weeping for Our Lord, and met St John. 'Where have you been, St John?' 'I was at Ave Salus.' 'You didn't see the good Lord there?' 'He's on the tree of the Cross, with his feet dangling, with his hands nailed down, with a little crown of hawthorn on his head.' Whoever recites this three times in the evening, and three times in the morning, will go to paradise when they die.

In 1827 this particular prayer had disappeared from the wall under a triple coat of whitewash. It has almost faded from the memory of a few young girls of that time who today are old women.

A large crucifix hanging on the wall completed the decoration of this refectory, whose only door, we believe we have already mentioned, opened on to the garden. Two narrow tables, each flanked by two wooden benches, formed two long parallel lines running from one end of the refectory to the other. The walls were white, the tables were black. These two colours of mourning constitute the only alternatives in a convent. The meals were unappetising and even the children's food was austere. A single dish, of meat and vegetables combined, or salt fish – this was luxury. And this plain fare, reserved for the pupils alone, was an exception. The children ate in silence under the eye of the mother on duty who, if a fly dared to buzz around in defiance of the rule, would noisily open and shut a wooden book from time to time. This silence was seasoned with the lives of the saints, read aloud from a little chair with a book-rest that stood at the foot of the crucifix. The reader was one of the senior girls, a different one each week. Set at regular intervals along the bare tables were glazed bowls in which the pupils washed their own mugs and cutlery, and into which they sometimes threw the odd scrap, tough meat or spoiled fish. This was punished. These bowls were called 'water basins'.

Any child who broke the silence made 'a cross for busy tongues'. Where? On the floor. She licked the pavement. The dust, to which all joys must come, was made to punish those poor little rose petals guilty of chattering.

There was in the convent a book of which only one copy has ever been printed and which it is forbidden to read. It is the Rule of St Benedict. A secret text that no profane eye should be allowed to see. *Nemo regulas, seu constitutiones nostras, externis communicabit.* *

One day the pupils succeeded in appropriating this book and began to read it avidly, their reading often interrupted by their dread of being caught, which kept making them slam the volume shut. From the great risk they had taken they derived only limited pleasure. A few unintelligible pages about the sins of young boys, that was the 'most interesting' thing they got out of it.

They played in the garden on a path lined with a few scraggy fruit trees. Notwithstanding the intense surveillance and the severity of the punishments, when the wind had shaken the trees they sometimes managed to filch an unripe apple or a spoiled apricot or a maggoty pear. A letter I have before me, a letter written twenty-five years ago by a former pupil, today one of the most elegant women in Paris, Madame la Duchesse de X, may be allowed to speak for itself. I quote verbatim: 'You hide your pear or your apple as best you can. When you go up to put the bedcover on before supper, you stuff them under your pillow and at night you eat them in bed, and when you cannot do that, you eat them in the privy.' This was one of their keenest pleasures.

On one occasion, again it was when the archbishop was visiting the convent, one of the young girls, Mademoiselle Bouchard, who had some connection with the Montmorency family, made a bet that she would ask for a day's holiday, unthinkable in so austere a community. The bet was accepted, but not one of those who made the bet with her believed she would do it. When the moment came, as the archbishop was passing in front of the pupils, to the indescribable horror of her companions Mademoiselle Bouchard stepped out of line and said, 'Monseigneur, a day's holiday.' Mademoiselle Bouchard was tall and radiant with the prettiest rosy little face in the world. Monsieur de Quélen smiled and said, 'My dear child, a day's holiday! By all means! Three days, if it please you. I grant three days.' The prioress could do nothing about it, the archbishop had spoken. To the convent's indignation but the boarding-school's delight. Telling responses.

This forbidding cloister was not so isolated behind its walls, how-

* 'No one shall divulge our rule or regulations to any outsiders.'

446

ever, that the life of the outside world, its passions, drama, and even romance did not make their way inside. To prove this, simply as a matter of record we will briefly describe a true and incontestable incident that in itself, it must be added, has no bearing on the story we are relating and no connection with it whatsoever. We mention this incident to complete the reader's mental picture of what the convent was like.

So, around that time there was in the convent a mysterious person, named Madame Albertine, who was not a nun and was treated with great respect. Nothing was known about her except that she was mad, and in the outside world she was thought to be dead. It was said that behind this story lay hasty arrangements that had had to be made for the sake of an important marriage.

This woman, of no more than thirty, dark-haired and rather beautiful, had a vacant look in her big dark eyes. Could she see? It was doubtful. She glided rather than walked. She never spoke. No one was quite sure whether or not she breathed. She had the pinched and blue-tinged nostrils of one who has already breathed her last. To touch her hand was like touching snow. She had a strange spectral gracefulness. Wherever she went, she brought a chill. One day a nun, seeing her go by, said to another sister, 'She's thought to be dead.' 'Perhaps she is,' replied the other.

Countless tales were told about Madame Albertine. She was the object of the pupils' perpetual curiosity. There was a gallery in the chapel called the Bull's-Eye. It was in this gallery, which had just one round window, a bull's-eye, that Madame Albertine attended the divine offices. She was usually on her own because from this gallery on the first floor it was possible to see the preacher or officiating priest, which was forbidden to the nuns. One day a young priest of noble birth spoke from the pulpit – Monsieur le Duc de Rohan, peer of France, an officer of the king's musketeers when he was Prince de Léon in 1815, and who died, after 1830, a cardinal and archbishop of Besançon. This was the first time Monsieur de Rohan had preached at the Petit-Picpus convent. Madame Albertine normally followed the sermons and services with a profound calm and in complete stillness. That day, as soon as she caught sight of Monsieur de Rohan, she half rose to her feet and said out loud in the silence of the chapel, 'Well, I never! Auguste!' The whole astounded community turned round, the preacher looked up, but Madame Albertine had fallen back motionless again. An intimation of the outside world, a glimmer of life, had momentarily passed across that cold and lifeless face, then all was gone, and the mad woman became a corpse again.

In the convent, however, those few words set wagging every tongue that could talk. What significance in that 'Well, I never! Auguste!' What revelations! Monsieur de Rohan's name was indeed Auguste. It was obvious that Madame Albertine came from the most elevated society since she knew Monsieur de Rohan, that she herself had been of high rank since she spoke so familiarly of such an important nobleman, and that there was some relationship between them, a family tie perhaps, but surely a very close relationship since she knew his first name.

Two very stern duchesses, Madame de Choiseul and Madame de Sérent, often visited the community, given access no doubt by virtue of the privilege of *Magnates mulieres**, and they brought terror to the school. All the poor young girls trembled and lowered their eyes when these two old ladies passed by.

Anyway, Monsieur de Rohan was the unwitting object of the girls' attention. At that time he had just been appointed vicar-general to the archbishop of Paris, pending a bishopric. It was one of his practices to come quite often and sing the offices in the Petit-Picpus nuns' chapel. None of the young recluses could see him because of the serge curtain, but he had a sweet and rather high-pitched voice they had learned to recognize and to single out. He had been a musketeer. And also, he was said to be extremely good-looking, with lovely chestnut-brown hair, in its rounded style very handsomely framing his head, and to have a magnificent broad black sash and the most elegantly cut black cassock. He kept the imaginations of all these sixteen-year-olds greatly occupied.

Not a sound from without made its way into the convent. But there was one year when the strains of a flute infiltrated it. This was an event, and the pupils of the time still remember it.

It was a flute that someone was playing near by. This flute always played the same tune, a tune very remote from the present, 'My Zétulbé, come reign o'er my soul', and it was to be heard two or three times a day.

The young girls spent hours listening to it, the vocal mothers became distraught, minds were exercised, punishments proliferated. This went on for several months. The girls were all more or less in love with the unknown musician. Each one dreamed that she was Zétulbé. The

---

* Citing an ordinance of 1207 by 'the legate Odo', Hugo uses this formula in fuller detail in *The Hunchback of Notre-Dame* (bk IV, ch. 5): '*aliquae magnates mulieres, quae sine scandolo evitari non possunt*' (some great ladies who cannot be refused without scandal).

sound of the flute came from the direction of Rue Droit-Mur. They would have given all, risked all, attempted all, to see if only for a second, to glimpse, to clap eyes on the 'young man' who played that flute so delightfully and who, without suspecting it, played on all these souls at the same time. There were some girls who slipped out by a service entrance and climbed up to the third floor on Rue Droit-Mur to try to see through the skylights. Impossible! One even thrust her arm through the grating above her head and waved her white handkerchief. Two were yet more audacious. They found a way up to a roof and ventured out on to it, and finally managed to see 'the young man'. He was a blind old émigré, a ruined gentleman, playing the flute in his garret in order to pass the time.

VI
The Little Convent

Within the precincts of the Petit-Picpus there were three totally distinct buildings, the main convent inhabited by the nuns, the boarding-school where the pupils dwelt, and lastly what was called 'the little convent'. This was a separate building with a garden, and there, living together, were all kinds of aged nuns from various orders, survivors of religious foundations destroyed by the Revolution, a collection of all the motley blacks, greys and whites of all possible communities and all possible varieties: what might be called, if such a coupling of words is permissible, a kind of harlequin convent.

From the days of the Empire all these poor dispersed and exiled women were allowed to come and take shelter here under the wings of the Bernardine-Benedictines. The government paid them a small pension, the Petit-Picpus nuns willingly took them in. It was a strange farrago. Each one followed her own rule. Sometimes the pupils from the boarding-school were allowed as a great treat to visit them, which is why those young minds have preserved a memory of Mère St-Basile, Mère Ste-Scolastique and Mère Jacob, among others.

One of these refugees was almost at home here. She was a nun of Ste-Aure, the only one of her order who had survived. At the beginning of the eighteenth century the nuns of Ste-Aure's old convent occupied this very house in Petit-Picpus that later belonged to the Benedictines of Martin Verga. Too poor to wear the magnificent habit of her order, which was a white robe with a scarlet scapulary, this saintly woman had piously dressed a little doll in it, which she loved to show off and bequeathed to the house when she died. In 1824 there was only one remaining nun of this order. Now all that remains of it is the doll.

Apart from these venerable nuns, some elderly society women had, like Madame Albertine, obtained permission of the prioress to come and live in retirement in the little convent. Among their number were Madame de Beaufort d'Hautpoul and Madame la Marquise Dufresne. Another was only ever known in the convent by the tremendous noise she made when she blew her nose. The pupils called her Madame Vacarmini*.

Around 1820 or 1821, Madame de Genlis, who was at that time publishing a small periodical called *L'Intrépide*, applied to take up residence in the Petit-Picpus convent. Monsieur le Duc d'Orléans recommended her. The hive was abuzz, the vocal mothers all aflutter. Madame de Genlis had written novels. But she declared that she was the first to abominate them, and besides, she was now in her fiercely devout phase. With the help of God, and of the prince too, she was admitted. She left after six or eight months, giving as her reason that there was no shade in the garden. The nuns were charmed by her. Although very old, she still played the harp, and extremely well.

When she went, she left her mark in her cell. Madame de Genlis was superstitious and a Latinist. These two words give a fairly good insight into her. Still visible a few years ago, stuck on the inside of a little cupboard in her cell in which she kept her silverware and her jewels locked up, were these five lines in Latin, written in her own hand in red ink on yellow paper, which in her opinion possessed the power to ward off robbers:

> *Imparibus meritis pendent tria corpora ramis:*
> *Dismas et Gesmas, media est divina potestas;*
> *Alta petit Dismas, infelix, infima, Gesmas;*
> *Nos et res nostras conservet summa potestas.*
> *Hos versus dicas, ne tu furto tua perdas.*†

---

* A character in *La Musicomanie* (Music Mania), an anonymous one-act comedy first staged in 1779, Vacarmini is an Italian whose name, constructed from the noun *vacarme*, meaning 'din', 'uproar', to which an italianizing ending has been added, is intended to present him in a ludicrous light.
† 'Three bodies of unequal merit hang from the branches: / Dismas and Gesmas and the divinity between them. / Dismas seeks the highest, wretched Gesmas the lowest. / May the Almighty protect us and our belongings. / Recite this verse that you might not lose your belongings by theft.' In an apocryphal text the two thieves crucified with Christ are named as Dismas and Gesmas, Dismas being the unnamed penitent thief in Luke 23:39–43.

These verses in sixth-century Latin raise the question whether the two thieves on Calvary were called Dismas and Gestas, as is commonly believed, or Dismas and Gesmas. The latter spelling might have undermined claims by the Vicomte de Gestas in the last century to be descended from the bad thief. However, the useful properties attached to these verses are an article of faith in the order of Hospitaller Sisters.

The convent-house church, constructed in such a way as to act as a complete divide separating the main convent from the boarding-school, was of course shared by the boarding-school, the main convent and the little convent. Even the public was admitted, by a kind of lazaretto entrance giving access from the street. But all was so arranged that none of the inhabitants of the cloister should see any face from the outside world. Imagine a church where the choir had been seized by a gigantic hand and reshaped in such a way as to form not, as in ordinary churches, an extension behind the altar but a sort of room or secret recess to the right of the officiating priest. Imagine this room to be screened off by the seven-foot-high curtain we have already mentioned. Cram into the gloom behind this curtain, in wooden stalls, the nuns' choir on the left, the schoolgirls on the right, the lay sisters and novices at the back, and you will have some idea of the Petit-Picpus religious community attending divine service. That recess, which was called the choir, was connected to the cloister by a corridor. Light came into the church from the garden. When the nuns attended services at which their rule commanded them to be silent, the public was alerted to their presence only by the banging of the miserere seats in the choirstalls as they tipped up and down.

VII
Some Figures in the Gloom

In the six years between 1819 and 1825 the prioress of Petit-Picpus was Mademoiselle de Blemeur, whose religious name was Mère Innocente. She belonged to the family of Marguerite de Blemeur, author of *Lives of the Saints of the Order of St Benedict*. She had been re-elected. She was a woman of about sixty years of age, short, stout, 'with a dreadful singing voice', says the letter we have already quoted. Otherwise an excellent woman, and the only cheerful one in the whole convent, and for that reason adored.

Mère Innocente took after her forebear Marguerite, the Madame Dacier of the order. She was well read, learned, clever, able, a historian with a curious mind, crammed with Latin, stuffed with Greek, full of Hebrew, and perhaps more Benedictine in scholarship than in devotion.

The sub-prioress, Mère Cineres, was an old Spanish nun who was almost blind.

The most important of the vocal mothers were Mère Ste-Honorine, treasurer, Mère Ste-Gertrude, chief novice mistress, Mère-St-Ange, assistant mistress, Mère Annonciation, sacristan, Mère St-Augustin, nurse, the only ill-natured one in the whole convent; then Mère Ste-Mechtilde (Mademoiselle Gauvain), very young with a beautiful voice, Mère des Anges (Mademoiselle Drouet), who had been in the convent of the Filles-Dieu and in the Trésor convent between Gisors and Magny, Mère St-Joseph (Mademoiselle de Cogolludo), Mère Ste-Adélaïde (Mademoiselle d'Auverney), Mère Miséricorde (Mademoiselle de Cifuentes, who was unable to withstand the austerities), Mère Compassion (Mademoiselle de la Miltière, received into the order at the age of sixty despite the regulations, very wealthy), Mère Providence (Mademoiselle de Laudinière), Mère Présentation (Mademoiselle de Sigüenza), who became prioress in 1847; and lastly Mère Ste-Céligne (sister of the sculptor Ceracchi), who went mad, and Mère Ste-Chantal (Mademoiselle de Suzon), who also went mad.

Still among the prettiest was a charming girl of twenty-three from Île Bourbon, a descendant of Chevalier Roze, who in the outside world was called Mademoiselle Roze and here took the name Mère Assomption.

Mère Ste-Mechtilde, who was in charge of singing and of the choir, was happy to include the pupils. She usually took a full set of them, that is to say seven, from ten to sixteen years old inclusive, an assortment of voices and sizes, and she would have them sing standing side by side in order of age, from the youngest to the oldest. This presented viewers with, as it were, a syrinx of young girls, a sort of living Pan pipe made of angels.

The lay sisters whom the pupils liked best were Soeur Ste-Euphrasie, Soeur Ste-Marguerite, Soeur Ste-Marthe, who was in her dotage, and Soeur Ste-Michel, whose long nose made them laugh.

All these women were kindly towards all these children. The nuns were hard only on themselves. There was no fire lit except in the school, and here the food was choice compared with that in the convent. Not to mention many other little comforts the nuns provided. Yet when a child passed close to a nun and spoke to her, the nun would never reply.

The effect of this rule of silence was that throughout the convent the power of speech had been withdrawn from human beings and given to inanimate objects. Sometimes it was the church bell that spoke, sometimes it was the gardener's bell. A very resonant gong-bell, placed beside the extern nun and audible all over the house, indicated by various sequences of bell-strokes, a kind of acoustic telegraph, all the daily activities that had to be performed, and if necessary it summoned to the parlour this or that occupant of the house. Each person and each thing had its own sequence. The prioress's was one and one, the sub-prioress's one and two. Six-five signalled the beginning of class, so that the pupils never talked of 'going to class' but of 'going to six-five'. Four-four was Madame de Genlis's sequence. It was very often heard. 'What a devil of a noise!'* said those who were uncharitable. Ten-nine bell-strokes announced a great event: the opening of the 'claustral door', a hideous slab of iron bristling with bolts, which turned on its hinges only for the archbishop.

As we have said, he and the gardener excepted, no man entered the cloister. The pupils saw two others: one, the old and ugly chaplain, Abbé Banès, of whom they were afforded a view from the choir through a grille; the other, the drawing-master Monsieur Ansiaux, who, in that letter of which a few lines have already been read, is called Monsieur Anciot and is described as 'a frightful old hunchback'.

We can see that all these men were carefully chosen.

Such was this peculiar house.

VIII
Post Corda Lapides†

After that brief outline of its spiritual composition, a few words giving some idea of its physical layout will not come amiss. The reader already has some idea of it.

The convent of Petit-Picpus-St-Antoine filled almost the whole of the vast quadrilateral marked out by the intersections of Rue Poncleau, Rue Droit-Mur, Petite-Rue-Picpus and the dead-end alleyway named on old maps as Rue Aumarais. These four streets

---

* In the French text, 'C'est le diable à quatre'. With Madame de Genlis's signature four rings in mind, Hugo here is playing on the expression *faire le diable à quatre*, meaning 'to create a great deal of noise and disorder' and said to derive from medieval morality plays featuring four characters – the devil and his lieutenants.

† Latin: Literally, 'After the hearts, the stones.'

surrounded this quadilateral like a moat. The convent consisted of several buildings and a garden. The main building, taken as a whole, was an assemblage of juxtaposed hybrid constructions that viewed from above had almost the exact shape of a gallows laid flat on the ground. The upright beam of the gallows occupied the whole of the stretch of Rue Droit-Mur between Petite-Rue-Picpus and Rue Polonceau. The short horizontal beam was a tall, grey, austere grilled façade on Petite-Rue-Picpus; carriage entrance no. 62 marked the end of it. Towards the centre of this façade was a low arched doorway, white with dust and ash, where spiders wove their webs and which opened only for an hour or two on Sundays and on the rare occasions when a nun's coffin left the convent. This was the public entrance to the church. The elbow of the gibbet was a square room used as a storeroom, which the nuns called 'the pantry'. In the main beam were the cells of the mothers, sisters and novices, in the short beam the kitchens, the refectory with the cloister behind it, and the church. Between entrance no. 62 and the corner of the closed-off Aumarais alleyway was the boarding-school, which could not be seen from without. The rest of the trapezoid quadrilateral formed the garden, which lay at a much lower level than Rue Polonceau. This meant the walls were a great deal higher on the inside than on the outside. The slightly cambered garden had at its centre on top of a mound a splendid fir tree, spiring and conical, from which radiated as from the peaked boss of a shield four wide paths, and laid out in pairs between the main radii were eight narrow paths, so that if the walled space had been circular the geometrical plan of these avenues and paths would have resembled a wheel overlaid with a cross. The paths, all ending at the very irregular walls of the garden, were of unequal length. They were bordered with currant bushes. At the bottom of the garden an avenue of tall poplars ran from the ruins of the old convent at the corner of Rue Droit-Mur to the little convent building at the corner of the Aumarais alleyway. In front of the little convent was what was called 'the little garden'. Add to this complex a courtyard, all kinds of various angles formed by the main buildings on the inside, prison-like walls, and for sole outlook and sole neighbourly presence the long black line of roofs bordering the other side of Rue Polonceau, and you will be able to form a complete mental picture of what the Bernardine convent of Petit-Picpus was forty years ago. This saintly house was built on the very site of a famous real-tennis court, dating from the fourteenth to the sixteenth century, that used to be called 'the eleven thousand devils' playground'.

As a matter of fact, all these streets were among the most ancient in Paris. The names – Droit-Mur and Aumarais – are very old; the streets that bear them are even older. Ruelle Aumarais was once called Ruelle Maugout, Rue Droit-Mur was once called Rue des Églantiers, for God brought forth flowers before man cut stone.*

IX
A Century under the Veil

Since we are giving details about what the Petit-Picpus convent once was, and since we have dared to open a window on that quiet sanctuary, the reader may allow us another small digression, unconnected with the substance of this book but telling, and helpful in making clear that even the cloister has its eccentric characters.

In the little convent there was a centenarian who came from Fontevrault Abbey. Before the Revolution she had even moved in court circles. She talked a great deal about Monsieur de Miromesnil, Keeper of the Seals under Louis XVI, and the wife of a Président Duplat, with whom she had been very intimate. It gave her pleasure and flattered her vanity to drop these two names all the time. She extolled the wonders of Fontevrault Abbey, saying it was like a town, and there were streets inside the monastery.

She spoke with a Picardy accent that amused the girls. Every year she solemnly renewed her vows, and when that moment came she would say to the priest, 'Monseigneur St François made his profession of vows to Monseigneur St Julien, Monseigneur St Julien made his to Monseigneur St Eusebius, Monseigneur St Eusebius made his to Monseigneur St Procopius, and so on and so forth, and now, mon père, it's my turn to take advantage of you.' And the girls would giggle, not up their sleeves but behind their veils, charming little stifled giggles that made the vocal mothers frown.†

On another occasion the centenarian was telling stories. She said that 'in her youth the Bernardine monks were a match for the musketeers'. That was the voice of a century speaking – the eighteenth century. She spoke of the custom, in Champagne and Burgundy, of the four wines. Before the Revolution whenever a person of distinction, a marshal of France, a prince, a duke and peer of the realm, passed through a town in Burgundy or Champagne, the city fathers would

---

* *Droit-Mur* means 'straight wall'. *Églantier* is the sweet briar, or wild rose.
† The nun's quaintness of expression, using the verb *bailler*, 'to give' or 'to pledge', which has a chivalric resonance, becomes comic when she inadvertently uses the verb in a turn of phrase that has a decidedly colloquial ring to it, suggesting deception.

come and greet him, and present him with four silver drinking-cups into which they had poured four different wines. On the first goblet an inscription read: 'monkey's wine'; on the second, 'lion's wine'; on the third, 'sheep's wine'; on the fourth, 'hog's wine'. These four legends expressed the four stages of intoxication through which the drunkard descends: the first, of merriment; the second, of ill temper; the third, of dullness; and the fourth, of brutishness.

She kept in a cupboard under lock and key a mysterious object she valued greatly. The rule of Fontevrault did not forbid this. She would not show this object to anyone. She used to closet herself away, which her rule allowed, and hide, whenever she wanted to contemplate it. If she heard a footstep in the corridor she would close the cupboard again as quickly as her old hands would permit. The moment the subject was raised with her, she who by nature was so willing to talk would fall silent. The most curious were baffled by her silence and the most persistent by her obstinacy. This was also a subject of gossip at any onset of idleness or boredom in the convent. What was this treasure belonging to the centenarian? What could be so precious and so secret? Some holy book, no doubt? Some priceless rosary? Some true relic? Speculation was rife. When the poor old woman died there was a greater rush to open her cupboard than was perhaps seemly. The object was found under three layers of cloth, like a consecrated paten. It was a Faenza dish representing little cupids taking flight, pursued by apothecaries' assistants armed with enormous syringes. The chase abounds in grimaces and comical postures. One of the charming little cupids is already well spiked. He is resisting, fluttering his tiny wings and still trying to fly, but the medic is laughing with satanic laughter. Moral: love conquered by the colic. This dish, a very curious one in fact, and one that possibly had the distinction of inspiring Molière, was still in existence in September 1845. It was for sale in a curiosity shop on Boulevard Beaumarchais.

This dear old lady did not want to receive any visits from the outside world because, she said, 'the parlour's too gloomy'.

X

The Origin of Perpetual Adoration

That almost sepulchral parlour, of which we have attempted to give some idea, is in any case an entirely local peculiarity that is not reproduced with the same severity in other convents. At the convent in Rue du Temple, in particular, which in truth belonged to another order, the black shutters were replaced by brown curtains; and the parlour itself was a salon with parquet flooring whose windows were framed by white muslin curtains and on whose walls all kinds of pictures were allowed – a portrait of a Benedictine nun with her face uncovered, painted bouquets and even a Turk's head.

The garden of the convent in Rue du Temple was where that famous horse-chestnut tree stood that was considered the finest and largest in France and among the good people of the eighteenth century had the reputation of being 'the ancestor of all the chestnut trees in the realm'.

As we have said, this convent in the Temple district housed Benedictines of Perpetual Adoration, Benedictines quite different from those related to Cîteaux. Their order of Perpetual Adoration is not very old, going back no more than two hundred years. In 1649 the Blessed Sacrament was desecrated on two occasions, a few days apart, in two churches in Paris, St-Sulpice and St-Jean-en-Grève, a rare and frightful sacrilege that shocked the whole city. Monsieur le prieur-grand vicaire of St-Germain-des-Prés ordered a solemn procession of all his clergy at which the papal nuncio officiated. But this expiation was insufficient for two venerable women, Madame Courtin, Marquise de Boucs, and the Comtesse de Châteauvieux. This outrage committed on 'the most sublime sacrament of the altar', though brief, preyed on these two saintly souls, and it seemed to them it could only be extenuated by 'Perpetual Adoration' in some monastic community of nuns. To this pious end both of them, one in 1652, the other in 1653, donated considerable sums of money to a Benedictine nun, Mère Catherine de Bar, known by the name of du St-Sacrement, for the purpose of founding a convent of the order of St Benedict. Permission for this foundation was first given to Mère Catherine de Bar by Monsieur de Metz, abbot of St-Germain, 'on condition that no woman might be admitted unless she contributed an income of three hundred francs a year, adding six thousand francs to the capital'. Following the abbot of St-Germain's lead, the king granted letters-patent, and in 1654 everything was ratified – abbot's charter and letters royal – by the court of accounts and by parliament.

Such were the origins and legal sanctification of the establishment of the Benedictines of Perpetual Adoration of the Blessed Sacrament in Paris. Their first convent was 'new-built' in Rue Cassette, with funds from Madame de Boucs and Madame de Châteauvieux.

As we can see, this order was not to be confused with the so-called Cistercian Benedictines. It came under the jurisdiction of the abbot of St-Germain-des-Prés in the same way that the nuns of the Sacred Heart come under the jurisdiction of the Jesuits' superior-general and the Sisters of Charity under that of the Lazarists' superior-general.

It was also completely different from the Bernardines of Petit-Picpus, the convent whose interior we have just described. In 1657 Pope Alexander VII, by special dispensation, authorized the Bernardines of Petit-Picpus to practise Perpetual Adoration like the Benedictine nuns of the Blessed Sacrament. But the two orders remained no less distinct.

XI
The End of the Petit-Picpus

Right from the start of the Restoration the Petit-Picpus convent was in decline, as part of the general demise of the order, which, like all religious orders after the eighteenth century, is disappearing. Contemplation, like prayer, is a human need. But like everything the Revolution has touched, it will change, and having been hostile to social progress it will become favourable to it.

The Petit-Picpus house was rapidly emptying. In 1840 the little convent was no more, the boarding-school was no more. There were no old women or young girls left. The former had died, the latter had gone away. *Volaverunt.**

The rule of Perpetual Adoration is so rigid, it is daunting. Vocations shrink from it, the order is not attracting recruits. In 1845 there were still the odd few here and there becoming lay sisters. But not cloistered nuns. Forty years ago the nuns numbered close on one hundred. Fifteen years ago they were no more than twenty-eight. How many are they today? In 1847 the prioress was young, a sign that the pool of choice is diminishing. She was not forty years old. As the number drops, the strain increases. What is required of each nun becomes more taxing. The day when there would be only a dozen bowed and aching shoulders to bear the heavy Rule of St Benedict could be seen approaching even then. The burden is relentless and remains the same, for few or for many. It is oppressive, it is overwhelming. And so they die. Two died in the days when the author of this book was still living in Paris. One was twenty-five years old, the other twenty-three – she, like Julia Alpinula, can say: *Hic jaceo. Vixi annos viginti et tres.*† It is because of this decline that the convent gave up educating girls.

We could not pass by this extraordinary unknown house of obscurity without entering it and taking inside our spiritual travelling companions, who are listening, maybe to the edification of some, as

---

* 'They have flown.'
† 'Here I lie. I lived twenty-three years.'

458

we tell our sad story of Jean Valjean. We have taken a look at this community, utterly steeped in those old practices that seem so novel today. This is the enclosed garden. *Hortus conclusus.* We have spoken of this remarkable place in detail, yet with respect, at least in so far as detail and respect are compatible. We do not understand everything, but we jeer at nothing. We are equally distant from the exaltations of Joseph de Maistre, who ends up sanctifying the executioner, and from the sneerings of Voltaire, who goes so far as to mock the crucifix.

A logical inconsistency on Voltaire's part, by the way, for Voltaire would have defended Jesus as he defended Calas. And even to those who deny supernatural incarnations, what does the crucifix represent? The killing of a man of wisdom.

In the nineteenth century religious thinking is undergoing a crisis. Some things can be unlearned, and rightly so, provided that when one thing is unlearned, another is learned. No vacuum in the human heart. Some demolitions occur, and a good thing too, but on condition that reconstruction follows.

Meanwhile, let us study things that are no more. We need to be familiar with them, if only to avoid them. The spurious things of the past assume false names and pass themselves off as the future. This spectre, the past, is liable to falsify its own passport. Let us be prepared for that pitfall. Let us be on our guard. The past has a face, superstition, and a mask, hypocrisy. Let us expose that face and tear off that mask.

As for convents, they pose a complicated question: a question of civilization, which condemns them, a question of liberty, which protects them.

BOOK SEVEN
PARENTHESIS

I
The Convent as Abstract Idea

This book is a drama whose main character is the infinite.

Man is the secondary character.

This being the case, since there was a convent along the way we had to enter it. Why? Because the convent, which is a feature of both East and West, of antiquity as well as of modern times, of paganism, Buddhism, Islam, as well as Christianity, is one of the optical devices through which man views the infinite.

This is not the place to develop certain ideas at unreasonable length; nevertheless, while abiding absolutely by our reservations, strictures and even censures, we must say that every time we encounter in man the infinite, well or ill understood, we have a feeling of respect. There is in the synagogue, the mosque, the pagoda, the wigwam, a hideous aspect that we loathe and a sublime aspect that we revere. What contemplation for the spirit and what boundless meditation – God reflected on the human wall!

II
The Convent as Historical Fact

From the viewpoint of history, reason and truth, monasticism is doomed.

When there are too many monasteries in a nation they are obstructions to the normal functioning of the system, otiose establishments, centres of idleness where centres of occupation should exist. Monastic communities are to the great social community what mistletoe is to the oak tree, what the wart is to the human body. Their prosperity and satisfied well-being are the land's impoverishment. Good in the first stage of civilizations, useful in bringing about the reduction of brutality through spirituality, the monastic regime is bad for nations in their maturity. Moreover, because it still continues to set the example when it grows lax and enters its era of dissoluteness, it becomes bad for all the reasons that made it beneficial in its era of untainted virtue.

Claustration has had its day. Useful in the early education of modern civilization, cloisters have been a hindrance to its growth and are harmful to its development. Good in the tenth century, debatable in the fifteenth, in the nineteenth century monasteries are detestable as an institution and as a method of cultivating human beings. The leprosy of monasticism has gnawed almost to the bone two great nations, Italy and Spain, one having been the beacon and the other the splendour of Europe for centuries, and at this present time these two illustrious peoples are only just beginning to recover, thanks to the healthy and vigorous therapy of 1789.

The convent, the old-fashioned convent for women in particular, as it still existed at the turn of this century in Italy, Austria and Spain, is one of the darkest manifestations of the Middle Ages. The cloister, that kind of cloister, is a point of intersection of diverse horrors. The Catholic cloister, properly speaking, is entirely filled with the black radiance of death.

The Spanish convent is the most dismal of all. There, beneath vaults filled with mists, beneath domes turbid with darkness, massive altars of Babel-like proportions rise in the gloom as high as cathedrals. There, enormous white crucifixes hang from chains in the shadows. There, stretched out naked on ebony, are great ivory Christs, not just blood-stained but bleeding, hideous and magnificent, with the bones of their elbows showing, the sinews of their knee-caps showing, the flesh of their wounds showing, crowned with silver thorns, nailed with nails of gold, with rubies for drops of blood on their brows and diamond tears in their eyes. The diamonds and rubies look wet, and elicit mourning from veiled figures in the darkness below, their sides sore from the hair shirt and the iron-tipped scourge, their breasts crushed in wicker cages, their knees chafed raw with prayer, women who think they are wives, spectres who think they are seraphs. Do these women think? No. Do they have any desire? No. Do they love? No. Do they live? No. Their nerves have turned to bone, their bones to stone. Their veil is woven darkness. Their breath beneath the veil is like some tragic exhalation of death. A ghost, the abbess sanctifies them and terrifies them. The immaculate is there, with a vengeance. Such are Spain's old monasteries. Dens of terrible devotion, lairs of virgins, savage places.

Catholic Spain was more Roman than Rome herself. The Spanish convent was the epitome of the Catholic convent. There was a touch of the oriental about it. The archbishop, the kizlar-agha* of heaven, kept confined and under surveillance this seraglio of souls reserved for God. The nun was the odalisque, the priest the eunuch. The devotees

---

* Turkish: Literally, 'lord of the girls', the chief black eunuch of the Ottoman sultan's harem.

were chosen in a dream and had possession of Christ. At night the handsome, naked young man came down from the cross and became the ecstasy of the convent cell. Guarded by high walls from all living distraction, the sultana-mystic had the crucified one for her sultan. One glance outside was an infidelity. The *in pace** replaced the leather sack. That which was cast into the sea in the East was cast under ground in the West. In both places women flailed their arms: for those, the waves; for these, a dungeon, on the one hand the drowned, on the other the buried. Monstrous parallel.

Unable to deny these things, the defenders of the past now shrug them off with a smile. A strange and convenient way of suppressing the revelations of history, of invalidating the interpretations of philosophy, of evading all disturbing facts and all serious questions, has become fashionable. Black propaganda, say the shrewd. Black propaganda, repeat the inane. Jean-Jacques a propagandist, Diderot a propagandist, Voltaire, on Calas, Labarre and Sirven, a propagandist. Someone has recently discovered that Tacitus was a propagandist, Nero was a victim, and really 'that poor Holofernes' deserves to be pitied.

Facts, however, are not easy to confound, and they remain obstinate. The author of this book has seen with his own eyes, twenty miles from Brussels, like something out of the Middle Ages, still there within everyone's reach at Villers Abbey, the manhole entrance to the oubliettes in the middle of the meadow that used to be the cloister's courtyard, and on the banks of the River Dyle four stone dungeons, half under ground, half under water. These were the *in pace*. Each of these dungeons has the remains of an iron door, a latrine, and a small grated window that on the outside is two feet above the river and on the inside six feet above the ground. A four-foot depth of river flows past the outside wall. The ground is always waterlogged. The occupant of the *in pace* had this waterlogged ground for his bed. In one of these dungeons there is a fragment of a neck iron riveted to the wall. In another, you can see a kind of square box made of four slabs of granite, too short for anyone to lie down in, too low to stand upright in. A human being was put inside this with a stone lid on top. This exists. You can see it. You can touch it. These *in pace*, these dungeons, these iron hinges, these neck shackles, this little high window with the river flowing right underneath it, this stone box sealed with a granite lid like a tomb, with this difference, that here the dead man was alive, this muddy ground, this latrine hole, these seeping walls – what propaganda!

* The Latin 'in peace', used to refer to a monastic prison cell.

On What Conditions We Can Respect the Past

For civilization, monasticism as it existed in Spain and as it still exists in Tibet is a kind of consumptive disease. It cuts off life. Quite simply, it causes depopulation. Claustration equals castration. It has been the scourge of Europe. Add to this the violence so often done to the conscience, coerced vocations, feudalism relying on the cloister, primogeniture directing surplus family members into the monastic life, the barbarities we have just been speaking of, the *in pace*, the sealed lips, the immured minds, so many ill-fated intellects confined in the dungeon of eternal vows, the taking of the habit, souls buried alive. Add to national debilitations individual tortures, and whoever you are you will shudder at the cowl and the veil, those two winding-sheets of human devising.

Nevertheless, in certain respects and in certain places, despite philosophy, despite progress, the spirit of the cloister lingers on, in the middle of the nineteenth century, and a bizarre new outbreak of asceticism now astounds the civilized world. The persistence of antiquated institutions in perpetuating themselves is like the stubbornness of stale scent clinging to your hair, the urgency of spoiled fish clamouring to be eaten, the oppression of childish garb expecting to clothe the adult, and the tenderness of corpses wanting to come back to kiss the living.

'Ungrateful wretch!' says the garment. 'I protected you in bad weather. Why will you have nothing more to do with me?' 'I come from the open sea,' says the fish. 'I was a rose,' says the perfume. 'I loved you,' says the corpse. 'I civilized you,' says the convent.

There is only one answer to this: once upon a time.

To dream of the indefinite protraction of defunct things and of embalmment as a way of governing mankind, to restore ravaged dogmas, regild shrines, patch up cloisters, re-bless reliquaries, revitalize superstitions, refuel fanaticisms, replace the handles on holy-water sprinklers and on sabres, recreate monasticism and militarism, to believe in the salvation of society by the multiplication of parasites, to force the past on the present – this seems strange. Still, there are theorists who propound these theories. Such theorists, and they are intelligent people, have a very simple method: they put a gloss on the past, a gloss they call 'social order', 'divine right', 'morality', 'family', 'respect for elders', 'ancient authority', 'sacred tradition', 'legitimacy', 'religion', and they go about shouting, 'Look! Take this, honest people.' This logic was known to the ancients. The haruspices practised it. They rubbed a black heifer with chalk and said, 'It's white.' *Bos cretatus**.

We ourselves respect the past in certain instances and in all cases grant it clemency, provided it consents to being dead. If it insists on being alive, we attack and try to kill it.

Superstitions, bigotries, false pieties, prejudices, these spectres, for all that they are spectres, cling to life. They have teeth and nails in their vaporousness, and they must be tackled head-on, and war must be waged against them, and it must be waged constantly. For it is one of the fates of humanity to be doomed to eternal battle against phantoms. Shades are difficult to throttle and destroy.

A convent in France in the middle of the nineteenth century is the equivalent of a parliament of owls confronting daylight. A cloister actually practising asceticism right in the heart of the city of 1789, 1830 and 1848, Rome flourishing in Paris, is an anachronism. In ordinary times, all it takes to disperse and dispel an anachronism is to make it spell out the date. But these are not ordinary times.

Let us fight.

Let us fight, but let us discriminate. The characteristic of truth is never to be extreme. What need has it to exaggerate? There is that which needs to be destroyed, and there is that which simply needs to be elucidated and examined. Well intentioned and serious examination, that is a force to be reckoned with! Let us not put to the torch where it is enough to bring light.

So, in the context of the nineteenth century, we are opposed to ascetic enclosure as a general proposition and among all peoples, in Asia as in Europe, in India as in Turkey. Whoever says convent, says swamp. Their tendency towards corruption is obvious, their stagnation unhealthy, their feverish ferment is infectious and etiolates nations. Their proliferation is becoming a plague of biblical proportions. We cannot think without horror of those lands overrun with fakirs, bonzes, santons, caloyers, marabouts, talapoins and dervishes, as with teeming vermin.

That said, the religious question remains. There are certain mysterious, almost awesome, aspects to this question. Allow us to confront it squarely.

---

* Latin: 'Chalk-whitened ox', for sacrificial purposes.

IV
The Convent from the Viewpoint of Principles

Men come together and live under one roof. By virtue of what right? By virtue of the right of association.

They shut themselves up in their communal home. By virtue of what right? By virtue of the right that every man has to open or shut his door.

They do not go out. By virtue of what right? By virtue of the right to come and go, which implies the right to stay at home.

There, at home, what do they do?

They keep their voices down and their eyes lowered, they work. They renounce the world, towns, sensual gratifications, pleasures, vanities, conceits, interests. They dress in coarse woollen or coarse linen. Not one of them has any personal possessions whatsoever. On entering the place, anyone who was rich becomes poor. What he has, he gives to all. The man who was what is called a nobleman, a gentleman or an aristocrat is the equal of the man who was a peasant. The cell is identical for everyone. All undergo the same tonsure, wear the same cassock, eat the same black bread, sleep on the same straw, die on the same ashes. With the same sackcloth on their backs, the same rope around their loins. If the rule adopted is to go barefoot, all go barefoot. There may be a prince among them. That prince is the same wraith as the rest. No more titles. Even family names are lost. They have only first names. All bow beneath the equality of baptismal names. They have annulled the blood-related family and within their community have formed a spiritual family. Their only relatives now are all of mankind. They help the poor, they care for the sick. They elect those whom they obey. They call each other 'my brother'.

You stop me, and you exclaim, 'But that's the ideal convent!'

It need only be the convent that might be, and I must give it its due.

That is why in the preceding book I spoke of a convent in respectful tones. Leaving aside the Middle Ages, leaving aside Asia, excluding the historical and political aspect, from the purely philosophical point of view, beyond crusading polemical imperatives, on condition that the monastery is completely voluntary and encloses only those who consent to it, I shall always treat the cloistered community with a certain diligent and in some respects deferential seriousness. Wherever there is community, there is commonality. Where there is commonality, there is legitimacy. The monastery is a product of the formula: Equality, Fraternity. Oh! what greatness there is in liberty! And what splendid powers of transfiguration! Liberty is all that is required to transform the monastery into a republic.

Let us continue.

Now these men, or these women, who live behind these four walls, they dress in rough homespun, they are equals, they call each other brothers. That is all very well. But do they do anything else?

Yes.

What?

They look into the darkness, they get down on their knees, and they put their hands together.

What is the significance of that?

V

Prayer

They pray.

To whom?

To God.

To pray to God: what do those words mean?

Is there an infinite beyond ourselves? Is that infinite one and indivisible, abiding, everlasting, necessarily substantial (since it is infinite, and if it were devoid of matter that would be a limitation on it), necessarily intelligent (since it is infinite, and if it lacked intelligence that would make it finite)? Does this infinite awaken in us the notion of essence, whereas we can only attribute to ourselves the notion of existence? In other words, is it not the absolute to which we are relative?

And while there is an infinite beyond ourselves, is there not at the same time an infinite within ourselves? Are these two infinites (what an alarming plural!) not superimposed one on top of the other? Does this second infinite not underlie, so to speak, the first? Is it not the mirror, reflection, echo of the first, an abyss concentric with another abyss? Is this second infinite also intelligent? Does it think? Does it love? Has it a will? If these two infinites are intelligent, they each have an element of will, and there is an I in the infinite above as there is an I in the infinite below. The I below is the soul, the I above is God.

To place the infinite below in contact with the infinite above by the medium of thought, that is called praying.

Let us not take anything away from the human mind. Suppression is bad. We must reform and transform. Certain faculties of mankind are directed towards the Unknown: thought, imagination, prayer. The

466

Unknown is an ocean. What is conscience? It is a compass in the Unknown. Thought, imagination, prayer, these are great mysterious radiances. Let us respect them. Where do these majestic radiances of the soul go? Into the darkness – that is to say, towards the light.

The greatness of democracy is to deny nothing and to repudiate nothing of humanity. Close to the rights of Man, alongside them at least, are the rights of the Soul.

To crush fanaticism and revere the infinite, that is the governing principle. Let us not restrict ourselves to bowing down before the tree of creation and contemplating its huge branches full of stars. We have a duty: to work on the human soul, to defend mystery against miracle, to adore the incomprehensible and reject the absurd, to admit as inexplicable only what we must, to purge belief, to cull religion of superstition. To decontaminate God.

VI
The Absolute Goodness of Prayer

As for the way to pray, all ways are good provided they are sincere. Turn your book over and become one with the infinite.

There is, as we know, a philosophy that denies the infinite. There is also a philosophy, of a pathological order, that denies the sun: this philosophy is called blindness.

To take a perception we lack and set it up as a source of truth, that is the hubris of a blind man!

What is curious are the self-important, superior and patronizing airs this groping philosophy adopts with regard to the philosophy that sees God. It is like hearing a mole exclaim, 'They make me feel sorry for them, with that sun of theirs!'

There are, as we know, renowned atheists of powerful intellect. Brought back to the truth by the very power of their intellect, fundamentally they are not very sure of being atheists. With them, it is little more than a matter of definition, and in any case, even if they do not believe in God, being great minds they prove the existence of God.

We salute them as philosophers while being severe critics of their philosophy.

Let us continue.

What is remarkable, too, is the propensity to play around with words. A metaphysical school of the north, a little fog-bound, thought it brought about a revolution in human understanding by replacing the word Force with the word Will.

It would indeed be fruitful to say 'the plant wills', instead of 'the plant grows', if we were to go on to say 'the universe wills'. Why? Because what would follow would be this: the plant wills, therefore it has an I; the universe wills, therefore it has a God.

For ourselves, although unlike this school we reject nothing a priori, yet we find it more difficult to admit that a plant has a will, which this school accepts, than that the universe has a will, which it denies.

You cannot deny the will of the infinite, that is to say God, unless you deny the infinite. This we have demonstrated.

Denial of the infinite leads straight to nihilism. Everything becomes 'a conceit of the mind'.

With nihilism no discussion is possible, for the logical nihilist doubts that his interlocutor exists and is not very sure that he himself exists.

From his point of view, it is possible that he himself may be just 'a conceit of his own mind'.

Only, he does not see that by the mere mention of that word 'mind', in one fell swoop he accepts everything he has denied.

In short, there is no line of thought open to a philosophy that forestalls everything with the monosyllable No.

To 'No', there is only one response: 'Yes.'

Nihilism is of no import.

There is no non-being. Zero does not exist. Everything is something. Nothing is nothing.

Man lives by affirmation much more than by bread.

It is not even enough to see and to tell. Philosophy must be a force of energy. To better mankind must be its endeavour and its effect. Socrates must enter Adam and produce Marcus Aurelius; in other words, out of the man of blissfulness bring forth the man of wisdom. Turn Eden into a Lyceum. Knowledge must be a tonic. The pursuit of pleasure – what a sorry purpose and what a paltry ambition! The brute beast pursues pleasure. The pursuit of thought, that is the soul's real triumph! To offer thought to mankind's thirst, to give as an elixir to all men the notion of God, to bring together within them conscience and knowledge, and by this mysterious conjunction to make them just, such is the function of real philosophy. Morality is a flourishing of truths. Contemplation leads to action. The absolute must be applicable. The ideal must be breathable, drinkable and eatable to the human mind. It is the ideal that has the right to say: 'Take this, this is my body, this is my blood.' Wisdom is a holy communion. It is on this condition that it ceases to be a sterile love of knowledge and becomes the one sovereign mode of inspiring human solidarity, and is elevated from philosophy to religion.

Philosophy must not be a mere belvedere built on mystery in order to gaze on it at leisure, for nothing more than the accommodation of curiosity.

Leaving the development of our ideas for another occasion, we simply say that we neither understand man as a point of departure, nor progress as a goal, without those two driving forces: faith and love.

Progress is the goal. The ideal is the paragon.

What is the ideal? It is God.

The ideal, the absolute, perfection, the infinite: identical words.

VII
Take Care in Censuring

History and philosophy have duties that are eternal and at the same time simple: to oppose Caiaphas as bishop, Draco as judge, Trimalchio as legislator, Tiberius as emperor. That is clear, straightforward and transparent, and presents no uncertainty. But the right to live apart, even with its dangers and abuses, needs to be recognized and respected. Coenobitism is a human problem.

When speaking of convents – those places of error but also of innocence, of misguidedness but also of good intentions, of ignorance but also of devotion, of torture but also of martyrdom – almost always you have to say yes and no.

A convent is a contradiction: with salvation as its object, with sacrifice as its means to achieve it. The convent is supreme egoism entailing supreme abnegation.

Abdicate in order to rule seems to be the motto of monasticism.

In the cloister you suffer to gain pleasure. You draw a bill of exchange on death. You anticipate celestial light in terrestrial darkness. In the cloister, hell is accepted in advance as a settlement against paradise.

The taking of the veil or the cowl is suicide repaid with eternity.

We do not think that on such a subject mockery is appropriate. Everything it involves is serious, the good as well as the bad.

The just man frowns, but never sneers. We understand anger, not malice.

VIII
Faith Rules

A few more words.

We criticize the Church when it is riddled with intrigue, we despise the spiritual in its attachment to the temporal, but everywhere we honour the thinking man.

We hail whoever kneels.

A faith: this is indispensable to man. Woe to anyone who believes nothing!

To be lost in thought is not to be idle. There is visible work and invisible work.

To contemplate is to toil, to think is to do. Folded arms are busy, joined hands are active. Gazing heavenward is industrious.

Thales remained motionless for four years. He founded philosophy.

In our opinion, coenobites are not lazy and recluses are not work-shy.

Meditating on darkness is a serious matter.

Without invalidating anything we have just said, we believe that the living ought to keep death constantly in mind. On this point the priest and the philosopher agree. *We must die.* The abbot of La Trappe echoes Horace.

To include in one's life some sense of mortality is the law of the sage. It is, too, the law of the ascetic. The ascetic and the sage come together in this respect.

There is material growth. We want it. There is also moral grandeur. We value it.

Unreasoning and mercurial minds say, 'What is the good of these motionless figures with an inclination for mystery? What use are they? What do they achieve?'

Honestly! Faced with the darkness that surrounds us and awaits us, not knowing what will become of us in the ultimate diaspora, we reply, 'There is probably no work more sublime than the work these souls do.' And we say further: 'There is probably no work more useful.'

Those who pray constantly are surely needed for those who never pray at all.

For us, the whole question lies in the amount of thought that goes into the praying.

Leibniz at prayer: there is greatness in that. Voltaire at worship: there is nobility in that. *Deo erexit Voltaire.**

We are for religion and against religions.

We are among those who believe in the abjectness of litanies and the sublimity of prayer.

Moreover, at this present moment, a moment that with luck will not characterize the nineteenth century, at this time when so many men are low-browed and not very high-minded, among so many mortals whose moral purpose is the pursuit of pleasure and who are taken up with material things, which are fleeting and fraudulent, anyone who goes into exile seems to us venerable. The monastery is a renunciation. Sacrifice based on a false premise is still sacrifice. Making a duty of an exacting misapprehension has its own grandeur.

To examine the truth from every angle exhaustively and impartially, the monastery, the female convent in particular – for in our century it is women who suffer most and in their monastic exile there is an element of protest – undeniably, in itself and ideally, has a certain grandeur.

This cloistered life, so austere, so bleak, a few of whose features we have just traced, is not life, for it is not liberty. It is not entombment, for it is not fulfilment. It is the strange place from where you see, as from a high mountain peak, on one side the abyss we are in now, on the other the abyss in which we shall be. It is the narrow, misty frontier separating two worlds, illuminated and obscured by both at the same time, where the feeble rays of life mingle with the wan rays of death. It is sepulchral semi-darkness.

We, who do not believe what these women believe, but who, like them, live by faith, have never been able to contemplate without a kind of compassionate and religious anguish, a kind of pity full of envy, those devout, quaking, trusting creatures, those humble, noble souls who dare to live on the very brink of mystery, waiting, between the world on which they have closed the door and a heaven that remains unopen, turned towards the invisible light with the sole joy of thinking they know where it is, aspiring to the abyss and the unknown, their eyes fixed on the still darkness, kneeling, overwhelmed, amazed, trembling, half raised at times by the deep breaths of eternity.

---

* 'Voltaire raised [this building] to God.' In 1760 Voltaire retired to his estate at Ferney, where he built a church for the villagers that bore this inscription.

BOOK EIGHT
CEMETERIES TAKE WHAT THEY ARE GIVEN

I
In Which There Is Discussion about How to Get into the Convent

This was the house where Jean Valjean had, as Fauchelevent put it, 'fallen from heaven'. He had scaled the wall of the garden at the corner of Rue Polonceau. That angels' hymn he had heard in the middle of the night was the nuns singing matins. That hall he had discerned in the gloom was the chapel. That phantom he had seen lying on the ground was the nun making reparation. That strangely jangling bell that had so startled him was the gardener's bell attached to old Fauchelevent's knee.

Once Cosette had been put to bed Jean Valjean and Fauchelevent, as we have seen, had a glass of wine and a piece of cheese for supper in front of a good blazing wood fire. Then, as the only bed in the hut was occupied by Cosette, each man threw himself down on a bale of straw.

Before he shut his eyes Jean Valjean said, 'I have to stay on here.'

This remark kept running through Fauchelevent's mind all night long. To tell the truth, neither of them slept.

Aware that he had been found out and that Javert was on his trail, Jean Valjean realized he and Cosette were doomed if they went back into Paris. Since the latest gust of wind that had buffeted him happened to have blown him into this cloister, Jean Valjean had only one thought: to remain here. Now, for a poor wretch in his position this convent was both the most dangerous and the safest of places. The most dangerous because, no men being allowed to enter it, if he were found inside he would be caught trespassing, and Jean Valjean would go straight from the convent to prison. The safest because, if there were some way of gaining acceptance and staying in this place, who would ever come looking for you here? To live in a place where you could not possibly be, that was salvation.

As for Fauchelevent, he was racking his brains. He began by owning that he was completely baffled. How did Monsieur Madeleine come to be here, with walls like these? There is no stepping over cloister walls. How did he get here with a child? You do not scale a perpendicular wall with a child in your arms. Who was this child? Where did they both come from?

Since Fauchelevent had been at the convent, he had heard nothing of Montreuil-sur-Mer and knew nothing of what had happened. Père Madeleine had that air about him that discourages questions. And besides, Fauchelevent said to himself, you don't question a saint. Monsieur Madeleine, for him, retained all his prestige. Only, from a few words Jean Valjean had let slip, the gardener thought he was able to infer that Monsieur Madeleine had probably been bankrupted in these hard times, and was being pursued by his creditors. Or else he was implicated in some political affair and was in hiding. Fauchelevent, who like many of our peasants in the north was an old Bonapartist at heart, was not at all unhappy about that. In hiding, Monsieur Madeleine had identified the convent as a refuge and it was quite natural he should wish to stay here. But the inexplicable thing, which Fauchelevent kept coming back to and could not work out, was how Monsieur Madeleine got here and how he got in with that little girl. Fauchelevent saw them, touched them, spoke to them, and did not believe it. The incomprehensible had just found its way into Fauchelevent's cabin. Fauchelevent was lost in conjecture and could see nothing clearly but this: Monsieur Madeleine saved my life. This sole certainty was sufficient, and decided his course. He said to himself: 'It's my turn now.' He added in his conscience: 'Monsieur Madeleine didn't spend so much time deliberating when it was a matter of getting under the cart so that I could be pulled out from under it.' He made up his mind to save Monsieur Madeleine.

Nevertheless, he put to himself various questions and gave various answers.

'After what he did for me, if he were a thief, would I save him?' Just the same. 'If he were an assassin, would I save him?' Just the same. 'Seeing as he is a saint, shall I save him?' Just the same.

But finding a way for him to stay in the convent – what a problem! Fauchelevent did not shrink in the face of this almost fantastic enterprise. This poor Picardy peasant with no other ladder than his devotion, his goodwill and a little of that old rustic cunning to be used in this instance to serve a generous purpose, undertook to scale the inaccessibilities of the cloister and the inhospitable ramparts of the Rule of St Benedict. Père Fauchelevent was an old man who had been selfish all his life and who now, at the end of his days, lame, crippled and with no further interest in the world, found pleasure in being grateful; and seeing a virtuous deed to be done, he leapt at it like a man who, at the moment of death, finding within reach a glass of good wine he has never tasted before, drinks it avidly. It might be added that the air he had been breathing in this convent for many years now had destroyed his self-centredness and had ended up making some sort of good deed necessary to him.

So he formed this resolution: to devote himself to Monsieur Madeleine.

We have just called him 'a poor Picardy peasant'. That description is accurate but incomplete. At this point in our story something of Père Fauchelevent's social background becomes useful. He was a peasant but he had been a copy clerk, which added casuistry to his cunning and insight to his naivety. Having for various reasons failed in his business, from being a copy clerk he had sunk to being a carter and a labourer. But despite oaths and lashings, essential to horses, apparently, something of the copy clerk survived in him. He had some natural wit. He did not say 'I's' or 'I 'as', he was chatty, a rarity in village life, and the other peasants said of him, 'He talks almost like a gentleman that wears a hat.' Fauchelevent was in fact one of that species which the supercilious and flippant vocabulary of the last century described as 'half burgher, half peasant'*, and in metaphors that rained down from the château on to the thatched cottage was labelled in the commoner category as 'urban-rustic; pepper and salt'. Though sorely tried and much worn down by fate, a poor threadbare old soul, as it were, Fauchelevent was still a man of impulse and very spontaneous, a precious quality that prevents a person from ever being wicked. His defects and his vices, for he did have some, were superficial. In short, he had the type of physiognomy that finds favour with the observer. That aged face had none of those disagreeable vertical lines on his forehead that denote malice or stupidity.

At daybreak after a vast amount of thinking, old Fauchelevent opened his eyes and saw Monsieur Madeleine sitting on his bale of straw, watching Cosette sleep.

Fauchelevent sat up and said, 'Now that you're here, how are you going to contrive to get in?'

This remark summed up the situation and roused Jean Valjean from his reverie.

The two fellows put their heads together.

'In the first place,' said Fauchelevent, 'you're going to start by not

---

* An allusion to La Fontaine's description – 'demi-bourgeois, demi-manant' – of the gardener in his fable 'Le Jardinier et son Seigneur' ('The Gardener and his Lord'; bk 4, fable 4).

setting foot outside of this room. Neither you nor the child. One step out into the garden, and we're done for.'

'You're right.'

'Monsieur Madeleine,' Fauchelevent went on, 'you've turned up at a very good moment, I mean to say a very bad moment. One of the nuns is very ill. That means no one will be paying much attention to what's going on over here. Apparently, she's dying. The forty-hours devotion is being observed. The whole community's distracted. It's all they can think about. The nun who's about to pass on is a saint. Actually, we're all saints here. The only difference between them and me is they say "our cell", and I say "my bunkdown". There'll be prayers for the dying and then prayers for the dead. We won't be disturbed here today but I can't answer for tomorrow.'

'Still, this hut is set back in a recess in the wall,' observed Jean Valjean, 'it's hidden by some sort of ruin, there are trees, it can't be seen from the convent.'

'And I tell you, the nuns never come near it.'

'Well, then?' said Jean Valjean.

The question mark that punctuated this 'Well, then' signified: It seems to me a person might remain hidden here.

It was this question mark that Fauchelevent responded to: 'There are the little girls.'

'What little girls?' asked Jean Valjean.

As Fauchelevent opened his mouth to explain what he had just said, the bell sounded once.

'The nun's died,' he said. 'That's the bell tolling.'

And he made a sign to Jean Valjean to listen.

The bell struck a second time.

'It's the death knell, Monsieur Madeleine. The bell will continue to strike once a minute for twenty-four hours until the body leaves the church. You see, it's the playing. At recreation a ball has only to roll this way and despite not being allowed to, they come after it, hunting and ferreting all around here. They're devils, those cherubs.'

'Who?' asked Jean Valjean.

'The little girls. You'd be very quickly discovered, believe me. They'd shriek, "Look! A man!" But there's no danger today. There'll be no recreation. It's going to be prayers all day. You can hear the bell. As I said, tolling once every minute. That's the death knell.'

'I understand, Père Fauchelevent. There are schoolgirls.'

And Jean Valjean thought to himself, 'That would be Cosette's education all taken care of.'

Fauchelevent exclaimed, 'My goodness, there are little girls all

475

right! And wouldn't they squeal at the sight of you! And wouldn't they run for their lives! Here, to be a man is to have the plague. You can see how they fasten a bell to my leg as if I were a wild animal.'

Jean Valjean fell deeper and deeper into thought. 'This convent would be our salvation,' he murmured.

Then he raised his voice. 'Yes, the difficulty is to stay here.'

'No,' said Fauchelevent, 'the difficulty is to get out.'

Jean Valjean felt the blood drain back to his heart.

'To get out!'

'Yes, Monsieur Madeleine. In order to get back in you must first get out.'

And after letting another toll of the bell go by Fauchelevent went on, 'You can't be found here like this. How did you get in? For me, because I know you, you fell from heaven. But for the nuns, you have to come through the door.'

All of a sudden a rather complicated ringing of another bell was heard.

'Ah!' said Fauchelevent. 'That's the vocal mothers being summoned. They're going into a chapter meeting. They always hold a chapter meeting when someone dies. She died at daybreak. It's usually at daybreak that people die. But couldn't you go out the same way you came in? Tell me, it's not that I want to ask any questions, but how did you get in?'

Jean Valjean turned pale. The very thought of going back into that terrible street made him shudder. Emerge from a forest full of tigers, and once you are out, imagine being advised by a friend that you should go back in there again! Jean Valjean pictured all the police still swarming over the neighbourhood, lookouts keeping watch, sentries posted everywhere, dreadful hands reaching for his collar, Javert perhaps at the crossroads.

'Out of the question!' he said. 'Père Fauchelevent, let's say I fell from above.'

'But so I believe, so I believe,' replied Fauchelevent. 'You've no need to tell me that. The good Lord must have picked you up in his hand to take a good look at you, and then let you go. Only, he meant to put you in a monastery for men. He made a mistake. Now there's another bell call. That's to tell the porter to go and notify the municipality and have them send the doctor for the dead to come and see that someone's died. All that's the formalities of dying. They don't much like that visit, the nuns don't. A doctor, now he doesn't believe in anything. He lifts the veil. Sometimes he even lifts something else.

How quickly they've called for the doctor this time! What's going on? I wonder. Your little one's still asleep. What's her name?'

'Cosette.'

'Your little girl, is she? That's to say, you must be her grandfather?'

'Yes.'

'For her, getting out of here will be easy. I have my own side gate leading into the courtyard. I knock. The porter opens. I have my basket on my back, the little one's inside it. I go out. Père Fauchelevent goes out with his basket, that's perfectly natural. You'll tell the child to keep very quiet. She'll be covered up. I'll leave her for however long is necessary with a dear old friend of mine who's deaf, a fruit-seller in Rue Chemin-Vert, where she has a little bed. I'll shout in the fruit-seller's ear that she's a niece of mine and to look after her for me till tomorrow. Then the little one will come back in with you. Because I'll get you back in. I'll have to. But how are you going to manage to get out?'

Jean Valjean shook his head.

'As long as no one sees me. That's all that matters, Père Fauchelevent. Find some way of getting me out like Cosette, in a basket, covered up.'

Fauchelevent scratched his ear lobe with the middle finger of his left hand, a sign of serious perplexity.

A third bell-ringing created a diversion.

'That's the doctor for the dead leaving,' said Fauchelevent. 'He's taken a look and said, "She's dead, sure enough." When the doctor has certified the passport for paradise, the undertakers send a coffin. If it's a mother, the mothers lay her out. If it's a sister, the sisters lay her out. After that, I do the nailing. That's part of my gardening duties. A gardener's a bit of a gravedigger. She's placed in a side room in the church that connects with the street and that no man may enter save the doctor of the dead. I don't count the coffin bearers and myself as men. It's in that chamber that I nail down the coffin. The coffin bearers come to fetch it, and drive on, coachman! That's how you go to heaven. They bring a box that has nothing inside it, they carry it off with something inside it. That's what a burial is. *De profundis.**'

A horizontal sunbeam settled on Cosette's face. In her sleep, with her lips parted, she looked like an angel drinking in the light. Jean

---

* The opening words of Psalm 130: 'De profundis clamavi ad te, Domine', 'Out of the depths have I cried unto thee, O Lord!' It is recited at funerals.

Valjean fell to gazing at her. He was no longer listening to Fauchelevent.

Not being listened to is no reason to stop talking. Untroubled, the trusty old gardener went rambling on. 'The grave's dug in Vaugirard Cemetery. They say it's going to be closed, that Vaugirard Cemetery. It's an ancient cemetery that doesn't meet the regulations, that's not got the right uniform, and is going to be pensioned off. That's a shame because it's convenient. I've a friend there, old Mestienne, the grave-digger. The nuns here have a privilege, it's to be taken to that cemetery at nightfall. There's a special order from the authorities for their bene-fit. But so much has happened since yesterday! Mère Crucifixion has died, and Père Madeleine—'

'Has been buried,' said Jean Valjean, smiling sadly.

Fauchelevent's answer turned on that word.

'I'll say! If you were here good and proper, that would be a real burial.'

For the fourth time the bell rang out. Fauchelevent snatched from the nail the knee-pad with a bell on it and buckled it back on his knee.

'That's me this time. The mother prioress is calling for me. Very well, I'm buckling my armour. Monsieur Madeleine, stay here and wait for me. Something's come up. If you're hungry, there's wine, bread and cheese.'

And he left the hut, saying, 'Coming! Coming!'

Jean Valjean watched him hurrying across the garden as fast as his gammy leg would allow him, casting a sidelong glance at his melon beds.

Less than ten minutes later, his knee-bell sending the nuns scatter-ing as he came by, old Fauchelevent tapped at a door and a soft voice replied, 'For ever and ever! For ever and ever!' That is to say, 'Come in.'

This door was the one leading into the parlour reserved for the gardener in the course of carrying out his duties. This parlour was next to the chapter room. The prioress sat on the only chair in the parlour, waiting for Fauchelevent.

II
Fauchelevent Faces Difficulty

It is typical of certain characters and certain professions, notably priests and members of religious communities, to look agitated and solemn at moments of crisis. When Fauchelevent came in, this twofold sign of preoccupation was imprinted on the face of the normally cheerful prioress, the charming and learned Mademoiselle de Blemeur, Mère Innocente.

The gardener gave an apprehensive bow and remained in the doorway of the cell. The prioress, who was saying her rosary, looked up and said, 'Ah! there you are, Père Fauvent.'

This abbreviation had been adopted in the convent.

Fauchelevent bowed again.

'Père Fauvent, I sent for you.'

'Here I am, reverend mother.'

'I've something to say to you.'

'And I, too,' said Fauchelevent with a boldness that inwardly frightened him, 'have something to say to the very reverend mother.'

The prioress stared at him.

'Ah! You have something to tell me.'

'A request to make.'

'Well, go on.'

Simple old Fauchelevent, former copy clerk, belonged to that category of peasants who have assuredness. A certain canny ignorance is a strength. People are not wary of it, and it wins them over. Fauchelevent had been in the convent a little over two years, and in that time he had done well in the community. Always by himself, and while busy at his gardening, he had hardly anything else to do than be curious. Distanced as he was from all these veiled women coming and going, he saw not much more in front of him than a flurry of shadows. Through his attentiveness and shrewdness he had succeeded in putting flesh on all these phantoms, and for him these dead women lived. He was like a deaf man whose sight grows keener or a blind man whose hearing becomes more acute. He applied himself to working out the significance of the various bell-ringings, and he succeeded, so that this taciturn and enigmatic cloister kept no secrets from him. This sphinx babbled all its secrets in his ear. Knowing all, Fauchelevent concealed all. This was his artfulness. The whole convent thought him stupid. A great merit in religion. The vocal mothers approved of Fauchelevent. His curiosity held its tongue. He inspired trust. Besides, he was dependable and never went out unless it was clearly necessary for the orchard or vegetable garden. His judicious behaviour counted in his favour. Nevertheless, he got two men talking: the porter at the convent, and he had detailed knowledge of the parlour; and the gravedigger at the cemetery, and he had specific knowledge about burials. So with regard to these nuns he had the benefit of a dual insight, into their life and into their death. But he did not take advantage. The community valued him. Old, lame, practically blind, probably a little deaf into the bargain, so many good qualities! It would have been hard to replace him.

With the confidence of one who feels appreciated, the good-hearted fellow embarked on a rather long-winded and very exhaustive rustic disquisition addressed to the reverend prioress. He talked at length about his age, his infirmities, the burden of years now weighing doubly heavy on him, the increasing demands of his work, the size of the garden, nights like the previous one, for example, when he had to lay down straw matting on the melon beds because of the moon, eventually leading up to this: that he had a brother (the prioress gave a start). A brother not at all young (another reaction from the prioress – reassured, however). That if it might be permitted, this brother could come and live with him, and help him, he was an excellent gardener, the community would be well served by him, better than by himself. That otherwise, if his brother were not admitted, as he the elder felt worn out and not up to the job, with great regret he would have to leave. And that his brother had a little girl that he would bring with him, who would be raised in godliness in this house and, who knows, would one day become a nun.

When he had finished speaking the prioress stopped running the rosary between her fingers and said to him, 'Could you between now and this evening procure a strong iron bar?'

'What for?'

'To serve as a lever.'

'Yes, reverend mother,' replied Fauchelevent.

Without another word the prioress rose and went into the adjoining room, which was the chapter room and where the vocal mothers were probably assembled. Fauchelevent was left on his own.

III
Mère Innocente

About a quarter of an hour went by. The prioress came back and sat in the chair again.

Both individuals seemed preoccupied. We reproduce as best we can the dialogue that took place.

'Père Fauvent?'

'Reverend mother?'

'You know the chapel?'

'I have a little cubicle there to hear mass and attend the offices.'

'And you have been in the choir when going about your work?'

'Two or three times.'

'There's a stone to be raised.'

'Heavy?'

'The flagstone that's at the side of the altar.'

'The stone that seals the crypt?'

'Yes.'

'This is a time when it would be good to have two men here.'

'Mère Ascension, who is as strong as a man, will help you.'

'A woman's never the same as a man.'

'We have only a woman to help you. We all do what we can. Although Dom Mabillon gives us four hundred and seventeen of St Bernard's letters while Merlonus Horstius gives us only three hundred and sixty-seven, I do not scorn Merlonus Horstius.'

'Neither do I.'

'Merit lies in working according to your capabilities. A cloister is not a stoneyard.'

'And a woman is not a man. My brother's the strong one!'

'And anyway, you'll have a lever.'

'That's the only kind of key that goes into doors like that.'

'There's a ring in the stone.'

'I'll put the lever through it.'

'And the stone is set to pivot.'

'That's fine, reverend mother. I'll open the crypt.'

'And the four mother precentors will help you.'

'And once the crypt is opened?'

'It must be closed again.'

'Will that be all?'

'No.'

'Give me your orders, very reverend mother.'

'Fauvent, we trust you.'

'I'm here to do whatever's to be done.'

'And to keep it all to yourself!'

'Yes, reverend mother.'

'Once the crypt is open—'

'I'll close it again.'

'But before that—'

'What, reverend mother?'

'Something must be lowered into it.'

There was a silence. After pursing her lower lip in what seemed like hesitation, the prioress broke that silence.

'Père Fauvent!'

'Reverend mother!'

'You know that one of the mothers died this morning?'

'No.'

'So you didn't hear the bell?'

'You don't hear anything at the bottom of the garden.'

'Really?'

'I only just manage to hear the bell when it rings for me.'

'She died at daybreak.'

'And then, this morning, the wind wasn't blowing in my direction.'

'It was Mère Crucifixion. One chosen by God.'

The prioress fell silent, moved her lips for a moment as though in mental prayer, and went on. 'Three years ago, just from having seen Mère Crucifixion at prayer, a Jansenist, Madame de Béthune, became orthodox.'

'Ah! yes, I can hear the bell tolling now, reverend mother.'

'The mothers have taken her to the room for the dead, which connects with the church.'

'I know.'

'No other man but you can or should enter that room. You make sure of that. A fine thing that would be, to see a man entering the room for the dead!'

'More often!'

'What?'

'More often!'

'What are you saying?'

'I'm saying more often.'

'More often than what?'

'Reverend mother, I'm not saying more often than what, I'm saying more often.'

'I don't understand you. Why do you say "more often"?'

'I was saying what you said, reverend mother.'

'But I didn't say "more often".'

At that moment nine o'clock struck.

'At nine o'clock in the morning and at every hour, praised and adored be the Most Blessed Sacrament of the altar,' said the prioress.

'Amen,' said Fauchelevent.

It was just as well the hour struck. It put an end to More Often. Otherwise, the prioress and Fauchelevent would probably never have extricated themselves from that tangle.

Fauchelevent wiped his brow.

The prioress had another little inward murmur, probably devo-

482

tional, then spoke aloud. 'In her lifetime Mère Crucifixion made converts. After her death she will perform miracles.'

'She will!' replied Fauchelevent, falling into step, and striving not to put a foot wrong again.

'Père Fauvent, the community has been blessed in Mère Crucifixion. Undoubtedly it is not granted to everyone to die like Cardinal de Bérulle while saying holy mass and to give up their souls to God while pronouncing these words: *Hanc igitur oblationem**. But without being quite so blessed, Mère Crucifixion had a very fine death. She remained conscious to the very end. She spoke to us, then she spoke to the angels. She gave us her last commands. If you had a little more faith, and you could have been in her cell, she would have cured your leg merely by touching it. She smiled. We sensed that she was being restored to life in God. There was something of paradise in that death.'

Fauchelevent thought this was a funeral oration that had come to an end. 'Amen,' he said.

'Père Fauvent, the wishes of the dead must be carried out.'

The prioress told a few beads on her rosary. Fauchelevent remained silent. She continued.

'On this question I've consulted several ecclesiastics working in the name of Our Lord who concern themselves most profitably with the practice of clerical life.'

'Reverend mother, from here you can hear the bell tolling much better than in the garden.'

'Besides, she's no ordinary dead woman, she's a saint.'

'Like yourself, reverend mother.'

'She'd been sleeping in her coffin for the past twenty years, by express permission of our holy father Pius VII.'

'The one who crowned the Emp—... Buonaparte.' For a clever man like Fauchelevent, this allusion was an unfortunate one. Luckily the prioress, entirely taken up with what was on her mind, did not hear it.

She continued. 'Père Fauvent?'

'Reverend mother?'

'St Diodorus, archbishop of Cappadocia, wanted to have this single

---

* The beginning of the eucharistic prayer in the canon of the mass, pronounced by the celebrant over the offerings of bread and wine before the consecration. 'Wherefore we beseech thee, O Lord, graciously to receive this oblation . . .'

word inscribed on his tomb: *Acarus*, which means "earthworm". And so it was. Is this not true?'

'Yes, reverend mother.'

'The blessed Mezzocane, abbot of Aquila, wished to be buried under the gallows. And so he was.'

'That's true.'

'St Terence, bishop of Portus at the mouth of the Tiber, asked that the sign put on the graves of parricides might be carved on his grave-stone in the hope that passers-by would spit on his tomb. And so it was. The dead must be obeyed.'

'Amen.'

'Even though Bernard Guidonis was bishop of Tuy in Spain, the body of Bernard Guidonis, who was born in France near Roche-Abeille, was taken to the Dominican church at Limoges as he had instructed and despite the king of Castile. Can this be denied?'

'Indeed not, reverend mother.'

'The fact is attested by Plantavit de la Fosse.'

Again a few beads of the rosary were told, silently. The prioress then spoke again.

'Père Fauvent, Mère Crucifixion will be buried in the coffin in which she has slept for the last twenty years.'

'Rightly so.'

'It's a continuation of sleep.'

'So I'll have to nail down that coffin with her inside it?'

'Yes.'

'And we'll leave aside the undertaker's coffin?'

'Precisely.'

'I'm here to serve the very reverend community.'

'The four mother precentors will help you.'

'In nailing down the coffin? I don't need their help.'

'No. In lowering it.'

'Where?'

'Into the crypt.'

'What crypt?'

'Under the altar.'

Fauchelevent started.

'The crypt under the altar?'

'Under the altar.'

'But—'

'You'll have an iron bar.'

'Yes, but—'

'Using the bar, you'll raise the stone by the ring.'

'But—'

'The dead must be obeyed. To be buried in the crypt under the altar of the chapel, not to be put in unholy ground, to remain in death where she had prayed in life, that was Mère Crucifixion's last wish. She asked it of us, that is to say, those were her instructions.'

'But it's forbidden.'

'Forbidden by men, ordered by God.'

'What if it were to become known?'

'We trust you.'

'Oh me, I'm a stone in your wall.'

'A chapter meeting is being held. The vocal mothers, whom I have just consulted again and who are deliberating, have decided that Mère Crucifixion shall in accordance with her wishes be buried in her own coffin under our altar. Imagine, Père Fauvent, if there were to be miracles worked here! What glory in God for the community! Miracles issue from tombs.'

'But reverend mother, if the representative of the health department—'

'Over the matter of burial St Benedict II resisted Constantine Pogonatus.'

'But the police superintendent—'

'Chonodamarius, one of the seven kings of the Alemanni who invaded Gaul during the reign of the emperor Constans, expressly recognized the right of nuns to be buried as nuns, that is to say beneath the altar.'

'But the prefectural inspector—'

'The world is nothing before the cross. Martin, the eleventh general of the Carthusians, gave this motto to his order: *Stat crux dum volvitur orbis**.

'Amen,' said Fauchelevent, unshakeable in this method of saving face whenever he heard Latin.

Any audience satisfies someone who has been silent for too long. On the day the rhetorician Gymnastoras left prison with many dilemmas and syllogisms bottled up inside him, he stopped in front of the first tree he came to, harangued it and made very great efforts to convince it. The prioress, usually subject to the dam of silence, and with her reservoir full to overflowing, stood up and exclaimed with the effusiveness of an opened sluice gate: 'I have on my right Benedict and

---

* 'The cross remains steady while the world turns', the motto of the contemplative Carthusian Order, founded in the eleventh century by St Bruno (*c.*1032–1101).

485

on my left Bernard. Who is Bernard? He was the first abbot of Clairvaux. Fontaine in Burgundy is blessed with having been his place of birth. His father was called Tescelin and his mother Alethe. He started out at Cîteaux and ended up at Clairvaux. He was ordained abbot by the bishop of Chalon-sur-Saône, Guillaume de Champeaux. He had seven hundred novices, and founded a hundred and sixty monasteries. He defeated Abelard at the Council of Sens in 1140, and Pierre de Bruys and his disciple Henry, and another kind of dissident called the Apostolicals. He silenced Arnold of Brescia, fulminated against the Jew-killing monk Radulf, dominated the Council of Reims in 1148, saw to it that the bishop of Poitiers Gilbert de la Porée was censured, that Éon de l'Étoile was condemned, settled the disputes of princes, instructed King Louis the Young, counselled Pope Eugenius III, formulated the rule of the Templars, preached the crusade, performed two hundred and fifty miracles during his lifetime and as many as thirty-nine in one day. Who is Benedict? He was the patriarch of Monte Cassino. He was the second founder of claustral holiness, he was the Basil of the West. His order has produced forty popes, two hundred cardinals, fifty patriarchs, sixteen hundred archbishops, four thousand six hundred bishops, four emperors, twelve empresses, forty-six kings, forty-one queens, three thousand six hundred canonized saints, and it has been going for fourteen hundred years. On the one hand St Bernard, on the other the representative of the health department! On the one hand St Benedict, on the other the inspector of public works! The state, public works, undertakers, regulations, administration, do we recognize any of that? Who's going to object to the way we're treated? Nobody! We don't even have the right to offer our dust to Jesus Christ! Your health department is a Revolutionary invention. God subordinated to the police superintendent – that's the age we live in. Silence, Fauvent!'

Fauchelevent did not feel very comfortable under this deluge.

The prioress continued. 'The monastery's right to bury their own is not in any doubt. Only the fanatical and the misguided deny it. We live in times of terrible confusion. People don't know what they should know, and they know what they shouldn't. They are ignoble and ungodly. There are in this age people who don't know the difference between the very great St Bernard and the Bernard of the Poor Catholics, a good churchman who lived in the thirteenth century. Others are so blasphemous as to compare Louis XVI's scaffold with the cross of Jesus Christ. Louis XVI was only a king. Let us be mindful of God! There is no right or wrong any more. Voltaire's name is known but not the name of César de Bus. Yet César de Bus counts among the blessed and Voltaire counts among the far from blessed. The last arch-bishop, Cardinal de Périgord, did not even know that Charles de Gondren was the successor to Bérulle, and François Bourgoing to Gondren, and Jean-François Senault to Bourgoing, and Père de la Ste-Marthe to Jean-François Senault. The name of Père Coton is known not because he was one of the three who promoted the foundation of the Oratory but because his name became an oath for the Huguenot king Henri IV.* What endears St Francis of Sales to the worldly is that he cheated at cards. And then religion is attacked. Why? Because there have been bad priests, because Sagittarius, bishop of Gap, was the brother of Salonius, bishop of Embrun, and because both of them rallied to Mummulus. What does that matter? Does that prevent Martin de Tours from being a saint and from having given half his cloak to a beggar? The saints are persecuted. People close their eyes to the truth. Darkness is the norm. The most ferocious beasts are blind beasts. No one takes hell seriously. Oh! this wicked nation! By order of the king today means by order of the Revolution. People no longer know what is due to the living or to the dead. It is forbidden to die a godly death. Burial is a civil matter. That's horrifying. St Leo II wrote two letters, one to Peter the notary, the other to the king of the Visigoths, for the express purpose of resisting and rejecting the authority of the exarch and the supremacy of the emperor in matters concerning the dead. Gautier, bishop of Châlons, stood up to Othon, Duc de Bourgogne, on this issue. The legal authorities of the past conceded this. We used to have a voice, in the chapter, even on matters of the day. The abbot of Cîteaux was councillor to the parliament of Burgundy by right of being general of the order. We do what we please with our dead. Is not the body of St Benedict himself in France at Fleury Abbey, known as St-Benoît-sur-Loire, even though he died in Italy at Monte Cassino on Saturday the twenty-first of March in the year 543? All this is indisputable. I abhor psalm-singers, I hate priors, I execrate heretics, but I should abominate even more anyone who were to maintain the contrary. You've only to read Arnold de Wyon, Gabriel Bucelin, Trithemius, Maurolycus and Dom Luc d'Achéry.'

The prioress drew breath, then turned to Fauchelevent.

'Père Fauvent, do we understand each other?'

---

* Confessor to Henri IV, the Jesuit priest Pierre Coton is supposed to have prevailed on the king to stop blaspheming by changing his favourite oath, 'Je renie Dieu', 'I deny God', to 'Je renie Coton', which became shortened to 'jarnicoton'.

'We do, reverend mother.'

'We may rely on you?'

'I'm at your command.'

'Very well.'

'I'm completely devoted to the convent.'

'We're agreed. You'll close the coffin. The sisters will carry it to the chapel. The office for the dead will be said. Then we shall return to the cloister. Between eleven o'clock and midnight you will come with your iron bar. All will be done in the utmost secrecy. In the chapel there will be only the four mother precentors, Mère Ascension and yourself.'

'And the sister at the post?'

'She won't turn round.'

'But she'll hear.'

'She won't listen. And anyway, what the cloister knows is not known to the world.'

There was another pause.

The prioress spoke again. 'You'll take off your bell. There's no need for the sister at the post to know you're there.'

'Reverend mother?'

'What, Père Fauvent?'

'Has the doctor for the dead paid his visit?'

'He's coming at four o'clock today. The bell to summon the doctor for the dead has already been rung. But don't you hear any of the bells?'

'I only pay attention to my own.'

'That's just as well, Père Fauvent.'

'Reverend mother, the lever will have to be at least six foot long.'

'Where will you find it?'

'Where there's no lack of gratings, there's no lack of iron bars. I have my scrap heap at the bottom of the garden.'

'About three-quarters of an hour before midnight, don't forget.'

'Reverend mother?'

'What?'

'If ever you were to have any other jobs like this, my brother's the strong man. An ox!'

'You'll be as quick as possible about it.'

'I don't move terribly fast. I'm crippled, that's why I could do with someone to help me. I limp.'

'Limping's not a sin and may be a blessing. Emperor Henry II, who opposed the anti-pope Gregory and re-established Benedict VIII, has two epithets, the Pious and the Lame.'

'Two overcoats* are a very good thing to have,' murmured Fauchelevent, who really was a little hard of hearing.

'Now that I think about it, Père Fauvent, let's take a whole hour. That's not too long. Be near the main altar with your iron bar at eleven o'clock. The office begins at midnight. It must all be done a good quarter of an hour before that.'

'I'll do everything to prove my devotion to the community. So that's settled. I'll nail down the coffin. At eleven o'clock precisely I'll be in the chapel. The mother precentors will be there. Mère Ascension will be there. Two men would be better. Still, never mind! I'll have my lever. We'll open the crypt, we'll lower the coffin, and we'll close up the crypt again. After that, no trace of anything. The government won't suspect a thing. Reverend mother, does that take care of everything?'

'No.'

'So what else is there?'

'There's still the empty coffin.'

This created a pause. Fauchelevent pondered. The prioress pondered.

'What will be done with the coffin, Père Fauvent?'

'It'll be buried.'

'Empty?'

Another silence. With his left hand Fauchelevent made the kind of gesture that dismisses a vexing question.

'Reverend mother, I'm the one who's to nail down the coffin in the church side room, and no one's allowed in there but me, and I'll cover the coffin with the pall.'

'Yes, but the coffin bearers, when they lift it into the hearse and lower it into the grave, will be able to tell there's nothing inside.'

'Oh, da—!' exclaimed Fauchelevent.

The prioress began to make the sign of the cross and glared at the gardener; '-mnation' remained lodged in his throat. He hastily improvised an expedient to make her forget the oath.

'I'll put earth in the coffin, reverend mother. That will create the effect of someone inside it.'

'You're right. Earth and man, they're one and the same. So you'll take care of the empty coffin?'

'I'll see to it.'

The prioress's face, troubled and clouded till then, cleared again.

---

* Fauchelevent has misheard the reverend mother, who spoke of two epithets (*surnoms*), not two overcoats (*surtouts*).

She signalled to him the way a superior dismisses an inferior. Fauchelevent made for the door. As he was about to go out the prioress raised her voice slightly: 'I'm pleased with you, Père Fauvent. Tomorrow after the burial, bring your brother to me, and tell him to bring his daughter.'

IV
In Which It Seems Jean Valjean Might Well Have Read Austin Castillejo

The strides of a cripple are like the leers of a one-eyed man: they do not reach their goal very swiftly. Besides, Fauchelevent was perplexed. It took him nearly a quarter of an hour to walk back to the shed in the garden. Cosette was awake. Jean Valjean had sat her by the fire. When Fauchelevent came in Jean Valjean was pointing to the gardener's basket on the wall and saying to her, 'Listen carefully, my little Cosette. We have to leave this house but we'll be coming back and we'll be very happy here. The old man who lives here is going to carry you away on his back in that. You'll wait for me at a lady's house. I'll come to fetch you. Above all, do as you're told and don't say anything, if you don't want Madame Thénardier to take you away again!'

Cosette nodded gravely.

At the sound of Fauchelevent pushing open the door Jean Valjean turned round.

'Well?'

'It's all sorted out, and nothing's sorted out,' said Fauchelevent. 'I've permission to bring you in. But before bringing you in you must be got out. That's where the difficulty lies. For the little one, it's easy.'

'You'll carry her out?'

'And she'll be quiet?'

'I guarantee it.'

'But you, Père Madeleine?'

And after a silence filled with some anxiety Fauchelevent cried out, 'But why not go out the way you came in!'

Like the first time, Jean Valjean merely said, 'Impossible.'

Talking more to himself than to Jean Valjean, Fauchelevent grumbled, 'There's something else that's worrying me. I said that I'd put earth in it. Now that I come to think about it, having earth inside instead of the body, it won't be the same, it won't do, it will shift, it will move about. The men will feel it. You see, Père Madeleine, the government will find out.'

Jean Valjean looked him straight in the eye and thought he was raving.

Fauchelevent went on, 'How the dev— . . . deuce are you going to get out? The thing is, it must all be done tomorrow. Tomorrow's when I'm supposed to bring you. The prioress is expecting you.'

Then he explained to Jean Valjean that it was a reward for a favour he, Fauchelevent, was doing the community. That it was part of his duties to assist with burials, that he nailed down the coffins and helped the gravedigger at the cemetery. That the nun who had died that morning had asked to be buried in the coffin that had served for her bed, and to be put in the crypt under the altar in the chapel. That this was forbidden by police regulations, but she was one of those dead to whom nothing is denied. That the prioress and the vocal mothers intended to fulfil the deceased's wishes. Never mind about the government. That he, Fauchelevent, was to nail down the coffin in the side room, lift the stone in the chapel and lower the corpse into the crypt. And that, by way of thanks, the prioress was to allow his brother into the house as a gardener and his niece as a pupil. That his brother was Monsieur Madeleine, and his niece was Cosette. That the prioress had told him to bring his brother the following evening, after the fake burial in the cemetery. But he could not bring Monsieur Madeleine in from outside if Monsieur Madeleine was not outside. That was the first problem. And then there was another problem: the empty coffin.

'What empty coffin?' asked Jean Valjean.

Fauchelevent replied, 'The authorities' coffin.'

'What coffin? What authorities?'

'A nun dies. The municipal doctor comes and says, "There's a nun that's died." The government sends a coffin. The next day it sends a hearse and coffin bearers to collect the coffin and bring it to the cemetery. The coffin bearers will come and lift the coffin. There'll be nothing inside it.'

'Put something in it.'

'A dead body? I haven't got one.'

'No.'

'What then?'

'A living person.'

'What living person?'

'Me!' said Jean Valjean.

Fauchelevent, who was sitting down, jumped up as if a firework had gone off under his chair.

'You!'

'Why not?'

Jean Valjean gave one of those rare smiles that came over him like a gleam of sunlight in a winter sky.

'You remember, Fauchelevent, that you said, "Mère Crucifixion's dead", and I added, "And Père Madeleine's buried." '

'Of course, you're joking. You're not being serious.'

'Very serious. I've got to get out of here?'

'Certainly.'

'I told you to find a basket and a covering for me too.'

'Well?'

'The basket will be of pine, and the covering a black pall.'

'For a start, it will be a white pall. Nuns are buried in white.'

'A white pall, then.'

'You're a man unlike other men, Père Madeleine.'

Seeing ideas such as these, which are nothing other than the wild and daring inventions of the prison hulks, emerge from the peaceable things surrounding him and become mixed up with what he called 'the convent's humdrum life' was astounding to Fauchelevent, in much the same way that the sight of a seagull fishing in the gutter would be to a passer-by on Rue St-Denis.

Jean Valjean went on, 'The problem is to get out of here without being seen. This is a way to do that. But explain to me first. What happens? Where is this coffin?'

'The empty one?'

'Yes.'

'Downstairs, in what's called the room for the dead. It stands on two trestles under the pall.'

'How long is the coffin?'

'Six foot.'

'What is this room for the dead?'

'It's a ground-floor room which has a barred window, looking on to the garden, that's closed behind a shutter from the outside, and two doors, one leading into the convent, the other into the church.'

'What church?'

'The church on the street, the church for everyone.'

'Have you the keys to those two doors?'

'No, I have the key to the convent door, the porter has the key to the church door.'

'When does the porter open that door?'

'Only to let in the coffin bearers when they come to fetch the coffin. Once the coffin's gone, the door's locked again.'

'Who nails the coffin down?'

'I do.'

'Who lays the pall over it?'

'I do.'

'Are you alone?'

'No other man except the police doctor can go into the room for the dead. That's even written on the wall.'

'When everyone's asleep tonight could you hide me in that room?'

'No. But I can hide you in a small dark closet off the room for the dead, where I keep my tools for burials. I look after it and I have the key to it.'

'What time will the hearse come for the coffin tomorrow?'

'About three o'clock in the afternoon. The burial will take place at Vaugirard Cemetery just before nightfall. It's a bit of a way from here.'

'I'll be hiding in your tool closet all night and all morning. What about food? I'll be hungry.'

'I'll bring you something.'

'You could come and nail down the coffin with me inside it at two o'clock.'

Fauchelevent recoiled and cracked his finger joints. 'But that's inconceivable!'

'Bah! What's inconceivable about taking a hammer and driving some nails into a plank of wood!'

What seemed appalling to Fauchelevent was, we repeat, common-place to Jean Valjean. Jean Valjean had been in worse straits than this. Any man who has been a prisoner knows the art of shrinking to fit the diameter of the escape hole. The prisoner is prone to escape, just as the sick man is prone to the crisis that kills or cures him. An escape is a cure. What will a man not consent to for the sake of being cured? To be nailed up inside a box and carried off like a parcel, to spend a long time in a confined space, to find air where there is none, to be sparing of breath for hours on end, to be capable of being stifled without dying – this was one of Jean Valjean's sinister talents.

Besides, this convict's ploy, of a coffin with a living person inside it, is also an emperor's ploy. If the monk Austin Castillejo is to be believed, it was by this device that Charles V, wanting to see La Plombes for the last time after his abdication, had her brought into the monastery of San Yuste and taken out again.

Having rallied a little, Fauchelevent exclaimed, 'But how will you manage to breathe?'

'I'll breathe.'

'In that box! Just to think of it suffocates me.'

'You must have a gimlet, you'll make a few holes around the mouth, here and there, and nail the top down not too tightly.'

'Fine! And what if you should happen to cough or sneeze?'

'A man escaping doesn't cough or sneeze.' And Jean Valjean added,

'Père Fauchelevent, there's a decision to be made: either be caught here or agree to be taken out in the hearse.'

Everyone has noticed the inclination of cats to stop and linger between double doors left standing ajar. Who is there who has not said to a cat, 'Come in, then!' There are men who, faced with a dilemma, also have a tendency to remain undecided between two resolutions, and risk getting crushed when fate suddenly slams the door shut on the incident.

The overly cautious, for all that they are cats, and because they are cats, sometimes put themselves in greater danger than the bold. Fauchelevent was a hesitant character of this sort. But despite himself, Jean Valjean's cool determination overcame him. He grumbled, 'The truth is, there's no other way.'

Jean Valjean went on, 'The only thing that worries me is what happens at the cemetery.'

'That's the very thing that doesn't bother me,' exclaimed Fauchelevent. 'If you're confident of getting through the experience of being in the coffin, I'm confident of getting you out of the grave. The gravedigger's a drunkard friend of mine. Père Mestienne. A veteran old soak. The gravedigger disposes of the dead, and I dispose of the gravedigger. I'll tell you what will happen. We'll get there shortly before dusk, three-quarters of an hour before the cemetery gates close. The hearse will drive directly up to the grave. I'll be following behind. That's my job. I'll have a hammer, a chisel and some pincers in my pocket. The hearse stops, the coffin bearers tie a rope around your coffin and lower you down. The priest says some prayers, makes the sign of the cross, sprinkles holy water, and he's off. I'm left alone with Père Mestienne. He's my friend, I tell you. There are two possibilities, he's either drunk or he's not. If he's not drunk, I say to him, "Come and have a drink while the Bon Coing's still open." I take him away, I get him drunk – it doesn't take long to get Père Mestienne drunk, he's always had a head start – I drink him under the table, I take his pass to get back into the cemetery and I return without him. Then you'll just be dealing with me. If he's drunk I say to him, "Go away, I'll do your work for you." Off he goes and I pull you out of the hole.'

Jean Valjean held out his hand and Fauchelevent was quick to respond with heart-warming rustic enthusiasm.

'That's settled, Père Fauchelevent. All will go well.'

'As long as nothing goes wrong,' thought Fauchelevent. 'Imagine how terrible that could be!'

V
To Be Immortal It Is Not Enough
to Be a Drunkard

The next day as the sun was setting, the passers-by on Boulevard du Maine, who were very few and far between, raised their hats as a hearse of the old-fashioned type went by, adorned with decorative skulls and bones and teardrops. This hearse contained a coffin covered with a white cloth with a huge black cross on it like a big dead body with its arms hanging over the sides. A black-draped carriage followed behind, in which could be seen a surpliced priest and a choirboy in his red skull-cap. Two coffin bearers in grey uniforms trimmed with black walked on the right and left of the hearse. An old man in labourer's clothing came limping after it. This procession was making its way to Vaugirard Cemetery.

The handle of a hammer, the blade of a cold chisel and the two handles of a pair of pincers could be seen protruding from the man's pocket.

Vaugirard Cemetery was an exception among Paris's cemeteries. It had its own particular practices, just as it had its carriage entrance and its side entrance, which old people in the neighbourhood, clinging to the old terms, still called the horsemen's entrance and the pedestrian entrance. The Bernardine-Benedictines of Petite-Rue-Picpus had obtained permission, as we have said, to be buried there, in the evening, in an isolated corner, this plot of land having formerly belonged to their community. The gravediggers, who because of this had to work in the cemetery at twilight in summer and in the dark in winter, were obliged to follow a special procedure. In those days the gates of the Paris cemeteries closed at sundown, and this being a municipal regulation, Vaugirard Cemetery was bound by it like the rest. The horsemen's entrance and the pedestrian entrance were two iron gates standing next to each other, alongside a lodge built by the architect Perronet and inhabited by the cemetery gatekeeper. These gates, therefore, swung inexorably on their hinges the moment the sun disappeared behind the Invalides dome. If any gravedigger were at that moment delayed inside the cemetery there was only one way he could get out: by using his gravedigger's pass, supplied by the burial authorities. A kind of letter-box was cut into the porter's window. The gravedigger dropped his pass into this box, the porter heard it fall, pulled the rope, and the pedestrian gate opened. If the man did not have his pass, he gave his name, the porter – who was sometimes in bed asleep – would get up, come out and identify the man, and open the gate with his key. The gravedigger would be let out, but paid a fine of fifteen francs.

With its exceptions to the rule, this cemetery upset the administrative order. It was closed down shortly after 1830. Montparnasse Cemetery next door, called the 'east cemetery', replaced it, and inherited that famous watering-hole in between, which had a quince painted on a wooden panel above it and stood on a corner with the drinkers' tables on one side and the graves on the other, under the shop sign 'Au Bon Coing'.*

Vaugirard Cemetery was what may be called a cemetery past its prime. It was falling into disuse. Mildew was overtaking it, flowers were deserting it. Wealthier citizens did not much care to be buried in Vaugirard, it suggested poverty. Père-Lachaise was the place! To be buried in Père-Lachaise is like having mahogany furniture. Its elegance is unmistakable. Vaugirard Cemetery was venerable ground, laid out in the style of an old-fashioned French garden. Straight paths, box, thuja, holly, old graves under old yew trees, very tall grass. It was macabre after dusk. It took on a very sinister aspect.

The sun had not yet set when the hearse with the white pall and black cross entered the avenue of Vaugirard Cemetery. The lame man following behind it was none other than Fauchelevent.

The burial of Mère Crucifixion in the crypt under the altar, getting Cosette out of the convent and Jean Valjean into the room for the dead – everything had gone smoothly and there had been no mishaps.

By the way, let us say that, as far as we are concerned, the burial of Mère Crucifixion under the altar in the convent is a truly venial matter. It is one of those transgressions that seem like a duty. The nuns had done it not only without any qualm but with the approval of their conscience. In the cloister, what is called 'the government' is only an interference with the rule, an interference that is always suspect. The rule comes first. As for the law, that remains to be seen. You men, make as many laws as you please, but keep them for yourselves. Caesar's due is never anything more than what is left over from God's due. A prince is nothing beside a principle.

Fauchelevent limped along behind the hearse feeling very satisfied. His two secrets, his twin conspiracies, one with the nuns, the other with Monsieur Madeleine, one for the convent, the other against it, had so far succeeded. Jean Valjean's equanimity was one of those powerful kinds of calm that are contagious. Fauchelevent was no longer doubtful of success. What remained to be done was nothing. In

---

* The word for 'quince', *coing*, is pronounced exactly the same as the word for 'corner', *coin*.

the last two years he had got that chubby-cheeked fellow good old Mestienne the gravedigger drunk at least ten times. He could work him like a puppet. He could do what he wanted with him. Fauchelevent could shape him to his will and his whim. Mestienne's head would fit the hat that Fauchelevent put on it. Fauchelevent felt utterly confident.

As the procession entered the avenue leading to the cemetery Fauchelevent glanced at the hearse and rubbed his big hands contentedly, saying under his breath, 'What a joke!'

The hearse stopped abruptly. They had reached the gate. The burial licence had to be shown. The undertaker's man conferred with the cemetery gatekeeper. During this exchange, which always involves a delay of one or two minutes, someone, a stranger, came and stood behind the hearse alongside Fauchelevent. He was some kind of labourer wearing a jacket with big pockets and he had a pick under his arm.

Fauchelevent stared at this stranger.

'Who are you?' he asked.

The man replied, 'The gravedigger.'

If you survived a cannon-ball hitting you right in the chest you would have the same expression on your face that Fauchelevent had.

'The gravedigger?'

'Yes.'

'You?'

'Me.'

'Old Mestienne is the gravedigger.'

'He was.'

'What do you mean, "he was"?'

'He's dead.'

Fauchelevent had expected anything but this, that a gravedigger should die. Yet it is true: even gravediggers die. By digging graves for other people they prepare their own.

Fauchelevent was left open-mouthed. He had hardly the strength to stammer, 'But that's not possible!'

'It is.'

'But,' he persisted feebly, 'the gravedigger is old Mestienne.'

'After Napoleon, Louis XVIII. After Mestienne, Gribier. Peasant, my name is Gribier.'

Completely ashen, Fauchelevent examined this Gribier.

He was tall, thin, pale-faced, utterly lugubrious. He looked like a failed doctor turned gravedigger.

Fauchelevent burst out laughing.

'Ah, what strange things happen! Old Mestienne's dead. Dear old Mestienne's dead, but long live dear old Lenoir! You know what dear old Lenoir is? It's a red wine at six sous the carafe. It's a carafe of Suresnes, by Jove! Real Paris Suresnes! Ah! So old Mestienne's dead! I'm sorry to hear it. He was a man who enjoyed life. But you're a man who enjoys life, too. Aren't you, comrade? We'll go and have a drink together presently.'

The man replied, 'I have some education. I completed three years' secondary schooling. I never drink.'

The hearse had started off again and was proceeding along the cemetery's main drive.

Fauchelevent had slowed down. He was limping much more from anxiety than from infirmity.

The gravedigger walked on ahead of him.

Fauchelevent again took stock of the unexpected Gribier.

He was one of those men who, though young, look old and, though lean, are extremely strong.

'Comrade!' cried Fauchelevent.

The man turned round.

'I'm the gravedigger from the convent.'

'My colleague,' said the man.

Uneducated but very astute, Fauchelevent realized he was dealing with a difficult customer, a smooth talker.

He muttered, 'So that's it, old Mestienne's dead.'

The man replied, 'Absolutely. The good Lord consulted his record for when payments fall due. Old Mestienne's time had come. Old Mestienne died.'

Fauchelevent repeated mechanically, 'The good Lord—'

'The good Lord,' said the man with authority. 'For philosophers, the Eternal Father. For Jacobins, the Supreme Being.'

'Shan't we get acquainted?' faltered Fauchelevent.

'We are already. You're a peasant, I am a Parisian.'

'People don't know each other until they've drunk together. He who empties his glass empties his heart. You must come and have a drink with me. There's no refusing that.'

'Work comes first.'

Fauchelevent thought: 'I'm doomed.'

Only another few turns of the wheel before they reached the side path leading to the nuns' corner.

The gravedigger spoke again. 'Peasant, I've seven kids that need feeding. Since they must eat, I must not drink.' And he added with the satisfaction of a serious-minded person delivering a well turned phrase, 'Their hunger is the enemy of my thirst.'

The hearse skirted a clump of cypress trees, left the main avenue, turned down a side path, set off across some rough ground, then plunged into a thicket. This signalled that they were very close to the burial plot. Fauchelevent slackened his pace but could not slow the hearse down. Fortunately, the loose soil, waterlogged with the winter rains, mired the wheels and made it heavy going.

He approached the gravedigger.

'They have such a nice drop of Argenteuil wine,' murmured Fauchelevent.

'Villager,' retorted the man, 'by rights I shouldn't be a gravedigger. My father was a porter at the Prytanée cadet school. He had intended me for Literature. But he suffered some setbacks. He made losses on the stock exchange. I was obliged to give up the profession of author. But I am still a public letter-writer.'

'So you're not a gravedigger, then?' said Fauchelevent, clutching at this straw.

'One doesn't rule out the other. I'm an incumbent of more than one post.'

Fauchelevent did not understand the word 'incumbent'.

'Come and have a drink,' he said.

A comment needs to be made here. However distressed he might be, Fauchelevent was suggesting a drink but he did not make himself clear on one point: who was to pay? Generally, Fauchelevent would suggest a drink and old Mestienne paid. The suggestion of a drink evidently resulted from the new situation created by the new gravedigger, and it needed to be made, but the old gardener left in some obscurity, not unintentionally, the proverbial moment of reckoning. Upset as he was, Fauchelevent was not anxious to be the one to pay.

The gravedigger went on with a superior smile, 'A man must eat. I agreed to fill the vacancy left by old Mestienne. When you've almost graduated, you're philosophical. I supplemented my handiwork with manual work. I have my letter-writer's stall in the Rue de Sèvres market. You know, the umbrella market? All the cooks in the Croix-Rouge neighbourhood come to me. I dash off their declarations of love to their soldier-boys. In the morning I write love letters, in the evening I dig graves. That's life, country cousin.'

The hearse rolled on. His anxiety reaching a peak, Fauchelevent looked around in every direction. Great drops of sweat were trickling from his brow.

'But it's impossible to serve two mistresses,' the gravedigger went on. 'I'll have to choose between the pen and the pick. The pick is ruining my hand.'

The hearse stopped. The choirboy descended from the draped carriage, then the priest. One of the small front wheels of the hearse had run a little way up a pile of earth, an open grave visible on the other side of it.

'What a joke!' Fauchelevent repeated in dismay.

VI
Inside the Wooden Box

Who was in the coffin? As we know: Jean Valjean.

Jean Valjean had taken steps to survive in there, and he could breathe, more or less.

It is a strange thing how much the mind that feels secure imparts a sense of security to the rest of the body. The whole scheme devised by Jean Valjean had been working out, and working out well, since the day before. He, like Fauchelevent, was counting on old Mestienne. He had no doubt about the outcome. Never more critical circumstances, never more utter calm.

The four sides of the wooden coffin emanated a kind of terrible peacefulness. It was as if something of the repose of the dead entered Jean Valjean's tranquillity. From inside that coffin he had been able to follow, and was following, every phase of the terrible drama he was staging with death.

Shortly after Fauchelevent had finished nailing the lid down, Jean Valjean had felt himself being carried out, then driven off. He could tell by the reduced jolting that they were going from cobblestones to an earthen surface, in other words they were leaving the streets and coming to the boulevards. From a dull sound he guessed they were crossing the Pont d'Austerlitz. At the first stop he realized they were entering the cemetery. At the second stop he said to himself: 'We're at the grave.'

Suddenly he sensed hands seizing the coffin, then a rough chafing against the wood. He realized this was a rope being tied round the coffin in order to lower it into the dug-out hole. Then some sort of dizziness came over him. The coffin bearers and the gravedigger had probably let the coffin tip and lowered it down head first. Once he felt horizontal and stationary, he recovered fully. He had just touched the bottom. He felt a certain coldness.

A voice rose above him, chilling and solemn. He heard Latin words he did not understand being recited over him, so slowly he was able to catch every one of them individually.

'*Qui dormiunt in terrae pulvere, evigilabunt; alii in vitam aeternam, et alii in opprobrium, ut videant semper.*'

A child's voice said, '*De profundis.*'

The solemn voice spoke again, '*Requiem aeternam dona ei, Domine.*'

The child's voice responded, '*Et lux perpetua luceat ei.*'

He heard something that sounded like the gentle patter of a few drops of rain on the wooden plank covering him. It was probably holy water. He thought: 'This will soon be over. A little more patience. The priest is going to leave. Fauchelevent will take Mestienne off drinking. I'll be left here. Then Fauchelevent will come back alone, and I'll get out. A good hour is what it will take.'

The grave voice resumed, '*Requiescat in pace.*'*

And the child's voice said, 'Amen.'

Jean Valjean strained his ears and heard something that sounded like retreating footsteps.

'That's them leaving,' he thought. 'I'm alone.'

All at once he heard above his head a sound that was like a clap of thunder to him. It was a spadeful of earth falling on the coffin.

A second spadeful came down. One of the holes through which he was breathing was now blocked. A third spadeful of earth came down. Then a fourth. There are some things that are too much for the strongest of men to bear. Jean Valjean lost consciousness.

VII
In Which We Find the Origin of the Saying '*Ne Pas Perdre la Carte*'†

This is what was happening above the coffin where Jean Valjean lay.

When the hearse had moved away, when the priest and the choir-boy had climbed back into the carriage and left, Fauchelevent, who did not take his eyes off the gravedigger, saw him bend over and grab his spade, which was standing upright, embedded in the pile of earth.

---

* From the office for the burial of the dead in the *Missel de Paris*: 'Those that sleep in the dust of the earth shall awake, some to everlasting life, and some to shame and everlasting contempt.' 'Out of the depths.' 'Eternal rest give unto her, O Lord.' 'And let perpetual light shine upon her.' 'May she rest in peace.'
† Literally, 'don't lose the card', i.e. 'don't lose the lead (or initiative)', as in a card game, or as here, 'don't lose your pass [*carte*]'.

Then Fauchelevent came to a drastic decision.

He placed himself between the grave and the gravedigger, crossed his arms and said, 'I'm paying!'

The gravedigger stared at him in astonishment and replied, 'What, peasant?'

Fauchelevent repeated, 'I'm paying!'

'For what?'

'The wine.'

'What wine?'

'The Argenteuil.'

'What Argenteuil?'

'At the Bon Coing.'

'Go to blazes!' said the gravedigger. And he threw a spadeful of earth on to the coffin.

The coffin resounded with a thud. Fauchelevent felt unsteady and about to fall headlong into the grave himself. He shouted in a voice that began to have the strangled rasp of death in it, 'Comrade! Before the Bon Coing closes!'

The gravedigger loaded more earth on to his shovel.

Fauchelevent said again, 'I'm paying.' And he seized the gravedigger's arm. 'Listen to me, comrade. I'm the convent's gravedigger, I'm here to help you. It's a job that can be done after dark. So let's go and have a drink first.'

And even as he spoke, even as he kept up this desperate nagging, he had this dour thought: 'And what if he *were* to drink – would he get drunk?'

'Provincial,' said the man, 'if you absolutely insist, I accept. We'll have a drink. After the work's done, never before.'

And he swung back his spade. Fauchelevent stopped him.

'It's Argenteuil wine at six sous.'

'That's enough!' said the gravedigger. 'A right bell clapper, you are. Ding dong, ding dong, that's all you can say. Give it a rest.'

And he threw in the second spadeful.

Fauchelevent had reached that point where a person no longer knows what he is saying.

'Oh, come along and have a drink,' he cried, 'since I'm paying!'

'When we've put the baby to bed,' said the gravedigger.

He threw in the third spadeful.

Then he dug his spade into the earth and added, 'You see, it's going to be cold tonight and the dear departed would cry out after us if we were to go off and leave her here without a blanket.'

At that moment, as he loaded his spade, the gravedigger bent over and his jacket pocket gaped open.

Fauchelevent's frantic gaze automatically looked into that pocket, and there it settled.

The sun was not yet obscured below the horizon. It was still light enough to be able to distinguish something white at the bottom of that gaping pocket.

All the brightness a Picard peasant's eye can hold gleamed in Fauchelevent's pupils. He had just had an idea.

Without the gravedigger noticing, all his concentration focused as it was on his spadeful of earth, Fauchelevent dipped his hand into Gribier's pocket from behind and pulled out of that pocket the white object lying at the bottom of it.

The gravedigger threw a fourth spadeful into the grave.

As he turned round to load the fifth, Fauchelevent looked at him with extreme calm and said, 'By the way, newcomer, have you got your pass?'

The gravedigger stopped what he was doing.

'What pass?'

'The sun's going down.'

'Good luck to it, and goodnight.'

'The cemetery gate's going to close.'

'So what?'

'Have you got your pass?'

'Ah! my pass,' said the gravedigger.

And he fumbled in his pocket.

Having fumbled in one pocket, he fumbled in the other. He moved on to his breast pockets, searched one, turned out the other.

'Well, no,' he said, 'I haven't got my pass. I must have forgotten it.'

'Fifteen francs fine,' said Fauchelevent.

The gravedigger turned green. Green is the pallor of the pale-faced.

'Oh, Jesus, my God, I don't believe it!' he exclaimed. 'Fifteen francs fine!'

'Three one-hundred-sou coins,' said Fauchelevent.

The gravedigger dropped his spade.

Fauchelevent's moment had come.

'Come now, novice,' said Fauchelevent, 'don't despair. There's no need to commit suicide and take advantage of the grave. Fifteen francs is fifteen francs, and besides, you can avoid paying it. I'm an old hand, you're new to the job. I know the tricks of the trade, the rules of the game, the ins and outs. I'm going to give you some friendly advice.

One thing's clear, the sun's going down, it's touching the dome, the cemetery is going to close in five minutes.'

'That's true,' replied the gravedigger.

'You haven't time in the next five minutes to fill the grave, it's devilish deep, this grave, and reach the gate in time to get out before it closes.'

'That's right.'

'In that case, fifteen francs fine to pay.'

'Fifteen francs.'

'But you *have* got time . . . Where do you live?'

'Just by the toll-gate, a quarter of an hour from here. Rue de Vaugirard, number 87.'

'You've got time, if you stir your stumps, to get out straight away.'

'That's correct.'

'Once outside the gate, you race home, you collect your pass, you come back to the cemetery, the gatekeeper lets you in. With your card, there's nothing to pay. And you bury your corpse. I'll look after it for you in the meantime and see that it doesn't run away.'

'You've saved my life, peasant.'

'Off you go!' said Fauchelevent.

Overwhelmed with gratitude, the gravedigger shook his hand and ran off.

When the man had disappeared into the thicket Fauchelevent listened until the sound of his footsteps died away, then he leaned over the grave and said in a low voice, 'Père Madeleine!'

No reply.

Fauchelevent gave a shudder. He rolled down into the grave rather than climbed down, threw himself at the head of the coffin and cried, 'Are you there?'

Silence in the coffin.

Breathless from trembling, Fauchelevent grabbed his cold chisel and hammer, and prised open the coffin lid. Jean Valjean's face appeared in the twilight, eyes closed, bloodless.

Fauchelevent's hair stood on end. He got to his feet, then close to collapsing on top of the coffin he fell back against the wall of the grave. He stared at Jean Valjean.

Jean Valjean lay there, deathly pale and still.

Fauchelevent murmured in a voice as faint as a sigh, 'He's dead!'

And drawing himself up, crossing his arms so violently that a clenched fist struck each shoulder, he cried, 'This is how I save him!'

Then the poor fellow began sobbing. And talking to himself, for it is a mistake to think that talking to oneself is not natural. Greatly disturbed emotions often speak aloud.

'It's old Mestienne's fault. Why did that fool go and die? Why did he have to snuff it when no one was expecting it? It's because of him Monsieur Madeleine's dead. Père Madeleine! He's in the coffin. And already lying in his grave. That's the end of it. Now, is there any sense in such things? Oh, my God! He's dead! And now what about the little girl, what am I going to do with her? What will the fruit-seller say? For a man like that to die like that, how in God's name is it possible? When I think how he got under that cart! Père Madeleine! Père Madeleine! By heaven, he suffocated, just like I said. He wouldn't believe me. Well, this is a pretty piece of mischief! He's dead, that good man, of all the good Lord's good people the very best of men! And his little girl! Oh! I'm not going back there for a start. I'm staying here. What a stupid thing to have done! What's the good of being two old men when you're two old fools! But how did he get inside the convent in the first place? That's how it all started. People shouldn't do things like that. Père Madeleine! Père Madeleine! Père Madeleine! Madeleine! Monsieur Madeleine! Monsieur le maire! He can't hear me. Now get yourself out of this one!'

And he tore at his hair.

A shrill creaking could be heard in the distance among the trees. It was the cemetery gate closing.

Fauchelevent bent over Jean Valjean, and all of a sudden he gave a kind of start and leapt back as far as anyone can leap back inside a grave. Jean Valjean's eyes were open and staring at him.

It is frightening to see a dead body, it is almost as frightening to see a resurrection. Fauchelevent grew petrified, pale, wild-eyed, overwhelmed by all these extremes of emotion, not knowing whether he was dealing with a living man or a dead one, and staring at Jean Valjean, who was staring at him.

'I fell asleep,' said Jean Valjean.

And he sat up.

Fauchelevent fell on his knees.

'Good sweet Virgin! Did you frighten me!'

Then he sprang to his feet and cried, 'Thank you, Père Madeleine!'

Jean Valjean had merely fainted. The fresh air revived him.

Joy is the ebbing of terror. Fauchelevent had almost as much difficulty in recovering his senses as Jean Valjean.

'So you're not dead! Oh! you are a teaser, you are! I called out to you so much, you came back. When I saw your eyes shut I said: "There! Now, he's suffocated!" I'd have gone raving mad, really and truly, fit for a straitjacket. They'd have put me in Bicêtre. What would you expect me to do if you'd died? And your little girl? The fruit-seller's the one that wouldn't have made any sense of it! The child's landed on her and the grandfather dies! What a to-do! Dear saints in heaven, what a to-do! Ah, you're alive, that's the crowning glory!'

'I'm cold,' said Jean Valjean.

This remark brought Fauchelevent right back to reality, with its urgent demands. Even restored to their senses, these two men without realizing it were troubled in spirit and felt a strangeness inside them, which was the sinister effect of the place.

'Let's get out of here quick!' cried Fauchelevent.

He fumbled in his pocket and pulled out a flask he had on him.

'But a little drop first!' he said.

The flask completed the work the fresh air had begun. Jean Valjean drank a mouthful of brandy and regained full possession of himself.

He climbed out of the coffin and helped Fauchelevent to nail the lid back down.

Three minutes later they were out of the grave.

Fauchelevent was calm about the rest. He took his time. The cemetery was closed. There was no fear of the gravedigger Gribier turning up. That 'novice' was at home busy looking for his pass, and certain not to find it at his lodgings since it was in Fauchelevent's pocket. With no pass, he could not come back into the cemetery.

Fauchelevent took the spade and Jean Valjean the pick, and together they buried the empty coffin.

When the grave had been filled in, Fauchelevent said to Jean Valjean, 'Let's go. I'll carry the spade, you bring the pick.'

Night was falling.

Jean Valjean had some difficulty in moving and walking. He had grown stiff in that coffin and had become a little corpse-like. The rigidity of death had taken hold of him inside that wooden box. He had, as it were, to thaw out from being in the grave.

'You're numb,' said Fauchelevent. 'It's a pity I'm crippled in one leg, otherwise we could play "step on your foot".'

'Bah!' replied Jean Valjean. 'A few steps, and my legs will be fine.'

They walked back along the paths the hearse had taken. When they came to the closed gate and the gatekeeper's lodge Fauchelevent, who held the gravedigger's pass in his hand, dropped it into the box, the porter pulled the rope, the gate opened, and they were out.

'How well everything's going!' said Fauchelevent. 'What a good idea that was of yours, Père Madeleine!'

They passed through the Vaugirard gate with no trouble at all. Anywhere near a cemetery, a spade and a pick act as two passports.

Rue Vaugirard was deserted.

'Père Madeleine,' said Fauchelevent, walking along and looking up at the houses, 'your eyes are better than mine. Tell me which is number 87.'

'This is it here,' said Jean Valjean.

'There's no one in the street,' said Fauchelevent. 'Give me your pick and wait a couple of minutes for me.'

Fauchelevent went into number 87, climbed to the very top, guided by the instinct that always leads the poor man to the garret, and in the gloom knocked at the door of an attic.

A voice replied, 'Come in.'

It was Gribier's voice.

Fauchelevent pushed open the door. The gravedigger's home was, like all such wretched dwellings, an unfurnished and cluttered hovel. A packing-case, a coffin perhaps, served as a chest, a butter-cooler served as a kitchen sink, a straw mattress served as a bed, the floor served as table and chairs. In one corner, in a heap on a tattered old scrap of carpet, were a thin woman and a gaggle of children. The whole wretched place showed signs of upheaval. It looked as though it had been hit by an earthquake all of its own. Lids were displaced, ragged clothing was scattered about, the jug was broken, the mother had been weeping, the children had probably been beaten: signs of a distraught and bad-tempered search. It was plain that the gravedigger had been frantically hunting for his pass and held everything in the garret, from the jug to his wife, responsible for its loss. He looked desperate.

But Fauchelevent was in too great a hurry to bring this adventure to a conclusion to notice this sorry side of his success.

He came in and said, 'I've brought you back your pick and spade.'

Gribier gazed at him, astounded. 'You here, peasant?'

'And tomorrow morning you'll find your pass with the gatekeeper at the cemetery.'

And he laid the spade and pick on the floor.

'What does this mean?' asked Gribier.

'What it means is that your pass fell out of your pocket, I found it on the ground after you left, I've buried the corpse, I've filled in the grave, I've done your work for you, the porter will give you your pass back, and you won't have to pay fifteen francs. So there you are, novice.'

'Thank you, villager!' exclaimed Gribier in amazement. 'Next time the drinks are on me.'

VIII
A Successful Interview

An hour later, in pitch darkness, two men and a child turned up at number 62 Petite-Rue-Picpus. The older man lifted the knocker and rapped. They were Fauchelevent, Jean Valjean and Cosette.

The two old fellows had gone to fetch Cosette from the fruit-seller's in Rue du Chemin-Vert, where Fauchelevent had left her the day before. Cosette had spent the past twenty-four hours completely baffled and trembling silently. She trembled so much, she did not cry. Nor had she eaten or slept. The worthy fruit-seller had plied her with a hundred questions without obtaining any response other than ever the same melancholy gaze. Cosette had given no hint of what she had seen and heard during the last two days. She could tell they were going through a crisis. She sensed deeply that she had to 'be good'. Who has not experienced the supreme power of those three words, delivered in a certain tone of voice in the ear of a terrified little person: 'Not a word!' Fear is mute. Besides, there is no one like a child for keeping a secret.

Only, when she saw Jean Valjean again after those dismal twenty-four hours, she let out such a cry of joy that any thinking person who heard it would have detected in that cry deliverance from an abyss.

Fauchelevent was from the convent and knew the passwords. Every door opened. And so it was that the tremendous twofold problem was resolved: of getting out and getting in.

The porter, who had his instructions, opened the little back door, still visible from the street twenty years ago, that led from the courtyard into the garden and was set in the wall at the far end of the courtyard facing the carriage entrance. The porter let all three of them in through this door, and from there they came to that special inner parlour where Fauchelevent had taken his orders from the prioress the day before.

The prioress was waiting for them, rosary in hand. A vocal mother stood beside her, veiled. A discreet candle lighted – one might almost say made a pretence of lighting – the parlour.

The prioress inspected Jean Valjean. There is no scrutiny like that of a downcast eye.

Then she questioned him. 'You're the brother?'

'Yes, reverend mother,' replied Fauchelevent.

'What's your name?'

Fauchelevent replied, 'Ultime Fauchelevent.'

He actually had a brother named Ultime, who had died.

'Where do you come from?'

Fauchelevent replied, 'From Picquigny, near Amiens.'

'How old are you?'

Fauchelevent replied, 'Fifty.'

'What is your trade?'

Fauchelevent replied, 'Gardener.'

'Are you a good Christian?'

Fauchelevent replied, 'Everyone in the family is.'

'This is your little girl?'

Fauchelevent replied, 'Yes, reverend mother.'

'You're her father?'

Fauchelevent replied, 'Her grandfather.'

The vocal mother murmured to the prioress, 'He answers well.'

Jean Valjean had not said a word.

The prioress studied Cosette and murmured to the vocal mother, 'She'll be ugly.'

The two mothers conferred for a few moments very quietly in the corner of the parlour, then the prioress turned and said, 'Père Fauvent, you shall have another knee-pad with a bell. Two are needed now.'

Indeed, the next day two bells could be heard in the garden, and the nuns could not resist the temptation to lift the corner of their veils. At the far end of the garden under the trees two men, Fauvent and another, could be seen digging side by side. An enormous event. Silence was broken to the point of telling each other, 'He's an assistant gardener.'

The vocal mothers added, 'He's a brother of Père Fauvent.'

Jean Valjean was indeed properly installed: he had his leather knee-pad with a bell on it, he was now official. His name was Ultime Fauchelevent.

The strongest determining factor in favour of his admission had been the prioress's observation about Cosette: 'She'll be ugly.' Having delivered her prognosis, the prioress immediately took a liking to Cosette and gave her a place in the school as a charity pupil.

There is nothing very logical about this. It is all very well having no mirror in the convent, women have an awareness about their faces. Now, girls who feel pretty are less likely to be recruited as nuns. A vocation being the more gladly accepted in inverse proportion to beauty, the ugly are a more hopeful prospect than the pretty. Hence a strong preference for the plain.

This entire escapade increased good old Fauchelevent's standing. He scored a triple success: with Jean Valjean, whom he rescued and took in; with the gravedigger Gribier, who said to himself 'He saved me that fine'; with the convent, which, thanks to him, by keeping Mère Crucifixion's coffin under the altar, evaded Caesar and satisfied God. There was a coffin with a body in it at Petit-Picpus, and a coffin without a body at Vaugirard Cemetery. Public order was no doubt seriously breached, but did not know it. As for the convent, its gratitude to Fauchelevent was great. Fauchelevent became the best of servants and the most precious of gardeners. On the archbishop's next visit the prioress recounted the affair to His Grace, partly confessing to it and also boasting of it. After leaving the convent the archbishop spoke of it with approval and very discreetly to Monsieur de Latil, confessor to Monsieur, later archbishop of Reims and cardinal. This admiration for Fauchelevent spread far and wide, for it reached Rome. We have seen with our own eyes a note addressed by the then reigning pope, Leo XII, to one of his relatives, a monsignor in the nuncio's office in Paris and named, like himself, Della Genga. These lines are to be read in it: 'Apparently there is in the Paris convent an excellent gardener who is a saintly man called Fauvent.' None of all this glory reached Fauchelevent in his hut. He went on grafting, hoeing, and covering up his melon beds, without being informed of his excellence and his saintliness. He had no more inkling of his renown than a Durham or Surrey bull whose picture is published in the *Illustrated London News* with this caption: 'Prize-winning bull at cattle show'.

IX
Cloistered

In the convent, Cosette continued to keep quiet.

Cosette quite naturally thought she was Jean Valjean's daughter. Besides, knowing nothing, there was nothing she could have said, and she would not in any case have said anything. As we remarked above, there is nothing like unhappiness for training children to be silent. Cosette had suffered so much that she was fearful of everything, even of speaking, even of breathing. A single word had so often brought an avalanche crashing down on her. She was only just beginning to feel secure since being with Jean Valjean. She quite quickly settled down in the convent. Only, she missed Catherine but dared not say so. Yet she did once tell Jean Valjean: 'Father, if I'd known, I'd have brought her with me.'

On becoming a boarder at the convent, Cosette had to start wearing the pupils' uniform. Jean Valjean was granted permission to have the clothes she no longer wore given back to him. This was the same mourning outfit he had dressed her in when she left the Thénardier inn. It was still not very worn. Jean Valjean locked up these garments, as well as her woollen stockings and shoes, together with a great quantity of camphor and all those aromatics that are so plentiful in convents, in a little valise that he managed to procure. He put this valise on a chair by his bed, and he always kept the key with him. 'Father,' Cosette asked him one day, 'what is that box that smells so good?'

Aside from the renown we have just mentioned, of which he knew nothing, old Fauchelevent was rewarded for his good action. In the first place it made him happy. He also had much less work to do, sharing it with someone else. Lastly, since he was very fond of snuff, he found that another advantage of having Monsieur Madeleine there was that he took three times as much snuff as he used to, and with infinitely more relish, seeing that Monsieur Madeleine treated him to it.

The nuns did not use that name, Ultime. They called Jean Valjean 'the other Fauvent'.

If these saintly women had had anything of Javert's sharpsightedness, they would eventually have noticed that whenever there was any errand to be done outside the convent for the upkeep of the garden, it was always the elder Fauchelevent, the old man, the invalid, the cripple, who went, and never the other. But whether eyes always fixed on God are incapable of spying or whether the nuns preferred to devote their attention to keeping an eye on each other, they did not notice this.

In fact it was just as well for Jean Valjean that he lay low and did not stir. Javert kept the neighbourbood under observation for more than a full month.

This convent was for Jean Valjean like an island surrounded by perilous depths. These four walls now constituted his world. Here, he saw enough of the sky for his own serenity, and enough of Cosette to be happy.

Life began to be very tranquil for him again.

He lived with old Fauchelevent in the hut at the bottom of the garden. This little cabin, built out of rubble, which was still there in 1845, consisted as we know of three rooms, completely stark with just the bare walls. The main room had been forced on Monsieur Madeleine by old Fauchelevent, for Jean Valjean had resisted in vain. Apart from the two nails on which to hang the knee-pad and the basket, the wall of this room was adorned with a royalist banknote of '93, set on the chimney-breast above the fireplace, of which an exact facsimile appears below:

This Vendean promissory note had been nailed to the wall by the previous gardener, a former Chouan counter-revolutionary who died in the convent and had been replaced by Fauchelevent.

Jean Valjean worked all day in the garden and was extremely useful there. He had in the past been a tree pruner and was glad to be a gardener again. Remember, he knew all kinds of secrets and lore about cultivating plants. He turned these to advantage. Almost all the trees in the orchard were wildings. He budded them and got them to bear excellent fruit.

Cosette was allowed to come and spend an hour with him every day. As the sisters were doleful and he was kind, the child made comparisons and adored him. At the appointed time she would run to the hut. When she came into that tumbledown cottage, she filled it with bliss. Jean Valjean brightened, and felt his own happiness increase with the happiness he gave to Cosette. What is delightful about the joy we inspire is that, far from growing dimmer, as all reflections do, it returns to us more radiant. At playtime, from afar, Jean Valjean watched Cosette running and playing, and he could distinguish her laughter from the laughter of the others.

For Cosette now laughed.

Cosette's face had to a certain extent even changed, as a result. The gloom had faded from it. Laughter is sunshine. It banishes winter from the human countenance.

Still not pretty, Cosette, it must be said, was becoming delightful. She would make wise little remarks in her sweet childish voice.

When playtime was over and Cosette had gone back into the house, Jean Valjean would gaze at her classroom windows, and he would get up at night to gaze at the windows of her dormitory.

God has his ways, after all. The convent contributed, like Cosette, to sustaining and completing in Jean Valjean the work of the bishop. It is certain that there is an aspect of virtue that leads to pride. There is a bridge there built by the devil. Jean Valjean was perhaps unwittingly quite close to that aspect and to that bridge when providence cast him into the Petit-Picpus convent. So long as he compared himself only with the bishop, he regarded himself as unworthy and remained humble. But for some time past he had been starting to compare himself with other men, and pride was germinating in him. Who knows? He might have ended up returning very slowly to hatred.

The convent stopped him on that downward slope.

This was the second place of captivity he had seen. In his youth, in what had been for him the beginning of life, and later on, very recently, he had seen another – a dreadful, terrible place whose harshness had always seemed to him the iniquity of justice and the criminality of the law. Now, after the prison hulks, he saw the cloister. And reflecting on how he had been an inmate of the prison and was now, so to speak, an observer of the cloister, he anxiously compared them in his mind.

Sometimes he would lean on his hoe and slowly sink into the fathomless convolutions of his musings.

He recalled his former companions. How wretched they were: they rose at dawn and toiled until dark. They were all but denied sleep. They lay on camp beds with mattresses only two inches thick allowed to them, in rooms that were heated only during the bitterest months of the year. They had to wear dreadful red tunics. As a concession they were allowed light trousers in the hot season and a woollen jacket in the cold season. They drank wine and ate meat only when they were 'on a job'. Without any names, referred to only by numbers and in a sense turned into ciphers, they lived with their eyes downcast, their voices lowered, their heads shorn, under the rod, in disgrace.

Then his mind reverted to the human beings before his eyes.

These human beings, too, lived with their heads shorn, their eyes downcast, their voices lowered, not in disgrace but amid the world's jeering, not with their backs bruised by the rod but with their shoulders lacerated by self-mortification. Their names, too, had died among men. They now existed only under an austere nomenclature. They never ate meat and they never drank wine. They often went without food until evening. They were dressed not in red tunics but in black woollen shrouds, heavy in summer, light in winter, unable to take anything off or to put on anything extra, without even the possibility, according to season, of thinner clothing or a woollen overcoat. And for six months of the year they wore serge vests that made them feverish. They lived not in rooms heated only during the coldest weather but in cells where no fire was ever lighted. They slept not on mattresses two inches thick but on straw. Lastly, they were not even left to sleep. Every night after a day of toil, just as they were falling asleep and beginning to get warm, they had to waken from the heaviness of their first sleep, get up and go and pray, kneeling on stone in a gloomy, freezing-cold chapel.

On certain days each of these human beings in turn had to remain twelve hours on end kneeling on the flagstones or lying on the ground, face down with arms outstretched in the form of a cross.

The others were men, these were women. What had those men done? They had stolen, raped, pillaged, killed, assassinated. They were outlaws, counterfeiters, poisoners, arsonists, murderers, parricides. What had these women done? They had done nothing.

On the one hand, highway robbery, fraud, theft, violence, debauchery, homicide, every kind of sacrilege, every type of outrage. On the other, one thing only: innocence. Perfect innocence – gathered up, almost, in a mysterious assumption, still earthly in its virtue, already heavenly in its saintliness.

On the one hand, whispered confidences about crimes committed, on the other, the public confession of sins. And what crimes! And what sins!

On the one hand, miasmic stenches, on the other, an ineffable perfume. On the one hand, a moral pestilence, incarcerated, under armed guard, and slowly devouring the afflicted. On the other, a pure conflagration of every soul in the one hearth. There, darkness. Here, shadow. But shadow filled with gleams of light and gleams filled with radiance.

Two places of slavery, but in the first, the possibility of being freed, a legal term always in sight, and even escape; in the second place a life sentence to be served, the only hope in the far distant future that glimmer of freedom men call death.

In the first the enslaved were fettered only by chains, in the other they were fettered by their faith.

What issued from the first? An all-encompassing curse, the gnashing of teeth, hatred, desperate viciousness, a cry of rage against human society, a jeer at heaven. What came from the second? Blessings and love. And in these two places, so alike and so unalike, these two species of human being, so different from each other, were devoted to the same task: expiation.

Jean Valjean well understood the expiation of the former, personal expiation, expiation for oneself. But he did not understand that of the latter, that of these blameless creatures free from sin, and he wondered with a shudder: 'Expiation of what? What expiation?'

A voice in his conscience replied: 'That most divine of human generosities, expiation for others.'

Here, all our own thinking is set aside. As narrator, we are simply putting ourselves in Jean Valjean's position and conveying his impressions from his point of view.

He had before his eyes the sublime pinnacle of self-sacrifice, the highest possible peak of virtue. Innocence that forgives men their wrong-doing and expiates that wrong-doing in their stead. Servitude endured, torture accepted, punishment craved by souls that have not sinned in order to spare the souls that have transgressed. Love of humanity steeped in love of God yet remaining distinct from it, and imploring. Frail, gentle creatures embracing the woe of those who are punished with the smile of those who are rewarded. And he remembered that he had dared to feel sorry for himself!

Often he would get up in the middle of the night to listen to the grateful song of those innocent creatures crushed by the rigours of their discipline, and his blood ran cold at the thought that those who were justly punished raised their voices to heaven only in blasphemy and, wretch that he was, that he had shaken his fist at God.

One striking thing, that like a whispered warning from providence itself made him deeply pensive: the climb, the barriers overcome, even the risk of death accepted, the dire and difficult ascent – all those same efforts he had made to get out of that other place of expiation, he had made in order to get into this one. Was this a symbol of his destiny?

This house was a prison too, and bore a bleak resemblance to the other place he had fled, and yet he had never conceived of anything like it.

Here again were gratings, bolts, iron bars, to imprison whom? Angels. Those high walls that he had seen around tigers he now saw around lambs.

This was a place of expiation and not of punishment. And yet it was more austere, more dismal and more pitiless than the other. These virgins were even more heavily bowed down than the convicts. A bitter cold wind, the wind that had chilled his youth, swept through the barred and padlocked pit of vultures. The blast of an even harsher and more biting wind prevailed in this cage of doves.

Why?

When he thought about these things, everything inside him was humbled before this sublime mystery. In these reflections pride vanished. He made all kinds of reassessments of himself: he felt lowly, and he wept many times. Everything that had entered his life over the last six months led him back to the bishop's saintly injunctions, Cosette through love, the convent through humility.

Sometimes in the evening at twilight, a time when the garden was deserted, he could be seen kneeling in the middle of the path running alongside the chapel, in front of the window he had looked through on the night of his arrival, turned towards the spot where he knew the sister who was making reparation lay prostrate in prayer. And so he prayed, kneeling before the sister. It was as if he dared not kneel directly before God.

He was slowly imbued with everything that surrounded him, this peaceful garden, these fragrant flowers, these children uttering joyful cries, these women of grave simplicity, this silent cloister, and little by little his soul became a creation of silence like this cloister, of perfume like these flowers, of peace like this garden, of simplicity like these women, of joy like these children. And then he reflected how it was two houses of God that had in turn taken him in at two critical moments in his life: the first when all doors were closed to him and human society rejected him, the second when human society started hounding him again and the prison hulks opened up before him once more. And that but for the first he would have fallen back into crime, and but for the second, back into torment.

His heart melted through and through in gratitude, and became ever more loving.

Thus a number of years went by; and Cosette grew up.

PART THREE

MARIUS

BOOK ONE
PARIS THROUGH
THE STUDY OF ONE
OF ITS ATOMS

I
Parvulus*

Paris has a child and the forest has a bird. The bird is called the sparrow, the child is called the *gamin*.

Paris, childhood: put together these two concepts, all furnace the one, all new light the other, strike these two sparks against each other and what this produces is a little being. *Homuncio*, Plautus would say.

This little being is joyous. He does not eat every day and he sees a show every evening if he feels like it. He has no shirt on his back, no shoes on his feet, no roof over his head. He is like the flies in the air that have none of all that. He is aged between seven and thirteen, lives in gangs, roams the streets, sleeps rough, wears an old pair of his father's trousers that come down over his heels, some other father's old hat that comes down below his ears, a single brace made of a strip of yellow cloth; he gads about, keeps his eyes peeled, scrounges, dawdles, breaks in tobacco pipes, swears like a trooper, haunts the tavern, associates with thieves, back-chats with whores, talks slang, sings dirty songs, and has not an ounce of wickedness in his heart. The fact is, he has in his soul a pearl, innocence, and pearls do not dissolve in the mire. So long as man is a child, God wants him to be innocent.

If you were to ask that huge city, 'What is that?' it would reply, 'That's my little one.'

---

* Latin for 'small', meaning here 'child'.

Some of His Characteristics

Paris's gamin is the giant's dwarf.

Let us not exaggerate, this guttersnipe-cherub does sometimes have a shirt, but then he has only one. He sometimes has shoes, but then they have no soles. He sometimes has a home, and he loves it, for there he finds his mother, but he prefers the street because there he finds freedom. He has his own games; his own mischief, founded on hatred of the respectable citizen; his own metaphors: being dead is called 'pushing up the daisies'; his own jobs: fetching hackney cabs, letting down carriage steps, charging pedestrians to get them from one side of the street to the other in heavy rain (what he calls creating *ponts des arts**); hollering speeches made by those in authority in favour of the French people; scrabbling between the cobblestones. He has his own coinage consisting of all the little bits of wrought copper that can be found on the public thoroughfare. This curious currency, which goes by the name of 'scrap', has a fixed and well regulated exchange rate within this little community of vagrant children.

Lastly, he has his own fauna, which he studiously observes in out-of-the-way corners: the ladybird, the death's-head plant-louse, the daddy-longlegs, the 'devil's coach-horse' – a black insect armed with two horns that conveys menace by twisting up its tail end. He has his own fabulous monster that has scales on its belly but is not a lizard, that has pustules on its back but is not a toad, that inhabits the nooks and crannies of old lime kilns and dried-out cisterns, a black, hairy, slimy creepy-crawly, sometimes slow-moving, sometimes fast, that makes no cry but stares, and is so terrible that no one has ever seen it. He calls this monster 'the salamander'. Hunting among stones for 'salamanders' is a dreadful kind of pleasure. Another pleasure is to lift up a cobblestone all of a sudden and see woodlice. Each area of Paris is famous for the interesting discoveries to be made there. There are earwigs in the storehouses at Les Ursulines, millipedes at the Panthéon, tadpoles in the Champ de Mars trenches.

As for witticisms, this child can match Talleyrand. He is no less cynical, but he is more honest. He is blessed with an unexpected sort of mirth. He baffles the shopkeeper with his fits of laughter. His range extends good-humouredly from high comedy to farce.

---

* The Pont des Arts iron footbridge across the Seine was built in 1802–4, taking its name from the Palais des Arts, as the Louvre was then called, whereas the artistry in the gamin's 'bridges' would be in their construction out of found objects.

A funeral procession goes by. Among those accompanying the deceased is a doctor. 'Well I never!' exclaims a gamin. 'Since when do doctors look after the dead?'

Another is in a crowd. A bespectacled and serious-looking gentleman, his watch chain festooned with charms, turns round indignantly. 'You rascal, you just pinched my wife!'

'Search me, monsieur! I haven't got her!'

III
He Is Likeable

In the evening, thanks to a few sous that he always manages to come by somehow, the *homuncio* goes to the theatre. On crossing that magic threshold he is transfigured. He was the gamin, he becomes the *titi**. Theatres are a kind of upturned ship with the keel in the air. It is in that keel that the titi congregates. The titi is to the gamin what the moth is to the grub: the same creature in flight, soaring high. His presence up there, with his radiant happiness, his tremendous enthusiasm and joy, his clapping hands like beating wings, is reason enough to call that constricted, fetid, dark, sordid, unhealthy, ghastly, dreadful keel 'the gods'.

Give a person the unnecessary and deprive him of the essential, what you have is the gamin.

The gamin is not without some literary instinct. His natural inclination, and we say this with all due regret, would not be for the classical style. He is not very academic by nature. So, to give an example, the popularity of Mademoiselle Mars among that small audience of rowdy children was seasoned with a touch of irony. The gamin called her 'Mademoiselle Muche'.†

This creature bawls, brawls, joshes and jibes, is young in years and old in experience, fishes in the gutter, hunts in the sewer, extracts merriment from filth, perks up life on the street, grins and bites, whistles and sings, cheers and jeers, tones down his hallelujahs with tra-la-las, chants all kinds of rhythms from the *De Profundis* to the carnival ditty, finds without seeking, knows what he is ignorant of, is Spartan even in his thieving, wise even in his foolery, lyrical even in his

---

* Like the gamin, another familiar term for a Parisian type.
† The joke may be that Mademoiselle Mars was a brunette, and there is a fly (*mouche*) called a *brune de mars* ('March brown fly'). A somewhat cryptic reference to *Muche* as a slang deformation of *Mars* appears in *Étude sur l'argot français* by Marcel Schwob and Georges Guieysse, Paris, 1889.

scurrilousness; he would squat down on Mount Olympus, he wallows in the dungheap and emerges from it covered with stars. The Parisian gamin is Rabelais as a boy.

He is not happy with his trousers if they have no fob-pocket.

He is not easily astonished, even less easily scared, he derides superstition, deflates bombast, scoffs at mystery, pokes his tongue out at ghosts, parodies pomposity, caricatures epic aggrandizement. It is not that he is prosaic, far from it, but he replaces the solemn view with the comically phantasmagorical. If Adamastor were to appear before him, the gamin would say, 'Well, if it isn't the bogeyman!'

IV
He Can Be Useful

Paris starts out with the gawper and ends up with the gamin, two types no other city is capable of producing: passive acceptance, content to look on, and inexhaustible initiative. Prudhomme and Fouillou. Paris alone has such specimens in its natural history. Monarchy is all there in the gawper. Anarchy is all there in the gamin.

This wan child of Paris's poorer neighbourhoods lives and develops in hardship, growing up physically stunted, a thoughtful witness to the social realities and human goings-on around him. He thinks he is blithe. He is not. He watches, ready to laugh. And not only to laugh. Whoever you may be, whether your name is Prejudice, Abuse, Ignorance, Oppression, Iniquity, Despotism, Injustice, Fanaticism, Tyranny, beware the gaping gamin.

This little lad will grow up.

Of what clay is he made? Of any old mud. A handful of dirt, a breath, and behold Adam. A god has only to pass by. One always does, in the case of the gamin. Fortune works on this little creature. By the word 'fortune' we want to suggest an element of fortuity. Ignorant, illiterate, bewildered, coarse, common, this pigmy moulded out of ordinary unrefined earth – will he be an Ionian or a Boeotian? Wait! *Currit rota.** Unlike the Latin potter, the spirit of Paris, that demon creator of children of accident and men of destiny, out of a kitchen jug makes an amphora.

---

* 'The wheel turns.' An allusion to Horace's *Ars Poetica*, lines 21–2: 'Amphora coepit / institui: currente rota cur urceus exit?' ('An amphora starts to be formed: why as the wheel turns is a kitchen jug the result?').

V

His Boundaries

The gamin loves the city. Having something of the sage in him, he also loves solitude. Like Fuscus, *urbis amator*. Like Flaccus, *ruris amator*.*

To take a contemplative stroll, that is to say to saunter, is for the philosopher a good use of time, particularly in the somewhat hybrid, rather ugly but bizarre and dual-natured countryside that surrounds certain cities, notably Paris. To study the outskirts is to study the amphibious. Where trees end and roofs begin, where grass ends and paving begins, where ploughed fields end and shops begin, where rutted tracks end and passions begin, where the divine murmur ends and the human uproar begins: therein lies extraordinary interest.

Hence the wool-gatherer's apparently aimless walks, in these not very attractive environs forever branded by the casual passer-by with the descriptive term 'dreary'.

He who writes these lines for a long time haunted the purlieus of the Paris gates, and this for him is a source of deep-seated memories. That bald turf, those stony paths, that chalk, that marl, that gypsum, those bleak monotonies of untilled and fallow land, early market-garden crops suddenly glimpsed in a hollow, that mixture of the feral and the respectable, those vast empty spaces where garrison drummers noisily learn their skills and give a kind of clumsy impression of battle, these spots unfrequented by day, death-traps by night, the ungainly windmill turning in the wind, the quarry pulley-wheels, the open-air cafés just by the cemeteries, the mysterious charm of high, grim walls squaring off huge wastelands basking in sunlight and full of butterflies – all this attracted him.

Hardly anyone on earth is familiar with these strange places – Glacière, Cunette, Grenelle's ghastly wall riddled with bullets, Mont-Parnasse, Fosse-aux-Loups, Les Aubiers on the banks of the Marne, Montsouris, Tombe-Issoire, Pierre-Plate at Châtillon where there is an old exhausted quarry, now used only for growing mushrooms and closed off at ground level by a trap-door of rotten planks. The Roman *campagna* is one concept, the outskirts of Paris another. To see in a landscape nothing but fields, houses or trees is to see only the surface. All aspects of things are notions of God. The place where a plain meets a city is always steeped in some indefinable pervasive

---

* An allusion to the opening lines of Horace's Epistle 10, addressed to Aristius Fuscus: 'Urbis amatorem Fuscum salvere iubemus / ruris amatores' ('We the country-lovers wish to salute Fuscus the town-lover'). Horace's full name was Quintus Horatius Flaccus.

melancholy. Nature and humanity speak to you simultaneously there. Local peculiarities become evident.

Anyone who, like us, has roamed those lonely wildernesses adjoining our *faubourgs* that might be called Paris's limbo has glimpsed here and there, in the most forsaken spot, at the most unexpected moment, behind a scraggy hedge or in the corner of a dank wall, rowdy groups of pallid, muddy, dusty, ragged, dishevelled children, crowned with cornflowers, playing hide-and-seek. These are all young runaways from poor families. The outer boulevard is their breathable environment, the periphery belongs to them. They make it their eternal playground. There, they innocently sing their repertory of dirty songs. There they are, or rather there they exist, far from all eyes, in the mild May or June sunlight, kneeling round a hole in the ground, flicking marbles with their thumbs, quarrelling over quarter-sous, carefree, on the wing, on the loose, happy. And no sooner do they catch sight of you than they remember they have a trade and must earn their living, and they offer to sell you an old woollen stocking filled with maybugs, or a bunch of lilacs. These encounters with strange children are one of the delights, at once charming and poignant, of the outskirts of Paris.

Sometimes among these gangs of boys there are little girls – their sisters? – almost young misses, thin, feverish, with weathered hands, and freckled, wearing spikes of rye and poppies in their hair, cheerful, frenetic, barefoot. You see some of them eating cherries in the wheat fields. In the evening you hear them laughing. In the warm brightness of high noon or glimpsed in the twilight, these groups linger in the wool-gatherer's mind and these visions mingle with his fantasies.

Paris, the centre, the outlying districts, the perimeter – for these children this constitutes the whole world. They never venture beyond it. They can no more leave the Parisian atmosphere than fish can leave water. For them, five miles beyond the gates there is nothing. Ivry, Gentilly, Arcueil, Belleville, Aubervilliers, Ménilmontant, Choisy-le-Roi, Billancourt, Meudon, Issy, Vanvre, Sèvres, Puteaux, Neuilly, Gennevilliers, Colombes, Romainville, Chatou, Asnières, Bougival, Nanterre, Enghien, Noisy-le-Sec, Nogent, Gournay, Drancy, Gonesse – here is where the universe ends.

VI
A Bit of History

During the period albeit so recent in which this book is set there was not, as there is now, a policeman at the corner of every street (a benefit this is not the time to go into). Paris was full of waifs and strays. The statistics give an average of two hundred and sixty homeless children rounded up annually by police patrols, on open land, on building sites and under the arches of bridges. One such bolt-hole of lasting notoriety yielded 'the swallows of the Pont d'Arcole'. We are in fact talking about the most dire of social symptoms. All the crimes of man begin in the vagabondage of the child.

Paris excepted, however. Relatively speaking, and notwithstanding that surviving memory we have just referred to, it is a fair exception. Whereas in any other city a vagabond child is a doomed man, whereas almost everywhere the child left to fend for itself is in a way consigned and abandoned to a kind of fatal submersion in public vices that destroy honesty and conscience in the child, we are adamant that, no matter how damaged and spoiled on the surface, inwardly the Paris gamin is virtually unscathed. Wonderful to relate, and clearly apparent in the splendid integrity of our popular revolutions, a certain incorruptibility ensues from the idea inherent in the air of Paris as from the salt inherent in the waters of the ocean. Inhaling Paris preserves the soul.

What we have just said in no way reduces the heartache you feel every time you come across one of these children, around whom you seem to see the fluttering ties of the broken family. In the present as yet very imperfect state of civilization they are not very unusual, these break-ups of families spilling their innards in the shadows, not really knowing what has become of their children, and abandoning their offspring on the public highway. Where they are left to their obscure fate. This is called – for this sad phenomenon has given rise to a common expression – 'being cast on to the streets of Paris'.

Incidentally, this abandonment of children was not discouraged by the former monarchy. An element of Egypt and Bohemia in the nether regions suited the upper echelons and served the interests of those in power. Virulent opposition to the education of children of the lower orders was an article of faith. What good are the 'semi-educated'? That was the watchword. Well, the stray child is the inevitable consequence of the uneducated child.

Besides, the monarchy sometimes had need of children, and then it would 'clean up' the streets.

Under Louis XIV, to go no further back, the king rightly wanted to create a fleet. A good idea. But let us consider how. Fleet there is none without not only the sailing-ship – plaything of the wind – but also, ready to tow it if need be, the vessel that goes where it pleases by the power of oar or steam. Galley ships were then to the navy what steamers are today. So galleys were necessary. But the galley moves only by virtue of the galley slave. So galley slaves were necessary. Colbert required the provincial commissioners and local parliaments to sentence to the galleys as many convicts as possible. The magistracy was very obliging in this matter. If a man kept his hat on when a procession went by – Huguenot behaviour – he was sent to the galleys. If you came across a child in the street – as long as he was fifteen years old and with nowhere to lay his head at night – you sent him to the galleys. Glorious reign, glorious century.

Under Louis XV children disappeared in Paris. The police abducted them, who knows for what mysterious purpose. Monstrous conjectures about the king's crimson baths were whispered in terror. Barbier naively mentions these things. It sometimes happened that the police, being short of children, took those who had fathers. These desperate fathers attacked the police. In such cases parliament intervened and they were hanged. Who? The police? No, the fathers.

VII
The Gamin Would Have His Own Place in India's Caste System

The brotherhood of the Parisian gamin virtually constitutes a caste. You might almost say: an exclusive caste.

This word *gamin* first appeared in print, and entered the literary language from the language spoken by the people, in 1834. It was in a short work entitled 'Claude Gueux' that the word appeared. There was a considerable outcry. The word survived.

The factors that contribute to the regard gamins have for each other are very varied. We have known and spent time with one who was greatly respected and greatly admired for having seen a man fall off the top of Notre-Dame's towers; another, for having managed to set foot inside the rear courtyard of Les Invalides where the statues from the dome had been temporarily deposited, and having 'filched' some lead off them; a third, for having seen a coach overturn; yet another, because 'a soldier he knew' had almost blinded some bourgeois or other.

Which explains this exclamation from a Parisian gamin: 'God Almighty, am I unlucky! To think I haven't yet seen anyone fall from the fifth floor' ('haven't' pronounced 'ain't' and 'fifth', 'fif') – a profound comment the vulgar herd laughs at without understanding.

Certainly, the following is a fine peasant riposte:

'Old So-and-So, your wife's died of her illness – why didn't you send for the doctor?'

'It can't be helped, monsieur, when it comes to dying, us poor folk have to shift for ourselves.'

But if all the peasant's sly passiveness is contained in that response, all the free-thinking anarchy of the outer-city street urchin is contained in this one: A man condemned to death is listening to his confessor in the tumbril. The Paris lad exclaims, 'He's talking to his holy man! Ah, the softie!'

A certain brazenness with regard to religion distinguishes the gamin. Being a free-thinker is important.

Attending executions counts as a duty. Pointing out the guillotine to his fellows, the gamin laughs. He has all sorts of nicknames for it: the Post-prandial, the Grouser, the Mother in the Blue Yonder (heaven), the Last Bite, and so on and so forth. In order not to miss anything of what is going on, he scales walls, hoists himself on to balconies, climbs trees, hangs from railings, clings to chimneys. The gamin is a born roofer as he is a born mariner. A roof inspires no more fear in him than a mast does. No entertainment is as good as La Grève. Sanson and Abbé Montès are truly popular names. The victim is jeered at by way of encouragement. He is sometimes admired. As a gamin himself, Lacenaire, on seeing the dreadful Dautun die bravely, made this remark, wherein lay his own future: 'I was jealous of him.' Among the gamin brotherhood, no one has heard of Voltaire but they know of Papavoine. 'Political criminals' share legendary status with assassins. What clothes they all wore at the last is part of gamin lore. Tolleron is known to have worn a fireman's cap, Avril an otter-skin cap, Louvel a bowler-hat; old Delaporte was bald and bare-headed; Castaing was all rosy, and very attractive; Bories had a romantic little beard; Jean Martin still had his braces on; Lecouffé and his mother sniped at each other. 'Don't spoil it all by squabbling!' a gamin yelled out to them. In order to see Debacker go by, another, dwarfed by the crowd, spots a lamp-post on the embankment and starts to shin up it. A gendarme posted there scowls. 'Let me climb up, m'sieur le gendarme,' says the gamin. And to mollify the policeman he adds, 'I won't fall.' 'As if I care whether you fall!' replies the gendarme.

Among gamins a memorable accident carries a lot of weight. You are held in the highest esteem if you happen to cut yourself very deeply, 'right to the bone'.

Putting your fists up is no small element in commanding respect. One of the things the gamin is apt to say is, 'Believe me, I'm real tough!' Being left-handed makes you very enviable. Being squint-eyed is something revered.

VIII
Concerning a Charming Remark
Made by the Last King

In summer he turns into a frog. And in the evening at nightfall, in front of the Pont d'Austerlitz and the Pont d'Iéna, he dives off the top of coal wagons and off the washerwomen's boats, head first into the Seine, in all possible contravention of the rules of both modesty and the law. However, the police are on the lookout, and the result is a highly dramatic situation that once gave rise to a memorable fraternal cry. This cry, famous around 1830, is a strategic warning from gamin to gamin. It scans like a verse from Homer, defying transcription almost as much as the Eleusinian chanting at the Panathenaean festival, and in it we recognize the ancient 'Evohe!'* This was it: 'Ohey, Titi, oheeey! 'ere comes trouble, there's bashers about, grab your stuff and run for it, cut through the sewer!'

Sometimes this brat – this is how he refers to himself – can read, sometimes he can write. He can always draw. He is eager to acquire, by who knows what mysterious pooling of knowledge, every talent that might serve the common good. From 1815 to 1830 he imitated the turkey's gobble. From 1830 to 1848 he scrawled pears on walls. One summer evening when Louis-Philippe was walking home, he saw one of them, a tiny little thing, just so high, sweating and straining to draw a gigantic pear on one of the pillars of the Neuilly gate with a piece of charcoal. With that good-heartedness inherited from Henri IV, the king helped the gamin to complete the pear and gave him a twenty-franc coin, saying, 'There's a pear on that too.'

The gamin loves uproar. He likes a certain state of violence. He loathes 'pastors'. One day one of these young scamps was thumbing his nose at the carriage gate of number 69 Rue de l'Université. 'Why do that at this entrance?' asked a passer-by. The lad replied, 'There's a pastor living here.' It was in fact the residence of the papal nuncio. However, whatever the gamin's Voltairian attitudes, if the occasion to serve as a chorister presents itself he may well accept, and in that case he serves mass politely. There are two things that cast him as Tantalus, things he always yearns for without ever attaining: to overthrow the government and to get his trousers mended.

The gamin in his prime is thoroughly acquainted with every policeman in Paris, and can always put a name to the face whenever he encounters one. He counts them off on his fingers. He studies their

---

* The Bacchic rallying cry among the followers of Dionysus.

habits and he keeps special notes on each one of them. The souls of the police are an open book to him. He will tell you straight off without hesitation: 'This one's slippery, that one's really vicious, this one's great, that one's laughable.' (All these words – slippery, vicious, great, laughable – have a particular meaning when he uses them.) 'This one thinks he owns the Pont-Neuf and stops "everyone" walking on the ledge outside the parapet. That one's forever twisting "people"'s ears', et cetera.

IX
The Old Spirit of Gaul

There was something of this child in Poquelin, son of Les Halles. There was something of him in Beaumarchais. The essence of the gamin is an aspect of the Gallic spirit. It sometimes combines with common sense to fortify it, as alcohol fortifies wine. Sometimes it is a weakness. Yes, Homer nods, but Voltaire might be said to play the gamin.* Camille Desmoulins came from the outer suburbs. Championnet, who strong-armed miracles, sprang from the streets of Paris. He had, as a small lad, 'flooded the porticoes'† of St-Jean de Beauvais and of St-Étienne du Mont. He was on close enough terms with St Genevieve's reliquary to be able to command St Januarius' phial.

The Paris gamin is respectful, ironic and insolent. He has horrible teeth because he is ill-nourished and his stomach aches, and beautiful eyes because he has spirit. In Jehovah's presence, he would hop up the steps of paradise. He is good at foot-boxing. There is no feat of which he is incapable. He plays in the gutter, and rises to the occasion when there is rioting. His boldness persists in the face of gunfire. Once a scamp, he is now a hero. Like the young Theban, he shakes the lion's pelt. Bara the drummer-boy was a Paris gamin. He cries 'Charge!' just as the horse in the Scriptures says 'Vah!'‡ And within a moment he is transformed from urchin to giant.

---

* An allusion to Horace, *Ars Poetica*, line 358: 'And I also become annoyed whenever the great Homer nods off', referring to Homeric lapses into repetition. For Voltaire, Hugo has invented the verb *gaminer*.
† An allusion to Racine's *Athalie*, Act I, sc. i, lines 7–8, referring to the crowd that emerges from the temple as 'flooding the porticoes'; the traditional schoolboy joke lies in a literal rather than a metaphorical interpretation of 'flooding'.
‡ A reference to Job 39:25. ' "Vah" is a word of exultation . . . because every bold preacher . . . rejoices in the triumph of victory', St Gregory the Great, *Morals on the Book of Job*, the second part of vol. 3, bk XXXI, p. 477, Oxford, 1850.

This child of the dungheap is also a child of idealism. Measure the range, from Molière to Bara.

Finally, to sum it all up, the gamin is a playful creature because he is unhappy.

X
Ecce *Paris*, Ecce Homo *

Again, to sum up, the gamin of Paris today, like the *graeculus*† of Rome in the past, is the people in its infancy but with the wrinkled brow of an aged world.

The gamin is a credit to the nation, and at the same time a sickness. A sickness that must be cured. How? By light.

Light is wholesome.

Light is animating.

All radiance of social beneficence emanates from science, literature, the arts, education. Create men, create men. Illuminate them so they may reflect warmth on you. Sooner or later the splendid issue of universal education will present itself with the irresistible authority of absolute truth, and then those who govern under the scrutiny of the French idea will have to make this choice: the children of France or the gamins of Paris, beacons in the light or will-o'-the-wisps in the dark.

The gamin embodies Paris and Paris embodies the world.

For Paris is a summation. Paris is the greatest achievement of the human race. This whole marvellous city is a compendium of ways of life past and present. Anyone who sees Paris fancies that he is seeing what underlies all of history, with the heavens and constellations in between. Paris has a Capitol, the Hôtel-de-Ville; a Parthenon, Notre-Dame; an Aventine Hill, the Faubourg St-Antoine; an Asinarium, the Sorbonne; a Pantheon, the Panthéon; a Via Sacra, the Boulevard des Italiens; a Tower of the Winds, public opinion; and for the Gemonian Steps it substitutes ridicule. The Parisian *majo* is called *un faraud*, the Parisian *trasteverino* is called *un faubourien*, the Parisian *hamal* is called *un fort de la halle*, the Parisian *lazzarone* is called *un pègre*, the

---

* 'Behold Paris, behold the man'.

† Literally, 'little Greek', a patronizing term used by the Roman master for the Greek slave, especially one who served as tutor.

Parisian cockney is called *un gandin*.* Everything that exists elsewhere exists in Paris. Dumarsais's thieving harridan can hold her own against Euripides' herb-seller. The discus-thrower Vejanus lives again in the tight-rope acrobat Forioso. Therapontigonus Miles would happily walk arm in arm with Grenadier Vadeboncoeur. The second-hand art dealer Damasippus would be in his element among Paris's bric-à-brac merchants. Vincennes would put the cuffs on Socrates just as the Agora would clap Diderot in gaol. Grimod de la Reynière has discovered roast beef cooked in dripping, just as Curtillus invented roast hedgehog. The trapeze that features in Plautus we see reappearing under the Arc de l'Étoile balloon. The sword-eater encountered by Apuleius at the Poecile Portico is a sabre-swallower on the Pont-Neuf. Rameau's nephew and Curculio the parasite are a perfect match. Ergasilus would have d'Aigrefeuille introduce him to Cambacérès. Rome's four young fops Alcesimarchus, Phaedromus, Diabolus and Argyrippus join the end-of-carnival parade from La Courtille into Paris in the Labatut post-chaise. Aulus Gellius would stop to watch Congrio no longer than would Charles Nodier to watch Pulchinello. Marton is no tigress, but Pardalisca was no dragon. Pantolabus the joker joshes the wastrel Nomentanus in the Café Anglais. Hermogenes is a tenor in the Champs-Élysées and Thrasius the beggar, dressed up as Bobèche, passes the hat round for him. The bore who buttonholes you in the Tuileries makes you repeat two thousand years later Thesprio's exclamation: *Quis properantem me prehendit pallio?*† Suresnes wine replicates the wine of Alba, Désaugier's glassful of red corresponds to Balatro's huge goblet. In the rain at night the same vaporous glimmerings emanate from Père-Lachaise and the Esquiline,

---

* Flourishing in the late eighteenth and early nineteenth centuries, the Spanish *majo* (female *maja*) was a working-class dandy who favoured an exaggeratedly Spanish traditional costume. The French *faraud* is a more fatuous kind of dandy. Matched in Paris by the *faubourien* inhabitant of the working-class *faubourgs*, the *trasteverino* inhabitant of Trastevere, on the far side of the Tiber, had the reputation of embodying the soul of the true Roman. The Turkish *hamal*, bent double under his load, has his equivalent in the beefy market porter of Paris. The Neapolitan scoundrel, the *lazzarone* and the Parisian *pègre* are both members of a similarly low-class fraternity of petty criminals. What is common to the cockney, as understood by the French, and the *gandin* is a kind of Jack-the-lad, cock-of-the-walk, preening self-confidence.

† 'Who is it that tugs me by the cloak when I'm in a hurry?', line 2 of Plautus' *Epidicus*, said by Thesprio to Epidicus.

and the pauper's grave bought for five years is the equivalent of the slave's hired coffin.

Try to think of something Paris does not have. Trophonius' cave contains nothing that is not in Mesmer's tub. Ergaphilas lives again in Cagliostro. The Brahmin Vasaphanta is reincarnated in the Comte de St-Germain. The cemetery of St-Médard works miracles just as good as those of the Umumiye mosque at Damascus.

Paris has an Aesop: he is Mayeux; and a Canidia: she is Mademoiselle Lenormand. Like Delphi, Paris takes fright at electrifying glimpses of visionary realities. It turns tables as Dodona turns tripods. It puts the grisette on the throne as Rome puts the courtesan there. And in the end, if Louis XV is worse than Claudius, Madame du Barry is better than Messalina. Paris combines in an extraordinary individual – who actually existed and with whom we were personally acquainted – Grecian nudity, Jewish tribulation and Gascon wit. It creates a mixture of Diogenes, Job and Pagliaccio the clown, clothes a spectre in back issues of *Le Constitutionnel*, and produces Chodruc-Duclos.

Although Plutarch says 'the tyrant rarely grows old', Rome became resigned under both Sulla and Domitian and readily watered its wine. The Tiber was a Lethe, if Varus Vibiscus' rather tendentious celebration of it is to be believed: *Contra Gracchos Tiberim habemus, Bibere Tiberim, id est seditionem oblivisci.** Paris consumes a million litres of water a day, but that does not prevent it from sounding the clarion call and rising up in arms.

Otherwise, Paris is easy-going. Majestically, it accepts everything. It is not too particular as regards Venus – its callipygian beauty is a Hottentot. It will forgive anything for the sake of a laugh. Ugliness cheers it, deformity tickles it, vice distracts it. Be a joker, and you can get away with being a scoundrel. Paris does not even object to the ultimate cynicism, hypocrisy. It is so literary that it does not hold its nose at Basile, and is no more scandalized by Tartuffe's prayer than Horace is offended by Priapus' 'eruption'. No trait of the universal face is missing from Paris's profile. The dancing at the Bal Mabille is no Polymnia-inspired ritual on the Janiculum, but the purveyor of frippery gloats with predatory intent over the flighty Parisienne

---

* 'Against the Gracchi we have the Tiber. To drink the Tiber is to forget sedition.' The Gracchi – Tiberius (163–133 BC) and his younger brother Gaius (154–121 BC) – were Roman tribunes who, in the context of increasing social unrest among the lower classes of society, attempted to introduce land reform in favour of the poor and met with overwhelming resistance from the Senate. Both Gracchi met with a violent end.

just as the procuress Staphyla eyed the virgin Planesium. The Combat gate is no Coliseum, but the fighting there is as ferocious as if Caesar were looking on. The Syrian hostess has more charms than Mère Saguet, but if Virgil haunted the Roman inn, David d'Angers, Balzac and Charlet have sat at the tables of the Parisian tavern. Paris reigns. Geniuses dazzle there, buffoons prosper. Adonai drives through it in his twelve-wheeled chariot of thunder and lightning. Silenus makes his entry seated on his ass. For Silenus read Ramponneau.

Paris is synonymous with Cosmos. Paris is Athens, Rome, Sybaris, Jerusalem, Pantin*. It is the epitome of all civilizations, all barbarisms too. Paris would be very aggrieved not to have a guillotine.

A modicum of the Place de Grève is a good thing. What would all this perpetual festivity be without such seasonings? Our laws have wisely made provision for it, and thanks to them the blade drips over this Mardi Gras.

XI
Jocularity Reigns

Paris knows no bounds. No other city has exercised this kind of dominion that sometimes baffles those it subjugates. 'To please you, O Athenians!' exclaimed Alexander. Paris does more than set the rules, it sets the fashion. Paris does more than set the fashion, it sets the pattern of daily life. Paris may be stupid if it pleases. It sometimes allows itself this luxury, and the universe is stupid along with it. Then Paris wakes up, rubs its eyes, says 'What a fool I am!' and bursts out laughing in the face of humankind. What a marvel is a city such as this! Strange that this grandeur and this buffoonery should sit well with each other, that all this majesty should not be troubled by all this parody, and that the same mouth could today sound the trumpet of doom and tomorrow the tootle-pipe! Paris has a lordly jocularity. Its frivolity has the force of a thunderbolt and its prankishness is invested with sovereignty. Its hurricane sometimes originates in a grimace. Its uprisings, its days of trial, its triumphs, its wonders, its glorious past resound throughout the universe, and its cock-and-bull stories as well. Its laughter is the mouth of a volcano that spills out over the whole world. Its quips are sparks. It imposes on other peoples its caricatures as well as its ideal. The greatest monuments of human civilization accept its ironies and lend their immortal fame to its mischievousness.

* Parisian argot for 'Paris'.

It is magnificent. It has a marvellous fourteenth of July that liberates the world. It makes all nations swear the Tennis Court Oath. Its night of the fourth of August dispels in three hours a thousand years of feudalism. It uses its reasoning as the muscle of unanimous will. It proliferates under all forms of the sublime. It infuses with its light Washington, Kosciuszko, Bolívar, Botsaris, Riego, Bem, Manin, López, John Brown, Garibaldi. Wherever the future is kindled, it is there: at Boston in 1773, at the Isla de León in 1820, at Pest in 1848, at Palermo in 1860. It whispers the mighty watchword 'Liberty' in the ears of the American abolitionists gathered at Harpers Ferry, and in the ears of the patriots of Ancona assembled in the shadows of Gli Archi, by the sea, in front of the Gozzi inn. It creates Canaris, it creates Quiroga, it creates Pisacane. It radiates greatness on earth. It is by going where prompted by its inspiration that Byron dies at Missolonghi and Mazet dies in Barcelona. It is the floor of the debating chamber under Mirabeau's feet, and the crater under Robespierre's. Its books, theatre, art, science, literature, philosophy, are the manuals of the human race. It has Pascal, Régnier, Corneille, Descartes, Jean-Jacques, Voltaire for every moment, Molière for every age. It makes its language one that is spoken universally, and this language becomes the Word. It constructs in all minds the idea of progress. The tenets of liberation that it forges are trusty swords for generations, and it is of the spirit of its thinkers and poets that, since 1789, all heroes of all nations are made. This does not stop it behaving like a gamin and, even while transfiguring the world with its light, this vast genius called Paris blackens the wall of the temple of Theseus with a charcoal sketch of Bouginier's nose and writes on the Pyramids 'Crédeville's a thief'.

Paris is always showing its teeth. When it is not snarling, it is laughing.

Such is Paris. From its smoking rooftops come the world's ideas. A heap of mud and stone, if you will, but above all a moral entity. It is more than great, its stature is immense. Why? Because it is daring.

To dare – that is the price of progress.

All sublime conquests are more or less prizes for audacity. For the Revolution to happen it is not enough that Montesquieu should anticipate it, Diderot advocate it, Beaumarchais announce it, Condorcet calculate it, Arouet pave the way for it, Rousseau design it. Danton has to dare it.

The cry: Be bold! is a *fiat lux*. For the advance of the human race we need to have noble lessons in courage, set permanently on the heights. Audacious deeds dazzle history and are one of mankind's great sources of light. Dawn shows daring when it breaks. To venture, to brave, to persist, to persevere, to be true to ourselves, to grapple with fate, to astound catastrophe by how little it makes us afraid, to challenge unjust power on the one hand, to scorn drunken victory on the other, to resist, to hold out – that is the example nations need and the light that electrifies them. The same tremendous flash of lightning extends from Prometheus' torch to Cambronne's mouth-blisterer.

XII
The Future Latent in the People

As for the Parisian populace, even when grown to manhood, it is ever the gamin. To portray the child is to portray the city. And that is why we have studied this eagle in this sparrow.

It is, we must emphasize, especially in the *faubourgs* that the Parisian race is in evidence. There, the thoroughbred. There, its true incarnation. There, this populace toils and suffers, and suffering and toil are the two faces of the grown man. There, among untold numbers of unidentified individuals is a proliferation of the strangest types, from the docker at La Râpée to the knacker of Montfaucon. 'Fex urbis!' exclaims Cicero.* 'Mob!' adds Burke indignantly. Rabble, multitude, riff-raff. These words are soon spoken. But even so, what does it matter? What do I care if they go barefoot! They cannot read? Too bad! Would you abandon them for that? Would you doom them to their plight? Cannot the light penetrate these masses? Let us return to that cry: Light! And let us keep calling for it! Light! Light! Who knows whether these opacities will not become transparent? Are not revolutions transfigurations? Go to it, philosophers, teach. Enlighten, illuminate, think aloud, speak aloud, run joyously in the full sunlight, become a friend of the market-place, announce the good news, hand out educational primers, proclaim rights, sing the 'Marseillaise' again and again, sow fervour, tear green boughs from the oak trees. Make a whirlwind of the idea. This multitude can be made sublime. Let us be capable of using this vast conflagration of principles and virtues that at certain moments crackles and blazes and quivers. These bare feet, bare arms, rags, this benightedness, degradation, darkness may be used for the conquest of the ideal. Look through the populace and you will see the truth. This vile sand you trample underfoot – let it be

* 'The excrement of the city', an allusion to Cicero's *Letter to Atticus*, I.16.11.

thrown into the furnace, let it melt and bubble there. It will turn into clear crystal, and it is thanks to this crystal that Galileo and Newton will discover the stars.

XIII
Young Gavroche

Eight or nine years after the events related in Part Two of this story, on Boulevard du Temple and around the Château-d'Eau area people noticed a little boy of eleven or twelve who would have quite accurately embodied the description given above of the archetypal gamin if, with the laughter of a child his age on his lips, his heart had not been totally bleak and empty. This child was well turned out in a pair of men's trousers, but he had not got them from his father, and a woman's jacket, but he had not got it from his mother. Somebody or other had clothed him in cast-offs, out of charity. Yet he did have a father and a mother. But his father gave no thought to him and his mother did not love him. He was one of those children, most deserving of all of pity, who have both father and mother and who are orphans.

This child never felt so happy as on the street. The pavements were less hard to him than his mother's heart.

His parents had kicked him out to make his way in life.

He had simply spread his wings.

He was a boisterous, pallid, resourceful, smart, cheeky lad, animated yet sickly-looking. He was always on the go, singing, playing tiddlywinks, scratching about in the gutter, stealing a little, but blithely, like cats and sparrows do, laughing when he was called a scamp, getting cross when he was called a guttersnipe. He had no home, no food, no warmth, no love, but he was cheerful because he was free.

When these poor creatures are men, almost invariably they are caught and crushed under the millstone of the social order, but as long as they are children, being small, they escape. The tiniest bolt-hole saves them.

Yet, neglected as this child was, occasionally, every two or three months, he would say, 'Now, I'm going to see ma!' Then he would turn his back on the boulevard, the Cirque, Porte St-Martin, go down to the embankment, cross the bridges, make for the *faubourgs*, reach La Salpêtrière – and arrive where? At that very same double number, 50–52, already known to the reader: at the Gorbeau tenement.

At that time the tenement, number 50–52, normally empty and forever decorated with the sign 'Rooms to let', happened to be inhabited, extraordinarily enough, by several individuals who in fact, typically of Paris, had no connection or relationship with each other. All belonged to that indigent class that starts with the lowliest petty bourgeois in financial straits and extends through one level of poverty to another, to the lowest depths of society, right down to those two beings with whom all the material things of civilization end up: the sewer-man who sweeps up the sludge, and the rag-and-bone man who salvages the rubbish.

The 'principal tenant' of Jean Valjean's day had died and had been replaced by another exactly like her. I am not sure which philosopher said, 'There is never any shortage of old women.'

This latest old woman was called Madame Burgon, and there was nothing remarkable in her life except a dynasty of three parrots that successively ruled her heart.

The most destitute of those who inhabited the tenement were a family of four, father, mother and two daughters already quite grown up, all four of them occupying the same garret, one of those cells we have already mentioned.

At first sight there was nothing very distinctive about this family except its extreme destitution. The father, when he rented the room, said his name was Jondrette. Some time after they moved in, which had very much resembled 'the moving-in of nothing at all', to borrow the principal tenant's memorable expression, this fellow Jondrette had said to this woman who, like her predecessor, was both doorkeeper and stair-sweeper, 'Mère so-and-so, if anyone should happen to turn up asking after a Pole or an Italian, or maybe even a Spaniard, that would be me.'

This family was the cheerful little ragamuffin's family. He would arrive there and find poverty and want, and what is even sadder, no smile: a cold hearth and cold hearts. When he arrived they would ask him, 'Where have you been?' He would reply, 'Out on the street.' When he left they would ask him, 'Where are you going?' He would reply, 'Out on the street.' His mother would say to him, 'What is it you've come here for?'

This child lived in this absence of affection like those etiolated plants that grow in cellars. It was not something he minded, and he did not hold it against anybody. He did not actually know how a father and mother should be.

What is more, his mother loved his sisters.

BOOK TWO
THE CONSUMMATE BOURGEOIS

I
Ninety Years Old with Thirty-two Teeth

Even today in Rue Boucherat, Rue de Normandie and Rue de Saint-onge there are a few residents from days past who remember a gent called Monsieur Gillenormand, and speak kindly of him. This gent was old when they were young. For those who look with melancholy on that profusion of blurry shadows called the past, this figure has not yet entirely disappeared from the maze of streets around the Temple that under Louis XIV were given the names of all the provinces of France, in exactly the same way as in our day the streets of the new Tivoli neighbourhood have been given the names of all the capitals of Europe – a development, by the way, that shows progress.

Monsieur Gillenormand, who was very much alive in 1831, was one of those men who become a curious sight only because they have lived a long time, and who are strange because they once looked like everyone else and now there is not another soul that looks like them. He was a funny old stick and truly a man of another age, a real dyed-in-the-wool and rather haughty bourgeois of the eighteenth century, wearing his pedigree bourgeois status in the same manner that marquises used to wear their marquisates. He was over ninety, walked straight-backed, talked loudly, saw clearly, drank his liquor neat, ate, slept and snored. He had all thirty-two of his teeth. He wore spectacles only for reading. He was of an amorous disposition but said he had completely and resolutely given up women for the past ten years. He was unable to please them any more, he said. He did not add 'I'm too old' but 'I'm too poor.' He would say, 'Ah! If I weren't ruined . . .' All he had left, in fact, was an income of about fifteen thousand francs. His dream was to come into an inheritance and have an income of a hundred thousand francs so that he could have mistresses. As you see, he was not of that delicate variety of octogenarian who, like Monsieur de Voltaire, has been dying all his life. His was not the longevity of a cracked pot. This hale old man had always enjoyed good health. He was shallow, quick, irascible. He flew into a rage over anything,

539

mostly in defiance of the truth. When contradicted he would raise his cane. He laid about him, as in the good old days. He had an unmarried daughter in her fifties. When he lost his temper he would give her a terrible tongue-lashing and would have gladly whipped her. He thought of her as being eight years old. He vigorously boxed his servants' ears and said, 'Ah! you good-for-nothing!' One of his oaths was 'Damned fiddle-faddler's fiddle-faddle!' He had some peculiar complacencies: he had himself shaved every day by a barber who had once gone crazy, and who detested him, being jealous of Monsieur Gillenormand on account of his own flirtatiously attractive wife. Monsieur Gillenormand admired his own discernment in all things and declared himself to be very shrewd. This is one of the things he would say: 'I really am quite perceptive. I can tell when a flea bites me which woman I got it from.' The words that he uttered most often were 'the man of feeling' and 'nature'. He did not give the latter word the great significance that our age has imparted to it. But he introduced it in his own way into his little homespun satires. 'In order that civilization might have a little of everything,' he would say, 'Nature even gives it some specimens of a charming ferocity. Europe has miniature versions of species from Asia and Africa. The cat is a drawing-room tiger, the lizard is a pocket-sized crocodile. The dancers at the Opéra are pink-skinned savages. They don't eat men, they bleed them. Or, magicians that they are, they transform them into oysters and swallow them. The Caribbeans leave only the bones, the dancers leave only the shell. Such are our ways. We do not devour, we gnaw. We do not kill off, we claw.'

II
A House to Match Its Occupant

He lived in the Marais, at 6 Rue des Filles-du-Calvaire. He owned the house. It has since been demolished and rebuilt, and the number has probably been changed in one of those revolutions in numbering systems the streets of Paris undergo. He occupied an old and spacious apartment on the first floor, between street and gardens, even the ceilings of which were covered with enormous Gobelins and Beauvais tapestries representing pastoral scenes. The designs on the ceilings and walls were repeated in miniature on the armchairs. He surrounded his bed with a huge nine-panelled screen in Coromandel lacquer. Long voluminous curtains hung at the casement windows and formed great heaped folds of extraordinary magnificence. The garden situated just below his windows was connected with the one at the corner by means of a flight of twelve or fifteen steps, which this old gent went up and down very nimbly. As well as a library next to his bedroom, he had a boudoir he set great store by, an elegant retreat whose walls were lined with a magnificent fabric of pale yellow with fleurs-de-lys and flower motifs, made on Louis XIV's galleys and commissioned from his convicts by Monsieur de Vivonne for his mistress. Monsieur Gillenormand had inherited it from a forbidding great-aunt on his mother's side, who had lived to be over a hundred. He was twice married. He conducted himself in a manner that was halfway between that of the courtier he had never been and the lawyer that he might have been. He was light-hearted, and affectionate when he wanted to be. In his youth he had been one of those men who are always deceived by their wives and never by their mistresses, because they are at once the most surly of husbands and the most solicitous of lovers. He was a connoisseur of painting. He had in his bedroom a marvellous portrait of some unknown person, painted by Jordaens, executed with bold brush-strokes, with countless details of a jumbled and seemingly haphazard kind. Monsieur Gillenormand's attire was not the apparel of Louis XV or even that of Louis XVI. It was the dandy's costume worn by the *incroyables** of the Directory period. He had thought of himself as quite young until then and had been a follower of fashion. His coat was of light wool with broad lapels, a long swallow-tail and big steel buttons. With this he wore knee-breeches and buckled shoes. He always tucked his hands into his fob-pockets. He would say authoritatively, 'The French Revolution is a bunch of scoundrels.'

III
Luc-Esprit

One evening at the Opéra at the age of sixteen he had the honour of being given the glad eye, simultaneously, by two famous beauties, then in their prime and celebrated by Voltaire, Camargo and Sallé. Caught in the crossfire, he had beaten a heroic retreat and fallen back on a young dancer, a little lass named Nahenry, who was sixteen, the same age as he was, a complete unknown, and with whom he was in love. He had memories galore. He would exclaim, 'How charming she looked, that Guimard-Guimardini-Guimardinette, the last time I saw her at Longchamps, her tresses in tightly curled ringlets, with her

---

* Literally, 'incredibles', young dandies of the Directory period, who also affected not to pronounce their rs, notably in a favourite catchphrase 'c'est inc[r]oyable' ('it's incredible').

turquoise fascinator studs on the heels of her shoes, in her gown of a colour worn by the newly successful, and a muff for flourishing!' As a youth he had worn a jacket of fine English cloth that he often spoke of with enthusiasm. 'I was dressed like a Turk of the Levantine Levant,' he would say. Madame de Boufflers, who happened to have seen him when he was twenty, described him as 'a delightful madcap'.

He was scandalized by all the names he saw in politics and in power, regarding them as low-class and bourgeois. He read the journals, 'the news papers, the gazettes', as he called them, stifling his explosions of laughter. 'Oh!' he would say. 'Who are these people! Corbière! Humann! Casimir Périer! Ministers, would you believe! Imagine this appearing in a newspaper: "Monsieur Gillenormand, minister"! It would be a joke. Well! They're so stupid, it would be taken seriously!' He would gaily call all kinds of things by their proper or improper name, and was not in the least constrained by the presence of ladies. He would say things that were coarse, obscene and scurrilous with an air of ineffable composure and unconcern that was elegant. It was in keeping with the unceremoniousness of the day. It is to be noted that the age of circumlocution in verse was the age of crudeness in prose. His godfather had predicted he would be a man of genius, and had given him these two significant names: Luc-Esprit.

IV
An Aspiring Centenarian

As a boy he had won prizes at school in Moulins, where he was born, and he had received the laurels from the hand of the Duc de Nivernais, whom he called the Duc de Nevers. Neither the Convention, nor the death of Louis XVI, nor Napoleon, nor the return of the Bourbons, nor anything else had been able to efface the memory of that coronation. The Duc de Nevers was for him the great figure of the century. 'What a charming nobleman,' he said, 'and how splendid he looked with his blue sash!' In the eyes of Monsieur Gillenormand, Catherine II had made amends for the crime of partitioning Poland by purchasing from Bestuchef, for three thousand roubles, the secret of the elixir of gold. He was animated on the subject. 'The elixir of gold,' he exclaimed, 'Bestuchef's yellow tincture, General Lamotte's drops – in the eighteenth century, at the cost of one louis for a half-ounce phial, this was the great remedy against the catastrophes of love, the cure against Venus. Louis XV sent two hundred phials of it to the pope.' He would have been greatly provoked and would have flown into a rage if he had been told that the elixir of gold is nothing but ferric chloride.

Monsieur Gillenormand adored the Bourbons and abhorred 1789. He was forever relating how he had escaped during the Terror and how it took a great deal of jollity and a great deal of wit to avoid having his head cut off. If any young man ventured to acclaim the Republic in his presence, he would turn blue and almost faint in his fury.

He sometimes alluded to his ninety years, saying, 'I certainly hope I shan't see ninety-three a second time.' On other occasions he hinted to people that he intended to live to be a hundred.

V
Basque and Nicolette

He had theories. This was one of them: 'When a man is passionately fond of women, and when he has a wife of his own he does not much care for, who is ugly, bad-tempered, lawfully wedded, fully entitled, well versed in the statute book, and jealous when occasion arises, there is only one way of dealing with the situation if he wants any peace, and that is to let his wife control the purse strings. This abdication sets him free. His wife then keeps herself occupied, develops a mania for handling cash, getting her fingers stained green in the process, undertakes the nurturing of sharecroppers and the training of tenant farmers, summons lawyers, directs notaries, harangues clerks, calls on magistrates, brings lawsuits, draws up leases, dictates contracts, feels supremely important, sells, buys, settles, promises and compromises, binds and annuls, cedes, concedes and retrocedes, arranges, disarranges, hoards, squanders. She does foolish things, to her tremendous and personal satisfaction, and this is a consolation. While her husband scorns her, she has the gratification of ruining her husband.' This theory Monsieur Gillenormand had applied to himself, and it had become his story. His wife, the second one, had administered his fortune in such a way that, when one fine day Monsieur Gillenormand found himself a widower, he was left with just enough to live on, after putting nearly everything into an annuity providing an income of fifteen thousand francs, three-quarters of which would terminate with his own demise. He had not hesitated, little concerned about leaving any legacy. Besides, he had noticed that unexpected things happened to patrimonies, for instance they became 'national assets'. He had witnessed the vicissitudes of the consolidated third of the public debt, and he had little faith in the public accounts. 'That's all Rue Quincampoix!' he said. As we have mentioned, the house in Rue des

Filles-du-Calvaire was his own property. He had two servants, 'a male and a female'. When a servant came to work for him Monsieur Gillenormand rechristened him. He gave the men the name of their province: Nîmois, Comtois, Poitevin, Picard. His latest valet was a fat, worn-out, wheezy man of fifty-five, incapable of running twenty paces but, since he was born in Bayonne, Monsieur Gillenormand called him Basque.* As for the female servants, in his household they were all called Nicolette (even the Magnon woman – of whom, more later). One day a first-rate cook, one of the very best, who came of honourable concierge stock, offered her services. 'How much do you want to be paid a month in wages?' asked Monsieur Gillenormand. 'Thirty francs.' 'What's your name?' 'Olympie.' 'You shall have fifty francs and you shall be called Nicolette.'

VI

Affording a Glimpse of La Magnon and Her Two Little Boys

With Monsieur Gillenormand, sorrow translated into anger. Being in despair made him furious. He harboured every prejudice and took every liberty. One of the things on which he built his public persona and his private satisfaction was, as we have indicated, to have remained a lady's man and lustily to pass for one. This he called having 'royal status'. This royal status sometimes attracted some unexpected reversions to the Crown. One day a newborn baby boy, bawling his head off and neatly wrapped in swaddling-clothes, was brought to his house in a flat basket, like an oyster basket. A servant-girl who had been sacked six months earlier accused him of fathering it. Monsieur Gillenormand had then already turned eighty-four. Indignation and uproar in the household. And who did that brazen hussy hope to convince of that? What a nerve! What a dreadful slander! Monsieur Gillenormand himself was not at all annoyed. He observed the bundle with the amiable smile of a fellow flattered by the slander and said to anyone who was listening, 'Well? So what? What of it? What's the matter? You're making such a fuss, and really behaving like ignoramuses. When he was eighty-five Monsieur le Duc d'Angoulême, the bastard son of His Majesty Charles IX, married a silly goose aged fifteen. Monsieur Virginal, Marquis d'Alluye, brother

* The name is inappropriate because a popular expression equates a Basque with speed. *Aller/courir comme un Basque*, 'to go/run like a Basque', means 'to move very quickly'.

of Cardinal de Sourdis, archbishop of Bordeaux, at the age of eighty-three had a son by one of Madame la Présidente Jacquin's chambermaids, a real love-child who became a Knight of Malta and a counsellor of state representing the old aristocracy. One of the great men of this century, Abbé Tabaraud, is the son of a man of eighty-seven. There is nothing out of the ordinary about any of these things. Just think of the Bible! On which I swear this little gentleman is not mine. Let him be taken care of. It's not his fault.' It was an accommodating solution. The woman in question, whose name was Magnon, sent him a second bundle the year after. It was another boy. This time Monsieur Gillenormand capitulated. He sent the two infants back to their mother, promising to pay eighty francs a month for their maintenance on condition the mother in question did not do it again. He added, 'I expect the mother to treat them well. I shall go and see them from time to time.' Which he did.

He had a brother who for thirty-three years was a priest and rector of the academy at Poitiers, and who died at the age of seventy-nine. 'I lost him when he was still young,' he said. This brother, who is little remembered, was a complacent miser who, being a priest, felt obliged to give alms to the poor that he encountered, though he never gave them anything but worthless Revolutionary coins or demonetized sous, thereby contriving to go to hell by following the path to paradise. As for Monsieur Gillenormand the elder, he did not stint in giving to the poor but gave gladly and nobly. He was benevolent, bluff, charitable, and had he been rich his natural bent would have been princely open-handedness. He wanted everything that involved him to be done in style – even swindles. One day, having been crudely and blatantly cheated over an inheritance by a bailiff, he made this solemn protest: 'Bah! That was indecently done! I'm truly ashamed of such fiddles. Everything has deteriorated during this century, even the crooks. By God! This is no way to rob a man of my standing. I've been robbed like a babe in the woods, in a shabby way. *Silvae sint consule dignae!*'*

As we have said, he was twice married. By his first wife he had a daughter, who had remained single, and by the second another daughter, who died at about the age of thirty. And for love or by chance or for some other reason, she had married a soldier of fortune who served in the armies of the Republic and of the Empire, won the Legion of Honour cross at Austerlitz and was made colonel at Waterloo. 'He's the bane of my family,' the old bourgeois would say. He

* Virgil, *Eclogue* 4, line 3: 'Si canimus silvas, silvae sint consule dignae' ('If we are to sing of woods, let them be woods worthy of a consul').

took an immense amount of snuff and had a particularly graceful way of flicking the ruffle at his throat with the back of his hand. He was no great believer in God.

VII
Rule: No Visitors before Evening

Such was Monsieur Luc-Esprit Gillenormand, who had lost none of his hair, which was grey rather than white and always worn in the 'poodle' style.* In short, and notwithstanding, a venerable man. He was like the eighteenth century: frivolous and grand. During the early years of the Restoration, Monsieur Gillenormand, who was still young then – he was only seventy-four in 1814 – lived in Faubourg St-Germain, Rue Servandoni, near St-Sulpice. He retired to the Marais only when he withdrew from society, well after he turned eighty. And after withdrawing from society, he found sanctuary in his habits. The principal one, in which he remained constant, was to keep his door categorically closed during the day and never to receive anyone before evening, no matter who it might be, on no matter what business. He dined at five o'clock, then his door was open. That was the custom of his age, and he stuck to it. 'Daytime is vulgar,' he said, 'and deserves only a closed shutter. Well-bred people display their wit when the heavens display their stars.' And he barricaded himself against the whole world, including the king. An old-fashioned refinement of his day.

VIII
Two Do Not Make a Matching Pair

We have just spoken of Monsieur Gillenormand's two daughters. They were born ten years apart. As children they were not at all similar, and in character and countenance they had been as little like sisters as could be. The younger one was a delightful soul, attracted to all that was light, devoted to flowers, poetry, music, soaring into glorious expanses, enthusiastic, ethereal, betrothed in her imagination even from childhood to some vague heroic figure. The elder had also her fanciful dream. She saw in her vision of the future some very wealthy

---

* *Oreilles de chien* (literally, 'dog's ears') or *chien barbet* ('poodle') was a hair-style in vogue among the *incroyables* for about two years at the end of the eighteenth century, with long tresses falling over the ears and the hair pinned up behind.

big fat army supplier, a splendidly stupid husband, a million francs made man; or else a prefect, receptions at the Prefecture, a gentleman usher with a chain of office around his neck, official balls, town-hall speeches, being 'Madame la Préfète' – this whirled round in her imagination. And so, as young girls, the two sisters let their minds wander, each in her own dream. Both had wings, one like an angel, the other like a goose.

No ambition is ever fully realized; here below, at least. There is no heaven on earth in our lifetime. The younger wedded the man of her dreams; but she died. The elder did not marry at all.

At the point when she enters the story we are relating, she was a sanctimonious old maid, an inveterate prude, one of the sharpest noses and dullest minds imaginable. One telling detail: outside of her immediate family, no one had ever known her first name. She was called 'the elder Mademoiselle Gillenormand'.

In terms of priggishness, the elder Mademoiselle Gillenormand would have needed no lessons from an English governess. She was modesty taken to extremes. She had a memory of a dreadful experience: one day a man had seen her garter.

Age had served only to intensify this unforgiving modesty. Her underbodice was never sufficiently opaque and never came up high enough. She wore an increasing number of clasps and pins where no one would have thought of looking. The peculiarity of prudery is to increase the guard in inverse proportion to the threat to the fortress.

Yet – can anyone explain these ancient mysteries of innocence? – she did not mind being kissed by an officer of the lancers: her great-nephew, named Théodule.

Despite this favoured lancer the label 'Prude', under which we have categorized her, was entirely appropriate. Mademoiselle Gillenormand was a kind of twilight soul. Prudery is half virtue, half vice.

To prudery she added bigotry, the perfect complement. She was a member of the confraternity of the Virgin, wore a white veil on certain feast-days, mumbled special prayers, revered 'the holy blood', worshipped 'the sacred heart', remained for hours in contemplation before a rococo Jesuit altar in a chapel that was closed to the ordinary faithful, and there allowed her soul to soar amid little marble clouds and through great rays of gilded wood.

She had a friend who went to the same chapel, an old maid like herself, called Mademoiselle Vaubois, who was thoroughly obtuse, next to whom Mademoiselle Gillenormand had the pleasure of being razor-sharp. Apart from Agnus Deis and Ave Marias, Mademoiselle Vaubois had no understanding of anything except different ways of making jam. A paragon of her type, Mademoiselle Vaubois was the white ermine of stupidity without a single fleck of intelligence.

Admittedly, Mademoiselle Gillenormand had benefited from getting older, improving rather than worsening. That is the way with passive natures. She had never been unkind, which is a relative goodness, and anyway, the years wear down sharp edges, and she had undergone the smoothing of time. She was sad with an obscure sadness whose secret she herself did not know. Her whole person was an expression of the dazed bewilderment of a life that was over without having begun.

She kept house for her father. Monsieur Gillenormand had his daughter with him as we have seen Monseigneur Bienvenu had his sister with him. These households consisting of an old man and an old maid are not unusual and always present that touching image of two frailties supporting each other.

Along with this old maid and this old man there was also in this house a child, a little boy, always trembling and silent in Monsieur Gillenormand's presence. Monsieur Gillenormand only ever spoke to this child in a stern voice and sometimes with his cane raised. 'Here, monsieur! Rascal, scamp, come closer! What have you got to say for yourself, young mischief-maker! Let me look at you! Little devil!' And so on. He idolized him.

This was his grandson. We shall return to this child.

BOOK THREE
GRANDFATHER AND GRANDSON

I
A Salon of the Past

When Monsieur Gillenormand lived in Rue Servandoni he frequented many very distinguished and very aristocratic salons where, although bourgeois himself, Monsieur Gillenormand was socially acceptable. As he had a double measure of wit, firstly his own wit and secondly the wit attributed to him, he was indeed sought after and welcomed with open arms. There was nowhere he would go unless he could hold sway. There are people determined at all costs to prevail and to have other people pay attention to them. Where they cannot be oracles, they play the fool. This was not in Monsieur Gillenormand's nature. His ascendancy over the royalist salons that he frequented cost him nothing in self-respect. He was everywhere an oracle. He held his own against Monsieur de Bonald, and even against Monsieur Bengy-Puy-Vallée.

Round about 1817 he invariably spent two afternoons a week at a house in his neighbourhood, in Rue Férou, the home of Madame la Baronne de T, a worthy and respectable person whose husband had been France's ambassador to Berlin under Louis XVI. Baron de T, who during his lifetime believed passionately in trances and magnetic visions, died bankrupt in exile, leaving as his sole asset ten manuscript volumes, gilt-edged and bound in red morocco leather, containing some very curious memoirs about Mesmer and his tub. Out of dignity Madame de T had not published the memoirs and maintained herself on a small income that had somehow been preserved. Madame de T stayed away from court, 'a very mixed society', as she said, living in noble isolation, proud and poor. A few friends gathered twice weekly around her widow's hearth, and this constituted a thoroughly royalist salon. They drank tea and, depending on whether the mood of the moment was elegiac or melodramatic, bemoaned or bewailed with horror the age, the Charter, the Buonapartists, the prostitution of the blue sash to bourgeois recipients or the Jacobinism of Louis XVIII, and spoke in hushed tones of the hopes raised by Monsieur, later Charles X.

Ribald songs in which Napoleon was called 'Nicolas' were greeted there with joyous rapture. Duchesses, some of the most refined and charming women in the world, went into ecstasies over verses such as the following, addressed to 'the federates':

> Tuck your shirt-tails in your trousers,
> Never let them flap about.
> Patriots with the white flag flying?
> Never let the word get out.

They delighted in making puns they believed to be devastating, in innocent wordplay they imagined to be virulent, in improvising four-line stanzas, even rhyming couplets – for instance, on the Dessolles ministry, a moderate cabinet that included Messieurs Decazes and Deserre:

> To restore the shaken throne to a firmer footing,
> Requires a change 'de sol [Dessolles], et de serre [Deserre] et
> de case [Decazes]'.*

Or they took the list of peers in the Upper House, 'that appallingly Jacobin chamber', and made combinations with the names on it to form phrases like the following: 'Damas, Sabran, Gouvion St-Cyr'†. All in jest.

In this social circle the Revolution was parodied. For some unknown reason they liked to foment the same violent feelings in reverse. They sang their own little version of 'Ça ira'‡:

> Ah! it'll come! it'll come! it'll come!
> Bonapartists from lamp-posts strung!

* 'Of soil, and of glasshouse and of dwelling'.
† 'Sabrant' ('sabring') being a homophone of 'Sabran': 'Damas *sabring* Gouvion St-Cyr'.
‡ *Ça ira* is an idiomatic expression meaning 'Things will work out' or 'We'll get there.' It was supposedly Benjamin Franklin's answer when asked in Paris how the American War of Independence was going. The refrain of this Revolutionary song – 'Ah! ça ira! ça ira! ça ira! / Les aristocrates à la lanterne!' (the salon members substitute the word 'Bonapartists' for 'aristocrats') – was so popular that it was sung as the refrain of another Revolutionary song, the 'Carmagnole'. Both songs were banned in 1799 when Napoleon became first consul.

Songs are like the guillotine – they cut indiscriminately, today this head, tomorrow that. Variations on a theme.

In the Fualdès affair, which dates from this time, 1816, they sided with Bastide and Jausion, because Fualdès was 'Buonapartist'. They referred to liberals as 'friends and brothers' – this was the ultimate insult.

Like certain church towers, Madame de T's salon had two weather-cocks. One of them was Monsieur Gillenormand, the other was the Comte de Lamothe-Valois, of whom people would whisper in each other's ears with a kind of respect: 'You know? He's the Lamothe of the necklace affair.' Political parties have these strange amnesties.

Let us add the following: among the bourgeoisie, positions of pres-tige are diminished by being too socially indiscriminate. You must be careful who you associate with. Just as there is a loss of heat in prox-imity to those who are cold, there is a dwindling of respect in the company of people who are scorned. However, the upper echelons of old considered themselves as much above this law as any other. Marigny, brother of La Pompadour, is an intimate of Monsieur le Prince de Soubise. Although? No, because. Vaubernier's sponsor du Barry is most warmly received by Monsieur le Maréchal de Richelieu. This society is Mount Olympus. Mercury and the Prince de Guéménée are at home here. A thief gains entry, provided he is a god.

There was nothing remarkable about the Comte de Lamothe, who in 1815 was an old man of seventy-five, except his taciturn and pom-pous manner, his cold and angular face, his perfectly polished manners, his coat buttoned up to his cravat, and his long legs always crossed in full-length loose-fitting trousers of a burnt-sienna colour. His face was the same colour as his trousers.

This Monsieur de Lamothe 'mattered' in this salon on account of his 'celebrity' and, strangely enough but true, because of the Valois name.

As for Monsieur Gillenormand, his prestige was thoroughly deserved. He had authority because he had authority. Frivolous as he was, and without its detracting at all from his jollity, he had a certain manner about him, commanding, dignified, honest, with a bourgeois arrogance. And his great age added to it. A man is not a century old with impunity. The years eventually create a venerable dishevelment around his head.

Moreover, he made comments that were absolute gems of old-style wit. Thus, when the king of Prussia, having restored Louis XVIII to the throne, came to pay the latter a visit under the name of Count von Ruppin, he was received by the descendant of Louis XIV rather as if he were the mere Margrave of Brandenburg and with the subtlest dis-respect. Monsieur Gillenormand approved: 'All kings who are not the king of France,' he said, 'are provincial kings.' One day the following exchange took place in his presence: 'What sentence did the editor of the *Courrier Français* receive?' 'Suspension.' 'Preferably by the neck,' commented Monsieur Gillenormand. Remarks of this nature create a reputation. At a *Te Deum* on the anniversary of the return of the Bourbons, he said on seeing Monsieur de Talleyrand pass by: 'There goes His Excellency the Devil.'

Monsieur Gillenormand was always accompanied by his daughter, that lanky spinster who by then had turned forty and looked fifty, and by a handsome little boy of seven, white, pink, fresh-faced, with happy and trusting eyes, who never appeared in that salon without hearing all those voices murmuring around him, 'How charming he looks! What a pity! Poor child!' This child was the one we referred to earlier. He was called 'poor child' because he had for a father 'a brig-and of the Loire'.

This brigand of the Loire was Monsieur Gillenormand's son-in-law, already mentioned, and whom Monsieur Gillenormand called 'the bane of his family'.

II
One of the Red Menaces of Those Days

Anyone who happened to pass through the little town of Vernon during this period, and who walked across that beautiful stone bridge – which, with luck, will soon be succeeded by some hideous iron cable bridge – might, if he had looked down over the parapet, have observed a man of about fifty years of age, in a leather cap, trou-sers, and a waistcoat of coarse grey cloth to which was sewn something yellow that had once been a red ribbon; he wore wooden clogs, and was tanned by the sun, his face almost black and his hair almost white, with a big scar running across his forehead and continuing down his cheek. Bowed, stooped, prematurely aged, he went about nearly all day long with a hoe or a sickle in his hand, in one of those walled plots that lie adjacent to the bridge and run along the left bank of the Seine like the links of a chain. Delightful enclosures full of flowers – if they were much bigger you would say, 'These are gardens', and if a little smaller, 'These are bouquets.' All these enclosures have the river at one end and a house at the other. Around 1817 the man in the waistcoat and wooden clogs whom we have just described occu-pied the smallest of these enclosures and the humblest of these houses.

He lived there alone, in solitude, silence and poverty, with a woman neither young nor old, neither beautiful nor ugly, neither peasant nor bourgeois, who was his servant. The patch of land he called his garden was famous in the town for the beauty of the flowers he cultivated there. He devoted himself to his flowers.

By dint of hard work, perseverance, attentiveness and buckets of water, he had, after the Creator, himself succeeded in creating, and contrived to produce, certain types of tulips and dahlias that seemed to have been forgotten by nature. He was ingenious; he had anticipated Soulange Bodin in creating little mounds of peat for the cultivation of rare and precious shrubs from America and China. In summer he was out in his garden from the crack of dawn, planting, pruning, weeding, watering the borders, walking among his flowers with a sad, gentle, kindly air, sometimes daydreaming and motionless for hours on end, listening to the song of a bird in a tree, the babble of a child inside a house, or else gazing transfixed at a dewdrop on the tip of a blade of grass, made jewel-like by the sun. He ate very frugally and drank more milk than wine. He would defer to a small child; his servant scolded him. He was diffident to the point of shyness, he rarely went out, and his only friends were the poor who tapped at his window, and his parish priest Abbé Mabeuf, a good-hearted old man. Yet if any of the town's inhabitants, or any strangers, any passers-by, curious to see his tulips and roses, rang at his little house, he would open the door with a smile. This was the brigand of the Loire.

Anyone who, at about the same time, had read military memoirs, biographies, *Le Moniteur* and bulletins of the Grand Army would have been struck by a name that cropped up fairly frequently, that of Georges Pontmercy. As a very young man, this Georges Pontmercy had been a soldier in the Saintonge regiment. The Revolution broke out. The Saintonge regiment formed part of the army of the Rhine. For even after the fall of the monarchy, the old regiments under the monarchy kept their names, which were those of their provinces, and were only restructured in brigades in 1794. Pontmercy fought at Speyer, Worms, Neustadt, Turckheim, Alzey and Mainz, where he was one of the two hundred who formed Houchard's rearguard. Behind the old rampart of Andernach he held out as twelfth man against the Prince of Hesse's entire corps, and only rejoined the main body of the army when the enemy's cannon had opened a breach from the string course on the parapet to the glacis. He served under Kléber at Marchiennes and at the battle for Mont-Palissel, where a biscayen bullet broke his arm. Then he crossed the border into Italy, and was one of the thirty grenadiers who defended the Col di Tenda with Joubert. Joubert was consequently made adjutant-general and Pontmercy sub-lieutenant. Pontmercy was under fire at Berthier's side that day at Lodi that prompted Bonaparte to say, 'Berthier has been gunner, trooper and grenadier.' He saw his former general fall at Novi at the very moment when, with sabre raised, Joubert shouted, 'Forward!' Embarked with his company, for campaign purposes, on a coastal vessel sailing from Genoa to some small port or other along the coast, he ran into a hornets' nest of seven or eight English naval ships. The Genoese captain wanted to throw the guns overboard, hide the soldiers between decks, and slip past in the dark as a merchant vessel. Pontmercy had the tricolour run up the flagpole and sailed proudly past the guns of the British frigates. Fifty miles on, his audacity increasing, from his coastal vessel he attacked and captured a large English transport ship carrying troops to Sicily, so loaded with men and horses that it was packed to the gunwales. In 1805 he was with the Malher division that took Günzburg from Archduke Ferdinand. At Wertingen, under a hail of bullets he took in his arms Colonel Maupetit, mortally wounded at the head of the 9th Dragoons. He distinguished himself at Austerlitz in that magnificent advance in echelon formation under enemy fire. When the cavalry of the Imperial Russian Guard crushed a battalion of the 4th Line, Pontmercy was one of those who took their revenge and routed the Guard. The emperor awarded him the cross. Pontmercy saw Wurmser, Melas and Mack taken prisoner, one after the other, at Mantua, Alexandria and Ulm. He was part of the 8th Corps of the Grand Army under Mortier's command, which took Hamburg. Then he was transferred to the 55th Line, which was the former Flanders regiment. At Eylau he was in the cemetery where the heroic captain Louis Hugo, uncle of the author of this book, alone with his company of eighty-three men held out for two hours against the enemy army's concentrated efforts. Pontmercy was one of the three who came out of that cemetery alive. He was at Friedland. Then he saw Moscow, then Beresina, then Lützen, Bautzen, Dresden, Wachau, Leipzig and the retreat through Gelnhausen; then Montmirail, Château-Thierry, Craonne, the banks of the Marne, the banks of the Aisne and the formidable position of Laon. At Arnay-le-Duc, as a captain, he sabred ten Cossacks and saved not his general but his corporal. He was hacked about on that occasion, and twenty-seven bone splinters were extracted from his left arm alone. Just eight days before the capitulation of Paris, he swapped posts with a comrade and joined the cavalry. He was what was called under the old regime 'two-handed'; that is to say he was equally adept, as a soldier, with sabre and musket, and as an officer, with cavalry squadron and infantry battalion. It is this aptitude, perfected by military training, that has led to the creation of some special forces, the dragoons, for example, who are mounted infantry. He accompanied Napoleon to the island of Elba. At Waterloo he headed a squadron of cuirassiers in Dubois's brigade. It was he who captured the colours of the Lüneburg battalion. He brought the flag and cast it down at the emperor's feet. He was covered with blood. He had been slashed across the face with a sabre as he seized the flag. A delighted emperor cried out, 'You're colonel now, baron, and officer of the Legion of Honour!' Pontmercy replied, 'Sire, on behalf of my widow I thank you.' An hour later he fell in the Ohain cutting. Now, who was this Georges Pontmercy? He was this same 'brigand of the Loire'.

We have already seen something of his history. After Waterloo, Pontmercy, who had been pulled out, remember, from Ohain's sunken road, managed to rejoin the army and crawled his way from one ambulance to the next to the cantonments on the Loire.

The Restoration had put him on half-pay, then sent him home; that is to say, he was placed under house arrest at Vernon. Regarding all that had taken place during the Hundred Days as not having happened, King Louis XVIII did not recognize his claim to being an officer of the Legion of Honour, nor his rank as colonel, nor his title of baron. He for his part neglected no opportunity to sign himself 'Colonel Baron Pontmercy'. He had only an old blue coat, and he never went out without fastening to it the rosette of an officer of the Legion of Honour. The crown prosecutor gave notice that the authorities would prosecute him for 'the unlawful wearing of this decoration'. When this notification was delivered to him through an officious intermediary, Pontmercy responded with a bitter smile, 'I don't know whether it's because I don't understand French any more or because you don't speak it, but the fact is, what you say doesn't make any sense to me.' Then he went out every day for a week wearing his rosette. They dared not challenge him. Two or three times the minister of war and the general chief of staff wrote to him using the following form of address: 'To Monsieur le Commandant Pontmercy'. He returned the letters unopened. Simultaneously, Napoleon in St Helena was treating in just the same way Sir Hudson Lowe's letters addressed to General Bonaparte. If you will forgive the expression, Pontmercy ended up with the same spittle in his mouth as his emperor.

Similarly, there were in Rome Carthaginian prisoners who refused to salute Flaminius and who had a little of Hannibal's spirit.

One morning, Pontmercy ran into the crown prosecutor in the street at Vernon, went up to him and said, 'Monsieur le procureur du roi, am I allowed to wear my scar?'

He had nothing, other than his meagre half-pay as cavalry major. He rented the smallest house he could find in Vernon. He lived there alone, as we have just seen. In the days of the Empire, in between wars, he found time to marry Mademoiselle Gillenormand. Furious at heart, the old bourgeois had given his consent, sighing and saying, 'The greatest families are forced to do likewise.' Madame Pontmercy, a wonderful woman, as it happened, in every respect, principled and exceptional and worthy of her husband, died in 1815, leaving a child. This child would have been a joy to the colonel in his solitude, but the grandfather had imperiously claimed his grandson, declaring that if the child were not handed over he would disinherit him. The father had yielded in the little one's interest and, not allowed to have his child, he had taken to loving flowers.

He had in fact forgone everything, neither agitating nor conspiring. He divided his thoughts between the innocent things he was doing and the great things he had done. He spent his time looking forward to a carnation or remembering Austerlitz.

Monsieur Gillenormand had no contact with his son-in-law. The colonel was for him 'a brigand' and he was for the colonel 'an old fogey'. Monsieur Gillenormand never spoke of the colonel other than occasionally to make derisive references to 'his barony'. It was expressly agreed that Pontmercy should never attempt to see his son or to speak to him, on pain of having the child returned to him disowned and disinherited. For the Gillenormands Pontmercy was a pariah. They intended to bring up the child as they pleased. Perhaps the colonel was wrong to accept these conditions but he submitted to them, believing he was doing the right thing and sacrificing no one but himself. Old Gillenormand's estate did not amount to much but the elder Mademoiselle Gillenormand's was considerable. This unmarried aunt was extremely wealthy by virtue of her mother's side of the family, and her sister's son was her natural heir.

The boy, whose name was Marius, knew he had a father, but that was all. No one ever said a word about him to the child. Nevertheless, in the social circles into which he was taken by his grandfather, the whisperings, innuendoes and winks eventually impinged even on the little boy's mind. He made some sort of sense of it in the end, and as he absorbed naturally by a kind of infiltration and slow penetration the ideas and opinions that were, so to speak, the air he breathed, he gradually came to think of his father only with shame and a heavy heart.

While he was thus growing up, the colonel would surreptitiously slip up to Paris every two or three months, on the sly, like an ex-convict violating the terms of his release, and go and station himself in St-Sulpice at the time of day when Aunt Gillenormand took Marius to mass. There, trembling with fear that the aunt might turn round, concealed behind a pillar, motionless, not daring to breathe, he would gaze at his child. This scarred veteran was afraid of that old maid.

It was this that brought about his friendship with the parish priest of Vernon, Monsieur l'Abbé Mabeuf. That commendable priest was the brother of a warden of St-Sulpice who had on several occasions noticed the man gazing at the child, and the scar on his cheek, and his eyes brimming with tears. A man who looked so much the man yet wept like a woman made an impression on the warden. The face stuck in his mind. One day, having gone to Vernon to see his brother, he passed Colonel Pontmercy on the bridge and recognized the man from St-Sulpice. The warden mentioned it to the priest, and on some pretext or other they both paid the colonel a visit. This visit led to others. Extremely reserved at first, the colonel eventually confided in them, and the priest and the warden at last came to know the whole story, and how Pontmercy was sacrificing his own happiness for his child's future. As a result the priest developed a deep regard and affection for him, and the colonel on his side developed a fondness for the priest. And besides, when both happen to be sincere and good-hearted, there is nothing like an old priest and an old soldier for understanding each other and getting along together. Fundamentally, they are the same man. One has served the country that is his in this world, the other has served the country that will be his in the next; that is the only difference.

Twice a year, on the first of January and on St George's Day, Marius wrote dutiful letters to his father, dictated by his aunt, that read as if they had been copied from some primer. This was all that Monsieur Gillenormand would allow. And the father replied with very loving letters that the grandfather stuffed into his pocket unread.

Requiescant*

Madame de T's salon was all that Marius Pontmercy knew of the world. It was the only opening through which he could look out on life. It was a gloomy opening, and through this small window he received more cold than warmth, more darkness than daylight. This child who was all joy and light on entering this strange world soon became unhappy in it and, what is even more incongruous at that age, solemn. Surrounded by all those peculiar and imposing individuals, he looked about with grave surprise. Everything conspired to increase this amazement. There were in Madame de T's salon some very venerable old noblewomen, whose names were Mathan, Noé, Lévis – pronounced 'Lévi' – and Cambis – pronounced 'Cambise'. These aged faces and these biblical names mingled in the child's mind with the Old Testament he was learning by heart, and when they were all there, seated in a circle around a dying fire, dimly lit by a green-veiled lamp, every now and then delivering utterances that were both majestic and opinionated, with their severe profiles, their hair grey or white, their long gowns of another age of which all that could be discerned were their lugubrious colours, little Marius stared at them with fear in his eyes, believing he saw not women but patriarchs and magi, not real beings but phantoms.

Consorting with these phantoms were several priests, regulars of this elderly salon, and a few noblemen: the Marquis de Sassenay, private secretary to Madame de Berry; the Vicomte de Valory, who under the pseudonym of Charles-Antoine published monorhymed odes; the relatively young Prince de Beauffremont, who had greying hair and a pretty, witty wife whose very low-cut dresses of scarlet velvet trimmed with gold braid defied this gloom; the Marquis de Coriolis d'Espinouse, in all of France the man best versed in 'proportionate politeness'†; the Comte d'Amendre, a fellow with a kindly chin; and the Chevalier de Port-de-Guy, a pillar of the Louvre library, the so-called royal collection. Monsieur de Port-de-Guy, bald and old-looking rather than old, would relate how in 1793, at the age of sixteen, he had been sent to the prison hulks for refusing to swear allegiance to the Republic, and

---

* Part of the liturgical formula *Requiescant in pace* ('May they rest in peace').
† An allusion to Saint-Simon's descriptions in his *Mémoires* of the theologian Fénelon: 'a politeness that, while being all-embracing, was always measured and proportionate', vol. 9, ch. 12 (1711); and 'an insinuating but noble and proportionate politeness', vol. 11, ch. 22 (1715).

had been shackled to an octogenarian, the bishop of Mirepoix, also a non-juror, but of the clergy, whereas he himself was a non-juring soldier. They were in Toulon. Their task was to go to the scaffold at night and collect the heads and bodies of those guillotined during the day. They carried on their backs those dripping headless trunks, and on the nape of their necks their red convict cloaks were caked with blood, dried in the morning, wet at night. There were many such tragic tales in Madame de T's salon, where cursing Marat meant applauding Trestaillon. A few deputies of the 'unfindable' kind played whist here: Monsieur Thibord du Chalard, Monsieur Lemarchant de Gomicourt, and the famous right-wing taunter Monsieur Cornet-Dincourt. The bailiff of Ferrette, with his short breeches and his thin legs, sometimes called in at this salon on his way to visit Monsieur de Talleyrand. He had been Monsieur le Comte d'Artois's companion in pleasure-seeking, and unlike Aristotle on his hands and knees under Campaspe, he had La Guimard crawling about on all fours, and so showed the world a philosopher avenged by a bailiff.

As for the priests, there were Abbé Halma, the one to whom Monsieur Larose, his collaborator at *La Foudre*, used to say, 'Bah! Who isn't fifty? Maybe the odd whippersnapper!'; Abbé Letourneur, preacher to the king; Abbé Frayssinous, who was not yet count, or bishop, or minister, or peer, and who wore an old cassock with buttons missing; and Abbé Keravenant, parish priest of St-Germain-des-Prés; also the pope's nuncio, at that time Monsignor Macchi, archbishop of Nisibis, later cardinal, remarkable for his long, pensive nose; and another monsignor with the following title: Abate Palmieri, domestic prelate, one of the seven apostolic protonotaries of the Holy See, canon of the illustrious Liberian basilica, the saints' advocate, *postulatore dei santi*, which relates to the process of canonization and more or less means master of requests for the department of paradise. Lastly, two cardinals, Monsieur de la Luzerne and Monsieur de Clermont-Tonnerre. Monsieur le cardinal de la Luzerne was a writer and was destined a few years later to have the honour of putting his name to articles in *Le Conservateur* alongside Chateaubriand. Monsieur de Clermont-Tonnerre was archbishop of Toulouse and often made trips to Paris to stay with his nephew, the Marquis de Tonnerre, who was minister for the navy and minister of war. The cardinal of Clermont-Tonnerre was a cheerful little old man who showed off his red stockings under his hitched-up cassock. His particular obsessions were a hatred of the *Encyclopaedia* and a passion for playing billiards, and on summer evenings in those days, people walking down Rue Madame where the Clermont-Tonnerre residence then stood would stop to listen to the clacking of billiard balls and the piercing voice of the cardinal crying out to his conclavist, Monseigneur Cottret, bishop *in partibus* of Caryste, 'Mark that up, abbé, it was a cannon shot.' The cardinal of Clermont-Tonnerre had been brought along to Madame de T's by his closest friend Monsieur de Roquelaure, former bishop of Senlis, and one of the Forty. Monsieur de Roquelaure was impressive on account of his great height and his assiduous attendance at the Academy. Every Thursday, through the glass door of the room adjacent to the library where the French Academy then held its meetings, curious onlookers could watch the former bishop of Senlis, usually on his feet, freshly powdered, in violet hose, with his back to the door apparently so as to give a better view of his embroidered collar. All these ecclesiastics, although most were as much courtiers as they were churchmen, added to the gravity of the de T salon, whose aristocratic credentials were enhanced by five peers of France: the Marquis de Vibraye, the Marquis de Talaru, the Marquis d'Herbouville, Vicomte Dambray and the Duc de Valentinois. This Duc de Valentinois, although Prince of Monaco, in other words a foreign sovereign prince, had so high an opinion of France and its peerage that he saw everything in relation to them. It was he who said, 'The cardinals are Rome's peers of France; the lords, England's peers of France.' However, as there must be revolution everywhere this century, this feudal salon was, as we have said, dominated by a bourgeois. Monsieur Gillenormand reigned there.

In this lay the essence and quintessence of Parisian monarchist society. Those who had made a reputation for themselves, even if they were royalist, were excluded. There is always an element of anarchy in renown. Chateaubriand turning up there would have produced the same effect as Père Duchesne. A few reformed Republicans, who rallied to the Restoration, did nevertheless find their way on sufferance into this orthodox world. Comte Beugnot was received there after mending his ways.

The 'noble' salons of today bear no resemblance to those of the past. The present Faubourg St-Germain has a whiff of heresy about it. Royalists nowadays are demagogues. To their credit, let us say.

In the elevated society of Madame de T's salon, taste was fastidious and supercilious beneath a great show of politeness. Here, customary usages included all kinds of unconscious affectations that were quintessentially *ancien régime*, buried, but alive. Some of these customary usages, especially in the matter of language, seem eccentric. Anyone who did not know better would have interpreted as provincial what was merely old-fashioned. A woman might be called 'madame la générale'. 'Madame la colonelle' was not entirely unknown. The charming Madame de Léon, in memory no doubt of the Duchesse de Longueville and the Duchesse de Chevreuse, preferred this form of address to her title of princess. The Marquise de Créquy was also called 'madame la colonelle'.

It was this superior little world that made it a point of etiquette at the Tuileries, when speaking to the king in private, always to address him as 'the king', in the third person, and never as 'your majesty', the designation 'your majesty' having been 'sullied by the usurper'. Here, they criticized events and individuals. They deplored the age they lived in, which saved them having to understand it. They offered each other mutual support in their bewilderment. They passed on to each other whatever light they could shed. Methuselah was Epimenides' informant. The deaf kept the blind up to date with what was going on. They declared null and void the time that had elapsed since Koblenz. Just as Louis XVIII was by the grace of God in the twenty-fifth year of his reign, likewise the emigrants were by natural right in the twenty-fifth year of their adolescence.

All was harmony, nothing was too animated. The spoken word was not much more than a whisper. The newspaper, to match the salon, might have been a papyrus. There were some young people, but they were somewhat lifeless. The domestic staff were time-worn. These completely superannuated individuals were waited on by servants who were just like them. They all looked as if they had lived a long time ago and were refusing to die. Conserve, conservation, conservative – that was more or less the entire lexicon. It was a matter of 'being in good odour'. Indeed, there were aromatic preservatives in the opinions of these venerable groups and their ideas had the scent of vetiver. It was a mummified society. The masters were embalmed, the servants were stuffed with straw. A worthy old émigrée marchioness who had lost her fortune and was left with just one maid continued to talk of 'my staff'.

What did they do at Madame de T's salon? They were ultra. To be ultra: this expression no longer has any meaning today, although what it represents may not have disappeared. It requires explanation.

To be ultra is to go to extremes. It is to attack the sceptre in the name of the throne and the mitre in the name of the altar. It is to ride your horse into the ground. It is to kick over the traces. It is to find fault with the bonfire for undercooking the heretic. It is to reproach the idol for its inadequate idolatry. It is to insult by being over-respectful. It is to find too little popery in the pope, too little royalty in the king, and too much light in darkness. It is to be dissatisfied, in the name of whiteness, with alabaster, snow, the swan, the lily. It is to be so much a supporter of things that you become their enemy. It is to be so strongly for, that you are against. The ultra spirit is especially characteristic of the first phase of the Restoration.

Nothing in history resembles that brief moment which begins in 1814 and ends around 1820 with the advent of Monsieur de Villèle, the pragmatist of the right. Those six years were an extraordinary interlude, at once uproarious and bleak, cheerful and gloomy, lit up as if by the radiance of dawn and at the same time overcast by the shadows of the great catastrophes still filling the horizon and slowly sinking into the past. There was in that light and that shadow a whole little world, old and new, comic and sad, youthful and aged, rubbing its eyes. A return is like nothing so much as a reawakening. This was a group that regarded France with resentment and that France regarded with scorn. The streets were full of good old marquises who had come out of hiding, returnees and revenants, the old aristocracy, amazed at everything; decent, noble gentlemen smiling because they were back in France, and weeping too, thrilled to see their country again, heartbroken not to find their monarchy in place; the nobility of the crusades decrying the nobility of the Empire, in other words the nobility of the sword; historic dynasties who had lost the sense of history, the sons of Charlemagne's comrades-in-arms despising Napoleon's comrades-in-arms. As we have just said, swords traded insults: the sword of Fontenoy was ludicrous and just an old museum piece; the sword of Marengo was loathsome and just a butcher's knife. Yesteryear belittled yesterday. There was no longer any appreciation of what was great, no sense of what was ridiculous. There was someone who called Bonaparte 'Scapin'. This world no longer exists. Let us say again, nothing of it survives. If we pick one of those figures at random and try mentally to bring him to life again he seems as strange to us as some antediluvian world. That is because he too has actually been swallowed up by a flood. He has disappeared under two revolutions. What tidal waves ideas are! How quickly they drown all that it is their mission to destroy and bury, and how swiftly they create tremendous depths!

Such was the physiognomy of the salons of those distant and innocent days when Monsieur Martainville had more wit than Voltaire.

These salons had their own literature and politics. There, they believed in Fiévée. Monsieur Agier's word was law. They discussed the writings of Monsieur Colnet, the journalist bookseller on the Quai Malaquais. Napoleon was quite the Corsican Ogre. Later, the introduction into history of a Monsieur le Marquis de Buonaparté, lieutenant-general of the king's armies, was a concession to the spirit of the age.

These salons did not long preserve their purity. As early as 1818 a few 'constitutional' monarchists (a disquieting distinction) began to spring up among them. The line they followed was to be royalist and to be apologetic about it. Whereas the ultras were very proud, these 'doctrinaires'* were a little shameful. They were capable of wit; they were capable of silence; their political dogma was suitably starched with arrogance; they were bound to succeed. They favoured inordinately, to their advantage in fact, white cravats and buttoned-up coats. The mistake, or the misfortune, of the 'doctrinaire' party was to create old young men. They adopted the attitude of sages. They dreamed of grafting restricted power on to the absolute principle of unrestraint. Against radical liberalism they urged, and sometimes with a rare intelligence, conservative liberalism. They were heard to say, 'Spare monarchism! It has done more than a little good. It has restored tradition, worship, religion, respect. It is loyal, brave, chivalrous, loving, dedicated. To the new greatness of the nation it has brought, albeit reluctantly, the age-old greatness of the monarchy. It is wrong in not understanding the Revolution, the Empire, glory, liberty, young ideas, young generations, the age. But this wrong it does us – have we not sometimes been guilty of the same wrong towards monarchism? The Revolution, whose heirs we are, must have understanding of everything. To attack monarchism is a contradiction of liberalism. What a mistake! And what blindness! Revolutionary France lacks respect for historic France, in other words its mother, in other words itself. After the fifth of September, the monarchy's nobility was treated as the Empire's nobility was treated after the eighth of July. They were unjust to the eagle, we are unjust to the fleur-de-lys. Must we always have something to outlaw! Does it serve any purpose to ungild Louis XIV's crown, to scrape away Henri IV's coat of arms? We jeer at Monsieur de Vaublanc who removed the Ns on the Pont d'Iéna! Well, what was he doing? What are we doing? Bouvines is as much ours as Marengo. The fleurs-de-lys are ours as well as the Ns. That is our patrimony. What is the good of diminishing it? We should not turn our back on our country in the past any more than in the present. Why not accept the whole of history? Why not love the whole of France?'

So it was that constitutional monarchists criticized and defended

* The name by which the political party of constitutional monarchists became known.

563

monarchism, which was unhappy at being criticized and furious at being defended. The ultras marked the first phase of monarchism, the Congregation characterized the second. Ardour gave way to cleverness. Let us end our brief summary there.

In the course of his narrative the author of this book has found in his path this curious moment of contemporary history. He has had to take a quick look at it in passing and describe some of the peculiar features of this now forgotten society. But he does it rapidly and without any bitter or derisive intent. Memories – fond and respectful memories, for they relate to his mother – tie him to this past. Besides, in all fairness this same little world had its own grandeur. We may smile at it, but we can neither despise nor hate it. It was the France of old.

Marius Pontmercy, like all other children, had some sort of education. When he was out of his Aunt Gillenormand's hands his grandfather entrusted him to a respectable tutor of the purest classical innocence. This developing young mind was passed on from a prude to a pedant. Marius had his school years, then became a law student. He was royalist, fanatical and austere. He had little love for his grandfather, whose levity and cynicism offended him, and his feelings towards his father were grim.

All in all, he was an ardent and cold-hearted boy, noble, generous, proud, religious, impassioned, callously self-respecting, ferociously pure.

IV
The End of the Brigand

The completion of Marius's classical studies coincided with Monsieur Gillenormand's retirement from society. The old man bade farewell to the Faubourg St-Germain and to Madame de T's salon, and came and settled in the Marais, in his house on Rue des Filles-du-Calvaire. There, in addition to the porter, he had as servants the Nicolette who succeeded La Magnon as chambermaid and that huffing and puffing Basque mentioned above.

In 1827, Marius had just turned seventeen. On returning home one evening he saw his grandfather holding a letter in his hand.

'Marius,' said Monsieur Gillenormand, 'you'll be going to Vernon tomorrow.'

'Why?' said Marius.

'To see your father.'

Marius shuddered. He had imagined everything but this, that he might one day have to see his father. Nothing could be more unexpected, more surprising and, it has to be said, more disagreeable to him. It was rapprochement forced on estrangement. It was not upsetting, no, it was irksome.

On top of his feelings of political antipathy, Marius was convinced that his father, the 'sabre-slasher', as Monsieur Gillenormand called him on his kinder days, did not love him. This was obvious from the way he had abandoned his son and left him to others. Feeling unloved, he did not love. 'Nothing simpler,' he said to himself.

He was so astounded that he did not question Monsieur Gillenormand.

The grandfather went on, 'Apparently he's ill. He's asking for you.' And after a pause he added, 'Go in the morning. I think there's a coach from Cour des Fontaines leaving at six o'clock that arrives in the evening. Take it. He says it's urgent.'

Then he crumpled the letter up in his hand and put it in his pocket. Marius might have set out that very evening and been with his father by the following morning. In those days a stage-coach from Rue du Bouloi made the journey to Rouen overnight and passed through Vernon. Neither Marius nor Monsieur Gillenormand thought to make enquiries.

The next day at dusk Marius arrived in Vernon. People were just beginning to light their candles. He asked the first person he met for 'Monsieur Pontmercy's house'. For he was, in his own mind, of the same opinion as the Restoration and was no more willing to recognize his father as either colonel or baron.

The house was pointed out to him. He rang the bell. A woman came to the door, holding a small lamp.

'Monsieur Pontmercy?' said Marius.

The woman just stood there.

'Is this the right address?' asked Marius.

The woman nodded.

'Can I speak to him?'

The woman shook her head.

'But I'm his son,' said Marius. 'He's expecting me.'

'He's not expecting you any more,' said the woman.

Then he noticed she was crying.

She pointed to the door of a room on the ground floor. He entered.

In this room, lit by a tallow candle on the mantelpiece, were three men, one standing, another kneeling, and one lying stretched out on the floor in his nightshirt. The one on the floor was the colonel.

The other two were a doctor and a priest, who was praying.

The colonel had been struck down with brain fever three days earlier. At the beginning of his illness, with a sense of foreboding he had written to Monsieur Gillenormand asking for his son. The illness had taken a turn for the worse. On the very evening of Marius's arrival in Vernon the colonel suffered a fit of delirium. Despite the serving-woman's efforts to prevent him, he had risen from his bed, crying, 'My son isn't going to arrive in time! I'm going out to meet him!' Then he left his bedroom and collapsed on the floor of the room next door. He had just breathed his last.

The doctor and the priest were summoned. The doctor arrived too late. The priest arrived too late. The son also arrived too late.

Discernible by the dim light of the candle, on the pale and recumbent colonel's cheek was a large teardrop that had trickled from his dead eye. The eye was extinguished but the tear was not yet dry. That tear represented his son's delay.

Marius gazed on that man he was seeing for the first and last time, on that venerable masculine face, those open, unseeing eyes, those white locks, those robust limbs on which brown lines were visible here and there – these were sabre scars – and red star shapes of some sort – these were bullet holes. He gazed on that gigantic scar that put the stamp of heroism on the face God had imprinted with kindness. He reflected that this man was his father, and that this man was dead, and he remained unmoved.

The sorrow he felt was the sorrow he would have felt in the presence of any other man he might have seen lying dead.

There was grief in that room, heartfelt grief. The serving-woman was lamenting in one corner, the priest was praying and could be heard sobbing, the doctor was wiping his eyes. Even the corpse was weeping.

This doctor, this priest and this woman stared at Marius in their distress without saying a word. He was the stranger there. Far too little affected, Marius felt ashamed and embarrassed at his own attitude. He had his hat in his hand. He dropped it on the floor to make them think sorrow drained him of the strength to hold it.

At the same time he felt a kind of remorse and despised himself for behaving like this. But was it his fault? He just did not love his father!

The colonel left nothing. The sale of his furniture barely paid the cost of his burial. The servant found a scrap of paper, which she handed to Marius. Written on it in the colonel's hand was the following: 'For my son. The emperor made me a baron on the battlefield of Waterloo. Since the Restoration disputes this title that I paid for with my blood, my son shall take it and bear it. It goes without saying, he will be worthy of it.'

Below this the colonel had added: 'At this same battle of Waterloo a sergeant saved my life. The man's name is Thénardier. I believe he has of late been the keeper of a small inn in a village outside Paris, at Chelles or Montfermeil. If my son ever meets him, he will do the best he can for Thénardier.'

Marius took this piece of paper and kept it, not because he felt duty-bound to his father but because of that vague respect for death that is always so compelling in the heart of man.

Nothing remained of the colonel. Monsieur Gillenormand had his sword and uniform sold to a second-hand clothes dealer. The neighbours plundered the garden and stripped it of its extraordinary flowers. The other plants became overgrown with brambles, or died.

Marius stayed only forty-eight hours in Vernon. After the burial he returned to Paris and resumed his law studies without giving any more thought to his father than if he had never lived. Within two days the colonel was buried, and in three days he was forgotten.

Marius wore a mourning band on his hat. That was all.

V

The Usefulness of Going to Mass to
Become a Revolutionary

Marius had kept up the religious habits of his childhood. One Sunday when he went to hear mass at St-Sulpice, at that same chapel of the Virgin where his aunt used to take him when he was little, being more distracted and absent-minded than usual that day, he took a place behind a pillar and without paying attention knelt at a seat of Utrecht velvet on the back of which was written this name: 'Monsieur Mabeuf, warden'. Mass had hardly begun when an old man came up to Marius and said, 'Monsieur, this is my place.'

Marius hastily stood aside and the old man took his seat.

After the mass had ended Marius was still standing a few paces away, lost in thought. The old man came up to him again and said, 'I beg your pardon, monsieur, for having disturbed you earlier. And for disturbing you again now, but you must have found me annoying, and I owe you an explanation.'

'Monsieur,' said Marius, 'there's no need.'

'But there is!' the old man went on. 'I don't want you to think ill of me. You see, I'm attached to this place. It seems to me the mass is better from here. Why? I'll tell you. It was to this spot that I saw a poor man come regularly, every two or three months, for many years, a fine father who had no other opportunity and no other way of seeing his child because he was prevented from doing so under the terms of a family agreement. He used to come at the time when he knew his son would be brought to mass. The lad never suspected his father was there. Perhaps he didn't even know he had a father, the little innocent! The father kept behind this pillar so he wouldn't be seen. He would gaze at his child and weep. He adored that child, poor man! I could see that. For me this spot has become almost sanctified, and I've developed the habit of coming here to hear mass. I prefer it to the stall where, as warden, I have a right to be. I even got to know that unfortunate gentleman a little. He had a father-in-law, a rich aunt, relatives, I don't quite remember, who threatened to disinherit the child if he, the father, saw him. He sacrificed himself so that his son might some day be rich and happy. They were kept apart on account of political opinions. Certainly, I'm in favour of political opinions, but there are people who don't know where to stop. My God! Just because a man was at Waterloo doesn't make him a monster. You don't keep a father away from his child for that. He was one of Bonaparte's colonels. He's now dead, I believe. He lived at Vernon, where I have a brother who's a priest, and his name was something like Pontmarie or Montpercy – my goodness, he had a fine sabre scar.'

'Pontmercy?' said Marius, turning pale.

'Exactly. Pontmercy. Did you know him?'

'Monsieur,' said Marius, 'he was my father.'

The old warden clasped his hands and exclaimed, 'Ah! you're the child! Yes, of course, he must be a man by now. Ah well, poor child, you can say you had a father who loved you dearly!'

Marius offered his arm to the old man and walked him home. The next day he said to Monsieur Gillenormand, 'I've arranged with a few friends to go hunting. Would you mind if I went away for three days?'

'Make it four!' replied his grandfather. 'Go and enjoy yourself.'

And he said quietly to his daughter with a wink, 'It'll be some sweetheart!'

VI
What Meeting a Churchwarden Can Lead To

Where Marius went, we shall see a little later.

Marius was away for three days, then he came back to Paris, went straight to the law school library and asked for back issues of *Le Moniteur*.

He read *Le Moniteur*, he read all the histories of the Republic and the Empire, the *Mémorial de Ste-Hélène*, every memoir, newspaper, bulletin, proclamation; he devoured them all. The first time he came across his father's name in the Grand Army bulletins, he had a fever for a whole week. He went to see the generals under whom Georges Pontmercy had served, Comte H among others. Churchwarden Mabeuf, whom he went back to visit, described life at Vernon, the colonel's retreat, his flowers, his solitude. Marius came to know everything about that rare, excellent and gentle man, that sort of lion-lamb that had been his father.

Meanwhile, busy with this research that took up his every moment and occupied his every thought, he hardly saw the Gillenormands at all. He would turn up for meals. Then they would look for him and he would be gone. Father Gillenormand smiled. 'Ah well, it's girls he's interested in now!' Sometimes the old man added, 'I'll be damned! I thought it was just a passing fancy, evidently it's a real passion!'

It was indeed a passion. Marius was learning to adore his father.

At the same time his ideas underwent an extraordinary change. There were numerous successive phases in this change. As this has been the experience of many minds of our time, we think it will be useful to follow these phases step by step and chart them all. He was bewildered by this history he had just begun to study. The first impression it made on him was dazzling.

Up until then the Republic, the Empire, had just been monstrous words to him. The Republic, a guillotine in the dusk. The Empire, a sabre in the dark. He had now taken a good look and, where he had expected to find only gloomy chaos, with a kind of extraordinary shock mingled with fear and joy he saw stars shining – Mirabeau, Vergniaud, Saint-Just, Robespierre, Camille Desmoulins, Danton – and a sun rising: Napoleon. He was utterly confused. He shrank back, blinded by the brightness of the light. Little by little, after his initial amazement, he grew accustomed to this radiance, he considered actions without experiencing a sense of vertigo, he examined individuals without experiencing a sense of dread. The Revolution and the Empire came brilliantly into perspective before the eye of his imagination. He saw these two separate complexes of events and of men encapsulated in two tremendous facts: the Republic in the supremacy of civil law restored to the masses, the Empire in the supremacy of the French idea imposed on Europe. He saw emerge from the Revolution the great figure of the people, and from the Empire the great figure of France. He avowed in his conscience that all this had been good.

What his dazzled admiration overlooked in this initial, far too synthetic assessment we do not consider necessary to point out here. It is the state of an evolving mind we are recording. Progress is not made overnight. That said, once and for all, applying as it does to what has already been said as well as to what follows, we continue.

He then realized that until that moment he had not understood his country any more than he had understood his father. He knew neither of them, and he had in a way kept himself in the dark. Now he could see. The one he admired, the other he adored.

He was full of regret and remorse, and reflected with despair that he could speak only to a grave, now, of all that he had in his soul. Oh! if his father had existed, if he had still had his father, if God in his compassion and goodness had granted that his father were still alive, how he would have gone running to him, how he would have rushed to him, how he would have cried out, 'Father! Here I am! It's me! I've the same feelings as you! I'm your son!' How he would have embraced his white head, bathed his hair in tears, contemplated his scar, squeezed his hands, adored his garments, kissed his feet! Oh! Why had his father died so soon, before his time, before justice was done, before his son loved him? Marius felt a never-ending ache in his heart, saying over and over again, 'Alas!' At the same time, he became more truly earnest, more truly serious, more sure of what he believed and what he thought. At every moment came glimmerings of the truth, to perfect his reasoning. There was some sort of inward development going on inside him. He felt a kind of natural expansion by virtue of these two things, both new to him – his father and his country.

Just as, when you have a key, everything opens, he was able to understand what he had previously hated, make sense of what he had previously abhorred. He could now plainly see the providential, divine and human significance of the great things he had been taught to detest and the great men he had been instructed to abominate. When he reflected on his former opinions, of only yesterday and yet seemingly to him already so far in the past, he was infuriated and he smiled.

From the rehabilitation of his father he naturally moved on to the rehabilitation of Napoleon – but this, to be truthful, was not achieved without a struggle.

From infancy he had been imbued with the way the men of 1814 judged Bonaparte. Well, all the prejudices of the Restoration, all its interests, all its instincts, tended to misrepresent Napoleon. It detested him even more than Robespierre, and it rather cleverly exploited the weariness of the nation and the hatred mothers had of him. Bonaparte had become a kind of monster, almost fabulous, and to portray him to the popular imagination, which as we said earlier is like the imagination of children, the men of 1814 presented a whole series of

frightening masks, from one that remains awe-inspiring in its frightfulness to one that in its frightfulness becomes a figure of fun, from
Tiberius to the bogey man. So, in speaking of Bonaparte, you were
free to sob or to snort with laughter provided there was an underlying
hatred. About 'that man', as he was called, Marius had never entertained any other ideas. They had combined with the tenacity that was
in his nature. There was within him a really stubborn little fellow who
hated Napoleon.

On reading history, on studying it especially through documents
and source materials, the veil hiding Napoleon from Marius's eyes
tore, little by little. He glimpsed something immense, and suspected he
had been mistaken until now about Bonaparte as well as all the rest.
Every day he was better able to see. And, slowly, almost reluctantly at
the outset, then with elation and as though drawn by an irresistible
fascination, he began to climb one by one first the dark steps, then the
dimly lit steps, finally the bright and splendid steps of enthusiasm.

One night he was alone in his small bedroom under the eaves. His
candle was lit. He was leaning on his elbows, reading, at the table by
his open window. All sorts of fanciful notions came to him from outer
space and mingled with his thoughts. What a spectacle the night is!
You hear muted sounds, not knowing where they are coming from,
you see Jupiter, which is twelve hundred times bigger than the earth,
glowing like an ember; the azure is black, the stars twinkle. It is
magnificent.

He was reading the Grand Army bulletins, those Homeric verses
written on the battlefield. He occasionally saw his father's name, and
always the name of the emperor. The whole great Empire became
apparent to him. He felt, as it were, a swelling tide rising within him.
At moments it was as if his father passed close by like a breeze, and
whispered in his ear. He became gradually abstracted. He thought he
heard drums, cannon, trumpets, the measured tread of battalions, the
thudding and distant gallop of cavalry. From time to time his eyes
turned heavenward and gazed at the stupendous constellations shining in the boundless depths of space, then he looked down at the book
again, and saw stirring there in confusion other stupendous things.
His heart was in his mouth. He was in a state of exhilaration, trembling, panting. All at once, without himself knowing what had got
into him and what he was obeying, he stood up, reached out of the
window with both arms, stared intently at the darkness, the silence,
the mysterious infinitude, the eternal immensity, and cried, 'Long live
the emperor!'

From that moment there was no going back. The Ogre of Corsica, the usurper, the tyrant, the monster who was his own sisters' lover, the charlatan who took lessons from Talma, the poisoner of Jaffa, the tiger, Buonaparté – all this vanished and gave way in his mind to an indeterminate and brilliant radiance, and, shining high out of reach within it, the pale marble phantom of Caesar. For his father, the emperor had been simply the well beloved captain, admired and devotedly served. For Marius, he was something more. He was the predestined master-builder of the French order, taking over from the Roman order in ruling the universe. He was the prodigious architect of a collapse, following on from Charlemagne, Louis XI, Henri IV, Richelieu, Louis XIV and the Committee of Public Safety; doubtless with his flaws, his lapses and even his criminality – in other words, a man – but majestic in his lapses, splendid in his flaws, strong in his criminality. He was the man of destiny who had compelled all nations to recognize 'the great nation'! Better still, he was the actual embodiment of France, conquering Europe by the sword he held, and the world by the light he cast. Marius saw in Bonaparte the dazzling apparition that will always rise up at the frontier and guard the future. Despot, but state-appointed, a dictator produced by a republic and encapsulating a revolution. Napoleon became for him the man-nation just as Jesus Christ is the man-God.

Evidently, like all new converts to a religion, he was elated by his conversion, threw himself into it, and went too far. That was his nature: once he started to follow his inclination it was almost impossible that he hold himself in check. A zealot's passion for the sword took hold of him and became embroiled in his mind with his enthusiasm for the idea. He did not realize that along with genius, and entangled with it, he was admiring might; in other words, he was setting up in the double niche of his idolatry on the one hand that which is divine, on the other that which is brutal. In several respects he was now misguided in a different way. He accepted everything. In seeking out the truth, there is a way of being misled. He had a kind of impulsive good faith that swallowed everything whole. On the new course he had taken, in condemning the wrongs of the old regime as in measuring the glory of Napoleon, he neglected attenuating circumstances.

In any case, a tremendous step had been taken. Where he had previously seen the fall of the monarchy, he now saw the advent of France. His orientation had changed. Where the sun had set, the sun now rose; west was now east. He had about-faced.

All these revolutions took place within him, and without his family having any idea of what was going on.

When by means of these mysterious workings he had shed his old

Bourbon and ultra skin entirely, when he had cast off the aristocrat, the Jacobite and the royalist, when he had become thoroughly revolutionary, deeply democratic and almost Republican, he went to an engraver on the Quai des Orfèvres and ordered a hundred calling-cards bearing this name: Baron Marius Pontmercy.

This was nothing but a very logical consequence of the change that had taken place in him, a change in which everything revolved around his father. Only, as he did not know anyone and he could not leave his cards with any porter, he put them in his pocket.

Another natural consequence was that as he grew closer to his father, to his memory and to the things the colonel for over twenty-five years had fought for, he felt correspondingly estranged from his grandfather. We have already said, Monsieur Gillenormand's temperament had long jarred on him. There already existed between them all the divergences between solemn youth and frivolous old man. Géronte's levity shocks and exasperates Werther's melancholy. As long as they shared the same political opinions and the same ideas, Marius had been able to meet Monsieur Gillenormand on that common ground as on a bridge. When this bridge collapsed, there was a gulf between them. And then, in addition to everything else, Marius had inexpressible feelings of outrage at the thought that it was Monsieur Gillenormand who for stupid motives had ruthlessly torn him away from the colonel, thus depriving the father of the child, and the child of the father.

So great was his devotion to his father that Marius had come to feel almost hostile towards his grandfather.

All the same, none of this, as we have said, showed outwardly. Only, he was increasingly chilly in his manner, laconic at mealtimes, and rarely in the house. When his aunt scolded him about it, he was very meek and gave as an excuse his studies, lectures, examinations, conferences, et cetera. His grandfather remained convinced of the infallibility of his diagnosis. 'Lovesick! I know what I'm talking about.'

Marius was away from home from time to time.

'Where does he go when he's not here?' said his aunt.

On one of these always very brief trips he went to Montfermeil, acting on the information his father had left him, and sought the one-time sergeant of Waterloo, the innkeeper Thénardier. Thénardier had gone bankrupt, the inn was closed, and no one knew what had become of him. Marius was away from the house for four days on this quest.

'He's certainly sowing his wild oats,' said his grandfather.

It was thought to have been observed that he was wearing on his chest, around his neck, underneath his shirt, something attached to a black ribbon.

VII

A Bit of Skirt

We have mentioned a lancer.

He was a great-great-nephew of Monsieur Gillenormand's on the paternal side, and led a garrison life, outside the family and far from any domestic hearth. Lieutenant Théodule Gillenormand had all the requisite elements to be what is called a fine-looking officer. He had 'a girl's waist', a triumphant manner of trailing his sword, and a handle-bar moustache. He came to Paris very rarely, so rarely that Marius had never seen him. The cousins knew each other only by name. Théodule was, as we think we have said already, his Aunt Gillenormand's favourite. She liked him better for seeing so little of him. Not seeing people means they can be assumed to have every perfection.

One morning the elder Mademoiselle Gillenormand returned to her room as greatly flustered as her sedateness would allow. Marius had just asked his grandfather's permission to make yet another little trip, adding that he meant to set out that very evening.

'Go ahead!' his grandfather replied, and raising both eyebrows to the top of his forehead Monsieur Gillenormand added to himself, 'He's developing a habit of sleeping in another bed.' Mademoiselle Gillenormand went back up to her room most intrigued, and on the staircase let out this exclamation: 'That's too bad!' And this question: 'But where is it that he goes?' She envisaged some more or less illicit amorous liaison, some shadowy woman, an assignation, a mystery, and she would not have minded prying a little more deeply. A mystery to savour is like a foretaste of scandal – saintly souls are not averse to it. In the secret compartments of bigotry there is a curiosity about scandal.

So she was possessed with a vague craving to learn of an affair.

In order to distract herself from this curiosity that was exciting her a little more than she was used to, she sought refuge in her talents and applied herself to buttonhole-stitching, in cotton thread on cotton, one of those Empire and Restoration embroideries with a lot of cabriolet-wheel motifs in them. Tedious work, peevish worker. She had been sitting there for several hours when the door opened. Mademoiselle Gillenormand looked up. Lieutenant Théodule stood before her, giving her the regulation salute. She squealed with delight. A person may be old, she may be a prude, she may be pious, she may be an aunt, but it is always a pleasure for her to see a lancer come into her room.

'You here, Théodule!' she exclaimed.

'Just passing through, aunt.'

'Well, give me a kiss, then.'

'There!' said Théodule.

And he kissed her. Aunt Gillenormand went to her writing-desk and opened it.

'You'll be staying with us for the rest of the week at least?'

'I'm off again this evening, aunt.'

'You don't mean it!'

'Absolutely!'

'Stay, my dear Théodule, please.'

'My heart says yes but my orders say no. It's simply this: the garrison's moving. We were at Melun, we're now at Gaillon. To get from our old posting to the new one we have to go through Paris. "I'm going to see my aunt," I said.'

'And this is for your trouble.' She put ten gold louis in his hand.

'You mean, for my pleasure, dear aunt.'

Théodule gave her a second kiss, and she had the delight of having her neck a little chafed by the braid on his uniform.

'Are you riding there with your regiment?' she asked him.

'No, aunt. I wanted to see you. I've got special leave. My batman's taking my horse. I'm travelling by coach. And by the way, I must ask you something.'

'What?'

'My cousin Marius Pontmercy is travelling too, is he?'

'How do you know that?' said his aunt, her curiosity instantly roused.

'As soon as I arrived I went to make a reservation for a seat in the front compartment.'

'Well?'

'A traveller had already come by to make a reservation for a seat next to the driver. I saw his name on the card.'

'What name?'

'Marius Pontmercy.'

'The wastrel!' exclaimed his aunt. 'Ah! your cousin isn't a steady lad like yourself. To think he's travelling overnight by coach!'

'Like me.'

'But with you it's duty, with him it's indulgence.'

'By Jove!' said Théodule.

At this point something happened to the elder Mademoiselle Gillenormand – she had an idea. Had she been a man, she would have slapped her forehead. She addressed Théodule bluntly, 'Your cousin doesn't recognize you, does he?'

'No. I've seen him, but he's never deigned to notice me.'

'So now you're going to travel together?'

'He'll be on top, I'm in the front compartment.'

'Where does this coach go?'

'Andelys.'

'So that's where Marius is going?'

'Unless, like me, he stops off on the way. I'm getting off at Vernon to catch the connection for Gaillon. I don't know anything about Marius's travel plans.'

'Marius! What an ugly name! What was the idea of calling him Marius? Whereas at least your name's Théodule!'

'I'd rather be called Alfred,' said the officer.

'Listen, Théodule.'

'I am listening, aunt.'

'Pay attention.'

'I am paying attention.'

'Are you sure?'

'Yes.'

'Well, Marius goes off on his own.'

'Uh huh!'

'He travels.'

'Ah hah!'

'He doesn't come home at night.'

'Oh hoh!'

'We'd like to know what's behind all this.'

Théodule replied with the composure of a hardened man, 'A bit of skirt.' And with that private chuckle denoting certainty, he added, 'A sweetheart.'

'Obviously!' cried the aunt, who thought she could hear Monsieur Gillenormand speaking, and felt her conviction grow irresistibly from that word 'sweetheart' delivered in almost exactly the same way by great-uncle and great-nephew.

She went on, 'You can do us a favour. Follow Marius for a bit. He doesn't recognize you, it'll be easy for you. Seeing there's a sweetheart, try to get a look at her. You write and tell us about it. It'll amuse his grandfather.'

Théodule did not have much appetite for this kind of spying, but he was very touched by the ten louis and thought he could see more where those came from. He accepted the commission and said, 'If that's what you want, aunt.' And he added to himself, 'Here I am, playing chaperone.'

Mademoiselle Gillenormand gave him a kiss. 'Now, you wouldn't get up to such mischief, Théodule. You respect discipline, you obey orders, you're a man of conscience and duty, and you wouldn't leave your family to go and see some hussy.'

The lancer gave the satisfied smirk of Cartouche being praised for his integrity.

Following this conversation, that same evening Marius took his place in the coach without suspecting there was someone set to spy on him. As for the spy, the first thing he did was to fall asleep. He slept soundly, with a clear conscience. Argus snored all night long.

At daybreak the coach driver shouted, 'Vernon! Vernon relay station! Travellers for Vernon!'

And Lieutenant Théodule woke up. 'Well,' he muttered, still half asleep, 'this is where I get off.'

Then, his memory gradually clearing as the result of wakening, he remembered his aunt, the ten louis, and the report he had undertaken to make of what Marius got up to. This set him off laughing.

'Perhaps he's not in the coach any more,' he thought, as he buttoned up the jacket of his undress uniform. 'He may have got off at Poissy, he may have got off at Triel. If he didn't get out at Meulan, he may have got out at Mantes, unless he got out at Rolleboise, or went on to Pacy, with the choice of taking a left turn for Évreux or a right turn for La Roche-Guyon. Don't think I'm going to run after him, aunt! What the devil am I to write and tell the old girl?'

At that moment a pair of black trousers climbing down from the seat above appeared in the window of the front compartment.

'Could this be Marius?' said the lieutenant.

It was Marius.

A young peasant girl, standing by the coach among the horses and postilions, was offering flowers to the travellers. 'Flowers for your ladies!' she cried.

Marius went up to her and bought the most beautiful flowers in her basket.

'Well now,' said Théodule, jumping down from his compartment, 'that's intriguing. Who the devil is he going to take those flowers to? She must be a damned pretty woman for such a fine bouquet. I want to see her.'

And no longer acting for someone else but out of personal curiosity, like dogs that hunt on their own account, he started to follow Marius.

Marius paid no attention to Théodule. Some elegant women got out of the coach. He did not look at them. He appeared not to see anything around him.

'He's in love!' thought Théodule.

Marius headed for the church.

'Excellent!' said Théodule to himself. 'The church! Of course! Assignations spiced with a little bit of a mass are the best. Nothing is so exquisite as a stolen glance in the presence of the good Lord.'

When he got to the church Marius did not go inside but turned off behind the apse. He disappeared round the corner of one of the buttresses.

'The tryst is outside,' said Théodule. 'Let's have a look at this sweetheart.'

And he made his way on his boot-tips to the corner that Marius had rounded.

There, he stopped, astounded.

With both hands over his forehead, Marius was kneeling in the grass on a grave. He had strewn his bouquet over it. At the far end of the grave, on a little mound that marked the head, was a black wooden cross with this name in white letters: 'COLONEL BARON PONT-MERCY'. Marius could be heard sobbing.

The sweetheart was a tomb.

VIII
Marble Versus Granite

It was here that Marius had come the first time he had left Paris. It was here that he had come every time Monsieur Gillenormand said, 'He's sleeping in another bed tonight.'

Lieutenant Théodule was totally nonplussed to find himself unexpectedly confronted with a tomb. It left him with an unpleasant and peculiar feeling he was incapable of analysing, and which consisted of respect for a grave mingled with respect for a colonel. He retreated, leaving Marius alone in the cemetery, and there was discipline in this retreat. Death appeared to him with large epaulettes, and he almost gave it the military salute. Not knowing what to write to his aunt, he decided not to write at all. And probably nothing would have resulted from the discovery made by Théodule about the object of Marius's affections if, by one of those mysterious coincidences that chance so frequently engineers, the scene at Vernon had not almost immediately had a kind of repercussion in Paris.

Marius returned from Vernon three days later, early in the morning, dropped in at his grandfather's, and, travel-worn after two nights spent in the coach and feeling the need to make up for his lack of sleep with an hour's swimming, he went quickly up to his room, taking time only to remove the coat he had been travelling in and the black ribbon he wore round his neck, and headed off to the baths.

Monsieur Gillenormand, who like all elderly folk in good health had got up early, heard him come in, and eagerly, as fast as his old legs could carry him, he climbed the stairs up to the attic where Marius lived, in order to embrace him and in so doing to question him and get some idea of where he had been.

But the young man took less time to descend than the octogenarian took to go up, and when old Gillenormand entered the attic room, Marius was no longer there.

The bed had not been disturbed, and lying unwarily on it were the coat and the black ribbon.

'So much the better,' said Monsieur Gillenormand.

And a moment later he entered the drawing room where the elder Mademoiselle Gillenormand was already seated, embroidering her cartwheels.

His entrance was triumphant.

Holding the coat in one hand and the neck-ribbon in the other, Monsieur Gillenormand cried, 'Victory! We're about to penetrate the mystery! We're going to learn the ultimate secret! We have our furtive friend's philanderings within our grasp! This is it! I have the portrait!'

Indeed, a black shagreen locket, rather like a medallion, hung from the ribbon. The old man held this locket and gazed at it for some time without opening it, with that look of voraciousness and ecstasy and anger of some poor starving wretch seeing, as it passes right in front of him, a wonderful meal not meant for him.

'For this here is obviously a portrait. I know what I'm talking about. It's worn on the heart with tender love. What fools they are! Probably some dreadful tart who'd make you shudder! Young men have such bad taste these days!'

'Let's see, father,' said the old maid.

The locket opened by pressing a spring. All they found inside was a carefully folded piece of paper.

' "From addressee to sender",' said Monsieur Gillenormand, with a burst of laughter. 'I know what it is. A love letter!'

'Ah! let's read it!' said the aunt.

And she put on her spectacles. They unfolded the paper and read the following: 'For my son. The emperor made me a baron on the battlefield of Waterloo. Since the Restoration disputes this title that I paid for with my blood, my son shall take it and bear it. It goes without saying, he will be worthy of it.'

What the feelings of father and daughter were cannot be described. They felt chilled as if by the breath from a skull. They exchanged not a word. Only Monsieur Gillenormand said in a low voice and as if talking to himself, 'It's that sabre-slasher's handwriting.'

The aunt examined the sheet of paper, turned it round in all directions, then put it back in the locket.

At the same moment a little oblong packet wrapped in blue paper fell out of one of the coat pockets. Mademoiselle Gillenormand picked it up and unfolded the blue paper. It was Marius's one hundred calling-cards. She handed one of them to Monsieur Gillenormand, who read: 'Baron Marius Pontmercy'.

The old man rang the bell. Nicolette came. Monsieur Gillenormand took the ribbon, the locket and the coat, threw the whole lot on to the floor in the middle of the room, and said, 'Take this stuff back where it came from.'

A full hour passed in the most profound silence. The old man and the old maid had sat down with their backs to each other and were thinking their own thoughts, which were probably the same. At the end of this hour Aunt Gillenormand said, 'A pretty state of affairs!'

A few moments later Marius appeared. He had just come home. Even before he stepped into the drawing room he saw his grandfather, holding one of his calling-cards in his hand. And with that air of sneering bourgeois superiority, which he used to devastating effect, Monsieur Gillenormand exclaimed at the sight of him: 'Well, well, well, well, well, you're a baron now! I present my compliments. What's the meaning of this?'

Marius reddened slightly and replied, 'It means I'm my father's son.'

Monsieur Gillenormand stopped laughing and said harshly, 'I'm your father.'

'My father,' Marius continued stiffly with eyes downcast, 'was a humble and heroic man, who proudly served the Republic and France, who was great in the greatest history that men have ever made, who lived in camp for a quarter of a century, under artillery fire and bullets by day, in the snow and mud and rain at night, who captured two flags, who suffered countless wounds, who died forgotten and neglected, and who committed only one wrong, which was to love too well two ingrates, his country and myself.'

This was more than Monsieur Gillenormand could bear to hear. At the word 'Republic' he stood up, or to be more accurate he leapt to his feet. Every word that Marius had just uttered had the effect on the old royalist's face of blasts of air pumped from a pair of bellows on to a burning ember. From dark, it turned to red, from red to purple, and from purple to incandescent.

'Marius!' he cried. 'You abominable child! I don't know what your father was! I don't want to know! I don't know anything about him and I don't know him! But what I do know is, there were never anything but miserable wretches among all those people, they were all villains, murderers, Revolutionaries, thieves! All of them, I say! All of them! I know of not one exception! All of them, I say! Do you hear, Marius! I'm telling you, you're no more a baron than is my slipper! They were all of them criminals who served Robespierre! All of them brigands who served Bu-o-na-parté. All of them traitors who betrayed, betrayed, betrayed their legitimate king! All of them cowards who ran away from the Prussians and the English at Waterloo! That's what I know! Whether the gentleman your father is among them, I don't know, I'm sorry, it can't be helped, that's all I have to say!'

It was Marius, in his turn, who was now the ember, and Monsieur Gillenormand, the bellows. Marius was shaking in every limb, he did not know what was to become of him, his brain was on fire. He was the priest who sees all his holy wafers thrown to the wind, the fakir who sees a passer-by spit on his idol. It was not possible that such things could be said with impunity in front of him. But what was he to do? His father had just been ridden roughshod over and trampled on, in his presence. But by whom? By his grandfather. How was he to avenge the one without attacking the other? It was impossible to insult his grandfather and it was equally impossible not to avenge his father. On the one hand was a sacred grave, on the other a hoary head. For a few moments he was reeling drunkenly, with all this whirling in his head. Then he looked up, stared intently at his grandfather and cried in a voice of thunder, 'Down with the Bourbons and with that fat swine Louis XVIII!'

Louis XVIII had been dead for four years, but he did not care.

Crimson as he was, the old man suddenly grew whiter than his hair. He turned to a bust of Monsieur le Duc de Berry that stood on the mantelpiece and bowed low towards it with a sort of peculiar majesty. Then, like a walking stone statue, he strode slowly and silently from the fireplace to the window and from the window to the fireplace, twice traversing the whole the room and making the parquet floor creak. The second time he leaned towards his daughter, who had witnessed this clash with the obtuseness of an old sheep, and said to her, smiling with a smile that was almost calm, 'A baron like this gentleman and a bourgeois like me cannot remain under the same roof.'

And all of a sudden drawing himself up, deathly pale, trembling, terrible, his brow seemingly magnified in the frightful blaze of his anger, he flung his arm towards Marius and shouted, 'Get out!'

Marius left the house.

The following day Monsieur Gillenormand said to his daughter, 'You will send six hundred francs every six months to that blood-thirsty revolutionist and you will never speak of him to me again.'

Left with a vast reserve of fury to expend and not knowing how to vent it, he continued to address his daughter formally as *vous* for more than three months.

Marius, for his part, had gone off feeling outraged. One incident that must be mentioned had further aggravated his indignation. There are always these little accidents of fate that complicate domestic dramas. As a result, resentments increase although no additional wrongs may have been done. While hurriedly carrying Marius's 'stuff' back to his room as instructed by his grandfather, Nicolette had without noticing dropped – probably on the attic staircase, which was dark – that black shagreen locket containing the note penned by the colonel. Neither the note nor the locket could be found. Marius was convinced that 'Monsieur Gillenormand' – from that day on he never called him anything else – had thrown 'his father's will' on the fire. He knew by heart the few lines written by the colonel and therefore nothing was lost. But the piece of paper, the handwriting, that sacred relic – all this was the very heart of him. What had been done with it?

Marius left without saying where he was going and without knowing where he was going, with thirty francs, his watch and a few clothes in an overnight bag. He climbed into a cab at a cab stand, hired it by the hour, and set off for the Latin quarter to take his chances.

What was to become of Marius?

BOOK FOUR
FRIENDS OF THE ABC

I
A Group That Came Close to Becoming Historic

In those days, a period of apparent passivity, a certain vague sense of revolutionary excitement prevailed. Murmurs rising from the depths of '89 and '93 were in the air. Callow youth, if we may be forgiven the expression, was spreading its wings. People were changing, almost unawares, just by virtue of the progress of time. The hand that advances around the clock-face advances, too, in people's souls. Each individual was taking whatever step forward was his to take. Royalists were becoming liberals, liberals were becoming democrats.

It was like a rising tide, complicated by countless undertows. It is in the nature of undertows to create turbulence, hence some very peculiar combinations of ideas. People adored both Napoleon and liberty. We are writing history here. These were the mirages of that period. Opinions go through phases. Voltairian monarchism, a peculiar variety, had in Bonapartist liberalism a no less strange counterpart.

Other schools of thought were more serious. This one sought to establish first principles. That one set great store by rights. There was enthusiasm for the absolute, with infinite materializations of it envisaged. The absolute by its very rigour turns minds skyward and sets them loose in the limitless blue. There is nothing like dogma for giving birth to dreams. And nothing like dreams for generating the future. Today's Utopia is tomorrow's flesh and blood.

Progressive opinions were subversive. An incipient secretiveness menaced 'the established order', which was suspicious and devious. A supremely revolutionary sign. In underground warfare, the hidden motives of the authorities and the hidden motives of the populace cross paths. The hatching of insurrections prompts the planning of *coups d'état*.

There were not yet in France at that time those vast underground organizations such as the German Tugendbund and Italian carbonarism, just the odd subversive enclave extending its reach. The Cougourde was first coming into being at Aix. There was in Paris, among other associations of this kind, the Society of Friends of the ABC.

What was this 'Friends of the ABC'? A society dedicated ostensibly to the education of children, in reality to the elevation of men.

Members declared themselves Friends of the ABC.* The *abaissé*† was the people. They were to be raised up. A pun not to be scoffed at. Puns sometimes have a serious bearing on politics. For instance, the *Castratus ad castra* that made an army general of Narses‡; or *Barbari et Barberini*§; or *Fueros y Fuegos*¶; or *Tu es Petrus et super hanc petram***, et cetera.

The Friends of the ABC were few in number. It was a secret society in embryo, we would say almost a clique, if cliques culminated in heroes. They met in Paris in two places, near Les Halles in a tavern called the Corinthe, of which we shall hear more later, and near the Panthéon in a little café on Rue St-Michel called Café Musain, which has now been pulled down. The first of these meeting-places was situated close to working men, the second, to students.

The secret meetings of the Friends of the ABC were usually held in a back room of Café Musain. This room, quite separate from the café itself, with which it was connected by an extremely long corridor, had two windows and an exit with a staircase hidden from view leading on to the little Rue des Grès. There was smoking and drinking, gambling and laughter. There was talking in very loud voices about all sorts of things, and in very low voices about other things. Nailed to the wall was an old map of France under the Republic, evidence enough to rouse the suspicions of any policeman.

Most of the Friends of the ABC were students who had an amiable understanding with a number of workers. Here are the names of the leading figures. They belong in some measure to history: Enjolras, Combeferre, Jean Prouvaire, Feuilly, Courfeyrac, Bahorel, Lesgle (or Laigle), Joly, Grantaire.

---

* In French, pronounced 'Ah-beh-seh'.

† Also pronounced 'Ah-beh-seh', and meaning 'one brought low'.

‡ The Byzantine general Narses (*c*.480–574) was a eunuch, a *castratus*, who became a military leader (*ad castrum* meaning literally, 'to the army camp'), under the emperor Justinian, conquering the Ostrogoth kingdom in Italy for Byzantium.

§ An allusion to the saying *Quod non fecerunt barbari, fecerunt Barberini* ('What the barbarians did not do, the Barberini did'), referring to Urban VIII, Maffeo Barberini (1568–1644), who is supposed to have plundered the Pantheon for the bronze needed for the baldachin that he commissioned Bernini to create for the basilica of St Peter.

¶ Spanish: Literally, 'Charters' (guaranteeing local rights and privileges) 'and Fires'.

** 'Thou art Peter [*Petrus*], and upon this rock [*petra*] I will build my church', Matthew 16:18.

So strong was their friendship, these young men were a kind of family to each other. All, apart from Laigle, were from the south.

This group was remarkable. It has vanished into the invisible depths that lie behind us. At the point we have now reached in this drama it is perhaps worth casting a ray of light on these young individuals before the reader sees them swallowed up into the darkness of a tragic episode.

Enjolras, the first name we have chosen to mention – it will be seen why later – was an only son, and well-off.

Enjolras was a charming young man, capable of being fearsome. Of angelic beauty, he was a grim-faced Antinous. Seeing the pensiveness reflected in his gaze, you would have thought he had already lived through the revolutionary apocalypse in some previous existence. That tradition was part of him, as of someone who had experienced it. He knew every little detail about that great cataclysm. He had a sacerdotal and warlike nature, at odds with his boyishness. He was both ministering and militant: in the immediate context, a soldier of democracy; above and beyond present circumstances, a priest of the ideal. He had fathomless eyes, slightly red eyelids, a full lower lip that was readily disdainful, a high forehead. A good deal of forehead in a face is like a good deal of sky in a landscape. Like certain young men at the beginning of this century and the end of the last who distinguished themselves at an early age, he was extraordinarily youthful, with a girlish bloom, though pale at times. Already a man, he seemed still a child. At twenty-two years old he looked only seventeen. He was serious; he seemed unaware that there was on earth a creature called woman. He had only one passion: rightfulness. Only one thought: to remove any obstacle to it. On the Aventine Hill he would have been Gracchus; in the Convention, he would have been Saint-Just. He barely perceived roses, he was oblivious of spring, he did not hear birds sing. Evadne's bared breast would have moved him no more than it would have moved Aristogeiton. For him, as for Harmodius, the only thing flowers were good for was to conceal the sword. He was stern in his delights. Before all but the Republic he chastely lowered his gaze. He was liberty's marmoreal lover. He was a fiercely inspired speaker with a hymnic thrill to his eloquence. He was liable to spread his wings unexpectedly. Woe betide any attempt to make a romantic conquest of him! If any grisette from Place Cambrai or Rue St-Jean-de-Beauvais, seeing that truant-schoolboy face, that pageboy neck, those long fair eyelashes and those blue eyes, that wind-tousled hair, those rosy cheeks, fresh lips, perfect teeth, had hankered after all this youthfulness in its prime and come to try her charms on Enjolras, a shocking, dreadful glance would have abruptly revealed the abyss to her and taught her not to confuse Ezekiel's awesome cherub with Beaumarchais's gallant Cherubino.

Alongside Enjolras, who represented the logic of revolution, Combeferre represented its philosophy. Between the logic of revolution and its philosophy there is this difference: its logic may lead to war whereas its philosophy can only lead to peace. Combeferre was both complement and corrective to Enjolras. He was less elevated and more accommodating. He wanted minds to be instilled with the broad principles of general ideas. He said, 'Revolution but with civilization.' And around the sheer mountain he opened up a vast blue horizon. Hence an element of accessibility and feasibility in Combeferre's whole outlook. Revolution was more sustainable with Combeferre than with Enjolras. Enjolras gave expression to its divine right and Combeferre to its natural right. The former aligned himself with Robespierre, the latter stood close to Condorcet. Combeferre shared the common experience of life more than did Enjolras. If these two young men had been granted a place in history, one would have been the righteous, the other the wise man. Enjolras was more manly. Combeferre was more human. *Homo* and *vir*, therein lay the subtle difference between them. Combeferre was gentle in the same way that Enjolras was severe, through natural purity of soul. He loved the word 'citizen' but preferred the word 'man'. He would gladly have used *hombre*, as the Spanish did. He read everything, went to the theatre, attended public lectures, learned from Arago about the polarization of light, was fascinated by a talk in which Geoffroy Saint-Hilaire explained the twin functions of the external carotid artery and the internal carotid artery, the one that leads into the face and the other that leads into the brain. He was well informed, keeping pace with scientific developments, comparing Saint-Simon with Fourier, deciphering hieroglyphics, splitting the stones that he found and studying geology, drawing a silkworm moth from memory, pointing out the incorrect French in the *Dictionnaire de l'Académie*, reading Puységur and Deleuze, affirming nothing, not even miracles, denying nothing, not even ghosts, dipping into old issues of *Le Moniteur*, pondering. He declared that the future lies in the hands of the schoolmaster, and devoted himself to educational matters. He wanted society to work unfailingly at raising moral and intellectual standards, popularizing science, putting ideas into circulation, developing the minds of young people; and he was afraid that the inadequacy of the methods currently employed, the woeful narrowness of literary outlook confined as it was to two or three so-called classic centuries, the tyrannical dogmatism of the official pedants, scholastic prejudices and learning by rote, would end up turning our schools into artificial oysterbeds. He was erudite, a purist, a polymath, meticulous, hard-working; and at the same time, his friends said, 'quixotically' thoughtful. He believed in every dream: the railways, the suppression of pain in surgical operations, the fixing of the image in the dark-room, the electric telegraph, dirigibles. Little daunted, moreover, by the bastions erected on all sides against humankind by superstition, despotism, and prejudice – he was one of those who think knowledge will eventually circumvent them. Enjolras was a leader, Combeferre was a guide. You would have wanted to fight with one and march with the other. It is not that Combeferre was not capable of fighting. He was not unwilling to grapple with any obstacle and tackle it by direct force and explosive power. But making the human race gradually conform to its destiny through the teaching of basic principles and the implementation of practical laws was more to his liking. And between the two types of brightness he was inclined to favour illumination over conflagration. A fire can certainly create a glow, but why not wait for daybreak? A volcano gives light, but dawn gives even better light. Maybe Combeferre preferred the pure white of the beautiful to the blaze of the sublime. A light obscured by smoke, progress bought by violence, only half satisfied this tender-hearted and serious-minded individual. The pitching of a nation headlong into the truth, a '93, appalled him. Yet he was even more averse to stagnation, he sensed in it putrefaction and death. All things considered, he preferred spume to miasma, the torrent to the cesspool, Niagara Falls to Montfaucon's lake. In short, he wanted neither halt nor haste. Whereas his turbulent friends, chivalrously enamoured of the absolute, adored splendid revolutionary adventures, and invited them, Combeferre was inclined to let progress take its course. Steady progress, passionless perhaps but pure, methodical but beyond reproach, stolid but undeterred. Combeferre would have gone down on his knees and joined his hands in prayer that the future might arrive in all its blamelessness and nothing disturb the immense and virtuous development of nations. Good must be innocent, he kept repeating. And indeed, if the greatness of revolution is to gaze steadily on the radiant ideal and fly towards it, thunderbolts notwithstanding, with fire and blood in your grip, the beauty of progress is to be untarnished. And between Washington who represents the one and Danton who embodies the other there is the same difference as that which sets apart the swan-winged angel from the eagle-winged angel.

Jean Prouvaire was a shade even gentler than Combeferre. He

called himself 'Jehan', out of that little touch of whimsy which was part of the powerful and far-reaching movement that gave rise to the much needed study of the Middle Ages. Jean Prouvaire was of an amorous disposition, tended pot-plants, played the flute, wrote poetry, loved the people, pitied women, wept for children, made no distinction between his trust in the future and his trust in God, reproached the Revolution for a royal beheading – that of André Chénier. His usually delicate voice could suddenly become manly. He was well read – indeed, something of a scholar – and little short of an orientalist. Above all, he was good. And quite naturally enough to anyone who knows how close goodness and greatness are to each other, as regards poetry he had a preference for the sublime. He knew Italian, Latin, Greek and Hebrew, and used this knowledge to read only four poets: Dante, Juvenal, Aeschylus and Isaiah. In French he preferred Corneille to Racine and Agrippa d'Aubigné to Corneille. He was fond of whiling away his time in meadows of wild oats and cornflowers, and clouds were almost as much the object of his concern as were events. He had two turns of mind, one directed towards man, the other towards God: study or contemplation. All day long he delved into social issues: remuneration for work, capital, credit, marriage, religion, freedom of thought, freedom in love, education, penal justice, poverty, the right of association, property, production and distribution, the earthly conundrum that casts in shadow the human ant-hill. And at night he gazed up at those enormous entities, the stars. Like Enjolras, he was wealthy and an only son. He spoke softly, kept his head bowed, his eyes lowered, smiled diffidently, dressed badly, behaved awkwardly, blushed at next to nothing, was extremely shy. Otherwise, fearless.

Feuilly was a fan-maker, an orphan without father or mother, who earned three francs a day for his toil and had but one thought: to free the world. He had one other preoccupation: to educate himself, which he also termed 'to free himself'. He had taught himself to read and write. Everything he knew he had taught himself. Feuilly was big-hearted. He had a huge embrace. This orphan had adopted nations. In the absence of his mother, his thoughts had dwelt on the motherland. He did not want any man on earth to be without a motherland. With the man of the people's profound and prophetic instinct he nurtured within himself what we now call the idea of national identity. He had studied history with the express purpose of being able to cry scandal in full possession of the facts. In this club of young Utopians mainly concerned with France, he represented the outside world. He had expert knowledge of Greece, Poland, Hungary, Romania, Italy. He was always bringing up these names, in and out of season, with the persistence of rightfulness. The assaults of Turkey on Crete and Thessaly, of Russia on Warsaw, of Austria on Venice, incensed him. That great iniquity of 1772 roused him above all others. There is no eloquence more supreme than righteous indignation, and that was the kind of eloquence he had. He was always talking about that infamous date 1772, about that noble and valiant people overcome by treachery, about that tripartite crime, about that monstrous attack – prototype and model for all those dreadful eliminations of states that have since struck down many a noble nation and, as it were, annulled their birth certificates. All today's social outrages derive from the partition of Poland. The partition of Poland is a theorem of which all present political crimes are the corollaries. Not a despot or a traitor for nearly a century who has not examined, endorsed, countersigned and initialled, *ne varietur*, the partition of Poland. When the record of modern treacheries is examined, this one comes first. The Congress of Vienna took account of this crime before perpetrating its own. The year 1772 was the kill, 1815 the division of the spoils. This was Feuilly's usual theme. This poor worker had made himself the guardian of justice, and justice rewarded him by making him great. For the fact is, there is perpetuity in rightfulness. Warsaw can no more be Tartar than Venice can be Teutonic. Monarchs waste their efforts and lose their honour in the enterprise. Sooner or later the submerged nation floats to the surface and reappears. Greece becomes Greece again, Italy is once more Italy. Rightfulness is everlastingly persistent in its protest against such doings. There is no statute of limitation on the theft of a nation. These great swindles have no future. A nation's identity cannot be removed like the initials from a pocket handkerchief.

Courfeyrac had a father who was called Monsieur *de* Courfeyrac. One of the misapprehensions of the bourgeoisie under the Restoration, with regard to aristocracy and nobility, was to believe in the particle. The particle, as everyone knows, means nothing. But in the days of *La Minerve* that poor *de* was so highly rated by the bourgeoisie that they felt an obligation to renounce it. Monsieur de Chauvelin insisted on being called Monsieur Chauvelin, Monsieur de Caumartin, Monsieur Caumartin, Monsieur de Constant de Rebecque, Benjamin Constant, Monsieur de Lafayette, Monsieur Lafayette. Courfeyrac did not want to lag behind, and called himself plain Courfeyrac.

As far as Courfeyrac is concerned we might almost leave it at that, and for the rest simply say 'For Courfeyrac, see Tholomyès.'

* Latin, meaning 'not to be altered', used on notarized legal documents.

Courfeyrac did indeed have that vivacity of spirit that might be called the waggish charm of youth. Later on, this fades, like a kitten's winsomeness, and all this appeal leads in the end (on two feet) to the bourgeois and (on four paws) to the tomcat.

This sort of waggishness is handed down by the generations that go through the educational institutions, passed on from one to the next by the successive intakes of young people, *quasi cursores**, and always more or less the same. So that, as we have just pointed out, anyone listening to Courfeyrac in 1828 might have thought they were hearing Tholomyès in 1817. Only, Courfeyrac was a decent lad. Beneath the apparent similarities in their outward dispositions, the difference between Tholomyès and him was considerable. The latent man inside the former was quite unlike the one inside the latter. There was in Tholomyès a public prosecutor, and in Courfeyrac a chivalrous knight.

Enjolras was the leader, Combeferre was the guide. Courfeyrac was the centre. The others gave more light, he gave more warmth. The fact is, he had all the qualities of a centre, roundedness and radiance.

Bahorel had been involved in the bloody disturbances of June 1822 that marked young Lallemand's funeral.

Bahorel was good-humoured and disreputable, brave, spendthrift, generous in his lavishness, eloquent in his chatter, brazen in his audaciousness, the damned finest fellow there ever could be, with gaudy waistcoats and fiery opinions. A great brawler – that is to say, he loved nothing so much as a quarrel, short of a riot, and nothing so much as a riot, short of a revolution. Always ready to smash a window-pane, then tear up cobblestones, then bring down a government, to see the effect. Eleven years a student, he sniffed around the law but did not apply himself to it. He had taken for his motto 'Never a lawyer', and for his heraldic device a bedside cabinet in which could be glimpsed a judge's hat. Every time he went past the law school, which was a rare occurrence, he buttoned up his frock-coat – the paletot had not yet been invented – and took health-protecting measures. Of the school porter he said, 'What a fine-looking old man!' and of the dean, Monsieur Delvincourt, 'What a phenomenon!' He found subject matter for songs in his lectures and opportunities for caricature in his professors. He consumed quite a considerable allowance, something like three

---

* An allusion to a line from *De Rerum Natura* by the first-century-BC poet Lucretius: 'et quasi cursores vitai lampada tradunt' ('and like runners they pass on the torch of life'), bk II, line 79.

thousand francs a year, doing nothing. His parents were peasants in whom he had been able to instil a respect for their son.

He used to say about them, 'They're not bourgeois, they're peasants, that's why they've got some intelligence.'

A man of fitful fancy, Bahorel spread his custom over several cafés. The others had habits, he had none. He sauntered. To stray is human, to saunter is Parisian. Basically, a penetrating mind and more of a thinker than he seemed.

He served as a link between the Friends of the ABC and other as yet amorphous groups that were to take shape later.

There was one bald head among this conclave of youngsters.

The Marquis d'Avaray, whom Louis XVIII had made a duke for having helped him into a hackney cab the day he emigrated, used to relate that as the king was disembarking at Calais on his return to France in 1814 a man handed him a petition.

'What is your request?' said the king.

'Sire, a stage-post office.'

'What is your name?'

'L'Aigle.'

The king frowned, glanced at the signature on the petition and saw the name written as 'LESGLE'. This scarcely Bonapartist spelling tickled the king and he began to smile.

'Sire,' continued the man with the petition, 'I had for ancestor a keeper of hounds, and the dogs earned him the nickname Lesgueules. That nickname is now my name. I'm called Lesgueules, by contraction Lesgle, and by corruption L'Aigle.' This made the king's smile broaden. He later gave the man the stage-post office of Meaux, intentionally or otherwise.*

The bald member of the group was the son of this Lesgle, or Lègle, and signed himself, Lègle (de Meaux). His comrades called him Bossuet for short.

Bossuet was a cheerful fellow who had bad luck. His speciality was being unable to succeed at anything. On the other hand, he laughed at everything. By the age of twenty-five he was bald. His father had finished up owning a house and a field but he, the son, had had nothing more urgent to do than to lose that house and field in an unsound speculative venture. He was left with nothing. He had learning and

---

* Meaux suggests itself as an appropriate post to give him because *l'aigle de Meaux* was already a familiar designation by which the great churchman Jacques-Bénigne Bossuet, bishop of Meaux, was known (which is why Lègle de Meaux is called Bossuet by his young Revolutionary comrades).

wit but he was a failure. Everything went wrong for him and everyone took advantage of him. Any endeavour he was involved in redounded badly on him. If he was chopping wood he would cut off a finger. If he had a mistress he would soon discover he had also a friend. Some mishap was always befalling him. Hence his cheerfulness. He used to say, 'I live under a roof of falling tiles.' Little could surprise him because for him the accidental was predictable, and he took his bad luck with equanimity and smiled at the taunts of fate like someone who could see the joke. He was poor, but his fund of good humour was inexhaustible. He was soon down to his last sou, never his last laugh. When he was visited by adversity he warmly greeted this old acquaintance. He was on intimate terms with catastrophe, and so familiar with misfortune he called it by its nickname. 'Hallo, Lady Jinx,' he would say.

These persecutions on the part of fate had made him inventive. He was full of resources. He had no money but he contrived, when he felt like it, to indulge in 'unbridled extravagance'. One night he went so far as to blow five gold louis on supper with some flibbertigibbet, which inspired him to make a memorable quip in the middle of that orgy: 'You five-louis whore, pull off my boots!'

Bossuet was heading slowly towards the profession of lawyer. He was pursuing his law studies just like Bahorel. Bossuet did not have much of a home, sometimes none at all. He would stay with one person, then another, most often with Joly. Joly was studying medicine. He was two years younger than Bossuet.

Joly was a young hypochondriac. What he had got out of medicine was to be more of an invalid than a doctor. At twenty-three he thought he was ailing and spent his life inspecting his tongue in the mirror. He maintained that man becomes magnetized like a needle, and in his room had positioned his bed with head to the south and foot to the north so that the circulation of his blood would not be countered at night by the globe's great magnetic current. During thunderstorms he would feel his pulse. Otherwise, the merriest of all. All these contradictions – being young and cranky, ailing and cheerful – happily coexisted, and the result was an eccentric and delightful individual whom his comrades, lavish with winged consonants, called 'Jol-l-l-ly'. 'With four Ls* you can take flight!' Jean Prouvaire said to him. Joly had a habit of touching his nose with the end of his cane, an indication of a shrewd mind.

* Pronounced *ailes*, meaning 'wings'.

All these very diverse young men, who when all is said and done cannot but be taken seriously, shared the same religion: Progress.

All were sons of the French Revolution by direct descent. The most flippant of them became solemn when mentioning that date, '89. Their flesh-and-blood fathers were or had been moderates, royalists, constitutional monarchists. Never mind. This muddle before their time had nothing to do with them. They were young. The pure blood of principle ran in their veins. They subscribed without any intermediary subtlety to incorruptible right and absolute duty.

Underground associates and initiates, they were secretly shaping the ideal.

Among all these impassioned hearts and earnest minds was one sceptic. How did he come to be there? By contiguity. This sceptic's name was Grantaire and he was in the habit of signing himself with this rebus: R.* Grantaire was a man who took great care not to believe in anything. Furthermore, he was one of the students who learned the most during their time in Paris. He knew that the best coffee was to be had at Café Lemblin and the best game of billiards at Café Voltaire, that good pancakes and pretty girls were to be found at the Ermitage on Boulevard du Maine, spatchcocked chickens at Mère Sauget's, an excellent fish stew at the Cunette toll-gate and a particularly drinkable white wine at the Combat gate. He knew the right place to go for everything. He was also adept at two types of foot-boxing, *savate* and *chausson*, knew a few dances, was very good at stick-fighting. And a heavy drinker into the bargain. He was extremely ugly. Vexed by his ugliness, the prettiest boot-stitcher of the day, Irma Boissy, delivered this verdict on him: 'Grantaire is impossible.' But Grantaire was unabashed in his self-complacency. He gazed fondly and intently at every woman, seeming to say about all of them, 'Mine if I wanted!', and trying to make his comrades believe he was much in demand.

All those words – justice for the people, rights of man, social contract, French Revolution, Republic, democracy, humanity, civilization, religion, progress – for Grantaire came very close to having no meaning whatsoever. He could not take them seriously. Scepticism, that dry rot of the intellect, had left him with not a single idea intact. He lived with irony. This was his fundamental premise: 'There's only one sure thing, my full glass.' He derided any self-sacrifice on the part of anyone, father or brother, Loizerolles or the younger Robespierre. 'A lot of good it's done them to end up dead!' he would cry. He used to say about the crucifix, 'That was a good piece of carpentry.' A womanizer

---

* Capital R, *grand R*, pronounced 'Grantaire'.

and a gambler, dissolute, often drunk, he liked to annoy these young idealists by constantly singing to himself, to the tune of 'Long Live Henri IV', 'I loves the girls and I loves good wine.'*

However, this sceptic had one obsession. This obsession was not an idea, nor a dogma, nor an art, nor a science. It was a man: Enjolras. Grantaire admired, loved and revered Enjolras. Which of this phalanx of absolutists did this doubting anarchist stand by? The most absolute. How did Enjolras enthral him? By his ideas? No. By his character. A phenomenon often observed. The sceptic attracted to the believer is as elementary as the law of complementary colours. We are drawn to what we lack. No one loves daylight as much as the blind man. The dwarfish girl idolizes the drum major. The toad's eyes always look skyward. Why? To watch the bird in flight. With insidious doubt creeping through him, Grantaire loved to watch faith soar in Enjolras. He needed Enjolras. Without being clearly aware of it, and without any notion of explaining it to himself, he was spellbound by that chaste, wholesome, steadfast, honest, rigorous, straightforward nature. By instinct, he admired his opposite. His weak, flaccid, inconsistent, sickly, distorted ideas fastened on Enjolras as to a backbone. His moral feebleness relied on that firmness. In Enjolras's company Grantaire once again became somebody. In fact he was himself made up of two apparently incompatible elements. He was ironic and he was well-meaning. His apathy cared. His mind dispensed with conviction but his heart could not do without friendship. A profound contradiction, for affection is belief. That was his nature. There are men who seemingly are born to be the verso, the inverse, the reverse. They are Pollux, Patroclus, Nisus, Eudamidas, Hephaestion, Pechméja. Their existence depends on being fronted by another man. Their names follow on and are never written without the conjunction 'and' in front of them. Their lives do not belong to them. They are the adjunct of a fate that is not theirs. Grantaire was one of these men. He was the reverse of Enjolras.

One might almost say that affinities begin with the letters of the alphabet. In that sequence, O and P are inseparable. You might just as well say O and P as Orestes and Pylades.

A true satellite of Enjolras, Grantaire lived within this circle of young men. He dwelt among them, only with them was he happy, he followed them everywhere. His pleasure was to watch these figures

* Two lines from a song called 'Vive Henri IV' ('Long Live Henri IV') from the three-act comedy *La Partie de Chasse de Henri IV* (Henri IV's Hunting Party) by the dramatist and librettist Charles Collé (1709–83).

come and go in a wine-induced haze. They put up with him because of his good humour.

In his belief, Enjolras looked down on this sceptic; and in his sobriety, on this drunkard. He spared him a little lordly pity. Grantaire was an unwanted Pylades. Always snubbed by Enjolras, spurned, rebuffed and back again for more, he said of Enjolras, 'What marmoreal magnificence!'

II
Bossuet's Funeral Oration for Blondeau

One particular afternoon, coinciding as we will shall see with events related in an earlier chapter, Laigle de Meaux was languidly leaning back against the doorpost of Café Musain. He looked like a caryatid on holiday, with nothing to support but his reverie. He was gazing at Place St-Michel. Leaning back against something is a way of lying down upright, to which thinkers are not averse. Laigle de Meaux was thinking, without despondency, about a little mishap that had befallen him at the law school two days earlier, one that altered his personal plans for the future, plans that were in any case rather vague.

Reverie does not prevent a cab from passing by, nor the daydreamer from noticing that cab. Laigle de Meaux, whose eyes were roaming in a kind of unfocused, leisurely way, in this state of semi-consciousness saw a two-wheeled vehicle moving through the square at walking pace in apparent indecision. Who was this cab stalking? Why was it going at walking pace? Laigle observed it more closely. In the cab next to the driver was a young man, and in front of the young man was a rather bulky travel-bag. The bag displayed to bystanders the following name inscribed in large black letters on a card sewn to the cloth: 'MARIUS PONTMERCY'.

This name prompted a change of attitude in Laigle. He straightened up and cried out to the young man in the cab, 'Monsieur Marius Pontmercy!'

The cab he called out to halted.

The young man, himself apparently deep in thought, looked up. 'Huh?' he said.

'You're Monsieur Marius Pontmercy?'

'Certainly.'

'I was looking for you,' Laigle de Meaux went on.

'What do you mean?' asked Marius. For he it was, having just left his grandfather's; and in front of him was a face he had never seen before. 'I don't know you.'

'And I don't know you,' replied Laigle.

Marius thought he had encountered some kind of joker, that this was the overture to some sort of horseplay. He was not in a very relaxed mood at that moment. He frowned.

Laigle de Meaux went on, undeterred. 'You weren't in school the day before yesterday.'

'That's possible.'

'That's for sure.'

'You're a student?' asked Marius.

'Yes, monsieur. Like yourself. The day before yesterday I happened to go into school. You know, you sometimes get these ideas. The professor was just calling the register. You must be aware of how very absurd they are about it. The third time your name's called and you don't respond, you're struck off the list. Sixty francs down the drain.'

Marius began to listen.

Laigle went on. 'It was Blondeau taking the roll-call. You know Blondeau, he's very sharp-nosed, and vicious with it, and he loves sniffing out absentees. He cunningly began with the letter P. I wasn't listening, since that letter didn't apply to me. The roll-call wasn't going badly. No names struck off. Everybody present. Blondeau was dejected. I said to myself: "Blondeau, my dear, you'll have not the most trifling execution to carry out today." All of a sudden Blondeau calls out, "Marius Pontmercy!" No one answers. Full of hope, Blondeau repeats more loudly, "Marius Pontmercy!" And he picks up his pen. Monsieur, I have feelings. I swiftly said to myself, "Here we have a decent fellow who's going to get struck off. This is a real human being, mind, who isn't conscientious. This isn't a good student. This isn't one of your desk-bound swotters, a student that studies, a pedant in the making, good at sciences, literature, theology and bookishness, one of those boring clever dicks that excel in every subject. This is an honourable idler who whiles away his time, who goes on country jaunts, who devotes himself to grisettes, who pays court to the fair sex, who at this very moment perhaps is with my mistress. Let's save him. Death to Blondeau!" At that moment Blondeau dipped into the ink his black pen for striking out names, let his predatory gaze wander around the lecture hall, and repeated for the third time "Marius Pontmercy!" I replied, "Present!" Which meant you weren't crossed off.'

'Monsieur—' said Marius.

'And I was,' added Laigle de Meaux.

'I don't understand,' said Marius.

Laigle continued. 'Nothing more straightforward. I was close to the rostrum to answer the roll-call and close to the door to make my escape. The professor stared at me with a certain intensity. Suddenly Blondeau, who must have that shrewd nose that Boileau spoke of,* skipped to the letter L. L is my letter. I'm from Meaux, and my name is Lesgle.'

'L'Aigle!' exclaimed Marius. 'What a fine name!

'Monsieur, Blondeau comes to this fine name, and calls out "Laigle!" I reply "Present!" Then Blondeau looks at me with the sweetness of a tiger, smiles, and says, "If you're Pontmercy, you're not Laigle." A turn of phrase invidious to you but inauspicious only to me. That said, he strikes me off.'

Marius exclaimed, 'Monsieur, I'm mortified—'

'First of all,' Laigle interrupted, 'allow me to embalm Blondeau in a few phrases of heartfelt praise. I assume he's dead. There'd be no great change for his thinness, his pallor, his coldness, his stiffness and his smell to undergo. And I say: *Erudimini qui judicatis terram*†. Here lies Blondeau, Blondeau the Nose, Blondeau *Nasica*‡, enforcer of discipline, *bos disciplinae*§, watchdog of the rule book, angel of the roll-call, who was uncompromising, stolid, precise, rigid, honest and frightful. God eliminated him as he eliminated me.'

Marius said, 'I'm so sorry—'

'Young man,' said Laigle de Meaux, 'let this serve as a lesson to you. In future, be conscientious.'

'I truly beg you a thousand pardons.'

'Don't ever again put yourself in the position of being responsible for having your fellow student struck off.'

'I'm devastated—'

Laigle burst out laughing. 'And I'm delighted. I was on the way to becoming a lawyer. Being struck off has saved me. I renounce the glories of the bar. I shan't defend the widow and I shan't attack the orphan. No more gown, no more studying. I already have my disbarment. And

---

* A punning allusion to Boileau's *Art Poétique* (lines 181–2): 'D'un trait de ce poème en bons mots si fertile, / Le Français, né malin, forma le Vaudeville' ('Out of one characteristic of this poem so fertile in witticisms, / The Frenchman, with his native cunning, created vaudeville'). *Né malin* ('born shrewd') is pronounced the same as *nez malin*, 'shrewd nose'.

† 'Be instructed, ye judges of the earth' (Psalm 2:10). Cited by Bossuet, bishop of Meaux, at the beginning of one of his most famous funeral orations (1670), dedicated to Henrietta Stuart, daughter of Charles I of England.

‡ Latin, meaning 'with a large or pointed nose'.

§ 'Ox of discipline', a turn of phrase evoking the *bos suetus aratro* ('ox accustomed to the plough') by which the seventeenth-century Bossuet, noted for his studiousness, was referred to by his contemporaries.

it's to you that I owe it, Monsieur Pontmercy. I intend to call on you and thank you formally. Where do you live?'

'In this cab,' said Marius.

'A sign of opulence,' said Laigle placidly. 'I congratulate you. You're paying a rent of nine thousand francs a year.'

At that moment Courfeyrac emerged from the café.

Marius smiled sadly. 'I've been in this rented accommodation for the past two hours and I'm eager to move out. But the fact of the matter is, I don't know where to go.'

'Monsieur, come and live with me,' said Courfeyrac.

'I should have priority,' observed Laigle, 'but I have no home to invite you to.'

'Shut up, Bossuet,' said Courfeyrac.

'Bossuet?' said Marius. 'But I thought your name was Laigle.'

'De Meaux,' replied Laigle. 'Metaphorically speaking, Bossuet.'

Courfeyrac climbed into the cab. 'Coachman,' he said, 'Hôtel de la Porte St-Jacques.'

And that very evening Marius was settled in a room at the Hôtel de la Porte St-Jacques next door to Courfeyrac.

III

Marius Bemused

Within a few days Marius was Courfeyrac's friend. Youth is the season of friendships quickly forged and wounds quickly healed. In Courfeyrac's company Marius breathed freely, something quite new for him. Courfeyrac asked no questions. He did not even think of it. At that age faces tell all straight away. Words are unnecessary. Of young men such as these you could say they have talkative faces. At a glance, they know each other.

One morning, however, Courfeyrac suddenly raised this query: 'By the way, have you any political view?'

'Certainly!' said Marius, almost offended by the question.

'What are you?'

'A Bonapartist democrat.'

'A safe mousy-grey,' said Courfeyrac.

The next day Courfeyrac took Marius along to Café Musain. Then he whispered in his ear with a smile, 'I must introduce you to the revolution.' And he led him into the room where the Friends of the ABC gathered. He presented him to his other comrades, saying in an undertone this single word that Marius did not understand: 'A novice.'

Marius had fallen into an intellectual hornets' nest. And although grave and silent, he was not the least equipped to defend himself.

A loner until then, and inclined by habit and personal preference to commune with himself or just one or two others, Marius was a bit bewildered by this swarm of young men around him. He was torn between all these various claims being made on him at once. The boisterous cut and thrust of these free spirits at work sent his thoughts into a spin. Sometimes in the confusion they went so far beyond him that he had difficulty recovering them. He heard philosophy, literature, art, history, religion being talked about in an unexpected way. He caught glimpses of unfamiliar viewpoints, and unable to put them in perspective he was unsure that it was not chaos he was seeing. In giving up his grandfather's opinions for his father's, he thought that had settled it for him. He now suspected, uneasily and without daring to admit it to himself, that it had not. The angle from which he saw everything was again beginning to shift. A certain unsteadiness was tilting all the horizons in his brain. A peculiar inner turbulence. It was almost painful.

It seemed that for these young men nothing was sacred. On every topic Marius heard remarkable things said that discomfited his still timorous mind.

At the sight of a theatre poster displaying the title of a tragedy from the old, so-called classical, repertoire, Bahorel cried, 'Down with the bourgeoisie's beloved tragedy!'

And Marius heard Combeferre reply, 'You're mistaken, Bahorel. The bourgeoisie likes tragedy, and on that score the bourgeoisie should be left alone. Tragedy in wigs has its own justification, and I'm not one of those who in the name of Aeschylus dispute its right to exist. There are in nature some crude designs; there are in creation some ready-made parodies: a beak that's not a beak, wings that aren't wings, flippers that aren't flippers, feet that aren't feet, a plaintive cry that makes you want to laugh – and there you have the duck. Now, since poultry and birds co-exist, I don't see why classical tragedy shouldn't play opposite ancient tragedy.'

On another occasion Marius happened to be walking down Rue Jean-Jacques-Rousseau, flanked by Enjolras and Courfeyrac.

Courfeyrac took his arm. 'Take note. This is Rue Plâtrière, now called Rue Jean-Jacques-Rousseau, on account of an unusual couple that lived here sixty years ago. They were Jean-Jacques and Thérèse. From time to time there were little ones born here. Thérèse brought them into the world, Jean-Jacques brought them to the foundling hospital.'

And Enjolras rebuked Courfeyrac. 'Not a word against Jean-Jacques! He's a man I admire. Even if he did disown his children, he adopted the people as his own.'

Not one of these young men mentioned that word 'the emperor'. Jean Prouvaire was the only one who sometimes said 'Napoleon', all the others said 'Bonaparte'. Enjolras pronounced it 'Buonaparte'.

Marius was vaguely surprised. *Initium sapientiae.**

IV
The Back Room of Café Musain

One of the conversations between these young men, conversations Marius witnessed and sometimes took part in, really shook up his thinking.

It took place in the back room of Café Musain. Nearly all the Friends of the ABC had convened that evening. The Argand lamp was solemnly lit. They talked of one thing and another, at low temperature but high volume. With the exception of Enjolras and Marius, who remained silent, each person held forth somewhat at random. Chatting among friends is sometimes characterized by this peaceful clamour. It was a game and a scramble as much as a conversation. Words were tossed about and caught. It was a kind of verbal puss-in-the-corner.

No woman was allowed into this back room except Louison, the café's washer-up, who passed through it from time to time to get from the scullery to the 'laboratory'.

A thoroughly inebriated Grantaire was deafening the corner he had taken over. Ranting and raving at the top of his voice, he shouted, 'I'm thirsty! Mortals, I have a dream: that the Heidelberg tun will have a fit of apoplexy, and I'm one of the dozen leeches that will be applied to it. I want to drink. I want to forget life. Life is I don't know whose hideous invention. It's over in no time and not worth the candle. You kill yourself living. Life's a stage set with very little that's real. Happiness is an old scenery flat painted on one side only. Ecclesiastes says: "All is vanity." I agree with that fellow, who probably never existed. Not wanting to go about stark-naked, Zero clothed himself in vanity. O vanity! Dressing everything up in big words! A kitchen is a laboratory, a dancer is a master, a tumbler is a gymnast, a boxer is a pugilist, a drug dispenser is a chemist, a wigmaker is an artist, a builder's mate is an architect, a jockey is a sportsman, a woodlouse is a

---

* From Psalm 111:10: 'The fear of the Lord is *the beginning of wisdom*.'

pterygibranchia. Vanity has a wrong side and a right side: the right side is idiotic, it is the savage with his glass beads; the wrong side is foolish, it is the philosopher in his rags. I weep at the one and laugh at the other. What are called honours and distinctions, and even honour and distinction themselves, are generally fake gold. Kings make a plaything of human pride. Caligula appointed a horse as consul. Charles II knighted a Sir Loin.* So now take pride of place between Consul Incitatus and Baron of Beef. As for people, their intrinsic merit is scarcely any worthier of respect. Listen to the fine things they say about their fellow men. White is vicious about white. If the lily could speak, what it would have to say about the dove! One sanctimonious old biddy gossiping about another is more venomous than the asp or the blue krait. It's a shame I'm an ignoramus, otherwise I'd be able to give you loads of examples, but I know nothing. However, I've always been witty. When I was a pupil of Gros, instead of messing about with paints I spent my time filching apples. Painting is an art of abstraction. So much for myself. As for the rest of you, you're no better than I am. I couldn't care less about your perfections, superiorities, qualities. Every virtue degenerates into a vice. Thrift is akin to avarice, generosity is close to extravagance, boldness borders on swagger, whoever says "very dutiful" is saying "a little holier than thou". There are just as many vices in virtue as there are holes in Diogenes' cloak. Whom do you admire, the man killed or his killer? Caesar or Brutus? Generally people are in favour of the killer. Long live Brutus! He killed a man! That's virtue for you. Virtue? Maybe, but madness too. These great men are strangely flawed. The Brutus who killed Caesar was fond of a statue of a little boy. This statue was by the Greek sculptor Strongylion, who also carved that figure of an Amazon known as the "Shapely-legged", Eucnemos, which Nero took with him on his travels. This Strongylion left only two statues that put Nero and Brutus in agreement with each other. Brutus was fond of one of them, Nero of the other. All history is nothing but endless repetition. One century is the plagiarist of the other. The battle of Marengo is a copy of the battle of Pydna. Clovis's Tolbiac and Napoleon's Austerlitz are as like each other as two drops of blood. I don't set great store by victory. Nothing is so dull-witted as winning the battle. True glory lies in winning the argument. Well, you just try to prove something! You settle

* According to folklore, Charles II is said to have given this name to an excellent cut of beef, which he knighted with a sword. A 'baron of beef', a term first recorded in Johnson's *Dictionary* (1775), is a joint consisting of a double sirloin attached to the bone.

for winning? What mediocrity! And for conquering? What pusil-
lanimity! Alas, vanity and cowardice everywhere. Everything obeys
success, even grammar. *Si volet usus*, says Horace.* So I scorn the
human race. Shall we descend from the general to the particular? You
want me to start admiring nations? Which nation, if you please? Is it
Greece? The Athenians, those Parisians of an earlier age, slew Phocion,
another Coligny, and fawned on tyrants to such an extent that Anacephorus said of Pisistratus, "His urine attracts bees." The most prominent
man in Greece for fifty years was that grammarian Philetas, who was
so small and puny he was obliged to weight his shoes with lead so as
not to be blown away by the wind. There was in the great square in
Corinth a statue carved by Silanion and recorded by Pliny. This statue
represented Epistates. What did Epistates do? He invented a wrestler's
leg hook. That sums up Greece and glory. Let us move on to other
candidates. Shall I admire England? Shall I admire France? France?
Why? Because of Paris? I have just told you my opinion of Athens.
England? Why? Because of London? I hate Carthage. And besides,
London, that metropolis of luxury, is the capital of destitution. In the
parish of Charing Cross alone there are a hundred people a year dying
of hunger. Such is Albion. And to cap it all, I've seen an Englishwoman dance wearing a coronet of roses and blue spectacles. So I
thumb my nose at England! And if I don't admire John Bull, shall I
admire Brother Jonathan? I don't much care for that slave-owning
brother. Take away "Time is money", and what's left of England?
Take away "Cotton is king", and what's left of America? Germany is
all lymph, Italy is all bile. Shall we go into raptures about Russia?
Voltaire admired it. He also admired China. I grant that Russia has its
attractions, among them strong despotism. But I pity the despots.
Their health is delicate. An Alexis beheaded, a Peter stabbed, a
Paul strangled, another Paul trampled, various Ivans assassinated by
having their throats cut, numerous Nicholases and Basils poisoned –
all this indicates that the palace of the emperors of Russia is in a
flagrantly unwholesome state. All civilized nations offer for the admiration of the thinking man this particular feature: war. Now war,
civilized war, reduces and subsumes all forms of banditry, from
the brigandage of Spanish irregulars in the gorges of Mount Jaxa
to marauding Comanches in Doubtful Pass. Bah! You'll tell me that
Europe's nonetheless better than Asia? I agree that Asia is a joke. But
I don't really see that you peoples of the West can afford to mock

* 'As usage dictates', Horace, *Ars Poetica*, line 71.

the Grand Lama, having included in your manners and refinements all the complicated squalors of majesty, from Queen Isabella's dirty shift to the Dauphin's commode. Gentlemen of the human race, I've nothing to say to you! Brussels is where the most beer is consumed, Stockholm the most brandy, Madrid the most chocolate, Amsterdam the most gin, London the most wine, Constantinople the most coffee, Paris the most absinthe. That's all you need to know. In short, Paris wins. In Paris even the rag-pickers are sybarites. Diogenes would just as soon have been a rag-picker on Place Maubert as a philosopher in Piraeus. Something else you should know: the rag-pickers' taverns are called *bibines*. The most famous are the Casserole and the Abattoir. So, O garden cafés, glee clubs, taverns, tap-houses, bars, bistros, music halls, dance halls, rag-pickers' drinking dens, caliphs' caravanserais, I am, I declare, a voluptuary, I eat at Richard's at forty sous a head, I must have Persian carpets in which to roll naked Cleopatra! Where is Cleopatra? Ah! It's you, Louison. Hallo.'

From his corner in the back room of the Café Musain, more than drunk, Grantaire held forth in this manner, detaining the washer-up on her way through.

Stretching out his hand towards him, Bossuet tried to silence him, but Grantaire was off again with renewed energy. 'Hands down, Aigle de Meaux! I'm utterly unimpressed by that gesture, of Hippocrates refusing Artaxerxes' trifles. You've no need to quieten me. Besides, I feel sad. What do you expect me to say? Man is no good, man is a monstrosity. The butterfly turned out well, man turned out badly. God failed with that one. A crowd is but a selection of uglinesses. All and sundry are wretches. Woman, thy name is infamy. Yes, I'm in a peevish mood, compounded with melancholy and nostalgia, plus hypochondria, and I sulk, I rage, I yawn, I'm fed up, I'm bored to death and I don't know what to do with myself! To hell with God!'

'Now shut up, capital R!' said Bossuet, who was discussing a point of law with no one in particular, and, practically up to his armpits in legal jargon, the sentence he was delivering concluded thus: 'and as for me, although I'm no legal authority, at most an amateur jurist, I would say this: that in accordance with Normandy custom, every year at Michaelmas except where other rights prevail a compensatory payment must be made in favour of the lord of the manor by each and every householder be he landowner in his own right or by right of inheritance and that this applies to all long leases, short leases, freeholds and contracts *bona fide, mala fide, de jure* and *de facto*.'

'Echo, plaintive nymph,' Grantaire sang under his breath.*

Just next to Grantaire, on an almost silent table, a sheet of paper, an inkpot and a pen between two glasses of wine indicated work in progress on a vaudeville play. This great enterprise was being discussed in an undertone by the two playwrights, bent over their task, heads touching.

'Let's start with the names. Once you've got the names, you hit on the subject.'

'That's right. You dictate. I'll write.'

'Monsieur Dorimon.'

'A gentleman of independent means?'

'Indeed.'

'His daughter, Célestine.'

'... tine. Next?'

'Colonel Sainval.'

'Sainval's hackneyed. I'd say Valsin.'

Beside the aspiring vaudevillians another group, they too taking advantage of the hubbub to talk quietly, were discussing a duel. An old hand, aged thirty, was counselling a youngster, aged eighteen, and explaining to him what sort of an adversary he was up against.

'Hell! You be careful. He's a fine swordsman. He strikes clean. He goes straight into the attack, no wasted feints, he has a strong wrist, he's light on his feet, he's quick, parries well and returns with mathematical precision, damn it, and he's left-handed.'

In the corner opposite Grantaire, Joly and Bahorel were playing dominoes and talking of love.

'You're a lucky one,' Joly was saying. 'You have a mistress who's always laughing.'

'That's a mistake on her part,' replied Bahorel. 'A man's mistress shouldn't laugh. It's an encouragement to be unfaithful to her. To see her looking cheerful relieves you of an uneasy conscience. If you see her looking sad, you feel guilty.'

---

* The line 'Écho, nymphe plaintive' is from a song of 1810 called 'Fleuve du Tage' ('The River Tagus') by Joseph Hélitas De Meun, with music by Jean-Joseph-Benoît Pollet (1755–1823). Berlioz published an arrangement of the song in 1819. The story of the nymph and the reason for her plaintiveness is told in Ovid's *Metamorphoses*, bk III, lines 359–401. Grantaire is picking up on the last two syllables of Bossuet's disquisition ending in singsong legalese: 'contrats domaniaires et domaniaux, hypothécaires et hypothécaux' (-*écaux*, pronounced 'echo').

'You heartless brute! A woman who laughs is such a delight! And you never quarrel!'

'That's because of the pact we've made. When we made our own little Holy Alliance we set boundaries for each other that we never cross. What lies on the northerly side belongs to Vaud, on the southerly side to Gex. Hence the peace.'

'Peace is happiness settling down.'

'And you, Jol-l-l-ly, what stage have you reached in your tiff with Mam'selle – you know who I mean?'

'She's cruelly unforgiving in her sulkiness towards me.'

'Yet you're pitifully thin in your lovesickness.'

'Alas!'

'If I were you I'd jilt her.'

'Easily said.'

'And done. Isn't Musichetta her name?'

'Yes. Ah! my poor Bahorel, she's a fine girl, very literary, with dainty feet and dainty hands, well-dressed, white and plump, with the eyes of a fortune-teller. I'm crazy about her.'

'Well then, my dear fellow, you must please her, be elegant, and get down on your knees. Buy yourself a good strong pair of twill trousers at Staub's. That helps.'

'How much?' shouted Grantaire.

The third corner was deeply involved in a poetical discussion. Pagan mythology was taking on Christian mythology. The subject of the discussion was Olympus, which Jean Prouvaire was defending out of sheer Romanticism. Jean Prouvaire was shy only when calm. Once excited, he sparkled, a kind of merriment marked his enthusiasm, and he was at once lyrical and light-hearted.

'Let's not insult the gods,' he said. 'The gods may not have gone away. Jupiter doesn't strike me as being dead. The gods are fanciful notions, you say. Well, even in nature, such as it is today, after these notions have taken flight, all the great old pagan myths are still there. Any mountain with the outline of a citadel, like the Vignemale, for example, is still to me Cybele's head-dress. I'm not convinced that Pan doesn't come at night and blow into the hollow trunks of willows, stopping up the holes by turns with his fingers. And I've always believed that Io has something to do with the Pissevache waterfall.'

In the last corner they were talking politics. The 1814 Charter was coming under criticism. Combeferre was weakly defending it, Courfeyrac energetically attacking it. On the table was an offending copy of the famous Touquet Charter. Courfeyrac had seized it and was waving it, accompanying his arguments with the rustling of this sheet of paper.

'Firstly, I want no kings. If only from the economic point of view I don't want them. A king is a parasite. Kings don't come free. Listen to this: the cost of kings. When François I died, France's national debt was thirty thousand francs a year. By the time Louis XIV died, it was two thousand six hundred million at twenty-eight francs to the marc, which was equivalent in 1760, by Desmarets's reckoning, to four thousand five hundred million, which today would be twelve thousand million. Secondly, with all due respect to Combeferre, the granting of a charter is a poor expedient for civilization to resort to. To ease the transition, smooth the change-over, minimize the upheaval, shift the nation from monarchy to democracy by the implementation of constitutional fictions – these are all odious justifications! No! No! Let us never illuminate the people with artificial light. Principles wilt and fade in your constitutional cellar. No vitiation! No compromise! No granting to the people by royal favour. In all such grants there is an Article 14. Alongside the hand that gives is the claw that takes back. I flatly reject your charter. A charter is a mask. It conceals a lie. A people that accepts a charter abdicates. What is rightful is rightful only in its integrity. No! No charter!'

It was winter. A couple of logs were crackling in the hearth. This was tempting, and Courfeyrac did not resist the temptation. He crumpled up the poor Touquet Charter in his fist and threw it on the fire. The paper blazed. Combeferre philosophically watched Louis XVIII's masterpiece burn, and confined himself to the remark, 'The charter that turned to ashes.'* And taunts, quips, gibes, that French thing called *entrain*†, that English thing called humour, good taste and bad, good reasons and bad, all the wild pyrotechnics of conversation, simultaneously rising in crossfire from all parts of the room, produced a kind of merry bombardment overhead.

* In the French: 'La chartre métamorphosée en flamme', evoking the title of La Fontaine's fable 18 (bk 2), 'La Chatte métamorphosée en Femme' (The Cat That Turned into a Woman), the moral of which is 'Nature will out!'
† Which might be translated as 'spiritedness'.

V
Broadening Horizons

The wonderful thing about the collision between young minds is that you can never predict the spark or anticipate the flash. What will the next moment bring? No one knows. The burst of laughter succeeds compassion. In the comic instant seriousness comes into play. Impulses are prompted by a chance word. Each individual's verve is paramount. A joke is enough to create an opening for the unexpected. These are exchanges that take abrupt turns, with sudden realignments of perspective. Fortuitousness is the scene-shifter in such conversations.

A sombre thought, bizarrely emerging from the verbal cut and thrust, suddenly arose from the confusion of wordplay in which Grantaire, Bahorel, Prouvaire, Bossuet, Combeferre and Courfeyrac were crossing swords with each other.

How does a phrase crop up in conversation? How does it suddenly make itself conspicuous to those who hear it? As we have just said, no one knows. All at once in the midst of the hubbub Bossuet concluded some tirade addressed to Combeferre with this date: 'The eighteenth of June 1815, Waterloo.'

At the name of Waterloo, Marius, who had his elbows resting on the table and a glass of water beside him, removed his hand from under his chin and began to stare intently at everyone in the room.

'By God!' exclaimed Courfeyrac ('By Jove' was falling into disuse at that time). 'It's strange, that number eighteen, and I'm struck by it. It's Bonaparte's fateful number. Put Louis in front of it and Brumaire after it, and you have the man's whole destiny – with this telling detail, that the end follows close on the heels of the beginning.'

Enjolras, who had not spoken until then, broke his silence and made this comment to Courfeyrac: 'You mean, atonement on the heels of the crime.'

To Marius, already deeply stirred by the unexpected reference to Waterloo, that word 'crime' exceeded the bounds of the acceptable.

He stood up, walked slowly over to the map of France displayed on the wall and at the bottom of which you could see an island in a separate box, put his finger on this box and said, 'Corsica. A little island that made France truly great.'

This came as an icy blast. Everyone stopped talking. There was a sense of something about to begin.

Bahorel was just striking a favourite pose in countering Bossuet. He abandoned it to listen.

Enjolras, whose blue gaze was not fixed on anyone and who seemed to be staring into space, without glancing at Marius replied, 'France needs no Corsica to be great. France is great by virtue of being France. *Quia nominor leo.**'

Marius felt no desire to back down. He turned to Enjolras, and his voice rang with a quiver that came from a visceral contraction inside him: 'God forbid I should belittle France! But to identify Napoleon with her is not to belittle her. Come, let's talk. I'm a newcomer among you but I confess you amaze me. Where do we stand? Who are we? Who are you? Who am I? Let's discuss the emperor. I hear you say Buonaparte, accenting the u like the royalists. I warn you, my grandfather goes one better. He says "Buonaparté". I thought you people were young. So where's your fervour? And what are you doing with it? Whom do you admire if you don't admire the emperor? And what more do you want? If you won't accept that great man, which great men will you accept? He had everything. He lacked nothing. His brain contained normal human faculties to the power of three. He was Justinian in law-making, he ruled with Caesar's authority, his conversation combined Pascal's lightning wit with the mighty thunder of Tacitus. He made history, and wrote it. His bulletins are *Iliad*s. He combined Newton's mathematics with Mohammed's metaphors. In the East, he left behind words as great as the pyramids. At Tilsit he taught emperors majesty, at the Academy of Sciences he challenged Laplace, in the Council of State he held his own against Merlin. He brought soul to the geometry of some and to the pettifogging of others. He was a jurist with lawyers and a star-gazer with astronomers. Like Cromwell blowing out every other candle, he went off to the Temple to bargain for a curtain tassel. He saw everything, he knew everything. Which did not prevent him, at his little child's cradle, from laughing with simple fatherly delight. And all at once Europe listened in alarm, armies went on the march, artillery parks mobilized, pontoon bridges extended across rivers, hosts of cavalry went galloping into the storm, everywhere cries, trumpets, thrones trembling; on the map the frontiers of kingdoms wavered; the sound could be heard of a superhuman sword being drawn from its sheath, and there, standing on the horizon, with

---

* 'Because my name is lion.' An allusion to a fable by the Roman writer Phaedrus, on which La Fontaine's 'La Génisse, la Chèvre et la Brebis en société avec le Lion' (The Heifer, the Goat and the Ewe in Company with the Lion) is based (bk 1, fable 6). In the sharing of spoils the lion has uncontestable reasons for ending up with all four shares – this reason being as persuasive as any other.

burning fire in his hand and radiance in his eyes and, in the midst of thunder, spreading his two wings, the Grand Army and the Old Guard: the archangel of war!'

Everyone remained quiet and Enjolras bowed his head. Silence always tends to give the impression of agreement, or of a sort of inability to disagree.

Almost without drawing breath, with increased fervour Marius went on: 'Let's be fair, my friends! What a splendid destiny for a nation to be the empire of such an emperor, when that nation is France and adds its own genius to the genius of that man! To come on to the scene and rule, to march and to triumph, to have every capital city mark the steps of your progress, to take grenadiers and make kings of them, to decree the demise of dynasties, to forge ahead with the transformation of Europe, to give the sense when you threaten that you have your hand on the hilt of God's sword; to follow, in the person of one man, Hannibal, Caesar, Charlemagne; to be the people of someone who with every dawn brings glorious news of a battle won, to have the cannon of Les Invalides as your morning alarm call, to cast into pits of light fabled words that blaze for ever – Marengo, Arcola, Austerlitz, Jena, Wagram! To keep filling the centuries' highest heavens with constellations of victories, with the French Empire to emulate the Roman Empire, to be the great nation and give birth to the Grand Army, to send your legions swooping across the whole earth as a mountain sends its eagles in all directions, to conquer, dominate, crush; to be in Europe a kind of gilded nation by virtue of being bathed in glory, to sound through history a fanfare of Titans, to conquer the world twice, by conquest and bedazzlement, that is sublime. And greater than this, what is there?'

'To be free,' said Combeferre.

Marius in turn bowed his head. That stark and coldly delivered word cut through his epic outpouring like a steel blade, and he felt it die away inside him. When he looked up, Combeferre was no longer there. Probably satisfied with his response to this deification, he had just departed, and everyone, with the exception of Enjolras, had followed him. The room had emptied. Left alone with Marius, Enjolras gazed at him solemnly. Marius, however, having somewhat rallied his thoughts, was not ready to admit defeat. There was something still seething inside him that would no doubt have translated into syllogistic arguments deployed against Enjolras, when suddenly someone could be heard singing on the stairs as he went. It was Combeferre, and this is what he was singing:

If Caesar had offered me glory and war,
But on pain of forsaking my mother's love,
I'd have told great Caesar his prizes to keep,
I love my mother more, tra-la, I love my mother more.

The fierce yet tender voice in which Combeferre sang this song gave it a sort of strange grandeur. Thoughtfully, looking up at the ceiling, Marius repeated almost mechanically, 'My mother?'

At that moment he felt Enjolras's hand on his shoulder.

'My mother, citizen', Enjolras said to him, 'is the Republic.'

VI
Res Angusta*

That evening left Marius deeply shaken and with a sad bewilderment in his soul. He felt what the earth may possibly feel when it is cut with the blade for the wheat seed to be planted in it. It feels only the wound. The thrill of germination and the joy of fruition do not come until later.

Marius was downcast. He had only just fashioned a faith for himself. Must he then reject it already? He assured himself he need not. He told himself he did not want to doubt, and he began to doubt in spite of himself. To stand between two religions, one of which you have not yet put behind you and the other that you have not yet embraced, is intolerable. And only bat-like souls are happy in such twilight zones. Marius's frank gaze demanded proper light. The shadows of doubt caused him distress. However much he might have wanted to stay where he was and stand by the position he held, he was irresistibly compelled to keep going, to advance, to question, to think, to go further. Where would this lead him? After having taken so many steps that had brought him closer to his father, he was afraid now to take any that would distance them from each other. With every thought that occurred to him his perplexity increased. The ground fell away from him on all sides. He was in accord with neither his grandfather nor his friends, being seen as headstrong by the former and reactionary by the latter, and he realized he was doubly isolated, from old and young alike. He stopped going to the Café Musain.

In this moral quandary he now gave very little thought to certain

* An allusion to Juvenal's Satire III, lines 164–5: 'Haud facile emergunt quorum virtutibus obstat res angusta domi' ('It is not easy for those to rise whose straitened circumstances stand in the way of their merits').

serious aspects of existence. The realities of life do not allow themselves to be forgotten, however. Suddenly, they came and nudged him. ·

The owner of the hotel entered Marius's room one morning and said, 'Monsieur Courfeyrac has vouched for you.'

'Yes.'

'But I must have my money.'

'Ask Courfeyrac to come and talk to me,' said Marius.

When Courfeyrac came, the hotel keeper left them. Marius told him what he had not thought to tell him before, that he was as good as alone in the world, with no relatives.

'What's to become of you?' said Courfeyrac.

'I've no idea,' replied Marius.

'What are you going to do?'

'I've no idea.'

'Have you any money?'

'Fifteen francs.'

'Do you want me to lend you some?'

'Never.'

'Have you any clothes?'

'These.'

'Have you any jewellery?'

'A watch.'

'Silver?'

'Gold. Here it is.'

'I know a clothes-dealer who will take your frock-coat and a pair of trousers.'

'Very well.'

'You'll then have only one pair of trousers, a waistcoat, a hat and a coat.'

'And my boots.'

'What! You won't go barefoot? What luxury!'

'It'll be enough.'

'I know a watch-maker who'll buy your watch.'

'That's good.'

'No, it's not good. What will you do after that?'

'Whatever I have to. As long as it's honest.'

'Do you know English?'

'No.'

'Do you know German?'

'No.'

'Too bad.'

'Why?'

'Because one of my friends in the book trade is publishing some sort of encyclopaedia for which you might have been able to translate articles from English or German. It's badly paid but it's a living.'

'I'll learn English and German.'

'And in the meantime?'

'In the meantime I'll live on my clothes and my watch.'

The clothes-dealer was sent for. He bought the garments for twenty francs. They went to the watch-maker's. He bought the watch for forty-five francs.

'That's not bad,' Marius said to Courfeyrac on their way back to the hotel, 'with my fifteen francs, that makes eighty.'

'And the hotel bill?' said Courfeyrac.

'Oh, I was forgetting about that,' said Marius.

'Hell!' exclaimed Courfeyrac. 'You'll have five francs to live on while you're learning English, and five while you learn German. That means getting a language under your belt very quickly or making a hundred sous go a very long way.'

Meanwhile, his Aunt Gillenormand, at heart quite a kind person in difficult moments, had finally tracked down Marius's lodgings. One morning on his return from the law school Marius found a letter from his aunt and six hundred francs in gold coin in a sealed box.

Marius returned the thirty louis to his aunt, with a polite letter declaring he was making his living and would be able to pay his own way in future. At the time he had three francs left.

His aunt did not tell his grandfather of this refusal for fear of thoroughly provoking him. Besides, had he not said, 'I never want to hear another word about that blood-thirsty revolutionist!'?

Marius moved out of the Hôtel de la Porte St-Jacques, not wanting to run into debt there.

BOOK FIVE
VIRTUE IN ADVERSITY

I
Marius in Penury

Life became hard for Marius. Using his clothes and his watch for food was nothing. There was much worse he had to stomach. Terrible hardship, consisting of days without bread, nights without sleep, no candle in the evening, no fire in the hearth, weeks without work, a future without hope, a coat worn through at the elbows, an old hat that makes young girls laugh, a door found locked at night because the rent has not been paid, the insolence of the doorman and the eating-house keeper, the sneering of neighbours, humiliations, dignity trampled underfoot, having to accept any kind of work, demoralization, bitterness, despondency. Marius learned how to swallow all this, and how it might often be all there was to swallow. At that time in a man's life when he needs self-respect because he needs love, he felt mocked because he was badly dressed and laughable because he was poor. At the age when youth swells the heart with an imperial pride he lowered his eyes more than once to his boots with holes in them, and he experienced the unjust disgrace and agonizing shame of poverty. Awesome and terrible test from which the weak emerge degenerate, the strong emerge sublime. Crucible into which fate casts a man whenever it wants a villain or a demigod.

For many great feats are performed in small struggles. There are dogged deeds of valour, overlooked, that hold out step by step in the darkness against the fatal onslaught of destitution and depravity. Noble and mysterious triumphs that no eye sees, no renown honours, no fanfare salutes.

Life, adversity, isolation, abandonment, poverty are battlefields that have their heroes, the obscure sometimes greater than the illustrious.

In such a way are steadfast and rare natures created. Almost always a stepmother, poverty is sometimes a mother. Deprivation begets strength of soul and of mind. Hardship is the wetnurse of pride. Adversity is a good milk for the noble in spirit.

There was a time in Marius's life when he swept his own landing, when he bought his sou's worth of Brie from the dairy, when he waited until dusk to go to the baker's to buy bread that he furtively carried back to his attic as though he had stolen it. Sometimes an awkward young man, shy and angry-looking, carrying books under his arm, was to be seen slipping into the butcher's shop on the corner, among the jeering housewives who crowded in with him. On entering he would remove his hat, the sweat beading on his brow, bow deeply to the astonished butcher-woman, give another bow to the butcher-boy, ask for a mutton cutlet, pay six or seven sous for it, wrap it up in paper, tuck it under his arm between two books, and be on his way. This was Marius. And that cutlet, which he cooked for himself, he lived on for three days.

On the first day he ate the meat, on the second he ate the fat, on the third he gnawed the bone.

His Aunt Gillenormand made several attempts to send him the six hundred francs. Marius kept sending them back, saying he needed nothing.

He was still in mourning for his father when that revolution we have spoken of occurred within him. From then on he adhered to wearing only black. But his black clothes did not adhere to him. The day came when he no longer had a coat. The trousers were still all right. What was to be done? Courfeyrac, for whom he had himself done a few good turns, gave him an old coat. For thirty sous Marius got it turned by some porter or other, which made it a new coat. But this coat was green. So Marius went out only after nightfall. This made his coat black. Wanting to be dressed always in mourning, he clothed himself in darkness.

While all this was going on he qualified as a lawyer. He was supposedly living in Courfeyrac's room, which was respectable and where a certain number of law books, propped up and augmented by a few odd volumes of novels, represented the library required by the regulations. He had his mail sent to Courfeyrac's address.

When Marius qualified he informed his grandfather in a letter coldly written but full of deference and respect. Tremulously, Monsieur Gillenormand took the letter, read it and threw it into the wastepaper basket, torn in four. Two or three days later Mademoiselle Gillenormand heard her father, who was alone in his room, talking out loud to himself. This happened whenever he was very upset. She listened. The old man was saying, 'If you weren't a fool, you'd know it was impossible to be both a baron and a lawyer.'

Marius in Poverty

It is the same with poverty as with everything else. It can become bearable. It eventually arranges itself and settles down. You vegetate, in other words you develop in some sort of stunted way, but enough to stay alive. This is the kind of existence Marius Pontmercy had fashioned for himself.

He had survived the worst. Ahead of him, the straits were becoming a little less narrow. By virtue of hard work, courage, perseverance and willpower he was managing to earn from his labours about seven hundred francs a year. He had learned German and English. Thanks to Courfeyrac, who had put him in touch with his friend the bookseller, Marius played the modest role of hack writer in the publishing side of the business. He produced advertising brochures, translated journals, annotated editions, compiled biographies, and so forth. Annual net income on average, seven hundred francs. He lived on this. How? Not badly. As we shall see.

At an annual cost of thirty francs Marius occupied in the Gorbeau tenement a cheerless room without a fireplace, described as a box-room, that in terms of furniture had only the strictly essential. This furniture belonged to him. He gave three francs a month to the old principal tenant to come and sweep and to bring him a little hot water every morning, with a fresh egg and a bread roll costing one sou. He breakfasted on this roll and this egg. Depending on whether eggs were dear or cheap, the cost of his breakfast varied between two and four sous. At six o'clock in the evening he would go down Rue St-Jacques to eat at Rousseau's, opposite Basset the stamp-dealer, on the corner of Rue des Mathurins. He did not have soup. He took a plate of meat at six sous, a half-portion of vegetables at three sous, and a dessert at three sous. And for three sous, as much bread as he wanted. As for wine, he drank water. When he paid at the desk, where, as fat as ever at that time and still in her prime, Madame Rousseau majestically presided, he gave the waiter a sou and Madame Rousseau gave him a smile. Then he went home. For sixteen sous he had had a smile and a meal.

This Rousseau restaurant, where so few bottles of wine and so many pitchers of water were emptied, was palliative rather than restorative. Today it no longer exists. The owner had a splendid nickname: he was called Aquatic Rousseau.*

* The noun *rousseau* denotes a sea bream or a type of pigeon.

So four sous for breakfast, sixteen sous for supper. His food cost him twenty sous a day, which came to three hundred and sixty-five francs a year. Add the thirty francs' rent and the thirty-six francs to the old woman, plus a few minor expenses: for four hundred and fifty francs Marius was fed, lodged and had his housekeeping done. His clothing cost him a hundred francs, his linen fifty, his laundry fifty. His total outgoings came to less than six hundred and fifty francs. That left him with fifty francs. He was rich. He sometimes lent ten francs to a friend. Courfeyrac had once been able to borrow sixty francs from him. As for heating, having no fireplace, Marius 'economized'.

Marius always had two suits of clothes: one old, 'for every day', the other brand-new, for special occasions. Both were black. He had only three shirts, one on him, the second in his chest of drawers, the third with the laundry woman. He replaced them as they wore out. They were usually ragged, which made him keep his coat buttoned up to the chin.

It had taken years for Marius to reach this flourishing state. Arduous years: difficult to get through, some of them, others difficult to get over. Not for a single day had Marius faltered. He had suffered everything in the way of privation. He had done everything except contract debts. He said in his own favour that he had never owed anyone a sou. To him, a debt was the beginning of slavery. He even told himself that a creditor is worse than a master, for the master is master only of your person whereas a creditor is master of your dignity and can give it a beating. Rather than borrow, he did not eat. There were many days when he had gone hungry. Sensing that all extremes are akin, and that, if you are not careful, being down on your luck can lead to low-mindedness, he kept a jealous watch on his pride. Some formality of expression or behaviour that in any other situation would have seemed to him polite, now seemed to him servile, and he bridled at it. He ventured nothing, not wanting to back down. There was in his face a kind of austere flush. He was shy even to the point of rudeness.

Through all his trials he felt encouraged and sometimes even sustained by a secret strength within him. The soul lends aid to the body and at certain moments uplifts it. It is the only bird that supports its own cage.

Besides his father's name another name was graven in Marius's heart, the name Thénardier. Given his fervent and solemn nature, Marius surrounded with a kind of halo the man to whom in his own mind he owed his father's life, that intrepid sergeant who had saved the colonel amid the cannon-balls and bullets of Waterloo. He never separated the memory of this man from the memory of his father, uniting them in his veneration. It was a sort of two-level form of worship – the high altar for the colonel, the lesser altar for Thénardier. What made his gratitude towards Thénardier all the more heartfelt was the idea of the hard times he knew Thénardier had fallen on and in which he had been swallowed up. Marius had learned at Montfermeil of the ruin and bankruptcy of the unfortunate innkeeper. He had since made extraordinary efforts to trace him and to try to find him in that black hole of poverty into which Thénardier had disappeared. Marius had scoured the whole region. He had gone to Chelles, Bondy, Gournay, Nogent, Lagny. For three years he had kept at it, spending on these searches the little money that he saved. No one had been able to give him any news of Thénardier. He was thought to have gone abroad. His creditors had also been looking for him, with less fond regard than Marius but just as assiduously, and had been unable to lay hands on him. Marius considered himself to be at fault and was almost angry with himself for his lack of success in his investigations. It was the only debt the colonel had left him, and Marius felt honour-bound to repay it. 'After all,' he thought, 'when my father lay dying on the battlefield Thénardier managed to find him through the smoke and the grapeshot and to carry him away on his shoulders, and yet he owed him nothing. And I who owe so much to Thénardier couldn't contrive to find him in that darkness where he languishes, and in my turn save him from death and restore him to life! Oh! I will find him!' Indeed, Marius would have given one of his arms to find Thénardier; and to rescue him from misery, his every drop of blood. To meet Thénardier, to do Thénardier any service whatsoever, to say to him, 'You don't know me but I know you! Here I am! Make use of me!' This was Marius's sweetest and most splendid dream.

III
Marius Attains Manhood

By that time Marius was twenty years old. It was three years since he had left his grandfather. On either side they held their ground, making no attempt at reconciliation and no attempt to see each other. In any case, what was the good of seeing each other? To battle it out? Which of them would have triumphed? Marius was the brass vase but old Gillenormand was the iron pot.

It must be said, Marius was mistaken about his grandfather's feelings. He had taken it into his head that Monsieur Gillenormand had never loved him, and that the only affection felt for him by this testy, difficult and spirited old gent, who cursed, railed, stormed and brandished his cane, was at most that affection at once capricious and stern of the dotards of classical comedy. Marius was wrong. There are fathers who do not love their children. There is no grandfather that does not adore his grandson. Deep down, as we have said, Monsieur Gillenormand idolized Marius. He idolized him after his own fashion, to the accompaniment of harsh words and even boxed ears. But once this child was gone he felt a black void in his heart. He insisted that no one was to mention the child to him, all the while secretly regretting he was so well obeyed. In the early days he hoped this Buonapartist, this Jacobin, this terrorist, this Septembrist, would return. But the weeks went by, the months went by, the years went by. To Monsieur Gillenormand's great despair the 'blood-thirsty revolutionist' did not reappear. 'Yet I couldn't do otherwise than turn him out,' the grandfather said to himself. And he wondered, 'Given another chance, would I do it again?' His pride instantly answered yes, but his aged head, which he shook in silence, replied sadly, no. He had his hours of despondency. He missed Marius. Old men need affection as they need the sun. For its warmth. Regardless of his strength of character, Marius's absence had changed something in him. Not for anything in the world would he have been willing to make any move towards 'that young whipper-snapper'. But he suffered. He never made any enquiries about him but he thought about him constantly. He lived more and more as a recluse in the Marais. He was still bright and vehement, as of old, but his brightness had a convulsive harshness to it as if it contained sorrow and anger, and his vehement outbursts always culminated in a kind of meek and dour dejection. He sometimes said, 'Oh! if he came back, what a good hiding I'd give him!'

As for his aunt, she was too little given to thinking to feel much love. Marius was no more than some kind of vague black figure to her now, and she had ended up worrying about him a lot less than about the cat or the parrot she probably had.

What increased old Gillenormand's secret suffering was that he kept it all locked up inside himself and let none of it show. His sorrow was like those recently invented furnaces that burn their own smoke.

Occasionally, some interfering busybody would speak to him about Marius and ask, 'What's your grandson doing?' Or 'What's become of the young gentleman?'

Sighing if he was very sad, or flicking his cuff if he wanted to appear cheerful, the elderly bourgeois gentleman would reply, 'Monsieur le Baron de Pontmercy is pettifogging somewhere or other.'

While the old man was regretful, Marius congratulated himself. As with all good-hearted people, misfortune had taken away his bitterness. He thought of Monsieur Gillenormand only with tenderness, but he was determined not to accept anything more from the man *who had been unkind to his father*. This was the now toned-down version of his initial indignation. He was, moreover, happy to have suffered and to be suffering still. For his father's sake. The harshness of his life satisfied and pleased him. He said to himself with a kind of joy that *it was the least he could do*. That it was an atonement. That otherwise he would have been punished in some other way, later on, for his sacrilegious heartlessness towards his father. And such a father! That it would not have been right for his father to have had all the suffering, and he none of it. That in any case, what were his own tribulations and hardship compared with the colonel's heroic life? That, in short, the only way for him to make it up to his father and to be like him was to meet penury with courage, as the other had met the enemy with valour. And that, surely, this was what the colonel meant by that phrase, 'He will be worthy of it.' Words that Marius continued to wear not on his chest, since the colonel's note had disappeared, but in his heart.

And besides, when his grandfather turned him out he had still been just a child; now he was a man. He felt this. Destitution, let us emphasize, had been good for him. The wonderful thing about poverty in youth, when it is effective, is that it directs the will entirely to effort, and the soul entirely to aspiration. Poverty instantly lays bare the materialistic life and renders it hideous. Hence, the ineffable impulse towards the life of the ideal. The wealthy young man has countless seductive and vulgar distractions, horse-racing, hunting, dogs, tobacco, gaming, good meals and all the rest. Pursuits that engage the baser aspects of the soul at the expense of its higher and more discerning aspects. It is a struggle for the impoverished young man to keep himself alive. He eats. When he has eaten he can only dream. He attends the spectacles that God provides at no cost. He observes the sky, space, stars, flowers, children, humankind among whom he suffers, creation amid which he shines. So closely does he observe humankind that he sees its soul, so closely does he observe creation that he sees God. He dreams, and he feels noble. He continues to dream, and he feels tender-hearted. From the egotism of the man who suffers he moves on to the compassion of the man who reflects. A wonderful feeling develops in him, self-forgetfulness and pity for all. Thinking of the countless joys that nature offers, gives, lavishes on the open-hearted while refusing them to hearts that remain closed, he, the millionaire in understanding, comes to feel sorry for the money millionaire. All hatred goes from his heart as a perfect light enters his soul. In any case, is he unhappy? No. A young man's penury is never misery. However poor, any young lad with his health, his strength, his brisk pace, his sparkling eyes, his blood that circulates its warmth, his black hair, his fresh cheeks, his red lips, his white teeth, his untainted breath, will always be the envy of an old emperor. And then, every morning he applies himself again to earning his bread, and while his hands earn bread, his backbone gains pride and his brain reaps ideas. His work finished, he returns to ineffable ecstasies, contemplations, joys. He lives with his feet among woes and impediments, on the streets, among thorns, sometimes in the mud, and with his head in the light. He is steadfast, serene, gentle, quiet, considerate, serious, content with little, kindly. And he thanks God for having given him these two riches that many a rich man lacks: work, which frees him, and thought, which dignifies him.

This is what Marius had undergone. To tell the truth, he even tended a little too much towards contemplation. From the day he could be more or less sure of earning his living, he had settled for that, considering it good to be poor, and cutting down on work in favour of thought. What this meant was that he sometimes spent all day long thinking, steeped and absorbed like a visionary in the silent delights of ecstasy and inward radiance. This is how he had formulated the problem of his life: to apply himself as little as possible to practical work in order to apply himself as much as possible to intangible work. In other words, to spare a few hours for real life and lavish the rest on the infinite. Believing he lacked for nothing, he did not realize that, interpreted in this way, contemplation ends up being one of the forms of idleness. That he had settled for mastering only the basic necessities of life, and that he was taking his rest too soon.

It was obvious that for such an energetic and generous nature this could only be a transitory phase, and that at the first collision with the inevitable complications of destiny Marius would wake up.

In the meantime, although he was a lawyer, and whatever old Gillenormand might have thought, he was not doing any lawyering, he was not even pettifogging. Reverie had deterred him from lawyering. Pursuing solicitors, haunting the law court, chasing cases – what a bore! Why do it? He saw no reason to change his livelihood! That obscure bookselling venture had in the end provided him with work he could depend on, work that was not very demanding and with which, as we have explained, he was satisfied. One of the booksellers he worked for, Monsieur Magimel, I believe, offered to take him into his own home, comfortably house him, set him up with a regular job and pay him fifteen hundred francs a year. To be comfortably housed! Fifteen hundred francs! Certainly. But to give up his freedom! To be a wage-slave! A kind of literary minion! To Marius's way of thinking, by accepting, his position would become at once better and worse, he would gain in comfort and lose in dignity. It was consummate, noble adversity turned into squalid, absurd constraint, rather as if a blind man were to become one-eyed. He declined.

Marius lived a solitary life. Because of that liking he had for remaining outside of everything, and also because he had been far too disconcerted by it, he had decidedly not joined the group presided over by Enjolras. They remained on good terms. They were ready to help each other in every possible way if need be, but nothing more. Marius had two friends: a young man, Courfeyrac, and an old man, Monsieur Mabeuf. The old man was dearer to him. In the first place Marius was indebted to him for the revolution that had occurred within him; and he was indebted to him for having known and loved his father. 'He removed my cataracts,' Marius said.

Certainly, this churchwarden had played a key role.

It was not, however, that Monsieur Mabeuf had been in this instance anything other than the calm and impassive instrument of providence. He had enlightened Marius by chance, and without knowing it, like a candle that someone brings along: he had been the candle and not the someone.

As for Marius's interior political revolution, Monsieur Mabeuf was totally incapable of comprehending it, wanting it, or directing it.

As we shall be encountering Monsieur Mabeuf again later, a few words will not come amiss.

IV
Monsieur Mabeuf

The day Monsieur Mabeuf said to Marius, 'Of course I approve of political opinions', he was expressing his true state of mind. All political opinions were alike to him, and he approved of them all indiscriminately, so that they would leave him in peace, in the same way that the Greeks called the Furies the Eumenides, 'the beautiful ones, the kindly ones, the gracious ones'. Monsieur Mabeuf's political opinion was his passionate love of plants, and especially of books. Like everyone else, he had his own -ist ending, without which no one could have existed at that time, but he was neither a royalist, a Bonapartist, a Chartist, an Orleanist or an anarchist – he was a book-specialist.

He did not understand how men could get involved in hating each other over such nonsense as the Charter, democracy, legitimacy, the monarchy, the Republic and the like, when there were in this world all sorts of mosses, grasses and shrubs they might be looking at, and stacks of folio volumes and even some in 32-mo that they might be leafing through. He was most anxious not to be idle. Having books did not prevent him from reading, being a botanist did not prevent him from being a gardener. When he met Pontmercy there had been that fellow feeling, between the colonel and him, that what the colonel did with flowers, he did with fruit. Monsieur Mabeuf had managed to produce pears, grown from seed, as tasty as the St Germain pear. It was one of his cross-fertilizations, apparently, that had resulted in the October mirabelle, now renowned, and no less perfumed than the summer mirabelle. He attended mass more out of good-heartedness than piety, and also because, loving men's faces but hating their noise, it was only in church that he found them gathered in silence. Feeling that he ought to do something connected with the Church he had chosen the career of churchwarden. In any case he had never succeeded in loving any woman as much as a tulip bulb or any man as much as an Elzevir edition. He was long past sixty when someone asked him one day, 'Were you never married?'

'I've forgotten,' he said.

When he sometimes happened to say – and who doesn't? – 'Oh! if I were rich!' it was not with his eye on a pretty girl, as was the case with old Gillenormand, but in contemplation of a rare book. He lived alone with an elderly housekeeper. He had a touch of gout in his hands, and when he was asleep his old fingers, stiffened with rheumatism, dug into the folds of his sheets. He had compiled and published a *Flora of the Environs of Cauterets*, with colour plates, quite a respected work, of which he owned the copper-plates, and which he sold himself. Two or three times a day people would come calling at his house in Rue Mézières to buy it. He earned as much as two thousand francs a year from the copies he sold. This was just about his entire fortune. Although poor, with patience and time and the sacrifices he made, he had the talent to build up a valuable collection of all kinds of rare editions. He never went out without a book under his arm and he often returned with two. The four rooms on the ground floor that together with a small garden constituted his lodgings had no decoration other than framed herbariums and engravings of the old masters. To him, the sight of a sword or a gun was chilling. He had never in his life been near a cannon, not even at Les Invalides. He had a reasonably good digestion, a brother who was a parish priest, completely white hair, not a tooth in his head, literally or metaphorically, a trembling in his whole body, a Picardy accent, a childlike laugh, a fearful nature, and the look of an old sheep. And besides that, no friend or close acquaintance among the living other than an old bookseller at Porte St-Jacques named Royol. His dream was to naturalize the indigo plant in France.

His housekeeper, too, embodied a kind of innocence. The poor old dear was a virgin. Her cat, Sultan, which could have miaowed Allegri's 'Miserere' in the Sistine Chapel, had claimed her heart and satisfied the amount of passion she had in her. None of her dreams had ever gone so far as to include a man. She had never been able to progress beyond her cat. Like the cat, she had whiskers. She prided herself on her caps – always white, they were. After mass on Sundays she would spend her time going through her linen chest and laying out on her bed dresses, bought ready to be sewn, that she never had made up. She could read. Monsieur Mabeuf had nicknamed her Mère Plutarque.

Monsieur Mabeuf had taken a liking to Marius because Marius, being young and gentle, gladdened his old age without alarming his timidity. Youth with gentleness has the effect on old folk of sun without wind. When Marius had had as much as he could take of military glory, gunpowder, marches and countermarches, and all those extraordinary battles in which his father had delivered and received such mighty sabre slashes, he went to see Monsieur Mabeuf, and Monsieur Mabeuf told him about the hero from the viewpoint of flowers.

His brother the parish priest died in about 1830 and almost immediately, as when night falls, the whole horizon darkened for Monsieur Mabeuf. A bankruptcy – of a lawyer – deprived him of the sum of ten thousand francs, which was everything he possessed both in his brother's right and in his own. The July Revolution brought a slump in the book trade. When times are hard the first thing that does not sell is a *Flora*. Sales of the *Flora of the Environs of Cauterets* dried up completely. Weeks went by without a single buyer. Sometimes Monsieur Mabeuf started at the sound of the doorbell.

'Monsieur,' Mère Plutarque would say sadly, 'it's the water-carrier.'

In short, one day Monsieur Mabeuf left Rue Mézières, resigned from his job as churchwarden, gave up St-Sulpice, sold not his books but some of his prints, those he was least attached to, and moved into a small house on Rue Montparnasse, where, though, he stayed only three months, and for two reasons. Firstly, the ground floor with garden cost three hundred francs and he dared not spend more than two hundred francs on his rent. Secondly, being next door to Fatou's shooting range, he heard pistol-shots all day long, which he could not bear.

He packed up his *Flora*, his copper-plates, herbariums, portfolios and books, and went to live near La Salpêtrière in some sort of thatched cottage in the village of Austerlitz, where for one hundred and fifty francs a year he had three rooms and his own garden with a hedge round it, and a well. He took advantage of this move to sell off nearly all his furniture. On the day he moved into these new lodgings he was very cheerful and put up the picture hooks himself on which to hang his engravings and herbariums, spent the rest of the day digging his garden, then in the evening, seeing Mère Plutarque looking doleful and pensive, he tapped her on the shoulder and said with a smile, 'Never mind! We have the indigo!'

Only two visitors, the bookseller from Porte St-Jacques and Marius, came to see him in his thatched cottage at Austerlitz, a contentious name that, to be truthful, was rather objectionable to him.

However, as we have just suggested, minds engrossed in wisdom or folly, or, as is often the case, both at the same time, are only very slowly pervious to matters of everyday life. Their own destiny is far removed from them. Resulting from this kind of concentration is a passivity, which, if there were any reasoning behind it, would seem philosophical. Such minds go into a decline, they sink, they languish, they even come to grief without really being aware of it. True, this always ends with an awakening, but a belated one. In the meantime it is as if they had no interest in the game that plays out between their happiness and their unhappiness. They who are themselves at stake watch the game with indifference.

Thus, as the darkness gathered, as all his hopes died, one by one, Monsieur Mabeuf remained serene, a little childishly, but profoundly so. His mind behaved like a swinging pendulum. Once wound up by an illusion, it kept going for a very long time, even after the illusion was gone. A clock does not stop dead the very moment the key is lost.

Monsieur Mabeuf had his innocent pleasures. These pleasures were inexpensive and unexpected. The merest chance provided them. One day Mère Plutarque was reading a novel in a corner of the room. She was reading aloud, thinking she understood better this way. To read aloud is to lend authority to your reading. There are people who read very loudly and seem to be vouching on their word of honour for what they are reading.

It was with this sort of energy that Mère Plutarque was reading the novel she held in her hand. Monsieur Mabeuf heard without listening.

As she was reading, Mère Plutarque came to this phrase, about a cavalry officer and a young beauty: '*La belle bouda et le dragon—*'*

* 'The beauty pouted and the dragoon—'

At this point she broke off to wipe her glasses.

'Buddha and the Dragon,'* Monsieur Mabeuf echoed quietly. 'Yes, it's true, there was a dragon that from the depths of its cave spouted flame from its mouth and burned the heavens. Many stars had already been incinerated by this monster, which also had the claws of a tiger. Buddha went into its den and managed to convert the dragon. That's a good book you're reading, Mère Plutarque. There's no legend more beautiful.'

And Monsieur Mabeuf fell into a delightful reverie.

V

Poverty, Misery's Good Neighbour

Marius was fond of this guileless old man who saw himself becoming slowly impoverished and who little by little came to wonder at it, yet without grieving. Marius would meet up with Courfeyrac and visited Monsieur Mabeuf. Quite rarely, however, twice a month at most.

Marius's pleasure was to take long walks by himself on the outer boulevards or in the Champ de Mars, or along the least frequented paths of the Luxembourg Gardens. He sometimes spent half a day contemplating a market-garden, the lettuce beds, the chickens on the dung-heap and the horse turning the water-wheel. Passers-by stared at him in surprise, and some regarded the way he was dressed with suspicion and thought him sinister-looking. He was only a poor young man aimlessly daydreaming.

It was on one of his strolls that he had come across the Gorbeau tenement, and tempted by its isolation and its cheapness he had taken a room in it. He was known there by no other name but Monsieur Marius.

Some of the old generals and old comrades of his father had invited him, when he met them, to come and see them. Marius had not declined their invitations. They were opportunities to talk about his father. So now and again he would call on Comte Pajol, General Bellavesne, General Fririon, or pay a visit to Les Invalides. There was music and dancing. On such evenings, Marius put on his new coat. But he never went to these receptions and dances except on days when it was freezing cold, because he could not afford a cab and did not want to turn up with his boots other than mirror-like.

He sometimes said, but without bitterness, 'Men are such that, in a drawing room, you can have mud sticking to you all over except on

* 'Bouddha et le Dragon', homophones of 'bouda et le dragon'.

your shoes. To be welcome there, only one thing is expected to be beyond reproach. Your conscience? No, your boots.'

All passions except those of the heart subside in idle musing. Marius's political fanaticisms were dispelled in this way. By satisfying and calming him the 1830 Revolution had helped in this. He remained the same, without the anger. He still had the same opinions; only, they had mellowed. Strictly speaking, he no longer had opinions – he had sympathies. To which party did he belong? Humanity. Among humanity he favoured France. Among the nation he favoured the people. Among the people he favoured women. That was mostly where his pity went. Now he preferred an idea to a deed, a poet to a hero, and he admired a book like Job more than an event like Marengo. And when after a day of pondering he returned in the evening along the boulevards and glimpsed, through the branches of the trees, fathomless space, nameless glimmerings, infinite reaches, obscurity, mystery, all that is merely human seemed very petty to him.

He thought he had come to understand what the truth of life and of human philosophy was, and indeed perhaps he had, and in the end he no longer looked at anything else but the sky, the only thing that truth can see from the bottom of her well.

This did not stop him from elaborating endless plans, schemes, blueprints, projects for the future. Any eye that might have looked inside Marius in this state of wishful thinking would have been dazzled by the purity of that soul. For had it been given to our eyes of flesh* to see into the conscience of others, our judgement of a man would be much sounder were it based on what he dreams rather than on what he thinks. There is will in thought, there is none in dreams. Dreams, which are wholly spontaneous, take on and retain the cast of our spirit, even in their vastness and their idealism. Nothing proceeds more directly and more sincerely from the very depths of our souls than our intuitive and boundless aspirations to the glories of destiny. In these aspirations, much more than in considered, reasoned, composed ideas, is the true character of every man to be found. Our fanciful dreams are what most resemble us. Everybody dreams of the unknown and the impossible according to his nature.

Sometime around the middle of that year 1831, the old serving-woman Marius employed told him that his neighbours, the wretched Jondrette family, were going to be thrown out on to the street. Mar-

* An allusion to the Book of Job 10:4: 'Hast thou eyes of flesh? or seest thou as man seeth?'

ius, who was out of the house almost all day and every day, hardly knew he had any neighbours.

'Why are they being evicted?' he asked.

'Because they don't pay their rent. They owe two quarters.'

'How much is that?'

'Twenty francs,' said the old woman.

Marius had thirty francs saved up in a drawer.

'Take this,' he said to the old woman, 'that's twenty-five francs. Pay the rent for those poor people, give them five francs, and don't tell them it came from me.'

VI
The Substitute

It just so happened that the regiment Lieutenant Théodule belonged to was sent to Paris on garrison duty. This gave Aunt Gillenormand another idea. She had first of all dreamed up the idea of getting Théodule to spy on Marius. Her new scheme was for Théodule to replace Marius.

In any event, and in case the grandfather should have the vague need of a young face around the house – these dawn rays are sometimes sweet to the decrepit – it was advisable to find another Marius. 'Very well,' she thought, 'it's a simple erratum like the ones I see in books. For Marius, read Théodule.'

A great-nephew is an approximation to a grandson. Failing a lawyer, a lancer will do.

One morning when Monsieur Gillenormand was reading *La Quotidienne* or some such, his daughter came into the room and said to him in her most saccharine voice, for she was talking about her favourite, 'Father, Théodule is going to call on you this morning to pay his respects.'

'Who's Théodule?'

'Your great-nephew.'

'Ah!' said the grandfather.

Then he resumed his reading, gave no more thought to his great-nephew, who was just some Théodule or other, and before long was feeling very bad-tempered, which almost always happened to him whenever he read. The paper in his hand, albeit royalist, that goes without saying, baldly gave notice for the following day of one of those minor events that were everyday occurrences in Paris at that time: the students of the schools of law and medicine were to assemble on Place du Panthéon at noon. For a debate. About one of the issues of the day: the artillery of the National Guard, and a clash between the minister of war and 'the citizens' militia' over the cannon parked in the courtyard of the Louvre. The students were to 'debate' the matter. It did not take much more than this to infuriate Monsieur Gillenormand.

He thought of Marius, who was a student, and who would probably go along with the others 'to debate, at noon, in Place du Panthéon'.

As he dwelt on this painful thought Lieutenant Théodule entered – not in uniform, which was clever, but discreetly shown in by Mademoiselle Gillenormand. The lancer had reasoned as follows: 'The old fossil hasn't put everything into a life annuity. So it's well worth dressing up as a salon fop from time to time.'

Mademoiselle Gillenormand said aloud to her father, 'Théodule, your great-nephew.'

And in an undertone to the lieutenant, 'Agree with everything.'

And she withdrew.

Little accustomed to such venerable meetings, the lieutenant stammered out with some timidity, 'Good day, uncle.' And he performed a complicated gesture of greeting composed of an automatic, involuntary attempt at a military salute that finished as a bourgeois bow.

'Ah! it's you. Very well, sit down,' said the old man.

That said, he forgot all about the lancer.

Théodule sat down and Monsieur Gillenormand stood up. Monsieur Gillenormand began to pace to and fro with his hands in his pockets, talking aloud and fiddling with his restless old fingers at the two watches he had in his two fob-pockets.

'That bunch of juveniles! Assembling on Place du Panthéon! My goodness! Young pups who were still suckling only yesterday! Squeeze their noses and milk would come out! And we're debating tomorrow at noon. What's the world coming to? What's the world coming to? It's clear we're heading towards the abyss. This is what the *descamisados* have brought us to! The citizen artillery! A debate on the citizen artillery! Going around jabbering in the open air about the National Guard and their popguns! And who's going to join them there? Just look what Jacobinism leads to! I'll wager anything you like, a million against damn all, there'll be no one there but old lags and freed convicts. Republicans and convicts are nose and handkerchief to each other. When Carnot said, "Where do you expect me to go, traitor?" Fouché replied, "Wherever you like, imbecile!" That's Republicans for you.'

'You're right,' said Théodule.

Monsieur Gillenormand half turned his head, saw Théodule, and carried on. 'When you think that mischief-maker has had the gall to become a Carbonaro! Why did you leave my house? To go and become a Republican! Bah! In the first place, the people want nothing to do with your Republic, they want none of it, they've got common sense, they know very well there have always been kings and there always will be. They know that, after all, the people are only the people. They don't give two hoots for your Republic, do you understand, you idiot? It's quite dreadful, this wilfulness! Becoming infatuated with Père Duchesne, making eyes at the guillotine, singing serenades and playing the guitar under the balcony of '93, they're such fools all these young fellows, they deserve to be horse-whipped! That goes for all of them. Without a single exception. Breathing the air in the street is enough to drive you mad. The nineteenth century is poison. Take any young pipsqueak, he grows a goatee beard, thinks he's a real somebody, and turns his back on his elderly relatives. It's Republican, it's Romantic. What does that mean, Romantic? Will someone be kind enough to explain? Every conceivable madness! A year ago it meant going to see *Hernani*. I ask you, *Hernani*! Antitheses! Abominations not even written in French! And now we have cannons in the court-yard of the Louvre. Such is the lawlessness of this age!'

'You're right, uncle,' said Théodule.

Monsieur Gillenormand resumed. 'Cannons in the courtyard of the Museum! What for? Cannons, would you believe? So you want to take a shot at the *Apollo Belvedere*? What have cartridges to do with the *Venus de' Medici*? Oh! the young men of today are all good-for-nothings! What a nonentity their Benjamin Constant is! And those who aren't villains are dolts! They do everything they can to be ugly, they're badly dressed, they're scared of women, their pathetic behav-iour in female company has the young hussies in gales of laughter. On my word of honour, the wretches behave as if they were ashamed of love. They're unsightly, and they complete the effect by being stupid. They repeat puns made by Tiercelin and Potier, they wear shapeless coats, stable lads' jackets, coarse linen shirts, thick woollen trousers, rough leather boots, and their blather matches their plumage. They could use their cant to resole their old shoes. And this incompetent rabble have political opinions, if you please! It should be strictly for-bidden to have political opinions. They invent systems, they reorder society, they demolish the monarchy, they throw out every law, they put the attic in place of the cellar and my porter in place of the king, they turn Europe upside down, they rebuild the world, and their love life consists of sneaking a look at a laundress's legs as she climbs into her cart. Ah! Marius! Ah! you devil! go and shout in the public square! Discuss, debate, take measures! Measures, they call them, for heaven's sake! It's disorder on a scale reduced to silliness. I've seen chaos, now I'm seeing muddle! Schoolchildren deliberating about the National Guard – you wouldn't see that among the Ojibwa or the Cadodache Indians! Savages that go about stark-naked with their heads dressed up like shuttlecocks, and carrying clubs, are less brutish than these young gentlemen! Overweening upstarts! And they're agreeing this and decreeing that! Deliberating and ratiocinating! It's the end of the world! Obviously it's the end of this wretched terraqueous globe! One last death rattle was needed, and France is now emitting it. Go on deliberating, my little mischief-makers! Such things will happen as long as they go on reading newspapers under the Odéon arcades. It costs them a sou, not to mention their common sense, intelligence, heart, soul and mind. They come away from there – and the next thing they're leaving home. All newspapers are a scourge, all of them, even *Le Drapeau Blanc*! Martainville was fundamentally a Jacobin. By heaven! you may well be able to boast of having driven your grand-father to despair!'

'It stands to reason,' said Théodule. And taking advantage of Monsieur Gillenormand's pausing to draw breath, the lancer added pompously, 'There should be no other newspaper than the *Moniteur*, and no other book than the army list.'

Monsieur Gillenormand continued, 'It's like that fellow Sieyès of theirs! A regicide ending up as a senator! For that's how they always end up. They make it a badge of honour to be called citizen and come to be addressed as monsieur le comte. Monsieur le comte, my eye! September assassins! Philosopher Sieyès! I will say this for myself, I've never taken any more notice of all those philosophers' philosophies than of the antics of the man who pulls faces in the Tivoli Gardens! I saw the senators one day walking along Quai Malplaquet in their purple velvet mantles and Henri IV-style hats. They were hideous. They looked like the monkeys at the tiger's court.* Citizens, I tell you, your progress is madness, your humanity's a dream, your Revolution's a crime, your Republic's a monster, your young and virginal France hails from the brothel, and I tell you all, whoever you might be,

* An allusion to Hugo's own poem 'Fable ou Histoire' (Fable or History) – a pastiche of La Fontaine's 'Le Loup devenu Berger' (The Wolf Turned Shepherd) and 'L'Âne vêtu de la peau du Lion' (The Donkey Dressed in the Lion's Skin) – included in *Les Châtiments*, a collection written in exile and published in 1853, which was directed against Napoleon III. See endnote p. 1377.

whether journalists or economists or lawyers, or greater experts in liberty, equality and fraternity than the blade of the guillotine! That's what I'll have you know, my fine fellows!'

'By God!' cried the lieutenant. 'Well said!'

Monsieur Gillenormand broke off in mid-gesture, turned, looked Lancer Théodule straight in the eye, and said, 'You're an idiot.'

BOOK SIX

THE CONJUNCTION OF
TWO STARS

I

The Nickname: A Way of Inventing Family Names

Marius was now a handsome young man of medium height, with thick jet-black hair, an intelligent high forehead, flared, sensuous nostrils, an air of sincerity and calm, and with something indefinable – proud, thoughtful, innocent – about his whole face. His profile, rounded in all its contours without any loss of definition, had a certain Germanic softness that has made its way into the French physiognomy by way of Alsace and Lorraine, and that complete absence of angularity that made the Sicambri so easily recognizable among the Romans, and distinguishes the leonine race from the aquiline. He was at that stage in life when the mind of the thinking man consists in nearly equal proportion of profundity and naivety. Given a serious situation, he had everything it takes to be stupid. With some fine tuning, he could be sublime. He was reserved, cold, courteous, not very congenial in his manner. Because his mouth was attractive, his lips the reddest of red and his teeth the whitest of white, his smile compensated for all the severity in his face. At certain moments, that chaste forehead and that voluptuous smile presented a peculiar contrast. He had narrow eyes and a broad vision.

During his time of greatest hardship he had noticed that young girls would turn round when he went by, and he would hurry away or hide, feeling mortified. He thought they were staring at him because of his old clothes, and laughing at them. The fact is, they stared at him because of his attractiveness and the yearnings it prompted in them.

This unspoken misunderstanding between him and the pretty passers-by had made him shy. He chose none of them, for the excellent reason that he fled from all of them. He went on like this indefinitely – stupidly, Courfeyrac said.

Courfeyrac also said to him, 'Don't aim for venerability' (they were now addressing each other as *tu* – such informality is soon adopted in youthful friendships). 'A piece of advice, my friend. Don't read so many books and spend a little more time looking at the lasses. O Marius, there's something to be said for the fair sex! Keep running away and blushing, and you'll turn into a boor.'

On other occasions Courfeyrac would meet him and say, 'Good morning, monsieur l'abbé!'

After Courfeyrac had made some remark of this kind, for the next week Marius would avoid women more than ever, young or old, and he would also avoid Courfeyrac.

Yet in all the boundlessness of creation there were two women Marius did not flee, and to whom he paid no attention whatsoever. To tell the truth, he would have been very much amazed if he had been told they were women. One was the bearded crone who swept his room and of whom Courfeyrac used to say, 'Seeing as his serving-woman has a beard, Marius doesn't have one.' The other was a little girl he saw very often and never looked at.

For more than a year Marius had noticed on an unfrequented path in the Luxembourg Gardens, the one that skirts the parapet of the tree nursery, a man and a very young girl, almost always seated side by side on the same bench, at the most deserted end of the path, towards Rue de l'Ouest. Whenever chance – which takes a hand in the walks of people whose gaze is turned inward – brought Marius along this path – and that was nearly every day – he found this pair there. The man was probably about sixty. He appeared sad and serious. His whole person had that robust and weary look of military men who have retired from service. If he had worn a decoration Marius would have said, 'He's a former officer.' He had a kindly but unapproachable air and he never met anyone's gaze. He wore blue trousers, a blue frock-coat and a broad-brimmed hat that still looked new, a black cravat and a Quaker shirt – that is to say, one that was dazzling white but of coarse linen. A grisette passing him one day said, 'That's a jolly smart widower.' He had very white hair.

The first time the young girl who accompanied him came and sat on the bench they seemed to have adopted, she was a slip of a thing of thirteen or fourteen years of age, so thin as to be almost ugly, awkward, unremarkable, but with some promise perhaps of having quite attractive eyes. Only, they were always raised with a kind of disagreeable self-confidence. Attired in the manner, at once old-maidish and childish, of girls who grow up in a convent, she wore a badly cut dress of black merino wool. They looked like father and daughter.

For two or three days Marius observed this elderly man who was not yet old and this little girl who was not yet a person, and then paid no more attention to them. They for their part appeared not even to notice him. They chatted together quietly, taking no interest in him. The girl would prattle on gaily. The old man said little, and from time to time he would settle on her his eyes filled with ineffable fatherliness.

Marius developed the unthinking habit of strolling along that path. He invariably found them there. This is what would happen:

Marius was most likely to come by from the end of the path furthest from their bench. He would walk the whole length of the path, pass in front of them, then turn round and go back the way he had come, then start all over again, from one end to the other. He would do this to-ing and fro-ing five or six times during his walk, and do this walk five or six times a week, and never once did they exchange a greeting, those people and he. Although, and perhaps because, they appeared to shun all glances, this individual and this young girl had naturally attracted the attention of the five or six students who strolled past the tree nursery now and then, the studious ones after lectures, the others after their game of billiards. Courfeyrac, who was among the latter, observed them for a while, but finding the girl ugly he very quickly made a point of keeping his distance. He fled from them, like a Parthian, firing a sobriquet as a parting shot. Struck solely by the child's dress and the old man's hair, he had dubbed the daughter Mademoiselle Lanoire* and the father Monsieur Leblanc†, and since no one knew who they were, in the absence of any other name this nickname stuck. The students would say, 'Ah! Monsieur Leblanc is on his bench.' And Marius, like the rest, found it convenient to call this unknown gentleman Monsieur Leblanc. We shall do likewise, and call him Monsieur Leblanc as a useful expedient in the telling of this tale.

So that first year Marius saw them nearly every day, at the same time. He found the man to his liking but the girl rather sullen.

II

Lux Facta Est

In the second year, at precisely the point that the reader has reached in the story, this Luxembourg habit was interrupted without Marius himself quite knowing why, and for nearly six months he did not go near his path. One day he eventually returned there. It was a cloudless

* 'Miss Black'.
† 'Mr White'.

summer morning and Marius was cheerful, as anyone is when the weather is fine. He felt as if he held in his heart all the birdsong he could hear and all the fragments of blue sky he could see through the leaves of the trees.

He went straight to 'his path', and when he reached the end of it he saw that familiar couple, still on the same bench. Only, when he came close, it was certainly the same man but it seemed to him it was no longer the same girl. The person he now saw was a tall and beautiful creature with all the loveliest of womanly curves at that very moment when they are still combined with all the most artless of childish graces. A fleeting and innocent moment that can only be conveyed by these three words: fifteen years old. This meant wonderful chestnut-brown hair with threads of gold, a brow seemingly made of marble, cheeks seemingly made of rose petal, a pale bloom, a flushed white-ness, exquisite lips on which the smile was a kind of radiance and the words spoken were a kind of music, a head such as Raphael would have given the Virgin Mary, set on a neck that Jean Goujon would have given to Venus. And so that there should be no defect in this bewitching face, her nose was not handsome, it was pretty. Neither straight nor curved, neither Italian nor Greek, it was the Parisian nose – that is to say, something spirited, delicate, irregular and pure, the despair of painters and the delight of poets.

When Marius passed close by her he could not see her eyes, which were always kept lowered. He saw only her long chestnut-brown eye-lashes steeped in shadow and modesty.

This did not prevent the beautiful child from smiling as she listened to the white-haired man talking to her, and nothing could be lovelier than that radiant smile with those downcast eyes.

In the first instance Marius thought she was another daughter of the same man, surely a sister of the other. But when the invariable pat-tern of his walk brought him close to the bench for the second time and he had scrutinized her, he realized it was the same girl. In six months the little girl had become a young woman. That was all. Noth-ing is more frequently encountered than this phenomenon. There is a moment when girls blossom in the twinkling of an eye, and all at once become roses. You left them yesterday as children, you come back today and find them disquieting.

This one had not only grown up, she had become the embodiment of an ideal. Just three days in April are enough for some trees to become covered in blossom. Six months had been enough for her to clothe herself in beauty. Her April had come.

You sometimes see people who, having been poor and shabby,

seem to wake up and all at once switch from penury to luxury, go on a spending spree, and suddenly start to sparkle, become lavish, magnificent. This is due to some injection of cash, yesterday was payment day. The young girl had received her half-year allowance.

And besides, she was no longer the convent girl with her felt hat, merino wool dress, school shoes and reddened hands. Along with beauty she had acquired taste. This person was well dressed with a kind of simple, costly and unaffected elegance. She wore a black damask dress, a cape of the same material, and a white crêpe hat. Her white gloves showed the daintiness of her hand toying with the Chinese ivory handle of a parasol, and her laced silk ankle-boot defined the smallness of her foot. When you passed by her, her entire outfit exuded a youthful and subtle fragrance.

As for the man, he was the same as ever.

The second time Marius came near her, the young girl looked up. Her eyes were a deep celestial blue, but in that veiled azure there was as yet only a child's gaze. She stared at Marius with indifference as she would have stared at the little boy running about under the sycamores, or the marble urn that cast a shadow on the bench. And Marius for his part continued his walk, thinking about something else.

He passed by the bench where the young girl was, another four or five times, but without even glancing in her direction.

On the days that followed he returned as usual to the Luxembourg Gardens. As usual he found 'father and daughter' there but paid no further attention to them. He thought no more about the girl now that she was beautiful than he had thought about her when she was ugly. He always passed very close to the bench where she sat, because that was his habit.

III
The Effect of Spring

One day the air was warm, the Luxembourg Gardens were suffused with shade and sunshine, the sky was as pure as if the angels had washed it that morning, the sparrows were twittering in the thick of the chestnut trees. Marius had wholly opened his soul to nature, he was not thinking of anything, simply living and breathing; he walked by the bench, the girl looked up at him, their eyes met.

What was in the girl's gaze on this occasion? Marius could not have said. Nothing and everything. It was a strange flash of brilliance.

She lowered her eyes, and he continued on his way.

What he had just seen was no longer the ingenuous and uncomplicated gaze of a child, it was a mysterious chasm that had opened up,
then abruptly closed again. There comes a day when every girl has
such a look. Pity the man who happens to be there!

That first glance of a soul as yet unknown to itself is like dawn
breaking in the sky. It is the awakening of something resplendent and
strange. Nothing can convey the dangerous charm of that unexpected
glimmering that all of a sudden vaguely illuminates an enchanting
darkness, and that comprises all present innocence and all future passion. It is a sort of undefined tenderness in waiting that accidentally
reveals itself. It is a trap that innocence unwittingly lays, in which it
catches hearts without intending to, and without knowing it. It is a
virgin with a woman's gaze.

It is rare that where that glance falls a deep reverie does not ensue.
All innocence and passion are concentrated in that heavenly and fateful beam that, more than the glad-eyeing of the most practised flirt,
has the magical power to bring about the sudden blossoming deep
within a soul of that ominous flower, full of perfumes and poisons,
which we call love.

That evening when he returned to his garret Marius took a look at
his clothes and noticed for the first time that he had been so slovenly,
so coarse, so inconceivably stupid as to go for his walk in the Luxembourg Gardens in his 'everyday' clothes, in other words, a hat that
was split near the hatband, heavy clodhoppers, black trousers with
faded knees and a black coat worn thin at the elbows.

IV
Start of a Great Sickness

The next day at the usual time Marius took out of his wardrobe his
new coat, his new trousers, his new hat and his new boots. He dressed
in the full panoply, put on gloves, a tremendous luxury, and set off for
the Luxembourg Gardens.

He passed Courfeyrac on the way and pretended not to see him.
When Courfeyrac got home he said to his friends, 'I just ran into Marius's new hat and new coat, with Marius inside them. He was probably
going to sit an exam. He looked a complete dolt.'

On arriving at the gardens Marius walked round the fountain and
stared at the swans. Then, for a long time, he stood in contemplation
in front of a statue with a head completely black with mildew, and a
missing hip. Near the fountain was a pot-bellied bourgeois of about
forty holding a five-year-old by the hand and saying to the little boy,

'Avoid extremes. Keep an equal distance, my son, from despotism and anarchy.' Marius listened to this bourgeois gentleman. Then he circled the fountain once again. At last he headed towards 'his path', slowly, and as if he were going there reluctantly. He looked as if he was being compelled to go there, and at the same time prevented from doing so. He was utterly unaware of any of this and thought he was behaving just as he did every day.

When he came to the path he saw at the other end of it Monsieur Leblanc and the young girl on 'their bench'. He buttoned up his coat, smoothed it down over his chest so there would be no wrinkles, examined with a certain satisfaction the glossy blackness of his trousers – and marched on the bench. There was in his approach something of an attack, and certainly a desire for conquest. So I say, he marched on the bench; as I would say, Hannibal marched on Rome.

In fact all his movements were quite unconscious, and he had in no way suspended his usual intellectual preoccupations nor those relating to his work. At that moment he was thinking that *The Baccalauréat Manual* was a stupid book, and that it must have been compiled by exceptional idiots for three of Racine's tragedies to be analysed in it as masterpieces of the human spirit, yet only one comedy by Molière. There was a high-pitched whistling in his ears. As he approached the bench he smoothed the folds of his coat and his eyes settled on the young girl. It seemed to him that she filled the whole end of the path with a bright blue haze.

As he drew nearer, his pace became slower and slower. When he got to a certain distance from the bench, and long before he had reached the end of the path, he stopped, and was himself at a loss to know why it was that he turned and retraced his steps. He did not even say to himself that he was not going right to the end. The girl could hardly have noticed him from so far away or seen how fine he looked in his new clothes. Yet he held himself very erect in case there should be anyone looking at him from behind.

He reached the far end, then walked back, and this time he came a little nearer to the bench. He even got to within the distance of three spaced-out trees, but there he felt some inexplicable impossibility of going any further, and he hesitated. He thought he had seen the young girl's face turn towards him. Nevertheless, with a tremendous manly effort he overcame his hesitation and kept going. A few seconds later he walked past the bench, erect and resolute, blushing to his ears, without daring to glance to left or right and, statesmanlike, his hand tucked into his coat. As he passed – 'right in the line of cannon-fire' – he felt a terrible thumping of his heart. She was wearing her damask gown and crêpe hat, as on the previous day. He heard an ineffable voice that must have been 'her voice'. She was chatting away quietly. She was very pretty. He sensed this although he made no attempt to look at her. 'Yet she couldn't help but have some respect and regard for me,' he thought, 'if she knew that I was actually the author of the dissertation on Marcos Obregón de la Ronda, which Monsieur François de Neufchâteau put at the front of his edition of *Gil Blas*, passing it off as his own.'

He carried on beyond the bench, went to the end of the path, which was very close by, then returned, passing in front of the lovely girl again. This time he was very pale. In fact there was nothing at all pleasant about the way he felt. He walked away from the bench and the girl, and while he had his back turned to her, he fancied she was watching him, and this made him stumble.

He did not attempt to go near the bench again. He stopped about halfway along the path, and there he sat down, which was something he never did, casting sidelong glances and thinking in the haziest depths of his mind that, after all, it was unlikely that anyone whose white hat and black gown he admired should be totally unimpressed by his glossy trousers and his new coat.

After a quarter of an hour he got to his feet as if he were about to start walking back towards that bench, with its aura of light. Yet he remained standing there, motionless. For the first time in fifteen months he said to himself that the gentleman who sat there every day with his daughter had no doubt noticed him too, and probably considered his persistent presence peculiar.

For the first time, also, he felt disrespectful in referring to this stranger, even in his own mind, by the nickname of Monsieur Leblanc.

He stood there like that for several minutes with his head bowed, drawing lines in the sand with a stick he was holding in his hand. Then he abruptly turned in the opposite direction, away from the bench, from Monsieur Leblanc and his daughter, and went home.

That day he forgot to go and eat. At eight o'clock in the evening he realized this, and as it was too late for Rue St-Jacques he said, 'Fancy that!' And he ate a piece of bread.

He went to bed only after he had brushed his coat and carefully folded it.

V

For Mame Bougon Thunder Strikes
in More Ways Than One

The next day Mame Bougon* – this is what Courfeyrac called the old caretaker-principal-tenant-housekeeper of the Gorbeau tenement; her name was actually Madame Burgon, as we have said, but he had no respect for anything, this hooligan Courfeyrac – Mame Bougon was astounded to see Monsieur Marius going out in his new coat again.

He returned to the Luxembourg Gardens, but went no further than his bench halfway along the path. He sat there as on the previous day, observing from a distance and seeing clearly the white hat, the black dress and above all the blue light. He did not stir from where he sat and only went home when the gates of the Luxembourg closed. He did not see Monsieur Leblanc and his daughter leave. He concluded they had made their way out of the garden by the gate on Rue de l'Ouest. When he thought about it later, several weeks afterwards, he could not for the life of him remember where he had dined that evening.

The next day, the third day, yet again Mame Bougon was thunderstruck. Marius went out in his new coat.

'Three days in a row!' she exclaimed.

She tried to follow him but Marius walked briskly, taking huge strides. It was like a hippopotamus trying to pursue an antelope. She lost sight of him within two minutes and came home panting, almost choked by her asthma, in a fury.

'Is there any sense,' she grumbled, 'in putting on your best clothes every day and making people run after you like that!'

Marius had gone to the Luxembourg Gardens. The girl was there with Monsieur Leblanc. Marius went as near as he could, pretending to be reading a book, but he was still a long way off; then he came back and sat on his bench where he spent four hours watching the sparrows hopping about on the path, which gave him the feeling they were making fun of him.

A fortnight elapsed in this way. Marius went to the Luxembourg Gardens no longer to take a stroll but always to sit in the same place, without knowing why. Once there, he did not stir. He put on his new coat every morning only so as to remain inconspicuous, and he would do the same all over again the next day.

She was without question amazingly beautiful. The only observa-

* 'Granny Grumpy'.

tion that might be made that constituted any kind of criticism was that the contradiction between her gaze, which was sad, and her smile, which was happy, gave her an air of slight distraction, which meant that at certain moments that sweet face, though nonetheless lovely, had a strangeness about it.

VI
Captivated

On one of the last days of the second week Marius was sitting on his bench as usual, holding in his hand an open book, not having turned a page for the last two hours. All at once he started. Something was happening at the other end of the path. Monsieur Leblanc and his daughter had just left their bench, the daughter had taken her father's arm, and both were slowly heading towards where Marius was, half-way along the path. Marius closed his book, then opened it again, then tried very hard to read. He was trembling. The aura of light was coming straight towards him. 'Oh my God!' he thought, 'I shall never have time to make the right impression.'

Meanwhile, the white-haired man and the girl continued moving towards him. It seemed to him this went on for ages and that it took only a second.

'What are they coming down here for?' he wondered. 'She's actually going to pass this way! Her feet will walk on this sand, on this path, right by me!'

He was thrown into confusion, he wished he was very handsome, he wished he had the Legion of Honour cross. He heard the quiet, regular sound of their footsteps approaching. He imagined Monsieur Leblanc glancing at him with annoyance.

'Is this gentleman going to speak to me?' he thought. He bowed his head. When he raised it again, they were very close to him. The girl walked by and as she passed she looked at him. She looked steadily at him with a pensive sweetness that thrilled Marius from head to foot. It was as if she were reproaching him for not having come to her in such a long time, and saying to him, 'I've come to you.'

Marius was dazzled by those eyes full of light and unfathomable depths. He felt his brain was on fire. She had come to him. How marvellous! And then the way she looked at him! She seemed to him more beautiful than he had ever yet seen her. Of a beauty that was wholly feminine and angelic, a perfect beauty that would have made Petrarch sing and brought Dante to his knees. He felt as if he were floating in the blue heavens. At the same time he was horribly upset because there was dust on his boots.

He felt sure she had also looked at his boots.

He followed her with his eyes until she disappeared. Then he began to walk about the Luxembourg Gardens like a madman. It is probable that at times he laughed to himself and talked out loud. He was so dreamy that every one of the children's nannies nearby thought he was in love with her.

He came out of the gardens, hoping to find her in the street.

He ran into Courfeyrac under the arcades of the Odéon and said to him, 'Come and have dinner with me.'

They went off to Rousseau's and spent six francs. Marius ate like a horse. He gave the waiter six sous.

Over dessert he said to Courfeyrac. 'Have you read the paper? What a fine speech Audry de Puyraveau gave!'

He was hopelessly in love.

After they had eaten he said to Courfeyrac, 'Let's go to the theatre – it's on me.'

They went to Porte-St-Martin to see Frédérick in *L'Auberge des Adrets*. Marius enjoyed himself enormously.

At the same time he was twice as unworldly as before. When they came out of the theatre he refused to look at a hat-shop girl's garter as she stepped over a gutter, and Courfeyrac came close to horrifying him by saying, 'I'd gladly add that woman to my collection.'

Courfeyrac invited him to lunch at the Café Voltaire the next morning. Marius went, and ate even more than on the previous evening. He was very thoughtful and very cheerful. He seemed to take every opportunity to burst out laughing. He warmly hugged some provincial nobody who was introduced to him. A group of students gathered round the table and talked of the professorial nonsense being dished out at the Sorbonne and paid for by the state, then the conversation turned to the shortcomings of Quicherat's dictionaries and his works on versification.

Marius interrupted the discussion to exclaim, 'All the same it's very gratifying to have the Legion of Honour cross!'

'That's odd!' Courfeyrac whispered to Jean Prouvaire.

'No,' replied Prouvaire, 'that's serious.'

It was indeed serious. Marius was at that delightful and fervent initial stage that marks the beginning of great passions. One look had achieved all this. When explosives have been laid in the mine, when the fire is ready to be lit, nothing is simpler. A look is a kindling spark.

And that was it. Marius loved a woman. His destiny was entering on the unknown.

A woman's look is like certain seemingly harmless yet powerful mechanisms. You pass by them every day without any fuss or bother, all unawares. A time comes when you even forget they are there. You come and go, let your mind wander, talk, laugh. Suddenly you feel caught. There is no escape. The mechanism holds you fast, the look has captured you. It has captured you, never mind how or in what way, by some vagrant part of your mind, during some momentary distraction. You are doomed. You will be entirely swallowed up. A concatenation of mysterious forces takes over. You struggle in vain. No one can help you now. You are going to pass through the mesh, from cog to cog, agony to agony, torture to torture, you, your mind, your fortune, your future, your soul. And depending on whether you are in the power of a vicious creature or of a noble heart, you will not emerge from this terrifying machine without being disfigured – by shame – or transfigured – by passion.

VII
Fortunes of the Letter U When a Subject of Conjecture

Solitariness, detachment from everything, pride, independence, a feeling for nature, having no humdrum job to do, an introspective life, secret struggles with chastity, open-hearted rapture before the whole of creation, had prepared Marius for this possession called passion. His devotion to his father had gradually become a religion, and like all religions it had retreated into the hinterland of his soul. Something was needed in the forefront. Love came along.

A whole month passed during which Marius went every day to the Luxembourg Gardens. At the appointed hour, nothing could detain him. 'He's on duty,' Courfeyrac would say.

Marius was in seventh heaven. Without any doubt the young girl was looking at him.

He had finally plucked up the courage to go nearer the bench. Yet, acting on both the instinctive timidity and the instinctive caution of a lover, he did not walk past it any more. He thought it advisable not to attract 'her father's attention'. With a downright Machiavellianism he contrived to stand behind trees and behind the pedestals of statues so as to be seen as much as possible by the girl and as little as possible by the old gentleman. Sometimes he would remain motionless for whole half-hours at a stretch in the shadow of some Leonidas or Spartacus, a book held in his hand, his eyes slightly raised over the edge of it, seeking out the beautiful girl, and she for her part with a vague smile turned her lovely profile towards him. She could not have been any more calm and natural as she chatted with the white-haired man, while her virginal and passionate gaze dwelt dreamily on Marius. An ancient ploy dating back to time immemorial, one that Eve knew from the first day of the world and that every woman knows from the first day of her life! With her lips she responded to one, and with her eyes to the other.

It is more than likely, however, that Monsieur Leblanc finally noticed something, for often when Marius arrived he stood up and began to walk about. He abandoned the place where they usually sat and adopted the bench next to the *Gladiator* at the other end of the path, as if to see whether Marius would follow them there. Marius did not realize, and made that mistake. The 'father' started to become unpredictable and no longer brought 'his daughter' every day. Sometimes he came alone. Then Marius did not stay. Another mistake.

Marius did not notice these warning signs. From the phase of timidity he moved on through a natural and inevitable progression to the phase of blindness. His love grew. He dreamed of her every night. And then he had a stroke of good fortune, adding oil to the fire, further obscuring his vision. One evening at dusk he found a handkerchief on the bench that 'Monsieur Leblanc and his daughter' had just left. A very ordinary handkerchief, without any embroidery on it, but white, of fine linen, and seeming to him to exude ineffable fragrances. He seized on it with rapture. This handkerchief was marked with the letters U F. Marius knew nothing about this beautiful girl – her family, her name, where she lived. These two letters were the first thing about her that he had managed to come by, adorable initials on which he immediately began to build his conjectures. U was evidently her first name. 'Ursule!' he thought. 'What a delightful name!' He kissed the handkerchief, breathed in its scent, placed it during the day on his heart, on his flesh, and at night fell asleep with it at his lips.

'I can smell her entire being in it!' he exclaimed.

This handkerchief belonged to the old gentleman, who had simply dropped it from his pocket. In the days that followed this lucky find, Marius never appeared in the Luxembourg Gardens without the handkerchief, kissing it and pressing it to his heart. The lovely child was completely baffled, and conveyed this to him by the discreetest of signs.

'What modesty!' said Marius.

Even War Veterans Can Be Happy

Since we have mentioned the word 'modesty' and since we have nothing to hide, we should say that on one occasion, however, in the midst of his raptures, 'his Ursule' gave him very serious grounds for complaint. It was one of the days when she prevailed on Monsieur Leblanc to leave the bench and stroll along the path. There was a brisk Prairial breeze blowing, stirring the tops of the plane trees. Father and daughter had just walked past Marius's bench, arm in arm. Marius had stood up behind them and was following them with his eyes, as was only to be expected of someone hopelessly in love.

All of a sudden a gust of wind, more lively than the rest and probably responsible for getting springtime's business done, rose up from the tree nursery, swept down the path, enveloped the young girl in a delicious shiver worthy of Virgil's nymphs and Theocritus' fawns, and lifted her dress, a dress more sacred than that of Isis, almost to the height of her garter. An exquisitely shaped leg appeared. Marius saw it. He was incensed, infuriated.

With a sublimely startled gesture the young girl swiftly batted down her dress, but he was nonetheless upset. True, he was alone on the path. But there might have been someone there. And what if there had been! Imagine such a thing! It was horrifying what she had just done! Alas, the poor child had done nothing. There was only one culprit, the wind. But the Bartolo that exists in Cherubino was quickening in some obscure part of him and, jealous of his own shadow, Marius was determined to be cross. So it is that the bitter and peculiar jealousy of the flesh awakens in the human heart and asserts itself even without justification. But leaving aside that jealousy, there was nothing at all agreeable to him about the sight of that lovely leg. Any other woman's white stocking would have given him more pleasure.

When 'his Ursule', having reached the end of the path, retraced her steps with Monsieur Leblanc and passed the bench on which Marius had sat down again, Marius darted a fierce and sullen look at her. The young girl stiffened, drawing herself back slightly, that movement accompanied by a raising of the eyebrows that signifies 'Now, what's the matter with him?'

This was their 'first tiff'.

Marius had scarcely finished this quarrel with her, conducted through glances, when someone came along the path. This was a very stooped, very wrinkled, very white-haired war veteran in a uniform dating back to Louis XV, the little oval of red cloth with crossed swords on his chest, the ordinary soldier's St Louis cross; and further decorated with an armless coat-sleeve, a silver chin and a wooden leg. Marius thought he discerned in this individual an air of great contentment. He even thought the old cynic hobbling by had given him a very brotherly and very cheerful wink, as if some chance occurrence had created an understanding between them and they had enjoyed some shared stroke of luck. Well, what made him so happy, war-ravaged wreck that he was? What were the goings-on between this wooden leg and that other leg? Marius's jealousy reached its peak. 'Perhaps he was there!' he said to himself. 'Perhaps he saw!' And he felt like killing the veteran.

With the help of time, all darts become blunted. However fair and justifiable, Marius's anger against 'Ursule' passed. He eventually forgave her, but it took a great effort. He sulked for three days.

Yet throughout all this and because of all this, his passion grew, driving him to distraction.

IX
Eclipse

We have just seen how Marius discovered, or thought he had discovered, that She was called Ursule.

Appetite comes with loving.* To know that her name was Ursule was already a great deal. But it was not very much. In three or four weeks Marius had consumed this blessing. He wanted another. He wanted to know where she lived.

He made his first mistake by falling into the trap of that bench near the *Gladiator*. He made a second by not staying in the Luxembourg Gardens when Monsieur Leblanc came alone. He made a third – a huge mistake. He followed 'Ursule'.

She lived in Rue de l'Ouest, in the quietest part of the street, in a new unpretentious-looking three-storey house.

From that moment on, Marius added to his happiness of seeing her at the Luxembourg the happiness of following her home. His hunger increased. He knew her name, her first name at least, a lovely name, a truly feminine name. He knew where she lived. He wanted to know who she was.

One evening after he had followed them home and seen them disappear through the carriage gateway he went in after them and said

* An allusion to Rabelais (bk I, ch. v): 'Appetite comes with eating, says Angeston, but the thirst goes away with drinking.'

pluckily to the porter, 'Was that the gentleman on the first floor that just came in?'

'No,' replied the porter. 'That was the gentleman on the third floor.'

Another advance made. This success emboldened Marius.

'At the front?' he asked.

'Good lord!' said the porter. 'The house doesn't go back any further, it all faces the street.'

'And what does the gentleman do for a living?' Marius went on.

'He's a man of independent means, monsieur. A very kind man, and though not rich he's good to the poor.'

'What's his name?' resumed Marius.

The porter looked up and said, 'Is monsieur a police spy?'

Marius went off quite shamefaced, but overjoyed. He was making progress.

'Right!' he thought. 'I know her name is Ursule, that she's the daughter of a gentleman, and she lives there, Rue de l'Ouest, on the third floor.'

The following day Monsieur Leblanc and his daughter made only a very brief appearance in the Luxembourg Gardens. It was still broad daylight when they left. Marius followed them to Rue de l'Ouest as he had now made a habit of doing. On arriving at the carriage entrance Monsieur Leblanc let his daughter go on ahead of him, then before stepping through himself he stopped, turned, and stared intently at Marius.

The next day they did not come to the Luxembourg. Marius waited in vain all day long. At nightfall he went to Rue de l'Ouest and saw light shining from the third-floor windows. He walked about below those windows until the light went out.

The next day, no one at the gardens. Marius waited all day, then went to do his evening stint beneath the windows. This took him to ten o'clock at night. His dinner went by the board. Fever feeds the sick man, and love the lover.

A week went by in this manner. Monsieur Leblanc and his daughter did not turn up again at the Luxembourg Gardens. Marius conjectured sadly about this. He dared not watch the carriage entrance during the day. He contented himself with going at night to gaze at the reddish glow in the windows. He saw shadows passing across them now and then, and his heart pounded. On the eighth day, when he arrived beneath the windows there was no light in them.

'Fancy that!' he said. 'The lamp's not been lighted yet. Although it's dark. Maybe they've gone out?'

He waited. Until ten o'clock. Until midnight. Until one in the morning. No light appeared in the third-floor windows and no one returned to the house. He went away feeling very gloomy.

The next day – because he existed only in terms of the next day, for him there was, so to speak, no today – the next day he found no one at the Luxembourg. It was what he expected. At dusk he went to the house. No light in the windows. The shutters were closed. The third floor was in total darkness.

Marius knocked at the carriage entrance, went in, and said to the porter, 'The gentleman on the third floor?'

'Moved out,' replied the porter.

Marius reeled and said weakly, 'How long ago?'

'Yesterday.'

'Where's he living now?'

'I've no idea.'

'So he didn't leave his new address?'

'No.' And looking up, the porter recognized Marius. 'Well, well!' he said. 'It's you again! So you really are a police sleuth then?'

BOOK SEVEN
PATRON-MINETTE

Mines and Miners

Human societies all have what is called in the theatre 'the third level down'. The ground on which society stands is everywhere mined, sometimes for good, sometimes for evil. These mine workings overlie each other. There are upper mines and lower mines. There is a top and a bottom in this obscure underground that occasionally gives way beneath civilization, and that our carelessness and indifference trample underfoot. In the last century the *Encyclopaedia* was a mine, practically open-cast. The shadows, those dark incubators of primitive Christianity, were only awaiting the opportunity to erupt under the Caesars and to inundate the human race with light. For in the sacred shadows is latent light. Volcanoes are full of a gloom capable of flaring into a blaze. All lava begins as darkness. The catacombs, where the first mass was said, were not just Rome's cellar, they were the world's underground.

Beneath the structure of society, that complicated marvel of a ramshackle edifice, are all sorts of excavations. There is the religious mine, the philosophical mine, the economic mine, the revolutionary mine. One person digs with an idea, another with numbers, another with anger. People call out and answer each other from one catacomb to another. Utopias make their way underground through these conduits. They branch out in all directions. They sometimes run into each other and make common cause. Jean-Jacques lends his pick to Diogenes, who lends him his lantern. Sometimes they fight among themselves. Calvin quarrels with Socinus. But nothing stops or interrupts the straining of all these energies towards their goal, and the immense activity going on simultaneously in these shadows, the to-ing and fro-ing, the climbing and descending, and climbing again, which slowly transforms the overlayer from the underlayer and the outside from the inside: a vast unseen multitudinous busyness. Society hardly even suspects this burrowing that leaves its surface intact and changes its viscera. Every underground level has its own different works going on and its own type of extraction. What emerges from all these deep delvings? The future.

The deeper down, the more mysterious the workers. Down to a level the social philosopher can identify, the work is good. Beyond that level it is dubious and variable. Lower still, it becomes terrible. At a certain depth the excavations become impenetrable to the spirit of civilization, the bounds of man's breathable environment have been exceeded. This may be the beginning of monsters.

The ladder of descent is a strange one, and each rung corresponds to a level where philosophy can gain a foothold and where one of its workers may be encountered, sometimes divine, sometimes perverted. Below Jan Hus, there is Luther. Below Luther, there is Descartes. Below Descartes, there is Voltaire. Below Voltaire, there is Condorcet. Below Condorcet, there is Robespierre. Below Robespierre, there is Marat. Below Marat, there is Babeuf. And so it goes on. Lower down, dimly perceptible at the boundary that separates the indistinct from the invisible, are other shadowy men who perhaps do not yet exist. The men of yesterday are spectres, those of tomorrow are larvae. The eye of the spirit somehow distinguishes them. The embryonic work of the future is one of the visions of philosophy.

A foetus world in limbo, what an extraordinary configuration!

Saint-Simon, Owen, Fourier are there also, in cross-tunnels.

Although, without knowing it, all these underground pioneers are linked by an invisible divine chain – they almost always think they are isolated but they are not – their works are very different, and the light of some contrasts with the flare of others. Some are otherworldly, others are tragic. Yet whatever the contrast, all these workers from the highmost to the most darksome, from the wisest to the maddest, have one thing in common, and it is this: disinterestedness. Marat, like Jesus, is self-abnegating. They set themselves aside, they leave themselves out, they do not think of themselves. They see something other than themselves. They have a look in their eyes, a look that seeks the absolute. The one has the entire heavens in his eyes; the other however enigmatic, still harbours beneath his brow the pale gleam of the infinite. Whatever he may do, venerate anyone who has this sign: the starry eye.

The dark eye is the other sign.

Therein is the beginning of evil. In the presence of anyone with unseeing eyes, reflect and tremble. The social order has its dark miners.

There is a point where delving deeper means entombment, and light is quenched.

Beneath all these mines we have just described, beneath all these galleries, beneath this whole vast vein-like subterranean network of progress and Utopia, much further down in the earth, deeper than Marat, deeper than Babeuf, deeper, much deeper, and without any connection with the upper levels, is the last tunnel. A terrible place. This is what we have called the third level down. It is the pit of darkness. It is the cavern of the blind. *Inferi**.

It connects directly with the abyss.

II
The Lowest Depths

There disinterestedness vanishes. The demon begins to take on some sort of shape. Every man for himself. The eyeless ego howls, fumbles, gropes, gnaws. Society's Ugolino is in this pit.

The savage figures prowling in this gulf – near-beasts, near-phantoms – are not concerned with universal progress, the concept and the word are unknown to them, they care only for individual gratification. They are barely conscious, and there is inside them a kind of terrifying blankness. They have two mothers, both stepmothers, ignorance and destitution. They have a guide, necessity, and an appetite for every type of indulgence. They are brutally voracious, that is to say, ravenous, not tyrant-like but tiger-like. These larvae move on from suffering to crime – inevitable progression, dizzying development, the logic of darkness. What creeps about in society's third level down is no longer the stifled claim to the absolute – it is the protest of matter. Man becomes dragon here. Going hungry, being thirsty – that is the starting-point. Embodying Satan – that is where it ends. Out of this cavern comes Lacenaire.

We have just seen, in Book Four, one of the chambers of the upper mine, of the great political, revolutionary and philosophical tunnel. There, as we have just said, everything is noble, honourable, admirable, honest. There, certainly, mistakes might be made, mistakes are made, but so much heroism is involved, any erring is to be respected. All the work done there has a name: Progress.

The moment has come to take a glimpse at other depths, hideous depths.

Let us say it again, underlying society there is – and there will be until the day ignorance is dispelled – the great cavern that is evil.

This cave underlies all others and is the foe of all. It is hatred without exception. This cave knows no philosophers. Its dagger has never

* Latin: 'The nether regions'. Also Italian, as in Dante's 'discesa agli inferi' ('descent into hell').

fashioned a quill. Its blackness has nothing to do with the sublime blackness of the inkwell. Never have the fingers of night that tense beneath this suffocating ceiling leafed through a book or opened a newspaper. To Cartouche, Babeuf is an exploiter. To Schinderhannes, Marat is an aristocrat. The object of this cave is the destruction of everything.

Everything. Including the upper tunnels, which it abhors. In its hideous busyness it not only undermines the present social order, it undermines philosophy, it undermines science, it undermines law, human thought, civilization, revolution, progress. It is called quite simply theft, prostitution, murder, assassination. It is darkness and it wants chaos. Its vault is shaped by ignorance.

All the others, those above, have but one object – to do away with it. It is towards this end that philosophy and progress strive by employing in unison every means at their disposal, by improving reality as well as by contemplating the absolute. Destroy the mine of Ignorance, and you destroy the underminer, Crime.

To put in a few words some of what we have been writing about: the only social peril is darkness.

Humanity is of one kind. All men are of the same clay. With no difference, here below at least, in their predetermined fate. The same obscurity before, the same flesh during, the same dust afterwards. But ignorance mingled with the stuff of humankind blackens it. This incurable blackness spreads inside man and there becomes Evil.

III
Babet, Gueulemer, Claquesous and Montparnasse

From 1830 to 1835 a gang of four ruffians, Claquesous, Gueulemer, Babet and Montparnasse, ruled Paris's third level down.

Gueulemer was a lowlife Hercules. His retreat was the Arche-Marion sewer. He was six feet tall with pectorals of marble, biceps of steel, a massive chest cavity, the torso of a colossus, a bird-like head. He looked like the Farnese *Hercules* dressed in twill trousers and a velveteen waistcoat. Being of such a sculptural build, Gueulemer might have subdued monsters – but had found it more expedient to be one. A low brow, broad temples, crow's-feet though not yet forty, short wiry hair, bristly cheeks, bearded like a wild boar – you can just picture the man. His muscles cried out for work, his stupidity would have none of it. This was a huge idle strength. He was a murderer through indolence. He was thought to be Creole. He had probably had some involvement in the attack on Marshal Brune, having been a porter at Avignon in 1815. With that training, he turned bandit.

Babet's slightness contrasted with Gueulemer's bulk. Babet was lean and canny. He was transparent but impenetrable. You could see daylight through his bones but nothing in his eyes. He declared himself a chemist. He had been a clown with Bobèche and a mountebank with Bobino. He had played in vaudeville at St-Mihiel. He was a man with designs, a fine talker, who underlined his smiles and put quotation marks around his gestures. He contrived to make a living as a street vendor, selling plaster busts and portraits of 'the head of state'. He also pulled teeth. He had been a showman of freaks at fairs and had his own booth, with trumpet, and this poster: 'Babet, Dentistry Artist, Member of the Academies, conducts physical experiments on metals and metalloids, extracts teeth, tackles stumps abandoned by fellow practitioners. Price: one tooth, one franc fifty centimes. Two teeth, two francs. Three teeth, two francs fifty. Take advantage of this bargain.' ('Take advantage of this bargain' meant 'Have as many pulled out as possible.') He had been married and had children. He did not know what had become of his wife and offspring. He had lost them the way a person loses a handkerchief. A rare exception in the shady world to which he belonged, Babet read the newspapers. Once, in the days when he had his family with him in his travelling booth, he read in *Le Messager* that a woman had just given birth to a viable infant with the muzzle of a calf, and he exclaimed, 'That's worth a fortune! My wife wouldn't have the wit to give me a child like that!'

He had since left all that behind him in order to 'take on Paris'. His expression.

What was Claquesous? He was night. He would wait until the sky had painted itself black before making an appearance. In the evening he would come out of some hole, which he would return to before daylight. Where was this hole? No one knew. In the pitch dark, he spoke to his accomplices only with his back turned to them. Was his name Claquesous? No. He would say, 'My name is Not-at-all.' If a candle was produced he put on a mask. He was a ventriloquist. Babet used to say, 'Claquesous is a nocturne for two voices.' Claquesous was elusive, vagrant, terrible. No one was sure whether he had a name, Claquesous being a nickname. No one was sure whether he had a voice, as his belly spoke more often than his mouth. No one was sure whether he had a face, as only his mask had ever been seen. He would vanish like a ghost, and seemed to appear out of the ground.

A lugubrious creature was Montparnasse. Montparnasse was a child, not twenty years of age, with an attractive face, lips like cherries, splendid black hair, the brightness of spring in his eyes. He had every vice and aspired to every crime. A diet of wickedness gave him an appetite for worse. He was the gamin turned lout, and the lout turned murderous robber. He was good-looking, effeminate, graceful, strong, languid, ferocious. He wore the brim of his hat turned up on the left to accommodate the tuft of hair in the fashionable style of 1829. He lived by robbery with violence. His frock-coat was of the best cut, but threadbare. Montparnasse was a fashion-plate, living in poverty and committing murder. The cause of all this adolescent's crimes was the desire to be well dressed. The first young working girl who told him he was handsome had cast the stain of darkness on his heart and had made a Cain of this Abel. Discovering he was good-looking, he wanted to be elegant. Now, the height of elegance is idleness. A poor man's idleness is crime. Few prowlers were so dreaded as Montparnasse. At eighteen he already had several killings behind him. More than one passer-by had lain in the shadow of this wretch, with arms outstretched, his face in a pool of blood. Curled, pomaded, nipped in at the waist, with a woman's hips, the chest and shoulders of a Prussian officer, murmured admiration from the boulevard trollops around him, cravat deftly knotted, a cudgel in his pocket, a flower in his buttonhole – such was this death-dealing dandy.

IV
The Make-up of the Gang

These four ruffians formed a kind of Proteus, snaking through the police and striving to escape Vidocq's inquisitive gaze 'under various guises, as tree, flame, fountain'*, swapping names and trading tricks, hiding in their own shadows, secret-keepers and asylums to each other, shedding their personalities as another would remove a false nose at a masked ball, sometimes so shrinking themselves as to be one sole individual, sometimes so multiplying themselves that Coco-Lacour himself mistook them for a throng.

These four men were not four men. They were a kind of mysterious four-headed robber operating all over Paris. They were the monstrous polyp of evil dwelling in society's crypt.

Thanks to their widespread coverage and their underlying network of contacts, Babet, Gueulemer, Claquesous and Montparnasse held

---

* A quotation from 'Ode to the Comte de Luc' by the poet Jean-Baptiste Rousseau (1671–1741): 'Just like the old shepherd of Neptune's flocks, / Proteus, from whom the sky, fortune's father, / hides no secrets, / under various guises, as tree, flame, fountain, / strives to escape the unsure sight / of indiscreet mortals'.

the exclusive contract for premeditated attacks in the *département* of the Seine. They perpetrated on the passer-by the underworld *coup d'état*. The men of nocturnal imagination who dreamed up these schemes came to them to have them carried out, supplying the four ruffians with a skeleton plot, which the latter took charge of staging. They worked from a synopsis. They were always in a position to provide the right personnel for any crime in need of a helping hand – and sufficiently lucrative. If there was some villainy afoot seeking manpower they would subcontract their accomplices to it. They had a troupe of shady actors available for every underworld drama.

They usually assembled at nightfall, their waking hour, on the flats by La Salpêtrière. There they conferred. They had the twelve hours of darkness before them. They settled on the use to be made of them.

Patron-Minette was the name given in underworld circles to the fellowship of these four men. In the fanciful popular parlance of old, which is dying out day by day, *patron-minette* means 'morning', just as *entre chien et loup** means 'evening'. Patron-Minette were probably so called because this was the time when their work ended, dawn being the moment when ghosts vanish and villains go their separate ways. These four men were known by this designation. When the assize judge visited Lacenaire in prison he questioned him about some misdeed that Lacenaire denied. 'Who did it, then?' asked the judge. Lacenaire gave the following reply, puzzling to the magistrate but clear to the police: 'Perhaps it was Patron-Minette.'

You can sometimes tell what a play is like from the cast of characters. Similarly, a gang can almost be appraised from the list of its members. These are the names – for such names survive in special reports – to which the principal associates of Patron-Minette answered:

Panchaud, alias Printanier, alias Bigrenaille.

Brujon. (There was a Brujon dynasty. We may return to them later.)

Boulatruelle, the road-mender who has already made a brief appearance.

Laveuve.

Finistère.

Homère Hogu, a negro.

Mardisoir.

Dépêche.

Fauntleroy, alias Bouquetière.

Glorieux, a freed felon.

Barrecarrosse, alias Monsieur Dupont.

---

* (When you cannot distinguish) 'between dog and wolf'.

Lesplanade-du-Sud.

Poussagrive.

Carmagnolet.

Kruideniers, alias Bizarro.

Mangedentelle.

Les-pieds-en-l'air.

Demi-liard, alias Deux-milliards.

El cetera, et cetera.

There are others no worse that we could mention.* These names have faces. They refer not merely to individuals but to types. Each of these names corresponds to a variety of those monstrous fungi found on the underside of civilization.

Not very keen on showing their faces, these individuals were not the kind of men to be seen out in the street. Exhausted by their nights of violence, during the day they would go off and sleep, sometimes in the lime kilns, sometimes in the abandoned quarries of Montmartre or Montrouge, sometimes in the sewers. They went to ground.

What has become of these men? They still exist. They have always existed. Horace speaks of them: *Ambubaiarum collegia, pharmacopolae, mendici, mimae.*† And as long as society is what it is, they will be what they are. Under the dark roof of their cellars they are forever being reborn of society's oozing slime. They keep returning, these ever identical spectres, only they no longer have the same name and are no longer inside the same skin.

Though individuals are extirpated, the tribe lives on.

They retain the same abilities. From swindler to prowler, the race remains pure. They can detect purses in pockets, they have a nose for watches in fobs. For them, gold and silver have a smell. There are unsuspecting bourgeois citizens who might be said to look like easy pickings. These men patiently pursue these innocents. At the passing of a stranger or of someone from the country they quiver like spiders.

Run into these men or catch a glimpse of them around midnight on a deserted boulevard, and they are terrifying. They seem to be not men, but forms made of living mist. They look as if they are usually at one with the shadows, are indistinct from them, have no other soul but the gloom, and it is only momentarily, for the purpose of living a

---

* An ironic allusion to a celebrated line from Hugo's play *Hernani*: 'J'en passe et des meilleurs' (Act III, sc. vi, the so-called portraits scene).

† 'Tribes of flute-players, pedlars of quack remedies, beggars, mountebanks', from the opening lines of Horace's *Satires* I:2.

monstrous life for a few minutes, that they have broken out of the darkness.

What is needed to make these noxious spirits disappear? Light. Floods of light. No bat withstands the dawn. Illuminate society's underside.

BOOK EIGHT

THE VILLAINOUS PAUPER

I

Looking for a Girl in a Hat, Marius Encounters a Man in a Cap

Summer passed, then autumn. Winter came. Neither Monsieur Leblanc nor the girl had set foot again in the Luxembourg Gardens. Marius now had only one thought: to see that sweet and adorable face once more. He kept searching, he searched everywhere. He found nothing. He was no longer Marius the impassioned dreamer, the man of resolve, ardent and steadfast, the bold challenger of destiny, the future-building intellectual, the youthful mind with so many plans, projects, ideas, so much pride and determination. He was a stray dog. He fell into a dark dejection. It was all over. Work was tedious to him, walking tired him. The vastness of nature, once so manifold, so full of brightness, voices, wise counsels, perspectives, horizons, lessons, now lay desolate before him. It seemed to him everything was gone.

He was still a thinker, for he could not be otherwise, but he no longer took pleasure in his thoughts. To all their incessant whispered suggestions he replied gloomily, 'What's the use?'

He reproached himself endlessly. 'Why did I follow her? I was so happy just to see her! She looked at me. Wasn't that wonderful? She appeared to love me. Wasn't that everything? What more did I want? After that, there's nothing else. I've been absurd. It's my fault', et cetera, et cetera. Courfeyrac, in whom he confided nothing (that was his nature) but who more or less guessed everything (and that was his nature), began by congratulating him on being in love – to Courfeyrac's great astonishment, it has to be said. Then, seeing Marius in this melancholy, he eventually said to him, 'I see that you are after all only human. Look, come to La Chaumière.'

Once, trusting in some lovely September sunshine, Marius allowed himself to be taken along by Courfeyrac, Bossuet and Grantaire to the public dance at Sceaux, hoping – what a pipe dream! – that he might perhaps find her there. He did not, of course, see the girl he was looking for. 'Yet this is the place where all lost women are to be found,' Grantaire grumbled privately. Marius left his friends at the dance and walked home alone, weary, feverish, his eyes blurred and sad in the dark; stunned by the noise and dust of the cheerful charabancs over-taking him, full of people singing on their way back from the festivities; feeling downhearted and, to clear his head, breathing in the pungent smell of the walnut-trees along the road.

He reverted to living more and more alone, distraught, disconsolate, totally obsessed with his inner anguish, pacing back and forth in his pain like a wolf in a trap, looking everywhere for the girl who was gone, besotted with love.

Another time, he had a chance encounter that made a curious impression on him. In the little streets around Boulevard des Invalides he passed a man dressed as a worker, in a long-peaked cap with locks of very white hair showing beneath it. Marius was struck by the magnificence of this white hair, and studied the man, who was walking slowly and as though lost in painful reflection. Strange to say, he thought he recognized Monsieur Leblanc. It was the same hair, the same profile in so as far as it could be seen under the cap, the same bearing, only sadder. But why these working man's clothes? What did this mean? What did this disguise signify? Marius was very surprised. When he recovered, his first impulse was to follow the man. Who was to know whether he might not at last have picked up the trail he had been seeking? In any case he must get a closer look at the man and clear up the mystery. But he thought of this too late, the man was not there any more. He had already turned into some little side street and Marius was unable to find him. This encounter preoccupied him for several days, then faded from his mind. 'After all,' he said to himself, 'it was probably just someone who looked like him.'

II
A Find

Marius was still living in the Gorbeau tenement. He paid no attention to anyone there.

As a matter of fact, during that period there were no other inhabitants in the house except for himself and those Jondrettes whose rent he had once paid without ever having spoken to father, mother or daughters. The other lodgers had moved away or died, or had been evicted for not paying the rent.

One day that winter the sun appeared briefly in the afternoon, but it was the second of February, Candlemas, according to ancient tradition the day whose treacherous sun, harbinger of six weeks' cold weather, inspired in Mathieu Laensberg these two lines, still rightly regarded as classic:

A glimpse or a glimmer of sun
And the bear goes back to its den.

Marius had just emerged from his. Night was falling. It was time to go for his evening meal, for alas, it could not be helped, he had started eating again! Oh, the frailties of ideal passions! He had just come out of his room, and Mame Bougon was at that very moment sweeping the doorstep and delivering this memorable monologue: 'What's cheap right now? Everything's expensive. Hardship's the only thing that comes cheap. You can get it for nothing, hardship!'

Marius slowly made his way up the boulevard towards the toll-gate, to get to Rue St-Jacques. He walked along, lost in thought and with his head bowed.

All of a sudden someone bumped into him in the fog. He turned round and saw two young girls dressed in rags, one tall and thin, the other a little shorter, rushing along breathlessly, in a fright, and looking as if they were running away. They were coming towards him, had not seen him, and collided with him as they passed. Marius could discern in the twilight their pallid faces, dishevelled heads, thin hair, hideous bonnets, tattered skirts and bare feet. They were talking to each other as they ran.

The taller one said in a very low voice, 'The bashers came along. They almost got me cornered.'

The other replied, 'I saw them. I scarpered!'

Marius understood from this unlovely argot that gendarmes or the police had almost caught these two children, and that the children had escaped.

They dived under the trees of the boulevard behind him, and there for a few instants appeared like a white blob in the dusk, then disappeared.

Marius had stopped for a moment. He was about to continue on his way when he noticed a little greyish bundle on the ground at his feet. He bent and picked it up. It was some sort of envelope that looked as if it had papers inside it.

'Well now,' he said, 'those poor girls must have dropped it.'

He retraced his steps, he called out, he could not find them. He thought they were already far away, put the package in his pocket and went off to eat.

On his way he saw in an alley off Rue Mouffetard a child's coffin covered with a black cloth, resting on three chairs and lit by a single candle. The two girls in the twilight came back into his mind.

'Poor mothers!' he thought. 'There's one thing sadder than seeing your children die – it's seeing them lead a bad life.'

Then these shadows that brought variety to his sadness slipped from his mind, and he lapsed into his usual preoccupations. He fell to thinking again about his six months of love and happiness in the open air, in the bright daylight beneath the beautiful trees of the Luxembourg Gardens.

'How bleak my life has become!' he said to himself. 'Young girls keep appearing before me. Only, before they were angels and now they're ghouls.'

III
Quadrifrons*

That evening, as he was undressing for bed, his hand happened to feel in his coat pocket the bundle he had picked up on the boulevard. He had forgotten about it. He thought it would be as well to open it, and that this bundle might possibly contain the address of those young girls – if indeed it belonged to them – and in any event the information necessary to return it to the person who had lost it.

He opened the envelope. It was not sealed, and contained four letters that were not sealed, either. The addresses had been written on them. All four of them stank of tobacco.

The first was addressed as follows: 'To Madame, Madame la marquise de Grucheray, the square opposite the Chamber of Deputies, number . . .'

In all likelihood he would find in it the information he sought, Marius said to himself, and anyway, seeing that the letter was not sealed, there was probably no harm in reading it.

This is how it was worded:

Madame la Marquise,

The virtue of mercy and piety is the one that most closely binds society. Allow your Christian spirit to rome and cast a look of compassion on this ill-fated Spaniard, victim of his loyalty and attachment to the sacred cause of legitimicy, which he has risked his life for, dedicated his fortune, intirely, to defend that cause, and today finds himself in the most pennurous circumstances. He has no doubt that your honrable self will make a contribution to maintain an existance extreemly distressing to a military man of education and honour with wounds aplenty. Relying in advance on your feelings of humanity and on the interest which Madame la marquise takes in such an unhappy nation. Their prayer will not be in vane, and their gratitude will preserve her delightful memry.

* Latin, meaning 'four-faced'.

661

I have the honour, Madame, to be respecfully yours,

Don Alvarez, captain español de caballerie,

a royalist refugee in France who is journying on behalf of his country and is without the meens to continue his journy.

No address was attached to the signature. Marius hoped to find the address in the second letter, which had these words written on it: 'To Madame, Madame la comtesse de Montvernet, Rue Cassette, No. 9'.
This is what Marius read in the letter:

Madame la comtesse

This is a poor mother of a family of six children the littelest one only eight months old. I been sick since the last one was born, abandoned by my husband five months ago, with no meens of support wot soever in the most dredful povurty.

In her hopes of Madame la contesse, she has the honour to be, madame, with deep respect,

Balizard's wife.

Marius turned to the third letter, which was, like the previous ones, a begging letter. This is what it said:

Monsieur Pabourgeot, voter, wholesale hosiery merchant, Rue St-Denis on the corner of Rue aux Fers.

I take the liberty of sending you this letter to beg you to grant me the inestummable favour of your simpathies and to interest yourself in a man of letters who has just submitted a play to the Théâtre-Français. The subject is historical and the action takes place in the Auvergne in the days of the Empire. The style, I think, is natural, concise, and may have some merit. There are songs to be sung in four places. The comic, the serious and the unexpected are combined with a variety of characters and with a light touch of romanticism running through the whole plot, which develops misteriously, and after remarkable vississitudes is eventually ressolved with several dramatic twists.

My chief aim is to satisfie the desire that increasingly motivates the man of our age, that is to say, FASHION, that caprishus and bizarre weathervane, changing at almost every new wind.

In spite of these qualities I have reason to fear the jealousy, the self-regard of fayvoured authors may contrive to exclude me from the theatre, for I am not unaware of the bitter cup of disappointment served to newcomers.

Monsieuer Pabourgeot, your deserved reputation as enlightened paytron of men of letters emboldens me to send my daughter to explain to you our pennurous situation, in want of warmth and sustinance in this winter season. When I say that with your kind permission I would like to dedicate to you my play and all those that I shall write in future, this goes to show how greatly I aspyre to the honour of being taken under your wing and of gracing my writings with your name. If you deign to favour me with even the most modest offering, I shall immediately devote myself to writing a tribbute in verse to repay my debt of gratitude to you. This tribbute, which I shall endeavour to make as perfect as possible, will be sent to you before being inserted at the beginning of the play and recited on stage.

To Monsieur and Madame Pabourgeot,

My most respectful complements,

Genflot, man of letters

P.S. Even just forty sous.

Excuse me for sending my daughter and not calling on you myself but owing to regrettable shortcomings in matters of dress I am, alas, unable to go out . . .

Finally, Marius opened the fourth letter. It was addressed: 'To the charitable gentleman at the church of St-Jacques-du-Haut-Pas'. It contained these few lines:

Charitable benefactor,

If you condesend to accompany my daughter you will see wretched misfortune, and I shall show you my certificates.

When you see these documents your genrous soul will be stirred with a sense of tender-hearted benevolence, for true philosophers always feel keen emotion.

In your compassion you will surely agree that an individuwal must be suffring the cruellest deprivation, and that it is very distressing to have to get the authorities to vouch for it in order to obtain any relief, as though that individuwal was not free to suffer and die of stavation while waiting for his destatution to be relieved. Fate is very hard on some and excessively indulgent and coddling towards others.

I look forward to your visit or to any contribution you may condesend to make. You are a man of true generosity and I have the honour to be respectfully,

your very humble and very obedient servant

P. Fabantou, actor

After reading these four letters Marius was not much further advanced than before. In the first place, not one of the signatories gave an address. And then they seemed to come from four different individuals – Don Alvarez, Balizard's wife, the poet Genflot and the actor Fabantou – but the strange thing about these letters was that all four were in the same handwriting. What conclusion was to be drawn from this, if not that they all came from the same person?

Besides which – and making the above surmise even more probable – all four were written on the same rough, yellowed paper, the tobacco smell was the same, and although some attempt had evidently been made to vary the style the same spelling mistakes recurred with the utmost unconcern, and Genflot the man of letters was no more exempt from them than the Spanish captain.

Striving to solve this little mystery was a waste of effort. Had it not been an accidental find, this might have seemed like some sort of practical joke. Marius was too miserable to take a joke, even one played on him by chance, or to join in a game with the boulevard as it seemingly wanted him to. He felt like the blindfolded player in a game of blind man's buff, with these four letters teasing him.

Nor was there anything to show that these letters belonged to the young girls Marius had bumped into on the boulevard. After all, they were obviously worthless bits of papers. Marius replaced them in the envelope, tossed the whole lot aside and went to bed.

At about seven in the morning, he had just got up and had his breakfast and was trying to settle down to work when someone knocked quietly at his door.

As he owned nothing he never locked his door except sometimes, very rarely, when he was working on something that needed to be done urgently. Even when he went out he left his key in the lock. 'You'll be robbed,' said Mame Bougon. 'Of what?' said Marius. Yet the fact is, one day, to Mame Bougon's great triumph, he was robbed of an old pair of boots.

Someone knocked again, very quietly as before.

'Come in,' said Marius.

The door opened.

'What is it, Mame Bougon?' said Marius, without looking up from the books and manuscripts he had on his table.

A voice, which was not that of Mame Bougon, replied, 'Excuse me, monsieur.'

It was a hollow, cracked, husky, hoarse voice, an old man's voice roughened with brandy and other liquor.

Marius's head spun round, and he saw a young girl.

IV
A Rose in Distress

A very young girl was standing in the half-open doorway. The garret's dormer window at which daybreak was appearing was directly opposite the door and shed a wan light on this figure. She was a gaunt, sickly-looking, emaciated creature, nothing but a chemise and skirt covering her shivering ice-cold nakedness. A piece of string for a belt, a piece of string to tie her hair, angular shoulders protruding from her chemise, a blonde and lymphatic pallor, grubby collar-bones, reddened hands, a slack-jawed and spoiled mouth with teeth missing, lacklustre eyes, brazen and venal, the stunted body of a girl with the gaze of a corrupt old woman. A cross between a fifty-year-old and a fifteen-year-old. One of those creatures who are at once frail and horrible, causing those who are not made to weep at the sight of them to shudder.

Marius had risen and was staring in a kind of stupor at this creature who was almost like the shadowy figures that appear in dreams.

What was so sad was that this young girl was not born to be ugly. She must have been even pretty as an infant. The charm of youth was still fighting the hideous premature agedness of debauchery and poverty. A lingering trace of beauty was fading from that sixteen-year-old's face like that pale sunlight quenched beneath ominous clouds at dawn on a winter's day.

It was a face not wholly unknown to Marius. He seemed to remember having seen it somewhere.

'What is it, mademoiselle?' he asked.

The young girl replied in her drunken convict's voice, 'There's a letter for you, Monsieur Marius.'

She called Marius by his name. He could not doubt that he was the person she wanted to speak to. But who was this girl? How did she know his name?

Without waiting to be told, she came in. She came in determinedly, inspecting the whole room and the unmade bed with a kind of assurance that was heart-breaking. Her feet were bare. Her long legs and scraggy knees showed through large holes in her skirt. She was shivering.

She had indeed a letter in her hand, which she gave to Marius.

Marius noticed in opening this letter that the huge thick wafer seal was still moist. The message could not have come from very far. He read:

My dear neighbour, young man!

I have learned of the good turn you have done me, by paying my rent six months ago. Bless you, young man. My eldest daughter will tell you that we have been without a morsul of bread for two days, four of us, and my wife sick. If I am not deceved in my thinking, I believe there is every reason to hope that your genrous heart will be touched by this account and will compel in you the desire to do me the favour of condesending to make a small charitable donation.

With the distinguished respect due to the benefactors of humanity,

Jondrette.

P.S. My eldest daughter will wait for your instructions, dear Monsieur Marius.

Amid the mysterious circumstances that had been preoccupying Marius since the previous evening, this letter was like a candle in a cellar. Suddenly all was clear. This letter came from where those others came. It was the same handwriting, the same style, the same spelling, the same paper, the same tobacco smell.

There were five letters, five stories, five signatures, and just one signatory. The Spanish Captain Don Alvarez, poor Mère Balizard, the dramatic poet Genflot, the old actor Fabantou were all four named Jondrette, if indeed Jondrette himself was named Jondrette.

Although Marius had been living in that old house for quite a long time already, he had, as we have said, only very rarely had occasion to see his very few neighbours, or even to catch a glimpse of them. His mind was elsewhere, and where the mind is so too are the eyes. He must have passed the Jondrettes in the corridor or on the stairs more than once, but they were just indistinct figures to him. He had taken so little notice of them that he had bumped into the Jondrette girls on the boulevard the night before without recognizing them, for obviously that is who they were, and it was with great difficulty that this one, who had just entered his room, stirred in him, amid feelings of distaste and pity, a vague recollection of having come across her elsewhere.

Now he saw it all plainly. He understood that his neighbour Jondrette turned his hand in his distress to exploiting the charity of benevolent individuals, that he got hold of addresses and wrote under assumed names to people he judged to be wealthy and compassionate, letters that his daughters delivered at risk and peril to themselves, for this father had sunk so low he was willing to expose his daughters to danger. He was playing a game with fate, putting them at stake. Marius grasped that, judging by how they were running away the night before, by their breathlessness, their terror and those words he had overheard, spoken in argot, these poor girls were probably engaged in other squalid activities; and that what had resulted from all that, in the midst of human society such as it is, were two wretched creatures that were not children nor girls nor women but some sort of monster, at once foul and innocent, created by penury.

Nameless, sexless, sorry creatures of indeterminate age no longer capable of good or evil, who emerge from childhood with already nothing left in this world, no freedom, no virtue, no responsibility. Souls fresh-blown yesterday, faded today, like those flowers dropped in the street, sullied and blighted by all kinds of filth until some wheel crushes them.

Nevertheless, while Marius stared at her in pained surprise, the young girl was moving all about the garret with the audacity of a ghost. She darted to and fro, not bothered about her nakedness. Occasionally her unfastened, torn chemise dropped almost down to her waist. She shifted the chairs, she moved the wash basin and jug on the chest of drawers, she touched Marius's clothes, she poked about in the corners.

'Oh!' she said. 'You've got a mirror!'

And as if she were alone she hummed snatches of satirical songs, frivolous refrains that in her hoarse, throaty voice sounded doleful. Beneath this brazenness a suggestion of something forced, uneasy, abashed was detectable. Effrontery is a display of shame.

Nothing was more dismal than the sight of her cavorting and, as it were, flitting about the room like a bird frightened by daylight or afflicted with a broken wing. You felt that under other circumstances, had she been brought up to lead a different life, the playful and uninhibited behaviour of this young girl might have been something sweet and charming. In the animal world, never does the creature born to be a dove turn into a bird of prey. That is something you see only among humans.

With such thoughts in his mind, Marius did not stop her. She came up to the table.

'Ah,' she said, 'books!'

A gleam came into her glazed eyes. She spoke again, and the tone of her voice expressed that pleasure in being able to boast of something, one to which no human being is immune.

'I can read!'

She grabbed the open book on the table and read quite fluently: 'General Bauduin received orders to capture with the five battalions in his brigade the château of Hougomont, which stands in the middle of the plain of Waterloo—'

She broke off.

'Ah! Waterloo! I know about that. It was a battle some time ago. My father was there. My father served as a soldier. We're Bonapartists good and proper in our family, we are! It was against the English, Waterloo.'

She put the book down, picked up a pen, and exclaimed, 'And I can write as well!'

She dipped the pen in the ink, and turning to Marius, said, 'Do you want to see? Look, I'm going to write something to show you.'

And before he had time to answer, she wrote on a sheet of blank paper lying in the middle of the table: 'The bashers are here.'

Then she threw down the pen. 'There're no spelling mistakes. You can look. We've had some education, my sister and me. We haven't always been the way we are now. We weren't meant—'

Here she stopped, fixed her dull gaze on Marius and burst out laughing, saying in a tone that contained every anguish stifled by every cynicism, 'Bah!'

And she began to hum these words to a merry tune:

> My belly's empty, pa.
> The cupboard's bare.
> I'm perishing cold, ma.
> No woollens to wear.
> Shiver, little lass.
> Grizzle, little lad.

She had no sooner got to the end of this verse than she exclaimed, 'Do you ever go to the theatre, Monsieur Marius? I do. I've got a little brother who's friends with the actors, and he sometimes gives me tickets. But I don't like the benches up in the gods. You feel cramped and uncomfortable up there. You sometimes get some rough customers. Some smelly customers, too.'

Then she considered Marius, adopted a strange air and said, 'You know, Monsieur Marius, you're a good-looking fellow?'

And the same thought occurred to them both at the same moment, making her smile and him blush. She came up close to him and laid her hand on his shoulder.

'You don't take any notice of me but I know you, Monsieur Marius. I pass you here on the staircase, and then I see you sometimes, when I'm wandering over that way, visiting someone by the name of Père Mabeuf who lives round Austerlitz. It really suits you, that untidy hair of yours.'

Her voice tried to be very soft but succeeded only in being very deep. Some of her words were lost in passing from her larynx to her lips, as on a keyboard that has notes missing.

Marius had quietly stepped back.

'Mademoiselle,' he said with that cold seriousness of his, 'I have here a packet that is yours, I believe. Allow me to return it to you.'

And he held out the envelope with the four letters enclosed.

She clapped her hands and cried, 'We searched everywhere!'

Then she grabbed the packet and opened the envelope, saying, 'God Almighty! Did we search, my sister and me! You were the one that found it! On the boulevard, of course? It must have been on the boulevard? You see, it fell when we ran. It was my little sister's fault. When we got home we hadn't got it any more. Since we didn't want to be beaten – there's no point, absolutely no point, no point at all in that – we said back home we'd delivered the letters to the various people and we'd drawn a blank. And here they are, those poor letters! So how did you know they were mine? Ah! yes, the handwriting. So it was you we bumped into last night. We couldn't see, could we! I said to my sister, "Was that a gentleman?" My sister said, "I think it was."'

Meanwhile, she had unfolded the petition addressed to 'the charitable gentleman at the church of St-Jacques-du-Haut-Pas'.

'Well fancy that!' she said. 'This is the one for that old man who goes to mass. In fact, now's the time. I'm going to take it to him. Perhaps he'll give us something for breakfast.'

Then she began to laugh again and added, 'If we have breakfast today, do you know what that means? It means we'll have had the day before yesterday's breakfast, the day before yesterday's dinner, yesterday's breakfast and yesterday's dinner, all in one go, this morning! And by God, if you don't like it, drop dead, you curs!'

This reminded Marius why the poor thing had come to him. He fumbled in his waistcoat pocket and found nothing there. The young girl carried on, and seemed to be talking as if no longer aware that Marius was there.

'Sometimes I go off in the evening. Sometimes I don't come back at night. Last winter, before we came here, we lived under the arches of the bridges. We huddled together so as not to freeze. My little sister cried. Water's so mournful! Whenever I thought of drowning myself I'd say, "No, it's too cold." I go out on my own when I want to, I sometimes sleep in a ditch. You know, at night, when I walk along the boulevard, I see the trees as gibbets, the houses look all huge and black like the towers of Notre-Dame, I imagine the white walls are the river and I say to myself, "Why, that's water there!" The stars are like smoking lanterns blown out by the wind, I'm in a daze, as if there were horses breathing in my ears. Although it's night I can hear barrel-organs and spinning-machines, or something. I think someone's throwing stones at me, I run away without knowing for sure, everything's spinning, spinning. It's very peculiar when you haven't eaten.'

And she stared at him with a look of bewilderment.

By digging deep into his pockets Marius had eventually come up with five francs and sixteen sous. It was all he had at that moment.

'This will get me my meal today, at any rate,' he thought, 'and we'll see about tomorrow.'

He kept the sixteen sous and handed the five francs to the girl. She grabbed the coin.

'Good!' she said. 'A bit of sunshine!'

And as if the sun had the capacity to melt avalanches of slang in her brain, she went on, 'Five francs! A shiner! A monarch! In this shack! Splendiferous! You're a true pal! My ticker's touched! Bravo, comrades! Two days' red! And belly timber! And hash! We'll treat ourselves! To good grub!'

She pulled her chemise up to her shoulders, gave Marius a low bow, then a familiar wave of the hand, and headed towards the door, saying, 'Good day, monsieur. Never mind. I'm off to find my old man.'

As she passed the chest of drawers she noticed a stale crust of bread mouldering there in the dust. She pounced on it and bit into it, muttering, 'That tastes good! It's hard! I'll break my teeth on it!'

Then she was gone.

V

The Providential Spy-hole

Marius had lived for five years in poverty, hardship, even distress, but he now realized he had not known true misery. True misery was what he had seen just now. It was this spectre that had just passed before his eyes. Anyone who has seen only a man in misery has seen nothing, he needs to see a woman in misery. Anyone who has seen only a woman in misery has seen nothing, he needs to see a child in misery.

When a man has been brought to the last extremity, he comes at the same time to his last resources. Woe to the defenceless beings around him! Work, wages, bread, warmth, courage, goodwill – he lacks all of these at once. The light of day seems to fail without, the moral light within. In this darkness man encounters the weakness of woman and child, and brutally exploits them for ignominious purposes.

Then every horror is conceivable. Despair is surrounded with flimsy walls, with vice or crime on the other side of all of them.

Health, youth, honour, the shy and saintly sensibilities of still untried flesh, the heart, virginity, modesty, that epidermis of the soul, are sinisterly manipulated by that groping after resources that meets with opprobrium and comes to terms with it. Fathers, mothers, children, brothers, sisters, men, women, girls, come together, and almost like a mineral formation become one, in that murky promiscuity of gender, relationship, age, infamy and innocence. They squat, back to back in the wretchedness of their fate. They eye each other mournfully. Oh, those poor people! How pale they are! How cold they are! They seem to be on a planet much further from the sun than ours.

This young girl was for Marius a kind of messenger from the dark. She revealed to him a whole hideous side of night.

Marius almost reproached himself for the daydreams and the love that had preoccupied him, preventing him until today from taking a look at his neighbours. Paying their rent was an automatic gesture, anyone else would have done the same. But he, Marius, should have done better. What! Only a wall separated him from these forsaken individuals, leading a groping existence in the dark, excluded from the rest of humanity; he rubbed shoulders with them, he was in a way the last link with the human race they were in contact with; he heard them living, or rather agonizing, alongside him, and he took no notice! Every moment of every day he could hear them through the wall, moving about, coming and going, talking, and he paid no attention! And in those words were groans, and he did not even listen. His mind was elsewhere, in dreams, impossible joys, fantasies of love, wild conceits. And meanwhile other human beings, his brothers in Jesus Christ, his brothers in the people, agonized beside him, agonized in vain! He was even part of their misfortune, and he made it worse. For had they had a different neighbour, a less fanciful and more attentive neighbour, an ordinary and charitable man, obviously their penury would have been noticed, their signals of distress would have been perceived, and perhaps long ago help would have been given to them and they would have been saved! They seemed very depraved, very corrupt, very debased – heinous, even – but rare are those who fall without sinking into vice. In any case, there is a point where the poor and the wicked become mixed up and lumped together in the one fateful word: *les misérables* – the wretched. Whose fault is this? And besides, should not charity be all the greater, the further into the depths the fall?

While lecturing himself in this way – for there were times when

Marius, like all truly honest souls, was his own tutor and scolded himself more than he deserved – he stared at the wall that separated him from the Jondrettes, as if he might be able to see through this partition with his eyes full of pity, and comfort those poor wretches. The wall was a thin layer of plaster held together on laths and beams, and as the reader has just learned, it allowed the sound of voices and words to be heard perfectly clearly. It took a dreamer like Marius not to have noticed this before. There was no paper pasted on this wall, either on the Jondrettes' side or Marius's. The coarse fabric of the building was exposed to view. Almost unconsciously Marius examined the partition. Sometimes the wandering mind examines, observes and scrutinizes in the same way as the thinking mind. Suddenly he was on his feet. He had just noticed up at the top, near the ceiling, a triangular hole resulting from three laths with a gap between them. The plaster that should have filled this gap was missing, and by climbing on to the chest of drawers you could see through this opening into the Jondrettes' garret. Commiseration has its curiosity, and so it should. This gap formed a kind of spy-hole. Spying on misfortune in order to relieve it is permissible.

'Let's take a look and see what these people are like,' thought Marius, 'and what their situation is.' He climbed on the chest of drawers, put his eye to the hole, and looked.

VI
The Wild Man in His Lair

Cities, like forests, have their dens, and inside them lurks whatever they have that is most savage and fearsome. Only, in cities, what lurks there is ferocious, foul and small, that is to say, ugly. In forests, what lurks there is ferocious, wild and big, that is to say, beautiful. Den for den, that of the beasts is preferable to that of men. Caves are better than slums.

What Marius saw was a slum. Marius was poor and his room was meagre, but just as his poverty was noble, his garret was clean. The room he looked down on was abject, dirty, fetid, squalid, dark, sordid. The only furniture, a straw-bottomed chair, a rickety table, some bits of old crockery and, in two corners, two indescribable pallets. The only source of light, a four-paned dormer window draped with spiders' webs. Just enough daylight came through this window to make a man's face appear like a ghost's. And like a face disfigured by some horrible disease, the walls were peeling and covered with welts and scars. A rheumy moisture seeped from them. Obscene drawings could be discerned, crudely sketched on them in charcoal.

The room Marius occupied had a dilapidated brick floor; this one was neither tiled nor planked. You walked directly on the old concrete of the tumbledown building, which had grown black underfoot. On this uneven floor – encrusted, as it were, with dirt; innocent only of the broom – were arbitrarily grouped constellations of old socks, worn-out shoes and frightful rags. This room also had a fireplace, so it was let for forty francs a year. There was everything in that fireplace, a stove, a cooking-pot, some broken planks, some tattered clothes hung on nails, a bird-cage, ashes, and even a little fire. The remains of two logs were smouldering sadly.

One thing that further added to the horror of this garret was that it was large. It had protrusions and angles and dark recesses, the underside of sloping roofs, bays and promontories. Hence ghastly fathomless corners where, it seemed, spiders as big as your fist, wood-lice the size of your foot and perhaps even some sort of monstrous human beings must be lurking.

One of the pallets lay by the door, the other by the window. Both were adjacent to the fireplace at one end, facing Marius.

In a corner near the hole Marius was looking through, a coloured engraving with 'THE DREAM' written in large letters underneath it was hanging on the wall in a black wooden frame. It represented a sleeping woman and in the woman's lap a sleeping child, an eagle in a cloud with a crown in its beak; and the woman, not even awake, waving the crown away from the child's head. In the background, Napoleon in a halo of glory rested against a big blue column with a yellow capital and bearing this inscription:

MARINGO

AUSTERLITS

IENA

WAGRAMME

ELOT

Standing on the floor, propped up against the wall underneath this picture, was a wooden panel of sorts, taller than it was wide. It could have been a painting turned face to the wall, a mounted canvas probably with some daub on the other side of it, a big mirror that had been taken down from some wall and left there, forgotten, waiting to be rehung.

Near the table, on which Marius saw a pen, ink and paper, sat a man of about sixty, small, thin, pale, gaunt, with a cunning, cruel, nervous look about him. A nasty piece of work. If Lavater had studied this face he would have identified in it the vulture crossed with the lawyer; the raptor and the pettifogger bringing out the worst in each other and complementing each other; the pettifogger making the raptor ignoble, the raptor making the pettifogger dreadful.

This man had a long, grey beard. He wore a woman's chemise that revealed his hairy chest and his bare arms covered with grey hairs. You could see below this chemise a pair of muddy trousers and boots with his toes sticking out of them. He had a pipe in his mouth and was smoking. There was no bread in the place, but there was still some tobacco left. He was writing, probably another letter like the ones Marius had read.

On the corner of the table could be seen a single shabby reddish-coloured volume whose size – the old 12mo of subscription libraries – revealed it to be a novel. Displayed on the cover was the following title printed in big capital letters: 'GOD, THE KING, HONOUR AND THE LADIES BY DUCRAY-DUMINIL. 1814'.

The man spoke out loud as he wrote, and Marius heard what he was saying.

'To think there's no equality even when you're dead! Just look at Père-Lachaise! The bigwigs, the ones who are rich, are at the top, on Allée des Acacias – that's paved! They can get there in a carriage. The nobodies, the people without, poor wretches in other words, they're put down at the bottom where there's mud up to your knees, in graves where it's damp. They're put there so they'll rot quicker! You can't go and see them without sinking into the ground.'

He paused, banged the table with his fist and, grinding his teeth, added, 'Oh! I'd devour those people!'

A big woman, who could have been aged forty or a hundred, was squatting by the fireplace on her bare heels. She, too, wore only a chemise and a knitted skirt patched with bits of old cloth. A coarse linen apron concealed half her skirt. Although this woman was bent and doubled up, you could tell she was tall. She was something of a giant next to her husband. She had hideous hair of a greying reddish-blonde that she gathered up now and again in her huge glistening hands with their flat fingernails. Lying open beside her on the floor was a volume of the same format as the other, probably of the same novel. On one of the pallets Marius could just see a pale, lanky young girl, sitting there half naked with her feet dangling, who looked as if she was not listening, apparently insentient, inanimate. Probably the younger sister of the one who had come to his room.

She looked eleven or twelve years old. On closer scrutiny you realized she must be fifteen. This was the child who had said on the boulevard the night before, 'I scarpered!'

She was of that puny type that remains underdeveloped for a long time, then suddenly shoots up. It is poverty that produces these sorry human plants. These creatures have no childhood or adolescence. At fifteen years of age they look twelve, at sixteen they look twenty. Little girls today, women tomorrow. They seem to take life in big strides so as to get through it faster. Right now this creature looked like a child.

There was no sign of any work going on in this place. No loom, no spinning-wheel, no implement of any kind. In one corner lay some dubious-looking bits of old iron. It is this dreary idleness that comes in the wake of despair and precedes the death throes.

Marius spent a while observing this grim interior, more terrifying than that of a tomb, for you could sense the human soul stirring here, and the pulse of life.

The garret, the cellar, the dungeon where some poor wretches crawl about at the very bottom of the social edifice is not quite the burial chamber, it is its antechamber. But like those rich people who display their greatest magnificence in the entrance hall of their palaces, death, in the next room, seems to place its most abject miseries in that vestibule.

The man had fallen silent, the woman said nothing, the young girl seemed not to be breathing. The scratching of pen on paper could be heard. Without ceasing to write, the man growled, 'Scum! Scum! All is scum!'

This variation on Solomon's dictum* drew a sigh from the woman.

'Calm down, sweetheart,' she said. 'Don't upset yourself, dearest. You're too good to write to all those people, my pet.'

Bodies huddle together in misery, as they do in the cold, but hearts grow apart. There was every indication this woman must have loved this man as much as she was capable of loving, but probably, in the mutual, daily accusations of blame for the dreadful hardship weighing on the whole family, that had been extinguished. She had nothing left for her husband but cinders of affection. Yet, as is often the case,

---

* Traditionally, Solomon was thought to be the author of the Book of Ecclesiastes, and therefore of the dictum, 'Vanity of vanities, all is vanity' (Ecclesiastes 1:2).

endearments had survived. Her lips spoke the words 'dearest', 'sweet-heart', 'my pet' and so forth, while her heart remained silent.

The man went on writing.

VII
Strategy and Tactics

Feeling heavy-hearted, Marius was about to climb down from the observatory of sorts that he had improvised, when a noise attracted his attention and made him stay where he was.

The door of the attic had just burst open. The eldest girl appeared on the threshold. She had on her feet a man's heavy shoes spattered with mud that had reached right up to her reddened ankles, and she was wrapped in a tattered old cloak that Marius had not seen her with an hour earlier but that she had probably left outside his door to make him feel sorrier for her, and that she must have collected when she went out. She came in, pushed the door shut behind her, paused to catch her breath, for she was panting, then cried with an expression of triumph and joy, 'He's coming!'

The father looked round, the woman turned round, the little sister did not stir.

'Who?' said the father.

'The gentleman!'

'The philanthropist?'

'Yes.'

'From the church of St-Jacques?'

'Yes.'

'The old man?'

'Yes.'

'And he's coming here?'

'He's following me.'

'You're sure?'

'I'm sure.'

'You mean he's coming right now?'

'In a cab.'

'In a cab! It's Rothschild!'

The father stood up.

'How can you be sure? If he's coming in a cab how is it you got here before him? You did give him the address at least? You did tell him it was the last door on the right at the end of the corridor? Let's hope he doesn't get it wrong! So you found him at the church? Did he read my letter? What did he say to you?'

'Whoa!' said the girl. 'Not so fast, old man! It was like this: I went inside the church, he was in his usual place, I greeted him politely and handed him the letter, he read it and said, "Where do you live, my child?" I said, "Monsieur, I'll take you there." He said, "No, give me your address, my daughter has some shopping to do, I'll take a cab and I'll get to your house at the same time as you." I gave him the address. When I told him which house it was he seemed surprised, and hesitated for a bit, then he said, "It makes no difference, I'll go." At the end of the mass I saw him leave the church with his daughter, and I saw them climb into a cab. And I did tell him, the last door on the right at the end of the corridor.'

'And what makes you think he'll come?'

'I just saw the cab turning into Rue du Petit-Banquier. That's what made me run.'

'How do you know it was the same cab?'

'Because I'd taken note of the number!'

'What was that number?'

'Four forty.'

'Good, you're a smart girl.'

The girl stared boldly at her father, and pointing to the shoes she had on her feet she said, 'A smart girl, maybe, but I tell you, I've had enough of these shoes, I won't wear them again. First for my own safety, second to keep clean. I don't know anything more maddening than soles that leak and go glup, glup, glup the whole way. I'd rather go barefoot.'

'You're right,' said her father in a smooth voice that contrasted with the young girl's brashness, 'but then you wouldn't be allowed inside the churches. The poor have to wear shoes. You can't go barefoot in the house of God,' he added bitterly.

Then returning to the subject that preoccupied him: 'And you're sure now, sure he's coming?'

'He's right behind me,' she said.

The man stiffened. There was some sort of brightness illuminating his face.

'Wife!' he cried. 'Do you hear? The philanthropist's coming. Put out the fire!'

The mother, dumbfounded, did not stir. With the agility of an acrobat the father grabbed a broken-lipped jug from the mantelpiece and threw water on the logs. Then to his elder daughter he said, 'You! Break up the seat of that chair!'

His daughter did not understand. He seized the chair and with one kick made a seatless chair of it. His leg went right through it. As he withdrew his leg he asked his daughter, 'Is it cold?'

'Very cold. It's snowing.'

The father turned to the younger girl sitting on the pallet near the window, and thundered at her, 'Quick! Get off that bed, you lazybones! Will you never do a thing! Break a window-pane!'

The child leapt off the bed, shivering.

'Break a window-pane!' he repeated.

The child was nonplussed.

'Do you hear me?' the father insisted. 'I told you to break a window-pane!'

With a kind of terrified obedience the child stood on tip-toe and struck at a pane with her fist. The glass broke and fell with a crash.

'Good,' said the father.

He was solemn and abrupt. His eyes swept rapidly over every corner of the garret. He looked like a general making his final preparations just as the battle is about to begin.

The mother, who had so far said nothing, now rose, and in words that came out sounding almost expressionless asked in a slow, dull voice, 'What are you trying to do, dear?'

'Get into bed,' replied the man. His tone of voice allowed for no discussion. The mother obeyed and threw herself heavily on to one of the pallets. Meanwhile, a sob could be heard from somewhere.

'What is it?' cried the father.

Without emerging from the shadows where she was cowering, the younger daughter showed her bleeding hand. She had cut herself breaking the window. She had gone over to her mother's bedside and was weeping silently.

It was now the mother's turn to sit up and cry, 'Now look what you've gone and done! She's cut herself breaking that window-pane of yours!'

'So much the better!' said the man. 'That was the idea.'

'What do you mean? So much the better?' replied his wife.

'Quiet!' retorted the father. 'I'm suppressing the freedom of the press.'

Then tearing at the woman's chemise he was wearing, he made a strip of cloth with which he hastily swathed the child's bleeding hand. That done, his eye fell with satisfaction on his torn chemise.

'And the chemise too,' he said. 'It all looks good.'

A chill wind was whistling at the window and blowing into the room. The fog came in from outside, spreading through the room like whitish cotton wool teased out by invisible fingers. Through the broken window-pane the snow could be seen falling. The cold weather promised by the Candlemas sunshine the day before had indeed arrived.

The father glanced around as if to make sure that he had not forgotten anything. He picked up an old shovel and spread ashes over the wet logs to hide them completely.

Then drawing himself up and leaning against the chimneypiece he said, 'Now we're ready for the philanthropist.'

VIII
The Ray of Light in the Slum

The older girl came up to him and laid her hand on her father's. 'Feel how cold I am,' she said.

'Bah!' replied the father. 'I'm much colder than that.'

The mother cried vehemently, 'You always have to go one better than everyone else! Even in suffering.'

'That's enough!' said the man.

Having been given a certain look the mother held her tongue. There was a moment of silence in the room. The older girl was nonchalantly brushing the mud off the bottom of her cloak, her little sister was still sobbing. The mother had taken the child's head in her hands and was covering it with kisses, saying under her breath, 'My treasure, please, it's nothing, don't cry, you're going to make your father angry.'

'No!' cried the father. 'On the contrary! Bawl! Bawl! It creates the right effect.'

Then, turning to the older girl, 'Well, where is he then? If he doesn't come now! I'd have put out my fire, wrecked my chair, torn my shirt and broken my window-pane all for nothing.'

'And hurt the child!' murmured the mother.

'You know,' the father went on, 'it's blasted cold in this hellish place! What if that man doesn't come! Oh! That's it! He's keeping us waiting! He says to himself, "Well now, they can wait for me! That's what they're there for." Oh! how I hate those rich folk! And how I could strangle them all! With jubilation, joy, enthusiasm, satisfaction! Those supposedly charitable men who pretend to be so pious, who go to mass, who hobnob with preachy priests, with churchy types, and think they're better than us, and come to humiliate us, and bring us clothes – well, that's what they call them! Old cast-offs worth nothing! And bread! That's not what I want, you heap of scum! It's cash! Ah! Never cash! Because they say we'd just go and drink it, that we're sots and idlers! What about them? What are they, then? And what have they been in their day! Thieves! They'd never have got rich, otherwise! Oh! Society ought to be taken by the four corners like a tablecloth and the whole lot tossed in the air! Everything would be destroyed, most likely, but at least no one would have anything, and so much the better! But what's keeping him, then, that churl of a charitable gentleman of yours? Will he come? Maybe the idiot's forgotten the address! I bet the old fool—'

At that moment someone tapped at the door. The man rushed to open it, exclaiming with deep bows and adoring smiles, 'Come in, monsieur! Do us the honour, virtuous benefactor, and your charming young lady too.'

A man of mature years and a young girl appeared in the doorway of the garret. Marius had not left his place. What he felt at that moment no human words can express.

It was She!

Anyone who has ever loved knows the full glorious implications contained in the three letters of that word: She.

She it was, indeed. Marius could hardly distinguish her through the luminous mist that suddenly came down over his eyes. It was that sweet creature who had gone missing, that star that had glimmered for six months, it was those eyes, that brow, that mouth, that lovely face that had vanished, leaving darkness in its wake. The vision had gone into eclipse and was now making its reappearance.

It made its reappearance in that dinginess, in that garret, in that ghastly slum, in that frightfulness.

Marius shook uncontrollably. What! It was she! The racing of his heart blurred his sight. He felt on the verge of dissolving into tears! What! He was seeing her again at last, after having searched for her for so long! It was as if he had lost his soul and had just found it again.

She was the same as ever, only a little pale. Her delicate face was framed by a purple velvet hood, her figure was shrouded in a fur-trimmed black satin cloak. Her tiny foot laced in a silk ankle-boot could be glimpsed under her full-length dress.

She was still accompanied by Monsieur Leblanc. She had taken a few steps into the room and had set down quite a large parcel on the table.

The older Jondrette girl had retreated behind the door and was staring dolefully at that velvet hood, that silk mantle and that lovely blessed face.

IX
Jondrette Almost Weeps

It was so dark, that hovel, that people coming in from outside felt as if they were entering a cellar. So the two newcomers stepped forward with a certain hesitation, barely able to make out the vague figures around them, whereas they themselves were perfectly visible to the eyes of the garret's inhabitants, accustomed to this gloom, and were subjected to their inspection.

With that sad but kindly expression in his eyes, Monsieur Leblanc approached Jondrette the father and said to him, 'Monsieur, in this parcel you'll find some new clothes, some woollen stockings and blankets.'

'Our angelic benefactor is more than generous,' said Jondrette, bowing right down to the ground. Then, leaning over to whisper quickly in his elder daughter's ear while the two visitors were examining the deplorable abode, he added, 'Eh? What did I say? Cast-offs! No cash! They're all the same! By the way, how was the letter to this old fool signed?'

'Fabantou,' replied the girl.

'The actor, good!'

Just as well that Jondrette asked, for at that very moment Monsieur Leblanc turned to him and said in the manner of someone trying to remember a name, 'I see that you are greatly to be pitied, Monsieur—'

'Fabantou,' replied Jondrette promptly.

'Monsieur Fabantou, yes, that's it, I remember now.'

'Actor, monsieur, and one who has had some success.'

At this point Jondrette evidently thought the moment had come to exert his influence over the 'philanthropist'. He cried out in a tone that at one and the same time had the ring of the charlatan's fairground patter and the humbleness of the mendicant who plies the highways.

'A pupil of Talma, monsieur! I'm a pupil of Talma! Fortune once smiled on me. Alas! It's now the turn of misfortune. You see, my charitable friend, no bread, no fire. My poor babes without a fire! My only chair in need of repair! A broken window-pane! In weather like this! My wife in bed! Sick!'

'Poor woman!' said Monsieur Leblanc.

'My child hurt!' added Jondrette.

Distracted by the arrival of these strangers, the child had started staring at 'the young lady' and had stopped sobbing.

'Cry, then!' Jondrette whispered to her. 'Go on, bawl!'

At the same time he pinched her sore hand. All this with a conjuror's dexterity. The little girl howled.

The adorable young lady that in his heart Marius called 'his Ursule' darted over to her.

'Poor dear child!' she said.

'Look at her bleeding wrist, my beautiful young lady,' Jondrette went on. 'It's the result of an accident that happened while working at a machine to earn six sous a day. She may have to have her arm cut off.'

'Really?' said the old gentleman in alarm.

Taking what had been said seriously, the little girl started bawling again even louder.

'Alas! yes, my charitable friend!' replied the father.

For several moments now Jondrette had been looking at 'the philanthropist' in a bizarre way. As he spoke he seemed to be studying the other man closely as if trying to summon up memories. Taking advantage of a moment when the newcomers were engrossed in questioning the child about her injured hand, he suddenly moved close to his wife, who lay in bed looking crushed and stupid, and said to her sharply and very quietly, 'Take a good look at that man!'

Then turning to Monsieur Leblanc, he continued his lament. 'You see, monsieur! All I have to cover myself is a chemise belonging to my wife! And all torn, at that! In the middle of winter! I can't go out for lack of a coat. If I had a coat of any kind I'd go and see Mademoiselle Mars, who knows me and is very fond of me. Isn't she still living in Rue de la Tour-des-Dames? You know, monsieur, we played together in the provinces. I shared her laurels. Célimène would come to my assistance, monsieur! Elmire would give alms to Belisarius! But no, nothing! And not a sou in the house! My wife ill, not a sou! My daughter seriously injured, not a sou! My wife suffers from breathlessness. It's her age, and her nervous system has also been affected. She needs help, and my daughter too! But the doctor! And the chemist! How am I to pay them? Not a centime. I'd go down on my knees for ten centimes, monsieur! That's what the arts are reduced to. And do you know, my dear young lady, and you, my generous patron, do you know? You who radiate virtue and goodness and who bring the odour of sanctity to that church where my daughter, who goes there to say her prayers, sees you every day – for I've brought up my children religiously, monsieur. I didn't want them to go on the stage. Ah! the little minxes! If I catch them stepping out of line! It's no joke as far as I'm concerned! I give them an earful about honour, morality, virtue! Ask them! They've got to keep to the straight and narrow. They have a father. They're not like those poor girls who start out with no family and end up married to the public. The ones that are Mam'selle Nobody and turn into Madame Everybody. Good Lord! None of that in the Fabantou family! I mean to bring them up virtuously, and for them to be honest and kind and believe in God. By heaven! – Well now, monsieur, my worthy friend, do you know what's going to happen tomorrow? Tomorrow is the fourth of February, the fateful day, the day when my landlord's patience finally runs out. If by this evening I haven't paid him, tomorrow my oldest daughter, myself, my wife with her fever, my child with her injury, all four of us will be evicted from here, cast out on to the street, on to the boulevard, without shelter, in the rain, in the snow. That's the fact of the matter, monsieur. I owe for four quarters, a whole year! That's to say, sixty francs.'

Jondrette was lying. Four quarters would have been only forty francs, and it could not be four he owed because not six months earlier Marius had paid for two.

Monsieur Leblanc pulled five francs out of his pocket and put them on the table.

Jondrette had time to mutter in his eldest daughter's ear, 'Bastard! What does he expect me to do with his five francs? That won't pay for my chair and window-pane! Come on, shell out!'

Meanwhile, Monsieur Leblanc had removed the heavy brown great-coat he was wearing over his blue frock-coat, and had thrown it over the back of the chair.

'Monsieur Fabantou,' he said, 'all I have with me are these five francs, but I'm going to take my daughter home and I'll come back this evening. It's this evening, isn't it, that you must pay by?'

Jondrette's face lit up with a strange expression. He replied eagerly, 'Yes, my respected friend. I must be at my landlord's at eight o'clock.'

'I'll be here at six and I'll bring you the sixty francs.'

'My benefactor!' Jondrette exclaimed with emotion. And he added under his breath, 'Take a good look at him, wife!'

Monsieur Leblanc took the beautiful girl's arm again and turned towards the door. 'Until this evening, my friends,' he said.

'Six o'clock?' said Jondrette.

'Six o'clock sharp.'

At that moment the overcoat lying on the chair caught the eye of the elder Jondrette girl. 'You're forgetting your coat, monsieur,' she said.

With a fearsome shrug of the shoulders, Jondrette glared at his daughter.

Monsieur Leblanc turned back and said with a smile, 'I'm not forgetting it, I'm leaving it.'

'O my patron!' said Jondrette. 'My august benefactor, I'm reduced to tears! Allow me to see you to your carriage.'

'If you come out,' replied Monsieur Leblanc, 'wear the coat. It's really very cold.'

Jondrette did not need to be told twice. He had the brown overcoat on in no time. And all three went out, Jondrette preceding the two strangers.

X

Licensed Cab Fare: Two Francs an Hour

Marius had missed nothing of this entire scene and yet he had actually seen nothing. His eyes had remained fixed on the girl, his heart had, so to speak, alighted on her and completely enveloped her from the moment she first stepped into that garret. The whole time she was there he had been in that state of ecstasy that suspends material perceptions and focuses the soul totally on a single particular. He contemplated not that girl but that luminescence, in a satin cloak and velvet hood. The star Sirius might have entered the room, and he would not have been any the more dazzled.

While the girl was opening the package, unfolding the clothing and blankets, questioning the sick mother with kindness and the injured child with sympathy, he watched her every movement, he tried to catch her words. He was familiar with her eyes, her brow, her beauty, her figure, the way she moved; he was not familiar with the sound of her voice. He thought he had once caught a few words in the Luxembourg Gardens but was not absolutely sure. He would have given ten years of his life to hear it, to be able to carry away in his heart a little of that music. But everything was drowned out by Jondrette's trumpetings and maudlin demonstrations. This brought genuine anger to Marius's rapture. He gazed longingly at her. He could not believe it really was that divine creature he was seeing among these vile beings in this monstrous slum. It was like seeing a hummingbird among toads.

When she left the room he had only one thought, to follow her, to remain on her trail, not to leave her without knowing where she lived, at least not to lose her again after having so miraculously found her. He jumped down from the chest of drawers and grabbed his hat. As he laid his hand on the door latch and was about to go out something occurred to him that stopped him. The corridor was long, the stair-

684

case steep, Jondrette talkative, Monsieur Leblanc probably not yet in his carriage. If he were to turn round in the corridor or on the staircase or on the doorstep, and were to catch sight of Marius in that house, obviously he would be alarmed and contrive to elude him once more, and that would be the end all over again. What was he to do? Wait a while? But in the meantime the carriage might drive off. Marius was in a quandary. At last he took the risk of emerging from his room.

There was no one in the corridor. He hurried to the staircase. There was no one on the stairs. He raced down and reached the boulevard in time to see a cab turning the corner of Rue du Petit-Banquier and heading back into Paris.

Marius ran in that direction. When he reached the corner of the boulevard he saw the cab speeding along Rue Mouffetard. The cab was already very distant, impossible to catch up with. What? Run after it? Out of the question. And besides, someone running after a cab as fast as his legs could carry him would certainly be noticed by those inside it, and the father would recognize him. At that moment, by an unbelievable stroke of wonderful good fortune, Marius saw a two-wheeled cab for hire passing along the boulevard. There was only one thing to do, take the lighter cab and follow the other. It was reliable, efficient, safe.

Marius waved to the cabman to stop and called out to him, 'By the hour!'

Marius was without a cravat, he had on his old work coat which had buttons missing, his shirt was torn along one of the folds across the chest.

The cabman stopped, winked, and extended his left hand towards Marius, gently rubbing his forefinger with his thumb.

'What is it?' said Marius.

'Pay in advance,' said the cabman.

Marius remembered he had only sixteen sous on him.

'How much?' he asked.

'Forty sous.'

'I'll pay when we get back.'

The driver's sole response was to whistle the tune of 'La Palisse' and whip his horse on.

Distraught, Marius watched the cab drive off. For the sake of twenty-four sous that he did not have, his joy, his happiness, his love were lost to him! He was plunged back into darkness. He had regained his sight, and now he was to be blind again. He thought bitterly and, it must be said, with deep regret of the five francs he had given away to that wretched girl that same morning. With those five francs he would have been saved, born again: he would have emerged from limbo and from darkness, escaped isolation and angst and bereavement for his lost love; he would have retied the black thread of his destiny to the beautiful gold thread that had just floated before his eyes and had broken once again! He returned to the house in despair.

He might have told himself that Monsieur Leblanc had promised to return that evening, and that he need only be better prepared this time to follow him, but so rapt in contemplation had he been that he barely heard this.

As he was about to climb the stairs he noticed on the other side of the boulevard, in a lonely spot by the wall on Rue de la Barrière-des-Gobelins, Jondrette, wrapped in the 'philanthropist's' overcoat, talking to one of those unnerving-looking fellows commonly called 'prowlers at the gates', shifty-looking characters whose talk is louche, who appear ill-intentioned and who fairly regularly sleep during the day, which suggests they work by night.

Those two men, standing there motionless, chatting together under flurries of falling snow, formed a pair that would surely have drawn a policeman's attention but that Marius scarcely noticed.

Still, sadly preoccupied as he was, he could not help noticing that the prowler at the gates whom Jondrette was talking to looked like a certain Panchaud, alias Printanier, alias Bigrenaille, that Courfeyrac had once pointed out to him and who was regarded locally as a pretty dangerous night stalker. We have come across this man's name in the preceding book. This Panchaud, alias Printanier, alias Bigrenaille, featured later in several criminal trials and has since become a celebrated scoundrel. At the time he was merely a notorious scoundrel. Today he is something of a legend among villains and cut-throats. He gained a following towards the end of the last reign. And in the evening, at nightfall, when groups would form and talk in whispers, he was the topic of conversation in the Lions' Den at La Force. In that prison, at the exact spot where the latrine sewer, used in 1843 in the unprecedented break-out in broad daylight of thirty prisoners, passes under the guards' patrol path, you may even read his name, 'PANCHAUD', audaciously carved by his own hand into the patrol-path wall above the latrine cover slab during one of his attempted escapes. In 1832, the police already had their eye on him, but his career had not yet seriously begun.

XI
Destitution Offers to Help Misery

Marius plodded up the stairs of the old house. Just as he was about to go back into his cell he became aware of the elder Jondrette girl behind him, following him down the corridor. The girl was a detestable sight to him. She was the one who had his five francs. It was too late to ask for them back, the two-wheeled cab was gone, the other was far away. She would not have given them back to him anyway. As for questioning her about where the people who had just been there lived, that was pointless. It was obvious she did not know, since the letter signed 'Fabantou' was addressed to 'the charitable gentleman at the church of St-Jacques-du-Haut-Pas'.

Marius went into his room and pushed the door to behind him. It did not close. He turned round and saw a hand holding the door open.

'What is it?' he asked. 'Who's there?'

It was the Jondrette girl.

'So it's you again,' said Marius almost harshly. 'What do you want with me?'

She looked pensive and did not reply. She no longer had the self-assurance of that morning. She had not entered the room, remaining in the shadows of the corridor, where Marius could see her through the half-open door.

'Come on now, won't you give me an answer?' said Marius. 'What do you want with me?'

She looked up at him with her dull eyes, a brightness of some sort seeming dimly to kindle in them, and said, 'Monsieur Marius, you look sad. What's the matter with you?'

'With me!' said Marius.

'Yes, you.'

'There's nothing the matter with me.'

'Yes, there is!'

'No, there isn't.'

'I know there is!'

'Leave me alone!'

Marius pushed the door again, but she continued to hold it open.

'Listen,' said she, 'you shouldn't be like this. Even though you're not rich you were a good sort this morning. Be a good sort again now. You gave me something to eat, now tell me what's wrong. It's clear you're unhappy. I don't want you to be unhappy. What's to be done about it? Can I be of help? Give me something to do. You needn't tell me your secrets, I'm not asking you to, but all the same perhaps I can be of use. I'm sure I can help you, because I help my father. If some-one's needed to take letters, to go inside houses, to make enquiries door to door, to find out an address, to follow a person, that's what I can do. So you can tell me what's wrong, and I'll go and speak to somebody. Sometimes if someone speaks to somebody, that's all it takes to find things out, and everything's put right. Let me help you.'

An idea flashed through Marius's mind. What straw will a man not clutch at to save himself? He moved nearer to the Jondrette girl.

'Listen—' he said, using the familiar *tu* form.

She interrupted him with a gleam of joy in her eyes. 'Oh yes, that's better, don't be stand-offish!'

'Well,' he went on, 'you brought that old gentleman with his daughter here.'

'Yes.'

'Do you know their address?'

'No.'

'Find out what it is for me.'

The Jondrette girl's eyes had turned from dull to joyful, now they darkened.

'That's what you want?' she said.

'Yes.'

'Do you know them?'

'No.'

'What you mean is, you don't know her but you want to know her,' she retorted.

In this switch from 'them' to 'her' there was some sort of insinu-ation and bitterness.

'Well, can you?' said Marius.

'Get you the lovely young lady's address?'

Again in those words 'the lovely young lady' there was an implica-tion that irritated Marius.

'Put it any way you like!' he said. 'The father and daughter's address. Their address, full stop!'

She stared at him intently. 'What will you give me?'

'Whatever you want.'

'Whatever I want?'

'Yes.'

'You'll have the address.' She bowed her head, then with an abrupt gesture she pulled the door and it closed.

Marius was left on his own. He collapsed on to a chair, his head and both elbows on his bed, almost dizzy, overwhelmed by thoughts he could not grasp. Everything that had happened since that morning, the angel's appearance, her disappearance, what this creature had just said to him, a wavering glimmer of hope amid immense despair, this is what confusedly filled his brain.

All at once he was jolted from his reverie. He heard Jondrette's harsh raised voice utter these words full of the strangest interest to him: 'I tell you, I'm sure of it, I recognized him.'

Of whom was Jondrette speaking? He had recognized whom? Monsieur Leblanc? The father of 'his Ursule'? What! Did Jondrette know him? Was Marius about to obtain in this sudden and unexpected manner all the information without which his life was darkness to him? Was he about to learn at last who it was he loved? Who that girl was? Who her father was? Was the great obscurity that hid them about to be dispelled? Was the truth about to be unveiled? Oh! Heavens above!

He leapt rather than climbed on to the chest of drawers and took up his position again at the little peep-hole in the partition wall.

He was looking once more into the Jondrettes' miserable lodgings.

XII
The Use Made of Monsieur Leblanc's Five-franc Piece

Nothing in the family's appearance had changed, except that the wife and daughters had been through the parcel and had put on the woollen stockings and sleeved vests. The two new blankets were thrown over the two beds.

Jondrette had evidently just returned. He was still breathless from being out of doors. His daughters were sitting on the floor by the fireplace, the older girl bandaging the younger one's hand. His wife was somehow slumped on the pallet close to the fireplace with an expression of amazement on her face. Jondrette was pacing the garret, striding back and forth. There was an extraordinary look in his eyes.

The woman, who seemed apprehensive and astounded by her husband, ventured to say to him, 'Really now? Are you sure?'

'I'm sure! It was eight years ago! But I recognize him! Ah! I recognize him. I knew him at once! You mean, it didn't leap out at you?'

'No.'

'But I told you: look closely. But it's that build, it's that face, scarcely any older-looking, there are some people who don't age,

I don't know how they manage it, it's the sound of that voice. He's better-dressed, that's all! Ah! you mysterious old devil, I've got you now!'

He stopped and said to his daughters, 'You two, clear out of here! Strange that it didn't leap out at you!'

They got up to obey. The mother stammered out, 'With that bad hand of hers?'

'The air will do it good,' said Jondrette. 'Get going!'

It was clear this was a man you did not argue with. The two girls took themselves off. Just as they were crossing the threshold the father caught the elder one by the arm, and said to her in a peculiar tone of voice, 'You be back here at five o'clock sharp. Both of you. I'll be needing you.'

Marius became even more attentive.

Left alone with his wife, Jondrette began to pace the room again and walked round it two or three times in silence. Then he spent a few minutes tucking into his trousers the bottom of the woman's chemise he was wearing.

Suddenly, he turned to the Jondrette woman, folded his arms and cried out, 'And shall I tell you something? The young lady—'

'Well?' retorted his wife. 'What about the young lady?'

Marius could be in no doubt, she was the one they were talking about. He listened with a burning anxiety. He was all ears, as if his life depended on it.

But Jondrette bent over and spoke to his wife in a whisper. Then he straightened up and concluded out loud, 'That's her!'

'Her?' said the wife.

'Her!' said the husband.

No expression could convey what was contained in the mother's 'Her?' It was a mixture of surprise, rage, hatred and anger, and all in an appalling tone of voice. All it took was a few words, the name no doubt, that her husband had whispered in her ear, for this big dozy woman to wake up, and from repulsive to become dreadful.

'Impossible!' she cried. 'To think that my girls are going barefoot and haven't got a single dress to wear! What! A satin cloak trimmed with fur, a velvet hood, ankle-boots and everything – more than two hundred francs' worth of clothes! So that anyone would think she was a lady! No, you've got it wrong! Why, in the first place the other one was a fright, and this one isn't bad-looking! She really isn't bad-looking! It can't be her!'

'I tell you it's her. You'll see.'

At such a categorical assertion the Jondrette woman turned her broad red pale-skinned face towards the ceiling and gazed up at it with a twisted expression. At that moment she seemed to Marius even more fearsome than her husband. A sow with the eyes of a tigress.

'What!' she said. 'If that horrible fine young lady who looked at my girls with pity in her eyes were that brat! Oh! If only I could give her a good kick in the guts wearing my clogs!'

She leapt from the bed and stood there for a moment, dishevelled, her nostrils flaring, her mouth half open, her clenched fists flung behind her. Then she slumped back on to the pallet. The man paced to and fro without paying any attention to his mate. After several moments' silence he moved towards the Jondrette woman and stopped in front of her, his arms folded, as before.

'And shall I tell you something else?'

'What?' she asked.

He answered in a low, curt voice, 'My fortune's made.'

The Jondrette woman stared at him with that look that says, 'Could the person talking to me be going mad?'

He went on, 'By heaven! It wasn't so very long ago I was a parishioner of the die-of-hunger-if-you-have-a-fire-die-of-cold-if-you-have-bread parish! I've had enough of misery! Mine and other people's! I'm not joking any more, I don't see anything funny about it any more – enough of this farce, for God's sake! No more messing about, Father Almighty! I want to eat my fill! I want to drink my fill! Make a pig of myself! Sleep! Do nothing! I just want my turn! Before I drop dead I want to be a bit of a millionaire!'

He took a turn round the hovel and added, 'Like some others.'

'What do you mean?' asked the woman.

He shook his head, winked, then raised his voice like some street-corner quack about to give a demonstration. 'What do I mean? Listen!'

'Shh!' muttered the woman. 'Not so loud! These are things that no one else should hear.'

'Bah! Who's going to hear? Our next-door neighbour? I saw him go out a little while ago. Besides, does he hear anything, that great numbskull? In any case, I saw him go out, I tell you.'

Nevertheless, by a kind of instinct Jondrette lowered his voice, yet not enough for his words to escape Marius. One favourable circumstance, which had made it possible for Marius not to miss anything of this conversation, was the snow that had fallen, deadening the sound of the carriages on the boulevard.

This is what Marius heard:

'Listen carefully. This Croesus is caught. All but! It's as good as done. Everything's fixed. I've seen some people. He'll come this evening at six o'clock. To bring his sixty francs, the bastard! Did you see how I came out with all that, my sixty francs, my landlord, my fourth of February! It's not even a quarter-day! Isn't that stupid? So he'll come at six! The time when our neighbour will be gone for his meal. Mère Burgon is in town washing dishes. There's no one in the house. The neighbour never comes home before eleven. The girls will keep a lookout. You'll give us a hand. He'll do as he's told.'

'And what if he doesn't?' asked his wife.

Jondrette made a sinister gesture and said, 'We'll do him in.' And he burst out laughing.

This was the first time Marius had seen him laugh. The laughter was cold and quiet and chilling.

Jondrette opened a cupboard by the fireplace and took out an old cap, which he put on his head after brushing it with his sleeve.

'I'm going out now,' he said, 'I've some more people to see. The best. You'll see how well it goes. I won't stay out any longer than I have to. It's a great stunt to pull. Stay inside.'

And with both hands thrust into the pockets of his trousers, he stood there for a moment thinking, then cried, 'You know, it's a great stroke of luck, after all, that he didn't recognize me! If he had, he wouldn't be coming back. He'd have slipped through our fingers! It's my beard that saved me! My Romantic beard! My nice little Romantic beard!'

And again he laughed. He went to the window. The snow was still falling and cutting across the grey of the sky.

'What filthy weather!' he said. Then wrapping the great-coat across his chest, 'This thing's too big for me. Never mind,' he added, 'it was a damn good thing he left it for me, the old crook! Otherwise, I wouldn't have been able to go out and everything would have come to nothing again! When you think what things can turn on!'

And pulling his cap down over his eyes, he left the room.

He had scarcely had time to take a few steps outside when the door opened again and his intelligent, feral face reappeared in the opening.

'I nearly forgot,' he said. 'Have a charcoal brazier burning.'

And he threw into his wife's apron the five-franc coin the 'philanthropist' had left with him.

'A charcoal brazier?' his wife queried.

'Yes.'

'How much charcoal?'

'Two good bushels.'

'That will come to thirty sous. With what's left over, I'll buy something to eat.'

'No, damn it.'

'Why not?'

'Don't go and spend the whole five francs.'

'Why not?'

'Because there's something I need to buy.'

'What?'

'Something.'

'How much will you need?'

'Where's the nearest ironmonger's?'

'Rue Mouffetard.'

'Ah! yes, I can picture it. The shop on the street corner.'

'Well, tell me how much you'll need for what you want to buy.'

'Fifty sous – three francs.'

'There won't be much left for dinner.'

'Today's not the day for eating. There's something better to do.'

'Whatever you say, love.'

At this remark from his wife Jondrette closed the door again, and this time Marius heard his footsteps receding along the corridor of the old house and hurrying down the staircase.

Just at that moment the church of St-Médard struck one o'clock.

XIII
Solus Cum Solo, in Loco Remoto,
Non Cogitabuntur Orare Pater Noster*

For all that he was a dreamer, Marius, as we have said, was a resolute and active kind of person. His habits of solitary meditation, while developing in him sympathy and compassion, had perhaps diminished his capacity for annoyance but had left intact his capacity for indignation. He had the kindliness of a Brahmin and the severity of a judge. He would take pity on a toad, but crush a viper. Now, it was a nest of vipers he had just been peering at, it was a coven of monsters he had right in front of him.

'These wretches must be stamped underfoot,' he said.

Not one of the enigmas he had hoped to see cleared up had been

---

* 'It is not to be expected that two men alone together in a remote place will be saying the Lord's Prayer.' This is a twist on an old saying, which Hugo uses in *The Hunchback of Notre-Dame* (bk VII, ch. 2), but instead of the usual formula *Solus cum sola . . .* ('A lone man together with a lone woman . . .') we have here *solus* and *solo*, both masculine forms, with a shift from a suggestion of sexual impropriety to one of criminal intent.

elucidated. On the contrary, they had all perhaps intensified. He knew nothing more about the lovely young girl of the Luxembourg Gardens and the man he called Monsieur Leblanc except that Jondrette recognized them. From the mysterious words that had been said only one thing was clear to him: the fact that an ambush was being laid, some obscure but terrible trap. That they were both in great danger, she probably, her father certainly. That they must be saved. That the Jondrettes' hideous machinations must be thwarted and this spider's web of theirs destroyed. He observed the Jondrette woman for a moment. She had pulled out of a corner an old sheet-metal brazier and was rummaging in the heap of old iron.

He climbed down from the chest of drawers as carefully as possible, taking care to make no noise.

In his dread of what was brewing and in the horror instilled in him by the Jondrettes, he felt a kind of joy at the idea that he might have the privilege of doing the one he loved such a service.

But how to go about it? Warn the individuals who were in danger? He did not know their address. They had momentarily reappeared before his eyes, then had been swallowed up again in the immense depths of Paris. Wait at the door for Monsieur Leblanc at six o'clock that evening when he was due to arrive, and alert him to the trap? But Jondrette and his men would see him waiting, it was a lonely spot, they would be stronger than him, they would find some way of seizing him or driving him away, and the man Marius was trying to save would be doomed. One o'clock had just struck. The trap was to be sprung at six. Marius had five hours.

There was only one thing to do.

He put on his decent coat, tied a neckerchief round his neck, took his hat and went out, making no greater sound than if he had been walking barefoot on moss.

In any case the Jondrette woman was still poking about among her old bits of iron.

Once out of the house, he made for Rue du Petit-Banquier.

He was about halfway along this street, near a very low wall that could be easily stepped over at certain points, running alongside wasteground. Given what was on his mind, he was walking slowly. The snow deadened the sound of his footsteps. All of a sudden he heard voices talking very close to him. He looked round. The street was deserted. Not a soul in sight. It was broad daylight. And yet he distinctly heard voices.

It occurred to him to look over the wall next to him. Sure enough, there were two men sitting in the snow, with their backs to the wall, talking in low voices. He did not recognize these two individuals. One was a bearded man in an overall, and the other a long-haired fellow in rags. The bearded man wore a tasselled cap, the other was bare-headed and had snow in his hair.

By sticking his head out above them Marius was able to hear.

The long-haired one nudged the other with his elbow and said, 'With Patron-Minette, it can't fail.'

'You think so?' said the bearded man.

'It's worth five hundred francs each, and the worst that can happen: five years, six years, ten years at most!'

The other replied with some hesitation, scratching under his cap, 'That's a fact, that is. You can't argue with something like that.'

'I tell you, this job can't fail,' replied the long-haired man. 'Old Man what's-his-name's gig will be ready and waiting.'

Then they began to discuss a melodrama they had seen the night before at the Gaîté Theatre. Marius continued on his way.

He had the feeling that the mysterious words of those men crouching in the snow and so strangely hidden behind that wall were perhaps not unconnected with Jondrette's heinous plot. That must be what 'this job' was.

He made for Faubourg St-Marceau and asked at the first shop he came to where there was a police station. He was directed to Rue de Pontoise, number fourteen. Marius headed off towards it.

Passing a baker's shop, he bought a roll for two sous and ate it, anticipating that he would not be getting his evening meal.

On his way he gave credit to Providence. He realized that if he had not given his five francs to the Jondrette girl in the morning, he would have followed Monsieur Leblanc's cab and in consequence would have known nothing, and nothing would have stood in the way of the Jondrettes' felony; Monsieur Leblanc would have been doomed, and no doubt his daughter along with him.

XIV
In Which a Policeman Gives a Lawyer Two Punches

When he got to number fourteen Rue de Pontoise he went upstairs and asked for the police commissioner.

'Monsieur le commissaire de police isn't here,' some sort of office boy told him, 'but there's an inspector standing in for him. Would you like to speak to him? Is it urgent?'

'Yes,' said Marius.

The office boy showed him into the commissioner's office. A tall man was standing there behind a grille, leaning against a stove and holding up with both hands the flaps of a huge triple-caped garrick coat. He had a square face, a thin, firm mouth, thick, very bushy greying whiskers, and a gaze capable of turning your pockets inside out. That gaze, it might well have been said, was not penetrating but searching.

In appearance, this man was not much less ferocious or fearsome than Jondrette. Sometimes the guard dog is no less terrible to encounter than the wolf.

'What do you want?' he said to Marius, omitting to add 'monsieur'.

'Monsieur le commissaire de police?'

'He's not here. I'm standing in for him.'

'It's about a very confidential matter.'

'Then speak.'

'And very urgent.'

'Then speak quickly.'

Calm and brusque, this man was both terrifying and reassuring. He inspired fear and he inspired confidence. Marius told him the story. That a person he knew only by sight was to be led into an ambush that very evening. That living in the room next door to the thieves' den, he Marius Pontmercy, a lawyer, had overheard the whole plot through the partition wall. That the villain who had devised the trap was a certain Jondrette. That he would have accomplices, probably marauders, among others a certain Panchaud, alias Printanier, alias Bigrenaille. That Jondrette's daughters were to keep a lookout. That there was no way of warning the man in danger, given that not even his name was known. And finally, that all this was to be carried out at six o'clock that evening in the most deserted part of Boulevard de l'Hôpital, in the house numbered 50–52.

At the mention of this number the inspector raised his head and said coldly, 'So it's the room at the end of the corridor?'

'Precisely,' answered Marius. And he added, 'Are you familiar with the house?'

The inspector remained silent for a moment. Then, warming the heel of his boot at the open stove, he replied, 'Apparently.'

He went on murmuring indistinctly, talking not so much to Marius as to his cravat. 'Patron-Minette must have a hand in this.'

This caught Marius's attention. 'Patron-Minette,' he said. 'I did hear that word mentioned.'

And he recounted to the inspector the conversation between the long-haired man and the bearded man in the snow behind the wall on Rue du Petit-Banquier.

The inspector muttered, 'The long-haired one must be Brujon, and the bearded one must be Demi-Liard, alias Deux-Milliards.'

He had lowered his eyes again, and was thinking.

'As for Old Man what's-his-name, I have an idea who he might be. Look, now I've scorched my coat. They always make these damned stoves burn too hot. Number 50–52. The old Gorbeau place.'

Then he looked at Marius.

'You saw only the bearded fellow and the long-haired man?'

'And Panchaud.'

'You didn't see some damned little fop hanging around?'

'No.'

'Or a huge towering hulk who looks like an elephant from the Jardin des Plantes?'

'No.'

'Or a sly one with something of the old clown about him?'

'No.'

'As for the fourth, no one ever sees him, not even his lieutenants or his agents or his henchmen. It's hardly surprising that you've not seen him.'

'No. And who are all these people?' asked Marius.

The inspector said in response, 'In any case, it's too early in the day for them.' He relapsed into silence, then went on, 'Number 50–52. I know the place. No way of hiding inside without our cast realizing it. Then all they have to do is cancel the show. They're so modest! They don't feel comfortable with an audience. None of that, none of that! I want to hear them sing, make them dance.'

Ending this monologue, he turned to Marius, and eyeing him intently asked, 'Are you afraid?'

'Of what?' said Marius.

'Of these men?'

'No more than you are!' retorted Marius brusquely; he had begun to notice he had not yet had the courtesy of a 'monsieur' from this bloodhound.

The inspector eyed Marius even more intently, and went on with a kind of sententious solemnity, 'Spoken like a brave man and an honest man. Courage has no fear of crime, and honesty no fear of authority.'

Marius cut him short. 'That's all very well, but what do you intend to do?'

The inspector confined himself to saying, 'The lodgers in that house have pass-keys to let themselves in when they come home at night. You must have one.'

'Yes,' said Marius.

'Have you got it with you?'

'Yes.'

'Give it to me,' said the inspector.

Marius extracted the key from his waistcoat, handed it to the inspector and added, 'If you take my advice, you'll come in force.'

The inspector gave Marius the kind of look that Voltaire would have given a provincial littérateur who might have suggested a rhyme to him. In a single movement he plunged both hands, which were enormous, into the two huge pockets of his garrick coat and pulled out two small steel pistols of the sort called 'punches'*. He handed them to Marius, saying rapidly and curtly, 'Take these. Go home. Hide in your room. So that you're assumed to be out. They're loaded. Each with two bullets. Keep an eye on them. There's a hole in the wall, you told me. The men will arrive. Let them carry on undisturbed for a while. When you think everything's gone as far as it should and it's time to put a stop to it, you fire a shot. Not too soon. The rest is my responsibility. A shot in the air, up into the ceiling, wherever you like. Above all, not too soon. Wait until the action has started. You're a lawyer, you know what that means.'

Marius took the pistols and put them in the side pocket of his coat.

'They bulge like that, it's too obvious,' said the inspector. 'Put them in your trouser pockets.'

Marius hid the pistols in his trouser pockets.

'Now,' said the inspector, 'nobody can afford to waste a minute. What time is it? Half-past two. Seven o'clock, was it?'

'Six,' said Marius.

'That gives me time enough,' said the inspector, 'but only just. Don't forget anything I've said to you. Bang! One pistol-shot.'

'Rest assured,' said Marius.

And as Marius was reaching for the door handle to leave the room, the inspector called out to him, 'By the way, if you need me between now and then, come here or send a message. Ask for Inspector Javert.'

XV
Jondrette Goes Shopping

A few moments later, at about three o'clock, Courfeyrac happened to be walking along Rue Mouffetard with Bossuet. The snow was falling more heavily than ever, filling the skies. Bossuet was just saying to Courfeyrac, 'Seeing all these snowflakes coming down, you'd think there was a plague of white butterflies in the heavens.'

All at once Bossuet caught sight of Marius walking up the street towards the toll-gate with a peculiar air about him.

* *Coups de poing.*

'Look!' exclaimed Bossuet. 'Marius!'

'I saw him,' said Courfeyrac. 'Let's not speak to him.'

'Why not?'

'He's busy.'

'With what?'

'Can't you see the way he's behaving?'

'What way?'

'Like someone who's following someone.'

'You're right,' said Bossuet.

'Just look at the expression on his face!' said Courfeyrac.

'But who the devil is he following?'

'Some flowery-bonneted sweetheart-minx! He's in love.'

'But I see no sweetheart or minx or flowery bonnet in the street,' remarked Bossuet. 'There are no women.'

Courfeyrac looked and exclaimed, 'He's following a man!'

A man in a grey cap, and whose grey beard was discernible even from behind, was indeed walking about twenty paces ahead of Marius.

This man was dressed in a brand-new overcoat that was too big for him and an awful pair of ragged trousers all filthy with mud.

Bossuet burst out laughing. 'Who on earth is that man?'

'That,' said Courfeyrac, 'is a poet. Poets are quite happy to go around wearing rabbit-skin-dealer's trousers with a peer of the realm's overcoat.'

'Let's see where Marius is going,' said Bossuet. 'Let's see where this man's going, let's follow them, eh?'

'Bossuet!' cried Courfeyrac. 'Aigle de Meaux! You're a dreadful beast! Follow a man who's following a man!'

They turned and went on their way.

Sure enough, Marius had seen Jondrette walking along Rue Mouffetard, and was spying on him.

Jondrette walked on without any inkling that he was already under observation. He left Rue Mouffetard, and Marius saw him go inside one of the most dreadful hovels on Rue Gracieuse. He remained there about a quarter of an hour, then returned to Rue Mouffetard. He stopped at an ironmonger's that there used to be in those days on the corner of Rue Pierre-Lombard – and a few minutes later Marius saw him emerge from the shop, holding in his hand a big cold chisel with a plain wooden handle, which he secreted under his overcoat. When he came to Rue Petit-Gentilly he turned left and quickly reached Rue du Petit-Banquier. Daylight was fading. The snow, which had let up for a while, had just started falling again. Right at the corner of Rue du Petit-Banquier, which was deserted as usual, Marius held back out of sight and did not follow Jondrette down the street. Just as well, because when Jondrette came alongside the low wall where Marius had heard the long-haired man and the bearded man talking he turned round to make sure no one was following him, and he did not see Marius. He then leapt over the wall and disappeared.

The wasteland that lay behind this wall gave on to a back yard belonging to a fellow of ill repute who had once had a carriage-hire business and who, having gone bankrupt, still had a few old rattle-traps in his sheds.

Marius thought it would be wise to take advantage of Jondrette's absence to return home. Besides, it was getting late. Every evening when Mame Burgon left to go and wash dishes in town she had the habit of locking the door to the house, which was always shut at dusk. Marius had given his key to the police inspector. It was therefore important that he should hurry back.

Evening had descended. Darkness had almost closed in. There was, on the horizon and in the vastness of space, only one spot left that was still lit by the sun, and that was the moon. It was rising, red, behind the low dome of La Salpêtrière.

Marius strode back to number 50–52. The door was still open when he arrived. He climbed the stairs on tip-toe and, hugging the wall, crept down the corridor to his room. This corridor, remember, was lined on both sides with garrets, all at present to let and empty. Mame Burgon usually left the doors open. As he went past one of these doors Marius thought he glimpsed in the unoccupied cell the white blur of the faces of four motionless men caught in the last of the light coming through a dormer window. Not wanting to be seen, Marius did not try to look closer. He managed to get back to his room without being noticed and without making a sound. Just in time. A moment later he heard Mame Burgon going off and locking the door of the house behind her.

XVI
Featuring a Song Sung to an English Tune Popular in 1832

Marius sat on his bed. It was probably about half-past five. Only half an hour lay between him and whatever was going to take place. He could hear the pounding of his arteries the way you can hear a watch ticking in the dark. He thought of that twofold advance being made in the shadows right then, crime moving forward on one side, justice coming up on the other. He was not afraid, but he could not envisage what was about to happen without a certain trepidation. As is the case with all those suddenly caught up in an amazing adventure, this whole day seemed like a dream to him, and to convince himself he was not in the grip of a nightmare he needed to feel the coldness of the two steel pistols in his trouser pockets.

It was no longer snowing. The moon emerged ever brighter from the mist, and its rays, combined with the white reflection of the snow that had fallen, gave the room a twilight appearance.

There was light in the Jondrette hovel. Marius saw the hole in the wall gleaming with a reddish brightness that was seemingly bloody to him.

The fact was, this brightness could not have been produced by a candle. Moreover, not a sound came from the Jondrettes' place, where no one stirred, no one spoke a word, not a whisper. The silence was chill and profound, and but for that light you might have thought you were next door to a tomb.

Marius quietly took off his boots and pushed them under his bed.

Several minutes went by. Marius heard the door downstairs swing open. A quick, heavy footstep climbed the staircase and went down the corridor. The door-latch to the hovel lifted with a clatter. It was Jondrette coming home.

All at once several voices were raised. The whole family was in the garret. Only, in the master's absence they were silent, like wolf cubs when the wolf is away.

'It's me,' he said.

'Hallo, pa,' yapped the girls.

'Well?' said the mother.

'It's all going to plan,' replied Jondrette, 'but my feet are devilish cold. So you've got yourself dressed up. Well done! You need to inspire trust!'

'All ready to go out.'

'You won't forget anything I told you. You'll remember what to do?'

'Don't fret.'

'Because . . .' said Jondrette. And he did not finish his sentence.

Marius heard him lay something heavy on the table, probably the chisel he had bought.

'Now then,' said Jondrette, 'have you eaten?'

'Yes,' said the mother. 'I had three big potatoes and some salt. I took advantage of the fire to cook them.'

'Good,' said Jondrette. 'Tomorrow I'll take you out to dinner. We'll have duck and all the trimmings. You'll dine like Charles the Tenth, every one of you. It's all going well!'

Then lowering his voice, he added, 'The mouse-trap's open. The cats are in place.'

He lowered his voice even more and said, 'Put that on the fire.'

Marius heard the clinking of tongs or some other iron utensil knocking against charcoal, and Jondrette went on, 'Have you greased the hinges of the door so they don't squeak?'

'Yes,' replied the mother.

'What time is it?'

'Nearly six. The half-hour just struck at St-Médard.'

'Hell!' said Jondrette. 'The girls must go and keep a lookout. Come here, you two, and listen.'

There was some whispering.

Jondrette raised his voice again: 'Has old Burgon left?'

'Yes,' said the mother.

'You're sure there's no one next door?'

'He hasn't been in all day and you know very well now's the time he has his evening meal.'

'You're sure?'

'Yes.'

'All the same,' said Jondrette, 'there's no harm in going to see whether he's there. My girl, take the candle and have a look.'

Marius dropped on to his hands and knees and crawled silently under his bed. Hardly had he got himself tucked away when he saw a light through the cracks in his door.

'P'pa,' cried a voice, 'he's out!'

He recognized the older girl's voice.

'Did you go in?' asked her father.

'No,' replied the girl, 'but his key's in the door, so he must be out.'

The father called out, 'Well, go in anyway!'

The door opened and Marius saw the older Jondrette girl come in with a candle in her hand. She looked just the same as that morning, only even more of a fright in this light.

She came straight up to the bed. Marius had a moment of unspeakable anxiety, but there was a mirror nailed to the wall by the bed, and that was what she came for. She stood on tip-toe and looked at herself in it. The sound of iron objects being moved around could be heard from the room next door.

She smoothed her hair with the palm of her hand and smiled in the mirror, singing quietly to herself in her cracked and sepulchral voice:

702

A whole week of love we had together!
Though happiness is so fleeting,
How could I regret our meeting?
The days of love should last for ever.
Last for ever, last for ever!

All the while, Marius was trembling. It seemed impossible to him that she could not hear his breathing.

She went over to the window and looked out, talking aloud in that half-crazed way she had.

'How ugly Paris is when it's dressed in a white shirt!' she said.

She came back to the mirror and again adopted affected poses, gazing at herself, alternately full in the face and in three-quarters profile.

'Hey there!' cried her father. 'What's keeping you?'

'I'm looking under the bed and under the furniture,' she replied, continuing to arrange her hair. 'There's no one here.'

'You ninny!' yelled her father. 'Get back here right now! And stop wasting time!'

'Coming! Coming!' said she. 'You get no time to yourself in this house!'

She sang under her breath:

You're leaving me in search of glory
Where'er you go my sad heart follows.

She cast a parting glance at the mirror and went out, shutting the door behind her.

A moment later Marius heard the two young girls going barefoot down the corridor, and Jondrette's voice shouting after them, 'Keep a sharp eye! One of you by the gate, the other on the corner of Rue du Petit-Banquier. Don't let the door of this house out of your sight for a moment, and as soon as you see something, get back here straight away! Quick as you can! You've got a key to let yourselves in.'

The older girl grumbled, 'Standing guard barefoot in the snow!'

'You shall have jasper-green silk ankle-boots tomorrow!' said the father.

They descended the staircase and a few seconds later the front door slammed shut, announcing that they were outside.

The only people left in the house now were Marius, the Jondrettes, and probably also the mysterious individuals glimpsed by Marius in the twilight behind the door of the unoccupied garret.

XVII
The Use Made of Marius's Five-franc Piece

Marius decided the moment had come to return to his observation post. In the twinkling of an eye and with the agility of his age, he was back at the hole in the partition wall.

He peered through it.

The interior of the Jondrette lodgings presented a peculiar sight, and Marius found an explanation for the strange brightness he had noticed. A candle was burning in a verdigrised candlestick, but that was not what really lit the room. The entire hovel was completely illuminated, as it were, by the reflection from a rather large sheet-metal brazier standing in the fireplace and filled with burning charcoal, the brazier the Jondrette woman had prepared that morning. The charcoal was glowing and the brazier was red-hot; a dancing blue flame enabled him to distinguish the shape of the chisel, bought by Jondrette in Rue Pierre-Lombard, that had been thrust into the burning embers and was turning red. In a corner by the door, and as if laid out for some intended purpose, two piles were to be seen, one of what looked like old iron, the other a heap of ropes. All this would have left anyone who did not know what was in store undecided between a very sinister interpretation and a very simple interpretation. Illuminated in this way, the hovel looked more like a smithy than the mouth of hell, but Jondrette in this light looked more like a demon than a blacksmith.

The heat from the brazier was such that the candle on the table was melting on that side and burning unevenly. An old copper dark-lantern, worthy of a Diogenes turned Cartouche, had been placed on the mantelpiece.

Standing in the hearth beside some half-burned logs, the brazier sent its smoke up the chimney, giving off no smell.

The moonlight entering through the four window-panes cast its whiteness into the blazing crimson garret, and to the poetic mind of Marius, a dreamer even at a time of action, it was like some heavenly notion mingling with the earth's monstrous dreams. A draught of air blowing through the broken pane helped to dispel the smell of charcoal and obscure the presence of the brazier.

The Jondrette den, if the reader can recall what we have said about the Gorbeau tenement, was very well appointed to serve as the scene of a black and violent deed, as the setting for a crime. It was the room set furthest back in the most isolated house on the loneliest boulevard in Paris. Had the ambush not yet existed, it would have been invented here.

The whole depth of a house and a great many uninhabited rooms separated this hovel from the boulevard, and its only window looked out on extensive undeveloped plots enclosed behind walls and fences. Jondrette had lighted his pipe, seated himself on the broken chair, and was smoking. His wife was talking to him in an undertone.

If Marius had been Courfeyrac, that is to say, one of those men who laugh at every opportunity in life, he would have burst out laughing when his gaze fell on the Jondrette woman. She wore a black feathered hat not unlike the heralds' hats at the coronation of Charles X, an immense tartan shawl over her knitted skirt, and the men's shoes that her daughter had scorned that morning. It was this outfit that had prompted Jondrette's exclamation, 'So you've got yourself dressed up! Well done! You need to inspire trust!'

As for Jondrette, he had not taken off the new overcoat Monsieur Leblanc had given him, which was too big for him, and his outfit continued to present that contrast between coat and trousers that in Courfeyrac's eyes constituted the archetypal poet.

Suddenly Jondrette raised his voice: 'Now that I think about it, in this weather he'll come in a carriage. Light the lantern, take it with you and go downstairs. Stand behind the front door. The moment you hear the carriage stop, open the door at once, he'll come upstairs, you light the way for him up the staircase and along the corridor, and while he's coming in, you get down there again as quick as you can, pay the coachman and send him away.'

'What about money?' said the woman.

Jondrette fumbled in his trouser pocket and handed her five francs.

'What's this?' she cried.

Jondrette replied with dignity, 'That's the monarch our neighbour gave us this morning.'

And he added, 'You know what? We need another two chairs in here.'

'What for?'

'To sit on.'

Marius felt a shiver run down his spine when he heard the Jondrette woman giving this placid reply: 'Well, for God's sake, I'll go and fetch the ones our neighbour has.'

And moving swiftly, she opened the door of the hovel and went out into the corridor.

Marius just did not have time to climb down from the chest of drawers, cross over to his bed and hide under it.

'Take the candle!' called Jondrette.

'No,' she said, 'that would be a nuisance, I've the two chairs to carry. The moon's bright.'

Marius heard the heavy hand of Mère Jondrette fumbling for his key in the dark. The door opened. He remained rooted to the spot with shock and amazement.

The Jondrette woman entered the room.

The dormer window let in a shaft of moonlight that fell between two big patches of shadow. One of these patches of shadow completely obscured the wall that Marius was backed against, so that he disappeared. Mère Jondrette looked up, did not see Marius, took the two chairs, the only ones Marius possessed, and went out, letting the door slam behind her.

She reappeared in the den.

'Here are the two chairs.'

'And here's the lantern,' said her husband. 'Get yourself down there quick.'

She hurried to obey, and Jondrette was left alone.

He arranged the two chairs on either side of the table, turned the chisel over in the burning coals, placed an old screen before the hearth, concealing the brazier, then went over to the corner where the pile of rope lay, and bent down as if to examine something. Marius then realized that what he had taken for a shapeless heap was a very well made rope-ladder, with wooden rungs and two hooks for attaching it. This ladder, and some large tools, really massive iron implements, jumbled up with the heap of old metal piled behind the door, had not been in the Jondrette hovel that morning and had evidently been brought there that afternoon during Marius's absence.

'Those are edge-tools,' thought Marius.

Had Marius been a little more expert in this area he would have recognized, in what he took to be edge-tools of some sort, certain implements capable of forcing a lock or jemmying a door and others capable of cutting or slicing, the two categories of sinister tool that burglars call 'claws' and 'clippers'.

The fireplace and the two chairs were right opposite Marius. With the brazier now screened, the room was lit only by the candle. The least crock on the table or on the mantelpiece cast a huge shadow. A sort of frightful and ominous calm prevailed in this room. There was a sense of anticipation, of something dreadful about to happen.

Jondrette had let his pipe go out, a serious sign of distraction, and had sat down again. The candlelight brought out the fierce, sharp angularity of his face. He kept scowling and brusquely gesturing with his right hand outspread, as if in response to some last words of advice in a grim interior monologue. In the course of one of these obscure responses to himself, he jerked the drawer of the table towards him, took out a long-bladed kitchen knife concealed inside it, and tested the edge on his fingernail. That done, he put the knife back in the drawer, which he pushed shut again.

As for Marius, he took hold of the pistol in his right-hand pocket, drew it out and cocked it. The pistol gave a clear, sharp click.

Jondrette started and half rose from his chair.

'Who's there?' he cried.

Marius held his breath.

Jondrette listened for a moment, then began to laugh and said, 'What a fool I am! It's the partition creaking!'

Marius kept the pistol in his hand.

XVIII
Marius's Two Chairs Are Set Facing Each Other

All of a sudden, the distant and melancholy vibration of a church bell made the window-panes rattle. Six o'clock was striking at St-Médard.

Jondrette counted off each stroke with a nod of his head. After the sixth stroke he snuffed the candle with his fingers. Then he began to walk around the room, listened for sound in the corridor, walked a little more, listened again.

'He'd better come!' he muttered. Then he returned to his chair.

He had hardly sat down again when the door opened. It was the Jondrette woman who opened it, and she stood in the corridor making a horrible ingratiating grimace, illuminated from below by one of the holes in the dark-lantern.

'Come in, monsieur,' she said.

'Come in, my benefactor,' said Jondrette, jumping to his feet.

Monsieur Leblanc appeared. He had an air of serenity that made him look peculiarly venerable. He laid four gold coins on the table.

'Monsieur Fabantou,' he said, 'this is for your rent and your immediate needs. After that, we'll see.'

'God bless you, my generous benefactor!' said Jondrette. And swiftly approaching his wife he said, 'Send the carriage away!'

She slipped out while her husband greeted Monsieur Leblanc profusely and offered him a chair. A moment later she was back, and whispered in his ear, 'It's done.'

The snow that had been falling non-stop since that morning was so deep, the cab had arrived without being heard, and it was not heard leaving.

Meanwhile, Monsieur Leblanc had sat down. Jondrette had taken the other chair, opposite Monsieur Leblanc.

Now, to picture to himself the scene that is to follow, the reader should bear in mind the icy darkness, the lonely, snow-covered wastes of La Salpêtrière that lay white in the moonlight like vast shrouds, the dim light from the street lamps casting their red glow here and there on those bleak boulevards, and the long rows of black elms, not a soul to be seen for perhaps more than a half a mile around; the Gorbeau tenement, its silence and horror and darkness never so great; in the midst of those lonely wastes, in the midst of those shadows, the vast Jondrette den lighted by a single candle; and in that miserable room two men seated at a table, Monsieur Leblanc placid, Jondrette smiling and terrible, and the Jondrette woman, the she-wolf, in a corner; and invisible behind the partition wall, Marius, standing there, missing not one word, not one movement, watching, pistol in hand.

In fact Marius had no fear, only a sense of horror. He clutched the pistol butt, and felt reassured. 'I can put a stop to this wretch whenever I want to,' he thought.

He was aware of the police somewhere out there, in hiding, waiting for the agreed signal and ready to leap into action.

He hoped, moreover, that this violent encounter between Jondrette and Monsieur Leblanc would result in some light being shed on all the things it was in his interest to know.

XIX
Beware the Dark Fringes

No sooner had Monsieur Leblanc sat down than he looked towards the pallets, which were unoccupied.

'How's the poor little girl who was hurt?' he enquired.

'In a bad way,' replied Jondrette with a heartbroken and grateful smile, 'very bad, my good monsieur. Her big sister has taken her to the Bourbe to be treated. You'll be seeing them, they'll be back soon.'

'Madame Fabantou seems to be better?' Monsieur Leblanc went on, glancing at the bizarre attire of the Jondrette woman, standing between him and the door as if already guarding the exit, and staring at him, her posture threatening, almost combatant.

'She's dying,' said Jondrette. 'But it can't be helped, monsieur. She has so much courage, that woman! She's not a woman, she's an ox!'

Touched by this compliment, simpering like some gratified monster, Jondrette's wife protested, 'You're always too good to me, Monsieur Jondrette!'

'Jondrette?' said Monsieur Leblanc. 'I thought your name was Fabantou.'

'Fabantou, alias Jondrette!' the husband came back quickly. 'A stage name!'

And directing a shrug at his wife, which Monsieur Leblanc did not see, he went on in an emphatic and wheedling tone of voice, 'Ah! the fact is, we've always got along so well together, this poor dear and myself! What would we be left with if we hadn't got that? It's so hard on us, my esteemed friend. We're willing and able but there's no work! I don't know how the government contrives it, but on my word of honour, monsieur, I'm no Jacobin, monsieur, I'm no anarchist. I don't wish anybody ill but if I were the ministers, on my most solemn word, things'd be different. To take an example, I wanted my girls to be taught the trade of box-making. You'll say to me, "What! A trade?" Yes! A trade! A simple trade! A livelihood! What a comedown, my benefactor! What degradation when you've been what we once were! Alas! We're left with nothing of our days of prosperity! Apart from just one thing, a picture that means a lot to me, but all the same I'm willing to part with it, for a man has to stay alive! Indeed, a man has to stay alive!'

While Jondrette was talking, with an apparent incoherence of sorts that in no way detracted from the shrewd and thoughtful expression of his physiognomy, Marius looked up and noticed at the far end of the room someone he had not seen before. A man had just entered so quietly, there had been no sound of the door opening. This man wore a purple knitted waistcoat – old, threadbare, stained, torn and gaping at every fold – wide velveteen trousers, wooden clogs on his feet, and no shirt. He was bare-necked, with bare tattooed arms and black-smeared face. He had sat down, in silence and with his arms folded, on the nearest bed, and since he was behind Jondrette he could be seen only indistinctly.

That, as it were, magnetic instinct that alerts the eye prompted Monsieur Leblanc to look about almost at the same moment as Marius did. He could not help but give a start of surprise, which did not escape Jondrette.

'Ah! I see!' exclaimed Jondrette, buttoning up his coat with an air of satisfaction. 'You're looking at your overcoat? It fits me, indeed it does!'

'Who is that man?' said Monsieur Leblanc.

'Pay no attention to him,' said Jondrette. 'He's a neighbour.'

The neighbour was a peculiar-looking individual. However, there are numerous chemical factories in the St-Marceau district. Many of the factory workers might have blackened faces. As it was, Monsieur Leblanc's entire being radiated a frank and fearless trust.

He went on, 'Forgive me, now what were you saying, Monsieur Fabantou?'

'I was telling you, monsieur, my dear patron,' replied Jondrette, placing his elbows on the table and gazing at Monsieur Leblanc with steady and commiserating eyes, rather like those of a boa constrictor, 'I was telling you that I have a picture to sell.'

There was a faint sound at the door. A second man had just entered and sat on the bed behind Jondrette. Like the first, he had bare arms and a mask of ink or soot. Although this man had literally slipped into the room, he was unable to do so without Monsieur Leblanc noticing.

'Don't mind them,' said Jondrette. 'They're part of the household. As I was saying, I still have a painting, a valuable painting . . . Here, take a look, monsieur.'

He got up and went over to the wall where the panel we have already mentioned was propped up. He turned the panel round, leaving it resting against the wall. It was indeed something that looked like a painting and it was more or less visible by the light of the candle. Marius could see nothing of it clearly, as Jondrette was standing between the picture and him. He could only half discern a crude daub and some sort of central figure depicted with the garish vulgarity of illustrations on fairground canvases and draught screens.

'What's that?' asked Monsieur Leblanc.

Jondrette exclaimed, 'The work of a master, a painting of great value, my benefactor! It means as much to me as my two daughters, it holds such memories for me! But I told you, and I won't go back on it, I'm so poor that I'd part with it . . .'

Either by chance or because he had begun to feel some incipient unease, while examining the picture Monsieur Leblanc's glance returned to the far end of the room. There were now four men, three seated on the bed, one standing by the doorpost, all four bare-armed, motionless, their faces smeared with black. One of the three on the bed was leaning back against the wall with his eyes closed, and appeared to be sleeping. This man was old, and his white hair with that blackened face was a ghastly sight. The other two looked young. One was bearded, the other had long hair. None of them wore shoes. Those without socks were barefoot.

Jondrette noticed that Monsieur Leblanc's eyes were fixed on these men.

'They're friends. Neighbours,' he said. 'Their faces are black because it's sooty work they do. They're sweeps and stove menders. Don't trouble yourself about them, my benefactor, but buy my picture. Take pity on my penury. I'll sell it to you for a reasonable price. How much do you think it's worth?'

'Well,' said Monsieur Leblanc, looking Jondrette straight in the eye and like a man put on his guard, 'it's some tavern sign. It's worth all of three francs.'

Jondrette replied smoothly, 'Have you got your wallet with you? I'd settle for three thousand francs.'

Monsieur Leblanc rose, stood with his back to the wall, and ran his eye around the room. He had Jondrette and the window on his left, and the Jondrette woman with the four men and the door on his right. The four men did not stir and seemed not even to notice him. Jondrette had begun to whine again, and with so vacant a look in his eye and in such a mournful tone that Monsieur Leblanc might have thought the person in front of him was quite simply a man driven mad with distress.

'If you don't buy my picture, dear benefactor,' said Jondrette, 'I'm destitute, there's nothing left for me but to throw myself in the river. When I think that I wanted my two girls to be taught middle-grade box-making, box-making for New Year gifts! Well! You need a table with a back-board so the glasses don't fall on the floor, you need a special stove, a pot with three compartments for the different strengths of glue needed, depending on whether it's to be used on wood, paper or cloth, a cardboard-cutter, a mould for shaping the cardboard, a hammer to fix the tacks, pincers – damn it, how should I know what else? And all that just to earn four sous a day! Working a fourteen-hour day! And every box handled by the box-maker thirteen times! And the paper to wet! And no marks to be made! And the glue to keep heated. Damn it, I tell you! Four sous a day! How is anyone expected to making a living?'

Jondrette spoke without looking at Monsieur Leblanc, who was watching him. Monsieur Leblanc's gaze was fixed on Jondrette, and Jondrette's gaze was fixed on the door. Marius's breathless attention went from one to the other. Monsieur Leblanc seemed to be wondering if this man was an imbecile. Jondrette repeated two or three times, with all sorts of variations of tone in the wheedling and whining range, 'There's nothing left for me but to throw myself in the river! I climbed down three steps by the Pont d'Austerlitz the other day with that in mind.'

All at once his lacklustre eyes lit up with a hideous blaze; this runt-ish man drew himself up, and became frightening. He took a step towards Monsieur Leblanc and thundered, 'All that's beside the point! Do you recognize me?'

XX
The Trap

The door of the garret had just flown open to reveal three men in blue overalls and wearing black paper masks. The first was thin and had a long iron-tipped cudgel; the second, who was a kind of colossus, was carrying a butcher's poleaxe for slaughtering cattle, which he held by the middle of the handle with the axe-head down. The third, a man with thick-set shoulders, not as thin as the first, not as massive as the second, was clutching in his fist an enormous key stolen from the door of some prison.

It appeared that the arrival of these men was what Jondrette had been waiting for. A rapid dialogue ensued between him and the man with the cudgel, the thin one.

'Is everything ready?' said Jondrette.

'Yes,' replied the thin man.

'Where's Montparnasse, then?'

'The leading man stopped to chat with your daughter.'

'Which one?'

'The eldest.'

'Is there a carriage at the door?'

'Yes.'

'Has the gig been got ready?'

'Yes.'

'With two good horses?'

'Excellent horses.'

'Is it waiting where I said it should wait?'

'Yes.'

'Good,' said Jondrette.

Monsieur Leblanc was very pale. He was looking at everything around him in that wretched place like a man who realizes full well his predicament, and his head, turning to all the faces surrounding him one by one, moved on his neck with an attentive and wondering slowness, but there was nothing in his manner resembling fear. He had improvised for himself a defence wall out of the table, and the man who only a moment ago had seemed just a kindly old gent had suddenly turned into some sort of athlete, laying his robust fist on the back of his chair in a gesture that was fearsome and unexpected.

So resolute and so brave in the face of such danger, this old man seemed to be one of those people who are courageous in the same way as they are kind – easily and simply. The father of a woman we love is never a stranger to us. Marius felt proud of this man he did not know.

Three of the bare-armed men, of whom Jondrette had said 'They're sweeps and stove menders', had helped themselves from the pile of old iron, one, to a pair of heavy shears, another, to a crowbar, the third, to a hammer, and had without uttering a word taken up a position barring the door. The old man remained on the bed, and had merely opened his eyes. The Jondrette woman had sat down beside him.

Marius decided that within a few seconds it would be time to intervene, and he raised his right hand towards the ceiling in the direction of the corridor, ready to fire his pistol.

Having concluded his exchange with the man carrying the cudgel, Jondrette turned back to Monsieur Leblanc and repeated his question, accompanying it with that terrible, low suppressed laugh of his, 'So you don't recognize me?'

Monsieur Leblanc looked him straight in the face, and replied, 'No.'

Then Jondrette came up to the table. He leaned over the candle, folding his arms, thrusting his fierce angular jaw towards Monsieur Leblanc's calm face, advancing as far as he could without Monsieur Leblanc backing away, and in this attitude of wild beast about to bite he cried, 'My name isn't Fabantou, my name isn't Jondrette, my name is Thénardier. I'm the innkeeper at Montfermeil! Do you hear? Thénardier! Now do you recognize me?'

An almost imperceptible flush passed across Monsieur Leblanc's brow, and with not a tremor in his voice, without raising it he replied with his customary serenity, 'No more than before.'

Marius did not hear this reply. Anyone who had seen him at that moment in that darkness would have seen that he was aghast, stupefied, thunderstruck. At that moment when Jondrette said, 'My name is Thénardier', Marius had trembled in every limb and collapsed against the wall as if he felt the cold blade of a sword run through his heart. Then his right arm, ready to fire the signal, had slowly dropped, and when Jondrette repeated 'Do you hear? Thénardier?' Marius's wilting fingers had almost let the pistol fall. By revealing who he was, Jondrette had left Monsieur Leblanc unmoved, but he had thrown Marius into turmoil. That name Thénardier, which seemed unknown to Monsieur Leblanc, was known to Marius. Remember what that name meant to him! That name he had worn on his heart, written in his father's will! He bore it in the depths of his mind, in the depths of his memory, in that sacred injunction: 'A man by the name of Thénardier saved my life. If my son ever meets him, he will do the best he can for him.' That name, remember, was one that his soul held in veneration, that in his filial devotion was associated with his father's name.

What! This was Thénardier, this was the innkeeper of Montfermeil he had for so long sought in vain! He had found him at last and – how could this be? – his father's saviour was a villain! That man, to whom Marius had a burning desire to dedicate himself, was a monster! The man to whom Colonel Pontmercy owed his deliverance was engaged in a crime whose precise nature Marius did not yet clearly apprehend but which looked like murder! And God Almighty! – who was his victim! What a twist of fate! What a bitter irony! His father had commanded him from where he lay in his coffin to do the best he could for this Thénardier, and for four years Marius had had but one thought in mind, to honour this debt of his father's, and just as he was about to ensure that a villain would be seized in flagrante delicto to face justice, destiny cried out to him, 'This is Thénardier!' At last he was going repay this man for saving his father's life amid a hail of grapeshot on the heroic battlefield of Waterloo – and he was going to repay him with the scaffold! He had sworn to himself that if ever he found this Thénardier he would approach him only by throwing himself at his feet. And now he had actually found him, but he was delivering him to the executioner! His father had said to him, 'Help Thénardier!' And he was responding to that adored and sainted voice by destroying Thénardier! Treating his father, in his tomb, to the spectacle of the execution on Place St-Jacques of the man who at the risk of his own life had wrested him from death. Executed because of his son, because of this same Marius to whom he had commended that man! And what a mockery for so long to have worn on his breast his father's last wishes, written in his own hand, and then, appallingly, to have done exactly the opposite! But on the other hand, to be witness to an ambush and not prevent it! What? Condemn the victim and spare the assassin! Could a person be bound by any debt of gratitude to such a wretch?

Every notion Marius had entertained for the last four years was as it were shot to pieces by this unexpected turn of events. He shuddered. Everything depended on him. He held in his hand the fate of these unwitting individuals playing out their parts beneath his gaze. If he fired his pistol Monsieur Leblanc was saved and Thénardier doomed. If he did not fire it Monsieur Leblanc would be sacrificed and – who knows? – Thénardier would escape. Be the undoing of one, or the downfall of the other! Remorse, either way. What should he do? What should he choose? Disregard the most pressing memories, so many solemn vows made to himself, the most sacred duty, the most venerated document! Disregard his father's will or allow a crime to be committed! It seemed to him that he could hear 'his Ursule' on the one hand, beseeching him for her father's sake, and the colonel on the other commending Thénardier to him. He felt as if he had gone mad. His knees were giving way beneath him. And he had not even time to think, so relentlessly fast was the scene before his eyes unfolding. It was like a whirlwind that he had thought was under his control and that he was now at the mercy of. He was on the verge of fainting.

Meanwhile, Thénardier – we shall refer to him by no other name from now on – was pacing up and down in front of the table in a kind of frenzied, crazed triumph.

He seized the candle in his fist and slammed it down on the mantelpiece so violently that the flame almost went out and the candle grease spattered on the wall.

Then, terrible in his fury, he turned to Monsieur Leblanc and spat out: 'Cooked! Roasted! Skewered! Done to a turn!'

And he started pacing again, in full flood.

'Ah!' he cried. 'At last I've found you, monsieur the philanthropist! Monsieur the threadbare millionaire! Monsieur who gives away dolls! Old fool! Ah! you don't recognize me! No, it wasn't you who came to Montfermeil, to my inn, eight years ago, on Christmas night of 1823! It wasn't you who carried away from my house Fantine's child, Alouette! It wasn't you who had a yellow coat! No! And a bundle of clothes in your hand like the one you brought to my house this morning! Fancy that now, wife! It seems he's always taking packages full of woollen stockings to people's houses! You old do-gooder! Are you a haberdasher, monsieur the millionaire? You saintly man, giving away your stock-in-trade to the poor! What a slippery customer! Ah! You don't recognize me? Well, I recognize you! I recognized you straight away, the minute you poked your nose in here. And now you're about to find out it isn't all roses, going into people's houses like that, on the grounds that they're inns, dressed all shabby, looking that much of a pauper anyone would've given you a sou, deceiving people, acting bountiful, taking away their livelihood, threatening them in the woods. And you don't get away with it just because later, when people are ruined, you bring them a coat that's too big and two miserable hospital blankets, you old scoundrel, you child-stealer!'

He stopped, and seemed to be talking to himself for a moment. It was as though his rage, like the Rhône, had disappeared down some hole. Then, as though he were concluding aloud things he had been saying to himself, he struck the table with his fist and shouted, 'With that innocent look of his!'

And he continued to harangue Monsieur Leblanc. 'Damn it! You made a fool of me in the past! You're the cause of all my woes! For fifteen hundred francs you got yourself a girl I had, from a rich family for sure, one who'd already brought me a lot of cash and would've kept me going for the rest of my life! A girl who would've compensated for all I lost on that vile watering-hole where some serious carousing went on and that, like a fool, I squandered everything I owned on! Oh! I wish all the wine that was drunk on my premises had poisoned those that drank it! Well, never mind! So you must have thought me a laughing-stock when you went off with Alouette! You had your cudgel in the forest. You had the advantage. My turn now. I'm the one who's got the upper hand today! The game's up, old man! Oh, am I laughing! Of course I'm laughing! He walked straight into the trap! I told him I was an actor, that my name was Fabantou, that I'd been on stage with Mam'selle Mars, with Mam'selle Muche, that my landlord insisted on being paid tomorrow, the fourth of February, and he didn't even notice that it's the eighth of January and not the fourth of February that's a payment date! Daft idiot! And those four wretched coins he brings me! The bastard! He didn't even have the decency to go as high as a hundred francs! And how he fell for my fawning! That did amuse me! "The old fool!" I said to myself. "Now I've got you! I was licking your boots this morning but I'll be sinking my teeth into you this evening!"'

Thénardier stopped. He was out of breath. His scrawny chest was puffing and blowing like a blacksmith's bellows. His eyes were full of that base delight of a weak, cruel and cowardly creature finally able to overcome what it had feared and insult what it had flattered, the glee of a dwarf that might place his foot on Goliath's head, the glee of a jackal beginning to tear to pieces a sick bull sufficiently moribund to be incapable of defending itself any more but sufficiently alive still to suffer.

Monsieur Leblanc did not interrupt him, but when he paused said, 'I don't know what you mean. You're mistaken. I'm a very poor man and anything but a millionaire. I don't know you. You're getting me mixed up with someone else.'

'Ah!' growled Thénardier. 'What humbug! You're sticking to that story! You're floundering, old man! Ah! You don't remember! You can't see who I am!'

'Forgive me, monsieur,' said Monsieur Leblanc in a polite tone of voice that was strangely powerful at such a moment, 'I see that you're a villain!'

Who has not noticed that hateful individuals have their own sensitivity, that monsters are ticklish! At this word 'villain' the Thénardier woman sprang from the bed, Thénardier grabbed his chair as if he was going to smash it to pieces.

'You stay where you are!' he shouted to his wife. And turning to Monsieur Leblanc he went on, 'Villain! Yes, I know that's what you call us, you rich folk! Well, it's true my business went bust, I'm in hiding, I've no food, I've no money, I'm a villain! I've not eaten for three days, I'm a villain! Ah! you lot keep your feet warm, you have shoes made by Sakoski, you have padded overcoats like archbishops, you live on the first floor in houses with caretakers, you eat truffles, you eat asparagus at forty francs a bunch in the month of January, and green peas, you gorge yourselves, and when you want to know whether it's cold you look in the newspaper to see what Engineer Chevallier's thermometer says. We're our own thermometers, we are! We don't need to go down to the embankment and look on the corner of the Tour de l'Horloge to find out how many degrees below zero it is. We feel the blood freezing in our veins and the ice reaching into our hearts, and we say: "There is no God!" And you come into our dens, yes, our dens, and call us villains! But we shall eat you, poor things! We'll devour you! Monsieur the millionaire, I'll have you know this: I had my own business, I was licensed, I was entitled to vote, I'm a respectable citizen, I am! And you may very well not be!'

Here Thénardier took a step towards the men who were standing by the door and added with a shudder, 'When I think that he dares come here and talk to me as if I were the lowest of the low!'

Then, addressing Monsieur Leblanc with renewed frenzy, 'And this too I'll have you know, monsieur the philanthropist! I'm not some shady customer! I'm not some nameless individual who comes along and abducts children from people's houses! I'm a French veteran, I should have been decorated! I was at Waterloo, I was! And in the battle I saved a general called Comte somebody-or-other. He told me his name but his damned voice was so weak I didn't hear. All I heard was "merci". I'd sooner have had his name than his thanks. It would have helped me to find him again. This picture you see here, it was painted by David in Brussels. You know what it represents? It represents me. David wanted to immortalize that feat of valour. I have that general on my back, and I'm carrying him through the grapeshot. That's the story! And he never did a thing for me, that general, he was no better than the others! But all the same I saved his life at the risk of my own, and I have pockets full of documents to prove it! I was a soldier at Waterloo, for God's sake! And now I've been good enough to tell you all that, let's get on with it, I want cash, I want a great deal of cash, I want enormous quantities of cash, or I'll kill you, God damn it!'

Marius had regained some control over his feelings of anguish and was listening. The last possibility of any remaining uncertainty had just vanished. This was, for sure, the Thénardier of the will. Marius shuddered at this accusation of ingratitude directed against his father and which he was so perniciously about to justify. It worsened his predicament. Besides, in all these words of Thénardier's, in his tone, in his gestures, in his eyes that set every word ablaze, in this eruption of an evil nature revealing all, in this mixture of swagger and abjectness, pride and pettiness, rage and stupidity, in this chaos of real grievances and false sentiment, in this malicious man's shameless relish of the pleasure of violence, in this brazen nakedness of an ugly soul, in this conflagration of every suffering combined with every hatred, there was something hideously evil and heart-breakingly true.

The picture by a master, the painting by David that he wanted Monsieur Leblanc to buy, was, as the reader will have surmised, none other than the sign from his tavern, painted, remember, by himself, the only relic he had preserved from the wreckage of Montfermeil.

Since he had stopped blocking Marius's field of vision, Marius could now observe this object, and in the daub he actually recognized a battle, a smoky background and a man carrying another man. This was the Thénardier and Pontmercy composition, the saviour sergeant and the colonel saved. Marius felt as if drunk. This picture in some way brought his father back to life, it was no longer the signboard of the tavern at Montfermeil, it was a resurrection, in which a tomb opened and a ghost arose from it. Marius heard his heart pounding at his temples, he had the cannon of Waterloo in his ears, his bleeding father indistinctly depicted on that sinister panel scared him, and it seemed to him this shapeless figure was staring at him.

Once Thénardier had caught his breath, he fixed his bloodshot eyes on Monsieur Leblanc and said to him in a low, curt voice, 'What have you to say before we knock the stuffing out of you?'

Monsieur Leblanc remained silent. In the midst of this silence a throaty voice delivered this ominous gibe from the corridor, 'If there's heavy work needs doing, I'm your man!'

It was the man with the poleaxe, who was looking forward to some fun.

At the same time an enormous face, bristling and grubby, with a frightful laugh that revealed not teeth but fangs, appeared in the doorway. It was the face of the man with the poleaxe.

'Why've you taken your mask off?' Thénardier shouted angrily.

'For a laugh,' replied the man.

For some moments Monsieur Leblanc had appeared to be following and watching every move made by Thénardier, who, blinded and dazzled by his own rage, paced about the den in the confidence of knowing that the door was guarded, that he was holding an unarmed man while armed himself and that they were nine against one, assuming the Thénardier woman counted for only one man. While rebuking the man with the poleaxe, he turned his back on Monsieur Leblanc.

Monsieur Leblanc seized this moment. He kicked the chair over, shoved the table back, then, before Thénardier had time to turn round, with amazing agility and in one bound he was at the window. To open it, to clamber on to the sill and climb over it, took a second. He was half out when six strong hands grabbed hold of him and forcibly dragged him back into the den. It was the three 'sweeps' who had pounced on him. At the same time, the Thénardier woman gripped him by the hair.

Hearing the scuffle, the other ruffians came running in from the corridor. The old man on the bed, who seemed befuddled with wine, got off the pallet and came staggering over with a road-mender's hammer in his hand.

One of the 'sweeps', on whose begrimed face the candle shed its light and whom Marius recognized in spite of the grime as Panchaud, alias Printanier, alias Bigrenaille, raised above Monsieur Leblanc's head some kind of bludgeon consisting of an iron bar with a leaden knob at either end.

Marius could not hold out against this spectacle. 'Father,' he thought, 'forgive me!' And his finger sought the trigger of his pistol.

The shot was about to go off when Thénardier's voice shouted, 'Don't harm him!'

The victim's desperate attempt, far from exasperating Thénardier, had calmed him. Inside him were two men, the vicious one and the crafty one. Up to that moment, in his overweening triumph, with his captured prey making no move, the vicious man had been dominant. When the victim struggled and seemed to want to fight back, the crafty man resurfaced and gained the upper hand.

'Don't harm him!' he repeated. And unwittingly, his first achievement was to stop the pistol going off and to paralyse Marius, for whom all urgency disappeared and who, faced with this new development, saw no harm in further delay. Who could tell? Something might turn up that would deliver him from the horrible alternatives of either letting Ursule's father perish or sealing the doom of the colonel's saviour.

A Herculean struggle was under way. With a punch full in the chest Monsieur Leblanc had sent the old drunk flying into the middle of the room, then with two backhanders had downed two more assailants and had one pinned under each knee. The wretches groaned under this pressure as if under a millstone of granite. But the other four had seized the formidable old man by both arms and the scruff of the neck, and held him crouched over the two floored 'sweeps'. Thus, over-powering some and overpowered by the others, crushing those below, smothered by those on top, vainly trying to shake off all the con-straints piled on top of him, Monsieur Leblanc disappeared beneath the heinous band of ruffians like a wild boar beneath a howling pack of mastiffs and bloodhounds.

They succeeded in throwing him back on the bed nearest the win-dow, and kept him at bay there. The Thénardier woman had not let go of his hair.

'You keep out of this,' said Thénardier. 'You'll tear your shawl.'

The Thénardier woman obeyed, as the she-wolf obeys the male, with a growl.

'The rest of you,' said Thénardier, 'search him!'

Monsieur Leblanc seemed to have given up resisting. He was searched. He had nothing on him except a leather purse containing six francs, and his handkerchief. Thénardier put the handkerchief into his own pocket.

'What! No wallet?' he said.

'And no watch,' replied one of the 'sweeps'.

'All the same,' the masked man who carried the big key murmured in a ventriloquist's voice, 'he's a tough old bastard.'

Thénardier went over to the corner by the door and picked up a bundle of ropes, which he threw at them.

'Tie him to the foot of the bed,' he said.

And noticing the old man who had been left sprawled across the room by the punch from Monsieur Leblanc and was not stirring, he asked, 'Is Boulatruelle dead?'

'No,' replied Bigrenaille, 'he's drunk.'

'Sweep him into a corner,' said Thénardier.

Two of the sweeps shoved the inebriate with their feet over to the heap of old iron.

'Babet,' Thénardier said quietly to the man with the cudgel, 'why did you bring so many. They weren't needed.'

'What can you do?' replied the man with the cudgel. 'They all wanted to be in on it. It's a bad time. There's nothing doing.'

The pallet Monsieur Leblanc had been thrown back on was a kind of hospital bed supported by four crude posts of barely finished wood. Monsieur Leblanc offered no resistance. The ruffians bound him securely to the bed-post furthest from the window and closest to the fireplace, upright, with his feet on the ground.

When the last knot had been tied Thénardier took a chair and came and sat almost facing Monsieur Leblanc. Thénardier was not like himself any more. Within a few moments his features had recomposed themselves, switching from unbridled violence to a calm and cunning mildness. Marius hardly recognized in that polite smile of the bureaucrat the almost bestial, foaming mouth of a moment ago. He viewed with amazement this extraordinary and unnerving metamorphosis, and he felt what a man would feel who saw a tiger turn into a lawyer.

'Monsieur . . .' said Thénardier – and dismissing with a gesture the ruffians who still had their hands on Monsieur Leblanc, 'Back off a bit and let me have a chat with monsieur.'

They all retreated towards the door.

He resumed, 'Monsieur, you shouldn't have tried to jump out of the window. You might have broken your leg. Now, if you don't mind, we're going to have a quiet chat. First of all, I have to tell you something I've noticed, which is that we've not yet heard so much as a peep out of you.'

Thénardier was right. True as it was, though, this detail had in his agitation escaped Marius. Monsieur Leblanc had uttered no more than a few words, without raising his voice. Even in his struggle with the six blackguards by the window he had maintained the most profound and peculiar silence.

Thénardier went on, 'My God! You might have cried thief and I wouldn't have thought it improper! Or murder! People do on occasion – and I wouldn't have taken it amiss. It's perfectly normal to create a bit of a rumpus when you find yourself with individuals that don't inspire enough trust. If you had, no one would have stopped you. You wouldn't even have been gagged. And I'll tell you why. This room's very out of the way. That's the only thing in its favour but it has got that. It's like a cellar. You might let a bomb off inside it, and at the nearest guard-house it'd sound like the snoring of a drunk. Here a cannon would make a pop and thunder a whisper. It's a handy place to live. But anyhow, you didn't cry out, and so much the better, I congratulate you on that, and I'll tell you what conclusion I draw. My dear monsieur, when you cry out, who comes? The police. And after the police? Justice. Well! You didn't cry out. That's because you're no keener than we are to have the police and justice turn up. That's because – I've long suspected it – you've an interest in hiding something. We ourselves have the same interest. So we can come to an understanding.'

As he went on in this way it seemed as though Thénardier, his gaze fixed on Monsieur Leblanc, was trying to plunge the daggers darting from his eyes into his prisoner's conscience. Moreover, his language, characterized by a kind of restrained, sly insolence, was guarded and almost considered, and in this wretch, who was no more than a ruffian just a moment ago, you were now aware of 'the man who studied for the priesthood'.

The silence the prisoner had maintained, that caution that extended even to the point of being oblivious to any concern for his own life, that resistance against the first impulse of nature, which is to cry out – all this, it has to be said, now that it had been remarked on, troubled Marius and came as a painful surprise to him.

Thénardier's very reasonable observation further intensified for Marius the mysterious obscurity shrouding that strange, grave character whom Courfeyrac had nicknamed Monsieur Leblanc. But whoever he might be, trussed up, surrounded by thugs, half buried, as it were, in a hole that every moment deepened beneath him inch by inch, in the face of Thénardier's fury as in the face of his suaveness, this man remained impassive. And Marius could not helping admiring, at such a time as this, that magnificently melancholy countenance.

This was obviously a person incapable of being scared and with no notion of what it was to feel panic-stricken. He was one of those men who in desperate circumstances overcome their bewilderment. No matter how dire his predicament, no matter how inescapable his doom, there was nothing here of the drowning man's anguish, with those ghastly eyes, open underwater.

Thénardier stood up in a matter-of-fact way, went to the fireplace, moved aside the screen, which he rested against the nearby pallet, and thus exposed the brazier full of glowing embers in which the prisoner could plainly see the white-hot chisel, spangled here and there with little flecks of scarlet.

Thénardier then returned to his seat beside Monsieur Leblanc.

'To continue,' he said. 'We can come to an understanding. Let's settle this amicably. I was wrong to lose my temper just now, I don't know what I was thinking of, I went much too far, I was talking wildly. For example, because you're a millionaire I told you I was demanding money, a lot of money, a huge amount of money. That would be unreasonable. Good God, for all that you're rich, you have your expenses, who hasn't? I don't want to ruin you, after all I'm no bloodsucker! I'm not one of those people who, because they're in a stronger position, take advantage of it to be ridiculous. Listen, I'll take a cut and make a sacrifice on my side. All I want is two hundred thousand francs.'

Monsieur Leblanc said not a word.

Thénardier went on, 'As you see, I take my wine with a fair amount of water. I don't know what your fortune stands at but I do know that money's no object to you, and a charitable man like yourself can well afford to give two hundred thousand francs to a family man down on his luck. You too are surely reasonable, you don't imagine I'd go to all this trouble and organize this evening, a well planned operation as all these gentlemen will agree, to end up asking you for enough to go and drink red at fifteen sous a glass and eat veal at Desnoyers's. Two hundred thousand francs, that's what it's worth. Once that little trifle is out of your pocket, I assure you, that'll be that, and you need have no fear anyone will lay a finger on you. You'll say: "But I haven't got two hundred thousand francs on me." Oh! I'm not unrealistic. I'm not expecting that. I ask only one thing of you. Be good enough to write down what I am about to dictate to you.'

Here Thénardier paused, then lingering on his words and casting a smile towards the brazier, he added, 'I warn you, I won't accept that you don't know how to write.'

A grand inquisitor might have envied that smile.

Thénardier pushed the table right up to Monsieur Leblanc and took the ink pot, a pen and a sheet of paper out of the drawer, which he left slightly open, with the long blade of the knife gleaming there. He placed the sheet of paper in front of Monsieur Leblanc.

'Write,' said he.

The prisoner finally spoke. 'How do you expect me to write? I'm tied up.'

'That's true,' said Thénardier, 'you're right, forgive me.' And turning to Bigrenaille, 'Untie the gentleman's right arm.'

Panchaud, alias Printanier, alias Bigrenaille, carried out Thénardier's order. When the prisoner's right arm was free Thénardier dipped the pen in the ink and handed it to him.

'Bear in mind, monsieur, that you're in our power, at our mercy, that no human strength can get you out of this, and we'd really hate to be compelled to resort to the unpleasantness of extreme measures. I don't know your name or your address, but I warn you that you'll stay tied up until the person sent to deliver the letter that you're about to write has returned. Now kindly write.'

'What?' said the prisoner.

'I'll dictate.'

Monsieur Leblanc took up the pen.

Thénardier began to dictate. ' "My daughter—" '

The prisoner shuddered and looked up at Thénardier.

'Put "My dear daughter",' said Thénardier.

Monsieur Leblanc obeyed.

Thénardier continued, ' "Come immediately—" ' He interrupted himself. 'You use *tu* when you address her, don't you?'

'Who?' asked Monsieur Leblanc.

'Damn it!' cried Thénardier. 'The child, Alouette.'

Monsieur Leblanc replied without showing the slightest emotion, 'I don't know what you mean.'

'Just carry on,' said Thénardier, and he went on dictating, ' "Come immediately. I need you urgently. The person who delivers this note is instructed to bring you to me. I'm depending on you. Come without any misgiving." '

Monsieur Leblanc had written all of this down.

Thénardier reconsidered. 'Cross out "Come without any misgiving". That might suggest everything was not quite straightforward and that there might be room for misgivings.'

Monsieur Leblanc crossed out the last four words.

'Now,' said Thénardier, 'sign it. What's your name?'

The prisoner laid down the pen and asked, 'Who's this letter for?'

'You know full well,' replied Thénardier. 'For the child. I just told you so.'

It was obvious that Thénardier was being evasive about naming the young girl in question. He said 'Alouette', he said 'the child', but he did not say her name. A cunning man's ploy to keep his secret from his accomplices. To say her name would have been to let them in on 'the whole story', and to tell them more than they needed to know.

He went on, 'Sign. What's your name?'

'Urbain Fabre,' said the prisoner.

Thénardier, with a cat-like movement, stuck his hand in his pocket and drew out the handkerchief that had been taken from Monsieur Leblanc. He held it up to the candlelight, looking for the initials on it.

'UF. That's right. Urbain Fabre. Well, sign it UF.'

The prisoner signed.

'As it takes two hands to fold the letter, give it to me, I'll fold it.'

That done, Thénardier said, 'Write the address. "Mademoiselle Fabre", at your house. I know you live not very far from here, somewhere near St-Jacques-du-Haut-Pas, because that's where you go to mass every day, but I don't know what street it is. I see that you understand your situation. As you haven't lied about your name, you won't lie about your address. Write it yourself.'

The prisoner remained thoughtful for a moment, then he took up the pen and wrote, 'Mademoiselle Fabre, care of Monsieur Urbain Fabre, Rue St-Dominique-d'Enfer, number 17'.

Thénardier seized the letter with a kind of feverish spasm.

'Wife!' he cried.

The Thénardier woman came rushing over.

'Here's the letter. You know what you have to do. There's a carriage downstairs. Get going, and be back as quick as you can.'

And addressing the man with the poleaxe, 'You! Seeing as you've taken your mask off, go along with the missus. You can ride on the back of the cab. You know where you left the gig?'

'Yes,' said the man. And leaving his poleaxe in a corner he followed after the Thénardier woman.

As they were going off, Thénardier poked his head out of the door, which was standing ajar, and shouted down the corridor, 'Whatever you do, don't lose that letter! Think of it as two hundred thousand francs you have on you!'

The Thénardier woman's rasping voice replied, 'You needn't fret. I've put it down my front.'

Not a minute had gone by when the crack of a whip was to be heard, the sound growing faint and rapidly dying away.

'Good!' growled Thénardier. 'They're off at a fair old pace. At that speed the missus'll be back in three-quarters of an hour.'

He pulled a chair up to the fireplace and sat down, folding his arms and presenting his muddy boots to the brazier. 'My feet are cold!' he said.

There were only five ruffians left in the den with Thénardier and the prisoner. Behind their black masks, or through the blacking smeared over their faces that turned them into colliers or negroes or demons, as fear dictated, these men looked sluggish and spiritless and gave the impression of carrying out a crime as if it were a chore, stolidly, without anger and without pity, with a kind of boredom. They huddled together in a corner like brute beasts, and remained silent. Thénardier warmed his feet. The prisoner had fallen back into taciturnity. A sombre calm had succeeded the furious uproar that had filled the garret a few moments before.

The candle, which had formed a lump of snuff on the end of the wick, barely lit the vast den, the brazier had lost its glow, and all those monstrous heads cast misshapen shadows on the walls and ceiling. No sound was to be heard except the quiet breathing of the drunken old man, who was fast asleep.

Marius waited, with everything adding to his anxiety. The mystery was more impenetrable than ever. Who was this 'child' that Thénardier had called Alouette? Was she his 'Ursule'? The prisoner had seemed unresponsive to that word 'Alouette', and had replied as naturally as could be, 'I don't know what you mean.' On the other hand, the two letters UF were explained: they stood for Urbain Fabre, and Ursule was no longer called Ursule. It was this that Marius saw most clearly. Some sort of ghastly fascination kept him nailed to the spot, where he was able to observe this whole scene from a commanding viewpoint. There he stood, almost incapable of thought or movement, as though overwhelmed by such dreadful things seen at close hand. He waited, hoping for something to happen, no matter what, unable to collect his wits and not knowing what to do.

'In any case,' he said, 'if she is Alouette, I'm sure to find out, for the Thénardier woman is going to bring her here. Then there are no two ways about it, I shall lay down my life if necessary, but I shall save her! Nothing will stop me!'

Nearly half an hour went by like this. Thénardier seemed absorbed in dark thoughts. The prisoner did not stir. Yet every now and then for some while Marius thought he heard a little faint sound coming from the prisoner's direction.

Suddenly Thénardier addressed the prisoner. 'Listen, Monsieur Fabre, I might as well tell you this now.'

These few words seemed to prelude some explanation. Marius strained to hear.

Thénardier went on: 'Be patient, my wife will be back shortly. I think Alouette is in fact your daughter and it seems to me quite right you should keep her. Now pay attention. My wife's going to fetch her with your letter. I told my wife to dress up, as you saw, so that your young lady would go along with her without any fuss. They'll both get into the carriage with my colleague behind. Somewhere beyond the gate there's a gig with two very good horses harnessed to it. Your young lady will be taken there. She'll get out of the carriage. My colleague will get into the gig with her, and my wife'll come back here to tell us it's done. As for the young lady, no harm will come to her. The gig will take her somewhere safe and just as soon as you've given me the small sum of two hundred thousand francs she'll be returned to you. If you have me arrested, my colleague will take care of Alouette. There you have it.'

The prisoner did not utter a word.

After a pause Thénardier continued, 'It's simple, as you see. No one's going to get hurt if you don't want anyone to get hurt. I'm giving it to you straight. I'm telling you so you know.'

He paused. The prisoner did not break the silence, and Thénardier went on, 'As soon as my wife gets back and tells me Alouette's on her way, we'll release you and you'll be free to go home to bed. As you see, our intention was not to cause harm.'

Frightful images went through Marius's mind. What! That young girl they were abducting was not going to be brought back? One of those monsters was going to carry her off into the dark? Where to? And what if it was her? – and it was all too clear that it was! Marius felt his heart stop beating. What was he to do? Fire the pistol? Put all these wretches in the hands of the law? But that dreadful man with the poleaxe would still be completely beyond reach with the young girl, and Marius thought about those words of Thénardier's, suspecting their deadly meaning: 'If you have me arrested, my colleague will take care of Alouette.'

Now, it was not just the colonel's written will that held him back, it was love itself, the danger to the one he loved. This appalling situation, which had already been going on for more than an hour, changed in complexion every moment. Marius had sufficient strength of mind to review in succession all the most distressing conjectures, seeking hope and finding none. The tumult of his thoughts contrasted with the funereal silence of that den.

In the midst of this silence came the sound of the door downstairs opening, then closing again. The bound prisoner stirred.

'Here comes the missus,' said Thénardier.

And no sooner had he spoken than the Thénardier woman rushed into the room, red-faced, breathless, panting, eyes ablaze, and slapping her huge hands on both thighs simultaneously she cried out, 'False address!'

The blackguard she had taken with her appeared behind her and came in to retrieve his axe.

She went on, 'Not a soul! Rue St-Dominique, number 17, no Monsieur Urbain Fabre! The name means nothing to anyone there!'

Choked, she paused, then continued, 'Monsieur Thénardier! That gaffer's been stringing you along! You're too good, you see! If it'd been me I'd've carved his face up to begin with! And if he'd fought back I'd have roasted him alive! He'd have had to talk, and tell us where the girl is and where he keeps his hoard! That's the way I'd have handled this! There's good reason for saying men are more foolish than women! Not a soul! Number 17! It's just a big carriage gate! No Monsieur Fabre in Rue St-Dominique! And not sparing the horses and tipping the coachman and all! I spoke to the porter and his wife, who's a thoroughly reliable woman, and they've never heard of him!'

Marius breathed again. Ursule or Alouette, the girl he no longer knew what to call – she was safe.

While his fuming wife ranted Thénardier sat on the table. For several moments he uttered not a word, swinging his right foot, which dangled, and staring at the brazier with a look of vicious rumination.

Finally he said to the prisoner in a measured and particularly ferocious tone of voice, 'A false address? What did you expect to gain by that?'

'Time!' cried the prisoner in a ringing voice.

And in the same instant he shook off his bonds. They had been cut. The prisoner was now tied to the bed by only one leg.

Before the seven men had time to gather their wits and throw themselves at him, he leaned over to the hearth, reached out his hand to the brazier, then straightened up again. And now Thénardier, the Thénardier woman and the ruffians, huddled in shock at the far end of the hovel, stared at him dumbfounded as he stood there, almost free, and striking a fearsome attitude with the red-hot chisel raised above his head, casting a sinister glow.

The subsequent judicial investigation into the ambush at the Gorbeau tenement recorded that a ten-centime coin, cut and worked in a special way, was found in the garret when the police raided it. This ten-centime coin was one of those marvels of ingenuity produced in the shadows, and for the shadows, by patience learned in the prison hulks – marvels that are nothing less than instruments of escape. These abominable yet delicate products of amazing skill are to the jeweller's work what the metaphors of argot are to poetry. There are the Benvenuto Cellinis of the prison hulks, just as there are the Villons of the language. The poor wretch who aspires to free himself contrives, sometimes without any tools, with just a pocket-knife or any old blade, to saw a coin into two thin discs, to hollow out these discs without damaging the impressions stamped on the coin, and to work a thread into the rim of the coin so that the discs can be put back together again. To be screwed and unscrewed at will. The thing is a box. In this box he hides a watch-spring, and this watch-spring, adeptly handled, cuts heavy shackles and iron bars. This wretched convict is believed to have only a coin in his possession. No! He has freedom! It was a ten-centime coin of this kind that during the later police search was found on the premises, open, in two pieces, under the bed near the window. They also found a tiny blue-steel saw that could be hidden inside the coin. It is likely that when the villains searched him the prisoner had this coin on him, which he managed to conceal in his hand, and then with his free right hand he unscrewed it and used the saw to cut the cords that tied him, which would explain the faint sound and the almost imperceptible movements that Marius had noticed.

Unable to bend down for fear of betraying himself, he had not cut the bonds on his left leg.

The villains had recovered from their initial surprise. 'Not to worry,' Bigrenaille said to Thénardier, 'he's still held by one leg and he won't get away. I guarantee that. I'm the one that lashed that trotter of his.'

Nevertheless the prisoner spoke out. 'You're miserable wretches, but my life isn't that much worth protecting. As for thinking that you'll make me talk, that you'll make me write what I don't want to write, that you'll make me say what I don't want to say . . .' He rolled up his left sleeve: 'Look!'

At the same time he stretched out his arm and laid on his bare flesh the glowing chisel that he held by the wooden handle in his right hand.

The sizzle of burning flesh could be heard and the smell that belongs to torture chambers spread through the hovel. Marius reeled, horror-stricken, the villains themselves shuddered, the strange old man's features barely contracted; and while the red-hot iron sank into the steaming wound, impassive and almost sublime he fixed on Thénardier his splendid gaze bearing no hatred, in which suffering dissolved into serene majesty.

When the flesh and the senses revolt against being subjected to physical pain, in those of a great and noble disposition this brings out the soul, to be seen on the brow, just as rebellions among the soldiery force the captain to show himself.

'Wretches!' he said. 'Have no more fear of me than I have of you!'

And drawing the chisel away from the wound he hurled it through the window, which had been left open. The horrible glowing implement disappeared, spinning into the darkness and falling to the ground far off, where it was quenched by the snow.

The prisoner said, 'Do what you will with me.'

He was unarmed.

'Seize him!' said Thénardier.

Two of the villains laid their hands on his shoulders and the masked man with the ventriloquist's voice stood in front of him, ready to smash his skull with his key at the slightest move.

At the same time Marius heard below him, at the foot of the partition but so close he could not see who was speaking, the following discussion conducted in low voices:

'There's only one thing left to do.'

'Finish him off.'

'That's right.'

It was the husband and wife conferring. Thénardier slowly walked over to the table, opened the drawer and took out the knife.

Marius worried the handle of his pistol. In an agony of indecision! For the last hour there had been two voices in his conscience, one telling him to respect his father's will, the other calling on him to rescue the prisoner. These two conflicting voices kept up an uninterrupted battle that was torture to him. Right up until then he had been vaguely hoping to find some way of reconciling these two duties, but no possible solution had emerged. However, the danger was now urgent, there was no more time to delay, a few paces from the prisoner was Thénardier, considering, knife in hand.

Marius looked round in panic, the automatic last resort of despair. Suddenly he gave a start.

At his feet, on the table, a beam of bright light cast by the full moon illuminated and seemed to point out to him a sheet of paper, on which he read the following line, written in big letters by the older Thénardier girl that very morning: 'THE BASHERS ARE HERE.'

An idea flashed into Marius's mind. This was what he was looking for, the solution to the dreadful problem that was torturing him: how to spare the assassin and save the victim. He knelt down on the chest of drawers, reached out his arm, grabbed the sheet of paper, quietly detached a chunk of plaster from the partition wall, wrapped the paper round it, and threw them both together through the hole in the wall into the middle of the den.

Just in time. Thénardier had conquered his last fears, or last scruples, and was advancing on the prisoner.

'Something fell!' cried the Thénardier woman.

'What is it?' asked her husband.

The woman darted forward and picked up the chunk of plaster wrapped in paper. She handed it to her husband.

'How did that get in here?' asked Thénardier.

'Honestly!' said the woman. 'How do you think it got in? It came in through the window, of course.'

'I saw it come in,' said Bigrenaille.

Thénardier rapidly unfolded the paper and held it up to the candle. 'It's Éponine's handwriting. Damn it!'

He signalled to his wife, who hurried over; he showed her the line written on the sheet of paper, then added in a lowered voice, 'Quick!

The ladder! Leave the bacon in the mousetrap and let's get out of here!'

'Without cutting the man's throat?' asked the Thénardier woman.

'We haven't time.'

'Which way?' said Bigrenaille.

'Through the window,' replied Thénardier. 'Since Ponine threw the stone through the window, that means the house isn't blocked off on that side.'

The masked man with the ventriloquist's voice put his huge key down on the floor, raised both arms in the air and opened and clenched his fists rapidly three times, without saying a word. It was like the signal for a ship's crew to clear the decks. The villains who were holding the prisoner let go of him. In the twinkling of an eye the rope ladder was unrolled out of the window and securely attached to the sill by the two iron hooks.

The prisoner paid no attention to what was going on around him. He seemed to be daydreaming or praying.

As soon as the ladder was fixed in place, Thénardier cried, 'Come on, wife!' And he rushed to the window.

But just as he was about to climb through it Bigrenaille seized him roughly by the collar. 'Not so fast, old man! After us!'

'After us!' yelled the villains.

'You're behaving like children,' said Thénardier, 'we're wasting time. We've got the law at our heels.'

'Well,' said one of the villains, 'let's draw lots for who goes first.'

'Are you mad!' Thénardier exclaimed. 'Are you crazy! What a bunch of idiots! You want to waste time, do you? Draw lots? By choosing the wet finger? Or the short straw! By writing down our names! And putting them in a hat!'

'Would you like my hat?' a voice called out from the doorway.

Everyone turned round.

It was Javert. He had his hat in his hand and was holding it out to them with a smile.

XXI
You Should Always Begin by Arresting the Victims

At dusk Javert had positioned his men and hidden himself behind the trees on Rue de la Barrière-des-Gobelins, which is directly opposite the Gorbeau tenement on the other side of the boulevard. He had begun by opening 'his bag' to bundle into it the two young girls detailed to keep watch on the approaches to the den. But he had only 'bagged' Azelma. As for Éponine, she was not at her post, she had disappeared, and he had not been able to round her up. Then Javert had settled down to wait, listening out for the agreed signal. The coming and going of the carriage had greatly disturbed him. At last he had grown impatient and, sure there was a criminals' den here, sure of having struck lucky, having recognized many of the villains who had gone inside, he had finally decided to go on up without waiting for the pistol-shot.

Remember, he had Marius's pass-key.

He arrived at just the right moment.

Dismayed, the villains scrambled for the weapons they had abandoned all over the place in the interests of escape. In less than a second these seven men, dreadful to behold, had grouped together and adopted a defensive stance, one with his poleaxe, another with his key, another with his cudgel, the rest with shears, crowbars and hammers. Thénardier had his knife in his hand. The Thénardier woman took up an enormous paving-stone that stood in the corner by the window and served her daughters as a stool.

Javert put his hat back on his head and took a couple of steps into the room, with his arms folded, his cane under one arm, his sword in its scabbard.

'Stop right there!' he said. 'You won't exit by the window, you'll exit by the door. It's less dangerous that way. There are seven of you, there are fifteen of us. Let's not descend to brawling like a bunch of Auvergne peasants. Let's have some co-operation.'

Bigrenaille drew out a pistol he had concealed under his overall and placed it in Thénardier's hand, whispering in his ear, 'It's Javert. I daren't fire at that man. What about you?'

'God damn it!' replied Thénardier.

'Well, you shoot then.'

Thénardier took the pistol and aimed at Javert.

Only three paces away, Javert gazed steadily at him and merely said, 'Now then, don't shoot. You'll miss.'

Thénardier pulled the trigger. He missed.

'Didn't I tell you!' said Javert.

Bigrenaille threw his bludgeon at Javert's feet. 'You're the devil supreme! I surrender.'

'And the rest of you?' Javert asked the other villains.

They responded, 'Us too.'

Javert went on calmly, 'That's it, well done, as I said, we're co-operating.'

732

'I have just one request,' said Bigrenaille, 'that I won't have to go without tobacco while I'm in solitary.'

'Granted,' said Javert.

And he turned and called out behind him, 'Come in now!'

A squad of police officers, swords in hand, and policemen armed with truncheons and clubs, poured in at Javert's summons. They pinioned the villains. Dimly lit by the single candle, this throng filled the den with shadows.

'Handcuff the lot of them!' shouted Javert.

'Just you try!' yelled a voice, which was not the voice of a man, but no one would ever have been able to tell it was a woman's.

The Thénardier woman had entrenched herself in one of the corners by the window, and it was she who had just let out this bellow. The policemen and agents fell back. She had thrown off her shawl but kept her hat on. Her husband, crouching behind her, was almost hidden under the discarded shawl; she was shielding him with her body, the paving-stone raised above her head, poised like a giantess about to hurl a rock.

'Keep away!' she shouted.

Everyone retreated towards the corridor. An empty space opened up in the middle of the garret.

The Thénardier woman cast a glance at the ruffians who had let themselves be pinioned, and muttered in a hoarse, throaty voice, 'Cowards!'

Javert smiled and stepped forward into the empty space that the Thénardier woman kept under her smouldering gaze.

'Don't come any closer,' she shouted, 'or I'll flatten you.'

'What a fighter!' said Javert. 'You've got the beard of a man, missus, but I've got the claws of a woman.'

And he continued to advance on her.

Dishevelled and terrifying, the Thénardier woman, legs apart, leaned back and furiously hurled the paving-stone at Javert's head. Javert ducked, the stone flew over him, struck the wall behind, knocked off a huge piece of plaster and, ricocheting from one corner to another across the luckily almost empty hovel, eventually came to rest at Javert's heels.

At the same moment Javert reached the Thénardier couple. One of his big hands clamped on the woman's shoulder, the other on her husband's head.

'Cuffs!' he shouted.

The policemen crowded back in and within a few seconds Javert's order had been carried out. Defeated, the Thénardier woman stared at her shackled hands and at those of her husband, dropped to the floor and cried out, weeping, 'My daughters!'

'They're in the clink,' said Javert.

Meanwhile, the police had spotted the drunk asleep behind the door, and were shaking him.

He woke up, mumbling, 'Is it all over, Jondrette?'

'Yes,' replied Javert.

The six handcuffed ruffians were on their feet. They were still in their spectral guise, three of them with blackened faces, three masked.

'Keep your masks on,' said Javert.

And inspecting them with the eye of a Frederick II reviewing a Potsdam parade, he said to the three 'sweeps', 'Good evening, Bigrenaille! Good evening, Brujon! Good evening, Deux-Milliards!'

Then turning to the three masked men, he said to the man with the poleaxe, 'Good evening, Gueulemer!'

And to the man with the cudgel, 'Good evening, Babet!'

And to the ventriloquist, 'Greetings, Claquesous!'

At that moment he caught sight of the villains' prisoner, who, keeping his head down, had not uttered a word since the police came in.

'Untie the gentleman!' said Javert. 'And no one's to leave!'

That said, in the manner of one whose authority is beyond question he sat at the table that still had the candle and writing-materials on it, drew a stamped sheet of paper from his pocket and began to write his report. When he had written the first lines, which were just the standard wording, he looked up.

'Bring forward the gentleman whom these gentlemen here had tied up.'

The policemen looked round.

'Well,' said Javert, 'where is he?'

The villains' prisoner, Monsieur Leblanc, Monsieur Urbain Fabre, the father of Ursule or Alouette, had disappeared. The door was guarded, but not the window. As soon as he was left untied and while Javert was drawing up his report, he had taken advantage of the confusion, the commotion, the crush, the darkness, and of a moment when attention was not fixed on him, to make a dash for the window. An agent ran to the casement and looked out. There was no one to be seen outside. The rope ladder was still swaying.

'Damn it!' Javert said to himself. 'He must have been the real prize.'

XXII

The Baby Boy Who Was Crying in Part Two

The day after these events took place in the house on Boulevard de l'Hôpital, a child who seemed to be coming from the direction of the Pont d'Austerlitz was walking up the right-hand side-lane in the direction of the Fontainebleau toll-gate. Darkness had fallen. This child was pale, thin, dressed in rags, wearing cotton trousers in the month of February, and he was singing at the top of his voice.

At the corner of Rue du Petit-Banquier a bent old woman was rummaging in a pile of rubbish by the light of a street lantern. The child bumped into her as he went by, then backed away, crying out, 'Hey! There was me thinking that was a huge, huge dog!'

He pronounced the word 'huge' the second time with a swell of his jeering voice that might be fairly well represented by capital letters: 'a huge, HUGE dog'.

The old woman straightened up in a fury. 'Cheeky brat!' she grumbled. 'If I hadn't been bending over, I can tell you where you'd have felt the end of my foot.'

The boy was already some way off. 'Kss! kss!' he goaded her. 'And you know what? Maybe I was right!'

Choking with indignation, the old woman drew herself up to her full height, and the red gleam of the lantern fell directly on her ghastly pale face, all sharp angles and wrinkles thrown into relief, crow's-feet down to the corners of her mouth. Her body disappeared into the shadows and only her head was visible. She looked like a mask of Decrepitude carved out by a light in the dark.

The boy considered her. 'Madame's is not my kind of beauty,' he said.

He went on his way and resumed his song:

> King Kicker went a-hunting,
> A-hunting after crow.
> On stilts he went a-hunting . . .

At the end of these three lines he paused. He had arrived outside number 50–52, and finding the door closed he began to kick it, delivering resounding and heroic kicks more indicative of the man's shoes he wore than the child's feet he had.

Meanwhile, the same old woman he had encountered at the corner of Rue du Petit-Banquier came hurrying up behind him, shouting and gesticulating wildly.

'What do you think you're doing? What do you think you're doing? God Almighty! Battering the door! Knocking the house down!'

The kicking continued.

The old woman was shouting herself hoarse. 'Is that how buildings are treated these days?'

All of a sudden she stopped. She had recognized the lad.

'Why, it's that little devil!'

'Well, if it isn't the old biddy,' said the boy. 'Good evening, Burgon-muche. I've come to see my kin.'

With a composite grimace – unfortunately lost in the dark – in which hatred admirably contrived to make the most of decrepitude and ugliness, the old woman responded, 'There's no one here, ragamuffin.'

'Bah!' retorted the boy. 'Where's my father, then?'

'At La Force.'

'You don't say! And my mother?'

'At St-Lazare.'

'Oh well! And my sisters?'

'At Les Madelonnettes.'

The lad scratched behind his ear, stared at Mame Burgon and said, 'Ah!'

Then he twirled on his heels, and a moment later the old woman, still standing on the doorstep, heard him singing in his clear young voice as he headed off under the elm trees, shivering in the winter wind.

> King Kicker went a-hunting,
> A-hunting after crow.
> On stilts he went a-hunting,
> And under you could go,
> And then to let you through, tra-la
> The payment was two sous, tra-la.

PART FOUR

THE RUE PLUMET IDYLL
AND
THE RUE ST-DENIS EPIC

BOOK ONE
A FEW PAGES OF
HISTORY

I
Well Cut

The two years immediately following the July Revolution – 1831 and 1832 – stand out as one of history's most distinctive and striking moments. Between the years that precede them and those that follow, these two years are like two mountains. They have a revolutionary grandeur. Precipitous faces can be discerned. The social masses, the very foundations of civilization, the solid grouping of overlapping and tenacious interests, the age-old contours of the previous French landscape keep appearing and disappearing through storm clouds of systems, passions and theories. These continual appearances and disappearances have been named 'resistance' and 'movement'. At intervals can be seen a glimmer of truth, that daylight of the human soul.

This remarkable period is quite a limited one and is already beginning to be far enough away from us that it might now be possible to determine its broad outlines.

That is what we shall try to do.

The Restoration had been one of those transitional periods hard to define, when exhaustion, rumblings and murmurings, dormancy and tumult prevail, periods that are nothing other than a great nation coming to the end of one stage in its progress before embarking on the next.

These periods are singular, and they mislead the politicians who want to exploit them. At first the nation wants nothing but rest. Its only thirst is for peace, its only ambition, to be small. Which is a translation of 'to keep quiet'. Of great events, great dangers, great adventures, great men, people have had enough, thank you very much, they have had more than enough. They would trade Caesar for Prusias and Napoleon for the king of Yvetot. 'What a good little king was he!' They have marched since daybreak, it is now evening after what has been for them a long, hard day; the first part of the way they went with Mirabeau, the second with Robespierre, the third with Bonaparte. They are worn out. Everybody is asking for a bed.

Self-sacrifice grown weary, heroism grown old, ambitions sated, fortunes made, all seek, crave, implore, beg – for what? A place to rest. They have it. Peace, tranquillity, leisure, are theirs. And they are happy. Yet at the same time certain realities surface, they present their credentials, and they too come knocking at the door. These realities are the result of revolutions and wars, they are, they exist, they are entitled to take their place in society, and they do. And most of the time these realities are just the quarter-masters and foragers sent in advance to make ready the accommodation of principles.

So this is how it appears to political philosophers:

As weary men demand rest, new realities demand guarantees. Guarantees are to new realities what rest is to men.

This is what England demanded of the Stuarts after the Protector. This is what France demanded of the Bourbons after the Empire.

These guarantees are a necessity of the times. They must be provided. Princes 'grant' them but in fact it is force of circumstance that supplies them. A profound truth, and useful to know, one the Stuarts were unaware of in 1660, and that the Bourbons had not even an inkling of in 1814.

The predestined family that returned to France when Napoleon fell had the fatal naivety to believe it was the family that was giving, and that what it had given it could take back again. That the House of Bourbon had divine right, France had nothing. And that the political right conceded in Louis XVIII's Charter was no more than a branch of that divine right lopped off by the House of Bourbon and graciously bestowed on the people until the day when it might please the king to have his gift back again. Still, from the offence caused by the gift, the Bourbons should have sensed it was not theirs to give.

This House was churlish towards the nineteenth century. It took every enhancement of the nation with a bad grace. To use the common expression, that is to say a popular and truthful expression, it pulled a long face. The people saw this.

It thought it had power because the Empire had been swept away before it, like a stage set. It did not notice that it had itself been established in the same way. It did not see that it was the work of the same hand that had removed Napoleon.

It thought it had roots because it identified itself with the past. It was wrong. It was part of the past, but the whole past was France. The roots of French society lay not in the Bourbons, but in the nation. These strong and hidden roots constituted not the right of a family but the history of a people. They were everywhere except beneath the throne.

The House of Bourbon was for France the illustrious and bloody nub of her history, but no longer the principal element in her destiny or the necessary foundation of her politics. People could do without the Bourbons. They had done without them for twenty-two years. There had been a break in continuity. Of this the Bourbons were oblivious. And how could they have suspected it, they who deluded themselves that Louis XVII reigned on the ninth of Thermidor and that Louis XVIII reigned on the day of the battle of Marengo? Never, since the beginning of history, had princes been so blind to reality and to that element of divine authority contained in reality and promulgated by it. Never had that earthly pretension called the right of kings so denied the right of a higher authority.

A great mistake, which led this family to withdraw the guarantees 'granted' in 1814, the 'concessions', as it called them. Deplorably, what it called its concessions were our conquests. What it called our infringements were our rights.

When it thought the time was ripe, the Restoration, imagining itself to be victorious over Bonaparte and well rooted in the country – that is to say, believing itself to be strong and deeply entrenched – took a gamble and abruptly declared itself. One morning it confronted France and, raising its voice, contested the collective right of the nation to sovereignty and the individual right of the citizen to liberty. In other words, it denied to the nation what made it a nation and to the citizen what made him a citizen.

This is the foundation of those famous decrees called the July Ordinances.

The Restoration fell.

It deserved to fall. Yet, to tell the truth, it had not been totally hostile to all forms of progress. Great things had been accomplished with the Restoration standing by.

Under the Restoration the nation had grown used to calm discussion, in which the Republic had been wanting, and to greatness in peace, in which the Empire had been wanting. A free and strong France had been an encouraging sight to the other peoples of Europe. The Revolution had spoken under Robespierre. The cannon had spoken under Bonaparte. Under Louis XVIII and Charles X came the turn of intelligence to speak. The wind dropped, the torch blazed again. The pure light of intellect could be seen flickering on the serene summits. A spectacle magnificent, useful and delightful to behold. For fifteen years these great principles, so old to the thinker, so new to the statesman, could be seen at work in full peacetime, in full public view: equality before the law, freedom of conscience, freedom of speech, freedom of the press, the accessibility of every office to all who had the capacity to hold it. So it went on until 1830. The Bourbons were an instrument of civilization that broke in the hands of Providence.

The fall of the Bourbons was full of grandeur, not on their side but on the side of the nation. They stepped down from the throne with gravity but without authority. Their descent into darkness was not one of those solemn disappearances whose legacy to history is a sombre emotion. It was neither the spectral calm of Charles I nor the eagle cry of Napoleon. They went, that is all. They laid down the crown and kept no aura. They were dignified, but they were not august. To some degree they fell short of the majesty of their misfortune. Charles X, who on the journey to Cherbourg had a round table cut down into a square one, appeared to be more anxious about the threat to etiquette than about the collapsing monarchy. This decline saddened both loyal men who loved them for themselves and serious men who honoured their ancestry. The people behaved admirably. Attacked one morning with armed force by a kind of royal insurrection, the nation sensed its strength was so great that it felt no anger. It defended itself, controlled itself, put things back in their place – government within the law, the Bourbons in exile, alas! – and stopped there. It removed old King Charles X from beneath the canopy that had sheltered Louis XIV and set him gently on the ground. Only with sadness and care did it lay hands on the royal personages. It was not one man, it was not a few men, it was France, all of France, France victorious and elated by her victory, who seemed to remember, and before the eyes of the whole world to act on, these solemn words of Guillaume du Vair after the day of the barricades: 'It is easy for those used to gleaning favours from the great and to hopping like a bird from bough to bough, from a blighted fortune to a flourishing one, to be disrespectful towards their prince in his adversity. But for myself, the fortune of my kings will always command respect, and especially that of the blighted ones.'

The Bourbons took with them respect but not regret. As we have just said, their misfortune was greater than they were. They disappeared over the horizon.

At once, the July Revolution had friends and enemies throughout the world. Some swooped on it with joy and enthusiasm, others turned their back on it, each according to his nature. In the first instance the princes of Europe, night-owls in this dawning light, shut their eyes, hurt and bewildered, and opened them again only to intimidate. Understandable fear, forgivable anger. This strange revolution was not much of a clash. Overthrown royalty had not even the honour of being treated as the enemy and having its blood spilled. In the eyes of despotic governments, always keen that freedom should blacken its own name, the July Revolution committed the crime of being momentous and remaining non-violent. In fact, nothing was attempted or plotted against it. The most discontented, the most vexed, the most agitated welcomed it. Whatever our self-interests and grudges may be, a mysterious respect is attendant on events wherein people sense the collaboration of someone working on a higher plane than man.

The July Revolution is the triumph of right in the overthrow of reality. A splendid thing.

Right overthrowing reality. Hence the magnitude of the 1830 Revolution, hence also its mildness. Right that triumphs has no need to be violent.

Right is that which is just and true.

Characteristic of what is right is to remain eternally beautiful and pure. Reality, even the most apparently inexorable, even the best-accepted by its contemporaries, if it exists only as reality and contains but too little right or none at all, is surely destined to become in the course of time distorted, squalid, perhaps even monstrous. Anyone wanting to take in at a glance how ugly reality can be, seen from a distance centuries later, should consider Machiavelli. Machiavelli is not an evil genius, or a demon, or a wretched and cowardly writer. He is simply the reality. And he is not just the Italian reality. He is the European reality, the reality of the sixteenth century. He seems hideous, and so he is, when confronted with the nineteenth-century moral conception.

This conflict between right and reality has been going on ever since societies came into being. To end this duel, to marry purity of concept with human actuality, to instil right in reality and reality in right, that is the work of the wise.

II
Stitched Together

But the work of the wise is one thing, the work of the astute, another.

The Revolution of 1830 quickly came to a halt.

As soon as a revolution runs aground the astute break up the beached vessel.

The astute in our century have conferred on themselves the title of statesmen, with the result that this word 'statesmen' has ended up becoming something of a slang word. After all, let us not forget that where there is only astuteness there is inevitably pettiness. To say 'the astute' is another way of saying 'the mediocre'.

Similarly, to say 'statesmen' is sometimes tantamount to saying 'traitors'.

According to the astute, then, revolutions like the July Revolution are severed arteries. Prompt ligature is needed. Too grandly proclaimed, right destabilizes. So, once right has been asserted, the state must be strengthened. After freedom is secured, thoughts must turn to authority.

At this point the wise have not as yet parted company with the astute, but they are beginning to be wary. Authority, agreed. But firstly, what is authority? Secondly, where does it come from?

The astute do not seem to hear this murmured objection, and press on with their scheme.

According to those politicians expert at putting the mask of necessity on advantageous fictions, the first requirement of a nation after a revolution, when that nation belongs to a monarchic continent, is to acquire a dynasty. That way, they say, it can have peace after its revolution, in other words time to dress its wounds and rebuild its house. A dynasty hides the scaffolding and shields the ambulance.

Now, it is not always easy to acquire a dynasty.

If need be, any man of genius or even any self-made adventurer will make a king. In the first case you have Napoleon, in the second, Iturbide.

But not just any family will make a dynasty. There is of necessity a certain element of antiquity in a lineage, and the stamp of centuries cannot be improvised.

If you put yourself – with all due reservations, of course – in the position of 'statesmen': after a revolution, what are the attributes of the king who emerges from it? He may be, and it is an advantage if he is, a revolutionary, that is to say, he personally took part in that revolution, he had a hand in it, he committed himself to it or distinguished himself in it, he handled the axe or wielded the sword of revolution.

What are the attributes of a dynasty? It must be national, that is to say, revolutionary at a distance, not through deeds done but ideas accepted. It must consist of the past and be historic, consist of the future and be sympathetic.

All this explains why first revolutions are satisfied with finding a man, Cromwell or Napoleon, and why second revolutions are absolutely determined to find a family, the House of Brunswick or the House of Orléans.

Royal houses are like those Indian fig trees whose every branch,

744

bending down to the earth, takes root and becomes another fig tree. Each branch may grow into a dynasty. On the sole condition that it bends down to the people.

That is the theory of the astute.

So the great art is this: to give success the ring of catastrophe so that those who profit by it may tremble also, to season with fear every step forward, to prolong the transition curve, thereby delaying progress, to dull the brightness of that dawn, to denounce and suppress the asperities of enthusiasm, to cut corners and trim claws, to stifle triumph and muffle right, to wrap the giant nation in flannel and very quickly put it to bed, to impose a diet on that exuberant health, to put Hercules on a convalescence regime, to dilute the event with expediency, to offer to spirits thirsting for the ideal that nectar diluted with tisane, to take precautions against undue success, to furnish the revolution with a sun-blind.

1830 put into practice this theory, which 1688 had already applied to England.

1830 is a revolution stopped in mid-course. Semi-progress. Quasiright. Well, logic takes absolutely no account of the more-or-less, as the sun takes no account of the candle.

Who stops revolutions in mid-course? The bourgeoisie.

Why?

Because the bourgeoisie is satisfied self-interest. Yesterday it represented appetite, today it represents repletion, tomorrow it will represent surfeit.

The phenomenon of 1814 after Napoleon recurred in 1830 after Charles X.

Some people have wanted wrongly to identify the bourgeoisie as a class. The bourgeoisie is simply the contented section of the people. The bourgeois is the man who now has time to sit down. A chair is not a caste.

But the very progress of the human race may be halted because of a desire to sit down too soon. This has often been the failing of the bourgeoisie.

A class is not made up of those with a failing. Selfishness is not one of the divisions of the social order.

Besides, we must be fair, even to selfishness: the state to which that part of the nation, the bourgeoisie, aspired after the upheaval of 1830 was not inertia, which involves indifference and laziness and includes a little shame. It was not sleep, which implies a momentary forgetfulness accessible to dreams. It was a state of pause – a halt.

'Halt' is a word that peculiarly combines a dual and almost contradictory meaning: troops on the march, that is to say, movement, and inaction, that is to say, rest.

A halt is the restoration of strength. It is armed rest in a state of alert. It is the new reality that posts sentinels and remains on guard. A halt implies fighting yesterday and fighting tomorrow.

It is the interval between 1830 and 1848.

What we here call fighting may also be called progress.

So the bourgeoisie as well as the statesmen needed a man who would represent that word 'halt'. An 'although–because'. A composite individual, signifying both revolution and stability, in other words, consolidating the present through the obvious compatibility of the past with the future.

This man was ready and waiting. His name was Louis-Philippe d'Orléans.

The two hundred and twenty-one made Louis-Philippe king. Lafayette was responsible for the consecration. He called it 'the best of republics'. Paris's Hôtel de Ville replaced Reims cathedral.

This substitution of a half-throne for the whole throne was 'the achievement of 1830'.

When the astute were done, the great iniquity of their solution became apparent. Absolute right was left out of the whole thing. Absolute right cried, 'I protest!' Then, ominously, it fell back into the shadows.

III
Louis-Philippe

Revolutions have a strong arm and a good hand, they strike hard and have the luck of the draw. Even incomplete, even bastardized and mongrelized and reduced to the state of minor revolution like the 1830 Revolution, they are nearly always left with enough providential far-sightedness to make it impossible they should ever come amiss. Their eclipse is never an abdication.

Yet we must not crow too loudly. Revolutions, too, make mistakes, and serious blunders have been known.

Let us return to 1830. In its aberration 1830 was lucky. In the institution that called itself 'order' after the truncated revolution, the king proved better than royalty. Louis-Philippe was a rare man.

Son of a father to whom history will surely grant extenuating circumstances, but as worthy of esteem as that father had been worthy of blame. Possessing all the private virtues and several of the public ones.

Mindful of his health, his fortune, his own person, his affairs, knowing the value of a minute and not always the value of a year. Sober, serene, peaceable, patient. A good fellow and a good prince. One who slept with his own wife and had footmen in his palace detailed to show respectable citizens the conjugal bed, a regular display of his private life that proved useful after the extra-conjugal spectacles of the senior branch in the past. Who had a command of all European languages, and rarer still all languages of all interest groups, and spoke them. An admirable representative of the 'middle class', but surpassing it and in every way superior to it. While appreciating his ancestry, having the extremely good sense to set greatest store by his own intrinsic worth, and on the actual question of his lineage being most particular to declare himself Orléans and not Bourbon. Very much the first Prince of the Blood while still only His Most Serene Highness, but ordinary citizen from the day he became His Majesty. Long-winded in public, succinct in private. Alleged, but not proven, to be a miser. Basically, one of those thrifty types with a readiness to be unsparing when the fancy takes them or when it is expected of them. Well read, but with little feeling for literature. A gentleman but no cavalier. Unpretentious, calm, strong. Adored by his family and his household. An engaging conversationalist, a statesman with no illusions, inwardly cold, ruled by immediate priorities, governing always in the short term, incapable of resentment or of gratitude, ruthless in deploying superiority against mediocrity, clever at getting parliamentary majorities to condemn those mysterious unanimities grumbling darkly beneath thrones. Expansive, sometimes imprudent in his expansiveness, but with marvellous adroitness in that imprudence. Rich in resourcefulness, with many faces and many masks. Instilling a fear of Europe in France and a fear of France in Europe! A man who undeniably loved his country but preferred his family. Valuing domination more than authority and authority more than dignity, a pernicious tendency in this respect: that in the interests of success, it sanctions guile and does not absolutely repudiate baseness. But advantageous in this: that it protects politics from violent upheaval, the state from fracturing, and society from catastrophe. Meticulous, punctilious, vigilant, careful, shrewd, indefatigable. Sometimes inconsistent and contradicting himself. Bold against Austria at Ancona, determined against England in Spain, bombarding Antwerp and paying off Pritchard. Singing the 'Marseillaise' with conviction. Incapable of despondency or lassitude, of any sense of the beautiful or the ideal, of reckless generosity, Utopianism, illusion, anger, vanity, fear. Possessing all manner of personal fearlessness, a general at Valmy, a soldier at Jemappes. Eight times targeted by regicides, and always smiling. Brave as a grenadier, courageous as a thinker, anxious only at the prospect of European turmoil, and unsuited for great political adventures. Always ready to risk his life, never his work. Disguising his will as influence so as to be obeyed for what he thought rather than as king. With a gift for observation but not for anticipation. Not much interested in people in the abstract but a good judge of men; that is to say, he relied on what he saw to make a judgement. A fluent speaker, of quick and discerning good sense, practical wisdom and prodigious memory. Drawing incessantly on this memory, his sole point of resemblance to Caesar, Alexander and Napoleon. Knowing facts, details, dates, proper names, ignorant of tendencies, passions, the various moods of the crowd, inward aspirations, the hidden and obscure stirrings within souls – in a word, everything that could be called the invisible currents of consciousness. Accepted at a superficial level, but not much in sympathy with the underlying France. Managing to survive through cunning. Governing too much and not ruling enough. His own first minister. Singularly successful at forging out of the pettiness of reality an obstacle to the greatness of ideas. Combining with a real creative capacity for civilization, order and organization a kind of bureaucratic and pettifogging attitude. Founder and promoter of a dynasty. With something of a Charlemagne and something of a lawyer about him. In short, a distinguished and exceptional individual, a prince who managed to exert authority despite France's misgivings and to show strength in spite of Europe's distrust. Louis-Philippe will be classed among the eminent men of his age, and would be ranked among the most illustrious rulers in history if he had cared a little for glory, and if his sense of what was great had been equal to his sense of what was useful.

Louis-Philippe had once been handsome, and in old age he remained personable. Not always winning the nation's approval, but always the crowd's. He was liked. He had that gift, charm. He lacked majesty. Although a king he wore no crown, and although elderly his hair was not white. He had the manners of the old regime and the habits of the new, a mixture of the aristocratic and the bourgeois that suited 1830. Louis-Philippe was the reign of transition. He kept to the old-style pronunciation and the old-style spelling, using them to express modern opinions. He loved Poland and Hungary, but he wrote *les polonois* and he said *les hongrais*.* He wore the uniform of

* Modern French spelling is *les polonais* ('the Poles'). *Les hongrois* ('the Hungarians') is pronounced as written, according to normal rules of French pronunciation.

the National Guard, like Charles X, and the Legion of Honour sash, like Napoleon.

He was not much of a church-goer, no huntsman, and never went to the Opéra. Incorruptible by the religious lobby, dog-handlers or ballet-dancers. This had something to do with his bourgeois popularity. He had no court. He would go out with his umbrella under his arm, and this umbrella for a long time contributed to his aura. He was a bit of a builder, a bit of a gardener, a bit of a doctor. He bled a postilion who fell off his horse. Louis-Philippe went nowhere without his surgical knife, any more than Henri III without his dagger. The royalists jeered at this ridiculous king, the first ever to shed blood as a cure.

Louis-Philippe cannot be held responsible for all the charges history lays against him. For some of these charges royalty is to blame, for some, the reign, and for some, the king. Three columns that each give a different total. Democratic rights suspended, progress reduced to a matter of secondary importance, street protests violently suppressed, insurrections quelled by military force, rioters fired on, Rue Transnonain, courts-martial, the takeover of the whole population by the enfranchised population, government by the privileged three hundred thousand – this is royalty's doing. Belgium refused, Algeria too harshly conquered and, like India by the English, with more barbarity than civilization, the breach of faith with Abd al-Qader, Blaye, Deutz bribed, Pritchard compensated – this is the regime's doing. A policy more family-based than national, this is the king's doing.

As we see, on balance, the king has less to answer for.

His great failing was this: he was modest in the name of France.

What was the reason for this failing?

We can explain it.

Louis-Philippe was a king who let fatherhood get the better of him. This incubation of a family intended to develop into a dynasty is fearful of everything and has no wish to be disturbed. Hence the inordinate want of courage, offensive to a people who have the fourteenth of July in their civilian history and Austerlitz in their military history.

Leaving aside those public duties that claim priority, it has to be said that his family deserved the deep affection Louis-Philippe had for them. They were an admirable bunch, the members of that family. Their virtues matched their talents. One of Louis-Philippe's daughters, Marie d'Orléans, won for her distinguished family's name a place among artists, as Charles d'Orléans had won for it a place among poets. She carved a statue of her soul and named it 'Joan of Arc'. Two of Louis-Philippe's sons drew from Metternich this demagogic praise: 'Few such young men are to be seen, and no such princes.'

This is the truth about Louis-Philippe, without holding anything back but also without being too critical.

To be Prince Equality, to carry within himself the contradiction between the Restoration and the Revolution, to have that disquieting revolutionary side that becomes reassuring in the man in power – this was Louis-Philippe's good fortune in 1830. Never was there a man better suited to an event. One was instilled in the other, and the incarnation came about: Louis-Philippe is 1830 made man. Moreover, he had in his favour that great recommendation for the throne, exile. He was banished, homeless, poor. He had worked for his living. In Switzerland, this heir to the richest princely domains in France had sold an old horse to buy food. At Reichenau he gave lessons in mathematics, while his sister Adélaïde embroidered and sewed. A king with such episodes in his past fired the bourgeoisie with enthusiasm. He had with his own hands demolished the last iron cage at Mont-St-Michel, built by Louis XI and used by Louis XV. He was Dumouriez's companion, he was Lafayette's friend. He had belonged to the Jacobin Club, Mirabeau had slapped him on the shoulder, Danton had addressed him as 'Young man!' As Monsieur de Chartres in '93 at the age of twenty-four, from the back of a dark booth he had followed the trial of Louis XVI, 'that poor tyrant', as he was so aptly named. The unseeing visionary Revolution, crushing royalty in the king and the king along with royalty, almost without noticing the man in the fierce destruction of the concept; the huge storm of the Assembly tribunal with public anger as interrogator, Capet not knowing what to reply, the ghastly bewildered swaying of that royal head in that grim blast, the relative innocence of all involved in that catastrophe, those who condemned as well as the one condemned – he had watched these things, he had gazed on this dizzying unfolding of events. He had seen the centuries appear before the court of the Convention, had seen the accused, the monarchy, looming fearsome in the shadows behind Louis XVI, that hapless passer-by made to answer for it. And lingering in his soul, a respectful dread of these immense dispensations of justice by the people, almost as impersonal as the justice of God.

The impression left on him by the Revolution was remarkable. His recollection of it was like a living imprint of those momentous years, minute by minute. One day, in the presence of a witness we cannot doubt, he corrected from memory every entry under the letter A in the alphabetical list of members of the Constituent Assembly.

Louis-Philippe was a king of total transparency. While he reigned there was press freedom, parliamentary freedom, freedom of conscience and freedom of speech. The September laws are an open book.

Although aware of the corrosive power of the light on privileges, he left his throne exposed to the light. History will recognize him for this honesty.

Like all historical figures who have left the stage, Louis-Philippe now faces judgement before the human conscience. The trial is still in progress.

For him, the hour has not yet struck when history speaks in its venerable and impartial voice. The moment has not yet come to deliver the final verdict on this king. The rigorous and illustrious historian Louis Blanc has himself recently tempered his initial assessment. Louis-Philippe was the chosen representative of those two approximations, called the two hundred and twenty-one and 1830, that is to say a quasi-parliament and a quasi-revolution. And in any case, from the vantage point that philosophy must occupy, our judgement of him now, as indicated above, would have to be subject to certain reservations in respect of the absolute democratic principle. In the eyes of the absolute, everything in disregard of these two rights – firstly the right of man, secondly the right of the people – is usurpation. But with these reservations, what we can say right now is that all in all, whichever way you look at him, Louis-Philippe, as a person and from the viewpoint of human kindness, will remain, to use the old language of an earlier history, one of the best princes who ever sat on a throne.

What has he against him? That throne. Take away Louis-Philippe the king, there remains the man. And the man is good. Sometimes good to the extent of being admirable. Often in the midst of the most serious difficulties, after a day of diplomatic conflict with the entire continent, he would return at night to his apartments and there, drained by exhaustion, shattered for want of sleep, what did he do? He picked up a file and spent the night reviewing a criminal case, believing it was one thing to stand up to Europe but a greater thing yet to save a man from the executioner. He would defy his minister of justice, dispute with the chief prosecutors – 'those legal windbags', as he called them – every inch of ground to which the guillotine laid claim. Sometimes heaps of files covered his table. He went through all of them. It caused him anguish to give up on those poor doomed wretches. One day he said to the same witness we mentioned earlier, 'I saved seven last night.' During the early years of his reign the death penalty was as good as abolished, and the re-erection of the scaffold was a violence done to the king. La Grève having disappeared with the senior branch of the royal family, a bourgeois Grève was instituted under the name of Barrière-St-Jacques. 'Pragmatists' felt the need of a quasi-legitimate guillotine. And this was one of the victories of Casimir

Périer, who represented the reactionary leanings of the bourgeoisie, over Louis-Philippe, who represented its liberal leanings. Louis-Philippe had annotated Beccaria in own hand. After the Fieschi conspiracy he exclaimed, 'What a pity I wasn't wounded! I might have issued a pardon!' On another occasion, alluding to the recalcitrance of his ministers, he wrote in connection with a political activist sentenced to death, who was one of the most generous figures of our day: 'His pardon is granted. It only remains for me to obtain it.' Louis-Philippe was as gentle-natured as Louis IX, and as good-hearted as Henri IV.

Now, goodness is that rare pearl in history, and for us the good almost take precedence over the great.

Louis-Philippe has been judged severely by some, perhaps harshly by others, and it is quite natural that a man, himself a phantom at present, who knew that king, should come and testify in his favour before history. This testimony, such as it is, is obviously and above all else completely disinterested. An epitaph written by a dead man is sincere. One shade may console another. Sharing the same darkness gives one sharer the right to praise his fellow sharer. And there is little fear it will ever be said of two tombs in exile: 'This one flattered the other.'

IV

Cracks in the Foundations

At this dramatic point in our narrative, which is going to delve deep into one of the tragic clouds that shroud the early reign of Louis-Philippe, it was important there should be no misunderstanding and it was necessary that this book should make known where it stood with regard to this king.

Louis-Philippe assumed royal authority without violence, without any direct action on his part, by virtue of a revolutionary change of tack, evidently quite at odds with the true goal of revolution but in which he, the Duc d'Orléans, had personally taken no initiative. He was born a prince and believed that he had been elected king. He had not given himself this mandate, he had not taken it. It had been offered to him and he had accepted it. Convinced – wrongly of course, but convinced – that the offer was rightfully made and dutifully accepted. That authority was therefore held in good faith. Now, with Louis-Philippe holding his authority in good faith, and democracy going on the offensive in good faith, we say in all conscience that whatever terror results from social conflict is not to be blamed either on the king or on democracy. A clash of principles is like a clash of elements. The ocean defends the water, the hurricane defends the wind, the king defends royalty, democracy defends the people. The monarchy, being relative, resists the absolute, which is the Republic. Society bleeds in this conflict, but what it suffers today will later be its salvation. And in any case, what we are not going to do here is incriminate the combatants. One of the two sides is obviously mistaken. Right does not stand like the Colossus of Rhodes on two shores at once, with one foot in the Republic and one foot in royalty. It is indivisible and all on one side. But those who are mistaken are sincere in their mistake. A blind man is no more culpable for his blindness than a Vendean is a bandit. So let us not blame these terrible clashes on anything other than the fatality of things. Whatever these storms may be, they are not entirely a matter of human responsibility.

Let us conclude this introduction.

The government of 1830 had a hard life from the outset. Born only yesterday, today it had to fight.

No sooner was it installed than it already felt vague movements of traction in the July contrivance so recently established and still so insecure.

Resistance was born the next day, perhaps it was even born the day before.

Month by month the hostility increased, turning from latent to blatant.

As we have said, little accepted by kings outside France, the July Revolution had been diversely interpreted within France.

God makes his will visible to men in events – an obscure text written in a mysterious language. Men produce instant translations, hasty, incorrect translations full of errors, gaps and misconstructions. Very few minds comprehend the divine language. The most discerning, most calm, most profound, decipher slowly, and by the time they come up with their text the task has long been completed – there are already twenty translations in the public arena. Each translation gives birth to a party and each misconstruction to a faction. And every party thinks it has the only true text, and every faction thinks it possesses the light.

Often, even the ruling power is a faction.

There are in revolutions those that swim against the tide. These are the old parties.

Revolutions deriving from the right to revolt, the old parties who cling to the principle of the God-given right of inheritance see themselves as having the right to revolt against revolution. Wrong. For in revolutions, it is not the people who are in revolt, it is the king. Revolution is precisely the opposite of revolt. Every revolution, being a normal occurrence, contains its own legitimacy, one that false revolutionaries sometimes dishonour, but a lasting legitimacy even when sullied, and surviving even when bloodied. Revolutions result not from accident but from necessity. A revolution is a return from the artificial to the real. It is because it must be so.

The old legitimist parties nonetheless attacked the 1830 Revolution with all the vehemence that springs from false reasoning. Fallacies make excellent projectiles. They struck shrewdly where it was vulnerable, finding its weak spot in its lack of logic: they attacked this revolution in its royalty. 'Revolution,' they cried, 'why this king?' Factions are blind, but their aim is true.

The Republicans too voiced this cry. But coming from them, the cry was logical. What was blindness in the legitimists was clearsightedness in the democrats. 1830 failed to meet its obligations to the people. Outraged democracy censured it for this.

Caught between the attack by the past and the attack by the future, the July establishment struggled. It represented the present moment, grappling with centuries of monarchy on the one hand and eternal right on the other.

Besides, in foreign affairs, now that it was revolution no longer and had become a monarchy, 1830 had to kowtow to Europe. Remaining at peace, that was an increased complication. A harmony that goes against the grain is often more onerous than a war. Out of this muted hostility, always kept muzzled but always growling, was born armed peace, that ruinous expedient of a self-doubting civilization. Whatever punishment it might incur, the July kingship bucked under the harness of the European governments. Metternich would gladly have hobbled it. Urged on in France by progress, in Europe it urged on those heel-dragging reactionaries, the monarchies. In tow, it towed.

Meanwhile at home, poverty, the proletariat, wages, education, the penal system, prostitution, the condition of women, wealth, destitution, production, consumption, distribution, exchange, currency, credit, capital's rights, labour's rights – all these problems multiplied, looming grimly over society.

Outside of the political parties properly speaking, another movement developed. In response to democratic ferment came philosophical ferment. The elite, like the masses, felt troubled – differently, but no less so.

Thinkers meditated while the ground, that is to say the people, penetrated by revolutionary currents, shook beneath them with vague epileptic-like tremors. These dreamers, some isolated, others in family gatherings and almost in spiritual fellowship, delved into social issues, peacefully but profoundly; impassive miners calmly extending their tunnels into the depths of a volcano, barely disturbed by the muffled shocks or by the glimpsed furnaces.

This calmness was not the least edifying spectacle of this unsettled period.

These men left to the political parties the question of rights; they occupied themselves with the question of happiness.

The well-being of man, that was what they wanted to extract from society.

They raised the importance of material issues – of agriculture, industry, commerce – almost to the status of religion. In the making of civilization, in a small way by God, largely by man, interests combine, amalgamate and compact to form really hard rock, according to a law of dynamics patiently studied by economists, those geologists of politics.

These men who grouped together under various names but who may all be referred to by the generic term 'socialists' strove to pierce that rock and bring forth the living waters of human happiness.

From the question of the scaffold to the question of war, the work they undertook embraced everything. To the rights of man, proclaimed by the French Revolution, they added the rights of woman and the rights of the child.

It will cause no surprise if for various reasons we do not here deal in depth from the theoretical viewpoint with the issues raised by socialism. We confine ourselves to outlining them.

Leaving aside cosmogonic visions, dreams and mysticism, all the problems the socialists considered can be reduced to two main problems.

First problem: how to produce wealth.

Second problem: how to share it out.

The first problem contains the issue of work.

The second contains the issue of wages.

The first problem is about the use of resources.

The second, about the distribution of benefits.

Effective use of resources results in national strength.

Fair distribution of benefits results in individual happiness.

Fair distribution should be understood to mean not equal but equitable distribution. The fundamental equality is equity.

These two things combined, national strength externally, individual happiness internally, result in social prosperity.

Social prosperity means the happiness of man, the freedom of the citizen, the greatness of the nation.

England solves the first of these two problems. She creates wealth admirably, she shares it out badly. This solution, which is only partial, leads inevitably to these two extremes: monstrous wealth, monstrous penury. All the benefits going to a few, all the hardship to the rest, that is to say, the people. Privilege, distinction, monopoly, feudalism are actually the fruits of labour. A false and dangerous situation, which bases national strength on private misery, which roots the greatness of the state in the sufferings of the individual. A badly constituted grandeur consisting of all the material elements but no moral element.

Communism and agrarian law think they are the solution to the second problem. They are wrong. Their distribution kills production. Equal allocation puts an end to competition. And consequently to work. It is a distribution carried out by a butcher who kills what he carves up. So these supposed solutions cannot be taken seriously. Killing wealth is not distributing it.

The two problems need to be solved together if they are to be solved properly. The two solutions need to be combined to provide a single solution.

Solve only the first of the two problems, and you will be Venice, or England. Like Venice, you will have artificial strength, or like England, material strength. You will be the villainous rich. You will perish under physical attack, as Venice has died, or through bankruptcy, as England will come to grief. And the world will let you come to grief and die because the world allows everything that is mere selfishness, everything that does not represent for humankind a virtue or an idea, to come to grief and die.

Of course these words 'Venice' and 'England' are used here to refer not to peoples but to social structures; the oligarchies superimposed on nations, not the nations themselves. Nations have our respect and our sympathy, always. Venice as a people will be reborn. England as an aristocracy will come to grief, but England as a nation is immortal. That said, let us continue:

Solve the two problems, encourage the rich and protect the poor, eliminate destitution, put an end to the unjust exploitation of the weak by the strong; curb the iniquitous envy, in the one who is making his way up, of the one who has arrived; set the wages for a job fairly and in the spirit of fellowship, foster the development of childhood with free compulsory education and make knowledge the foundation of manliness, develop minds while keeping hands busy; be at once a powerful nation and a family of happy individuals; democratize property not by abolishing it but by making it universal, so that every citizen without exception may be a property owner, something

756

easier to achieve than people think. In short, learn how to produce wealth and how to distribute it, and you will have both material greatness and moral greatness. And you will be worthy of calling yourself France.

This is what socialism, apart from a few misguided sects, said. This is what it sought to achieve, this is the idea it forged in people's minds.

Admirable efforts! Inspired endeavours!

These doctrines, these theories, this kind of opposition, the statesman's unforeseen need to take philosophers into account, partial insights into confused states of affairs, a new system of politics to be created in chime with the old world without being too much out of tune with the revolutionary ideal, a situation in which Lafayette had to be used to defend Polignac, the clear intimation of progress beyond the rioting; parliament and the mob; a balance to be maintained between the rivalries surrounding him, his faith in the Revolution, perhaps a kind of ambiguous resignation born of the vague acceptance of some ultimate higher authority, his desire to remain true to his ancestors, his sense of family, his sincere respect for the people, his own honesty – these things exercised Louis-Philippe almost painfully, and at times, strong and courageous as he was, they overwhelmed him with the difficulty of being king.

He felt beneath his feet a dreadful disintegration; not, however – France being more France than ever – a crumbling into dust.

An accumulating darkness shrouded the horizon. A strange shadow, reaching nearer and nearer, gradually extended over men, things, ideas, a shadow arising out of anger and out of the way things were organized. Everything that had been hastily stifled was astir, in ferment. At times the conscience of the honest man caught its breath, so great was the unrest in the air, with fallacies and truths intermingled. Mentally, people trembled in the social unease like leaves at the approach of a storm. The electric tension was such that at certain moments anyone who came along, any stranger, shed light. Then the twilight gloom closed in again. At intervals, deep rumblings gave an indication of just how much thunder there was in the clouds.

Barely twenty months had passed since the July Revolution, the year 1832 had begun in an ominous atmosphere of impending doom. The people suffering hardship, workers going hungry, the last Prince de Condé dying in suspicious circumstances, Brussels getting rid of the Nassaus as Paris had got rid of the Bourbons, Belgium offering herself to a French prince and giving herself to an English prince, Nicholas's Russian hatred, two demons of the south at our back, Ferdinand in Spain, Miguel in Portugal; the earth trembling in Italy, Metternich extending his reach over Bologna, France defying Austria at Ancona, from the north the somehow sinister sound of a hammer nailing Poland back into her coffin, eyes all over Europe watching France with annoyance, England, a dubious ally, ready to give a push to any teetering and to pounce on what should fall, the peerage taking advantage of Beccaria to deny to the law the heads of four guilty men, the fleurs-de-lys erased from the king's carriage, the cross removed from Notre-Dame, Lafayette marginalized, Laffitte ruined, Benjamin Constant dying in poverty, Casimir Périer dying from exhaustion in office; political and social disorder breaking out simultaneously in the two capitals of the kingdom, one the city of thought, the other the city of toil, in Paris civil war, in Lyon 'servile war', in both cities the same blazing furnace, the crater's crimson glow on the brow of the people, the south turned fanatic, the west unsettled, the Duchesse de Berry in the Vendée, plots, conspiracies, uprisings, cholera – to the grim clamour of ideas was added the grim turmoil of events.

V

Facts behind History of Which History Is Unaware

By the end of April the whole situation had deteriorated. The unrest was coming to a head. Ever since 1830 there had been the odd little riot, which was quickly suppressed only to erupt again, indicating a vast smouldering conflagration. Something terrible was brewing. Glimpses emerged of a possible revolution, its features still blurred and ill lit. France eyed Paris. Paris eyed Faubourg St-Antoine.

Faubourg St-Antoine, having slowly heated up, was coming to the boil.

The wine shops of Rue de Charonne were sober and agitated, although, applied to wine shops, this combination of adjectives seems odd.

Here, the government was purely and simply being called into question. There was open discussion of whether to fight or to keep the peace. There were back rooms of shops where working men were made to swear that 'they would be on the street at the first cry of alarm', and 'they would fight regardless of how many the enemy numbered'. Once the oath had been taken, a man seated in the corner of the wine shop 'spoke in a resonant voice', saying, 'Now, understand, you're sworn to it!' Sometimes people went upstairs to a private room on the first floor and there scenes that were almost masonic took place. The initiate was made to swear 'to serve the cause and likewise fathers of families'. That was the formula.

758

'Subversive' pamphlets – 'They were very critical of the government,' says a secret report of that time – were read in the public rooms.

Such comments as this were to be heard: 'I don't know the names of the leaders. The likes of us won't know the day until two hours beforehand.' One workman said, 'There are three hundred of us, if we each contribute ten sous that'll be one hundred and fifty francs for making powder and shot.' Another said, 'I'm not asking for six months, I'm not even asking for two. We'll be a match for the government in less than a fortnight. With twenty-five thousand men we can take them on.' Another said, 'I don't go to bed because I'm making cartridges all night.' From time to time 'well dressed' men 'in civilian clothes', apparently 'in charge', came 'swaggering' along, and shook hands with 'the ringleaders', and then went away again. They never stayed more than ten minutes. Meaningful remarks were exchanged in low voices: 'The moment's ripe, it's about to happen.' 'Everyone there was buzzing with it', to borrow the expression actually used by one of those present. The excitement was such that one day, in the middle of the wine shop, a worker exclaimed, 'We have no weapons!' In an unwitting travesty of Bonaparte's proclamation to the army in Italy, one of his comrades replied, 'The soldiers have!' 'Anything more secret', adds one report, 'they did not communicate to each other.' It is hard to understand what else they could be hiding after having said what they said.

These meetings were sometimes regular. Some were attended by never more than eight or ten individuals, and always the same ones. Other meetings, anyone who wanted to could attend, and the place was so full there was standing room only. Some came to them out of enthusiasm and passion, others because 'it was on their way to work'. As during the Revolution, there were in these wine shops patriotic women who embraced newcomers.

Other telling facts came to light.

A man would enter a shop, drink, and leave with the remark, 'Wine merchant, what's owing, the Revolution will pay.'

In a wine shop opposite Rue de Charonne revolutionary representatives were appointed. Their names were drawn out of a hat.

Some workers met at the house of a fencing-master who fought bouts at Rue de Cotte, where there was a trophy of arms formed of wooden broadswords, singlesticks, batons and foils. One day the buttons were removed from the foils. One worker said, 'There are twenty-five of us, but I don't count because I'm regarded as a mindless automaton.' This mindless automaton turned out later to be Quénisset.

Whatever was being planned gradually acquired some strange notoriety. One woman sweeping her doorstep said to another, 'For a long time a lot of work's been going into making cartridges.' Proclamations addressed to the National Guard in the *départements* were out there on the street for the public to read. One of these proclamations was signed: 'Burtot, wine merchant'.

One day outside the door of a wine and spirits merchant in Lenoir market, a man with a fringe beard and an Italian accent climbed on to a stone post and read aloud a peculiar document that seemed to emanate from some occult power. Groups formed around him, and applauded. The passages that most stirred the crowd were collected and noted down. 'Our views are suppressed, our proclamations torn up, our bill-stickers ambushed and thrown into prison.' 'The recent collapse in the cotton trade has won many moderates over to us.' 'The future of nations is being forged within our humble ranks.' 'We have to think in these terms: action or reaction, revolution or counter-revolution. For in these times no one believes in inertia or immobility any more. For the people, or against the people – that is the question. There is no other.' 'The day when we're no good to you any more send us packing, but until that day help us to march on.' And all this in broad daylight.

Other yet more audacious things that happened were by reason of their very audacity suspect to the people. On the fourth of April 1832, a man in the street climbed on to a cornerstone on Rue Ste-Marguerite and shouted, 'I'm a Babeufist!' But behind Babeuf the people thought they detected Gisquet.

Among other things this man said, 'Abolish private property! The left-wing opposition is cowardly and treacherous. It preaches revolution when it's convenient. It's democratic to avoid defeat and royalist to avoid a fight. The Republicans are fairweather friends. Distrust the Republicans, citizen workers.'

'Shut up, citizen spy!' yelled one worker.

This cry put an end to his speech.

Mysterious incidents occurred.

One day as the light was fading, over by the canal, a worker came across a 'well dressed man' who said to him, 'Where are you going, citizen?' 'Monsieur,' replied the worker, 'I haven't had the honour of making your acquaintance.' 'I know very well who you are,' said the man, adding, 'Don't be alarmed, I'm the committee representative. You're suspected of not being entirely reliable. You know, if you were to give anything away, we have our eye on you.' Then he shook hands with the worker and went off, saying, 'We'll meet again soon.'

The police, who were keeping their ears open, overheard some peculiar exchanges, not only in the wine shops but in the street.

'Get yourself recruited as quick as you can,' said a weaver to a cabinet-maker.

'Why?'

'There's some shooting to be done.'

Two individuals in tattered clothing exchanged these extraordinary remarks fraught with apparent *jacquerie*: 'Who rules us?'

'Monsieur Philippe.'

'No, it's the bourgeoisie.'

The reader is mistaken if he thinks we use the word *jacquerie* disapprovingly. The Jacques were the poor.

On another occasion, one man was heard to say to another as they passed by, 'We have a good plan of attack.'

All that was caught of a private conversation between four men crouching in a ditch at the Trône toll-gate circus was this: 'We'll do what we can to see he doesn't go walking around Paris any more.'

Who was *he*? Ominous obscurity.

'The chief leaders', as they were referred to locally, remained in the background. It was believed they met for consultation in a wine shop near St-Eustache corner. A man by the name of Aug. —, head of the Tailors' Benevolent Society, Rue Mondétour, was supposed to be the chief intermediary between the leaders and Faubourg St-Antoine. All the same, these leaders always remained very much in the shadows and no firm evidence could dent the extraordinary pride inherent in this reply later made by a defendant before the Court of Lords: 'Who was your leader?' 'I knew of none and I recognized none.'

So far this was a matter of not much more than words, transparent but vague words, sometimes idle talk, rumours, hearsay. Other evidence started turning up.

While nailing some wooden fencing round a plot on which a house was being built in Rue de Reuilly, a carpenter found on the ground a piece of a torn-up letter on which the following lines were still legible: 'The committee must take measures to prevent recruitment from the sections by different societies ...' And as a postscript: 'We have learned of guns in Rue du Faubourg-Poissonnière, number 5B, totalling some five or six thousand, in a courtyard at a gunsmith's. The section has no weapons.'

What excited the carpenter and made him show the thing to his neighbours was the fact that a few paces away he picked up another piece of paper, also torn, and even more significant. Because of the historical interest of these strange documents we reproduce below the way it was laid out:

Q	C	D	S	*Learn this list by heart. Then tear it up.*
				The men included will do the same when
				you have given them their orders.
				Brotherly greetings.
				L.
				u og a¹ fe

It was only later that the people who at the time were let into the secret of this find learned what those four capital letters stood for: quinturions, centurions, decurions and scouts, and the meaning of those letters *u og a¹ fe*, which represented a date and translated as the fifteenth of April 1832. Under each capital letter were inscribed names followed by very distinctive notes. Like this:

> Q: Bannerel. 8 guns, 83 cartridges. Trustworthy.
> C: Boubière. 1 pistol, 40 cartridges.
> D: Rollet. 1 foil, 1 pistol, 1 pound of explosive.
> S: Teissier. 1 sword, 1 cartridge box. Meticulous.
>   Terreur. 8 guns. Brave, etc.

Finally, still within that same enclosure the carpenter found a third piece of paper on which was pencilled, but very legibly, this enigmatic list of sorts:

> Unity. Blanchard. Arbre-Sec. 6.
> Barra. Soize. Salle-au-Comte.
> Kosciuszko. Aubry the butcher?
> J. J. R.
> Caius Gracchus.
> Right of appeal. Dufond. Bakery.
> Fall of the Girondists. Derbac. Maubuée.
> Washington. Pinson. 1 pist. 86 cart.
> Marseillaise.
> Sov. of the people. Michel. Quincampoix. Sword.
> Hoche.
> Marceau. Plato. Arbre-Sec.
> Warsaw. Tilly, street seller of the *Populaire*.

The honest bourgeois in whose keeping this list had remained knew its significance. It would seem the list was a complete roster of the Society of the Rights of Man sections in the fourth *arrondissement*, with the names and addresses of the section leaders. Now that all these shadowy details are no more than history, they can be published. It should be added that the Society of the Rights of Man seems to have been set up after the date when this piece of paper was found. Perhaps this was just an early draft.

However, after the talk and the things overheard, after the written indicators, material evidence began to appear.

At an old curiosity shop in Rue Popincourt seven sheets of grey paper, all folded in four lengthwise, were found in a chest of drawers and seized. These sheets lay on top of twenty-six squares of this same grey paper folded into cartridge shapes, and a card on which was to be read the following:

Saltpetre	12 ounces.
Sulphur	2 ounces.
Charcoal	2 and a half ounces.
Water	2 ounces.

The police report of the seizure stated that the drawer gave off a strong smell of gunpowder.

A mason returning home after his day's work left a small package on a bench near the Pont d'Austerlitz. This package was taken to the police station. It was opened and in it were found two printed pamphlets signed 'Lahautière', a song entitled 'Workmen, Join Forces' and a tin full of cartridges.

One worker drinking with a comrade made the latter feel how hot he was; the other man felt a pistol under his waistcoat.

In the loneliest part of the boulevard between Père-Lachaise and the Trône toll-gate some children playing in a ditch found, under a pile of wood shavings and vegetable peelings, a bag containing a bullet mould, a wooden cartridge roll, a wooden bowl with gunpowder residue in it, and a little cast-iron pot with clear traces of molten lead on the inside.

A police raid at five o'clock in the morning on the home of a certain Pardon, later a member of the Barricade-Merry section, who was killed in the April 1834 uprising, found him standing by his bed, holding in his hand some cartridges he was making.

Around the time when workers take their break, two men were seen meeting between the Picpus gate and the Charenton gate on a little patrol path running between two walls, near a wine shop with a Siamese skittles pitch in front of it. One drew a pistol from beneath his overall and handed it to the other. As he was handing it over he noticed some damp had got into the powder from the sweat on his chest. He primed the gun and added more powder to what was already in the pan. Then the two men parted.

A certain Gallais, later killed in Rue Beaubourg during the April disturbances, boasted of having in his house seven hundred cartridges and twenty-four flints.

The government one day received a warning that there had just been an issue of weapons to the neighbourhood along with two hundred thousand cartridges. The next week, thirty thousand cartridges were distributed. Strangely enough, the police were unable to seize any of them.

An intercepted letter read, 'The day is not far off when eighty thousand patriots will be under arms within the space of four hours.'

All this unrest was overt, you might almost say peaceful. The impending insurrection was calmly readying for the storm, right there in front of the government. There was no lack of oddity about this still underground but already perceptible crisis. Bourgeois citizens were talking to workers about what was afoot. People said, 'How's the uprising?' in the same tone of voice in which they might have said, 'How's your wife?'

A furniture dealer on Rue Moreau asked, 'Well, when are you going to attack?'

Another shopkeeper said, 'The attack will be launched soon. I know. A month ago there were fifteen thousand of you, now there are twenty-five thousand.' He offered his gun, and a neighbour offered a small pistol that he wanted to sell for seven francs.

In fact, revolutionary excitement was mounting. No corner of Paris, or of France, was free of it. Everywhere the artery was throbbing. Like those membranes that result from certain inflammations and develop in the human body, the network of secret societies began to spread all over the country. From the Friends of the People, an association both public and secret, sprang the Society of the Rights of Man, which dated one of its bulletins 'Pluviôse, year 40 of the Republican era', and which was destined to survive even assize-court rulings that it should be dissolved, and did not hesitate to give its sections telling names such as these:

Pikes.

Alarm bell.

Signal cannon.

Phrygian cap.

21st January.

Beggars.

Vagrants.

Onward march.

Robespierre.

Level.

'Ça Ira'.

Out of the Society of the Rights of Man came the Society of Action. These were impatient individuals who broke away and went racing ahead. Other associations sought to recruit members from the main original societies. Section members complained they were being torn apart. So there was the Gallic Society and the Municipalities Organization Committee. There were the Associations for the Freedom of the Press, for Individual Freedom, for the Education of the People, against Indirect Taxation. Then there was the Society of Egalitarian Workers, which was divided into three factions: the Egalitarians, the Communists, the Reformers. Then the Army of the Bastilles, a kind of militarily organized cohort – four men commanded by a corporal, ten by a sergeant, twenty by a sub-lieutenant, forty by a lieutenant; there were never more than five men who knew each other. A creation combining caution with audacity, and seemingly stamped with the genius of Venice. The central committee, which was at the head of the organization, had two limbs, the Society of Action and the Army of the Bastilles. Among these Republican bodies there were stirrings of a legitimist association, the Knights of Faithful Allegiance. It was denounced and repudiated.

The Parisian societies branched out into the main cities. Lyon, Nantes, Lille and Marseille had their own Society of the Rights of Man, the Carbonarists, and the Free Men. Aix had a revolutionary society called the Cougourde. We have already mentioned this name.

In Paris, Faubourg St-Marceau was hardly any less febrile than Faubourg St-Antoine, and the schools were no less restless than the *faubourgs*. A café in Rue St-Hyacinthe and the Seven Billiards wine shop in Rue des Mathurins-St-Jacques served as meeting-places for students. The Society of the Friends of the ABC, affiliated with the

Friendly Society of Angers and the Cougourde of Aix, met as we have seen in Café Musain. These same young men also gathered, as we have already mentioned, at the tavern called Corinthe near Rue Mondétour. These meetings were secret. Others were as public as could be, and their audacity may be judged by this extract from an interrogation conducted during one of the later trials: 'Where was this meeting held?' 'In Rue de la Paix.' 'At whose house?' 'In the street.' 'Which sections were at this meeting?' 'Only one.' 'Which one?' 'Manuel.' 'Who was the section leader?' 'I was.' 'You are too young to have taken that grave decision to attack the government on your own authority. Where did your instructions come from?' 'The central committee.'

The army was mined at the same time as the population, as uprisings at Belfort, Lunéville and Épinal later proved. The fifty-second regiment, the fifth, the eighth, the thirty-seventh, and the twentieth light cavalry were to be counted on for support. In Burgundy and the southern towns liberty trees were planted – that is to say, poles with red caps on top of them.

Such was the situation.

And, as we said at the outset, this situation was more intense and felt more acutely in the Faubourg St-Antoine neighbourhood than in any other section of the population. This was the sore spot.

A seething mass of people, a hive of plucky, angry industry, this old neighbourhood was quivering with anticipation and yearning for upheaval. Everything was in turmoil – not that that was any excuse to stop working. It would be impossible to convey any idea of that characteristic energy and grimness. Hidden under the attic roofs of this neighbourhood are heart-breaking miseries. There are, too, exceptional and fiery intellects. It is particularly dangerous in respect of hardship and intellect for extremes to meet.

Faubourg St-Antoine had yet other reasons for unrest, being adversely affected by the commercial crises, bankruptcies, strikes, the unemployment inherent in great political disturbances. In times of revolution poverty is both cause and effect. The blow it strikes rebounds on it. Full of proud courage, with the highest capacity for latent heat, always ready to take up arms, prone to violent outbursts, volatile, intense, mined, this population seemed to be just waiting for a spark to fall. Whenever certain fiery particles drift across the horizon driven by the wind of events, it is impossible not to think of Faubourg St-Antoine and the extraordinary accident of fate that has placed at the gates of Paris this powder-keg of suffering and ideas.

The wine shops of Faubourg St-Antoine, which have cropped up more than once in the brief description the reader has just encountered, have a historic notoriety. Here, in troubled times, people get more drunk on words than on wine. There is a sort of prophetic spirit and an emanation of the future in the air, swelling hearts and exalting souls. The wine shops of Faubourg St-Antoine are like those taverns on Mount Aventine built above the sibyl's cave and communicating with the sacred effusions from the deep, taverns whose tables were almost tripods and where what Ennius calls 'the sibylline wine' was drunk.

Faubourg St-Antoine is a proletarian reservoir. Revolutionary upheaval creates cracks in it from which the sovereignty of the people flows. This sovereignty may do harm, it makes mistakes like any other, but even when misled it remains great. It could be described, like the blind Cyclops, as *ingens**.

Depending on whether the idea in the air was good or bad, whether it was a day of fanaticism or of enthusiasm, in '93 it was sometimes savage hordes, sometimes heroic bands, that set out from Faubourg St-Antoine.

Savage. Let us explain what we mean by this word. These ragged, roaring, ferocious, irate men, with clubs raised and pikes held high, who in those Genesis days of revolutionary chaos hurled themselves on the old Paris turned upside down – what did they want? They wanted an end to oppression, an end to tyranny, an end to strife, work for men, education for children, social goodwill towards women, liberty, equality, fraternity, bread for all, an idea for all, a paradise made of this world, progress. And that good, sweet blessed thing, progress, they demanded fearsomely, driven to extremity, to utter distraction, half-naked, with bludgeon in hand and a roar in their throats. They were savages, yes, but savages of civilization.

They asserted rightfulness, with a fury. They wanted, through fear and trembling if need be, to force the human race towards paradise. They seemed barbarians, and they were saviours. Wearing the mask of darkness, they clamoured for light.

Facing these men, ferocious men admittedly, and terrifying, but ferocious and terrifying for the sake of good, are other men, smiling, braided, gilded, beribboned, star-spangled, in silk stockings, white plumes, yellow gloves and shiny shoes, who with their elbows resting on a velvet table beside a marble chimneypiece gently insist on the preservation and perpetuation of the past, of the Middle Ages, of divine right, of fanaticism, of ignorance, of slavery, of the death penalty,

* An allusion to Virgil's description of the Cyclops (*Aeneid*, bk III, line 658): 'monstrum horrendum, informe, ingens, cui lumen ademptum' ('a hideous monster, shapeless, *huge*, deprived of light').

of war; glorifying quietly and politely the sword, the stake and the scaffold. As for us, if we had to make a choice between the barbarians of civilization and the civilized representatives of barbarism, we would opt for the barbarians.

But, thank heavens, another choice is possible. A sheer drop is no more unavoidable ahead of us than behind. Neither despotism nor terrorism. We want the gentle incline towards progress.

God sees to that. Making slopes gentler – that is the whole principle on which God operates.

VI
Enjolras and His Lieutenants

Around this time, bearing in mind what was likely to happen, Enjolras carried out a mysterious sort of census.

They were all gathered together at Café Musain.

Intermingling with his words a few half-puzzling but revealing metaphors, Enjolras said, 'We ought to know where we stand and who we can count on. If we want fighters they need to be prepared. Have something to fight with. That can't do any harm. There is always more chance of passers-by being gored when there are bulls on the road than when there are none. So let's do a little assessment of the herd. How many are we? Not that this is work we're going to put off till tomorrow. Revolutionaries should always feel a sense of urgency, progress has no time to lose. Let's beware of the unexpected. Don't let's be taken by surprise. We need to review all the alliance-building we've done and see whether it's holding up. That's something that needs to be checked today. Courfeyrac, you'll go and see the polytechnic students. It's their day off. Today being Wednesday. Feuilly, you'll visit our friends at La Glacière, won't you? Combeferre has promised to go over to Picpus. That's quite a lively hotspot over there. Bahorel will pay a visit to Estrapade. Prouvaire, the masons are cooling. You report back to us from the Rue de Grenelle-St-Honoré lodge. Joly will go to Dupuytren's clinical lecture and take the pulse of the medical school. Bossuet will take a little turn around the law courts and chat with the law students. I'll deal with the Cougourde.'

'That's everything taken care of,' said Courfeyrac.

'No.'

'What else is there?'

'Something very important.'

'What's that?' asked Courfeyrac.

'The Maine toll-gate,' replied Enjolras.

768

Enjolras remained for a moment as if deep in thought, then resumed, 'There are marble-workers, painters and sculptors' assistants at the Maine toll-gate. They're an enthusiastic bunch but with a tendency to blow cold. I don't know what's come over them recently. They've something else on their mind. They're losing their spark. They spend their time playing dominoes. It's high time someone went and gave them a bit of a firm talking-to. Richefeu's is where they meet. You'll find them there between twelve and one o'clock. Those embers need blowing on. For that, I'd been counting on that dreamer Marius, who on the whole is sound, but he no longer comes. I need someone for the Maine toll-gate. I haven't anyone else.'

'What about me?' said Grantaire. 'I'm here.'

'You?'

'Yes, me.'

'You? Rally Republicans! You? In defence of principles, fire up hearts that have grown cold!'

'Why not?'

'Are you capable of being good for something?'

'I have the vague ambition to be,' said Grantaire.

'You don't believe in anything.'

'I believe in you.'

'Grantaire, will you do me a favour?'

'Anything. Polish your boots.'

'Well, don't meddle in our affairs. Go and sleep off the effects of your absinthe.'

'You're heartless, Enjolras.'

'As if you'd be the man to send to the Maine gate! As if you were capable of it!'

'I'm capable of going down Rue des Grès, crossing Place St-Michel, heading off along Rue Monsieur-le-Prince, taking Rue de Vaugirard, passing the Carmelite convent, turning into Rue d'Assas, proceeding to Rue du Cherche-Midi, leaving the Military Court behind me, wending my way along Rue des Vieilles-Tuileries, striding across the boulevard, following Chaussée du Maine, walking through the toll-gate and going into Richefeu's. I'm capable of that. My shoes are capable of that.'

'Do you know them at all, those comrades who meet at Richefeu's?'

'Not very well. But we're on friendly terms.'

'What will you say to them?'

'I'll talk to them about Robespierre, of course! And about Danton. About principles.'

'You?'

'Yes, me. But I'm not being given the credit I deserve. When I put my mind to it, I'm terrific. I've read Prudhomme, I'm familiar with the *Social Contract*, I know by heart my constitution of the year II. "The liberty of the citizen ends where the liberty of another citizen begins." Do you take me for a brute beast? I have in my drawer an old promissory note from the time of the Revolution. The rights of man, the sovereignty of the people, for God's sake! I'm even a bit of an Hébertist. I can keep coming out with some wonderful things, watch in hand, for a whole six hours by the clock.'

'Be serious,' said Enjolras.

'I mean it,' replied Grantaire.

Enjolras thought for a few moments, and with the gesture of a man who had come to a decision, 'Grantaire,' he said gravely, 'I agree to try you out. You'll go to the Maine toll-gate.'

Grantaire lived in furnished lodgings very close to Café Musain. He went out, and came back five minutes later. He had gone home to put on a Robespierre-style waistcoat.

'Red,' he said as he came in, gazing intently at Enjolras.

Then, with an energetic pat of his hand, he pressed the two scarlet lapels of the waistcoat to his chest.

And stepping close to Enjolras he said in his ear, 'Don't worry.'

He resolutely jammed on his hat, and off he went.

A quarter of an hour later the back room of Café Musain was deserted. All the Friends of the ABC were gone, each his own way, each to his separate task. Enjolras, who had saved the Cougourde for himself, was the last to leave.

Members of the Cougourde of Aix who were in Paris used to meet on Issy plain, in one of the many abandoned quarries in that part of the city.

As Enjolras headed towards this meeting-place he reviewed the whole situation. The gravity of the circumstances was obvious. When events symptomatic of a kind of latent social disease move sluggishly, the slightest complication arrests and obstructs them. A phenomenon resulting in collapse and renewal. Enjolras discerned a revolutionary brightness beneath the overcast reaches of the future. Who knows? Perhaps the moment was at hand. The people reasserting their right – what a glorious spectacle! The Revolution was majestically taking hold of France once again and saying to the world, 'The story continues!' Enjolras was pleased. Things were hotting up. He had at that very moment a powder trail of friends scattered all over Paris. With Combeferre's shrewd and philosophical eloquence, Feuilly's cosmopolitan enthusiasm, Courfeyrac's wit, Bahorel's mirth, Jean Prouvaire's melancholy, Joly's erudition, Bossuet's sarcasm, he mentally orchestrated a kind of explosion of electric sparks that set alight almost everywhere at once. Everyone doing his bit! The result would surely repay the effort. It was going well. This made him think of Grantaire.

'Well now,' said he to himself, 'the Maine toll-gate doesn't take me far out of my way. Why not go on to Richefeu's? Just to see what Grantaire's doing, and how he's getting on.'

One o'clock was striking from the Vaugirard bell-tower when Enjolras reached the Richefeu smoking-den. He pushed open the door, went inside, folded his arms, let the door close again behind him, bumping his shoulders, and viewed the room full of tables, men and smoke.

A voice rose out of this haze along with lively interjections from another voice. It was Grantaire engaged in dialogue with some opponent.

Grantaire was sitting opposite another person at a table of St-Anne marble strewn with sawdust and arrayed with dominoes. He was banging his fist on the marble, and this is what Enjolras heard:

'Double six.'

'Four.'

'You swine! I haven't any left.'

'You're doomed. Two.'

'Six.'

'Three.'

'One.'

'My turn.'

'Four points.'

'Hard won.'

'Your turn.'

'I've made a terrible mistake.'

'You're doing fine.'

'Fifteen.'

'Plus seven.'

'That makes twenty-two.' (Pondering.) 'Twenty-two!'

'You weren't expecting that double six. If I'd put it down at the beginning it would have changed the whole game.'

'Two, would you believe?'

'One.'

'One! Well now, five.'

'I haven't any fives.'

'You're the one that just played, I think?'

'Yes.'

'A blank.'

'If he doesn't have all the luck! Ah! You're a lucky one, you are!'
(Pondering at length.) 'Two.'

'One.'

'One! Well then, five.'

'No fives, no ones. That's a problem for you.'

'Domino!'

'Well, I'll be—!'

BOOK TWO
ÉPONINE

I
Alouette's Meadow

Marius was there to see the unexpected outcome of the ambush he had put Javert on to, but Javert had no sooner left the Gorbeau tenement, taking his prisoners away in three cabs, than Marius in turn slipped out of the house. It was still only nine o'clock in the evening. Marius went over to Courfeyrac's. Courfeyrac was no longer the peaceable resident of the Latin quarter; he had gone to live in Rue de la Verrerie 'for political reasons'. This neighbourhood was one of those where insurrection was apt to establish itself in those days. Marius said to Courfeyrac, 'I've come to sleep at your place.' Courfeyrac pulled off one of the two mattresses on his bed, laid it on the floor, and said, 'There you are.'

The next day, as early as seven o'clock in the morning, Marius returned to the house, paid his rent and what he owed Mame Bougon, had his books, bed, table, chest of drawers and two chairs loaded on to a handcart and went away without leaving his address, so that when Javert came back later that morning to question Marius about what had happened the day before he found only Mame Bougon. 'Moved out!' she told him.

Mame Bougon was convinced Marius was some sort of accomplice of the robbers caught during the night.

'Who'd have thought it?' she cried in the company of other caretakers in the neighbourhood. 'A young man as harmless as a girl, by the looks of him!'

Marius had two reasons for doing this sudden flit. Firstly, he now had a horror of this house where he had seen at such close quarters, fully developed, at its most repulsive and most ferocious, a social ugliness perhaps even more dreadful than the villainous rich man: the villainous pauper. Secondly, he did not want to take part in whatever trial would probably ensue and to have to testify against Thénardier.

Javert thought the young man whose name he did not remember had taken fright and fled, or might not even have been at home at the time of the ambush. Yet he did make some effort to find him, without success.

A month went by, then another. Marius was still staying with Courfeyrac. He had learned from a student lawyer, who spent a lot of time hanging about the law courts, that Thénardier was in solitary confinement. Every Monday Marius had five francs paid to the clerk of La Force prison, for Thénardier.

Not having any money, Marius borrowed the five francs from Courfeyrac. This was the first time in his life he had ever borrowed money. These regular five francs were a twofold enigma, to Courfeyrac who lent them and to Thénardier who received them. 'Who can they be going to?' thought Courfeyrac. 'Where can they be coming from?' Thénardier wondered.

Marius was in any case devastated. Once again everything was closed to him. He could see nothing in front of him any more. His life was plunged back into that mystery where he was left groping his way. In that obscurity he had for a moment seen again very close at hand the young girl he loved, the old man who seemed to be her father, those unknown persons who were his sole interest and his sole hope in this world. And just when he thought he had them in his grasp all these shadows had been blown away. Even the most frightful shock had produced not one spark of certainty or truth. No conceivable explanation. Now he did not even know the name he had thought he knew. Certainly, it was no longer Ursule. And Alouette was a nickname. And what was to be made of the old man? Was he in fact hiding from the police? The white-haired workman Marius had run into near Les Invalides came back to mind. That worker and Monsieur Leblanc, it now seemed likely, were one and the same. So he disguised himself? There were heroic aspects and ambiguous aspects to this individual. Why had he not called for help? Why had he fled? Was he the young girl's father, yes or no? And was he really the man Thénardier thought he had recognized? Could Thénardier have been mistaken? So many insoluble problems. None of this, it is true, detracted in the slightest from the angelic charms of the young girl from the Luxembourg Gardens. A sorry plight: Marius had passion in his heart and darkness before his eyes. He was driven, he was drawn and he could not move. Everything was gone except love. Even love's instincts and sudden enlightenments he had lost. Ordinarily this flame burning within us also illuminates us a little, and casts some useful light around us. But Marius was no longer even aware of these quiet promptings of passion. He never said to himself, 'What if I went there? What if I tried this?' The girl he could no longer call Ursule must be somewhere. Nothing suggested to Marius whereabouts he should look for her. His whole life could now be summed up in a nutshell: total uncertainty in impenetrable obscurity. He still yearned to see her again but had no expectation of doing so.

To make matters worse, poverty returned. He felt that chill blast very close to him, at his back. In all his tribulations, and already quite some time ago, he had stopped working, and nothing is more dangerous than to stop working. It is a habit you lose. A habit easy to give up and difficult to resume.

A certain amount of daydreaming does you good, like a narcotic in small doses. It sedates the sometimes severe fevers of the toiling intellect and produces in the mind a cool and gentle mist that softens the over-harsh contours of pure thought, fills in the gaps and intervals here and there, creates cohesion and smooths the sharp edges of ideas. But too much daydreaming drags you down and overwhelms you. Woe to the intellectual kind of worker whose thinking completely subsides into daydreaming! He thinks he will easily regain lost ground, and he tells himself that after all they both amount to the same thing. Wrong!

Thought is the exertion of the intellect, daydreaming is its indulgence. To replace thought with daydreaming is to mistake a poison for sustenance.

Marius, remember, had started out like this. Passion had intervened and given him the final push into flights of fancy without purpose or substance. A person in such a state leaves the house only to go daydreaming. Idle pastime. Stagnant and turbulent abyss. And with less and less work came more and more needs. This is a law. Man, when he is a dreamer, is naturally lavish and lax. The relaxed mind cannot keep a tight grip on life. There is good and bad in this style of life, for while laxity is pernicious, generosity is kind-hearted and wholesome. But the generous and noble pauper who does not work is doomed. Resources run out, necessities arise.

An inevitable downhill slope on which the most honest and the most steadfast no less than the weakest and the most depraved are doomed, ending up at one of these two pitfalls: suicide or crime. Keep going out to daydream, and the day comes when you go out to drown yourself. Too much daydreaming results in the likes of Escousse and Lebras.

Marius was slowly walking down this slope with his eyes fixed on the girl he could not see any more. That sounds strange, what we have just written, and yet it is true. The memory of an absent person lights up the shadows of the heart. The greater the absence, the more radiant it is. The despairing soul in darkness sees this light on its horizon, the star of inner night. She was Marius's only thought. He could think of nothing else. He was vaguely aware that his old coat was becoming unseemly and that his new coat was becoming an old one, that his

775

shirts were wearing out, his hat was wearing out, his boots were wearing out, that is to say his life was wearing out, and he said to himself, 'If I could only see her before I die!'

He had one sweet fancy left to him: that she had loved him, that her glance had told him so, that she did not know his name but she knew his soul, and wherever she was, whatever that mysterious place might be, perhaps she still loved him. Who knows whether she was not thinking of him as he was thinking of her? Sometimes, in those inexplicable moments experienced by every loving heart with cause only for sadness and yet feeling an obscure frisson of joy, he would say to himself, 'Those are her thoughts reaching me!' Then he would add, 'Perhaps my thoughts are reaching her.'

This conceit, at which he would shake his head a moment later, managed nevertheless to cast into his soul rays of light at times resembling hope. Now and then, especially at that hour of the evening that dreamers find most melancholic, he would jot down, in a notebook containing nothing else, the purest, most impersonal, most ideal of the musings with which love filled his mind. He called this 'writing to her'.

You must not think he was deranged. Quite the contrary. He had lost the ability to work or to direct himself resolutely towards any fixed goal, but he had more perspicacity and integrity than ever. Marius saw in a calm, true, albeit peculiar light what passed before his eyes, even the most unimportant of men and events. He was exactly right in what he said about everything with a kind of honest disconsolation and candid dispassion. Almost detached from hope, his judgement floated aloft.

In this state of mind nothing escaped him, nothing deceived him, and he was discovering at every moment the essence of life, humanity, destiny. Blessed is he, even in his suffering, to whom God has given a soul worthy of love and sorrow! He who has not seen the things of this world and the hearts of men by this dual light has seen nothing real and knows nothing.

The soul that loves and suffers is in a state of sublimity.

Otherwise, the days went by and there were no new developments. It just seemed to him that the dismal interval he had yet to endure grew shorter every moment. He thought he could already clearly discern the brink of the bottomless drop.

'So will I not see her again before then!' he kept saying to himself.

When you go up Rue St-Jacques, past the toll-gate, and follow the old inner boulevard to the left for a while, you come to Rue de la Santé, then La Glacière, and shortly before the little Gobelins River you reach a kind of field, which is the only spot along the whole monotonous length of the boulevards encircling Paris where Ruysdael would be tempted to sit down.

There is an indefinable charm about the place, a green meadow with clothes drying in the wind from lines strung out across it, an old market-garden farmhouse built in the days of Louis XIII, its large roof quaintly studded with dormer windows, some ramshackle fencing, a small pond lying amid poplar trees, women, laughter, voices. On the horizon the Panthéon, the tree of the Deaf-Mutes School, the Val-de-Grâce – black, squat, fantastical, witty, magnificent – and the severe square tops of the towers of Notre-Dame in the background.

As it is a place worth seeing, no one goes there. Scarcely a cart or a carrier once in a quarter-hour.

It so happened that Marius's solitary walks brought him to this patch of land by this pond. That day, unusually on that boulevard, there was a passer-by. Vaguely struck by the attractiveness of this near-wilderness, Marius asked this person, 'What is this place called?'

The person replied, 'This is Alouette's Meadow.' And he added, 'It was here that Ulbach killed the shepherdess of Ivry.'

But after that word 'Alouette' Marius heard nothing more. There are in the state of daydream these sudden crystallizations that it takes only a single word to produce. All thought suddenly condenses around a single idea and is no longer capable of any other perception. 'Alouette' was the name that in the depths of Marius's melancholy had replaced 'Ursule'. 'Well,' he said with the kind of unreasoning amazement typical of these mysterious asides, 'this is her meadow. I shall learn here where she lives.'

It was absurd, but not to be resisted.

And he came every day to this Alouette's Meadow.

II
Prison Incubators of Embryonic Crime

Javert's triumph at the Gorbeau tenement seemed complete, but it was not.

In the first place, and this was his main concern, Javert had not taken the prisoner prisoner. The murder victim who flees is more suspect than the murderer, and the likelihood was that this individual, so valuable a prize to those ruffians, was no less a good catch to the authorities. Furthermore, Montparnasse had eluded Javert.

He would have to wait for another opportunity to lay his hands on that 'devil's dandy'. For having encountered Éponine as she stood watch under the trees on the boulevard, Montparnasse had gone off with her, preferring to be a Némorin with the daughter rather than a Schinderhannes with the father. Just as well for him. He was free. As for Éponine, Javert had her 'nicked' later. Poor consolation. Éponine had joined Azelma at Les Madelonnettes.

Finally, on the way from the Gorbeau tenement to La Force, one of the chief arrests made, Claquesous, vanished. No one knew how it had happened, the police who were with him were 'completely baffled', he had vaporized, slipped out of the thumb-cuffs and slithered through chinks in the carriage – the cab was cracked, and it leaked. All they could say was that when they got to the prison Claquesous was gone. It was either a case of magic or the police had something to do with it. Had Claquesous melted into the shadows like a snowflake in water? Had there been some unavowed connivance with his custodians? Was this man part of the dual enigma of order and disorder? Was he concentric to both law-breaking and law enforcement? Did this sphinx have his forelimbs in crime and his hindlimbs in authority? Javert did not approve of arrangements of this kind and would have taken exception to such a compromise. But his squad included other inspectors besides himself, and they were perhaps, although his subordinates, more initiated than he was into the secrets of the Prefecture. And Claquesous was such a villain, he might make a very good agent. To feel so much at home in the dark as to be able to elude detection is excellent for robbers and admirable for the police. Such double-dealers do exist. All the same, having gone missing, Claquesous was not tracked down again. Javert appeared to be more annoyed than surprised by this.

As for Marius, 'that innocent of a lawyer who probably took fright' and whose name Javert had forgotten, Javert attached very little importance to him. Besides, you can always track down a lawyer. But was he actually a lawyer?

The investigation had begun. The examining magistrate thought it as well not to put one of the men from the Patron-Minette gang in solitary confinement, hoping to encourage some loose talk. This man was Brujon, the long-haired fellow from Rue du Petit-Banquier. He was released into the Cour Charlemagne and the warders kept a watchful eye on him.

The name Brujon is one that is remembered at La Force. In that frightful yard known as the Cour du Bâtiment-Neuf, which the administration called the Cour St-Bernard and the robbers called the Lions' Den, on that scaly, peeling wall rising roof-high on the left, by an old rusty iron door that led to the former chapel of the La Force ducal residence which had become a dormitory for criminals, up to twelve years earlier there could still be seen, crudely etched into the stone with a nail, a sort of prison fortress and beneath it this signature: 'BRUJON, 1811'.

The Brujon of 1811 was the father of the Brujon of 1832.

The latter, of whom we were only able to catch a glimpse in the Gorbeau ambush, was a very cunning and extremely crafty young lad with a bewildered and pathetic look about him. It was because of this bewildered look that the magistrate had released him, thinking he would be more useful in the Cour Charlemagne than in solitary confinement.

Being in the hands of justice is no obstruction to robbers. A little thing like that is not going to bother them. To be in prison for one crime is no reason not to start on another. These are artists who are already showing one picture at the Salon but even so are working on a new painting in their studios.

Brujon seemed to be dazed by the prison. He was sometimes to be seen standing for hours on end at the canteen hatch in the Cour Charlemagne, staring like an idiot at that grubby canteen price list that began with 'garlic: 62 centimes' and ended with 'cigar: 5 centimes'. Or else he spent his time shivering, his teeth chattering, saying he had a fever and asking whether one of the twenty-eight beds in the fever ward was vacant.

Then out of the blue, in the latter part of February 1832, it was discovered that numbskull Brujon had had three different messages delivered by the prison's messengers, not in his own name but in the name of three of his comrades, which had cost him fifty sous in all, a huge expense that attracted the attention of the chief prison warder.

Enquiries were made, and by consulting the price list for the delivery of messages posted in the inmates' visiting-room it was possible to establish that the fifty sous could be broken down as follows: three messages – one to the Panthéon, ten sous; one to the Val-de-Grâce, fifteen sous; and one to the Grenelle toll-gate, twenty-five sous. This last was the most expensive category on the whole price list. Now, the Panthéon, the Val-de-Grâce and the Grenelle toll-gate just happened to be the home patches of three extremely dangerous marauders: Kruideniers alias Bizarro, Glorieux, a freed felon, and Barrecarrosse, who were brought to the attention of the police by this incident. It was thought likely these men were members of Patron-Minette, two of whose leaders, Babet and Gueulemer, had been put away. It was assumed that in Brujon's messages, which had been delivered not to addresses of buildings but to people waiting in the street, there must have been instructions about some planned crime. Further evidence was obtained. The three prowlers were arrested, and that, it was thought, put paid to whatever Brujon had been plotting.

One night about a week after these measures had been taken, a warder on his rounds, who was checking on the lower dormitory in the Bâtiment-Neuf, was just about to drop his tally in the box – this was the method used to make sure the warders did their job properly; every hour a tally had to be dropped in all the boxes on the dormitory doors – and through a peep-hole into the dormitory this warder saw Brujon sitting up in bed writing something by the light of the wall-lamp. The warder went in, Brujon was put in solitary confinement for a month, but what he had written could not be found. The police were unable to find out any more about it.

What is certain is that the next day a 'postilion' was thrown from the Cour Charlemagne into the Lions' Den, over the five-storey build-ing separating the two yards.

What the prisoners call a 'postilion' is a cleverly kneaded ball of bread that is sent 'to Ireland', that is to say, over the roofs of a prison, from one courtyard to another. Etymology: over England, from one country to another, 'to Ireland'. This little ball falls in the yard. Whoever picks it up opens it and finds a note inside addressed to some prisoner in the yard. If it is a prisoner that finds it he delivers the note to its destination. If it is a warder, or one of those prisoners secretly turned traitor who are called 'sheep' in prisons and 'foxes' in the prison hulks, the note is taken to the clerk and handed over to the police.

On this occasion the postilion reached its destination, although the person for whom the message was intended was at that moment in solitary. This person was none other than Babet, one of the four chiefs of Patron-Minette.

The postilion contained a rolled-up piece of paper with only these two lines on it: 'Babet. There is a job worth doing in Rue Plumet. A gate with a garden behind it.'

This is what Brujon had been writing that night.

Notwithstanding searches conducted by male and female prison staff, Babet managed to send the note from La Force to a 'good friend' of his who was locked up inside La Salpêtrière. This woman in turn passed the note on to someone else she knew, a certain Magnon, who was being closely watched by the police but had not yet been arrested.

This Magnon, whose name the reader has already encountered, had some dealings with the Thénardiers about which more will be said later, and by going to see Éponine she could serve as a go-between for La Salpêtrière and Les Madelonnettes.

It just so happened that at that very point, for lack of evidence with regard to his daughters in the Thénardier investigation, Éponine and Azelma were released.

When Éponine came out, the woman by the name of Magnon, who was waiting for her at the gate of Les Madelonnettes, handed her Brujon's note to Babet, telling her to 'look into it'.

Éponine went to Rue Plumet, identified the gate and the garden, watched the house, spied, lay in wait, and a few days later brought to the Magnon woman, who lived in Rue Clocheperce, a biscuit that she in turn conveyed to Babet's mistress in La Salpêtrière.

In the obscure symbolism of prison language a biscuit means 'Nothing doing.'

The result was that less than a week later, when Brujon and Babet passed each other on the parapet walk of La Force, one of them on his way to the inquiry, the other on his way back, Brujon asked, 'Well, what about Rue P?' And Babet replied, 'Biscuit.'

So it was that this embryonic crime, fathered by Brujon in La Force, was aborted. However, this abortion had consequences completely unconnected with Brujon's plan. As we shall see.

Often you think you are tying up a loose end and in doing so you get caught up in something else.

III

Père Mabeuf's Visitation

Marius no longer visited anyone, but he sometimes happened to run into Père Mabeuf.

As Marius slowly made that dismal descent down what might be called the steps to the cellar leading to lightless depths where those favoured by fortune can be heard walking overhead, elsewhere Monsieur Mabeuf was making a similar descent.

The *Flora of Cauterets* was simply not selling any more. The experiments with indigo had been unsuccessful in the little garden at Austerlitz, which got no sun. Monsieur Mabeuf could cultivate in it only those few rare plants that like damp and shade. Yet he did not lose heart. He had acquired in the Jardin des Plantes a corner plot with a suitable exposure, to carry out his trials with indigo 'at his own expense'. For this purpose he had pawned the copper-plates of his *Flora*. He had reduced his lunch to two eggs, and one of these he would leave for his old servant whose wages he had not paid for the last fifteen months. And often, lunch was his only meal of the day. He no longer laughed with his childlike laugh, he had grown morose and

781

he did not receive visitors any more. It was just as well that Marius no longer thought of calling on him. Sometimes, when Monsieur Mabeuf was on his way to the Jardin des Plantes, the old man and the young man would pass each other on Boulevard de l'Hôpital. They did not speak, and nodded sadly to each other. Heart-breaking that a time should come when poverty creates estrangement! Once two friends, now two passers-by.

The bookseller Royol was dead. Monsieur Mabeuf's life was confined to his books, his garden and his indigo: these were the three forms that happiness, pleasure and hope had taken for him. This was all he needed to survive. He said to himself, 'When I've made my balls of blue, I'll be rich, I'll redeem my copper-plates from the pawn-shop, I'll drum up interest in my *Flora* again by putting a lot of money into it and advertising in the newspapers, and I'll buy a copy, I know exactly where, of the 1559 edition of Pedro de Medina's *Art of Navigation* with wood-cut illustrations.' In the meantime he worked all day at his indigo plot and in the evening he came home to water his garden and read his books. Monsieur Mabeuf was by then very nearly eighty.

One evening he had a peculiar visitation.

He had come home while it was still light. Mère Plutarque, whose health was deteriorating, was ill in bed. He had dined on a bone with a little meat left on it and a piece of bread he had found on the kitchen table, and he had sat down on an overturned boundary-stone that served as a bench in his garden.

Near this bench rose a big, very dilapidated hut of sorts, a construction of beams and planks, typical of old orchards, with a rabbit hutch below and a fruit loft above. There were no rabbits in the hutch but there were a few apples in the loft. The remains of the winter supply.

Monsieur Mabeuf had started leafing through and reading, with the aid of his glasses, two books that fascinated him and even, a much more serious thing at his age, worried him. His natural timidity made him susceptible to a certain acceptance of superstitions. The first of these books was the famous treatise by Judge Delancre, *Of the Inconstancy of Demons*, the other was the quarto volume by Mutor de la Rubaudière, *On the Devils of Vauvert and the Goblins of the Bièvre.**

---

* Legendary evil spirits were supposed to haunt the medieval ruined castle of Vauvert in Paris, giving rise to the idiomatic expression *au diable vauvert*, meaning 'in the back of beyond'. There is a play here, too, on the name Gobelins, the great family of tapestry-makers closely associated with the nearby Bièvre River in Paris, sometimes called *le ruisseau des Gobelins* ('the Gobelins river'), and *gobelins*, meaning 'goblins'.

This second old book interested him all the more because his garden had been one of the sites haunted by goblins in the past. The twilight had begun to bleach the heights above and darken all below. Even as he read, over the top of the book he held in his hand Père Mabeuf surveyed his plants, a magnificent rhododendron among others, which was one of his consolations. There had been four days of dryness, of wind and sunshine, without a drop of rain. Stems were sagging, buds drooping, leaves falling, everything needed watering – the rhododendron looked particularly sad. Père Mabeuf was one of those for whom plants have souls. The old man had laboured all day at his indigo plot, he was utterly exhausted, but he stood up, laid his books on the bench, and all stooped and unsteady on his feet he tottered over to the well; but when he had grasped the chain he could not even pull it hard enough to unhook it. Then he turned and looked up in anguish towards the sky, which was filling with stars.

The evening had that serenity that overcomes man's woes with an indefinable joy, mournful and eternal. The night promised to be as dry as the day had been.

'Stars everywhere!' thought the old man. 'Not the tiniest cloud! Not a drop of water!'

And his head, which had been upturned for a moment, dropped down on his chest.

He raised it again and looked once more at the sky, murmuring, 'A drop of dew! A little pity!'

He tried once again to unhook the well chain, and could not.

At that moment he heard a voice speaking, 'Père Mabeuf, would you like me to water your garden?'

At the same time there was a sound as of some creature of the wild moving in the hedge, and he saw emerge from the shrubbery a tall, thin girl who stood before him, staring at him boldly. She looked not so much a human being as some evening-flowering manifestation.

Before Père Mabeuf, who was easily scared and, as we have said, quick to take fright, could utter a syllable in reply, this being whose movements had in the dusk a kind of bizarre abruptness had unhooked the chain, lowered and retrieved the bucket and filled the watering-can, and the old boy saw this apparition, barefoot, in a ragged skirt, darting among the flowerbeds, distributing life all around her. The sound of the watering-can on the leaves filled Père Mabeuf's soul with delight. It seemed to him the rhododendron was happy now.

When the first bucketful had been emptied, the girl drew a second, then a third. She watered the whole garden.

There was something about the sight of her walking down the paths – where she appeared as a completely black figure with her shawl all in tatters fluttering about her long arms – that resembled a bat.

When she was done Père Mabeuf went up to her with tears in his eyes, and laid his hand on her forehead.

'God shall bless you,' he said, 'you're an angel because you care for flowers.'

'No,' she replied, 'I'm the devil, but I don't mind.'

Without waiting for or hearing her reply, the old man exclaimed, 'What a pity I'm such a poor wretch and that I can't do anything for you!'

'You can do something,' she said.

'What?'

'Tell me where Monsieur Marius lives.'

The old man did not understand. 'Who's Monsieur Marius?' He looked up and his glassy eyes seemed to be searching for something that had disappeared.

'A young man who used to come here.'

Meanwhile, Monsieur Mabeuf had been probing his memory.

'Ah, yes!' he exclaimed. 'I know who you mean. Now wait a moment! Monsieur Marius – Baron Marius Pontmercy, for heaven's sake! He lives – or rather, he doesn't live there any more – ah well, I don't know.'

As he was speaking, he bent down to pin back a rhododendron branch. 'Listen, I remember now,' he went on. 'He very often comes along the boulevard and heads off towards La Glacière. Rue Croule-barbe. Alouette's Meadow. Go over in that direction. He's not hard to find.'

When Monsieur Mabeuf straightened up there was no one there. The girl had vanished.

He was really a little frightened.

'Truly,' he thought, 'if my garden hadn't been watered, I'd think that was a spirit of some sort.'

When he was lying in bed an hour later this came back to him, and as he dozed off, in that uncertain moment when, like the fabulous bird that changes into a fish in order to swim across the sea, thought gradually takes the form of a dream to traverse sleep, he said to himself in confusion, 'Actually, that was very like Rubaudière's account of goblins. Could she have been a goblin?'

IV
Marius's Visitation

One morning a few days after this visitation of a 'spirit' to Père Mabeuf – it was a Monday, the day when Marius would borrow a five-franc coin from Courfeyrac for Thénardier – Marius had put this five-franc coin in his pocket, and before taking it to the clerk's office he had gone 'for a little walk', hoping this would help him settle down to work on his return. In fact, this was ever the way. As soon as he got up in the morning, he would sit down in front of a book and a sheet of paper to dash off some translation. His job at that time was to produce a French version of a celebrated German dispute, the Gans–Savigny controversy. He would take Savigny, he would take Gans, read four lines, try to write one, not succeed, he would see a star that came asterisk-like between himself and the page, and he would rise from his chair, saying, 'I'll go out. That will get me started.'

And off he would go to Alouette's Meadow. There he would more than ever see the star; and less than ever, Savigny and Gans.

He would come home, try to resume his work, and fail. Impossible to repair a single one of the broken threads in his brain. Then he would say to himself, 'I shan't go out tomorrow. It stops me working.' And he would go out every day.

He lived more in Alouette's Meadow than in Courfeyrac's lodgings. His real address was Boulevard de la Santé, the seventh tree after Rue Croulebarbe.

That morning he had moved away from that seventh tree and sat down on the parapet by the Gobelins River. Cheerful sunlight shone through the bright, glossy, newly unfurled leaves.

He was thinking of 'Her'. And his wandering thoughts, turning to reproach, came back to himself. He reflected dolefully on the idleness, paralysis of spirit, that was overtaking him, and on that darkness before him, growing denser moment by moment so that already he could not even see the sun any more.

Yet, through this painful emergence of hazy notions that did not even constitute a monologue, so debilitated was his capacity for action, which he no longer had even the strength of will to lament any more, through this melancholy self-absorption sensations from the outside world did reach him.

He heard behind him, below him, on both banks of the river, the Gobelins washerwomen beating their laundry, and above his head the birds chattering and singing in the elm trees. On the one hand the sound of freedom, carefree happiness, winged idleness, on the other the sound of toil. What profoundly bemused him, and made him almost pensive, was that both were joyous sounds.

All of a sudden in the midst of his dejected ecstasy he heard a familiar voice saying, 'Ah! Here he is!'

He looked up and recognized that poor child who had come to his room one morning, the elder of the Thénardier daughters, Éponine. He knew her name now. Strange to say, she looked poorer and prettier – developments that in both respects seemed impossible. She had made a twofold advance, towards the light and towards destitution. As on the day when she had so resolutely entered his room, she was barefoot and in rags; only, her rags were two months older now, the holes were larger, her tattered clothes filthier. It was the same husky voice, the same forehead, weatherbeaten and lined, the same free-ranging, distracted and unsettled gaze. There was in her face, more than there had been in the past, that indefinable fearfulness and pitifulness that time spent in prison adds to poverty.

She had bits of straw and hay in her hair, not on account of being driven mad like Ophelia by the contagion of Hamlet's madness, but because she had slept in some stable loft.

And with all that, she was beautiful. What a morning star is youth!

Meanwhile, she stood there before Marius with a hint of joy on her pallid face and something that resembled a smile.

For several moments it was as if she were incapable of speech.

'So I've found you!' she said at last. 'Père Mabeuf was right, it was on this boulevard! How I've looked for you! If you only knew! You know I've been inside? A fortnight! They let me go, seeing they had nothing on me, and besides I'm not old enough to be held criminally responsible. I'm two months shy of it. Oh! how I've looked for you! For the past six weeks! So you don't live there any more?'

'No,' said Marius.

'Oh! I understand. Because of what happened. They're nasty, those snatches. You moved out. Now why wear an old hat like that! A young man like you ought to have fine clothes. You know, Monsieur Marius, Père Mabeuf calls you Baron Marius something or other. You're not a baron, are you? Barons are old folk, they go to the Luxembourg and sit in front of the château to get the most sun, and they read the *Quotidienne* that costs a sou. I once took a letter to a baron who was like that. He was more than a hundred years old. Tell me, where do you live now?'

Marius did not reply.

786

'Ah,' she went on, 'you've got a hole in your shirt! I must mend it for you.'

She resumed with an expression that gradually clouded over, 'You don't look happy to see me.'

Marius said nothing. She too remained silent for a moment, then exclaimed, 'But I could make you look happy if I wanted to!'

'What?' said Marius. 'What do you mean by that?'*

'Ah! you used not to be so formal,' she said.†

'Very well, what do you mean?' he said.‡

She bit her lip. She seemed to hesitate, as though torn by some sort of inner conflict. Finally she appeared to come to a decision.

'Never mind, it won't make any difference. You look sad, I want you to be happy. Just promise to laugh. I want to see you laugh and hear you say, "Oh, now that's good." Poor Monsieur Marius! You know, you promised you'd give me whatever I wanted—'

'Yes! But go on, tell me!'

She looked Marius straight in the eye and said, 'I've got the address.'

Marius turned pale. All the blood drained back to his heart.

'What address?'

'The address you asked me for!' She added, as if it were costing her some effort, 'The address – you know the one?'

'Yes!' stammered Marius.

'Of that young lady.' Having said this, she sighed deeply.

Marius leapt up from the parapet where he had been sitting and frantically grabbed her hand.

'Oh! Well then? Show me the way! Tell me! Ask whatever you want of me! Where is it?'

'Come with me,' she replied. 'I don't really know the street or the number. It's way over in the other direction from here, but I certainly know which house it is, I'll take you there.'

She withdrew her hand and went on in a tone of voice that would have cut to the heart anyone watching – but Marius, now enraptured, in transports of delight, did not even notice – 'Oh! how happy you are!'

Marius's brow clouded. He seized Éponine by the arm. 'Swear to me something!'

---

* He addresses her as *vous*.

† Although regretting his formality, she still addresses him as *vous*: 'Ah! vous me disiez tu!'

‡ Here he is using the familiar *tu*.

787

'Swear?' she said. 'What are you talking about? You want me to swear?' And she laughed.

'Your father! Promise me, Éponine! Swear to me you won't tell your father this address!'

She turned to him with a look of amazement. 'Éponine! How do you know my name's Éponine?'

'Promise me what I said!'

But she seemed not to hear him. 'Now, that's lovely, that is! You called me Éponine!'

Marius held her by both arms.

'For heaven's sake, answer me! Listen to what I'm saying. Swear to me you won't tell your father the address that you know!'

'My father?' she said. 'Ah yes, my father! You needn't worry. He's locked up. In any case, as if I care about my father!'

'But you haven't promised!' exclaimed Marius.

'Now let go of me!' she said with a burst of laughter. 'You're shaking me so hard! Yes! Yes! I promise! I swear! What's it to me? I won't tell my father the address. There! Satisfied? Is that what you wanted?'

'Or anyone else!' said Marius.

'Or anyone else.'

'Now take me there,' said Marius.

'Right now?'

'Right now.'

'Come along. Oh! how happy he is!' she said.

After a few steps she stopped.

'You're following me too closely, Monsieur Marius. Let me go on ahead, and you hang back so it doesn't look as if you're following me. A respectable young man like you shouldn't be seen with a woman like me.'

No language could convey everything contained in that word 'woman', as spoken by that child.

She went on a dozen paces, then stopped again. Marius caught up with her. She spoke to him out of the corner of her mouth, without turning towards him. 'By the way, you know you promised me something?'

Marius fumbled in his pocket. All he had in the world was the five francs intended for old Thénardier. He took them and put them in Éponine's hand.

She opened her fingers and let the coin fall to the ground. And gazing at him sombrely, she said, 'I don't want your money.'

BOOK THREE
THE HOUSE IN RUE PLUMET

I
The House with a Secret Entrance

Towards the middle of the last century, a High Court judge in the Paris parliament who was keeping a mistress on the sly – for in those days aristocrats were open about their mistresses and the bourgeoisie were secretive about theirs – had 'a little house' built in Faubourg St-Germain, on that deserted street Rue Blomet, now called Rue Plumet, not far from the spot then known as the Combat des Animaux.

This house was a two-storey villa, with two rooms on the ground floor, two bedrooms on the first floor, a kitchen downstairs, a dressing room upstairs, an attic under the roof, and in front of it all a garden with a big iron gate giving on to the street. This garden measured about an acre. This was all that could be seen by passers-by. But behind the villa was a narrow courtyard and at the far end of the courtyard a low two-roomed building with a cellar, a kind of contingency measure for keeping a child and a wet-nurse out of sight, if need be. This building connected from the rear, via a concealed door operated by a secret opening mechanism, with a long, narrow, winding passage. Paved, open to the sky, bounded by two high walls and hidden with extraordinary cunning, as if lost between the perimeter fencing of allotments and market-gardens whose every twist and turn it followed, this passage eventually led to another door, also with a secret lock, that opened some five hundred yards away almost in another neighbourhood, at the lonely end of Rue de Babylone.

This is where the High Court judge, Monsieur le Président, would let himself in, so that even if anyone had been spying on him and following him, and had noticed that Monsieur le Président would mysteriously go somewhere every day, they could not have suspected that going to Rue de Babylone meant going to Rue Blomet. Thanks to some canny land purchases, the clever judge had been able to have this secret passage built on his own property, and consequently without any interference. Later on he had sold off in small parcels, for allotments and market-gardens, the plots of land bordering the passage, and the owners of these plots on either side thought that what they saw before them was a party wall, and did not even suspect the existence of that long strip of paving, winding through their flowerbeds and orchards between two walls. Only the birds could see this curiosity. The warblers and tits of the last century probably chattered a great deal about Monsieur le Président.

Stone-built in the Mansart style, wainscoted and furnished in the Watteau style, rococo whimsy on the inside, old-fashioned restraint on the outside, secluded behind triple ranks of flowers – there was something discreet, attractive and solemn about the house, as befits a caprice of love and the law.

This house and this passage, which have now disappeared, were still in existence fifteen years ago. In '93 a boiler-maker bought the house in order to demolish it, but as he was unable to pay the purchase price the nation declared him bankrupt. So it was the house that demolished the boiler-maker. After that, the house was left uninhabited and slowly fell into ruin, just like any other dwelling no longer instilled with life by man's presence. It remained furnished with its old furniture and perpetually for sale or to let, and the ten or twelve people a year who passed by Rue Plumet were alerted to the fact by a yellowing and illegible sign that had been hanging on the garden wall since 1810.

Towards the end of the Restoration these same passers-by might have noticed that the sign had disappeared, and indeed that the first-floor shutters were open. The house was in fact occupied. Half-curtains hung at the windows, indicating there was a woman about.

In the month of October 1829 an elderly man had turned up and rented the house, just as it was, including of course the building in the back yard and the passage that led to Rue de Babylone. He had the secret opening mechanisms of the two doors to this passage mended.

The house, as we have just mentioned, was still more or less furnished with the judge's old furniture. The new tenant ordered some repairs, added whatever was lacking here and there, replaced some paving-stones in the yard, some tiles in the flooring, some treads in the staircase, some wood blocks in the parquet and some panes of glass in the casement windows, and finally moved in with a young girl and an elderly maidservant, without any fuss, more like someone stealing in than a man entering his own home. This did not set the neighbours chattering, by reason of there being no neighbours.

This rather retiring tenant was Jean Valjean, the young girl was Cosette. The servant was a woman called Toussaint, whom Jean Valjean had saved from the poorhouse and from destitution. She was old, from the country, and a stammerer, three qualities that made Jean Valjean decide to take her on. He had rented the house under the name of Monsieur Fauchelevent, gentleman of independent means. In the episode related earlier, the reader was probably even less slow than Thénardier to recognize Jean Valjean.

Why had Jean Valjean left the Petit-Picpus convent? What had happened? Nothing had happened.

Remember, Jean Valjean was happy in the convent, so happy that his conscience eventually became troubled. He saw Cosette every day. He felt more and more a sense of paternity begin to grow and develop in him. He cherished that child. He told himself that she was his, that nothing could take her away from him, that it would be like this indefinitely. She would surely become a nun, being gently encouraged to do so every day; and, that being the case, the convent was now her universe, as it was his. He would grow old here and she would grow up here. She would grow old here and he would die here. In short – blissful expectation! – no separation was possible. Reflecting on this resulted in his falling into a state of perplexity. He questioned himself. He wondered if all this happiness really belonged to him, if it was not made up of someone else's happiness – this child's happiness which he in his old age was confiscating and appropriating – and if this was not robbery. He told himself, this child had a right to experience life before renouncing it, that to deprive her in advance of all the joys of life, and to some extent without consulting her, under the pretext of sparing her from all its tribulations, to take advantage of her ignorance and her isolation in order to foster in her a spurious vocation, was to pervert the nature of a human being and to lie to God. And who knows if Cosette, understanding all this some day and wishing she had not become a nun, would not come to hate him? A last thought, this; almost selfish and less heroic than the others, but one that was intolerable to him. He decided to leave the convent.

He made that decision. Sorrowfully, he admitted that it had to be done. As for objections, there were none. Five years' disappearance, staying within these four walls, had inevitably destroyed or dispersed any elements of fear. He could return among men without qualms. He had grown old, and everything had changed. Who would recognize him now? And then, if the worst came to the worst, there was a danger only to himself, and he had no right to condemn Cosette to the cloister because he had been condemned to the prison hulks. Besides, what is danger where duty is involved? After all, nothing prevented him from being careful and taking precautions. As for Cosette's education, it was almost concluded and complete.

Once his mind was made up he awaited his opportunity. It soon presented itself. Old Fauchelevent died.

Jean Valjean asked for an interview with the reverend prioress and told her that, having come into a small inheritance on the death of his brother that meant he did not have to work any more to earn his living, he was giving up his duties at the convent and taking his daughter away with him. But seeing that Cosette was not going to be taking her vows, it was not right she should have received her education for nothing, and he humbly begged the reverend prioress to allow him to give to the community, as payment for the five years Cosette had spent there, the sum of five thousand francs.

So it was that Jean Valjean left the Convent of Perpetual Adoration.

When he left he personally carried under his arm, and would entrust it to no one else, that little travelling-case to which he always had the key about him. This travelling-case intrigued Cosette because of the smell of preservative balms that wafted from it.

Let us say straight away, from then on he never parted with this valise. He always kept it in his bedroom. It was the first and sometimes the only thing that he took with him whenever he moved house. Cosette would laugh about it and she called this travelling-case 'the inseparable', saying 'I'm jealous of it.'

Be that as it may, Jean Valjean did not go back out into the world without deep anxiety.

He found the house in Rue Plumet, and secluded himself there. He now called himself Ultime Fauchelevent.

At the same time he rented two other apartments in Paris so as to attract less attention than if he were to remain always in the same neighbourhood, to be able to make himself scarce if need be at the slightest misgiving and, in short, never again to find himself utterly defenceless as on the night when he had so miraculously eluded Javert. These two apartments were two extremely modest lodgings of humble appearance in two parts of town very distant from each other, one in Rue de l'Ouest, the other in Rue de l'Homme-Armé.

Every so often he would go and spend a month or six weeks sometimes in Rue de l'Homme-Armé, sometimes in Rue de l'Ouest, with Cosette, leaving Toussaint behind. He relied on the caretakers for service when he was there and gave the impression he was a gentleman of independent means from the suburbs with a little pied-à-terre in town. This model of virtue had three addresses in Paris in order to evade the police.

National Guardsman Jean Valjean

However, strictly speaking, he lived in Rue Plumet, where he had arranged his life as follows.

Cosette and the servant occupied the villa. She had the large bed-room with the painted panels, the dressing room with the gilded mouldings, the judge's drawing room furnished with tapestries and huge armchairs. She had the garden. Jean Valjean had installed in Cosette's bedroom a canopied bed of antique three-coloured damask and a beautiful old Persian carpet bought from Mère Gaucher in Rue du Figuier-St-Paul, and to offset the austerity of these magnificent antiques he had included in this miscellany all the charming little fur-nishings that delight young girls – ornament stand, bookcase, gilt-edged books, writing-case, blotter, work table inlaid with mother-of-pearl, silver-gilt dressing-table set, Japanese porcelain water jug and bowl. Long three-coloured damask curtains with a red background, like the curtains round the bed, hung at the upper-floor windows. On the ground floor were tapestry hangings. Cosette's little house was heated from top to bottom throughout the winter. He himself inhabited that sort of porter's lodge in the courtyard at the back, with a mattress on a trestle-bed, a deal table, two straw-bottomed chairs, an earthenware water jug, a few old books on a shelf, his cherished valise in one corner, and never a fire. He dined with Cosette and for him there would be a loaf of black bread on the table. He had said to Toussaint when she came to them, 'The young lady is the mistress of the house.' 'And you, m-m-m-monsieur?' Toussaint replied in astonishment. 'Better by far than being master, I'm the father.'

Cosette had been schooled in housekeeping at the convent and she was in charge of the household expenses, which were very mod-est. Every day Jean Valjean would take Cosette's arm and go for a walk with her. He took her to the Luxembourg Gardens, to the least frequented avenue, and every Sunday he took her to mass at St-Jacques-du-Haut-Pas because it was very far away. Since this was a very poor neighbourhood he was very charitable, and those in need would flock around him in the church – this is what had earned him that letter from Thénardier 'To the charitable gentleman at the church of St-Jacques-du-Haut-Pas'. He liked to take Cosette to visit the poor and the sick. No stranger ever entered the house in Rue Plumet. Tous-saint did the shopping, and Jean Valjean went himself to fetch water from a standpipe on the boulevard near by. Wood and wine were stored in a kind of semi-underground roughcast recess, which was right by the Rue de Babylone doorway and had formerly served Monsieur le Président as a grotto, for in the days of pleasure retreats and 'little houses' no love affair was complete without a grotto.

In the side door on Rue de Babylone was one of those slots for posting letters and newspapers into a box. Only, as the three inhabitants of the house in Rue Plumet received no newspapers or letters, the entire usefulness of that box, once a lovers' go-between and the recipient of a courting lawyer's confidences, was now limited to tax-collector's notices and guard-duty orders.

For Monsieur Fauchelevent, gentleman of independent means, was in the National Guard. He had not been able to slip through the fine mesh of the 1831 census. The municipality's information-gathering at the time had extended even to the Petit-Picpus convent, a kind of impenetrable and saintly cloud from which in the eyes of the authorities Jean Valjean emerged as a venerable man and consequently fit for guard duty.

Three or four times a year Jean Valjean donned his uniform and did his service. Very willingly, in fact. It was for him a perfect disguise that allowed him to mix with other people while leaving him on his own. Jean Valjean had just turned sixty, the legal age of exemption, but he looked no more than fifty. Besides, he had no desire to evade his sergeant-major or to wrangle with Comte de Lobau. He had no official status in society. He was concealing his name, concealing his identity, concealing his age, he was concealing everything. And as we have just said, he was a willing National Guardsman. To be like anyone else who paid his taxes – that was his sole ambition. The ideal to which this man aspired was, inwardly, an angel, outwardly, a respectable citizen.

Yet let us mark one detail. When Jean Valjean went out with Cosette he dressed as we have seen, and looked much like a retired officer. When he went out alone, and this was usually at night, he was always dressed in a workman's jacket and trousers, with a cap that hid his face. Was this caution or humility? Both. Cosette was accustomed to this mysterious aspect of his life and hardly noticed her father's peculiarities. As for Toussaint, she revered Jean Valjean and thought well of everything he did. One day her butcher, who had barely set eyes on Jean Valjean, said to her, 'He's a strange one.' She replied, 'He's a s-s-s-saint.'

Neither Jean Valjean nor Cosette nor Toussaint ever came in or went out except by the door on Rue de Babylone. Unless they were glimpsed through the garden gate it would have been hard to tell that they lived in Rue Plumet. This gate was always closed. Jean Valjean let the garden run wild in order not to attract attention.

In this, he was possibly mistaken.

III
Foliis ac Frondibus *

The garden thus left to itself for more than half a century had become attractive and remarkable. Passers-by of forty years earlier would stop to gaze at it without suspecting the secrets it hid in its fresh and verdant depths. More than one daydreamer of that period had many a time allowed his eyes and thoughts to pry indiscreetly between the bars of that buckled and ramshackle ancient padlocked gate, attached to two green and moss-grown pillars, bizarrely crowned with a pediment of indecipherable arabesques.

There were one or two mildewed statues, a stone bench in one corner, several trellises rotting on the wall, from which they had become detached with the passage of time, and no paths or lawn surviving, couch grass everywhere. Gardening had taken its leave, and nature had returned. Weeds ran riot, a wonderful treat for any poor corner of land. The display of gillyflowers was glorious. Nothing in this garden obstructed the sacred struggle for life of all things. Awesome growth was in its element here. The trees had stooped towards the brambles, the brambles had climbed towards the trees, the plant had reached up, the branch had bowed down, what creeps over the earth had sought what flourishes in the air, what flutters in the wind had dipped towards what trails in the moss. Tree trunks, boughs, foliage, fibres, tufts, tendrils, suckers, thorns were intermingled, intertwined, conjoined, inextricable. There, in that three-hundred-square-foot enclosure, under the well pleased eye of the Creator, vegetation in deep and close embrace had celebrated and fulfilled the holy mystery of its own fraternity, symbol of human fraternity. This garden was no longer a garden, it was a colossal thicket, that is to say, something as impenetrable as a forest, as densely populated as a city, as tremulous as a nest, as tenebrous as a cathedral, as aromatic as a bouquet, as lonely as a tomb, as much a living thing as a crowd.

During Floréal this huge wilderness, free behind its bars and within

---

* 'In foliage and leafy branches', an allusion to Lucretius' *De Rerum Natura*, bk V, line 972.

795

its four walls, went into rut, part of the secret process of universal germination; it quivered in the rising sun, almost like an animal breathing in rushes of cosmic love and feeling the April sap rising and bubbling in its veins; and shaking its extraordinary green mane in the wind, it scattered over the damp earth, the worn statues, the crumbling steps to the house and even the pavement of the deserted street, starry flowers, beads of dew, fecundity, beauty, life, joy, fragrances. At noon countless white butterflies would take refuge here; and it was a heavenly sight to see, whirling about in the shade, flurries of those living snows of summertime. There, in those merry green shadows, a throng of innocent voices spoke sweetly to the soul, and anything the twitterings had forgotten to say was made up for by the hummings. In the evening, a haze of reverie rose from the garden to envelop it. A shroud of mist, a calm and celestial sadness, lay over it. Such a heady perfume of honeysuckle and convolvulus emanated from everywhere, like an exquisite and subtle poison. You could hear the last cries of the tree-creepers and the wagtails as they dozed off among the branches. You could sense that sacred intimacy between birds and trees: by day the wings gladden the leaves, by night the leaves protect the wings.

In winter the thicket was dark, wet, shaggy and shivering, and allowed a glimpse of the house. Instead of blossom on the branches and dew on the blossom you saw the long silvery ribbon-trails of slugs on the cold thick carpet of yellow leaves. But always, in all its guises, in all seasons, spring, winter, summer, autumn, this tiny enclosure exuded melancholy, contemplation, solitude, freedom, the absence of man, the presence of God. And the rusty old gate seemed to say, 'This garden belongs to me.'

No matter that the streets of Paris lay all around, that the splendid classical mansions of Rue de Varennes were within a few steps of there, the Invalides dome close by, the Chamber of Deputies not far off; no matter that the carriages of Rue de Bourgogne and Rue St-Dominique made a great show of passing through the neighbourhood; no matter that yellow, brown, white, red omnibuses drove past each other at the nearest crossroads – Rue Plumet was the wilderness. And the death of its former proprietors, a revolution that had taken place, the collapse of old fortunes, absence, oblivion, forty years of neglect and isolation were enough to bring back to this place of privilege the bracken, mullein, hemlock, yarrow, foxgloves, tall grasses, great crimped plants whose broad leaves were sheets of pale green, lizards, beetles, quick restless insects; and to bring forth from the depths of the earth this ferocious and untamed grandeur of sorts, and to let it reappear within these four walls; and enough for nature, which thwarts man's petty arrangements and wherever it takes over takes over completely, in the ant as well as in the eagle, eventually to thrive as robustly and majestically in a small insignificant Paris garden as in a virgin forest of the New World.

In fact nothing is insignificant, as anyone susceptible to the deep insights of nature knows. Although no ultimate satisfaction is given to philosophy, either in restricting cause or in limiting effect, the contemplator falls into boundless ecstasies on account of all these disintegrating forces culminating in unity. Everything has a bearing on everything else.

Algebra applies to the clouds, the star's radiance benefits the rose. No thinker would dare to say the scent of hawthorn is irrelevant to the constellations. Who, then, can calculate a molecule's destiny? How do we know the creation of worlds is not determined by falling grains of sand? Who, then, is conversant with the reciprocal ebb and flow of the infinitely great and the infinitely small, the repercussions of causes in the abysses of being and the avalanches of creation? A mite matters. The small is great and the great is small. Everything is bound by necessity in equilibrium. Dreadful for the mind to envisage. There are extraordinary relations between creatures and things. In that inexhaustible whole, from the sun to the aphid, none scorns the other. Each has need of the other. Light carries terrestrial perfumes into the blue not without full knowledge of what it is doing. Darkness distributes stellar essence to sleeping flowers. All birds that fly have attached to one leg the thread of infinity. Germination embraces in its complexity the explosion of a meteor and the breaking of the eggshell by the peck of the swallow's beak, and is equally responsible for the birth of an earthworm and the coming of Socrates. Where the telescope ends, the microscope begins. Which of the two has the greater vision? You choose. A patch of mould is a constellation of flowers. A nebula is an ant's nest of stars. Similarly promiscuous and yet more extraordinary are things of the mind and facts of matter. Elements and principles mix, come together, wed, multiply by agency of each other, until the material and the moral worlds achieve the same clarity. The existential phenomenon is in perpetual convolution. In vast cosmic interchanges universal life, disseminated and indivisible, comes and goes in unknown quantities, drawing everything into the unseen mystery of emanations, making use of everything, wasting not one dream, not one sleeping moment, sowing the seed of some tiny creature here, reducing to smithereens an astral body there, weaving and wavering, making of light a force and of thought an element, disintegrating everything except that geometric point, the ego; reducing everything to the soul atom; bringing everything to fulfilment in God; implicating all activities, from the highest to the lowest, in the obscurity of a dizzying mechanism, connecting the flight of an insect with the movement of the earth, subordinating – who knows? if only by the application of the same law – the comet whirling in the firmament to the protozoa wriggling in the drop of water. A mind-made machine. A vast intermeshed apparatus whose prime motor is the gnat and whose ultimate wheel the Zodiac.

IV
The Convent Grille Replaced by Garden Railings

It was as if this garden, created in the past to conceal dissolute secrets, had been transformed and adapted to protect chaste secrets. There were no longer any arbours, lawns, pergolas, grottoes; there was a magnificent dishevelled obscurity draped over everything, like a veil. Paphos had turned into Eden. Some suggestion of repentance had purified this retreat. This flower-seller now offered her flowers to the soul. Once greatly compromised, this flirtatious garden was restored to virginity and to modesty. A judge with the assistance of a gardener, one of them who thought he was following on from Lamoignon and the other who thought he was following on from Le Nôtre, had shaped it, trimmed it, prettified it, decked it out, fashioned it for illicit romance. Nature had reclaimed it, filled it with shade, and arranged it for love.

There was in this seclusion a heart just ready for it. Love had only to show itself. Here was a temple to it composed of greenery, grass, moss, the sighs of birds, soft shadows, swaying branches, and a soul formed of sweetness, faith, simplicity, hope, yearning and illusion.

Cosette had emerged from the convent still a child, almost. A little over fourteen, she was at that 'awkward age'. As we have already mentioned, apart from her eyes she was plain-looking rather than pretty. Though none of her features was ugly, she was gawky, skinny, at once shy and bold; in short, a big little girl.

Her education had come to an end. In other words, she had been taught religion, and even devotion – most of all, devotion. Then 'history', that is to say what is so called in the convent; geography, grammar, participles, the kings of France, a little music, how to draw a face. But that apart, she knew nothing, which is a charm and a danger. A young girl's spirit should not be kept in obscurity, this later giving rise, as in a camera obscura, to chimeric images too rudimentary and too intense. She should be gently and discreetly enlightened, rather by the reflection of realities than by their direct, harsh glare. An effective and graciously austere half-light that dissipates childish fears and prevents falls. Only maternal instinct, that wonderful intuition in which virginal memories and womanly experience play their part, knows how this half-light should be created and of what it should consist. There is no substitute for this instinct. In the shaping of a young girl's spirit all the nuns in the world are not equal to a mother.

Cosette had no mother. She just had many mothers, plural. As for Jean Valjean, he certainly had within him at one and the same time every fondness and every tender care, but he was only an old man who knew nothing at all. Now, in this educational enterprise, in this serious matter of preparing a woman for life, what knowledge is needed to combat that vast ignorance called innocence!

There is nothing like the convent for priming a young girl for passion. The convent directs the mind towards the unknown. Retreating into itself, the heart unable to reach out delves within, and unable to blossom digs deep. Hence fantasies, assumptions, conjectures, half-envisaged romances, hoped-for intrigues, fabulous constructs, edifices built wholly in the inner dark of the mind, sombre and secret abodes where the passions, once through the gate and let inside, immediately take up residence. The convent is a repression that must be lifelong if it is to triumph over the human heart.

On leaving the convent Cosette could have found nothing more pleasant and more dangerous than the house in Rue Plumet. It was a continuation of solitude, with the beginnings of freedom: an enclosed garden, but nature here was aggressive, exuberant, voluptuous, and scented; the same daydreams as in the convent but with glimpses of young men, behind railings but on the street.

Yet, we say it again, when she first came here she was still only a child. Jean Valjean left this neglected garden to her. 'Do whatever you like with it,' he told her. This amused Cosette. She turned over every tuft and every stone, she hunted for 'creatures'. Here she played, until the time came for dreaming. She loved this garden for the insects she found in the grass beneath her feet, until the time came to love it for the stars she would see through the boughs above her head.

And besides, she loved her father, that is to say Jean Valjean, with all her heart, with an innocent filial passion that made the old man a cherished and delightful companion to her. Remember, Monsieur Madeleine used to read a great deal. Jean Valjean continued to do so. He had come to be a good conversationalist. He had the hidden riches and the eloquence of a truthful and humble mind that has improved itself. He retained just enough abrasiveness to season his kindness. He was tough-spirited and soft-hearted. When there were just the two of them together, talking in the Luxembourg Gardens, he would give long explanations of everything, drawing on what he had read, drawing also on what he had suffered. As she listened, Cosette's eyes vaguely wandered.

This simple man answered to the needs of Cosette's intellect, just as this garden run wild answered to the needs of her games. When she had been chasing after butterflies she would come up to him, short of breath, and say, 'Oh! Have I been running!' He would kiss her forehead.

Cosette adored the old man. She was always at his heels. Wherever Jean Valjean was, that was where she wanted to be. Since Jean Valjean lived neither in the house nor in the garden, she was happier in the paved rear courtyard than in the flower-filled enclosure, and in his little hut furnished with straw-bottomed chairs than in the large drawing room with upholstered armchairs and tapestry hangings on the walls behind them. Smiling with happiness at being disturbed, Jean Valjean sometimes said to her, 'Now, go back to your house! Leave me by myself for a while!'

She would scold him in that delightfully affectionate way so charming in a daughter addressing her father.

'Father, it's very cold here. Why don't you put in a carpet and a stove?'

'My dear child, there are so many people who are more deserving than I am and who don't even have a roof over their heads.'

'Then why do I have a fire and every other comfort?'

'Because you're a woman and a child.'

'Pah! So men must be cold and uncomfortable?'

'Some men.'

'Very well, I'll just come and see you so often you'll have to have a fire here too.'

And she also said to him, 'Father, why do you eat such nasty bread?'

'Because, my daughter.'

'Well, if you eat it, I'll eat it too.'

Then, so that Cosette should not have to eat black bread, Jean Valjean ate white bread.

Cosette only dimly remembered her early childhood. She prayed morning and evening for the mother she had not known. The Thénardiers stayed with her in a dreamlike way, as two hideous figures. She remembered that she had been to fetch water from the forest 'one day, in the dark'. She thought that was somewhere very far away from

Paris. It seemed to her she had started out living in a chasm, and it was Jean Valjean who had pulled her out of it. Her childhood seemed to her a time when there had been nothing around her but millipedes, spiders and snakes. Since the notion of being Jean Valjean's daughter and of his being her father was not very clear to her, when in the evening before falling asleep her thoughts ran on, she imagined that her mother's soul had entered the old man and come to stay close to her.

When he was seated she would rest her cheek against his white hair, and quietly shedding a tear say to herself, 'This man could be my mother!'

Although this might be a strange thing to say, in the profound ignorance of a girl brought up in a convent, maternity being in any case absolutely unintelligible to virginity, Cosette had ended up with the notion that she had had as little of a mother as it was possible to have. She did not even know her mother's name. Whenever she happened to ask Jean Valjean, Jean Valjean remained silent. If she repeated her question he responded with a smile. Once, she insisted. The smile turned to tears.

This silence of Jean Valjean's shrouded Fantine in darkness. Was it caution? Was it respect? Was this a fear of surrendering that name to the vagaries of a memory other than his own?

So long as Cosette was a little girl, Jean Valjean had gladly talked to her about her mother. When she became a young woman, it was impossible for him to do so. It was as if he dared not any more. Was it because of Cosette? Was it because of Fantine? He felt a kind of religious horror at allowing that shadow to enter Cosette's mind and at giving the dead woman a place in their life together. The more sacred this shadow was to him, the more formidable it seemed. He thought of Fantine and felt crushed by silence. He saw indistinctly something in the half-light that looked like a finger placed to someone's lips. Had all the modesty that was in Fantine, and of which during her lifetime she had been violently bereft, returned, outraged, after her death to settle over her, to protect the peace of that dead woman and to guard her fiercely in her grave? Was Jean Valjean unknowingly influenced by this? We, who believe in death, are not among those who would reject this mysterious explanation. Hence the impossibility, even for Cosette's sake, of uttering that name 'Fantine'.

One day Cosette said to him, 'Father, I saw my mother in a dream last night. She had two big wings. My mother must have come close to saintliness in her life.'

'Through martyrdom,' replied Jean Valjean.

This apart, Jean Valjean was happy.

When Cosette went out with him she leaned on his arm, proud, happy too, in the fullness of her heart. At all these marks of affection, an affection so exclusive and so satisfied with him alone, Jean Valjean felt his spirit melt with delight. The poor man shuddered with an overwhelming angelic joy. He assured himself with elation that it would be like this for the rest of his life. He told himself he had not really suffered enough to deserve such radiant bliss, and he thanked God in the depths of his soul for having allowed the miserable wretch that he was to be so loved by this innocent creature.

V

The Rose Realizes She Is a Weapon of War

One day Cosette happened to look in her mirror and said to herself, 'Goodness me!' She almost thought she was pretty. This threw her into a strange confusion. Until that moment she had never given any thought to her face. She would see herself in the mirror but not look at herself. And besides, she had so often been told she was plain. Only Jean Valjean would say gently, 'Not at all! Not at all!' Whatever the truth of it, Cosette had always believed she was plain, and had grown up in that belief with the resignation that comes easily to children. Now, suddenly, her mirror was telling her the same as Jean Valjean: 'Not at all!' She did not sleep that night. 'Suppose I were pretty!' she thought. 'How odd it would be if I were pretty!' And she remembered those companions of hers whose beauty attracted attention in the convent, and she said to herself, 'Imagine! If I were to be like Mademoiselle so-and-so!'

The next morning she looked at herself, not by accident this time, and she felt doubtful. 'Whatever was I thinking?' she said. 'No, I'm plain.' She had slept badly, that was all, she had rings round her eyes and she was pale. She had not felt very happy the day before at the thought of being beautiful, but she was sad now at the thought of not being so. She did not look at herself again, and for more than a fortnight she tried to do her hair with her back to the mirror.

In the evening after dinner more often than not she did some tapestry or some other needlework she had been taught at the convent, and Jean Valjean read beside her in the drawing room. Once, she looked up from her needlework and was quite taken aback by the way her father was anxiously gazing at her.

On another occasion, when she was walking in the street, she thought someone behind her she could not see said, 'Pretty woman!

But badly dressed.' 'Well,' she thought, 'that's not me. I'm well dressed and ugly.' She was then wearing her plush hat and merino gown.

Then one day she was in the garden and she heard poor old Toussaint saying, 'Monsieur, have you noticed how pretty mademoiselle's becoming?' Cosette did not hear what her father replied – Toussaint's words came as something of a shock to her. She hurried from the garden, went up to her room, ran over to the looking-glass – it was three months since she last looked at herself in it – and she gave a cry. She was dazzled by herself.

She was beautiful and a joy to behold. She could not help agreeing with Toussaint and her mirror. Her figure had filled out, her complexion glowed, her hair shone, an unfamiliar brilliance lit up her blue eyes. A total conviction about her beauty came to her instantaneously, with a daylight clarity. Besides, other people noticed it, Toussaint spoke of it, obviously she was the one the passer-by had been talking about, it was now beyond doubt. She went back down to the garden, thinking herself a queen, hearing birds singing – this was winter – seeing golden skies, the sun in the trees, flowers on the bushes, bewildered, beside herself, in unutterable rapture.

Jean Valjean, for his part, felt a deep and indefinable pang in his heart. The fact is, he had for some time now been watching with terror this beauty on Cosette's sweet face, appearing every day more radiant. A delightful dawn for everyone else, dismal for him.

Cosette had been beautiful for quite a long time before she became aware of it. But that unexpected light, slowly brightening and gradually enveloping the young girl's whole person, hurt Jean Valjean's doleful eyes from the very first day. He sensed this brought change to a happy life, so happy he dared not tinker with it for fear of spoiling it. This man who had lived through every hardship, who was still all bloodied with fate's bruises, who had been almost wicked and had become almost a saint, who having dragged the chain of the convicted felon was now dragging the invisible but heavy chain of perpetual infamy, this man whom the law had not released and who could be seized again at any moment and dragged back from the obscurity of his virtue to the broad daylight of public opprobrium – this man accepted all, excused all, forgave all, and asked only one thing of providence, of man, of society, of its laws, of nature, of the world: that Cosette might love him!

That Cosette might continue to love him! That God would not prevent that child's heart from coming to him and staying with him. Loved by Cosette, he felt healed, rested, soothed, gratified, recompensed, crowned. Loved by Cosette, he was happy! He asked for nothing more! Had anyone said to him, 'Do you want anything better?' he would have replied, 'No.' If God had asked him, 'Do you want to go to heaven?' he would have replied, 'I'd be worse off there.'

Anything that could affect this situation, even superficially, made him quake, as being the start of something new. He had never had much idea about a woman's beauty, but he knew instinctively it was terrible.

Out of the depths of his ugliness, his old age, his misery, his reprobacy, his disconsolation, he looked on appalled at this beauty, a beauty ever more triumphant and glorious, blossoming beside him, before his very eyes, on the child's innocent and awesome brow.

He said to himself, 'How beautiful she is! What's to become of me?'

And herein lay the difference between his love and a mother's love. What he saw with anguish a mother would have seen with joy.

It was not long before the first symptoms showed. The very next day after she had said to herself, 'I'm definitely beautiful!' Cosette began to pay attention to what she wore. She recalled that passer-by's remark, 'Pretty but badly dressed', an oracular utterance that wafted past her and was gone, after planting in her heart the desire to look attractive, one of the two seeds destined later on to fill a woman's whole life. Love is the other.

Confident of her beauty, the feminine spirit within her came entirely into its own. She acquired a horror of merino and felt ashamed of wearing plush. Her father had never refused her anything. She immediately knew everything there was to know about hats, gowns, mantles, ankle-boots, cuffs, what cloths were suitable, what colours were flattering, that knowledge that makes the Parisian woman something so charming, so deep, and so dangerous. The words 'captivating woman' were invented for the Parisienne.

In less than a month little Cosette in that secluded retreat in Rue de Babylone was not only one of the prettiest women in Paris, which is something, but one of the 'best-dressed', which is a great deal more. She would have liked to encounter her 'passer-by' to see what he would say and 'to let him know!' The truth is, she was ravishing in every respect, and she had a wonderful ability to distinguish a Gérard hat from an Herbaut hat.

Jean Valjean watched these ravages with anxiety. He who felt he would only ever be able to crawl, to walk at most, saw a winged Cosette emerging.

However, just by studying the way Cosette dressed, a woman would have known she had no mother. Some little proprieties, some particular conventions, were not observed by Cosette. A mother, for instance, would have told her that a young girl never wears damask.

The first day that Cosette went out in her black damask gown and mantle and her white crêpe hat she came – bright, radiant, rosy, proud, dazzling – and took Jean Valjean's arm.

'Father,' she said, 'how do I look?'

Jean Valjean replied in a voice that sounded like the bitter voice of envy. 'Charming!'

He was no different from usual during their walk. On their return home he asked Cosette, 'Won't you ever wear that dress and that bonnet of yours again? You know the ones.'

This took place in Cosette's room. Cosette turned to the rail in the wardrobe where her schoolgirl cast-offs were hanging.

'That frightful outfit!' she said. 'Father, what earthly good is that to me? Oh, the very idea, no, I shall never wear those horrors again. With that thing on my head, I look like a crazy old woman.'

Jean Valjean sighed deeply.

From that moment on he noticed that Cosette, who in the past always wanted to stay at home, saying, 'Father, I enjoy being here with you more', was now always asking to go out. After all, what is the use of having a pretty face and a lovely dress if nobody gets to see them?

He also noticed that Cosette no longer had the same fondness for the back yard. Now she liked spending more time in the garden and was not unhappy to stroll past the gate. The retiring Jean Valjean did not set foot in the garden. He stayed in his back yard, like a dog.

Knowing she was beautiful, Cosette lost the grace of being unaware of it – exquisite grace – for beauty enhanced by naivety is beyond expression, and nothing is so adorable as a creature of radiant innocence going about holding the key to paradise and not knowing it. But what she lost in ingenuous grace she gained in pensive and serious charm. Imbued with the joys of youth, innocence and beauty, her whole person emanated a splendid melancholy.

It was at this point, after six months had gone by, that Marius saw her again in the Luxembourg Gardens.

VI

The Battle Begins

Cosette occupied her shadows, as Marius occupied his, all set to be ignited. With its mysterious and inexorable patience, destiny slowly brought together these two individuals, thoroughly charged and pining away with the raging electricities of passion, these two souls bearing love like two clouds bearing thunderbolts, who were bound to meet and converge in a glance like clouds in a flash of lightning.

The glance has been so over-exploited in romantic novels, it has eventually been discredited. You hardly dare say nowadays that two people fell in love because they looked at each other. Yet that is the way, and the only way, that people fall in love. The rest is just that, and comes afterwards. Nothing is more real than the great shock two souls give each other by exchanging that spark.

At that particular moment when Cosette unknowingly cast the glance that disturbed Marius, Marius had no idea that he also had cast a glance that disturbed Cosette. It caused her the same pain and the same pleasure.

She had been seeing him and observing him for a long time already, in that way that young girls have of seeing and observing while looking elsewhere. Marius still found Cosette plain when she had already begun to find Marius handsome. But as he paid no attention to her, she was quite indifferent to this young man.

Still, she could not help telling herself that he had a fine head of hair, fine eyes, fine teeth, a delightful tone of voice when she heard him conversing with his comrades, that admittedly he walked with a slouch but with a gracefulness of his own, that he seemed not at all stupid, that everything about his appearance was noble, gentle, simple and proud; in short, he looked poor but distinguished.

The day when their eyes met and at last suddenly conveyed to each other those first obscure and ineffable things that glances impart falteringly, Cosette did not immediately understand. She returned pensively to the house in Rue de l'Ouest where Jean Valjean, as was his custom, had come to spend six weeks. On waking the next morning she thought of that strange young man, for so long cool and indifferent, who now seemed to be paying attention to her, and it did not seem to her in the least that this attention was welcome. On the contrary, she was a little cross with this disdainful Apollo. An underlying hostility stirred within her. She sensed, and this gave her a wholly childish joy, that she was at last to have her revenge.

Knowing that she was beautiful, she was well aware, although in some indistinct way, that she had a weapon. Women wield their beauty the way children play with knives. They hurt themselves with it.

Remember Marius's misgivings, his agitation, his fears. He remained on his bench and did not come near. Which annoyed Cosette. One day she said to Jean Valjean, 'Father, let's take a little stroll that way.' Seeing that Marius was not coming to her, she went to him. In such cases every woman is like Mohammed. And strange to say, the first symptom of true love in a young man is timidity; in a young girl, it is boldness. This is surprising, and yet nothing is more natural. It is the two sexes tending towards each other and taking on each other's characteristics.

That day Cosette's glance infatuated Marius, and Marius's glance made Cosette tremble. Marius went away confident and Cosette disquieted. From that day, they adored each other.

The first thing Cosette felt was a deep and obscure sadness. It seemed to her that from one day to the next her soul had turned black. She no longer recognized it. The whiteness of young girls' souls, which is made up of coldness and mirth, is like snow. It melts in the sun of love.

Cosette did not know what love was. She had never heard the word mentioned in its earthly sense. In the books of profane music that entered the convent, *amour* was replaced by *tambour** or *pandour†*. This gave rise to puzzles that exercised the imaginations of the older girls: puzzles such as 'Ah, how delightful is the drum!' or 'Pity is no brigand.' But Cosette was too young when she left the convent to have cared much about that 'drum'. So she did not know what name to give to whatever it was she was now feeling. Is anyone the less ill for not knowing the name of their illness?

She loved with all the more passion for not knowing that she loved. She could not tell whether it was good or bad, useful or dangerous, essential or fatal, eternal or transient, permissible or forbidden. She loved. It would have come as a great surprise if anyone had said to her, 'You're not sleeping? But that's not allowed! You're not eating? Why, that's very bad! You feel breathless and you have palpitations? But that's unacceptable! You blush and turn pale when a certain human being dressed in black appears at the end of a certain garden path? But that's dreadful!' She would not have understood and she would have replied, 'How can I be blamed for something I can't help and that I'm at a loss to understand?'

It so happened that the love that visited itself on her was exactly the kind of love best suited to the state of her heart. It was a sort of distant adoration, a silent contemplation, the deification of a stranger. It was the apparition of adolescence to adolescence, a dream transformed into romance and still a dream, the longed-for phantom at last materialized and made flesh but as yet without name, without fault, without blemish, without demands, without any shortcoming. In

---

* 'Drum'.
† 'Brigand'.

a word, the distant lover still idealized, a chimera invested with form. Any closer and more palpable encounter would have affrighted Cosette at this initial stage when she was still half immersed in the magnifying mists of the cloister. She had all the fears of a child combined with all the fears of a nun. The spirit of the convent, with which she had been imbued for five years, was still slowly evaporating from her whole being, causing all around her to quiver. In such circumstances it was not a lover she needed, it was not even an admirer, it was a vision. She began adoring Marius as something charming, luminous, impossible.

Since extreme innocence verges on extreme flirtatiousness, she smiled at him, quite openly.

She looked forward every day to when it was time for their walk, she would encounter Marius, feel unspeakably happy and truly believed she was expressing everything in her mind when she said to Jean Valjean, 'How delightful this Luxembourg Garden is!'

Marius and Cosette appeared to each other as if in the dark. They did not speak to each other, they did not greet each other, they did not know each other. They saw each other. And like the stars of heaven, millions of miles apart, they existed by gazing at each other.

So it was that Cosette developed, and little by little became a woman, beautiful and loving, conscious of her beauty and ignorant of her love. And in all innocence, a flirt into the bargain.

VII
Sadness, and Yet Greater Sadness

All situations have their instincts. Old and eternal Mother Nature gave Jean Valjean covert warning of Marius's presence. Jean Valjean shuddered in his innermost psyche. Jean Valjean saw nothing, knew nothing, and yet he studied with persistent attention the darkness around him, as though he sensed on one side something taking shape, and on the other something disintegrating. Marius, too, having been warned, and – as the good Lord in his profundity has decreed – warned by that same Mother Nature, did all he could to avoid being seen by 'the father'. Yet Jean Valjean did occasionally catch sight of him. Marius's behaviour was not in the least natural any more. He was shifty in his wariness and inept in his boldness. He no longer came very close, as in the past. He sat at a distance and remained in ecstasies. He had a book and pretended to be reading. Pretending to whom? He used to come in his old coat, now he wore his new one every day. It was not quite certain that his hair had not been curled, he had the most peculiar look in his eyes, he wore gloves. In short, Jean Valjean cordially detested this young man.

Cosette gave nothing away. Without knowing exactly what it was, she had the distinct feeling that something had come over her and that it had to be hidden.

To Jean Valjean, there was an unwelcome parallel between the dress sense that Cosette had acquired and the habit this stranger had developed of wearing new clothes. It was a coincidence perhaps, no doubt, certainly, but an ominous coincidence. He never breathed a word about this stranger to Cosette. One day, however, he could not contain himself, and with the vague despair of one suddenly taking a sounding of his misery he said to her, 'Now there's a pretentious-looking young man!'

The year before, Cosette, a carefree little girl, would have replied, 'Why, no, he's agreeable-looking.' Ten years later, with love for Marius in her heart, she would have replied, 'Pretentious and insufferable-looking! You're quite right!' At this moment in her life with her heart in its present state, she confined herself to saying with the utmost calm, 'That young man there?'

As if she were seeing him for the first time in her life.

'How stupid I am!' thought Jean Valjean. 'She hadn't yet noticed him. I'm the one that's pointed him out to her.'

Oh, the naivety of the old! The canniness of the young!

It is another law of those youthful years of suffering and torment, of first love's desperate struggles to overcome initial obstacles, that the young woman does not allow herself to be caught in any trap and the young man falls into every single one. Jean Valjean had launched a secret war against Marius of which Marius, with the sublime stupidity of his passion and of his years, was oblivious. Jean Valjean targeted him with a multitude of subterfuges. He changed his schedule, he moved to another bench, he forgot his handkerchief, he came alone to the Luxembourg Gardens. Marius blundered headlong into every snare. And to all those question marks posted in his path by Jean Valjean he ingenuously answered yes. Yet Cosette remained immured in her apparent unconcern and imperturbable calm, so much so that Jean Valjean came to this conclusion: 'That young whippersnapper is madly in love with Cosette but Cosette is not even aware of his existence.'

Nonetheless his heart ached with apprehension. Cosette could fall in love at any moment. Does not everything start with indifference?

Only once did Cosette slip up and alarm him. After they had been sitting on the bench for three hours he rose to leave, and she said, 'Already?'

Jean Valjean had not stopped going for walks in the Luxembourg Gardens, not wanting to do anything out of the ordinary and above all afraid of putting Cosette on her guard. But during those hours so sweet to the two lovers, while Cosette bestowed her smile on the enraptured Marius, who was aware of only that and now saw nothing else in the world but an adored and radiant face, Jean Valjean glared at Marius with a terrible glint in his eyes. There were moments when he who had come to believe he was no longer capable of any malevolent feeling had the sense, if Marius was there, of becoming fierce and brutal again, and he felt those old depths in his soul that had once contained so much anger reopening and rising up against that young man. He almost had the feeling that unknown craters were re-forming inside him.

Look! There he was, that creature! What was he here for? He had come sniffing about, prying, trying his luck! He had come to say, 'Well? Why not?' He had come prowling around his life – the life of Jean Valjean – prowling around his happiness, intending to snatch it away from him!

Jean Valjean raged on. 'Yes, that's it! What's he after? An opportunity! What does he want? A little fling! A little fling! And I? What! Am I to have been first the most wretched of men, then the most unhappy, to have spent sixty years of my life on my knees, to have endured every conceivable hardship, to have grown old without ever having been young, to have lived without family, without relatives, without friends, without a wife, without children, to have left my blood on every rock, on every bramble, on every milestone, along every wall, to have been kind although others have been cruel to me, and good although others have been wicked, am I to have become an honest man again, despite everything, to have repented for the evil I've done and forgiven the evil that's been done to me, and just when I get my reward, when it's over, when I've reached my goal, when I have what I want, it's settled, it's as it should be, I've paid for it, I've earned it – all this is to go, all this is to vanish and I'm to lose Cosette, and I'm to lose my life, my joy, my soul, because some great booby has chosen to come and idle away his time in the Luxembourg Gardens!'

Then his eyes filled with an extraordinary baleful gleam. This was no longer a man glaring at a man, this was no longer an enemy glaring at an enemy. This was a guard dog glaring at a thief.

The rest we know. Marius continued to be reckless. One day he followed Cosette to Rue de l'Ouest. Another day he spoke to the porter. The porter himself then spoke, and said to Jean Valjean, 'Monsieur, that inquisitive young man who was asking about you – now, who would he be?'

The next day Jean Valjean cast that glance at Marius that Marius finally noticed. A week later Jean Valjean had moved house. He vowed never to set foot again either in the Luxembourg Gardens or in Rue de l'Ouest. He returned to Rue Plumet.

Cosette did not complain, she said nothing, she asked no questions, she sought no explanation. She was already at the point when you are afraid of being found out and giving yourself away. Jean Valjean had no experience of these miseries, the only ones that are delightful and the only ones unknown to him. So he did not understand the grave significance of Cosette's silence. But he did notice that she was sad, and he became gloomy. It was inexperience on either side pitted against each other.

Once he put her to the test. He asked Cosette, 'Do you want to come to the Luxembourg Gardens?'

Cosette's pale face brightened. 'Yes,' she said.

They went. Three months had elapsed. Marius did not go there any more. Marius was not there.

The next day Jean Valjean asked Cosette again, 'Do you want to come to the Luxembourg Gardens?'

She replied sadly, softly, 'No.'

Jean Valjean was pained by this sadness, grieved by this softness.

What was going on in that mind? One so young and already so impenetrable. What evolution was taking place there? What was happening to Cosette deep down inside her? Sometimes, instead of getting into bed and going to sleep Jean Valjean remained seated beside his bed with his head in his hands, and spent all night long wondering, 'What is on Cosette's mind?' and dwelling on the things she might be dwelling on.

Oh! with what mournful glances did he look back, during those moments, on the cloister, that chaste summit, that realm of angels, that inaccessible glacier of virtue! How he contemplated with despairing delight that convent garden full of unseen flowers and cloistered virgins, where every fragrance and every soul rises straight to heaven! How he adored that Eden now closed off to him for ever, which he had willingly, insanely, left behind to descend to this! How he regretted his self-denial and his lunacy in having brought Cosette back into the world, poor self-sacrificing hero, caught out and overthrown by his very devotion to her! How he kept asking himself, 'What have I done?'

However, none of this showed in his dealings with Cosette. No ill-temper, no harshness. Always the same serene and kindly face. Jean Valjean was more loving and more paternal than ever in his behaviour towards her. If there was anything that gave any intimation of less joy, it was his greater indulgence.

And meanwhile Cosette pined. She suffered from Marius's absence as she had rejoiced in his presence, oddly, without really understanding why. When Jean Valjean stopped taking her out for their customary walks, a woman's instinct murmured vaguely in the depths of her heart that she must not seem to care about the Luxembourg Gardens, and that if it was a matter of indifference to her, her father would take her there again. But days, weeks, months went by. Jean Valjean tacitly accepted Cosette's tacit consent. She regretted it. It was too late. The day she went back to the Luxembourg Gardens, Marius was not there any more. So Marius was gone. That was the end of it, what could she do? Would she ever find him again? She felt a heartache that nothing could relieve, and which became more intense every day. She no longer knew whether it was winter or summer, sunshine or rain, whether the birds were singing, whether it was the time of year for dahlias or daisies, whether the Luxembourg Gardens were more attractive than the Tuileries Gardens, whether the linen that came back from the laundress was starched too much or too little, whether Toussaint had done well or badly with her shopping; and she remained despondent, lost to the world, mindful of one thing only, her eyes vague and staring like those of someone gazing in the dark at the pitch-blackness into which an apparition has vanished.

And for Jean Valjean she let nothing show either, except her pallor. For him she kept the same sweet face. Her pallor was more than enough to worry Jean Valjean. Sometimes he would ask her, 'What's the matter?'

She would reply, 'Nothing.'

And after a silence, since she could tell that he too was sad, she would say, 'And is there anything the matter with you, father?'

'Me?' he said. 'Nothing at all.'

These two human beings who had loved each other so exclusively, with a love so touching, and had for so long lived each for the other, now suffered side by side, each on account of the other, without telling each other, without blaming each other, and smiling.

VIII
The Chain Gang

The more unhappy of the two was Jean Valjean. Youth, even in its sorrows, always has its own brightness.

At times Jean Valjean suffered so much he became childish.

It is a characteristic of grief to bring out the child in the man. He had the unconquerable feeling that Cosette was slipping away from him. He wanted to fight back, to detain her, to win her over with something tangible and eye-catching. Such notions – childish notions, as we have just said, and at the same time typical of old age – by their very childishness gave him a fairly accurate idea of the influence of finery on young girls' imaginations. He once happened to see a general ride past in the street, on horseback, in full dress uniform, Comte Coutard, the commander of Paris. He envied that gilded man. What an advantage it would be, he said to himself, to be able to wear that outfit, which was something that could not be ignored, and if Cosette saw him like that she would be dazzled, then he would give his arm to her and when they passed in front of the Tuileries gates the guard would present arms to him, and that would keep Cosette satisfied and she would think no more of looking at young men.

In the midst of these sad reflections came an unexpected jolt.

Since moving to Rue Plumet they had, in the isolated life they led, developed a habit: they sometimes made an outing of going to watch the sun rise, the kind of quiet pleasure suited to those embarking on life and to those leaving it.

For anyone who likes solitude, going for a walk in the early morning is the same as going for a walk at night, with the added cheerfulness of nature. The streets are deserted and the birds are singing. Cosette liked to rise with her namesake the lark. These early-morning excursions were planned the night before. He proposed, she agreed. It was planned like a conspiracy, they would set out before daybreak, and for Cosette this was all part of the fun of it. Young people enjoy these innocent eccentricities.

Jean Valjean's inclination was, as we know, to go to out-of-the-way places, lonely spots, forgotten parts. In those days there were around the gates of Paris, almost part of the city, fields of a sort, of poor quality, where scraggly corn grew in summer, and which in the autumn after harvest looked not so much as if they had been reaped as stripped bare. Jean Valjean liked to frequent these fields. Cosette did not mind going there. To him it meant solitude, to her, freedom.

There she became a little girl again, she could run about and almost play, she would take off her hat, rest it on Jean Valjean's lap, and gather posies. She observed the butterflies on the flowers but did not catch them. Kindness and tenderness come with love, and the young girl who has a fluttering, fragile ideal inside her pities the butterfly's wing. She wove garlands of poppies that she placed on her head, and suffused with the sunlight shining through them and turning them to blazing crimson, they formed a crown of burning embers above that fresh rosy face.

Even after their life had taken a sad turn, they kept up their habit of early-morning walks.

So tempted by the perfect serenity of the autumn of 1831, they set out one October morning and found themselves at daybreak near the Maine toll-gate. It was not dawn, it was that moment just before dawn, a moment of tentative delight. A few constellations here and there in the deep, pale heavens, the earth very black, the sky very white, a shiver passing through the blades of grass, everywhere the mysterious thrill of the morning twilight. A lark, apparently lost among the stars, sang from an amazing height, and it was as if this hymn of the infinitesimal to the infinite stilled the immensity. To the east, the dark mass of the Val-de-Grâce stood out against the steel-bright horizon. Sparkling Venus rose from behind that dome, looking like a soul escaping from some dark edifice.

All was peace and quiet. No one on the highway. Just the occasional glimpse, down by the roadside, of a labourer on his way to work.

Jean Valjean was sitting on some planks that had been left at the gate of a timber-yard, in the side-lane running parallel to the highway. He was looking towards the road, with his back to the breaking light. He had forgotten about the sunrise. He had fallen into one of those intense introspections in which the whole mind is absorbed, imprisoning even the gaze, and which are tantamount to four walls. There are sessions of thought that may be called vertical. When you are deeply immersed in them, it takes time to resurface. Jean Valjean had sunk into one of these reveries. He was thinking about Cosette, about the happiness that could be if nothing came between him and her, about the light with which she filled his life, a light that was the breath of his soul. He was almost happy in his reverie. Cosette, standing beside him, watched the clouds turn pink.

All at once Cosette exclaimed, 'Father, there seem to be people coming from over there.' Jean Valjean looked up.

Cosette was right.

The road leading to the old Maine toll-gate is, as everyone knows, a continuation of Rue de Sèvres, and is cut across at right-angles by the inner boulevard. At the intersection, where the road and the boulevard meet, could be heard a noise difficult to explain at that time of day, and some kind of lumbering mass appeared. A thing of no recognizable shape, coming from the boulevard, was turning into the road.

It grew larger, it seemed to be moving in an orderly fashion, though it bristled and juddered. It seemed to be a vehicle but you could not distinguish what it was carrying. There were horses, wheels, shouts. Whips cracked. Gradually, although steeped in shadow, the outlines gained definition. It was indeed a vehicle that had just turned from the boulevard on to the highway and was heading towards the toll-gate, where Jean Valjean was sitting close by. A second vehicle, like the first, came following after, then a third, then a fourth. Seven carts appeared, one after the other, the horses' heads touching the rear of the cart in front. Dark figures stirred on these carts, you could see glints in the half-light as of drawn swords, you could hear a rattling that sounded like the movement of chains, it came closer, the voices grew louder. It was a fearsome thing of the kind that emerges from the cavern of dreams.

Drawing nearer, it took shape, a ghostly dimness becoming faintly discernible behind the trees. The mass whitened. The slowly gathering daylight cast a pale glimmer on this writhing welter, at once live and sepulchral; the heads of those dark figures became the faces of corpses. And this is what it was:

Seven carts were following each other along the road. The first six had a peculiar structure. They were like coopers' drays. They consisted of a kind of long ladder placed on two wheels and forming shafts at the front end. Each dray, or rather each ladder, had four horses harnessed to it, one behind the other. Drawn on these ladders were strangely clustered groups of men. In the faint light you could not see these men, you just had an impression of them. Twenty-four to each vehicle, twelve on each side, back to back, facing out towards passers-by, their legs dangling in the air – that is how these men were travelling. And they had something that clinked behind their backs, which was a chain, and something shiny round their necks, which was an iron collar.

Each man had his own iron collar but the chain was for all of them. So that whenever these twenty-four men happened to get off the dray and walk on the ground, they were seized with a kind of inexorable unity and had to snake along with the chain for a backbone, somewhat like a millipede. At the back and the front of each vehicle stood two men armed with muskets, each with one end of the chain under his foot. The iron collars were sturdy. The seventh vehicle, a huge wagon with sides to it but no canopy, had four wheels and six horses and carried a clanking pile of iron boilers, cast-iron pots, braziers and chains, with several men bound hand and foot lying among them. These men appeared to be sick. This open-slatted wagon was fitted with dilapidated hurdles that looked as if they had been used in olden-day tortures.

These vehicles kept to the middle of the road. On each side marched a double column of villainous-looking guards, in the tricorn hats that folded flat worn by soldiers under the Directory, stained and dirty and ragged, kitted out in veterans' uniforms and undertakers' breeches, grey and blue striped, almost in tatters, with red epaulettes, yellow shoulder belts, bayonets, muskets and cudgels. Soldier ruffians, they were. These bully boys seemed to combine the abjectness of the beggar with the authority of the executioner. The one who appeared to be their leader was holding a horsewhip. All these details, lacking definition in the half-dark, became ever more distinct as it grew lighter. At the head and rear of the convoy rode mounted police, grim-faced, swords in hand.

This procession was so long that when the first vehicle reached the toll-gate, the last was only just turning off the boulevard.

A crowd, emerging out of nowhere and gathering in no time, as happens frequently in Paris, thronged both sides of the road, and watched. You could hear the shouts of people calling for each other in the nearby lanes, and the wooden clogs of the market-gardeners flocking to see the spectacle.

The men huddled on the carts were jolted along in apathetic silence. They were leaden-hued with the morning chill. All wore duck-cloth trousers and wooden clogs on their bare feet. The rest of their attire depended on the vagaries of destitution. Their items of clothing were horribly ill-assorted. Nothing is more dismal than motley rags. Battered felt hats, oilcloth caps, hideous woollen skullcaps and beside the fatigue shirt a black coat worn through at the elbows. Many had women's hats, others wore punnets on their heads. Hairy chests could be seen, and through the torn garments tattoos were discernible: temples of love, flaming hearts, cupids. Skin infections and unhealthy red blotches were also to be observed. Two or three had a straw rope attached to the crossbars of the dray and suspended beneath them like a stirrup that supported their feet. One of them held in his hand and raised to his mouth something that looked like a black stone, which he seemed to be biting into. It was bread that he was eating. Here were none but dry eyes, dull eyes, or eyes with an evil glint in them. The escort troop cursed, the men in chains breathed not a word. From time to time you could hear the sound of a cudgel blow landed on shoulder blades or skulls. Some of these men yawned. Their raggedness was terrible. Feet dangled, shoulders swayed, heads banged together, fetters rattled, eyes blazed fiercely, fists clenched or opened inertly like the hands of corpses. Bursts of laughter came from a gaggle of children behind the convoy.

Whatever it was, this column of vehicles was lugubrious. It was obvious that tomorrow, in an hour's time, there could be a sudden downpour, that it would be followed by another and another, and these threadbare garments would be soaked; that, once wet, these men would not dry off again, once chilled they would not warm up again. Their duck trousers would be stuck to their bones by the drenching, water would fill their shoes, whip lashings would be unable to stop jaws chattering, the chain would continue to hold them by the neck, their feet would continue to dangle. And it was impossible not to shudder at the sight of these human beings, shackled like this; like the trees and the stones, passive beneath the cold clouds of autumn, exposed to the rain, to the icy wind, to all the fury of the elements.

The cudgel blows spared not even the sick, who lay still, tied up with ropes, on the seventh wagon, looking as if tossed there like sacks full of misery.

Suddenly the sun appeared. A tremendous brightness spilled from the east and seemed to set all these savages alight. Tongues were loosened. There was an explosion of sniggering, swearing and singing. The broad horizontal beam cut the whole column in two, illuminating heads and bodies, leaving feet and wheels in obscurity. Thoughts could be read on faces. It was a dreadful moment. Demons seen with their masks removed, brutal souls laid bare. Lit up, this mob remained sinister-looking. A cheerful few had quill pipes in their mouths which they used to blow vermin over the crowd, picking on the women. Dawn accentuated with dark shadows these appalling profiles. There was not one of these creatures who was not deformed by misery. And so monstrous a sight seemed to dim the sun's brightness to a glimmer of lightning.

The cartload at the head of the column had broken into song, and with frenetic jocularity were belting out the lyrics of a then famous medley by Désaugiers, 'The Vestal Virgin'. The trees rustled mournfully. In the side-lanes running parallel to the highway, respectable citizens listened with idiotic delight on their faces to these bawdy songs sung by spectres.

All manner of distress appeared in this procession in a chaotic jumble. Here were facial angles of every kind, old men, adolescents, bald heads, grey beards, the cynically monstrous, the sullenly resigned, the savagely grimacing, the dementedly posturing. Brutish faces with caps on their heads. Young, girlish faces with corkscrew curls at the temples. Baby faces, ghastly by very reason of their babyishness. Thin and all but dead skeletal faces. There was a black man to be seen on the first cart. Perhaps he had been a slave and could compare chains. That frightful leveller of the down-and-out, ignominy, gave uniformity to these faces. At that degree of degradation everyone in the direst depths underwent the direst transformations, and ignorance turned to stupor was the equal of intelligence turned to despair. There was nothing to choose between these men, who looked like prime scum. It was clear that whoever was responsible for organizing this dreadful cortège had not sorted them in any way. These creatures had been fettered and thrown together pell-mell, probably in alphabetical disorder, and loaded haphazard on to these carts. Yet horrors combined always end up producing a composite result. Every added wretchedness contributes to a sum total. From each chain gang emerged a common identity, and each cartload had its distinctive character. After one that sang came one that yelled. A third begged. One was distinguished by a gnashing of teeth. Another threatened bystanders, another cursed and swore. The last was as silent as the tomb. Dante might have thought he was seeing the seven circles of hell in procession.

A procession of the damned on their way to their endless torments, haplessly conveyed not on the Apocalypse's fearsome fiery chariot but more grimly on the tumbril of infamy.

One of the guards, who had a hook on the end of his cudgel, from time to time made as if to stir these human dung-heaps. An old woman in the crowd pointed them out to a little boy of five years old and said to him, 'Let that be a lesson to you, young rascal!'

As the singing and swearing swelled, the man who appeared to be the escort captain cracked his whip and at this signal a terrible volley of blows, sounding like hail, fell blindly, wildly, on the seven cartloads. Many roared and foamed with rage, to the even greater delight of the youngsters who came running, like a cloud of flies on these wounds.

Jean Valjean's gaze had become frightful. His eyes were unseeing. There was that deep glassiness in them that in some poor wretches replaces sight, that is seemingly unaware of reality, and in which blaze reflections of terror and catastrophe. He was not observing a spectacle. He was enduring a vision. He wanted to get to his feet, to run away, to escape. He could not move a muscle. Sometimes, the things you see grab you and hold you fast. He remained transfixed, paralysed, stunned, wondering in his confused inexpressible anguish what this macabre persecution signified and where this hellish entourage that was hounding him had come from. All of a sudden he clapped his hand to his forehead in the customary gesture of those suddenly remembering. He recalled that this was indeed the regular route, that this detour was always made to avoid any possibility of encountering royalty on the road to Fontainebleau, and that thirty-five years ago he had himself passed through this gate.

In her own way Cosette was no less appalled. She did not understand. It took her breath away. What she saw did not seem possible. At length she cried out, 'Father, what on earth is in those carts?'

Jean Valjean replied, 'Convicts.'

'Where are they going?'

'To the prison hulks.'

At that moment the volley of blows dealt by numerous hands intensified, including swipes with the flat of the sword. It was a kind of frenzy of whips and clubs. The convicts cringed, a hideous submission was extorted by this punishment, and with the look of chained wolves in their eyes all fell silent. Cosette trembled in every limb. She persisted, 'Father, are they men?'

'Sometimes,' said the poor wretch.

This was indeed the chain gang that set out before daybreak from Bicêtre and was taking the Le Mans road in order to avoid Fontainebleau, where the king was. This detour added three or four days to the dreadful journey, but to spare the royal personage the sight of such an ordeal it could well be extended.

Jean Valjean went home devastated. Such encounters come as a shock and the memory they leave is like a cataclysm.

Yet Jean Valjean did not notice that on the way back with Cosette to Rue de Babylone she put other questions to him about what they had just seen. Perhaps he was too wrapped up in his own despondency to hear her speaking and to reply to her. But as Cosette left him that evening to go to bed he heard her say quietly, and as though talking to herself, 'I think if I were ever to cross paths with one of those men, oh dear God, I'd die, just from looking him in the face.'

Luckily it happened that the next day there were celebrations in Paris in connection with some official occasion or other – a review in the Champ de Mars, water tournaments on the Seine, theatrical performances in the Champs-Élysées, fireworks at the Arc de l'Étoile, illuminations everywhere. Going against habit, Jean Valjean took

Cosette to these festivities so as to distract her from the chilling memory of the day before and to blot out with the joyous tumult of all Paris the abomination that had passed before her. The review, which gave added zest to the festivities, made it perfectly natural to go about in uniform. Jean Valjean put on his National Guard uniform with the vague inward feeling of a man taking refuge. In any case this trip seemed to achieve its purpose. Cosette, who made a rule of pleasing her father and for whom, after all, any spectacle was a novelty, welcomed this distraction with the free and easy good grace of adolescence, and did not wrinkle her nose too disdainfully at being served up this slice of merriment called a public holiday. So much so that Jean Valjean may well have believed he had succeeded, and that the hideous vision had left no lasting impression.

One morning a few days later the sun was shining brightly, and in another departure from the rules that Jean Valjean seemed to have imposed on himself, and a departure too from the habit of remaining in her room that Cosette's sadness had led her to adopt, they were both out on the garden steps. Cosette stood in her dressing-gown with that early-morning carelessness of appearance that is enchanting in a young girl, enveloping her rather like a cloud settled over a heavenly body. And with the light around her head, rosy from a good night's sleep and watched lovingly by the fond old man, she was plucking the petals from a daisy. Cosette was unacquainted with that charming folklore tradition, 'He loves me, he loves me not' – who would have told her about it? She was toying with the flower instinctively, innocently, with no inkling that to pluck the petals from a daisy is to peel open a heart. If there were a fourth, smiling, Grace called Melancholy she would have borne a resemblance to that Grace. Jean Valjean gazed, spellbound, at those little fingers on that flower, forgetting everything in the radiance this child possessed. A robin chirped in the bushes near by. White clouds scudded across the sky so gaily that they looked as if they had just been set free. Cosette continued intently plucking at her flower. She seemed to be musing on something, but it must have been something pleasant. Suddenly she looked back over her shoulder with the delicate languor of a swan, and said to Jean Valjean, 'Father, what exactly are the prison hulks?'

BOOK FOUR
HELP FROM BELOW MAY BE HELP FROM ON HIGH

I
External Wound, Internal Healing

So a shadow was gradually cast over their life.

They were left with only one distraction that in the past had been a joy to them, which was to take bread to those who were hungry and clothing to those who were cold. In these visits to the poor, on which Cosette often accompanied Jean Valjean, they recovered some vestige of their old uninhibitedness with each other. And sometimes, when the day had gone well, when there had been much hardship relieved and many little children restored and comforted, Cosette was quite cheerful in the evening. It was at this time that they paid their visit to the Jondrette den.

The very day after that visit Jean Valjean appeared at the villa, in the morning, calm as usual but with a large, extremely inflamed suppurating wound on his left arm that looked like a burn, and for which he gave some vague explanation. This wound meant that he was kept indoors with a fever for more than a month. He refused to see a doctor. Whenever Cosette tried to persuade him, he would say, 'Call the dog-doctor.'

Cosette dressed his wound morning and evening, looking heavenly and so angelic in her pleasure to be of use to him that Jean Valjean felt all his old happiness returning, his fears and anxieties dissipating, and he gazed at Cosette, saying, 'Oh, what a welcome injury! Oh, what a blessing in disguise!'

Seeing her father ill, Cosette had forsaken the villa and once more found the little hut and the back yard to her liking. She spent nearly all day, every day, with Jean Valjean and read to him the books he chose. Mostly travel books. Jean Valjean took on a new lease of life. His happiness was restored with an ineffable radiance. The Luxembourg Gardens, the young stranger lingering about, Cosette's coolness towards him, all these dark clouds in his soul dispersed. Eventually he was saying to himself, 'I imagined it all. I'm an old fool.'

Such was his happiness that the Thénardiers' shocking discovery, made in the Jondrette den, and coming so unexpectedly, had as it were washed over him. He had managed to escape. He had left no trail. What did the rest matter to him! He thought no more about it except to feel sorry for those miserable wretches. 'Now they're in prison and unable to do any more harm,' he thought, 'but what a pitiful family and in such dire straits!' As for the hideous vision at the Maine toll-gate, Cosette had made no further mention of it.

Cosette had been taught music at the convent by Soeur Ste-Mechtilde. She had the voice of a lark. A lark with a soul. And sometimes in the evening, in the wounded man's humble abode, Cosette sang sad songs that were a delight to Jean Valjean.

Spring came. The garden was so lovely at that time of year that Jean Valjean said to Cosette, 'You never set foot in it, I wish you'd go out there and enjoy it.'

'Whatever you say, father,' said Cosette.

And to obey her father she resumed her walks in the garden, more often than not by herself, for as we have noted, Jean Valjean, no doubt fearful of being seen through the railings, hardly ever ventured into it.

Jean Valjean's injury had been a diversion.

When Cosette saw that her father was in less pain, that he was recovering and seemed happy, she felt a contentment she did not even notice, so gently and naturally did it come over her. Then it was the month of March. The days were getting longer, winter was on its way out; and winter always takes with it something of our sadness. Then came April, the dawning of summer, fresh as every dawn, bonny as every infancy, a little tearful at times like the new-born babe that it is. Nature during this month has a luminous beauty that distils from the sky, the trees, the meadows and the flowers into the heart of man.

Cosette was still too young not to be affected by that April joy, which bore a likeness to her. Imperceptibly and without her being conscious of it, the gloom departed from her spirit. In spring, light reaches into sad souls, just as light reaches into cellars at noon. Already, Cosette was actually no longer very sad. She may not have realized it, but nevertheless that is how it was. When she managed to drag her father into the garden for a quarter of an hour after breakfast in the morning, at about ten o'clock, and walked in front of the steps with him in the sunshine, supporting his injured arm, she was quite unaware that she was continually laughing and that she was happy.

Seeing her regain her rosiness and her bloom, Jean Valjean was elated.

'What a blessing in disguise!' he kept repeating to himself.

And he felt grateful to the Thénardiers.

Once his wound had healed, he resumed his solitary twilight rambles.

It would be a mistake to think you can go walking about like that, on your own, in uninhabited parts of Paris, without incident.

II

Mère Plutarque at No Loss to Explain an Extraordinary Phenomenon

It was evening and little Gavroche had not eaten. He remembered he had not had a meal the day before, either. This was becoming tiresome. He made up his mind to try for some supper. He went out on the prowl in those unfrequented parts beyond La Salpêtrière. That is where you strike lucky. Where there is no one, there is something to be found. He eventually came to an outlying locality that he thought was the village of Austerlitz.

On one of his earlier saunterings he had noticed an old garden there, with an old man and an old woman often in it, and in that garden a decent-sized apple tree. Next to this apple tree there was a kind of ill-secured fruit loft from which a person might obtain an apple for himself. An apple constitutes supper, an apple means life. What was Adam's undoing might be Gavroche's salvation. The garden was bordered by a lonely unpaved lane with scrubland on either side of it, the houses as yet unbuilt; between them was a hedge.

Gavroche made for this garden. He found the lane, he recognized the apple tree, he located the fruit loft, he examined the hedge. A hedge is no obstacle. The light was fading, not a soul to be seen, the time was right. Gavroche started to make his break-in, then suddenly stopped. Someone was talking in the garden. Gavroche peered through one of the gaps in the hedge.

A couple of paces away at the foot of the hedge on the other side, exactly where the breach he was planning to make would have landed him, was an overturned stone that formed a kind of bench, and on this bench was sitting the old man he had seen in the garden, with the old woman standing in front of him. The old woman was grumbling. Not much of a one for discretion, Gavroche listened.

'Monsieur Mabeuf!' said the old woman.

'Mabeuf!' thought Gavroche. 'What a funny name!'

There was no response from the old man. The old woman repeated, 'Monsieur Mabeuf!'

Without looking up, his eyes still fixed on the ground, the old man made the effort to reply, 'What is it, Mère Plutarque?'

'Mère Plutarque!' thought Gavroche. 'Another funny name.'

Mère Plutarque went on, and the old man could not but take part in the conversation.

'The landlord's not happy.'

'Why not?'

'He's owed rent for the last three quarters.'

'In three months' time he'll be owed four quarters.'

'He says he'll turn you out on to the street.'

'I'll go.'

'The greengrocer wants to be paid. She won't deliver any more logs. How will you keep warm this winter? We won't have any wood.'

'There's the sun.'

'The butcher won't give credit, he'll not let us have any more meat.'

'That's just as well. Meat doesn't agree with me. It's too indigestible.'

'What will we eat?'

'Bread.'

'The baker wants a payment on account and is saying, "No money, no bread."'

'Very well.'

'What will you eat?'

'We have the apples from the apple tree.'

'But Monsieur, it's just not possible to go on living like this, without any money.'

'I haven't any.'

The old woman went off, and the old man was left by himself. He fell to thinking. Gavroche too was thinking. It was almost dark.

The first result of Gavroche's thinking was that instead of climbing through the hedge, he squatted under it. The branches thinned out a little at the bottom of the bushes.

'Look at this!' Gavroche exclaimed to himself. 'A little snuggery!' And he tucked himself into it. His back was almost against Père Mabeuf's bench. He could hear the eighty-year-old breathing.

Then, to feed his hunger, he tried to sleep.

A cat-nap, with one eye open. Even as he dozed, Gavroche remained on the lookout.

The blanched sky of twilight cast its whiteness on the earth, and the lane showed as a pale line between two rows of dark bushes.

Suddenly, on this strip of whitishness, two figures appeared, one in front, the other some distance behind.

'Two people,' muttered Gavroche.

Stooped and pensive, dressed plainer than plain, the first figure appeared to be some respectable gentleman of advanced years, walking slowly because of his age, enjoying an evening stroll beneath the stars.

The second figure was straight-backed, assured, slim. This figure matched its pace to that of the first, but in its deliberate slowness could be sensed a litheness and an agility. Along with something grim and disquieting about it, this figure had the full turnout of what was then called a dandy. The hat was stylish, the frock-coat black, well cut, probably of fine cloth and close-fitting at the waist. The head was held upright with a kind of robust grace, and beneath the hat the pallid profile of a young man was discernible in the twilight. This profile had a rose in its mouth. This second figure was very familiar to Gavroche. It was Montparnasse.

As for the other one, he could not have said anything about him, except that he was some old gent.

Gavroche immediately began to pay attention.

One of these two individuals obviously had designs on the other. Gavroche was well placed to see what happened. The little snuggery had become a very convenient hiding-place.

Montparnasse on the prowl, at such a time, in such a place – this was ominous. In his gamin entrails Gavroche felt moved to pity for the old man.

What could he do? Intervene? One weakling coming to the aid of another! That would give Montparnasse good reason to laugh. Gavroche had no illusions – this dangerous eighteen-year-old ruffian would make short work of them both, the old man first, then the child.

While Gavroche was deliberating, the attack took place. It was swift and ugly. The tiger attack on the wild ass, the spider attack on the fly. Montparnasse suddenly tossed aside the rose, rushed at the old man, collared him, grabbed him, clung to him, and Gavroche was hard put to stifle a cry. A moment later one of these men was underneath the other, overpowered, groaning, struggling, with a knee of marble on his chest. Only it was not quite what Gavroche had expected. The one on the ground was Montparnasse. The one on top of him was the elderly gent.

All this unfolded just a few feet away from Gavroche.

The old man had been attacked and had fought back, and fought back so terrifyingly that, in the blink of an eye, assailant and assailed had reversed roles.

'There's a fine veteran!' thought Gavroche.

And he could not refrain from clapping. But his applause was wasted. It was inaudible to the combatants, intent on each other and mutually deafened, their laboured breath mingling in the fray.

Silence fell. Montparnasse stopped struggling. Gavroche whispered to himself, 'Is he dead?'

The elderly gent had uttered no word, voiced no cry. He rose, and Gavroche heard him say to Montparnasse, 'On your feet!'

Montparnasse picked himself up but the old boy held him fast. Montparnasse looked humbled and enraged, like a wolf caught by a sheep.

Gavroche watched and listened, straining his ears as much as his eyes. He was enjoying himself immensely.

He was rewarded for his conscientious anxiety as spectator. He managed to catch this exchange to which the darkness lent an indefinably tragic dimension.

The old boy asked the questions. Montparnasse replied.

'How old are you?'

'Nineteen.'

'You're strong and healthy. Why don't you work?'

'It's boring.'

'What are you by trade?'

'An idler.'

'Be serious. Can anything be done for you? What would you like to be?'

'A thief.'

A silence ensued. The old man seemed lost in thought. He stood still and did not loose his hold on Montparnasse.

Every few moments the young villain, strong and limber as he was, wriggled convulsively like an animal caught in a snare. Giving a jerk, attempting a leg-trip, desperately twisting his limbs, he tried to escape. The old man did not seem to notice; and with the supreme indifference of absolute strength, with only one hand he held him by both arms.

The old man's abstraction went on for some time, then gazing steadily at Montparnasse he raised his voice slightly, and in the shadows where they were he addressed a kind of sermon to him, of which not a single syllable escaped Gavroche.

'My boy, through laziness you're letting yourself in for the most arduous kind of existence. Ah! You profess to be an idler! Prepare yourself for work. Have you ever seen a machine that's to be feared? It's called a rolling-mill. You need to be wary of it, it's a crafty and ravenous thing. If it gets hold of your coat flap it'll have all the rest of you! That machine is idleness. Stop while there's still time and save yourself! Otherwise, you're done for. Before long you'll be caught up in the mechanism. And once caught, there's no hope for you. Knuckle down, lazybones! No more rest for you! The iron hand of implacable toil has laid hold of you. Earn your living, have a job, assume responsibility – that's not what you want! To be like others – that bores you! Well, one way or another, the rule of work prevails. Whoever spurns it as boring will suffer it as punishment. You don't want to be a worker; you'll be a slave. Work only lets go of you on the one hand to reclaim you on the other. You don't want to be its friend; you'll be its serf. Ah! You'd not have the honest weariness of men; you shall have the sweat of the damned. Where others sing, you will groan. You'll see from afar, from the lower depths, other men at work. They will seem to you to be resting. The ploughman, the reaper, the sailor, the blacksmith will appear to you bathed in light, like the blest in paradise. What satisfaction in the anvil! To drive the plough, to bind the sheaf – that's a pleasure. The ship sailing free in the wind, what a joy! You, idler – dig, haul, heave, shift yourself! Pull against your harness, you're now a beast of burden under the yoke of hell! Ah! To do nothing, that was your aim. Well, not a week, not a day, not an hour free from exhaustion. You'll not be able to lift anything without anguish. Every minute that passes will wrench your muscles. What to others is a feather will be a rock to you. The simplest things will become an uphill challenge. Life will turn into a nightmare around you. Coming and going and breathing, each of these a terrible grind. Your lungs will feel like a hundred-pound weight. To walk here rather than there will be a problem to resolve. Any ordinary person who wants to go out simply pushes open the door – and that's it, he's outside. But if you want to go out, you'll have to make a hole in the wall. To go down into the street, what does everyone else do? Everyone else goes downstairs. You, though, you'll tear up the sheets on your bed, you'll make a rope of them strip by strip, then you'll climb out of your window and you'll hang by that thread over an abyss, and it will be dark, a storm raging, rain falling, a hurricane blowing, and if the rope's too short you'll have only one way to get down – by falling. Falling blindly into the abyss, from any height, on to what? On to what is below, the unknown. Or you'll climb up a chimney at the risk of burning. Or you'll crawl through a sewer pipe at the risk of drowning. Not to mention the holes that have to be concealed, the stones that have to be removed and put back twenty times a day, the plaster that has to be hidden in your straw pallet. Faced with a lock, the respectable citizen has in his pocket a key made by a locksmith. If you, though, want to get past it you're condemned to a tremendous feat of labour: you'll take a ten-centime coin, you'll slice it into two discs. With what tools? You'll improvise. That's up to you. Then you'll hollow out the inside of these discs, being very careful to preserve the outside, and you'll work into the rim a screw-thread so they can be fitted closely together like a base and a lid. With the top and bottom screwed together like this, there won't be anything suspicious about it. To the guards, for you'll be watched, it'll just be a coin. To you it will be a box. What will you put in this box? A tiny piece of steel. A watch-spring that you'll have cut teeth into, which will be a saw. With this saw, the length of a pin and hidden in a coin, you'll have to cut the lock pin, the bolt latch, the padlock shackle, the bar that you'll have on the window and the fetter you'll have on your leg. This masterpiece wrought, this feat accomplished, all these miracles of craft and skill and dexterity and patience performed, what will be your recompense if it becomes known you are the author of them? Solitary confinement. That's the future. Laziness and dissipation – what dangerous precipices! Don't you know, to do nothing is a fateful choice to make? To sponge on the fabric of society! To be useless, in other words pernicious! That leads straight to the depths of misery. Woe to anyone that wants to be a parasite! He'll be vermin! Ah! So you choose not to work? Ah! You've only one thing in mind: to drink well, eat well, sleep well. You'll drink water, you'll eat black bread, you'll sleep on a plank with your limbs shackled in irons that at night will feel cold on your flesh. You'll break those irons, you'll flee. Fine. You'll crawl on your belly in the undergrowth and you'll eat grass like the beasts of the forest. And you'll be recaptured. And then you'll spend years in a dungeon, chained to a wall, groping for a drink from your mug, gnawing on some foul loaf a dog wouldn't touch, eating beans that worms have eaten before you. You'll be a wood-louse in a cellar. Ah! Have pity on yourself, poor child, even now so young, not twenty years ago a nursling, and no doubt your mother's still alive! I beg you, listen to me. You want fine black cloth and patent-leather shoes, you want to curl your hair and dress your curls with scented oils, to please women, to look good. Your hair will be completely shorn, you'll wear a red shirt and wooden clogs. You want a ring on your finger; you'll have an iron collar round your neck. If you look at a woman, you'll get a beating. And you'll go in there aged twenty and you'll come out at fifty! You'll go in there young and pink and fresh-faced, with your bright eyes and your full set of white teeth and a young man's fine head of hair. You'll come out broken, bent, wrinkled, toothless, horrible-looking, white-haired! Ah! my poor child, you're going astray. Idleness is misguiding you. The hardest work of all is thieving. Believe me, don't take on that arduous task of being an idler. It's not easy to become a rogue. It's less difficult to be an honest man. Now go away and think about what I've told you. By the way, what was it you wanted of me? My purse? Here you are.'

And releasing him, the old man put his purse in Montparnasse's hand, where Montparnasse weighed it for a moment. Then, with the same automatic wariness as if he had stolen it, he carefully slipped it into the back pocket of his coat.

When all this was said and done, the old gent turned away and calmly resumed his stroll.

'Silly old fool!' muttered Montparnasse.

Who was this old gent? The reader has probably guessed.

Astounded, Montparnasse watched him disappear into the twilight. This preoccupation proved costly for him.

As the old man walked away Gavroche came closer.

Gavroche had reassured himself with a sidelong glance that Père Mabeuf was still sitting on his bench, perhaps asleep. Then the gamin had emerged from his bush and begun to creep up in the dark behind the motionless Montparnasse. The boy got right up to him like this without being seen or heard, delicately introduced his hand into the back pocket of that frock-coat of fine black cloth, took hold of the purse, withdrew his hand and, creeping back again, slipped away into the shadows like a grass-snake. Montparnasse, who had no reason to be on his guard and who for the first time in his life was thinking, noticed nothing. When Gavroche got back to where Père Mabeuf was on the other side, he threw the purse over the hedge and ran off as fast as his legs could carry him.

The purse fell on Père Mabeuf's foot. This disturbance woke him. He bent down and picked up the purse. He was baffled by it, and opened it. It was a purse with two compartments; in one there was some small change, in the other six twenty-franc coins.

Greatly flustered, Monsieur Mabeuf referred the matter to his housekeeper.

'It's a godsend,' said Mère Plutarque.

BOOK FIVE
WHICH DOES NOT END
THE WAY IT BEGAN

I
Loneliness and the Barracks Combined

Cosette's heartache, so keen and so intense four or five months before, without her even realizing it, was on the mend. Nature, spring, youthfulness, love for her father, the cheerfulness of the birds and the flowers day by day, drop by drop, gradually instilled in that soul so young and virginal an indefinable something almost like forgetting. Was the fire burning out completely? Or were there merely layers of ash forming? The truth is, she now felt hardly any sense of suffering or feverishness.

One day she suddenly thought of Marius. 'Goodness me!' she said. 'I don't think about him any more.'

That same week she noticed going past the garden gate a very handsome officer of the lancers, with a wasp waist, a splendid uniform, girlish cheeks, a sabre under his arm, a waxed moustache and a shiny chapska. Along with fair hair, prominent blue eyes, a vain, insolent, attractive round face – quite the opposite of Marius. And a cigar in his mouth. Cosette thought this officer probably belonged to the regiment barracked in Rue de Babylone.

The next day she saw him go by again. She noted the time. From then on – was it by chance? – she saw him go by nearly every day.

The officer's comrades noticed in that 'neglected' garden, behind that sorry-looking rococo gate, quite a pretty creature who was almost always there when the handsome lieutenant went by. This lieutenant is not unknown to the reader: his name was Théodule Gillenormand.

'Hey!' they said to him. 'There's a girl who's taken a fancy to you, go on, look at her.'

'Have I time', replied the lancer, 'to look at all the girls who look at me?'

This was precisely when Marius was going into a serious decline and anticipating death, saying, 'If I could only see her before I die!' Had his wish been realized, had he seen Cosette at that moment gazing at a lancer, he would have been unable to utter a word and died of grief.

Whose fault was it? No one's.

Marius was the sort of person who becomes immersed in sorrow and settles into it. Cosette was one of those who sink into it, and emerge from it.

Besides, Cosette was going through that dangerous time, a fateful stage for feminine fancy left to its own devices, when the heart of a lonely young girl is like those vine tendrils that cling, as chance dictates, to the capital of a marble column or to the doorpost of a tavern.

A short decisive moment, critical for every orphan girl whether she be rich or poor, for wealth is no protection against a bad choice. Bad matches are made in the highest circles. The truly bad match is one of souls. And just as many an unknown young man, without name, without birth, without fortune, is a marble column supporting a temple of noble sentiments and noble ideas, so many a man of the world, monied and content, with polished boots and varnished words, if looked at not on the outside but on the inside, which is what is in store for his wife, is nothing more than a pillar of stupidity harbouring violent, despicable and bibulous passions: the doorpost of a tavern.

What was there in Cosette's heart? Stilled or dormant passion, uncommitted love, something limpid, sparkling, clouded at a certain depth, darkness below. The image of the handsome officer was reflected on the surface. Was there a memory deep down? In the very deepest depths? Possibly. Cosette did not know.

A peculiar incident occurred.

II
Cosette's Fears

During the first fortnight in April, Jean Valjean went away on a trip. As we know, this was something that would happen from time to time, at very long intervals. He would be gone for a day or two, three days at most. Where did he go? No one knew, not even Cosette. Once only, on one of his departures, she had accompanied him in a cab that stopped at the end of a little blind alley on the corner of which she read: 'Impasse de la Planchette'. There he climbed out and the cab took Cosette back to Rue de Babylone. It was usually when the household needed money that Jean Valjean made these little journeys.

So Jean Valjean was away. He had said, 'I'll be back in three days.'

That evening Cosette was alone in the drawing room. To pass the time she had opened her piano-organ and, accompanying herself, had begun to sing the chorus from *Euryanthe*, 'Die Thale dampfen, die

Höhen glühn', perhaps the loveliest of all music. When she had finished, she remained pensive.

Suddenly she thought she heard someone walking in the garden. It could not be her father, he was away. It could not be Toussaint, she was in bed. It was ten o'clock at night. She went over to the drawing-room shutter, which was closed, and laid her ear to it. What she heard sounded like a man's footsteps, as if he were treading very lightly.

She quickly went up to the first floor, to her own room, opened a small vent in her shutter, and looked into the garden. There was a full moon. It was no more difficult to see than if it had been daylight. There was no one there.

She opened the window. The garden was absolutely peaceful, and all that could be seen of the street was deserted, as usual.

Cosette thought she had been mistaken in believing she had heard that noise. It was a hallucination produced by that magnificent, melancholy chorus of Weber's, opening up before her mind bewildering depths, shimmering before her eyes like a dizzying forest, a hallucination in which she could hear the snap of dead branches beneath the uneasy tread of the huntsmen glimpsed in the twilight.

She thought no more about it.

Besides, Cosette was by nature not very easily frightened. There was gypsy blood in her veins, the blood of the barefoot adventuress. Remember, she was more of a lark than a dove. She was wild and brave at heart.

The next day, not so late, about dusk, she was strolling in the garden. Amid the confused thoughts preoccupying her she did think that from time to time she heard a sound similar to the sound of the night before, as of someone walking in the dark under the trees not very far away from her; but she told herself that nothing so closely resembles a footstep in the grass as the natural rustling of two branches, and she took no notice. Besides, she could see nothing.

She emerged from 'the shrubbery'. She had only to cross a small green lawn to regain the steps. As she came out of the shrubbery the moon, which had just risen behind her, cast Cosette's shadow in front of her, on to this lawn.

Cosette stopped dead, terror-stricken.

The moon distinctly outlined on the turf beside her shadow another shadow, a particularly startling and terrible shadow, with a round hat. It was the shadow of a man who must have been standing on the fringes of the bushes a few paces behind Cosette.

For a moment she was powerless to speak, or cry, or call out, or move, or look behind her. Eventually she summoned up all her courage and resolutely turned round. There was no one there. She looked on the ground. The shadow was gone.

She went back into the shrubbery, boldly searched high and low, went all the way to the gate, and found nothing.

She felt truly chilled. Was this another hallucination? What! Two days in a row! One hallucination, fair enough, but two? What was disturbing was that the shadow was certainly no ghost. Ghosts do not wear round hats.

Jean Valjean came home the next day. Cosette told him what she thought she had seen and heard. She expected to be reassured and that her father would shrug and say to her, 'You're a silly little girl.'

Jean Valjean looked worried. 'It can't be anything,' he said.

Making some excuse, he left her and went into the garden, and she saw him examining the gate very carefully.

During the night she woke up. This time she was sure, she distinctly heard someone walking very close to the steps beneath her window. She ran to the shutter flap and opened it. There was indeed a man in the garden, holding a big stick. Just as she was about to scream, the moon lit up the man's profile. It was her father. She went back to bed, saying to herself, 'He really is worried, then!'

Jean Valjean spent that night and the two following nights in the garden. Cosette saw him through the vent in her shutter.

The third night – the moon was on the wane and beginning to rise later, it might have been one o'clock in the morning – she heard a great burst of laughter and her father's voice calling her, 'Cosette!'

She jumped out of bed, put on her dressing-gown and opened the window.

Her father was down below on the lawn.

'I'm waking you up to set your mind at rest,' he said. 'Look. There's your shadow with the round hat.'

And he pointed out to her a projected shadow outlined on the lawn by the moonlight, one that did indeed look rather like the figure of a man wearing a round hat. It was the silhouette of a capped metal chimney rising above a neighbouring roof.

Cosette joined in his laughter, shedding all her ominous conjectures, and the next morning at table with her father she joked about the sinister garden haunted by the shadows of stove pipes.

Jean Valjean's peace of mind was fully restored. As for Cosette, she did not give much thought as to whether the stove pipe was in the same direction as the shadow she had seen, or thought she had seen, and whether the moon had been in the same part of the sky. She did not wonder about the peculiarity of a stove pipe that is afraid of being

833

caught out in the open and draws back when someone looks at its shadow, for the shadow had vanished when Cosette turned round, and Cosette had felt very sure of this. Cosette's fears were completely allayed. The demonstration seemed conclusive to her and put out of her mind the idea that there could be anyone walking in the garden in the evening or at night.

A few days later, however, another incident occurred.

III
Enhanced by Toussaint's Comments

In the garden, by the railings on the street, there was a stone bench, protected from prying eyes by a hedge, but just within reach, through the railings and the hedge, of the arm of a passer-by.

One evening after sunset during that same month of April, Jean Valjean had gone out, and Cosette had sat down on this bench. The wind freshened in the trees. Cosette was daydreaming. An indeterminate sadness gradually came over her, the invincible sadness that evening brings and which may come – who knows? – from an insight that time of day gives into the mystery of the tomb.

Fantine was perhaps in those shadows.

Cosette rose, slowly took a turn around the garden, walking on the dew-drenched grass and saying to herself, in the depths of that sort of melancholy somnambulism in which she was immersed, 'You really need wooden clogs in the garden at this hour. You'll catch a chill.'

She returned to the bench. As she was about to sit on it, she noticed in the place that she had vacated a rather large stone that had obviously not been there the moment before.

Cosette considered this stone, wondering what it meant. All of a sudden it occurred to her that this stone had not ended up on this bench all by itself, that someone had put it there, that an arm had slipped through the railing, and this idea scared her. This time her fear was genuine. No room for any doubt, the stone was there. She did not touch it. She fled, not daring to look behind her, and took refuge in the house. The french window that gave on to the steps she immediately shuttered, bolted and locked.

She asked Toussaint, 'Is my father back yet?'

'Not yet, mademoiselle.'

(We have already noted Toussaint's stutter once and for all. Allow us not to dwell on it any further. We are loath to make a song and dance about any handicap.)

Jean Valjean, a man given to reflection and to nocturnal strolls, often did not come home until quite late at night.

'Toussaint,' Cosette went on, 'you are careful to bar the shutters properly at night, on the garden side at least, and to make sure those little iron things are inserted into those little rings for pinning them?'

'Oh, you needn't worry, mademoiselle.'

Toussaint would be as good as her word, Cosette well knew, but she could not help adding, 'It's just that it's so isolated out here.'

'Well, that's true,' said Toussaint. 'You'd be killed before you could utter a word. And what with monsieur not sleeping in the house either. But never fear, mademoiselle, I close the windows as if this were a prison. Women on their own! Of course it makes you shudder! Can you imagine? Seeing men coming into your room at night, telling you to "Shut up!" and starting to cut your throat. It's not so much the dying – everyone dies, it's only natural, we all know we've got to die – but it's the horror of feeling those people touching you. And then their knives, they probably don't cut well! Oh dear God!'

'Say no more,' said Cosette. 'Just close everything up.'

Terrified by Toussaint's improvised melodrama and perhaps also by the recollection of those apparitions of the other week that now came back to her, Cosette dared not even say to the old woman, 'Go and look at the stone someone has put on the bench!' for fear of opening the door into the garden and letting 'the men' get inside. She made sure all the doors and windows were secured, sent Toussaint to check over the whole house from the attic to the cellar, locked herself in her bedroom, drew the bolts, looked under her bed, got into it, and slept badly. All night long she saw that stone, as big as a mountain and full of caves.

Waking at sunrise – the characteristic of sunrise is to make us laugh at all our night terrors, and our laughter is always commensurate with the fear we have felt – Cosette regarded her terror as a nightmare, and said to herself, 'What could I have been thinking of? It's like those footsteps I thought I heard in the garden at night the other week! It's like the shadow of the stove pipe! Am I now going to become a coward?' The warm glow of sunshine coming through the vents in her shutters, turning the damask curtains crimson, so reassured her that everything faded from her mind, even the stone.

'There was no more a stone on that bench than there was a man in a round hat in the garden. I imagined the stone, like everything else.'

She got dressed, went down into the garden, ran to the bench, and felt herself break into a cold sweat. The stone was there. But this lasted only a moment. What is dread by night is curiosity by day.

'Pah!' said she. 'Let's have a look, then.'

She picked up that stone, which was quite large. There was something underneath it that looked like a letter. It was a white envelope. Cosette snatched it up. There was no address on one side, no seal on the other. Yet, although open, the envelope was not empty. Sheets of paper could be glimpsed inside it.

Cosette peered at them. This was no longer dread, this was no longer curiosity. This was the onset of anxiety.

Cosette pulled out of the envelope what it contained, a little booklet, with every page numbered and each with a few lines written on it in very small and, Cosette thought, rather delicate handwriting.

Cosette looked for a name. There was none. A signature. There was none. Who was it for? For her, probably, since a hand had placed the envelope on her bench. Who was it from? An irresistible fascination came over her. She tried to avert her eyes from the pages trembling in her hand, she looked up at the sky, at the street, at the acacias all bathed in light, at the pigeons flying over a neighbouring roof; and then suddenly her gaze fell, darting to the handwritten booklet, and she said to herself she must know what was inside it.

This is what she read.

IV

A Heart beneath a Stone

The universe reduced to a single being, a single being expanding to encompass God, that is love.

Love is the angels' greeting to the stars.

How sad the soul is, when sad for love's sake!

What emptiness in the absence of the person who fills the world with their sole being! Oh! how true it is that the beloved becomes God. It would be understandable if God were jealous, had not the Almighty Father obviously made creation for the soul and the soul for love.

With just the glimpse of a smile beneath a lilac-trimmed white crêpe hat, the soul gains entrance to the palace of dreams.

God is behind everything but everything hides God. Things are black, human beings are opaque. To love someone is to make them transparent.

Certain thoughts are prayers. There are moments when, whatever position the body might be in, the soul is on its knees.

Parted lovers beguile absence with a thousand fanciful devices that nevertheless have their own reality. They are prevented from seeing each other, they cannot write to each other. They find a host of mysterious ways to communicate. They send each other the song of birds, the scent of flowers, the laughter of children, the light of the sun, the sighs of the wind, the radiance of the stars, all creation. And why not? All the works of God are made to serve love. Love is sufficiently powerful to entrust the whole of nature with its messages.

O springtime! You are a letter that I write to her.

The future belongs much more to hearts than to minds. Loving, that is the only thing that can occupy and fill eternity. The infinite requires the inexhaustible.

Love partakes of the soul itself. It is of the same nature. A divine spark, like the soul, it is likewise incorruptible, indivisible, imperishable. It is a burning flame within us, immortal and infinite, which nothing can contain and nothing can extinguish. We can feel it burning even in the marrow of our bones, and we can see its glow reaching into the depths of heaven.

O love! Mutual adoration! The delight of two minds that understand each other, two hearts given in exchange for each other, two gazes that fathom each other's depths! Blissful happiness, you will come to me, will you not! Secluded walks with just the two of us together! Glorious blessed days! I have sometimes dreamed that now and then hours detached themselves from the lives of angels and inserted themselves in the fate of mankind here below.

God can add nothing to the happiness of those who love, other than to give them everlastingness. After a lifetime of love – an eternity of love: that is indeed an increase. But to increase in its actual intensity the ineffable bliss that love already imparts to the soul in this world is impossible, even to God. God is the plenitude of heaven. Love is the plenitude of man.

You look at a star for two reasons, because it is bright and because it is impenetrable. You have beside you a sweeter radiance and a greater mystery: woman.

For all of us, whoever we may be, there are those who are as the breath of life to us. Without them, without air, we suffocate. Then we die. To die for want of love is dreadful. Suffocation of the soul!

When love has melted and conjoined two beings in sacred and angelic unity, for them the secret of life has been discovered. They are but the two terms of the same destiny. They are but the two wings of the same spirit. Love, and you soar!

The day when a woman walking in front of you casts light as she goes on her way, you are lost, you are in love. There is only one thing you can do: think of her so intently that she is compelled to think of you.

What love initiates only God can bring to completion.

True love despairs and exults in losing a glove or finding a handker-chief, and has need of eternity for its devotion and its hopes. It comprises both the infinitely great and the infinitely small.

If you are a stone, be a lodestone. If you are a plant, be a sensitive one.* If you are human, be love.

Nothing satisfies love. Lovers have happiness, they want paradise; they have paradise, they want heaven.

O you who love each other, all this is contained in love. You need only know how to find it there. Love has contemplation just as much as heaven does. And in addition, it has sensual delight.

'Does she still come to the Luxembourg Gardens?' 'No, monsieur.' 'This is the church where she attends mass, is it not?' 'She doesn't come here any more.' 'Does she still live in this house?' 'She's moved away.' 'Where has she moved to?' 'She didn't say.'

What a dire thing it is for a man not to know the address of his soul!

Love has its childishness, other passions have their small-mindedness. Shame on the passions that belittle man! All honour to the one that makes a child of him!

* A lodestone is 'une pierre d'aimant', *aimant* meaning both 'magnet' and 'lov-ing'. The sensitive plant is another name for *Mimosa pudica*.

It is a strange thing, this – did you know? I live in darkness. There is someone who went away, taking with her the sky.

Oh! to lie side by side in the same tomb, holding hands, and gently to caress each other's fingers now and then in the shadows, that would satisfy me for eternity!

You who suffer because you love, love yet more. To die of love is to live by love.

Be in love. A transfiguration of starry darkness is implicit in this torture. There is ecstasy in the agony.

O joy of the birds! It is because they have a nest that they sing.

Love is a heavenly breath of the air of paradise.

Deep hearts, wise spirits, take life as God has made it. It is a long ordeal, an incomprehensible preparation for an unknown destiny. This destiny, the true one, begins for a man with his first step inside the tomb. Then something appears to him, and he begins to discern finality. Finality, think about that word. The living see infinity. Finality reveals itself only to the dead. Meanwhile, love and suffer, hope and contemplate. Woe, alas! to any that have loved only bodies, forms, appearances! Death will deprive them of everything. Try to love souls; you will be reunited with them.

I met in the street a very poor young lover. His hat was old, his coat was worn. He had holes at his elbows. Water filled his shoes, and stars filled his soul.

What a glorious thing, to be loved! And more glorious yet, to love! The heart becomes heroic through passion. So that it consists only of what is pure, and is founded only on what is elevated and noble. An unworthy thought can no more be conceived by it than a nettle can spring up out of a glacier. Inaccessible to passions and to ordinary feelings, rising above the clouds and shadows of this world, above follies, falsehoods, hatreds, vanities, miseries, the serene and lofty soul inhabits the blue heavens and feels nothing but the deep underlying perturbations of destiny, as the mountain peak feels the earthquake.

If there were not someone who loved, the sun would be extinguished.

V
Cosette after the Letter

Reading this, Cosette gradually fell into a daydream. Just as she looked up from the last line of the booklet, the handsome officer – it was his usual time – went past the gate, triumphantly. Cosette found him repulsive.

She returned to studying the booklet. It was lovely handwriting, thought Cosette. All penned by the same hand, but with different inks – sometimes very black, sometimes pale as when water has been added to the inkwell – and therefore on different days. So this was a mind that had unburdened itself, sigh by sigh, irregularly, unmethodically, indiscriminately, erratically, at random. Cosette had never read anything like it. This manuscript, in which she saw much more clarity than obscurity, gave her the impression of a sanctuary whose door stood ajar. Each one of these mysterious lines glowed before her eyes and bathed her heart in a strange light. The education she had received had always talked to her about the soul and never about love, rather as one might talk about the firebrand and not the flame. This fifteen-page manuscript suddenly and sweetly revealed to her all about love, sorrow, destiny, life, eternity, the beginning, the end. It was as if a hand had opened and suddenly thrown her a clutch of luminous rays. She sensed in these few lines a passionate, ardent, generous, honest nature, an inspired will, a boundless sorrow and a boundless hope, a heavy heart and a rapturous ecstasy. What was this manuscript? A letter. A letter without an address, without a name, without a date, without a signature, urgent and self-abnegating, an enigma composed of truths, a message of love to be delivered by an angel and read by a virgin, an out-of-this-world assignation, the love letter of a phantom to a shadow. It came from one, calm and despondent in his absence, who seemed ready to take refuge in death, sending to another, in her absence, the secret of fate, the key of life, love. This had been written with a foot in the grave and a finger in heaven. These lines, spilled on to the page one by one, were what might be called droplets from a soul.

Now, who could these pages come from? Who could have penned them? Cosette did not hesitate for a second. One man only!

It was he!

There was a return of daylight to her soul. Everything was clear again. She felt an extraordinary joy and a deep anguish. He was the one! He it was who had written to her! He was there! It was his arm that had slipped through the railing! While she had forgotten him, he had found her again! But had she forgotten him? No, never! She was crazy to have thought so for a single moment. She had always loved him, always adored him. The fire had been banked down and had smouldered for a while, but – she saw it plainly now – it had only gone deeper, and now it was bursting into flame again and taking hold of her entirely. This booklet was like a spark that had fallen from that other soul into her own, and she felt the blaze rekindled. She absorbed every one of those handwritten words. 'Oh yes!' she said. 'How well I recognize it all! It's everything I'd read in his eyes.'

As she came to the end of it for the third time, Lieutenant Théodule passed in front of the gate once more and his spurs rattled on the pavement. Cosette could not but look up. She found him dull, inane, stupid, feckless, conceited, disagreeable, impertinent, and very ugly. The officer thought he should smile at her. She turned away, ashamed and indignant. She would gladly have thrown something at him.

She fled, went back inside the house, and shut herself in her room to reread the manuscript, to learn it by heart, and to daydream. When she had read it thoroughly, she kissed it and tucked it into her bodice.

Her fate was sealed. Cosette had fallen into deep, seraphic love again. Eden's abyss had just reopened.

All day long Cosette was in a kind of daze. She could scarcely think, her ideas were all tangled inside her brain, she was incapable of conjecturing; she hoped, tremulously – what? – vague things. She dared make no promises to herself, and wanted to deny herself nothing. Her face would turn pale and shivers would run through her body. At times it seemed as if she were in a dream. She said to herself, 'Is this real?' Then she felt for the cherished paper beneath her gown, she pressed it to her heart, she felt the edges of it on her flesh. And had Jean Valjean seen her at that moment he would have quaked before that luminous and unfamiliar joy brimming in her eyes. 'Oh yes!' she thought. 'This is surely his! It comes from him. For me.'

And she told herself that some intervention by the angels, some celestial blessing, had given him back to her.

O transfiguration of love! O dreams! This celestial blessing, this intervention by the angels, was that ball of bread tossed by one thief to another over the roofs of La Force prison, from the Cour Charlemagne into the Lions' Den.

VI
Old Folk Are Designed to Be Out
at the Right Time

When evening came Jean Valjean went out. Cosette dressed. She arranged her hair the way it most suited her and put on a gown with a bodice that had been given one snip of the scissors too many, and this more revealing, lower-cut neckline was, as young girls say, 'a little indecent'. It was not in the least indecent, but it was more attractive than it would have been otherwise. She took all this trouble over her appearance without knowing why.

Did she mean to go out? No. Was she expecting a visitor? No. At dusk, she went out into the garden. Toussaint was busy in her kitchen, which looked out on to the back yard.

She set off walking beneath the boughs, brushing them aside from time to time because some hung very low.

And so she came to the bench. The stone was still there. She sat down and laid her soft white hand on this stone as though wanting to caress it and thank it.

Suddenly she had that indefinable feeling you get, even without seeing, when someone is standing behind you. She looked round and jumped up.

There he was.

He was bare-headed. He looked pale and wasted. His black coat was barely discernible. Dusk cast a wan light on his fine brow and hid his eyes in shadow. Beneath a veil of incomparable tenderness, he had something of death and darkness about him. His face was illuminated by the light of the dying day and by the mind of a departing soul. This seemed not yet to be the ghost, but already no longer the man.

His hat had been thrown into the bushes, a few feet away.

On the verge of fainting, Cosette did not cry out. She stepped back slowly, for she felt drawn forward. He did not stir. By virtue of some enveloping sense of sadness beyond words, she was aware of the expression in his eyes that she could not see.

Cosette, retreating, backed into a tree, and leaned against it. Had it not been for that tree, she would have fallen.

Then she heard his voice, the voice she had never really heard before, which rose above the rustling of the leaves and murmured, 'Forgive me for being here. My heart is bursting, I couldn't go on living the way I was, I had to come. Have you read what I left here on this bench? Do you recognize me at all? Don't be afraid of me. It's already a while ago now, you remember the day you looked at me in the Luxembourg Gardens by the *Gladiator*. And the day when you walked past me? The sixteenth of June and the second of July, it was. It will soon be a year ago now. I haven't seen you for such a long time. I asked the woman who hires out chairs, and she told me she didn't see you any more. You lived in Rue de l'Ouest, on the third floor at the front of a new building – you see what I know! I followed you. What else could I do? And then you disappeared. I thought I saw you go by once when I was reading the newspapers under the Odéon arcades. I ran after you. But no. It was someone who had a hat like yours. I come here at night. Don't be afraid, no one sees me. I come to gaze at your windows from close by. I tread very softly so you won't hear me, for you might be frightened. The other evening I was behind you, you turned round, I fled. Once I heard you singing. I was happy. Do you mind if I hear you singing through the shutters? No, you don't mind, do you? You see, you're my angel! Let me come here occasionally. I think I'm going to die. If you only knew! I adore you! Forgive me, I'm talking to you, I don't know what I'm saying, perhaps I'm annoying you, am I annoying you?'

'Oh dear mother!' she said.

And she sank down, as if she were dying.

He caught her, she fell, he took her in his arms, he pressed her close, unconscious of what he was doing. Himself reeling, he supported her. It was as though his head was thick with smoke. Light flickered through his eyelashes. His thoughts melted away. He felt he was performing some religious rite and that he was committing an act of desecration. Yet he had not the least desire for this lovely woman whose form he felt against his chest. He was overwhelmed with love.

She took his hand and laid it on her heart. He felt the paper that was kept there. 'You love me, then?' he stammered.

She replied in a voice so low it was no more than a barely audible whisper, 'Hush, my beloved! You know I do!'

And she hid her crimson face upon the chest of the proud and elated young man.

He dropped on to the bench, she beside him. They were now wordless. The stars were beginning to twinkle. How was it their lips met? How is it that the bird sings, that snow melts, that the rose unfolds its petals, that May comes into bloom, that dawn brightens behind the dark trees on the quivering crest of the hills?

One kiss was all.

Both trembled, and gazed at each other in the shadows, their eyes sparkling. They did not feel the night chill, or the cold stone, or the damp earth, or the wet grass. They gazed at each other, and their hearts were full of thoughts. They had taken hold of each other's hands without knowing it.

She did not ask him, she did not even wonder, where and how he had found a way into the garden. It seemed so natural that he should be there!

From time to time Marius's knee touched Cosette's, and they both felt a frisson. Now and then Cosette stammered out a word. Her soul trembled on her lips like a drop of dew on a flower.

Little by little they began to talk. An outpouring followed the fullness of their silence. Overhead, the night was serene and splendid. These two beings, pure as spirits, told each other everything, their dreams, their raptures, their ecstasies, their fantasies, their yearnings, how they had adored each other from afar, how they had longed for each other, their despair when they had stopped seeing each other. In perfect intimacy, which already nothing could add to, they confided to each other the greatest secrets and mysteries about themselves. With ingenuous trust in their illusions, they shared with each other everything that love, youth and the last vestiges of childhood within them put into their heads. These two hearts poured themselves into each other, so that after an hour it was the young man who possessed the young girl's soul and the young girl who possessed the young man's. They were imbued with each other, enraptured, dazzled by each other.

When they had finished, when they had told each other everything, she laid her head on his shoulder and asked him, 'What's your name?'

'My name is Marius,' he said. 'And yours?'

'My name is Cosette.'

BOOK SIX
YOUNG GAVROCHE

I
The Wind's Mischief

Since 1823, when the tavern at Montfermeil was going under and gradually foundering – not in the abysmal depths of bankruptcy but in a squalid puddle of petty debts – the Thénardier couple had had two more children, both male. That made five: two girls and three boys. That was a lot.

While they were still young and very small, by a peculiar stroke of luck the Thénardier woman disencumbered herself of the last two.

'Disencumbered' is the right word. There was only a fraction of natural feeling in that woman. A phenomenon of which there is more than one example, as a matter of fact. Like the Maréchale de La Mothe-Houdancourt, the Thénardier woman was a mother only to her daughters. Her maternal instincts ended there. Her hatred of the human race began with her sons. Towards her boys she was downright cruel, and her heart was a bleak stone wall to them. As we have seen, she detested the eldest. She could not bear the sight of the other two. Why? Because. The most terrible of motives, the most indisputable of responses. Because. 'I don't need a gaggle of children,' said this mother.

Let us explain how the Thénardiers had managed to unburden themselves of their youngest children, and even to make a profit out of them.

That Magnon woman, mentioned a few pages earlier, was the very same who had got old Gillenormand to support the two children she had. She lived on Quai des Célestins, at the corner of that ancient Rue du Petit-Musc of ill-repute, which has done its best to put itself in good odour.* Remember the great croup epidemic that ravaged the Seine's riverside districts in Paris thirty-five years ago, and which science took advantage of to test on a large scale the efficacy of alum inhalations, replaced today so effectively by the external use of tincture of iodine. During this epidemic, when they were still at a very

---

* *Petit-Musc*, meaning 'little musk deer', is a deformation of the street's earlier name *Put-y-musse*, meaning 'where whores hide'.

young age, the Magnon woman lost both her boys on the same day, one in the morning, the other in the evening. This was a blow. These children were precious to their mother. They represented eighty francs a month. Those eighty francs were paid very punctually in the name of Monsieur Gillenormand by the collector of his rents, Monsieur Barge, a retired bailiff in Rue du Roi-de-Sicile. Once the children were dead, that was the end of the income. La Magnon sought a way round this. In that shady freemasonry of villainy to which she belonged, everything is common knowledge, no one betrays a secret, and everybody helps each other out.

La Magnon needed two children. The Thénardiers had two children. The same sex, the same age. A good arrangement for her, a good investment for them. The little Thénardiers became the little Magnons. The Magnon woman left Quai des Célestins and went to live in Rue Clocheperce. In Paris, the identity that ties an individual to his own self is ruptured from one street to the next.

Not having been advised of anything, the registry office raised no objection and the substitution took place without the least bother. Only, for this loan of his children Thénardier demanded ten francs a month, which the Magnon woman promised him, and even paid. It goes without saying that Monsieur Gillenormand continued to fulfil his obligations. He came to see the children every six months. He did not notice the change. 'Monsieur,' La Magnon said to him, 'they look so much like you!'

Thénardier, who freely adopted aliases, took this opportunity to become Jondrette. His two daughters and Gavroche had hardly had time to register that they had two little brothers. At a certain level of wretchedness a kind of spectral indifference takes over, and you see human beings as ghostly presences. Those closest to you are often no more than vague shadowy forms, barely distinct from life's nebulous background and easily reabsorbed by the invisible.

On the day she handed over her two little ones to the Magnon woman, with the very explicit intention of renouncing them for ever, that evening the Thénardier woman felt, or appeared to feel, a scruple. She said to her husband, 'But it's abandoning your own children, this is!'

Magisterial and phlegmatic, Thénardier cauterized her scruple with this comment, 'Jean-Jacques Rousseau went further!'

The mother's scruple gave way to anxiety. 'But what if the police were to come and bother us? Tell me, Monsieur Thénardier – now, what we've done, is that allowed?'

Thénardier replied, 'Everything's allowed. Nobody'll see anything wrong in it. In any case, with children who haven't got a sou, it's in nobody's interest to investigate.'

La Magnon was a kind of belle of the criminal world. She took pains over her appearance. She shared her lodgings, furnished in a wretchedly genteel manner, with a Frenchified Englishwoman who was a clever thief. Having some very wealthy connections on her side, this Englishwoman, the naturalized Parisienne, was closely linked with the coins from the library and with Mademoiselle Mars's diamonds, and later achieved notoriety in the criminal record-books. She was called Mam'selle Miss.

The two little boys the Magnon woman had come by had no reason to complain. With the eighty francs to recommend them they were looked after, like everything that is exploited. Neither badly clothed nor badly fed, treated almost like 'little gentlemen', they were better off with their bogus mother than with their real one. La Magnon acted the fine lady and spoke properly in front of them.

Several years went by in this way, giving Thénardier high hopes for the future. There came a day when he said to the Magnon woman as she handed over his monthly ten francs, 'Their "father" will have to provide for their education.'

Suddenly these two poor children, who had been fairly protected until then, even in their misfortune, were catapulted into life and forced to fend for themselves.

A mass arrest of criminals like the one at the Jondrette den, inevitably compounded by investigations and subsequent imprisonments, is a veritable disaster for that ugly, hidden counter-society that underlies the society that is in the public eye. An incident of this kind brings all sorts of catastrophes to that shady world. The Thénardiers' downfall led to the Magnon woman's downfall.

One day, shortly after La Magnon had handed Éponine the note about Rue Plumet, the police made a sudden raid on Rue Clocheperce. La Magnon was seized, as well as Mam'selle Miss, and a clean sweep made of the whole suspect household. While this was going on, the two little boys were playing in the back yard and saw nothing of the round-up. When they tried to get back into the house they found the door locked and the house empty. A cobbler in a workshop opposite called them over and gave them a note that 'their mother' had left for them. On the piece of paper there was an address: 'Monsieur Barge, rent collector, 8 Rue du Roi-de-Sicile'. 'You don't live here any more,' the man in the workshop told them. 'Go there. It's very near by. The first street on the left. Use this note to ask the way.'

The two children set off, the older one leading the younger, and holding in his hand the note that was to guide them. He was cold and, being numb, his little fingers had not much grip and were not holding the note very tightly. At the corner of Rue Clocheperce a gust of wind tore it from him, and as darkness was falling the child was unable to find it again.

They began to wander aimlessly through the streets.

II

In Which Little Gavroche Takes Advantage
of the Great Napoleon

Spring in Paris is quite often windswept, with harsh, bitter northerlies that leave you not exactly frozen, but chilled. These north winds that mar the most beautiful days have the very same effect as those draughts of cold air that get into a warm room through chinks in a window or a door that is not properly closed. It is as though winter's cheerless door has been left ajar and the wind is blowing through it. In the spring of 1832, which was when the first great epidemic of this century broke out in Europe, the northerlies were more raw and biting than ever. It was a door even icier than winter's that stood ajar. It was the door of the tomb. In these northerlies you felt the blast of cholera.

From a meteorological viewpoint, these cold winds had the peculiarity of not precluding considerable electric tension. There were at this time frequent storms erupting, accompanied by thunder and lightning.

One evening when these northerlies were blowing a gale, so that January seemed to have returned and respectable citizens had put on their winter coats again, young Gavroche, still cheerfully shivering in his rags, was standing as though entranced in front of a wig-maker's shop near Orme-St-Gervais. He was arrayed in a woman's woollen shawl, picked up who knows where, of which he had made a muffler for himself. Little Gavroche seemed lost in deep admiration of a revolving wax bride, in a low-necked dress with orange-blossoms in her hair, displayed between two lamps in the window and bestowing her smile on passers-by. But he was actually observing the shop to see whether he might not be able 'to lift' a cake of soap from the window, which he would then go and sell for a sou to a 'hair-dresser' in the city outskirts. He had often managed to breakfast off one such cake. He called this type of work, for which he had a special aptitude, 'shaving barbers'.

While contemplating the bride and eyeing the cake of soap, he was muttering to himself: 'Tuesday. It wasn't Tuesday. Was it Tuesday? Perhaps it was Tuesday. Yes, it was Tuesday.'

What this monologue was about, it was never known. If by chance it referred to the last time he had eaten, that was three days earlier, for it was now Friday.

In his shop, warmed by a good stove, the barber was shaving a customer and casting a sideways glance from time to time at this foe, this chilled and cheeky gamin who had both hands in his pockets but whose mind was evidently bared.

While Gavroche was considering the bride, the shop window and the Windsor soaps, two children of different heights, quite neatly dressed and even younger than he was, one who looked about seven years of age, the other five, timidly turned the handle and entered the shop, asking for something or other, charity perhaps, in a plaintive murmur that sounded more like a wail than an entreaty. They both spoke at once, and their words were unintelligible because sobs choked the younger one's voice and the older one's teeth chattered with the cold. The barber turned round with fury in his face, and without letting go of his razor, expelling the older one with his left hand and the younger one with his knee, he pushed them both out into the street and shut the door on them, saying, 'Letting in the cold for no good reason!'

The two children set off again, in tears. In the meantime clouds had gathered. It began to rain.

Young Gavroche ran after them and said, 'What's the matter with you brats?'

'We've nowhere to sleep,' replied the older one.

'Is that all?' said Gavroche. 'As if that was a problem! Is that anything to cry about? What ninnies!'

And tempering his rather facetious superiority by adopting a tone of kindly authority and gentle protectiveness, he said, 'Come along with me, bratlings!'

'Yes, monsieur,' said the older one.

And the two children followed him as they would have followed an archbishop. They had stopped crying. Gavroche led them up Rue St-Antoine in the direction of the Bastille.

As he went, Gavroche cast an indignant backward glance at the barber's shop.

'That cold fish has no heart,' he muttered. 'He's an Englisher.'

A streetwalker, seeing the three of them trailing one behind the other, Gavroche leading the way, gave vent to boisterous laughter. This laughter was disrespectful of the group.

'And good day to you, Mam'selle Omnibus,' Gavroche said to her.

A moment later the wig-maker came back to mind, and he added, 'I've got the wrong animal, he's not a fish, he's a snake. Barber, I'll go and fetch a locksmith and have him put a rattle on your wig-tail!'

This wig-maker had made him aggressive. Striding over a gutter, he called out to a bearded lady door-keeper with her broom in her hand, whom Faust might well have encountered on the Brocken.

'Madame,' he said, 'so you're taking your horse for a ride?'

And with that, he spattered the polished boots of a passer-by.

'You pest!' shouted the furious passer-by.

Gavroche poked his nose over his shawl.

'Monsieur has a complaint?'

'About you!' said the man.

'The office is closed,' said Gavroche, 'I'm not taking any more complaints.'

However, continuing up the street, he noticed, blue with cold under an archway, a beggar-girl of thirteen or fourteen, so scantily clad that her bare knees showed. The young girl was getting to be too grown-up for that. Growing up catches you out that way – just when nakedness becomes indecent your skirt becomes short.

'Poor girl!' said Gavroche. 'Without even a pair of breeches. Here, take this at least.'

And unwinding all that good wool he had round his neck, he threw it over the beggar-girl's thin, purple shoulders, where the muffler became a shawl again. The young girl stared at him in astonishment and received the shawl in silence. At a certain level of hardship, the pauper no longer laments the ill that befalls him, no longer gives thanks for the good.

That done, 'Brrr!' said Gavroche, shivering more than St Martin, who at least kept half his cloak for himself.

At this brrr! the downpour, turning nastier, intensified. Those wicked skies punish good deeds.

'Now then!' exclaimed Gavroche. 'What's the meaning of this? It's raining again! Lord, if it goes on like this, I'm cancelling my subscription.'

And he set off again.

'Never mind,' he said, casting a glance at the beggar-girl, who was huddling under the shawl, 'at least one of us is well covered.'

And looking up at the clouds he exclaimed, 'So there!'

The two children followed close on his heels.

As they were passing one of those heavy lattice grilles that indicate a baker's shop – for bread, like gold, is put behind iron bars – Gavroche turned round, 'Ah, by the way, young 'uns, have we eaten?'

'Monsieur,' replied the older one, 'we've had nothing to eat since earlier this morning.'

'So you've neither father nor mother?' Gavroche went on grandly.

'Begging your pardon, monsieur, we have papa and mama, but we don't know where they are.'

'Sometimes that's just as well,' said Gavroche, who was a thinker.

'We've been wandering about for the past two hours,' the older one went on, 'we looked for things at the bottom of boundary-posts, but we didn't find anything.'

'I know,' said Gavroche, 'it's the dogs that eat everything.'

He went on after a pause, 'So we've lost our parents. We don't know what we've done with them. That won't do, lads. It's silly, mislaying old folk like that. Ah well! We still need to line our bellies.'

He asked no more questions. What was more natural than to be homeless? The elder of the two youngsters, almost completely restored to the ready blitheness of childhood, exclaimed, 'All the same, it's odd! Mama told us she'd take us to church on Palm Sunday to get a blessed sprig of box.'

'Would you believe it?,' said Gavroche.

'Mama,' the older one went on, 'is a lady who lives with Mam'selle Miss.'

'What's-her-name,' said Gavroche.

Meanwhile, he had come to a halt and for the last few minutes had been patting and searching all kinds of little pockets that he had in his ragged clothing. At last he looked up with an expression striving to be merely satisfied but that was actually triumphant.

'Keep calm, little nippers. This will get the three of us something to eat.'

And from one of his pockets he pulled out a sou. Without giving the two youngsters time to stand gaping, he pushed both of them in front of him into the baker's shop, and put his sou on the counter, crying, 'Five centimes' worth of bread, my man!'

The baker – it was the master baker himself – picked up a loaf and a knife.

'In three pieces, my man!' said Gavroche. And he added with dignity, 'There are three of us.'

And seeing that after assessing his three customers the baker had picked up a loaf of black bread, he stuck his finger right up his nose with an inhalation as imperious as if he had a pinch of Frederick the Great's snuff on the end of his thumb, and challenged the baker outright with an indignant, 'Wossat?'

Those of our readers who might be tempted to identify in this challenge that Gavroche delivered to the baker a Russian or a Polish word,* or one of those savage cries the Ioway Indians and the Botocudos hurl at each other from one riverbank to another across the empty wastes, are advised that it is a word that they (our readers) use every day, and which takes the place of the phrase 'What is that?' The baker understood perfectly and replied, 'Why, it's bread, very good second-grade bread.'

'You mean *larton brutal*†!' Gavroche remonstrated, calmly and coldly disdainful. 'Some white bread, my man! Some *larton savonné*‡! It's my treat.'

The baker could not help smiling, and as he cut the white bread he viewed them in a sympathetic way that shocked Gavroche.

'Hey, baker's boy!' he said. 'Don't think you've got the measure of us!'

All three of them placed end to end would have hardly added up to six feet.

When the bread was cut the baker put the sou in the till, and Gavroche said to the two children, 'Now polish that off!' The little boys stared at him in bewilderment.

Gavroche began to laugh. 'Of course! They wouldn't understand, they're too young.'

And he said, 'Eat!'

At the same time he held out to each of them a piece of bread.

And thinking that the older one, who seemed worthier of conversing with him, deserved some special encouragement and must be relieved of any hesitation in satisfying his appetite, he added, as he handed him the largest piece, 'Stick that down your muzzle.'

There was one piece smaller than the others. He took this for himself.

The poor children were famished, Gavroche included. Tearing at

---

* The French version of what Gavroche says, 'Keksekça?' (for 'Qu'est-ce que c'est que cela?'), looks more like a Russian or Polish word than the English 'Wossat?'

† Footnoted by Hugo: 'Pain noir', 'black bread' [*brutal* meaning 'coarse' and *larton* argot for 'bread'].

‡ Literally, 'soaped bread'.

their bread hungrily, they were crowding the baker's shop, and now that they had paid their money he looked at them crossly.

'Back out on to the street,' said Gavroche.

They set off once more in the direction of the Bastille.

Now and then, when they passed in front of lighted shop windows, the youngest one stopped to look at the time on a toy watch hanging from a string around his neck.

'Now there's a real dolt, and no mistake,' said Gavroche.

Then he muttered to himself pensively, 'All the same, if I had kids I'd look after them better.'

As they were finishing their pieces of bread and coming up to the corner of that dismal Rue des Ballets, at the end of which you can see the low, hostile gate of La Force prison, someone said, 'Hey, Gavroche, isn't it?'

'Hey, Montparnasse, isn't it?' said Gavroche.

It was a man who had just spoken to the gamin, and that man was none other than Montparnasse, disguised in blue specs but recognizable to Gavroche.

'Lord!' said Gavroche. 'You've got a coat the colour of a linseed poultice and blue spectacles like a doctor. That's style for you! I'll say!'

'Shh!' went Montparnasse. 'Not so loud.'

And he jerked Gavroche aside, out of the light from the shops.

The two little ones followed on automatically, holding hands.

When they were under the arch of a carriage entrance, hidden from view and sheltered from the rain, 'You know where I'm going?' said Montparnasse.

'To Mount-Weeping Abbey*,' replied Gavroche.

'Very funny!' And Montparnasse went on, 'I'm going to find Babet.'

'Ah!' exclaimed Gavroche. 'So she's called Babet.'

Montparnasse lowered his voice, 'Not she, he.'

'Ah! Babet.'

'Yes, Babet.'

'I thought he was in clink.'

'He got out,' replied Montparnasse.

And quickly he told the gamin that, having been transferred to the Conciergerie, Babet had made his escape that very morning by

---

* The abbey of Mont-à-Regret – literally, 'Mount-with-Regret' – footnoted by Hugo: 'À l'échafaud', 'to the scaffold', i.e. the guillotine.

taking a left turn instead of a right in the corridor to the interrogation room.

Gavroche admired this skilfulness. 'What a dentist!' he cried.

Montparnasse added a few details about Babet's escape, concluding, 'And that's not all!'

While listening, Gavroche had grasped a cane that Montparnasse was holding in his hand. Without thinking, he pulled on the upper part and the blade of a dagger appeared.

'Oh!' he exclaimed, hastily pushing the dagger back inside. 'You've brought along your plain-clothes officer.'

Montparnasse winked.

'Gosh!' said Gavroche. 'So you're going to have a run-in with the bashers?'

'You never know,' Montparnasse replied, as if he did not care. 'It's always good to have a blade on you.'

Gavroche pressed him, 'So what're you doing tonight?'

Montparnasse came over all serious again and mumbled, 'Things.' And abruptly changing the conversation: 'By the way!'

'What?'

'Something happened the other day. Imagine. I run into this gent. He gives me a sermon as well as his purse. I put it in my pocket. A minute later I feel in my pocket. Nothing there.'

'Except the sermon,' said Gavroche.

'What about you,' said Montparnasse, 'where are you off to now?'

Gavroche pointed to his two dependants and said, 'I'm going to put these children to bed.'

'To bed where?'

'At my place.'

'Where's that?'

'At my place.'

'So you have lodgings?'

'Yes, I have.'

'And where are your lodgings?'

'Inside the elephant,' said Gavroche.

Though not one to be easily surprised, Montparnasse could not hold back an exclamation. 'Inside the elephant!'

'That's right, inside the elephant!' retorted Gavroche. 'Woddabowdit?'

This is another word in the language that no one writes and everyone speaks. 'Woddabowdit' means 'What about it?'

The gamin's profound remark calmed Montparnasse and brought

him back to his senses. He seemed to think better of Gavroche's lodgings.

'Of course,' he said. 'Yes, the elephant. Comfortable, is it?'

'Very,' said Gavroche. 'I tell you, real cosy. There're no draughts like under the bridges.'

'How do you get in?'

'I get in.'

'So there's a hole?' asked Montparnasse.

'Sure there is! But you mustn't tell anyone. It's between the front legs. The *coqueurs** haven't seen it.'

'And you climb in? Yes, I see.'

'There's a knack to it, upsadaisy and you're there.'

After a pause Gavroche added, 'I'll get a ladder for these young 'uns.'

Montparnasse burst out laughing. 'Where the devil did you pick up those kids?'

Gavroche replied simply, 'They're nippers that a hairdresser gave me as a present.'

Meanwhile, Montparnasse had become pensive. 'You recognized me very easily,' he murmured.

He took out of his pocket two small objects that were actually just two quill tips wrapped in cotton, and stuck one up each nostril. This gave him a different nose.

'That changes the look of you!' said Gavroche. 'Makes you less ugly. You should keep them like that all the time.'

Montparnasse was a good-looking lad, but Gavroche was a joker.

'Seriously,' said Montparnasse, 'how do I look?'

The sound of his voice was also different. In a twinkling Montparnasse had become unrecognizable.

'Oh! Do Porrichinelle† for us!' cried Gavroche.

The two children, who had so far not been listening, busy as they were with sticking their fingers up their noses, came over on hearing this name and stared at Montparnasse with stirrings of joy and admiration.

Unfortunately, Montparnasse was worried.

He laid his hand on Gavroche's shoulder and said to him, emphasizing his words, 'Listen to me, lad, I've something to tell you! If I was standing in the square with my *dogue*, my *dague* and my *digue*, and I was to be offered fifty centimes, I wouldn't turn a blind eye to it, no

---

* Footnoted by Hugo: 'Mouchards, gens de police', 'Grasses, police informers'.

† A childish mispronunciation (also a dialect form) of *Polichinelle* (Pulchinello).

indeed I wouldn't, sorely tempted would I be, but a diabolical quandary I'd find myself in.'

This peculiar statement produced a remarkable effect on the gamin. He turned sharply, his little beady eyes looking round with keen attention, and noticed a police officer standing with his back to them a few paces away. Gavroche let out an 'Ah! I see!' that he immediately repressed, and shaking Montparnasse's hand, he said, 'Well, good night. I'm off to my elephant with my young 'uns. Supposing you were to need me some night, that's where you'd come and find me. I'm just above the ground floor. There's no porter. Ask for Monsieur Gavroche.'

'All right,' said Montparnasse.

And they parted, Montparnasse heading off in the direction of La Grève, and Gavroche towards the Bastille. The little five-year-old, dragged along by his brother, who was being dragged along by Gavroche, looked back several times to watch 'Porrichinelle' walking away.

The obscure statement by which Montparnasse had warned Gavroche of the presence of the policeman contained no other talisman than assonance – *dy* repeated five or six times in different forms. This syllable, *dy*, uttered not in isolation but artfully blended into the words of a sentence, means 'Take care, we can't talk freely any more.'* There was, besides, in Montparnasse's sentence, a literary beauty that was lost on Gavroche, that 'my *dogue*, my *dague* and my *digue*', an expression in the argot of the Temple district meaning 'my dog, my knife and my wife', greatly in vogue among clowns and buffoons during that golden age when Molière was writing and Callot was doing his drawings.

Twenty years ago, in the south-west corner of Place de la Bastille, near the canal basin dug out of the ancient moat of the fortress-prison, you could still see a bizarre monument that has already faded from the memories of Parisians and which deserved to leave some lasting impression, for it was the brainchild of 'a member of the Institute, the general-in-chief of the army of Egypt'.

We say 'monument', although it was only a preparatory model. But

---

* The assonant syllable in the French text is *deeg*: 'Écoute ce que je te *dis*, garçon, si j'étais sur la place, avec mon dogue, ma dague et ma *dig*ue, et si vous me pro*dig*uiez *dix* gros sous, je ne refuserais pas *d'y* goupiner, mais nous ne sommes pas le mar*di* gras'. When the text is translated directly into English that repetition is lost, so I have slightly reworded the text with the recurring syllable *dy* (rhyming with *why*).

this model itself, an extraordinary specimen, the grandiose carcass of one of Napoleon's ideas, which two or three successive gusts of wind have carried away and removed further from us each time, had become historic and acquired some sort of permanence that contrasted with its provisional appearance. It was an elephant forty feet high, built of timber and masonry, carrying on its back a tower that looked like a house, once painted green by some handyman and now painted black by the heavens, the rain and the passage of time. In this unfrequented and exposed corner of the square, the broad brow of this colossus, its trunk, its tusks, its tower, its enormous rump, its four pillar-like legs, at night formed an astonishing and awesome silhouette against the starry sky. There was no knowing what it meant. It was in the manner of a symbol of popular strength. It was dark, enigmatic, huge. It was some sort of visible mighty phantom standing next to the invisible spectre of the Bastille.

Few strangers visited this edifice, no passer-by gave it a glance. It was falling to pieces. With every season, bits of plaster came away, forming hideous wounds in its sides. The 'city fathers', as the locals elegantly refer to the municipal authorities, had forgotten it since 1814. There it stood in its corner, looking glum, sickly, in a bad way, surrounded by a rotting fence, constantly pissed on by drunken coachmen. Its belly was full of cracks, a wooden batten stuck out of its tail, weeds grew high around its legs. And as the level of the square had been rising all around it for thirty years, by that slow and continuous process that imperceptibly raises the floor of big cities, it stood in a hollow, and the earth underneath appeared to be giving way. It was foul, despised, repellent and superb, an ugly sight to respectable people, a doleful sight to the reflective mind. There was something about it suggestive of rubbish that is about to be swept away, and of majesty that is about to be beheaded.

As we have said, at night its appearance changed. Night is the true element of everything that is shadow. As soon as dusk fell, the old elephant was transfigured. It cut a tranquil and formidable figure in the dreadful serenity of the dark. Being of the past, it belonged to the night. This obscurity went with its grandeur.

This crude, squat, heavy, forbidding, austere, almost misshapen but certainly majestic monument, stamped with a kind of magnificent and untamed gravity, has disappeared, and the gigantic stove of sorts, adorned with its pipe, that has replaced the sombre fortress with its nine towers, more or less as the bourgeoisie replaces the feudal classes, is left to reign in peace. It is quite natural that a stove should be the symbol of an era in which power resides in a cooking-pot. This era will pass, it is already passing. People are beginning to understand that while there might be power in a boiler, there can be no authority except in a brain. In other words, what lead and drive the world are not locomotives, but ideas. Harness locomotives to ideas, fair enough, but do not mistake the horse for the rider.

Be that as it may, to return to Place de la Bastille, the architect of this elephant had succeeded in creating something significant out of plaster. The architect of the stove pipe has succeeded in creating something insignificant out of bronze.

This stove pipe, which has been given a portentous name – it is called 'the July Column' – this misconceived monument of an abortive revolution was still encased in 1832 in a great sheath of scaffolding – we ourselves were sorry to see it go – and fenced off behind a vast wooden enclosure that made the isolation of the elephant complete.

It was towards that corner of the square, with only the reflection of a distant street lamp to cast a dim light on it, that the gamin guided his two 'young 'uns'.

May we slip a word in at this point, and remind you that we are talking about reality here? Twenty years ago a child that had been caught asleep inside the elephant of the Bastille was brought before the magistrates' court on charges of vagabondage and damage to a public monument. Bearing that in mind, let us continue.

As they neared the colossus, appreciating the effect that the infinitely great can produce on the infinitely small, Gavroche said, 'Don't be frightened, kids!'

Then he slipped through a gap in the fence into the elephant enclosure and helped the youngsters to clamber through the hole. A little scared, the two children followed Gavroche without a word and entrusted themselves to providence in the shape of this ragged little fellow who had given them bread and promised them shelter.

Lying by the fence was a ladder that was used during the day by the workmen in the neighbouring timber-yard. Gavroche lifted it with remarkable strength, and propped it against one of the elephant's forelegs. Near where the ladder ended, a kind of black hole in the belly of the colossus was discernible.

Gavroche showed his guests the ladder and the hole, and said to them, 'Climb up and go inside.'

The two little boys exchanged terrified glances.

'You kids are scared!' exclaimed Gavroche. And he added, 'You'll see!'

He grasped the rough-surfaced leg of the elephant and in a twinkling, without bothering to use the ladder, he had reached the opening. He crept in like an adder slipping into a crevice, and disappeared, then a moment later the two children saw his pale face appear as a bleary whitishness at the edge of the shadow-filled hole.

'Well, climb up then, you nippers!' he exclaimed. 'You'll see how cosy it is! Up you come!' he said to the older one. 'I'll reach down for you.'

The little ones nudged shoulders. The gamin frightened and at the same time reassured them, and besides, it was raining heavily. The older one decided to risk it. Watching his brother climb up, leaving him on his own between the legs of this great beast, the younger one very much wanted to cry, but dared not.

Unsteadily, the older boy mounted the rungs of the ladder. Gavroche coaxed him up with the blandishments of a fencing-master to his pupils or of a mule-driver to his mules.

'Don't be scared! That's it! Keep going! Put your foot there! Your hand here! Go on!'

And when the child was within reach, he grabbed him briskly and vigorously by the arm, and pulled the youngster towards him.

'Got you!' he cried.

The child was through the hole.

'Now,' said Gavroche, 'you just wait for me. Monsieur, be so good as to sit yourself down.'

And going out the way he had come in, he slipped down the elephant's leg with the agility of a marmoset, landed on his feet in the grass, grabbed the five-year-old round the waist and planted him right in the middle of the ladder, then began to climb up after him, shouting up to the older one, 'I'm going to push, you're going to pull.'

And in no time the little lad was up the ladder, pushed, dragged, pulled, bundled and stuffed into the hole before he knew what had happened to him, and Gavroche, coming in behind him, kicked away the ladder, which fell on to the grass, and began to clap his hands, crying, 'We're in! Long live General Lafayette!'

Once this outburst was over, he added, 'This is my home, kids.'

And this was indeed Gavroche's home.

O unforeseen usefulness of the useless! The benevolence of big things! The kindliness of giants! This huge monument that contained an idea of the emperor's had become a refuge to a street urchin. The lad had been taken in and sheltered by the colossus. Respectable citizens who walked past the elephant of the Bastille in their Sunday best were fond of saying as they viewed it contemptuously with their bulging eyes, 'What purpose does that serve?' The purpose of saving from

859

the cold, frost, hail and rain, of sheltering from the winter wind, of sparing from having to sleep in the mud, which causes fever, and having to sleep in the snow, which causes death, a young creature with no mother, no father, no food, no winter clothes, no roof over his head. The purpose of providing a safe haven to the innocent spurned by society. The purpose of lessening the failings of society. It was a retreat open to one against whom all doors were shut. It was as if the poor old mastodon, swarming with vermin and falling into oblivion, covered with warts, mould and ulcers, ramshackle, worm-eaten, abandoned, condemned, as if this colossal beggar of sorts, in the middle of the crossroads, vainly beseeching a kindly glance, had taken pity on that other beggar, the poor little pygmy who went about with no shoes on his feet, no roof over his head, blowing on his fingers, dressed in rags, living on scraps. That was the purpose the elephant of the Bastille served. That idea of Napoleon's, scorned by men, had been taken up by God. What would have been merely illustrious had become sublime. In order to realize what he had in mind the emperor would have needed porphyry, brass, iron, gold, marble. For God, the tumbledown assemblage of wooden planks, girders and plaster sufficed. The emperor had had a dream of inspired genius. In that fabulous Titanic elephant, armed, raising its trunk, carrying its tower, and with life-giving water joyously gushing all around it, he wanted to embody the people. God had done something greater: he had housed a child in it.

The hole through which Gavroche had entered was a crack barely visible from the outside, concealed as it was, as we have said, in the elephant's belly, and so narrow that it was only cats and children and not much more that could slip through it.

'Let's begin,' said Gavroche, 'by telling the porter we're not at home.'

And plunging into the darkness with the confidence of someone with an intimate knowledge of his living quarters, he took a plank and covered the hole with it.

Gavroche dived back into the darkness. The children heard the spurt of the match inserted into the phosphoric box. The chemical match did not yet exist. At that time the Fumade lighter represented progress.

A sudden brightness made them blink. Gavroche had just managed to light one of those bits of cord dipped in resin, called 'cellar rats'. The cellar rat, which smoked more than illuminated, made the inside of the elephant dimly visible.

Gavroche's two guests looked around them, and felt something rather similar to what anyone shut up inside the great Heidelberg tun would feel, or better still what Jonah must have felt in the biblical belly of the whale. A whole gigantic skeleton appeared, in which they were enveloped. Above, a long brown beam set at regular intervals with massive curved ribs represented the vertebral column with its ribcage, stalactites of plaster hung from them like viscera, and vast spiders' webs stretching from one side to the other looked like dusty diaphragms. You could see here and there in the corners big blobs of blackishness that seemed to be alive, scuttling about, abrupt and startled in their movements.

Debris that had fallen from the elephant's back into its belly had filled up the cavity so that it was possible to walk about as if there were a floor inside.

The younger child huddled up close to his brother and whispered, 'It's dark.'

This remark prompted an exclamation from Gavroche. The petrified look of the two kids called for a shake-up.

'What are you grousing about?' he cried. 'Are we joking? Are we being fussy? You're not expecting the Tuileries? Where are your manners? I warn you, I'm not the type that's going to put up with any nonsense. Now, tell me, just who do you think you are?'

A little chivvying is a good way of dealing with fear. It is reassuring. The two children moved closer to Gavroche.

Touched in a fatherly way by this trustfulness, Gavroche switched 'from grave to light'*, and addressed the youngest: 'Nitwit,' he said, delivering the insult in an affectionate tone of voice, 'it's outside that it's dark. Outside it's raining, in here it isn't. Outside it's cold, in here there's not the tiniest bit of wind. Outside there are heaps of people, in here there's no one. Outside there's not even a moon, in here there's my candle, for goodness' sake!'

The two children began to look at their lodgings with less terror. But Gavroche did not give them much more time to dwell on them.

'Get a move on,' he said.

And he herded them towards what we are very glad to be able to call the far end of the room. There was his bed. Gavroche's bed was the whole works. That is to say, it had a mattress, a blanket, and an

---

* A quotation from Boileau's *Art Poétique*, canto 1, lines 75–6: 'Heureux qui, dans ses vers, sait d'une voix légère / Passer du grave au doux, du plaisant au sévère.' In Dryden's translation: 'Happy who in his verse can gently steer / From grave to light, from pleasant to severe.'

alcove with curtains. The mattress was a straw mat, the blanket a rather long strip of grey woollen stuff – it was very warm and almost new.

This is what the alcove consisted of: three fairly long poles, fixed firmly into the rubble underfoot – that is to say, in the elephant's belly – two in front and one behind, and roped together at the top so as to form a pyramidal structure. This structure supported a lattice of wire-netting that was simply but artfully laid over it and held in place with wire fastenings so that it completely encased the three struts. A row of heavy stones kept this lattice pinned to the floor all the way round, so that nothing could get under it. The lattice was none other than a piece of the copper mesh used to cover aviaries in zoos. Gavroche's bed was behind this mesh, as in a cage. The whole thing looked like an Eskimo's tent. It was this mesh that took the place of curtains.

Gavroche shifted the stones that kept the wire-netting pinned down in front, and the two overlapping flaps of the trellis opened up.

'Down on all fours, kids!' said Gavroche.

He helped his guests carefully make their way into the cage, then crawled in after them, pulled the stones back in place, and sealed the opening again.

All three were stretched out on the mat. Small as they were, none of them could have stood upright in the alcove. Gavroche still had the cellar rat in his hand.

'Now, get some shut-eye,' he said. 'I'm going to put out the light from our candelabra.'

'Monsieur,' the older of the two brothers asked Gavroche, pointing to the netting, 'what's that?'

'That', Gavroche said solemnly, 'is for the rats. Get some shut-eye!'

Yet he felt obliged to say a few words more for the education of these young creatures. He went on, 'It comes from the Jardin des Plantes. It's for the wild animals. Z'a (there is a) whole storeroom full of it. Juzz'afta (you just have to) climb over a wall, crawl through a window and get past a door. There's as much as you want.'

While talking, he wrapped one end of the blanket round the little one, who murmured, 'Oh, that's lovely and warm!'

Gavroche eyed the blanket with satisfaction.

'That's from the Jardin des Plantes too,' he said. 'I pinched it from the monkeys.'

And pointing out to the eldest the mat on which he was lying, a very thick and well made mat, he added, 'That was the giraffe's.'

After a pause he continued, 'The animals had all this. I took it away from them. They didn't mind. I told them: "It's for the elephant."'

He fell silent again, and then went on, 'You climb over walls and you couldn't care less about the government. So there!'

The two children stared with a timorous and astounded respect at this intrepid and resourceful creature, a vagabond like them, all on his own like them, a little nobody like them, about whom there was something wretched yet all-powerful, who seemed supernatural to them, and whose face was a composite of an old fairground tout's every grimace combined with the most ingenuous and charming smile.

'Monsieur,' said the older one timidly, 'you're not afraid of the police, then?'

Gavroche replied simply, 'Kid, you don't say "police", you say "bashers".'

The little one had his eyes open but said nothing. As he was on the edge of the mat, the older one being in the middle, Gavroche tucked the blanket under him as a mother might have done, and plumped up the mat under his head with some old rags to make a pillow for the lad. Then he turned to the elder one.

'We're cosy as can be in here, eh?'

'Oh, yes!' replied the older one, gazing at Gavroche with the expression of a rescued angel.

The two poor little children, who had been wet through, began to warm up again.

'Well, then,' Gavroche went on, 'why were you crying?'

And pointing to the little one, Gavroche said to his brother, 'I'm not talking about a mite like that, but crying at your age, it's stupid. It makes you look like a cry-baby.'

'Well, we had nowhere to stay,' replied the child.

'Kid!' said Gavroche. 'You don't say nowhere "to stay", you say nowhere "to doss".'

'And besides, we were afraid of being all on our own at night.'

'You don't say "night", you say "darktime".'

'Thank you, monsieur,' said the child.

'Listen,' Gavroche went on, 'you must never ever snivel again over nothing. I'll take care of you. You'll see what fun we'll have. In summer we'll go to La Glacière with Navet, a comrade of mine, we'll swim in the canal basin, we'll run stark-naked on the barges in front of the Pont d'Austerlitz – that riles the washerwomen. They shout and holler, if you only knew how funny they are! We'll go and see the skeleton man. He's alive! In the Champs-Élysées. He's as thin as anything, that character. And then I'll take you to the theatre. I'll take you to see Frédérick Lemaître. I've got tickets, I know some actors, I was even in a play once. We were little kids, and we ran under a sheet, and that made the sea. I'll get you a job at my theatre. We'll go and see the savages. They're not real savages, these ones. They wear pink maillots that wrinkle, and you can see where their elbows've been darned with white thread. After that, we'll go to the Opéra. We'll go in with the hired clappers. The hired clappers at the Opéra are very select. I wouldn't go with the clappers on the boulevards. At the Opéra, imagine, there's some who pay twenty sous, but they're boobies. Wet rags we call them. And then we'll go and watch the guillotine at work. I'll show you the executioner. He lives in Rue des Marais. Monsieur Sanson. There's a letter-box in his front door. Oh! we'll have terrific fun!'

At that moment a drop of wax fell on Gavroche's finger and brought him back to the realities of life.

'Drat!' he said. 'We're using up the wick. Careful now! I can't spend more than a sou a month on lighting. When you go to bed, you have to sleep. We haven't time to read Monsieur Paul de Kock's romances. Besides, the light might show through the cracks in the carriage entrance, and the bashers would only have to see it.'

'And a spark might fall on the straw,' the older boy timidly remarked, being the only one who dared talk to Gavroche and engage in a conversation with him, 'we must be careful not to burn the house down.'

'You don't say "burn the house down",' said Gavroche, 'you say "fry the gaff".'

The storm intensified. Amid the claps of thunder you could hear the rain beating down on the colossus's back.

'Bamboozled you, rain!' said Gavroche. 'I like hearing it come bucketing down the legs of the house. Winter's a fool. It's wasting its reserves, it's wasting its time, it can't wet us, and that's making it grumble, the silly old water-carrier.'

This allusion to the thunder, which as a nineteenth-century philosopher Gavroche accepted with all its consequences, was followed by a great flash of lightning so dazzling that something of it penetrated the crack in the elephant's belly. Almost at the same instant, the thunder rumbled, very angrily. The two little ones cried out and sat up so abruptly the trellis very nearly came apart. But Gavroche turned his fearless face to them and took advantage of the clap of thunder to burst out laughing.

'Steady on, children. Don't wreck the place! Now that's what I call thunder. And that was no piddling lightning! Bravo, God! That was almost as good as at the Ambigu.'

With that, he set the netting to rights, gently pushed the two children down on to the bed, pressing on their knees so they were lying full length, properly stretched out, and exclaimed, 'Since the good Lord is lighting his candle, I can blow mine out. Children, you must go to sleep now, my young humans. It's very bad not to sleep. It makes your trap pong, or as they say in polite society, it makes your gob stink. Wrap up well in the blanket! I'm putting the light out. All right?'

'Yes,' murmured the elder, 'I'm fine. I feel as if I've got feathers under my head.'

'You don't say "head",' cried Gavroche, 'you say "block"!'

The two children cuddled up together, Gavroche made sure they were lying comfortably on the mat, drew the blanket up to their ears, then for the third time repeated his instruction expressed in esoteric language, 'Get some shut-eye!'

And he snuffed out the candle stub.

No sooner was the light extinguished than the netting the three children were lying under was disturbed by a strange shaking. A multitude of mysterious scrabblings that produced a metallic sound, as if claws and teeth were gnawing at the copper wire. This was accompanied by all sorts of little squealings.

Hearing this din above his head and frozen with terror, the five-year-old lad nudged his older brother but the older brother was already 'getting some shut-eye', as Gavroche had told him to. So the little one, beside himself with fear, dared to address Gavroche, but very quietly and with bated breath.

'Monsieur?'

'Huh?' said Gavroche, who had just closed his eyes.

'What's that?'

'It's rats,' replied Gavroche. And he laid his head down on the mat again.

Indeed the rats, in their teeming thousands inside the elephant carcass, were those live black blobs that we have already mentioned; and they had been kept at a distance by the flame of the candle as long as it was alight. But as soon as this cavern, their city, as it were, was restored to darkness, scenting what good old Perrault the storyteller calls 'fresh meat'* they had come swarming over Gavroche's

---

* An allusion to the story of Tom Thumb, 'Le Petit Poucet', in Perrault's *Tales of Mother Goose*, in which the Ogre smells the presence of Petit Poucet and his brothers.

tent, climbed to the top of it, and were biting at the mesh as though trying to penetrate this new type of mosquito net.

Still the little one could not sleep, and he had another question.

'Monsieur?'

'Huh?' said Gavroche.

'What's rats?'

'They're mice.'

This explanation somewhat reassured the child. He had seen white mice before, and he was not afraid of them. Nevertheless, he piped up yet again.

'Monsieur?'

'Huh?' said Gavroche.

'Why haven't you got a cat?'

'I did have one,' replied Gavroche, 'I brought one back but they ate it.'

This second explanation undid the work of the first, and the little one started trembling again. The dialogue between him and Gavroche resumed for the fourth time.

'Monsieur?'

'Huh?'

'Who was it that got eaten?'

'The cat.'

'And who was it that ate the cat?'

'The rats.'

'The mice?'

'Yes, the rats.'

Dismayed by these mice that ate cats, the child went on, 'Monsieur, would those mice eat us?'

'Wouldn't they just!' said Gavroche.

The child was now utterly terror-stricken.

But Gavroche added, 'Don't be afraid. They can't get in. And besides, I'm right here! Look, hold my hand. Hush now and get some shut-eye!'

As he spoke, Gavroche reached across the boy's brother and took the little lad's hand. The child kept the hand clasped closely to him and felt reassured. Courage and strength are mysteriously transmitted. Silence re-established itself around them once more. The sound of their voices had frightened off the rats. No matter that they would be in a frenzy again a few minutes later, the three youngsters were fast asleep and heard nothing more.

The hours of night went by. Darkness covered the vast Place de la

Bastille. A winter wind blustered, mingled with rain. Patrols searched doorways, alleyways, secluded areas and dark corners, looking for nocturnal vagrants, and silently passed by the elephant. Standing motionless, open-eyed in the dark, the monster appeared to be dreaming as if contented with its good deed, sheltering from the heavens and from men the three poor sleeping children.

In order to understand what is to follow, remember that at that time the Bastille guard-house was situated at the other end of the square, and that what took place near the elephant could be neither seen nor heard by the night watch.

As the hour immediately before dawn drew to a close, a man came running out of Rue St-Antoine, across the square, round the perimeter of the July Column enclosure, and slipped through the fence until he was right under the elephant's belly. If any light had been cast on that man, you would have been able to tell from how thoroughly drenched he was that he had spent the night in the rain. Once under the elephant, he could be heard to make a peculiar cry that belonged to no human language and that only a parakeet could have imitated. Twice he repeated this cry, of which the following spelling can barely convey any notion: 'Kirikikiew!'

At the second cry a bright and cheerful young voice responded from the elephant's belly, 'Yes!'

Almost immediately the plank blocking up the hole moved aside, letting out a child who slid down the elephant's leg and landed nimbly next to the man. It was Gavroche. The man was Montparnasse.

As for his cry 'Kirikikiew!', this was probably what the child meant when he said, 'Ask for Monsieur Gavroche.'

On hearing it, he had woken with a start, crawled out of his 'alcove', pushing the netting aside a little, which he had carefully closed up again, then he had opened the trap-door and descended.

In the dark, the man and the child silently acknowledged each other.

Montparnasse confined himself to saying, 'We need you. Come and give us a hand.'

The lad asked for no further elucidation. 'I'm ready,' he said.

And both headed off towards Rue St-Antoine, where Montparnasse had come from, swiftly winding their way through the long line of market-gardeners' carts that come down to market at that time of day.

Huddled in their wagons, half asleep among the salads and vegetables, cloaked up to the eyebrows on account of the beating rain, the market-gardeners did not even glance at these strange passers-by.

The Vicissitudes of Escape

This is what had taken place that same night at La Force:

An escape had been planned jointly by Babet, Brujon, Gueulemer and Thénardier, although Thénardier was in solitary confinement. Babet had pulled it off for himself that same day, as we know from what Montparnasse told Gavroche.

Montparnasse was supposed to help them from outside.

During a month spent in a punishment cell, Brujon had had time firstly to weave a rope, secondly to work out a plan. In the old days those harsh places where under prison discipline the convict is left to himself were composed of four stone walls, a stone ceiling, a stone-flagged floor, a camp bed, a grated window and an iron-clad door, and were called dungeons. But the dungeon was judged to be too dreadful. Nowadays they are composed of an iron door, a grated window, a camp bed, a stone-flagged floor, four stone walls and a stone ceiling, and they are called punishment cells. They get a little daylight around noon. The drawback with these cells, which, as we can see, are not dungeons, is that people who should be made to work are left to daydream.

So Brujon daydreamed, and he came out of the punishment cell with a rope. As he was considered very dangerous in the Cour Charlemagne, he was put in the New Building. The first thing he found in the New Building was Gueulemer, the second was a nail. Gueulemer meant crime. A nail meant freedom.

It is time we formed a complete picture of Brujon. With an apparently delicate constitution and a deeply cultivated languidness, Brujon was a well mannered, intelligent bruiser and thief, who had a gentle look in his eyes and a ghastly smile. The look in his eyes was intentional, his smile was natural.

In pursuit of his art his first studies focused on roofs. He made great strides in the business of lead-stripping, whose practitioners strip roofs and take gutters to pieces by the process known as 'double-padding'*.

What made this point in time a thoroughly favourable one for an attempted escape was that right then roofers were re-laying and re-pointing a section of the prison's roof tiles. Cour St-Bernard was no longer totally isolated from Cour Charlemagne and Cour St-Louis. Up

---

* With the stolen sheets of lead wrapped round the thief as padding: '*au gras-double*', in Hugo's words.

there were ladders and scaffolding – in other words, bridges and stairways to freedom.

There was nothing in the world more dilapidated and more full of cracks than the New Building. It was the prison's weak spot. The walls were so eroded by saltpetre that the dormitory vaults had to be lined with wood because of loose grit falling on the prisoners in their beds. Despite this decrepitude, the mistake was made of confining in the New Building those facing the most serious charges, of detaining here 'the hard cases', as they say in prison parlance.

The New Building contained four dormitories, one on top of the other, and a garret called the Bel-Air. A large chimney flue, probably from some ancient kitchen of the Ducs de la Force, went from the ground floor, rising through four storeys, dividing all the dormitories in two with the kind of flattened pillar it created, and out through the roof.

Gueulemer and Brujon were in the same dormitory. As a precaution, they had been put on the lower floor. As chance would have it, the heads of their beds were up against the chimney. Thénardier was directly above them in that garret known as Bel-Air.

Any passer-by who stops on Rue Culture-Ste-Catherine, past the firemen's barracks, in front of the carriage entrance to the bath-house, sees a courtyard full of flowers and shrubs in wooden tubs, and at the far end, with two wings extending from it, a little white rotunda brightened up with green shutters, Jean-Jacques's bucolic dream. Not more than ten years ago, above that rotunda rose a huge, stark, hideous black wall, which it backed on to. This was the wall of La Force's perimeter walkway.

That wall beyond the rotunda was Milton towering above Berquin.

High as this wall was, there was a still darker roof beyond, which could be seen looming above it. This was the roof of the New Building, in which were to be noted four dormer windows, reinforced with bars. These were the Bel-Air windows. A chimney came out of this roof; this was the chimney that went through the dormitories.

Bel-Air, that garret in the New Building, was a kind of large mansarded hall, locked behind triple bars and iron-clad doors with huge studs all over them. When you entered from the north end, you had on your left the four dormer windows and on your right, facing the windows, four square cells, quite spacious, set apart from each other, with narrow corridors between them, brick-built to chest height, then with iron bars up to the roof.

Thénardier had been in solitary confinement in one of these cells since the night of the third of February. No one was ever able to discover how, and with whose complicity, he managed to procure and hide a bottle of that wine said to have been invented by Desrues, which has a narcotic added to it and was made famous by the Sleep-inducers gang.

There are in many prisons treacherous employees, part-time gaol-ers, part-time thieves, who are involved in escapes, who sell their disloyal services to the police, pocketing their dishonestly gotten gains. So on the very same night that young Gavroche picked up the two stray children, Brujon and Gueulemer, knowing that Babet, who had escaped that morning, was waiting for them in the street together with Montparnasse, quietly got up and, with the nail that Brujon had found, began to make a hole in the chimney by the end of their beds. The detritus fell on Brujon's bed, so could not be heard. The wet thun-dery squalls shook the doors on their hinges, creating a terrible and useful din inside the prison. Those prisoners who woke up pretended to go back to sleep, letting Gueulemer and Brujon get on with it. Bru-jon was deft, Gueulemer was strong. Before any sound reached the guard, who was bedded down behind the bars of the cell from which the dormitory was kept under surveillance, the hole in the wall had been made, the chimney climbed, the iron grating over the top of the chimney flue forced open, and the two dangerous criminals were on the roof. The wind and rain intensified, the roof was slippery.

'*Quelle bonne sorgue pour une crampe!*'* said Brujon.

A chasm six feet broad and eighty feet deep separated them from the perimeter walkway. At the bottom of this chasm they could see a sentry's musket gleaming in the dark. They fastened one end of the rope that Brujon had woven in his dungeon to the stumps of those iron bars over the chimney that they had just bent back, threw the other end over the perimeter walkway, in one bound leapt across the chasm, clung to the coping on the wall, straddled it, slid one after the other down the rope on to a little roof adjoining the bath-house, pulled the rope after them, jumped down into the bath-house court-yard, crossed it, then pushed open the porter's hatch next to which hung the door-pull, used the door-pull to open the carriage entrance, and found themselves out in the street.

It was not three-quarters of an hour since they had got out of bed in the dark, nail in hand, scheme in mind.

A few moments later they had joined Babet and Montparnasse, who were lurking near by.

* Footnoted by Hugo: 'Quelle bonne nuit pour une évasion!', 'What a good night for an escape!'

In pulling their rope down after them, they had broken it, and a bit was left attached to the chimney on the roof. That apart, they had suffered no other loss or injury except having almost entirely chafed the skin off their hands.

That night Thénardier had been tipped off, nobody could explain how, and was not asleep. Around one o'clock in the morning, it being a very dark night, he saw on the roof, in the wind and rain, two shadows pass in front of the dormer window opposite his cage. One stopped at the window long enough to take a look inside. It was Brujon. Thénardier recognized him, and understood. He did not need to be told any more.

Thénardier, identified as a cut-throat and detained on charges of organizing a night-time ambush with threat of violence, was kept under armed surveillance. A sentry, relieved every two hours, was posted in front of his cage with a loaded musket. Bel-Air was lit by a wall-lamp. The prisoner had on his feet a pair of fetters weighing fifty pounds. Every day at four o'clock in the afternoon a guard escorted by two mastiffs – this was still the practice at that time – entered his cage, left beside his bed a two-pound loaf of black bread, a jug of water, a bowlful of thinnish gruel with a few beans swimming in it, inspected his fetters and tapped the bars. This man with his mastiffs came back twice during the night.

Thénardier had obtained permission to keep a kind of iron spike that he used to nail his bread to a crack in the wall, 'to save it from the rats,' he said. As Thénardier was kept under watch this spike was not thought to present any risk. However, it was later remembered that one of the gaolers had said, 'It would be better to let him have just a wooden spike.'

At two o'clock in the morning there was a change of guard, and the sentry, who was an old soldier, was replaced by a conscript. A few moments later the man with the dogs paid his visit, then went away without having noticed anything except perhaps how very young the 'soldier-boy' was, and what a 'country bumpkin' he looked. Two hours afterwards, at four o'clock, when the relief guard came along, the conscript was found asleep next to Thénardier's cage where he had fallen to the ground in a heap. As for Thénardier, he was no longer there. His broken fetters lay on the floor. There was a hole in the ceiling of his cage and another hole in the roof above. A wooden plank had been torn off his bed and probably carried away, for it was never found. A half-empty bottle containing the remains of the drug-laced wine that had put the soldier to sleep was also seized from the cell. The soldier's bayonet had disappeared.

When this discovery was made it was assumed that Thénardier was completely out of range. The truth is, he was no longer in the New Building, but he was still in grave danger. He had not yet made his get-away.

On reaching the roof of the New Building, Thénardier had found the remains of Brujon's rope hanging from the bars of the grating that had closed off the chimney flue, but as this piece of rope was much too short he was not able to escape over the perimeter walkway, as Brujon and Gueulemer had done.

When you turn off Rue des Ballets into Rue du Roi-de-Sicile, you come almost at once to a squalid gap. In the last century there was a house here, of which all that remains is the back wall, the wall of a real barn of a place, rising between the adjoining buildings to third-floor level. This ruin is recognizable by the two large square windows still to be seen in it. The one in the middle, nearest the right-end gable, is barred with a worm-eaten beam, set strut-wise inside it. Through these windows you used to be able to see a grim high wall that was a section of La Force's perimeter wall.

The space the demolished house has left on the street is half filled with a fence of rotten planks, shored up by five stone posts. Hidden inside the enclosure is a small shack built up against the ruin left standing. The fence has a gate in it that a few years ago closed only on a latch.

It was on top of this ruin that Thénardier ended up a little after three in the morning.

How had he got there? That is what no one has ever been able to explain or understand. The lightning must have been both a help and a hindrance to him. Had he made use of the roofers' ladders and scaffolding to get from roof to roof, enclosure to enclosure, section to section, to the Cour Charlemagne buildings, then on to the Cour St-Louis buildings, the perimeter wall, and from there to the ruin on Rue du Roi-de-Sicile? But that route posed problems that would have seemed to make it impossible. Did he use the wooden plank from his bed as a bridge from the Bel-Air roof to the perimeter walkway, and crawl flat on his stomach along the coping of the outer wall all around the prison to the ruined building? But the perimeter wall of La Force formed a crenellated and irregular line. It rose and fell, it went down by the firemen's barracks, then it went up by the bath-house, intermediary structures cut across it; it was not the same height above Hôtel Lamoignon as above Rue Pavée, there were sheer drops and right-angled corners everywhere. And besides, the sentries would have seen the fugitive's dark silhouette. So this way too, how Thénardier man-

872

aged it remains more or less inexplicable. Impossible to escape either way. Inspired by that tremendous thirst for liberty that turns precipices into ditches, iron bars into willow hurdles, a sluggard into an athlete, a gouty cripple into a bird, stupidity into instinct, instinct into intelligence and intelligence into genius, had Thénardier come up with a third way? No one has ever found out.

You cannot always make sense of the miracles of escape. The man making his bid for freedom, let us say it again, is a man inspired. There is something of the shooting star and the streak of lightning in the mysterious shimmer of escape. The striving for deliverance is no less amazing than that winging towards the sublime. And it is said of an escaped thief, 'How did he manage to scale that wall?' just as it is said of Corneille, 'How did he come by that "He should have died"?'*

However that may be, dripping with perspiration, drenched with rain, his clothes in shreds, his hands raw, elbows bleeding, knees grazed, Thénardier had reached what in the concrete imagery of their language children call the 'knife-edge' of the ruin's wall, had stretched out full length on it, and there his strength had failed him. A sheer drop three storeys high separated him from the pavement.

The rope he had was too short.

There he waited, pale, exhausted, all hope that he had had now gone, still cloaked in darkness but telling himself that it was about to get light. Terror-stricken at the thought of hearing within a few moments the neighbouring clock of St-Paul strike four, the time when there would be a change of guard and the sentry would be found asleep under the roof with a hole in it. Staring blankly at the glimmer of the street lamps, at the dark wet pavement appallingly far below, beckoning and terrible, the paving that was both death and freedom.

He wondered whether his three fellow escapees had succeeded, whether they had waited for him and would come to his aid. He listened. Apart from one patrol, no one had passed in the street since he had been there. Nearly all the market-gardeners going to market, from Montreuil, Charonne, Vincennes, Bercy, come down Rue St-Antoine.

Four o'clock struck. Thénardier shuddered. A few moments later, from the prison came that frantic and confused clamour that follows

---

* Corneille's *Horace*, Act III, sc. vi: Julie: 'What would you have wanted him to do against three?' Horace the Elder: 'He should have died.' At this point in the play Horace the Elder, knowing that two of his sons have been killed in the defence of Rome, believes that his third, Horace the Younger, has fled the mortal fray. Horace's response in this instance – 'Qu'il mourût' – has been hailed by French critics, most notably Voltaire, as sublime.

the discovery of an escape. He could hear the sound of doors opening and shutting, the squeal of gates on their hinges, the commotion in the guard-house, the raucous shouts of the turnkeys, the clatter of gun butts on the yard flagstones. Lights went upstairs and downstairs at the barred windows of the dormitories, a torch ran along the roof ridge of the New Building, the firemen from the barracks next door had been called in. Their helmets, caught by torchlight in the rain, passed to and fro along the rooftops. At the same time Thénardier saw in the direction of the Bastille a pale tinge ominously bleaching the lower part of the sky.

He was on top of a wall ten inches wide, stretched out under the downpour, an abyss to right and left, incapable of moving, overcome by vertigo at the possibility of falling and by horror at the certainty of being arrested, and his mind, like the pendulum of a clock, swung from one of these thoughts to the other: 'Dead if I fall, caught if I stay.'

With the street still in complete darkness, in his anguish he suddenly saw a man slinking along close to the walls and coming from the direction of Rue Pavée; the man stopped at the gap above which Thénardier was, as it were, suspended. This man was joined by a second, walking just as warily, then by a third, then by a fourth. When these individuals were assembled, one of them lifted the latch of the gate in the fence, and all four of them entered the enclosure with the shack in it. They were standing directly below Thénardier. These men had obviously chosen this recess so that they could talk without being seen by passers-by or by the sentry guarding the La Force wicket-gate a few steps away. It must be said that the rain kept this sentry confined to his cabin. Unable to distinguish their faces, Thénardier listened to what they were saying with the desperate attention of a poor wretch who feels himself doomed.

Thénardier saw something resembling hope pass before his eyes: these men were talking in slang.

The first said in a low but distinct voice, '*Décarrons. Qu'est-ce que nous maquillons icigo?*'*

The second replied, '*Il lansquine à éteindre le riffe du rabouin. Et puis les coqueurs vont passer, il y a là un grivier qui porte gaffe, nous allons nous faire emballer icicaille.*'†

These two words, *icigo* and *icicaille*, which both mean 'here', the first belonging to the argot used by the toll-gates, the second to the argot of the Temple district, were rays of light to Thénardier. From *icigo* he recognized Brujon, who was a prowler at the gates, and from *icicaille* Babet, who, among all his other jobs, had been a second-hand dealer at the Temple.

The old-fashioned slang of the golden age is no longer spoken except in the Temple district, and Babet was actually the only person to speak it in a really pure form. Had it not been for that *icicaille*, Thénardier would not have recognized him, for he had completely disguised his voice.

In the meantime, the third man had chipped in. 'There's no hurry yet, let's wait a bit. How do we know he doesn't need us?'

From this, in ordinary French, Thénardier recognized Montparnasse, who distinguished himself by understanding all kinds of slang and speaking none.

As for the fourth, he remained silent, but his huge shoulders gave him away. Thénardier was in no doubt. It was Gueulemer.

Brujon replied almost impetuously, but still in a low voice: '*Qu'est-ce que tu nous bonis là? Le tapissier n'aura pas pu tirer sa crampe. Il ne sait pas le truc, quoi! Bouliner sa limace et faucher ses empaffes pour maquiller une tortouse, caler des boulins aux lourdes, braser des faffes, maquiller des caroubles, faucher les durs, balancer sa tortouse dehors, se planquer, se camoufler, il faut être mariol! Le vieux n'aura pas pu, il ne sait pas goupiner.*'*

Babet added, still in that classic, restrained slang that Poulailler and Cartouche spoke, and which is to the brazen, new, raffish, ribald slang used by Brujon what the language of Racine is to the language of André Chénier, '*Ton orgue tapissier aura été fait marron dans*

---

be coming by. There's a soldier posted on guard, we're going to get ourselves arrested here.'

* Footnoted by Hugo: '*Qu'est-ce que tu nous dis là? L'aubergiste n'a pas pu s'évader. Il ne sait pas le métier, quoi! Déchirer sa chemise et couper ses draps de lit pour faire une corde, faire des trous aux portes, fabriquer des faux papiers, faire des fausses clefs, couper ses fers, suspendre sa corde, se cacher, se déguiser, il faut être malin! Le vieux n'aura pas pu, il ne sait pas travailler*', 'What are you saying? The innkeeper hasn't managed to escape. It's not his line of business, after all! Ripping up your shirt and tearing up your bedsheet to make a rope, making holes in doors, forging false papers, making skeleton keys, cutting your fetters, slinging your rope, hiding, disguising yourself, you've got to be smart! The old man won't have been up to it, it's work he doesn't know how to do.'

l'escalier. Il faut être arcasien. C'est un galifard. Il se sera laissé jouer l'harnache par un roussin, peut-être même par un roussi, qui lui aura battu comtois. Prête l'oche, Montparnasse, entendus-tu ces criblements dans le collège? Tu as vu toutes ces camoufles. Il est tombé, va! Il en sera quitte pour tirer ses vingt longes. Je n'ai pas taf, je ne suis pas un taffeur, c'est colombé, mais il n'y a plus qu'à faire les lézards, ou autrement on nous la fera gambiller. Ne renaude pas, viens avec nousiergue, allons picter une rouillarde encible.'*

'You don't desert your friends when they're in trouble,' grumbled Montparnasse.

'*Je te bonis qu'il est malade!*' retorted Brujon. '*À l'heure qui toque, le tapissier ne vaut pas une broque! Nous n'y pouvons rien. Décarrons. Je crois à tout moment qu'un cogne me ceintre en pogne.*'†

Montparnasse was holding out only feebly now. The fact was, with that honour among thieves of never abandoning each other, these four men had been lurking around La Force all night long, regardless of the danger, in the hope of seeing Thénardier appear on the top of some wall. But with the night turning out to be only too dreadful – it was a downpour to empty the streets – with the cold creeping up on them, their rain-drenched clothes, their leaking shoes, the alarming hue and cry that had just broken out in the prison, the hours gone by, the patrols on the streets, hope fading, fear returning – everything urged

---

* Footnoted by Hugo: 'Ton aubergiste aura été pris sur le fait. Il faut être malin. C'est un apprenti. Il se sera laissé duper par un mouchard, peut-être même par un mouton, qui aura fait le compère. Écoute, Montparnasse, entends-tu ces cris dans la prison? Tu as vu toutes ces chandelles. Il est repris, va! Il en sera quitte pour faire ses vingt ans. Je n'ai pas peur, je ne suis pas un poltron, c'est connu, mais il n'y a plus rien à faire, ou autrement on nous la fera danser. Ne te fâche pas, viens avec nous, allons boire une bouteille de vieux vin ensemble', 'Your innkeeper must have been caught in the act. You've got to be smart. He's a novice. He must've been taken in by a snitch, perhaps even a nark who pretended to be a crony. Listen, Montparnasse, you hear that shouting in the prison? You've seen all those candles. He's been recaptured, believe me! He'll end up doing his twenty years. I'm not scared, I'm no coward, everyone knows that, but there's nothing more to be done, otherwise we'll be made to pay for it. Don't cut up rough, come with us, let's go and drink a bottle of vintage wine together.'

† Footnoted by Hugo: 'Je te dis qu'il est repris. À l'heure qu'il est, l'aubergiste ne vaut pas un liard. Nous n'y pouvons rien. Allons-nous-en. Je crois à tout moment qu'un sergent de ville me tient dans sa main', 'I tell you, he's been caught. By now, the innkeeper's not worth a quarter-sou. There's nothing we can do about it. Let's get going. I keep thinking a policeman's got me in his grasp.'

them to retreat. Montparnasse himself, who was perhaps something of a son-in-law to Thénardier, was giving up. Another moment, and they would be gone.

Thénardier was panting on his wall like the shipwrecked survivors of the *Medusa* on their raft, watching the vessel they had sighted disappear over the horizon.

He dared not call out to them, a cry overheard might ruin everything. He had an idea, one last idea, one glimmer of an idea. He drew from his pocket Brujon's bit of rope that he had untied from the chimney of the New Building, and threw it down inside the fenced area.

This rope fell at their feet.

'*Une veuve!*'* said Babet.

'*Ma tortouse!*'† said Brujon.

'It's the innkeeper,' said Montparnasse.

They looked up. Thénardier poked his head out a little.

'Quick!' said Montparnasse. 'Have you got the other bit of rope, Brujon?'

'Yes.'

'Knot the two bits together, we'll throw him the rope, he can fix it to the wall, he'll have enough to let himself down.'

Thénardier ventured to raise his voice. 'I'm frozen stiff.'

'We'll get you warmed up.'

'I can't move.'

'Slide down, we'll catch you.'

'My hands are numb.'

'Just tie the rope to the wall.'

'I can't.'

'One of us must climb up,' said Montparnasse.

'Three storeys!' exclaimed Brujon.

An old flue built of plaster, which had once served a stove that used to be lit in the shack, snaked up the wall almost to where they could see Thénardier. This flue, full of cracks and very shaky in those days, has since fallen down, but traces are still visible. It was very narrow.

'Someone could climb up through that,' said Montparnasse.

'Through that pipe?' exclaimed Babet. '*Un orgue*‡, never! It'd have to be *un mion*§.'

---

* Footnoted by Hugo: 'Une corde (argot du Temple)', 'A rope (Temple slang)'.
† Footnoted by Hugo: 'Ma corde (argot des barrières)', 'My rope (toll-gate slang)'.
‡ Footnoted by Hugo: 'Un homme', 'A man'.
§ Footnoted by Hugo: 'Un enfant (argot du Temple)', 'A child (Temple slang)'.

'It'd have to be *un môme**,*' said Brujon.

'Where can we find a nipper?' said Gueulemer.

'Wait,' said Montparnasse. 'I've got the answer!'

Cautiously, he opened the gate in the fence a fraction, made sure no one was coming along the street, stepped out warily, shut the gate behind him, and made off towards the Bastille.

Seven or eight minutes went by, eight thousand centuries to Thénardier. Babet, Brujon and Gueulemer did not break the silence. The gate opened again at last and Montparnasse appeared, breathless, and he had Gavroche with him. The rain continued to keep the street totally deserted.

Little Gavroche entered the enclosure and gazed calmly at these villainous characters. Water dripped from his hair.

Gueulemer spoke to him. 'Are you a man, lad?'

Gavroche shrugged and replied, '*Un môme comme mézig est un orgue, et des orgues comme vousailles sont des mômes.*'†

'*Comme le mion joue du crachoir!*'‡ cried Babet.

'*Le môme pantinois n'est pas maquillé de fertille lansquinée,*'§ added Brujon.

'What do you want me to do?' asked Gavroche.

Montparnasse answered, 'Climb up that pipe.'

'With this *veuve*¶,' said Babet.

'And *ligoter la tortouse***,' continued Brujon.

'*Au monté du montant,*'†† went on Babet.

'*Au pieu de la vanterne,*'‡‡ added Brujon.

'And then?' said Gavroche.

'That's it!' said Gueulemer.

The gamin examined the rope, the flue, the wall, the windows, and

---

* Footnoted by Hugo: 'Un enfant (argot des barrières)', 'A child (toll-gate slang)'.

† Footnoted by Hugo: 'Un enfant comme moi est un homme et des hommes comme vous sont des enfants', 'A child like me is a man and men like you are children.'

‡ Footnoted by Hugo: 'Comme l'enfant a la langue bien pendue!', 'That child's got a ready tongue!'

§ Footnoted by Hugo: 'L'enfant de Paris n'est pas fait en paille mouillée.' Literally, 'The Paris child is not made of wet straw' – i.e. he is made of sterner stuff.

¶ Footnoted by Hugo: 'Cette corde', 'This rope'.

** Footnoted by Hugo: 'Attacher la corde', 'Tie the rope'.

†† Footnoted by Hugo: 'Au haut du mur', 'To the top of the wall'.

‡‡ Footnoted by Hugo: 'À la traverse de la fenêtre', 'To the crossbar of the window'.

made that sound with his lips, scornful beyond words, that means 'Is that all!'

'There's a man up there you'll be rescuing,' said Montparnasse.

'You'll do it?' said Brujon.

'Thickhead!' replied the child as if he thought this was an absurd question. And he took off his shoes.

Gueulemer picked up Gavroche by one arm, put him on the roof of the shack, whose worm-eaten planks sagged beneath the child's weight, and handed him the rope that Brujon had knotted together again during Montparnasse's absence. The gamin made his way over to the flue, where thanks to a wide crack reaching up to the roof he could easily get inside. Just as he was about to climb up, Thénardier, who saw salvation and survival approaching, leaned over the edge of the wall. The first glimmerings of daylight blanched his forehead, streaming with sweat, his ashen cheekbones, his sharp feral nose, his bristling grey beard, and Gavroche recognized him.

'Fancy that! It's my father! Oh, not that it makes any difference.'

And taking the rope in his teeth, he resolutely began his ascent.

He reached the top of that standing ruin, straddled the old wall as if it were a horse, and knotted the rope firmly to the window's upper crossbar.

A moment later Thénardier was down in the street.

As soon as he touched the pavement, as soon as he felt out of danger, he was no longer tired, or cold, or trembling. The terrible things he had been through vanished like smoke, all that strange and ferocious intelligence reawakened, found itself free, up and ready to go.

The first thing this man said was 'Now, who are we going to eat?'

There is no need to explain the meaning of this horribly transparent word, whose connotations are to kill, murder and rob. To eat, in its true sense: to devour.

'Let's lie low,' said Brujon. 'We can settle this quickly and part company at once. There was a promising-looking job in Rue Plumet – deserted street, isolated house, garden gate falling to pieces, women on their own.'

'Well, why not?' asked Thénardier.

'*Ta fée** Éponine went to look it over,' replied Babet.

'And she brought Magnon a biscuit,' added Gueulemer. '*Rien à maquiller là.*'†

---

* Footnoted by Hugo: 'Ta fille', 'Your daughter'. Literally, 'Your fairy'.

† Footnoted by Hugo: 'Rien à faire là', 'Nothing doing there'.

'The girl's not *loffe**,' said Thénardier. 'Still, we'll have to see.'

'Yes, yes,' said Brujon, 'we'll have to see.'

None of these men seemed any longer aware of Gavroche's presence. During this discussion he had sat down on one of the boundary-posts by the fence. He waited for a few moments – perhaps his father might turn to him – then he put on his shoes again and said, 'Is that all? You men don't need me any more? You're out of trouble now. I'm off. I've got to go and get my kids up.'

And off he went. The five men emerged from behind the fence one after the other.

When Gavroche had disappeared round the corner of Rue des Ballets, Babet took Thénardier aside.

'Did you notice that nipper?' he asked.

'What nipper?'

'The nipper that climbed up the wall and brought you the rope.'

'Not particularly.'

'Well, I don't know, but it looked like your son.'

'Bah!' said Thénardier. 'You think so?'

And off he went.

---

* Footnoted by Hugo: 'Bête', 'Stupid'.

BOOK SEVEN
SLANG

I
Origins

*Pigritia** is a terrible word. It breeds a world, *la pègre*, for which read 'thieving', and a hell, *la pégrenne*, for which read 'hunger'.

Idleness is mother, then, to a son, theft, and a daughter, hunger. What are we talking about here? Slang.

What is slang? It is both a nation and its linguistic expression. It is thieving in its two guises: people and language.

When thirty-four years ago the narrator of this weighty and sombre tale introduced, in the middle of a work written with the same purpose as this one,† a thief talking slang, there was amazement and uproar. 'What? Why? Slang? But slang is dreadful! It's the language of the chain gangs, the prison hulks, gaols, of everything that's most abhorrent in society!' And so on and forth.

We have never understood objections of this kind.

Later, two influential novelists, one a profound observer of the human heart, the other an intrepid friend of the people, Balzac and Eugène Sue, like the author of *The Last Day of a Condemned Man* in 1828 allowed their villains to speak in the language that comes naturally to them, and the same protests were made.

Again people said, 'Why do authors want to force this outrageous patois on us? Slang is awful! Slang makes you shudder!'

Who is denying it? Of course it does.

Since when has it been wrong to delve too deep when probing a wound? To go too far in sounding the depths of an abyss or of a society? We have always thought it was sometimes an act of courage, at the very least a useful and simple deed deserving the sympathy and respect that a duty undertaken and fulfilled merits. Why not explore everything? Why not study everything? Why stop along the way? It is the lead on the sounding line that is supposed to stop, not the person taking the sounding.

---

* Latin, 'laziness' or 'idleness'.
† Footnoted by Hugo: '*Le Dernier jour d'un condamné*', '*The Last Day of a Condemned Man*'.

Certainly, it is neither an attractive nor an easy task to go trawling through the lower depths of the social order, where terra firma ends and the ooze begins, to go delving into that viscous ocean, to chase after, catch and land that abject idiom, all aquiver and running with slime in the light of day, that pustular vocabulary whose every word is like a foul coil of some monster of the mire and murk. Nothing is more dismal than to contemplate the seething horror of slang exposed like this to the light of the intellect. It does indeed resemble some dread beast destined for darkness that has just been dragged out of its bog. It seems like some ghastly, living, bristling undergrowth that shivers, stirs, shakes, craves a return to the gloom, threatens and glares. This word is like a claw, another like a dull and bleeding eye. This phrase seems to move like a crab's pincer. All, alive with that hideous vitality of things that have ordered themselves in disorder.

Now, since when has horror ruled out research? Since when has disease driven away the doctor? Can you imagine a naturalist refusing to study the viper, the bat, the scorpion, the centipede, the tarantula, and throwing them back into the darkness whence they came, saying, 'Ugh! how ugly!' The thinker who recoiled from slang would be like a surgeon recoiling from an ulcer or a wart; like a philologist reluctant to examine some feature of language; like a philosopher reluctant to investigate a fact of humanity. For, it must be said for the benefit of those who do not know, slang is both a literary phenomenon and a social consequence. What is slang in its true sense? Slang is the language of wretchedness.

You might stop us at this point. You might generalize its usage, which is one way of lessening its significance. You might say to us that every trade, every profession – you could almost add, every level in the social hierarchy and every area of knowledge – has its own slang. The merchant who says 'Montpellier in stock, fine-quality Marseille', the broker who says 'bring forward', 'premium', 'on maturity', the gambler who says *'tiers et tout'* and 'a flush of spades', the bailiff of the Channel Islands who says, 'The feoffor distraining his estate cannot claim the fruits of that estate while the defaulter holds the property by hereditary entitlement', the playwright who says his play was 'given the goose'*, the actor who says, 'I was roasted', the philosopher who says 'phenomenal triplicity', the huntsman who uses the expressions 'breaking cover' and 'going to ground', the phrenologist who says

---

* The turn of phrase that Hugo uses here – *'on a égayé l'ours'* (literally, 'we cheered up the bear') – is footnoted by him: 'On a sifflé la pièce' ('The play was booed'). To be given the goose, or the bird, is an old theatrical expression with the same meaning.

'amativity', 'combativity', 'secretivity', the footsoldier who talks of 'column', 'line' and 'square', the cavalryman who talks of 'cuirassiers', 'dragoons', 'hussars' and 'uhlans', the fencing-master who says 'tierce', 'quart', 'retreat', the printer who says 'bold', 'roman' and 'italic': all of them – printer, fencing-master, cavalryman, footsoldier, phrenologist, huntsman, philosopher, actor, playwright, bailiff, gambler, broker and merchant – are talking slang.* The painter, the notary, the hairdresser and the cobbler, in using their own special words for 'apprentice', are all talking slang. Strictly speaking, and to stretch a point, all the different ways of saying 'left' and 'right', the sailor's 'port' and 'starboard', the scene-shifter's 'prompt side' and 'opposite prompt', the verger's 'epistle side' and 'gospel side', are slang. There is the slang of affectation today just as there was the slang of affectation in the salons of the seventeenth century. The Hôtel Rambouillet was not so far removed from the Cour des Miracles. There is a duchesses' slang, evidenced by this sentence contained in a love letter from a very grand lady – and a very attractive woman she was too – of the Restoration period: *Vous trouverez dans ces potains-là une foultitude de raisons pour que je me libertise.*†

Diplomatic codes are slang. When the papal chancery uses 'twenty-six' to mean 'Rome', 'grkztntgzyal' for 'dispatch', and 'abfxustgrnogrkzutuXI' for 'Duke of Modena', it is using slang. The physicians of the Middle Ages who for 'carrot', 'radish' and 'turnip' said *opoponax, perfroschinum, reptitalmus, dracatholicum angelorum, postmegorum* were talking slang. The sugar producer who says '*vergeoise*', 'clayed', 'clarified', 'plug', 'broken', 'refined', 'bastard', 'sucrose', 'caramelized', 'loaf' – this honest manufacturer is talking slang. A certain school of criticism of twenty years ago that said that 'Half of Shakespeare is wordplay and puns' was also talking slang. The poet and artist who in their considered judgement would describe Monsieur de Montmorency as 'bourgeois' if he knew nothing about poetry and

---

* Hugo has the footsoldier talking of his '*clarinette*' ('clarinet'), a slang term for 'rifle' or 'gun', and the cavalryman of his '*poulet d'Inde*' ('turkey'), a slang term for 'horse'; 'column', 'line' and 'square', and 'cuirassiers', 'dragoons', 'hussars' and 'uhlans' are the translator's substitutions. And Hugo has the printer saying '*parlons batio*' ('let's talk *batio*'), also spelled *batiau*, the expression *parler batio* meaning 'to talk shop' in the typographical world; 'the printer who says "bold", "roman" and "italic" ' is the translator's substitution.

† Footnoted by Hugo as 'Vous trouverez dans ces commérages-là une multitude de raisons pour que je prenne ma liberté', 'You will find in such tittle-tattle a multitude of reasons why I should liberate myself'.

statues are talking slang.* The classicist Academician who calls flowers 'Flora', fruits 'Pomona', the sea 'Neptune', love 'the fiery passions', beauty 'alluring charms', a horse 'a steed', the white or tricolour cockade 'the rose of Bellona', the tricorn hat 'Mars' triangle' – that Academician is talking slang. Algebra, medicine, botany all have their own slang. The language spoken on board ship, a language so comprehensive and so picturesque that merges with the whistling in the rigging, the sound of loud-hailers, the thud of poleaxes, the rolling of the vessel, the gusting wind, the cannon, that wonderful language of the sea spoken by Jean Bart, Duquesne, Suffren and Duperré – this whole vibrant and heroic slang is to the uncouth slang of thievery what the lion is to the jackal.

Doubtless. But whatever anyone might say, this understanding of the word 'slang' is an extension of its meaning that not everyone will accept. We ourselves keep to the old, specific, distinct and determinate sense of the word, and restrict slang to slang. True slang, pure slang, if those two words can be used together, that age-old slang that was a world unto itself, we say again, is nothing other than the ugly, shifty, artful, treacherous, virulent, cruel, devious, vile, deep, inevitable language of destitution. Beyond the utmost degradation and the utmost adversity there is an ultimate destitution that rebels and decides to wage war against all that belongs to the world of prosperity and prevailing interests, a dreadful war in which, now cunning, now violent, at once pernicious and ferocious, it attacks the social order with pinpricks through vice and with cudgel-blows through crime. For the requirements of this war, destitution has invented a language of combat, which is slang.

To preserve and save from oblivion, from the abyss, if only a fragment of any language that man has spoken and that would otherwise be lost – that is to say, one of the elements, good or bad, contributing to the composition and the complexity of civilization – is to broaden the terms of social observation, to serve civilization itself. As Plautus served it, intentionally or not, by making two Carthaginian soldiers speak Phoenician. As Molière served it, by making so many of his characters speak the Levantine language and all sorts of dialects. At this point objections are raised yet again. Phoenician, excellent! Levantine, hurrah! Even dialect, fair enough! These are languages that have been associated with nations or provinces. But slang! What is the good of preserving slang? What is the good of keeping slang alive?

---

* The Montmorencys are one of France's oldest and most illustrious aristocratic dynasties; the term 'bourgeois' is used here in the sense of 'philistine'.

To this we have only one thing to say. Surely, if the language that a nation or a province has spoken is worthy of interest, something even more worthy of attention and study is the language spoken by misery.

It is the language spoken in France, for instance, for more than four centuries, not only by a particular kind of misery, but misery in general, all possible human misery.

Furthermore, and we must emphasize this, studying social disorders and afflictions, and drawing attention to them in order to remedy them, is not a task that admits of any choice. The historian of manners and ideas has a mission no less demanding than the historian of events. The latter has to deal with the surface of civilization, conflicts between crowned heads, the births of princes, the marriages of kings, battles, parliaments, great public figures, open revolution, all that is external. The other historian has to deal with the internal, the underside, the people who toil, suffer and wait; the oppressed woman, the child in distress, the covert war between man and man, the unknown aggressions, the prejudices, the iniquities condoned, the undeclared repercussions of the law, the secret developments of souls, the indistinct tremors of multitudes, the starving, the barefoot, the bare-armed, the disinherited, the orphans, the wretched and the depraved, all those spectral life-forms lurking in the shadows. With a heart full of both charity and severity, as brother and as judge, he must go down into those impenetrable vaults where skulking in a heap together are those who bleed and those who strike, those who weep and those who curse, those who go hungry and those who devour, those who endure evil and those who inflict it. Do these historians of hearts and souls have lesser responsibilities than historians of external facts? Does anyone think that Alighieri has less to say than Machiavelli? Is the underside of civilization any less important than the upper side, for being deeper and darker? Do we really know the mountain when we do not know the cavern?

And incidentally, it needs to be said, from a few words above a clear-cut distinction between the two categories of historian might be inferred that does not exist in our mind. There is no good historian of the evident, the manifest and the remarkable, of the public life of nations, who is not also to some extent the historian of their underlying and hidden life. And there is no good historian of the nation from within who does not understand, when necessary, how to be the historian of the nation from without. The history of manners and ideas permeates the history of events, and vice versa. They are phenomena of two different orders, which complement each other, which are always interrelated, and often follow from each other. All the features that providence draws on the surface of a nation have their dark but distinct parallels below, and all convulsions below produce upheavals above. True history being implicated in everything, everything is the business of the true historian.

Man is not a circle with a single centre. He is an ellipse with two focal points: one actions, the other ideas.

Slang is nothing but a dressing room where language, having to perform some wicked deed, disguises itself. There, it clothes itself in word masks, in metaphor rags. So it becomes horrendous.

It is scarcely recognizable. Is that really French, the great human language? There it is, ready to come on stage and share the scene with crime, all set to play any part in evil's repertory. It no longer walks, it hobbles. It limps on a crutch from the Cour des Miracles, a crutch that can be turned into a cudgel. It is called fraudulence. Its face has been painted by every hideous spectre serving as its dresser. It slithers along and gathers itself up, a reptilian duplicity of movement. It is now fit for all roles, to be made two-faced by the faker, verdigrised by the poisoner, blackened by the arsonist's soot. And the murderer lends his rouge.

When you listen from respectable folk's side of society's door, you overhear the exchanges of those on the outside. You distinguish questions and answers. Without understanding it you discern a hideous murmur, almost with a human ring to it but closer to yelping than to speech. It is slang. The words are distorted and characterized by an indescribable, fantastic bestiality. It sounds like hydras talking.

This unintelligibility in the shadows, grating and whispering, adds mystery to the darkness. It is dark in adversity, it is darker still in crime. These two darknesses combined constitute slang. Obscurity in the atmosphere, obscurity in deeds, obscurity in voices. Terrible and toad-like, language that comes and goes, hops, crawls, slavers, and moves about monstrously in that vast grey fog created by rain, gloom, hunger, vice, mendacity, injustice, nakedness, suffocation and winter, broad daylight to the wretched.

Pity those who are punished. Alas! Who are we, after all? Who am I who speak to you now? Who are you, listening to me? Where do we come from? And is it quite certain we did nothing before we were born? The earth is not without some resemblance to a gaol. Who knows whether man is not a previous offender against divine justice?

Take a close look at life. It is so organized that everywhere there is a sense of punishment.

Are you what is called a happy man? Well, you are sad every day.

Every day has its great sorrow or petty anxiety. Yesterday you were trembling for the health of someone dear to you, today you fear for your own; tomorrow it will be financial worries, the next day some back-biter's slander, the day after that a friend's misfortune. Then the weather, then something broken or lost, then a pleasure that your conscience and your backbone begrudge you. Another time, what is going on in the world. Not to mention heartache. And so on and so forth. One cloud clears, another forms. Hardly one day in a hundred that is entirely joyous, entirely sunny. And you are one of that small number who are happy! As for the rest of mankind, stagnant night is upon them.

Reflective minds rarely use those terms, 'the happy' and 'the unhappy'. In this world, the antechamber to another, of course, no one is happy.

The real human division is this: the enlightened and the benighted.

To reduce the numbers of the benighted, to increase the numbers of the enlightened, that is the object. That is why we cry: Education! Science! To teach someone to read is to light a fire! Every spelled-out syllable sparkles!

And he who says 'light' does not necessarily say 'joy'. People suffer in the light. An excess of it burns. The flame is enemy to the wing. To burn without ceasing to fly, that is the marvel of genius.

Even if you have knowledge and even if you have love, you will still suffer. Each day begins with tears. The enlightened weep, if only for the benighted.

II

Roots

Slang is the language of the benighted.

Confronted with this enigmatic dialect, a rebel dialect and one that is also stigmatized, the intellect is stirred in its darkest depths, social philosophy is spurred to its most painful reflections. Here is punishment made manifest. Every syllable gives the impression of having been branded. The words of the spoken language seem, as it were, wrinkled and shrivelled by the brander's red-hot iron. Some appear still to be smoking. A certain phrase has the same effect on you as a thief's shoulder with the fleur-de-lys burned into it, suddenly exposed to view. The mind almost resists expression in such recalcitrant terms. The metaphors are sometimes so shameless that you sense they are no stranger to the iron collar.

Yet despite all this and because of all this, this strange patois is entitled to its own pigeon-hole in that great impartial records office called literature, where there is room for the tarnished quarter-sou as well as for the gold coin. Like it or not, slang has its own syntax and its own poetry. It is a language. While from certain verbal distortions we can tell it was gabbled by Mandrin, we sense from some magnificent turns of phrase that Villon spoke it.

Mais où sont les neiges d'antan?*That line, so exquisite and so celebrated, is a line of slang. *Antan* – from *ante annum* – is a Thunes slang word meaning 'the past year', and by extension 'times past'. Thirty-five years ago, when the great chain gang of 1827 set off, you could still read this maxim, scratched with a nail on the wall of one of the cells at Bicêtre by a Thunes king condemned to the prison hulks: *Les dabs d'antan trimaient siempre pour la pierre du Coësre.* This means 'The kings in times past always had themselves anointed.' In the mind of that king, anointment meant being condemned to the prison hulks.

The word *décarrade*, which describes the departure of a heavy vehicle at a gallop, is attributed to Villon, and is worthy of him. This word strikes sparks, summing up entirely with masterly onomatopoeia La Fontaine's admirable line: 'Six strong horses were pulling a coach.'†

From a purely literary point of view, few studies would prove more intriguing and more fruitful than the study of slang. It is a whole language within a language, a kind of morbid excrescence, a malign graft that has produced growth, a parasite that has its roots in the old Gallic stem and whose pernicious foliage creeps all over one side of the language. This is what we might call the first impression, the crude impression of slang. But for those who study the language as it should be studied, that is to say as geologists study the earth, slang is like a veritable alluvium. Depending on how far you delve into slang, beneath demotic Old French you find Provençal, Spanish, Italian, the Levantine language of the Mediterranean ports, English and German, three varieties of Romance languages, Gallo-Romance, Italo-Romance and Romanian, Latin, and finally Basque and Celtic. A bizarre formation that goes deep down, a subterranean edifice constructed by all the wretched, collectively. Every outcast race has added its stratum, every

---

* Translated by Dante Gabriel Rossetti (1828–82) as 'Where are the snows of yesteryear?' this is a line from Villon's 'Ballade des dames du temps jadis' (in Rossetti's translation, 'Ballad of Dead Ladies'), part of his great work *Le Testament*.

† 'Six forts chevaux tiraient un coche.' From La Fontaine's fable 10, bk 7, 'Le Coche et la Mouche' (The Coach and the Fly).

individual suffering has left its stone, every heart has invested its pebble. A host of wicked, lowly or angry souls who went through life and have vanished into eternity are here, almost intact and in some way still visible in the form of some monstrous word.

You want Spanish? Old Gothic slang was rife with it. There is *boffete*, a 'smack in the face', which comes from *bofetón*; *vantane*, 'window' (later *vanterne*), which comes from *vantana*; *gat*, 'cat', which comes from *gato*; *acite*, 'oil', which comes from *aceite*. You want Italian? Here is *spade*, 'sword', which comes from *spada*; *carvel*, 'boat', which comes from *caravella*. You want English? Here is *bichot*, from 'bishop'; *raille*, 'spy', which comes from *rascal*, *rascallion*; *pilche*, 'case', which comes from *pilcher*, 'scabbard'. You want German? Here is *caleur*, 'waiter', from *Kellner*; *hers*, 'master', from *Herzog* ('duke'). You want Latin? Here is *frangir*, 'to break', from *frangere*; *affurer*, 'to steal', from *fur*; *cadène*, 'chain', from *catena*. There is one word that with a kind of mysterious power and authority crops up in every language of the continent. It is the word *magnus*; Scotland turns it into that country's 'mac', which denotes the chief of the clan; Mac-Farlane, Mac-Callummore, 'the great Farlane', 'the great Callummore'*; slang turns it into *meck* and later *meg*, that is to say, 'God'. You want Basque? Here is *gahisto*, 'devil', which comes from *gaïztoa*, 'evil'; *sorgabon*, 'goodnight', which comes from *gabon*, 'good evening'. You want Celtic? Here is *blavin*, 'handkerchief', which comes from *blavet*, 'gushing water'; *ménesse*, 'woman' (as a pejorative), which comes from *meinec*, 'full of stones'; *barant*, 'brook', from *baranton*, 'fountain'; *goffeur*, 'locksmith', from *goff*, 'blacksmith'; *guédouze*, 'death', which comes from *guenn-du*, 'white-black'. Finally, you want history? Slang calls an écu a *maltaise*, a reminder of the currency used on the Maltese galleys.

Apart from the philological origins that have just been noted, slang has other, even more natural roots, ones that grow, so to speak, straight out of the mind of man.

Firstly, the sheer invention of words. Herein lies the mystery of language. Painting with words that, who knows how or why, convey images. This is the primitive foundation of all human languages, what may be called their granite. Words of this kind proliferate in slang, instant words, entirely invented, impossible to say where or by whom, with no etymologies, no analogies, no derivatives, isolated, barbarous, sometimes hideous words, which have a remarkable expressiveness

---

* Footnoted by Hugo: 'It must be noted, however, that *mac* in Celtic means "son".'

889

and vitality. 'The executioner', *le taule*; 'the forest', *le sabri*; 'fear' or 'flight', *taf*; 'the lackey', *le larbin*; 'general', 'prefect' or 'minister', *pharos*; 'the devil', *le rabouin*. There is nothing more strange than these words that both mask and reveal. Some, *le rabouin*, for example, are at once grotesque and dreadful, and put you in mind of a Cyclopean grimace.

Secondly, metaphor. It is characteristic of a language that wants to say all and to conceal all to be rich in imagery. Metaphor is a riddle in which the thief plotting an attack, the prisoner planning an escape, takes refuge. No language is more metaphorical than slang: *dévisser le coco**, 'to wring someone's neck'; *tortiller†*, 'to eat'; *être gerbé‡*, 'to be condemned'; *un rat§*, 'a bread thief'; *il lansquine*, 'it is raining', a striking antiquated image that carries its date of origin within it, assimilating the long oblique shafts of rain with the thick slanting pikes of the lansquenets, and which reduces to a single verb the imagery contained in the popular expression, 'it's raining halberds'¶. Sometimes, as slang moves from the first era to the second, primitive and barbaric words give way to the use of metaphor. The devil ceases to be *le rabouin* and becomes 'the baker', 'the man feeding the oven'. This is witty but less grand, a bit like Racine after Corneille, like Euripides after Aeschylus. Certain slang phrases that belong to both eras and have a barbaric and at the same time metaphorical cast are phantasmagorical: *Les sorgueurs vont sollicer des gails à la lune*, 'The prowlers go stealing horses by night.' This presents itself to the mind as so many spectres. You do not know what you are seeing.

Thirdly, expediency. Slang lives off the language. It does what it likes with it, it draws on it at random and, where need arises, it is often content to alter it in a crude and summary fashion. Occasionally, with ordinary words distorted in this way and the addition of words of pure slang, picturesque phrases are created in which you can sense the mixture of the two elements just mentioned, sheer invention and metaphor: *Le cab jaspine, je marronne que la roulotte de Pantin trime dans le sabri*, 'The dog is barking, I suspect that the coach for Paris is passing through the woods.' *Le dab est sinve, la dabuge est merloussière, la fée est bative*, 'The bourgeois gent is stupid, his bourgeois wife is sly, their daughter is pretty.' More often than not, so as

---

* Literally, 'to unscrew the coconut'.
† Literally, 'to twirl'.
‡ Literally, 'to be bound into sheaves'.
§ Literally, 'a rat'.
¶ *Il pleut des hallebardes*, for which probably the closest English equivalent visually would be 'it's raining stair-rods'.

to baffle anyone listening, slang merely adds indiscriminately to every word of the language a sort of ignominious tail, an ending in *-aille*, *-orgue*, *-iergue* or *-uche*. Thus: *Vousiergue trouvaille bonorgue ce gigotmuche?* 'Is this leg of mutton to your liking?' Which is what Cartouche said to a turnkey in order to find out whether the sum offered for his escape was satisfactory. The *-mar* ending is a fairly recent addition.

Being the language of corruption, slang itself is soon corrupted. Moreover, since it is always trying to dissimulate, as soon as it gets the feeling it can be understood, it changes. Unlike any other vegetation, contact with a ray of light kills it. So slang goes on endlessly decomposing and recomposing itself, an obscure and rapid process that never stops. It covers more ground in ten years than the standard language in ten centuries. Thus *le larton** becomes *le lartif*; *le gail†* becomes *le gaye*; *la fertanche‡* becomes *la fertille*; *le momignard* becomes *le momacque§*; *les siques¶*, *les frusques*; *la chique***, *l'égrugeoir*; *le colabre††*, *le colas*. The devil is first of all *gahisto*, then *le rabouin*, then 'the baker'; the priest is *le ratichon*, then 'the boar'; the dagger is 'the twenty-two'‡‡, then *le surin*, then *le lingre*; the police are *railles*, then *roussins*, then *rousses*, then 'shoelace-sellers', then *coqueurs*, then *cognes*; the executioner is *le taule*, then *Charlot*, then *l'atigeur*, then *le becquillard*. In the seventeenth century, 'to fight' was *se donner du tabac*; in the nineteenth it is *se chiquer la gueule*.§§ There have been twenty different phrases between these two at either end. To Lacenaire, Cartouche would have been talking double Dutch. Like the men who utter them, all the words in this language are perpetually on the run.

* Footnoted by Hugo: 'Pain', 'Bread'.
† Footnoted by Hugo: 'Cheval', 'Horse'.
‡ Footnoted by Hugo: 'Paille', 'Straw'.
§ Deformations of *le môme*, a colloquial term for 'youngster' that entered the language in the nineteenth century.
¶ Footnoted by Hugo: 'Hardes', 'Clothes'.
** Footnoted by Hugo: 'L'église', 'The church'.
†† Footnoted by Hugo: 'Le cou', 'The neck'.
‡‡ A term deriving from the 22-centimetre hunting knife that was the preferred weapon of nineteenth-century ruffians.
§§ A homonym of *tabac* meaning 'tobacco', *tabac* in the sense of 'fighting' or 'beating', as in the expression *se donner du tabac*, 'to give each other a beating', probably derives from *taper* ('to hit'). However, the tobacco association probably influenced the later slang expression *se chiquer la gueule* (*chiquer* meaning 'to chew tobacco', so literally, 'to chew each other's face').

Yet from time to time, and because of this very mobility, ancient slang reappears and renews itself. It has its bastions where it holds its own. The Temple preserved the slang of the seventeenth century. Bicê-tre, when it was a prison, preserved the slang of Thunes. There you could hear the -*anche* ending of the old-time Thuners. *Boyanches-tu?* 'Are you drinking?' *Il croyanche.* 'He believes.' But perpetual motion remains the rule.

If the philosopher manages for a moment to pin down this infin-itely volatile language so as to observe it, he becomes immersed in sad if profitable reflections. No study is more effective and more fruitful in its instructiveness. There is not one metaphor in slang, not one ety-mology, that does not contain a lesson. Among these people, 'to beat' means 'to feign'. And in that sense you 'beat' an illness. Ruse is their strength.

For them, the idea of man is inseparable from the idea of dark-ness. Night is called *la sorgue*; 'man', *l'orgue*. Man is a derivative of night.

They have developed the habit of regarding society as an atmos-phere that kills them, like some lethal force, and they speak of their freedom as you would speak of your health. A man under arrest is 'a sick man', a convict is 'a dead man'.

What is most terrible for the prisoner entombed within those four stone walls is a kind of glacial chastity. He calls the dungeon the *castus*. In that dismal place life outside always appears in the most cheerful light. The prisoner has irons on his feet. You may think that what is in his mind is that feet are for walking? No, what is in his mind is that feet are for dancing. So when he manages to saw through his fetters, his first thought is that now he can dance, and he calls the saw *un bistringue*, 'a dance-hall'. 'A name' is *un centre*, 'a centre' – a deep association of ideas. The villain has two heads, one that rules his actions and guides him all his life, and the other that he has on his shoulders the day he dies. He calls the head that counsels crime *la sorbonne*, 'the brain-box', and the head that expi-ates it *la tronche*, 'the block'. When a man no longer has anything but rags on his body and vice in his heart, when he has reached that state of dual degradation, moral and material, that characterizes the twofold meaning of the word *gueux*, 'wretch', he is ripe for crime. He is like a well sharpened knife. He has two cutting edges, his indi-gence and his wickedness. So slang does not say *un gueux*, it says *un réguisé*, 'one who has been resharpened'. What are the prison hulks? Damnation's furnace, a hell. The convict calls himself *un fagot*, 'a bundle of firewood'. And finally, what name do offenders give to prison? 'The college.' A whole penitentiary system can be built on that word.

The robber too has his cannon fodder, the ripe for robbing – you, me, any passer-by: the *pantre*. (*Pan* meaning 'all'.)

You want to know where most of the songs of the prison hulks originate, those ballads that in the specialist vocabulary are called *lirlonfa**? Listen to this:

At the Châtelet in Paris there was a big long cellar. This cellar was eight feet below the level of the Seine. It had neither windows nor air-vents, the only opening was the door. Men could enter, air could not. This cellar had a stone vault for a ceiling and ten inches of mud for a floor. It had been flagged, but under the seeping water the flagstones had crumbled and cracked. Eight feet above the ground a long massive beam ran right across this basement. From this beam at regular intervals hung chains three feet long, and at the end of these chains were iron collars. Men who had been condemned to the prison hulks were put in this cellar until the day of departure for Toulon. They were shoved under this beam, where each had waiting for him, swinging in the dark, his restraints. The chains, those dangling arms, and the iron collars, those open hands, caught these wretches by the throat. They were shackled, and left there. As the chains were too short, they could not lie down. They stood motionless in that cellar, in that darkness, below that beam, virtually hanged, having to make unbelievable efforts to reach their bread or their jug, with the vault overhead, mud halfway up their legs, their own excrement running down the backs of their legs, racked with exhaustion, sagging at the hips and at the knees, clinging to the chains with their hands in order to rest, only able to sleep standing up, and woken at every moment by the strangling collar. Some did not wake. To eat, using their heels they nudged up their shins to within reach of their hands the bread that was thrown to them in the mud. How long did they remain like this? One month, two months, sometimes six. One was there a year. It was the ante-chamber to the prison hulks. People were put there for a hare stolen from the king. What did they do in this hellish tomb? What can be done in a tomb – they suffered agonies; and what can be done in hell – they sang. For where there is no further hope, there is still singing. In the waters off Malta, when a galley was approaching, the

---

* A word of uncertain meaning and etymology, from the refrain of a prison song cited in Hugo's *Dernier jour d'un condamné*.

singing could be heard before the sound of the oars. Poor Survincent the poacher, who had been through the Châtelet prison cellar, used to say, 'It was the rhymes that kept me going.' The futility of poetry. What good is rhyme? It was this cellar that gave birth to nearly all the songs in argot. From this dungeon in Paris's Grand-Châtelet came that melancholy refrain of Montgomery's galley: *Timaloumisaine, timou-lamison*. Most of these songs are lugubrious. Some are cheerful. One is tender:

> Here is the theatre
> Of the little dart-thrower.*

No matter what you do, you will never destroy that everlasting vestige of man's heart, love.

In this world of dark deeds you give nothing away. Secrecy is common to all. In the eyes of these poor wretches, it is the one thing on which unity is founded. To violate this secrecy is to rip out of each member of that ferocious community some part of his being. In the forceful language of slang, the expression for being an informer is *manger le morceau*, to 'take the bite'. As if the informer took for himself a little of everyone's substance and fed on a morsel of everyone's flesh.

What is 'a smack in the face'†? Commonplace metaphor replies: *C'est voir trente-six chandelles‡*. Here slang intervenes and makes its contribution, substituting *camoufle* for *chandelle*. At which point the conventional language gives *camouflet* as a synonym for 'a smack in the face'. So by a kind of bottom-up infiltration, with the help of metaphor whose trajectory defies computation, slang climbs from the thieves' den up to the Academy; and Poulailler saying, 'I light my *camoufle*' prompts Voltaire to write, 'Langleviel La Beaumelle deserves a hundred *camouflets*.'

To conduct an investigation into slang is to make a discovery each step of the way. Examination and study of this strange language lead to the mysterious point of intersection between conventional society and the society of the damned.

Slang is the word made felon.

That the intellectual element in man could be brought so low, that it should be dragged down and pinioned there by the obscure tyran-

---

* *Icicaille est le théâtre / Du petit dardant.* The last words footnoted by Hugo: 'Archer. Cupid.'
† In the French text, 'un soufflet'.
‡ Literally, 'It's seeing thirty-six candles', or in the English idiom, 'seeing stars'.

nies of fate, that it should be bound by who knows what shackles in that abyss, is cause for dismay.

Oh, the poor minds of the wretched!

Alas! will no one come to the aid of the human soul in that darkness? Is its destiny to await for ever the spirit, the liberator, the great rider of Pegasean steeds and of griffons, the combatant who in the hues of dawn shall descend from the azure carried on two wings, the radiant knight of the future? Shall it ever in vain call to its rescue ideality's lance of light? Is it condemned to hear the dreadful coming of evil through the thick of the abyss and to catch ever closer glimpses, beneath the hideous water, of that dragon's head, that froth-spewing maw, that serpentine undulation of claws and coils and bulges? Must it remain there, without a glimmer, without hope, abandoned to that terrible oncoming, vaguely sniffed out by the monster, shuddering, dishevelled, arms twisting, for ever chained to the rock of night, a forlorn Andromeda, white and naked in the shadows!

III
Weeping Slang and Laughing Slang

As we see, slang as a whole, the slang of four hundred years ago like the slang of today, is permeated with that dark symbolic spirit that gives all words at times a doleful tone, at times a suggestion of menace. You sense in them the old, fierce sadness of those vagrants in the Cour des Miracles who played card games with their own special playing-cards, a few of which have been preserved. The eight of clubs, for instance, was represented as a huge tree with eight enormous trefoil leaves, like some fantastic representation of a forest. At the foot of this tree you see a lighted fire at which three hares are roasting a huntsman on a spit, and behind that, over another fire, hangs a steaming pot with a dog's head emerging from it. Nothing could be more lugubrious than these painted reprisals on a pack of playing-cards for smugglers burned at the stake and counterfeiters boiled in cauldrons. All the various forms that thought took in the realm of slang – even songs, even jokes, even threats – had this impotent, defeated quality. The songs – and the tunes of some have been collected – were all pathetically meek and pitiful.

The thief is always 'the poor thief', *le pauvre pègre*, and he is always the hare in hiding, the mouse running for its life, the bird flying away. He barely complains, he merely sighs. One of his laments has come down to us: *Je n'entrave que le dail comment meck, le daron des orgues, peut atiger ses mômes et ses momignards et les locher*

895

*criblant sans être atigé lui-même.** Whenever he has time to think, the poor wretch cowers before the law and grovels before society. He lies flat on his stomach, he begs, he appeals for pity. You sense that he recognizes his wrong-doing.

Towards the middle of the last century a change occurred. Prison songs and thieves' ditties took on an insolent and jovial expression, as it were. The plaintive *maluré* was replaced by the *larifla*.† In the eighteenth century, in nearly all the galley, prison and chain-gang songs, you find a baffling and diabolical merriment. You hear this strident and skipping refrain that seems to glow with a phosphorescent brightness and to ring out in the forest like the piping of a will-o'-the-wisp:

> *Mirlababi surlababo*
> *Mirliton ribonribette*
> *Surlababi mirlababo*
> *Mirliton ribonribo.*

This was sung while cutting a man's throat in a cellar or in some out-of-the-way spot.

Of serious significance. In the eighteenth century the age-old melancholy of these dismal classes disappears. They begin to laugh. They mock the *grand meg* and the *grand dab*, the 'guvnor' and the 'boss'. Under Louis XV, they call the king of France 'the Marquis de Pantin'. And now they are almost gay. A kind of tenuous light emanates from these wretches, as if their consciences no longer weighed on them. These deplorable tribes of darkness no longer possess merely a desperate audacity of action, but a reckless audacity of mind too. A sign that they are losing the sense of their own criminality and that they feel they have support of a kind, even among intellectuals and thinkers, who are not themselves aware of lending any such support. A sign that theft and pillage are beginning to find their way into doctrines and sophisms in such a way as to lose a little of their ugliness – while passing on a great deal of it to those sophisms and doctrines. A sign,

---

* Footnoted by Hugo: 'Je ne comprends pas comment Dieu, le père des hommes, peut torturer ses enfants et ses petits-enfants et les entendre crier sans être torturé lui-même', 'I don't understand how God, the father of men, can torture his children and his grandchildren and hear them cry out without himself feeling tortured.'
† Like *lirlonfa*, these are refrain words of uncertain derivation and little meaning – folderols, like 'hey nonny no'.

in fact, if nothing arises to divert it, of some extraordinary and imminent fruition.

Now, just a moment. Who is it that we are accusing here? Is it the eighteenth century? Its philosophy? Certainly not. The work of the eighteenth century is good and sound. The Encyclopaedists led by Diderot, the physiocrats led by Turgot, the free-thinkers led by Voltaire, the Utopians led by Rousseau – these are four sacred legions. The great advance towards the light that humanity has made is due to them. They are the four vanguards of the human race, directed towards the four cardinal points of progress. Diderot towards beauty, Turgot towards usefulness, Voltaire towards truth, Rousseau towards justice. But alongside and below the *philosophes* came the sophists, poisonous vegetation mixed in with the healthy growth, hemlock in the virgin forest. While the century's great books of deliverance were burned by the authorities on the main steps of the law court, now-forgotten writers were publishing under royal licence who knows what strangely subversive texts, eagerly read by the wretched. Some of these publications, bizarrely enough sponsored by a prince, are to be found in the Secret Library. These underlying but unknown facts escaped notice on the surface. It is sometimes in the very obscurity of a fact that its danger lies. It is obscure because it is underground. Of all these writers, the one who was perhaps the most dangerous in his undermining among the masses was Restif de la Bretonne.

This kind of work, going on all over Europe, wreaked more havoc in Germany than anywhere else. During a certain period in Germany, evoked by Schiller in his famous drama *The Robbers*, theft and pillage rose up in protest against property and labour, embracing certain rudimentary ideas, erroneous and specious, apparently true but actually absurd; they cloaked themselves in these ideas, disappeared under them, as it were, assumed an abstract name, acquired the status of a theory, and in that way circulated among the honest, suffering, labouring masses, without even the knowledge of the foolhardy chemists who had prepared the mixture, without even the knowledge of the masses who accepted it. Whenever this kind of thing happens, it is a serious matter. Suffering breeds anger, and while the prosperous classes blind themselves or fall asleep, either way closing their eyes to it, the hatred of the poorer classes lights its torch at some overlooked and embittered or ill-natured mind and sets about examining society. Hatred's examination is a terrible thing.

Hence, if worse comes to worst, those terrifying disturbances that used to be called *jacqueries*, compared to which purely political unrest is child's play, and which are not just the struggle of the oppressed against the oppressor but the revolt of hardship against well-being. Then everything collapses.

Jacqueries are the people in seismic ferment.

It was this peril, which might well have been imminent in Europe towards the close of the eighteenth century, that the French Revolution, that immense act of integrity, forestalled.

The French Revolution, which is none other than the ideal armed with the sword, took a stand, and by the same decisive move closed the door on wickedness and opened the door to good.

It clarified the issue, promoted the truth, dispelled the miasma, restored the century to health, crowned the people.

It could be said that the French Revolution created man a second time, by giving him a second soul, his rights.

The nineteenth century has inherited and profited by its work, and today the social catastrophe we alluded to above is simply impossible. Blind is the person who denounces it! Foolish the person who fears it! Revolution is the vaccine against *jacquerie*.

Thanks to the Revolution, social conditions have changed. Feudal and monarchical diseases are no longer in our blood. There is nothing of the Middle Ages left in our constitution. We no longer live in the days when terrifying inward seethings would erupt, when you would hear the passage of a dull rumbling beneath your feet, when mole hills of a sort appeared on the surface of civilization, when cracks opened up in the ground, when the roofs of caverns fissured and when suddenly you might see monstrous heads rise up out of the earth.

Revolutionary awareness is moral awareness. The sense of right, once developed, develops the sense of duty. The universal law is liberty, which ends where the liberty of others begins, according to Robespierre's admirable definition. Since '89, the entire people has flourished in the sublimated individual. There is not a pauper who, given his rights, has not his ray of sunshine; the starving man senses within himself the integrity of France. The dignity of the citizen is an interior armour. Whoever is free is scrupulous. Whoever votes, rules. From that follows incorruptibility. From that follows the aborting of unhealthy feelings of envy. From that follows eyes heroically lowered in the face of temptation. Revolutionary recovery is such that on a day of deliverance, a fourteenth of July, a tenth of August, there is no longer any rabble. The first cry of the growing throngs of the enlightened is 'Death to thieves!' Progress is an honest man. Neither the ideal nor the absolute steal pocket handkerchiefs. By whom were the wagons containing the riches of the Tuileries escorted in 1848? By the rag-pickers of Faubourg St-Antoine. Tatters stood guard over treasure.

This ragged crew were made magnificent by virtue. In those wagons, in those barely closed chests, some even half open, among countless dazzling caskets was that ancient crown of France encrusted with diamonds, surmounted by that royal gemstone, the Regent diamond, worth thirty million francs. Barefoot, they guarded that crown.

So no more *jacquerie*. To the calculating, a regrettable blow. That was an old fear that has had its day and can no longer be exploited in politics. The great red spectre has lost its momentum. Everyone knows it now. The scarecrow no longer scares. The birds show no respect for it, dung-beetles settle on it, the bourgeoisie laugh at it.

IV
The Two Duties: To Watch and to Hope

That being the case, has all social danger evaporated? Of course not. No *jacquerie*. Society may rest assured on that score, the blood will not go to its head any more. But it should be careful how it breathes. Apoplexy is no longer to be feared, but consumption is a danger. Social consumption is called misery.

You can die from wasting away as well as from being struck down.

Let us never tire of repeating this: think above all of the woeful, disinherited multitudes, comfort them, bring air and light to them, love them, broaden their horizons magnificently, lavish on them all manner of education, give them the example of toil, never the example of idleness; lessen the weight of the individual burden by promoting the notion of the common objective, restrict poverty without restricting wealth, create vast areas of public activity for the people; have, like Briareus, a hundred hands to reach out in all directions to the weak and the oppressed; direct the collective power towards that great obligation to open workshops for all hands, schools for all aptitudes, laboratories for all intellects; raise wages, reduce hardship, balance the account between debit and credit; in other words match enjoyment to effort and satisfaction to need; in short, see to it that the social mechanism provides, for the benefit of those who suffer and of those who are in darkness, more light and more well-being. This – let sympathetic souls not forget it – is the primary fraternal obligation. This – selfish hearts should know – is the primary political necessity.

And it needs to be said, even all that is only a start. The real issue is this: work cannot prevail as law without being a right.

We will not dwell on this, this is not the place.

If nature is called providence, society ought to be called prudence.

Intellectual and moral growth are no less indispensable than material betterment. Knowledge is a viaticum. Thought is essential. Truth, like wheat, is sustenance. Reason, starved of learning and wisdom, is debilitated. Let us pity both minds and stomachs that do not eat. If there is anything more heart-breaking than a body starving for want of bread, it is a hungry soul dying for want of enlightenment.

Progress as a whole is tending towards the solution. One day we shall be amazed. As the human race moves upward, the lower strata will quite naturally emerge from the distress zone. Poverty will disappear through a simple rise in the standard of living.

This solution would be a blessing, and it would be wrong to have any doubts about it.

At the moment, it is true, the past is very strong. It is reviving. This rejuvenation of a corpse is astounding. Back on its feet again, here it comes. It looks victorious. This defunct is a conqueror, it arrives with its legion – superstitions – with its sword – despotism – with its banner – ignorance. Recently, it has won a dozen battles. It is advancing, threatening, laughing, it is at our gates. For our part, let us not despair. Let us sell the field on which Hannibal is encamped.

What have we, who believe, to fear?

Ideas are no more able to retreat than rivers to reverse their flow.

But let those set against the future think about it. By saying no to progress, it is not the future they are condemning, but themselves. They are giving themselves a serious illness. They are infecting themselves with the past. There is only one way of rejecting Tomorrow, which is to die.

Now, what we want is no death – that of the body, as late as possible, that of the soul, never.

Yes, the enigma will surrender its key, the sphinx will speak, the problem will be resolved. Yes, the People, the eighteenth century's work in progress, will be completed by the nineteenth. Anyone who would doubt this is a fool! Future fulfilment, imminent fulfilment of universal well-being, is a phenomenon of divine fate.

Tremendous collective impetuses direct human affairs and bring them all within a given time to the logical state: that is to say, equilibrium; that is to say, equity. A force of heaven and earth combined, deriving from humanity, governs it. This force is a worker of miracles, for which marvellous outcomes are no harder to achieve than extraordinary adventures. Assisted by science, which is the work of man, and by events, the work of another, this force is not greatly alarmed by these contradictions in the posing of problems, which to the ordinary person seem impossibilities. It is no less able to create a solution from the reconciliation of ideas than to learn a lesson from the reconciliation of facts. And anything can be expected of that mysterious power of progress that one fine day brings East and West face to face in a tomb and has imams conversing with Bonaparte inside the Great Pyramid.

In the meantime, no halt, no hesitation, no pause in the great onward march of minds. Social philosophy is essentially the science of peace. Its object is – and its result must be – to dispel anger by the study of antagonism. It examines, scrutinizes, analyses, then it reconstructs. It proceeds by a process of reduction, excising all hatred.

A society destroyed by the winds raging against mankind is something that has been seen more than once before. History is full of nations and empires that have foundered. Customs, laws, religions – some fine day that something unknown, the hurricane, passes over and sweeps them all away. The civilizations of India, Chaldea, Persia, Assyria, Egypt, have disappeared one after the other. Why? We do not know. What are the causes of these disasters? We do not know. Could these societies have been saved? Are they to blame? Did they persist in some fatal depravity that was their undoing? How great is the element of suicide in these terrible deaths of nations and races? Questions without answers. Obscurity shrouds these doomed civilizations. They must have been shipping water, for they sank. There is nothing more we can say. And it is with a kind of terror that far across that ocean we call the past, in the wake of those colossal waves that are the centuries, we watch those immense vessels go down – Babylon, Nineveh, Tarsus, Thebes, Rome – under the fearful blast blowing from every gaping mouth of darkness. But darkness there, light here. We know nothing of the maladies of those ancient civilizations, we know only the complaints of our own. Over all of it we have the right to shine a light; we contemplate its beauties, we expose its deformities. Where there is pain, we probe. And the sickness once diagnosed, study of the cause leads to discovery of the remedy. Our civilization, the work of twenty centuries, is both monster and marvel. It is worth saving. Saved it will be. Bringing comfort to it is already a great deal. Bringing enlightenment is a great deal more. All the work undertaken by modern social philosophy must concentrate on that goal. Today's thinker has a great duty, to apply the stethoscope to civilization.

We repeat, this use of the stethoscope is encouraging. And it is with this insistence on encouragement that we want to conclude these few pages, a serious interlude in a heart-rending drama. Beneath social mortality we sense human imperishability. Just because it has the odd wound in the form of craters, and the odd skin eruption in the form of fumaroles, just because a volcano comes to a head and ejects its pus, the globe does not die. Disease in the population does not kill mankind.

And yet anyone who does the ward-rounds of society shakes his head at times. The strongest, the most tender-hearted, the most logical, have their moments of weakness.

Will there be a future? We feel we might almost ask ourselves this question when we see so much terrible darkness. Grim confrontation between the selfish and the wretched. In the selfish, prejudices, the ignorance of a superior education, appetite fed by overindulgence, the insensitivity of an indurating prosperity, fear of suffering that in some extends to an aversion to those who suffer, relentless complacency, an ego so inflated it denies access to the soul. In the wretched, greed, envy, a hatred of seeing others enjoying themselves, the convulsions of the human beast within them seeking satisfaction, hearts befogged, sadness, need, fatalism, ignorance impure and simple.

Must we continue to raise our eyes to heaven? Is the pinpoint of light we glimpse there the kind that fades away? It is dreadful to see the ideal thus lost in the depths, small, isolated, almost imperceptible, twinkling, but surrounded by those great menacing darknesses monstrously banked up around it; yet no more in danger than a star swallowed up by cloud.

BOOK EIGHT
ENCHANTMENT AND DESPAIR

I
All Is Light

It must be clear to the reader that Éponine, having recognized through the railing the girl who was living at that address on Rue Plumet where Magnon had sent her, had firstly warded off the villains from Rue Plumet and then taken Marius there; and after several days' ecstasy in front of that railing, impelled by that force that draws the iron to the magnet and a lover towards the stones of which his beloved's house is built, Marius had finally entered Cosette's garden as Romeo entered Juliet's garden. This was even easier for him than for Romeo. Romeo had to scale a wall, Marius had just slightly to force one of the rickety railings that wobbled in its rusty socket the way old people's teeth do. Marius was slim, and slipped through easily.

As the street was always deserted, and in any case as Marius only went into the garden at night, he was in no danger of being seen.

From that blessed and sacred moment when a kiss pledged these two souls to each other, Marius came here every evening. If at this point in her life Cosette had fallen in love with a dissolute and not very scrupulous man it would have been her ruin, for there are generous natures that surrender themselves and Cosette was one of them. One of the generosities of women is to yield. Love so great that it is absolute involves some sort of divine blindness to propriety. But what dangers you run, O noble souls! Often you give your heart, we take your body. You are left with your heart, and there in the shadows you gaze on it, quaking. There is no half way with love. It means either ruin or salvation. This is the dilemma of all human existence. And no fate poses this dilemma, ruin or salvation, more inexorably than love. Love means life unless it means death. Cradle, and also coffin. The same emotion says yes and no in the human heart. Of all things God has made, the human heart is the one that sheds the most light and alas! the most darkness.

God willed that the love Cosette encountered was a love that saves.

Every night throughout the month of May in that year of 1832, there in that poor neglected garden, behind that shrubbery that grew every day denser and more fragrant, were to be found two creatures embodying every kind of purity and innocence, brimming over with all the joys of heaven, closer to archangels than to human beings, chaste, honest, elated, radiant and resplendent to each other in the shadows. It seemed to Cosette that Marius wore a crown, and to Marius that Cosette had a halo. They sat close to each other, gazed at each other, held hands, clung to each other, but there was a distance that they preserved. Not that they respected it; they were unaware of it. Marius sensed a barrier, Cosette's purity, and Cosette sensed a stay, Marius's integrity. The first kiss had also been the last. Marius had not since ventured beyond brushing with his lips Cosette's hand, or her shawl, or a lock of her hair. Cosette was to him a perfume, not a woman. She was the air he breathed. She refused nothing, and he asked for nothing. Cosette was happy and Marius was satisfied. They lived in that state of rapture that might be termed the dazzling of one soul by another. It was that ineffable first embrace between two virginities in the realm of the ideal. Two swans meeting on the Jungfrau.

At that stage of love, a stage when sensuality is totally silenced by the all-powerfulness of ecstasy, Marius, pure and seraphic Marius, would have been more capable of visiting a common prostitute than of lifting Cosette's dress ankle-high. Once, in the moonlight, Cosette stooped to pick something up from the ground, her bodice gaped slightly, revealing a glimpse of the rise of her bosom. Marius averted his eyes.

What took place between these two individuals? Nothing. They adored each other.

When they were there at night that garden seemed a living and sacred place. All the flowers opened around them and wafted their incense over them, while they in turn, amid the flowers, opened their hearts in profuse outpourings. In sap-filled delirium the voluptuous and vigorous vegetation quivered around these two innocents, and they uttered words of love that set the trees rustling.

What words were these? Whispers. Nothing more. These whispers were enough to stir and thrill all this nature. A magic power, and one hard to understand if you were to read in a book those sweet nothings meant to be carried away like smoke and dispersed by the breeze beneath the leaves. From these murmurings of two lovers, take away that melody emanating from the soul and accompanying them like a lyre, and what is left is just a shadow. 'Is that all?' you say. Well, yes. Childish prattle, repetitions, laughter over nothing, frivolities, inanities, the most utterly sublime and profound things imaginable! The only things worth saying and the only things worth listening to!

The man who has never heard these inanities, these banalities, the man who has never uttered them, is a sorry fool.

Cosette said to Marius, 'You know –' (in all this, and despite that heavenly modesty, and without either of them being able to say how it came about, they were *tu* to each other) '– you know, my name is Euphrasie.'

'Euphrasie? But your name is Cosette.'

'Oh! Cosette is a rather ugly name that was given to me when I was little. But my real name is Euphrasie. Don't you like that name, Euphrasie?'

'Yes. But Cosette isn't ugly.'

'Do you like it better than Euphrasie?'

'Well – yes.'

'Then I like it better too. It's true, it's pretty, Cosette. Call me Cosette.'

And the smile she added transformed this conversation into an idyll worthy of some celestial grove.

On another occasion, gazing intently at him, she exclaimed, 'Monsieur, you're handsome, you're charming, you're witty, you're far from stupid, you're much more learned than I am, but I challenge you with this: I love you!'

And to Marius, in very heaven, this sounded like poetry sung by a star.

Or she would give him a gentle tap because he was coughing and say, 'Don't cough, monsieur. I won't have anyone coughing here without my permission. It's very naughty to cough, and worry me. I want you to be well because in the first place if you weren't well I'd be very unhappy. What else would you expect?'

And this was quite simply divine.

Once Marius said to Cosette, 'Just imagine, for a while I thought your name was Ursule.'

This made them laugh all evening.

During another of their conversations he happened to burst out, 'Oh, one day in the Luxembourg Gardens I felt like finishing off a disabled veteran!'

But he stopped short, and went no further. He would have had to talk to Cosette about her garter, and that was impossible. It touched on the unknown, the flesh, before which that great innocent love recoiled with a kind of sacred terror.

Marius imagined life with Cosette just like this, without anything more: coming every evening to Rue Plumet, moving aside the obliging old railing in the judge's gate, sitting close to each other on this bench, gazing through the trees at the twinkling of oncoming night, accommodating his trouser knee to the fullness of Cosette's gown, caressing her thumbnail, calling her *tu*, taking turns to smell the scent of the same flower, for ever, without end. Meanwhile, the clouds passed above their heads. Every time the wind blows it carries away more human dreams than clouds in the sky.

Nor was this chaste, almost shy, love totally without courtship. 'To pay compliments' to the woman you love is the first stage in caressing her, a tentative half-daring. A compliment is something like a kiss through a veil. There is, albeit concealed, a sweet element of sensual delight to it. The heart shrinks from sensual delight only to love the more. Marius's endearments, steeped in fancy, were azure-tinted, so to speak. The birds when they fly up towards the angels must hear such words. Yet they also contained life, humanity, all the reality of which Marius was capable. It was what is said in the arbour, a prelude to what will be said in the bedchamber, a lyrical effusion, strophe and sonnet intermingled, the pretty exaggerations of wooing, all the little subtleties of adoration arranged in a bouquet and exuding a heavenly, delicate, subtle fragrance, an ineffable heart-to-heart billing and cooing.

'Oh,' murmured Marius, 'how beautiful you are! I daren't look at you. Which is why I'm contemplating you. You're a gift from God. I don't know what's wrong with me. The hem of your gown, when the tip of your shoe peeps out from under it, throws me into confusion. And then, what a captivating brilliance when your mind reveals even a fraction of itself! There's astonishing wisdom in what you say. At times I think you're a dream. Say something, I'm listening, I'm lost in wonder. Oh Cosette! how strange and delightful this is, I'm truly beside myself. You're wonderful, mademoiselle. I study your feet with a microscope and your soul with a telescope.'

And Cosette replied, 'After all the time that's gone by since this morning I love you a little more than before.'

Questions and answers ranged as far they could in this dialogue, always settling on love, like those self-righting elderwood tumbler dolls on their weighted bases.

Cosette was all simplicity, ingenuousness, transparency, whiteness, candour, radiance. You might have said of Cosette that she was brightness. She gave to everyone who saw her a sense of April and of daybreak. There was a dew in her eyes. Cosette was the dawn light condensed into the form of a woman.

It was quite natural that Marius should wonder at her, adoring her as he did. But the truth is, this little schoolgirl fresh from the convent spoke with remarkable insight and at times said all kinds of true and discerning things. Her chatter was conversation. She was never wrong about anything, and her views were sound. A woman feels and speaks with the infallibility of a heart's tender instinct. No one knows better than a woman how to say things that are both sweet and profound. Sweetness and profundity, that is the essence of woman, that is the essence of heaven.

In this state of complete happiness tears kept coming to their eyes. A crushed ladybird, a feather fallen from a nest, a broken hawthorn branch, stirred their pity; and their rapture, sweetly imbued with melancholy, seemed to ask nothing better than to weep. The supreme symptom of love is a tenderness at times almost unbearable.

And alongside this – all these contradictions are love's lightning display – they were quick to laugh with delightful abandon, and so comfortable with each other they sometimes seemed almost like two boys. Giddily chaste hearts may be unaware of it, but nature, unforgettable, is always there. She is there with her brutish and sublime objective, and whatever the innocence of souls, in even the most discreet tête-à-tête you sense that marvellous and mysterious nuance that distinguishes a couple in love from two close friends.

They idolized each other.

The constant and the immutable are abiding. You are sweethearts, you smile at each other, laugh together, purse your lips at each other, intertwine your fingers, call each other *tu*, and it makes no difference to eternity. Two lovers seclude themselves in the evening, in the twilight, where they cannot be seen, with the birds and the roses; they bewitch each other in the darkness, their hearts in their eyes, they murmur, they whisper, while the vast movements of stars fill the infinite.

II
In a Daze of Perfect Happiness

They lived in a daze, bewildered with happiness. They did not notice the cholera taking its toll on Paris during that very same month. They confided in each other as much as they could, but this had gone scarcely beyond giving their names. Marius told Cosette he was an orphan, that his name was Marius Pontmercy, that he was a lawyer, that he lived by writing things for booksellers, that his father had been a colonel, and that the man was a hero; that he, Marius, had fallen out with his grandfather, who was wealthy. He also said something about being a baron, but this made no impression on Cosette. Marius, a baron? She did not understand. She did not know what that word meant. Marius was Marius. For her part, she told him that she had been brought up at the Petit-Picpus convent; that her mother, like his, was dead; that her father was called Monsieur Fauchelevent, that he was a very good man, that he was very generous to the poor but was himself poor, and that he denied himself everything while denying her nothing.

Strange to say, within the harmony, as it were, that Marius inhabited since he had been seeing Cosette, the past, even the very recent past, had become so distant and confused that what Cosette told him satisfied him completely. It did not even occur to him to mention to her what had happened that night at the Gorbeau place, the Thénardiers, that burn, her father's strange behaviour and his peculiar disappearance. Marius had for the time being forgotten all this. He did not even know by the time evening came what he had done that morning, where he had eaten or who had spoken to him. He had a singing in his ears that made him deaf to any other thought. He existed only during the time he was seeing Cosette. Then, since he was in heaven, it was quite natural he should forget about earth. Both were languid with the indefinable weight of intangible delights. Such is life for those sleepwalkers we call lovers.

Alas! Who has not experienced all these things? Why does there come a time when you emerge from this heavenly bliss, and why does life go on afterwards?

Loving almost replaces thinking. Love is an ardent forgetfulness of everything else. So, expecting passion to be logical is pointless. There is no more an absolute logic in the human heart than there is a perfect geometrical figure in celestial mechanics. For Cosette and Marius nothing else existed except Marius and Cosette. The universe around them had fallen away. They lived in a golden moment. There was nothing before, nothing after. Marius barely remembered Cosette had a father. There was in his mind a blotting-out and a bedazzlement. So what did they talk about, these lovers? As we have seen, about flowers, swallows, the setting sun, the rising moon, all the important things. They told each other all, bar all. Lovers' all is nothing. But about her father, the actual facts, that squalid den, those villains, that episode – what was the good of talking about them? And was he quite sure that nightmare had been real? There were the two of them, they adored each other, that was all. Nothing else existed. This fading-away of hell behind us is probably inherent in reaching paradise. Have we seen demons? Are there any? Have we trembled? Have we suffered? We are sure of nothing any more. A rose tint overlies everything.

And such was life for these two individuals, in very heaven, with all the semblance of unreality that exists in nature. Neither at the nadir nor at the zenith, between man and the seraphim, above the mire, below the ether, up in the clouds. Scarcely flesh and blood; soul and ecstasy from head to foot. Already too purified to walk the earth, still too instilled with humanity to disappear into the blue, suspended like atoms before precipitation. Seemingly removed from destiny. Knowing nothing of this rut that is yesterday, today, tomorrow. Wonderstruck, rapturous, walking on air. At times weightless enough to take off into infinity, almost primed for eternal flight.

So beguiled, they lived in a waking sleep. O splendid trance of ideal-stricken reality! Sometimes, beautiful as Cosette was, Marius closed his eyes to her. The best way to look at the soul is with closed eyes.

Marius and Cosette were not wondering where this would lead, they felt they had arrived. It is a strange presumption of men to expect love to lead somewhere.

III
An Incipient Shadow

Jean Valjean was completely unsuspecting.

A little less dreamy than Marius, Cosette was cheerful, and this was enough to make Jean Valjean happy. The thoughts Cosette had, her tender concerns, the image of Marius that filled her heart, detracted nothing from the matchless purity of her chaste and smiling lovely face. At her age, the virgin carries her love as the angel carries its lily. Jean Valjean was, therefore, untroubled. And besides, when two lovers understand each other, it always works out very well for them. Any third party who might disturb their love is kept in total darkness by means of a few precautionary measures, ever the same for all lovers. So no opposition to Jean Valjean from Cosette. He wanted to go for a walk? Yes, father dearest. He wanted to stay at home? Of course. He wanted to spend the evening with Cosette? She was delighted. As he always retired at ten o'clock Marius did not come into the garden on those occasions until after that time, when from the street he heard Cosette open the french window on to the terrace. It goes without saying, Marius was never to be encountered by day. Jean Valjean did not even remember that Marius existed. There was just one occasion when he said to Cosette one morning, 'Why, your back's all covered with white.' Overcome with feeling the night before, Marius had pressed Cosette against the wall.

Once her work was done, Old Toussaint, who went to bed early, thought only of sleeping, and like Jean Valjean she was completely unaware of what was going on.

Marius never set foot in the house. When he was with Cosette they hid in a recess by the steps so they could not be seen or heard from the street, and there they sat, for sole conversation often contenting themselves with squeezing each other's hand twenty times a minute while gazing at the branches of the trees. At such moments a thunderbolt might have struck thirty paces away and they would not have noticed it, so deeply was the reverie of one engrossed and immersed in the reverie of the other.

Limpid purities. Hours of sheer whiteness, almost completely identical. This kind of love is a collection of lily petals and doves' feathers.

The whole garden lay between them and the street. Every time Marius came in or out, he carefully realigned the railing in the gate so there was no sign of anything out of place. He usually left at about midnight and went back to Courfeyrac's place.

Courfeyrac said to Bahorel, 'Would you believe it? Marius is now coming home at one o'clock in the morning!'

Bahorel replied, 'What do you expect? Inside every seminarian there's a firecracker.'

Sometimes Courfeyrac would fold his arms, adopt a serious look and say to Marius, 'You're getting into bad habits, my boy!'

A practical man, Courfeyrac did not take kindly to this reflection in Marius of an invisible paradise. He was little given to any out-of-the-ordinary passion. It exasperated him, and there were times when he would issue Marius with summonses to return to reality.

One morning he delivered this rebuke: 'My dear fellow, you give me the impression right now of being on the moon, in the realm of dreams, in a state of delusion, whose capital is Soap-Bubble City. Now, be a good chap – what's her name?'

But nothing could induce Marius to talk. He would sooner have had his fingernails torn out than let either of the two sacred syllables constituting that ineffable name Cosette be prised out of him. True love is as luminous as the dawn and as silent as the tomb. And Courfeyrac saw this change in Marius: he was now radiantly taciturn.

During that lovely month of May, Marius and Cosette experienced immense pleasures: that of arguing and of addressing each other as *vous* solely for the greater pleasure of using *tu* again afterwards; of talking at great length in the most minute detail about people in whom they had not the slightest interest – further proof that in that delightful opera called love the libretto counts for almost nothing; for Marius, the joy of listening to Cosette talk about clothes; for Cosette, of listening to Marius talk about politics; the joy of hearing the carriages on Rue de Babylone pass by as they sat with their knees touching; of gazing at the same planet in space or the same glow-worm in the grass; of remaining silent together, a yet greater pleasure than talking. And so on.

Meanwhile, various complications were looming.

One evening Marius was making his way to his assignation along Boulevard des Invalides. He usually walked with his head down. As he was about to turn the corner of Rue Plumet he heard someone say very close by, 'Good evening, Monsieur Marius.'

He looked up, and recognized Éponine.

This had a peculiar effect on him. He had not once thought of that girl since the day she had taken him to Rue Plumet. He had not seen her again, and she had gone out of his mind completely. He had cause only for gratitude towards her, he owed her his present happiness, and yet it was galling to him to meet her.

It is a mistake to think that, when pure and happy, passion leads a man to a state of perfection. We have noted already, it simply leads him into a state of oblivion. A man in this condition forgets to be bad, but he also forgets to be good. Gratitude, duty, unwelcome memories of fundamental importance, are forgotten. At any other time Marius would have behaved quite differently towards Éponine. Completely taken up with Cosette, he had not even fully realized that this Éponine was called Éponine Thénardier and bore a name written in his father's will, that name for which only a few months ago he would have so zealously sacrificed himself. We present Marius as he was. In the splendour of his love, even his father was fading somewhat from his heart.

In some confusion, he replied, 'Ah, is that you, Éponine?'

'Why address me as *vous*? Have I offended you?'

'No,' he replied.

Certainly, he had nothing against her. Far from it. Only, now that he said *tu* to Cosette he felt he could not do otherwise than say *vous* to Éponine.

As he remained silent she exclaimed, 'Tell me now—'

Then she stopped. It seemed this creature who had been so jaunty and so bold in the past was at a loss for words. She tried to smile and could not.

'Well?' she said.

Then she fell silent again and remained with her eyes downcast.

'Good evening, Monsieur Marius,' she said briskly all of a sudden, and off she went.

IV

A Cab Drives in English and Barks in Slang

The next day was the third of June, the third of June 1832, a date that needs to be mentioned because of the grave events that at the time hung like storm clouds on the Paris horizon. At nightfall, Marius was going the same way as the day before with the same thoughts of rapture in his heart when he caught sight of Éponine through the trees on the boulevard. Two days in succession was too much. He abruptly changed direction, turned off the boulevard, took a different route and made his way to Rue Plumet via Rue Monsieur.

Consequently, Éponine followed him to Rue Plumet, something she had not done before. Until then she had contented herself with watching him pass along the boulevard without ever seeking to make contact with him. Only the previous evening had she tried to speak to him.

So without his being aware of it, Éponine followed him. She saw him shift the railing and slip into the garden.

'Fancy that!' she said. 'He's going into the house!'

She went up to the gate, tested the railings one by one, and easily identified the railing Marius had displaced. In a gloomy voice she murmured under her breath, 'Now, none of that, Lisette!'*

She sat at the foot of the gatepost, right next to the railing, as if she were guarding it. It was just where the gate met the adjoining wall. Here was a dark nook where Éponine could disappear completely.

Thus she remained for more than an hour, without moving an inch or uttering a sound, consumed by her thoughts. Around ten o'clock in the evening one of the two or three passers-by on Rue Plumet, an elderly gent, hurrying home late through this deserted and ill-reputed part of town, was passing by the garden gate when on reaching the corner where the gate met the wall he heard a low, threatening voice saying, 'I wouldn't be surprised if he came here every evening.'

The passer-by glanced round, saw no one, dared not peer into that dark corner, and felt very fearful. He quickened his pace.

This individual rightly hurried, for just a few moments later six men, walking separately and at some distance from each other, hugging the walls, and who might have been mistaken for a night patrol, entered Rue Plumet.

The first to arrive at the garden gate halted, and waited for the

---

* Here Hugo uses a catchphrase, *Pas de ça, Lisette*, that dates back to the eighteenth century. It is still used today.

others. A moment later all six were assembled. These men began to talk in subdued voices.

'This is the place,' said one of them, '*icicaille.*'

'Is there a *cab** in the garden?' asked another.

'I don't know. In any case, I brought† a meatball we can give it to eat‡.'

'You got some putty to break the window with§?'

'Yes.'

'It's an old gate,' said a fifth, who had a voice like a ventriloquist's.

'So much the better,' said the one who had spoken second. 'It won't squeal¶ so much under the *bastringue*** and it won't be so hard to cut through††.'

The sixth, who had not yet opened his mouth, now began to inspect the gate just as Éponine had done an hour earlier, grasping each railing in turn and carefully shaking it. In due course he came to Marius's loose railing. As he was about to seize hold of it a hand shot out of the dark and clamped down on his arm, he felt himself being catapulted backwards by a shove to the chest, and a hoarse, restrained voice said, 'There's a *cab*.'

At the same time he saw the pale figure of a girl standing in front of him. The man experienced that shock the unexpected always delivers. He bristled horribly. There is no more formidable sight than that of a wild beast disturbed. Its fear is fearsome. He recoiled and stammered out, 'Who is this baggage?'

'Your daughter.'

Éponine it was, speaking to Thénardier.

At Éponine's appearance the other five, that is to say Claquesous, Gueulemer, Babet, Montparnasse and Brujon, had approached noiselessly, unhurriedly, without a word, with that sinister stealth characteristic of these men of the night.

---

* Footnoted by Hugo: 'Chien', 'Dog'.

† In the French text 'levé'. Footnoted by Hugo: 'Apporté. De l'espagnol *llevar*', 'Brought: from the Spanish *llevar*'.

‡ In the French text 'morfiler'. Footnoted by Hugo: 'Manger', 'To eat'.

§ In the French text 'frangir la vanterne'. Footnoted by Hugo: '*Casser un carreau* au moyen d'un emplâtre de mastic qui, appuyé sur la vitre, retient les morceaux de verre et empêche le bruit', '*To break a window* with the aid of a layer of putty that, applied to the window-pane, holds the pieces of glass together and prevents any noise.'

¶ In the French text 'criblera'. Footnoted by Hugo: 'Criera', '(Will) squeal'.

** Footnoted by Hugo: 'La scie', 'The saw'.

†† In the French text 'faucher'. Footnoted by Hugo: 'Couper', 'To cut'.

Discernible in their hands were horrific-looking tools of some kind. Gueulemer held one of those curved crowbars that prowlers call *fanchons*.

'What the hell are you doing here? What do you want with us? Are you crazy?' Thénardier cried out, in so far as anyone can cry out when speaking in a low voice. 'Why've you to come get in the way when we're working?'

Éponine burst out laughing and threw her arms around his neck.

'I'm here, my dear pa, because I'm here. Isn't sitting on the ground allowed these days? You're the one that oughtn't to be here. Why've you come, seeing as this place is a biscuit? I told Magnon that. It's no good for you. But give me a hug, my dear pa! It's such a long time since I last saw you! So you're out now?'

Thénardier tried to free himself from Éponine's arms, grumbling, 'All right. You've hugged me. Yes, I'm out. I'm not inside. Now, clear off.'

But Éponine did not let go, and redoubled her displays of affection.

'But how did you manage that, pa dear? You must be very clever to have got yourself out of there. Tell me all about it! And ma? Where's ma? Now give me news of ma.'

Thénardier replied, 'She's fine, I don't know, let me alone, clear off, I tell you.'

'I don't want to clear off just yet,' said Éponine, pouting like a spoiled child. 'You're turning me away when I haven't seen you for four months and I've hardly had time to give you a hug.'

And she caught her father around the neck again.

'Now this is stupid!' said Babet.

'Let's get on with it!' said Gueulemer. 'The bloodhounds may come by.'

The ventriloquist's voice recited these lines:

New Year's Day is the right time
For hugging ma and pa – not now.

Éponine turned to the five villains.

'Why, it's Monsieur Brujon. Hallo, Monsieur Babet. Hallo, Monsieur Claquesous. Don't you recognize me, Monsieur Gueulemer? How are you, Montparnasse?'

'Yes, everybody recognizes you!' said Thénardier. 'Hallo, goodbye, now get along with you! Leave us alone!'

'This is the time of day for foxes, not birds,' said Montparnasse.

'You can see we've got a job to do here*,' added Babet.

Éponine took Montparnasse's hand.

'Careful!' he said. 'You'll cut yourself, I've got an unsheathed *lingre*†.'

'My dear Montparnasse,' Éponine replied very softly, 'you should trust people. I'm my father's daughter, after all. Monsieur Babet, Monsieur Gueulemer, I'm the one who was given this job to look into.'

It is remarkable that Éponine was not using slang. Since meeting Marius she had become incapable of speaking that dreadful language.

She squeezed Gueulemer's rough, fat fingers in her skeletally weak and bony little hand, and went on, 'As you well know, I'm no fool. Usually I'm taken at my word. I've been useful to you before. Well, I asked around. You'll be taking an unnecessary risk, you see. There's nothing for you in this house, I swear.'

'There are women on their own here,' said Gueulemer.

'No. Those people have moved out.'

'Well, the candles haven't!' said Babet.

And through the tree-tops he pointed out to Éponine a light moving about in the villa's mansard roof. It was Toussaint, who had stayed up late hanging some washing to dry.

Éponine made a last-ditch effort.

'Well,' she said, 'they're very poor people, there's nothing to steal here.'

'Go to hell!' cried Thénardier. 'When we've turned the place upside down and put the cellar where the attic belongs and the attic in place of the cellar, we'll tell you what there is inside and whether it's *des balles, des ronds ou des broques*‡.'

And he pushed her aside.

'My dear friend Monsieur Montparnasse,' said Éponine, 'you're a decent lad, I beg you not to go in there.'

'You be careful, you're going to cut yourself,' replied Montparnasse.

Thénardier said in that authoritative tone of voice he had, 'Make yourself scarce, my girl, and let the men get on with their business!'

Éponine released Montparnasse's hand which she had seized again, and said, 'So you mean to go into that house?'

---

* In the French text 'goupiner icigo'. Footnoted by Hugo: 'Travailler ici', 'To work here'.

† Footnoted by Hugo: 'Couteau', 'Knife'.

‡ Footnoted by Hugo: 'Des francs, des sous ou des liards', 'Francs, sous or quarter-sous'.

'You bet!' sniggered the ventriloquist.

Then she backed up against the gate, confronting the six villains who were armed to the teeth and looking like demons in the dark, and she said in a low, steady voice, 'Well, I won't let you.'

They stopped in their tracks, astounded. The ventriloquist did stop sniggering, however.

She went on, 'Friends! Now, listen carefully. It's not going to happen. Now I'm doing the talking. For a start, if you go into that garden, if you touch this gate, I'll scream, I'll go banging on doors, I'll wake up the neighbourhood, I'll have all six of you rounded up, I'll call the police.'

'She would, too,' Thénardier said quietly to Brujon and the ventriloquist.

She tossed her head and added, 'Starting with my father!'

Thénardier came nearer.

'Not so close, old man!' she said.

He stepped back, muttering under his breath, 'Now, what's got into her?' And he added, 'Bitch!'

She began to laugh in a dreadful way.

'Please yourself, you won't get in. I can't be the daughter of a dog seeing as I'm the daughter of a wolf! There are six of you. What's that to me? You're men. Well, I'm a woman. You don't frighten me, that's for sure. I'm telling you, you won't get inside this house because I don't want you to. If you come any nearer I'll bark. I told you, I'm the *cab*. I couldn't care less about you. Now be on your way, I've had enough of you ! Go anywhere you like, but don't come here, I won't let you! You use your knives, I'll use my feet, it's all the same to me. So come on, then!'

She took a step towards the villains; she was terrifying. She started laughing again.

'Good God! I'm not scared. This summer I'll be hungry, this winter I'll be cold. Daft, these jokers are, thinking they're going to be able to frighten a girl! Frightened? Of what? Oh yeah, ever so frightened! Just because you've got pathetic fancy women who hide under the bed when you raise your voice! Well, I'm not scared of anything!'

She fastened her steady gaze on Thénardier and said, 'Not even of you!'

Then, letting her blazing eyes wander over the villains, this spectre went on, 'What do I care if I'm picked up off the pavement of Rue Plumet tomorrow morning, knifed to death by my father, or found a year from now in the nets at St-Cloud or on the Île des Cygnes among rotten old cork floats and drowned dogs?'

Seized by a dry cough, she was forced to break off, her weak, narrow chest wheezing as she breathed.

She resumed. 'I just have to shout and there'll be folk here in no time! There's six of you, but I've got everybody with me.'

Thénardier made a move towards her.

'Get back!' she cried.

He halted, and said to her softly, 'All right. I won't come any nearer, but you keep your voice down. You want to stop us working, then, my girl? But we've got to earn our living! Don't you feel kindly towards your father any more?'

'I've got no time for you,' said Éponine.

'But we've got to live, we've got to eat—'

'Drop dead!'

That said, she sat at the foot of the gatepost, singing to herself:

> Those bygone days
> Of my youthful charms
> And my winning ways.

With her elbow on her knee and her chin in her hand, she swung her foot with an air of indifference. Her thin shoulder blades showed through her tattered dress. The nearby street lamp lit up her face, and the attitude she struck. You would never expect to see anything more resolute, or more surprising.

Dumbfounded and dejected at being thwarted by a girl, the six cut-throats went and stood in the shadow cast by the lantern to confer, their deliberations accompanied by shrugs of fury and humiliation.

In the meantime she watched them with an air that was both calm and wild.

'Something's got into her,' said Babet. 'For some reason. Is she in love with the *cab*? It's a pity, though, to miss out on this one. Two women, an old man living in a back yard. Those are quite good curtains on the windows. The old boy must be a *guinal**. I think we're on to a good thing here.'

'Well, you lot go on in there,' cried Montparnasse, 'and get on with the job! I'll stay here with the girl, and if she gives me any trouble . . .'

He revealed the unsheathed knife he had up his sleeve, making it glint in the light of the street lamp.

Thénardier said not a word and seemed willing to go along with anything.

* Footnoted by Hugo: 'Un juif', 'A Jew'.

Brujon, who was something of an oracle and who, as we know, had 'set the job up', had not yet spoken. He seemed thoughtful.

He had the reputation of stopping at nothing, and he was known to have one day burgled a police station out of sheer bravado. He also made up verses and songs, which gave him great authority.

Babet questioned him. 'Nothing to say, Brujon?'

Brujon remained silent a moment longer, tossed his head this way and that, then finally made up his mind to speak: 'The thing is, this morning I came across two sparrows fighting, this evening I bump into an argumentative woman. That's bad. Let's be off.'

And off they went.

As they were going Montparnasse muttered, 'All the same, if you'd wanted, I'd've finished her off.'

Babet replied, 'Not me. I don't raise my hand against a woman.'

At the corner of the street they stopped, and in an undertone held this enigmatic conversation:

'Where are we going to sleep tonight?'

'Under Pantin*.'

'Got the key to the gate with you, Thénardier?'

'Of course.'

Éponine, who did not take her eyes off them, saw them go back the way they had come. She stood up and began to creep after them, keeping close to the walls and the houses. She followed them like this as far as the boulevard. There they parted, and she saw those six men plunge into the darkness, where they seemed to melt away.

V

Things of the Night

After the villains had gone, Rue Plumet resumed its quiet night-time appearance.

What had just taken place in this street would have been no surprise in a forest. Stands of trees, underwoods, thickets, rampant and tangled branches, overgrown weeds, are inherently sinister. There, the teeming wilderness glimpses the sudden apparitions of the invisible. What lies beneath man perceives through the mist what lies beyond him. And things unknown to us in our lifetime confront each other in the dark. Bristling and farouche, nature takes fright at the approach of certain things in which it believes it detects the supernatural. The forces of darkness are familiar with each other and there are between

* Footnoted by Hugo: 'Paris'.

them mysterious counter-balances. Tooth and claw fear the ungraspable. Bloodthirsty bestiality, ravenous, voracious appetites in search of prey, instincts armed with talons and jaws, beginning and ending only in the belly, watch and anxiously scent the shrouded spectral form on the prowl, standing impassively in the vagueness of its quivering robe and seemingly, to them, animated by a ghastly, deathly life force. These brute beasts of mere matter are obscurely afraid of dealing with the great unknown condensed into some strange being. A black figure barring the way stops the creature of the wild in its tracks. What emerges from the graveyard intimidates and confounds what emerges from the den. The ferocious is afraid of the sinister. Wolves back away from any encounter with a ghoul.

VI
In a Return to Reality Marius
Gives Cosette His Address

While this she-dog in human form kept guard at the gate, and the six villains were being seen off by a girl, Marius was at Cosette's side.

Never had the sky been starrier or more spellbinding, the trees more tremulous, the plant smells more pervasive. Never had the birds fallen asleep among the leaves with a sweeter sound. Never had all the harmonies of cosmic serenity better answered the inward music of love. Never had Marius been happier, more smitten, more enraptured. But he had found Cosette sad. Cosette had been weeping. Her eyes were red.

This was the first cloud in that wonderful dream.

Marius's first words had been, 'What is it?'

And she had replied, 'I'll tell you.'

Then she sat on the bench by the steps; and while, all atremble, he took his place beside her, she went on, 'My father told me this morning to make preparations, he has some business to attend to, and we might be going away.'

Marius shuddered from head to foot.

When you are at the end of your life, dying means going away, when you are at the beginning of it, going away means dying.

Every day for the last six weeks, little by little, slowly, by degrees, Marius had taken possession of Cosette. Complete possession, but in a totally abstract sense. As we have already explained, with first love, the soul is taken long before the body. Later the body is taken long before the soul, sometimes the soul is not taken at all. The Faublas and the Prudhommes would add, 'Because there isn't one.' But happily, that piece of sarcasm is a blasphemy. Marius's possession of Cosette, then, was a spiritual possession, but he enveloped her with his entire soul and jealously laid claim to her with incredible conviction. He possessed her smile, her breath, her perfume, the deep radiance of her blue eyes, the softness of her skin when he touched her hand, the charming birthmark she had on her neck, all her thoughts. They had agreed never to sleep without dreaming of each other, and they had kept their word. So he possessed all of Cosette's dreams. He stared incessantly at the fine hairs on the back of her neck, lightly touching them with his breath and assuring himself there was not one of those little hairs that did not belong to him, Marius. He contemplated and adored the things she wore – her ribbon bow, her gloves, her cuffs, her ankle-boots – as sacred objects of which he was master. He dreamed he was lord of those pretty tortoiseshell combs she wore in her hair and, passion declaring itself in suppressed and confused stutterings, he even told himself that there was not one lacing in her gown, not one stitch in her stockings, not one pleat in her bodice, that was not his. At Cosette's side he felt close to his own property, his chattel, his despotic ruler and his slave. It was as if so fused were their souls that had they wished to reclaim them it would have been impossible to tell them apart. 'This one is mine.' 'No, it's mine.' 'I assure you, you're mistaken. That's undoubtedly me.' 'What you mistake for yourself is me.' Marius was something that formed part of Cosette, and Cosette was something that formed part of Marius. Marius felt Cosette living within him. To have Cosette, to possess Cosette – this to him was inseparable from breathing. It was in the context of this belief, this delirium, this virginal possession of an absolute and extraordinary nature, this supremacy, that those words 'We're going away' were sprung on him and the blunt voice of reality screamed, 'Cosette doesn't belong to you!'

Marius woke up. As we have said, for six weeks he had been leading a life divorced from reality. Those words – going away! – brought him back to reality with a vengeance.

He was lost for words. Cosette felt only that his hand was very cold. It was her turn to say to him, 'What is it?'

He replied, his voice so low that Cosette barely heard him, 'I don't understand what you said.'

She explained, 'This morning my father told me to pack all my things and be ready to leave, that he would give me his linen to put in a trunk, that he had to make a trip, that we were going away, that we would need a large trunk for me and a small one for him, and to have all this ready within a week from now, and that we might be going to England.'

'But that's outrageous!' exclaimed Marius.

It is certain that in Marius's mind at that moment, no abuse of power, no violence, no abomination by the worst of tyrants, no deed of Busiris, Tiberius, or Henry VIII could have equalled in ferocity this: Monsieur Fauchelevent taking his daughter off to England because he had business there.

He asked in a faint voice, 'And when will you leave?'

'He didn't say when.'

'And when will you return?'

'He didn't say when.'

Marius rose and said coldly, 'Cosette, will you go?'

Cosette turned to him her lovely eyes filled with anguish, and replied in a kind of bewilderment, 'Where?'

'To England. Will you go?'

'Why are you saying *vous* to me?'

'I'm asking you whether you will go.'

'What do you expect me to do?' she said, clasping her hands together.

'Then you will go?'

'Well, if my father's going?'

'Then you will go?'

Cosette clutched Marius's hand and squeezed without replying.

'Very well,' said Marius. 'Then I'll go elsewhere.'

Cosette sensed rather than understood the meaning of these words. She turned so pale that her face showed white in the darkness. She stammered out, 'What do you mean?'

Marius stared at her, then slowly raised his eyes to heaven, and replied, 'Nothing.'

When he lowered his gaze he saw Cosette smiling at him. The smile of a woman you love has a radiance that can be seen in the dark.

'How silly we are! Marius, I have an idea.'

'What is it?'

'You'll come too if we go away! I'll tell you where! Come and join me wherever I am!'

Marius was now a man fully awake. He had returned to reality. He cried out to Cosette, 'Go away with you! Are you mad? But that costs money and I haven't any! Go to England? But I now owe – I don't know – more than ten louis to Courfeyrac, a friend of mine that you don't know! But I have an old hat that's not worth three francs, I've a coat that has buttons missing down the front, my shirt's all torn, I've holes at my elbows, my boots let in water. For the last six weeks I haven't thought about it and I haven't told you. Cosette, I'm an impoverished wretch. You see me only at night and you give me your love. If you saw me in daylight you'd give me a sou! Go to England! Huh! I haven't enough to pay for a passport!'

He threw himself against a nearby tree and on the point of collapse, with both arms above his head, his forehead against the bark, feeling neither the wood grazing his skin nor the fever throbbing at his temples, he stood there motionless – the statue of despair.

He remained like that for a long time. You could spend eternity in such depths of misery. At last he turned round. He heard behind him a soft, sad, stifled little sound.

It was Cosette sobbing.

She had been weeping at Marius's side for more than two hours while he was rapt in thought.

He turned to her, fell on his knees, and slowly prostrating himself took the tip of her foot peeping out from under her gown and kissed it. She let him do so in silence. There are moments when, like a mournful goddess, a woman accepts with resignation the religion of love.

'Don't cry,' he said.

She murmured, 'When I may be going away and you can't come!'

He went on, 'Do you love me?'

'I adore you!' she sobbed – those words of paradise that never sound more enchanting than when said through tears.

He continued in a tone that was an inexpressible caress, 'Don't cry. Now will you do that for me, will you not cry?'

'Do you love me?' she said.

He took her hand.

'Cosette, I've never given my word of honour to anyone because my word of honour frightens me. I sense that my father is very close by. Well, I give you my most sacred word of honour that if you go away I shall die.'

There was in the way he spoke these words such a solemn, quiet melancholy that Cosette trembled. She felt that chill you get at the passing-by of something sombre and real. Seized with dread, she stopped weeping.

'Now, listen,' he said, 'don't expect me tomorrow.'

'Why not?'

'Don't expect me until the day after tomorrow.'

'Oh? Why not?'

'You'll see.'

'A day without seeing you! But that's impossible!'

'Let's sacrifice one day for the sake of perhaps spending the rest of our lives together.'

And Marius added under his breath, as if to himself, 'He's a man rigid in his habits and he only ever receives visitors in the evening.'

'Which man are you talking about?' asked Cosette.

'Me? I didn't say anything.'

'So what is it you're hoping for?'

'Wait until the day after tomorrow.'

'That's what you want?'

'Yes, Cosette.'

She took his head in her hands, standing on tip-toe to raise herself to his height and searching his gaze, looking for hope in his eyes.

Marius said, 'Now that I think of it, you ought to know my address, things can happen, you never know, I'm living with that friend called Courfeyrac, Rue de la Verrerie, number sixteen.'

He rummaged in his pocket, pulled out a penknife, and with the blade he wrote in the plaster on the wall '16 Rue de la Verrerie'. Meanwhile, Cosette had been looking into his eyes again.

'Tell me what you have in mind. Marius, you do have something in mind. Tell me what it is. Oh! tell me, so that I don't have a sleepless night.'

'What I have in mind is this: that God can't possibly want to part us. Expect me the day after tomorrow.'

'What will I do until then?' said Cosette. 'You're out and about, you come and go! Men are so lucky! I'm going to be left all on my own! Oh, how miserable I'm going to be! Tell me, what is it you'll be doing tomorrow evening?'

'I'll be trying for something.'

'Then I'll be thinking of you from now until then and praying to God that you succeed. I won't ask any more questions, since you don't want me to. You're my master. I'll spend tomorrow evening singing that music from *Euryanthe* that you love, that you came and heard one night from behind my shutters. But the day after tomorrow you must come early. I'll be expecting you after dark, at nine o'clock sharp, I'm warning you. Oh dear God! How sad it is when the days are long! Have you got that? On the stroke of nine I'll be in the garden.'

'And so will I.'

And with not another word between them, prompted by the same thought, impelled by those electric currents that put two lovers in constant communication with each other, both revelling in the delight even of their sorrow, they fell into each other's arms without noticing that their lips met, while their raised eyes, filled with tears and brimming with ecstasy, contemplated the stars.

When Marius left, the street was deserted. This was just when Éponine was following the villains to the boulevard.

While Marius was brooding, his head pressed against the tree, an idea had crossed his mind, an idea, alas! that he himself considered far-fetched and impossible. He had made a desperate resolve.

VII
Interaction between an Old Heart and a Young One

Old Gillenormand by this time had already turned ninety-one. He still lived with Mademoiselle Gillenormand in Rue des Filles-du-Calvaire, number six, in the old house that belonged to him. He was, remember, one of those antiquated old men who await death straight-backed, burdened by age but unbowed, whom even sorrow cannot bend.

Yet for some time his daughter had been saying, 'My father is in decline.' He no longer railed against the maids, he no longer struck the staircase landing so vigorously with his cane when Basque was slow to open the door for him. The July Revolution had barely incensed him for six months now. He had read in *Le Moniteur* almost with equanimity that combination of words: Monsieur Humblot-Conté, peer of France. The fact is, the old man was filled with despondency. He did not buckle, he did not capitulate, it was no more in his physical nature than in his moral nature to do so. But he felt himself inwardly weakening. For four years he had been waiting for Marius, steadfastly – that is the right word – convinced that the cheeky young scamp would ring at his door sooner or later. Now he was reduced at certain bleak moments to telling himself that if Marius were to keep him waiting much longer . . .

It was not death he could not bear, it was the idea that perhaps he would never see Marius again. Never to see Marius again – until that day, not for a moment had this even entered his mind. Now this idea was beginning to dawn on him, and it chilled him. As is always true of genuine and natural feelings, absence had only increased his grandfatherly love for the ungrateful child who had gone off like that. It is during December nights, when the temperature drops below zero, that you most think of the sun. Monsieur Gillenormand was above all incapable, or so he thought, of taking a single step – he, the grandfather – towards his grandson. 'I'd sooner die,' he said. He considered himself completely blameless, but could not think of Marius without deep affection and the unspoken despair of an old man on the threshold of darkness.

He was beginning to lose his teeth, which added to his misery.

Though he would not admit it to himself, for it would have made him furious and ashamed, Monsieur Gillenormand had never loved a mistress as he loved Marius.

He had arranged for an old portrait of his other daughter, the one who had died, Madame Pontmercy, a portrait painted when she was eighteen, to be placed in his room, facing his bed, as the first thing he wanted to see when he woke up. He was constantly looking at that portrait. One day as he was studying it he happened to say, 'I think it captures a likeness.'

'Of my sister?' Mademoiselle Gillenormand responded. 'Yes, of course.'

The old man added, 'And of him too.'

Once, as he sat with his knees pressed together and his eyes almost closed in an attitude of dejection, his daughter ventured to say to him, 'Father, are you still as angry as ever?'

She paused, not daring to go any further.

'With whom?' he asked.

'With poor Marius.'

He raised his aged head, laid his wrinkled, wasted hand on the table, and exclaimed in his angriest and most ringing tone of voice, 'Poor Marius, you say! That gentleman is a rascal, a scoundrel, a heartless, soulless, ungrateful little egotist, a conceited and disagreeable wretch!'

And he turned away so that his daughter would not see the tear he had in his eye. Three days later he broke a silence that had lasted four hours to say bluntly to his daughter, 'I made a point of asking Mademoiselle Gillenormand never to speak of him to me.'

Aunt Gillenormand gave up any further attempt at reconciliation and made this profound diagnosis: 'My father was never very fond of my sister after that foolishness of hers. It's clear he detests Marius.'

'After that foolishness of hers' meant 'after she married the colonel'.

However, as anyone might have surmised, Mademoiselle Gillenormand had failed in her ploy to substitute her favourite, the officer of the lancers, for Marius. The replacement, Théodule, had not been a success. Monsieur Gillenormand had not accepted the exchange of one for the other. A hole in the heart is not mended with a stop-gap. Théodule, for his part, while scenting the prospect of inheriting, balked at the chore of currying favour. The old gent bored the lancer and the lancer offended the old gent. Lieutenant Théodule was lively,

I dare say, but a chatter-box; frivolous but vulgar, enjoying the pleasures of life but keeping bad company. He had mistresses, it is true, and he had a great deal to say about them, that is also true, but he spoke badly of them. All his good qualities had some shortcoming. Monsieur Gillenormand lost patience with the tales of his undistinguished amorous adventures around the barracks in Rue de Babylone. And then, Lieutenant Gillenormand sometimes came in uniform, wearing the tricolour cockade. This rendered him quite simply unacceptable. Old Gillenormand eventually said to his daughter, 'I've had enough of Théodule. You can see him if you like. I don't much care for warriors in peacetime. I'm not sure I don't prefer a sabre-slasher to a sabre-sporter. The clash of blades in battle is less dismal, after all, than the clatter of scabbards on the pavement. And besides, swaggering around like a swashbuckler and primping like a woman, wearing a corset under your cuirass, is doubly ridiculous. If you're a real man, you keep an equal distance from blustering and from mincing. Neither bully boy nor pretty boy. You can keep that Théodule of yours for yourself.'

It was no use his daughter saying to him, 'But he's your great-nephew, after all', as it turned out that Monsieur Gillenormand, a grandfather to his very fingertips, was not in the least a great-uncle. Since he was discriminating and made comparisons, essentially Théodule had served only to make him regret Marius all the more.

One evening – it was the fourth of June, which did not prevent old Gillenormand from having a very good fire going in his fireplace – he had dispatched his daughter with her sewing to the next room.

He was alone in his own room with its pastoral décor, his feet on the fire-dogs, half surrounded by his huge nine-panelled Coromandel screen, elbows resting on the table where two lighted candles burned under a green shade, sunk into his tapestry-upholstered armchair, with a book in his hand but not reading. He was dressed in his usual style, as a post-Revolutionary dandy, and looking like an old portrait of Garat. This would have had people running after him in the street, but whenever he went out his daughter bundled him up in a great quilted overcoat of the kind bishops wear, which concealed his clothes. Except for getting up and going to bed, he never wore a dressing-gown when he was at home. 'It gives the impression of being old,' he said.

Old Gillenormand was thinking of Marius fondly and bitterly, and as usual the bitterness was dominant. This soured tenderness always ended up by boiling over and turning into indignation. He had reached that point when you try to come to terms with the situation and to accept what is tearing you apart. He was in the process of explaining to himself that there was no longer any reason why Marius should return, that if he was ever going to return he would have already done so, that all hope of it was to be abandoned. He was trying to get used to the idea that it was all over, and that he would die without having seen 'that gentleman' again. But his whole nature rebelled. His old fatherliness could not consent to it. 'How could he not come back!' he said. This was his doleful refrain.

His bald head had dropped down on to his chest and he was staring vaguely at the ashes in his hearth with an angry and mournful gaze.

When he was most deeply absorbed in these thoughts, his old servant Basque came in and asked, 'Is Monsieur able to receive Monsieur Marius?'

The old man sat bolt upright, drained of colour like a corpse galvanized by an electric shock. All the blood had flowed to his heart. He stammered, 'Monsieur Marius who?'

'I don't know,' replied Basque, intimidated and disconcerted by his master's manner. 'I didn't see him. It was Nicolette who just came and told me, "There's a young man here – say it's Monsieur Marius."'

Old Gillenormand muttered in a low voice, 'Show him in.'

And he remained in the same attitude, his head shaking, his eyes riveted on the door. It opened again. A young man entered. It was Marius.

Marius stopped in the doorway as if waiting to be told to come in.

His near-wretched attire was not noticeable in the gloom created by the lampshade. All that could be made out clearly was his calm, grave but strangely sad face.

Several moments went by before old Gillenormand, dazed with astonishment and joy, could see anything but a brilliance of the kind that accompanies the presence of an apparition. He was close to fainting. He saw Marius through a dazzling light. It was Marius, it really was Marius.

At last! After four years! He captured him, as it were, whole, in a single glance. He found him handsome, noble, distinguished, matured, a grown man, decent-looking, charming in manner. He felt like opening his arms to him, calling his name, rushing towards him; his heart melted in rapture, affectionate words swelled his breast to bursting. Finally all his tenderness came to the surface and reached his lips and, by virtue of a contrariness that was the very essence of his nature, what came out was harshness. He said abruptly, 'What are you doing here?'

Marius replied in confusion, 'Monsieur—'

Monsieur Gillenormand wished Marius had thrown himself into his arms. He was angry with Marius and with himself. He sensed that he was being abrupt and that Marius was being cold. It was vexing and unbearably disquieting for the old man to feel so loving and tearful on the inside and to be capable only of harshness on the outside. His bitterness returned. He interrupted Marius in a curmudgeonly tone, 'So why are you here?'

That 'so' meant 'if you don't come and hug me'. Marius looked at his grandfather, whose pallor gave him a face of marble.

'Monsieur—'

'Have you come to ask my forgiveness? Have you realized you were in the wrong?'

He thought he was encouraging Marius in the right direction and that 'the child' was going to relent. Marius shuddered. It was the disowning of his father that was being asked of him. He lowered his eyes and replied, 'No, monsieur.'

'Well then,' exclaimed the old man impetuously, with a sorrow keenly felt and full of anger, 'what do you want of me?'

Marius put his hands together, took a step forward, and said in a weak and trembling voice, 'Monsieur, have pity on me.'

These words stirred Monsieur Gillenormand. Delivered sooner, they would have softened him, but they came too late. The grandfather rose. He rested on his cane with both hands, his lips were white, his head unsteady, but his tall figure reared above Marius, bowed before him.

'Pity on you, monsieur? The young stripling asks the old man of ninety-one for pity! You're starting out in life, I'm departing it. You go to the theatre, to dances, to the café, to the billiard-hall, you're clever, women like you, you're a handsome fellow. Whereas I'm huddled by the fire at the height of summer. You're rich with the only riches there are, I have all the poverties of old age, infirmity, isolation! You have your thirty-two teeth, a good stomach, keen eyes, strength, appetite, health, mirth, a thick crop of black hair. I don't even have white hair any more, I've lost my teeth, my legs are going and I'm losing my memory. There are three street names I constantly get muddled up, Rue Charlot, Rue du Chaume and Rue St-Claude. That's what I've come to. You have the whole future, full of sunshine, ahead of you, I'm beginning not to be able to see beyond the end of my nose, so far into the darkness am I. You're in love, that goes without saying, not a soul loves me, and you ask me for pity! Damn it, Molière didn't think of that. If that's the kind of joke you gentlemen lawyers crack at the law courts, I sincerely congratulate you. You're very amusing.'

And the octogenarian* repeated in a low-pitched, angry voice, 'So what do you want of me?'

'Monsieur,' said Marius, 'I know that my presence is objectionable to you but I've come only to ask one thing of you, and then I'll go away at once.'

'You're an idiot!' said the old man. 'Who's telling you to go away?'

This was the translation of those fond words he had deep down inside him: 'Now, come along, ask my forgiveness! Come along, throw your arms round my neck!' Monsieur Gillenormand sensed that in a few minutes Marius was going to leave him, that his unpleasant welcome was discouraging Marius, that his harshness was driving him away – he told himself all this, adding to his grief, but as his grief turned instantly to anger his harshness intensified. He wished that Marius understood this, and Marius did not understand, which infuriated the old man.

He resumed, 'What! You treated me, your grandfather, with disrespect, you left my house to go who knows where, you broke your aunt's heart, you went off, as anyone would guess, it's more agreeable, to lead a bachelor life, to sow your wild oats, to come home at all hours, to amuse yourself. You've given me no sign of life, you've been incurring debts without even telling me to settle them for you, you've become a roisterer and a hell-raiser, and you come to see me after four years and that's all you have to say to me!'

This brutal way of forcing a grandson to be affectionate resulted only in Marius's silence. Monsieur Gillenormand folded his arms, a gesture that was particularly imperious in him, and bitterly berated Marius.

'Let's get this over with. You've come to ask me for something, you say? Well, what? What is it? Speak up!'

'Monsieur,' said Marius, with the look of a man who senses he is about to plunge into a precipice, 'I've come to ask your permission to marry.'

Monsieur Gillenormand rang the bell. Basque opened the door.

'Send for my daughter.'

A second later the door reopened, Mademoiselle Gillenormand did not come in but made herself visible. Marius stood silent, his arms dangling, looking like a criminal. Monsieur Gillenormand paced the room, back and forth. He turned to his daughter and said, 'Nothing

---

* As in the French text, but we have been told that Monsieur Gillenormand has turned ninety-one, and is therefore a nonagenarian.

important. It's Monsieur Marius. Say good day to him. Monsieur wants to get married. That's all. You can go.'

The rough, curt sound of the old man's voice revealed a strange intensity of emotion. The aunt stared at Marius with a frightened expression, seemed hardly to recognize him, let not a gesture nor a syllable escape her, and disappeared at her father's behest quicker than a straw before the hurricane.

Meanwhile, old Gillenormand had returned to lean back against the mantelpiece.

'To marry! At the age of twenty-one! You've got it all planned! There's just the small matter of asking permission! A formality. Sit down, monsieur. Well now, you've had a revolution since I last had the honour of seeing you. The Jacobins got the upper hand. You must have been delighted. Are you not a Republican now that you've become a baron? You can reconcile that. The Republic comes with the barony. Did you win any July distinctions? Did you have any part in the attack on the Louvre, monsieur? Quite near here, in Rue St-Antoine, opposite Rue des Nonnains-d'Hyères, there's a cannon-ball embedded in the wall on the third floor of a house with this inscription on it: '28th July 1830'. Go and take a look. It's an impressive sight. Ah! they do some fine things, those friends of yours. By the way, aren't they putting a fountain in place of the monument to Monsieur le Duc de Berry? So you want to get married? To whom? Without being indiscreet, may one ask to whom?'

He paused, and before Marius had time to answer he added aggressively, 'Come now, you have a situation? Your fortune's made? How much do you earn practising as a lawyer?'

'Nothing,' said Marius with an almost fierce determination and firmness.

'Nothing? All you have to live on is the twelve hundred francs' allowance I give you?'

Marius did not reply.

Monsieur Gillenormand went on, 'Ah, I see, the girl is rich, then?'

'As rich as I am.'

'What! No dowry?'

'No.'

'Expectations?'

'I believe not.'

'Completely unprovided for! And what does the father do?'

'I don't know.'

'And what's her name?'

'Mademoiselle Fauchelevent.'

'Fauchewhat?'

'Fauchelevent.'

'Bah!' the old man snorted.

'Monsieur!' cried Marius.

Monsieur Gillenormand interrupted him in the tone of a man talking to himself, 'Just as I thought, twenty-one years old, no situation, twelve hundred francs a year, and Madame la baronne Pontmercy will be going out to buy a couple of sous' worth of parsley from the greengrocer.'

'Monsieur,' Marius repeated in the frenzy of seeing his last hope disappear, 'I beg you! I implore you in the name of heaven, with my hands together, monsieur, I throw myself at your feet, allow me to marry her!'

The old man gave a burst of strident, doleful laughter, coughing and speaking through it.

'Ha-ha-ha! You said to yourself: "By God, I'm going to visit that old duffer, that silly old fool! What a pity I'm not yet twenty-five! Then I'd have simply sent him notification of my marriage! I wouldn't have bothered with him! Never mind, I'll say to him: 'You old relic, you're exceedingly happy to see me, I want to get married, I want to marry some Mam'selle Nobody, daughter of some Monsieur Who-knows-what, I've no shoes, she hasn't a stitch of clothing, that's fine, I want to throw away my career, my future, my youth, my life, I want to plunge into misery with a woman around my neck, it's what I want, and you must agree to it!' And the old fossil will agree." Of course, my lad, whatever you want, tie yourself to your millstone, marry your Pousselevent, your Coupelevent . . . Never, monsieur, never!'

'Father!'

'Never!'

At the tone in which that 'Never!' was uttered, Marius lost all hope. He slowly crossed the room, his head bowed, reeling, more like someone dying than someone taking his leave. Monsieur Gillenormand followed him with his eyes, and just when the door opened and Marius was about to leave the room, he darted forward with that sprightliness of domineering and spoiled old men, grabbed Marius by the collar, dragged him back into the room, threw him into an armchair and said to him, 'Tell me all about it!'

It was that single word 'father', blurted out by Marius, that had brought about this revolution. Marius stared at him in bewilderment. Monsieur Gillenormand's changing face now expressed nothing but plain, unutterable goodwill. The patriarch had given way to the grandfather.

'Come along, now, speak, tell me about your amorous escapades, chatter away, I want to know everything! Heavens above! Young men are so idiotic!'

'Father!' Marius resumed.

The old man's whole face lit up with an indescribable radiance.

'Yes, that's right, call me father, and you'll see!'

There was now something so kind, so gentle, so open and so paternal in this bluffness that in his sudden transition from despair to hope Marius was as if stunned and elated by it. He was sitting by the table, the candle-light revealing the shabbiness of his clothes, which old Gillenormand now observed with amazement.

'Well, father,' said Marius.

'Now then!' interrupted Monsieur Gillenormand. 'You really haven't a sou? You're dressed like a thief!'

He rummaged in a drawer, took out a purse and laid it on the table. 'There you are, that's two hundred and fifty francs, buy yourself a hat.'

'Father,' Marius continued, 'my dear father, if you only knew! I love her. You can't imagine, the first time I saw her was at the Luxembourg Gardens, she used to go there. At first I didn't take much notice of her and then, I don't know how it came about, I fell in love with her. Oh! how unhappy that made me! Well, now I see her every day, at her home, her father doesn't know, and would you believe it, they're going away, we see each other in the evenings, in the garden, her father intends to take her to England, so I said to myself, "I'll go and see my grandfather and talk to him about it. I'd go mad first, I'd die, I'd fall ill, I'd throw myself in the river. I simply must marry her, since I'd go mad otherwise. Well, that's the whole truth, I don't think I've left anything out. She lives where there's a garden behind a gate on Rue Plumet. It's over towards Les Invalides.'

Old Gillenormand had sat down beside Marius, beaming. While listening to him and savouring the sound of his voice, he savoured at the same time a long-drawn pinch of snuff. At the words 'Rue Plumet' he stopped inhaling and let the remainder of the snuff fall on his knees.

'Rue Plumet! You said Rue Plumet? Now let's see! Isn't there a barracks near there? Of course, that's it. Your cousin Théodule mentioned it to me. The lancer, the officer. A young filly, my dear fellow, a young filly! Yes, by God, Rue Plumet. It used to be called Rue Blomet. It all comes back to me now. I've heard talk of that girl behind the railings in Rue Plumet. In a garden. A Pamela. Not a bad choice. She's very well turned out, I'm told. Between ourselves, I think that booby of a lancer courted her a little. I don't know how far it went. Anyway, it doesn't matter. Besides, he's not to be believed. He's a braggart, Marius! I think it's very acceptable that a young man like you should be in love. It's natural at your age. I like you better for being in love than for being a Jacobin. I like you better for running after a woman – good heavens, twenty women – than for being enamoured of Monsieur de Robespierre. For my part, I give myself credit for the fact that the only sans-culottes I ever liked were women!* Pretty girls are pretty girls, damn it! There's no denying that. As for your sweetheart, she's seeing you in secret, keeping her father in the dark. That's the way these things are done. I had affairs like that too. More than one. You know how to deal with it? You don't take it too seriously. You don't go making a tragedy of it. You don't decide to get wed with monsieur le maire in his sash presiding. You just stick to being a clever lad. You're sensible. "So, Lightly touch and quickly go" and no getting married. You come and look up your grandfather, who's a good fellow at heart and always has a few rolls of gold coins in some old drawer. You say to him, "Grandfather, it's like this." And your grandfather says, "It's only natural!" The young must live and the old must die. I've been young, and you'll be old. Now, my boy, you pass that on to your grandson. Here's two thousand francs. Enjoy yourself, by God! Best thing you can do! That's the way to deal with it. There's no reason to get married. You understand?'

Paralysed and incapable of uttering a syllable, Marius shook his head. The old man burst out laughing, winked an aged eye, gave him a slap on the knee, squarely met his gaze in a mysterious and gleeful manner, and said to him with the most indulgent of shrugs, 'Make her your mistress, silly boy!'

Marius blenched. He had understood nothing of what his grandfather had just said. All that harping on about Rue Blomet, Pamela, the barracks, the lancer, had passed Marius by like some phantasmagoria. None of that could have anything to do with Cosette, who was pure as a lily. The old man was raving. But his ravings had concluded with words that Marius had understood, and which were a deadly insult to Cosette. Those words 'Make her your mistress' ran through the austere young man's heart like a sword.

He rose, picked his hat up from the floor and strode resolutely towards the door. There he turned, bowed deeply to his grandfather, straightened up, head held high, and said, 'Five years ago you insulted

* A racy *bon mot* from Monsieur Gillenormand. The sans-culottes were the Revolutionaries from the lower classes, those without breeches (*sans culottes*), who wore instead the longer *pantalon* (full-length trouser); the women he has in mind would of course wear neither.

933

my father. Today you insult my wife. I won't ask for you for anything ever again, monsieur. Farewell.'

Dumbfounded, old Gillenormand opened his mouth, reached out his arms, tried to get to his feet, and before he could utter a word the door had closed and Marius was gone.

For several moments the old man remained motionless and as though thunderstruck, unable to speak or to breathe, as though a hand were tightening around his throat. At last he tore himself from his armchair, ran to the door – in so far as a ninety-one-year-old is capable of running – opened it and cried, 'Help! Help!'

His daughter appeared, then the servants.

In a pitifully rasping voice he said, 'Run after him! Bring him back! What did I do? He's mad! He's gone! Oh my God! Oh my God! This time he'll never come back again!'

He went to the window overlooking the street, threw it open with his trembling old hands, leaned as far out as he could while Basque and Nicolette held him from behind, and shouted, 'Marius! Marius! Marius! Marius!'

But already Marius was out of earshot and at that very moment was turning the corner of Rue St-Louis.

Two or three times the octogenarian raised both hands to his temples with an expression of anguish, staggered backwards and collapsed into an armchair, pulseless, voiceless, tearless, shaking his head and moving his lips with an air of stupidity, his eyes and his heart now empty but for something deep and mournful that resembled night.

BOOK NINE

WHERE ARE THEY GOING?

I
Jean Valjean

That same day, around four o'clock in the afternoon, Jean Valjean was sitting alone on one of the most deserted slopes of the earthworks around the Champ de Mars. Whether it was out of prudence or a desire for some time to himself, or quite simply owing to one of those barely perceptible changes in habit that gradually make their way into any life, he now rarely went out with Cosette. He wore his workman's jacket and coarse grey cotton trousers, and his long-peaked cap concealed his face. He was now calm and happy with regard to Cosette. What had for a while frightened and disturbed him had been dispelled. But for the last week or two, anxieties of a different kind had arisen. One day, while walking along the boulevard, he had caught sight of Thénardier. Thanks to his disguise, Thénardier had not recognized him, but since then Jean Valjean had seen him several times and he was now convinced that Thénardier was prowling around the neighbourhood. This was enough to bring him to a major decision. There was every danger in having Thénardier around.

Furthermore, Paris was unsettled. Political unrest had this drawback for anyone who had something in his life to hide: namely, that the police had become extremely uneasy and extremely suspicious, and that while trying to track down a man like Pépin or Morey they might very well detect a man like Jean Valjean.

From all these points of view he was anxious.

Finally, something inexplicable that had just come to his attention and by which he was still thoroughly shaken had added to his alarm. Up before the rest of the household the morning of that same day, and strolling in the garden before Cosette's shutters were open, he had suddenly noticed these words scratched on the wall, probably with a nail: '16 Rue de la Verrerie'.

It was very recent, the grooves in the old black mortar were white, a tuft of nettles at the foot of the wall was covered with a dusting of fresh plaster. It had probably been written during the night. What was it? An address? A signal for others? A warning to him? In any event, it was obvious that the garden had been broken into and strangers had been there. He recalled these bizarre incidents that had already upset the household. From these elements his mind tried to build up a picture. He carefully refrained from telling Cosette about what was written on the wall with a nail, for fear of frightening her.

Having weighed up all these considerations, Jean Valjean had decided to leave Paris, and even France, and to go to England. He had let Cosette know. He wanted to be gone within a week. He had sat down on that slope at the Champ de Mars, turning over in his mind all sorts of ideas, Thénardier, the police, that strange line written on the wall, this journey and the difficulty of getting a passport.

In the midst of these ruminations he noticed from a shadow cast by the sun that someone had just come to a halt on the crest of the slope immediately behind him. He was about to turn round when a piece of paper folded in four fell on his knees as if some hand above his head had dropped it. He took the piece of paper, unfolded it and read these words pencilled in capital letters: 'MOVE HOUSE'.

Jean Valjean leapt up, there was no one on the slope now. He looked around and noticed a person of some sort, bigger than a child but smaller than a man, in a grey shirt and velveteen trousers the colour of dust, climbing over the parapet and slipping into the trench around the Champ de Mars.

Jean Valjean went home straight away, with much on his mind.

II
Marius

Marius had left Monsieur Gillenormand's house feeling devastated. He had gone there with very little hope. He came away in immense despair.

And yet – those who have observed the first stirrings of the human heart will understand this – the officer, the lancer, the booby, cousin Théodule, had cast no shadow on his mind. Not the slightest. It might seem that the poet-dramatist could hope for a few complications resulting from this revelation sprung on the grandson by the grandfather. But what would be gained in drama would be lost in truth. Marius was at the age when you believe nothing bad about a person, later comes the age when you believe everything. Suspicions are nothing but wrinkles. The first blush of youth has none. What devastates Othello glances off Candide. Suspect Cosette? There are countless crimes Marius would more readily have committed.

He began to wander the streets, something to which those who suffer are prone. He thought of nothing he could later remember. At two o'clock in the morning he went home to Courfeyrac's place and threw himself fully dressed on his mattress. The sun was shining when he fell into that dreadful leaden sleep that allows your thoughts to keep going round inside your head. When he woke up he saw Courfeyrac, Enjolras, Feuilly and Combeferre standing in the room with their hats on, all ready to go out and in a great hurry.

Courfeyrac said to him, 'Are you coming to General Lamarque's funeral?'

It was as if Courfeyrac were speaking to him in Chinese.

He went out some time after them. He put in his pocket the pistols Javert had given him at the time of the third of February affair and that remained in his possession. These pistols were still loaded. It would be difficult to say what obscure notion he had in mind when he took them with him.

All day long he roamed about aimlessly. It rained on and off, he did not notice. For his midday meal he bought a roll for one sou at a baker's, put it in his pocket and forgot about it. Apparently, he bathed in the Seine without being aware of it. There are times when you feel as if you have a conflagration inside your head. It was one of those times for Marius. There was nothing he any longer hoped for, nothing he feared – this was an overnight development. He looked forward to the evening with feverish impatience, he had only one clear idea, that at nine o'clock he would see Cosette. This ultimate happiness was now his whole future; followed by darkness. Now and again, as he walked along the most deserted boulevards of Paris, he seemed to hear strange noises. Raising his head, he would emerge from his reverie and say, 'Are people fighting?'

At nightfall, at nine o'clock sharp, as he had promised Cosette, he was in Rue Plumet. Approaching the gate, he forgot about everything else. He had not seen Cosette for forty-eight hours. He was about to see her again. Every other thought faded and he felt only an incredible, intense joy. Those minutes that last centuries always have at the time that superlative and wonderful quality of completely filling the heart.

Marius shifted the railing and hurried into the garden. Cosette was not where she usually waited for him. He made his way through the bushes and went to the alcove by the flight of steps. 'She's waiting for me there,' he said. Cosette was not there. He looked up and saw that the shutters of the house were closed. He walked around the garden, the garden was deserted. Then he came back to the house and, crazed with love, delirious, terror-stricken, in a frenzy of grief and anxiety, like a master who returns home at a late hour he banged on the shutters. He banged and banged again, at the risk of seeing the window open and her father's grim face appear and ask him, 'What do you want?' That was nothing compared with what he now envisaged. He had finished banging, he raised his voice and called Cosette.

'Cosette!' he shouted. 'Cosette!' he repeated urgently.

There was no reply. It was all over. No one in the garden. No one in the house.

Marius fixed his desperate eyes on that dismal house, as dark and silent as a tomb and even emptier. He gazed at the stone bench where he had spent so many precious hours beside Cosette. Then he sat on the steps, his heart filled with tenderness and determination. He blessed his love in the depths of mind and said to himself that since Cosette was gone there was nothing left for him but to die.

Suddenly he heard a voice that seemed to come from the street, calling through the trees.

'Monsieur Marius!'

He got to his feet.

'Huh?'

'Monsieur Marius, are you there?'

'Yes.'

'Monsieur Marius,' the voice continued, 'your friends are expecting you at the barricade on Rue de la Chanvrerie.'

This voice was not wholly unfamiliar to him. It sounded like Éponine's, rough and husky. Marius ran to the gate, pushed the loose railing aside, stuck his head through and saw someone who looked to him like a young man, running off and disappearing into the twilight.

III
Monsieur Mabeuf

Jean Valjean's purse did Monsieur Mabeuf no good. In his venerable, childlike austerity, Monsieur Mabeuf had not accepted the gift from the night sky. He could not admit that gold coins might be minted out of stars. He had not guessed that what had fallen from the sky came from Gavroche. He had taken the purse to the local police station as a lost article placed by the finder at the disposal of possible claimants. The purse was indeed lost. It goes without saying that no one claimed it, and it did not help Monsieur Mabeuf.

And Monsieur Mabeuf had continued to decline.

His experiments with indigo had been no more successful in the

Jardin des Plantes than in his garden at Austerlitz. The year before he had owed his housekeeper her wages. Now, as we have seen, he owed a year's rent. After thirteen months had gone by, the pawnshop had sold the plates of his *Flora*. Some coppersmith had made cooking-pots out of them. Once his copper-plates were gone, and now unable even to complete the incomplete copies of the *Flora* still in his possession, he had sold for a pittance to a second-hand dealer the printed plates and text, as oddments. Nothing remained to him of his life's work. He began to eat up the money from those copies. When he saw that this meagre resource was running out, he gave up his garden and let it grow wild. Before this, a long time before, he had given up the two eggs and the morsel of beef he ate from time to time. He dined on bread and potatoes. He had sold the last of his furniture, then any spare bedding, clothing, blankets, then his herbariums and his prints. But he still had his most precious books, among them several of great rarity, including a 1560 edition of *Les Quadrains Historiques de la Bible*, a *Concordance des Bibles* compiled by Pierre de Besse, Jean de La Haye's *Les Marguerites de la Marguerite* with a dedication to the Queen of Navarre, Sieur de Villiers-Hotman's *De la Charge et Dignité de l'Ambassadeur*, a *Florilegium Rabbinicum* of 1644, a *Tibullus* of 1567 with this splendid inscription: *Venetiis, in aedibus Manutianis**, and lastly a Diogenes Laertius printed in Lyon in 1644 containing the famous variants of Vatican manuscript 411, dating from the thirteenth century, as well as those of the two Venice manuscripts 393 and 394 so fruitfully examined by Henri Estienne, and all the passages in Doric dialect that are only to be found in the celebrated twelfth-century manuscript belonging to the library of Naples. Monsieur Mabeuf never lit a fire in his room and went to bed at sundown so as not to burn any candles. It was as if he no longer had any neighbours – they avoided him when he went out, this he was aware of. The wretchedness of a child is of concern to a mother, the wretchedness of a young man of concern to a young girl, the wretchedness of an old man is of concern to no one. It is of all distresses the coldest. Still, Père Mabeuf had not entirely lost his childlike serenity. His eyes brightened slightly when they rested on his books, and he smiled when he viewed the Diogenes Laertius, which was a unique copy. His glass-doored bookcase was the only piece of furniture beyond the absolutely essential that he had kept.

One day Mère Plutarque said to him, 'I've no money to buy dinner.'

---

* Latin: 'Venice at the Aldine Press'.

What she called dinner was a loaf of bread and four or five potatoes.

'On credit?' suggested Monsieur Mabeuf.

'You know very well I won't be given any.'

Monsieur Mabeuf opened his bookcase, gazed at all his books one after another for a long time, as a father forced to sacrifice one of his children would gaze on them before making a choice, then abruptly seized one, put it under his arm and went out. He came back two hours later, now with nothing under his arm, laid thirty sous on the table and said, 'Get something for dinner.'

That was when Mère Plutarque saw a dark veil that was never to lift again come down over the old man's guileless face.

The next day, the day after, every day, it had to be done again and again. Monsieur Mabeuf went out with a book and returned with a coin. As the book dealers could see he was obliged to sell, they bought from him for twenty sous what he had paid twenty francs for. Sometimes at the very same bookshop. Volume by volume, the whole library went the same way. He said at times, 'After all I'm eighty', as if he had some secret hope of reaching the end of his days before reaching the end of his books. His sadness increased. Yet one day he had something to be happy about. He had gone out with a Robert Estienne that he sold for thirty-five sous on Quai Malaquais, and he returned with an Aldus that he bought for forty sous in Rue des Grès.

'I owe five sous,' he said to Mère Plutarque, wreathed in smiles. That day he went without dinner.

He belonged to the Horticultural Society. His plight became known there. The president of the society came to see him, promised to talk to the minister of agriculture and commerce about him, and did so.

'But of course!' exclaimed the minister. 'I should think so too! An elderly scholar! A botanist! A harmless old man! Something must be done for him!'

The next day Monsieur Mabeuf received an invitation to dinner from the minister. Trembling with joy, he showed the letter to Mère Plutarque.

'We're saved!' he said.

On the day appointed, he went to the minister's house. He noticed that his ragged cravat, his big old loose-fitting coat and his shoes polished with eggwhite astonished the ushers. No one spoke to him, not even the minister. About ten o'clock in the evening he was still waiting for a word of conversation when he heard the minister's wife, a beautiful woman in a low-cut gown he had not dared approach, asking, 'Who is that old gentleman?' He returned home on foot at midnight in the pouring rain. He had sold an Elzevir to pay for a cab to go there.

He had adopted the habit of reading a few pages of his Diogenes Laertius every night before he went to bed. He knew enough Greek to enjoy the particularities of the text he owned. He had now no other pleasure. Several weeks went by. Then Mère Plutarque suddenly fell ill. There is one thing sadder than having no money to buy bread from the baker, and that is having no money to buy drugs from the pharmacy. One evening the doctor prescribed a very expensive potion. Moreover, the illness was worsening, which meant nursing was needed. Monsieur Mabeuf opened his bookcase. There was nothing inside it. The last volume had gone. All he had left was the Diogenes Laertius.

He put that unique copy under his arm and went out. It was the fourth of June 1832. He went to Royol's successor at Porte St-Jacques and came home with one hundred francs. He put the pile of five-franc coins on the old serving-woman's bedside table and returned to his room without saying a word.

The next day at the crack of dawn he sat on the boundary-post in his garden and could be seen over the top of the hedge all morning, not moving, his head bowed, his eyes staring vaguely at the withered flowerbeds. From time to time it rained. The old man seemed not to notice. In the afternoon extraordinary noises erupted in Paris. They sounded like gunshots and the shouting of a multitude.

Père Mabeuf looked up. He saw a gardener passing by and asked, 'What's going on?'

The gardener, carrying his spade on his shoulder, replied, as calm as you please, 'They're rioting.'

'What! Rioting?'

'Yes. People are fighting.'

'What are they fighting about?'

'Ah, well may you ask!' exclaimed the gardener.

'Whereabouts?' said Monsieur Mabeuf.

'Over by the Arsenal.'

Père Mabeuf went back into the house, took his hat, automatically searched for a book to put under his arm, found none, said 'Ah! of course!' and set off, looking dazed.

BOOK TEN
THE FIFTH OF JUNE 1832

I
A Superficial Analysis

What makes for rioting? Everything and nothing. A gradual build-up of electricity, a sudden spark, an uncontained force, a gust of wind. This gust of wind encounters individuals who think, minds that dream, souls that suffer, passions that burn, wretchedness that howls, and carries them away with it.

Where?

Wherever it blows. Right through the state, right through any laws, right through the prosperity and insolence of others.

Convictions goaded, enthusiasms thwarted, indignations stirred, instincts for war repressed, young hearts inflamed, well meaning fanaticisms, curiosity, the desire for change, a thirst for the unexpected, the susceptibility that makes us happy to read the poster for a new play and delighted to hear the whistle for a scene change at the theatre; vague hatreds, grudges, disappointments, every vanity that feels cheated by destiny; dissatisfactions, futile dreams, unattainable ambitions; whoever sees in social collapse hope of escape; finally, that inflammable substratum, the peat beneath it all, the mob – such are the elements of rioting.

To rioting belong what is mightiest and what is lowliest: the totally excluded lurking on the outside waiting for an opportunity, gypsies, vagrants, tramps, those who sleep at night amid a wilderness of houses but with no other roof than the cold clouds of heaven, those who look to chance and not to toil for their daily bread, the nobodies of poverty and obscurity, the ragged and the barefoot.

Whoever harbours in his soul a secret rebellion against something the state or life or fate has done to him is close to rioting, and at the first sign of it he starts to quiver, and to feel caught up in the vortex.

Rioting is a kind of whirlwind in the social atmosphere that develops suddenly in certain climatic conditions, that whirls, rises, races, thunders, rips, razes, crushes, demolishes, uproots, carrying away with it the great-hearted and the small-minded, the manly and the weak-spirited, the tree trunk and the wisp of straw.

It is an ill wind both to anyone caught up in it and to anyone that obstructs it! It dashes one against the other.

It imparts to those seized by it some sort of extraordinary power. It fills whoever happens to come along with the force of events. It turns everything into a projectile. It makes a cannon-ball of a piece of rubble and a general of a street porter.

If certain oracles of political cunning are to be believed, from the viewpoint of those in power, a little rioting is to be desired. Theory: rioting bolsters those governments it does not overthrow. It tests the army, it rallies the bourgeoisie, it flexes the muscles of the police, it ascertains the resilience of the social structure. It is exercise. It is almost healthy. Authority is the better for a riot just as a human being is the better for a rub-down.

Rioting, thirty years ago, was seen in yet another light.

For everything there is a theory that declares itself to be 'common sense'; Philinte as opposed to Alceste; mediation offered between truth and falsehood: justification, censure, a somewhat lordly extenu-ation that, because it contains a mixture of blame and excuse, considers itself wisdom and is often just pedantry. A whole school of politics called 'the happy medium' derives from this. Between cold water and hot, this is the party of the lukewarm. In its entirely super-ficial pseudo-profundity, which analyses the effects without looking at the causes, with its semi-scientific superiority this school condemns public unrest.

Judging by what we hear from this school, 'The riots that attended what happened in 1830 deprived that great event of some of its purity. The July Revolution had been a good, populist squall, quickly followed by blue skies. The riots brought back overcast skies. They caused this Revolution, initially so remarkable for its unanimity, to degenerate into disagreement. In the July Revolution, as in all fitful progress, there had been latent cracks – the riots made them perceptible. People might say, "Ah! this is broken." After the July Revolution a sense of deliverance was all they felt. After the riots it was a sense of catastrophe.

'All rioting closes shops, brings down stock prices, alarms the stock exchange, interrupts trade, interferes with business, triggers bankruptcies; money dries up; private wealth is unnerved, public credit shaken, industry dismayed, capital funding withdrawn, work underpaid, fear everywhere; repercussions in every town. Hence eco-nomic disaster. It has been calculated that the first day of rioting costs France twenty million, the second day forty, the third day sixty. A three-day uprising costs one hundred and twenty million: that is to say, looking at only the financial consequences, the equivalent of a naval disaster, either from shipwreck or a lost battle, entailing the total destruction of a fleet of sixty men-of-war.

'No doubt, historically, riots have a beauty of their own. The street battle is no less grandiose and no less stirring than the guerrilla war in the countryside: in one is the soul of the forest, in the other the essence of cities; one has its Jean Chouan, the other its Jeanne. The rioting lit up in red, but magnificently, all the most distinctive innate features of the Parisian character, generosity, loyalty, a rowdy cheerfulness, students showing that with intelligence comes bravery, the National Guard steadfast, shopkeepers entrenched, street urchins embattled, a scorn for death in passers-by. School clashed with legion. After all, the only difference between the combatants was one of age. They were of the same stock. They were the same stoical men, dying at twenty for their ideas, at forty for their families. Always unhappy in civil war, the army countered daring with prudence. While demonstrating a demotic fearlessness, the riots were also the proving ground of bourgeois courage.

'That's all well and good. But was it worth the bloodshed? And add to the bloodshed a darkened future, progress jeopardized, anxiety among the best of men, honest liberals in despair, foreign absolutism rejoicing in the Revolution's self-inflicted wounds, the defeated of 1830 gloating and saying, "We told you so!" Add to that, Paris possibly all the greater for it but France most certainly diminished. Add to that, for we must tell the whole story, the massacres that too often disgraced the victory of order turned ferocious over liberty gone mad. When all is said and done, rioting has been disastrous.'

So speaks that approximation of wisdom which the bourgeoisie, that approximation of the people, is so ready to settle for.

For our part, we reject that too broad and consequently too convenient term, 'rioting'. We distinguish between one popular movement and another. We do not ask ourselves whether a riot costs as much as a battle. In the first place, why a battle? Here the question of war arises. Is war less dreadful than the disaster of an uprising? And besides, are all uprisings disasters? And so what if the fourteenth of July cost a hundred and twenty million? Securing the throne for Philip V of Spain cost France two thousand million. Even at the same price, we would prefer the fourteenth of July. In any case, we reject these figures that seem like reasons but are only words. Given an uprising, we examine it for what it is. In everything it says, the 'doctrinaire' argument set out above deals only with the effect. We are in search of the cause.

We shall take a closer took.

The Root of the Matter

There is riot, and there is insurrection. These are two kinds of anger. One is unjustified, the other is justified. In democratic states, which alone are based on justice, it sometimes happens that a minority usurps power. Then the whole community rises up and the necessary vindication of its rights may go as far as the taking-up of arms. In all matters that result from collective sovereignty, any war of the community against the minority is insurrection, any attack by the minority against the community is riot. Depending on whether the Tuileries houses a king or the Convention, the palace is justly or unjustly attacked. The same cannon aimed at the crowd, on the tenth of August is in the wrong, and on the fourteenth of Vendémiaire in the right. Apparently similar, fundamentally different, the Swiss defend the illegitimate, Bonaparte defends the legitimate. What universal suffrage has done in its freedom and in its sovereignty cannot be undone by the street. The same holds true in matters of pure civilization. Clear-sighted today, the instinct of the masses may be blurred tomorrow. The same fury is legitimate when directed against Terray and absurd when directed against Turgot. The smashing of machines, the pillaging of warehouses, the tearing-up of rail track, the destroying of docks, the misguidedness of multitudes, the people's refusal to give progress a fair hearing, Ramus assassinated by students, Rousseau driven out of Switzerland by stoning, that is riot. Israel against Moses, Athens against Phocion, Rome against Scipio, that is riot. Paris against the Bastille, that is insurrection. The soldiers against Alexander, the sailors against Christopher Columbus – this is the same reprobate rebellion. Why? Because Alexander does for Asia by the sword what Christopher Columbus does for America with the compass. Alexander, like Columbus, discovers a world. These worlds gifted to civilization bring with them such an increase in light that any resistance, in this case, is reprehensible. Sometimes the people perverts loyalty to itself. The mob is traitor to the people. Is there anything stranger, for example, than that long and bloody protest of the salt smugglers, a justified rebellion of long duration that at the decisive moment, on the day of salvation, at the very hour of demotic victory, allies itself with the throne, turns into the Chouan uprising and switches, from insurrection against, to rioting for! Oh, the dismal achievements of ignorance! The salt smuggler escapes the royal gallows and, with the end of a rope left hanging round his neck, dons the white cockade. 'Death to the salt-tax collectors!' gives birth to

'Long live the king!' St Bartholomew killers, September slaughterers, Avignon butchers, Coligny's assassins, Madame Lamballe's assassins, Brune's assassins, Miquelets, Verdets, Cadenettes, Companions of Jehu, Knights of the Armband – here you have rioting. La Vendée is one big Catholic riot.

The sound of rightfulness on the move is recognizable, and it does not always emerge from the tremors of the tumultuous masses. There are mad rages, there are cracked bells, not all tocsins ring with the sound of bronze. The impulse of passion and ignorance is different from the impetus of progress. Rise up, certainly, but in order to grow in stature. Show me which way you are going. There is no insurrection that is not forward-moving. Any other sort of uprising is bad. Every violent step backwards is rioting. Retreat is an act of violence against the human race. Insurrection is an outburst of truth's rage. The paving-stones displaced by insurrection strike the spark of rightfulness. Rioting is left with only the dirt on those stones. Danton against Louis XVI is insurrection. Hébert against Danton is riot.

This is why, if insurrection in certain cases can be, as Lafayette says, the most sacred of duties, rioting can be the most deadly offence.

There is also some difference in the intensity of heat. Insurrection is often a volcano, riot often just a flash in the pan.

Insurgency, as we have said, sometimes takes place within the ranks of those in power. Polignac is a rioter. Camille Desmoulins is a ruler.

Sometimes insurrection is resurrection.

Given that universal suffrage as the solution to everything is a totally modern development, and that all history pre-dating it was for four thousand years filled with the violation of rights and the oppression of peoples, each period in history brings with it the protest of which it is capable. Under the Caesars there was no insurrection, but there was Juvenal.

The *facit indignatio* replaces the Gracchi.*

Under the Caesars there is the Syene exile, there is also the author of the *Annals*.

Not to mention the great Patmos exile, who also launches a damning protest against the real world in the name of the ideal world, who creates a tremendous satire out of a vision and casts on Rome-

---

* From Juvenal's Satire I, line 79: 'facit indignatio versum' ('Indignation inspires poetry'). Juvenal is traditionally believed to have been exiled to Syene in Egypt for having insulted an actor who was a favourite of the emperor, either Trajan or Domitian.

Nineveh, on Rome-Babylon, on Rome-Sodom, the blazing reflection of the Apocalypse.

John on his rock is the sphinx on its pedestal. We may not understand what he says – he is a Jew, and it is all in Hebrew – but the author of the *Annals* is a Latin-speaker, to be more specific, a Roman.

Since the Neros rule by darkness, they must be depicted likewise. A simple etching would be pallid. Into the incisions must be poured a concentrated, biting prose.

Despots have their effect on thinkers. Fettered speech is fearsome speech. The virtuosity of a writer's style increases twofold, threefold, when a master imposes silence on the people. Out of this silence comes a certain mysterious plenitude that filters into the mind and sets like bronze. Historical repression produces conciseness in the historian. The granite solidity of some celebrated prose is nothing other than a density created by the tyrant's oppression.

Tyranny puts the writer under the constraint of diametric contractions, which create increased strength. Ciceronian rhetoric, barely adequate against Verres, would be ineffectual against Caligula. The less rotund the phrase, the harder it hits. Tacitus thinks with his fists up.

The integrity of a great heart, condensed into justice and truth, is devastating.

It is worth noting, in passing, that Tacitus does not overlap historically with Caesar. The Tiberiuses were reserved for him. Caesar and Tacitus are two successive phenomena; a meeting between the two mysteriously avoided, it seems, by him who in the staging of the centuries directs the exits and entrances. Caesar is great, Tacitus is great. God spares these two greatnesses by not pitting them against each other. In hitting out against Caesar, the judge might hit too hard and be unjust. That is not God's will. The great wars of Africa and Spain, the pirates of Sicily crushed, civilization brought to Gaul, to Brittany, to Germany, all this glory makes up for the Rubicon. There is here a kind of delicacy on the part of divine justice, hesitating to unleash the formidable historian on the illustrious usurper, sparing Caesar from Tacitus and granting extenuating circumstances to genius.

Certainly, despotism remains despotism even under the despot who is a genius. There is corruption under illustrious tyrants, but the moral scourge is ghastlier under infamous tyrants. Under their rule nothing veils their shamefulness, and the critics, whether Tacitus or Juvenal, more usefully denounce to the world at large this indefensible ignominy.

Rome smells worse under Vitellius than under Sulla. Under Claudius and Domitian there is a low-class deformity corresponding to the

947

ugliness of the tyrant. The baseness of the slaves derives directly from the despot. Miasmic fumes emanate from those cringing consciences in which the master is reflected; the authorities are depraved; hearts are small, consciences are dull, souls are servile. It is so under Caracalla, it is so under Commodus, it is so under Heliogabalus, while under Caesar the only smell that comes from the Roman senate is that particular smell of bird droppings that distinguishes the eagle's eyrie.

Hence the seemingly late arrival of the Tacituses and the Juvenals. It is when the evidence is there that someone turns up to demonstrate it.

But Juvenal and Tacitus, like Isaiah in biblical times, like Dante in the Middle Ages, are individuals. Riot and insurrection are the multitude, which is sometimes right and sometimes wrong.

In the most common cases riot results from a physical fact; insurrection is always a moral phenomenon. Riot is Masaniello. Insurrection is Spartacus. Insurrection is close to the mind, rioting close to the belly. Gaster gets angry, but Gaster is certainly not always wrong. In cases of famine, riot – as at Buzançais, for instance – has a starting-point that is genuine, stirring and just. Yet it is still riot. Why? Because although right in essence, it took the wrong form. Vicious in its legitimacy, violent in its strength, it hit out at random. It went trampling about like a blind elephant, leaving in its wake the corpses of old men, women and children. Without knowing why, it spilled the blood of the innocent and the harmless. Feeding the masses is a good objective, massacring them is a bad expedient.

All armed protests, even the most legitimate, even the tenth of August, even the fourteenth of July, begin with the same unrest. Before rightfulness emerges, there is foaming and tumult. At the outset insurrection is riot, just as a river is a mountain torrent. Ordinarily it ends in that ocean called revolution. Having its source in those lofty mountains that rise above the moral horizon – justice, wisdom, reason, rightfulness – and made of the ideal's purest snow, after a long descent from rock to rock, after reflecting the sky in its transparency, swollen by a hundred tributaries in a majestic, triumphal progress, insurrection sometimes peters out suddenly in some bourgeois quagmire, as the Rhine ends in marshland.

All that belongs to the past; the future is different. What is wonderful about universal suffrage is that it nips riot in the bud and, by giving the vote to insurrection, disarms it. The disappearance of war, war on the streets as well as war on the frontiers, is the inevitable progression. Whatever today might be, tomorrow brings peace.

Be that as it may, insurrection, riot, and how the former differs from the latter – the true bourgeois knows nothing of such nuances. In his mind all is sedition, resistance pure and simple, the dog rebelling against its master, an attempt to bite that must be punished with the chain and the kennel, barking, yapping – until the day when the dog's head, suddenly grown bigger, appears dimly out of the shadows as the face of a lion.

Then the bourgeois shouts, 'Long live the people!'

In the light of this explanation, what does the unrest of June 1832 signify for history? Is it a riot? Is it an insurrection?

It is an insurrection.

It may be that in this presentation of a dreadful event we will sometimes speak of rioting, but merely to describe what was happening on the surface and always maintaining the distinction between form and essence, riot and insurrection.

In the sudden outbreak and grim suppression of this 1832 uprising there was so much grandeur that even those who see it as mere riot cannot speak of it without respect. For them it is like a vestige of 1830. Imaginations once stirred, they say, are not calmed in a day. A revolution does not come to an abrupt halt. Inevitably there are always ripples in its aftermath before a return to a state of rest, like a mountain descending to the plain. There are no Alps without their Jura, no Pyrenees without their Cantabrian range.

This distressing crisis in contemporary history, which Parisians remember as 'the time of the riots', is without doubt a moment typical of the stormy days of this century.

One last word before we take up the story.

The facts that are about to be related belong to that dramatic and vivid reality the historian sometimes neglects for want of time and space. Here, however, we insist, is life, the beating pulse, quivering humanity. The small details, we believe we have already said, are so to speak the foliage of great events and become lost in the remoteness of history. The so-called time of riots abounds in details of this nature. For reasons different from those of history, judicial investigations have not revealed all, and have perhaps not been exhaustive. So we are going to bring to light, add to the known and published particulars, things that were not known, facts overlooked because of the forgetfulness of some, the deaths of others. Most of the actors in these mighty scenes are no more. From the very next day they were silent. But of what we will relate we may say: 'We saw it.' We will alter a few names, for history recounts and does not indict, but we will depict things that are true. In the context of the book we are writing, we will be showing one side only of just a single episode, and surely the least known, from the days of the fifth and sixth of June 1832. But we will do it in such way that the reader may perceive, under the dark veil we are going to lift, the true face of this dreadful civil crisis.

III
A Funeral: An Opportunity for Rebirth

In the spring of 1832, although cholera had for three months dampened spirits and quelled their excitement with a sort of bleak calm, for a long while now Paris had been ready to erupt. As we have said, a city is like a cannon. Once it is loaded, a stray spark is all that is needed to set it off. In June 1832 that spark was the death of General Lamarque.

Lamarque was a man of renown and a man of action. He had shown in succession, under the Empire and under the Restoration, the two kinds of bravery needed for those two periods, bravery on the battlefield and bravery on the floor of the debating chamber. He was eloquent in the way that he had been valiant; in his words you sensed the sword. Like his predecessor Foy, having distinguished himself as a military commander he distinguished himself as a champion of liberty. He sat between the left and the extreme left, loved by the people because he welcomed the possibilities of the future, loved by the masses because he had served the emperor well. Along with Comtes Gérard and Drouet, he was one of Napoleon's marshals *in petto*. The treaties of 1815 grieved him like a personal insult. He hated Wellington with a blunt hatred that pleased the crowd. And for seventeen years, scarcely attentive to intervening events, he had majestically retained the sadness of Waterloo. At the last, in his dying hour, he clasped to his breast a sword that had been presented to him by the officers of the Hundred Days. Napoleon died with the word 'army' on his lips, Lamarque with the word 'country'.

His anticipated death was dreaded by the people as a loss and by the government as an occasion. This death was mourned. Like everything bitter, mourning may turn to revolt. That is what happened.

On the eve and the morning of the fifth of June, the day set for Lamarque's funeral, Faubourg St-Antoine, which the cortège was to pass through, took on an ominous cast. This network of rowdy streets filled with rumours. People armed themselves as best they could. Joiners carried off claw-hammers from their workbenches 'to break down doors'. One of them had made himself a dagger out of a slipper-maker's hook by breaking off the hook and sharpening the end of it.

950

Another, in his feverish impatience 'to attack', had been going to bed fully dressed for the past three days. A carpenter named Lombier met a comrade who asked him, 'Where are you going?' 'Well, I've no weapons.' 'So?' 'I'm going to my workshop to fetch my compass.' 'What are you going to do with that?' 'I don't know,' said Lombier.

A certain Jacqueline, a man of enterprise, called out to any workman passing by, 'Come over here!' He treated them to ten sous' worth of wine and said, 'Are you employed?' 'No.' 'Go to Filspierre, between the Charonne toll-gate and the Montreuil toll-gate, you'll find employment there.'

At Filspierre's they found cartridges and weapons. Certain well known leaders were 'doing the rounds', that is to say, running from one house to another to assemble their men.

At Barthélemy's near the Trône toll-gate, at Capel's Petit-Chapeau, the drinkers greeted each other with sombre expressions. They were overheard saying, 'Where's your pistol?' 'Under my smock. And yours?' 'Under my shirt.' In Rue Traversière, in front of the Roland workshop, and in Cour de la Maison-Brûlée in front of Bernier the tool-maker's workshop, groups whispered together. Noteworthy as the most ardent among them was a certain Mavot, who never lasted more than a week in any workshop, the master craftsmen always sacking him 'because they had to have words with him every day'. Mavot was killed the next day on the barricade in Rue Ménilmontant. Pretot, who was also to die in the fighting, was Mavot's right-hand man, and to the question 'What's your objective?' he replied, 'Insurrection.' Workmen met at the corner of Rue de Bercy to wait for a certain Lemarin, revolutionary agent for Faubourg St-Marceau. Watchwords were exchanged almost openly.

So on the fifth of June, a day of sunshine and rain, General Lamarque's funeral procession passed through Paris, the official military honours somewhat increased as a precaution. Two battalions, drums draped and arms reversed, ten thousand National Guardsmen with their swords at their sides, escorted the coffin. The hearse was drawn by young men. Veteran officers from Les Invalides followed immediately behind, bearing laurel branches. Then came a strange, excited, countless multitude, local sections of the Friends of the People, the Law School, the School of Medicine, refugees of all nationalities, Spanish, Italian, German and Polish flags, horizontal tricolours, every conceivable banner, children waving green branches, stonecutters and carpenters who were on strike at the time, printers recognizable by their paper caps walking two by two, three by three, shouting, nearly all of them brandishing sticks, some of them swords, unorganized and yet united in spirit, now a tumultuous mob, now a column. Insurgent groups chose leaders for themselves. A man armed with a perfectly visible pair of pistols seemed to be conducting a review of others who were dividing into columns before him. In the side lanes running parallel to the boulevards, in the branches of the trees, on balconies, at windows, on the rooftops was a seething mass of men, women and children. Their eyes were filled with anxiety. An armed throng went by, a frightened throng looked on.

As for the government, it watched. It watched with its hand on the hilt of its sword. Four squadrons of carabineers, their cartridge pouches filled, their carbines and musketoons loaded, could be seen mounted in Place Louis XV, with bugles at their head, all ready to march. In the Latin quarter and at the Jardin des Plantes the Municipal Guard were spread out in echelon formation from street to street. At the Halle-aux-Vins a squadron of dragoons, at La Grève half the 12th Light Infantry, the other half at the Bastille, the 6th Dragoons at the Célestins, the courtyard of the Louvre full of artillery. The remainder of the troops were standing by in their barracks, not to mention the regiments from the Paris vicinity. The apprehensive authorities held suspended over the menacing multitude twenty-four thousand soldiers in the city and thirty thousand in the outskirts.

Various rumours circulated in the procession. There was talk of legitimist intrigues; there was talk of the Duc de Reichstadt, whom God had marked out for death at the very moment the crowd were nominating him for the Empire. One as yet unidentified individual announced that two foremen had been persuaded to throw open to the people at the appointed time the gates of an arms factory. The dominant expression on the uncovered brows of most of those present was excitement mingled with grievance. Also to be seen here and there among that multitude in the grip of such violent but noble feelings were the faces of real criminals and appalling wretches saying, 'Let's loot!' There are certain disturbances that stir up the beds of marshes and cloud the water with mud. A phenomenon to which police forces 'who know their business' are no strangers.

The funeral procession made its way with feverish slowness along the boulevards from the house of the deceased to the Bastille. Now and then it rained. The rain made no difference to this multitude. Several incidents marked the progress of the cortège – the coffin borne round the Vendôme column, stones thrown at the Duc de Fitzjames seen on a balcony wearing his hat, the Gallic cockerel torn off a populist flag and dragged through the mud, a policeman wounded with a sword at the Porte St-Martin, an officer of the 12th Light Infantry saying out loud, 'I'm a Republican', Polytechnic students who had been gated turning up to shouts of 'Long live the Polytechnic! Long live the Republic!' Filing down from Faubourg St-Antoine, long columns of dangerous-looking types, drawn by curiosity, joined the procession at the Bastille, and the crowd began to simmer with a terrible kind of ferment.

One man was heard to say to another, 'You see that fellow with a red beard? He's the one who'll give the word for when to fire.' Apparently this red-beard was back again later in the same role at another riot, the Quénisset affair.

The hearse went past the Bastille, followed the canal, crossed the little bridge and reached the esplanade at the Pont d'Austerlitz. There it halted. A bird's-eye view of the crowd at that moment would have looked like a comet, its head at the esplanade and its tail extending along Quai Bourdon, spreading out over the Bastille and reaching down the boulevard to the Porte St-Martin. A circle formed around the hearse. The vast crowd fell silent. Lafayette spoke and bade Lamarque farewell. This was a touching and solemn moment, all heads were uncovered, all hearts felt a pang. Suddenly, in the middle of the group a man on horseback dressed in black appeared with a red flag – others say with a pike and a red liberty cap on top of it. Lafayette turned away. Exelmans left the procession.

This red flag raised a storm, and was swallowed up by it. From Boulevard Bourdon to the Pont d'Austerlitz one of those clamours like an ocean swell swept through the multitude. Two tremendous cries went up: 'Lamarque to the Panthéon! Lafayette to the city hall!' To cheers from the crowd, some young men harnessed themselves and began to draw Lamarque in the hearse across the Pont d'Austerlitz and Lafayette in a carriage along Quai Morland.

Among the crowd that surrounded and cheered Lafayette people noticed and pointed out to each other a German named Ludwig Snyder, who has since died at the age of over a hundred and who took part in the war of 1776, fighting at Trenton under Washington and at Brandywine under Lafayette.

Meanwhile, moving off on the left bank, the municipal cavalry proceeded to bar the bridge, and emerging from the Célestins barracks on the right bank the dragoons deployed along Quai Morland. The people drawing Lafayette suddenly caught sight of them round the bend on the embankment and shouted, 'The dragoons! The dragoons!' The dragoons advanced at walking pace, in silence and with an air of grave expectation, their pistols in their holsters, their swords in their scabbards, their musketoons in their rifle buckets.

Two hundred paces from the little bridge they halted. The carriage carrying Lafayette made its way towards them, their ranks parted, allowed it to pass, and closed up behind it. At that moment the dragoons and the crowd met. The women fled in terror.

What took place in that fateful minute? No one can say. It was the dark moment when two clouds merge. Some say that over by the Arsenal a bugle giving the signal to charge was heard, others that a child stabbed a dragoon with a dagger. The fact is that suddenly three shots were fired. The first killed the leader of the squadron, Cholet, the second killed a deaf old woman who was closing her window on Rue Contrescarpe, the third clipped the shoulder of an officer. A woman screamed, 'They're starting too soon!' And at that instant a squadron of dragoons that had remained in the barracks were seen emerging at a gallop with bared swords from Rue Bassompierre and down Boulevard Bourdon, sweeping all before them.

The inevitable follows, the storm breaks, stones rain down, rifles are fired, many rush down to the bottom of the embankment to cross that little branch of the Seine that is now filled in; the timber-yards of Île Louviers, a vast ready-made citadel, are taken over by combatants; posts are pulled up, pistol-shots fired, a barricade takes shape; the young men forced back go running across the Pont d'Austerlitz with the hearse and charge the Municipal Guard, the carabineers come at a rush, the dragoons wield their swords, the crowd scatters in all directions, the rumour of war flies to every part of Paris. The cry 'To arms!' goes up, people run, trip over, flee, fight back. Anger spreads rioting the way wind spreads fire.

IV
The Disturbances of the Past

There is nothing more extraordinary than the first paroxysms of a riot. Everything erupts everywhere at the same time. Was it anticipated? Yes. Was it planned? No. Where does it originate? On the street. Where does it strike from? Out of the blue. Here the insurrection is of the nature of a conspiracy, there of an improvisation. Anyone with any initiative seizes control of a current in the crowd and directs it wherever he wants. The outbreak is fraught with terror combined with a kind of ominous gaiety. First of all there is noisy confusion, shops close, vendors' stalls vanish, then come isolated gunshots; people flee; rifle butts strike at carriage gateways; servants are heard laughing in the courtyards of houses and saying, 'There's going to be trouble!'

With not a quarter-hour gone by, this is what was taking place almost simultaneously at twenty different points in Paris.

In Rue Ste-Croix-de-la-Bretonnerie some twenty bearded, long-haired young men went into a wine shop and came out a moment later carrying a horizontal tricolour covered in a mourning veil; they were led by three armed men, one with a sword, one with a rifle, the third with a pike.

In Rue des Nonnains-d'Hyères, a well dressed bourgeois citizen who had a paunch, a deep voice, a bald head, a high forehead, a black beard and one of those unruly moustaches that cannot be tamed, was openly offering cartridges to passers-by.

In Rue St-Pierre-Montmartre some bare-armed men were carrying a black flag on which these words could be read in white letters: 'Republic or Death'. In Rue des Jeûneurs, Rue du Cadran, Rue Montorgueil, Rue Mandar, groups appeared waving flags on which were to be seen in gold letters the word 'Section' with a number. One of these flags was red and blue with a barely perceptible white stripe in between.

An arms factory on the Boulevard St-Martin was looted, as well as three gunsmiths' shops, the first in Rue Beaubourg, the second in Rue Michel-le-Comte, the other in Rue du Temple. Within a few minutes innumerable hands in the crowd seized and carried off two hundred and thirty rifles, nearly all double-barrelled, sixty-four swords and eighty-three pistols. So that more people should be armed, one would take the gun, another the bayonet.

Opposite Quai de la Grève, young men armed with muskets took up positions inside places occupied by women, to fire their guns. One of them had a flintlock musket. They rang at the door, went in, and started making cartridges. One of these women said later, 'I didn't know what cartridges were, it was my husband who told me.'

One group broke into a curiosity shop in Rue des Vieilles-Haudriettes and seized some yataghans and Turkish firearms.

The body of a mason who had been shot dead lay in Rue de la Perle.

And then on both sides of the river, on the embankments, on the boulevards, in the Latin quarter, round Les Halles, men panting for breath, workmen, students, section members read proclamations, shouted 'To arms!', smashed street lanterns, unhitched carriages, took up street paving, battered down the doors of houses, uprooted trees, ransacked cellars, rolled out barrels, heaped up cobblestones, rubble, furniture, planks of wood, made barricades.

They forced bourgeois citizens to help them in this. They went into women's homes, made them hand over the swords and guns of their absent husbands, and they chalked on the door, 'Weapons collected'. Some signed 'in their own names' receipts for the guns and swords, and said, 'Send someone to fetch them tomorrow from the city hall.' On the streets, they disarmed solitary watchmen and National Guardsmen on their way to their local headquarters. Officers had their epaulettes torn off. In Rue du Cimetière-St-Nicolas, a National Guard officer, pursued by a gang armed with clubs and foils, just managed to take refuge in a house that he was unable to leave until after dark, and then only in disguise.

In the St-Jacques district, students swarmed out of their lodgings and headed up Rue St-Hyacinthe to Café du Progrès or down to Café des Sept-Billards in Rue des Mathurins. There, young men standing on the corner-posts outside the door distributed weapons. The timber-yard in Rue Transnonain was plundered to build barricades. At one point only did the residents resist, at the corner of Rue Ste-Avoye and Rue Simon-le-Franc, where they themselves destroyed the barricade. At one point only did the insurgents yield: after firing on a detachment of the National Guard they abandoned a barricade begun in Rue du Temple and fled down Rue de la Corderie. The detachment found in the barricade a red flag, a packet of cartridges and three hundred bullets. The National Guardsmen tore up the flag and carried away the tatters on the tips of their bayonets.

Everything we are here recounting slowly and in sequence took place all over the city at once, in the midst of a vast tumult, like myriad flashes of lightning in one clap of thunder.

In less than an hour, in the Les Halles district alone, twenty-seven barricades sprang up out of the ground. At the centre was that famous house number 50, the fortress of Jeanne and his one hundred and six companions, flanked on one side by a barricade in St-Merry and on the other by a barricade in Rue Maubuée, and which commanded three streets, Rue des Arcis, Rue St-Martin and Rue Aubry-le-Boucher, in front of it. There were two right-angled barricades, one running from Rue Montorgueil and back along Rue de la Grande-Truanderie, the other from Rue Geoffroy-Langevin and back along Rue Ste-Avoye. Not to mention countless barricades in twenty other Paris neighbour-hoods in the Marais, on Mont-Ste-Geneviève; one in Rue Ménilmontant where you could see a carriage gate torn off its hinges; another near the Petit Pont by the Hôtel-Dieu, constructed with a carriage that had been unharnessed and overturned, three hundred yards from the police headquarters.

At the Rue des Ménétriers barricade, a respectably dressed man was distributing money among the workers. At the Rue Greneta barricade, a horseman appeared and handed to the person who seemed to be in charge of the barricade what looked like a roll of silver coins. 'That's to cover expenses,' he said, 'wine, et cetera.' A fair-haired young man, without a cravat, went from barricade to barricade delivering passwords. Another, with his sword unsheathed and a blue police cap on his head, positioned sentries. Inside the barricades, wine shops and porters' lodges were converted into guard-houses. In fact, the riot was conducted according to the most skilful military tactics. The narrow, winding, irregular lanes, full of twists and turns, were admirably chosen, the area round Les Halles in particular, a network of streets more intricate than a forest. The Society of Friends of the People, it was said, had taken charge of the insurrection in the Ste-Avoye district. When searched, a man killed in Rue du Ponceau was found to be carrying a map of Paris.

What had actually directed the course of the riot was a kind of strange impetuousness in the air. The insurrection had suddenly built barricades with one hand and with the other seized nearly all the garrison posts. In less than three hours, like a trail of powder igniting, the insurgents had stormed and occupied, on the right bank, the Arsenal, the city hall on Place Royale, the whole of the Marais, the Popincourt arms factory, Galiote, Château-d'Eau and all the streets near Les Halles; and on the left bank, the veterans' barracks, Ste-Pélagie, Place Maubert, the Deux-Moulins powder magazine and all the toll-gates. At five o'clock in the evening they were in control of the Bastille, Lingerie, Blancs-Manteaux, their scouts had reached Place des Victoires and were threatening the Bank, the Petits-Pères barracks and the Post Office. A third of Paris was controlled by the rioters.

In every respect the fighting was extraordinarily determined; and with the commandeering of weapons, the house searches, and gunsmiths' shops being quickly overrun, the result was that the conflict that had begun with stone-throwing continued with gunfire.

About six o'clock in the evening Passage du Saumon became a battlefield. The rioters were at one end and the troops at the other. They were firing at each other from the gates at either end. An observer, a dreamer, the author of this book, who had gone to see the volcano from close up, found himself in the passage, caught in the crossfire. All he had to protect him from the bullets were the projecting half-columns that separated the shops. He was in this perilous position for almost half an hour.

Meanwhile the call to arms was sounded, the National Guardsmen hastily dressed and armed themselves, the legions turned out from their municipal headquarters, the regiments turned out from their barracks. Opposite Passage de l'Ancre a drummer was stabbed. Another, in Rue du Cygne, was attacked by thirty young men who punctured his drum and took his sword. Another was killed in Rue Grenier-St-Lazare. In Rue-Michel-le-Comte three officers were killed, one after the other. Several Municipal Guards, wounded in Rue des Lombards, retreated.

In front of Cour Batave, a detachment of National Guardsmen found a red flag bearing this inscription: 'Republican revolution, no. 127'. Was this indeed a revolution?

The insurrection turned the centre of Paris into a sort of stronghold, huge, impenetrable, and labyrinthine. This was the seat of the trouble, this was obviously the key to it all. Everything else was just skirmishes. What proved that this was where everything would be decided was the fact that as yet there was no fighting going on here.

In some regiments the soldiers were undecided, which added to the dreadful uncertainty of the crisis. They recalled the popular acclaim that had greeted the neutrality of the 53rd line regiment in July 1830. Two fearless men who had proved themselves in the great wars, Marshal Lobau and General Bugeaud, were in command, Bugeaud under Lobau. Huge patrols, composed of line battalions contained within entire companies of National Guardsmen and led by a senior police officer wearing his sash of office, went off to reconnoitre the streets in rebellion. The insurgents, for their part, placed lookouts at crossroads and audaciously sent patrols outside the barricades. Each side was watching the other. The government, with an army at its disposal, hesitated. Darkness was about to fall and St-Merry's bell began to toll. The then minister of war, Marshal Soult, who had been at Austerlitz, observed this with a sombre air.

These old hands, accustomed to disciplined action and whose only resource and guide is that battle-compass tactics, are completely disoriented in the presence of this vast ferment called public anger. The winds of revolution are not easy to deal with.

The National Guards from the outskirts came rushing pell-mell. A battalion of the 12th Light came at the double from St-Denis, the 14th of the line arrived from Courbevoie, the artillery troops from the Military School had taken up position at Carrousel, cannons were sent from Vincennes.

Isolation settled on the Tuileries. Louis-Philippe was filled with serenity.

V
Paris's Originality

Over the last two years, as we have said, Paris had seen more than one insurrection. As a rule, outside the insurgent neighbourhoods, nothing is more weirdly calm than the way Paris appears during a riot. Paris very quickly adapts to everything – it is only a riot . . . And Paris has so much going on that it is not bothered by so small a matter. These colossal cities are alone capable of offering such spectacles. These vast precincts are alone capable of simultaneously containing civil war and an indefinable bizarre tranquillity.

Ordinarily, when the insurrection begins, when the shopkeeper hears the drum, the call to arms, the alarm, all he says is, 'There seems to be a bit of a rumpus in Rue St-Martin.'

Or, 'Faubourg St-Antoine.'

Often he adds carelessly, 'Somewhere in that direction.'

Later on, when the rending and ominous racket of rifle shots and volleys of gunfire is heard, the shopkeeper says, 'So, it's hotting up, then? Yes, it's hotting up!'

A moment later, if the rioting is coming closer and gaining strength, he hurriedly shuts up his shop and rapidly dons his uniform, that is to say, he makes sure his merchandise is safe and puts his life at risk.

There is an exchange of fire in a square, a passage, a blind alley, barricades are taken, lost and retaken, blood flows, the façades of houses are peppered with gunfire, bullets kill people in their beds, bodies are left lying on the pavement. A few streets away the click-clack of billiard balls can be heard in the cafés.

Bystanders laugh and chat within a few yards of these war-fraught streets. Theatres open their doors and stage light comedies. Cabs circulate. Passers-by go out to dinner – sometimes in the very neighbourhood where the fighting is taking place. In 1831 gunfire was suspended to let a wedding party go by.

During the twelfth of May insurrection of 1839, in Rue St-Martin, a feeble old man pulling a handcart with a tricolour rag attached to it, and carrying carafes filled with some sort of liquid, went to and fro between the barricade and the troops, impartially offering glasses of liquorice water, now to government, now to anarchy.

Nothing could be stranger. And this is the distinctive characteristic of Paris uprisings, not to be found in any other capital. What is needed for this are two things, the size of Paris and its gaiety. What is needed is the city of Voltaire and of Napoleon.

This time, however, when arms were taken up on the fifth of June 1832, the great city sensed something that was perhaps more powerful than itself. It was afraid. Everywhere, in the most distant and most 'uninvolved' neighbourhoods, doors, windows and shutters were to be seen closed in the middle of the day. The courageous armed themselves, cowards hid. The unconcerned passer-by going about his business disappeared. Many streets were so deserted, it might have been four o'clock in the morning. Alarming details spread abroad, dire news was rife. That *they* were in control of the Bank. That at the St-Merry cloister alone there were six hundred of them entrenched and embattled inside the church. That the troops were not to be depended on. That Armand Carrel had been to see Marshal Clauzel and the marshal had said, 'Get yourself a regiment first.' That Lafayette was ill but had nevertheless told them, 'I'm at your disposal. I'll follow you wherever there's room for a chair.' That you needed to be on your guard. That at night there would be people looting isolated houses in deserted corners of Paris (here, you could detect the imagination of the police at work, that Ann Radcliffe element in the government). That a battery position had been established in Rue Aubry-le-Boucher. That Lobau and Bugeaud were conferring and that at midnight or daybreak at the latest, four columns would march simultaneously on the centre of the uprising, the first coming from the Bastille, the second from Porte St-Martin, the third from La Grève, the fourth from Les Halles. That perhaps, too, the troops would evacuate Paris and withdraw to the Champ de Mars. That no one knew what would happen – but this time, for sure, it was serious. Marshal Soult's indecisiveness was giving cause for concern. Why did he not attack at once? Certainly, he was deeply preoccupied. The old lion seemed to scent in this obscurity some unknown monster.

Evening came, the theatres did not open. The patrols went round looking nervous. Passers-by were searched. Suspects were arrested. By nine o'clock there had been more than eight hundred arrests. The Prefecture of Police was overcrowded, the Conciergerie was overcrowded, La Force was overcrowded. At the Conciergerie in particular, that long underground gallery known as Rue de Paris was strewn with bales of straw, and lying on them were a heap of prisoners being valiantly rallied by the man from Lyon, Lagrange. All this straw rustled by all these men produced the sound of a downpour. Elsewhere prisoners lay crammed together in courtyards out in the open. Anxiety was everywhere, and a certain trepidation rather unusual for Paris.

People barricaded themselves in their houses, wives and mothers fretted. The constant refrain was 'Oh my God! He's not home yet!'

Audible in the distance were no more than a few rare carriages rolling by. Out on their doorsteps people listened to the clamour, the shouting, the disturbance, muffled and indistinct sounds, things that prompted them to say, 'It's the cavalry' or 'That's wagons thundering about'; trumpets, drums, volleys of rifle-fire and above all that doleful tolling of St-Merry's bell. Everyone was waiting for the first cannon to be fired. Armed men appeared at street corners, then disappeared, shouting, 'Get inside!' And people rushed to bolt their doors. They said, 'How will it all end?' With every passing moment, as darkness fell, Paris seemed to take on a more lurid hue from the tremendous blaze of the riot.

BOOK ELEVEN
THE ATOM EMBRACES THE STORM

I
Some Light on the Sources of Gavroche's Poetry – and an Academician's Influence on It

At that moment during the insurrection when the people and the troops suddenly came up against each other in front of the Arsenal, the forward motion of the multitude following the hearse all the way down the boulevards – pressing, as it were, on the head of the procession – was thrown into reverse, causing a terrifying backward surge. The crowd swayed, broke ranks; everybody ran, bolted, fled, some with cries of attack, others with the pallor of flight. The great river filling the boulevards divided in the blink of an eye, overflowed to right and left and went rushing down two hundred streets at once like water pouring from an opened sluice gate. At that moment a ragged child, coming down Rue Ménilmontant, holding in his hand a branch of laburnum blossom he had just picked on the heights of Belleville, caught sight of an old saddle pistol on display outside a bric-à-brac shop. Throwing his branch of blossom to the ground, he cried, 'Mère Thingummy, I'm borrowing this what's-it of yours!'

And off he ran with the pistol.

Two minutes later a stream of terrified bourgeois citizens fleeing down Rue Amelot and Rue Basse ran into the child brandishing his pistol and singing:

> It's dark at night,
> The day is bright;
> An unsigned scrawl
> Written on the wall,
> Has got you all
> Worried.
> Toodle-toot!

It was little Gavroche on his way to war.

On the boulevard he noticed the pistol had no hammer.*

This verse that he marched along to, and all the other songs he would happily sing, given the opportunity – who were they written by? We do not know. Who can tell? By him, perhaps. In any event, Gavroche knew all the popular tunes in circulation, and he added his own chirpings to them. That impish little urchin created a medley of the voices of nature and the voices of Paris. He combined the repertory of birds with the repertory of workshops. He knew some artists' apprentices, a tribe close to his own. He had apparently been apprenticed for three months to a printer. One day he had run an errand for Monsieur Baour-Lormian, one of the Forty. Gavroche was a gamin of letters.

Gavroche actually had no idea that on that dreadful rainy night when he had offered two little lads the hospitality of his elephant, it was to his own brothers that he had been the agent of providence. His brothers in the evening, his father the next morning – that is what that night had brought him. After leaving Rue des Ballets at daybreak, he had hurried back to the elephant, contrived to get the two youngsters out, shared with them whatever breakfast he had concocted and had then gone off, entrusting them to that good mother, the street, who had more or less brought him up. When they parted, he arranged to meet them at the same spot that evening, and left them with these words of farewell: 'I'm hooking it, in other words I'm scooting, or as they say at court, I'm off. If you don't find pa and ma, kids, come back here this evening. I'll fix you some supper and put you to bed.' Picked up by some policeman and put in the cells, or stolen by some travelling showman, or having simply lost their way in that immense Chinese puzzle that is Paris, the two children had not returned. The lower depths of today's social world are full of such lost trails. Gavroche had not seen them again. Ten or twelve weeks had gone by since that night. He had happened more than once to scratch his head and say, 'Where the devil are my two children?'

Meanwhile, he had come, pistol in hand, to Rue du Pont-aux-Choux. He noticed there was only one shop open in this street and, come to think of it, it was a pastry shop. Here was a heaven-sent opportunity to eat another apple turnover before setting off into the unknown. Gavroche stopped, patted down his sides, fumbled in his

* Hugo is setting up a joke here for Gavroche to hark back to at the beginning of the next chapter, the hammer of a pistol being *un chien*, also meaning 'a dog'.

purse pocket, turned his other pockets inside out, found nothing, not even a sou, and cried out, 'Help!'

It is hard to miss out on the very last pastry.

Gavroche nevertheless continued on his way.

Two minutes later he was in Rue St-Louis. While crossing Rue du Parc-Royal he felt the need to be compensated for the unattainable apple turnover, and he gave himself the huge pleasure of ripping down theatre posters in broad daylight.

A little further on, seeing a group of portly individuals go by, who looked to him like men of property, he shrugged and spat out at random this mouthful of philosophical bile: 'These property owners, my, but they're fat! They stuff themselves! They wallow in good dinners. Ask them what they do with their money. They can't tell you. They gobble it up, that's what! It's all fill your belly and gone with the wind.'*

II

Gavroche on the March

Brandishing a hammerless pistol in the middle of the street is such a public undertaking that Gavroche felt his ardour increase with every step. In between snatches of the 'Marseillaise' he cried out, 'Everything's fine. My left hand hurts a lot, my rheumatism's playing up, but I'm happy, citizens. Our respectable citizens will just have to brace themselves, I'm going to hit them with subversive ditties. What's a police spy? A bloodhound. Crikey! Let's have no lack of respect for bloodhounds. What wouldn't I give to have one myself.† I've just come from the boulevard, my friends, things are hotting up, coming to the boil, simmering. It's time to skim the pot! Forward, men! May the ploughed fields be flooded with impure blood!‡ I'm ready to serve my country, my mistress I shall see no more, hey, ho, hey nonny no! But never mind! Long live joy! Let's fight, blast it! I'm fed up with despotism.'

* Gavroche puns on the well known line by Villon, the refrain of his 'Ballade en Vieil Langage François' (Ballad in Old French) from *Le Testament*: 'Autant en emporte le vent', usually translated as 'Gone with the wind'. Gavroche substitutes the word *ventre* ('belly') for *vent* ('wind'). 'Wind' is, as it happens, appropriately suggestive in this context.

† To the question 'What's a police spy?' the answer in the French text is *un chien*, 'a dog', also meaning 'a gun-hammer'. It is with this in mind that Gavroche's comment 'What wouldn't I give to have one myself?' is to be understood. Gavroche returns to the theme at the end of this chapter when one dog, a very thin poodle, distracts his attention from another – the hammerless pistol.

‡ An allusion to the refrain of the 'Marseillaise'.

A lancer in the National Guard was riding by when at that moment his horse fell under him. Gavroche laid his pistol on the paving, helped the man up, then helped to get the horse back on its feet. After which he picked up his pistol and continued on his way.

In Rue de Thorigny all was peace and quiet. This apathy, typical of the Marais, contrasted with the great clamour all around. Four old crones were gossiping in a doorway. Scotland has its trios of witches, Paris has its quartets of old gossips, and Bonaparte could be hailed in Carrefour Baudoyer with a 'Thou shalt be king hereafter' quite as direfully as Macbeth on the blasted heath. The croaking voices would be more or less the same.

The gossips of Rue de Thorigny were interested only in their own affairs. Three of them were doorkeepers and the fourth was a rag-picker, with her basket and her hooked stick.

The four of them seemed to be standing at the four corners of old age: senility, decrepitude, ruin and desolation.

The rag-picker was humble. In this outdoor world the rag-picker pays her respects and the doorkeeper offers protection. This is because what is put out on the street is as the doorkeeper dictates, rich pickings or lean, depending on the whim of whoever creates the pile of sweepings. There may be kindness in the broom.

This rag-picker was a grateful recipient and she smiled – how she smiled! – at the three doorkeepers.

What they said to each other were things like this:

'So now, is that cat of yours still vicious?'

'Lord! Cats, as you know, are the natural enemies of dogs. It's the dogs that take on so.'

'People as well.'

'But cats' fleas don't go after people.'

'It's not that, it's that dogs are dangerous. I remember one year there were so many dogs, it had to be reported in the papers. That's when there were those big sheep at the Tuileries that drew the king of Rome's little carriage. Remember the king of Rome?'

'It was the Duc de Bordeaux I liked.'

'I remember Louis XVII, I do. I preferred Louis XVII.'

'Meat's so dear these days, Mère Patagon!'

'You're telling me it is! Butcher's shops are a scandal. A frightful scandal. All they have is offal.'

Here the rag-picker intervened. 'Mesdames, business is bad. Rubbish heaps are thin pickings. No one throws anything away any more. Everything gets eaten.'

'There are those worse off than you, Vargoulême.'

'Aye, that's true,' replied the rag-picker deferentially, 'I've got a trade.'

There was a pause, and surrendering to that fundamental need in man to show off, the rag-picker added, 'When I get home in the morning I go through what I've collected, I do my salting' (she probably meant 'sorting').* 'I end up with different piles in my room. I put the rags in a basket, peelings in a bucket, linen in my cupboard, woollens in my chest, old papers in the corner by the window, anything good to eat in my bowl, bits of glass in the fireplace, slippers behind the door, and bones under the bed.'

Just behind them, Gavroche had stopped to listen. 'What's this? You old girls talking politics?' he said.

He came under a broadside attack, a fourfold jeering.

'Here's another mischief-maker.'

'Now what's that he's got in his paw? A pistol!'

'The little brat! I ask you!'

'Can't rest without challenging authority.'

Gavroche's only retaliation was to thumb his nose disdainfully, spreading his hand wide.

The rag-picker cried, 'Cheeky little guttersnipe!'

The one who answered to the name of Mame Patagon clapped her hands in indignation.

'There's going to be trouble, that's for sure. The errand boy next door who's got a little beard, I used to see him go by every morning with a girl in a pink bonnet on his arm, today I saw him go by, he had a gun on his arm. Mame Bacheux says there was a revolution last week at – at – at – where the veal comes from! – at Pontoise. And now look at him there with his pistol, horrible little ragamuffin! I've heard the Célestins barracks is full of guns. How else can the government be expected to deal with scoundrels who've got nothing better to do than think up ways of making trouble, when it was just beginning to settle down a bit after all the terrible things that've happened? God help us! That poor queen I saw going by in the tumbril! And all this is going to make tobacco even dearer. It's a disgrace! And I'll make sure I'm there to see you guillotined, you rascal!'

'You're snivelling, old girl,' said Gavroche. 'Blow your nozzle.'

And off he went. When he was in Rue Pavée, the rag-picker came back into his mind and he soliloquized: 'You're wrong to insult Revolutionaries, Mère Rubbish-Heap. This pistol is for your own good. So's you'd have more good things to eat in your basket.'

---

* The rag-picker speaks of her *treillage*, 'wire fencing' or 'trellis work', instead of *triage*, 'sorting'.

All of a sudden he heard someone shouting behind him. It was the doorkeeper Patagon, who had followed him and was shaking her fist from a distance, yelling, 'A little bastard, that's all you are.'

'You know, I couldn't care less!' said Gavroche.

Shortly afterwards he passed by Hôtel Lamoignon. There he voiced this cry: 'Forward into battle!'

And he was seized with a fit of melancholy. He gazed reproachfully at his pistol, as if trying to make it relent. 'I go off,' he said, 'but you don't!'

One dog may distract attention from another. A very thin poodle happened to pass by. Gavroche felt sorry for it.

'Poor doggy,' he said, 'you must have swallowed a barrel, all the hoops are showing inside you.'

Then he headed off towards Orme-St-Gervais.

III
A Hairdresser's Righteous Indignation

The worthy hairdresser who had chased away the two youngsters Gavroche had welcomed into the elephant's fatherly bowels was at that moment in his shop, shaving an old soldier who had been awarded the Legion of Honour for his service under the Empire. They were chatting. Naturally, the hairdresser had spoken to the veteran about the riot, then about General Lamarque, and Lamarque had led them on to the emperor. A conversation between barber and soldier that Prudhomme, had he been present, would have embellished with artistic flourishes and entitled *Dialogue between the Razor and the Sword*.

'Monsieur, how well did the emperor mount his horse?' said the barber.

'Badly. He didn't know how to fall. So he never fell.'

'Did he have handsome horses? He must have had handsome horses!'

'On the day he gave me the cross I noticed his mount. It was a fleet-footed mare of pure white. She had very wide-set ears, a sway back, a fine head with a black star marking, a very long neck, strongly defined knees, prominent ribs, a sloping shoulder and powerful hindquarters. A little over fifteen hands.'

'A fine horse,' remarked the hairdresser.

'It was His Majesty's beast.'

The hairdresser felt that after that remark a short silence was appropriate, which he observed. He then went on, 'The emperor was wounded only once, is that not so, monsieur?'

The old soldier replied with the quiet authority of one who was there, 'In the heel. At Ratisbon. I never saw him so well turned out as on that day. Like a newly minted coin.'

'And you, monsieur le vétéran, you must have been frequently wounded?'

'Me?' said the soldier. 'Oh! nothing much to speak of. I took two sabre blows on the back of my neck at Marengo, a bullet in my right arm at Austerlitz, another in my left hip at Jena, a bayonet wound – just there – at Friedland, seven or eight lance thrusts here, there and everywhere at Borodino, at Lützen an exploding shell crushed one of my fingers. Ah! and then at Waterloo, a biscayen bullet in the thigh. That's all.'

'How splendid,' exclaimed the hairdresser, in Pindaric tones, 'to die on the field of battle! On my word of honour, sooner than die on a sick bed, slowly, day by day, with drugs, poultices, the syringe and the doctor, I'd much sooner take a cannon-ball in the belly!'

'You're a man after my own heart,' said the soldier.

He had barely finished speaking when a tremendous crash shook the shop. A front window had suddenly shattered. The barber turned pale.

'My God!' he cried. 'There's one now!'

'What?'

'A cannon-ball.'

'Here it is,' said the soldier.

And he picked up something that rolled on the floor. It was a pebble.

The hairdresser rushed over to the broken window and saw Gavroche running off towards the St-Jean market as fast as his legs would carry him. With the two little lads on his mind, Gavroche could not resist the desire to pay his respects to the hairdresser as he went past his shop and had thrown a stone at his window-pane.

'You see!' shrieked the hairdresser who had turned from white to purple. 'That's mischief-making for mischief's sake. What harm's anyone ever done to that little guttersnipe?'

IV

The Child Is Amazed by the Old Man

In the St-Jean market, meanwhile, where the guard-post had already been disarmed, Gavroche had just met up with a band led by Enjolras, Courfeyrac, Combeferre and Feuilly. One way or another, they were armed. Bahorel and Jean Prouvaire had caught up with them, adding to their number. Enjolras had a double-barrelled hunting rifle, Combeferre a rifle bearing a National Guard legion number and two pistols in his belt that could be seen under his unbuttoned coat, Jean Prouvaire an old cavalry musketoon, Bahorel a carbine, Courfeyrac brandished an unsheathed sword-cane, and Feuilly with a naked sabre in his hand marched at their head shouting, 'Long live Poland!'

They reached Quai Morland, cravatless, hatless, breathless, rain-drenched, with a gleam in their eyes. Gavroche approached them and said, 'Where are we going?'

'Come along,' said Courfeyrac.

Marching behind Feuilly, or rather leaping, a fish in the stream of the riot, came Bahorel. He wore a scarlet waistcoat and had a barrage of words at the ready. His waistcoat dismayed a passer-by, who cried out with the utmost alarm, 'Here come the reds!'

'The reds, the reds!' replied Bahorel. 'A daft thing to be afraid of, bourgeois! I don't myself tremble in front of a poppy, Little Red Riding Hood inspires no terror in me. Believe me, bourgeois, leave the fear of red to horned beasts.'

He caught sight of a patch of wall with the most peaceable announcement in the world posted on it: a permission to eat eggs, a Lenten notice addressed by the archbishop of Paris to his 'flock'.

'Flock!' Bahorel exclaimed. 'A polite way of saying geese.'

And he tore the notice off the wall. This won Gavroche over. From that moment on, Gavroche began to study Bahorel.

'That was a mistake, Bahorel,' remarked Enjolras. 'You should have left that notice alone. That's not what we're here for. You're wasting your anger. Husband your resources! Potshots are no more to be fired from the heart than from the gun.'

'Each to his own, Enjolras,' retorted Bahorel. 'This episcopal prose offends me, I want to eat eggs without being given permission to do so. You're the passionately cold type. I'm enjoying myself. Besides, I'm not squandering anything, I'm getting myself fired up. *Hercle!** If I tore down that notice, it was only to whet my appetite.'

Gavroche was struck by that word, *Hercle*. He took every opportunity to educate himself and he felt respect for this tearer-down of posters. He asked him, 'What does that mean, *Hercle*?'

Bahorel replied, 'It means "God damn it" in Latin.'

Just then Bahorel recognized a pale young man with a black beard

---

* A Latin oath invoking the god Hercules.

watching them go by from a window, probably a friend of the ABC. He cried out to him, 'Quick, cartridges, *para bellum*.*'

'*Bel homme* – yes, indeed, a handsome man!' said Gavroche, who now understood Latin.

They acquired a noisy following, students, artists, young men associated with the Cougourde d'Aix, labourers, dock-workers, armed with sticks and bayonets, some like Combeferre with pistols tucked into their trousers. Among this advancing band was an extremely aged-looking man. He carried no weapon, and although apparently lost in thought he was hurrying so as not to be left behind. Gavroche noticed him.

'Wossat?' he said to Courfeyrac.

'Some old man.'

It was Monsieur Mabeuf.

V

The Old Man

Let us explain what had happened.

Enjolras and his friends were on Boulevard Bourdon near the grain stores when the dragoons charged. Enjolras, Courfeyrac and Combeferre were among those who escaped down Rue Bassompierre, shouting, 'To the barricades!' They came across an old man making his way along Rue Lesdiguières.

What attracted their attention was that this fellow was zigzagging as if he were drunk. Furthermore, although it had been raining all morning and was raining quite heavily at that very moment, he had his hat in his hand. Courfeyrac recognized Père Mabeuf. He knew him from the many times he had accompanied Marius to the old man's front door. Familiar with the book-loving old warden's quiet and more than retiring habits, and astonished to see him in the midst of this tumult, a few steps away from the cavalry charges, almost in the thick of a barrage of gunfire, hatless in the rain and wandering about among the bullets, he went up to him, and the twenty-five-year-old rioter and the octogenarian had this exchange.

'Monsieur Mabeuf, go home.'

'Why?'

'There's going to be fighting.'

'That's fine.'

---

* From the Latin adage *Si vis pacem, para bellum* ('If you want peace, prepare for war'). Gavroche misinterprets what he hears as Latin for *bel homme*, 'handsome man'.

'Sabre cuts and gunfire, Monsieur Mabeuf.'

'That's fine.'

'Cannon-fire.'

'That's fine. Where are you people going?'

'We're going to bring the government down.'

'That's fine.'

And he began to follow them. After that, he uttered not a word. Suddenly he had become firm of foot. Some workers offered him an arm, he refused with a shake of the head. He advanced almost to the front row of the column, in his movements looking like a man on the march, in his expression like a man asleep.

'My! But the old boy's enraged!' murmured the students. The rumour spread through the ranks that he was a former member of the Convention, an old regicide.

The crowd turned into Rue de la Verrerie.

Little Gavroche marched in front, singing at the top of his voice, which made him into a kind of bugle.

This is what he sang:

> The moon's now rising in the sky.
> Shall we go to the woods near by?
> Charlot asked Charlotte.

> Tou, tou, tou,
> For Chatou,
> I've only one God, one king, one sou, one shoe.

> Drinking the early-morning dew
> From thyme leaves – a heady brew –
> Made two sparrows tipsy.

> Zi zi zi
> For Passy
> I've only one God, one king, one sou, one shoe.

> Those poor little chicks
> Were as tight as ticks
> Gladdening a tiger in its den.

> Don, don, don
> For Meudon.
> I've only one God, one king, one sou, one shoe.

One cursed, the other swore.
Shall we go to the woods no more?
Charlot asked Charlotte.

Tin, tin, tin
For Pantin.
I've only one God, one king, one sou, one shoe.

They headed towards St-Merry.

VI
Recruits

The band kept growing. As they came to Rue des Billettes a tall man with greying hair joined them; his bold and doughty demeanour was noted by Courfeyrac, Enjolras and Combeferre, but none of them knew him. Gavroche, who was busy singing, whistling, humming, running on ahead and banging on the shutters of shops with the butt of his hammerless pistol, paid no attention to this man.

They happened to pass Courfeyrac's front door in Rue de la Verrerie.

'That's lucky,' said Courfeyrac, 'I forgot my purse and I've lost my hat.' He left the band and raced upstairs to his lodgings. He grabbed an old hat and his purse. He also grabbed a large square chest the size of a large travelling-bag that was concealed in his dirty laundry.

As he came rushing back downstairs the caretaker called out to him, 'Monsieur de Courfeyrac!'

'Caretaker, what's your name?'

The caretaker was nonplussed.

'Why, you know perfectly well, I'm the concierge. My name's Mère Veuvain.'

'Well, if you call me Monsieur *de* Courfeyrac again, I shall call you Mère *de* Veuvain. So now tell me, what is it?'

'There's someone here wanting to speak to you.'

'Who?'

'I don't know.'

'Where?'

'In my lodge.'

'To hell with them!' said Courfeyrac.

'But they've been waiting for you more than an hour,' said the caretaker.

At the same time a young worker of some kind, small, thin, pale and freckled, wearing a shirt with holes in it and patched fustian trousers, looking more like a girl dressed up as a boy than a man, came out of the lodge and said to Courfeyrac in a voice that, for that matter, sounded not in the least a woman's voice, 'Monsieur Marius, if you please?'

'He's not here.'

'Will he be back this evening?'

'I've no idea.'

And Courfeyrac added, 'Speaking for myself, I shan't be back.'

The young man stared at him and said, 'Why not?'

'Because.'

'Well, where are you going?'

'What's it to do with you?'

'Do you want me to carry your chest?'

'I'm going to man the barricades.'

'Do you want me to go with you?'

'If you like!' replied Courfeyrac. 'No one's stopping you, the streets belong to everyone.'

And he ran off to rejoin his friends. When he caught up with them, he gave one of them the chest to carry. It was not until a good quarter of an hour later that he noticed that the young man had indeed followed them.

A rabble does not determine precisely where it goes. As we have explained, it is at the mercy of the wind. They went beyond St-Merry, and without really knowing how they ended up there, they found themselves in Rue St-Denis.

BOOK TWELVE
CORINTHE

I
The History of Corinthe from Its Foundation

Nowadays Parisians entering Rue Rambuteau from the direction of Les Halles who notice on their right, opposite Rue Mondétour, a basket-weaver's shop that has for its sign a basket in the shape of the emperor Napoleon the Great with this inscription:

> NAPOLEON IS MADE
> ENTIRELY OF WILLOW

little suspect the terrible scenes that took place on this very spot barely thirty years ago.

Here was Rue de la Chanvrerie, written Chanverrerie in ancient title deeds, and here stood the famous tavern called Corinthe.

Bearing in mind everything that has been said about the barricade erected here, eclipsed though it was by the St-Merry barricade, it is on this famous Rue de la Chanvrerie barricade, now fallen into deep obscurity, that we are going to shed a little light.

If we may for the sake of clarity be allowed to avail ourselves of the simple device we have already used in connection with Waterloo, those who want to picture to themselves with reasonable accuracy the blocks of houses that stood at that time near Pointe St-Eustache at the north-east corner of Paris's Les Halles, where today Rue Rambuteau begins, have only to imagine a letter N with Rue St-Denis running along the top of it and Les Halles along the base, and the two vertical legs representing Rue de la Grande-Truanderie and Rue de la Chanvrerie, with Rue de la Petite-Truanderie running obliquely between them. The old Rue Mondétour cut across the three strokes of the N at the most crooked angles. So much so that within an area of some two hundred square yards, between Les Halles and Rue St-Denis on the one hand and Rue du Cygne and Rue des Prêcheurs on the other, the labyrinthine criss-crossings of these four streets contrived to divide up the houses into seven oddly shaped islets of different sizes, lying this way and that, as though at random, and barely separated from each other by narrow chinks, like blocks of stone in a quarry.

We say narrow chinks, and it would be impossible to give any better idea of those dark, cramped, crooked lanes lined with eight-storey tenement buildings. These tenement buildings were so decrepit that in Rue de la Chanvrerie and Rue de la Petite-Truanderie the façades were shored up with beams running across from one house to another. The street was narrow and the gutter wide, anyone on foot walked on paving that was always wet, past cellar-like shops, thick, iron-ringed boundary-posts, inordinate piles of rubbish, portals fitted with huge, age-old grilles. All this Rue Rambuteau swept away.

That name 'Mondétour' wonderfully conjures up the convolutions of this whole warren. A little further on they were even better conveyed by 'Rue Pirouette', which ran into Rue Mondétour.

Anyone coming from Rue St-Denis into Rue de la Chanvrerie saw it gradually narrow ahead of him as if he had entered an elongated funnel. At the end of the street, which was very short, he would find the way barred towards Les Halles by a tall row of houses, and he might have thought he was in a blind alley had he not noticed to right and left two dark cuttings by which he could escape. This was Rue Mondétour, leading to Rue des Prêcheurs on the one side and to Rue du Cygne and Rue de la Petite-Truanderie on the other. At the bottom of this blind alley, as it were, on the corner of the right-hand cutting, a house not so tall as the others was to be observed, forming a kind of promontory on to the street.

It was in this house, only two storeys high, that a celebrated tavern had been happily located for over three hundred years. This tavern brought a joyous sound to the very place old Théophile evoked in these two lines of verse:

> There swings the dreadful skeleton
> Of some poor lover who hanged himself.

It was in a good position, the business was passed on from father to son.

In the days of Mathurin Régnier this tavern was called the Pot-aux-Roses*, and as rebus puzzles were then in fashion it had for its sign a pillar† painted pink ‡. In the last century the worthy Natoire, one of those imaginative masters today scorned by the formal school, having several times made merry in this tavern at the very table where Régnier

---

* Meaning 'plant-pot of roses'.
† In the French: 'poteau', a homophone of *pot-aux*.
‡ In the French: 'rose', also meaning 'a rose plant'.

had caroused, to show his gratitude painted a bunch of Corinth grapes on the pink pillar. In his delight the tavern-keeper altered the sign and beneath the bunch of grapes had these words emblazoned in gold: 'Au Raisin de Corinthe'. Hence the name 'Corinthe'. Nothing is more natural to drunkards than ellipsis. Ellipsis is the zigzagging of the spoken word. Corinthe gradually displaced the Pot-aux-Roses. No longer even knowing about the tradition, the last tavern-keeper of the dynasty, Père Hucheloup, had the pillar painted blue.

A downstairs room where the bar was, an upstairs room with a billiard table, a wooden spiral staircase going through the ceiling, wine on the tables, smoke on the walls, candles at midday, that was the kind of tavern it was. A staircase under a trap-door in the room on the ground floor led to the cellar. On the second floor were the Hucheloup family's quarters, reached by a staircase – more ladder than staircase – with only a hidden door in the large first-floor room for an entrance. Under the roof, two garrets for the serving-maids. The kitchen shared the ground floor with the bar-room.

Père Hucheloup might have been born a chemist, but the fact is he was a cook. You could not only drink in his tavern, you could also eat. Hucheloup had invented a splendid dish not to be had anywhere else. It was stuffed carp, which he called *carpes au gras*. It was eaten by the light of a tallow candle or a lamp dating from the time of Louis XVI, on tables with oilcloth nailed to them for a tablecloth. People would come a long way for it. One fine morning Hucheloup had seen fit to notify passers-by of his 'speciality'. He had dipped a brush in a pot of black paint, and as he had his own individual spelling as well as his own individual cuisine, he concocted this remarkable inscription on his wall: *Carpes ho gras**.

One winter the downpours and hailstorms had freakishly erased the *s* on the end of the first word and the *g* at the beginning of the third, leaving *Carpe ho ras*. Time and rain assisting, a humble culinary advertisement had become a profound maxim.†

So it was that, not knowing French, Père Hucheloup displayed a knowledge of Latin, drew philosophy from cooking and, simply wanting to banish Lent, proved himself a match for Horace. And, what was impressive, this wording also meant 'Come into my tavern.'

None of this exists today. The Mondétour maze was gutted and

---

* *Ho gras* is an incorrect phonetic transcription of *au gras*, meaning 'with a rich filling, usually of meat'.
† *Carpe horas*: Latin for 'Seize the hours', a variation on Horace's *carpe diem*, 'seize the day' (bk 1, Ode 11, line 8).

largely opened up as long ago as 1847, and by now is probably no more. Rue de la Chanvrerie and Corinthe have disappeared beneath the paving-stones of Rue Rambuteau.

As we said, Corinthe was one of the meeting-places, if not assembly points, of Courfeyrac and his friends. It was Grantaire who discovered Corinthe. He went in because of the *carpe horas* and returned because of the *carpes au gras*. You could drink, you could eat, you could shout, for which you paid little, badly, or not at all; you were always welcome. Père Hucheloup was a good man.

A good man, as we said, Hucheloup was a mustachioed tavern-keeper: the jolly kind. He always looked bad-tempered, seemingly set on intimidating his customers, grumbling at the people who came in, and was apparently more inclined to pick a quarrel with them than to serve them soup. And yet, we abide by what we have already said – everyone was always welcome. This eccentricity attracted custom, bringing in young men who would say to each other, 'Come and see Père Hucheloup grouch.' He had been a fencing-master. All of a sudden he would burst out laughing. Loud-mouthed, easy-going. Comic at heart, and outwardly tragic. He wanted nothing better than to frighten you, rather like those snuff-boxes in the shape of a pistol. The explosive sneeze. He had an extremely ugly, bearded wife, Mère Hucheloup.

About 1830, Père Hucheloup died. With him went the secret of the stuffed carp. His inconsolable widow kept the tavern going. But standards dropped and the food became atrocious; the wine, which had always been bad, was abominable. Courfeyrac and his friends nevertheless continued going to Corinthe – out of pity, said Bossuet.

Widow Hucheloup was short-winded and misshapen, with some rustic memories. These she rescued from banality by her pronunciation. She had her own way of saying things that added piquancy to her reminiscences of village life in the springtime. In the old days, she said, she loved to hear 'the robber redbreasts singing in the orphan bushes'.

The upstairs room where 'the restaurant' was, was a big, long room crammed with stools, trestles, benches, chairs and tables and an old lopsided billiard table. It was reached by the spiral staircase that led up to a square hole like a ship's hatchway in a corner of the room.

Illuminated by a single narrow window and a lamp that was always lit, this room had an attic-like appearance. Every piece of four-legged furniture behaved as if it had but three. The whitewashed walls had no decoration other than the following verse in tribute to Mame Hucheloup:

She's a wonder at ten paces, frightening at two,
With a wart on her wobbly nose.
You're in constant dread that one good blow –
And into her mouth it goes!

This was scrawled in charcoal on the wall.

Looking very like it, Mame Hucheloup passed to and fro in front of this verse from morning till night without turning a hair. Two serving-maids, called Matelote and Gibelotte* and who had never been known by any other names, helped Mame Hucheloup to set on the tables the jugs of red wine and the various broths served to the hungry in earthenware bowls. Fat, round, red-haired and strident, once the deceased Hucheloup's favourite concubine, Matelote was uglier than any mythological monster. Yet, just as it befits the servant always to give precedence to her mistress, she was less ugly than Mame Hucheloup. Lanky, delicate, lymphatically pale, with rings round her eyes and drooping lids, always drained and exhausted, afflicted with what might be called chronic lassitude, the first to get up and the last to retire, Gibelotte waited on everyone, even the other serving-maid, with meekness and in silence, smiling through her fatigue with a vague, sleepy kind of smile.

There was a mirror above the bar.

Anyone entering the restaurant room would read the following line chalked on the door by Courfeyrac: 'Enjoy if you can and eat if you dare.'†

II
Preliminary Jollities

As we know, L'aigle de Meaux lived at Joly's more than anywhere else. Home to him was as a branch to a bird. The two friends lived together, ate together, slept together. They shared everything, even Musichetta occasionally. They were what among junior monks are called *bini*‡. On the morning of the fifth of June they went to eat at Corinthe. Joly, with his nose all blocked, had a heavy cold that Laigle was beginning to share. Laigle's coat was threadbare but Joly was smartly dressed.

---

* Meaning 'fish stew' and 'rabbit stew', respectively.
† An allusion to a line written by Corneille (1606–64): 'Devine, si tu peux, et choisis, si tu l'oses' ('Guess if you can, and choose if you dare'), from his tragedy *Héraclius* (Act IV, sc. iv).
‡ *Bini* is Latin for 'two by two', junior monks (Hugo uses the term *frères chapeaux*) being required to process in pairs behind the senior dignitaries.

It was about nine o'clock in the morning when they stepped through the door of Corinthe. They went up to the first floor. Matelote and Gibelotte welcomed them.

'Oysters, cheese and ham,' said Laigle.

And they sat down at a table. The tavern was empty. There were just the two of them. Recognizing Joly and Laigle, Gibelotte put a bottle of wine on the table.

They were just starting on the oysters when a head appeared through the staircase hatchway and a voice said, 'I was passing by. From out in the street I catch a delicious smell of Brie. In I come.'

It was Grantaire. Grantaire took a stool and sat at the table. Seeing Grantaire, Gibelotte put two bottles of wine on the table. That made three.

'Are you going to drink those two bottles?' Laigle asked Grantaire.

Grantaire replied, 'Everyone here's a genius, it's only you that's ingenuous. No man has ever wondered at two bottles.'

The others had begun by eating, Grantaire began by drinking. Half a bottle was rapidly consumed.

'You must have a hole in your belly!' said Laigle.

'You certainly have one at your elbow,' said Grantaire.

And having emptied his glass, he added, 'I have to tell you, Laigle of the funeral oration, your coat is old.'

'I should hope so too,' said Laigle. 'It means we're a happy couple, my coat and I. It has adapted to all my physical quirks, it's not in any way uncomfortable, it has moulded itself to my deformities, it allows me complete freedom of movement, I'm aware of it only because it keeps me warm. Old coats are just like old friends.'

'That's right,' cried Joly, joining in the conversation, 'an old goat's an old bate.'*

'Especially for a man with a blocked nose,' said Grantaire.

'Grantaire, have you come from the boulevard?' asked Laigle.

'No.'

'We just saw the head of the funeral procession go by, Joly and I.'

'It's a barvellous sight,' said Joly.

'How quiet this street is!' cried Laigle. 'Who would suspect that Paris was in turmoil? It's obvious this part of town used to be all convents! Du Breul and Sauval list them, Abbé Lebeuf as well. All round here, they were. The place was teeming with the calced, the discalced,

---

* With his blocked nose, Joly's statement that an old coat (*un vieil habit*) is an old friend (*un vieil ami*, or as he pronounces it, *un vieil abi*) sounds like a tautology (the pronunciation of *habit* and *abi* being identical).

the tonsured, the bearded, greys, blacks, whites, Franciscans, Minims, Capuchins, Carmelites, little Augustinians, great Augustinians,* old Augustinians . . . They were thick on the ground.'

'Let's not talk about monks,' said Grantaire, interrupting, 'it makes you want to scratch yourself.'

Then he exclaimed, 'Ugh! I've just swallowed a bad oyster. Now I've another attack of hypochondria coming on. The oysters are off, the servants are ugly. I hate the human race. I came along Rue Richelieu earlier, past the big public library. That pile of oyster-shells they call a library puts me off thinking. All that paper! All that ink! All that scribbling! The amount that's been written! Which numbskull was it that said man was a featherless biped?† And then I ran into a pretty girl I know, as lovely as springtime, who deserves to be called Flora, and she's delighted, ecstatic, overjoyed, in seventh heaven, poor thing, because yesterday some dreadful banker all pitted with smallpox deigned to take a fancy to her! Alas! women are susceptible to practicalities no less than to good looks; cats chase mice as well as birds. Not two months ago that young woman was a good girl living in a garret. She fitted little brass rings – or whatever they're called – into the eyelets of corsets. She sewed, she had a trestle-bed, she sat at home with a jar of flowers, she was content. Now she's a banker's consort. This transformation took place last night. I met the victim this morning, looking utterly delighted. The awful thing is, the little hussy is as pretty today as she was yesterday. Her patron didn't show on her face. Roses are better or worse off than women in this respect: the traces that pests leave on them are visible. Ah! there's no morality on this earth, I call to witness the myrtle, symbol of love, the laurel, symbol of war, the silly old olive, symbol of peace, the apple tree that almost choked Adam on one of its pips, and the fig tree, grand-papa of petticoats. As for rightfulness, do you want to know what rightfulness is? The Gauls want Clusium, Rome protects Clusium and asks the Gauls what wrong Clusium has done them. Brennus replies, "The wrong that Alba did you, the wrong that Fidenae did you, the wrong the Aequi, the Volsci and the Sabines did you. They were your neighbours. The Clusians are ours. We have the same understanding of what it means to be neighbours as you do. You stole Alba, we're taking Clusium." Rome said,

---

* The French Petits-Augustins ('Little Augustinians') were the Discalced Augustinians; the Grands-Augustins ('Great Augustinians') were the Hermits of St Augustine.

† Man may be featherless – *sans plume* – but he is not without a (quill) pen – *sans plume*.

"You will not take Clusium." Brennus took Rome. Then he cried, "*Vae victis!*"* That's what rightfulness is. Ah! so many predators in this world! So many eagles! So many eagles! It gives me gooseflesh.'

He held out his glass to Joly, who refilled it, then he drank and went on, scarcely interrupted by this glass of wine that no one, not even he himself, had noticed.

'Brennus, who takes Rome, is an eagle. The banker who takes the grisette is an eagle. No more sense of decency here than there. So let's not believe in anything. There's only one reality: drinking. Whatever your opinion, whether you favour the lean cockerel like the canton of Uri, or the fat cockerel like the canton of Glarus, it doesn't matter. Drink. You talk to me about the boulevard, the funeral procession, et cetera. So now there's going to be another revolution, is there? This paucity of resources on the part of the good Lord amazes me. He has to keep greasing the rails of events. There's a hitch, things aren't going smoothly. Quick, a revolution! The good Lord's hands are always black with that filthy grease. If I were in his place I'd keep things simpler, I wouldn't be tinkering with the works the whole time, I'd deal firmly with the human race, I'd keep things going, knitted together stitch by stitch, without breaking the yarn, I wouldn't have anything special in reserve, I wouldn't have any emergency measures to fall back on. What you people call progress is driven by two motors, men and events. But sad to say, from time to time something out of the ordinary is called for. In terms of events as well as men, the usual players are unsatisfactory. With men, geniuses are needed; with events, revolutions. Great accidents are mandatory. They're indispensable to the order of things. And seeing the appearance of comets, you'd be tempted to think that heaven itself has to recruit actors from outside the company. Just when you least expect it God placards a meteor on the wall of the firmament. Some weird star turns up, with a huge tail trailing after it. And as a result Caesar dies. Brutus stabs him with a knife and God attacks him with a comet. Suddenly, there you have it! An aurora borealis, a revolution, a great man. Ninety-three writ large, Napoleon given star billing, and the comet of 1811 at the top of the poster. Oh! such a beautiful blue poster all spangled with unexpected bursts of light! Boom! Boom! An extraordinary spectacle. Look up, you idiots. Everything's unruly, star and drama alike. Good God, this is all too much and not enough! Seemingly magnificent, these resources, for all that they're exceptional, are poor indeed. My friends, providence is reduced to expediency. A revolution proves what? That

* 'Woe to the vanquished!' For more historical details, see endnote p. 1402.

981

God has been found wanting. He engineers a *coup d'état* because continuity between present and future is thereby resolved, and because God himself has not been able to make the two ends meet. In fact, this confirms me in my conjectures about the state of Jehovah's wealth. And seeing so much distress, up on high as well as down below, so much meanness, grasping avarice, thievery and privation in heaven and on earth, from the bird without a grain of millet to myself without an income of a hundred thousand a year; seeing the fate of humanity, which is very shabby, and even the fate of royalty, which hangs by a thread (witness the demise of the Prince de Condé); seeing winter, which is nothing but a rent in the celestial heights through which the wind blows; seeing so much raggedness in morning's first flush of crimson on the crest of the hills; seeing those fake pearls, the dewdrops; seeing those paste diamonds, the frost; seeing humanity in tatters and events all patched up, and so many spots on the sun and so many holes in the moon; seeing so much pauperism everywhere, I suspect God isn't rich. He keeps up appearances, it's true, but I sense the strain. He stages a revolution the way a merchant with empty coffers gives a ball. Gods shouldn't be judged on appearances. Beneath the divine gilding I detect an impoverished universe. There's a shortfall in creation. That's why I'm unhappy. Look, it's the fifth of June, it's almost dark. I've been waiting for daylight to come since morning. It hasn't come yet and I bet it won't come before the day is out. That's negligence of a kind you'd expect of an ill-paid shop assistant. Yes, everything's badly organized, nothing's co-ordinated with anything else, this old world is out of kilter, I'm siding with the opposition. Everything is skewed, the universe is perverse. It's like with children, those who want them haven't any, and those who don't want them have. Result: I'm upset. Besides, this bald-head Laigle de Meaux is a painful sight to me. It's humiliating to think I'm the same age as this coot. All the same, I criticize but I'm not rude. The universe is what it is. I'm speaking here with no ill intent, and for conscience's sake. Be assured, Eternal Father, of my sincere regard. Ah! by all the saints of Olympus and all the gods of paradise, I wasn't cut out to be a Parisian, that's to say forever to-ing and fro-ing like a shuttlecock, batted this way and that, between idlers and carousers. I was meant to be a Turk watching oriental beauties all day long performing those exquisite Egyptian dances as lascivious as a chaste man's dreams, or a peasant from the Beauce, or a Venetian nobleman surrounded by Venetian noblewomen, or some German princeling providing the German Confederation with half a footsoldier and whiling away the time drying his socks on a hedge, that's to say, his frontier. Those are the destinies for which I was born! Yes, a Turk, I said, and I'll stand by that. I don't understand why Turks are generally looked down on. There's some good in Mohammed. All due respect to the inventor of seraglios with houris and paradises with odalisques! Let's not insult Islam, the only religion graced with a henhouse! At this point, I insist on having a drink. The earth's a great absurdity. And it appears that all these imbeciles are going to fight each other, to get themselves killed, to massacre each other, at the height of summer, in the month of Prairial, when they could be going off into the countryside with some creature on their arm to relish the vast aromatic cup of tea that is new-mown hay! People really are exceedingly foolish. An old broken lantern I saw in a curiosity shop earlier gives me pause for thought: it might be time to enlighten the human race. Yes, I'm back in the doldrums. That's how it is when an oyster and a revolution go down the wrong way! I become miserable again. Oh! what a dreadful old world – of drudgery and beggary and debauchery and butchery – and we get used to it!'

And after this fit of eloquence Grantaire had a well earned fit of coughing.

'Sbeaking of revolution,' said Joly, 'abbarently Barius is badly in love.'

'Do we know who with?' asked Laigle.

'Doh.'

'No?'

'Doh, I said.'

'Marius in love!' exclaimed Grantaire. 'I can just see it. Marius is a haze and he must have found himself a mist. Marius belongs to the poet breed. Whoever says poet, says madman. *Timbraeus Apollo.**
Marius and his Marie, or his Maria, or his Mariette or his Marion – they must make quaint lovers. I can tell what it's like. Ecstasies where kissing's forgotten. Chaste on earth but coupling in the infinite. They're sensual souls. They lie together among the stars.'

Grantaire was about to start on his second bottle and possibly his second harangue when a newcomer emerged from the square staircase opening. It was a boy less than ten years of age, ragged, very small, sallow-complexioned, with a little pointed face, bright-eyed, very long-haired, rain-soaked, and happy-looking.

* Timbra, near Troy, was one of the places where Apollo was worshipped. The French *timbré*, from *timbre* meaning 'bell' or 'quality of tone', is also used figuratively to mean 'cracked' in the sense of 'crazy'.

Unhesitatingly choosing between the three, the child addressed Laigle de Meaux.

'Are you Monsieur Bossuet?' he asked.

'That's my nickname,' replied Laigle. 'What is it you want?'

'Well, a tall fair-haired fellow on the boulevard said to me, "You know Mère Hucheloup?" I said, "Yes, Rue Chanvrerie, the old man's widow." He said, "Go over there. You'll find Monsieur Bossuet there, and you give him this message from me: A B C." It's some kind of joke, isn't it? He gave me ten sous.'

'Joly, lend me ten sous,' said Laigle. And turning to Grantaire, 'Grantaire, lend me ten sous.'

That made twenty sous, which Laigle handed to the child.

'Thank you, monsieur,' said the little boy.

'What's your name?' asked Laigle.

'Navet, Gavroche's friend.'

'Stay with us,' said Laigle.

'Eat with us,' said Grantaire.

The child replied, 'I can't, I'm in the procession, I'm the one that's shouting "Down with Polignac!"'

And off he went, dragging his feet, which is the most respectful of all possible salutations.

When the child had gone, Grantaire spoke.

'That's the gamin pure and simple. There are many varieties of the gamin species. The gamin lawyer is called the errand boy, the gamin cook is called the scullion, the gamin baker is called the baker's assistant, the gamin footman is called the boot-boy, the gamin seaman is called the cabin-boy, the gamin soldier is called the drummer-boy, the gamin artist is called the apprentice, the gamin shopkeeper is called the counter-jumper, the gamin courtier is called the minion, the gamin king is called the dauphin, the gamin god is called the bambino.'

Laigle, meanwhile, was thinking. He said to himself, 'A B C, that means Lamarque's funeral.'

'The tall fair-haired fellow,' said Grantaire, 'that's Enjolras tipping you off.'

'Shall we go?' said Bossuet.

'It's raining,' said Joly. 'I've sworn to go under fire, not water. I doh'd wanda catch cold.'

'I'm staying here,' said Grantaire. 'I prefer a meal to a hearse.'

'Conclusion: we stay,' said Laigle. 'Well then, let's drink. Besides, we can miss the funeral without missing the riot.'

'Ah! Count be in for the riot!' cried Joly.

Laigle rubbed his hands. 'So we're going to make adjustments to the 1830 Revolution. It's a bit of a tight fit for the people.'

'I don't really care about your revolution,' said Grantaire. 'I've no strong feelings against this government. It's the crown moderated by the nightcap. It's a sceptre with an umbrella on the end of it. In fact, come to think of it, today, in this weather, Louis-Philippe could use his royalty in two ways, he could wield the sceptre end against the people and open the umbrella end against the skies.'

The room was dark, any daylight was entirely blotted out by large clouds. There was no one in the tavern or on the street, everyone having gone 'to see the disturbances'.

'Is it noon or midnight?' cried Bossuet. 'You can't see a thing. Gibelotte, some light.'

Grantaire was drinking morosely.

'Enjolras despises me,' he muttered. 'Enjolras said, "Joly's ill, Grantaire's drunk." He sent Navet to Bossuet. If he'd come to fetch me I'd have followed him. Too bad for Enjolras! I shan't go to his funeral.'

Once this decision was made, Bossuet, Joly and Grantaire did not stir from the tavern. By two o'clock in the afternoon the table they were sitting at was covered with empty bottles. They had two candles burning, one in a candle-holder of completely green copper, the other in the neck of a cracked carafe. Grantaire had waylaid Joly and Bossuet with wine. Bossuet and Joly had put Grantaire back on the road to cheerfulness.

Since noon Grantaire himself had moved on from wine, no great source of dreams. Among serious drinkers wine has only limited success. In the matter of drunkenness, there is white magic and black magic. Wine is only white magic. Grantaire was an adventurous drinker of dreams. As a prospect, the blackness of extreme drunkenness, far from deterring him, attracted him. He had forsaken the bottles and taken to the tankard. The tankard is the abyss. With neither opium nor hashish to hand, and wanting to fill his head with twilight, he had resorted to that dreadful mixture of brandy, stout and absinthe that produces such terrible lethargies. It is of these three vapours, beer, brandy and absinthe, that the leadenness of the soul is made. They are three darknesses in which the celestial butterfly drowns. And in a vaporous layer vaguely condensed into a bat's wing, three silent Furies take shape, Nightmare, Night and Death, hovering over sleeping Psyche.

Grantaire was not yet at that dire stage, far from it. He was extremely merry, and Bossuet and Joly no less so. They clinked glasses.

To the eccentric emphasis he laid on words and ideas, Grantaire added a singularity of gesture. With dignity, he rested his left fist on his knee, his arm forming a right-angle; and astride his stool, with his cravat untied, his full glass in his right hand, he addressed these solemn words to the fat serving-maid Matelote.

'Let the doors of the palace be thrown open! Let everyone be a member of the French Academy and have the right to embrace Madame Hucheloup. Let's drink!'

And turning to Mame Hucheloup, he added, 'Ancient woman sanctified by custom, come here, that I may gaze on you!'

And Joly cried out, 'Batelote and Gibelotte, doh'd give Grantaire any bore to drink. He's spending buhney like water. Since this borning he's already recklessly squandered two francs and ninety-five centibes.'

And Grantaire went on, 'Who was it that fetched down the stars without my permission and put them on the table as candles?'

In his extreme drunkenness Bossuet had retained his composure. He was seated on the sill of the open window, getting his back wet in the falling rain, and observing his two friends.

Suddenly he heard a commotion behind him, people running, cries of 'To arms!' He turned round and in Rue St-Denis, at the end of Rue de la Chanvrerie, he saw Enjolras passing by with a rifle in his hand, and Gavroche with his pistol, Feuilly with his sabre, Courfeyrac with his sword, Jean Prouvaire with his musketoon, Combeferre with his rifle, Bahorel with his carbine, and the whole armed and tumultuous rabble following on behind.

Rue de la Chanvrerie was scarcely the length of a carbine's range of fire. Bossuet improvised a loud-hailer with his two hands around his mouth and yelled, 'Courfeyrac! Hey, there! Courfeyrac!'

Courfeyrac heard the shout, saw Bossuet and walked a few paces into Rue de la Chanvrerie, shouting a 'What do you want?' while a 'Where are you going?' came from the opposite direction.

'To build a barricade,' replied Courfeyrac.

'Well, this is a good place! Build it here!'

'You're right, Aigle,' said Courfeyrac.

And at a signal from Courfeyrac the riotous crowd swept down Rue de la Chanvrerie.

Darkness Starts to Descend on Grantaire

It was indeed ideally located, wider at the top of the street and narrowing to a dead end at the bottom, with Corinthe creating a choke point, Rue Mondétour easy to bar to right and to left, no attack possible except from Rue St-Denis, that is to say, frontally and exposed. Bossuet in his cups had fasting Hannibal's eye.

At the irruption of the mob terror had taken hold of the whole street. Not a passer-by that did not make himself scarce. Quick as a flash, down at the bottom, to right, to left, shops, workshops, doors, windows, blinds, skylights, shutters of every size had closed, from ground floor to rooftop. To absorb the gunfire, a terrified old woman had with two clothes-drying poles fixed a mattress in front of her window. The tavern alone remained open, and for a very good reason: the rabble had come rushing in.

'Oh my God! Oh my God!' sighed Mame Hucheloup.

Bossuet had gone downstairs to meet Courfeyrac.

Joly, who was standing at the window, cried out, 'Courfeyrac, you should have brought an ubbrella. You'll catch a cold.'

Meanwhile, within a few minutes, twenty iron bars had been wrenched from the grating in front of the tavern, forty yards of cobblestones had been ripped up from the street; Gavroche and Bahorel seized a passing cart belonging to a lime-maker named Anceau, and overturned it. This cart contained three barrels full of lime, which they placed beneath the piles of cobblestones. Enjolras opened up the trap-door to the cellar and all Widow Hucheloup's empty casks were set alongside the barrels of lime. With fingers accustomed to painting the delicate ribs of fans, Feuilly buttressed the barrels and the cart with two massive heaps of rubble. Rubble improvised like everything else and taken from who knows where. Support beams were torn from a neighbouring house front and laid on the casks. When Bossuet and Courfeyrac turned round, half the street was already blocked with a rampart higher than a man. There is nothing like the hand of the common people for building anew out of what has been demolished.

Matelote and Gibelotte mingled with the workers. Gibelotte went to and fro loaded with rubble. Her lassitude contributed to the barricade. She served up cobblestones just as she would have served wine, sleepily.

An omnibus drawn by two white horses passed by the end of the street.

Bossuet climbed over the cobblestones, ran, stopped the driver, made the passengers descend, offered his hand to 'the ladies', dismissed the conductor and came back with the vehicle, leading the horses by the bridle.

'No omnibus,' he said, 'goes past Corinthe. *Non licet omnibus adire Corinthum.*'*

A moment later the unhitched horses wandered off down Rue Mondétour, and the omnibus lying on its side completed the blocking of the street.

Distraught, Mame Hucheloup had taken refuge upstairs.

She gazed vacantly with unseeing eyes, quietly whimpering. Her cries of horror dared not emerge from her throat. 'It's the end of the world,' she murmured.

Joly planted a kiss on Mame Hucheloup's fat, red, wrinkled neck, and said to Grantaire, 'My dear fellow, I've always regarded a woman's neck as an infinitely delicate thing.'

But Grantaire was soaring to extreme heights of rhapsody. When Matelote came back upstairs Grantaire grabbed her by the waist and burst into great gales of laughter at the window.

'Matelote is ugly!' he cried. 'Matelote is the perfection of ugliness! Matelote is a chimera. This is the secret of her birth: a Gothic Pygmalion, who made gargoyles for cathedrals, one fine morning fell in love with the most horrible of them. He begged Love to bring it to life, and Matelote was the result. Look at her, citizens! She has chrome-yellow hair like Titian's mistress, and she's a good girl. I guarantee she'll fight well. Every good girl contains a hero. As for Mère Hucheloup, she's an old warrior. Look at the moustache she has! She's inherited it from her husband. In a word, a trooper! She too will fight. These two alone will be the terror of the outskirts! Comrades, we shall overthrow the government as sure as there are fifteen intermediate acids between margaric acid and formic acid. Not that it matters to me in the least. Gentlemen, my father always detested me because I couldn't understand mathematics. All I understand are love and liberty. Good old Grantaire, that's me! Never having had money, I never became accustomed to it, so I've never felt the need of it, but if I'd been rich there would have been no more poor! Believe me! Oh, if kind hearts had fat purses, how much better things would be! Imagine Jesus Christ with

* An allusion to a Latin saying attributed to Horace (*Epistles* I:17, line 36: 'Non cuivis homini contingit adire Corinthum', 'It is not every man's lot to go to Corinth'). Bossuet is playing on the word 'omnibus', the new form of public transport in Paris (since 1828), and the aptly named tavern.

Rothschild's fortune! He would do so much good! Matelote, kiss me! You're voluptuous and shy! You have cheeks that invite a sister's kiss and lips that cry out for a lover's.'

'Put a cork in it!' said Courfeyrac.

Grantaire replied, 'I'm official magistrate and master of poetry!'

Enjolras, who was standing on the ridge of the barricade, gun in hand, raised his stern, handsome face. As we know, there was something of the Spartan and the Puritan in Enjolras. He would have perished at Thermopylae with Leonidas and burned down Drogheda with Cromwell.

'Grantaire,' he shouted, 'go and wallow in your drunkenness elsewhere! This is a place for the spirited, not for the sot. You're a disgrace to the barricade!'

This tetchy remark had a striking effect on Grantaire. It was as if a glass of cold water had been thrown in his face. He suddenly seemed to sober up. He sat down at a table by the window, rested his elbows on it, gazed at Enjolras with an indescribable tenderness and said to him, 'You know, I believe in you.'

'Go away!'

'Let me sleep here.'

'Go and sleep somewhere else!' shouted Enjolras.

But still staring at him with fond and blurry eyes, Grantaire replied, 'Let me sleep here – until I die.'

Enjolras threw him a disdainful look. 'Grantaire, you haven't the will to do anything – to believe, to think, to live, to die.'

Grantaire replied solemnly, 'You'll see.'

He stammered out a few more unintelligible words, then his head fell heavily on to the table and – a fairly common effect of the second phase of sobering-up into which Enjolras had unceremoniously and abruptly precipitated him – a moment later he was asleep.

IV

An Attempt to Console Widow Hucheloup

Thrilled with the barricade, Bahorel cried, 'The street shows to much better advantage with that end of it cut off!'

Even as he proceeded to half-demolish the tavern, Courfeyrac sought to console the widowed proprietress.

'Mère Hucheloup, weren't you complaining the other day that you'd been officially reported and charged with an offence because Gibelotte shook a bedside rug out of your window?'

'My dear Monsieur Courfeyrac, yes indeed. Oh my God, are you going to put that table of mine as well on to that monstrosity of yours? And what's more, the government fined me a hundred francs for that rug, and also for a jar of flowers that fell from the attic into the street. Isn't that outrageous?'

'Well, Mère Hucheloup, we're seeing to it that you get your revenge.'

Mère Hucheloup seemed not really to understand how she benefited from this. She was being given redress in the same way as that Arab woman who, having been struck by her husband, went and complained to her father, crying for vengeance and saying, 'Father, you must pay my husband back, injury for injury.' The father asked, 'Which cheek did he strike?' 'The left cheek.' The father struck her on the right cheek and said, 'There now. Go and tell your husband, he slapped my daughter but I slapped his wife.'

The rain had stopped. New recruits had arrived. Workmen had brought with them under their overalls a barrel of powder, a basket containing bottles of vitriol, two or three carnival torches and a hamper filled with outdoor tallow candles, 'left over from the king's name-day festivities', the festivities being recent, having taken place on the first of May. It was said that these supplies came from a grocer named Pépin, in Faubourg St-Antoine. The only street lantern in Rue de la Chanvrerie, the corresponding lantern in Rue St-Denis and all the lanterns in the surrounding streets – Mondétour, Cygne, Prêcheurs, Grande- and Petite-Truanderie – had been smashed.

Enjolras, Combeferre and Courfeyrac directed everything. Two barricades were now being constructed simultaneously, both of them abutting on the Corinthe building at right-angles to each other, the larger one blocking Rue de la Chanvrerie, the other blocking Rue Mondétour on the Rue du Cygne side. This latter barricade, which was very narrow, was constructed only of casks and cobblestones. About fifty workers were there to man them, some thirty of whom were armed with guns, for they had borrowed the entire stock of a gunsmith's shop on the way.

No more motley or bizarre crew than this. One wore a short jacket, carried a cavalry sabre and two saddle-pistols, another was in his shirtsleeves, a round hat, with a powder-horn hanging at his side; a third had padded his chest with nine sheets of brown paper and was armed with a saddler's awl. One shouted, 'Let's kill to the last and die on the end of our bayonets!' This fellow had no bayonet. Another wore over his coat the leather slings and belts and cartridge pouch of a National Guardsman, the cartridge pouch cover decorated with this inscription in red wool: 'Public order'. A great many guns bearing legion numbers, few hats, no cravats, lots of bare arms, some pikes. Add to this all ages, all types; pale, puny young men and tanned dock-workers. All were eager to waste no time, and while helping each other they talked about their prospects – help would come at about three o'clock in the morning, they were sure of a regiment, Paris would rise up – fearsome words combined with a kind of hearty good-humour. They might have been brothers. They did not know each other's names. That is the beauty of great danger, it brings out the fraternity of strangers.

A fire had been lit in the kitchen, and jugs, spoons, forks, all the tavern's pewter-ware was being melted down in a bullet mould. The drinking continued while all this was going on. Firing caps and buck-shot lay scattered on the tables among the glasses of wine. In the billiard room Mame Hucheloup, Matelote and Gibelotte, variously affected by terror, one of them dazed, another breathless and the third wide awake, were tearing old dish-cloths into bandage strips. Three insurgents were helping them, three strapping lads, long-haired, bearded and mustachioed, who picked off stray threads with the deli-cate fingers of a linen maid and made them tremble.

The tall man that Courfeyrac, Combeferre and Enjolras had noticed when he joined the mob at the corner of Rue des Billettes was working on the small barricade and making himself useful there. Gav-roche was working on the main one. As for the young man who had been waiting for Courfeyrac at his lodgings and had asked after Mon-sieur Marius, he disappeared round about the time when the omnibus was overturned.

Utterly elated and radiant, Gavroche had taken charge of the oper-ation. He went to and fro, clambering up and down and back up again, a continuous chattering, sparkling presence. He seemed to be there for everyone's encouragement. Did he have an incentive? Yes, indeed, his poverty. Did he have wings? Yes, indeed, his joy. Gavroche was a whirlwind. He was never out of sight, he was always within hearing. He filled the air, being everywhere at once. He had a kind of almost irritating ubiquity. With him around, no possibility of slack-ing. The enormous barricade felt him on its rump. He bothered the time-wasters, inspired the indolent, heartened the weary, provoked the thoughtful, injected some with cheerfulness, others with energy, others with anger, spurred all to action, prodded a student, nagged a workman, settled, paused, took off again, flew over the hustle and

bustle, darted from one group to another, hummed, buzzed and harassed the whole team, gadfly to the vast Revolutionary coach.*

Perpetual motion was in his little arms and a perpetual clamour in
his little lungs.

'Come on! More cobblestones! More barrels! More what's-its! Where
can we can find some? A hodful of plaster to stop up this hole! It's very
small, this barricade of yours. It needs building up. Put everything on it,
dump everything on it, chuck everything on it. Bring the house down! A
barricade's the same as Mère Gibou's tea†. Look, there's a glass door!'

At this the workers protested. 'A glass door? What do you expect
us to do with a glass door, pipsqueak?'

'Pipsqueaks yourselves!' retorted Gavroche. 'A glass door's just
the thing for a barricade! It doesn't stop it being attacked but it makes
it hard to capture. So you've never been pinching apples over a wall
with broken glass in it? A glass door'll cut the corns off the National
Guard's feet when they try to climb the barricade! Lord! Glass is
vicious. You certainly haven't got much imagination, comrades.'

He was also furious about his hammerless pistol. He went from
one person to another, demanding, 'A gun, I want a gun! Why won't
anyone give me a gun?'

'You? A gun!' said Combeferre.

'Well!' said Gavroche. 'Why not? I had one in 1830 when we had
that argument with Charles X.'

Enjolras shrugged.

'When the men have all they need, we'll give them to children.'

Gavroche turned round haughtily and replied, 'If you're killed
before me I'll take yours.'

'Gamin!' said Enjolras.

'Beardless boy!' said Gavroche.

An elegant dandy who had lost his way and was wandering past
the end of the street created a diversion. Gavroche shouted out to him,
'Come and join us, young man! Or are you not going to do anything
for this dear old country?'

The dandy fled.

---

* Another allusion to La Fontaine's 'Le Coche et la Mouche' (see page 888), in
which the fly takes all the credit for getting the coach up the hill – here, though,
perhaps with some justification.
† An allusion to *Madame Gibou et Madame Pochet, ou le Thé chez la ravaudeuse*
(Madame Gibou and Madame Pochet, or The Hotch-potch Tea), a comedy by
Théophile Dumersan (1780–1849), first staged in 1832: the tea is made with oil,
vinegar, garlic, eggs, flour and a splash of brandy all boiled up together.

V
Preparations

Contemporary newspapers that said the Rue de la Chanvrerie barricade, that 'almost impregnable edifice' as they called it, reached the height of a first-floor building were mistaken. The fact is, it did not exceed an average height of six or seven feet. It was built so that the combatants were able at will either to disappear behind the road block or to command it, and even climb up on top of it by means of a quadruple row of piled-up cobblestones arranged as steps on the inside. On the outside, the front of the barricade, composed of heaps of cobblestones and casks with connecting beams and planks jammed into the wheels of Anceau's cart and the overturned omnibus, was a spiked entanglement. A gap had been left, wide enough for a man to pass through, between the wall of the houses and the end of the barricade furthest from the tavern, so it was possible to get out. The shaft from the omnibus had been stood upright and was held in position with ropes, and a red flag fastened to this shaft flew above the barricade.

The little Mondétour barricade, hidden behind the tavern building, was not visible. The two barricades together formed a genuine redoubt. Enjolras and Courfeyrac had not thought it necessary to barricade the other section of Rue Mondétour that offers a way out to Les Halles via Rue des Prêcheurs, no doubt wanting to preserve the possibility of communicating with the outside, and having little fear of being attacked from that dangerous and awkward Ruelle des Prêcheurs.

With the exception of this outlet, left open and constituting what Folard would have called in strategic terms a communication trench, and taking into account also the narrow gap leading into Rue de la Chanvrerie, the area inside the barricade, where the tavern formed a salient angle, presented an irregular quadrilateral closed on all sides. There was a distance of some twenty paces between the main barricade and the tall buildings at the end of the street, so it could be said that the barricade was backed by these houses, all inhabited but shut up from top to bottom.

All this work was done without interruption in less than an hour, and without any sighting of bearskin or bayonet by this handful of bold men. The few bourgeois citizens still venturing into Rue St-Denis at this stage of the riot would glance down Rue de la Chanvrerie, catch sight of the barricade, and quicken their pace.

Once the two barricades were completed, and the flag flying, a table was dragged out of the tavern and Courfeyrac climbed on to it.

Enjolras brought out the square chest, and Courfeyrac opened it. This chest was full of cartridges. At the sight of the cartridges there was a tremor among the bravest, and a momentary silence. A smiling Courfeyrac distributed them.

Each man received thirty cartridges. Many had powder, and began to make more with the bullets that were being cast. As for the barrel of powder, it was set on a table apart, by the door, and kept in reserve.

The alarm continued incessantly to sound throughout Paris, but it had ended up as no more than a monotonous noise to which they no longer paid attention. This noise alternately approached and receded, in mournful undulations.

All together they loaded their rifles and carbines, unhurriedly and with a solemn gravity. Enjolras went and placed three lookouts outside the barricades, one in Rue de la Chanvrerie, the second in Rue des Prêcheurs, the third at the corner of Rue de la Petite-Truanderie.

Then, barricades built, positions assigned, guns loaded, sentries posted, alone in those menacing streets that no one any longer walked down, surrounded by those silent and seemingly lifeless houses revealing no quiver of human activity, enveloped in the deepening twilight that was beginning to fall, in the heart of that gloom and silence in which there could be sensed something approaching, and which had something indefinably tragic and terrifying about them; isolated, armed, resolute, calm, they waited.

VI
Waiting

During those hours of waiting, what did they do?

We must say, since this is history.

While the men made bullets and the women made bandages, while a large pot full of melted-down pewter and lead, destined for the bullet-mould, smoked above a glowing brazier, while the sentries kept watch, at support arms, on the barricade, while Enjolras, who could not be distracted, kept watch on the sentries, Combeferre, Courfeyrac, Jean Prouvaire, Feuilly, Bossuet, Joly, Bahorel and a few others sought each other out and gathered together, as during their most tranquil student days when they would sit and talk; and in one corner of this tavern turned fortified enclosure, a few steps from the redoubt they had built, with their carbines loaded and primed and resting on the backs of their chairs, these fine young men, so close to their final hour, began to recite a love poem.

Which poem? This one:

Remember the sweet life we led,
When we were both so young,
When to look our best and be in love
Was our heart's sole desire?

When your years added to mine
Amounted to less than forty,
And, in our humble dwelling, all
Was springtime to us, even winter.

Happy days! Manuel, proud and wise,
Paris, seated at sacred banquets!
When Foy fulminated, and a pin
In your corsage pricked me.

All eyes were on you. A lawyer, I,
With no case to plead, and you so lovely,
Roses turned to look, it seemed,
When I took you to the Prado for dinner.

How beautiful she is! I heard them say.
How fragrant! Such flowing locks!
Like a peeping bud in her charming bonnet.
Beneath that cloak she must have wings.

Your soft arm held tight in mine,
We went our wandering way, seeming
To passers-by the sweet month of April
Wedded to the fair month of May.

We hid in happiness behind closed doors,
Devouring the forbidden fruit called love.
And even before my lips had spoken,
Already your heart replied, 'I'm yours.'

The Sorbonne was the setting for our idyll
Where from dusk till dawn I adored you.
So by the map of Tenderness do lovers
Find their way in the Latin quarter.

O Place Maubert! O Place Dauphine!
When you drew a stocking over your slender leg,
A bright star I'd see beneath the eaves
In our fresh and vernal garret.

Plato have I read but not a word remember.
More about heaven's goodness I learned
From a flower you gave me than from anything
Lamennais or Malebranche ever said.

O gilded garret! where I laced you!
Watched you, up and about at break
Of day in your chemise, gazing
On your young face in an old looking-glass!

How could anyone forget those heavenly
Auroral days of ribbons and flowers,
Of gauze and moire, of love's falterings
In a charming language all of its own?

A pot of tulips was our garden.
You draped the window with a petticoat.
The clay bowl I took for myself
And gave you the porcelain cup.

Those great calamities that made us laugh!
Your scorched muff, your lost boa!
Divine Shakespeare's cherished portrait
Sold one evening to pay for supper!

I was a poor beggar and you so kind.
I'd kiss your arms and you'd not mind.
A copy of Dante served as our table,
On a bagful of chestnuts we happily dined.

That first time in my blissful garret
That I stole a kiss from your burning lips
Left you all dishevelled and flushed,
Left me white, my faith restored.

Do you recall our countless pleasures,
And all those shawls now turned to rags?
Oh! many the sighs that have escaped
Our heavy hearts and heavenwards have flown!

The time, the place, these recollections of youth, a few stars beginning
to twinkle in the sky, the deathly quiet of those deserted streets, the
imminence of the inexorable drama that was about to unfold lent a
pathetic charm to these verses softly murmured in the twilight by Jean
Prouvaire, who, as we have said, was a gentle poet.

Meanwhile, a tallow candle had been lit on the small barricade,
and on the main barricade one of those wax torches of the kind you
see on Shrove Tuesday at the front of carts crammed with masked
revellers on their way to La Courtille. These torches, as we have seen,
came from Faubourg St-Antoine.

The torch had been placed in a sort of cage made of paving-stones,
enclosed on three sides to shelter it from the wind and arranged in
such a way that all the light fell on to the flag. The street and the barricade remained steeped in darkness, and nothing could be seen except
the red flag strikingly illuminated as if by an enormous dark-lantern.

This light lent to the scarlet flag an indescribably terrible crimson
hue.

VII

The Man Recruited in Rue des Billettes

It was well after dark, and nothing came. All that could be heard were
an indistinct clamour and at intervals volleys of gunfire, but few and
far between, unsustained and distant. This extended lull was a sign
that the government was biding its time and gathering its forces. These
fifty men were waiting on sixty thousand.

Enjolras felt in the grip of that impatience that overcomes men of
character on the threshold of dire events. He went in search of Gavroche, who had settled down to make cartridges in the bar room by
the wavering light of two candles placed on the counter for safety's
sake in case of any powder lying on the tables. These two candles cast
no brightness outside. The insurgents had also been careful not to
have any light on the upper floors.

Gavroche was deeply preoccupied at that moment – not with his
cartridges, as it happened. The man from Rue des Billettes had just
entered the bar room and had sat down at the most shadowy table.

He had been allotted a full-size large-calibre rifle that he kept between his legs. Distracted by countless 'amusing' things, until that instant Gavroche had not even seen the man.

When he came in, Gavroche instinctively followed him with his eyes, admiring his gun. Then, when the man was seated, the gamin abruptly stood up. Anyone watching the man up to that moment would have seen him observing the barricade and the band of insurgents, all with close attention. But since entering the room he had fallen into a reflection of sorts and seemed no longer to notice anything going on around him. The gamin approached this pensive individual and began to tip-toe around him the way people do when they are afraid of waking someone up. At the same time there passed over his childish face, at once so cheeky and so earnest, so skittish and so intense, so cheerful and so heart-breaking, all the grimaces of an old man signifying 'Bah!' 'Impossible!' 'My eyesight's playing me up!' 'I'm dreaming!' 'Could it be—?' 'No, it's not!' 'But it must be!' 'But it can't be!' and so on. Gavroche rocked on his heels, clenched both fists in his pockets, made bird-like motions with his neck, invested all the sagacity of his lower lip in an extraordinary pout. He was astounded, doubtful, incredulous, convinced, amazed. He wore the expression of the chief eunuch finding a Venus among the unprepossessing offerings in the slave market, and displayed the attitude of an amateur recognizing a Raphael in a pile of worthless daubs. All his faculties were at work, the shrewd instinct and the scheming intelligence. Obviously, this was an important moment for Gavroche.

It was at the height of his preoccupation that Enjolras came up to him.

'You're small,' said Enjolras, 'you'll not be seen. Go outside the barricades, keep close to the houses, take a bit of a wander round the streets, and come back and tell me what's going on.'

Gavroche straightened up, standing four-square. 'So young'uns do have their uses! Just as well! I'll go! In the meantime, trust to young'uns, be wary of grown-ups.'

Then raising his head and lowering his voice, Gavroche added, indicating the man from Rue des Billettes, 'You see that tall fellow over there?'

'Well?'

'He's a nark.'

'Are you sure?'

'It's not two weeks since he twisted my ear and pulled me off the ledge of the Pont Royal, where I was taking the air.'

Enjolras promptly deserted the gamin and very quietly murmured a few words to a dock-worker from the Port au Vin who happened to be there. The man left the room and came back almost at once, accompanied by three others. Without doing anything that might attract his attention the four men – four burly dock-hands – went and stood behind the table at which the man from Rue des Billettes sat, resting on his elbows. They were ready to pounce on him.

Then Enjolras went up to the man and asked, 'Who are you?'

At this abrupt question the man started. He gazed deep into Enjolras's clear eyes, where he appeared to read his mind. He smiled a smile that conveyed the utmost disdain, forcefulness and resolve, and replied with supercilious gravity, 'I see how it is . . . Oh, yes indeed!'

'You're a nark?'

'I'm an officer of the law.'

'And your name?'

'Javert.'

Enjolras signalled to the four men. In the twinkling of an eye, before Javert had time to turn round, he was collared, pinioned to the ground, and searched.

They found on him a little round card, pasted between glass, that had the French coat of arms with the motto 'Surveillance and Vigilance' embossed on one side, and this identification on the other: 'JAVERT, inspector of police, aged fifty-two', and the signature of the prefect of police at the time, Monsieur Gisquet.

He had, in addition, his watch and his purse, which contained several gold coins. His purse and watch they let him keep. Feeling behind the watch, they found at the back of his fob-pocket a sheet of paper in an envelope, which Enjolras unfolded and on which he read these lines, written in the prefect of police's own hand: 'As soon as his political mission is accomplished, Inspector Javert will conduct a special investigation to ascertain whether it is true that agitators are plotting to make trouble on the right bank, down by the Seine, near the Pont d'Iéna.'

Having completed their search, they set Javert on his feet again, tied his arms behind his back, and bound him to the famous pillar in the middle of the bar room that had long ago given the tavern its name.

Gavroche, who witnessed the whole scene and approved of everything with a silent nod of his head, stepped up to Javert and said to him, 'So the mouse has caught the cat.'

All this was done so quickly that it was over by the time anyone else noticed. Javert had not uttered a cry.

Seeing Javert tied to the pillar, Courfeyrac, Bossuet, Joly, Combeferre and the men dispersed among the two barricades came running up.

With his back to the pillar and with so much rope tied round him that he could not move at all, Javert held up his head with the fearless serenity of a man who has never lied.

'He's a nark,' said Enjolras. And turning to Javert, 'You'll be shot two minutes before the barricade is taken.'

Javert replied in his most imperious tone, 'Why not straight away?'

'We're saving our powder.'

'Then finish me off with a knife.'

'Nark,' said the handsome Enjolras, 'we're judges, not assassins.'

Then he called Gavroche. 'Hey you! Get on with it! Do what I told you!'

'I'm off!' cried Gavroche.

And pausing as he was about to leave, 'By the way, his gun you'll give to me!' And he added, 'I'll let you keep the musician, but I want the clarinet.'

The gamin gave a military salute and cheerfully slipped through the gap in the main barricade.

VIII
Several Question Marks over One Le Cabuc Whose Name May Not Have Been Le Cabuc

The tragic description we have embarked on would not be complete, the reader would not see in accurate and true relief those great moments of social parturition and revolutionary birth where exertion combines with convulsion, were we to omit in our depiction an incident full of epic and savage horror that occurred almost directly after Gavroche's departure.

Mobs, as we know, are like snowballs and gather as they roll a great many unruly men. These men do not ask each other where they come from. Among those along the way who had joined the rabble led by Enjolras, Combeferre and Courfeyrac was an individual wearing a docker's jacket with worn shoulders, who was gesticulating and shouting and looked like some sort of wild drunkard. Very drunk, or pretending to be, this man, named or nicknamed Le Cabuc, in fact a complete stranger to those who claimed to know him, had sat down with several others at a table they had dragged outside the tavern. This Cabuc, while encouraging those he was with to drink, seemed to be thoughtfully considering the large house behind the barricade, whose five storeys commanded the whole street and faced Rue St-Denis. All at once he exclaimed, 'You know, comrades, it's from that house we need to be firing. If we were up at those windows, it would be the devil for anyone coming up the street!'

'Yes, but the house is shut up,' said one of the drinkers.

'Let's knock!'

'They won't open.'

'Let's break down the door!'

Le Cabuc runs to the door, which has an extremely heavy knocker, and knocks. The door does not open. He knocks a second time. No one answers. A third time. The same silence.

'Is there anyone in there?' shouts Le Cabuc.

Nothing stirs.

Then he grabs a rifle and starts to batter the door with his rifle butt. It was an old portal, arched, low, narrow, of solid oak, reinforced on the inside with sheet metal and an iron frame, a real prison postern. The pounding with the rifle butt made the house tremble but did not shake the door.

All the same, it probably disturbed the inhabitants, for in the end light was seen at a small square dormer window on the third floor, which opened, and at this window appeared a candle and the bewildered and terrified face of a grey-haired old man, who was the porter.

The man banging at the door stopped.

'Gentlemen,' said the porter, 'what is it?'

'Open up!' said Le Cabuc.

'Gentlemen, that's impossible.'

'Come on, open up!'

'Out of the question, gentlemen.'

Le Cabuc took his gun and took aim at the porter, but as he was down below, and as it was very dark, the porter did not see him.

'Will you open, yes or no?'

'No, gentlemen.'

'Did you say no?'

'I said no, my good—'

The porter got no further. The shot was fired. The bullet went in under his chin, passed through his jugular and out at the back of his neck. The old man collapsed without even a sigh. The candle fell over and went out, and all that could be seen was a motionless head lying on the window-sill and a little whitish smoke drifting up to the roof.

'There!' said Le Cabuc, standing the butt of his rifle on the pavement again.

He had hardly uttered this word when he felt a hand laid on his shoulder with the weight of an eagle's talon, and he heard a voice saying, 'On your knees!'

The murderer turned and saw before him the cold, white face of Enjolras. Enjolras held a pistol in his hand.

He had come at the sound of the gunfire. With his left hand he grabbed Le Cabuc by his collar, overall, shirt and braces.

'On your knees!' he repeated.

And with sovereign command, the slight young man of twenty bent the sturdy, thickset housebreaker like a reed and brought him to his knees in the mud. Le Cabuc tried to resist, but he seemed to have been seized by a superhuman hand.

Pale and dishevelled, his throat bared, Enjolras, with his womanly face, had at that moment something of ancient Themis about him. His flaring nostrils, his downcast eyes, gave to his implacable Greek profile that expression of wrath and that expression of chastity that for the ancient world are appropriate to justice.

Everyone from the barricade had come running, then they had all drawn up in a circle, at a distance, feeling there was nothing they could say about what they were going to see.

Defeated, Le Cabuc no longer made any attempt to struggle, and trembled in every limb. Enjolras released him and drew out his watch.

'Prepare yourself,' he said. 'With prayer or reflection. You have one minute.'

'Mercy!' murmured the murderer. Then he hung his head and mumbled a few inarticulate oaths.

Enjolras did not take his eyes off his watch. He let one minute go by, then put his watch back in his pocket. That done, he took Le Cabuc by the hair as the latter clutched at his knees howling, and placed the barrel of the pistol to his ear. Many of those intrepid men who had so calmly embarked on the most terrifying of enterprises turned away.

The gunshot was heard, the assassin fell forward on to the pavement, Enjolras drew himself up and looked around, his gaze severe and assured.

Then he nudged the corpse with his foot and said, 'Throw that out.'

Three men lifted the wretch's body as it twitched in the last involuntary post-mortem spasms, and flung it over the small barricade into the Mondétour alleyway.

Enjolras remained pensive. An indefinable grandiose sombreness slowly pervaded his awesome serenity. All at once he raised his voice. There was silence.

'Citizens,' said Enjolras, 'what that man did is dreadful and what I have done is terrible. He shot someone, that is why I killed him. I had to do it because insurrection must have its discipline. Assassination is even more of a crime here than elsewhere. We are under the gaze of the Revolution, we are the priests of the Republic, we are the sacrificial offerings that must be made, and there must be no possible cause for denigration of our struggle. I have, therefore, judged that man and sentenced him to death. As for myself, obliged to do what I have done but abhorring it, I have also judged myself and you will see presently to what I have sentenced myself.'

Those who were listening shuddered.

'We will share your fate!' cried Combeferre.

'So be it,' said Enjolras. 'One word more. In executing this man I've obeyed necessity. But necessity is a monster of the old world, and necessity's name is Fate. Now, the law of progress is that monsters should disappear before angels, and that Fate should give way to fraternity. This is a bad moment to mention the word "love". I mention it anyway, and I glorify it. Love, the future belongs to you. Death, I make use of you but I hate you. Citizens, in the future there will be neither darkness nor thunderbolts, neither savage ignorance nor bloody retaliation. As there will be no more Satan, there will be no more Michael. In the future there will be no killing, the earth will be radiant, the human race will love. The day will come, citizens, when all will be concord, harmony, light, joy and life – it will come. And it's so that it does come that we are going to die.'

Enjolras fell silent. His chaste lips closed and he remained for some time standing, still as marble, on the spot where he had shed blood. His fixed gaze made those around him talk quietly.

Jean Prouvaire and Combeferre silently shook hands; and leaning against each other at the corner of the barricade, contemplated with a compassionate admiration that grave young man, executioner and priest, of crystalline light and also of adamantine rock.

Let us say right now that later, after the event, when the bodies were taken to the morgue and searched, a police agent's identity card was found on Le Cabuc. The author of this book held in his hands, in 1848, the special report on this subject made to the prefect of police in 1832.

We would also add that, if a strange but probably well founded police tradition is to be believed, Le Cabuc was Claquesous. The fact is that after the death of Le Cabuc there was no further mention of Claquesous. Claquesous left no trace after his disappearance; he would seem to have blended into the invisible. His life had been shadows, his end was night.

The whole rebel group was still under the shock of this tragic case so swiftly investigated and so swiftly concluded when Courfeyrac saw again, on the barricade, the slip of a young man who had come asking for Marius at his lodgings that morning.

At nightfall this lad, with his bold and carefree manner, had come to join the insurgents.

BOOK THIRTEEN
MARIUS ENTERS INTO DARKNESS

I
From Rue Plumet to the St-Denis Neighbourhood

The voice that through the dusk had summoned Marius to the Rue de la Chanvrerie barricade sounded to him like the voice of destiny. He wanted to die, the opportunity presented itself. He knocked at the door of the tomb, a hand in the gloom offered him the key. In the darkness of despair, these grim opportunities that open up are tempting. Marius pushed aside the gate that had so often let him through, left the garden behind him, and said, 'Let's go.'

Mad with grief, with no longer a sense of anything fixed or stable in his mind, incapable now of accepting anything from fate after those two months spent in the delirium of youth and love, overcome at one and the same time by all the bleak fancies of despair, he had but one desire: to make a speedy end of it all. He set off, walking quickly. It just so happened that he was armed, having Javert's pistols on him.

The young man he thought he had glimpsed had disappeared from sight down one of the streets.

Marius, who had come out of Rue Plumet on to the boulevard, crossed the Esplanade and the Pont des Invalides, the Champs-Élysées, Place Louis XV, and reached Rue de Rivoli. The shops there were open, the gas-lights were burning under the arcades, women were in the shops making purchases, people were eating ices in Café Laiter and pastries in the English tea room. Just a few post-chaises were setting out at a gallop from Hôtel des Princes and Hôtel Meurice.

Marius cut through Passage Delorme into Rue St-Honoré.

There the shops were closed, shopkeepers chatted on their doorsteps, the doors ajar behind them, there were people about, the street lanterns were lit; from the first floor up, all the windows were alight as usual. There was cavalry on Place du Palais-Royal.

Marius proceeded along Rue St-Honoré. As he left the Palais-Royal behind him there were fewer lighted windows, the shops were shut up, no one was chatting in the doorways, the street became darker and at the same time the crowd grew denser. For those gathered along the way now amounted to a crowd. No one could be seen speaking in this throng and yet there arose from it a deep, subdued murmur.

Near the Arbre-Sec fountain there were 'assemblies', motionless, sinister-looking groups that amid the coming and going were like stones in flowing waters.

At the top of Rue des Prouvaires the crowd was stationary. Huge, resistant, solid, compact, it formed an almost impenetrable mass, crammed together and talking to each other in an undertone. Here were hardly any black coats or round hats. Smocks, overalls, caps, grimy faces and unkempt hair. This multitude swayed confusedly in the nocturnal mist. Its whisperings had the hoarse accents of agitation. Although not a soul stirred, the sound of tramping in the mud could be heard. Beyond this dense crowd, in Rue du Roule, Rue des Prouvaires and the continuation of Rue St-Honoré, there was not a single window where a candle glowed. Single and ever-diminishing rows of lanterns ran down those streets. The lanterns of those days looked like big red stars hanging from ropes, and cast a shadow on the pavement in the shape of a huge spider. These streets were not deserted. Here, stacks of rifles were discernible, and the stir of bayonets, and troops bivouacking. No one drawn by curiosity went beyond this boundary. Here, traffic ceased. Here, the crowd ended and the army began.

Marius had the will of a man who has given up hope. He had been summoned, he had to go. He managed to get through the crowd and through the troops' makeshift camp, he slipped past the patrols, he avoided the sentries. He made a detour, reached Rue de Béthisy, and headed for Les Halles. From the corner of Rue des Bourdonnais onwards, there were no lanterns.

Having crossed the area occupied by the crowd, he reached the other side of the troop line. Here he came to something frightening. Not one passer-by, not one soldier, not one light, no one. Loneliness, silence, darkness, an unaccountably penetrating chill. Starting down a street was like stepping into a cellar.

He kept going. He went a few paces. Someone ran past him. Was it a man? A woman? More than one person? He could not have said. Whoever it was had passed by and was gone.

Circling this way and that, he came to a little lane that he thought was Rue de la Poterie. About halfway down this lane he walked into an obstacle. He reached out his hands. It was an overturned cart. His foot recognized puddles, hollows in the ground and scattered piles of cobblestones. There was a skeleton barricade here that had been abandoned. He climbed over the cobblestones and found himself on the other side of the road block. He made his way along, keeping close to the kerb-posts, guiding himself by the walls of the houses. A little beyond the barricade he thought he discerned something white in front of him. He drew nearer, it took on a shape. It was two white horses, the omnibus horses unhitched that morning by Bossuet. They had been straying all day from street to street and had finally stopped there, with that weary patience of brute beasts that no more understand the actions of man than man understands the actions of providence.

Marius left the horses behind him. As he came to a street that must be, he thought, Rue du Contrat-Social, a gunshot from who knows where, fired into the dark at random, whistled close by him and the bullet went through a brass shaving-dish hanging above his head outside a barber's shop. In 1848, on Rue du Contrat-Social, at the corner of the Piliers des Halles, that shaving-dish with a hole in it could still be seen.

This gunshot was a sign of life, still. From that moment on he came across no other.

This entire route was like a dark descending stairway.

Nevertheless, Marius pressed on.

II
An Owl's View of Paris

Any bat-winged or owl-winged individual that might have hovered over Paris at that moment would have viewed a bleak spectacle below.

That whole ancient district of Les Halles, which is like a city within a city, with Rue St-Denis and Rue St-Martin cutting through it and crisscrossed by countless little lanes, and which the insurgents had made their redoubt and parade ground, would have appeared to such a being like a huge black hole sunk into the centre of Paris. To gaze on that was to look down into an abyss. Thanks to the shattered street lanterns, thanks to the closed windows, all light, all life, all sound, all movement ceased here. Keeping watch everywhere, and maintaining order, was the riot's invisible police force – that is to say, the night. To hide in immense obscurity its small numbers, to multiply every combatant by the possibilities this obscurity contains, are the necessary tactics of insurrection. At nightfall, every window where a candle was lighted had been hit by a bullet. The light was extinguished, sometimes the inhabitant killed. So nothing stirred. Here inside the houses was nothing but terror, bereavement, bewilderment, and in the streets a kind of awed horror. The long rows of windows and upper storeys, the irregular outlines of chimneys and roofs, and the vague reflections glistening on the wet and muddy pavements – not even these were discernible. Any eye looking down from above on that mass of shadow might perhaps have caught a glimpse here and there, at remote intervals, of paler patches throwing into relief bizarre broken lines, the contours of peculiar constructions, something resembling glimmers of light coming and going amid the ruins. That is where the barricades were located. The rest was a dark lake, vaporous, oppressive, dismal, and rising above it the still and gloomy silhouettes of the tower of St-Jacques, the church of St-Merry, and two or three more of those great edifices of which man makes giants and night makes phantoms.

All around this deserted and unnerving labyrinth, in neighbourboods where the free movement of Parisians had not been completely eliminated and where a few rare street lanterns still cast light, the aerial observer might have been able to perceive the metallic gleam of sabres and bayonets, the muffled rumbling of artillery and the seething restlessness of silent battalions swelling from minute to minute – a fearsome belt that was slowly tightening and closing in on the insurrection.

The besieged district was now no more than a kind of monstrous cavern. Everything here seemed asleep or motionless, and, as we have just seen, whichever street you came to afforded nothing but darkness.

A grim darkness, full of pitfalls, full of unknown and dreadful collisions, a darkness terrifying to penetrate and appalling to be in, where those who entered shuddered at those who awaited them, where those who waited shuddered at those who were to come. Invisible combatants entrenched at every street corner, deadly ambushes concealed in the depths of night. This was the end. No hope now of any other light but the flash of guns, of any other encounter but the swift and sudden appearance of death. Where? How? When? Impossible to tell, but it was certain and inevitable. The government and the insurrection, the National Guard and the workers' societies, the bourgeoisie and the uprising, would grope their way towards each other in this place marked out for the conflict. All faced the same imperative. The only outcome now possible: to be killed or to emerge as victors. So extreme was the situation, so potent the darkness, that the most timid felt seized with resolve and the most daring smitten with terror.

Furthermore, on both sides equal fury, desperation, determination. For these, to advance was to die, and no one thought of retreating. For those, to stay was to die, and no one thought of fleeing.

By the next day it must all be over, triumph must lie either here or there; the insurrection must be a revolution, or a skirmish. The government understood this, as did all other parties. Every last bourgeois was aware of it. Hence a sense of anguish pervaded the impenetrable gloom of this neighbourhood where all would be decided. Hence a growing apprehension around that silence out of which a catastrophe would emerge. Here, there was only one sound to be heard, a sound as harrowing as the death-rattle, as menacing as a curse, the bell of St-Merry's. Nothing was more chilling than the clangour of that distraught and desperate bell tolling in the darkness.

As often happens, nature seemed to have complied with what men were going to do. Nothing upset the deadly harmony in all of this. The stars had disappeared, melancholy swathes of heavy clouds filled the entire horizon. There was a black sky above these dead streets, like an immense winding-sheet unfurled above this immense tomb.

While here on the site that had already witnessed so many Revolutionary incidents, preparations were under way for another supremely political battle; while young men, secret societies and schools, in the name of principles, and the middle classes, in the name of vested interests, closed in on each other in order to clash and to grapple with each other and to bring each other down; while everyone hastened and courted the final decisive moment of the crisis; far away and beyond this fateful district, in the deepest of the fathomless pits of that squalid old Paris that lies hidden beneath the splendour of the happy and affluent Paris, could be heard the muffled grumblings of the people's sullen voice.

A dreadful and hallowed voice that comprises the brute beast's roar and the word of God, which terrifies the weak and gives warning to the wise, which comes from below like the voice of the lion and at the same time from on high like the voice of thunder.

III
The Brink

Marius had reached Les Halles.

There, everything was yet quieter, darker and more still than in the neighbouring streets. It was as though the chill peacefulness of the tomb had issued from the earth and spread out beneath the sky.

A red glow, however, outlined against this dark background the high rooftops of the houses that closed off Rue de la Chanvrerie on the St-Eustache side. It was the reflection of the torch burning on the Corinthe barricade. Marius headed towards this red glow. It led him to the Marché-aux-Poirées, and he saw the dark opening of Rue des Prêcheurs. Along it he started. The insurgents' lookout, posted at the other end of the street, did not see him. He sensed he was very close to what he had come in search of, and he proceeded on tip-toe. So he came to the corner of that short stretch of the Mondétour alleyway that was, remember, the only communication route Enjolras had preserved with the outside world. At the last house on the left, he poked his head round the corner and looked down that section of Mondétour.

A little beyond the dark corner of the lane where it met Rue de la Chanvrerie, casting a broad blanket of shadow in which he himself was shrouded, he saw a glimmer of light on the pavement, a bit of the tavern and, behind, a tallow candle flickering in some kind of shapeless wall, and men crouched down with guns on their knees. All this was twenty yards away from him. It was the inside of the barricade.

The houses lining the lane on the right concealed from him the rest of the tavern, the main barricade and the flag.

Marius had only one more step to take. Then the poor young man sat on a kerb-post, folded his arms and thought of his father.

He thought of that heroic Colonel Pontmercy who had been such a proud soldier, who had guarded France's frontier under the Republic and had reached as far as Asia's frontier under the emperor; who had seen Genoa, Alexandria, Milan, Turin, Madrid, Vienna, Dresden, Berlin, Moscow; who had left on all the fields of victory in Europe drops of that same blood that ran in Marius's veins; who in the exercise of discipline and command had grown white-haired before his time; who had lived with his sword-belt buckled, his epaulettes slipping over his chest, his cockade blackened with gunpowder, his brow creased by his helmet, in hut, camp, bivouac, field hospital; and who after twenty years had returned from the great wars with his cheek scarred and a smile on his face, unassuming, placid, admirable, pure-hearted as a child, having done everything for France and against her, nothing.

Marius said to himself that his day had now come, that his hour had struck, that after his father he too was going to prove brave, intrepid, bold; to rush towards the bullets, to present his chest to the bayonets, to shed his blood, to meet the enemy, to seek death; that he in turn was going to wage war and fight on the battlefield, and this battlefield he was going to fight on was the street, and this war he was about to wage was civil war!

He saw civil war gaping before him like an abyss, an abyss into which he was about to fall. Then he shuddered.

He thought of his father's sword, which his grandfather had sold off to some second-hand dealer, and whose loss he so painfully regretted. He told himself that it had done well, that chaste and valiant sword, to elude him and disappear into the dark in vexation. If it had escaped like that, it was because it was intelligent and foresaw the future. It was because it anticipated the riot, the gutter war, the street war, the bursts of gunfire from basement windows, the attacks from behind on both sides. It was because, coming from Marengo and Friedland, it did not want to go to Rue de la Chanvrerie. It was because after what it had done with the father, this it did not want to do with the son! He told himself that if that sword were here, if having inherited it from his father on his deathbed he had dared to claim it and carry it away with him for this night fight between fellow Frenchmen at a crossroads, it would surely burn his hands and start to blaze before him like the sword of the angel! He told himself he was glad it was not here and that it had disappeared, that it was right, it was fitting, that his grandfather had been the true guardian of his father's glory. It was far better that the colonel's sword should have been auctioned off, sold to the old-clothes dealer, thrown out as scrap, rather than that it should draw blood from the flesh of his own country.

And then he began to weep bitterly.

Indeed, it was dreadful. But what was he to do? Live without Cosette – that he could not do. Now that she had left, he was bound to die. Had he not given her his word of honour that he would die? She had left, knowing that. The fact was that she was happy for Marius to die. And besides, it was obvious she did not love him any more since she had gone away without telling him, without a word, without sending him a letter, although she knew his address! What was the use of living, what had he to live for now? And then, for goodness' sake, to have come this far and to go back now! To have come this close to danger, and to run away from it? To have come and taken a look inside the barricade, and to turn tail? To turn tail all atremble, saying, 'Actually, I'm going to call it a day, I've had a look, that's enough, this is civil war, I'm off!' To desert the friends who were expecting him? Who perhaps had need of him! Who were a handful against an army! To renege on everything at once, on love, on friendship, on his word! To give his cowardice the excuse of patriotism! But that was impossible, and if his father's ghost were here in the shadows and saw him turn back, he would whip his hide with the flat of his sword and cry, 'Get to it, coward!'

Tormented by his vacillating thoughts, he hung his head.

Suddenly, he raised it again. A wonderful mental adjustment, as it were, had just taken place within him. There is an expansion of thought that comes with proximity to the grave. Being close to death enables you to see clearly. The prospect of the action in which he felt he might be about to engage seemed to him no longer deplorable, but magnificent. By some sort of inner working of the soul, street warfare was suddenly transfigured in his mind's eye. All the turbulent questions raised in his state of abstraction came crowding back, but without troubling him. He left none unanswered.

Come now, why should his father be angered? Are there not cases where insurrection attains the dignity of duty? What dishonour to the son of Colonel Pontmercy would there be in this present conflict? This is not Montmirail or Champaubert any more, it is something different. It is no longer about a sacred territory but about a sacred ideal. The country may well groan, but humanity applauds. Anyway, is it true that the country is groaning? France bleeds, but freedom smiles. And seeing freedom's smile, France forgets her wound. Moreover, taking an even loftier view of things, why should we be talking about civil war?

Civil war? What does that mean? Is there such a thing as foreign war? Is not all war between men war between brothers? War is defined only by its objective. There is no such thing as foreign or civil war, there is only unjust war and just war. Until the day when the great human pact is made, war may be necessary – at least the war that is the urgent future striving against the ever dawdling past. What is there, in such a war, to take exception to? War does not become a disgrace, the sword does not become a dagger, except when it murders rightfulness, progress, reason, civilization, truth. Then, whether civil war or foreign war, it is iniquitous. The word for it is 'crime'. Without that sacred thing justice, by what right does one form of war despise another? By what right should Washington's sword repudiate Camille Desmoulins' pike? Leonidas against the stranger, Timoleon against the tyrant, which is the greater? One is the defender, the other the liberator. Shall any resort to arms within the city limits be condemned without regard to its purpose? Then brand with infamy Brutus, Marcel, Arnould von Blankenheim, Coligny. Skirmish war? Street war? Why not? Such was the war of Ambiorix, Artevelde, Marnix, Pelagius. But Ambiorix fought against Rome, Artevelde against France, Marnix against Spain, Pelagius against the Moors – all against the foreigner. Well, monarchy is the foreigner, oppression is the foreigner, divine right is the foreigner. Despotism violates the moral frontier just as invasion violates the geographical frontier. To drive out the tyrant or to drive out the English is in both cases to retake your own territory. There comes a time when to protest is no longer enough. After philosophy, action is needed. Direct force achieves what the mind first envisages. *Prometheus Bound* initiates, Aristogeiton concludes. The *Encyclopaedia* enlightens souls, the tenth of August galvanizes them. After Aeschylus, Thrasybulus. After Diderot, Danton. The multitudes tend to accept the master. Their mass creates a sediment of apathy. A crowd readily coheres in obedience. Men need to be stirred, driven, bullied by the very benefit they derive from their deliverance, their eyes need to be stung by the truth, they need to have light hurled at them in tremendous handfuls. They themselves need to be a little thunderstruck by their own salvation. This bedazzlement will rouse them. Hence the need for alarm signals and wars. Great combatants must rise up, enlighten nations by their audacity and shake up this sorry humanity kept in darkness by divine right, imperial glory, force, fanaticism, irresponsible power and absolute majesty; this stupefied throng lost in contemplation of these sinister triumphs of the night in their twilight splendour. Down with the tyrant! But just who are you talking about? Do you call Louis-Philippe a tyrant? No, no more than Louis XVI. They are both what history usually calls good kings. But principles are indivisible, the logic of truth is rectilinear, truth is inherently unaccommodating. So no compromises. All violation against man must be curbed. There is divine right in Louis XVI, there is 'because a Bourbon' in Louis-Philippe. Both represent to some degree a seizure of rights, and in order to do away with universal usurpation they must be opposed. This is essential, France being always the trailblazer. When the master falls in France, he falls everywhere. In short, to re-establish social truth, to give liberty back her throne, to give the people back to the people, to give sovereignty back to man, to reinvest France with the purple of authority, fully to reinstate equity and reason, to suppress any form of antagonism by restoring self-determination to every individual, to destroy the obstacle that royalty presents to boundless universal concord, and to bring the human race back in line with rightfulness – what cause more just, and consequently what war more noble? Such wars build peace. An enormous fortress of prejudice, privilege, superstition, mendacity, extortion, abuse, violence, iniquity and darkness still stands on this earth with its towers of hatred. It must be pulled down. This monstrous mass must be overthrown. To triumph at Austerlitz is grand, to storm the Bastille is magnificent.

There is no one who has not noticed in himself that the soul – and the wonderful complexity of its pervasive oneness is hereby demonstrated – has this strange capacity for reasoning almost calmly in the direst extreme, and it often happens that disconsolate passion and profound despair in the very throes of their bleakest monologues deal with issues and weigh up arguments. Logic marries with turmoil, and the syllogistic thread runs through the dismal tumult of thought without breaking. This was Marius's state of mind.

BOOK FOURTEEN
THE GRANDEURS OF DESPAIR

I
The Flag: Act One

Still no sign of anything coming. Ten o'clock had struck at St-Merry's. Enjolras and Combeferre had gone to sit down, rifles in hand, close to the gap in the main barricade. They did not speak to each other, they listened, trying to catch even the faintest and most distant sound of movement.

Suddenly, in the midst of that ominous calm was distinctly heard a clear, cheerful young voice that seemed to come from Rue St-Denis, and it began singing to the popular old tune of 'Au clair de la lune' this poem, concluding with a cry something like a cock-crow:

> My nose is a-dripping,
> My dear friend Bugeaud,
> Let me tell your gendarmes
> Something they should know.
> Dressed in navy great-coat
> And feathered shako
> Here comes the outer city,
> Co-cocorico.

They shook hands.

'That's Gavroche,' said Enjolras.

'He's giving us a warning,' said Combeferre.

Running footsteps disturbed the deserted street, an individual more agile than a clown was seen climbing over the omnibus, and Gavroche jumped down inside the barricade, all out of breath, saying, 'My gun! They're here!'

An electric shiver ran through the whole barricade, and the sound of hands reaching for guns could be heard.

'Do you want my rifle?' Enjolras said to the gamin.

'I want the big gun,' replied Gavroche. And he took Javert's rifle. Two lookouts had fallen back and returned almost at the same time as Gavroche. They were the lookouts at the end of the street and on Rue de la Petite-Truanderie. The sentry on Ruelle des Prêcheurs remained at his post, which meant nothing was coming from the direction of the bridges and Les Halles.

Rue de la Chanvrerie, of which barely a few cobblestones were visible in the reflection of light projected on to the flag, presented to the insurgents the appearance of a huge black entrance hall opening on to nebulousness.

Everyone had taken up position, ready for action.

Forty-three insurgents, including Enjolras, Combeferre, Courfeyrac, Bossuet, Joly, Bahorel and Gavroche, were kneeling inside the main barricade, their heads level with the top of the barrier, the barrels of their guns and rifles trained on the cobblestones as if through loop-holes; alert, silent, ready to fire. Six, commanded by Feuilly, were positioned at the windows of Corinthe's two upper storeys, with their guns aimed.

Another few minutes went by. Then from the direction of St-Leu the sound of footsteps could be heard distinctly – regular, thudding, numerous. This sound, faint at first, then clear, then heavy and rever-berating, approached slowly, without cease, uninterrupted, with a calm and terrible continuousness. Nothing else could be heard. It was at once silence and the sound of the Commendatore's statue, but that tread of stone had something tremendous and manifold about it that gave rise to the idea of a throng and at the same time the idea of a ghost. It sounded like the terrifying statue of Legion on the march. The tread came nearer. Nearer still it came, then stopped. The breath-ing of many men at the end of the street seemed to be audible. Yet nothing could be seen – except, just discernible in that pitch-darkness beyond, a multitude of metallic lines, as fine as needles and almost imperceptible, moving restlessly like those indescribable phosphores-cent patterns that you see beneath your closed eyelids in the first mists of sleep, just as you drift off. These were bayonets and gun barrels dimly lit by the distant reflection of the torch.

There was another pause, as if both sides were waiting. Suddenly from out of this dark a voice shouted, a voice that was all the more sinister because no one could be seen; it was as if the dark itself were speaking. 'Who goes there?'

At the same time could be heard the clatter of guns being readied.

Enjolras replied in a proud, ringing tone, 'The French Revolution!'

'Fire!' cried the voice.

A flash of light turned all the street façades crimson, as if the door of a furnace had opened and quickly closed again.

A tremendous blast exploded over the barricade. The red flag fell. The discharge was so fierce and so dense it had cut through the flag pole, that is to say, the very tip of the omnibus's shaft. Bullets ricocheting from the cornices of the houses struck inside the barricade and wounded several men.

The effect of this opening volley was chilling. The attack was ruthless, of a kind to give pause to the boldest. It was evident they were dealing with an entire regiment, at least.

'Comrades!' shouted Courfeyrac, 'let's not waste our powder. Let's wait until they're in the street before we return fire.'

'And first of all,' said Enjolras, 'let's raise the flag again!'

He picked up the flag, which had fallen at his feet.

The jangle of cleaning-rods in guns could be heard outside. The troops were reloading their weapons. Enjolras went on: 'Who here has the courage? Who's going to set up the flag on the barricade again?'

Not a soul responded. To climb on to the barricade when it was undoubtedly about to come under fire again could only mean death. The bravest is reluctant to condemn himself. Even Enjolras shuddered. 'Is no one to volunteer?' he repeated.

II

The Flag: Act Two

Since they had arrived at Corinthe and begun to build the barricade, hardly any further notice had been taken of Père Mabeuf. Yet Monsieur Mabeuf had not left the gathering. He had gone into the tavern downstairs and sat behind the counter. There he had, as it were, turned in on himself in self-obliteration. He seemed to see no more, to think no more. Courfeyrac and others had spoken to him two or three times, warning him of the danger, telling him to go home, but apparently without being heard. When he was not being spoken to, his mouth moved as though he were replying to someone, and as soon as anyone addressed him his lips became still and his eyes looked lifeless. Several hours before the barricade was attacked he had assumed an attitude that he had not since abandoned, his two hands on his knees and his head thrust forward as though he were looking over a precipice. Nothing had been able to draw him out of this posture. It was as if his mind were not inside the barricade. When everyone had gone to take up position, ready for action, there remained in the downstairs room only Javert tied to the pillar, one insurgent with his sword drawn keeping an eye on Javert, and Mabeuf himself. At the moment of the attack, when the blast came, he felt the physical shock and it appeared to rouse him. He rose abruptly, crossed the room and just as Enjolras repeated his call 'Is no one to volunteer?' the old man was seen coming out of the tavern.

His appearance produced a sort of commotion among the various groups. A shout went up: 'It's the voter! It's the member of the Convention! It's the representative of the people!'

He probably did not hear.

He walked straight up to Enjolras, the insurgents making way before him with a religious awe. He snatched the flag from Enjolras, who fell back, paralysed, and then, since no one dared stop him or help him, this old man of eighty – head shaking, but firm-footed – began slowly to ascend the flight of cobblestones set into the barricade. So solemn and so noble was this, that all around him cried, 'Bravo!' With every step he climbed, the effect was terrifying: rising out of the darkness, and magnified in the blood-red light of the torch, his white hair, his age-worn face, his broad brow, bald and wrinkled, his sunken eyes, his amazed and gaping mouth, his old arm holding high the red banner – it might have been the spectre of '93 emerging from the earth, holding the flag of the Terror in his hand.

When he reached the top step, when this trembling and fearsome phantom, standing on that pile of rubble in front of twelve hundred invisible guns, drew himself up in the face of death, and as if he were the mightier of the two, the whole barricade assumed in the darkness a colossal, supernatural appearance. There was one of those silences that occur only in the presence of marvels.

In the midst of this silence the old man waved the red flag and shouted, 'Long live the Revolution! Long live the Republic! Fraternity! Equality! And Death!'

Those behind the barricade heard a low and rapid whispering, like the murmur of a priest rushing through a prayer. It was probably a police official giving legal advice at the other end of the street. Then the same ringing voice that had shouted, 'Who goes there?' shouted, 'Remove yourself!'

Monsieur Mabeuf, pale, drawn, his eyes lit up with the woeful glints of frenzy, raised the flag above his head and repeated, 'Long live the Republic!'

'Fire!' cried the voice.

A second volley, like artillery fire, rained down on the barricade.

The old man sagged to his knees, then rose again, dropped the flag and toppled on to the street, dropping like a stone, flat on his back, arms outstretched, crucifix-like. Rivulets of blood seeped from beneath him. Pale and sad, his old face seemed to be gazing up at the sky.

One of those emotions greater than man, causing a person to forget even to defend himself, overcame the insurgents, and they approached the body with an appalled respectfulness.

'What men those regicides were!' said Enjolras.

Courfeyrac leaned towards Enjolras's ear. 'This is something only you need to know, and I don't want to dampen anyone's enthusiasm, but that man was anything but a regicide. I knew him. He was called Père Mabeuf. I don't know what got into him today. But he was a decent old buffer. Just look at his face.'

'The face of an old buffer and the courage of Brutus,' replied Enjolras.

Then he raised his voice. 'Citizens! This is the example the old give to the young. We hesitated, he presented himself! We drew back, he stepped forward! That's what those who tremble with old age teach those who tremble with fear! This elder is a hero to his country. He had a long life and a magnificent death! Now, let's protect his body, let each one of us defend this old man in death as he would his own living father, and may his presence among us make the barricade impregnable!'

A grim and emphatic murmur of assent followed these words.

Enjolras bent down, lifted the old man's head and fiercely kissed his brow. Then, handling this corpse with tender care as if afraid of hurting it, having freed the arms, he removed the coat, showed everyone the bloodied holes in it and said, 'This is now our flag.'

III
Gavroche Would Have Done Better to
Accept Enjolras's Rifle

A long black shawl belonging to Hucheloup's widow was thrown over Père Mabeuf. Six men made a litter of their rifles, laid the body on it, and with their heads bared carried it with solemn deliberation to the large table in the downstairs room of the tavern.

These men, utterly intent on the grave and sacred thing they were doing, were no longer thinking about their perilous situation.

When the corpse passed by the ever impassive Javert, Enjolras said to the spy, 'Your turn before long!'

Meanwhile, young Gavroche, the only one who had not left his post and had remained on guard, thought he saw some men creeping up to the barricade. Suddenly he cried, 'Watch out!'

Courfeyrac, Enjolras, Jean Prouvaire, Combeferre, Joly, Bahorel, Bossuet, all came thundering out of the tavern. Already it was almost too late. They saw glinting ranks of bayonets swaying above the barricade. Towering Municipal Guardsmen were infiltrating, some climbing over the omnibus, others through the gap, driving back the gamin, who retreated before them but did not flee.

This was a critical moment. It was that dreadful first minute of flooding when the river level rises to the height of the embankment and the water begins to seep through the cracks in the dyke. Another second, and the barricade would have been taken.

Bahorel rushed at the first Municipal Guardsman coming in and killed him, shooting him with his rifle at point-blank range. The second killed Bahorel with a thrust of his bayonet. Another had already brought down Courfeyrac, who was crying 'Help!' The tallest of all, a veritable colossus, came at Gavroche with bayonet fixed. The gamin took Javert's enormous gun in his little arms, resolutely levelled it at the giant and pulled the trigger. Nothing happened. Javert had not loaded his gun. The guardsman burst out laughing and raised his bayonet over the child.

Before the bayonet touched Gavroche, the gun slipped from the soldier's hands. A bullet had struck the guardsman in the middle of his forehead, and he fell on his back. A second bullet hit the other guardsman – the one who had attacked Courfeyrac – right in the chest and sent him sprawling on to the street.

It was Marius, who had just entered the barricade.

IV
The Powder Keg

Still hidden at the corner of Rue Mondétour, irresolute and shivering, Marius had witnessed the first phase of the fighting. Yet he had not been able to withstand that mysterious and supreme light-headedness that might be termed 'the call of the abyss'. Faced with imminent peril, faced with that grievous enigma the death of Monsieur Mabeuf, faced with Bahorel killed, Courfeyrac crying 'Help!', that child threatened, friends to be rescued or avenged, all hesitation vanished, and he had rushed into the fray with his two pistols in his hands. With the first shot he saved Gavroche and with the second he saved Courfeyrac.

At the sound of firing, at the cries of the guards hit, the besiegers had scaled the fortification, on the top of which rose a host, now visible to below the waist, of Municipal Guardsmen, soldiers of the line and National Guardsmen from the outer city, with guns in hand. They already covered more than two-thirds of the barrier, but they did not jump down inside the enclosure, as if they were wavering, afraid of some trap. They looked down inside the dark barricade as you would look into a lions' den. Only their bayonets, their bearskin caps and the upper part of their anxious and angry faces were reflected in the torchlight.

Marius now had no weapon, he had thrown aside his discharged pistols, but he had noticed the powder keg in the bar room by the door.

As he turned away, looking in that direction, a soldier took aim at him. Just as the soldier was targeting Marius, a hand was laid over the end of the gun barrel and blocked it. It was someone who had darted forward, the young worker in fustian trousers. The shot was fired, went through the hand and perhaps the worker too, since he fell, but the bullet did not hit Marius. All this shrouded in smoke, half glimpsed rather than seen.

Marius, who was on his way into the bar room, scarcely noticed. Yet he had vaguely seen that gun barrel aimed at him and the hand that blocked it, and he had heard the shot. But at such moments the things you see are uncertain and fast-moving, and you stop for nothing. You feel obscurely impelled towards yet deeper darkness, and everything is hazy.

The insurgents, taken by surprise but undaunted, had rallied. Enjolras shouted, 'Wait! Don't fire at random!' Indeed, in the initial confusion they might injure one another. Most of them had gone up to the first-floor window and the dormer windows, from where they looked down on the assailants. The most determined, with Enjolras, Courfeyrac, Jean Prouvaire and Combeferre, had proudly taken up an exposed position with their backs to the houses behind, facing the ranks of soldiers and guards on the crest of the barricade.

All this was done unhurriedly, with that strange and menacing gravity that precedes conflicts. Both sides had their weapons levelled at each other at point-blank range. They were so close, they were within speaking distance of each other. When the situation had reached the point when a spark was about to set things off, an officer wearing a gorget and large epaulettes levelled his sword and said, 'Lay down your arms!'

'Fire!' replied Enjolras.

The two volleys went off simultaneously, and everything disappeared in smoke. An acrid and suffocating smoke in which the dying and the wounded crawled with weak and muffled groans.

When the smoke cleared, the combatants were to be seen on both sides, fewer in number but still in the same positions, reloading their weapons in silence. Suddenly, a voice like thunder was heard shouting, 'Get back, or I'll blow up the barricade!'

All turned in the direction from where the voice came.

Marius had gone into the bar room, picked up the powder keg, then he had taken advantage of the smoke and the sort of murky fog that filled the fortified enclosure to creep along the barricade to that niche of cobblestones in which the torch was set. Pulling the torch out, putting the powder keg in and pushing the pile of stones under the barrel, which immediately broke open with a kind of dreadful obedience – all this had taken Marius no more time than it takes to bend down and stand up again. And now National Guardsmen, Municipal Guardsmen, officers, soldiers, all huddled at the other end of the barricade, stared at him in astonishment as he stood with his foot on the cobblestones, torch in hand, his proud face lit up with a deadly resolve, tilting the torch flame towards that enormous pile in which the broken powder keg could be discerned, and uttering that terrifying cry, 'Get back, or I'll blow up the barricade!'

Marius on the barricade after the octogenarian was a vision of the young revolution following that apparition of the old.

'Blow up the barricade!' said a sergeant. 'And yourself with it!'

Marius replied, 'And myself with it!'

And he brought the torch closer to the powder keg.

But already there was no one left on the barricade. Abandoning their dead and wounded, the assailants surged back in disorder and confusion towards the far end of the street, and there melted back into the night. It was a rout.

The barricade was cleared.

V

The End of Jean Prouvaire's Verses

Everyone gathered around Marius. Courfeyrac flung his arms around his neck.

'You're here!'

'What luck!' said Combeferre.

'You arrived just in time!' said Bossuet.

'If it weren't for you, I'd be dead!' Courfeyrac went on.

'If it weren't for you, I'd have copped it!' added Gavroche.

Marius asked, 'Who's in charge?'

'You are!' said Enjolras.

All day long Marius's mind had been a furnace, now it was a whirlwind. This whirlwind inside him gave him the impression of being on the outside and of carrying him away. He felt already at an immense distance from life. Those two bright months of love and joy ending abruptly at this frightful precipice, Cosette lost to him, this barricade, Monsieur Mabeuf getting himself killed for the Republic, himself the leader of the insurgents, all this seemed to him a dreadful nightmare. He had to make a mental effort to remind himself that everything around him was real. Marius had not lived long enough to know that nothing is more imminent than the impossible, and that what you must always expect is the unexpected. He watched the drama of his own life like someone watching a play he cannot follow.

With his mind in this haze, he did not recognize Javert, tied to his pillar, who had not so much as moved his head during the entire attack on the barricade, and who watched the rebellion seething around him with the resignation of a martyr and the majesty of a judge. Marius did not even notice him.

Meanwhile, the besiegers were staying put. They could be heard milling about at the end of the street but they did not venture into it, either because they were awaiting orders or because they were awaiting reinforcements before storming this impregnable stronghold again. The insurgents posted sentries, and some of them who were medical students set about treating the wounded.

The tables – with the exception of the two reserved for bandages and cartridges, and the one on which Père Mabeuf lay – had been thrown out of the tavern. They had been added to the barricade, and replaced in the bar room with mattresses from the beds of Widow Hucheloup and her serving-women. On these mattresses they laid the wounded. As for the three poor creatures who lived at Corinthe, no one knew what had become of them. However, they were eventually found hiding in the cellar.

One distressing realization was to cast a pall over the joy of the reclaimed barricade.

Roll call was taken. One of the insurgents was missing. And who was it? One of those held most dear. One of the most valiant. Jean Prouvaire. They looked for him among the wounded. He was not there. They looked for him among the dead. He was not there. Clearly, he had been taken prisoner.

Combeferre said to Enjolras, 'They have our friend, but we have their agent. Do you set great store by this spy's death?'

'Yes,' replied Enjolras. 'But not as much as by Jean Prouvaire's life.'

This took place in the bar room by Javert's pillar.

'Well then,' said Combeferre, 'I'll tie a handkerchief to my cane as a flag of truce and go and offer to exchange our man for theirs.'

'Listen,' said Enjolras, laying his hand on Combeferre's arm.

From the end of the street came an ominous clatter of firearms.

They heard a male voice cry out, 'Long live France! Long live the future!'

They recognized Prouvaire's voice.

There was a flash of light and a blast of gunfire.

Silence fell again.

'They've killed him!' cried Combeferre.

Enjolras looked at Javert, and said to him, 'Your friends have just shot you.'

VI
After the Agony of Life, the Agony of Death

A characteristic of this type of warfare is that any attack on the barricades is almost always frontal, and assailants generally refrain from skirting a position, either because they are concerned about ambushes or because they are afraid of getting caught up in a maze of streets. So all the insurgents' attention was focused on the main barricade, which was obviously the position under constant threat and where fighting would surely start again. But Marius remembered the smaller barricade and went there. It was deserted, guarded only by the candle flickering among the cobblestones. The Mondétour alleyway and the connecting stretches of La Petite-Truanderie and Le Cygne were perfectly quiet.

As Marius turned to go, having made his inspection, he heard his name uttered feebly in the darkness.

'Monsieur Marius!'

He was startled, for he recognized the voice that had called to him through the railings in Rue Plumet two hours earlier. Only, this voice was now a mere whisper.

He looked round and saw no one. Marius thought he had been mistaken, that it was a hallucination, something his mind had added to the extraordinary realities jostling around him. He took a step away from this secluded corner where the barricade was.

'Monsieur Marius!' repeated the voice.

This time there could be no doubt, he heard it distinctly. He looked and saw nothing.

'At your feet,' said the voice.

He stooped, and saw in the darkness a figure dragging itself towards him. It was crawling on the ground. It was this figure that had spoken to him.

The tallow candle allowed him to make out an overall, torn fustian trousers, bare feet, and something that looked like a pool of blood.

Marius discerned a pale face lifted towards him and saying, 'You don't recognize me?'

'No.'

'Éponine.'

Marius dropped down at once. It was indeed that poor child. She was dressed as a man.

'How do you come to be here? What are you doing here?'

'I'm dying,' she said to him.

There are words and things that happen that rouse people from their torpor. Marius cried out as if jolted, 'You're wounded! Wait, I'll carry you inside! They'll look after you. Is it serious? How should I pick you up so as not to hurt you? Where are you injured? Help! My God! But why have you come here?'

And he tried to slip his arm under her to lift her.

She gave a feeble cry.

'Did I hurt you?' asked Marius.

'A little.'

'But I only touched your hand.'

She raised her hand to Marius's gaze, and in the middle of that hand Marius saw a black hole.

'What happened to your hand?' he said.

'A bullet went through it.'

'How?'

'Did you see a gun aimed at you?'

'Yes, and a hand that blocked it.'

'That was my hand.'

Marius shuddered.

'What madness! Poor child! But so much the better, if that's all, it's nothing. Let me carry you to a bed. They'll dress your wound, you don't die of being shot in the hand.'

She murmured, 'The bullet went through my hand but it came out through my back. There's no point in moving me from here. I'll tell you how you can treat me better than any surgeon. Sit down beside me on this stone.'

He obeyed. She laid her head in Marius's lap, and without looking at him said, 'Oh! that's lovely! How good it feels! There! I'm not in pain any more.'

She remained silent for a moment, then with an effort turned her face and looked at Marius.

'You know, Monsieur Marius, it annoyed me that you went into that garden, which was stupid since I was the one who showed you the house, and in any case I really should have told myself that a young man like you—'

She broke off, and setting aside the bleak thoughts that were surely in her mind, she resumed with a heart-rending smile, 'You found me ugly, didn't you?' She went on, 'You're doomed, you see! No one will leave the barricade now. I tell you, I was the one who brought you here! You're going to die. I'm certainly counting on it. And yet when I saw you being aimed at, I put my hand over the mouth of the gun barrel. That's so strange! But that's because I wanted to die before you. When I was hit by that bullet, I dragged myself here, no one saw me, no one picked me up. I was waiting for you, I said, "Won't he ever come!" Oh, if you only knew, I was chewing at my overall, I was in so much pain! I'm fine now. Do you remember the day I came into your room and I looked at myself in your mirror, and the day when I met you on the boulevard along by the washerwomen? How the birds were singing! That was a long time ago. You gave me five francs and I told you, "I don't want your money." You did pick up your coin, I hope? You're not rich. I didn't think of telling you to pick it up. The sun was shining brightly, it wasn't cold. Do you remember, Monsieur Marius? Oh! I'm so happy! Everyone's going to die.'

She had a look about her that was crazed, earnest, pathetic. Her torn overall exposed her bare neck.

As she spoke, she pressed her wounded hand to her breast where there was another hole, from which blood flowed in momentary spurts like a gush of wine from an open bunghole.

Marius gazed on this poor creature with deep compassion.

'Oh,' she said suddenly, 'it's coming back, I can't breathe!'

She grasped her overall and bit on it, and her limbs stiffened on the ground.

Just then the voice of that young cock sparrow Gavroche rang out from inside the barricade. The child had climbed on to a table to load his gun and was cheerfully singing a song that was very popular at the time:

> The sight of Lafayette,
> Causes great upset.
> Gendarmes, run, run, run!

Éponine raised herself and listened, then murmured, 'That's him.' And turning to Marius, 'My brother's here. He mustn't see me. He'd scold me.'

'Your brother?' said Marius, who was thinking with the bitterest,

1026

most heartfelt grief about the obligations towards the Thénardiers that his father had bequeathed to him. 'Who's your brother?'

'The little boy.'

'The one singing?'

'Yes.'

Marius gave a start.

'Oh! don't go,' she said, 'it won't be long now.'

She was sitting almost upright but her voice was very low and came in broken gasps. At intervals the death rattle interrupted it. She brought her face as close as she could to Marius's. She added, with a strange expression, 'Listen. I don't want to deceive you. I've got a letter in my pocket for you. Since yesterday. I was told to bring it to you. I kept it. I didn't want it to reach you. But perhaps you'll be cross with me because of that when we meet again, before long. People do meet again, don't they? Take your letter.'

She seized Marius's hand convulsively with her wounded hand, but she seemed not to notice the pain any more. She put Marius's hand in the pocket of her overall. Inside it, Marius could indeed feel some paper.

'Take it,' she said.

Marius took the letter.

She gave a nod of satisfaction and assent.

'Now, promise me, in return—'

And she stopped.

'What?' asked Marius.

'Promise me!'

'I promise.'

'Promise to kiss me on the forehead when I'm dead. I shall feel it.'

She let her head drop back into Marius's lap, and her eyes closed. He thought this poor soul was gone. Éponine remained motionless. Suddenly, just when Marius thought she had fallen asleep for ever, she slowly opened her eyes, where the dark depths of death appeared, and said to him in a tone whose tenderness seemed already to come from another world, 'And then, you see, Monsieur Marius, I think I was a little in love with you.'

She tried to smile again, and died.

VII
Gavroche, Great Calculator of Distances

Marius kept his promise. He placed a kiss on that pale brow beaded with cold sweat. This was no betrayal of Cosette, it was a gentle and pensive farewell to a poor unfortunate soul.

Not without a tremor had he taken the letter Éponine gave him. He sensed at once this was a matter of importance. He was impatient to read it. Man's heart is so fashioned, the poor child had barely closed her eyes before Marius was thinking about opening that sheet of paper. He laid her gently on the ground and walked away. Something told him that he could not read this letter in the presence of that body.

He went up to a candle in the bar room. It was a little note folded and sealed with a woman's elegant care. The address was in a woman's hand and read: 'To Monsieur, Monsieur Marius Pontmercy, care of Monsieur Courfeyrac, 16 Rue de la Verrerie'.

He broke the seal and read:

> My beloved, alas! my father is determined to leave without delay. This evening we shall be at 7 Rue de l'Homme-Armé.
> In a week's time we shall be in England.
>   COSETTE, 4 June

Such was the innocence of their love that Marius was not even familiar with Cosette's handwriting.

What had happened may be told in a few words. Éponine was responsible for everything. Following that evening of the third of June, her intention had been twofold: to thwart her father and those villains in their designs on the house in Rue Plumet, and to keep Marius away from Cosette. She had swapped her ragged clothes for those of the first young joker to come along who found it amusing to dress up as a woman while Éponine disguised herself as a man. It was she who in the Champ de Mars had given Jean Valjean that explicit warning: 'Move house.' Jean Valjean had actually gone home and said to Cosette, 'We're leaving this evening and going to Rue de l'Homme-Armé with Toussaint. Next week, we'll be in London.' Shocked by this unexpected blow, Cosette had hastily written a few lines to Marius. But how was the letter to be delivered? She never went out alone, and Toussaint, surprised at such an errand, would certainly have shown the letter to Monsieur Fauchelevent. In her perplexity Cosette had caught sight through the railings of Éponine dressed as a man, who now prowled around the garden incessantly. Cosette had called 'this young workman' to her and handed over five francs and the letter, saying, 'Take this letter straight away to its destination.' Éponine put the letter in her pocket. The next day, on the fifth of June, she went to Courfeyrac's and asked for Marius, not to deliver the letter but, something every jealous and loving heart will understand, 'just to see'. There she waited for Marius, or at least for Courfeyrac – still, just to see. When Courfeyrac told her 'We're going to the barricades' an idea entered her mind. To cast herself into that death as she would have cast herself into any death, and to ensure that Marius did likewise. She had followed Courfeyrac and made sure of where the barricade was being built. And quite certain, since Marius had received no warning and she had intercepted the letter, that he would be at the meeting-place he came to every evening at nightfall, she had gone to Rue Plumet, waited for Marius there, and made that appeal to him in the name of his friends that she thought would bring him to the barricade. She was counting on Marius's despair when he failed to find Cosette. She had not been mistaken. She herself returned to Rue de la Chanvrerie. We have just seen what she did there. She died feeling that tragic joy of jealous hearts who drag their beloved into death with them, and who say, 'No one shall have him!'

Marius covered Cosette's letter with kisses. So she did love him! The thought momentarily occurred to him that he need not now die. Then he said to himself, 'She's going away. Her father is taking her to England, and my grandfather is against our marriage. There's no change in our fate.' Dreamers like Marius are given to such extremes of despondency, resulting in decisions prompted by despair. The weariness of living is unbearable. The sooner death comes, the better.

Then he remembered he still had two duties to fulfil: to inform Cosette of his death and send her a last farewell, and to save from the impending catastrophe in the making that poor child, Éponine's brother and Thénardier's son.

He had a notecase on him, the same one that had contained the notebook in which he had written down so many reflections on love for Cosette. He tore out a page and wrote these few lines in pencil: 'Our marriage was impossible. I asked my grandfather, he was against it. I am without money, and so are you. I came running, you were already gone from the house. You know the vow I made to you, I abide by it. I am to die. I love you. When you read this, my soul will be close by, smiling on you.'

Having nothing to seal this letter with, he contented himself with folding the sheet of paper in four and wrote this address on it: 'To Mademoiselle Cosette Fauchelevent, care of Monsieur Fauchelevent, 7 Rue de l'Homme-Armé'.

Having folded the letter, he remained thoughtful for a moment, took out his notecase again, opened it and with the same pencil wrote these four lines on the first page: 'My name is Marius Pontmercy. Take my body to my grandfather, Monsieur Gillenormand, 6 Rue des Filles-du-Calvaire, in the Marais.'

He put his notecase back in his coat pocket, then called for Gavroche. On hearing Marius's voice, the gamin came running, with an expression of cheerful devotion on his face.

'Will you do something for me?'

'Anything,' said Gavroche. 'For goodness' sake! Truly, but for you, I was done for.'

'You see this letter?'

'Yes.'

'Take it. Leave the barricade right now' (Gavroche began to scratch his ear uneasily) 'and tomorrow morning deliver it to its destination, to Mademoiselle Cosette, at the house of Monsieur Fauchelevent, 7 Rue de l'Homme-Armé.'

The heroic child replied, 'But meanwhile the barricade'll be taken and I shan't be here.'

'All the signs are, the barricade won't come under attack again before daybreak, and it won't be taken before midday tomorrow.'

The fresh respite granted to the barricade by the assailants was indeed continuing. It was one of those lulls, frequent in nocturnal battles, that are always followed by an intensification of the fighting.

'Well then,' said Gavroche, 'what if I take your letter tomorrow morning?'

'It'll be too late then. The barricade will probably be closed off, all the streets will be guarded, and you won't be able to get out. Go now.'

Gavroche could think of no reply to this, and stood there wavering, sadly scratching his ear. Suddenly, with one of those birdlike motions of his, he took the letter.

'All right,' he said.

And off he ran down the Mondétour lane.

An idea had occurred to Gavroche that had decided him, but he did not mention it for fear that Marius might raise some objection.

The idea was this: 'It's barely midnight, Rue de l'Homme-Armé isn't far. I'll take the letter straight away and I'll be back in time.'

BOOK FIFTEEN
RUE DE L'HOMME-ARMÉ

I
The Tell-tale Blotter

What are the upheavals of a city compared to the turbulences of the soul? Man is of yet greater depth than the people. At that very same time Jean Valjean was in the grip of terrible turmoil. Every chasm had reopened inside him. Like Paris, he too was trembling on the brink of a tremendous revolution, in obscurity. A few hours were all it had taken. His fate and his consciousness were suddenly overshadowed. It might well have been said of him, as of Paris: two principles confront each other. The white angel and the black angel are going to grapple with each other on the bridge over the abyss. Which of the two will hurl the other down into it? Who will win?

The evening before that fifth of June, Jean Valjean, accompanied by Cosette and Toussaint, had moved into Rue de l'Homme-Armé. A twist of fate awaited him there.

Cosette had not left Rue Plumet without some show of resistance. For the first time since they had lived side by side, Cosette's will and Jean Valjean's had proved to be distinct from each other, and had, if not clashed, at least been at variance. There had been objection on one side and inflexibility on the other. The bald advice 'Move house', thrown at Jean Valjean by a stranger, had alarmed him so far as to make him uncompromising. He thought he had been tracked down and was being followed. Cosette had to give way.

Both had arrived at Rue de l'Homme-Armé tight-lipped, without exchanging a word, entirely absorbed in their own private concerns, Jean Valjean so anxious that he failed to notice Cosette's sadness, Cosette so sad that she failed to notice Jean Valjean's anxiety.

Jean Valjean had brought Toussaint along, something he had never done during his previous absences. He envisaged the possibility that he might not return to Rue Plumet, and he could neither leave Toussaint behind nor tell her his secret. In any event, he felt that she was loyal and trustworthy. Between master and servant betrayal starts with curiosity. Now, Toussaint, as though predestined to be Jean Valjean's servant, was not curious. Speaking in that Barneville peasant dialect of hers, she stammered out, '*Je suis de même de même, je chose mon fait, le demeurant n'est pas mon travail.'* (That's the way I am, I get on with my work, the rest is none of my business.*)

In this departure from Rue Plumet, which had been almost a flit, Jean Valjean had taken with him nothing but the little perfumed valise, nicknamed 'the inseparable' by Cosette. Packed trunks would have meant porters, and porters are witnesses. A cab had come to the door on Rue de Babylone, and they had left.

It was with difficulty that Toussaint had obtained permission to pack a little linen and some clothes and a few toiletry items. Cosette had taken only her writing-case and her blotter.

For the greater privacy and concealment of their disappearance, Jean Valjean had contrived not to leave the villa in Rue Plumet until dusk, which gave Cosette time to write her note to Marius. They arrived at Rue de l'Homme-Armé after dark. They went to bed in silence.

The lodgings in Rue de l'Homme-Armé were situated overlooking a back yard, on the second floor, and comprised two bedrooms, a dining room and adjoining kitchen, and a room under the eaves with a trestle-bed that was allotted to Toussaint. The dining room also served as a reception room, and the two bedrooms were separated by it. The apartment was fully equipped with all the essentials.

People's apprehensions are allayed almost as easily as they are raised. Human nature is like that. Jean Valjean was no sooner at Rue de l'Homme-Armé than his anxiety lifted and gradually faded. There are calming places that have some sort of automatic effect on the mind. An unfrequented street, peaceful residents, Jean Valjean felt almost a contagion of tranquillity in that little lane in ancient Paris, a lane so narrow it is barred to carriages by a horizontal beam resting on two posts, silent and unhearing in the midst of the city hubbub, in a twilight shadow at midday and incapable, as it were, of emotion between its two rows of tall centuries-old houses that keep their counsel like the veterans they are. There was in that street an undisturbed oblivion. There, Jean Valjean breathed again. How could anyone possibly find him?

The first thing he did was to put 'the inseparable' beside him.

He slept well. Night brings counsel. We might add, night brings calm. The next morning he woke up almost cheerful. He found the dining room delightful – it was hideous, furnished with an old round table, a low sideboard with a tilted mirror above it, a dilapidated arm-

---

* As glossed in the French text: 'Je suis ainsi; je fais ma besogne; le reste n'est pas mon affaire.'

chair and several dining chairs piled with Toussaint's bundles. Visible through a hole in one of these bundles was Jean Valjean's National Guard uniform.

As for Cosette, she had Toussaint bring some broth to her room, and did not appear until evening.

At about five o'clock, to-ing and fro-ing, kept very busy by this little house move, Toussaint placed a cold chicken on the dining table, which out of deference to her father Cosette consented to look at.

Having done so, pleading a persistent migraine, Cosette said goodnight to Jean Valjean and shut herself up in her bedroom. Jean Valjean ate a chicken wing with some appetite and, elbows resting on the table, his peace of mind gradually restored, he began to feel safe again.

While he was having this frugal meal he was vaguely aware two or three times of Toussaint's stammering, saying to him, 'Monsieur, there's trouble, there's fighting going on in Paris.' But engrossed in countless schemes, he paid no attention. To tell the truth, he had not heard.

He got up and began to pace from the door to the window and from the window to the door, feeling increasingly calm.

With this calm, Cosette, his sole concern, came back to mind. Not that he was upset by this migraine, a little fit of temperament, a young girl's moodiness, a temporary cloud – it would be all over in a day or two. But he was thinking about the future, and as usual thinking about it with tenderness.

After all, he saw no obstacle to a resumption of their happy life. At certain times everything seems impossible, at others times everything seems easy. For Jean Valjean this was one of those good times. They generally succeed the bad ones as day follows night, by that law of succession and contrast that is at the very foundation of nature and which superficial minds call 'antithesis'. In this peaceful street where he had taken refuge Jean Valjean shrugged off all that had lately been troubling him. It was precisely because he had seen many dark shadows that he now began to perceive a little blue sky. To have left Rue Plumet without complications and without incident was one step in the right direction.

Perhaps it would be wise to travel abroad, if only for a few months, to go to London. Well then, they would. Whether in France or in England, what difference did it make, as long as he had Cosette with him? Cosette was his nation. Cosette was all that was necessary to his happiness. The idea that he himself was not perhaps all that was necessary to Cosette's happiness, this idea that had once caused him fever and insomnia, did not even occur to him. All his past sufferings were in remission, and he was full of optimism. Cosette, being with him, seemed to be his, an optical illusion everyone has experienced. He arranged in his own mind, with all kinds of self-indulgences, his departure for England with Cosette; and in his daydreams, whichever way he looked, he saw his happiness restored.

As he slowly paced to and fro, his gaze suddenly encountered something strange. He saw in front of him, distinctly legible in the tilted mirror above the sideboard, these four lines:

My beloved, alas! my father is determined to leave without delay.
This evening we shall be at 7 Rue de l'Homme-Armé.
In a week's time we shall be in England.
COSETTE, 4 June

Jean Valjean stopped, aghast.

On arrival Cosette had placed her blotter on the sideboard in front of the mirror, and totally rapt in her sorrowful plight she had forgotten about it, not even noticing that she had left it wide open – and open at precisely the page on which she had pressed down, to blot dry, the four lines she had written and entrusted to the young workman passing by in Rue Plumet. The writing had imprinted itself on the blotter. The mirror reflected the writing.

This produced what in geometry is called a symmetric image, so that the backwards writing on the blotter was reversed in the mirror, and appeared the right way round. And Jean Valjean had before his eyes the letter Cosette had written to Marius the day before. It was simple, and it was devastating.

Jean Valjean went up to the mirror. He reread the four lines but he did not believe them. They seemed to him to appear in a flash of lightning. It was a hallucination. It was impossible. It was not there.

Little by little his perception cleared. He looked at Cosette's blotter and a sense of concrete reality returned to him. He picked up the blotter and said, 'This is where it comes from.' He feverishly examined the four lines imprinted on the blotter. The reversal of the letters turned them into a bizarre scrawl, and he saw no sense in them. Then he said to himself, 'But this doesn't mean anything, there's nothing written here.' And with inexpressible relief he drew a deep breath. Who has not experienced such foolish joys in dreadful moments? The soul does not give in to despair without having exhausted every illusion.

He held the blotter in his hand and contemplated it, stupidly happy, almost ready to laugh at the hallucination he had been taken in by. Suddenly his eyes fell on the mirror again, and again he saw the vision. The four lines were traced with inexorable distinctness. This time it was no mirage. The recurrence of a vision is a reality, it was plain, it was the inverted writing displayed correctly in the mirror. He understood.

Jean Valjean reeled, dropped the blotter and collapsed into the old armchair by the sideboard, his head bowed, glassy-eyed, distraught. He told himself there could be no mistake about it, that the light of the world had been eclipsed for ever, and that Cosette had written this to someone. Then he heard rising from the depths of his soul, terrible once more, a deep roar. Try taking from the lion the dog that it has in its cage!

Oddly and sadly enough, at that moment Marius had not yet received Cosette's letter. Chance had treacherously brought it to Jean Valjean before delivering it to Marius.

Jean Valjean was until that day unvanquished by any ordeal. He had suffered appalling tribulations. No onslaught of ill fortune had been spared him. Armed with every punishment and every form of social contempt, the ferocity of fate had victimized and hounded him. He had accepted when necessary every extremity. He had sacrificed his regained inviolability as a man, given up his freedom, risked his life, lost everything, endured everything; and he had remained selfless and stoical to the point that it might have been thought he was detached from himself, like a martyr. Inured to destiny's every conceivable assault, his conscience might have seemed for ever impregnable. Well, anyone who had been able to see deep down inside him would have been forced to conclude that at that moment it was weakening.

The truth is that of all the tortures he had suffered during that lengthy persecution to which he was doomed, this was the most terrible. Never had he been so lacerated. He felt the mysterious stirring of all his latent sensibilities. He felt agonized in every last fibre of his being. Alas! the supreme test, or rather, the only test, is the loss of the beloved.

Poor old Jean Valjean did not, of course, love Cosette other than as a father, but we have already pointed out that into this fatherhood the very aridity of his life had introduced every type of love. He loved Cosette as his daughter, he loved her as his mother, he loved her as his sister. And since he had never had a sweetheart or a wife, since nature is a creditor that cannot be denied, that sentiment too, the most inalienable of all, was mingled with the rest; ill-defined, unknowing, pure with the purity of blindness, unconscious, celestial, angelic, divine, not so much a sentiment as an instinct, not so much an instinct as an attraction, imperceptible and invisible, but real. And there was in his immense tenderness for Cosette love in the true sense of the word, like the vein of gold that lies, hidden and virgin, within the mountain.

Remember, we have already commented on this state of the heart. No marriage was possible between them, not even that of souls. And yet it is unquestionable that their destinies were wedded to each other. Apart from Cosette, that is to say, apart from the duration of her childhood, throughout his long life Jean Valjean had known nothing of what love might be. No series of passions or affections had produced in him those successive greens, tender green on dark, that can be seen in foliage that lasts through winter and in men who last into their fifties. In short, and we have dwelt on this more than once, all taken together, this whole inner complexity, resulting in great virtuousness, made of Jean Valjean in the end a father for Cosette. A strange father, forged out of the grandfather, the son, the brother and the husband contained in Jean Valjean. A father in whom there was even a mother. A father who loved Cosette, who adored her, and for whom that child was light, home, family, country, paradise.

So when he saw that it was all over, that she was escaping from him, absconding, slipping out of his hands; that it was nothing but mist, but water; when he had before his eyes this crushing proof – another is the object of her love, another is what she wants of life, there's now a beloved, I'm only her father, I no longer exist – when he could doubt no longer, when he said to himself, 'She's going away and leaving me!', the pain he felt was beyond endurance. To have done all that he had done and be reduced to this! What? To count for nothing! Then, as we have just said, a shudder of revolt ran through him from head to foot. He felt to the very roots of his hair the immense reawakening of egotism; and the self in the abyss that was this man howled.

There is such a thing as internal collapse. Despairing certitude does not infiltrate a human being without displacing and disrupting certain profound elements that sometimes constitute the man himself. Grief, when it reaches this pitch, routs all strength of conscience. These are deadly crises. Few of us emerge from them true to ourselves and steadfast in our duty. When the limit of endurance is exceeded, the most unshakeable virtue is undermined. Jean Valjean picked up the blotter again and convinced himself once more. He remained hunched and as though paralysed over those undeniable four lines, his gaze transfixed. And such were the shadows that gathered inside him, it might have been thought that here was a soul in total collapse from within. Through the magnifying power of introspection, he examined this revelation with apparent calm – and a terrifying calm, at that, for it is a dangerous thing when a man's calm attains the coldness of a statue.

He measured the dreadful step that his destiny had taken without his even suspecting it. He recalled his fears of the summer before, so foolishly quelled. He recognized the precipice; it was the same as ever. Only, Jean Valjean was no longer on the edge of it, he was at the bottom.

Extraordinarily and poignantly enough, he had fallen over the edge without noticing. All the light in his life had gone and there he was, thinking he could still see the sun.

His instinct was unfaltering. He put together certain circumstances, certain dates, certain of Cosette's blushes and pallors, and he said to himself: 'That's who it is.' Despair's divination is a kind of mysterious bow that never misses its mark. He hit on Marius at his very first guess. He did not know the name but he found the man instantly. He saw distinctly, dredged up by his ruthless memory, the unknown prowler in the Luxembourg Gardens, that wretched philanderer, that romantic idler, that imbecile, that coward, for it is cowardly to come and make eyes at young girls who have at their side their fathers who love them.

After he had firmly established in his mind that behind the present situation was this young man and that everything followed from that, he, Jean Valjean, a man regenerated, a man who had worked so hard on his soul, a man who had made such efforts to resolve into love all life, all misery and all unhappiness, looked inside himself and saw there a spectre: hatred.

Great sorrows bring desolation. They sap the essence of being. Any man they enter feels something go out of him. To be visited by them in youth is dismal, later on it is dire. Alas, if despair is a dreadful thing when the blood is hot, when the hair is black, when the head is erect on the body like the flame on the torch, when the scroll of destiny is still almost fully unrolled; when the heart, filled with a desirable love, may still find its heartbeats echoed in another; when there is still time for reparation; when there are all those women, all those smiles, the whole future, the entire horizon; when still in the full force of life – what is it like in old age, when the years rush on, ever more wan, to that twilight hour when you begin to see the stars from the grave?

While his thoughts ran on, Toussaint came in.

Jean Valjean stood up and asked her, 'Whereabouts is it? Do you know?'

Baffled, Toussaint could only answer, 'I beg your pardon?'

Jean Valjean elaborated, 'Didn't you tell me just now there's fighting going on?'

'Ah! yes, monsieur,' replied Toussaint. 'It's over towards St-Merry.'

There is a certain automatic impulse that, unknown even to ourselves, comes from the innermost recesses of our mind. It was no doubt driven by such an impulse of which he was barely conscious that Jean Valjean, five minutes later, found himself in the street.

He was bare-headed, sitting on the boundary-post at the entrance to his building. He seemed to be listening. Night had fallen.

II
The Gamin, Enemy of the Light

How much time did he spend like that? What was the ebb and flow of his thoughts in this tragic introspection? Did he draw himself up again? Did he remain slumped? Had he been bowed beyond breaking-point? Could he still straighten up and regain his footing on something solid in his conscience? He himself would probably have been unable to say.

The street was deserted. A few anxious citizens hurrying home scarcely noticed him. In times of peril, every man for himself. The lamp-lighter came as usual to light the lantern that was located exactly opposite the entrance to number seven, and went away again. To anyone who had observed him there in the shadows, Jean Valjean would not have looked like a living man. He sat there, on the boundary-post at the entrance, as still as a revenant made of ice. There is a frozenness in despair. The alarm bell and indistinct clamorous noises could be heard. In the midst of all this tempestuous bell-ringing and rioting the clock of St-Paul struck eleven, solemnly and unhurriedly. For the alarm bell belongs to man; time belongs to God. The striking of the hour had no effect on Jean Valjean. Jean Valjean did not stir. But at about that moment there was a sudden blast from the direction of Les Halles. A second blast, even more violent, followed. It was probably that attack on the barricade in Rue de la Chanvrerie that we have just seen repelled by Marius. At this double volley of gunfire, whose fury seemed augmented by the stupor of the night, Jean Valjean started. He stood up, facing in the direction the noise had come from. Then he dropped back on to the post, folded his arms, and his head sank slowly on to his chest again.

He resumed his gloomy dialogue with himself.

All of a sudden he looked up. Someone was walking in the street, he heard footsteps near by. By the light of the lantern he saw, coming from the end of the street that leads to the Archives, a young, pale, radiant figure.

Gavroche had just arrived in Rue de l'Homme-Armé. He was looking up in the air, apparently in search of something. He certainly saw Jean Valjean, but took no notice of him.

After looking up in the air, Gavroche looked lower down. He raised himself on tip-toe, feeling for the ground-floor doors and windows. They were all shut, bolted and padlocked. Having found the frontages of five or six houses barred in this manner, the gamin shrugged and his first reaction was expressed to himself in these terms: 'Blast!'

Then he began to look up in the air again.

Jean Valjean, who the moment before, given his state of mind, would neither have spoken to anyone nor even have answered, felt irresistibly impelled to talk to this child.

'What's the matter with you, little fellow?' he said.

'What's the matter with me is I'm hungry,' Gavroche replied bluntly. And he added, 'Little fellow yourself!'

Jean Valjean fumbled in his fob-pocket and pulled out a five-franc piece. But Gavroche, who was of the wagtail species and darted from one thing to the next, had just picked up a stone. He had noticed the street lamp.

'Now fancy that!' he said. 'You've still got your lanterns here. You're going against the rule, my friends. It's public disorder. Let's break it!'

He threw the stone at the lantern, and the glass made such a noise on impact that the respectable citizens cowering behind their curtains in the house opposite cried out, 'It's ninety-three all over again!'

The lantern swung violently, then the light went out. The street was suddenly dark.

'That's right, old street,' said Gavroche, 'put your night-cap on.' And turning to Jean Valjean, 'What do you call that huge building you've got at the end of the street? It's the Archives, isn't it? I ought to have a go at those big fat pillars and make a nice barricade out of them.'

Jean Valjean went over to Gavroche. And talking to himself under his breath he said, 'Poor creature, he's hungry.' And he put the five-franc coin in the boy's hand.

Gavroche looked up, amazed at the size of this coin. He stared at it in the dark, and the whiteness of the coin dazzled him. He knew of five-franc coins, from hearsay. He liked the sound of them. He was delighted to see one at close quarters. He said, 'Let's examine the beast.'

He contemplated it for several moments, enraptured. Then, turning to Jean Valjean, he held out the coin towards him and said majestically, 'Bourgeois, I prefer to smash lanterns. Take back your fierce beast. I can't be bribed. It's got five claws but it can't scratch me.'*

'Have you a mother?' asked Jean Valjean.

Gavroche replied, 'More likely than you are to have one.'

'Well,' returned Jean Valjean, 'keep that money for your mother!'

Gavroche was touched. Besides, he had just noticed that the man who was talking to him had no hat, and this inspired confidence.

'Honest?' he said. 'It's not to stop me breaking lanterns?'

'Break whatever you like.'

'You're a decent chap,' said Gavroche. And he put the five-franc coin into one of his pockets. His confidence growing, he added, 'You live in this street?'

'Yes, why?'

'Can you tell me where number seven is?'

'What do you want with number seven?'

Here the child stopped himself, afraid he had said too much. He ran his fingernails briskly through his hair and confined his response to 'Ah, well now!'

An idea flashed through Jean Valjean's mind. Anguish has such moments of insight. He said to the lad, 'Are you the person who's bringing me the letter I'm expecting?'

'You?' said Gavroche. 'You're not a woman.'

'The letter's for Mademoiselle Cosette, isn't it?'

'Cosette,' muttered Gavroche. 'Funny name. Yes, I think it's that.'

'Well,' Jean Valjean went on, 'I'm the one who'll see that she gets it. Give it to me.'

'In that case, you must know I've been sent from the barricade.'

'Of course,' said Jean Valjean.

Gavroche stuck his hand in another of his pockets and drew out a piece of paper folded in four.

Then he gave a military salute.

'Respect the dispatch,' he said. 'It comes from the provisional government.'

---

* A slang term for a five-franc coin was *un tigre à cinq griffes* ('a five-clawed tiger'), perhaps deriving from the Napoleonic five-franc coins that were countermarked after 1815 with the head of a caged lion.

'Give it to me,' said Jean Valjean.

Gavroche held the piece of paper above his head. 'Don't you go thinking it's a love letter. It's for a woman, but it's for the people. We fight, we do, and we respect the ladies. We're not like society, where popinjays send cocottes billets-doux.'

'Give it to me.'

Gavroche continued, 'True, you seem like an honest man to me.'

'Give it to me! Quickly!'

'Here.'

And he handed the piece of paper to Jean Valjean.

'And hurry up, Monsieur Chose, Mam'selle Chosette's waiting.'*

Gavroche was pleased with this little joke.

Jean Valjean went on, 'Is it to St-Merry the reply's to be sent?'

'That,' cried Gavroche, 'would be like making one of those loaves called a "bloomer"! This letter comes from the Rue de la Chanvrerie barricade, and I'm going back there. Good evening, citizen.'

That said, Gavroche set off again, or rather he winged his way back to where he had come from like an escaped bird returning home. As if piercing a hole in it, he shot off into the darkness with the undeviating speed of a projectile. That little street, l'Homme-Armé, became silent and desolate once again. In a twinkling that strange child, with dream and shadow in his make-up, had plunged into the gloom of those rows of dark houses and disappeared into the obscurity like smoke. And you might have thought he had melted away into nothingness if, a few minutes after his disappearance, an explosion of shattering glass and the glorious clatter of a lantern falling on to the street had not once again rudely awakened the indignant bourgeois residents. It was Gavroche making his way along Rue du Chaume.

---

* Cosette's unusual name inspires Gavroche to form a diminutive of the feminine noun *une chose* ('thing') and call her 'Mam'selle Chosette' (Little Miss Whatsit), making Jean Valjean 'Monsieur Chose'.

While Cosette and Toussaint Sleep

Jean Valjean went back inside with Marius's letter.

He groped his way upstairs, glad of the dark, like an owl with its prey in its clutches, quietly opened and shut the front door, listened out for any sound, ascertained that in all likelihood Cosette and Toussaint were asleep, and used up three or four matches before he could draw a spark from the Fumade lighter, his hand was trembling so much: there was thievery in what he had just done. At last the candle was lit. He sat with his elbows resting on the table, unfolded the piece of paper and read.

In the throes of violent emotion you do not read, you wrestle, as it were, with the piece of paper you are holding, you grip it as if it were your victim, you handle it roughly, you dig into it the fingernails of your anger or your joy. You race through to the end, you jump back to the beginning. Your attention is feverish. It broadly, more or less, grasps the essential. It seizes on one point, and all the rest disappears. In Marius's note to Cosette, Jean Valjean saw only these words, 'I am to die . . . When you read this, my soul will be close by . . .'

In the presence of these lines he felt horribly dazed. He remained for a moment as if crushed by the change of emotion taking place inside him. He stared at Marius's note with a kind of drunken bewilderment. He had this brilliant vision before his eyes, the death of a hated individual.

He uttered a dreadful cry of inward joy. So it was all over. The solution had come sooner than anyone might have dared hope. The individual who was such an unwelcome intrusion in his life was going to vanish. The man was going, of his own accord, freely, willingly. Without Jean Valjean having to do anything about it, without his having to take any blame for it, 'that man' was going to die. He might even be dead already. Here his feverishness made some calculations. 'No, he's not dead yet. The letter was obviously written to be read by Cosette tomorrow morning. Since those two volleys of gunfire we heard between eleven o'clock and midnight there's been nothing more. The barricade won't be seriously attacked until daybreak. But it makes no difference, from the moment "that man" became involved in this war, he was doomed. He's caught up in the works.' Jean Valjean felt liberated. So he was going to be left alone with Cosette. The rivalry was over. The future was beginning again. He had only to keep this note in his pocket. Cosette would never know what had become of 'that man'. 'Just let things take their course. That man can't escape. If he's not already dead, he's going to die for sure. What luck!'

Having said all this to himself, his mood darkened. Then he went downstairs and woke up the porter.

About an hour later Jean Valjean went out, dressed in his National Guard uniform, and armed. The porter had easily been able to find in the vicinity what he needed to be fully equipped. He had a loaded rifle and a cartridge pouch filled with cartridges. He headed off in the direction of Les Halles.

IV
Gavroche Overzealous

In the meantime, Gavroche had had an adventure.

Having conscientiously stoned the street lantern in Rue du Chaume, Gavroche turned into Rue des Vieilles-Haudriettes, and seeing 'not a mouse stirring' thought this was a good moment to start singing at the top of his voice. Far from being slowed down by his singing, his pace was quickened. On his way past the sleeping, or terrorized, houses, he began to dispense these inflammatory verses:

> A tittle-tattle bird in the bushes
> Is putting it about that yesterday
> Atala went off with a Russian.

> Where fair maids go.
> With a hey and a ho.

> My friend Pierrot is ranting and raving,
> Because, on seeing me the other day,
> Mila rapped on her window, waving.

> Where fair maids go.
> With a hey and a ho.

> Brazen hussies have a way with them.
> To the charm that worked its poison on me
> Monsieur Orfila would surely succumb.

> Where fair maids go.
> With a hey and a ho.

Love and its tiffs, I love. Agnes
I love, and Pamela. Igniting my desire
Lisa herself was burned by the fire.

Where fair maids go.
With a hey and a ho.

When first I first saw Susette and Zeila
Many moons ago, my heart became
Entangled in the folds of their mantillas.

Where fair maids go.
With a hey and a ho.

When Lola's head you crown with roses,
In the darkness where you shine, Love,
For that honour I'd go to blazes.

Where fair maids go.
With a hey and a ho.

In front of her mirror, Jeanne dresses!
I lost my heart one fine day.
To Jeanne, I think, it made its way.

Where fair maids go.
With a hey and a ho.

Emerging at night, after dancing quadrilles,
I show off Stella to the stars above,
Saying, 'Gaze on her, if you will!'

Where fair maids go,
With a hey and a ho.

Gavroche accompanied his singing with a great deal of pantomime. The refrain relies on gesture. An inexhaustible repertory of masks, his face produced grimaces more convulsive and more fantastic than the mouthings of a hole in a sheet in a high wind. Unfortunately, as he was alone and in the dark this was both unseen and invisible. There are such lost gems.

He stopped dead.

'Let's cut the love song short,' he said.

His catlike eyes had just discerned in a recessed carriage entrance what in painting is called a 'composition study', in this case featuring a human figure and an object: the object was a handcart, the human figure was that of an Auvergnat asleep in it.

The shafts of the handcart were resting on the pavement, and the Auvergnat's head was resting on the floor of the cart. His body was curled up on this tilted plane, his feet touching the ground.

With his experience of the things of this world, Gavroche recognized a sot. This was some local street porter who had drunk too much and was sleeping too soundly.

'That's what summer nights are for,' thought Gavroche. 'The Auvergnat drops off in his cart. We take the cart for the Republic, and leave the Auvergnat to the monarchy.'

A bright idea had just occurred to him: 'That cart would make a very useful addition to our barricade!'

The Auvergnat was snoring.

Gavroche gently tugged at the cart from behind and at the Auvergnat from the forward end, that is to say, by the feet. And a minute later the insensible Auvergnat lay flat on the ground. The cart was freed.

Used to encountering the unexpected from every quarter, Gavroche was always fully equipped. He fumbled in one of his pockets and drew out of it a scrap of paper and the stub of a red pencil filched from some carpenter.

He wrote: 'French Republic. In receipt of your cart.' And he signed it 'Gavroche'.

That done, he put the piece of paper in the pocket of the still-snoring Auvergnat's fustian jacket, grabbed the barrow with both hands and went tearing off in the direction of Les Halles, pushing the cart in front of him and making a glorious and triumphant racket.

This was dangerous. There was a guard-post at the royal printing works. Gavroche did not think of this. This guard-post was manned by National Guardsmen from the outskirts. With signs of waking, the squad began to stir, and heads were raised from camp-beds. Two street lanterns broken one after the other, that song bawled out – this was a lot to put up with for such craven streets that want to be off to sleep at sunset and that snuff out their candles so early. For the past hour the lad had been kicking up a shindy in that peaceful district, like a fly in a bottle. The sergeant from the outskirts listened. He waited. He was a prudent man.

The frantic rattling of the cart marked the limit to how long he could wait, and the sergeant was obliged to attempt a reconnaissance.

'There's a whole gang of them out there!' he said. 'Let's be careful.'

It was clear that the Hydra of Anarchy was out of its box and wreaking havoc on the neighbourhood. Treading softly, the sergeant ventured out of the guard-post.

Suddenly, just as he was about to emerge from Rue des Vieilles-Haudriettes pushing his handcart, Gavroche found himself face to face with a uniform, a plumed shako and a gun. For the second time he stopped dead.

'Well, look who's here,' he said. 'Hallo, law and order.'

Gavroche's dumbfoundedness was always short-lived and quickly overcome.

'Where are you going, guttersnipe?' shouted the sergeant.

'Citizen,' said Gavroche, 'I haven't called you "bourgeois" yet. Why are you insulting me?'

'Where are you going, troublemaker?'

'Monsieur,' retorted Gavroche, 'you may have had a sense of humour yesterday but you've not got one this morning.'

'I asked you where you're going, vandal?'

Gavroche replied, 'That's a nice way to talk. Honest, no one would guess you were as old as you are. You ought to sell every hair on your head for a hundred francs apiece. That would bring you five hundred francs.'

'Where are you going? Where are you going? Where are you going, scoundrel?'

Gavroche responded, 'What nasty words! You need to wash your mouth out.'

The sergeant levelled his bayonet.

'For the last time, will you tell me where you're going, wretch?'

'General,' said Gavroche, 'I'm going to fetch a doctor for my wife who's in labour.'

'To arms!' shouted the sergeant.

Saving yourself by means of what has been your undoing is the masterstroke of resourceful men. Gavroche assessed the whole situation at a glance. It was the handcart that had got him into trouble, it was up to the handcart to protect him.

Just as the sergeant was going to blast away at Gavroche, the cart, turned into a projectile and launched with all the gamin's might, came thundering at him, and the sergeant, hit right in the stomach, toppled backwards into the gutter while his gun went off in the air.

At the sergeant's cry the men in the guard-post had come rushing out helter-skelter. The shot prompted a general burst of random firing, which was followed by a reloading of weapons and then repeated. This shooting blindfold, as it were, went on for a good quarter-hour, and several panes of glass paid the price.

Meanwhile, Gavroche, who had gone tearing back the way he had come, stopped five or six streets away and sat panting on the boundary-post at the corner of Rue des Enfants-Rouges. He listened out.

After catching his breath for a few moments he turned towards where the gunfire was raging, raised his left hand to nose level and made three forward chopping movements, while slapping the back of his head with his right hand – a superlative gesture in which the Parisian gamin brotherhood has condensed French irony, and which is obviously effective since it has already lasted half a century.

His mirth was marred by one bitter reflection.

'Yes,' said he, 'I'm bursting and rolling and writhing with glee, but I'm losing my way, I'll have to take a roundabout route. Just hope I get to the barricade in time!'

Then he went running off again. And as he ran, he said, 'Now then, where was I?'

As he darted down the streets he picked up his song where he had left off, and his singing faded away into the darkness:

> But there are prisons still remaining,
> To which I intend to put an end
> And as well to all else pertaining.
>
> Where fair maids go,
> With a hey and a ho.
>
> Anyone fancy a game of skittles?
> For when the great ball rolled
> Little was left standing of the old world.
>
> Where fair maids go,
> With a hey and a ho.
>
> Wield your crutches, you fine old people,
> Against the monarchy's flaunting and flouncing.
> Let's give the Louvre a regular trouncing!
>
> Where fair maids go,
> With a hey and a ho.

> We did storm those palace gates;
> And Charles the Tenth, then King of France,
> Lost his grip and came unstuck.
>
> Where fair maids go,
> With a hey and a ho.

The guard-post's show of force was not without result. The handcart was conquered, the drunkard incarcerated. The former was impounded, and the military tribunals later attempted to bring charges against the latter as an accessory. The public prosecutor's department of the day demonstrated in this case its indefatigable zeal in defence of society.

Gavroche's adventure, preserved in Temple-district lore, is one of the most terrible memories of the old bourgeois residents of the Marais, and entitled in their recollections: 'Night-time attack on the guard-post at the royal printing works'.

PART FIVE

JEAN VALJEAN

BOOK ONE
THE WAR WITHIN
FOUR WALLS

I

The Scylla of Faubourg St-Antoine and the
Charybdis of Faubourg du Temple

The two most memorable barricades that the observer of social ills might mention do not belong to the period in which the plot of this book is set. Those two barricades, both symbols, in two different guises, of a dire situation, rose up out of the earth at the time of the fateful insurrection of June 1848, the greatest street battle history has ever seen.

It sometimes happens that, even contrary to principles, even contrary to liberty, equality and fraternity, even contrary to universal betterment, even contrary to government by all for all; from the depths of its anguish, its despondency, its destitution, its fevers; from the depths of its hardship, its morbidity, its ignorance, its darkness, that great despairing body the rabble protests, and the populace wages war against the people.

Beggars attack the general rule of law. The mob rebels against the Demos.

These are grim days. For there is always a certain element of rightfulness even in this madness, there is suicide in this duel. And these words that are intended to be insults – 'beggars', 'rabble', 'mob', 'populace' – indicate alas! that the blame lies with those who rule rather than with those who suffer, with the privileged rather than with the deprived.

For our own part, we never use these words without sorrow and without respect, for when philosophy fathoms the facts to which they correspond, it often finds much greatness alongside the wretchedness. Athens lived under mob rule. The sea-beggars were the making of Holland. The populace saved Rome more than once. And the rabble followed Jesus Christ.

There is no thinker who has not sometimes contemplated the splendours of the lower depths.

It was of this rabble that St Jerome was no doubt thinking, and of all these poor people, and of all these vagabonds, and of all these wretches from among whom came the apostles and the martyrs, when he uttered these mysterious words: *Fex urbis, lex orbis.**

The lashing-out of this mob that suffers and bleeds, its wrong-headed violence against the principles that are its life, its assaults on lawfulness are populist *coups d'état* and must be quelled. The man of probity dedicates himself to this, and out of his very love for the mob he fights against it. But even while opposing it, how excusable he feels it to be! Even while resisting it, how he reveres it! This is one of those rare moments when, in doing what must be done, you sense something perplexing that would almost dissuade you from going any further. You persist, you must. But in your satisfied conscience there is sadness, and in the carrying out of your duty there is heartache.

June 1848, let us hasten to say, was an exceptional event, and almost impossible to categorize in the philosophy of history. Everything we have just said must be set aside when it comes to this extraordinary uprising in which there was a sense of the sacred anxiety of labour claiming its rights. It had to be combated, as a matter of duty, for it attacked the Republic. But fundamentally, what was June 1848? A revolt of the people against itself.

Where the subject is not lost from sight, there is no digression. So may we be permitted to detain the reader's attention for a moment on the two absolutely unique barricades we have just mentioned, which characterized this insurrection.

One blocked the entrance to Faubourg St-Antoine, the other made Faubourg du Temple inaccessible. Those who saw these two appalling masterpieces of civil war looming over them, beneath the bright blue June sky, will never forget them.

The St-Antoine barricade was monstrous. It was three storeys high and seven hundred feet wide. Running from corner to corner, it barred the vast approach to this faubourg, that is to say, three streets. Gullied, jagged, indented, craggy, battlemented with a huge notch, buttressed with piles that were themselves bastions, throwing out headlands here and there, powerfully shored up by the two great promontories that were the district's houses, it rose like a Cyclopean dyke at the end of the formidable square that had seen the fourteenth of July. Nineteen barricades were ranged at intervals in the streets extending behind this principal barricade. At the mere sight of it, you sensed in the *faubourg* the immense, agonizing suffering that had reached that ultimate moment when hardship is set to become a catastrophe. Of what was that barricade made? The destruction of three

* 'The dregs of the city [make] the law of the world.'

six-storey houses, purposely demolished, said some. All that stupendous anger, said others. It had the deplorable aspect of all of hatred's edifices: ruin. You might say: Who built this? You might just as well say: Who destroyed this? It was the improvisation of ferment. Here! This door! This grating! This weatherboard! This window-frame! This broken brazier! This cracked pot! Hand it all over! Throw it all on! Push, roll, dig, dismantle, overturn, bring everything down! It was the collaboration of cobblestone, rubble-stone, wooden beam, iron bar, broken tile, bottomless chair, cabbage-stalk, rags, tags, tatters, and execration. It was huge and it was small. It was the abyss directly parodied by the chaos, the mass beside the atom, the torn-down wall and the broken pudding bowl, an ominous fraternization among all kinds of debris. Sisyphus had thrown his rock in there, and Job his pot shard. In a word, dreadful. It was the acropolis of the wretched. Overturned barrows gave the slope ruggedness. An enormous dray-cart lay across it, axle skywards, and looked like a scar on that battered façade. An omnibus, cheerfully hoisted by muscle strength alone to the very top of the pile, as though the architects of this monstrosity wanted to add to terror a gamin's mischievousness, offered its unhitched shaft to what horses of the air no one knows. This gigantic heap, the alluvium of rioting, brought to mind the image of an Ossa on Pelion of all revolutions: '93 on '89, the ninth of Thermidor on the tenth of August, the eighteenth of Brumaire on the twenty-first of January, Vendémiaire on Prairial, 1848 on 1830. This site was worth the effort, and this barricade deserved to appear on the very spot where the Bastille disappeared. If the ocean made dykes, this is how it would build them. The fury of the surging torrent was imprinted on this shapeless mass. What surging torrent? The mob. You fancied you saw a petrified pandemonium. You fancied you heard the enormous sinister bees of violent progress buzzing over this barricade, as if they had their hive there. Was this an overgrown thicket? Was it a bacchanalian orgy? Was it a fortress? Vertigo seemed to have constructed it, with panache. There was something of the cesspool in that redoubt, and something of Olympia in that welter. You could see, in a jumble that spoke of despair, roof rafters, bits of attic with wallpaper on them, window-frames with all their panes planted in the wreckage, awaiting the cannon, detached chimneys, wardrobes, tables, benches, a howling topsy-turvy, and those countless destitute things, rejected even by the beggar, invested with both fury and nothingness. A people's tatters, you would have said, tatters of wood, iron, bronze, stone, as if Faubourg St-Antoine had swept them there, in front of its door, with some colossal broom, making its barricade out of its poverty. Blocks of wood like executioner's blocks, broken chains, wooden frames braced in the shape of a gibbet, horizontal wheels projecting from the wreckage, brought to this edifice of anarchy the dismal image of the old tortures suffered by the people. The St-Antoine barricade made a weapon of everything. Everything that civil war can hurl at society came out of here. This was not fighting, this was paroxysm. The rifles that defended this redoubt, among which were a few blunderbusses, fired fragments of broken crockery, gaming chips, coat-buttons, even the castors off night-stands – dangerous projectiles on account of the brass in them. This barricade was frenzied. It threw up at the clouds an indescribable din. At certain moments, to provoke the army, it resorted to crowd and tumult, and was crowned with a mass of blazing faces, filled with a seething multitude, its crest spiked with guns, sabres, cudgels, axes, pikes and bayonets. A huge red flag on it flapped in the wind. Shouts of command could be heard, songs of attack, the rolling of drums, the sobbing of women and lugubrious bursts of laughter from the famished. Enormous and alive it was, and crackles and sparks emitted from it, as from the back of some electric beast. The spirit of revolution clouded this summit from which roared the voice of the people, which is like the voice of God. A strange majesty emanated from this Titanic mound of rubble. It was a heap of detritus and it was Sinai.

As we said earlier, it attacked in the name of the Revolution – what? – the Revolution. This barricade – this unpredictability, disorder, alarm, misunderstanding, uncertainty – was confronting the Constituent Assembly, the sovereignty of the people, universal suffrage, the nation, the Republic. And it was the 'Carmagnole' defying the 'Marseillaise'.

Senseless but heroic defiance – for hero this old *faubourg* is.

The *faubourg* and its redoubt stood by each other. The *faubourg* sheltered behind the redoubt, the redoubt was backed by the *faubourg*. The vast barricade extended like a cliff on which the strategy of the generals who served in Africa was dashed. Its caverns, its excrescences, its warts, its protuberances grimaced, so to speak, and grinned beneath the smoke. Canister-shot disappeared into the shapelessness. Shells sank into it, were swallowed up and lost in it. All that bullets succeeded in doing was to make holes in it. What was the use of cannonading chaos? And the regiments, accustomed to the most fearsome sights of war, gazed uneasily on that wild beast of a redoubt, a bristling boar of mountainous size.

Not half a mile away, at the corner of Rue du Temple where it joins the boulevard near the Château-d'Eau, if you boldly stuck your head out of the Dallemagne shop-front, which formed one of the projecting points, you could see in the distance, beyond the canal, at the very top of the street that climbs the slopes of Belleville, a strange wall reaching the façades' second storey, a kind of link between the houses on the right and the houses on the left, as though the street had risen up to the height of its highest wall in order to close itself off abruptly. This wall was built of cobblestones. It was plumb-straight, perfectly aligned, precise, perpendicular, squared, level. It probably had no cement but, as with some Roman walls, without detriment to its sturdy architecture. You could tell how thick it was from its height. The coping was exactly parallel with the base. Discernible at intervals in its grey surface were almost invisible loopholes, like black threads. These loopholes were equally spaced. The street was deserted as far as the eye could see. All windows and doors were closed. Rising at the end of the street, this barrier created a dead end. A wall, still and quiet. No one to be seen, nothing to be heard. Not a cry, not a sound, not a breath. A sepulchre.

This terrible thing was bathed in the dazzling June sunlight.

It was the Faubourg du Temple barricade.

As soon as you arrived on the scene and caught sight of it, it was impossible, even for the boldest, not to become thoughtful before this mysterious apparition. It was tightly laid, with staggered joints inter-locked; rectilinear, symmetrical, and louring. Here was the scientific and the sinister. You sensed that the man in charge of this barricade was a surveyor, or a spectre. You looked at it and you spoke in hushed tones.

From time to time, if anyone – soldier, officer or representative of the people – ventured to cross the deserted road, a faint high-pitched whistling sound was heard and that individual would fall dead or wounded, or, if he escaped, you would see a bullet embed itself in a closed shutter, in the gap between two rubble-stones or in the plaster of a wall. Sometimes a biscayen ball. For the men on the barricade had made themselves two small cannons out of two lengths of cast-iron gas piping, plugged at one end with tow and fire-clay. No needless waste of gunpowder. Nearly every shot struck home. There were a few corpses here and there, and pools of blood on the cobbles. I remember a white butterfly coming and going in the street. Summer does not abdicate.

The carriage entrances in the vicinity were crowded with casualties.

You felt targeted by someone you could not see, and you realized the whole length of the street was taking aim.

Massed behind the kind of humpback formed by the arched bridge leading over the canal into Faubourg du Temple, grave and reflective, the soldiers of the attack column watched this dismal redoubt, this stillness, this impassiveness whence came death. Some crawled on their bellies to the top of the bridge's arch, taking care that their shakos did not show above it.

The valiant Colonel Monteynard admired this barricade with a shudder. 'Look how it's built!' he said to a political representative. 'Not one cobblestone juts out beyond another. Porcelain, that is!' At that moment a bullet shattered the cross on his breast, and he fell.

'The cowards!' people said. 'Why don't they show themselves! Let's see them! They daren't! They're hiding!'

The Faubourg du Temple barricade, defended by eighty men, attacked by ten thousand, held out for three days. On the fourth, as at Zaatcha, as at Constantine, the attackers forced their way into the houses, they came over the rooftops, the barricade was taken. Not one of the eighty cowards thought of fleeing, all were killed there, with the exception of the leader, Barthélemy, of whom we shall say more presently.

The St-Antoine barricade was thunderous tumult, the Temple barricade was silence. There was between these two redoubts the difference between the awesome and the sinister. One seemed a maw, the other a mask.

Allowing that the gigantic and tenebrous June insurrection was created out of rage and enigma, you sensed in the first barricade the dragon, and behind the second, the sphinx.

These two fortresses had been erected by two men, one named Cournet, the other Barthélemy. Cournet made the St-Antoine barricade, Barthélemy the Temple barricade. Each barricade was the reflection of the man who built it.

Cournet was a tall man; he had broad shoulders, a red face, a crushing fist, a bold heart, a staunch spirit, a sincere and terrible gaze. Intrepid, energetic, irascible, tempestuous, the most cordial of men, the most formidable of fighters. War, strife, conflict – he was in his element in these situations, and they put him in good humour. He had been a naval officer, and from his gestures and his voice you could tell that he thrived on the ocean and had survived the storm. He took the hurricane into battle with him. There was in Cournet something of Danton without the genius, as there was in Danton something of Hercules without the divinity.

Thin, scrawny, pale, taciturn, Barthélemy was a kind of tragic gamin; struck by a policeman whom he then waylaid and killed, at seventeen he was sent to the prison hulks. He came out and built this barricade.

Later, fatefully enough, in London, where both were political refugees, Barthélemy killed Cournet. It was a fatal duel. Some time afterwards, caught up in one of those mysterious intrigues where passion is involved, calamities in which French justice sees extenuating circumstances and English justice sees only death, Barthélemy was hanged. The bleak social edifice is so designed that, thanks to material poverty, thanks to moral darkness, this hapless individual of some intelligence, an intelligence that was certainly intense, possibly great, started out in the prison hulks in France and ended up on the gallows in England. Barthélemy only ever raised one flag – the black flag.

II
In a Desperate Plight,
*What Else Can You Do But Talk?** *

Sixteen years are significant in the clandestine education of riot, and June 1848 was a great deal wiser than June 1832. So the Rue de la Chanvrerie barricade was only a primitive version, a barricade in embryo compared with the two colossal barricades we have just described, but for its time it was formidable.

The insurgents under Enjolras's supervision – for Marius no longer paid attention to anything – had made good use of the night. The barricade had been not only repaired but enlarged. It had been made two feet higher. Iron bars stuck in between the cobblestones looked like couched lances. All sorts of added debris brought from all around gave it a more intricately meshed exterior. The redoubt had been cleverly reworked into a defence wall on the inside and a tangled thicket on the outside.

The cobblestone staircase that made it possible, as with a citadel wall, to climb the barricade had been restored.

The barricade had been put to rights, the bar room cleared, the kitchen taken over for the treatment of casualties, the tending of the wounded completed, the powder that had been spilled on the ground and on the tables gathered up, bullets cast, cartridges made, linen torn into strips, the weapons of the fallen redistributed, the inside of the redoubt tidied, the wreckage collected, the corpses removed.

They heaped the dead in the Mondétour alleyway, which they still

---

* An allusion to La Fontaine's fable 14, bk 2, 'Le Lièvre et les Grenouilles' (The Hare and the Frogs): 'A hare in its resting-place pondered / (For what else can you do in a resting-place but ponder?)' The fearful hare realizes that it scares the frogs, and concludes that there is no coward on earth who cannot find another more cowardly than himself.

controlled. The paving there was for a long time red. Among the dead were four National Guardsmen from the city outskirts. Enjolras had their uniforms put aside.

Enjolras recommended two hours' sleep. Advice from Enjolras was a command. Still, only three or four of them took his advice. Feuilly devoted those two hours to carving this inscription into the wall opposite the tavern: 'LONG LIVE THE MASSES!'

These four words, chiselled into the masonry with a nail, could still be read on that wall in 1848.

The three women took advantage of the respite of darkness to disappear for good, which meant the insurgents were able to breathe more easily. The women managed to take refuge in some neighbouring house.

Most of the wounded were able and still willing to fight. On a sickbed of mattresses and bales of straw, in the kitchen that had become a first-aid post, were five seriously wounded men, two of whom were Municipal Guards. The Municipal Guards were treated first.

There was nothing left in the bar room but Mabeuf under his black pall and Javert tied to his pillar.

'This is the mortuary,' said Enjolras.

Right at the back of this room, dimly lit by the scant light of a single candle, with the mortuary table behind the pillar like a horizontal bar, Javert standing and Mabeuf lying there created the effect of a sort of big indistinct crucifix.

The omnibus shaft, although shortened by the hail of gunfire, was still left sufficiently intact for a flag to be hung from it.

Enjolras, who had that quality in a leader of always doing what he said he would do, attached to this pole the old man's bullet-riddled and bloodstained coat.

No meal was to be had now. There was neither bread nor meat. The fifty men on the barricade, in the sixteen hours they had spent there, had soon exhausted the tavern's meagre supplies. At a given moment, every barricade that holds out inevitably becomes the raft of the *Medusa*. They had to resign themselves to hunger. It was the early hours of the sixth of June, that Spartan day when surrounded by insurgents asking for bread in the St-Merry barricade, to all those combatants crying 'Something to eat!', Jeanne replied, 'Why? It's three o'clock. We'll be dead by four.'

As they could no longer eat, Enjolras would not allow drinking. He banned wine and rationed the brandy.

They had found in the cellar fifteen full bottles, tightly sealed. Enjolras and Combeferre examined them. When he came up again

Combeferre said, 'It's old stock that Père Hucheloup, who started out as a grocer, had.' 'It must be really good,' remarked Bossuet. 'It's lucky Grantaire's asleep. If he were up and about, we'd have a job saving those bottles.' Despite the murmuring, Enjolras placed his veto on the fifteen bottles, and so that no one touched them and they would be treated as sacred, he had them placed under the table on which Père Mabeuf lay.

About two o'clock in the morning they counted how many they numbered. There were still thirty-seven of them.

It began to grow light. Replaced in its cobblestone niche, the torch had just been put out. The interior of the barricade, that little court-yard of sorts claimed from the street, was steeped in shadow, and in the dreadfulness of that ghostly half-light looked like the deck of a ship in distress. The combatants in their comings and goings were dark figures moving about. Above this terrifying pocket of obscurity the upper floors of the silent houses began to loom wanly. Right at the top, the chimneys were growing paler. The sky was of that lovely inde-terminate shade that might be white and might be blue. Birds in flight gave cries of joy. Facing east, the tall building behind the barricade had a rosy reflection on its roof. At the third-storey window, the morning breeze ruffled the grey hair on the dead man's head.

'I'm delighted the torch has been put out,' Courfeyrac said to Feuilly. 'That torch flickering in the wind was upsetting me. It was as if it were afraid. The light of torches is like the wisdom of cowards: it casts a poor light because of its unsteadiness.'

Dawn wakens the wits as well as the birds. All were chattering.

Seeing a cat prowling on the tiles, Joly waxed philosophical.

'What is the cat?' he exclaimed. 'It's a correction. The good Lord, having made the mouse, said, "Oh dear, that was a mistake!" And he made the cat. The cat is the mouse's erratum. Mouse plus cat are the revised and corrected proofs of creation.'

Surrounded by students and artisans, Combeferre was talking about the dead, Jean Prouvaire, Bahorel, Mabeuf and even Cabuc, and about Enjolras's stern sorrow. He said, 'Harmodius and Aristogei-ton, Brutus, Chaerea, Stephanus, Cromwell, Charlotte Corday, Sand, have all had their moment of anguish after the event. Our hearts are so tremulous and human life is such a mystery that in a case of murder even for the public good, of murder even in the cause of freedom – if such a thing exists – remorse for having killed a man exceeds the joy of having served the human race.'

And a moment later, such are the circuitous routes of conversa-tional exchange, with Jean Prouvaire's verses providing the transition,

Combeferre was comparing the translators of the *Georgics*, Raux with Cournand, Cournand with Delille, referring to the few passages translated by Malfilâtre, particularly the portents at Caesar's death. And with that word 'Caesar', the conversation returned to Brutus.

'Caesar,' said Combeferre, 'was justly brought down. Cicero was harshly critical of Caesar, and he was right to be. That harshness is no diatribe. When Zoilus insults Homer, when Maevius insults Virgil, when Visé insults Molière, when Pope insults Shakespeare, when Fréron insults Voltaire, it is an old law of envy and hatred that is being observed. Genius attracts insult, great men are always more or less subject to carping. But Zoilus and Cicero are two different matters. Cicero metes out justice by the intellect just as Brutus metes out justice by the sword. For my own part, I condemn this latter form of justice, the blade, but antiquity allowed it. Caesar, violator of the Rubicon, bestowing as if they derived from him the dignities that derived from the people, not rising for the Senate, acted, as Eutropius says, like a king and almost like a tyrant, *regia ac poene tyrannica*. He was a great man. Too bad. Or so much the better – the lesson is all the more edifying. His twenty-three wounds affect me less than the spitting in Jesus Christ's face. Caesar is stabbed by the senators. Christ is treated with contempt by lackeys. In the greater outrage you sense the deity.'

Up above the other speakers, on top of a pile of paving-stones, Bossuet, rifle in hand, cried out, 'O Cydathenaeum, O Myrrhinus, O Probalinthus, O graces of the Aeantis! Oh, who will grant that I may deliver Homer's verses like a Greek of Laurium or Aedapteon?'

III

Enlightenment and Gloom

Enjolras had undertaken a reconnaissance sortie. He had slipped out through the Mondétour alleyway, keeping close to the houses.

The insurgents, frankly, were full of hope. The way they had repulsed the night attack made them almost scornful in advance of the dawn attack. They waited for it smiling. They were no more doubtful of their success than of their cause. Moreover, help was of course going to come. They were counting on it. With that tendency to prophesy success that is one of the strengths of the French fighter, they divided the day that was about to begin into three definite phases. At six o'clock in the morning a regiment 'they had been working on' would come over to their side; at noon, the whole of Paris would rise up; at sunset, revolution.

They heard the tolling of St-Merry's, which had not for one minute fallen silent since the previous day, proof that the other barricade, the main one, Jeanne's, was still holding out.

All these hopes were exchanged between one group and another in a sort of eager and frightful whispering that resembled the buzzing of a hive of bees on the warpath.

Enjolras reappeared. He was back from his grim, eagle's excursion into the outer darkness. He listened for a moment to all this joy, with his arms folded, one hand over his mouth. Then, fresh and rosy in the increasingly pale light of dawn, he said, 'The whole Paris army is out. The weight of a third of that army is being brought to bear on the barricade where you are. As well as the National Guard. I identified the shakos of the 5th of the Line and the colours of the 6th Legion. You'll be attacked in an hour's time. As for the people, yesterday they were in ferment, but this morning they're not stirring. Nothing to expect, nothing to hope for. Neither a regiment, nor still less a *faubourg*. You've been abandoned.'

These words, falling on that buzzing among the groups, had the effect of the first raindrop of a storm on a swarm of bees. Everyone fell silent. There was a moment of unutterable quiet in which death might have been heard passing over.

That moment was brief. A voice from the groups' obscurest depths cried out to Enjolras, 'So be it. Let's raise the barricade to a height of twenty feet, and all of us stay here. Citizens, let our dead bodies protest. Let's demonstrate that, while the people may abandon the Republicans, the Republicans do not abandon the people.'

These words dispelled from everyone's mind the oppressive gloom of individual anxieties. They were met with enthusiastic cheering.

No one ever knew the name of the man who had spoken them. He was some unacknowledged worker, unidentified, forgotten, a passing hero, that nameless champion always involved in human crises and social turning-points who at a given moment says the decisive word in a superlative way, and then disappears into the shadows, having momentarily, in a flash of lightning, represented the people of God.

This unshakeable resolve was so much in the air on the sixth of June 1832 that almost at the very same time the insurgents on the St-Merry barricade were raising that shout that has gone down in history and was recorded in the subsequent legal proceedings: 'What does it matter whether anyone comes to our aid or not? Let every last one of us be killed here.'

As we can see, the two barricades, though physically separated, were communicating with each other.

IV
Five Fewer, One More

After the nameless man advocating 'the protest of the dead bodies' had spoken, thereby giving expression to the common feeling, from every mouth came a strangely satisfied and terrible cry, grim in meaning and triumphant in tone, 'Long live death! We shall all stay!'

'Why all?' said Enjolras.

'All! All!'

Enjolras went on: 'The position is good, the barricade is solid. Thirty men are enough. Why sacrifice forty?'

They replied, 'Because not one is willing to leave.'

'Citizens,' cried Enjolras, and there was in his voice an almost irritated resonance, 'the Republic is not rich enough in men to be needlessly extravagant with them. Vainglory is wasteful. If it is the duty of some to leave, that duty must be fulfilled like any other.'

Enjolras, principle incarnate, had over his co-religionists an omnipotence of the kind that emanates from the absolute. Yet that omnipotence notwithstanding, a murmur arose. A leader to his very fingertips, Enjolras, seeing there was murmuring, insisted.

He said disdainfully, 'Let those who are afraid of being not more than thirty say so.'

The murmuring intensified.

'Anyway,' said a voice in one group, 'leaving is easier said than done. The barricade is surrounded.'

'Not on the side of Les Halles,' said Enjolras. 'Rue Mondétour is free, and you can reach the Marché des Innocents via Rue des Prêcheurs.'

'And there,' said another voice, 'you'll be captured. You'll run into some picket of line troops or guards from the outskirts. They'll see a man going by wearing overalls and a cap. "You there, where have you come from? Weren't you on the barricade?" And they'll look at your hands. "You smell of gunpowder." Executed.'

Without replying, Enjolras tapped Combeferre's shoulder, and they both went into the bar room.

They came out again a moment later. Enjolras held in his two outstretched hands the four uniforms he had put aside. Combeferre followed him, carrying the leather belts and shakos.

'In this uniform,' said Enjolras, 'mingle with the ranks and you escape. That's four, at least.'

And he threw the four uniforms down on the ground from which the cobblestones had been removed.

Among those stoical listeners there was not the slightest wavering. Combeferre began to speak.

'Come now, we must have a little pity,' he said. 'You know what's at issue here? What's at issue is women. Just consider. Are there women, yes or no? Are there children, yes or no? Are there mothers rocking cradles with their foot, and a whole brood of little ones around them, yes or no? Any one of you who has never seen the breast of a nursing woman, raise his hand. Ah! you want to get yourselves killed, and as I stand here talking to you, I do too. But I don't want to sense around me the spectres of women wringing their hands. Die, that's fine, but don't cause others to die. Suicides like the one that is about to take place here are sublime, but suicide has a narrow compass that is not to be broadened. And as soon as it affects your family, suicide is murder. Think of the fair-haired youngsters, and think of the white-haired old folk. Listen. A little while ago, Enjolras has just told me, he saw at the corner of Rue du Cygne a lighted casement, a candle at a humble fifth-floor window, and on the glass the quivering shadow of someone's head, that of an old lady who appeared to have been sitting up all night, waiting. Perhaps she's the mother of one of you. Well, that man should leave, and hurry home to tell his mother, "Mother, here I am!" He needn't worry, the job here will get done anyway. When it's your work that's supporting your family, you've no right to sacrifice yourself. Desertion of your family, that is. And those who have daughters, and those who have sisters! What are you thinking of? You get yourselves killed, then you're dead, fine – and tomorrow? Young girls with nothing to eat, that's terrible. A man begs, a woman sells. Ah! these delightful creatures, so charming and so gentle, who wear flowery bonnets, who sing, who chatter, who fill the house with chastity, who are like a living fragrance, who prove the existence of angels in heaven by the purity of virgins on earth, this Jeanne, this Lise, this Mimi, these adorable and respectable individuals who are a blessing to you, who are your pride, oh my God, they'll go hungry! What can I say to you? There is a market for human flesh, and it's not with your ghostly hands fluttering around them that you'll prevent them from becoming part of it! Think of the street, think of the pavement thronged with passers-by, think of the shops and the women to-ing and fro-ing in front of them, revealingly clothed, women who have gone to the bad. Those women, too, were pure once. Think of your sisters, those of you who have them. Misery, prostitution, police patrols, St-Lazare, that's what they'll be reduced to, those lovely delicate girls, those fragile marvels of modesty, kindness and beauty, fresher than lilacs in the month of May. Ah, you've got yourselves killed! Ah, you're not there any more! That's fine. You wanted to deliver the people from royalty, and you hand your young girls over to the police. Friends, beware! Have some compassion! We're not given to thinking about women very much. Poor women! We put our trust in the fact that women don't get the education that men do, we prevent them from reading, we prevent them from thinking, we prevent them from being involved in politics. Will you prevent them from going to the morgue this evening to identify your bodies? Now then, those who have families must do the decent thing, shake hands with us and go, and leave us here to deal with this on our own. I know that it takes courage to go, it's hard, but the harder it is, the more praiseworthy. You say: "I have a gun, I'm at the barricade, too bad, I'm staying here." "Too bad" is easily said. My friends, there is a tomorrow, you won't be here for that tomorrow, but your families will. And the suffering! Look, a fine healthy child with apple cheeks, who babbles, who prattles, who chatters, who laughs, whose smell you breathe in when you kiss him – you know what happens to him when he's abandoned? I've seen one like him, a tiny little thing, just so high. His father was dead. He was taken in out of charity by poor people, but they had no bread for themselves. The child was always hungry. It was winter. He didn't cry. You'd see him go up to the stove, where there was never any fire, and the stove pipe was sealed, you know, with yellow clay. The child would pick off a bit of this clay with his little fingers and eat it. His breathing was raspy, his face ashen, his legs weak, his stomach swollen. He said nothing. When you spoke to him, he didn't answer. He died. He was brought to the Necker Hospital to die – that's where I saw him. I was house-physician at that hospital. Now, if there are any fathers among you, fathers whose joy it is to go for a stroll on Sundays holding their child's little hand in their own good strong hand, let every one of those fathers picture to himself that child as his own. That poor little mite, I remember him, I seem to see him now, when he lay naked on the autopsy table, his ribs protruding under his skin like the grass-covered mounds in a cemetery. There was some sort of mud found in his stomach. There was ash in his teeth. Now, let's examine our consciences and allow our hearts to advise us. Statistics demonstrate that the mortality rate among abandoned children is fifty-five per cent. I repeat, what is at issue here is women, what is at issue is mothers, what is at issue is young girls, what is at issue is little kiddies. Is it you we're talking about? We know what you are. We know that you're all courageous men, by God! We know that you all set your minds on the joy and the honour of sacrificing your life for the great cause. We know that you feel you've been chosen to die usefully and magnificently, and that each one of you is determined to have his share of the glory. Good for you! But you're not alone in this world. There are others you have to think of. You must not be selfish.'

All bowed their heads sombrely.

Strange contradictions of the human heart in its most sublime moments. Combeferre, who was saying these things, was not an orphan. Mindful of other men's mothers, he forgot his own. He was going to get himself killed. He was 'selfish'.

Deprived of sustenance, feverish, all his hopes exhausted, one after the other, mired in grief, most dismal of all plights, overwhelmed by violent emotions and sensing that the end was coming, Marius had plunged deeper and deeper into that visionary stupor that always precedes the hour of death willingly accepted.

A physiologist might have studied in him the growing symptoms of that febrile state of absorption known to science, and analysed by it, which is to suffering what voluptuousness is to pleasure. Despair, too, has its ecstasy. Marius had reached that stage. It was as if he were watching everything from the outside. As we said, things happening right in front of him seemed to him far away. He could get a sense of the overall picture but he could not see any details. He saw people coming and going through a blazing brightness. He heard voices speaking as if from the bottom of a pit.

However, he was moved by this. This scene had a point to it that pierced even him, and roused him. He had only one thought now, to die, and he did not want to be distracted from it. But in his morbid somnambulism he thought that in going to his doom there was no ban on saving someone else.

He spoke up.

'Enjolras and Combeferre are right,' he said. 'No unnecessary sacrifice. I agree with them, and there's no time to lose. Combeferre has said what matters. There are some among you who have families, mothers, sisters, wives, children. They should step forward.'

No one stirred.

'Married men and family breadwinners, step forward!' repeated Marius.

He had great authority. Enjolras was certainly leader of the barricade, but Marius was its saviour.

'I command you,' cried Enjolras.

'I entreat you,' said Marius.

Then, stirred by Combeferre's speech, unsettled by Enjolras's command, moved by Marius's entreaty, these heroic men began to denounce each other.

'It's true,' said one young man to an older one, 'you're the father of a family. Go.'

'You'd better go yourself,' replied the man, 'you have two sisters to provide for.'

And an extraordinary argument broke out. Each vied to be the one who would not be turned away from the tomb.

'Hurry,' said Courfeyrac, 'in another quarter of an hour it will be too late.'

'Citizens,' said Enjolras, 'this is the Republic, here universal suffrage rules. You yourselves nominate those who are to leave.'

They obeyed. After a few minutes, five were unanimously selected and came forward.

'Five of them!' exclaimed Marius.

There were only four uniforms.

'Well then,' the five responded, 'one of us must stay.'

And each vied to be the one who stayed, finding reasons for the others not to stay. The generous quarrel began afresh.

'You have a wife who loves you.'

'You have your aged mother.'

'You've lost both father and mother, what's to become of your three little brothers?'

'You're the father of five children.'

'You have a right to live, you're only seventeen, it's too early for you to die.'

These great Revolutionary barricades were venues for heroism. The improbable was natural here. These men did not surprise each other.

'Be quick,' repeated Courfeyrac.

Voices in the groups shouted to Marius, 'You say who's to stay!'

'Yes,' said the five, 'you choose. We'll do as you say.'

Marius no longer believed himself capable of any feeling. Yet, at the thought of selecting a man to die, the blood drained back to his heart. He would have turned pale, if he could have been any paler than he was.

He moved towards the five, who smiled at him; and every one of them, his eyes filled with that great blaze to be seen far back in history over Thermopylae, cried out to him, 'Me! Me! Me!'

And stupidly, Marius counted them. There were still five! Then he looked down on the four uniforms.

At that moment a fifth uniform dropped on top of the other four, as if from heaven. The fifth man was saved.

Marius looked up and recognized Monsieur Fauchelevent. Jean Valjean had just arrived inside the barricade.

Either because he had made inquiries, or by instinct, or by chance, he came by way of the Mondétour alleyway. Thanks to his National Guard uniform, he had passed unhindered.

The lookout posted by the insurgents in Rue Mondétour had no need to raise the alarm for a lone National Guardsman. He let the latter turn into the street, saying to himself, 'He's probably another supporter, or at worst a prisoner.' This was too serious a moment for the lookout to allow his attention to be diverted from his duties or from his observation post.

When Jean Valjean had entered the redoubt, no one had noticed him, all eyes being fixed on the five chosen men and the four uniforms. Jean Valjean himself had seen and heard, and he silently took off his coat and threw it on the pile with the rest.

The ferment was indescribable.

'Who is this man?' asked Bossuet.

'He's a man who saves others,' replied Combeferre.

Marius added in a solemn voice, 'I know him.'

This guarantee satisfied everyone.

Enjolras turned to Jean Valjean. 'Citizen, welcome.' And he added, 'You know we're going to die.'

Without replying, Jean Valjean helped the insurgent he was saving to put on his uniform.

V

The Outlook from the Top of the Barricade

The plight of all, in that fateful hour and in that implacable place, had as issue and pinnacle Enjolras's supreme melancholy.

Enjolras had within him the plenitude of the Revolution. He was incomplete, however, in so far as the absolute can be. He was too much like Saint-Just, and not enough like Anacharsis Cloots. Yet in the Society of the Friends of the ABC his mind had eventually come under the influence of Combeferre's ideas. He had for some time been gradually departing from the narrowness of dogma and giving way to the expansiveness of progress, and he had come to accept, as a definitive and magnificent evolution, the transformation of the great French Republic into a vast human republic. As for the direct means to achieve it, given a violent situation, he chose violence. In that, he never varied. And he was still of that epic and fearsome school encapsulated in this word: 'ninety-three'.

Enjolras was standing on the cobblestone staircase, with one of his elbows resting on the barrel of his gun. He was thinking. He shuddered, as if at passing emanations; places of death have these oracular effects. In that inward-turned gaze were smouldering fires. All at once he raised his head; with his blond hair swept back like that of the angel on the dark chariot of stars, it had the look of a lion's mane fanned out in a flaming aureole.

And Enjolras cried: 'Citizens, do you visualize the future? The streets of cities bathed in light, green branches on the doorsteps, nations become sisters, men become just, old men blessing the young, the past cherishing the present, total freedom for thinkers, full equality for believers, for religion the firmament, God the unmediated priest, human conscience the altar, no more hatred, fraternity in workshop and school, reputation for sole punishment and reward, work for all, rights for all, peace for all, no more bloodshed, no more wars, happy mothers! The taming of matter is the first step. The creation of the ideal is the second. Reflect on what progress has already accomplished. Long ago, seeing before them the hydra that breathed on the waters, the dragon that vomited fire, the griffin that was the monster of the air, flying with the wings of an eagle and the claws of a tiger – fearsome beasts that were superior to man – the earliest human races looked on in terror. Yet man laid his traps, the sacred traps of intelligence, and with them eventually caught these monsters.

'We have tamed the hydra, and it is called the steamer. We have tamed the dragon, and it is called the locomotive. We are on the verge of taming the griffin, it is already in our possession, and it is called the balloon. The day when this Promethean work is done and man has finally harnessed to his will the threefold chimera of antiquity – hydra, dragon and griffin – he will be master of water, fire and air, and he will be to the rest of living creation what the ancient gods once were to him. Courage, and ever onward! Citizens, what lies ahead of us? Science made the principle of government, force of circumstance become the sole police force, natural law having its own inherent sanction and penalty and promulgating itself by evidence, a dawning of truth corresponding to the dawning of day. Ahead lies the unity of peoples, ahead lies the unity of mankind. No more fictions, no more parasites. Reality governed by truth, that is the goal. Civilization will hold its conclaves at Europe's summit, and later the centre of continents, in a great assembly of intelligence. Something of the like has already been seen. The amphictyons held two sittings a year, one at Delphi, site of the gods, the other at Thermopylae, site of heroes. Europe will have her amphictyons, the globe will have its amphictyons. France carries in its womb this sublime future. This is the gestation of the nineteenth century. What Greece began is worthy of being completed by France.

'Listen to me, Feuilly, valiant worker, man of the people, man of the peoples. I revere you. Yes, you see the future clearly, yes, you are right. You had neither father nor mother, Feuilly. You adopted humanity as your mother and right as your father. You're going to die here – in other words, to triumph. Citizens, whatever happens today, by our defeat just as much as by our victory, what we are going to achieve is a revolution. As fires light up a whole city, so revolutions give light to the whole human race. And what revolution shall we bring about? I've just told you, the revolution of Truth. From the political point of view there is only one principle: man's sovereignty over himself. This sovereignty of the self over the self is called Liberty. In the formation of an alliance between two or three of these sovereignties is the beginning of the State. But in this alliance there is no abdication. Each sovereignty concedes a certain amount of itself to form the sovereign law to which all are subject. That amount is the same for all. This uniformity of the concession each individual makes to all is called Equality. The sovereign law to which all are subject is nothing other than the protection of all deriving from the right of each individual. This protection of all over each individual is called Fraternity. The point of intersection between all these allied sovereignties is called Society. This intersection being a juncture, the point in question is a nexus. Hence what is called "the social bond". Some say "social contract", which is the same thing, the word "contract" being etymologically formed from the notion of binding. Let's be clear what we mean by equality. For, if liberty is the summit, equality is the base. Equality, citizens, doesn't mean vegetation all of one height, a society of huge blades of grass and tiny oak trees, a collective of mutually emasculating jealousies. It is, in civil terms, all who have the same aptitude having the same opportunity; in political terms, all votes having the same weight; in religious terms, all consciences having the same right. Equality has an agency: free and compulsory education. The right to the alphabet, that's where to start. Primary schooling imposed on all, secondary schooling offered to all, that's the rule of law. From identical schooling will come an equal society. Yes, teaching! Light! Light! Everything comes from light, and returns to it. Citizens, the nineteenth century is a great century, but the twentieth century will be a happy one. Nothing like the history of old – not any more. There'll be no reason then to fear, as we do today, conquest, invasion, usurpation, rivalry between armed nations, civilization interrupted by a marriage of kings, a birth within the hereditary tyrannies, a partition of peoples by congress, dismemberment brought about by the collapse of a dynasty, a conflict between two religions coming up against each other, like two goats of darkness on the bridge of infinity. There'll be no reason to fear famine, exploitation, prostitution as a result of poverty, destitution as a result of unemployment, and the sword, and the scaffold, the battles, and all the banditry of chance in the forest of incidents. You might almost say there will be no more incidents. People will be happy. Just as the terrestrial globe fulfils its own law, so too will the human race. Harmony will be re-established between soul and star. The soul will revolve around the truth, as the star revolves around light. Friends, the present moment in which I'm speaking to you is a grim moment. But these are the terrible costs of the future. A revolution is a toll. Oh! the human race will be delivered, raised up, consoled! On this barricade, we assure it of that. From where will the cry of love come, if not from the height of sacrifice? Oh my brothers, this is the juncture between those who think and those who suffer. This barricade is made not of cobblestones, or rafters, or ironmongery. It's made of two piles – a pile of ideas and a pile of woes. Here, misery meets the ideal. Here, day embraces night and tells it: "I'm going to die with you, and you are going to be born again with me." Faith springs from embracing every desolation. Sufferings bring here their agony, and ideas their immortality. This agony and this immortality are about to combine and constitute our death. Brothers, he who dies here dies in the radiance of the future, and we go to a grave pervaded through and through by the light of dawn.'

Enjolras broke off rather than stopped talking. His lips moved silently as if he were continuing, talking to himself, which meant that, trying to hear more, they watched him attentively. There was no applause, but the whispering went on for a long time. The spoken word being breath, the thrilling of minds is like the rustling of leaves.

VI
Marius Haggard, Javert Laconic

Let us convey what was going on in Marius's mind.

Remember what his mental state was. As we have just been reminded, nothing was real to him any more. His perceptions were blurred. Marius, it must be emphasized, was under the shadow of the great dark wings that spread out over those in their death throes. He felt he had entered the tomb, it seemed to him he was already on the other side of the wall, and he could no longer see the faces of the living other than through the eyes of one who was dead.

How was it that Monsieur Fauchelevent was there? Why was he there? What had he come for? Marius did not ask himself all these questions. For our despair has the characteristic of enveloping others as well as ourselves, so it seemed logical to him that everyone should come here to die.

Only, he felt a pang in his heart when he thought of Cosette.

In any case, Monsieur Fauchelevent did not speak to him, did not look at him, and did not even seem to hear him when Marius spoke up to say, 'I know him.'

As far as Marius was concerned, this attitude of Monsieur Fauchelevent was a relief to him, and if such a word may be used for such impressions we would say, pleasing to him. He had always found it quite impossible to speak to this enigmatic man who was for him both ambiguous and imposing. Moreover, he had not seen him for a very long time, which for someone of Marius's timid and reserved nature made it even more impossible.

The five chosen men left the barricade by way of the Mondétour alleyway. They looked just like National Guards. One of them went away weeping. Before leaving, they embraced those who were staying.

When the five men restored to life had gone, Enjolras turned his attention to the man sentenced to death. He went into the bar room. Javert, tied to his pillar, was thoughtful.

'Need anything?' Enjolras asked him.

Javert replied, 'When will you kill me?'

'You'll have to wait. Right now we need all our cartridges.'

'Then I'll have something to drink,' said Javert.

Enjolras himself fetched a glass of water, and as Javert was bound hand and foot he held the glass for him.

'Is that all?' said Enjolras.

'It's uncomfortable against this pillar,' replied Javert. 'You didn't show much consideration leaving me here all night. Tie me if you want, but you could surely lay me down on a table, like him.'

And he nodded in the direction of Monsieur Mabeuf's body.

There was, remember, at the end of the room a big, long table on which they had been casting bullets and making cartridges. Now that all the cartridges were made and all the powder used up, this table was free.

At Enjolras's command, four insurgents untied Javert from the pillar. While they were untying him, a fifth held a bayonet to his breast. His arms were left tied behind his back, and thin, strong whipcord was put round his feet, allowing him to take fifteen-inch steps like those going to the scaffold; and he was walked to the table at the end of the room where he was laid down, closely bound around the middle of his body.

As an extra precaution, to the complexity of knots that made escape impossible they added, by means of a rope secured around his neck, the kind of restraint, in prisons called a martingale, that goes from the nape of the neck, divides over the belly and returns to the hands after passing between the legs.

While they were trussing up Javert, a man standing at the threshold studied him with peculiar attention. The shadow cast by this man made Javert turn his head. He looked up and recognized Jean Valjean. Without a flicker of emotion he proudly closed his eyes and said only, 'It's so simple.'

VII
The Situation Worsens

It was rapidly growing lighter. But no window or door opened, not even a chink. It was dawn, but not an awakening. As we said earlier, the far end of Rue de la Chanvrerie, opposite the barricade, had been evacuated by the troops. It appeared to be clear, and in its sinister quiet lay open to passers-by. Rue St-Denis was as silent as the Avenue of the Sphinxes at Thebes. Not a living soul at the crossroads that lay bleached in reflected sunlight. There is nothing so mournful as this brightness of deserted streets.

Nothing could be seen, but something could be heard. There was at a certain distance some mysterious movement going on. It was obvious the critical moment was approaching. As on the previous evening, the lookouts fell back, but all of them this time.

The barricade was stronger than when the first attack took place. Since the five had left, it had been built up even higher.

On the advice of the lookout who had been watching the area of Les Halles, Enjolras, for fear of a surprise attack from behind, took a serious decision. He had the Mondétour alleyway, which had been left open until then, barricaded. For this an additional stretch of paving, the length of several houses, was taken up. Consequently, the barricade, walled off on three streets, on Rue de la Chanvrerie straight ahead, on Rue du Cygne and de la Petite-Truanderie to the left, on Rue Mondétour to the right, really was almost impregnable. True, those on the inside were inevitably confined. Now it had three fronts but no exit.

'A fortress mousetrap,' said Courfeyrac, laughing.

Enjolras had some thirty cobblestones – 'pulled up unnecessarily', said Bossuet – stacked near the door of the tavern.

So profound was the silence now in the direction from which the attack was to come that Enjolras had everyone return to battle stations. A ration of brandy was distributed to each individual.

There is nothing more curious than a barricade preparing for an assault. Everyone chooses a place for himself, as if at the theatre. Settling down, shouldering and elbowing each other. There are some who create stalls for themselves out of cobblestones. Here is an awkward corner of wall; move away from it. Here is a bastion that may afford protection; shelter behind it. The left-handed are valuable – they take places that are awkward for others. Many contrive to fight seated, wanting to be at their ease for killing and comfortable for dying. In the dreadful war of June 1848, one insurgent, who was a formidable marksman and fought from a rooftop terrace, had a high-backed armchair brought up there for him. He was sitting in it when he was hit by canister-shot.

As soon as the leader has given the order to clear the decks for action, all disorderly movement ceases. No more wrangling with each other, no more factions, no private conversations, no separate group. Whatever is in everyone's mind converges and turns into anticipation of the attack. A barricade preceding danger: chaos; in danger: discipline. Peril creates order.

As soon as Enjolras had taken up his double-barrelled rifle and positioned himself at a battlement of sorts that he had reserved for himself, everyone fell silent. A flurry of little sharp cracks rang out along the cobblestone wall. It was the cocking of guns.

Now the men stood prouder and more confident than ever. Extreme sacrifice strengthens. They had no hope left, but they had despair. Despair, the ultimate weapon that sometimes brings victory. Virgil said so.* Out of drastic resolve comes supreme resourcefulness. To embark on death is sometimes the way to avoid foundering. And the coffin lid becomes a life-saver.

As on the previous evening, all attention was focused, we might almost say brought to bear, on the end of the street, now visible in the daylight.

There was not long to wait. Renewed stirring was clearly detectable in the St-Leu district, but this was not the same sort of movement that had characterized the first attack. The spilling of chains, the

---

* 'Moriamur et in media arma ruamus. / Una salus victis, nullam sperare salutem' ('Let us die and hurl ourselves into the midst of battle. / The only salvation for the defeated is to have no hope of salvation'), *Aeneid*, bk II, lines 353–4.

unnerving progress of some juddering mass, the clink of brass boun-
cing on the pavement – a sort of orderly commotion – announced that
some sinister piece of ironware was approaching. There was a tremor
in the entrails of those quiet old streets, laid out and built for the fruitful circulation of interests and ideas, and not meant for the monstrous
rumble of war.

The fixedness with which all the combatants kept staring at the far
end of the street grew ferocious. A cannon appeared.

Artillerymen pushed the gun up. It was in its firing trunnion-holes.
The limber had been detached. Two men supported the gun-carriage,
with four at the wheels, others followed with the ammunition chest.
The lighted match could be seen smoking.

'Fire!' shouted Enjolras.

The whole barricade fired, the detonation was terrible. An avalanche of smoke enveloped both cannon and men, obliterating them.
After a few seconds the cloud dispersed, and the cannon and the men
reappeared. Slowly, precisely, unhurriedly, the gun crew finished rolling the cannon into position, opposite the barricade. Not one of them
had been hit. Then the chief gunner, pressing down on the breech in
order to raise the elevation, began to aim the cannon with the gravity
of an astronomer training a telescope.

'Bravo, cannoneers!' cried Bossuet.

And the whole barricade applauded. A moment later, squarely sited
right in the middle of the street, straddling the gutter, the piece was in
firing position. A tremendous maw gaped over the barricade.

'Now the fun starts!' said Courfeyrac. 'What a brute! After the
flick of the fingers, the bunched fist. The army's reaching out for us
with its big paw. The barricade's going to be seriously shaken. Rifle-
fire gropes, cannon-fire grabs.'

'It's an eight-pounder, new model, bronze,' added Combeferre.
'The proportion ten parts tin to a hundred parts copper has only to be
exceeded by a fraction, and those guns are liable to explode. Too
much tin makes them too brittle. They end up with pits and cavities
inside the barrel. To avoid that danger and to be able to increase the
charge, it might be better to return to the fourteenth-century tech-
nique of hooping, encircling the piece on the outside from the breech
to the trunnions with a series of weldless steel bands. Meanwhile, any
defect is dealt with as best it can be. Any pits or cavities in the cannon
barrel are detected by means of a "cat's paw". But there's a better
method, with Gribeauval's *étoile mobile*.'

'In the sixteenth century,' remarked Bossuet, 'cannons were rifled.'

'Yes,' replied Combeferre, 'that increases ballistic power but diminishes accuracy. Furthermore, at short range, the trajectory lacks the desired stability, it curves too much, the projectile's path is no longer straight enough to allow it to hit all intervening objects – an essential requirement in battle and one whose importance increases with the enemy's proximity and the rapidity of fire. This lack of stability in the trajectory of the projectile fired from the rifled cannon of the sixteenth century was due to the weakness of the charge. Weak charges for that sort of weapon are dictated by ballistic considerations, such as preserving the gun-carriage. In short, the cannon, despot that it is, can't do everything it wants to. Strength is a great weakness. A cannon-ball travels only fifteen hundred miles an hour. Light travels a hundred and eighty thousand miles a second. Such is the superiority of Jesus Christ over Napoleon.'

'Reload your weapons,' said Enjolras.

How would the barricade hold up under cannon-fire? Would it be breached? That was the question. While the insurgents reloaded their guns, the artillerymen loaded the cannon.

Anxiety in the redoubt was intense. The gun went off, the detonation resounded.

'Here!' cried a cheerful voice.

And just as the cannon-ball came down on the barricade, so too did Gavroche drop down inside it. Arriving from the Rue du Cygne side, he had nimbly climbed over the secondary barricade facing the Petite-Truanderie maze.

Gavroche's impact inside the barricade was greater than the cannon-ball's.

The cannon-ball disappeared in the jumble of rubble. At most it smashed an omnibus wheel and finished off Anceau's old cart. Seeing which, the barricaders started to laugh.

'Carry on!' Bossuet shouted to the artillerymen.

VIII

The Gunners Have to Be Taken Seriously

Gavroche was the centre of attention. But he had no time to tell his story. Quaking, Marius took him aside.

'What are you doing here?'

'Well!' said the child. 'What about you?'

And, his eyes widened by the proud gleam within them, he steadily held Marius's gaze with a heroic brazenness.

It was in a severe tone that Marius went on. 'Who told you to come back? Did you at least deliver my letter to its destination?'

Gavroche was not without a touch of remorse regarding that letter. In his hurry to return to the barricade, he had got rid of it rather than delivered it. He was obliged to admit to himself that he had entrusted it somewhat lightly to that stranger, not even having been able to see his face clearly. True, the man was bareheaded, but that was insufficient. In short, he chided himself about it and feared Marius's reprimands. To get out of trouble, he adopted the simplest strategy: he lied abominably.

'Citizen, I delivered the letter to the porter. The lady was asleep. She'll get the letter when she wakes.'

Marius had two objectives in sending that letter: to bid farewell to Cosette and to save Gavroche. He had to settle for half of what he wanted.

Were the sending of his letter and the presence of Monsieur Fauchelevent in the barricade connected? he wondered.

He pointed out Monsieur Fauchelevent to Gavroche.

'Do you know that man?'

'No,' said Gavroche.

As we have just recalled, Gavroche had seen Jean Valjean only in the dark.

The vague and pathological suspicions that had started to form in Marius's mind faded. What did he know of Monsieur Fauchelevent's opinions? Monsieur Fauchelevent was probably a Republican. If so, his presence in this conflict was quite simple.

Meanwhile, Gavroche was already at the other end of the barricade, shouting, 'My gun!' Courfeyrac saw to it that he got it back.

Gavroche warned 'the comrades', as he called them, that the barricade was surrounded. He had had great difficulty in reaching it. A line battalion with their arms piled up in Petite-Truanderie had them under observation on the Rue du Cygne side. On the opposite side, Rue des Prêcheurs was held by the Municipal Guard. In front of them they had the bulk of the army.

Having conveyed this information, Gavroche added, 'You've my permission to give them a thrashing.'

Meanwhile, at his battlement, listening out, Enjolras kept watch.

Doubtless not very happy with their roundshot, the assailants had not repeated it.

A company of line infantry had occupied the end of the street behind the gun. The soldiers were taking up the roadway and using the cobblestones to build a low defence wall, a kind of epaulment no more than eighteen inches high, facing the barricade. At the corner to the left of this epaulment could be seen the head of a column formed by a battalion from the city outskirts, massed in Rue St-Denis.

On the alert, Enjolras thought he detected that distinctive sound made when canister-shells are taken out of ammunition chests, and he saw the chief gunner alter the aim and move the mouth of the cannon slightly leftwards.

Then the cannoneers began to load the gun. The chief gunner himself seized the linstock and brought it to the touch-hole.

'Heads down, close to the wall!' shouted Enjolras. 'And all of you, on your knees along the barricade!'

Scattered in front of the tavern, the insurgents who had left their battle stations when Gavroche turned up made a desperate rush for the barricade. But before Enjolras's order could be carried out, the gun went off with the terrifying rattle of canister-shot. Which is exactly what it was.

The blast had been directed at the gap in the redoubt, had ricocheted against the inside wall, and this terrible ricochet had resulted in two dead and three wounded. If this went on, the barricade could no longer be held. Canister-shot was finding its way in. There was a murmur of dismay.

'Let's stop the second blast, at least!' said Enjolras.

And lowering his rifle, he took aim at the chief gunner, who at that moment was bent over the breech, making one last correction to the laying of the gun.

This chief gunner was a handsome artillery sergeant, extremely young, blond, with a very kindly face and the look of intelligence fitting in one who was in charge of this fateful and dangerous weapon of horror which, if ever more refined, must eventually kill off war.

Combeferre, standing beside Enjolras, observed the young man.

'The pity of it!' said Combeferre. 'How appalling such slaughter is! Well, when there are no more kings, there'll be no more war. Enjolras, you're aiming at that sergeant, you're not looking at him. Believe it or not, he's a charming young man, he's brave, you can see he's capable of thought – they're very educated, these young artillerymen – he has a father, a mother, a family, he probably has a sweetheart, he's twenty-five at most, he could be your brother.'

'He is,' said Enjolras.

'Yes,' replied Combeferre, 'and mine too. So let's not kill him.'

'Don't interfere. What must be, must be.'

And a tear trickled slowly down Enjolras's marble cheek.

At the same time he pressed the trigger of his rifle. There was a flash. The artilleryman spun round twice, his arms stretched out in front of him, his head tipped back, as though gasping for breath; then he fell sideways on to the gun and lay there motionless. A stream of blood could be seen gushing from the middle of his back. The bullet had gone straight through his chest. He was dead.

He had to be carried away and replaced. This was indeed a few minutes gained.

IX
Using Those Old Poaching Skills and the Infallible Shot That Had Some Bearing on a Conviction in 1796

An exchange of opinion took place inside the barricade. The cannon was going to start firing again. With those canister-shells, they would be unable to hold out for as much as fifteen minutes. A buffer against them was absolutely essential.

Enjolras issued this command: 'We need to put a mattress there.'

'We have none spare,' said Combeferre, 'the wounded are lying on them.'

Jean Valjean, who was sitting apart on a boundary-stone at the corner of the tavern with his gun between his knees, until that moment had not been involved in anything that was happening. He seemed not to hear the combatants saying around him, 'There's a gun doing nothing.'

Responding to Enjolras's directive, he rose.

Remember, when the crowd arrived in Rue de la Chanvrerie, an old woman, anticipating bullets, had put her mattress in front of her window. This window, an attic window, was in the roof of a six-storey house a little beyond the barricade. The mattress, set crosswise, was supported underneath by two poles for hanging out washing and held up by two ropes that from a distance looked like two pieces of string, attached to nails in the window-frame. These ropes could be seen distinctly against the sky, like two hairs.

'Can someone lend me a double-barrelled rifle?' said Jean Valjean.

Enjolras, who had just reloaded his, handed it to him. Jean Valjean took aim at the attic window and fired. One of the two mattress ropes was severed. The mattress now hung by just a single thread. Jean Valjean fired another shot. The second rope whipped against the window-pane. The mattress slipped between the two poles and fell into the street. The barricade applauded. Every voice cried out, 'A mattress!'

'Yes,' said Combeferre, 'but who will go and fetch it?'

Sure enough, the mattress had fallen outside the barricade, between the besiegers and the besieged. Now, the death of the artillery sergeant having infuriated the troop, the soldiers for the past several minutes had been lying flat on their stomachs behind the line of cobblestones they had set up, and to compensate for the enforced silence of the cannon, quieted while its gun crew was being reorganized, had opened fire on the barricade. So as to save their ammunition, the insurgents did not reply to this rifle-fire. The fusillade was deflected by the barricade, but the street, filled with its bullets, was an inferno.

Jean Valjean went through the gap, out into the street under the hail of bullets, reached the mattress, picked it up, loaded it on to his back and returned to the barricade.

He himself plugged the mattress into the gap. He wedged it there against the wall so that the artillerymen could not see it.

That done, they waited for the canister-shot. It was not long in coming.

With a roar, the cannon vomited its pack of pellets. But there was no ricochet. The canister-shot aborted on the mattress. The envisaged effect had been achieved. The barricade was saved.

'Citizen,' Enjolras said to Jean Valjean, 'the Republic thanks you.'

Bossuet, marvelling, laughed. 'It's outrageous that a mattress should have so much power!' he cried. 'A triumph of yielding over battering! But never mind, all glory to the mattress that nullifies a cannon!'

X
Dawn

At that moment Cosette woke up.

Her room was narrow, neat, modest, with a long, east-facing casement window looking out on the back courtyard of the house.

Cosette knew nothing of what was going on in Paris. She had not been out the day before and had already retired to her room when Toussaint said, 'There seems to be trouble.'

Cosette had slept not many hours, but soundly. She had been having sweet dreams, which might have had something to do with the fact that her little bed was very white. Someone who was Marius had appeared to her in a blaze of light. She woke with the sun in her eyes, which at first gave her the impression of this being a continuation of her dream.

Her first thought on emerging from this dream was joyful. Cosette felt completely reassured. Like Jean Valjean a few hours earlier, she was undergoing that reaction of a spirit that is dead set against unhappiness.

She began to hope with all her might, without knowing why. Then her heart sank. It was three days since she had last seen Marius. But she said to herself that he must have received her letter, that he knew where she was, and that he was so clever he would find some way of reaching her. Today, for sure, perhaps that very morning. It was broad daylight, but by the very horizontal slant of the light she thought it was early; all the same, she had better get up, to receive Marius.

She felt she could not live without Marius; and consequently, that was sufficient, Marius would come. No objection was allowed. All this was certain. It was monstrous enough already to have suffered for three days. Three days without Marius was horrible of the good Lord. This cruel teasing from on high was a trial that was now over. Marius was going to arrive, and he would bring good news. That is the nature of youth. It quickly dries its eyes. It finds sorrow pointless and does not accept it. Youth is the smile of the future in the face of the unknown, which is its own self. It is natural for youth to be happy. It is as though it breathes hope.

Anyway, Cosette could not remember what Marius had said to her about this absence that was to last only one day, and what explanation he had given her for it. Everyone has noticed how niftily a coin that you drop on the ground rolls away and hides, and how cunningly it makes itself unfindable. There are thoughts that play the same trick on us. They curl up in a corner of our brains. And that's it, they are gone. Impossible to call them to mind. Cosette was rather cross with her memory for the futile little effort it made. She told herself it was very naughty and unforgivable of her to have forgotten anything Marius had said.

She got out of bed and performed two ablutions, of body and soul, washing herself and saying her prayers.

It is just about acceptable for a reader to be taken into a bridal chamber, but not into a young virgin's room. Verse would scarcely dare to do so, prose must not.

It is the retreat of a still-unopened flower, it is a whiteness in the shade, it is the inner sanctum of a closed lily that so long as the sun has not looked on it must not be looked on by a man. A woman in bud is sacred. That innocent bed with the covers thrown back, that adorable semi-nudity fearful of itself, that white foot taking refuge in a slipper, that bosom concealing itself in front of a mirror as if that mirror were an eye; that chemise hurriedly pulled on, at the creaking of a piece of furniture or the passing of a carriage, so as to hide a shoulder; those ribbons tied, those hooks fastened, those laces drawn, those tremors, those little shivers of cold and modesty, that exquisite fluster in every movement, that almost winged agitation where there is nothing to fear, the successive layers of clothing as charming as the dawn clouds – it is quite improper for any of this to be recounted, and it is already going too far even to mention it.

A man's eye must be even more reverential at a young girl's rising than at the rising of a star. The possibility of attainment should turn into increased respect. The down on the peach, the bloom on the plum, the prismatic snow crystal, the powdery butterfly-wing, are coarse things beside that chastity that does not even know it is chaste. A young girl is only a glimmer of a dream, and not yet a statue. Her bedchamber is hidden in the shadowy part of the ideal. The indiscreet feel of a glance violates this vague half-light. Here, to gaze upon is to profane.

We shall, therefore, show none of all that delightful little bustle that accompanied Cosette's awakening.

An oriental tale relates that the rose was made white by God, but that Adam having watched as it opened, it was ashamed and turned crimson. We are among those who feel awed in the presence of young girls and of flowers, finding them sacred.

Cosette dressed very quickly, combed and arranged her hair, which was an extremely simple matter in those days when women did not fill out their curls and tresses with pads and rolls, and did not put crinolines on their heads. Then she opened the window and let her eyes roam all about her, hoping to light upon some little bit of the street, the corner of a building, a patch of cobblestones, and to be able to watch out for Marius coming that way. But nothing of what was outside could be seen. The rear courtyard was enclosed by fairly high walls, with a view only of a few gardens. Cosette declared these gardens to be hideous: for the first time in her life, she found flowers ugly. The smallest stretch of gutter at the crossroads would have been much more to her liking. She opted to look up at the sky, as if she thought Marius might also come from there.

Suddenly she burst into tears. Not because of some fickleness of feeling; but, her hopes dashed by despondency, because of her plight. She had a vague sense of something dreadful. Things do, after all, affect the atmosphere. She told herself that she was sure of nothing, that to lose sight of each other was to lose each other. And the idea that Marius could actually return to her from the heavens seemed to her no longer delightful, but macabre.

Then, such are these clouds, calm returned to her – and hope, and a smile of sorts that was unconscious but trusting in God.

Everyone else in the building was still in bed. A provincial silence reigned. Not a single shutter was open. The porter's lodge was closed. Toussaint was not up, and Cosette quite naturally thought her father was asleep. She must have suffered a great deal, and been suffering still, for she told herself that her father had been unkind. But she was relying on Marius. The eclipse of such a light was quite impossible. She prayed. Now and then she heard some sort of dull thuds a certain distance away, and she said, 'How odd that anyone should be opening and shutting carriage gates so early.' It was the cannon-fire battering the barricade.

A few feet below Cosette's window, on the wall's blackened old cornice, was a swifts' nest. The nest's roundness projected a little beyond the cornice, so that from above it was possible to look into this little paradise. The mother was there, her wings fanned out over her brood. The father flitted about, flying off, then coming back again with food and kisses in his beak. The dawning light gilded this thing of gladness; here, joyful and awesome, was that great law, Multiply; and that sweet mystery flourished in the glory of the morning. Her hair in the sunlight, her soul lost in reverie, illuminated by love within and by dawn without, Cosette leaned over as if instinctively, and almost without daring to admit to herself that she was thinking at the same time of Marius, began to observe these birds, this family, this male and this female, this mother and her young, with the profound discomfiture that a nest imparts to a virgin.

XI

The Shot That Never Misses and Kills No One

The assailants' onslaught continued. Rifle-fire and canister-shot alternated, without actually causing much damage. Only the Corinthe's upper façade suffered. Riddled with canister-shot and bullets, the window on the first floor and the dormer windows in the roof were slowly being destroyed. The combatants who had been posted there had been forced to take cover. This, in fact, is a tactic for attacking barricades: to sustain fire so as to exhaust the insurgents' ammunition if they make the mistake of firing back. When you can tell from the slackening of their response that they have run out of gunpowder and bullets, you take them by storm. Enjolras had not fallen into this trap. The barricade held its fire.

At every volley, Gavroche thrust his tongue in his cheek, a sign of utter contempt.

'Go on,' he said, 'let rip! We need bandages.'

Courfeyrac jeered at the canister-shot for its neglible effect and addressed the cannon: 'You're overextending yourself, old boy!'

There is as much intrigue involved in battle as there is in the ball-room. It is likely that this silence from the redoubt began to unnerve the besiegers and make them fear some unexpected turn of events, and they may well have felt the need to see through this mound of cobble-stones, to know what was going on behind this impassive wall that was being fired on but not responding. Suddenly, the insurgents noticed a helmet glinting in the sunlight on a neighbouring roof. A fireman stood resting against a tall chimney-stack, apparently there as a lookout. He had a view right down inside the barricade.

'There's an unwelcome observer,' said Enjolras.

Jean Valjean had returned Enjolras's rifle but he had his own gun.

Without a word, he took aim at the fireman, and a second later the helmet, struck by a bullet, fell clattering into the street. The panic-stricken soldier was quickly gone.

A second observer took his place. This one was an officer. Jean Valjean, who had reloaded his gun, took aim at the newcomer and sent the officer's helmet to join the soldier's. The officer did not persist, and speedily withdrew. This time the warning was understood. No one else appeared on the roof, and spying on the barricade was given up as a bad job.

'Why didn't you kill the man?' Bossuet asked Jean Valjean.

Jean Valjean did not reply.

XII
Disorder Upholds Order

Bossuet muttered in Combeferre's ear, 'He didn't answer my question.'

'He's a man who does good deeds with a gun,' said Combeferre.

Those who have retained some memory of this already distant period know that the outer-city National Guard proved its mettle against the insurrections. It fought particularly fiercely and valiantly in the days of June 1832. Any self-respecting tavern-keeper in Pantin, Des Vertus or La Cunette whose 'establishment' was closed down by the riots grew bold as a lion at the sight of his deserted dance-hall and got himself killed so as to preserve the order represented by the out-skirts' pleasure gardens. In those days, at once bourgeois and heroic, when ideas had their crusaders, mercenary interests had their champions. The prosaic nature of the motive detracted nothing from the valour of the gesture. Diminishing stacks of gold and silver coin had bankers singing the 'Marseillaise'. Men would lyrically shed their blood for the sake of trade, and with Lacedaemonian fervour defend that great *patria* in miniature, the shop.

Basically, it must be said, there was nothing to laugh about, this was all very serious. These were social elements in conflict with each other, pending the day when they will be in harmony.

Another sign of the times was anarchy combined with governmentalism (the barbarous term for the establishment party).

People were in favour of order with unruliness. Suddenly, the drum would beat a call to arms, at a command given on impulse by some colonel of the National Guard. On the spur of the moment, some captain would leap into action; some National Guardsman would fight 'by conviction' and on his own account. In the moments of crisis during 'those days', men were guided not so much by their leaders as by their instincts. In that army for law and order were some real irregulars: those of the sword like Fannicot, those of the pen like Henri Fonfrède.

Civilization, unfortunately represented at that time more by a conglomeration of interests than by a group of principles, was, or believed itself to be, in peril. It sounded the alarm. Each individual, taking centre stage, defended it, aided it and protected it as he saw fit. And all and sundry took it upon themselves to save society.

Zeal sometimes went as far as extermination. A platoon of National Guardsmen would on its own authority set itself up as a court martial, and would sit in judgement and execute within five minutes any insurgent taken prisoner. It was an ad hoc body of this sort that had killed Jean Prouvaire. That ferocious Lynch law for which no party is entitled to castigate any other, since it is applied by the republic in America as well as by the monarchy in Europe. This Lynch law was fraught with misapprehension. On one day of rioting, a young poet named Paul-Aimé Garnier was chased in Place Royale with a bayonet at his back, and only escaped by taking refuge in the carriage gateway of number six. People shouted, 'That's another of those Saint-Simonians!' And they tried to kill him. The fact was, he was carrying under his arm a volume of the Duc de Saint-Simon's memoirs. A National Guardsman had read the words 'Saint-Simon' on the book and shouted, 'Death to the Saint-Simonian!'

On the sixth of June 1832, a company of National Guards from the city outskirts, commanded by the above-mentioned Captain Fannicot, out of sheer caprice and wifulness contrived to get themselves decimated in Rue de la Chanvrerie. Peculiar as the incident was, it was confirmed by the judicial investigation into the insurrection of 1832.

Captain Fannicot, a bold and impatient bourgeois, a sort of *condottiere* of law and order, one of those we have just characterized, a fanatical and unruly governmentalist, could not resist the temptation to open fire prematurely or his ambition of capturing the barricade on his own, that is to say, with his company. Infuriated by the successive appearance of the red flag and the old coat that he mistook for the black flag, he openly criticized the generals and senior officers who were still deliberating, who thought that the moment had not yet come for a decisive assault, and were letting the insurrection 'stew in its own juices', to use the celebrated expression of one of them. He himself thought the barricade was ripe, and since whatever is ripe ought to fall, he gave it a try.

He commanded men as resolute as himself, 'wild men', a witness said. His company, the one that had shot the poet Jean Prouvaire, was at the head of the battalion posted at the corner of the street. Just when it was least expected, the captain sent his men against the barricade. This move, carried out with more eagerness than strategy, cost Fannicot's company dear. Before it was two-thirds down the street it met with a volley of fire from the barricade. Four of them, the most audacious, who were running ahead, were struck down within point-blank range at the very foot of the redoubt, and this courageous mob of National Guards, very brave men but lacking in military tenacity, had to fall back, after some hesitation, leaving fifteen corpses in the street. That momentary hesitation gave the insurgents time to reload their weapons, and a second and most deadly volley overtook the company before it could regain shelter at the corner of the street. At one point it was caught in the crossfire, sustaining casualties inflicted by its own artillery, which, not having received the order, had not stopped firing. The intrepid and reckless Fannicot was one of those killed by this shelling. He was killed by the cannon, that is to say, by law and order.

More furious than serious, this attack annoyed Enjolras. 'The fools!' he said. 'They're getting their own men killed and using up our ammunition for nothing.'

Enjolras spoke like the true insurgency general that he was. Insurrection and repression do not fight with equal weapons. Soon drained, insurrection has only a certain number of shots to fire and a certain number of combatants to expend. An empty cartridge box, a man killed, cannot be replaced. Having the army at its disposal, repression keeps no count of men, and having Vincennes, it keeps no count of shots. Repression has as many regiments as the barricade has men, and as many arsenals as the barricade has cartridge boxes. So these are conflicts of one against a hundred, which always end with the crushing of the barricade – unless revolution, suddenly breaking out, throws into the balance its archangel's flaming sword. This does happen. Then the whole place is up in arms, the streets erupt, the people's redoubts are everywhere, Paris thrills in its sovereignty, the *quid divinum* emerges, a tenth of August is in the air, a twenty-ninth of July is in the air, a wonderful light appears, the gaping jaws of might draw back, and the lion that is the army sees standing serenely before it the prophet that is France.

XIII
Fleeting Glimmers

In the chaos of sentiments and passions that defend a barricade, there is everything: bravery, youth, integrity, enthusiasm, idealism, conviction, the addiction of the gambler and, above all, intermittent hopefulness.

One of those vague frissons of such intermittent hope suddenly ran through the Chanvrerie barricade at the most unexpected moment.

'Listen,' came an abrupt cry from Enjolras, always on the alert, 'I think Paris is rousing itself.'

It is unquestionable that during the morning of the sixth of June there was for an hour or two some sort of renewed outbreak of insurrection. The persistent tolling of St-Merry's revived some fanciful notions. Attempts were made to build barricades in Rue du Poirier and Rue des Gravilliers. At the St-Martin gate, a lone young man armed with a rifle attacked a squadron of cavalry. Out in the open, in the middle of the boulevard, he went down on one knee, brought his weapon up to his shoulder, fired, killed the squadron commander, then turned away, saying, 'That's another one who won't do us any more harm.' He was cut down with the sword. In Rue St-Denis, a woman fired on the Municipal Guard from behind a lowered blind. The slats of the blind could be seen vibrating at every shot. A fourteen-year-old child was arrested in Rue de la Cossonnerie with his pockets full of cartridges. Several police stations were attacked. At the entrance to Rue Bertin-Poirée, a very lively and quite unexpected volley of gunfire greeted a regiment of cuirassiers, General Cavaignac de Baragne marching at their head. In Rue Planche-Mibray bits of old broken crockery and household utensils were thrown down from the rooftops on to the soldiers. A bad sign. And when this incident was reported to Marshal Soult, Napoleon's old lieutenant grew thoughtful, remembering Suchet's words at Saragossa: 'When old women empty their chamber-pots on our heads, we're doomed.'

These general symptoms that presented themselves just when the uprising was thought to have been localized, this renewed outbreak of feverish anger, these sparks flying here and there above those dense masses of combustibility called the Paris *faubourgs* – all this had the military chiefs worried. There was a rush to quench these embryonic fires. The attack on the Maubuée, Chanvrerie and St-Merry barricades was delayed until these sparks had been snuffed out, so as to have nothing but the barricades to deal with, to be able to finish everything off at one fell swoop. Columns were sent out into the ferment, sweeping through the main streets, probing the little streets to right and left, now slowly and cautiously, now charging down them. Troops broke open the doors of buildings from where shots had been fired. At the same time cavalry manoeuvres dispersed gatherings on the boulevards. This repression was not implemented without some uproar or without that tremendous commotion typical of clashes between the army and the people. This is what Enjolras had noted in the intervals between cannon- and rifle-fire. Moreover, at the end of the street he had seen casualties passing by on stretchers, and he said to Courfeyrac, 'Those casualities are none of our doing.'

That hope was short-lived; that glimmer, quickly eclipsed. In less than half an hour what was in the air was gone, like a flash of lightning without thunder, and the insurgents felt descending on them again that cloak of lead, as it were, which the people's indifference casts over forsaken diehards.

The general unrest that seemed to have been brewing had come to nothing, and the minister of war's attention and the generals' strategy could now concentrate on the three or four barricades left standing.

The sun was coming up over the horizon.

An insurgent called out to Enjolras, 'We're hungry here! Are we really going to die like this, without getting anything to eat?'

Still at his battlement, without taking his eyes off the end of the street Enjolras nodded.

XIV
In Which You Will Read the Name of
Enjolras's Mistress

Seated on a paving-stone beside Enjolras, Courfeyrac continued to jeer at the cannon, and every time that sinister cloud of projectiles called canister-shot passed overhead, making its monstrous sound, he greeted it with an outburst of sarcasm.

'You're wearing your lungs out, you poor old brute, it makes me feel sorry for you, you're shouting yourself hoarse! That's not thunder, that's a cough!'

And everyone around him laughed.

Courfeyrac and Bossuet, whose valiant good humour increased with the danger, like Madame Scarron, replaced nourishment with wit, and in the absence of wine dispensed cheerfulness to all.

'I admire Enjolras,' said Bossuet. 'His impassive temerity astounds me. He lives alone, which makes him perhaps a little sad. Enjolras complains of his greatness, which binds him to widowerhood. The rest of us more or less all have mistresses who drive us mad, that is to say, embolden us. When a man is like a tiger in love, the least he can do is fight like a lion. This is one way of taking our revenge for our lady grisettes' infidelities. Orlando gets himself killed to annoy Angelica. All our heroism comes from our women. A man without a woman is a pistol without a hammer. It's the woman that fires the man. Well, Enjolras has no woman. He's not in love, and he manages to be intrepid. It's an extraordinary thing for someone to be as cold as ice and as ardent as fire.'

Enjolras seemed not to be listening, but anyone near him would have heard him mutter to himself, '*Patria*'.

Bossuet was still laughing when Courfeyrac cried out, 'Something new!' And assuming the tone of an usher who announces arrivals, he added, 'My name is Eight-Pounder.'

A new character had indeed just come on the scene. It was a second gun. The artillerymen rapidly manoeuvred the heavy ordnance into place, ready to fire alongside the first gun. This was the beginning of the end.

A few minutes later the two guns, briskly operated, were firing at the redoubt directly in front of them; the artillery was supported by rifle-fire from troops of the line and units from the outskirts.

Another cannonade could be heard some way off. At the same time that the two guns were blasting away at the Rue de la Chanvrerie redoubt, two other cannons, one set up in Rue St-Denis, the other in Rue Aubry-le-Boucher, were bombarding the St-Merry barricade. The four cannons echoed each other lugubriously.

The dark dogs of war were responding to each other's barking.

Of the two guns now battering the Rue de la Chanvrerie barricade one was firing canister-shells, the other cannon-balls.

The gun firing cannon-balls was elevated a little, and the line of fire was calculated so that the cannon-ball hit of the upper ridge of the barricade, took the top off it, and brought down on the insurgents a hail of shot-like shattered cobblestones.

The object of this method of firing was to drive the insurgents back from the top of the redoubt and force them to huddle together on the inside. In other words, this heralded the assault.

Once the insurgents were driven back from the top of the barricade by cannon-ball and from the windows of the tavern by canister-shot, the attacking columns would be able to venture into the street without being picked off, perhaps even without being seen, quickly scale the redoubt as on the preceding evening and – who knows? – take it by surprise.

'The harassment from those guns has simply got to be reduced,' said Enjolras, and he shouted, 'Fire on the artillerymen!'

All were ready. The barricade, which had so long been silent, erupted in a frenzy, firing seven or eight volleys in succession with a kind of rage and joy. The street filled with blinding smoke and after a few minutes, through this flame-streaked haze, two-thirds of the gunners could be dimly made out lying under the wheels of the cannons. Those left standing continued with an austere calm to operate the guns, but the rate of fire had slackened.

'That's better,' Bossuet said to Enjolras. 'Success!'

Enjolras shook his head and replied, 'Another quarter of an hour of this success, and there won't be as many as a dozen cartridges left in the barricade.'

Gavroche apparently overheard this remark.

XV
Gavroche Outside

Courfeyrac suddenly caught sight of someone at the foot of the barricade, outside in the street, under the bullets.

Gavroche had taken a bottle basket from the tavern, slipped out through the gap, and was placidly emptying into his basket the full cartridge pouches of the National Guardsmen who had been killed on the redoubt's rampart.

'What are you doing there?' asked Courfeyrac.

Gavroche looked up. 'I'm filling my basket, citizen.'

'Can't you see the gunfire?'

Gavroche replied, 'Well, it's raining. So what?'

Courfeyrac shouted, 'Come back inside!'

'In a minute,' said Gavroche.

And with a bound, he was off down the street.

Remember, Fannicot's company had left behind a trail of bodies. Some twenty corpses lay scattered here and there on the cobblestones down the whole length of the street. Twenty cartridge pouches for Gavroche. A supply of cartridges for the barricade.

The smoke hung in the street like a fog. Anyone who has seen a cloud lying in a mountain gorge between two sheer cliff-faces can imagine this smoke trapped and, as it were, its density increased by two dismal rows of tall buildings. It slowly drifted upwards and was constantly replaced, creating a gradual obscurity that dimmed even broad daylight. Short as the street was, the combatants could hardly see each other from one end to the other.

This obscurity, probably welcomed and taken into account by the commanders who were to direct the assault on the barricade, was useful to Gavroche.

Under cover of this veil of smoke and thanks to his small size, he was able to make his way quite far down the street without being seen. He emptied the first seven or eight cartridge pouches without much danger.

He crawled on his stomach, galloped on all fours, carried his basket in his teeth, twisted, crept, wriggled, wormed his way from one dead body to another, and emptied the cartridge box or pouch like a monkey opening a nut.

On the barricade, which he was still quite close to, they dared not call him back for fear of attracting attention to him.

On one body, that of a corporal, he found a powder flask.

'For when supplies run dry,' he said, putting it in his pocket.*

Ever advancing, he reached the point where the fog of the fusillade thinned out. So that the sharpshooters of the line, on the lookout behind their cobblestone defence wall, and the sharpshooters from the outskirts massed at the corner of the street, suddenly pointed out to each other something moving in the smoke.

Just as Gavroche was removing the cartridges from a sergeant lying near a boundary-stone, a bullet hit the dead body.

'I'll be blowed!' exclaimed Gavroche. 'Someone's trying to kill my corpses.'

A second bullet struck a spark on the cobblestones beside him. A third overturned his basket. Gavroche looked and saw that this was the outer city firing.

He stood up straight, his hair caught in the wind, his hands on his

---

* A powder flask in French is *une poire* (literally, 'a pear', from the shape) *à poudre*. Gavroche is playing on the expression *garder une poire pour la soif* (literally, 'to put aside a pear for thirstiness' sake', i.e. to keep something in reserve for hard times to come).

hips, his eyes fixed on the National Guardsmen who were firing, and he sang:

> They're so ugly in Nanterre,
> For that, blame Voltaire;
> And numbskulls in Palaiseau,
> For that, blame Rousseau.

Then he picked up his basket, put back into it the cartridges that had fallen out, not losing a single one; and advancing towards the gunfire, he went and emptied another cartridge pouch. A fourth bullet missed him, yet again. Gavroche sang:

> I'm no lawyer, I swear,
> For that, blame Voltaire;
> I'm just a little sparrow,
> For that, blame Rousseau.

A fifth bullet succeeded only in extracting from him a third verse.

> I'm devil-may-care,
> For that, blame Voltaire;
> A pauper I am, though,
> For that, blame Rousseau.

This went on for some time.

It was a dreadful and enchanting spectacle. Gavroche under fire was teasing the rifles. He seemed to be enjoying himself tremendously. Here was the sparrow pecking at the bird-hunters. To every volley he responded with another verse. They kept firing at him, and they kept missing. The National Guardsmen and the soldiers laughed as they took aim. He would lie down, spring to his feet, hide in the corner of a doorway, then skip off, disappear, reappear, scamper away, come back, respond to the gunfire by thumbing his nose at it, and all the while pillaging cartridges, emptying pouches and filling his basket. Breathless with anxiety, the insurgents followed him with their eyes. The barricade trembled. He sang. He was not a child, he was not a man, he was a strange gamin-fairy. He might have been described as the invulnerable dwarf of the fray. The bullets chased after him, he was nimbler. He played some ghastly game of hide-and-seek with death. Every time the spectre's noseless face came near, the gamin flicked it away.

One bullet, however, better aimed or more treacherous than the others, finally struck that will-o'-the-wisp child. Gavroche was seen to stagger, then he collapsed. The whole barricade gave a cry. But there was something of Antaeus in that pygmy. Touching the street for the gamin was like touching the ground for the giant. Gavroche had fallen only to rise again. He sat up, a long trickle of blood streaked his face, he raised both arms in the air, looked in the direction from where the shot had come, and began to sing:

> I've fallen down, I declare,
> For that, blame Voltaire,
> In the gutter, brought so low,
> For that, blame . . .

He did not finish. A second bullet from the same marksman cut him short. This time he fell face forward on to the paving and moved no more. That great little soul had just flown.

XVI
How Being a Brother Turns into Being a Father

At that same moment, in the Luxembourg Gardens – for the eyes of the drama must be everywhere – there were two children holding hands. One might have been seven years old, the other five. Having got wet in the rain, they were walking along the paths in the sunshine. The older one led the little one. They were pale and ragged. They had a look of wild birds about them. The younger one said, 'I'm really hungry.'

The older one, already somewhat protective, led his brother with his left hand and in his right hand carried a small stick.

They were alone in the gardens. The gardens were deserted, the gates had been closed by order of the police because of the insurrection. The troops who had been bivouacked there had gone off to deal with the unrest.

How did those children come to be there? Perhaps they had escaped from some guard-room whose door was left ajar. Perhaps somewhere in the vicinity, at the Enfer toll-gate or on Esplanade de l'Observatoire, or at the nearby crossroads dominated by the façade of a building on which could be read *invenerunt parvulum pannis involutum**, there

---

* 'They shall find a child wrapped in swaddling clothes', an allusion to Luke 2:12, in which the angel who appears to the shepherds in Bethlehem, announ-

was an itinerant entertainers' booth from which they had fled. Perhaps they had eluded the garden wardens at closing time the previous evening and spent the night in one of those shelters where people read newspapers? The fact is, they were wandering about and apparently at liberty. To be wandering about and apparently at liberty is to be lost. These poor little ones were indeed lost.

These two children – the reader will remember them – were the very same ones that Gavroche had taken under his wing. Children of the Thénardiers, hired out to La Magnon, passed off as Monsieur Gillenormand's, and now leaves fallen from all those rootless branches and skittered over the ground by the wind. The clean clothes they wore in La Magnon's day, and which served her as a warranty with regard to Monsieur Gillenormand, had become ragged.

These individuals were now included in the figures for 'Abandoned Children' registered, rounded up, lost and found again by the police on the streets of Paris.

Only because of the confusion of a day like that were those poor little mites in those gardens. If the wardens had spotted them, they would have driven such riff-raff out. Little paupers do not go into public gardens. Yet it ought to be considered that, as children, they have a right to flowers.

These two were here thanks to the gates being closed. They were here in contravention of the regulations. They had slipped into the gardens and stayed. Closed gates do not mean that wardens are off duty, surveillance is supposed to continue, but it slackens, and takes a rest. And the wardens, they too affected by the public anxiety and more concerned about what was going on outside than inside, were no longer watching the gardens and had not seen the two trespassers.

It had rained the day before and even a little during the morning. But in June, showers do not matter. You can hardly tell, an hour after a storm, that this fair beauty, the day, has wept. The earth in summer dries as quickly as a child's cheek.

At the time of the solstice the light of high noon is, as it were, aggressive. It takes in everything. It overlies the earth and attaches itself to it with a kind of suction. It is as if the sun were thirsty. A shower is a glass of water, a downpour is immediately imbibed. In the morning everything was dripping, in the afternoon everything is dusty.

cing the birth of Christ, gives them this sign. The foundling foundation that Hugo is referring to was housed in what had been a convent with a chapel dedicated to the Holy Childhood of Jesus Christ, bearing this inscription.

There is nothing so wonderful as foliage washed by the rain and dried by the sun – it is a warm freshness. The gardens and meadows, with water in their roots and sunshine in their flowers, become incense-holders, releasing all their fragrances at once. Everything smiles, sings, offers itself. You feel gently intoxicated. Springtime is a temporary paradise, the sun helps man to be patient.

There are those who ask for nothing more, who, being alive and having the azure of heaven, say, 'That's enough!' Stargazers absorbed in the wonder of nature, drawing from their idolatrous worship of it an indifference to good and evil. Contemplators of the cosmos, radiantly unmindful of man, who do not understand that anyone would bother about the hunger of these people, the thirst of those others, the nakedness of the poor in winter, the lymphatic curvature of a little spine; about the pallet, the garret, the prison cell or the rags of shivering young girls, when they could be daydreaming beneath the trees. Serene and terrible spirits, pitilessly content. Strangely enough, for them, the infinite suffices. Of that great need of man for the finite, which admits of human embrace, they know nothing. To the finite, which admits of progress, that sublime toil, they give no thought. The indefinite, born of the combination, human and divine, of infinite and finite, goes unnoticed by them. Provided they are face to face with immensity, they smile. Never joy, always ecstasy. To lose themselves is what they live for. For them, the history of humanity shows only the distribution of individual lots. The overall view is missing. The truly all-important is left out. 'What's the use of worrying about man, that mere detail? Man suffers, that may be so. But just look at Aldebaran rising! The mother has no more milk, the new-born babe is dying, of that I know nothing, but just observe this marvellous rosette formation of a slice of pinewood examined under the microscope! Compare the most beautiful Mechlin lace with that!' These thinkers forget about loving. The Zodiac has such an impact on them that it prevents them from seeing the weeping child. God eclipses their souls. There is a type of mind like this, at once great and small. Horace was one, so was Goethe, La Fontaine perhaps. Magnificent egoists of the infinite, calm spectators of sorrow who fail to see Nero if the weather is fine, from whom the sun hides the execution pyre, who would look for an effect of the light in a guillotining, who hear neither the cry, nor the sob, nor the groan, nor the tolling bell; for whom everything is fine since there is a month of May, who as long as there are clouds of crimson and gold overhead declare themselves content, and are determined to be happy until starlight and birdsong come to an end.

These are dark radiances. They have no idea that they are to be pitied. As indeed they are. He who sheds no tears does not see. These people are to be admired and pitied, as you would pity and admire a being embodying both night and day, with no eyes beneath its eyebrows but with a star in the middle of its forehead.

The indifference of these thinkers is, according to some, a superior philosophy. That may well be. But in this superiority there is infirmity. It is possible to be immortal and yet to be crippled: witness Vulcan. It is possible to be more than man and less than man. Imperfect immensity exists in nature. Who knows whether the sun is not blind?

But then what? In whom are we to trust? *Solem quis dicere falsum audeat?** So even certain geniuses, certain humans Most High, man-stars, could be mistaken? What is set on high, at the pinnacle, the summit, the zenith, what casts so much light on earth, might have limited vision, poor vision, no vision at all? Is this not cause for despair? No. But then what is there above the sun? The deity.

Lonely and unfrequented at about eleven o'clock in the morning on the sixth of June 1832, the Luxembourg Gardens were delightful. Exchanging sweet fragrances, the quincunxes and ornamental borders dazzled each other in the light. Crazed in the midday brilliance, the branches seemingly strove to embrace each other. There was in the sycamores a hullaballoo of linnets, sparrows exulted, woodpeckers hopped up chestnut trees, giving little pecks with their beaks at holes in the bark. The flowerbeds accepted the legitimate royalty of lilies. The noblest of perfumes is one that emanates from whiteness. The peppery smell of carnations was in the air. Marie de' Medici's old crows were playing lovebirds in the tall trees. The sun gilded, encrimsoned and set alight the tulips; every type of flame turned into flowers – tulips are nothing else but this. All around the banks of tulips danced the bees, sparks from those flame-flowers. All was charm and delight, even the impending rain. This threatened rain, from which the lilies of the valley and the honeysuckle were to benefit, was no cause for disquiet. The danger of low-flying swallows was enchanting. Anyone there breathed in happiness. Life smelled fragrant. All this nature exuded candour, comfort, caress, succour, paternity, dawn. The thoughts that fell from heaven were as sweet as a child's small hand to one's kiss.

White and naked, the statues under the trees were robed in shadow rent with light. These goddesses were clothed all in tatters of sunshine. Sunbeams hung from them on every side. Around the ornamental

* 'Who dares to say the sun lies?', Virgil's *Georgics*, bk I, lines 463–4, a motto often used on sundials.

pond the ground was already so dry, it was almost scorched. There was enough breeze to raise here and there little flurries of dust. A few yellow leaves, left from last autumn, gamin-like, merrily chased each other.

This abundance of light had something indescribably reassuring about it. Life, sap, heat, fragrances overflowed. Beneath creation could be sensed the vastness of the source. In all these exhalations imbued with love, in this back-and-forth of reverberation and reflection, in these extraordinarily unstinting sunbeams, in this endless outpouring of liquid gold, could be sensed the prodigality of the inexhaustible. And behind this splendour, as behind a curtain of flame, could be glimpsed God, that millionaire of stars.

Thanks to the sand, there was not a speck of mud. Thanks to the rain, there was not a fleck of ash. The bouquets had just been washed. All the velvets, all the satins, all the varnishes, all the golds that spring from the earth in the form of flowers were flawless. This magnificence was immaculate. The great silence of joyful nature filled the garden. A celestial silence compatible with all sorts of music, cooing nests, humming swarms, fluttering breezes. The full harmony of the season was expressed in gracious accord, with spring's entrances and exits taking place in requisite order. The lilacs were finishing, the jasmines beginning. Some flowers were late, some insects early. The vanguard of June's red butterflies fraternized with the rearguard of May's white ones. The plane trees were growing their new bark. The breeze created billows in the magnificent enormity of the chestnut trees. It was splendid. Looking through the railings, an old soldier in the nearby barracks remarked, 'Spring's presenting arms in full dress uniform.'

The whole of nature was breakfasting. Creation was at table. It was time to eat. The great blue tablecloth was spread in the sky, and the great green tablecloth on the earth. The sun cast a brilliant light. God was serving the universal meal. Every creature had its forage or fodder. The wood pigeon found hempseed, the chaffinch found millet, the goldfinch found chickweed, the robin found worms, the bee found flowers, the fly found infusoria, the greenfinch found flies. Certainly, there was some feeding off each other, that is the mystery of evil mingled with good; but not a single creature had an empty stomach.

The two little strays had come close to the pond and, a little disturbed by all this light, they tried to hide, an instinct of the poor and the weak in the presence of magnificence, even when that magnificence is impersonal. And they lurked behind the swan-house.

Now and then, at intervals, when the wind dropped, could be heard a vague confusion of shouts, rumblings, tumultuous rattlings of a sort – volleys of gunfire – and dull thuds – cannon discharges. There was smoke above the rooftops in the direction of Les Halles. A church bell rang in the distance, like a summons.

The children seemed not to notice these sounds. The little one repeated faintly from time to time, 'I'm hungry.'

At almost the same moment as the children, another couple approached the pond. This couple consisted of a fellow aged fifty leading by the hand a lad of six. Father and son, no doubt. The six-year-old was holding a big brioche.

In those days some of the houses on Rue Madame and Rue d'Enfer had a key to the Luxembourg Gardens, which the residents could use when the gates were closed, a privilege since withdrawn. This father and son probably came from one of those houses. The two little paupers saw 'this gentleman' approaching, and concealed themselves a little more.

The man was a respectable citizen. The very same one, perhaps, that Marius in his fever of love had heard one day, near the same pond, counselling his son 'to avoid excess'. He had an affable and superior manner, and a mouth that, never closing, always smiled. This mechanical smile, produced by too much jaw and too little flesh, shows teeth rather than soul. The child, having taken only a bite of his unfinished brioche, seemed full. The lad was dressed for the sake of the insurrection in National Guardsman's uniform, and for the sake of prudence the father had remained in his bourgeois clothes.

Father and son had come to a halt by the pond, where the two swans were disporting themselves. The respectable citizen appeared to have a special admiration for the swans. He resembled them in so far as he walked like them. Right now, the swans were swimming, which is their main talent, and they looked superb.

If the two little paupers had listened and if they had been old enough to understand, they might have taken to heart the words of a serious man.

The father was saying to his son, 'The wise man is content with little in life. Look at me, my son. I don't like ostentation. You never see me in clothes trimmed with gold and precious stones. I leave that false brilliance to badly ordered souls.'

At this point the muffled shouting coming from the direction of Les Halles intensified, with more tolling of bells and more uproar.

'What's that?' asked the child.

The father replied, 'It's a saturnalian orgy of violence.'

Suddenly he caught sight of the two little ragamuffins, standing motionless behind the green swan-house.

'Here's where it starts,' he said. And after a pause he added, 'Anarchy is entering this garden.'

Meanwhile, his son took a bite of his pastry, spat it out, and abruptly began to cry.

'What are you crying for?' asked his father.

'I'm not hungry any more,' said the child.

The father's smile broadened. 'You don't need to be hungry to eat a brioche.'

'I'm fed up with my brioche. It's stale.'

'You don't want any more?'

'No.'

The father pointed to the swans. 'Throw it to those waterfowl.'

The child hesitated. You may not want any more of your brioche, but that is no reason to give it away.

The father went on, 'Be humane. You must show pity towards animals.'

And taking the pastry from his son, he threw it into the pond. The brioche landed quite close to the edge. The swans were far away, in the centre of the pond, busy with some prey. They had seen neither the bourgeois citizen nor the brioche.

Sensing that the pastry was in danger of not being noticed, and upset by this pointless waste, the bourgeois citizen resorted to telegraphically waving his arms about, which finally attracted the swans' attention.

They noticed something afloat, changed tack like the ships that they are, and slowly made their way towards the brioche with the unruffled majesty that befits white creatures.

'The swans understand signals,' said the bourgeois, delighted with his wit.*

At that moment the distant tumult of the city suddenly swelled again. This time it was sinister. There are some gusts of wind that speak more clearly than others. The one blowing at that moment brought distinct drum-beats, an uproar, concerted gunfire, and the dismal responses of the tolling bell and the cannon. This coincided with a black cloud that suddenly hid the sun.

The swans had not yet reached the brioche.

'Let's go home,' said the father, 'the Tuileries are being attacked.'

He grasped his son's hand again. Then continued, 'The distance from the Tuileries to the Luxembourg is no greater than the distance

---

* The witticism lies in the fact that swans (*cygnes*) and signals (*signes*) are homophones in French.

separating royalty from the peerage. It's not far. The bullets are going to come showering down.'

He looked up at the cloud.

'And rain too perhaps. The sky's joining in. The cadet branch is doomed. Let's get home quickly.'

'I'd like to see the swans eat the brioche,' said the child.

The father replied, 'That would be foolhardy.'

And he led his little bourgeois away. Hankering after the swans, the son looked back towards the pond until a corner of the quincunxes concealed it from him.

Meanwhile, the two little waifs had approached the brioche at the same time as the swans. It was floating on the water. The younger one eyed the cake, the elder one eyed the respectable citizen, who was walking away.

Father and son entered the labyrinth of paths that led to the great flight of steps by the cluster of trees over towards Rue Madame.

As soon as they had disappeared from view, the older lad quickly lay flat on his stomach on the curved edge of the pond and, clinging to it with his left hand, leaning over the water, almost falling in, with his right hand he reached his stick out towards the brioche. Seeing the enemy, the swans came hurrying, and in hurrying created an effect with their breasts that was useful to the little angler. The water in front of the swans backed up, and one of those gentle concentric ripples gently nudged the brioche towards the child's stick. Just as the swans arrived, the stick touched it. The child delivered a sharp swipe, drew in the brioche, frightened away the swans, grabbed the brioche, and stood up. The pastry was wet. But they were hungry and thirsty.

The older boy broke the brioche into two pieces, one big and one small, took the small one for himself, gave the big one to his brother and said to him, 'Ram that down your muzzle.'

XVII
Mortuus Pater Filium Moriturum Expectat*

Marius had dashed out of the barricade, Combeferre had followed him. But it was too late. Gavroche was dead. Combeferre brought back the basket of cartridges. Marius brought back the child.

Alas! he thought, what the father had done for his father, he was doing for the son. Except that Thénardier had brought his father back alive. He was bringing the child back dead.

---

* 'The dead father awaits the son who is to die.'

When Marius re-entered the redoubt with Gavroche in his arms, his face, like the child's, was streaming with blood. As he stooped to pick up Gavroche, a bullet had grazed his skull. He had not noticed.

Courfeyrac untied his cravat and bandaged Marius's forehead with it. They laid Gavroche on the same table where Mabeuf lay, and spread the black shawl over both corpses. It was big enough for the old man and the child. Combeferre distributed the cartridges from the basket he had brought back. This gave each man fifteen shots to fire.

Jean Valjean was still in the same place, motionless at his boundary-post. When Combeferre offered him his fifteen cartridges, he shook his head.

'We have a real eccentric here,' Combeferre said quietly to Enjolras. 'He contrives not to fight inside this barricade.'

'Which doesn't prevent him from defending it,' replied Enjolras.

'Heroism has its originals,' said Combeferre.

And Courfeyrac, who overheard, added, 'He's another Père Mabeuf in a different guise.'

It should be noted that the gunfire battering the barricade barely disturbed the interior. Those who have never experienced the vortex of this kind of warfare cannot imagine the peculiar moments of tranquillity that intersperse these convulsions. People wander about, chatting, joking, whiling away the time. Someone we know heard a combatant say to him under a hail of grapeshot, 'We could be at a bachelors' luncheon!'* The Rue de la Chanvrerie redoubt, we repeat, seemed very calm within. Every vicissitude and every phase was spent, or was about to be. Having been critical, the situation was now ominous, and from ominous was probably about to become hopeless. As their plight worsened, the barricade became ever more steeped in the crimson glow of heroism. Enjolras ruled over it gravely, in the attitude of a young Spartan dedicating his naked sword to the sombre spirit Epidotes.

Combeferre, with an apron round his waist, was dressing the wounded. Bossuet and Feuilly were making cartridges with the powder flask Gavroche had recovered from the dead corporal, and Bossuet was saying to Feuilly, 'We'll soon be taking the coach to another planet.' On the few paving-stones he had reserved for himself close to Enjolras, with the carefulness of a young girl putting in order a little cabinet of trinkets Courfeyrac was neatly laying out a complete arsenal: his sword-cane, his rifle, two saddle pistols and a cudgel. Jean Valjean stared silently at the wall in front of him. One workman was

* An allusion to the title of a comic opera of 1806.

fastening on to his head with a piece of string Mère Hucheloup's big straw hat – 'For fear of sunstroke,' he said. The young men of the Cougourde d'Aix were chatting cheerfully among themselves, as though eager to speak their patois for the last time. Joly, who had taken down Widow Hucheloup's mirror, was examining his tongue in it. A few combatants, having discovered some crusts of more or less mouldy bread in a drawer, were eagerly devouring them. Marius was anxious about what his father was going to say to him.

XVIII
The Vulture Turned Prey

We want to insist on a psychological characteristic of barricades. Nothing that distinguishes this amazing street warfare should be omitted.

Regardless of that strange interior calm of which we have just spoken, for those inside it the barricade remains nonetheless unreal.

There is something of the apocalypse in civil war, all the mists of the unknown commingle with those wild blazes, revolutions are sphinx-like, and anyone who has lived through the experience of a barricade thinks he has lived a dream.

What you feel in these places – we have shown it in relation to Marius and we shall see the consequences of it – is both more and less than life. Once you have come out of a barricade, you no longer know what you have seen there. You have been terrible, you are unaware of it. You have been surrounded by militant ideas with human faces. You had your head in the light of the future. There were sprawling corpses and standing phantoms. The hours were immensely long and seemed like the hours of eternity. You have lived in death. Shadows have passed by. What was it? You saw hands with blood on them. It was fearsomely deafening; it was also appallingly silent. There were open mouths crying out, and other open mouths that made no sound. You were in smoke, in darkness perhaps. You think you touched on the sinister seeping from unknown depths. You observe something red on your fingernails. You remember nothing.

Let us return to Rue de la Chanvrerie. Suddenly, between two volleys of fire, the distant sound could be heard of a clock striking the hour.

'It's noon,' said Combeferre.

The twelfth stroke had not sounded when Enjolras drew himself up to his full height, and from the top of the barricade issued this thundering directive, 'Take the cobblestones into the house! Build up the sills of the casement window and the dormer windows with them. Half of you men to arms, the other half to the cobblestones! Not a minute to lose!'

A squad of firemen, shouldering their axes, had just appeared in battle array at the end of the street.

This could only be the head of a column. Of what column? Obviously, the assault column. The firemen whose task it is to demolish the barricade must always precede the soldiers who have to scale it.

Obviously, the moment that Monsieur Clermont-Tonnerre in 1822 called 'the final push' was imminent.

Enjolras's order was carried out with the disciplined speediness essential to ships and barricades, the only two combat sites where escape is impossible. In less than a minute, two-thirds of the cobblestones that Enjolras had had piled up at Corinthe's door had been taken up to the first floor and the attic, and before a second minute had elapsed, the casement window on the first floor and the dormer windows in the roof were half walled up with these cobblestones, expertly stacked on top of each other. A few loop-holes carefully contrived by Feuilly, the chief engineer, allowed gun barrels to pass through. This reinforcement of the windows could be achieved all the more easily since the canister fire had ceased. The two cannons were now firing cannon-balls at the centre of the barrier in order to make a hole in it and, if possible, open up a breach for the assault.

When the cobblestones destined for the last stand were in place, Enjolras had the bottles he had put aside, under the table on which Mabeuf lay, carried up to the first floor.

'So who will drink that?' Bossuet asked him.

'They will,' replied Enjolras.

Then they barricaded the downstairs window, and placed in readiness the iron cross-beams used to bar the tavern door at night from the inside. The fortress was complete. The barricade was the rampart, the tavern was the keep.

With the remaining cobblestones they filled in the gap.

As the defenders of a barricade are always obliged to be sparing of their ammunition, and as the assailants know this, the assailants go about their business with a kind of irritating leisureliness, expose themselves to fire prematurely, but in appearance more than in reality, and take their time. The preparations for attack are always made with a certain methodical slowness. After which, the lightning-strike.

This slowness allowed Enjolras to review everything and to see that everything was perfect. He felt that since such men were going to die, their death ought to be a masterpiece.

He said to Marius, 'We're the two leaders. I'm going give the final orders inside. You stay outside and keep watch.'

Marius took up an observation post on the ridge of the barricade. Enjolras had the door to the kitchen nailed up – this was the first-aid post, remember.

'No splattering over the wounded,' he said.

He issued his final instructions in the bar room in a curt but supremely calm voice. Feuilly listened and replied for all.

'On the first floor have some axes ready to cut off the staircase. Are they in place?'

'Yes,' said Feuilly.

'How many?'

'Two hatchets and an axe.'

'Good. There are twenty-six combatants left standing. How many guns?'

'Thirty-four.'

'Eight too many. Keep those eight guns to hand, loaded like the rest. Swords and pistols in belts. Twenty men on the barricade. Six stationed at the dormer windows and at the window on the first floor so as to fire on the assailants through the loop-holes in the cobble-stones. Let's have no worker here who's not put to good use. Presently, when the drum sounds the charge, the twenty down below are to rush to the barricade. The first to get there will be the best-placed.'

Once these arrangements had been made, he turned to Javert and said, 'I haven't forgotten about you.'

And laying a pistol on the table, he added, 'The last man out of here will put a bullet in this spy's head.'

'Here?' a voice asked.

'No, let's not get this corpse muddled up with our own. The smaller barricade in Mondétour lane can be climbed over. It's only four feet high. The man's securely bound. He'll be taken there and executed.'

There was at that moment someone more impassive than Enjolras. It was Javert. Then Jean Valjean appeared. He was among the groups of insurgents. He emerged and said to Enjolras, 'You're in command?'

'Yes.'

'You thanked me a while ago.'

'In the name of the Republic. The barricade has two saviours: Marius Pontmercy and yourself.'

'Do you think I deserve some reward for that?'

'Certainly.'

'Well, I request one.'

'What is it?'

'To be the one who blows that man's brains out.'

Javert looked up, saw Jean Valjean, gave an almost imperceptible start, and said, 'Quite so.'

As for Enjolras, he had begun to reload his rifle. He let his eyes wander around. 'No objections?'

And he turned to Jean Valjean. 'Take the spy.'

Sitting down at the end of the table, Jean Valjean did indeed take possession of Javert. He picked up the pistol, and a quiet click announced that he had cocked it. Almost at the same moment, trumpets sounded.

'Look out!' yelled Marius from the top of the barricade.

Javert began to laugh with that noiseless laugh that was characteristic of him, and staring intently at the insurgents, he said to them, 'You're no better off than I am.'

'Everyone out!' shouted Enjolras.

The insurgents rushed out in disorder, followed by this parting shot – if we may be allowed the expression – from Javert: 'See you soon!'

XIX
Jean Valjean Takes His Revenge

When Jean Valjean was left alone with Javert, he untied the rope binding the prisoner round his middle and knotted under the table. After this, he motioned to him to stand up. Javert obeyed with that indefinable smile in which is condensed the supremacy of fettered authority.

Jean Valjean took Javert by the martingale as you would take a beast of burden by the breast-harness, and dragging him along behind, emerged from the tavern slowly, because Javert, with his trammelled legs, could take only very small steps. Jean Valjean had the pistol in his hand.

In this manner they crossed the barricade's inner quadrangle. Intent on the imminent attack, the insurgents had their backs turned.

Positioned to one side, on the far left of the barricade, Marius alone saw them pass. On this pair, victim and executioner, was cast the sepulchral light that he carried in his soul.

With some difficulty, but without loosening his grip for a single instant, Jean Valjean made Javert, bound as he was, scramble over the defence barrier in the Mondétour lane. Once clear of this obstacle, they found themselves alone together in the lane. No one could see them any more now. They were round the corner, hidden from the insurgents. A few paces away, the corpses that had been removed from the barricade formed a terrible pile.

Among the heap of dead bodies could be singled out a livid face, hair falling loose, a pierced hand and the half-naked breast of a woman. It was Éponine.

Javert gave this body a sideways look, and with the utmost calm said quietly, 'I think I know that girl.'

Then he turned to Jean Valjean.

Jean Valjean thrust the pistol under his arm and fixed on Javert a look that needed no words to say, 'Javert, it is I.'

Javert replied, 'Take your revenge.'

Jean Valjean drew a knife from his pocket and opened it.

'A blade!' exclaimed Javert. 'You're right. It suits you better.'

Jean Valjean cut the martingale Javert had round his neck, then he cut the cords around his wrists, then stooping down he cut the string with which his feet were tied, and straightening up he said, 'You're free.'

Javert was not easily surprised. But for all his self-control, he could not help giving a start. He remained dumbfounded and motionless.

Jean Valjean went on. 'I don't think I'll be getting out of here. But if by chance I do, I go by the name of Fauchelevent, Rue de l'Homme-Armé, number seven.'

Javert gave a tigerish grimace that opened one corner of his mouth a fraction, and muttered between his teeth, 'Take care.'

'Go,' said Jean Valjean.

Javert responded, 'Fauchelevent, you said, Rue de l'Homme-Armé?'

'Number seven.'

Javert repeated in a low voice, 'Number seven.'

He buttoned up his coat, restored some military stiffness to his shoulders, turned round, folded his arms, resting his chin on one hand, and started walking in the direction of Les Halles. Jean Valjean followed him with his gaze.

Having taken a few steps, Javert turned round and shouted to Jean Valjean, 'You annoy me! I'd rather you killed me!'*

Javert himself did not notice that he was no longer addressing Jean Valjean with disrepectful familiarity.

'Go, now,' said Jean Valjean.

Javert slowly walked away. A moment later he turned the corner of Rue des Prêcheurs.

---

* Javert here uses the *vous* form in addressing Jean Valjean.

When Javert had disappeared, Jean Valjean fired his pistol into the air. Then he returned to the barricade and said, 'It's done.'

Meanwhile, this is what had happened:

More intent on what was going on outside than inside, Marius had not until then looked closely at the spy tied up in the gloomy depths of the bar room.

When he saw him in broad daylight, climbing over the barricade to go to his death, he recognized him. A sudden recollection came to mind. He remembered the inspector from Rue de Pontoise and the two pistols he had given him, which he, Marius, had used at this very barricade. And not only did he recall his face, he recalled his name.

However, like all his thoughts, this recollection was hazy and confused. It was not an assertion of fact that he made to himself, but a question that he put to himself: 'Is that not the inspector of police who told me his name was Javert?'

Perhaps there was still time to intervene on behalf of this man. But he had first to find out whether it was indeed Javert.

Marius called out to Enjolras, who had just positioned himself at the other end of the barricade, 'Enjolras!'

'What?'

'What is that man's name?'

'What man?'

'The police agent. Do you know his name?'

'Yes, he told us.'

'What is it?'

'Javert.'

Marius stiffened.

At that moment they heard the pistol-shot. Jean Valjean reappeared and cried, 'It's done.'

A sinister chill went through Marius's heart.

XX
The Dead Are Right, the Living Are Not Wrong

The barricade's death throes were about to begin.

Everything contributed to the tragic majesty of that supreme moment: countless mysterious rumblings in the air, the breathing of armed masses out of sight and on the move in the streets, the intermittent gallop of cavalry, the trundling of artillery, the crossfire of rifle volleys and cannonades in the labyrinth that is Paris, the smoke of battle rising all gilded above the rooftops, distant cries of some vaguely terrible nature, ominous flashes everywhere; the tolling of St-Merry's bell, become a sobbing sound; the mildness of the season, the splendour of the sky filled with sunshine and clouds, the beauty of the day and the dreadful silence of the houses.

For since the day before, the two rows of houses in Rue de la Chanvrerie had become two hostile blank walls. Doors closed, windows closed, shutters closed.

In those days, so different from the present, when the time had come and the people wanted to see an end to a situation that had gone on for too long, to a charter 'granted' or a state unrepresentative of society; when universal anger pervaded the atmosphere, when the city consented to the tearing-up of its cobblestones, when the whispering in its ear of insurrection's watchword made the bourgeoisie smile, then the local population, imbued with rioting, as it were, was the combatants' auxiliary force, and the house made common cause with the improvised fortress propped up against it. When the time was not ripe, when the insurrection was not positively welcomed, when the general population disowned the movement, the combatants were doomed; the city became a desert surrounding the revolt, hearts froze against its protagonists, places of asylum were closed to them, and the street lent itself to the army as a conduit for the taking of the barricade.

A population cannot be made to advance more quickly than it wants to by being taken by surprise. Woe betide anyone who tries to force its hand! A population does not allow itself to be manipulated. So it leaves the insurrection to its own devices. The insurgents become plague-carriers. A house is an escarpment, a door is a rejection, a façade is a wall. This wall sees, hears, and is set in its opposition. It could open up a crack and save you. But no. This wall is a judge. It looks down on you and condemns you. How grim these shuttered houses are! They look dead, they are alive. Life persists inside them, suspended, as it were. No one has emerged from them for twenty-four hours, but no one is out. Within this rock, people move about, go to bed, get up. They are at home with their families. They eat and drink. The terrible thing is, they are afraid! Fear is the excuse for this deadly lack of hospitality, adding an element of panic, an extenuating circumstance. Sometimes – and this has been witnessed – fear even becomes violent. Terror can turn to fury, as prudence can turn to rage. Hence that very profound term, 'the enraged moderates'. There are blazing eruptions of the utmost terror from which, like an ominous smoke, rises anger. 'What do these people want? They're never satisfied. They put law-abiding citizens at risk. As if we haven't had enough revolutions! What have they come here for? Let them fend for themselves. So much the worse for them. It's their own fault. They're only getting what they deserve. It's nothing to do with us. Look at our poor street, riddled with bullets. They're a bunch of good-for-nothings. Whatever you do, don't open the door.' And the house takes on the appearance of a tomb. The insurgent in front of that house is about to die. He sees the bullets and the drawn swords closing in on him. If he cries out, he knows that someone is listening but no one will come. There are walls here that could protect him, there are men here who could save him, and these walls have ears of flesh, and these men have hearts of stone.

Who is to blame?

No one, and everyone.

The imperfect times in which we live.

It is always at its own risk and peril that Utopia turns into insurrection, and changes from philosophical protest into armed protest, from Minerva into Pallas. The Utopia that loses patience and turns to riot knows what awaits it. Almost always it arrives too soon. Then it resigns itself, and instead of triumph it stoically accepts catastrophe. It serves those who deny it without complaining, and even exonerates them, and its magnanimity lies in consenting to being abandoned. It is indomitable in the face of obstacle and forgiving towards ingratitude.

And come to that, is it ingratitude?

Yes, from the viewpoint of the human race.

No, from the viewpoint of the individual.

Progress is in man's disposition. The common life of humankind is called Progress, the collective stride of humankind is called Progress. Progress moves forward. It makes the great human and terrestrial journey towards the celestial and the divine. It makes halts so as to rally the flock that lags behind, it takes breaks for contemplation in the presence of some splendid land of Canaan suddenly unveiling its horizon, it has nights when it sleeps. And it is one of the thinker's painful anxieties to see darkness lying upon the human soul, and to feel Progress sleeping in the shadows without being able to waken it.

'Maybe God is dead,' Gérard de Nerval said one day to the writer of these lines, confusing progress with God, and mistaking the interruption of movement for the death of the Essence.

Whoever despairs is wrong. Progress awakes again without fail, and all things considered it might be said to have moved on even while asleep, for it has grown. Back on its feet, it looks taller. To be always peaceful depends no more on progress than on the river. Raise no barriers against it, throw no boulders into it. Obstacles make the waters foam and humanity seethe. This gives rise to turmoil. But after this turmoil, it has to be recognized that some headway has been made. Until order has been established, order being nothing other than universal peace, until harmony and unity reign, progress will be marked by revolutions along the way.

What, then, is progress? We have just said what it is. The enduring life of peoples.

Now it sometimes happens that the momentary life of individuals offers resistance to the eternal life of humankind.

Let us acknowledge, without bitterness, that the individual has his own personal interest and may without doing anything wrong declare that interest and defend it. The present has its forgivable quotient of selfishness. The momentary life has its rights, and is not bound to keep endlessly sacrificing itself to the future. The generation currently taking its turn on the earth is not obliged to shorten its stay for the sake of generations who are its equals, after all, and will have their turn later. 'I exist,' murmurs that someone whose name is Everyman. 'I'm young and I'm in love, I'm old and I want to rest, I'm a family man, I work, I'm doing well, I'm successful, I have houses to let, I have money invested in government bonds, I'm happy, I have a wife and children, I love all this, I want to live, let me be.' Hence, at certain times, an intense cold chills humankind's noble pioneers.

In any case, let us admit that, when it makes war, Utopia forsakes its radiant sphere. The truth of tomorrow, which it is, borrows its method of operation, armed conflict, from the untruth of yesterday. The future, which it is, behaves like the past. The pure ideal, which it is, becomes an act of violence. It complicates its heroism with a violence for which it is rightly accountable, an opportunistic and expedient violence that goes against principle and for which it is inevitably punished. The Utopian insurrection fights upholding the old military code. It shoots spies, it executes traitors, it does away with living beings and casts them into uncharted darkness. It resorts to death, which is a serious matter. It is as if Utopia had no more faith in radiance, in its irresistible and incorruptible force. It strikes with the sword. Now, no sword cuts only one way. Every blade is double-edged. Whoever wounds with one edge wounds himself on the other.

With that reservation, made in all severity, it is impossible for us not to admire the glorious combatants of the future, the advocates of Utopia, whether or not they succeed. Even when they come to grief they are to be revered, and it is perhaps in failure that they have greater majesty. Victory, when in accord with progress, deserves the approbation of the masses, but a heroic defeat deserves their compassion. The one is magnificent, the other sublime. For those of us who prefer martyrdom to success, John Brown is greater than Washington, and Pisacane is greater than Garibaldi.

Someone has to take the part of the vanquished.

Those great strivers for the future are hard done by when they fail.

Revolutionaries are accused of sowing terror. Every barricade seems an outrage. Their theories are condemned, their purpose is suspected, their ulterior motives are feared, their moral conscience is discredited. They are accused of erecting, constructing and assembling against the prevailing social order a whole heap of hardships, woes, iniquities, grievances, causes for despair, and of tearing up from the lower depths swathes of darkness in order to throw up battlements and fight from behind them. People shout, 'You're tearing up the paving-stones of hell!' They might well reply, 'That's because our barricade is made of good intentions.'

Of course, the peaceful solution is best. Admittedly, all things considered, anyone seeing the paving-stone thinks of the bear*, and it is a good intention that makes society uneasy. But it is up to society to save itself. We appeal to its own good intentions. No violent remedy is necessary. Study amicably the ills that it suffers, diagnose them, then cure them. That is what we invite it to do.

Be that as it may, even when fallen, especially when fallen, they are noble, these men, who throughout the universe, with their eyes fixed on France, fight for the great enterprise with the inflexible logic of the ideal. They give their lives freely for progress. They carry out the will of providence. They do a sacred deed. At the appointed hour, with as little self-regard as an actor who comes in on cue, following the divine script, they enter the tomb. And this hopeless conflict, this stoic demise, they accept, in order to bring to glorious and universal fulfilment the magnificent and irresistibly human movement begun on the fourteenth of July 1789. These soldiers are priests. The French Revolution is an act of God.

Furthermore – and this distinction should be added to the distinctions already made in another chapter – there are insurrections that are welcomed, which are called revolutions; there are insurrections that are not welcomed, which are called disturbances. An insurrection that catches fire is an idea that in the people's view has passed its test.

---

* An allusion to La Fontaine's fable 10, bk 3, 'L'Ours et l'Amateur des Jardins' (The Bear and the Gardener), about a bear who, wanting to spare his new friend the gardener from the annoyance of a fly on the end of his nose, drops a paving-stone on it.

If the people blackball it, the idea comes to nothing, the insurrection is snuffed.

Going to war at every summons and every time Utopia wishes is not how the masses behave. Nations do not always and at every moment have the temperament of heroes and martyrs.

They are practical. A priori, they are averse to insurrection; first, because it often results in catastrophe; second, because it always has an abstraction as its point of departure.

For it is always for the sake of the ideal, and the ideal alone – and this is a fine thing – that those who sacrifice themselves make that sacrifice. Insurrection is fervour. Fervour may become anger, hence the resort to arms. But every insurrection that targets a government or a regime aims higher. So, for instance, let us be clear about this, what the leaders of the 1832 insurrection, and in particular the young firebrands of Rue de la Chanvrerie, were fighting against was not exactly Louis-Philippe. Most of them, speaking candidly about this middle-of-the-road king, halfway between monarchy and revolution, gave him credit for his qualities. No one hated him. But in Louis-Philippe they were attacking the cadet branch of divine right as they had attacked the senior branch in Charles X. And what they wanted to overthrow in overthrowing kingship in France was, as we have explained, the usurpation of one man's sovereignty by another and the encroachment of privilege on right throughout the entire universe. Paris without a king has as consequence a world without despots. This is the way they reasoned. Their goal was no doubt distant, vague perhaps, and ever receding as they strove towards it; but noble.

That is the way it is. And people sacrifice themselves for these visions, which for those who are sacrificed are almost always illusions, but illusions imbued on the whole with all human certainty. Insurgents poeticize insurrection and see it in a golden light. They throw themselves into these tragic affairs, elated by what they are going to do. Who knows? They might succeed. They are few in number, they are up against a whole army, but they are defending right, natural law, the sovereignty of each individual over himself that allows of no abdication, justice, truth. And if need be, they will die like the three hundred Spartans. They think not of Don Quixote, but of Leonidas. And they forge on, and once committed there is no going back, they press forward, heads down, in hope of an unprecedented victory, the fulfilment of the revolution, progress once again set free, the advancement of the human race, universal deliverance, and if the worse comes to the worst, Thermopylae.

This taking-up of arms for the sake of progress often fails, and we

IIII

have just explained why. The crowd is resistant to the zeal of champions. These lumbering masses, the multitudes, which are weak by reason of their very unwieldiness, are fearful of risk, and there is in the ideal an element of risk.

Moreover, let us not forget, there are interests involved, interests not very favourable to the ideal and to finer feelings. Sometimes the belly paralyses the heart.

It is the greatness and beauty of France that she becomes less paunchy than other nations. She more readily tightens her belt. She is the first awake, the last to fall asleep. She leads the way. She is a pioneer.

This is owing to her being artistic.

The ideal is nothing other than the culmination of logic, just as the beautiful is nothing other than the pinnacle of truth. Artistic nations are also important nations. To love beauty is to yearn for light. This is why the torch of Europe, that is to say of civilization, was first carried by Greece, who passed it on to Italy, who passed it on to France. Divine trail-blazing nations! *Vitai lampada tradunt.**

Remarkably enough, the poetry of a people determines its progress. The degree of civilization is measured by the degree of imagination. But a civilizing nation must remain a virile nation. Corinth, yes. Sybaris, no. To become effeminate is to become degenerate. A nation must be neither dilettante nor virtuoso, but it must be artistic. In the matter of civilization, it is not refinement that is wanted but sublimation. It is with this proviso that the human race is given the template of the ideal.

The modern ideal finds its pattern in art, and its means of implementation is science. It is through science that the august vision of the poets – social beauty – will be realized. Eden will be recreated by A plus B. At the point that civilization has now reached, precision is a necessary element of the magnificent, and artistic feeling is not only served but brought to perfection by the scientific medium. Dreams must be calculating. Art, the conqueror, must have science, the foot-slogger, for support. The sturdiness of the mount is important. The modern spirit is the genius of Greece with the genius of India as its vehicle: Alexander riding the elephant.

Races fossilized by dogma or corrupted by lucre are unfit to guide civilization. Genuflecting before idols, or before gold, atrophies the muscles for walking and the will that provides motivation. Absorption in religious ritual or money-making dims a people's radiance,

* 'They pass on the torch of life', Lucretius, *De Rerum Natura*, bk II, line 79.

lowers its horizons by degrading it, and deprives it of its understanding of the universal goal, that understanding at once human and divine that makes missionaries of nations. Babylon has no ideal. Carthage has no ideal. But even across the great dark expanse of the centuries, Athens and Rome have and retain aureoles of civilization.

France is a nation of the same quality as Greece and Italy. She is Athenian in terms of beauty and Roman in terms of greatness. Moreover, she is good. She gives of herself. She is more often than other nations in the mood for dedication and self-sacrifice. But the mood is one that comes and goes. And this is the great peril for those who run when France wants merely to walk, or who walk when she wants to stop. France has her relapses into materialism, and at certain moments there is nothing reminiscent of French greatness about the ideas that clog that sublime intellect, ideas the size of a Missouri or a South Carolina. What can anyone do about it? The giant plays at being a dwarf. Immeasurable France has her wilful pettinesses. That is all.

There is no objection to be made to this. Peoples, like stars, have the right to go into eclipse. And everything is fine, as long as the light returns and eclipse does not degenerate into permanent darkness. Dawn and resurrection are synonymous. The reappearance of light is indistinguishable from the enduring quality of the self.

Let us state these facts calmly. Death on the barricade, or the tomb in exile, are for self-sacrifice an acceptable eventuality. The true name of self-sacrifice is unselfishness. Let the abandoned be abandoned, let the exiled be exiled, and let us confine ourselves to entreating great nations not to draw back too far when they draw back. They must not, on the pretext of a return to sanity, sink too low.

Matter exists, the moment exists, interests exist, the belly exists, but the belly must not be the sole fount of wisdom. Momentary life has its rights, we admit, but enduring life has its rights also. Alas! to have climbed does not preclude falling. This can be seen in history more frequently than anyone would wish. A nation is illustrious, it relishes the ideal, then it eats from the gutter and thinks it tastes good. And if asked how it is that it forsakes Socrates for Falstaff, it replies, 'It's because I love statesmen.'

One word more before returning to the fray.

A battle like the one we are now giving an account of is nothing other than a convulsive approach towards the ideal. Trammelled progress is sickly, and has these tragic epileptic fits. This affliction of progress, civil war, we have had to contend with along the way. Both act and interlude, it is one of the fateful developments in that drama whose central character is a social outcast and whose real title is *Progress*.

Progress!

This cry that we often raise is the expression of our entire way of thinking, and at the point in this drama we have now reached – the idea it contains having more than one ordeal yet to undergo – we may perhaps be permitted, if not to lift the veil, at least to allow its light to shine through clearly.

The book before the reader's eyes at this moment is from start to finish, in its entirety and in its detail – whatever the inconsistencies, the exceptions and the failings – the progression from evil to good, from wrong to right, from night to day, from craving to conscience, from putrefaction to life, from bestiality to duty, from hell to heaven, from nothingness to God. Point of departure: matter. Point of arrival: spirit. Hydra at the outset, angel at the last.

XXI
Heroes

Suddenly the drum beat the charge.

It was a hurricane attack. The night before, the barricade had been approached in the dark, as by a boa, silently. Now, in broad daylight, in this broad-mouthed street, surprise was decidedly impossible; indeed, sheer might had now unmasked itself, the cannon had begun roaring, the army hurled itself at the barricade. Fury was now skilful deployment. With massed support, heard though not seen, and reaching far back, a powerful column of line infantry, interspersed at regular intervals with National and Municipal Guardsmen on foot, to the beating of drum, to the blaring of bugle, bayonets levelled, pioneers leading the way, came pouring into the street at a run, imperturbable under fire, and with the force of a bronze battering-ram against a wall charged the barricade.

The wall held firm.

The insurgents blasted away. Glints of light crested the scaled barricade, and so furious was the assault that for a moment it was swarming with assailants. But it shook off the soldiers as a lion shakes off dogs, and was covered with besiegers only as the cliff is covered with foam, to reappear a moment later looming dark and formidable.

Forced to fall back, the column remained massed in the street, exposed but terrifying, and responded to the redoubt with tremendous rifle-fire. Anyone who has seen a firework display will recall that sheaf arrangement of flares, called a bouquet. Imagine this bouquet, no longer vertical but horizontal, with a pellet or a bullet or a bis-cayen ball at the tip of its every spray of fire, meting out death with its clusters of gun reports. The barricade lay beneath it.

Equal resolve on both sides. The bravery here was almost barbaric, and complicated by a kind of heroic ferocity that began with self-sacrifice. Those were the days when a National Guardsman fought like a Zouave. The military wanted to get this over with, the insurrec-tion wanted to put up a fight. Acceptance of death in the prime of youth and the prime of health whips fearlessness into a frenzy. In that hour of death, the stature of everyone engaged in this conflict grew. The street was strewn with corpses.

The barricade had Enjolras at one end and Marius at the other. Enjolras, who had mental command of the whole barricade, keeping himself in reserve and under cover. Three soldiers fell, one after the other, beneath his embrasure without even having noticed him. Mar-ius was fighting out in the open. He was offering himself as a target, exposed above the top of the redoubt to below the waist. There is no more reckless spendthrift than the miser who takes the bit between his teeth. There is no man in action more terrifying than a stargazer. Mar-ius was fearsome and pensive. He fought in battle as in a dream. He might have been a phantom firing a gun.

The besieged were running out of cartridges but not out of witti-cisms. In the vortex of death in which they found themselves, they laughed.

Courfeyrac was bare-headed.

'So what have you done with your hat?' Bossuet asked him.

Courfeyrac replied, 'They finally shot it off me with cannon-balls.'

Or they made arch remarks.

'Can you understand those men,' Feuilly exclaimed bitterly (citing names, names that were not unknown, that were even famous, some associated with the army of old), 'who promised to join us and vowed to help us, and who gave their word of honour, men who are our generals and who've deserted us!'

And Combeferre confined himself to replying with a grim smile, 'There are people who observe the rules of honour the way you observe the stars, from a great distance.'

The inside of the barricade was so thickly strewn with spent car-tridges it looked as if it had been snowing.

The assailants had the numbers. The insurgents had the position. They were at the top of a wall, blasting down at point-blank range on the soldiers stumbling over the dead and wounded and trapped on the slope. Constructed the way it was and admirably buttressed, this barricade was indeed one of those instances where a handful of men can hold a legion in check. Nevertheless, constantly reinforced and expanding under the shower of bullets, the attacking column came inexorably nearer, and now, little by little, step by step, slowly but surely the army closed in on the barricade, like the screw on a wine-press.

The assaults came one after another. The horror intensified.

Then, on that heap of cobblestones, in that Rue de la Chanvrerie, a battle broke out worthy of one of the walls of Troy. These gaunt, ragged, exhausted men who had not eaten for twenty-four hours, who had not slept, who had only a few shots left to fire, who felt their empty pockets for cartridges, nearly all of them wounded, their heads or arms bound in blackened bandages stained the colour of rust, with holes in their clothes from which the blood flowed, barely armed, with inferior rifles and old jagged-edged swords – these men became Titans. Ten times the barricade came under attack, was assaulted, scaled, and never captured.

To have any idea of this conflict you would have to imagine a bevy of courageous hearts set alight, and then watch the conflagration. It was not a fight, it was the inside of a furnace, where mouths breathed flame, faces looked extraordinary, the human form seemed to embody the impossible, the combatants blazed; and awesome to behold in that red smoke was the coming and going of those salamanders of the fray. The successive and simultaneous scenes of this spectacular carnage we shall not attempt to depict. The epic alone has the right to fill twelve thousand lines with the account of a battle.

It was like that hell of Brahmanism, the most dreadful of the seventeen abysses, which the Veda calls the Forest of Swords.

They fought hand to hand for every inch of ground, using pistols, swords, fists, at a distance, at close quarters, from above, from below, from everywhere, from the roofs of the houses, from the windows of the tavern, from the vents in the cellar, a few of them having slipped down there. They were one against sixty. Half demolished, Corinthe's façade was hideous. The window, tattooed with canister-shot, had lost its panes and casement frame, and having been feverishly walled up with cobblestones it was now no more than a shapeless hole. Bossuet was killed. Feuilly was killed. Courfeyrac was killed. Stabbed in the chest three times with a bayonet as he helped a wounded soldier, Combeferre had time only to look skywards, and died.

Marius, who was still fighting, was so riddled with wounds, particularly to his head, that his face could not be seen for all the blood and looked as if it were covered with a red handkerchief.

Enjolras alone was unscathed. Whenever he was left unarmed he would hold out his hand to right or left, and one of the insurgents would put some sort of blade into it. He was left at the last with the stump of a fourth sword – one more than François I at Marignano.

Homer says: 'Diomedes slays Axylus, son of Teuthranis, who dwelt in blessed Arisba; Euryalus, son of Mecistaeus, kills Dresus; and Opheltius, Aesepius, and that Pedasus whom the naiad Abarbarea bore to the blameless Bucolion; Ulysses strikes down Pidytes of Percote; Antilochus, Ablerus; Polypaetes, Astyalus; Polydamas, Otus of Cyllene; and Teucer, Aretaon. Melanthius dies by Euripylus' spear. Agamemnon, king of the heroes, defeats Elatus, born in the city whose steep slopes are bathed by the babbling river Satnoeis.'* In our own epic poems of old, Esplandian attacks the giant Marquis Swantibor with a double-headed axe of fire, and the latter defends himself by hurling uprooted towers at the knight. Our ancient wall-frescoes show us two dukes, the Duc de Bretagne and the Duc de Bourbon, in their heraldic armour emblazoned with their coats of arms, on horseback and challenging each other, battle-axe in hand, masked in iron, booted in iron, gloved in iron, the one caparisoned in ermine, the other draped in azure; Bretagne with his lion between the two horns on his crown, Bourbon helmeted with a huge visored fleur-de-lys. But in order to be magnificent it is not necessary to wear the ducal helmet, like Yvon, or to brandish a living flame, like Esplandian; or like Phyleus, father of Polydamas, to have brought back from Ephyra a strong suit of mail, presented as a gift by that lord of men, Euphetes. It is enough to give one's life in defence of a belief or in service of a cause. This poor innocent soldier, yesterday a Beauce or Limousin peasant, with his cabbage-cutting knife at his side, who hangs around the nursemaids in the Luxembourg Gardens, this pale young student bent over an anatomical illustration or a book, a blond adolescent who trims his beard with scissors – take them both, infuse them with a sense of duty, confront them with each other in Carrefour Boucherat or Cul-de-Sac Planche-Mibray, and let the one fight for his flag and the other for his ideal, and let both imagine they are fighting for their country. The struggle will be tremendous. And the shadow that this soldier-boy and this young medic project as they fight it out on humanity's great epic battlefield will equal the shadow cast by Megaryon, king of tiger-teeming Lycia, wrestling with mighty Ajax, equal of the gods.

* A résumé of lines 12–35 of Homer's *Iliad*, bk 6, describing the raging battle between the Trojans and the Greeks.

XXII
Inch by Inch

When there were no other leaders left alive except, at either end of the barricade, Enjolras and Marius, the centre, which Courfeyrac, Joly, Bossuet, Feuilly and Combeferre had for so long defended, gave way. Without opening up a passable breach, the cannon had cut a sizeable notch in the middle of the redoubt. There, the top of the wall had disappeared under the cannon-ball and dropped away, and the debris that had fallen, some within, some without, piling up on either side of the barricade, had ended up creating two shelves, as it were, one on the inside, the other on the outside. The shelf on the outside offered a rising slope to oncomers.

Here a final assault was attempted, and this assault succeeded. The bristling mass of bayonets came at a steady run, unstoppable; and the dense battlefront of the attacking column appeared through the smoke at the top of the escarpment. This time, it was decisive. The group of insurgents defending the centre fell back in frantic disorder.

Then the grim love of life stirred in some. With this forest of guns taking aim at them, several no longer wanted to die. This is a moment when the instinct for self-preservation gives vent to howling, when the beast reappears in the man. They were backed up against the tall six-storey house that formed the rear of their redoubt. That house could offer salvation. The building was barricaded and walled up, as it were, from top to bottom. There was time, before the soldiers were inside the redoubt, for a door to open and close, a split second would be enough, and to those desperate men, for the door of that house suddenly to open a crack and instantly to close again meant life. Behind that house were streets, possible escape, open expanses. They started banging at the door with the butts of their guns, and kicking at it, calling out, shouting, begging, with hands pressed together. No one opened. From the dormer window on the third floor, the head of the dead man gazed down on them.

But Enjolras and Marius, and seven or eight others rallied around them, sprang forward to protect the men. Enjolras shouted to the soldiers, 'Don't come any nearer!' And one officer having failed to obey, Enjolras had killed him. He was now in the little inner courtyard of the redoubt, with his back against the Corinthe building, sword in one hand, rifle in the other, holding open the door to the tavern, which he was barring to the assailants. 'There's only one open door, this one!' he shouted to the desperate insurgents. And shielding them with his body, single-handedly confronting a whole battalion, he let them slip in behind him. All of them dashed inside.

Executing with his rifle, which he was now using like a cane, what stick-fighters call a 'covered rose' around his head, Enjolras fended off the bayonets around and in front of him, and was the last to go in. And there was a terrible moment when the soldiers were trying to get in and the insurgents were trying to shut them out. The door was closed with such violence that, as it slammed shut, the five severed fingers of a soldier who had been clinging to the door-frame could be seen stuck on the inside of it.

Marius was left outside. A gunshot had just broken his collar-bone; he felt himself fainting and falling. At that moment, with eyes already shut, he felt the jolt of a strong hand grabbing hold of him; and losing consciousness, he scarcely had time for this thought as it mingled with a final memory of Cosette: 'I'm taken prisoner. I shall be shot.'

Not seeing Marius among those who had taken refuge in the tavern, Enjolras had the same thought. But they were now at the moment when each individual has time to reflect only on his own death. Enjolras fixed the bar across the door and bolted it, double-locked and padlocked it, while those outside battered at it furiously, the soldiers with the butts of their rifles, the sappers with their axes. The assailants were concentrated at that door. It was the siege of the tavern that was now beginning.

The soldiers, it must be said, were full of anger.

The death of the artillery sergeant had upset them, and then, more sinister, in the few hours preceding the attack it had been rumoured among them that the insurgents were mutilating their prisoners and that there was the headless body of a soldier in the tavern. This kind of dire rumour is the usual accompaniment of civil war, and it was a false report of this kind that would later cause the catastrophe of Rue Transnonain.

When the door was barricaded, Enjolras said to the others, 'Let's sell ourselves dearly.'

Then he approached the table on which lay Mabeuf and Gavroche. Straight and stiff under the black cloth two figures could be seen, one large, the other small, and the two faces were roughly contoured beneath the shroud's bleak folds. A hand emerged from under that pall and hung down towards the ground. It was the old man's.

Enjolras bent down and kissed that venerable hand, just as he had kissed the old man's forehead the day before. These were the only two kisses he had bestowed in his life.

To cut this long story short, the barricade had fought like one of the gates of Thebes; the tavern fought like one of the houses of Saragossa. Such resistances are obdurate. No quarter is given. No truce possible. Men are willing to die, provided they can kill. When Suchet says, 'Capitulate', Palafox replies, 'From cannon warfare to knife warfare.' The storming of the Hucheloup tavern lacked nothing – neither the cobblestones raining down from the windows and the roof on to the besiegers and provoking the soldiers by causing horrible injuries, nor the gunshots fired from the cellars and the dormer windows, nor the ferocity of the attack, nor the fierceness of the defence, nor finally, when the door gave way, the frenzied madness of the killing. Getting their feet entangled in the panels of the door that had been broken down and thrown to the ground, the assailants came rushing into the tavern to find not a single fighter there. The spiral staircase, cut down with an axe, lay in the middle of the downstairs room; there were a few wounded men breathing their last, anyone who had not been killed was on the first floor, and from there, through the hole in the ceiling that had been the staircase opening, a tremendous firing now broke out. These were the last of their cartridges. When they were used up, when these warriors facing death had no powder or bullets left, each took hold of two of the bottles set aside by Enjolras, mentioned earlier, and they held off the ascent of their attackers with these fearsomely fragile bludgeons. They were bottles of nitric acid. We relate these sombre facts of carnage as they were. The besieged, alas! use everything as a weapon. Greek fire brought no disgrace on Archimedes, boiling pitch brought no disgrace on Bayard. All war is terror, and there is nothing to choose between one form and another. Although constrained and directed upwards from below, the besiegers' rifle-fire was deadly. The hole in the ceiling was soon ringed with the heads of the slain, with long, red rivulets streaming from them. The pandemonium was indescribable. Stifling, burning smoke created near-night above this conflict. There are no words to describe this degree of horror. These were no longer men taking part in the now infernal struggle. These were no longer giants against Titans. This was more Milton and Dante than Homer. Fiends attacked, phantoms resisted.

It was monstrous heroism.

XXIII
Sober Orestes and Drunken Pylades

Giving each other a leg up, making use of the skeletal remains of the staircase, scaling the walls, clinging to the ceiling, lashing out at the last of those resisting round the very edge of the opening, a score of besiegers – soldiers, National and Municipal Guardsmen, mingled together pell-mell, most disfigured by face wounds in their terrible ascent, blinded by blood, driven wild with fury – finally came bursting into the room on the first floor. Only one man was left standing there, Enjolras. Without cartridges, without a sword, all he had left in his hand was the barrel of his rifle, having broken the butt on the heads of those coming in. He had placed the billiard table between his assailants and himself. He had retreated into the corner of the room, and there, with a proud gaze, head held high, with that stump of a weapon in his hand, he was still unnerving enough to create an empty space around him.

A cry was raised, 'He's the leader! It was he who slew the gunner. Just as well he's taken up position over there. He can stay there. Let's shoot him where he stands!'

'Go ahead and shoot me,' said Enjolras.

And flinging aside the stump of his rifle and folding his arms, he offered them his chest.

The courage to die bravely always affects men. As soon as Enjolras folded his arms, accepting his end, the deafening noise of the fighting ceased in that room, and the chaos suddenly subsided into a kind of sepulchral solemnity. The menacing majesty of the disarmed and motionless Enjolras seemed to weigh on that tumult, and this young man, who alone had not a single injury, proud, bloodied, charming, with the indifference of the invulnerable, seemed merely by the authority of his tranquil glance to constrain this sinister rabble to kill him with respect. His beauty, at that moment enhanced by pride, was resplendent, and as if it were no more possible for him to be tired than to be wounded after the dreadful twenty-four hours that had just elapsed, he was pink and rosy. It might have been of him that the witness was speaking who later told the court martial, 'There was one insurgent I heard referred to as Apollo.'

A National Guardsman who had taken aim at Enjolras lowered his gun, saying, 'I feel as if I'm going to be shooting a flower.'

Twelve men formed a firing squad in the corner opposite Enjolras, and in silence readied their guns.

Then a sergeant cried, 'Take aim!'

An officer intervened. 'Wait.'

And addressing Enjolras, he said, 'Do you want to be blindfolded?'

'No.'

'Was it you who killed the artillery sergeant?'

'Yes.'

A few moments earlier Grantaire had woken up.

Grantaire, remember, had been asleep since the day before, in the upper room of the tavern, seated on a chair, slumped over a table.

He embodied with every fibre of his being the old metaphor 'dead drunk'. The hideous potion of absinthe, stout and brandy had plunged him into lethargy. His table being small and of no use for the barricade, he had been left with it. He was still in the same posture, his chest slouched over the table, his head resting on his arms, surrounded by glasses, beer mugs and bottles. He had slept the sluggish sleep of the torpid bear and the sated leech. Nothing had disturbed him, neither the gunfire, nor the cannon-balls, nor the canister-shot that came through the window into the room where he was, nor the extraordinary commotion of the assault. He merely responded to the cannonade now and then by snoring. He seemed to be waiting there for a bullet that would save him the trouble of waking up. Several corpses lay around him, and at first glance nothing distinguished him from those deep sleepers in death.

Noise does not rouse a drunkard, it is silence that wakens him. This peculiarity has been observed more than once. The collapse of everything around him increased Grantaire's prostration. Devastation lulled him. That cessation of tumult, as it were, around Enjolras was a jolt to this heavy slumber. It had the same effect as a carriage going at full gallop that suddenly stops dead. The dozing passengers are wakened. Grantaire straightened up with a start, stretched out his arms, rubbed his eyes, stared, yawned, and understood.

Drunkenness that comes to an end is like a curtain tearing apart. Everything it concealed can be seen, in total, at a single glance. Everything suddenly offers itself to memory, and the drunkard who knows nothing of what has happened during the last twenty-four hours, even before his eyes are fully open, is aware of how things stand. Thoughts return to him with sudden lucidity. The fuddle of drunkenness, a kind of vapour that blinds the brain, dissipates and gives way to the clear, obsessive, sharply defined claims of reality.

The soldiers, their eyes fixed on Enjolras, had not even noticed Grantaire, tucked away as he was in a corner and as though screened by the billiard table; and the sergeant was about to repeat his order

'Take aim!' when all at once they heard a loud voice cry out beside them, 'Long live the Republic! So say I!'

Grantaire was on his feet. The tremendous conflagration of all that fighting he had missed, in which he had played no part, appeared in the glittering eyes of the transfigured drunkard.

'Long live the Republic!' he repeated, then strode across the room and went to stand next to Enjolras, facing the guns.

'Make it two at the same time,' he said.

And turning to Enjolras, he said to him deferentially, 'With your permission?'

Enjolras pressed his hand, smiling. He was still smiling when the burst of gunfire came.

With eight shots through him, Enjolras was left backed up against the wall as if the bullets had pinned him there. He simply bowed his head. Grantaire fell dead at his feet.

A few moments later the soldiers dislodged the last of the insurgents, who had taken refuge at the top of the house. They fired through a wooden lattice into the attic. There was fighting under the eaves. Bodies were thrown out of the windows, some of them still alive. Two light-infantrymen, trying to right the shattered omnibus, were slain by two shots fired from the garret windows. A man in an overall was pushed out, bayoneted in the stomach, and lay groaning on the ground. A soldier and an insurgent slid together down the tiles of the sloping roof, would not let go of each other, and fell, locked in a ferocious embrace. Similar fighting in the cellar. Shouts, shots, a furious trampling. Then silence. The barricade was captured.

The soldiers began searching the houses near by in pursuit of the fugitives.

XXIV
Prisoner

Marius was indeed a prisoner. The prisoner of Jean Valjean.

The hand that had caught him from behind as he fell, and whose sudden grasp he had felt as he lost consciousness, was that of Jean Valjean.

Jean Valjean had taken no part in the fighting except to expose himself to it. Had it not been for him, no one in that last phase of that desperate struggle would have thought of the wounded. Thanks to him, like an angel of mercy everywhere present among the carnage, those who fell were picked up, carried to the bar room, and their wounds dressed. In between, he repaired the barricade. But nothing that could be seen as an act of hostility or aggression, or even as self-defence, proceeded from his hands. He kept his own counsel, and he gave help. He himself had suffered only a few scratches. The bullets had avoided him. If suicide formed any part of what he had hoped to find in this place of death, on that count he had not succeeded. But we doubt that he had in mind suicide, an irreligious act.

In the thick fog of battle, Jean Valjean did not appear to see Marius. The fact is, he never took his eyes off him. When a gunshot felled Marius, Jean Valjean pounced with the agility of a tiger, fell on him as if on prey, and carried him off.

The vortex of the attack was at that moment so violently concentrated on Enjolras and the door to the tavern that no one saw Jean Valjean, supporting in his arms the unconscious Marius, cross the denuded floor of the barricade and disappear around the corner of the Corinthe building.

This corner, remember, formed a kind of promontory into the street. It shielded a few square feet of ground from cannon-balls, gun-fire and the eyes of onlookers. There is sometimes a room that does not burn in a fire, and in the most tumultuous seas, in the lee of a headland or deep in a rock-bound cove, an oasis of tranquillity. It was in that sort of a recess in the barricade's inner quadrangle that Éponine had breathed her last.

There Jean Valjean halted, let Marius slip to the ground, leaned back against the wall and cast his eyes around him. The situation they were in was dreadful.

For the moment, for two or three minutes perhaps, this stretch of wall offered shelter, but how to get away from this massacre? He recalled the plight in which he had found himself in Rue Polonceau eight years before, and how he had contrived to escape. It was difficult then, today it was impossible. He had before him this implacable and unresponsive six-storey house whose only inhabitant seemed to be the dead man hanging out of the window. To his right he had the fairly low barricade that closed off Rue de la Petite-Truanderie. Climbing over this obstacle looked easy, but visible over the top of the barricade was a line of bayonet tips. It was soldiers of the line posted beyond the barricade, on the lookout. It was obvious that to cross the barricade was to go to meet a firing squad, and that any head ventured above the top of that wall of cobblestones would serve as a target for sixty rifle shots. To his left he had the battlefield. Death lay behind the corner of that wall.

What could he do? Only a bird could have found a way out of there.

And a decision had to be made quickly, some expedient found, some course adopted. There was fighting going on a few steps away from him. Fortunately, everyone was intent on a single point, the door to the tavern, but if it occurred to any one soldier to go round to the back of the house, or to attack it from the side, they were done for.

Jean Valjean stared at the house in front of him, he stared at the barricade beside him, then he stared at the ground with the violence of total desperation, at a complete loss, as though he would have liked to drill a hole with his eyes.

By dint of staring, something vaguely distinguishable in such a state of anguish came into focus and took shape at his feet, as if it were within the power of a gaze to make the thing desired appear. A few paces away, at the foot of the small barricade so ruthlessly guarded and watched from the outside, he noticed, under a collapsed heap of cobblestones that partly concealed it, an iron grating, laid flat, flush with the ground. This grating, made of strong horizontal bars, was about two feet square. The surround of cobblestones that had kept it in place had been torn up, and it was as if it had been forced loose. Through the bars a dark opening could be glimpsed, something resembling a chimney flue or a cistern cylinder. Jean Valjean darted forward. His old expertise in escape flooded his mind like an illumination. Clearing away the cobblestones, lifting the grating, heaving Marius, inert as a dead body, on to his shoulders, and with that weight on his back, using his elbows and knees to help him, climbing down into that well-shaft of sorts, which was fortunately not very deep, letting the heavy iron hatch drop into position above his head, thereby setting the cobblestones rolling back on top of it, finding his footing on flag-stones ten feet below the surface – all this was performed as if a frenzy, with the strength of a giant and the swiftness of an eagle. It took a few minutes, at most.

Jean Valjean found himself, with Marius still unconscious, in a kind of long underground corridor. Profound peace, absolute silence, night.

The sensation he had experienced when escaping from the street into the convent came back to him. Only, today it was not Cosette that he was carrying, it was Marius.

Barely could he hear now, but as an indistinct murmur above him, the tremendous tumult of the tavern being taken by storm.

BOOK TWO

THE BOWELS OF LEVIATHAN

I
The Land Impoverished by the Sea

Paris pours twenty-five million a year down the drain. Literally. How, and in what manner? Day and night. To what purpose? To no purpose. With what in mind? With nothing in mind. Why? For no reason. By means of what organ? By means of its intestine. What is its intestine? Its sewer.

Twenty-five million is the most conservative estimate produced by specialized scientific calculations.

Having long proceeded by trial and error, science now knows that the most effective fertilizer is human manure. The Chinese, let us confess to our shame, knew this before we did. No Chinese peasant – it is Ekeberg who tells us this – goes to town without bringing back on either end of his bamboo pole two buckets full of what we call 'filth'. Thanks to human manure, the earth in China is still as youthful as in the days of Abraham. The Chinese wheat yield is up to a hundred per cent of the seed sown. There is no guano that can compare as a fertilizer with the excrement of a capital city. A city is the mightiest of dung-beetles. Using the city to manure the plain would be a sure success. If our gold is dung, our dung inversely is gold.

What is done with this gold-dung? It is swept into the abyss.

Fleets of vessels are sent at great expense to the South Pole to collect the droppings of petrels and penguins, and the substance of incalculable wealth that we have to hand we pour into the sea. All the human and animal manure that the world wastes, if it were put back into the land instead of being thrown into the sea, would suffice to feed the world.

Those heaps of excrement at boundary-posts, those cartloads of muck jolted through the streets at night, those frightful vats at the municipal dumps, those fetid seepings of subterranean sludge that the pavements hide from you – do you know what they are? They are the meadow in flower, green grass, serpolet, thyme and sage, they are game, they are cattle, they are the satisfied lowing of oxen in the evening; they are fragrant hay, golden wheat, bread on your table; they are warm blood in your veins, they are health, they are joy, they are life. Such is the will of that mysterious process of creation that is transfiguration on earth and transfiguration in heaven.

Return the stuff to the great crucible, your plentiful abundance will follow. The nutrition of the plains produces food for man.

You are free to waste this wealth – and to consider me ridiculous into the bargain. That will be the triumph of your ignorance.

According to statistical calculations, France alone pours away into the Atlantic through the mouths of her rivers half a billion every year. Note this: with those five hundred million we could cover one-quarter of our budget expenditure. So clever is man, he prefers to throw those five hundred million down the drain. It is the very substance of the people that the wretched evacuation of our sewers into the rivers, and the gigantic evacuation of our rivers into the ocean, carry away, now drop by drop, now in torrents. Every belch of our cesspools costs us a thousand francs. This has two consequences: impoverished land and contaminated water. Hunger emanating from the fields and disease emanating from the rivers.

It is common knowledge, for instance, that the Thames is at this moment poisoning London. As for Paris, it has become necessary of late to move most of the sewer outlets downstream, below the last bridge.

A bi-tubular mechanism equipped with valves and scouring sluices and operating by suction and expulsion, an elementary system of drainage as simple as human lungs and already fully functional in many communities in England, would suffice in order to bring into our towns the clean water of the countryside and to send back into the countryside the enriched water of the towns; and this easy exchange, of paramount simplicity, would allow us to keep for ourselves the five hundred million now being thrown away. People have other things on their minds.

The present system, meaning to do good, does harm. The intention is good, the outcome is unfortunate. We think we are purging the city, and we are enfeebling the population. A sewer is a misapprehension. When drainage – with its dual functionality, restoring what it takes away – has everywhere replaced the sewer – a simple depletory flush system – then this, combined with the realities of a new social economy, will increase tenfold the productiveness of the land, and the problem of destitution will be significantly alleviated. Add the elimination of parasitisms, and it will be resolved.

Meanwhile, public wealth goes into the river, and wastage occurs. Wastage is the word. In this way Europe is ruining itself by depletion.

As for France, we have just cited the figures. Now, Paris containing one twenty-fifth of the total French population, and Parisian guano being the richest of all, valuing Paris's share of the loss at twenty-five million of the half-billion that France annually denies itself is an understatement of the truth. Those twenty-five million, used for welfare relief and recreation, would double the splendour of Paris. The city sends them down into the sewers. So it could be said that Paris's great extravagance, its spectacular entertainment, its Folie-Beaujon, its festive orgy, its cascades of gold by the handful, its pomp, its luxury, its magnificence, is its sewer system.

So it is that, blinded by an inadequate political economy, we drown the well-being of all, leaving it to be carried off downstream and to disappear into the abyss. There should be St-Cloud nets put in place to catch the public fortune.

Economically, the matter can be summed up thus: Paris is a wastrel.

This model city, Paris, this paradigm of well designed capitals of which every nation strives to have its own copy, this metropolis of the ideal, this celebrated home of initiative, enterprise and endeavour, this centre and abode of intellect, this nation-city, this hive of the future, this marvellous combination of Babylon and Corinth would, from the viewpoint we have just indicated, make a Fokien peasant shrug his shoulders.

Imitate Paris, and you will ruin yourself. Besides, Paris is itself an imitator, and particularly in this immemorial and senseless waste.

This surprising ineptitude is not new. This is no recent folly. The ancients acted in the same way as the moderns. 'The sewers of Rome,' says Liebig, 'have absorbed all the well-being of the Roman peasant.' When the Roman countryside had been ruined by the Roman sewer, Rome depleted Italy, and after she had put Italy in her sewer, she put in Sicily, then Sardinia, then Africa. The sewer of Rome has engulfed the world. This cloaca offered engulfment to the city and to the universe. *Urbi et orbi.** Eternal city, unfathomable sewer.

In this as in other things Rome sets the example. Paris follows this example with all the stupidity characteristic of intellectual cities.

For the purposes of the operation on which we have just expounded, Paris has underneath it another Paris, a Paris of sewers, which has its

* 'To the city and to the world', the formula used in papal messages and blessings.

streets, its crossroads, its squares, its blind alleys, its arteries and its circulation – of muck, that is – without the human dimension.

For there must be no flattering, not even of a great people. Where there is everything, there is also ignominy alongside sublimity. And if Paris contains Athens, the city of light, Tyre, the city of might, Sparta, the city of virtue, Nineveh, the city of wonder, it also contains Lutetia, the city of mud.

In fact, therein lies the hallmark of its power, and Paris's colossal sump embodies, among monuments, that strange ideal embodied in humanity by a few men such as Machiavelli, Bacon and Mirabeau: abject grandeur.

If the eye could penetrate the surface, subterranean Paris would have the appearance of a huge madrepore coral. A sponge scarcely has more channels and chambers than the mound of earth fifteen miles in circumference on which the ancient city stands. Not to mention the catacombs, which are a separate cavern, not to mention the tangled network of gas pipes, leaving aside the vast distribution system of piped running water that feeds the stand-post hydrants, the sewers alone constitute an enormous murky network beneath both river-banks, a maze whose guiding thread is its incline.

There in the dank mist appears the rat, to which Paris seems to have given birth.

II

The Ancient History of the Sewer

Imagine Paris removed like a lid; a bird's-eye view of the underground network of sewers will reveal a large bough, so to speak, grafted on to the river on either side. On the right bank, the orbital sewer will be this bough's main trunk, the secondary drains will be the smaller branches, and the dead-end ducts will be the twigs.

This is only a simplified and half-accurate diagram, the right-angle, which is the usual angle in subterranean ramifications of this kind, being very rare in vegetation.

You will form a more accurate picture of this strange geometrical plan if you suppose that you are looking at some bizarre oriental alphabet, lying flat on a dark background, all jumbled up, and the misshapen letters welded together in apparent confusion and as if haphazardly, sometimes end to end, sometimes at angles to each other.

Sumps and sewers played a great role in the Middle Ages, in Late Antiquity and in that ancient Orient. The plague was born of them, despots died in them. The masses regarded these beds of putrefaction, monstrous cradles of death, with an almost religious fear. The vermin pit of Benares is no less dizzying than the lions' den of Babylon. According to rabbinical texts, Tiglath-Pileser swore by the sump of Nineveh. It was from the sewer of Münster that Jan van Leiden made his false moon appear, and it was from the cesspit of Kekscheb that his oriental counterpart, Mokanna, veiled prophet of Khorassan, made his false sun appear.

The history of men is reflected in the history of waste dumps. The Gemonian Steps told the story of Rome. Paris's sewer system has been an extraordinary thing over time. It has been a burial place, it has been a place of sanctuary. Crime, intelligence, social protest, freedom of conscience, thought, theft, everything that human laws pursue or have pursued has lain hidden in that warren: the Maillotins in the fourteenth century, the coat-snatchers in the fifteenth, the Huguenots in the sixteenth, Morin's visionaries in the seventeenth, the *chauffeurs* in the eighteenth. A hundred years ago the nocturnal thrust of the dagger emerged from it, the endangered scoundrel crept into it. Woodland had its caves, Paris had its sewer. The criminal underworld regarded the sewer as an annexe of the Cour des Miracles, and at night that Gallic *picareria**, sly and vicious, would creep back under the Maubuée vomitorium as to a bedchamber.

It was quite natural that those whose place of work in the daytime was Pick-pocket Alley or Cut-throat Lane should have as their nighttime abode Chemin-Vert Culvert or Hurepoix Catchment Drain. Places rife with memories. All sorts of phantoms haunt these long desolate corridors. Everywhere, putridness and miasma. Now and again, an air-well, where Villon on the inside talks to Rabelais on the outside.

The sewer in ancient Paris is the meeting-place of all things exhausted and of all things tried. Political economy sees detritus in it, social philosophy sees residue.

The sewer is the city's conscience. Everything converges here, and is brought face to face here. In this ghastly place there are shadows but there are no more secrets. Each thing has its true form, or at least its definitive form. The pile of filth has this in its favour: it does not lie. Artlessness has taken refuge here. There is Basil's mask, but you can see the cardboard and the ties, and the inside as well as the outside, and it is made more obvious by honest mud. Scapin's false nose is close by. Once civilization has no further use for its bits of grubbiness, they fall into this pit of truthfulness, where the great social downward

---

* From *pícaro*, Spanish for 'cunning rogue' (and hence 'picaresque', describing the adventures of such an anti-hero), *pícareria* is a confederacy of rogues.

slide ends; they are swallowed up by it, but they are on display. This farrago is a confession. No more false appearances here, no possible plastering-over; filth takes off its shirt; stark nakedness, all illusions and mirages dispelled, nothing other than what is, showing the ugly face of what is finished with. Reality and disappearance. Here, the bottom of a bottle admits to drunkenness, a basket handle tells of domestic service; there, the apple core that once had literary opinions reverts to being an apple core; the effigy on the ten-centime coin is plainly turning green, Caiaphas's spittle meets Falstaff's vomit, the gold coin from the gambling den strikes the nail from which the suicide's rope hangs, a grey foetus rolls away, wrapped in the sequins that danced at the Opéra last Mardi Gras; a justice's cap that passed judgement on men wallows next to a putridness that was a trollop's skirt. This is more than fraternity, this is intimacy. Everything that used to pretty itself is now besmirched. The last veil is torn off. A sewer is a cynic. It tells all.

We like this sincerity in foulness, it is restful to the soul. When you have spent your time on earth enduring the spectacle of the airs and graces assumed by reasons of state, solemn oaths, political wisdom, human justice, professional integrity, the rigours of high office, the robes of incorruptibility, it is a relief to go into a sewer and see the filth that belongs there.

It is also instructive. We said earlier, history passes through the sewer. The St Bartholomews filter into it, drop by drop, between the paving-stones. Great public assassinations, political and religious massacres, pass through this underground realm of civilization, and shove their corpses down here. To the eye of anyone given to reflection, all history's murderers are here in the hideous murk, on their knees, with a piece of their shroud for an apron, dismally cleaning up their doings. Louis XI is here with Tristan, François I with Duprat, Charles IX with his mother, Richelieu with Louis XIII, Louvois is here, Le Tellier is here, Hébert and Maillard are here, scratching at the stones and trying to make the traces of their actions disappear. Beneath these vaults you hear the brooms of those spectres. Here, you breathe in the overwhelming fetidness of social catastrophes. You see in the corners reddish glimmerings. Terrible waters flow there, in which bloodied hands have been washed.

The social observer must enter these shadows. They are part of his laboratory. Philosophy is the microscope of the mind. Everything wants to flee it, but nothing escapes it. Dodging is useless. Which side of yourself do you show when dodging? The shameful side. Philosophy trains its honest gaze on evil and does not let it escape into the void. In the fading-away of things that disappear, in the dwindling of things that vanish, it recognizes everything. It reconstructs the purple from the rag and the woman from her tatters. Out of the sewer it reconstructs the city. Out of the mud it reconstructs morality. From the shard it deduces the amphora or the pitcher. From the imprint of a fingernail on a piece of parchment it recognizes the difference between the Jewry of the Judengasse and the Jewry of the Ghetto. In what remains, it finds what has been – good, evil, falsehood, truth, the bloodstain from the law courts, the ink-blot from the cavern, the drop of candle grease from the brothel, ordeals suffered, temptations welcomed, orgies spewed up, the kink that characters have acquired in abasing themselves, the trace of prostitution in souls whose coarseness made them capable of it, and in the jerkins of Rome's street porters the imprint of Messalina's elbow.

III
Bruneseau

Paris's sewer was legendary in the Middle Ages. In the sixteenth century Henri II attempted a survey that came to nothing. Not a hundred years ago, Mercier tells us, the sewer system was abandoned, and left to itself to survive as best it could.

That was ancient Paris, consigned to disputes, indecision and uncertainty. For a long time it was quite stupid. Later, '89 showed how cities come to their senses. But in the good old days the capital had little idea. It did not know how to manage its affairs either morally or materially, and was no more capable of sweeping away filth than abuses. Everything was an obstacle, everything was debatable. The sewer, for example, followed no route. People could no more find their bearings down there than they could understand each other in the city. Above ground the unintelligible, below ground the unchartable. Beneath the confusion of tongues was the confusion of tunnels. Underlying Babel was the Labyrinth.

Sometimes the Paris sewer took to overflowing, as though this unappreciated Nile were suddenly seized with anger. There were, disgusting to relate, inundations of sewerage. At times, this stomach of civilization failed to digest properly, resulting in a reflux from the cloaca into the city's gullet, and Paris got an after-taste of its own excreta. There was something to be said for these bouts of remorse on the part of the sewer. They were warnings – taken very badly, in fact. The city was outraged that its filth should be so bold, and would not tolerate its return. Flush it away more effectively.

The inundation of 1802 is still a vivid memory to Parisians in their eighties. The filth spread crosswise over Place des Victoires, where the statue of Louis XIV stands. It entered Rue St-Honoré by the two man-holes in the Champs-Élysées, Rue St-Florentin by the St-Florentin drain, Rue Pierre-à-Poisson by the Sonnerie drain, Rue Popincourt by the Chemin-Vert drain, Rue de la Roquette by the Rue de Lappe drain. It filled the gutter running down the middle of Rue des Champs-Élysées to a depth of well over twelve inches. And, to the south, the outlet into the Seine backed up, sending it into Rue Mazarine, Rue de l'Échaudé and Rue des Marais, where after covering a hundred and twenty yards it stopped just a few paces short of the house where Racine had lived, showing greater respect for the seventeenth-century poet than for the king. It reached its maximum depth in Rue St-Pierre, where it rose three feet above the flagstones of the gutter, and its max-imum expanse in Rue St-Sabin, where it stretched over two hundred and sixty yards.

At the beginning of this century the Paris sewers were still a place of mystery. Filth will never be well thought of, but in this instance such was its ill-repute that it was regarded with dread. Paris knew in some confused way that there was underneath it a terrible cavern. People spoke of it as of that monstrous pit of Thebes teeming with fifteen-foot-long centipedes and that might have served Behemoth for a bathtub. The sewermen's great boots never ventured beyond certain well known points. It was still very close to the time when waste-carts, on top of which Sainte-Foix fraternized with the Marquis de Créqui, discharged their loads directly into the sewers. As for any flushing, responsibility for that task was entrusted to downpours of rain, which clogged rather than cleared. Rome still allowed its waste dump a little poetry, calling it the Gemonian Steps. Paris insulted its cloaca and called it the Stink-Hole. Science and superstition concurred in their horror. The Stink-Hole was no less loathsome to hygiene than to legend. Paris's bogeyman flourished under the fetid vault of the Mouf-fetard drain. The corpses of the Marmousets had been thrown into the Barillerie drain. Fagon had attributed the terrible malignant fever of 1685 to the great long stretch of the Marais open drain, which remained uncovered in Rue St-Louis, almost opposite the sign of the Gallant Messenger, until 1833. The mouth of the Rue de la Mortel-lerie drain was famous for the vermin that came out of it. With the sharp points of its iron grating suggestive of a row of teeth, it was like a dragon's maw in that deadly street, breathing hell over men. The popular imagination enlivened the grim Parisian sump with who knows what hideous mixture of infinitudes. The sewer was bottomless. The sewer was a barathrum. The idea of exploring these leprous regions did not even occur to the police. To probe this unknown, to fathom this darkness, to go exploring this abyss – who would have dared? It was terrifying. Yet someone did volunteer. The sewer had its Christopher Columbus.

One day in 1805, during one of the emperor's rare appearances in Paris, the minister of the interior, some Decrès or Crétet or other, attended the master's *petit lever*. The sound of their swords being trailed after them by all those extraordinary soldiers of the great Republic and the great Empire could be heard from Place du Carrousel. Napoleon's doorway was choked with heroes, men from the Rhine, the Escaut, the Adige and the Nile, companions of Joubert, Desaix, Marceau, Hoche, Kléber, Fleurus balloonists, Mainz grenadiers, Genoa bridge-builders, hussars the Pyramids had gazed on, artillerymen bespattered by Junot's cannon-ball, cuirassiers who had taken by assault the fleet lying at anchor in the Zuyderzee. Some had followed Bonaparte across the bridge at Lodi, others had been with Murat in the trenches at Mantua, others had gone ahead of Lannes along the sunken road at Montebello. There in the courtyard of the Tuileries was the whole army of that time, represented by a section or a unit, guarding Napoleon in his sleep. And it was the magnificent epoch when the Grand Army had Marengo behind it and Austerlitz ahead of it. 'Sire,' the minister of the interior said to Napoleon, 'yesterday I saw the most intrepid man in your Empire.' 'What man was that?' said the emperor brusquely. 'And what has he done?' 'Sire, he's intending to do something.' 'And what is that?' 'To visit the sewers of Paris.'

This man existed, and his name was Bruneseau.

IV
Unknown Details

The visit took place. It was a formidable campaign, a nocturnal battle against pestilence and asphyxiation. It was at the same time a journey of discovery. A few years ago one of the survivors of this expedition, an intelligent workman, very young at the time, was still recounting some of the curious details that Bruneseau felt obliged to leave out of his report to the prefect of police, as a discredit to the administrative style. Disinfection procedures were very rudimentary in those days. Bruneseau had hardly gone beyond the first intersections of that subterranean network when eight of the twenty workmen refused to go

any further. The operation was complicated. The visit involved cleaning. So there was cleaning to be done, and at the same time surveying:
noting water inlets, counting gratings and outlets, detailing the branch
structure, indicating the currents where the waters divided, identifying
the respective perimeters of the various sewage basins, probing the
smaller drains grafted on to the main drain, measuring the maximum
height of each drain and the width, at the base of the vault as well as
at floor level, and lastly plotting the level of every water inlet relative
to both drain floor and street. Progress was arduous. It was not
uncommon for the ladders descending into the sewers to plunge into
three feet of sludge. The lamps guttered in the miasmic fumes. Every
now and then a sewerman was carried out unconscious. At certain
points, a precipitous drop. The ground had given way, the paving had
collapsed, the drain had turned into a soak-pit. There was nothing
solid left. A man suddenly disappeared. He was rescued with the
greatest difficulty. On the advice of Fourcroy they lighted, at regular
intervals, in duly sanitized locations, big wire-mesh containers filled
with resin-soaked tow. The wall was covered in some places with
gnarled fungi that looked like tumours. The very stone itself seemed
diseased in this unbreathable atmosphere.

In his exploration Bruneseau followed the direction of the flow. At
the head of the two Grand-Hurleur channels he deciphered on a projecting stone the date 1550. This stone marked the furthest that
Philibert Delorme, charged by Henri II with visiting Paris's subterranean network, had reached. This stone was the sixteenth century's
mark on the sewer. Bruneseau found the seventeenth century's handiwork in the Ponceau drain and the Rue Vieille-du-Temple drain,
vaulted between 1600 and 1650, and the eighteenth century's handiwork in the western section of the collector channel, which was
enclosed and vaulted in 1740. These two vaultings, especially the one
that was less old, of 1740, were more cracked and decrepit than the
masonry of the orbital sewer, which dated from 1412, when the
Ménilmontant fresh-water brook was elevated to the rank of Paris's
main sewer, a promotion similar to that of a peasant appointed chief
valet to the king, something like Gros-Jean transformed into Lebel.

In a few places, particularly beneath the court of justice, were identified what were thought to be the cavities of ancient dungeons
actually built into the sewer. Hideous oubliettes. An iron neck-collar
hung in one of these cells. They were all walled up. There were some
bizarre finds, including the skeleton of an orang-utan that had vanished from the Jardin des Plantes in 1800, a disappearance probably

connected with the famous and indisputable apparition of the devil in Rue des Bernardins in the last year of the eighteenth century. The poor devil had ended up drowning in the sewer.

Beneath the long arched corridor that ends at Arche-Marion, a perfectly preserved rag-picker's basket excited the admiration of the experts. Everywhere, the sludge, which the sewermen had learned how to deal with intrepidly, abounded in valuable objects, gold and silver jewellery, precious stones, coins. Any giant that had sifted this cesspool would have had the riches of centuries in his sieve. Where the two branches of Rue du Temple and Rue Ste-Avoye divided, a curious Huguenot copper medal was found, showing a pig wearing a cardinal's hat on one side and a wolf with a tiara on its head on the other.

The most surprising discovery was made at the entrance to the main sewer. This entrance had once been closed off by a grating, of which nothing but the hinges remained. From one of these hinges, arrested there in its passage, no doubt, hung a dirty shapeless rag, fluttering in the dark, not quite completely disintegrated. Bruneseau brought his lantern up close and examined this tattered oddment. It was of very fine batiste, and discernible in one corner, less frayed than the others, was a heraldic coronet embroidered above these seven letters: LAVBESP. The coronet was the coronet of a marquis, and the seven letters stood for 'Laubespine'. It was realized that what they had before their eyes was a piece of Marat's shroud. Marat in his youth had had an amorous intrigue. It was around the time that he held the post of physician to the household of the Comte d'Artois. From that affair with a great lady – a matter of historical record – he was left with this bedsheet. Casualty of fate, or souvenir. At his death, this being the only linen of any fineness that he had in his house, it was used to wrap his body. In cerements that had known carnal pleasure old women had shrouded for burial the tragic Friend of the People.

Bruneseau passed on. That rag was left where it was, just as it was. Out of contempt or respect? Marat deserved both. And besides, the mark of destiny that it bore was enough to make anyone hesitate to touch it. In any case, burial things are best left in the place they themselves have chosen. In short, it was a strange relic. A marquise had slept in it. Marat had rotted in it. It had been through the Panthéon and ended up with the rats in the sewer. This remnant of the bedchamber, whose every fold Watteau would once have joyfully depicted, had come to be worthy of Dante's steady gaze.

The visit to Paris's underground waste-disposal network lasted a full seven years, from 1805 to 1812. Along the way Bruneseau designated, directed and brought to completion some major works. In

1808 he lowered the floor of the Ponceau and, creating new routes everywhere, in 1809 he extended the sewers under Rue St-Denis to the Fontaine des Innocents, in 1810 under Rue Froid-Manteau and La Salpêtrière, in 1811 under Rue Neuve-des-Petits-Pères, Rue du Mail, Rue de l'Écharpe, Place Royale, and in 1812 under Rue de la Paix and Chaussée-d'Antin. At the same time he had the whole network disinfected and sanitized. In the second year of his work Bruneseau was joined by his son-in-law Nargaud.

So it was that at the beginning of this century the old society attended to its hidden underside and put its sewers to rights. At least that was one thing cleaned up.

Full of twists and turns, creviced and fissured, in need of repaving, potholed, suddenly veering off at bizarre angles, rising and descending without any logic, fetid, feral, fearsome, steeped in darkness, its flagstones and walls scarred and gashed, horrendous – looking back, that is what Paris's ancient sewer was like. Tunnels branching off in every direction, ducts criss-crossing, junctions, multiple intersections, radial-patterned like mining trenches, with dead ends, blind alleys, saltpetre-lined vaults, foul sumps, scabrous seepings from the walls, dripping ceilings, blackness – nothing equalled the horror of this old waste-disposal crypt, Babylonian alimentary canal, cavern, catacomb, alley-riddled abyss, gigantic burrow where in the mind's eye that enormous blind mole, the past, is seen prowling through the shadows in filth that was once magnificence.

This, we repeat, was the sewer of old.

V
Present-day Progress

Today the sewer is clean, stark, straight, as it should be. It almost realizes the ideal of what is meant in England by the word 'respectable'. It is decent and drab; well laid out; you might almost say 'well turned out'. It has the look of a tradesman who has come up in the world. It is almost light enough to see. The sludge observes a decorum. At first sight it might easily be mistaken for one of those underground passageways that were once so common and so useful to fleeing monarchs and princes, in the good old days 'when the people loved their kings'. The present sewer is a fine sewer, where the pure style prevails. Driven out of poetry and having apparently taken refuge in architecture, the classic rectilinear alexandrine verse seems inherent in every stone of this long and palely shadowed vault. Every drain is an arcade. The Rue de Rivoli is emulated, even in the sewer. The fact is, if the geometrical

1137

line has a place anywhere it is certainly in a city's sewerage system. Here, everything must conform to the shortest route. The sewer has acquired a certain official status nowadays. Even police reports, in which it sometimes figures, are no longer disrespectful when referring to it. The words that characterize it in administrative language are formal and dignified. What used to be called a 'passage' is now called a 'gallery'. What used to be called a 'hole' is now called an 'inspection chamber'. Villon would no longer recognize his old bolt-hole. This network of cellars has its immemorial population of rodents, pullulating more than ever. From time to time a seasoned old sewer-rat dares to show its head at the window and observes the Parisians. But even these vermin are tamed, satisfied as they are with their subterranean palace. The sewer has nothing of its earlier barbarism. The rain that used to foul the sewer now flushes it. But do not be too trusting. Noxious fumes still inhabit it. It is more hypocritical than irreproachable. The Prefecture of Police and the health commission have done their best, but despite all the sanitization measures it exudes a faintly suspect smell, like Tartuffe after confession.

What we can agree on is that since, all things considered, mucking-out is a tribute the sewer pays to civilization, and from that point of view Tartuffe's conscience is an advance on the Augean Stables, there has certainly been some improvement in Paris's sewer system.

This is more than progress, it is a transformation. Between the old sewer and the present sewer there has been a revolution. Who brought about this revolution? The man forgotten by everyone and whose name we have mentioned, Bruneseau.

VI
Future Progress

The excavation of Paris's sewer has been no small task. The last ten centuries have worked on it without being able to complete it any more than they have been able to finish building Paris. Indeed, the sewer suffers all the repercussions of Paris's expansion. It is a kind of hidden multi-tentacled polyp that, as the city grows above it, grows in the earth beneath. Every time the city opens up a new street, the sewer extends an arm. The old monarchy constructed only twenty-five thousand four hundred and eighty yards of sewers. That was the situation in Paris on the first of January 1806. We shall have more to say about that era in due course. From then onwards the enterprise was effectively and energetically resumed and pursued. Napoleon built five thousand two hundred and fifty yards – these figures are interesting;

Louis XVIII, six thousand two hundred and forty; Charles X, eleven thousand eight hundred and fifty; Louis-Philippe, ninety-seven thousand three hundred and fifty-three; the Republic of 1848, twenty-five thousand five hundred and seventy; the present regime, seventy-seven thousand one hundred; in all, to date, two hundred and forty-eight thousand eight hundred and forty-three yards, close on one hundred and fifty miles of sewers; Paris's vast entrails. An obscure, ever-expanding network, an immense and unnoticed engineering operation.

As we can see, Paris's subterranean labyrinth is today more than ten times what it was at the beginning of the century. It is difficult to imagine all the perseverance and effort it has taken to bring this sewer system to the point of relative perfection that it has now reached. It was with great difficulty that the old monarchic administration, and during the last ten years of the eighteenth century the Revolutionary municipal authorities, managed to lay the fifteen miles or so of sewer that existed before 1806. All sorts of obstacles hindered this operation, some to do with the nature of the terrain, others inherent in the Parisian working-class population's own prejudices. Paris is built on a site strangely resistant to the mattock, the hoe, the drill, to human intervention. There is nothing more difficult to cut through and penetrate than this geological stratum on which stands the marvellous historical structure called Paris. As soon as any kind of work starts on this layer of alluvial deposits, subterranean obstructions abound, such as liquid clay, fresh-water springs, hard rock and that soft, deep mud for which the scientific term is 'ooze'. The pickaxe makes arduous progress through calcareous layers alternating with very thin veins of clay and beds of schist, whose folia are encrusted with oyster-shells coeval with the pre-adamite oceans. Sometimes a rivulet suddenly bursts through a vault under construction and drenches the labourers working on it. Or loose mudstone is suddenly exposed and comes pouring down in a raging torrent, breaking the strongest supporting beams as if they were made of glass. Quite recently, at La Villette, where the main sewer had to be routed under the St-Martin Canal without interrupting navigation and without draining the canal, a crack opened up in the canal basin, and water suddenly poured into the underground tunnel, overwhelming the power of the pumps. They had to use a diver to find the crack, which was in the Grand Bassin lock, and it was not without great difficulty that the crack was filled in. Elsewhere, near the Seine, and even quite far from the river – for instance, at Belleville, Grande-Rue and Passage Lunière – you come across quicksands that suck you in, where a man can disappear before your eyes. Add to that, asphyxiation by noxious fumes, being buried under cave-ins, and the ground suddenly giving way. Add to that, typhus, to which the workmen slowly succumb. In our own day, after having excavated the Clichy gallery, with a shelf for carrying a water main from the Ourcq – work that was carried out in an open trench over thirty-two feet deep; after cave-ins, and by means of often foul excavations and of underpinning, having vaulted the Bièvre from Boulevard de l'Hôpital down to the Seine; after having constructed the sewer line from Barrière Blanche to Chemin d'Aubervilliers in four months, working day and night at a depth of thirty-six feet, in order to save Paris from the torrential flood-waters of Montmartre and so as to provide drainage for those twenty-two acres of fluvial marshland that lie stagnating by Barrière des Martyrs; after having built underground, without a trench – something that had not been seen before then – twenty feet below the surface, a sewer in Rue Barre-du-Bec, Foreman Monnot died. After having vaulted over three thousand yards of sewers all over the city, from Rue Traversière-St-Antoine to Rue de Lourcine, after having dealt with the storm-water flooding of Carrefour Censier-Mouffetard by installing the Arbalète drain, after having built the St-Georges sewer on stone bedding and concrete in shifting sands, after having overseen the formidable task of lowering the floor of the Notre-Dame-de-Nazareth sewer, Engineer Duleau died. There is no official reporting of such acts of bravery, more useful though they are than the senseless slaughter on battlefields.

The sewers of Paris in 1832 were far from being what they are today. Bruneseau provided the initial impetus, but it took cholera to bring about the vast reconstruction that has been carried out since. It is surprising, for example, that in 1821 part of the orbital sewer, called the Grand Canal as in Venice, was still an open drain festering in Rue des Gourdes. It was not until 1823 that the city of Paris found in its pocket the two hundred and sixty-six thousand and eighty francs six centimes needed to cover this foulness. The three soak-wells of Combat, La Cunette and St-Mandé, with their outflows, cesspools, appliances and purification systems, date from only 1836. Paris's intestinal network has been rebuilt and, as we have said, increased in extent more than tenfold within the last quarter of a century.

Thirty years ago, at the time of the fifth–sixth of June insurrection, there was still in many places more or less the original sewer. A great number of streets, now cambered, then had a gutter running down the middle of them. Very often to be seen in the declivity into which the sides of a street or a crossroads sloped were large square gratings with thick iron bars that gleamed from being polished by the feet of the crowd, dangerous and slippery for vehicles and liable to bring down horses. The official language of the Bridges and Highways Authority gave these declivities and gratings the expressive name *cassis*. In 1832, in countless streets – Rue de l'Étoile, Rue St-Louis, Rue du Temple, Rue Vieille-du-Temple, Rue Notre-Dame-de-Nazareth, Rue Folie-Méricourt, Quai aux Fleurs, Rue du Petit-Musc, Rue de Normandie, Rue Pont-aux-Biches, Rue des Marais, Faubourg St-Martin, Rue Notre-Dame-des-Victoires, Faubourg Montmartre, Rue Grange-Batelière, the Champs-Élysées, Rue Jacob, Rue de Tournon – the old Gothic sewer still cynically displayed its innards. These were long stretches of stone-lined drains under gratings, sometimes edged with boundary-posts-a monumental check.

In 1806 the extent of Paris's sewers was still comparatively close to the figure recorded in 1663: five thousand three hundred and twenty-eight *toises**. After Bruneseau, by the first of January 1832, it was forty-four thousand yards. Between 1806 and 1831, an average of eight hundred and twenty yards were constructed every year. Since then, eight and a half, even eleven, thousand yards of galleries have been constructed every year, of small masonry materials with hydraulic-lime mortar on a concrete base. At some two hundred francs a yard, the one hundred and fifty miles of sewers of present-day Paris represent in the region of fifty million francs.

Apart from the economic progress we mentioned at the beginning, there are serious problems of public hygiene relating to this enormous issue of Paris's sewer.

Paris is sandwiched between two layers, a layer of water and a layer of air. The layer of water, lying fairly deep underground but already tapped by two borings, is supplied by the layer of greensand lying between the chalk and the Jurassic limestone. This layer may be represented as a disc of some sixty miles' radius. A multitude of rivers and brooks seeps into it. In a glass of water from the Grenelle well you are drinking the Seine, the Marne, the Yonne, the Oise, the Aisne, the Cher, the Vienne and the Loire. This layer of water is wholesome, it comes from heaven in the first place, then from the earth. The layer of air is insalubrious; it comes from the sewer. All the noxious fumes of the sewer are inhaled in the city's respiration; hence this bad breath. The air taken from above a dung-heap, it has been scientifically proved, is purer than the air taken from above Paris. In due course, with the help of progress, as machines improve and our knowledge

---

* A pre-Revolutionary unit of measurement equivalent to 1.944 metres or 2.126 yards. The metric system was first adopted in France in 1793.

increases, the layer of water will be used to purify the layer of air. That is to say, to clean the sewer. We know that by 'cleaning the sewer' we mean returning the muck to the earth, putting dung back in the soil and manure back in the fields. As a result of this measure there will be a reduction in poverty and an improvement in health for the whole social community. At present, the spread of disease around Paris, taking the Louvre as the hub of this pestilential wheel, extends for one hundred and twenty-five miles.

It might be said that for ten centuries the sewer has been Paris's disease. The sewer is the vice that Paris has in its blood. The people's instinct has never been wrong about this. The occupation of sewer-man used to be almost as dangerous, and almost as loathsome to the people, as the occupation of knacker, regarded with horror and for so long left to the executioner. High wages were necessary to induce a builder to disappear into that fetid warren. The shaft-sinker's ladder hesitated to plunge into it. It was said proverbially, 'To descend into the sewer is to step into the grave.' And as we have said, all sorts of frightful legends shrouded in terror this colossal cesspit, this dreaded stink-hole that bears traces of the revolutions of the globe as well as of the revolutions of man, and where vestiges of all cataclysms are to be found, from the seashells of the Flood to Marat's rag.

BOOK THREE

THE MIRE, YET THE SOUL

I

The Sewer and Its Surprises

Jean Valjean, it turned out, was in the sewers of Paris.

Yet another resemblance between Paris and the sea: he who plunges into it, as into the ocean, may disappear.

The transition was extraordinary. In the very heart of the city Jean Valjean had found a way out of the city; and in the twinkling of an eye, the time taken to lift a manhole cover and close it again, he had passed from broad daylight to total darkness, from midday to midnight, from tumult to silence, from the maelstrom of thunderous explosions to the stagnancy of the tomb and, by a twist of fate far more remarkable even than that of Rue Polonceau, from the most extreme peril to the utmost safety.

Suddenly dropping into a cellar, disappearing into Paris's secret dungeon, leaving that street where death was ubiquitous for this tomb of sorts where there was life – that was a strange moment. He remained as if bewildered for a few seconds, listening, stupefied. The pitfall of safety had suddenly opened beneath him. Celestial goodness had, in a manner of speaking, caught him by treachery. Wonderful ambushes laid by providence!

Only, the wounded man did not stir, and Jean Valjean did not know whether what he was carrying down that hole was dead or alive.

His first sensation was blindness. Suddenly, he could no longer see anything. He also felt that within a moment he had become deaf. He could no longer hear anything. As we have said, thanks to the depth of earth that separated him from it, the frenzied orgy of murder that raged a few feet above reached him only faintly and indistinctly, like a deep and distant murmur. He felt solid ground under his feet. That was all. But it was enough. He extended one arm and then the other, touched the walls on both sides, and realized the corridor was narrow. He slipped, and realized the flagged surface was wet. He cautiously put one foot forward, fearing a hole, a drain-well, some abyss. He found that the paving continued. A whiff of foulness signalled to him what place he was in.

After a few moments he was no longer blind. A little light came down the air-well he had slipped into, and his eyes had adjusted to this cellar. He began to discern something. The passage in which he had gone to ground – no other expression better describes the situation – ended in a wall behind him. It was one of those blind alleys for which the technical term is 'lateral sewer'. In front of him was another wall, a wall of blackness. The light from the air-well gave out ten or twelve paces from the point where Jean Valjean stood, and cast the merest deathly pallor on a few yards of the damp sewer wall. Beyond, the opacity was massive. To penetrate it seemed horrifying, and entering it like being swallowed up. Yet it was possible for a man to force his way through that wall of fog, and it had to be done. Indeed, it had to be done quickly. That grating, Jean Valjean thought, that he had noticed under the cobblestones might also be noticed by the soldiers; everything depended on that accident of fate. They too might descend, and search this air-well. There was not a minute to lose. He had put Marius down on the ground, now he gathered him up – that again is the appropriate term – settled him back on his shoulders, and set off. He resolutely entered that darkness.

The truth is, they were less out of danger than Jean Valjean thought. Perils of another kind, and no less great perhaps, awaited them. After the blistering maelstrom of the fighting, the cavern of miasmas and pitfalls; after chaos, the cloaca. Jean Valjean had fallen from one circle of hell into another.

When he had gone fifty paces he had to stop. A problem presented itself. The corridor ended at another passageway that cut across it. There was a choice of direction. Which way should he go? Should he turn left or right? How was anyone to find his bearings in this pitch-black labyrinth? This labyrinth, as we have already mentioned, had a guiding thread, its incline. To follow the incline was to go down to the river. Jean Valjean realized this immediately.

He told himself he was probably in the sewer of Les Halles, that if he chose to go left and followed the incline, within fifteen minutes he would come to some outlet on the Seine between Pont-au-Change and Pont-Neuf; that is to say, he would appear in broad daylight in the busiest part of Paris. Perhaps he would come out at a grating in the middle of a crossroads. Astounding the bystanders with the spectacle of two bloodied men emerging from the ground under their feet. The police turning up, the local guardsmen called to arms. They would be arrested before they were out. It was better to head back into the labyrinth, trust in that blackness and rely on providence to find a way out. Going in the upward direction, he turned to the right.

When he had turned the corner of the gallery, the distant glimmer of the air-well disappeared, the curtain of darkness fell over him once more and he was blind again. Still he kept going, as quickly as he could. Marius's two arms were wrapped around his neck and his feet dangled behind him. He held both arms with one hand, and felt his way along the wall with the other. Marius's cheek was touching his and, being bloody, stuck to it. He felt a warm trickle, coming from Marius, dripping on to him and soaking into his clothes. But a damp warmth at his ear, which the wounded man's mouth was touching, indicated breathing, and therefore life. The passage Jean Valjean was now following was not as narrow as the first. He trudged along it with considerable difficulty. The rains of the preceding day had not yet entirely run off and had created a little stream running down the middle of the sewer floor, forcing him to keep close to the wall so as not to have his feet in the water. So he progressed, darkly. He was like the creatures of the night, groping in the invisible, lost underground in veins of shadow.

Yet little by little, either because distant air-wells sent a little unsteady glimmering into this opaque fog or because his eyes were adjusting to the dark, he regained some dim level of vision and began once again to perceive indistinctly now the wall he was touching, now the vault he was walking under. The pupil dilates in the dark and eventually finds light there, just as the soul dilates in misfortune and eventually finds God.

Finding his way was no easy task. The layout of the sewers reflects, as it were, the layout of the streets above. There were in Paris at that time two thousand two hundred streets. Imagine, underneath them, that forest of shadowy branches called the sewer. The network of sewers existing at that time, placed end to end, would have reached a length of twenty-seven miles. We said earlier that, thanks to exceptional activity in the last thirty years, the present network extends to no less than one hundred and fifty.

Jean Valjean started out under a misapprehension. He thought he was under Rue St-Denis, and unfortunately for him he was not. Under Rue St-Denis there is an old stone sewer that dates from Louis XIII and runs directly to the main sewer, the so-called Great Sewer, with only one turning to the right, at the level of the old Cour des Miracles, and a single junction, with the St-Martin sewer, where the four passages meet at a crossroads. But the Petite-Truanderie drain, whose entrance was near the Corinthe tavern, has never connected with the Rue St-Denis sewer. It leads into the Montmartre sewer, and that is the one Jean Valjean had entered. There were plenty of opportunities for getting lost down there. The Montmartre sewer is one of the most labyrinthine of the old network. Fortunately, Jean Valjean had left behind him the Les Halles sewer, which on the map looks like a tangled host of topgallant masts. But before reaching the orbital sewer, which alone could lead him to some exit that was far enough away to be safe, there lay ahead of him more than one unwelcome encounter and more than one street corner – for streets they are – inviting him in the dark like a question mark: first, on his left, the huge Plâtrière sewer, a kind of Chinese puzzle, with its chaos of Ts and Zs confused, extending under the Post Office and under the wheat market roundhouse right down to the Seine, where it ends in a Y; second, on his right, the curving corridor of Rue du Cadran with its three teeth that are so many blind alleys; third, on his left, the Mail branch, complicated by a kind of fork almost at the mouth of it, zigzagging its way to the great underground chamber of the Louvre outlet, divided up into subsections with offshoots in every direction; and last, the dead-end passage of Rue des Jeûneurs, not to mention little recesses here and there.

If Jean Valjean had had the faintest notion of everything we have just described, he would have soon realized, merely by the feel of the wall, that he was not in the Rue St-Denis underground gallery. Instead of the old ashlar stonework, instead of the earlier style of architecture, regal and majestic even in the sewer, with paving and walls of granite and fat-lime mortar costing four hundred francs a yard, he would have felt beneath his hand contemporary cheapness, economic expediency, buhrstone with hydraulic-lime mortar on a concrete base, which costs two hundred francs a yard, the so-called 'small' bourgeois masonry. But he knew nothing of all this.

He kept going, anxious but calm, seeing nothing, knowing nothing, at the mercy of fate; that is to say, in the hands of providence.

Gradually, it has to be said, a vague horror came over him. The gloom that enveloped him penetrated his spirit. He was walking within a riddle. This cloacal aqueduct is dreadful. It is vertiginously convoluted. Being trapped inside this sinister Paris is a dismal experience. Jean Valjean was obliged to find his way, and almost to fabricate it, without seeing it. In this unknown, every step he ventured might be his last. How would he get out of here? Would he find an exit? Would he find it in time? Would this colossal underground sponge with its stone pores allow itself to be penetrated and invaded? Would they encounter some unexpected concentration of inextricable darkness? Would they be baffled by the inescapable, and thwarted by the impassable? Would Marius die down here from loss of blood, and he of hunger? Having lost their way down here, would they both end up as two skeletons in some corner of this black night? He did not know. He asked himself all this and was unable to reply. The bowels of Paris are an abyss. Like the prophet, he was in the belly of the monster.

Suddenly, he was taken aback. At the most unexpected moment, and having been walking in a straight line all the time, he noticed the ground was no longer rising. The water of the rivulet was following at his heels instead of coming towards him from the tips of his toes. The sewer was now descending. Why? So was he all of a sudden going to arrive at the Seine? There was great danger in this, but the danger of turning back was even greater. He pressed on.

It was not towards the Seine that he was going. The ridge of higher ground on Paris's right bank drains on one side into the Seine, and on the other into the Great Sewer. The crest of this ridge that determines the parting of the waters follows a very capricious line. In the Ste-Avoye sewer the highest point, which is where the flow divides, is beyond Rue Michelle-Comte; in the Louvre sewer it is near the boulevards; and in the Montmartre sewer, near Les Halles. It was this highest point that Jean Valjean had reached. He was heading towards the orbital sewer. He was going the right way, but he did not know it.

Every time he came to a junction he would feel round the edges of the opening, and if he found that it was not as wide as the corridor he was in he did not enter it but continued on his way, rightly judging that any passage that was narrower must come to a dead end and could only lead him further from his goal, that is to say, an outlet. So it was that he avoided the quadruple trap, represented by the four mazes we have just listed, that he was faced with in the darkness.

At a certain moment he realized that he was leaving behind, down here, the Paris that was paralysed by the rioting, where the barricades had stopped all movement, and that he was now beginning to make his way under the normal, lively Paris. Overhead he suddenly heard what sounded like thunder, distant but continuous. It was the rattling of carriages.

He had been walking for about half an hour, at least according to his own calculation, and he had not yet thought of taking a rest. He had merely switched hands to hold on to Marius. The darkness was more intense than ever, but its very intensity reassured him.

All at once he saw his shadow in front of him. It was outlined against a faint, almost imperceptible flush that tinged with crimson the floor at his feet and the vault above his head, and to his right and to his left stole across the two slimy walls of the corridor. Astounded, he turned round.

Shafting through the thick darkness behind him, in the part of the corridor he had just passed through and at what seemed to him a vast distance, blazed some sort of dreadful star that seemed to be staring at him.

This was the sinister star of the police rising up in the sewer. Moving about in some confusion behind that star were eight or ten figures. Black, upright, indistinct, terrifying.

II
An Explanation

On the sixth of June, a search of the sewers had been ordered. It was feared that the vanquished might have taken refuge in them, and Prefect Gisquet was to flush out hidden Paris, while General Bugeaud conducted a sweep of public Paris; a twofold combined operation that called for a twofold strategy from the armed forces, represented above ground by the army and below ground by the police. Three units of police and sewermen explored the subterranean network of Paris, one on the right bank, the second on the left bank, the third in the heart of the city. The police were armed with rifles, truncheons, swords and daggers.

What was shining in Jean Valjean's direction at that moment was the lantern of the right-bank patrol.

This patrol had just visited the curving gallery and three blind alleys that run under Rue du Cadran. While the patrol with its lantern was checking those blind alleys, Jean Valjean had come across the entrance to the gallery, identified it as being narrower than the main corridor, and had not taken that turning. He had continued on his way. When the police emerged from the Cadran gallery, they thought they heard the sound of footsteps coming from the direction of the orbital sewer. These were in fact Jean Valjean's footsteps. The sergeant leading the patrol had raised his lantern and the squad were peering earnestly into the murk in the direction from where the sound came.

It was an indescribable moment for Jean Valjean.

Fortunately, though it was easy for him to see the lantern, it was not easy for the lantern to see him. The lantern was light and he was shadow. He was very far off, and blended into the darkness of the place. He shrank back against the wall and halted.

He did not, in any event, realize what was moving back there. Sleep deprivation, want of food and emotional stress had made him as well slip into a hallucinatory state. He saw a brightness, and round that brightness some spectral figures. What was it? He did not understand.

Jean Valjean having stopped, the noise stopped. The patrolmen listened and heard nothing, they looked and saw nothing. They conferred. There was in those days at that point in the Montmartre sewer a kind of 'service' crossroads, which has since been dispensed with on account of the small interior lake that a build-up of torrential rains during heavy storms formed there. The patrol was able to huddle together at that crossroads. Jean Valjean saw those spectral figures form some sort of circle. Those bulldog heads came together and whispered.

What this conference held by the guard-dogs concluded was that they had been mistaken, there had been no noise, there was no one there, it was pointless going into the orbital sewer, it would be a waste of time, but they ought to hurry over to St-Merry. If there was anything to be done or any *bousingot* to track down, it was in that neighbourhood.

From time to time, parties mend their old insults. In 1832 the word *bousingot* was the interim term between the word *jacobin*, which was by then down at heel, and the word *demagogue*, then almost unused, which has since rendered such excellent service.

The sergeant gave the order to veer left down towards the Seine. Had it occurred to them to separate into two groups and cover both directions, Jean Valjean would have been caught. Everything hung on that. It is likely that, anticipating circumstances in which there would be fighting and the insurgents numerous, the Prefecture had issued orders that the patrol was not to separate. The patrol went on its way, leaving Jean Valjean behind. Of all this movement Jean Valjean perceived nothing but the disappearance of the lantern that suddenly turned back.

Before moving off, to set the police mind at rest, the sergeant fired his rifle towards the route they were giving up on, in Jean Valjean's direction. The detonation re-echoed around that underground warren like a rumbling of those Titanic guts. A bit of mortar that fell into the rivulet and made the water splash a few paces away from Jean Valjean told him that the bullet had struck the vault above his head.

Slow and measured footsteps on the sewer floor resounded for a while, growing fainter and fainter with their ever-increasing distance. The group of black figures was swallowed up. A gleam of light wavered and swayed, casting on the arched ceiling a diminishing reddish glow, then vanished. Deep silence returned, pitch-blackness returned, blindness and deafness laid claim to the dark once more, and Jean Valjean, not yet daring to move, remained for a long time with his back to the wall, his ears strained and his pupils dilated, watching the disappearing phantom patrol.

III
The Tailed Man

The police in those days must be given credit for fulfilling their duty with regard to highway regulation and surveillance – unperturbed, even in the gravest of political crises. A riot was no excuse, in their eyes, for allowing malefactors free rein or for neglecting society because the government was in peril. Ordinary duties were duly carried out, unaffected by additional duties. In the midst of a huge political emergency, under threat of a potential revolution, without allowing himself to be distracted by insurrection and barricades, a policeman 'tailed' a thief.

It was precisely something of this kind that was taking place on the afternoon of the sixth of June, down by the riverside on the right bank of the Seine, a little beyond Pont des Invalides.

There is no riverbank there now. The appearance of the place has changed.

On that riverbank two men, a certain distance apart, seemed to be keeping an eye on each other, one avoiding the other. The one in front was trying to get away, the one behind was trying to catch up with him.

It was like a game of chess played from afar and in silence. Neither seemed to be in a hurry, and both walked slowly, as if each were afraid that to show too much haste would make the other quicken his pace. It put you in mind of an appetite following its prey without appearing to do so deliberately. The prey was crafty and on its guard.

The appropriate distinction in physical proportions between hunted ferret and hunter dog was observed. The one trying to escape was a short-necked, puny-looking individual. The one trying to catch him, a tall strapping fellow, had a tough look about him and must have been a tough man to deal with.

The former, feeling he was the weaker, was avoiding the latter, but avoiding him in an intensely furious manner. Anyone able to observe him would have seen in his eyes the grim hostility of one on the run, and all the menace that there is in fear.

The riverbank was deserted. There were no passers-by, not even a boatman or a dock-hand on the barges moored here and there.

These two men were not easily visible except from the opposite embankment, and to anyone observing them from that distance the man in front would have looked an unkempt, tattered, shady character, anxious and shivering in a threadbare overall; and the other, of conventional appearance and of some official standing, wearing the frock-coat of authority buttoned to the chin. The reader would perhaps recognize these two men if given a closer look at them.

What was the objective of the pursuer? Probably to succeed in clothing the pursued more warmly.

When a man dressed by the state pursues a man in rags, it is in order to make him too a man who is dressed by the state. Only, the colour is all-important. To be dressed in blue is glorious. To be dressed in red is disagreeable. There is a purple of the lower orders. It was probably some disagreeableness and some purple of this sort that the pursued wanted to avoid.

If the pursuer was letting him walk on ahead and was not yet arresting him, it was to all appearances in the hope of seeing him end up at some assignation of significance and with some group that would make a good catch. This delicate operation is called 'tailing'.

What makes this conjecture altogether likely is that the buttoned-up man, on catching sight from the riverbank of a cab passing by empty on the embankment, signalled to the coachman. The coachman understood, obviously recognized who he was dealing with, turned round and from up on the embankment began to follow the two men at walking pace. This was not noticed by the ragged and disreputable-looking individual walking ahead of them.

The cab drove past the trees on the Champs-Élysées. Whip in hand, the driver could be seen, gliding along, head and shoulders above the parapet.

One of the police's secret instructions to their officers contains this provision: 'Always have a cab within reach, in case of need.'

While tactically manoeuvring on each side with a strategy not to be faulted, these two men were approaching a ramp between the embankment and the shoreline, which at that time allowed cab drivers arriving from Passy to come down to the river to water their horses. This ramp has since been removed in the interests of visual harmony. Horses die of thirst, but the eye is satisfied.

It was conceivable that the man in the overall was going to climb this ramp to try to escape into the Champs-Élysées, adorned with trees but on the other hand with a strong police presence, and where the other would have help at hand.

This point on the embankment is not at all far from the house transported from Moret to Paris in 1824 by Colonel Brack, and known as François I's house. There is a guard-house very close by.

To the great surprise of his tracker the man under surveillance did not go up by the watering-ramp. He continued walking on the riverbank, alongside the embankment. Clearly, his position was becoming critical. Unless he jumped into the Seine, what was he going to do?

No way of getting up on to the embankment from this point on, no more ramps, and no steps. And they were now very close to the spot, marked by the bend in the Seine near the Pont d'Iéna, where the river-bank, becoming ever narrower, ended in a thin spit of land that disappeared into the water. There he was inevitably going to find himself trapped between the sheer wall to his right, the river to his left and ahead of him, and the law at his heels.

True, this end of the riverbank was hidden from sight by a pile of debris six or seven feet high, from some demolition or other. But did the man hope to conceal himself effectively behind this heap of rubble, just by going behind it? That would have been an infantile move. It was certainly not what he had in mind. The innocence of thieves does not extend that far.

This pile of debris formed a kind of mound at the water's edge with a promontory extending to the wall of the embankment.

The man being followed arrived at this hillock and went round it, so he could no longer be seen by the other.

Not being able to see, the other could not be seen. He took advantage of this to abandon all dissimulation and to walk very quickly. In a few moments he reached the mound of rubble and skirted it. He came to a halt on the other side, astounded. The man he was after was no longer there. Absolutely no sign of the man in the overall.

From the rubbish heap, the riverbank extended no more than about thirty paces, then it dipped down into the water lapping against the wall of the embankment. The fugitive could not have thrown himself into the Seine or climbed up the embankment without being seen by the man following him. What had become of him?

The man in the buttoned-up frock-coat walked to the end of the riverbank and remained there for a moment, lost in thought, his fists fitfully clenched, his gaze searching. All of a sudden he slapped his forehead. He had just noticed, at the point where the land ended and the water began, a big, low, arched iron grating, fitted with a heavy lock and three massive hinges. This grating, a kind of doorway cut into the foot of the embankment, opened on to the river as much as on to the riverbank. A blackish rivulet flowed under it. This rivulet discharged into the Seine.

Beyond its heavy, rusted bars some sort of dark vaulted corridor could be discerned.

The man folded his arms and gave the grating a look of reproach.

A look proving insufficient, he tried giving it a push. He shook it.

It stood fast. It had probably just been opened, although strangely enough for such a rusty grating no sound had been heard. But it had certainly been closed again. This suggested that the man to whom this door had just opened had not a picklock but a key.

This realization suddenly dawned on the man who was trying to shift the grating, and evoked from him this indignant comment: 'That's really something! A government key!'

Then, straight away calming down, he expressed a whole host of inner thoughts with this outburst of almost ironically delivered monosyllables: 'Well! Well! Well! Well!'

That said, in the hope of who knows what, either of seeing the man come out again or others go in, with the patient obsession of a pointer dog he took up a watchful position behind the heap of rubble.

As for the cab, which took its cue from all his movements, it had come to a halt on the embankment above him, close to the parapet. Anticipating a lengthy wait, the coachman slipped over the muzzle of his horses the wet-bottomed bag of oats so familiar to Parisians, who, let it be said in passing, are themselves sometimes similarly treated by their governments. The rare passers-by on the Pont d'Iéna, before going on their way, turned round to look momentarily at these two motionless details in the landscape: the man on the riverbank, the cab on the embankment.

IV
He Too Has His Cross to Bear

Jean Valjean had resumed his progress and had not stopped again since.

This progress became more and more arduous. The height of these vaults varies. The average height is about five feet six inches, and was calculated for the size of a man. Jean Valjean was forced to bend forward so as not to bump Marius against the ceiling. He had to keep crouching down, then straightening up, constantly feeling his way along the wall. The humidity of the stone and the sliminess of the floor offered poor purchase for either hand or foot. He stumbled along inside the city's ghastly dung-pit. The intermittent glimmers of light from the air-wells appeared only at very long intervals, and so wanly that full sunlight seemed like moonlight. All the rest was murk, miasma, opacity, darkness. Jean Valjean was hungry and thirsty, most of all thirsty, and this, like the sea, was a place full of water where a man cannot drink. His strength, which as we know was extraordinary, and thanks to his chaste and sober life very little diminished by age, was nevertheless beginning to fail. He was growing weary, and his ebbing strength increased the weight of his burden. Marius, perhaps dead, had the weight of an inert body. Jean Valjean held him so that his chest was not constricted and he could breathe as freely as possible. Jean Valjean felt rats scampering between his legs. One of them took such fright, it bit him. He felt the occasional breath of air coming through the vents at the mouths of the sewer, reviving him.

It might have been three in the afternoon when he reached the orbital sewer. He was at first astonished at this sudden widening out. All at once he found himself in a gallery whose two walls his outstretched hands could not reach, beneath a ceiling that his head did not touch. The main sewer is, in fact, eight feet wide and seven feet high.

At the point where the Montmartre sewer connects with the main sewer two other underground galleries, those of Rue de Provence and of Rue de l'Abattoir, join them to form a crossroads. Someone less shrewd would have hesitated between these four alternative routes. Jean Valjean selected the broadest, that is to say, the orbital sewer. But then, the same question – to go uphill or down? The situation was growing urgent, he thought, and he must now get to the Seine, whatever the risk. In other words, go downhill. He turned left.

It was a good thing he did. For it would be a mistake to think that the orbital sewer has two outlets, one over towards Bercy, the other towards Passy, and that it is, as its name suggests, the underground ringway of Paris's right bank. The main sewer, which, it should be remembered, is none other than the old Ménilmontant brook, if you follow it upstream comes to a dead end, that is to say, at its old starting-point, its source, at the foot of the Ménilmontant rise. It has no direct communication with the branch sewer that collects Paris's waste waters from the Popincourt district and flows out into the Seine through the Amelot sewer above the ancient Île Louviers. That branch sewer, which is complementary to the collecting sewer, is separated from it, under Rue Ménilmontant itself, by a ridge that marks the divide between the waters upstream and downstream of it. If Jean Valjean had gone up that gallery, he would have ended up after untold effort, worn out, on his last legs, in the dark, at a solid wall. It would have spelled his doom.

At best, by retracing his steps a little and turning into the Filles-du-Calvaire corridor, provided he did not hesitate at the underground intersection of Carrefour Boucherat, taking the St-Louis tunnel, then the St-Gilles passageway on the left, then turning right and avoiding the St-Sébastien gallery, he might have been able to reach the Amelot sewer, and from there – as long as he did not get lost in the kind of F-shape under the Bastille – make his way to the outlet into the Seine near the Arsenal. But for that he would have had to be thoroughly familiar with the enormous madrepore that was the sewer, in all its ramifications and all its passageways. Now, we must reiterate, he knew nothing of this terrifying network in which he was trying to find his way. And if anyone had asked him where he was, he would have replied, 'In the dark.'

His instinct served him well. Going downhill was indeed potential salvation.

He went past the two corridors on his right that branched off in a claw shape under Rue Laffitte and Rue St-Georges, and the long forked corridor of Chaussée-d'Antin.

A little beyond a tributary that was probably the Madeleine branch sewer, he halted. He was very tired. Quite a large air-well, probably the manhole in Rue d'Anjou, cast an almost bright light. With the gentleness of movement that a brother would have shown towards his wounded sibling, Jean Valjean set Marius down on the sewer ledge. Marius's bloodstained face appeared under the white light from the air-well as if at the bottom of a tomb. His eyes were closed, his hair stuck to his temples like the dried bristles of paint-brushes with red paint on them, his hands limp and lifeless, his limbs cold, coagulated blood in the corners of his mouth. A clot of blood had collected in the knot of his cravat, his shirt was getting into his wounds, the cloth of his coat was rubbing the gaping gashes in the living flesh. Parting the garments with his fingertips, Jean Valjean laid his hand on Marius's chest. His heart was still beating. Jean Valjean tore the shirt, bandaged the young man's wounds as best he could and stemmed the flow of blood. Then bending over Marius (still unconscious and barely breathing), he gazed at him in that half-light with an inexpressible hatred.

In disturbing Marius's clothes he had found two things in his pockets, the bread forgotten about from the night before, and Marius's notecase. He ate the bread and opened the notecase. On the first page he found the four lines written by Marius. Remember: 'My name is Marius Pontmercy. Take my body to my grandfather, Monsieur Gillenormand, at 6 Rue des Filles-du-Calvaire, in the Marais.'

Jean Valjean read these four lines by the light of the air-well, and remained for a moment as if entirely self-absorbed, repeating under his breath: 'Rue des Filles-du-Calvaire, number 6, Monsieur Gillenormand.' He put the notecase back in Marius's pocket. He had eaten, he had recovered his strength. He lifted Marius on to his back again, settled his head carefully on his right shoulder, and set off once more down the sewer.

Following the Ménilmontant valley floor, the main sewer is about five miles long. Over a considerable part of its course it is paved.

This guiding light – the names of Paris's streets – by which we are illuminating for the reader Jean Valjean's underground progress, Jean Valjean himself did not have. There was nothing to tell him which zone of the city he was passing through, nor the distance he had covered. Only the increasing pallor of the pools of light he encountered from time to time told him that the sunlight was receding from the streets and the day would soon be drawing to a close. And the rumbling of carriages overhead having become intermittent instead of continuous, then having almost ceased, he concluded that he was no longer under central Paris but was approaching some lonely area near the outer boulevards or the furthest embankments. Where there are fewer houses and fewer streets, the sewer has fewer air-wells. The gloom thickened round Jean Valjean. He nevertheless kept going, groping his way in the dark.

This darkness became suddenly terrible.

V
With Sand as with Women, There Is a Fineness That Is Treacherous

He could feel he was now walking in water, and that he no longer had paving underfoot, but mud.

It sometimes happens, along certain coasts of Brittany or Scotland, that a man, a traveller or a fisherman, walking on the strand at low tide far away from the shoreline, suddenly notices that for the past several minutes he has been making his way with some difficulty. The beach is like pitch beneath his feet, his soles stick to it, it is not sand any more, it is bird-lime. The strand is perfectly dry but at every step taken, as soon as he lifts his foot, the indentation it leaves fills with water. Moreover, his eye has noticed no change. The immense beach is uniform and tranquil, the sand all looks the same, nothing distinguishes the ground that is solid from the ground that no longer is. The gleeful little cloud of sand-hoppers continue frenetically leaping about the passer-by's feet. The man keeps going, forges on, bears landwards, tries to get closer inshore. He is not anxious. Anxious about what? Only, he feels somehow as if his feet are getting heavier with every step he takes. All at once he sinks. He sinks two or three inches. He is certainly not following a good course. He stops to get his bearings.

Suddenly he glances at his feet. His feet have vanished. They are covered by the sand. He pulls his feet out of the sand, he tries to retrace his steps, he turns back, he sinks in deeper than before. The sand is up to his ankles, he wrenches himself out of it and flings himself to the left, the sand comes halfway up his shins, he flings himself to the right, the sand comes up to his knees. Then he realizes with indescribable terror that he is caught in quicksand, and that he has beneath him that appalling medium in which a man can no more walk than a fish can swim. He throws aside his burden, if he has one, he lightens himself like a ship in distress. It is already too late, the sand is above his knees.

He yells, he waves his hat or his handkerchief, the sand is gaining on him more and more. If the beach is deserted, if the land is too far away, if the sandbank is too notorious, if there is no hero in the vicinity, it is all over, he is condemned to be swallowed up. He is condemned to that terrible, long, certain, relentless burial, impossible either to delay or to hasten, that lasts for hours, that goes on interminably, that takes you standing, free, in good health, that drags you down by your feet, that with every exertion you make, with every shout you utter, draws you a little lower, that seems to punish you for your resistance by tightening its hold, that slowly sucks a man into the ground while leaving him time to watch the horizon, the trees, the verdant countryside, the smoke from the villages on the plain, the sails of the ships on the sea, the birds that fly and sing, the sun, the sky. Being swallowed by quicksand is the tomb turning into a tide and creeping up from the depths of the earth towards a living man. Every minute spells inexorable interment. The poor wretch tries to sit, lie down, crawl. Every move he makes buries him deeper. He draws himself up, he sinks, he feels himself being engulfed, he screams, implores, cries out to the heavens, flails his arms, despairs. Now he is up to his waist in the sand. The sand reaches his chest. All that is left of him are his head and shoulders. He throws up his hands, groans in a frenzy, digs his fingernails into the beach, tries to get a grip on this mollescence, puts his weight on his elbows so as to wrest himself from that soft sheath, and sobs frantically; the sand rises. The sand reaches his shoulders, the sand reaches his throat, only his face is visible now. His mouth cries out, the sand fills it. Silence. His eyes are still staring, the sand closes them. Night. Then his forehead narrows, a tuft of hair quivers above the sand; a hand emerges, breaks through the surface, flaps and flutters, and disappears. Dreadful obliteration of a man.

Sometimes the horseman is swallowed up with his horse, sometimes the carter is swallowed up with his cart. Everything founders on that strand. It is like being lost at sea, but not in water. It is land drowning a man. Land, infiltrated by the ocean, becomes a deathtrap. It presents itself as a plain and opens up like a wave. The abyss has such treacheries.

This sinister fate, always possible on this or that seashore, was also possible thirty years ago in the sewers of Paris. Before the major works begun in 1833, Paris's underground network was subject to sudden subsidences.

Water would seep into certain particularly friable underlying strata. The sewer bed, whether flagged as in the old sewers or of hydraulic lime on concrete as in the new tunnels, having nothing to take its weight, dipped. A dip in a floor of this kind means a crevice. A crevice means the ground giving way. The sewer floor collapsed over a certain distance. This chasm, this gulf of mire, was called in specialist terminology an underground sink-hole. What is an underground sink-hole? It is the quicksands of the seashore unexpectedly encountered underground. It is the beach of Mont St-Michel inside a sewer. The ground, being waterlogged, dissolves, as it were. All its molecules are suspended in a soft medium. It is not earth and it is not water. Sometimes to a very great depth. There can be nothing more appalling than such an encounter. If water predominates, death is quick, it is a submersion. If earth predominates, death is slow, it is a sinking.

Can anyone imagine such a death? If sinking into the ground is terrible on the seashore, what is it in the sewer? Instead of fresh air, the full light of day, that clear horizon, those spacious sounds, those free-moving clouds and their life-giving rain, those vessels seen in the distance, that hope in every guise, passers-by likely, help possible right up to the last minute – instead of all this: deafness, blindness, a black vault, the inside of a tomb already prepared, death in the lidded mire, a slow smothering by muck, a stone coffin where asphyxia opens its claws in the filth and takes you by the throat; foulness mingled with the death-rattle, sludge instead of the strand, hydrogen sulphide instead of the hurricane, excrement instead of the ocean! And the shouting, and gnashing of teeth, and writhing, and struggling, and agonizing, and this enormous city overhead, aware of nothing!

The unspeakable horror of dying like that! Death sometimes redeems its atrociousness with a certain terrible dignity. In burning at the stake, in going down in a shipwreck, there can be grandeur. In the flames as in the foaming sea, a proud bearing is possible. There, a person is transfigured as he perishes. But not here. Death is filthy. It is humiliating to die. The last wavering visions are abject. Mire is synonymous with shame. It is mean, ugly, squalid. To die in a butt of malmsey, like Clarence, that is one thing; in a cesspit, like Escoubleau – that is horrible. To struggle in that is ghastly, an ignominious floundering in the throes of death. It is dark enough to be hell and muddy enough to be just a bog, and the dying man cannot tell whether he is going to become a spectre or a toad.

Everywhere else the tomb is sinister, here it is monstrous.

The depth of the sink-holes, their extent and their density, all varied in relation to the better or worse quality of the subsoil. Sometimes an underground sink-hole was three or four feet deep, sometimes eight or ten. Occasionally it was bottomless. Here, the mire was almost solid, there, almost liquid. A man would have taken a day to disappear into the Lunière sink-hole, whereas he would have been swallowed up in five minutes by the Phélippeaux quagmire. Mud supports a greater or lesser weight, depending on its density. A child is saved where a man is doomed. The first law of salvation is to get rid of whatever you are carrying. To throw aside his toolbag or bucket or hod – that was the first thing every sewerman who ever felt the ground give way beneath him did.

The underground sink-holes had various causes: the friability of the soil, some sort of landslip at a depth beyond the reach of man; heavy summer downpours; incessant winter rains; continuous drizzle. Sometimes the weight of surrounding houses on marl or sandy soil exerted pressure on the vaults of the underground tunnels and made them buckle, or the sewer floor ruptured and split open under this crushing force. The settling of the Panthéon destroyed some of the cellars in the Montagne Ste-Geneviève in this way, over a century ago. When a sewer caved in under the pressure of the houses, the disturbance sometimes translated into a kind of saw-tooth crack between the paving-stones in the street above. This rift snaked along the whole length of the cracked vault, and then, the damage being visible, it could be swiftly remedied. It also happened that often the interior devastation was not revealed by any scar on the outside. To the sewermen's misfortune. Going into the collapsed sewer unwarily, they could meet their doom. Ancient records mention several sewermen who were swallowed up in sink-holes in this way. They give several names. Among others, that of the sewerman who was engulfed by subsidence under the catchment drain in Rue Carême-Prenant, a certain Blaise Poutrain. This Blaise Poutrain was the brother of Nicolas Poutrain, who was the last grave-digger at the cemetery known as the Charnier des Innocents, in 1785, when the cemetery closed.

There was also that young and charming Vicomte d'Escoubleau we spoke of just now, one of the heroes of the siege of Lerida, where they launched their attack wearing silk stockings and with violins leading the way. Surprised one night when visiting his cousin the Duchesse de Sourdis, Escoubleau drowned in a quagmire in the Beautreillis sewer, where he had taken refuge to escape from the duke. When informed of this death, Madame de Sourdis asked for her smelling-bottle, and so busy was she sniffing her salts that she forgot to weep. In such cases, there is no love that can be counted on. The sewer quells it. Hero refuses to wash Leander's body. Thisbe holds her nose at Pyramus and says, 'Phew!'

VI
The Underground Sink-hole

Jean Valjean was confronted with an underground sink-hole.

This sort of subsidence was a common occurrence at that time in the subsoil under the Champs-Élysées, which presents difficulties for hydraulic works and is a poor medium for underground constructions on account of its excessive fluidity. This fluidity exceeds the looseness of the sands of even the St-Georges district, which only concrete bedding has been able to overcome, and the clayey gas-contaminated strata of the Martyrs district, which are so liquid that the only way a passage could be created under the Martyrs tunnel was by means of a cast-iron pipe. When in 1836 the old stone sewer under Faubourg St-Honoré, in which we now see Jean Valjean, was demolished in order to rebuild it, the quicksand that is the subsoil of the Champs-Élysées all the way down to the Seine presented such an obstacle that the operation lasted nearly six months – to the loud protests of riverside dwellers, particularly riverside dwellers with private mansions and carriages. The construction work was more than difficult, it was dangerous. True, there were four and a half months of rain, and the Seine was in flood three times.

The underground sink-hole that Jean Valjean encountered was caused by the downpour of the preceding day. Rainwater had gathered in a dip in the paving, which was ill-supported by the underlying sand. Once there had been some infiltration, subsidence followed. The destabilized sewer floor had collapsed into the quagmire. Over what distance? Impossible to say. The darkness was denser here than elsewhere. It was a mudpit in a black cavern.

Jean Valjean felt the paving give way beneath him. He entered this sludge. There was water on the surface, ooze down below. He had to get through it. It was impossible for him to retrace his steps. Marius was fading, and Jean Valjean exhausted. Besides, where else was he to go? Jean Valjean pressed on. In fact, for the first few steps the quagmire seemed not very deep. But as he progressed, his feet sank deeper. He soon had ooze up to his calves and water above his knees. He walked on, using both arms to hold Marius as far above the water as he could. The ooze now came up to his knees, and the water up to his waist. Already there was no turning back. He was sinking deeper and deeper. Dense enough to carry the weight of one man, this sludge could obviously not support two. Separately, Marius and Jean Valjean would probably have made it. Jean Valjean ploughed on, carrying a man who was dying or was perhaps a corpse.

The water came up to his armpits. He felt he was going under. He could barely move in the depth of mud he was in. The density that offered support was also the obstacle. He was still holding Marius above him; and exerting extraordinary strength, he kept going. But he was sinking. He had only his head above the water now and his two arms holding up Marius. In old paintings of the Flood there is a mother holding her child like this.

He sank deeper still, tipping his head back to escape the water and so as to breathe. To anyone who had seen him in that gloom he would have looked like a mask floating on darkness. He could dimly see above him Marius's drooping head and ghastly-pale face. He made a desperate effort, and thrust his foot forward. His foot struck something solid. A firm foothold. Just in time.

He straightened up, and twisted round and rooted himself with a kind of fury on this firm foothold. It felt to him like the first step on a staircase leading back to life.

This firm footfold, encountered in the ooze at the very last moment, was the beginning of the upward slope of the sewer floor, which had given way without fracturing and sagged beneath the water like an unbroken plank. Well laid paving is cambered and has such resilience. Partly submerged but solid, this section of the floor was a proper ramp; and once on this ramp, they were saved. Jean Valjean climbed the slope and reached the other side of the quagmire.

As he emerged from the water, he tripped over a stone and fell to his knees. He found this appropriate, and he remained there for a while, his soul rapt in who knows what words addressed to God.

He stood up, shivering, chilled, stinking, bowed beneath this dying man he was carrying, dripping all over with filth, his soul filled with a strange brightness.

Sometimes When You Think You Have Reached Your Destination, You Have Run Aground

He set off once more.

However, although he had not lost his life in the sink-hole, he seemed to have lost his strength there. That supreme effort had exhausted him. His weariness was now so great that he was obliged to catch his breath, and every three or four steps he leaned against the wall. Once he had to sit down on the ledge to change Marius's position, and he thought he would be there for good. But though his strength was gone, his willpower was not. He got up again.

He walked on desperately, almost rapidly, covering some hundred paces in this way, without raising his head, almost without drawing breath, and abruptly hit a wall. He had come to a bend in the sewer, and arriving at the corner with his head down, he had walked straight into the wall. He looked up, and there in front of him at the end of the tunnel, far away, very far away, he perceived light. It was not that terrifying light this time; it was good white light. It was daylight. Jean Valjean could see the exit.

A soul in torment who, from within the furnace of hell, suddenly saw the way out would feel what Jean Valjean felt. With the vestiges of its burned wings it would fly frantically towards the radiant gateway. Jean Valjean no longer felt fatigue, he no longer felt Marius's weight, he recovered his legs of steel, he ran rather than walked. The closer he came to it, the more and more distinct the exit appeared. It was a rounded arch, not as high as the gradually descending vault and not as wide as the gallery that narrowed as the vault grew lower. The tunnel ended like the inside of a funnel, the narrowing, a design fault, copied from the entrances to prisons, logical in a place of detention, illogical in a sewer, and which has since been rectified.

Jean Valjean reached the exit. There he halted. It was indeed the exit, but there was no possibility of getting out.

The archway was closed off by a sturdy grating, and the grating, which to all appearances rarely swung on its rusty hinges, was secured to its stone frame by a heavy lock, red with rust, that looked like an enormous brick. You could see the keyhole, and the strong bolt deeply recessed in the iron plate. It was obviously double-locked, one of those gaol locks with which old Paris was so readily unsparing.

Beyond the grating was the open air, the river, the light of day, the riverbank (very narrow, but wide enough to walk along and get away from here), the distant embankments, Paris (that engulfing immensity in which a man so easily escapes detection), the broad horizon, freedom. To the right downstream could be seen the Pont d'Iéna, to the left, upstream, the Pont des Invalides. It would have been a good place to wait till night to slip away. This was one of the loneliest spots in Paris: the riverbank opposite Gros-Caillou. Flies went in and out through the bars of the grating.

It might have been half-past eight o'clock in the evening. The light was fading.

Jean Valjean laid Marius alongside the wall, on the dry part of the sewer floor, then walked up to the grating and clutched the bars in both hands. The shaking he gave it was frenzied, to no effect at all. The grating did not move. Jean Valjean grabbed the bars one after the other, hoping to be able to rip out the least firmly fixed and use it as a lever to lift up the gate or break the lock. Not one bar so much as shifted. The teeth of a tiger are no more firmly set in their sockets. No lever, no way of exerting pressure. The obstacle was invincible. The gate impossible to open.

So must it end here? What could he do? What was to become of them? Go back, retrace the terrifying route he had already taken – he had not the strength for it. Besides, how was he to go back through that quagmire from which they had escaped only by a miracle? And after the quagmire, was there not the police patrol, which they surely would not evade twice? And then, where was he to go? What direction to take? Following the incline was no guarantee of being able to get out. Even if they were to reach another outlet, they would find it blocked by a manhole cover or a grating. Undoubtedly, every exit was likewise shut off. Chance had loosened the grating by which they had entered, but of course every other sewer mouth was closed.

They had succeeded only in escaping into a prison. It was all over. Everything that Jean Valjean had done was useless. God was against it.

They were both caught in death's huge sinister web, and Jean Valjean sensed the dreadful spider scuttling along those black threads quivering in the dark.

He turned his back on the grating and dropped to the paving, cast down rather than seated, close to the still motionless Marius and his head bowed between his knees. This was the last drop of anguish.

Of whom was he thinking in his deep despondency? Neither of himself nor of Marius. He was thinking of Cosette.

VIII
The Torn Coat Flap

In the midst of this utter despair a hand was laid on his shoulder and a low voice said to him, 'Fifty-fifty.'

Someone there, in this gloom? Nothing is more dreamlike than despair. Jean Valjean thought he was dreaming. He had heard no footsteps. Was it possible? He looked up. A man stood before him.

This man was dressed in an overall. He was barefoot, holding his shoes in his left hand. He had evidently removed them so as to be able to approach Jean Valjean unheard.

Jean Valjean had not a moment's uncertainty. However unexpected this encounter, the man was known to him. The man was Thénardier.

Although startled awake, as it were, Jean Valjean, being used to sudden alarms and to dealing with unexpected blows that demanded quick reactions, instantly regained complete presence of mind. Besides, the situation could not possibly get any worse – a certain degree of distress can gain no more in intensity – and Thénardier himself could add nothing to the blackness of this night.

There was an expectant pause.

Raising his right hand to his forehead as a shade against the light, Thénardier then brought his eyebrows together by narrowing his eyes, which, together with a slight pursing of the mouth, marks the shrewd attention of a man who is trying to identify another. He did not succeed. Jean Valjean, as we have just said, had his back to the light, and in any case was so besmirched, so filthy and so bloodstained that in the full brightness of day he would have been unrecognizable. By contrast, with the light from the grating falling directly on him – a sepulchral leaden light, it is true, but clear in its leadenness – Thénardier, to use a striking commonplace metaphor, 'jumped out' at Jean Valjean. This inequality of circumstance was enough to ensure some advantage to Jean Valjean in that mysterious duel that was going to take place between the two predicaments and the two men. The encounter took place between Jean Valjean obscured and Thénardier unmasked.

Jean Valjean realized straight away that Thénardier did not recognize him.

They considered each other for a moment in that gloom, as though sizing each other up. Thénardier was the first to break the silence.

'How are you going to get out?'

Jean Valjean did not reply.

Thénardier continued, 'Impossible to force the gate. But you've got to get away from here.'

'That's true,' said Jean Valjean.

'Well, then, fifty-fifty.'

'What do you mean?'

'You killed your man. That's fine. I've got the key.' Thénardier pointed to Marius. He went on, 'I don't know you, but I want to help you. You must be a friend.'

Jean Valjean began to understand. Thénardier took him for a murderer.

Thénardier resumed, 'Listen, comrade. You didn't kill that man without seeing what he had in his pockets. You give me my half, I'll open the gate for you.' And half pulling out a big key from under his tattered overall, he added, 'You want to see what the key to freedom looks like? There you are.'

Jean Valjean was 'left stupefied', as old Corneille put it,* so much so that he doubted whether what he was seeing was real. It was providence appearing in horrible guise and the good angel coming out of the ground in the form of Thénardier.

Thénardier stuffed his hand into a big pocket hidden under his overall, pulled out a rope and offered it to Jean Valjean.

'Here,' he said, 'I'll give you the rope into the bargain.'

'A rope? What for?'

'You'll also need a stone, but you'll find one outside. There's a heap of rubble out there.'

'A stone? What for?'

'Since you're going to throw the sap in the river, you need a stone and a rope, idiot, otherwise he'd float on the surface.'

Jean Valjean took the rope. There is no one who does not similarly respond automatically.

Thénardier snapped his fingers as if a thought had suddenly occurred to him. 'Now then, comrade, how did you manage to get through that sink-hole back there? I haven't dared risk it myself. Phew! you stink.'

After a pause he added, 'I'm asking you questions, but you're right not to answer. It's good training for when you're up in front of the examining magistrate. Besides, if you say nothing, you're in no danger of speaking too loud. All the same, just because I can't see your face

---

* An allusion to Corneille's *Cinna* (1640), Act V, sc i: 'Je demeure stupide', words spoken by Cinna when the emperor Augustus reveals to him that he has full knowledge of Cinna's plot to assassinate him.

and I don't know your name, you'd be wrong to think I don't know who you are and what you want. The hell I don't! You've knocked that gentleman about a bit, now you'd like to hide him away somewhere. You need the river, that great concealer of misdemeanours. I'm going to get you out of trouble. Helping one of the lads when he's in difficulty, that's my pleasure.'

While congratulating Jean Valjean on remaining silent, he was clearly trying to make him talk. He nudged his shoulder in an attempt to get a look at him in profile, and exclaimed, yet without allowing his voice to rise, 'Talking of that sink-hole, you're a fine one! Why didn't you throw your man in there?'

Jean Valjean kept quiet. Pulling right up to his Adam's apple the rag that served him as a cravat, a gesture that puts a finishing touch to a serious-minded man's air of capability, Thénardier went on, 'As it happens, you may've acted wisely. The workmen coming tomorrow to fill in the hole were bound to find the blockhead you'd left behind there, and little by little, step by step, they might've picked up your scent and caught up with you. Someone's been through the sewer. Who? Where did he get out? Did anyone see him come out? The police are very sharp. The sewer's treacherous and gives you away. A find like that's out of the ordinary, it attracts attention, very few people take to the sewers to conduct their business, whereas the river belongs to everyone. The river's the real graveyard. After a month they fish your man out of the nets at St-Cloud. Well, so what? It's a dead body! Who killed him? Paris. And the law doesn't even investigate. You did well.'

The more talkative Thénardier was, the more uncommunicative was Jean Valjean.

Thénardier nudged his shoulder again. 'Now let's settle this thing. Share and share alike. You've seen my key, show me your money.'

Thénardier was intense, tigerish, shifty, slightly menacing, yet amicable. There was one strange thing: Thénardier's behaviour was not straightforward. He did not look entirely at ease. While not affecting any air of mystery, he kept his voice down. From time to time he placed his finger on his lips and muttered 'Shh!' It was difficult to work out why. There was no one there but the two of them. Jean Valjean thought that other ruffians might be in some hidey-hole not very far off, and that Thénardier was not anxious to share with them.

Thénardier went on, 'Let's settle this. How much did the sap have in his pockets?'

Jean Valjean went through his own pockets.

It was his habit, remember, always to have some money on him. The grim life of expediency to which he was condemned made this a rule. On this occasion, however, he was caught unprepared. When putting on his National Guardsman's uniform the night before, immersed in his lugubrious thoughts, he had forgotten to take his wallet. He had only a few coins in his waistcoat pocket. This amounted to about thirty francs. He turned his thoroughly mud-drenched pocket inside out, and laid on the sewer-floor ledge one twenty-franc gold coin, two five-franc and five or six ten-centime pieces.

With a meaningful twist of his neck, Thénardier thrust out his lower lip.

'You killed him for not very much,' he said.

With utter familiarity he started patting both Jean Valjean's and Marius's pockets. His main concern being to keep his back to the light, Jean Valjean let him do as he wanted. While he had his hands on Marius's coat, Thénardier, with the skill of a conjuror and unnoticed by Jean Valjean, tore off a strip, which he concealed under his overall, probably thinking this piece of cloth might later serve to identify the murder victim and the murderer. However, he found no more than the thirty francs.

'It's a fact,' he said, 'between the both of you you've got no more than that.'

And forgetting his agreement – 'fifty-fifty' – he took it all.

He hesitated a little over the ten-centime coins. On second thoughts, he took them as well, muttering, 'What of it! It's knifing people for too little.'

Having done that, once again he pulled out the big key from under his overall.

'Now, comrade, you'd better go! It's like the fair here, you pay on the way out. You've paid, now get out.' And he started laughing.

In helpfully lending this key to a stranger and making someone other than himself go out through that gate, had he the pure and disinterested intention of rescuing a murderer? That is something we may well doubt.

Thénardier helped Jean Valjean to set Marius back on his shoulders, then tip-toed, barefoot, up to the grating, beckoning to Jean Valjean to follow him; he looked out, placed his finger over his lips, and remained for several seconds as if uncertain. His inspection over, he placed the key in the lock. The bolt slipped back and the gate swung open. There was no squeaking, no creaking. It was very quiet. It was obvious that this gate and those hinges, having been carefully oiled, opened more frequently than would have been thought. This quietness was sinister. It was suggestive of furtive comings and goings, of the silent entrances and exits of men of the night, of the stealthy footsteps of crime. The sewer was evidently in collusion with some mysterious gang. This taciturn grating was a fence for stolen goods.

Thénardier opened the gate a fraction, just wide enough to let Jean Valjean slip out, closed the grating behind him, turned the key twice in the lock and plunged back into the dark, making no more noise than a breath of air. He seemed to walk on the velvet paws of a tiger. A moment later that hideous providence had returned to the invisible. Jean Valjean found himself outside.

IX
To the Expert Eye, Marius Looks Dead

He let Marius slip down on to the riverbank. They were outside! The noxious vapours, the darkness, the horror lay behind him. Salubrious, pure, live, joyous, freely breathable air flooded over him. All around, silence, but the lovely silence of a sunset in unclouded blue skies. Dusk had fallen. Night was coming, that great liberator, friend to all those who need a mantle of darkness to find a way out of their distress. The sky offered itself on all sides as a vast calm. The river came up to his feet with the sound of a kiss. The dialogue between the nests bidding each other goodnight in the elm trees on the Champs-Élysées could be heard overhead. A few stars, dimly pricking the pale blue of the high heavens and visible only to reverie, created tiny twinklings, scarcely perceptible in the immensity. Above Jean Valjean's head evening was unfolding all the delights of the infinite.

It was that indecisive and exquisite time of day that says neither yes nor no. It was already dark enough to be able to disappear from sight within a short distance, and still light enough to be able to recognize someone at close quarters.

Jean Valjean was for several seconds irresistibly overwhelmed by that awesome and gentle serenity. There are such moments of oblivion. Suffering stops harassing the wretched. Everything is lost in thought. Peace envelops the dreamer like the night. And beneath the radiant twilight, imitating the illumination in the sky, the soul is filled with stars. Jean Valjean could not help but contemplate that vast clear darkness above him. Meditating on the majestic silence of the eternal heavens, he was bathed in ecstasy and prayer. Then abruptly, as if a sense of duty came back to him, he bent down towards Marius, and cupping some water in the hollow of his hand he gently splashed a few drops on the young man's face. Marius's eyelids remained closed, yet breath passed between his parted lips.

Jean Valjean was about to dip his hand in the river again when all at once he felt an indefinable unease, that sense of having someone you cannot see standing behind you. We have already referred elsewhere to this feeling, which everyone has experienced. He turned round.

As before, there was indeed someone behind him.

A man of tall stature, wrapped in a long frock-coat, with his arms folded and holding in his right hand a truncheon with its lead knob showing, was standing a few paces behind Jean Valjean as he crouched over Marius.

The shadows playing their part, it was like some kind of apparition. A suggestible man would have been fearful because of the twilight, a level-headed man because of the truncheon. Jean Valjean recognized Javert.

The reader has no doubt guessed that Thénardier's pursuer was none other than Javert. After his unexpected departure from the barricade, Javert had gone to police headquarters and given an oral report to the chief himself in a brief meeting with him, then immediately resumed his duties, which involved in particular – remember, from the note that was found on him – surveillance of the riverbank on the right side of the Seine near the Champs-Élysées, which had for some time past aroused the attention of the police. There he caught sight of Thénardier and followed him. The rest we know.

And, of course, that grating so obligingly opened for Jean Valjean was an act of cunning on Thénardier's part. Thénardier sensed that Javert was still there. The marked man has an instinct that never deceives him. Some bone had to be thrown to that sleuth-hound. A murderer, what a godsend! It was the sacrifice that had to be made. By sending Jean Valjean outside in his stead, Thénardier gave the police another quarry, made them leave off pursuing him, saw to it that he was forgotten about in a bigger operation, repaid Javert for his waiting – which always flatters a spy – earned himself thirty francs, and could count on making his own escape with the help of this diversion.

Jean Valjean had exchanged one plight for another.

These two encounters, coming one after the other, first Thénardier and then Javert – that was hard.

Javert did not recognize Jean Valjean, who, as we said, no longer looked like himself. Javert kept his arms folded, with an imperceptible movement made sure he had a firm grip on his truncheon, and said in a curt, calm voice, 'Who are you?'

'It's me.'

'And who's that?'

'Jean Valjean.'

Javert put his truncheon between his teeth, flexed his knees, leaned forward, placed his two powerful hands on Jean Valjean's shoulders, clamping them like two vices, took a good look and recognized him. Their faces were almost touching. Javert's gaze was terrible.

Jean Valjean remained inert in Javert's clutches, like a lion submitting to the claws of a lynx.

'Inspector Javert,' he said, 'you've got me now. In fact, I've considered myself your prisoner since this morning. I wouldn't have given you my address if I was going to try to escape from you. Take me in. Just grant me one thing.'

Javert seemed not to hear. He kept staring at Jean Valjean. His puckered chin pushed his lips up towards his nose, a sign of fierce speculation. At length he released Jean Valjean, straightened up in one stiff movement, took a firm hold of his truncheon again, and as if in a dream murmured rather than voiced this question, 'What are you doing here? And who is this man?'

He continued not to use the familiar *tu* form in addressing Jean Valjean.

Jean Valjean replied, and the sound of his voice appeared to rouse Javert, 'As a matter of fact, he's just what I wanted to talk to you about. Deal with me as you will, but help me first to take him home. That's all I ask of you.'

Javert's face contracted as it always did when anyone seemed to think him capable of some concession. However, he did not say no.

He bent down again, pulled out of his pocket a handkerchief, which he dipped in the water, and wiped Marius's bloodstained brow.

'This man was at the barricade,' he said in an undertone and as though talking to himself. 'He's the one they called Marius.'

A first-class spy who, when he thought he was to die, had observed everything, listened to everything and taken everything in; who spied even at the very last, and resting his elbows on the first step of the sepulchre, had taken notes.

He seized Marius's hand, feeling for his pulse.

'He's wounded,' said Jean Valjean.

'He's dead,' said Javert.

Jean Valjean replied, 'No. Not yet.'

'So you brought him here from the barricade?' remarked Javert.

He must have been deeply preoccupied not to dwell on this harrowing rescue through the sewers, and not even to notice Jean Valjean's silence after his question.

Jean Valjean, for his part, seemed to have but one thought. He spoke up again, 'He lives in the Marais, Rue des Filles-du-Calvaire, with his grandfather . . . I can't remember the name.'

Jean Valjean fumbled in Marius's coat, pulled out the notecase, opened it at the page on which Marius had written in pencil, and held it out to Javert.

There was still enough indeterminate light in the air to be able to read by. Besides, Javert had in his eye the feline phosphorescence of night birds. He deciphered the few lines written by Marius, and muttered, 'Gillenormand, Rue des Filles-du Calvaire, number six.'

Then he cried, 'Coachman!'

Remember, there was a cab waiting, just in case.

Javert kept Marius's notecase.

A moment later the cab, which came down via the watering-ramp, was on the riverbank. Marius was laid on the back seat, and Javert sat next to Jean Valjean on the front seat.

The door was closed and the carriage was rapidly on its way, returning along the embankment towards the Bastille.

They left the embankment and turned into the streets behind. The coachman, a black silhouette on his box, whipped his thin horses. Glacial silence inside the cab. Marius, motionless, his body propped up in the corner, his head falling forward on to his chest, his arms dangling, his legs stiff, appeared to be waiting for nothing else but a coffin. Jean Valjean seemed made of shadow, and Javert of stone. And in that vehicle full of darkness, whose interior, every time it passed in front of a street lantern, was luridly bleached as if by intermittent lightning, chance brought together, in what seemed a macabre confrontation, the three tragic stillnesses: the corpse, the spectre and the statue.

X
The Return of the Suicidally Prodigal Son

At every bump in the road a drop of blood fell from Marius's hair. It was dark when the carriage arrived at number six, Rue des Filles-du-Calvaire.

Javert alighted first, checked at a glance the number above the carriage gate, and raising the heavy wrought-iron knocker, fashioned in the old style as a billy-goat and a satyr face to face, he gave it a forceful rap. One side of the gate opened a fraction, and Javert gave it a push. The porter half appeared, yawning, vaguely awake, with a candle in his hand.

The whole household was asleep. People go to bed early in the Marais, especially on days of rioting. This good old neighbourhood, terrified by revolution, takes refuge in sleep, just as children, when they hear the bogeyman coming, quickly hide their heads under the blanket.

Meanwhile Jean Valjean and the coachman were lifting Marius out of the carriage, Jean Valjean supporting him under the armpits, and the coachman, under the knees.

While carrying Marius like this, Jean Valjean slipped his hand under the young man's clothes, which were considerably torn, felt his chest, and satisfied himself that his heart was still beating. It was actually beating a little less feebly, as if the movement of the cab had brought about a certain reassertion of life.

Javert called out to the porter in a tone appropriate for the government to take in the presence of a seditious individual's porter.

'Someone by the name of Gillenormand?'

'This is the place. What do you want with him?'

'We've brought his son.'

'His son?' said the porter in bewilderment.

'He's dead.'

Following behind Javert, ragged and filthy, Jean Valjean, whom the porter observed with some horror, shook his head at him in denial. The porter did not seem to understand either what Javert had said or Jean Valjean's shake of the head.

Javert continued, 'He was on the barricade, and here he is.'

'On the barricade!' cried the porter.

'He got himself killed. Go and wake his father.'

The porter did not stir.

'Go on!' Javert insisted. And he added, 'There'll be a funeral here tomorrow.'

For Javert, the incidents that occurred from day to day in the public domain were clearly categorized, which is where anticipation and supervision start, and every eventuality had its own compartment; the potential incidents were in separate drawers, as it were, from which they emerged in variable quantities depending on the occasion; on the street, there were fighting, rioting, carnival festivities and funerals.

The porter confined himself to waking Basque. Basque woke Nicolette. Nicolette woke Aunt Gillenormand. As for the grandfather, they let him sleep on, thinking that he would anyhow find out about it soon enough.

Marius was carried up to the first floor without having been seen, as it happened, by anyone else in the rest of the building, and laid on an old sofa in Monsieur Gillenormand's antechamber. And while Basque went to fetch a doctor and Nicolette opened the linen presses,

Jean Valjean felt Javert tapping him on the shoulder. He understood and went back downstairs, Javert's footsteps following behind him.

The porter watched them leave as he had watched them arrive: in a drowsy state of shock. They climbed back into the cab, and the coachman on to his box.

'Inspector Javert,' said Jean Valjean, 'grant me one more favour.'

'What is it?' Javert asked gruffly.

'Let me go home for a minute. Then do with me as you will.'

Javert remained silent for a few moments, with his chin buried in the collar of his frock-coat, then he lowered the front window.

'Driver,' he said, 'Rue de l'Homme-Armé, number seven.'

XI
A Shift in the Absolute

They remained tight-lipped all the rest of the way.

What did Jean Valjean want? To finish what he had begun. To alert Cosette, to tell her where Marius was, perhaps to give her some other useful information, to make, if he could, some final arrangements. As for himself, as for what related to him personally, it all was over. He was in Javert's custody and he was offering no resistance. Any other man in such a situation might perhaps have vaguely thought of the rope that Thénardier had given him, and of the bars of the first prison cell he would enter. But ever since the bishop there had been in Jean Valjean, we must emphasize, a deep religious aversion towards all violence, even against himself.

Suicide, that mysterious assault on the unknown that may to a certain extent comprise the death of the soul, was impossible to Jean Valjean.

At the turning into Rue de l'Homme-Armé, the cab halted, this street being too narrow for carriages to enter. Javert and Jean Valjean got out.

The coachman humbly pointed out to 'monsieur l'inspecteur' that the Utrecht velvet in his carriage was all stained with blood, by the murder victim, and with mud, by the murderer. That was the situation as he understood it. Some compensation was due to him, he added. At the same time, drawing his logbook out of his pocket, he begged the inspector to have the goodness to write in it 'a few words to vouch for it'. Javert pushed aside the book the coachman held out to him and said, 'How much is owing, including the time you were kept waiting as well as the fare?'

'There's seven and a quarter hours,' replied the coachman, 'and my velvet was brand-new. Eighty francs, monsieur l'inspecteur.'

Javert drew from his pocket four napoleons and sent the cab away.

Jean Valjean thought it was Javert's intention to take him on foot to the Blancs-Manteaux police station or the one in Rue des Archives, both of which are close by. They started down the street. It was, as usual, deserted. Javert followed Jean Valjean. They came to number seven. Jean Valjean knocked. The door opened.

'All right,' said Javert. 'Go on up.'

He added with a strange expression, and as if it cost him an effort to say it, 'I'll wait for you here.'

Jean Valjean looked at Javert. This was hardly Javert's usual way of doing things. However, resolved as Jean Valjean was to give himself up and make an end of it, he could not be greatly surprised that Javert should now have a kind of arrogant confidence in him, the confidence of the cat that allows the mouse a freedom within the reach of its claws. He pushed open the door, entered the building; and to the porter who, having turned in for the night, had pulled the door's release cord from his bed, he called out 'It's me!' And he went upstairs.

When he reached the first floor, he paused. Every *via dolorosa* has its stations along the way. The window on the landing, which was a sash-window, was open. As in many old houses, the staircase looked out on the street, with light coming in from there. The street lantern, directly opposite, illuminated the stairs, which saved on lighting costs.

Either to get some air or without thinking, Jean Valjean stuck his head out of this window. He leaned out over the street. It is short, and the lantern illuminated it from end to end. Jean Valjean was astonished and bewildered. There was no one there.

Javert had gone.

XII
The Grandfather

Basque and the porter had carried Marius – still lying motionless on the sofa where he had been laid on arrival – into the drawing room. The doctor who had been sent for came quickly. Aunt Gillenormand was up and about.

Aunt Gillenormand went to and fro, wringing her hands in distress, incapable of doing anything other than saying, 'Good Lord! Is it possible?' From time to time she added, 'There's going to be a lot of blood spilled.' When she got over her initial horror, a certain philosophical view of the situation established itself in her mind and was expressed by this exclamation: 'It was bound to end this way!' She did not go as far as the usual 'I told you so!' prompted by occasions of this kind.

On the doctor's orders a trestle-bed had been set up beside the sofa. The doctor examined Marius, and having ascertained that his pulse was still beating, that there was no deep wound to his chest and that the blood at the corners of his mouth came from the nasal cavity, he had him laid flat on the bed, without a pillow, with his head at the same level as his body and even a little lower, and his chest bared to facilitate his breathing. Seeing that Marius was being undressed, Mademoiselle Gillenormand retired to her room and settled down to saying her rosary.

There was no internal injury to his torso. A bullet, stopped by his notecase, had been deflected over his ribs, making a gash that looked hideous but was not deep and therefore not dangerous. In the long underground trek the broken collar-bone had been completely dislocated, and there was some serious damage there. His arms were sabre-slashed. No laceration disfigured his face, but his head seemed covered with lesions. What would result from those head wounds? Did they stop at the scalp, or did they cut into the skull? It was impossible to tell yet. A worrying symptom was that they had caused loss of consciousness, and people do not always recover from that kind of unconsciousness. Moreover, the wounded man was exhausted by loss of blood. From the waist down, the lower part of his body had been protected by the barricade.

Basque and Nicolette tore up strips of linen and prepared bandages. Nicolette sewed them, Basque rolled them. Not having any lint, the doctor had instead stopped the bleeding with pads of wadding. Next to the bed, three candles burned on a table where the case of surgical instruments lay open. The doctor bathed Marius's face and hair with cold water. A bucketful was red in an instant. The porter, with his tallow candle in his hand, provided light.

The doctor seemed sadly thoughtful. From time to time he shook his head, as if replying to some unspoken question he had asked. A bad sign for the patient, these mysterious dialogues the doctor was having with himself.

Just as the doctor was wiping Marius's face and lightly touching with his finger his still-closed eyes, a door opened at the end of the drawing room and a tall, pale figure appeared. It was the grandfather.

The rioting had for the past two days greatly preoccupied, upset and outraged Monsieur Gillenormand. He had not been able to sleep the previous night, and he had been feverish all day long. That evening he had gone to bed very early, with instructions that the whole house should be well barred, and, tired out, he had dozed off.

Old men sleep lightly. Monsieur Gillenormand's bedroom was next to the drawing room, and whatever precautions might have been taken, the noise had wakened him. Surprised by the streak of light he saw under his door, he had got out of bed and groped his way towards it.

With one hand on the handle of the half-open door, his head a little bent forward and doddering, his body wrapped in a straight, white, close-fitting dressing-gown, like a shroud, he stood on the threshold, astounded. He looked like a ghost gazing into a tomb.

He saw the bed, and on the mattress that young man: bleeding, white with the whiteness of wax, eyes closed, mouth open, lips pale, naked to the waist, slashed all over with crimson wounds, motionless, starkly lit.

The grandfather shuddered from head to foot as much as ossified limbs would allow; a kind of vitreous sheen veiled his eyes whose corneas were yellowed because of his great age; his whole face acquired in an instant the ashen angularity of a skeleton's skull, his arms hung loose as though a spring had broken, and his amazement was conveyed by the outspread fingers of his two aged hands all atremble; his knees were bent, exposing through the front of his dressing-gown his poor bare legs bristling with white hairs, and he murmured, 'Marius!'

'Monsieur,' said Basque, 'the young gentleman has just been brought back. He joined the barricade, and—'

'He's dead!' cried the old man in a terrible voice. 'Ah! The brigand!'

Then a kind of sepulchral transfiguration straightened this centenarian, and he stood as erect as a young man.

'Monsieur,' he said, 'you are the doctor. Start by telling me one thing. He's dead, isn't he?'

The doctor, in the utmost anxiety, remained silent.

Monsieur Gillenormand wrung his hands with a dreadful burst of laughter. 'He's dead! He's dead! He's dead! He's got himself killed on the barricades! Out of hatred for me! It was to defy me that he did it! Ah! the blood-thirsty killer! That's how he comes back to me! Bane of my life, he's dead!'

He went to the window, threw it wide open as if he felt stifled, and standing there before the dark began talking to the night in the street outside. 'Stabbed, sabred, butchered, slashed to ribbons, hacked to pieces! You see that, the wretch ! He knew full well that I was waiting for him and that I had his room ready, and that I'd put beside my bed his portrait from when he was a little boy! He knew full well that he had only to come back, and that I've been yearning for him for years, and that I sat at my fireside with my hands on my knees, not knowing what to do; and that I was at my wits' end. You knew full well, yes you did, that you had only to come home and say, "I'm back", and you would be master of the house, that I would obey you, and that you could do whatever you wanted with your old numbskull of a grandfather! You knew that full well, and you said, "No, he's a royalist, I shan't go back!" And you went and joined the barricades, and you got yourself killed out of spite! To take your revenge for what I said to you about Monsieur le Duc de Berry! That's what's so appalling! Go off to bed and sleep peacefully. He's dead. This is what I wake up to!'

The doctor, beginning to be concerned about both parties, left Marius for a moment, and went over to Monsieur Gillenormand, and took him by the arm.

The grandfather turned, gazed at him with eyes that seemed enlarged and bloodshot, and said to him placidly, 'Monsieur, I thank you. I'm calm, I'm a man, I saw the death of Louis XVI, I know how to bear events. What's frightful is the thought that it's your newspapers that do all the harm. You'll have your scribblers and talkers, your lawyers and orators and tribunes, your discussions, and progress, and leading lights, and rights of man and freedom of the press – and this is how your children will be brought home to you! Ah! Marius! It's dreadful! Killed! Dead before me! A barricade! Ah, the rogue! Doctor, you live in this neighbourhood, I believe? Oh! I know you well. I see your cabriolet going by from my window. I'm going to tell you something. You'd be wrong to think I'm angry. You don't get angry with a dead man. That would be stupid. This is a child I raised. I was already old when he was still very young. He played in the Tuileries Gardens with his little spade and his little chair, and so that the keepers wouldn't complain I'd go along after him filling in with my walking-stick the holes that he dug in the earth with his spade. One day he shouted, "Down with Louis XVIII!" And off he went. It's not my fault. He was all rosy and blond. His mother died. Have you noticed that all little children are blond? Why is that so? He's the son of one of those brigands of the Loire. But children are innocent of their fathers' crimes. I remember when he was just so high. He couldn't pronounce his Ds properly. He had a way of talking that was so quiet and unintelligible, he sounded like a bird. I remember once, in front of the Farnese *Hercules*, people stood round in an admiring circle, marvelling at him, he was so handsome, that child! He had a face of the kind you see in paintings. I used to scold him, I'd frighten him with my walking-stick, but he knew very well it was only a joke. In the morning when he came into my room I'd grumble, but it was as if he brought the sunshine. You can't defend yourself against those youngsters. They get hold of you, they latch on, and they never let go. The truth is, there was never such a darling child. Now, what have you got to say for your Lafayettes, your Benjamin Constants and your Tirecuir de Corcelles, who get him killed? This can't be allowed to happen!'

He approached Marius, still ghastly-pale and motionless and to whom the doctor had returned, and began once more to wring his hands. The old man's white lips moved as though unconsciously, letting out words that were barely audible, like whisperings in the last agony: 'Ah! heartless lad! Ah! clubbist! Ah! wretch! Ah! Septembrist!' Reproaches in the low voice of a dying man, addressed to a corpse.

Little by little, as internal eruptions inevitably have to come to the surface, the words came in sentences again, but the grandfather seemed no longer to have the strength to utter them; his voice, so faint and hollow, sounded as if it came from the other side of an abyss:

'It's all the same to me, I too am going to die. And to think there's not a lass in Paris who wouldn't have been delighted to make this wretch happy! A young rogue who, instead of having fun and enjoying life, went off to fight and got himself shot down like a brute! And for whom? Why? For the Republic! Instead of going dancing at La Chaumière, as young people have a moral obligation to! What's the use of being twenty years old? The Republic! Such damned silliness! Poor mothers, go ahead and produce fine boys! Well, he's dead. That will make two funerals under the same carriage gate. So you got yourself into that state for the sake of General Lamarque's handsome eyes! What had that General Lamarque ever done for you? A slasher! A blatherer! To get yourself killed for a dead man! As if that isn't enough to drive anyone crazy! Make some sense out of that! At twenty! And without looking back to see if he wasn't leaving something behind! There are now poor old men reduced to dying all alone. Croak in your corner, troglodyte! Well, as it happens, so much the better, it's what I was hoping for, it'll kill me off. I'm too old, I'm a hundred, I'm a hundred thousand years old, by rights I should have been dead long ago. This blow will see to it. So it's all over, what a blessing! What's the good of making him inhale ammonia and all that parcel of drugs? You're wasting your efforts, you idiot doctor! Believe me, he's dead, well and truly dead. I'd know, being dead myself. He's not done things by halves. Yes, this age is vile, vile, vile, and that's what I think of you, of your ideas, your systems, your masters, your oracles, your doctors, your good-for-nothing writers, your rascally philosophers, and of all the revolutions that for the past sixty years have been scaring the gatherings of crows in the Tuileries! And since you were pitiless in getting yourself killed like this, I shan't even grieve over your death, do you hear, murderer!'

At that moment Marius slowly opened his eyes, and his gaze, still clouded with lethargic amazement, rested on Monsieur Gillenormand.

'Marius!' cried the old man. 'Marius! My little Marius! My child! my darling boy! You're opening your eyes, you're looking at me, you're alive, thank you!'

And he fainted.

BOOK FOUR
JAVERT DERAILED

Javert had slowly walked away from Rue de l'Homme-Armé.

For the first time in his life he walked with his head bowed, and also for the first time in his life with his hands behind his back. Until that day, of Napoleon's two attitudes only the one that expresses resolution, arms folded across the chest, had Javert ever adopted. The one that expresses uncertainty – hands behind the back – was unknown to him. Now, a change had come about. Slow and sombre, his entire person bore the imprint of anxiety.

Down the silent streets he went. However, he was following a route. He took a short cut down to the Seine, reached Quai des Ormes, walked along the embankment, passed La Grève, and stopped some distance from the Place du Châtelet police station, at the corner of Pont Notre-Dame. There, between Pont Notre-Dame and Pont au Change on the one hand, and Quai de la Mégisserie and Quai aux Fleurs on the other, the Seine forms a kind of square lake, with rapids running through it.

This point in the Seine is dreaded by boatmen. There is nothing more dangerous than these rapids, in those days constricted and made turbulent by the piles of the now demolished watermill on the bridge. The two bridges, so close together, increase the peril. The water races with tremendous force under the arches. It churns there in huge and terrible swirls, it accumulates and backs up. The flow puts a strain on the bridges' piers as though trying to pull them down with great liquid ropes. Men who fall in here never reappear. The best of swimmers drown here.

Javert rested both elbows on the parapet, his chin in both hands, and automatically digging fingernails into his thick side-whiskers, he pondered.

A change, a revolution, a catastrophe had occurred deep down inside him, and there was cause for self-examination. Javert was suffering horribly. Several hours ago Javert had ceased to be a simple man. He felt troubled. That mind, so limpid in its blindness, had lost its transparency. There was a cloudiness in that crystal. Javert was aware in his conscience of a division of duty, and he could not conceal it from himself. When he had so unexpectedly encountered Jean Valjean on the banks of the Seine, there had been inside him something of the wolf recapturing its prey and of the dog finding its master again.

He saw ahead of him two paths, both equally straight, but he saw two of them. And that terrified him, having never in all his life known but one straight line. And to his deep anguish these two paths went in opposite directions. One of these straight lines excluded the other. Which of the two was the right one? His predicament was beyond words.

To owe his life to a criminal, to accept that debt and to settle it, in spite of himself to be on an equal footing with a former convict, and to repay him for one service with another service, to allow himself to be told 'Go', and in turn to say 'Remain free'; to sacrifice duty, that universal obligation, to personal considerations, and to sense in those personal considerations something that was also universal and perhaps of a higher nature, to betray society in order to remain true to his conscience: that all these absurdities should come about and be heaped on top of him – it was this that defeated him.

One thing astounded him: that Jean Valjean should have spared him. And one thing scared him rigid: that he, Javert, should have spared Jean Valjean.

What had become of him? He searched and could not find himself.

What was to be done now? It was bad to hand Jean Valjean over. It was bad to let Jean Valjean go free. In the first instance, the policeman sank lower than the man sentenced to the prison hulks, in the second, a convict rose above the law and trampled it underfoot. In both cases, Javert was himself disgraced. In every course that could be taken, there was ruin. Destiny comes, at certain points, to a sheer drop above the impossible, beyond which life is nothing but a precipice. Javert had come to one of those sheer drops.

One of his anxieties was that he was being made to think. The very violence of all these conflicting emotions forced it on him. Thinking was something he was unused to, and something peculiarly painful for him.

In thinking, there is always a degree of inner conflict, and it angered him to have that inside him.

Thinking about any subject outside the narrow sphere of his duties would have been, for him, in any event, futile and stressful. But thinking on the day that had just gone by was a torture. However, he really had to examine his conscience after such upsets and give an account of himself, to himself.

What he had just done made him shudder. He, Javert, contrary to all police regulations, contrary to the whole social and legal system, contrary to the entire criminal code, had seen fit to rule in favour of a release.

This had suited him. He had substituted his own affairs for those of the public. Was that not unspeakable? Every time he confronted this nameless deed he had committed, he trembled from head to foot. What must he bring himself to do? There was only one course open to him: to rush back to Rue de l'Homme-Armé and have Jean Valjean imprisoned. It was clear that this was what he ought to do. He could not.

Something was barring his way. Something? What? Is there anything in the world other than tribunals, sentences that have to be carried out, the police and the authorities? Javert was bewildered.

An inviolable convict! A condemned criminal beyond the reach of the law! And that, by Javert's own doing!

That these two men, Javert and Jean Valjean, both creatures of the law, the man meant to enforce it and the man meant to submit to it, should have come to the point of both putting themselves above the law – was that not shocking?

What! Such enormities could happen and no one would be punished! Jean Valjean, outweighing the entire social order, was to remain free, and he, Javert, was to go on eating the government's bread!

His reflections gradually took a terrible turn.

In those reflections he might also have reproached himself with regard to the insurgent brought home to Rue des Filles-du-Calvaire, but he gave no thought to that. The lesser fault was lost in the greater. Besides, that insurgent was obviously a dead man and, legally, death puts an end to any pursuit.

Jean Valjean, that was the load he had on his mind.

Jean Valjean confounded him. All the axioms that his whole life had hinged on gave way before that man. Jean Valjean's generosity towards him crushed Javert. Other things that he remembered, and that he had once treated as lies and nonsense, now came back to him as facts. Monsieur Madeleine reappeared behind Jean Valjean, and the two figures were superimposed on each other so that they now formed just the one figure, who was to be revered. Javert felt that something terrible was infiltrating his soul: admiration for a convict. Respect for a felon condemned to the prison hulks, is that possible? He shuddered at it, and could not escape it. In vain did he struggle, he was compelled to acknowledge in his heart of hearts the sublimity of that wretch. It was abhorrent.

A beneficent wrong-doer, a compassionate, gentle, forbearing convict, ready to help, returning good for evil, returning forgiveness for hatred, choosing pity rather than vengeance, preferring to doom himself rather than to doom his enemy, saving one who had struck out against him, kneeling on the heights of virtue, more akin to the angels than to man. Javert was forced to admit to himself that this monster existed.

Things could not go on like this.

Of course – and this we stress – he had not yielded without resistance to this monster, this vile angel, this frightful hero, by whom he was almost as much outraged as astounded. Twenty times, as he sat in that carriage face to face with Jean Valjean, the legal tiger had roared within him. Twenty times he had been tempted to fall on Jean Valjean, to seize him and devour him, in other words to arrest him. Indeed, what could be simpler? To cry out at the first police station they passed, 'Here's an ex-convict in violation of his parole!' To call the gendarmes and say to them, 'This man is yours!' Then to walk away, to leave this reprobate there, to ignore the rest and not have any more to do it. This man is for ever a prisoner of the law. The law will do with him what it will. What could be more just? Javert had said all this to himself. He had wanted to go further, to act, to apprehend the man and, then as now, he had not been able to. And every time his hand had convulsively reached up towards Jean Valjean's collar, as if restrained by an enormous weight that hand had dropped down again, and in the recesses of his mind he had heard a voice, a strange voice shouting at him, 'That's right! Deliver up your saviour! Then have Pontius Pilate's basin brought to you, and wash your filthy paws!'

Then his thoughts turned back to himself; and beside Jean Valjean, increased in stature, he saw himself, Javert, diminished. A convict was his benefactor!

But then, why had he allowed this man to let him live? He had the right to be killed inside that barricade. He should have exercised that right. It would have been better to summon the other insurgents to his aid against Jean Valjean, to contrive to get himself shot.

His supreme anguish was the loss of certainty. He felt he had lost his moorings. The law was no more than a broken stick in his hand. He had scruples of an unfamiliar kind to deal with. Taking place inside him was an emotional epiphany completely distinct from any legal considerations, his sole yardstick until then. Persisting in his former integrity was no longer enough. A whole order of unexpected factors was emerging, and getting the better of him. A whole new world was revealing itself to his soul: kindnesses accepted and repaid, self-sacrifice, mercy, leniency, severity constrained by pity, consideration for individuals, no more outright condemnation, no more damnation, the possibility of a tear in the law's eye, some sort of justice as laid down by God running contrary to justice as laid down by men. He perceived in the shadows the awesome rising of an unknown moral sun. He was horrified and dazzled by it. An owl with an eagle's-eye view forced upon it.

It was true, then, he told himself, there were exceptional cases, authority could lose face, the rules could fall short in some situations, not everything fitted into the text of the Penal Code, the unforeseen commanded obedience, the virtue of a convict could set a trap for the virtue of a functionary, the monstrous could be divine; destiny laid such ambushes, and he reflected with despair that he himself had not been safe from surprise.

He was forced to acknowledge that kindness existed. This convict had been kind. And he himself, extraordinarily enough, had just been kind. So he was becoming depraved. He thought himself cowardly. He horrified himself.

The ideal, for Javert, was not to be human, to be grand, to be sublime; it was to be irreproachable. Well, in this he had just failed.

How had he come to such a pass? How had all this happened? He himself could not have told. He clasped his head in both hands, but, try as he might, he could not explain it.

He had certainly always intended to turn Jean Valjean over to the law, Jean Valjean being its captive, and he, Javert, its slave. Not for a single instant while he held him had he admitted to himself that he had it in mind to let him go. It was in some sense unwittingly that his hand had opened and released him.

Glimpses of all sorts of new conundrums opened up before his eyes. He asked himself questions, and he answered them, and his answers frightened him. He asked himself, 'This convict, this desperado, whom I've pursued, indeed persecuted, and who has had me at his mercy, and who could have avenged himself and should have done so in consideration of both his grievance and his safety – what has he done by not taking my life, by sparing me? His duty? No. Something more. And I, in turn, by sparing him, what have I done? My duty? No. Something more. So there is something above duty?' Here he took fright. His scales were thrown out of kilter. One pan dropped into the abyss, the other flew heavenward, and Javert was no less terrified by the one on high than by the one below. Without being in the least what is called Voltairian, or philosophical, or sceptical – on the contrary, by instinct respectful towards the established Church – he knew it only as a venerable fragment of the social whole. Order was his dogma, and for him it sufficed. Since reaching manhood and becoming a servant of the state, he had made of the police more or less his entire religion, being – and we are using the words here without the least irony and in their most serious sense – being, as we have said, a spy as other men are priests. He had a superior, Monsieur Gisquet. Until that day he had barely given any thought to that other superior, God.

He was now suddenly conscious of this new chief, God, and he felt disturbed.

He was disorientated by this unexpected presence. He did not know what to do about this superior, aware as he was that the subordinate is always supposed to defer, that he must neither disobey nor find fault, nor argue, and that, in the presence of a superior who too greatly perplexes him, the inferior has no other option but to resign.

But how was a person to set about handing in his resignation to God?

In any event, and it was this that he kept coming back to, for him one fact overshadowed everything else, which was that he had just committed a terrible offence. He had just closed his eyes to a recidivist in violation of his parole. He had just set a felon free. He had just robbed the legal system of a man belonging to it. This he had done. He no longer understood himself. He was not sure of being himself. Even the reasons for his action escaped him, all it did was make him dizzy. He had lived until that moment by that blind faith that breeds a grim integrity. This faith was deserting him, this integrity was failing him. Everything he had believed was disintegrating. Truths he did not want to recognize obsessed him unrelentingly. He must from now on be a different man. He suffered the strange pangs of a conscience that has suddenly undergone a cataract operation. He saw what he shrank from seeing. He felt drained, useless, out of joint with his past life, dismissed, dissolved. Authority was dead within him. He no longer had any reason for being.

A terrible state of affairs! To be emotional!

To be of granite, and to doubt! To be the statue of retribution, cast all of a piece in the mould of the law, and suddenly to realize that beneath your torso of bronze you have something absurd and unruly that is almost like a heart! To reach the point of returning good for good, although you have told yourself, until today, that that particular good is evil! To be the guard dog, and to start licking! To be ice, and to melt! To be pincers, and to turn into a hand! Suddenly to feel your fingers opening up! To let go! The horror of it!

The man-missile not knowing his way any more, and drawing back!

To be compelled to admit this to yourself: infallibility is not infallible, there can be error in dogma, all has not been said when a penal code has spoken, society is not perfect, authority is complicated by an element of vacillation, a creaking of the immutable is possible, judges are men, the law may err, tribunals may be mistaken! To see a crack in the immense blue glass of the firmament!

What was going on inside Javert was the Fampoux of a rectilinear conscience, the derailment of a soul, the shattering of an integrity irresistibly propelled in a straight line and dashed against God. Certainly, it was strange. That the stoker of order, the engine driver of authority, mounted on the unseeing, fixed-track iron horse, could be unseated by a burst of light! That the inflexible, the straight, the precise, the geometrical, the unfeeling, the perfect might be capable of deflection! That there should be for the locomotive a road to Damascus!

God, always within man and, being the true conscience, defying the false, forbidding the spark to die out, commanding the ray to remember the sun, directing the soul to recognize the real absolute when confronted with the fictitious absolute, inalienable humanity, unallowable human feeling, that splendid phenomenon, perhaps the finest of all our inner marvels – did Javert understand this? Did Javert perceive this? Was Javert conscious of this? Evidently not. But under the pressure of its incomprehensibility, its undeniability, he felt his skull cracking open.

He was not so much transfigured by this miracle as a victim of it. In all this he saw only an immense difficulty in being. It seemed to him his breathing was now constricted for evermore. To have the unknown looming over him, he was not used to that.

Until now, all that he had had above him had been, to his eyes, a clear, plain, limpid surface. Nothing unknown or obscure there. Nothing that was not defined, systematized, pinned down, precise, exact, circumscribed, confined, closed. No surprises. Authority was something flat. No falling within it, no dizziness in the face of it. The only unknown Javert had ever seen was down below. The irregular, the unexpected, the disorderly opening-up of chaos, the possibility of sliding into an abyss – this was something to do with the nether regions, with the intractable, the wicked, the wretched. Now Javert tipped his head back, and he was suddenly terrified by this extraordinary apparition: a chasm on high.

What! This was the total demolition of selfhood! This was utter confoundment! What was to be trusted? Convictions held were now in ruins!

What! The chink in society's armour could be found by a magnanimous wretch! What! An honest servant of the law could suddenly find himself caught between two crimes, the crime of letting a man escape and the crime of arresting him! There was no complete certainty in the orders the state gave to its official! In duty there could be deadlocks!

What! All this was real! Was it true that an old ruffian, bowed under the sentences against him, might draw himself up again and ultimately be in the right? Was this believable? Were there cases, then, in which the law, in the face of crime transfigured, had to stand back, stammering its apologies?

Yes, indeed! And Javert was seeing this! And Javert was touching this! And not only was he unable to deny it, he was collaborating in it. These were actual facts. It was shocking that realities could come to be so monstrous.

If realities did their duty, they would just be proofs of law. It is God who dispenses realities. So was anarchy now going to descend from on high?

This being the case – and everything that might have curbed and corrected his impression was effaced by the exaggeration of anguish and by the distortion of dismay, and society and the human race and the universe were now reduced in his eyes to hideously simplified contours – this being the case, then, punishment, the final sentence, the force of law, the rulings of sovereign courts, the magistrature, the government, prevention and repression, official wisdom, legal infallibility, the principle of authority, all the dogmas on which political and civil security rest, sovereignty, justice, the logic following from the law as it stands, the social absolute, the public truth – all this was rubble, debris, chaos. He himself, Javert, order's watchman, incorruptibility in the service of the police, society's guard-dog saviour – defeated and felled. And standing above all this ruin, a man wearing a green cap, and a halo around his head. Such was the cataclysm that had overtaken him, such was the frightful vision he had in his soul.

And this could be endured? No.

A dire state, if ever there were one. There were only two ways out of it. One was to go resolutely to Jean Valjean and return to gaol the man from the prison hulks. The other . . .

Javert left the parapet and, this time with head held high, strode towards the police station identified by a lantern on a corner of Place du Châtelet.

When he got there he saw a policeman through the window, and went inside. Policemen recognize each other as colleagues just by the way they push open the door of a guard-room. Javert gave his name, showed his card to the police officer, and sat down at the guard-room table, on which a candle was burning. On the table lay a pen, a lead inkpot and some notepaper for any particulars that might need to be taken down and for night-patrol reports.

This table, which always comes with its straw-bottomed chair, is an institution. It exists in every police station. It is invariably graced with a boxwood saucer filled with sawdust and a cardboard pin-cushion box full of red sealing-wafers; it is the ground floor of official style. It is with this table that the literature of the state begins.

Javert took the pen and a sheet of paper, and began to write. This is what he wrote:

A FEW OBSERVATIONS FOR THE BENEFIT OF THE SERVICE.

First: I humbly commend this to Monsieur le Préfet's attention.

Second: prisoners, coming back from questioning, take off their shoes and stand barefoot on the flagstones while they are being searched. A number of them return to gaol coughing. This incurs hospital expenses.

Third: tailing procedures are good, with relays of agents posted at intervals, but in major cases it would be better that at least two agents were never to lose sight of each other, so that if for any reason one agent happens to fail in his duty, the other will be watching him and can take his place.

Fourth: it is not clear why the special regulations of Les Madelonnettes prison prohibit inmates from having a chair, even if paying for it.

Fifth: at Les Madelonnettes there are only two security bars separating the canteen, so the canteen woman can let the prisoners touch her hand.

Sixth: the so-called barkers, prisoners who summon the other inmates to the visiting room, make them pay two sous to have their names called out distinctly. This is robbery.

Seventh: for one loose thread, the prisoner in the weaving-shed is docked ten sous. This is an abuse on the part of the contractor since the cloth is nonetheless good.

Eighth: it is a nuisance that visitors to La Force have to cross the young-sters' courtyard in order to reach the Ste-Marie-l'Égyptienne visiting room.

Ninth: there is no doubt that every day gendarmes are to be heard in the courtyard of police headquarters talking about the interrogation of pris-oners by the magistrates. For a gendarme, who ought to be held in the highest esteem, to repeat what he has heard in the criminal investigation chambers is a serious indiscipline.

Tenth: Madame Henry is an honest woman. Her canteen is very clean. But it is wrong that a woman should be keeper of the solitary-confinement cells. This is unworthy of the Conciergerie of a great civilization.

Javert wrote these lines in his steadiest and neatest handwriting, omitting not a single comma and making the paper screech under the firmness of his pen. He signed below the last line:

JAVERT

Senior Inspector

Place du Châtelet police station

7 June 1832, about one o'clock in the morning

Javert dried the fresh ink on the sheet of paper, folded it like a letter, sealed it, wrote on the back 'Note for the administration', laid it on the table and left the police station. The grated glass-panelled door swung shut behind him.

He made his way back diagonally across Place du Châtelet, reached the embankment, and returned with automatic precision to the very spot from which he had walked away a quarter of an hour earlier. There, he rested his elbows on the parapet and found himself once more in the same pose on the same flagstone. It was as if he had not stirred.

There was complete darkness. It was that sepulchral moment after midnight. A ceiling of cloud hid the stars. The sky was no more than a sinister density. In the houses on Île de la Cité not a single light still showed. There was no one about. All that could be seen of the streets and embankments was emptiness. Notre-Dame and the towers of the law courts seemed features of the night. A street lantern cast its red glow on the edge of the embankment. The silhouettes of the bridges, lying one behind the other, appeared distorted in the mist. Rains had swollen the river.

The spot where Javert had rested his elbows was situated, remember, directly above the rapids in the Seine, over that dreadful spiral of swirling waters, turning and unturning like an endlessly driven screw.

Javert bent his head and looked down. All was black. Nothing was distinguishable. A sound of raging foam could be heard, but the river was invisible. Now and again in those vertiginous depths a gleam of light appeared and dimly coiled, water having that power, in the most complete darkness, of capturing light from who knows where and transforming it into a snake. The light vanished and all became indistinguishable again. Down there, immensity seemed to gape. What lay below was not water, it was an abyss. The wall of the embankment, sheer, blurred, misted with spray, suddenly lost from sight, seemed like an escarpment of the infinite.

Nothing could be seen, but the hostile chill of the water and the

1189

mustiness of the wet stones could be felt. A frenzied exhalation rose from that abyss. The swollen river sensed rather than seen, the tragic murmur of the torrent, the grim hugeness of the bridge's arches, the imaginable fall into that dark void, all this gloom was full of horror.

For a few minutes Javert remained motionless, watching this tenebrous orifice. He gazed on the invisible with a seemingly attentive fixity. There was the sound of the rushing waters. Abruptly, he took off his hat and placed it on the edge of the embankment. A moment later a tall black figure, which from a distance some tardy passer-by might have taken for a phantom, appeared standing on the parapet, leaned over the Seine, then straightened up again and dropped into the blackness below. There was a heavy splash. And the shadows alone were privy to the convulsions of that mysterious figure after it had disappeared under the water.

BOOK FIVE
GRANDFATHER AND GRANDSON

I
Returning to the Tree with the Band of Zinc

Some time after the events we have just related, Sieur Boulatruelle experienced great excitement.

Sieur Boulatruelle is that road-mender of Montfermeil whom we have already encountered in the shadowy parts of this book.

Boulatruelle, the reader may recall, was a man with various unsettling preoccupations. He was a stone-breaker, and a blight to travellers on the highway. A navvy and a thief, he had a dream. He believed there was treasure buried in the forest of Montfermeil. He hoped some day to find money in the ground at the foot of a tree. In the meantime he was happy to seek it in the pockets of wayfarers.

However, he was being careful for now. He had just had a narrow escape. As we know, he had been rounded up with the other ruffians in Jondrette's garret. A vice may have its uses: his drunkenness had saved him. It could never be clarified whether he was there as robber or as robbed. A ruling of no case to answer, based on his well established state of inebriation on the evening of the ambush, secured his release. And he was off back to the woods. He had returned to the Gagny–Lagny road to do his road-building for the state under administrative supervision, looking downcast and extremely pensive, a little put off thieving, which had almost done for him; but turning to wine, which had just saved him, only with increased fondness.

As for the great excitement he had experienced shortly after his return to his road-mender's turf-roofed hut, it was this:

One morning a little before daybreak, on his way to work as usual (and maybe also to his lurking-place), through the branches Boulatruelle caught sight of a man he saw only from behind, but whose physique, it seemed to him from a distance and in the half-light, was not entirely unfamiliar to him. Although a drunkard, Boulatruelle had an accurate and lucid memory, a defensive weapon indispensable to anyone slightly at odds with the law.

'Where the devil have I seen the likes of that man before?' he wondered.

But he was unable to come up with any answer, except that there was a resemblance here to someone of whom he had a vague impression in his mind.

Anyway, leaving aside the identity he was unable to pin down, Boulatruelle made some calculations and deductions. This man was not local. He had just arrived here. On foot, evidently. No public transport passes through Montfermeil at that time of day. He had walked all night. Where did he come from? Not very far away. For he had neither haversack nor bundle. From Paris, no doubt. Why was he in these woods? Why was he here at such an early hour? What had he come to do here?

Boulatruelle thought of the treasure. By delving deep into his memory he vaguely recalled having already been on similar alert many years before with regard to someone who, it seemed to him, could be this very same man.

While pondering, he had naturally enough, but not very cleverly, bowed his head beneath the very weight of his ponderings. When he looked up again, there was no sign of anyone. The man had melted away into the forest and into the half-light.

'Damn it!' said Boulatruelle. 'I'll track him down. I'll find out what his business is. He's out and about at the crack of dawn for a purpose, this fellow, and I'll get to the bottom of it. No one has any secrets in my forest that can be kept from me.'

He took up his pickaxe, which was very sharp.

'This,' he muttered, 'is something to search the ground with – and to search a man with.'

And, as though tying one thread to another thread, following step by step as closely as he could the route the man must have taken, he set off through the woods.

After he had gone some hundred paces, the beginnings of daylight helped him. Footprints here and there in the sand, trampled grasses, crushed heather, young branches in the underwood bent back and straightening out again with a graceful slowness like the arms of a pretty woman stretching when she wakes, showed him a kind of trail. He followed it, then lost it. Time wore on. He went deeper into the forest and came to a kind of mound. An early-morning huntsman passing by on a path in the distance, whistling the tune of 'Guilleri'*,

* 'Compère Guilleri' is a traditional song about a hunter who climbs a tree to look for his dogs. (The branch breaks and Guilleri falls to the ground.)

gave him the idea of climbing a tree. Although old, he was agile. Right there was a very tall beech tree, worthy of Tityrus and of Boulatruelle. Boulatruelle climbed the beech tree as high as he could.

It was a good idea. Scanning the solitude over in the direction where the forest is completely wild and overgrown, Boulatruelle suddenly caught a glimpse of the man.

He had no sooner caught a glimpse than he lost sight of him.

The man entered, or rather slipped into, a clearing some distance away screened by tall trees, but Boulatruelle knew it very well, having noticed an ailing chestnut tree there near a big pile of millstones, with a band of zinc nailed on to the bark. This clearing is the one that used to be called Blaru's Piece. The heap of stones, intended for who knows what purpose and to be seen there thirty years ago, is doubtless still there now. Nothing matches the longevity of a pile of stones, except that of a fence made of wooden planks. They are there temporarily. No wonder they last!

Boulatruelle, with a joyful alacrity, dropped rather than climbed down from the tree. The lair was located, it was a matter of catching the beast. The famous dreamed-of treasure was probably there.

It was no small matter to reach that clearing. By the beaten paths, which make countless tiresome zigzags, it took a good quarter of an hour. Making a bee-line through the thicket, which is particularly dense there, very thorny and very punishing, it took a full half-hour. Boulatruelle made the mistake of not realizing this. He believed in the bee-line, a convincing optical illusion but the undoing of many a man. Through the thicket, bristly as it was, seemed to him the way to go.

'Let's take the wolves' Rue de Rivoli,' he said.

Given to crookedness, Boulatruelle on this occasion misguidedly went straight.

He plunged resolutely into the tangle of undergrowth.

He had to deal with holly bushes, nettles, hawthorn, briars, thistles and extremely prickly brambles. He was very scratched.

At the bottom of the gully he found there was water to get across.

At last, forty minutes later, he reached the Blaru clearing, sweating, drenched, out of breath, torn to shreds, ferocious.

Nobody in the clearing.

Boulatruelle rushed to the heap of stones. It was still in place. It had not been moved.

As for the man, he had vanished into the forest. He had made his escape. Where to? In what direction? Into which thicket? Impossible to tell.

And, distressingly enough, behind the pile of stones, in front of the tree with the band of zinc on it, there was freshly turned earth, a pick that had been forgotten or abandoned, and a hole.

This hole was empty.

'Thief!' shouted Boulatruelle, shaking his fist at the horizon.

II
Emerging from Civil War,
Marius Prepares for Domestic War

For a long time Marius was neither dead nor alive. For several weeks he had a fever accompanied by delirium and by some rather serious cerebral symptoms, caused more by the trauma of his wounds than by the wounds themselves.

In the morbid loquacity of feverishness and with the grim persistence of anguish, he repeated Cosette's name for whole nights on end. The extent of some of his injuries posed a serious danger, with always the possibility, under certain atmospheric conditions, of the suppuration of large wounds being reabsorbed and consequently killing the patient. At every change of weather, at the slightest storm, the physician became anxious. 'It's most important the patient has no emotional excitement whatsoever,' he kept saying. The dressing of the wounds was complicated and difficult, the fixing of compresses and bandages by adhesive plaster not yet having been invented. Nicolette used up a sheet 'as big as a ceiling', she said, for lint. It was no easy matter for the chlorinated lotions and silver nitrate to defeat gangrene. As long as there was any danger Monsieur Gillenormand, distraught at his grandson's bedside, was, like Marius, neither dead nor alive.

Every day, sometimes twice a day, a white-haired gentleman, very well dressed – such was the description given by the porter – came to ask for news of the patient, and left a large packet of lint dressing.

Eventually, on the seventh of September, four months to the day after that woeful night when Marius was brought home, dying, to his grandfather's, the doctor declared he was confident that Marius would pull through. He was on the road to recovery. But Marius had to remain more than another two months reclining on a chaise-longue because of complications resulting from the fracture of his collarbone. There is always a last wound like that, that will not heal and, to the patient's great frustration, keeps him in bandages interminably.

However, this long illness and this long convalescence saved him from prosecution. In France there is no anger, even governmental anger, that six months does not quench. In the present state of society, everyone is so much to blame for any rioting that there is a certain need to turn a blind eye afterwards.

Let us add that the scandalous Gisquet decree, which called on doctors to report casualties to the police, having provoked public outrage – and not only the outrage of the public but of the king, first and foremost – the casualties were shielded and protected by that outrage. And with the exception of those who had been taken prisoner while actually fighting, the courts martial dared not pursue any of them. So Marius was left in peace.

Monsieur Gillenormand experienced every anguish to begin with, and then every ecstasy. It was very difficult to prevent him spending every night with the patient. He had his big armchair installed at Marius's bedside. He insisted that his daughter take the finest linen in the house to make compresses and bandages. As a sensible person of some seniority, Mademoiselle Gillenormand contrived to spare the fine linen while letting the grandfather believe he was being obeyed. Monsieur Gillenormand would not allow anyone to explain to him that for making lint, cambric is not as good as coarse linen, and new cloth not as good as worn cloth. He stayed for the dressing of all wounds, while Mademoiselle Gillenormand modestly absented herself. When the dead flesh was being cut away with scissors, he would say, 'Ow! Ow!' Nothing was more touching than seeing him, with the gentle tremor of his advanced years, holding a cup of herbal tea to the patient's lips. He plied the doctor with questions. He did not notice that he always kept asking the same ones.

The day the doctor told him that Marius was out of danger, the old man was delirious. He gave his porter a tip of three gold coins, each worth twenty francs. Retiring to his bedroom that evening, he danced a gavotte, clicking his thumb and forefinger like castanets, and he sang the following song:

> Jeanne was born at Fougère,
> A true shepherd-maid's haunt.
> I so adore her taunting
> Petticoat.
>
> Love, you dwell within her;
> By a cunning device, lies
> Buried deep in her eyes
> Your quiver.

I sing of the one I love
More than Diane herself,
My Breton Jeanne, and her
Firm bosom.

Then he knelt on a chair, and Basque, who was watching through the half-open door, felt sure that he was praying.

Until then, he had scarcely believed in God.

At each new stage of recovery, which became more and more marked, the grandfather went into raptures. All sorts of things that he did automatically were full of light-heartedness. He went up and down the stairs without knowing why. A woman living near by, and a pretty one at that, was quite amazed to receive a big bouquet one morning. It was Monsieur Gillenormand who had sent it to her. The jealous husband made a scene. Monsieur Gillenormand tried to sit Nicolette on his lap. He called Marius 'Monsieur le baron'. He cried, 'Long live the Republic!'

He kept on asking the doctor, 'There's no danger any more, is there?' He watched Marius with the eyes of a grandmother. He gazed at him fondly while he ate. He no longer recognized himself, he no longer mattered, Marius was master of the house; there was abdication in his joy, he was his grandson's grandson.

In his gladness he was the most venerable of children. Fearful of tiring or bothering the convalescent, he would go behind him to smile at him. He was cheerful, happy, delighted, charming, youthful. His white hair added a gentle dignity to the cheerful radiance of his visage. When grace is combined with wrinkles, it is enchanting. There is a sort of dawning in the full bloom of old age.

As for Marius, while allowing himself to be bandaged and nursed, he had one thing only on his mind: Cosette. Since the fever and delirium had left him, he had not mentioned that name again, and it might have been supposed he no longer thought of her. He kept quiet for the very reason that his soul resided in her.

He did not know what had become of Cosette. The whole Rue de la Chanvrerie affair was a blur in his memory. Almost indistinguishable shadows floated in his mind, Éponine, Gavroche, Mabeuf, the Thénardiers, all his friends calamitously embroiled in the smoke of the barricade. Monsieur Fauchelevent, turning up so strangely in that bloody venture, was to him like a riddle in a storm. He could not account for his own life. He knew neither how nor by whom he had been saved, and no one around him knew. All that anyone had been able to tell him was that he had been brought back at night in a cab to

Rue des Filles-du-Calvaire. Past, present, future were now no more than the fog of some vague idea within him. But in that fog there was one fixed point, one clear and precise outline, something of granite, a resolve, a will: to find Cosette. For him, the idea of life could not be separated from the idea of Cosette. He had decided in his heart that he would not accept one without the other, and he was unshakeably determined to demand – of his grandfather, of fate, of hell, of anyone who wanted to force him to live – the return of his lost Eden.

He did not hide the obstacles from himself.

One detail not to be overlooked: he was not won over and was little mollified by all his grandfather's displays of concern and tenderness. For a start, he did not know about all of them. Then, in his perhaps still feverish reveries the patient distrusted this loving kindness as a strange and novel thing, intended to subjugate him. He remained cold to it. The grandfather's poor old smile was utterly wasted on him. Marius told himself that it was fine as long as he, Marius, kept his mouth shut and did not assert himself, but when it came to Cosette he would be shown a completely different face, and his grandfather's true attitude would reveal itself. Then things would turn nasty: a resurgence of family quarrels, a clash of positions, every sarcastic remark and every objection all at once, Fauchelevent, Coupelevent, wealth, poverty, wretchedness, a millstone round his neck, the future. Violent resistance. Outcome: refusal. Marius was steeling himself in advance.

And then, as he regained life, his old grievances resurfaced, old sores reopened in his memory, his thoughts returned to the past, Colonel Pontmercy came between Monsieur Gillenormand and Marius himself again, he told himself there was no hope of any true kindness from someone who had been so unjust and so cruel towards his father. And with the return of his health came a kind of bitterness towards his grandfather. The old man suffered in silence.

Without actually giving any sign of it, Monsieur Gillenormand noticed that not once since having been brought home and having regained consciousness had Marius called him 'father'. True, he did not say, 'monsieur'. But by a certain way of turning his phrases he contrived to say neither one nor the other.

Obviously, a crisis was brewing.

As almost always happens in such circumstances, to prime himself Marius skirmished before giving battle. This is called 'seeing how the land lies'. One morning it happened that, apropos of a newspaper he chanced to pick up, Monsieur Gillenormand spoke slightingly about the Convention and let slip a royalist remark about Danton, Saint-Juste and Robespierre. 'The men of '93 were giants,' said Marius severely. The old man kept quiet and breathed not a word for the rest of that day.

Marius, who still had in mind the inflexible grandfather of his early years, saw in this silence a profound concentration of anger that foreshadowed a bitter struggle, and in the innermost recesses of his psyche he stepped up his preparations for conflict.

In the event of refusal, he decided, he would tear off his dressings, dislocate his collar-bone, expose whatever open wounds he still had and reject all food. His wounds were his ammunition. To have Cosette or to die.

With the cunning patience of the sick he waited for the right moment. That moment came.

III
Marius Attacks

One day, while his daughter was tidying up the flasks and cups on the marble-topped dresser, Monsieur Gillenormand bent over Marius and said to him in his fondest tone of voice, 'You see, Marius, my dear, in your place I'd eat meat now rather than fish. A fried sole is excellent at the start of convalescence, but to set the patient on his feet a good cutlet is what's needed.'

Marius, who had regained almost all his strength, mustered it, sat up straight, rested his two clenched fists on the sheets of his bed, looked his grandfather in the eye, adopted a fearsome expression and said, 'That brings me to something I have to tell you.'

'Which is?'

'That I want to get married.'

'All arranged,' said his grandfather. And he burst out laughing.

'What do you mean, all arranged?'

'Yes, all arranged. You shall have your little sweetheart.'

Dumbfounded and overwhelmed with amazement, Marius trembled in every limb.

Monsieur Gillenormand went on, 'Yes, you shall have your dear beautiful girl. She comes every day in the shape of an old gentleman to ask after you. She's been spending the whole time, ever since you were hurt, weeping and making lint. I've made inquiries. She lives in Rue de l'Homme-Armé, at number seven. Ah! There we have it! Ah! You want her! Well, you shall have her! You've been caught out. You had your little scheme, you said to yourself, "I'm going to come right out and tell that grandfather, that Regency and Directory old fossil, that antiquated dandy, that Dorante turned Géronte. He too has sown his wild oats, and had his love affairs and his grisettes, and his Cosettes. He's done his own prancing about, he's spread his own wings and tasted the joys of spring, he really needs to remember that. Let's just see. To battle!" Ah! you take the old goat by the horns. That's fine. I offer you a cutlet and your answer is "By the way, I want to get married." There's a change of subject for you! Ah! you reckoned on some wrangling! You didn't realize I was an old coward. What do you say to that? You're cross? To find your grandfather even more foolish than yourself, you didn't expect that. The riot act you were supposed to read me, your honour, is wasted, that's upsetting. Well, too bad, rage away! I'm doing what you want – that shuts you up, you imbecile! Listen. I've done some investigating, I'm a crafty one as well. She's delightful, she's respectable, it's not true about the lancer, she's made heaps of lint, she's a jewel, she adores you. If you had died, there would have been three of us, her coffin would have accompanied mine. It certainly occurred to me, as soon you were better, to plant her at your bedside with no more ado, but it's only in novels that young ladies are brought just like that to the bedside of handsome wounded lads they care about. It's not done. What would your aunt have said? You were stark-naked three-quarters of the time, my dear boy. Ask Nicolette, who hasn't left you for a moment, if it was possible to have a woman here. And then, what would the doctor have said? That's no cure for fever, a pretty girl. Anyway, never mind, there's nothing more to be said, it's settled, it's done, it's all sorted out, take her. That's how ferocious I am. You see, I saw that you didn't love me. I said: "Now, what could I do to make that brute love me?" I said, "Look, I've got my little Cosette right here, I'm going to give her to him, then he'll surely have to love me a little, or I'll know the reason why." Ah! You thought the old man was going to rant and rage and shout no, and raise his cane at all that loveliness. Not a bit of it. Cosette, agreed. Love, agreed. I couldn't ask for more. Monsieur, please get married. Be happy, my beloved child.'

That said, the old man burst out sobbing.

And he took hold of Marius's head and clasped it with both arms to his aged chest, and both began to weep. This is one form of supreme happiness.

'Father!' cried Marius.

'Ah! So you do love me!' said the old man.

There was an unutterable moment. They felt choked and could not speak.

Eventually the old man stammered out, 'That's it! He said the word. He called me "father"!'

Marius freed his head from his grandfather's arms and said gently, 'But father, now that I'm well, I think I could see her.'

'All arranged, you'll be seeing her tomorrow.'

'Father!'

'What?'

'Why not today?'

'Very well, today. Today it is. You've called me "father" three times, that's well worth the price. I'm going to see to it. She'll be brought to you. All arranged, I tell you. This has already been put into verse. It's the ending of the elegy "Le Jeune Malade" by André Chénier, André Chénier who was murdered by the cut-thr—, by the giants of '93.'

Monsieur Gillenormand thought he discerned a slight frown on Marius's brow – but, to be honest, Marius was not actually listening to him any longer and was thinking much more of Cosette than of 1793.

Trembling at having introduced André Chénier so inopportunely, the grandfather went on hurriedly, ' "Murdered" isn't the right word. The fact is, the great revolutionary geniuses, who were not wicked, there's no doubt about that, who were heroes, of course, found that André Chénier something of nuisance, and they had him guillot—, that's to say, in the interests of public safety those great men asked André Chénier on the seventh of Thermidor if he wouldn't mind going—'

With his own sentence catching in his throat, Monsieur Gillenormand could not go on. Unable either to finish it or retract it while his daughter was arranging the pillow behind Marius, overwhelmed by all this emotion, the old man rushed from the bedroom as fast as his age would allow, pushed the door shut behind him and found himself – purple, choking, foaming at the mouth, his eyes popping out of his head – face to face with the dependable Basque, who was polishing boots in the anteroom. He grabbed Basque by the collar and shouted in fury, right in his face, 'By the devil's hundred thousand tittle-tattlers, those ruffians assassinated him!'

'Who, monsieur?'

'André Chénier!'

'Yes, monsieur,' said Basque, terror-stricken.

Mademoiselle Gillenormand Does Not in the End Disapprove of Monsieur Fauchelevent's Arrival with Something under His Arm

Cosette and Marius saw each other again. How that meeting went it is not for us to say. There are some things we should not attempt to describe, the sun being one of them.

The whole family, including Basque and Nicolette, were assembled in Marius's room when Cosette came in. She appeared on the threshold. She seemed to be surrounded by a halo of light. Just at that moment the grandfather was about to blow his nose. He stopped short, with his nose in his handkerchief, looking over at Cosette.

'Adorable!' he exclaimed.

Then he noisily blew his nose.

Cosette was elated, enraptured, scared, in heaven. She was as bewildered with happiness as it is possible to be. She stammered, all pale, all flushed, wanting to throw herself into Marius's arms and not daring to, ashamed of showing her love in front of all these people. People have no pity for happy lovers, staying when the lovers most wish to be alone. Yet lovers have no need at all of other people.

Coming in with Cosette, following behind her, was a white-haired man, grave-faced yet smiling, but with a vague and heart-rending smile. It was 'Monsieur Fauchelevent'. It was Jean Valjean.

He was 'very well dressed', as the porter had said, his clothes all black, all new, and with a white cravat.

The porter would never have recognized in this impeccable bourgeois, in this probable lawyer, the terrifying corpse-bearer who had turned up at his door on the night of the seventh of June, tattered, muddy, hideous, haggard, his face masked with blood and filth, carrying an unconscious Marius, whom he held by the armpits. Yet his porter's instinct was aroused. When Monsieur Fauchelevent had arrived with Cosette, the porter could not help remarking privately to his wife, 'I don't know why I keep thinking I've seen that face before.'

In Marius's room, Monsieur Fauchelevent remained to one side, as it were, by the door. He had under his arm a package much like an octavo-sized volume, wrapped in paper. The wrapping-paper was greenish and looked mildewed.

'Does that gentleman always carry books under his arm like that?' Mademoiselle Gillenormand, who did not like books, asked Nicolette in an undertone.

'Well,' replied Monsieur Gillenormand in the same tone, having overheard her, 'he's a scholar. So what? Is that his fault? Monsieur Boulard, whom I knew, never went anywhere without a book under his arm either, and always had some old volume clutched to his heart like that.'

And bowing, he said aloud, 'Monsieur Tranchelevent—'

Old Gillenormand did not do it intentionally, but carelessness about proper names was an aristocratic mannerism of his.

'Monsieur Tranchelevent, I have the honour of asking you, on behalf of my grandson, Baron Marius Pontmercy, for Mademoiselle's hand in marriage.'

'Monsieur Tranchelevent' bowed.

'That's settled,' said the grandfather.

And turning to Marius and Cosette, with both arms extended in blessing, he cried, 'Permission to adore each other!'

They did not need to be told twice. It could not be helped! The cooing began. They spoke to each other quietly. Marius, propped up on his elbow on his chaise-longue, Cosette standing beside him.

'Oh my God!' murmured Cosette. 'I'm seeing you again! It's you! It is you! To go and join in the fighting like that! Why? It's dreadful. For the past four months I've been dead. Oh! how wicked it was of you to have taken part in that battle! What had I done to you? I forgive you, but you're not to do it again. A little while ago, when they came to fetch us, I still thought I was going to die, but to die of joy. I'd been so miserable! I didn't take time to dress properly, I must look a fright! What will your relatives say, seeing me with my collar all crumpled? Well, say something! You're letting me do all the talking. We're still in Rue de l'Homme-Armé. Apparently your shoulder was terrible. They told me, you could get your whole hand into it. And then, apparently you had your flesh cut away with scissors. That's the really ghastly thing. I cried my eyes out. It's strange that a person can suffer like that. Your grandfather looks very kindly. Don't move, don't put your weight on your elbow, be careful, you'll hurt yourself. Oh! how happy I am! So that's the last of our sorrows! I'm completely bemused. I wanted to tell you things that I can't remember at all now. Do you still love me? We live in Rue de l'Homme-Armé. There's no garden. I made lint the whole time – look, monsieur, you see? It's your fault I have callused fingers.'

'Angel!' Marius kept saying.

'Angel' is the only word in the language that cannot wear thin. No other word could withstand being so mercilessly used by lovers.

Then, as there were others present, they fell silent and said not another word, confining themselves to very gently touching hands.

Monsieur Gillenormand turned to all those who were in the room and cried, 'Now, speak up, the rest of you! Make some noise, everybody! Come on, a little hubbub, damn it! So that these children can chatter together in peace.'

And going over to Marius and Cosette, he said to them in a very low voice, 'You needn't stand on ceremony with each other.'*

Aunt Gillenormand looked on with amazement at this irruption of light into her old-fashioned home. There was nothing aggressive about this amazement. It was not at all the scandalized and envious gaze of a lone owl at the sight of two turtle-doves; it was the baffled gaze of a poor fifty-seven-year-old innocent. It was a life unlived seeing that triumph, love.

'Mademoiselle Gillenormand,' her father said to her, 'I told you this would happen.'

He remained silent for a moment, and added, 'Gaze on the happiness of others.'

Then he turned to Cosette.

'What a lovely girl! What a lovely girl! A Greuze, she is. So you're going to have that all to yourself, you clever rascal! Ah! my boy, you had a narrow escape from me, you're lucky, if I were fifteen years younger we'd be drawing swords to see which of us should have her. Well now! I'm in love with you, mademoiselle. It's only natural. It's what you're entitled to. Ah! what a wonderful, charming little wedding this is going to be! Our parish is St-Denis-du-St-Sacrement, but I'll get a dispensation so that you can be married at St-Paul. The church is better. It was built by the Jesuits. It's more attractive. It's opposite Cardinal de Birague's fountain. The masterpiece of Jesuit architecture is at Namur. It's called St-Loup. You must go there after you're married. It's worth the journey. Mademoiselle, I'm with you entirely, I want girls to marry, that's what they're for. There's a certain St Catherine I'd like to see not ever wearing a bonnet.† To remain a virgin is a fine thing, but of cold comfort. The Bible says: "Multiply." In order to save the nation, we need Jeanne d'Arc. But to create the nation, we need Mère Gigogne. So get married, young ladies. I really don't see the point of remaining a spinster! I know they have their own separate chapel in church, and there's the Society of the Virgin to fall back on,

---

* He urges them to address each other as *tu*. 'Tutoyez-vous. Ne vous gênez pas.'

† Monsieur Gillenormand is alluding to the expression *coiffer Sainte-Catherine*, 'to don St Catherine's bonnet', meaning 'to become an old maid'. St Catherine of Alexandria is the patron saint of single women and milliners.

but heavens alive! An attractive husband worth his salt, and by the end of the year a chubby fair-haired baby boy, eager for your milk, with good rolls of fat on his thighs, kneading your breast with his little pink hands, like the smiling dawn – that's surely better than holding a candle at vespers and chanting "Turris eburnea"*!'

The grandfather pirouetted on his ninety-year-old heels, and was off again like a released spring.

'"So, abandoning the daydreams with which you have long tarried,
    Is it true, then, Alcippe, you are shortly to be married?"†

By the way!'

'What is it, father?'

'Didn't you have a close friend?'

'Yes, Courfeyrac.'

'What has become of him?'

'He's dead.'

'That's just as well.'

He sat down beside them, made Cosette sit down, and took their four hands in his wrinkled old hands.

'She's delightful, this darling girl. She's a masterpiece, this Cosette! She's a mere child and a great lady. She will be only a baroness, that's a travesty – she's a born marchioness. Those eyelashes of hers! Get it firmly into your heads, children, that you've made the right choice. Love each other. Be fools in love. Love is the foolishness of men and the wit of God. Adore each other. But oh, what a shame!' he added, suddenly downcast. 'It's only just occurred to me! More than half of what I own is in annuities. So long as I live, there's no problem, but after my death, some twenty years from now, ah! my poor children, you'll be penniless! Your beautiful white hands, madame la baronne, will be spoiled trying to make ends meet.'

At this point they heard a deep, calm voice saying, 'Mademoiselle Euphrasie Fauchelevent has six hundred thousand francs.'

It was Jean Valjean's voice.

He had not yet uttered a single word, no one even seemed aware that he was still there; he stood motionless behind all these happy people.

---

* 'Tower of ivory', an invocation from the Marian 'Litanies of Loreto' (*Litaniae laurentanae*).

† A slight reworking of the first two lines of Boileau's Satire X, published in 1694, in which the poet satirizes the weaknesses and failings of women.

'Who on earth is this Mademoiselle Euphrasie?' asked the grand-father in bewilderment.

'That's me,' replied Cosette.

'Six hundred thousand francs?' said Monsieur Gillenormand.

'Minus fourteen or fifteen thousand francs maybe,' said Jean Valjean.

And he laid on the table the package that Aunt Gillenormand had taken for a book. Jean Valjean himself opened the package. It was a bundle of banknotes. They were divided up and counted out. There were five hundred one-thousand-franc notes and one hundred and sixty-eight five-hundred-franc notes. In all, five hundred and eighty-four thousand francs.

'That's a good book,' said Monsieur Gillenormand.

'Five hundred and eighty-four thousand francs!' murmured the aunt.

'That certainly helps matters, doesn't it, Mademoiselle Gillenormand?' said the grandfather. 'This lucky devil Marius has managed to find in the tree of dreams a little dove who's a millionairess! So now, trust in young people's love for each other! Students find student sweethearts with six hundred thousand francs. Cherubino does a better job than Rothschild.'

'Five hundred and eighty-four thousand francs!' Mademoiselle Gillenormand repeated under her breath. 'Five hundred and eighty-four! Well, you might as well say six hundred thousand!'

As for Marius and Cosette, all this time they were gazing at each other. They paid hardly any attention to this detail.

V

Deposit Your Money in a Forest Rather Than with a Notary

The reader has no doubt understood without the need for any lengthy explanation that after the Champmathieu affair, Jean Valjean, thanks to his first escape, which lasted a few days, was able to reach Paris in time to withdraw from Laffitte the money earned by him under the name of Monsieur Madeleine at Montreuil-sur-Mer. And fearing that he might be recaptured, which is indeed what happened to him shortly afterwards, he had buried and hidden that money in the forest of Montfermeil, in the place known as Blaru's Piece. The sum of six hundred and thirty thousand francs, all in banknotes, was not very bulky and contained in a box. Only, in order to protect the box from the damp, he had placed it in an oak casket filled with chestnut-wood shavings. In the same casket he had placed his other treasure, the bishop's candlesticks. Remember, he had taken the candlesticks with him when escaping from Montreuil-sur-Mer. The man seen one evening for the first time by Boulatruelle was Jean Valjean. Later, every time Jean Valjean needed money, he went to fetch it from Blaru's Piece. Hence the absences we have mentioned. He kept a pick somewhere in the undergrowth, in a hiding-place known only to him. When he saw Marius recovering, sensing that the time was approaching when this money might be useful, he had gone to fetch it. And it was Jean Valjean again that Boulatruelle had seen in the woods, but on that occasion, in the morning and not in the evening. Boulatruelle inherited the pick.

The actual sum of money was five hundred and eighty-four thousand five hundred francs. Jean Valjean kept the five hundred francs for himself. 'Afterwards, we'll see,' he thought.

The difference between that sum and the six hundred and thirty thousand francs withdrawn from Laffitte represented ten years' expenditure, from 1823 to 1833. The five years spent in the convent had cost only five thousand francs.

Jean Valjean put the two silver candlesticks on the mantelpiece, where they gleamed – to Toussaint's great admiration.

Moreover, Jean Valjean knew that he was rid of Javert. It had been said in his presence, and he had checked the report in *Le Moniteur*, which had published the story, that a police inspector named Javert had been found drowned under a laundry boat between the Pont au Change and the Pont-Neuf, and that a handwritten note left by this man, who was otherwise irreproachable and highly thought of by his superiors, pointed to a fit of mental aberration and suicide.

'The fact is,' thought Jean Valjean, 'since he let me go free, having got hold of me, he must have been already mad.'

VI
The Two Old Men Do Everything, Each in His Own Way, to Make Cosette Happy

All the preparations for the wedding were made. The doctor, on being consulted, ruled that it could take place in February. It was then December. A few rapturous weeks of perfect happiness went by.

The grandfather was not the least happy of all. He would spend a quarter of an hour at a time gazing at Cosette.

'My, what a pretty girl!' he would cry. 'And she looks so sweet and so kind-hearted! There's no denying it, she's the most charming girl I've ever seen in my life. Later on, she'll have violet-scented virtues. In a word, she's a goddess! A man cannot but live nobly with such a creature. Marius, my boy, you're a baron, you're rich, don't take up lawyering, I beg you.'

Cosette and Marius had been transported suddenly from the tomb to paradise. The transition was rather abrupt, and they would have been nonplussed had they not been wonderstruck by it.

'Do you understand any of this?' said Marius to Cosette.

'No,' replied Cosette, 'but I think the good Lord is looking after us.'

Jean Valjean did everything, smoothed everything, harmonized everything, made everything easy. He hastened towards Cosette's happiness with as much eagerness and apparent joy as Cosette herself.

As he had been mayor, he was able to solve a delicate problem, the secret of which he alone was acquainted with: Cosette's civil status. Plainly to state her origins – who knows? – might have prevented the marriage. He saved Cosette from any difficulty. He fabricated for her a family of dead people, a sure way of not raising any objections. Cosette was the last survivor of an extinct family. Cosette was not his daughter but the daughter of another Fauchelevent. Two Fauchelevent brothers had been gardeners at the Petit-Picpus convent. A visit was made to this convent, providing a wealth of the most reliable information and the most respectable references. The good nuns, little suited and little inclined to fathom questions of paternity, and seeing no harm in it, had never quite known of which of the two Fauchelevents Cosette was the daughter. They said what was wanted and they said it earnestly. An affidavit establishing legal identity was drawn up. Cosette became, in law, Mademoiselle Euphrasie Fauchelevent. She was declared an orphan, both motherless and fatherless. Jean Valjean contrived matters so that he was appointed, under the name of Fauchelevent, as Cosette's guardian, with Monsieur Gillenormand as her deputy guardian.

As for the five hundred and eighty-four thousand francs, they were a legacy left to Cosette by a deceased person who wished to remain anonymous. The original legacy was five hundred and ninety-four thousand francs, but ten thousand francs had been spent on Mademoiselle Euphrasie's education, of which five thousand francs had been paid to the convent. This legacy, lodged with a third party, was to be handed over to Cosette on her coming of age or when she married. All of this was evidently very acceptable, especially with a sum of over half a million involved. There were certainly a few peculiarities here and there, but they went unnoticed. The eyes of one of the interested parties were blindfolded by love, those of the others by the six hundred thousand francs.

Cosette learned that she was not the daughter of this old man she had for so long called father. He was just a relative. Another Fauchelevent was her real father. At any other time she would have felt devastated. But at this ineffable moment of her life it was no more than a slight shadow, a little overcasting, and she had so much to make her happy that this cloud quickly passed. She had Marius. Now that the young man was here, the old man faded into the background. Such is life.

And then, Cosette had long ago grown used to observing mysteries around her. Anyone who has had a mystifying childhood is always prepared to make certain sacrifices. But she continued to call Jean Valjean father.

Cosette, in seventh heaven, was very taken with old Gillenormand. It is true that he showered her with compliments and with presents. While Jean Valjean established for Cosette a normal place in society and an unassailable civil status, Monsieur Gillenormand attended to the bridal gift-basket. He enjoyed nothing so much as being extravagantly generous. He gave Cosette a gown of Binche guipure lace that he had inherited from his grandmother.

'These fashions are coming back into vogue,' he said, 'antique things are now all the rage, and the young women of my old age dress like the old women of my childhood.'

He plundered his respectable pot-bellied Coromandel-lacquered chests of drawers that had not been opened for years. 'Let's get these dowagers to spill their secrets,' he said, 'let's see what they've been hoarding away inside them.' He boisterously despoiled the bulging drawers full of clothes belonging to all his wives, all his mistresses and all his female ancestors. Pekins, damasks, lampas, painted moires, gowns of coruscating Tours grosgrain, Indian cotton handkerchiefs embroidered with a washable gold thread, lengths of reversible Lyon silk, Genoese and Alençon lace, antique jewellery, ivory sweet-containers decorated with microscopic battles, trinkets, ribbons – on Cosette he lavished everything. Enchanted, desperately in love with Marius and wildly grateful to Monsieur Gillenormand, Cosette dreamed of boundless happiness, clothed in satin and velvet. Her bridal gift-basket appeared to her to be upheld by seraphim. Her soul flew off into the blue on wings of Mechlin lace.

The lovers' rapture was matched, as we said, only by the grandfather's ecstasy. It was as if a fanfare was sounding in Rue des Filles-du-Calvaire.

Every morning, a new offering of bric-à-brac from the grandfather to Cosette. She was surrounded by a glorious array of finery of every conceivable kind.

One day Marius, who despite his happiness was given to serious conversation, said apropos of some incident or other, 'The men of the Revolution are so great, they already have the prestige of ages past, like Cato and Phocion, and every one of them seems to have an aura of antiquity.'

'Tea!' exclaimed the old gentleman. 'Thank you, Marius. That's exactly what I was trying to think of.'

And the next day a magnificent gown of tea-coloured moire antique was added to Cosette's bridal gifts.

The grandfather drew a lesson from this fancy stuff.

'Love's all very well, but you must have this too. You must have the unnecessary as well as happiness. Happiness is just the essential. Season it generously with the superfluous. A palace and her heart. Her heart and the Louvre. Her heart and the great water features of Versailles. Give me my shepherdess, and have her be a duchess. Bring me Phyllis crowned with cornflowers, and allow her an income of a hundred thousand francs. Unfold for me beneath a marble colonnade an endless prospect of the pastoral. I accept the pastoral along with the magic of marble and gold. Happiness on its own is like dry bread. You eat, but you don't dine. I want the superfluous, the unnecessary, the extravagant, the exorbitant, that which is of no use. I remember seeing in Strasbourg Cathedral a clock as tall as a three-storey house that struck the hours – that had the goodness to strike the hours but did not look as if that was what it was made for. And having struck midday or midnight – midday, the hour of the sun, midnight, the hour of love – or any other hour you like, it gave you the moon and the stars, the earth and the sea, birds and fishes, Phoebus and Phoebe, and a whole procession of things that came out of a niche, and the twelve Apostles, and the emperor Charles the Fifth, and Eponina and Sabinus, and loads of little gilded men, playing the trumpet into the bargain. Not to mention the enchanting chimes it kept scattering into the air at all moments, no one knew why. Can a plain, ugly dial that merely tells the time equal that? I personally go for Strasbourg's great clock, and I like it better than the Black Forest cuckoo clock.'

Monsieur Gillenormand raved especially about the wedding, and all the extravagances of the eighteenth century tumbled out in his lyrical ebullience.

'You know nothing of the art of festivity! Nowadays you don't know how to organize a day of pleasure!' he exclaimed. 'Your nineteenth century is etiolated. It lacks excess. It's ignorant of opulence, it's ignorant of nobility. It is in every respect shorn bare. Your Third Estate is dull, colourless, odourless and shapeless. What your bourgeois ladies who "establish" themselves, as they say, dream of: a pretty boudoir freshly decorated in rosewood and calico. Make way! Make way! Sieur Skinflint is marrying Mademoiselle Pinchpenny. Sumptuousness and splendour? A gold louis stuck to a candle! That's the age we live in! I want to get back to before the Sarmatians. Ah! even in 1787 I predicted that all was lost, the day I saw the Duc de Rohan – Prince de Léon, Duc de Chabot, Duc de Montbazon, Marquis de Soubise, Vicomte de Thouars, peer of France – driving to Longchamps in a rattletrap! It has borne fruit. In this century people do business, they speculate on the stock exchange, they earn money and they're stingy. They're groomed and polished on the surface. They're impeccably turned out, washed, soaped, scraped, shaved, combed, waxed, smoothed, rubbed, brushed, cleaned on the outside, irreproachable, like a polished stone, discreet, neat and tidy, and at the same time – heaven knows! – in the depths of their consciences lurk dung-heaps and cesspools from which a cow-girl who uses her fingers to blow her nose would shrink. I confer on these present times this motto: Grubby Cleanliness. Don't be cross, Marius, give me permission to speak. I'm not saying anything bad about the people, you see, there's plenty I could say about your people, but I think it advisable to give the bourgeoisie a bit of a drubbing. I'm one of them. Spare the rod and spoil the child. So I'll be blunt. People today get married but they don't know how to do it any more. Ah! it's true, I miss the graciousness of the old ways. I miss everything about them. That elegance, that chivalry, that courtesy and delicacy of manner, that delightful refinement everyone possessed, music forming part of the wedding festivities, harmonic strains above, percussive rhythms below, the dances, the joyous faces at the table, the refined madrigals, the ballads, the fireworks, the hearty laughter, the big ribbon bows and everything else that goes with it. I miss the bride's garter. The bride's garter is cousin to Venus' girdle. What does the Trojan War revolve around? Helen's garter, by Jove! Why are they fighting? Why does the divine Diomedes smash down on Meriones' head that great ten-pointed bronze helmet? Why do Achilles and Hector trade great pike blows with each other? Because Helen let Paris take her garter! Given Cosette's garter, Homer would have penned the *Iliad*. He would have put in his poem a garrulous old fellow like me, and he would have called him Nestor. My friends, once upon a time, in the good old days, people married well. They drew up a good contract, then they had a good feast. On Cujas's departure, Camacho would arrive. But for heaven's sake, it's just that the stomach is an agreeable beast that claims its due and wants to celebrate the wedding too. You'd have a good meal, and you'd be sitting at table with a lovely dining companion wearing no insert in her décolleté and only moderately concealing her charms. Oh! those wide, laughing mouths! And how merry people were in those days! Youth was a bouquet of flowers. No young man was complete without a spray of lilacs or a bunch of roses. Even warriors would be shepherds. And anyone who happened to be a captain of dragoons contrived to call himself Florian. Every man strove to look attractive, decking himself out in his finery. A bourgeois looked like a flower, a marquis looked like a precious stone. None wore footstraps, none wore boots. All were dashing, glossy, gleaming, golden, all of a flutter, charming, stylish – which did not prevent them from carrying a sword at their sides. Humming-birds with beaks and claws. It was the era of *Les Indes Galantes*. One aspect of that century was daintiness, the other was magnificence. And by gosh! people enjoyed themselves. Today, people are serious. The bourgeois is miserly, his wife is a prude. Your century is an unhappy one. The Graces would be hounded for showing too much flesh. Alas! beauty is concealed as if it were ugliness. Since the Revolution, everyone wears trousers, dancing-girls included. A dancer has to be serious. Your rigadoons are stiff. Stateliness is all. A man would be very vexed not to have his cravat up to his chin. The ideal of any twenty-year-old whippersnapper getting married is to resemble Monsieur Royer-Collard. And you know how you end up, with that kind of stateliness? Looking insignificant. Let me tell you this: joy is not only joyous, it is grand. So be merrily in love, for goodness' sake! And when you do marry, marry with the excitement and giddiness and hullabaloo and hurly-burly of happiness! Solemnity in church, that's fine. But as soon as mass is over, by heaven! the bride should be caught up in a delightful whirl. A marriage should be royal and magical. It should parade its ceremony from Reims cathedral to the pagoda of Chanteloup. I abhor a niggardly wedding. Gracious me! Dwell on Olympus for that one day at least. Be gods. Ah! people could be sylphs, deities of pleasure and laughter, Argyraspides. They are clodhoppers. My friends, every bridegroom should be Prince Aldobrandini. Take advantage of that unique moment in life to soar with the swans and eagles into the empyrean, even if you do have to fall back the next day among the bourgeoisie of frogs.* Don't stint on nuptials, don't clip their splendour, don't scrimp on the day that you shine. A wedding isn't housekeeping. Oh, if I had a free hand, it would be glorious! Violins would be heard playing among the trees.

---

* An allusion to La Fontaine's fable 12, bk 6, 'Le Soleil et les Grenouilles' (The Sun and the Frogs), in which the frogs lament the wedding of the Sun, as Aesop once lamented the wedding of a tyrant, for fear of offspring: one sun is barely tolerable, but half a dozen will dry the seas and spell the doom of all water-dwelling species.

This is my plan: sky-blue and silver. I'd have the rural divinities take part in the festivities, I'd summon the dryads and nereids. The nuptials of Amphitrite, a rosy mist, naked nymphs with lovely tresses, an Academician reciting poems to the goddess, a chariot drawn by sea monsters.

"Triton trotted on before, drawing from his conch-shell
Sounds so enchanting he enchanted one and all!"

Now, I tell you, that's a plan for a celebration if ever there was one – or else, dash it all, I'm no judge!'

While the grandfather, in full lyrical flow, listened to himself, Cosette and Marius revelled in gazing freely at each other.

Aunt Gillenormand observed all this with her imperturbable placidness. Within the last five or six months she had had a number of excitements. Marius coming home again, Marius brought back covered in blood, Marius brought back from a barricade, Marius dead, then alive, Marius reconciled, Marius engaged to be married, Marius marrying a pauper, Marius marrying a millionairess. The six hundred thousand francs had been the last surprise. Then, her otherworldliness, like that of a young girl taking her first communion, returned to her. She went to church regularly, said her rosary, read her prayerbook, whispered Hail Marys in one corner of the house while 'I love you' was being whispered in another, and saw Marius and Cosette indistinctly, as two shadows. She, though, was the shadow.

There is a certain state of passive asceticism in which the soul, neutralized by torpor, a stranger to what may be called the business of living, has no perception, earthquakes and catastrophes aside, of any human sensation, pleasant or painful. That kind of devotion, as old Gillenormand said to his daughter, is equivalent to a cold in the head. You scent nothing of life. No bad smell, nor any good one.

Anyway, the six hundred thousand francs settled the old maid's indecision. Her father had acquired the habit of taking so little account of her that he did not consult her about consenting to Marius's marriage. He acted impetuously, as was his way, having but a single thought, despot turned slave that he was: to satisfy Marius. As for the aunt, that she existed and that she might have an opinion had not even occurred to him, and for all that she was a sheep, this offended her. Feeling somewhat mutinous in her heart of hearts but outwardly impassive, she said to herself, 'My father has settled the question of marriage without me. I shall settle the question of inheritance without him.' She was in fact rich, and her father was not. So she decided for herself. It is probable that if the match been a poor one, she would have left the couple poor. 'So much the worse for his nibs my nephew! He's marrying a pauper, let him be a pauper!' But Cosette's half-million pleased the aunt and altered her attitude with regard to this pair of lovers. Six hundred thousand francs commands respect, and it was obvious that she could not do otherwise than leave her fortune to these young people, seeing that they did not need it now.

It was arranged that the couple should live with the grandfather. Monsieur Gillenormand was absolutely insistent on giving up his room to them, the finest room in the house. 'It will rejuvenate me,' he said. 'It's something I've been planning to do for a long time. I've always had this idea of doing up my room.' He furnished this room with a multitude of charming old curios. He had the ceiling and walls hung with bolts of some extraordinary cloth that he had and which he thought came from Utrecht, with velvet auriculas on a satin ground of buttercup-yellow.

'It was with this cloth,' he said, 'that the Duchesse d'Anville's bed at La Roche-Guyon was draped.'

On the mantelpiece he set a Dresden china figurine holding a muff against her naked stomach.

Monsieur Gillenormand's library became the lawyer's chambers that Marius needed – chambers, remember, being a requirement of the Bar Council.

VII
Dreamlike Visions Mingled with Happiness

The lovers saw each other every day. Cosette came with Monsieur Fauchelevent. 'It's the wrong way round like this,' said Mademoiselle Gillenormand, 'having the intended bride come to the groom's house to be courted.' But Marius's convalescence had introduced the habit, and the armchairs at Rue des Filles-du-Calvaire, better for tête-à-têtes than the straw-bottomed chairs at Rue de l'Homme-Armé, firmly established it. Marius and Monsieur Fauchelevent would see each other, but they were barely on speaking terms. It was as if this had been agreed. Every young girl needs a chaperone. Cosette could not have come without Monsieur Fauchelevent. For Marius, Monsieur Fauchelevent was the condition attached to Cosette. He accepted it. By addressing political issues, vaguely and without going into detail, from the viewpoint of the general improvement of the lot of all, they managed to say a little more than yes and no to each other. Once, on the subject of education, which Marius wanted free and compulsory, propagated in every form, made available to all like fresh air and sunshine – in short, to be enjoyed by the entire population – they were of one mind, and almost conversed. Marius noted on that occasion that Monsieur Fauchelevent spoke well, and even with a certain nobility of language. Yet in some indefinable way he was wanting. There was in Monsieur Fauchelevent something less than a man of the world, and something more.

Inwardly and at the back of his mind Marius plied with all sorts of unasked questions this Monsieur Fauchelevent, whom he saw as simply benign and cold. There were moments when he doubted his own recollections. There was a gap in his memory, a black hole, a chasm gouged by four months of agony. Many things had been lost in it. He even wondered if he really had seen Monsieur Fauchelevent, so serious and so calm a man, at the barricade.

Moreover, this was not the only bewilderment that past appearances and disappearances had left in his mind. It should not be assumed that he was free from all those obsessions of memory that compel us, even when happy, even when content, to look back mournfully. The head that does not turn towards vanished horizons contains neither thought nor love. At times Marius would bury his face in his hands, and the tumultuous and ill-defined past would pass through the mental twilight in his brain. Once again, he saw Mabeuf fall, he heard Gavroche singing under fire, he felt beneath his lips Éponine's cold forehead. Enjolras, Courfeyrac, Jean Prouvaire, Combeferre, Bossuet, Grantaire, all his friends rose up before him, then faded away. Were all those dear, sad, brave, charming, tragic individuals merely figments of his imagination? Had they actually existed? The rioting had wrapped everything in its smoke. Those great fevers create great illusions. He questioned himself. He pinched himself. All those vanished realities made him dizzy. So where were they all? Was it really true that everything was gone? Everything had dropped away into darkness, except him. Everything seemed to have disappeared as if behind a theatre curtain. In life, there are such curtains that come down. God moves on to the following act.

And was he himself actually the same person? He, the pauper, was now rich. He, the forsaken, had a family. He, the forlorn, was to marry Cosette. He felt as if he had passed through a tomb, and that he had gone into it black and had come out white. And the others had remained in that tomb. At certain moments all those individuals from the past, a haunting presence, formed a circle around him, and saddened him. Then he thought of Cosette, and regained his serenity. But nothing less than this happiness was needed to efface that catastrophe.

Monsieur Fauchelevent almost had a place among those dead.

Marius found it hard to believe that the Fauchelevent at the barricade was the same as this Fauchelevent of flesh and blood, so solemnly seated beside Cosette. The first was probably one of those recurrent nightmares that visited him in his hours of delirium. However, both men being reserved by nature, there was no possibility of Marius putting any question to Monsieur Fauchelevent. The idea did not even occur to him. We have already mentioned this characteristic detail.

Two men who share a secret and by a kind of tacit agreement exchange not a single word on the subject – this is not as unusual as is generally believed. Only once did Marius make some attempt. He introduced Rue de la Chanvrerie into the conversation, and turning to Monsieur Fauchelevent said to him, 'You know that street well?'

'What street?'

'Rue de la Chanvrerie.'

'The name of that street means nothing to me,' replied Monsieur Fauchelevent in an utterly natural tone of voice.

The reply, which related to the name of the street and not to the street itself, seemed more conclusive to Marius than it was.

'I must have dreamed it,' he thought. 'I had a hallucination. It was someone who looked like him. Monsieur Fauchelevent wasn't there.'

VIII
Two Men Impossible to Find

Marius's delight, great as it was, did not wipe from his mind some other preoccupations. While the wedding preparations were under way and he awaited the appointed time, he had some difficult and meticulous research into the past carried out.

He owed several debts of gratitude. He owed a debt of gratitude on behalf of his father, and he was indebted on his own account. There was Thénardier; and there was the unknown man who had delivered him, Marius, to Monsieur Gillenormand. Marius was bent on finding these two men, not intending simply to marry, to be happy and to forget them, and fearing that these unpaid debts of gratitude might cast a shadow over his life, now so bright. It was impossible to leave behind him all these painful arrears, and before joyfully embarking on the future he wanted to settle with the past.

That Thénardier was a villain detracted nothing from the fact that he had saved Colonel Pontmercy. Thénardier was a scoundrel for everyone except Marius. And Marius, unaware of what had actually taken place on the battlefield of Waterloo, was unaware also of this peculiar detail: that with regard to Thénardier his father was in the strange position of owing him his life without owing him any gratitude.

None of the various agents that Marius employed managed to pick up Thénardier's trail. All trace of him seemed to have been obliterated. The Thénardier woman had died in prison during the investigation of the case. Thénardier and his daughter Azelma, the only two surviving members of that sorry group, had plunged back into the shadows. The chasm of the Social Unknown had silently closed again over those individuals. Leaving nothing to be seen on the surface, not even that quivering, that trembling, those mysterious concentric circles indicating where something has fallen in and that a sounding may be taken there.

Now that the Thénardier woman had died, now that criminal charges against Boulatruelle had been dismissed, that Claquesous had disappeared and the principal defendants had escaped from prison, the trial for the ambush at the Gorbeau tenement had more or less collapsed. The affair had remained quite mystifying. The court had to be content with two small-fry appearing in the dock: Panchaud alias Printanier alias Bigrenaille, and Demi-Liard alias Deux-Milliards, who had been condemned after an extensive hearing to ten years in the prison hulks. A life sentence of penal servitude was passed *in absentia* on their escaped accomplices. Also *in absentia*, Thénardier, the ringleader, was sentenced to death. This sentence was all that remained of Thénardier, casting its sinister light over that buried name like a candle beside a coffin. Moreover, by driving Thénardier back into the furthest depths for fear of being recaptured, this sentence added to the thickening shadows that kept the man hidden.

As for the other person, as for the unidentified man who had saved Marius, the researches at first yielded some result, then suddenly came to nothing. The cab that had brought Marius back to Rue des Filles-du-Calvaire on the evening of the sixth of June was successfully found. The coachman declared that on the sixth of June, at the command of a police officer he had 'stood by' from three o'clock in the afternoon until nightfall on Quai des Champs-Élysées, above the outlet to the Great Sewer; that around nine o'clock in the evening, the grating of the sewer that leads out on to the riverbank opened; that a man emerged from it, carrying on his shoulders another man, who was seemingly dead; that the police officer, who was keeping watch there, had arrested the man who was alive and taken charge of the dead man; that at the command of the police officer, he, the coachman, had taken 'the whole lot of them' in his carriage; that they had first driven to Rue des Filles-du-Calvaire; there they had dropped off the dead man; that the dead man was Monsieur

Marius, and he, the coachman, certainly recognized him, even though 'this time' he was alive; that they had then climbed back into his carriage, he had whipped up his horses, and a few paces from the gate to the Archives someone had shouted to him to stop; that there, in the street, he was paid off, and the police officer had taken the other man with him; that he knew nothing more; that it was a very dark night.

Marius, as we said, remembered nothing. All he recalled was having been seized from behind by a strong hand just as he was falling backwards into the barricade. Then, everything went blank for him. He had regained consciousness only at Monsieur Gillenormand's.

He was lost in conjecture.

He could not doubt his own identity. Yet how was it possible that having fallen in Rue de la Chanvrerie, he had been picked up by the police officer on the banks of the Seine near the Pont des Invalides? Someone had carried him from the district of Les Halles to the Champs-Élysées. How? Through the sewer. Unbelievable devotion!

Someone? Who?

It was this man that Marius was searching for. Of this man who was his saviour, not a trace, not the slightest indication. Nothing.

Although having to be very cautious in this regard, Marius extended his investigations as far as police headquarters. The inquiries made there led to no more elucidation than those made elsewhere. Police headquarters knew less than the cabman. They had no knowledge of any arrest having been made on the sixth of June at the mouth of the Great Sewer. They had received no police report of this incident, which was regarded at police headquarters as a cock-and-bull story. The invention of the story was attributed to the cabman. A cabman who wants a tip is capable of anything, even imagination. Yet the incident had certainly occurred, and Marius could not doubt it unless he doubted his own identity, as we have just said.

Everything about this strange enigma was inexplicable.

That man, that mystery man, whom the cabman had seen emerge from the Great Sewer grating carrying the unconscious Marius on his back, and whom the police officer, lying in wait, had arrested there and then for the crime of rescuing an insurgent, what had become of him? What had become of the officer himself? Why had this officer remained silent? Had the man succeeded in escaping? Had he bribed the officer? Why did this man not give Marius, who was totally indebted to him, some sign of life? His lack of self-interest was no less extraordinary than his devotion. Why did that man not reappear? Perhaps he was above recompense, but no one is above gratitude. Was he dead? What kind of man was he? What did he look like? No one could tell him. The cabman replied, 'It was a very dark night.' Basque and Nicolette, aghast, had eyes only for their young master, who was all covered in blood. The porter, whose candle had lighted Marius's dramatic arrival, was the only one who had noticed the man in question, and this is the description he gave of him: 'a dreadful-looking man'.

In the hope that they would prove useful to his investigations, Marius ensured that the bloodstained clothes he had on his body when he was brought back to his grandfather's house were kept. On examination of the coat, it was noticed that one flap was bizarrely torn. There was a piece missing.

One evening, Marius was talking in the presence of Cosette and Jean Valjean about this whole peculiar story, about the countless inquiries he had made and the fruitlessness of his efforts. The coldness in 'Monsieur Fauchelevent's' face irritated him. He exclaimed with an intensity that had almost a ring of anger, 'Yes, that man, whoever he might be, was sublime. Do you know what he did, monsieur? He intervened like an archangel. He must have thrown himself into the thick of the fighting, rescued me from it, opened the sewer, dragged me into it, carried me through it! He must have gone over three and a half miles through atrocious underground tunnels, bent double, weighed down, in the dark, in the filth, over three and a half miles, monsieur, with a corpse on his back! And with what object? With the sole object of saving that corpse. And that corpse was myself. He said to himself, "There may still be a glimmer of life here. I'll risk my own existence for this merest flicker!" And his existence he risked not once but twenty times! And every step was a danger. The proof being, that on emerging from the sewer he was arrested. You know, monsieur, that man did all this. And with no expectation of any reward. What was I? An insurgent. What was I? A defeated nobody. Oh! if Cosette's six hundred thousand francs were mine—'

'They are yours,' Jean Valjean interjected.

'Well,' Marius went on, 'I would give them away to find that man.'

Jean Valjean remained silent.

BOOK SIX

THE SLEEPLESS NIGHT

I

The Sixteenth of February 1833

The night of the sixteenth to the seventeenth of February 1833 was a night blessed with joy. Above was a clear sky. It was Marius and Cosette's wedding night.

It had been a wonderful day.

It was not the fairy-tale wedding dreamed of by the grandfather, a fantastic spectacle with a riot of cherubim and cupids above the heads of the bridal pair, a marriage scene to grace a door panel, but it was charming and delightful.

The style of marriage was not the same in 1833 as it is today. France had not yet borrowed from England that supreme delicacy of abducting your wife, absconding on leaving the church, going into hiding, shameful of your happiness, and combining with the enchantments of the Song of Songs the behaviour of a bankrupt. People had not yet fully grasped how chaste, delicate and seemly it is to bundle your beloved into a jolting post-chaise, punctuating the mystery of your paradise with clattering hooves, taking as your nuptial bed a bed at an inn, and leaving behind you, in some commonplace room at so much a night, the most sacred of life's memories to share company with the intimacies between the coach driver and the serving-girl.

In this second half of the nineteenth century in which we are now living, the mayor and his sash, the priest and his chasuble, the law and God are no longer sufficient. We must also have the postilion of Lonjumeau: blue waistcoat with red facings and jingling buttons, emblem-bearing armband, knee-breeches of green leather, oaths directed at Norman horses with plaited tails, imitation gold braid, waxed hat, a good deal of powdered hair, an enormous whip and stiffened boots. France does not yet take elegance as far as the English nobility does, to the point of pelting the newly-weds' post-coach with a hail of shabby slippers and worn-out shoes, in memory of Churchill, later Marlborough, or Malbrouck, who was assailed on his wedding-day by an aunt's fury that was to bring him good luck. Old shoes and slippers do not, as yet, form part of our nuptial celebrations. But – patience. With good taste becoming more widespread, we shall come to it.

In 1833, an age ago, marriage was not something that was rushed through.

Strange to say, people still had the idea in those days that a wedding was an intimate and social celebration, that a patriarchal banquet did not spoil a domestic ceremony; that even excessive gaiety, as long as it was sincere, did happiness no harm, and that it was after all a good and venerable thing for the joining of these two destinies, from which a family would result, to begin at home, and for the married couple to have as witness to their union the nuptial chamber.

Also, people had the audacity to marry in their own homes.

So the marriage took place, following this now obsolete practice, at Monsieur Gillenormand's house.

As simple and commonplace as the business of getting married might be, what with the banns to be published, the documents to be drawn up, the register office and the church, there is always some complication. There was no possibility of being ready before the sixteenth of February.

Now – we note this detail for the pure satisfaction of being precise – the sixteenth happened to be Shrove Tuesday. Misgivings, doubts, particularly on the part of Aunt Gillenormand.

'Shrove Tuesday!' exclaimed the grandfather. 'So much the better. There's a proverb, "A Mardi Gras wedding brings dutiful offspring." No need to worry. The sixteenth will do fine! Do you want to postpone, Marius?'

'No, certainly not!' replied the groom-to-be.

'On with the wedding!' said the grandfather.

So, regardless of the public merry-making, the marriage took place on the sixteenth. It rained that day, but there is always a little patch of blue in the sky attendant on happiness, which lovers see even when the rest of creation is under an umbrella.

The day before, Jean Valjean had handed over to Marius, in the presence of Monsieur Gillenormand, the five hundred and eighty-four thousand francs. Since the terms of the marriage were to establish joint ownership of the whole estate, the settlement documents were straightforward.

Toussaint was of no further use to Jean Valjean. Cosette inherited her and promoted her to the rank of lady's maid. As for Jean Valjean, there was a beautiful furnished room in the Gillenormand house especially for him, and Cosette said to him so irresistibly, 'Father, I beg you', that she had more or less extracted a promise that he would come and occupy it.

A few days before the day fixed for the marriage, Jean Valjean had an accident. He somehow injured the thumb on his right hand. It was not serious, and he had not allowed anyone to tend to it or dress it, or even to see his injury, not even Cosette. It did, however, compel him to swathe his hand in a bandage and to wear his arm in a sling, and prevented him from signing anything. Monsieur Gillenormand, as Cosette's deputy guardian, had signed instead.

We shall not take the reader either to the register office or to the church. It is hardly ever the case that two lovers are accompanied so far; it is customary to turn your back on the drama as soon as it puts the flower in the bridegroom's buttonhole. We shall confine ourselves to noting an incident that took place, although unnoticed by the wedding party, on the way from Rue des Filles-du-Calvaire to the church of St-Paul.

The north end of Rue St-Louis was at that time being repaved. It was closed off above Rue du Parc-Royal. The wedding carriages could not drive directly to St-Paul. There was no alternative but to take a different route, and the simplest way was via the boulevard. One of the guests remarked that it was Mardi Gras, and there would be traffic congestion on that road. 'Why?' asked Monsieur Gillenormand. 'Because of the maskers.' 'Excellent,' said the grandfather. 'Let's go that way. These young people are getting married. They are about to embark on the serious part of life. To see a bit of masquerading will prepare them for that.'

They went by way of the boulevard. The first of the wedding coaches contained Cosette and Aunt Gillenormand, Monsieur Gillenormand and Jean Valjean. Still separated from his betrothed, according to custom, Marius followed behind, in the second. On emerging from Rue des Filles-du-Calvaire, the wedding cortège joined the long procession of vehicles in an endless circuit from the Madeleine to the Bastille and from the Bastille to the Madeleine.

Maskers thronged the boulevard. For all that it rained intermittently, Paillasse, Pantaloon and Gille were undeterred. In that good-humoured winter of 1833, Paris had disguised itself as Venice. You do not see Mardis Gras like that any more. Now that everything in existence is an extended carnival, there is no longer any carnival.

The side-lanes were crowded with passers-by and the windows with the curious. The terraces above the colonnades in front of the theatres were lined with spectators. Besides watching the maskers they were watching that procession, typical as much of Mardi Gras as of Longchamps, of vehicles of every kind – hackney cabs, landaus, charabancs, carrioles, cabriolets – driving in orderly fashion, as close as could be to each other in strict accordance with police regulations, and as if moving on rails. Whoever rides in these vehicles is both spectator and spectacle. Police kept these two interminable parallel lines moving in opposite directions along the side-lanes of the boulevard, and saw to it that nothing obstructed the two-way flow of the two streams of carriages, one coming down, the other going up, one heading towards Chaussée-d'Antin, the other towards Faubourg St-Antoine. The emblazoned vehicles of France's peers and ambassadors occupied the central carriageway, circulating freely. Certain merry and magnificent pageant wagons, notably the Fatted Ox, enjoyed the same privilege. In this Parisian mirth, England cracked her whip: Lord Seymour's post-chaise, bedevilled with a vulgar nickname, passed by with much to-do.

In those two lines, alongside which Municipal Guards went rushing like sheepdogs, good old family conveyances, packed with great-aunts and grandmothers, displayed at their doors clusters of fresh-faced children in costume, seven-year-old pierrots, six-year-old pierrettes, delightful little creatures, feeling themselves officially part of the public festivities, imbued with the dignity of their harlequinade and behaving with the gravity of state functionaries.

From time to time a hold-up occurred somewhere in the procession, and one or other of the two lines on either side halted until the hitch was disentangled. One impeded carriage was enough to paralyse the whole line. Then they would start moving again.

The wedding carriages were in the line heading towards the Bastille and driving along the right-hand side of the boulevard. At the top of Rue du Pont-aux-Choux there was a temporary stoppage. Almost at the same moment, the other line, heading towards the Madeleine, also stopped. At that point in the line there was a maskers' carriage.

These carriages of maskers – or cartloads, to be more precise – are very familiar to Parisians. If they failed to appear on Mardi Gras or at a mid-Lent festival it would be taken as a bad sign and people would say, 'There's something behind this. There's probably going to be a change of government.' A crowd of Cassandras, Harlequins and Columbines jolting along above pedestrian passers-by, every conceivable grotesque from the Turk to the savage, strong-men holding up marchionesses, fishwives who would have made Rabelais block his ears just as the Maenads made Aristophanes lower his eyes, wigs of tow, pink leggings, dandified hats, clownish spectacles, Simple Simon tricorn hats with butterfly teaser attached, jeers at those on foot, hands on hips, bold stances, bare shoulders, masked faces, shamelessness unleashed, a chaotic array of insolence paraded around by a coachman crowned with flowers: such was this institution.

Greece had need of Thespis' wagon, France has need of Vadé's hackney cab.

Everything can be parodied, even parody. The Saturnalia, that contortion of ancient beauty, increasingly exaggerated, ends up as Mardi Gras. And the Bacchanalia, in times past crowned with vine leaves, bathed in sunshine and revealing marble breasts in divine semi-nakedness, now debased in the wet shabbiness of the north, has ended up being called Misrule.

The tradition of maskers' carriages harks back to the earliest days of the monarchy. Louis XI's accounts allocate to the palace bailiff 'twenty sous, minted at Tours, for three coaches of street masqueraders'. In our day, these gaggles of rowdy creatures are usually carted about in some lumbering old *coucou* carriage, riding on the top of it, or else the unruly crew is crowded into a hired landau with its hoods thrown back. Twenty of them in a carriage for six. They are on the inside seats, on the folding seat, on the rims of the hoods, on the shaft. They even straddle the carriage lamps. They are standing, lying down, sitting, knees drawn up, legs dangling. The women sit on the men's laps. This crazy pyramid can be seen from a distance above the teeming mass of heads. These carriage-loads form mountains of mirth in the middle of the throng. Collé, Panard and Piron derive from such as these, enriched by slang. The fishwives' catechism is spewed out at the people from up there. Their carriage, now monstrous with excess of cargo, has an air of conquest about it. Uproar rides in front, pandemonium behind. There is yelling, shrieking, bawling, bellowing, convulsing with joy. Merriment roars, sarcasm flares, jollity flaunts itself like regal purple, two old nags draw this apotheosis of farce, the triumphal chariot of Laughter.

A laughter too cynical to be candid. And indeed, this laughter is suspect. This laughter has a mission. It is supposed to prove to the Parisians the authenticity of Carnival.

These vulgar conveyances, about which there is a sense of some indefinable darkness, set the philosopher thinking. There is a government dimension to this. Here, you can put your finger on a mysterious kinship between public men and 'public women'*.

Of course, it is sad that a conglomeration of depravity should yield a sum total of mirth, that degeneracy mounted on disgrace should titillate the masses, that espionage upholding prostitution should amuse the rabble while insulting them, that the mob should like to watch this monstrous living pile of tawdriness, half smut, half glitter, go rolling by, barking and singing, on the four wheels of a carriage; that people

* *Une femme/fille publique* is a prostitute.

should clap their hands at this splendour created out of every shame, that the multitudes would have no fun if the police did not parade among them these twenty-headed hydras of glee, as it were. But what can anyone do? These cartloads of filth bedecked with ribbons and flowers are both insulted and condoned by public laughter. Everyone's laughter is the accomplice of universal degradation. Certain pernicious festivities cause the disintegration of the people and turn them into hoi polloi. And hoi polloi, like tyrants, need their jesters. The king has Roquelaure, the people have Paillasse. Whenever it is not the sublime capital, Paris is the crazy capital. Carnival is part of politics. There is no denying it, Paris gladly gets its comedy from the disreputable. It asks of its masters – when it has masters – only one thing: 'Put a painted face on the mire for me.' Rome was of the same mind. Rome loved Nero. Nero was a colossal roisterer.

By chance, as we have just said, one of these shapeless clusters of masked men and women, trundled along in a vast carriage, stopped on the left-hand side of the boulevard while the wedding train stopped on the right. The carriage the maskers were travelling in saw right opposite it on the other side of the boulevard the carriage containing the bride.

'Look!' said a masker. 'A wedding party.'

'A fake one,' retorted another. 'The real party, that's us.'

And, being too far off to heckle the wedding party, and in any case afraid of police intervention, the two maskers looked elsewhere.

The whole carriage-load of maskers had their work cut out a moment later when the multitude began to jeer at them – which is the way a crowd embraces masquerades – and the two maskers who had just spoken had to stand up to the throng along with their comrades, needing every barb in Les Halles' repertoire to respond to the great mouthfuls they were getting from the people. A frightful exchange of metaphors between the maskers and the crowd ensued.

Meanwhile, two other maskers in the same carriage, an elderly-looking Spaniard with an enormous nose and an enormous black moustache, and a gaunt fishwife, a very young girl, with a mask over her eyes, had also noticed the wedding party, and while their companions and the passers-by were exchanging insults they were speaking to each other in low voices.

What they said was drowned by the tumult, and lost in it. The gusts of rain had drenched the open carriage. The February wind is not warm. In replying to the Spaniard, the fishwife in her skimpy dress shivered, laughed and coughed.

This was their conversation:

'Now fancy that!'

'What, *daron**?'

'Do you see that old boy?'

'What old boy?'

'Over there, in the wedding caravan† in front, on this side.'

'The one with his arm in a black scarf?'

'Yes.'

'Well?'

'I'm sure I know him.'

'Ah!'

'Je veux qu'on me fauche le colabre, et n'avoir de ma vioc dit vousaille, tonorgue ni mézig, si je ne colombe pas ce pantinois-là.'‡

'Today Paris belongs to those who call it Pantin.'

'If you lean over, can you see the bride?'

'No.'

'And the groom?'

'There's no groom in that caravan.'

'Bah!'

'Unless it's the other old boy.'

'Go on, lean right over, try and see the bride.'

'I can't.'

'All the same, that old boy that's got something wrong with his paw, I know him, I'm sure of it.'

'What's the good of knowing him?'

'There's no telling. It could just turn out to be useful!'

'As if I cared about old codgers!'

'I know him.'

'Know him all you like.'

'How the devil has he got in on the party?'

'Well, we're in on it, too.'

'Where's it coming from, that wedding party?'

'How should I know?'

'Listen.'

'What?'

---

* Footnoted by Hugo: 'père', 'father'.

† In the French 'roulotte', meaning any kind of 'cart', or 'trailer', or 'caravan'. Footnoted by Hugo: 'voiture', 'carriage'.

‡ Footnoted by Hugo: 'Je veux qu'on me coupe le cou, et n'avoir de ma vie dit vous, toi, ni moi, si je ne connais pas ce parisien-là', 'I would that my head was cut off, and that never in my life had I said "you" [plural/formal], "you" [singular/informal], or "me", if I don't know that Parisian over there'.

'You'd better do something.'

'What?'

'Get down off our caravan and tail* that wedding party.'

'What for?'

'To find out where it's going and who's in it. You being young, hurry up and get down, *ma fée*†, run!'

'I can't leave the carriage.'

'Why not?'

'I've been hired.'

'Blast!'

'I owe my day's work as fishwife to the Prefecture.'

'You're right.'

'If I leave the carriage the first inspector that sees me's going to arrest me. As you well know.'

'Yes, I know.'

'Today I'm in Pharos‡' pay.'

'All the same. That old man's plaguing me.'

'Old men plague you. And you're not even a young girl!'

'He's in the first carriage.'

'What of it?'

'In the bride's caravan.'

'So?'

'So he's the father.'

'What do I care?'

'I tell you, he's the father.'

'He's not the only father in the world.'

'Listen!'

'What?'

'I can only go about masked. Here I'm hidden, no one can see me. But tomorrow, there'll be no more maskers. It's Ash Wednesday. I'll risk being run in§. I'll have to go to ground again. But you're free.'

'Not that free.'

'More than I am, anyhow.'

'Well, so what?'

'You've got to try and find out where that wedding party's going.'

'Where it's going?'

'Yes.'

---

* In the French text 'filer'. Footnoted by Hugo: 'suivre', 'to follow'.

† Footnoted by Hugo: 'fille', 'daughter/girl'.

‡ Footnoted by Hugo: 'le gouvernement', 'the government'.

§ In the French text 'tomber'. Footnoted by Hugo: 'être arrêté', 'to be arrested'.

'I know that.'

'Where's it going, then?'

'To the Cadran-Bleu.'

'It's not that way, for a start.'

'Well, La Râpée, then.'

'Or somewhere else.'

'It's free to go anywhere. Wedding parties can go anywhere.'

'That's not the point. I tell you, you've got to try and find out for me whose wedding that is that the old boy's with, and where they live.'

'Oh sure! Are you joking? That'll be easy to track down, a week later, a wedding party that went through Paris on Mardi Gras. A *tiquante** in a haystack! Very likely, that is!'

'Never mind, you've got to try. Understand, Azelma?'

The two lines on either side of the boulevard started moving again, in opposite directions, and the maskers' carriage lost sight of the bride's 'caravan'.

II
Jean Valjean Still Has His Arm in a Sling

To have one's dream come true. Who is granted that? There must be elections for it in heaven. Unknowingly, we are all candidates. The angels vote. Cosette and Marius were elected.

At the register office and in church, Cosette was dazzling and charming. It was Toussaint, assisted by Nicolette, who had dressed her.

Cosette wore over a white taffeta petticoat her Binche guipure-lace dress, with an English point-lace veil, a necklace of fine pearls and a coronet of orange blossom. All in white, and in this whiteness she was radiant. It was a consummation of exquisite purity and its transfiguration into brilliance. She might have been described as a virgin in the process of becoming a goddess.

Marius's splendid hair was lustrous and perfumed. Visible here and there, beneath the thick curls, were pale lines, scars from the barricade.

Superb, with head held high, incorporating more than ever in his dress and in his manner all the elegant distinction of Barras's day, the grandfather led Cosette to the altar. He was standing in for Jean Valjean, who, with his arm in a sling, was unable to offer his hand to the bride.

---

* Footnoted by Hugo: 'épingle', 'pin'.

Jean Valjean, dressed in black, followed behind, smiling.

'Monsieur Fauchelevent,' the grandfather said to him, 'this is a marvellous day. I vote for an end to affliction and sorrow. There must be no more sadness anywhere from now on. By heaven! I decree joy! Suffering has no right to exist. Really, it's an insult to the azure of the skies that there should be any unhappy men. The problem doesn't lie with man, who is fundamentally good. The seat and ministry of all human miseries is hell, in other words the devil's Tuileries. Well now, here I am, talking like a demagogue! For myself, I've no longer any political opinions. Let all men be rich, that's to say, happy, I'll confine myself to that.'

When, with all the ceremonies completed, after having declared every possible yes before the mayor and before the priest, after having signed the registers at the town hall and the sacristy, after having exchanged rings, after having knelt side by side in the smoke from the censer under the white moire canopy, and hand in hand, admired and envied by all, Marius in black, she in white, preceded by the master of ceremonies in colonel's epaulettes striking the flagstones with his halberd, between serried ranks of marvelling onlookers, they emerged from the wide-open church door, ready to climb back into their carriage – now, when it was all over, Cosette still could not believe it. She stared at Marius, she stared at the crowd, she stared at the sky: it seemed that she might be afraid of waking. Her amazed and anxious look gave her an indefinable charm. For the return home they both took the same carriage, Marius seated beside Cosette. Monsieur Gillenormand and Jean Valjean opposite them. Taking a step backwards and removing herself from the foreground, Aunt Gillenormand was in the second vehicle.

'My children,' said the grandfather, 'you're now monsieur le baron and madame la baronne, with an income of thirty thousand francs.'

And Cosette, leaning as close as could be to Marius, caressed his ear with this angelic whisper: 'So it's true. I've taken your name. You and I are one.'

These two creatures were resplendent. At that irrevocable and irrecoverable moment, at the dazzling intersection of all youth and all joy, they were the realization of Jean Prouvaire's verses. The ages of the two of them together did not add up to forty. It was a marriage of sublimity. These two children were two lilies. They were not seeing each other, they were contemplating each other. Cosette beheld Marius in a nimbus. Marius beheld Cosette on an altar.

And on that altar and in that nimbus, the two apotheoses somehow essentially blending, in a haze for Cosette, in a burning blaze for Marius, was the abstract ideal, the actual reality, the meeting of kiss with dream, the nuptial pillow.

All the torment they had suffered was returning to them in exultation. It seemed to them that their sorrows, sleeplessness, tears, anguish, terrors, despair, had become caresses and rays of light and were making yet more blissful the coming moments of bliss. And that their griefs were but so many handmaidens now putting the finishing touches to their joy. How good it is to have suffered! Their unhappiness was the halo to their happiness. The long agony of their love was culminating in an ascension.

The same enchantment dwelt in both souls, subtly distinguished by sensual pleasure in Marius and by modesty in Cosette. They whispered to each other, 'We'll go back to see our little garden in Rue Plumet.' The folds of Cosette's gown lay on Marius.

Such a day is an ineffable mixture of dream and certainty. Possession and conjecture. There is still time ahead to imagine what is to come. It was an indescribable emotion, that day, to be there at noon and to be dreaming of midnight. The rapture of these two hearts spilled over on to the crowd and gladdened passers-by.

People stopped outside St-Paul in Rue St-Antoine to see, through the carriage window, the orange blossom quivering on Cosette's head.

Then they returned home to Rue des Filles-du-Calvaire. Triumphant and radiant, side by side with Cosette, Marius climbed the staircase where he had been dragged up, dying. The poor, gathered at the door for their share of the purses, blessed them. There were flowers everywhere. The house was no less perfumed than the church: after the incense, roses. They thought they heard voices singing in the infinite, they had God in their hearts, destiny appeared to them like a ceiling of stars, they saw above their heads the glow of sunrise. Suddenly the clock struck. Marius gazed at Cosette's lovely bare arm and at the rosy charms vaguely discernible through her lace bodice, and Cosette, seeing Marius's gaze, blushed to the roots of her hair.

A good number of the Gillenormand family's old friends had been invited. Cosette was mobbed, everyone wanting to be the first to call her madame la baronne.

Officer Théodule Gillenormand, now a captain, had come from Chartres, where he was garrisoned, to attend the wedding of his cousin Pontmercy. Cosette did not recognize him.

Used to being found attractive by women, he, for his part, no more remembered Cosette than he remembered any other woman.

'How right I was not to believe that story of the lancer!' old Gillenormand said to himself.

Cosette had never been more affectionate towards Jean Valjean. She was at one with old Gillenormand. While he built joy into aphorisms and maxims, she exuded love and kindness like a perfume. Happiness wants the whole world to be happy.

When she spoke to Jean Valjean, her voice regained the inflections it had had when she was a little girl. She caressed him with her smile.

A banquet had been laid out in the dining room. Light as bright as day is the necessary accompaniment of great joy. Mist and obscurity are not acceptable to those who are happy. They do not consent to be sombre. Night, yes; shadows, no. If there is no sunlight, sunlight must be created.

The dining room was a kaleidoscope of brilliance. In the centre, above the glittering white table, a baguette crystal Venetian chandelier with all kinds of coloured birds – blue, violet, red and green – perched among the candles; round the chandelier, girandole candelabras, on the walls, three-branched and five-branched mirrored sconces; mirrors, crystal, glass, tableware, porcelain, majolica, earthenware, gold plate, silverware – everything sparkled and rejoiced. The empty spaces between the candelabras were filled with bouquets, so where there was not a light, there was a flower.

Softly playing Haydn quartets in the antechamber were three violins and a flute.

Jean Valjean was sitting on a chair in the drawing room behind the door, its opened leaf almost concealing him. A few moments before everyone took their seats at table, as if on a sudden impulse Cosette came and gave him a deep curtsey, holding out her bridal gown with both hands, and with a tenderly mischievous glance asked him, 'Father, are you pleased?'

'Yes,' said Jean Valjean, 'I am pleased!'

'Well, then, laugh.'

Jean Valjean began to laugh.

A few moments later Basque announced that dinner was served.

The guests, preceded by Monsieur Gillenormand with Cosette on his arm, entered the dining room and settled around the table in the requisite order.

Two large armchairs were positioned to the right and left of the bride, the first for Monsieur Gillenormand, the other for Jean Valjean. Monsieur Gillenormand took his seat. The other armchair remained empty.

They looked around for 'Monsieur Fauchelevent'. He was no longer there. Monsieur Gillenormand called Basque over.

'Do you know where Monsieur Fauchelevent is?'

'Indeed, Monsieur,' replied Basque. 'Monsieur Fauchelevent instructed me to tell monsieur that he was in some pain from his injured hand and would be unable to dine with monsieur le baron and madame la baronne. That he begged to be excused, and he would come tomorrow. He's just left.'

That empty armchair cast a momentary chill on the jollity of the wedding banquet. But, regardless of Monsieur Fauchelevent's absence, Monsieur Gillenormand was there, and the grandfather beamed for two. He declared that Monsieur Fauchelevent had done well to retire early if he was in pain, but it was a mere 'scratch'. This declaration sufficed. Besides, what is one dark corner in such an abundance of joy? Cosette and Marius were in one of those selfish and blissful moments when a person has no other faculty but the perception of happiness. And anyway, Monsieur Gillenormand had an idea. 'Heavens! This armchair is empty. Come over here, Marius. Your aunt will allow it, even though she has a claim on you. This armchair's for you. It's legitimate, and it's charming. Fortunatus beside Fortunata.'

Applause from the whole table. Marius took Jean Valjean's place beside Cosette, and as things turned out, Cosette, at first sad at Jean Valjean's absence, ended by being happy about it. As long as Marius was the replacement, Cosette would not have regretted the absence of God. She put her own sweet little foot, shod in white satin, on top of Marius's.

With the armchair occupied, Monsieur Fauchelevent was out of mind; nothing was missing. And five minutes later the whole table, from one end to the other, was laughing with all the ebullience of forgetfulness.

At dessert, on his feet, with a glass of champagne in his hand, half filled so that the ninety-two-year-old's trembling did not make it spill, Monsieur Gillenormand toasted the married couple.

'You can't escape two sermons!' he exclaimed. 'This morning you had the priest's, this evening you shall have your grandfather's. Listen, I'm going to give you a piece of advice: adore each other. I'm not beating about the bush, I'm coming straight to the point: be happy. The only creatures of wisdom are turtle-doves. Philosophers say: "Moderate your joys." I say: "Give free rein to your joys. Be fiendishly smitten. Be frantically in love." The philosophers talk nonsense. I'd like to ram their philosophy down their throats. Can there be too many perfumes, too many rosebuds coming into bloom, too many nightingales singing, too many green leaves, can there be in life too much dawn light? Can lovers love each other too much? Can they be too attractive to each other? Beware, Estelle, you're too pretty! Beware, Némorin, you're too handsome! What an absurdity! Is it possible to be too enchanting, too beguiling, too charming towards each other? Is it possible to be too much alive? To be too happy? Moderate your joys? Nothing of the kind! Down with philosophers! Wisdom is rejoicing. Rejoice, and let us rejoice. Are we happy because we are good, or are we good because we are happy? Is the Sancy diamond called the Sancy because it belonged to Harlay de Sancy or because it weighs a hundred and six carats? What do I know? Life is full of such problems. The important thing is to have the Sancy, and to be happy. Let us be happy without quibbling. Let us blindly obey the sun. What is the sun? It's love. Whoever says love, says woman. Ahah! Now there's an almighty power: womankind. Ask that demagogue Marius if he's not the slave of that little tyrant Cosette. And of his own free will, the craven fellow! Womankind! Regardless of any Robespierre, woman reigns. I'm no royalist any more, except as regards that particular royalty. What is Adam? The realm of Eve. No '89 for Eve. There used to be the royal sceptre surmounted with a fleur-de-lys, there used to be the imperial sceptre surmounted with a globe, there used to be Charlemagne's iron sceptre, there used to be Louis the Great's gold sceptre – the revolution bent them between thumb and forefinger like worthless straws. Broken, done with, destroyed. No more sceptre. But go on, have a revolution against that little patchouli-scented embroidered handkerchief! I'd like to see it. Try! Why is it resistant? Because it's just a piece of frippery. Ah, you're the nineteenth century? Well, what of it? We were the eighteenth century. And we were as foolish as you are. Don't imagine, because your killer of young men is called *Cholera morbus* and your *bourrée* is called the *cachucha*, that you've changed very much in the universe. Basically, women must always be loved. I defy you to find any way out of that. These she-devils are our angels. Yes, love, women, kisses, it's a circle I defy you to escape. And as for myself, I should be only too happy to re-enter it. Which of you has seen the star Venus rising in the infinite, calming all beneath her, looking down on the waves like a woman, the great charmer of the abyss, the Célimène of the ocean? The ocean, now there's a churlish Alceste. Well, grumble as he may, when Venus appears he can't help but smile. That brute beast is tamed. We're all like that. Anger, fury, thunderbolts, foam up to the ceiling. A woman comes on the scene, a star rises, and we're grovelling! Marius was fighting six months ago. Today he's getting married. Well done! Yes, Marius, yes, Cosette, you're right. Be bold in existing for each other, caress each other, make us burst with rage that we can't do likewise, idolize each other. Gather in your two beaks all the little wisps of happiness that there are on earth, and build yourselves a nest for life out of them. By God, to love, to be loved, the splendid miracle of being young! Don't think you invented it. I've dreamed, I've imagined, I've sighed. I, too, have had a moonlight soul. Love is a child six thousand years old. Love is entitled to a long white beard. Methuselah is a youngster compared with Cupid. It is by being in love that, for sixty centuries, men and women have got by. The devil, who is cunning, started to hate man. Man, who is even more cunning, started to love woman. That's how he's done himself more good than the devil has done him harm. This clever tactic dates all the way back to the Garden of Eden. It's an old trick, my friends, yet as new a find as ever. Take advantage of it. Be Daphnis and Chloe until you become Philemon and Baucis. See to it that when you are together you lack for nothing, and that Cosette is for Marius the sun, and Marius is for Cosette the universe. May fair weather, for you, Cosette, be your husband's smile. May rain, for you, Marius, be your wife's tears. And may it never rain in your household. You've landed the winning number in the lottery: love in matrimony. You've won the big prize, look after it well, keep it under lock and key, don't squander it, adore each other, and never mind the rest. Believe what I'm telling you. It's good sense. Good sense cannot lie. Be a religion to each other.

'Every man has his own way of adoring God. Heavens above! the best way to adore God is to love your wife. "I love you!" That's my catechism. Whoever loves is orthodox. Henri IV's oath places sanctity between feasting and drunkenness. *Ventre-saint-gris!** Mine is not the religion of that oath. Women have been left out. This amazes me in an oath coming from Henri IV. My friends, long live women! I'm old, so I'm told. It's amazing how young I'm feeling right now. I'd like to go and listen to shepherd's pipes playing in the woods. These children, contriving to be beautiful and happy – that makes me tipsy. I'd get married myself if anyone would have me. It's impossible to imagine that God could have made us for anything else but this: to idolize, to preen, to be a dove, to be a peacock, to bill and coo from morning till night, to admire ourselves in our own little woman, to be proud, triumphant, to strut – that's the aim of life. That, if you please, is what we thought in our day, when we were young. Ah, heavens alive! there were such lovely women then, such pretty little faces, such budding beauties! I made my conquests among them. So love

---

* *Ventre* meaning 'belly' or 'stomach' and *gris* a familiar word for 'inebriated'. For the derivation of the oath see endnote p. 1415.

each other. Without love between each other, I really don't see what point there would be in having spring, and I personally would ask the good Lord to pack up all the beautiful things he shows us and take them away, and put the flowers, the birds and the pretty girls back in his box. My children, this fond old man gives you his blessing.'

The evening was lively, merry, congenial. The grandfather's supreme good humour set the tone for the entire celebration, and everyone took their cue from this nigh-on-centenarian conviviality. There was a little dancing, there was a deal of laughter. It was a delightful wedding. Le Bonhomme Jadis* could have been invited. Indeed, he was present in the person of old Gillenormand.

There was hurly-burly, then silence. The bridal couple disappeared. A little after midnight the Gillenormand house became a temple.

Here we stop. On the threshold of wedding nights stands a smiling angel with a finger to its lips. The soul goes into spiritual contemplation before this sanctuary where the celebration of love occurs.

There must be glimmerings of light above such houses. The joy they contain must escape as brightness through the stones of the walls, and appear as faint streaks in the dark. It is impossible that this sacred and fateful celebration does not cast into the infinite a celestial radiance. Love is the sublime crucible in which the fusion of man and woman takes place. The one being, the triple being, the final being, the human trinity proceeds from it. This birth of two souls in one must thrill the darkness. The lover is priest; the ravished virgin is awestruck. Something of that joy ascends to God. Where there is true marriage, that is to say, where there is love, there is an element of the ideal. A nuptial bed creates a glimpse of dawn among the shadows. If it were given to the eye of flesh to perceive the awesome and enchanting visions of the higher life, it is probable that we should see a throng of dark heads around the luminous house, figures of the night, unknown winged creatures, elusive wayfarers of the invisible, bending down, giving their blessings, pointing out to each other the virgin wife, sweetly awed, with the reflection of human bliss on their divine faces. If in that superlative moment the newly-weds, dazed with sensual pleasure and believing themselves to be alone, were to listen, they would hear in their bedroom the rustling of a confusion of wings. Perfect happiness implies fellowship with the angels. That obscure little bedchamber has

* Staged for the first time in 1852, Le Bonhomme Jadis (Old Mister Times-Past) is a play by Henry Murger (1822–61), in which an old man plays matchmaker to a young couple.

the whole heavens for its ceiling. When two mouths, sanctified by love, come together in procreation, it is impossible that above that ineffable kiss there would not be a quivering amid the immense mystery of the stars.

These are the true joys. No other joy, save these. Love is the only ecstasy. All the rest is weeping.

To love, or to have loved, is enough. Ask for nothing more. There is no other pearl to be found in life's shadowy convolutions. To love is an achievement.

III
The Inseparable Companion

What had become of Jean Valjean?

Straight after having laughed, at Cosette's sweet bidding, when no one was paying him any attention, Jean Valjean got up and slipped away unnoticed to the antechamber. This was the very room he had entered eight months earlier, blackened with mud, blood and gunpowder, bringing the grandson back to his grandfather. The old panelling was garlanded with foliage and flowers. Musicians were seated on the sofa where Marius had been laid. Basque, in black coat, knee-breeches, white stockings and white gloves, was arranging circlets of roses around each of the dishes to be served. Jean Valjean showed him his arm in a sling, told him to explain his absence, and left.

The casement windows of the dining room looked out on to the street. Jean Valjean remained for several minutes standing motionless in the dark beneath those windows ablaze with light. He listened. The hubbub reached his ears. He heard the grandfather giving his loud, grandiloquent speech, the violins, the clink of plates and glasses, the bursts of laughter, and in all that merry din he distinguished Cosette's sweet, happy voice.

He left Rue des Filles-du-Calvaire and returned to Rue de l'Homme-Armé.

To get back there he went via Rue St-Louis, Rue Culture-Ste-Catherine and Rue Blancs-Manteaux. It was a slightly longer route, but it was the one that for the past three months he had been in the habit of taking with Cosette every day between Rue de l'Homme-Armé and Rue des Filles-du-Calvaire, avoiding the crowds and the muddiness of Rue Vieille-du-Temple.

This route that Cosette had taken excluded, for him, any other.

Jean Valjean arrived back home. He lighted his candle and went upstairs. The apartment was empty. Not even Toussaint was still there. Jean Valjean's footsteps resounded in the rooms more than usual. All the cupboards were open. He went into Cosette's bedroom. There were no sheets on the bed. The ticking-covered pillow, without pillowcase or lace trimmings, was lying on the folded blankets at the foot of the stripped mattress, on which no one was ever to sleep again. All the little feminine objects dear to Cosette had been taken away. Nothing remained except the heavy furniture and the four walls. Toussaint's bed was stripped too. Only one bed was made up and seemed to be expecting someone: that was Jean Valjean's bed.

Jean Valjean looked at the walls, closed a few cupboard doors, and moved back and forth from one room to another. Then he found himself back in his own room, and put his candle down on a table.

He had taken his arm out of the sling and was using his right hand as if it did not hurt.

He drew near his bed, and his eyes rested – was it by chance? was it intentionally? – on 'the inseparable' of which Cosette had been jealous, the little case he always had with him. On arriving at Rue de l'Homme-Armé on the fourth of June, he had put it on a little round table at his bedside. He approached this table with a kind of animation, took a key from his pocket, and opened the valise.

He slowly drew from it the garments in which, ten years earlier, Cosette had left Montfermeil: first the little black dress, then the black shawl, then the good stout pair of child's shoes that Cosette could almost still have worn, so small were her feet; then the good thick fustian vest with sleeves, the knitted petticoat, the apron with pockets, then the woollen stockings. These stockings that prettily retained the shape of a little leg were scarcely any longer than Jean Valjean's hand. All of these things were black. It was he who had brought these clothes for her to Montfermeil. As he removed them from the case, he laid them on the bed. He was thinking. He was remembering. It was winter, a very cold December, she was shivering, half naked and in rags, her poor little feet all reddened in their wooden clogs. He, Jean Valjean, had her taken out of those rags and dressed in these mourning clothes. The mother lying in her grave must have been pleased to see her daughter wearing mourning for her, and above all to see that she was warmly clad. He thought of the forest of Montfermeil. They had passed through it together, Cosette and he. He thought of what the weather had been like, of the leafless trees, the birdless forest, the sunless sky. It was delightful, all the same. He arranged the tiny garments on the bed, the shawl next to the petticoat, the stockings beside the shoes, and he looked at them one by one. She was only so high, she carried her big doll in her arms, she put her gold coin in the pocket of that apron, she laughed, they walked along together hand in hand, she had no one in the world but him.

Then his venerable white head fell forward on to the bed, that stoical old heart broke; his face buried itself, so to speak, in Cosette's clothes, and anyone who had passed by on the stairs at that moment would have heard tremendous sobs.

IV
Immortale Jecur*

The terrible struggle of old, of which we have already seen several phases, began once more.

Jacob wrestled with the angel for only one night. Alas! how many times have we seen Jean Valjean forced to grapple with his conscience in the dark, and struggling frantically against it!

A desperate struggle! At certain moments it is the foot that slips; at other times the ground that gives way. How many times had that conscience, passionately devoted to goodness, fastened on him and overpowered him! How many times had unrelenting truth held its knee against his chest! How many times, floored by the light, had he begged for mercy! How many times had that implacable light, shone within him and over him by the bishop, compelled him to be dazzled when he wanted to be blinded! How many times, in combat, had he got back on his feet, clung to the rock, resorted to sophistry, been dragged through the dust, sometimes overthrowing his conscience, sometimes overthrown by it! How many times, after an equivocation, after delivering a specious and perfidious argument dictated by selfishness, had he heard his angry conscience cry in his ear, 'Trying to pull a fast one? You wretch!' How many times had his rebellious mind groaned convulsively in the face of clear duty! Offering resistance against God! Sweating in agony! What secret wounds that only he could tell were bleeding! What abrasions to his pitiful existence! How many times had he risen, bleeding, bruised, broken, enlightened, with despair in his heart, with serenity in his soul! And vanquished, he felt himself the victor. And having wrenched him

* A quotation from Virgil's *Aeneid*, bk 6, line 598: the 'immortal liver' on which the vulture continually fed, inflicting everlasting torment on the giant Tityus. Prometheus, chained to a rock, is similarly punished and preyed on by an eagle, in Hesiod's *Theogony*, lines 521–5.

apart, tortured him with red-hot pincers, broken him on the wheel, his conscience, standing over him – formidable, luminous, calm – said, 'Now, go in peace!'

But after such a grim struggle, what a dismal peace, alas!

Yet that night Jean Valjean felt he was fighting his last battle. He was faced with an agonizing question.

Predestined fates do not all follow a direct route. They do not run straight before the one who is predestined. They have dead ends, blind alleys, obscure turnings, daunting crossroads offering several alternative routes. Jean Valjean at that moment had come to a halt at the most perilous of these crossroads.

He had reached the ultimate parting of the ways between good and evil. He had this shadowy intersection before his eyes. Yet again, as had already happened to him in other sad vicissitudes, two paths lay before him, one tempting, the other appalling. Which one was he to take?

Pointing to the one that appalled was the mysterious forefinger that we all perceive whenever we stare into the dark.

Once again Jean Valjean faced a choice between the dreadful haven and the alluring ambush. Is it, then, true? A soul may be cured, but not of its fate? What an horrendous thing! An incurable destiny!

This is the question he was faced with:

How was Jean Valjean to behave with regard to Cosette and Marius's happiness? It was he who had wanted that happiness, it was he who had created it. He himself had plunged it into his own entrails; and reflecting on it at that moment, he could feel the kind of satisfaction felt by an armourer who, on pulling from his chest a knife all reeking with blood, recognizes on it his own trademark.

Cosette had Marius, and she was his. They had everything, even wealth. And this was Jean Valjean's doing.

But now that it existed, now that it was there, what was he, Jean Valjean, to do about this happiness? Would he impose himself on it? Would he treat it as if it belonged to him? Granted, Cosette belonged to another, but would he, Jean Valjean, retain as much of Cosette as he could? Would he remain the kind of father he had been until now – little seen, but respected? Would he feel no concern about going into Cosette's house? Would he, without saying a word, bring his past to that future? Would he present himself there, as if by right, and with a pall of darkness hanging over him take a seat at that glowing hearth? Would he, smiling, take the hands of those innocents in his own two tragic hands? Would he warm his feet, with the infamous shadow of the law trailing behind them, at the Gillenormand drawing room's peaceful fireside? Would he share his fate with Cosette and Marius? Would he deepen the blackness on his own brow, and the shadow on theirs? Would he bring to their two shares of happiness his third share of catastrophe? Would he continue to say nothing? In a word, would he be destiny's sinister mute alongside these two happy creatures?

Only a person used to the vagaries of fate will dare look up when certain questions appear before him in all their horrible starkness. A choice between good and evil lies behind this stern question mark. What are you going to do? asks the sphinx.

Jean Valjean was used to being put to the test. He stared intently at the sphinx. He examined every facet of the inexorable problem.

That dear soul Cosette was this castaway's raft. What was he to do? Cling to it, or let go?

If he clung to it, he escaped disaster, he returned to the sunlight, he let the briny water drip from his garments and his hair; he was saved, he lived.

Were he to let go? In that case, the abyss.

Thus, painfully, he debated in his mind. Or to be more accurate, he struggled, he lashed out furiously within himself, now against his will, now against his conviction.

It was a blessing for Jean Valjean to have been able to weep. It may have brought him light. But the beginning was ferocious. A storm broke inside him, more furious than that previous storm that had driven him to Arras. The past came back to him, seen from the present. He compared, and he sobbed. Once the floodgate of tears had opened, the man was convulsed with despair.

He felt thwarted.

Alas! in this all-out fight between our selfishness and our duty, when we give ground step by step before our uncompromising ideal, bewildered, frenzied, incensed to find ourselves yielding, disputing the territory, hoping for possible escape, seeking a way out, what sudden and sinister resistance from the wall at our back!

To feel the sacred shadow standing in our way! The inexorable. Invisible. What an obsession!

So no one is ever done with conscience. Make the best of it, Brutus. Make the best of it, Cato. Being God, conscience is fathomless. Into this well you throw your lifetime's work, you throw your fortune, your riches, you throw your success, your liberty or your country, you throw your well-being, your rest, your joy! More! More! More!

Empty the vessel! Tip up the urn! In the end you must throw in your heart.

Somewhere in the mists of times past there is a hellish vat like that.

Is it not forgivable eventually to refuse? Can the inexhaustible be thus entitled? Is it not beyond human capacity to endure endless chains? Who would blame Sisyphus or Jean Valjean for saying, 'Enough!' The compliance of matter is limited by friction. Is there no limit to the compliance of the soul? If perpetual motion is impossible, can perpetual self-sacrifice be demanded?

The first step is nothing, it is the last step that is hard. What was the Champmathieu affair compared with Cosette's marriage and all that it entailed? What is that – returning to the prison hulks – compared with this – being reduced to nothingness?

Oh, first downward step, how sombre! Oh, second step, how black! How was a man not to turn back this time?

Martyrdom is sublimation, corrosive sublimation. It is a torture that consecrates. You can consent to it for the first hour. You seat yourself on the red-hot iron throne, you place on your head the red-hot iron crown, you take the red-hot iron globe, you accept the red-hot iron sceptre, but the fiery mantle is yet to be donned. And is there not a moment when the poor wretched flesh revolts and you abdicate suffering?

At length, Jean Valjean attained the calm of exhaustion.

He pondered, he reflected, he considered the alternatives in the mysterious balance of light and dark. Impose his penal servitude on those two radiant children, or be the author of his own irrevocable engulfment? Cosette sacrificed on the one hand, he himself on the other.

What choice did he make? What decision did he come to? What was his ultimate response to fate's interrogation, which cannot be suborned? Which door did he decide to open? Which side of his life did he resolve to close off and condemn? Of all the bottomless precipices that surrounded him, which did he choose? To which extreme did he resign himself? To which of these abysses did he give the nod?

His dizzying deliberations went on all night long.

He was there until daylight, in the same attitude, bent over on that bed, prostrate – perhaps crushed, alas! – beneath the enormity of fate; fists clenched, arms extended at right-angles to his body, like one crucified, removed from the cross and thrown face down on the ground. For twelve hours, the twelve hours of a long winter's night, he remained there, frozen, without lifting his head and without uttering a word. He was as still as a corpse, while his mind slithered and soared, now like the hydra, now like the eagle. Seeing him motionless like that, anyone would have thought he was dead. All of a sudden he shuddered convulsively, and his mouth, pressed to Cosette's clothes, kissed them, and the onlooker saw that he was alive.

Who? Which onlooker? – since Jean Valjean was alone, and there was no one else there.

The Onlooker in the shadows.

BOOK SEVEN

THE LAST DROP IN
THE CHALICE

I
The Seventh Circle and the Eighth Heaven

The day after a wedding is a quiet one. People respect the self-absorption of the happy couple. And their belated sleep too, a little. The bustle of visits and congratulations does not begin until later. On the morning of the seventeenth of February it was a little past midday when Basque, while busy 'doing the antechamber', with a cloth and feather duster under his arm, heard a light tap at the door. The caller did not ring the bell, which was considerate on such a day. Basque opened the door and saw Monsieur Fauchelevent. He ushered him into the drawing room, still cluttered and topsy-turvy, and looking like the battlefield of the previous day's celebrations.

'My goodness, monsieur,' remarked Basque, 'we did wake up late.'

'Is your master up?' asked Jean Valjean.

'How is monsieur's arm?' replied Basque.

'Better. Is your master up?'

'Which one? The old one or the new one?'

'Monsieur Pontmercy.'

'Monsieur le baron?' said Basque, drawing himself up.

A man is a baron most of all to his servants. Something of his being so redounds on them. They have what a philosopher would call the reflected glory of the title, and that flatters them. A militant Republican, as he had proved, Marius was now a baron – it needs to be said in passing – in spite of himself. A small revolution had taken place within the family with regard to this title. By this time it was Monsieur Gillenormand who prized it and Marius who had no use for it. But Colonel Pontmercy had written: 'My son will bear my title.' Marius obeyed. And besides, the woman in her beginning to emerge, Cosette was delighted to be a baroness.

'Monsieur le baron?' Basque repeated. 'I'll go and see. I'll tell him that Monsieur Fauchelevent is here.'

'No. Don't tell him it's me. Tell him that someone wants to speak to him in private, and don't give any name.'

'Ah!' said Basque.

'I want to surprise him.'

'Ah!' Basque reiterated, giving himself the second 'Ah!' as an explanation of the first.

And he went out of the room. Jean Valjean was left on his own.

The drawing room, as we have just said, was in total disorder. It seemed as if anyone listening carefully might still have been able to hear the faint hubbub of the wedding. On the parquet floor were all kinds of flowers that had fallen from garlands and head-dresses. The burned-down candles added wax stalactites to the chandeliers' crystals. Not a single piece of furniture was in its rightful place. In various corners three or four armchairs, drawn up together in a circle, appeared to be continuing a conversation. The general effect was pleasing. There is a certain lingering charm about the aftermath of a celebration. It had been a happy occasion. On those untidy chairs, among those fading flowers, beneath those extinguished lights, thoughts had been joyful. Sunshine was replacing chandelier, brightly entering the drawing room.

Several minutes went by. Jean Valjean remained motionless on the spot where Basque had left him. He was very pale. His eyes were deep-set, and so sunken in their sockets by sleeplessness that they almost disappeared. His black coat had the tired creases of a garment that has been worn all night. The elbows were white with the fluff left on cloth from rubbing against bedlinen. Jean Valjean stared at the window outlined by the sun on the parquet floor at his feet.

There was a sound at the door, he looked up. Marius came in, head high, a smile on his lips, an ineffable radiance on his face, a clear forehead, a triumphant look in his eye. He had not slept, either.

'It's you, father!' he exclaimed, on seeing Jean Valjean. 'That idiot Basque was being so mysterious! But you've come too early. It is only half-past twelve. Cosette's sleeping.'

That word 'father', said by Marius to Monsieur Fauchelevent, conveyed supreme happiness. As we know, there had always been aloofness, coldness and constraint between them, an iciness that needed to be broken or to melt. Marius felt so elated that the aloofness lessened, the ice dissolved, and Monsieur Fauchelevent was for him, as for Cosette, a father.

He went on, the words pouring out of him, which is characteristic of these divine transports of joy.

'How glad I am to see you! If you only knew how much we missed you yesterday! Good morning, father. How is your hand? Better, isn't it?'

And satisfied with the comforting reply he had given himself, he continued.

'The two of us have talked about you a great deal. Cosette is so fond of you! Don't forget you have a room here. We want no more of Rue de l'Homme-Armé. We want no more of it at all. How could you go and live in a street like that, a street that's seedy, and surly, and ugly, that has a barrier at one end, where it feels cold, a street you can't enter? You'll come and live here. And from today. Or you'll have Cosette to reckon with. She intends to have us under her thumb, I warn you. You've seen your room, it's right next to ours, it looks out over the gardens. The lock's been fixed, the bed's made, it's all ready, you just have to move in. Cosette has put by your bed a big old wing-backed chair covered with Utrecht velvet, and said to it, "Reach your arms out to him." In the acacia bushes outside your windows there's a nightingale that comes every spring. It'll be there in another two months. You'll have its nest on your left and ours on your right. At night it will sing, and in the daytime Cosette will talk. Your room faces due south. Cosette will put your books in it for you, your Captain Cook's *Voyage* and the other one, by Vancouver – all your belongings. I believe there's a small case that you're attached to, I've arranged a little place of honour for it. You've won over my grandfather, he likes you. We shall live together. Do you play whist? My grandfather will be overjoyed if you play whist. It'll be you that takes Cosette out for a walk on the days when I'm in court, you'll give her your arm, you know, the way you used to in the Luxembourg Gardens. We're absolutely determined to be very happy. And you shall be included in our happiness, do you hear, father? Now, you're lunching with us today?'

'Monsieur,' said Jean Valjean, 'I have something to tell you. I am an ex-convict.'

The limits of perceptibility can be transcended just as much for the mind as for the ear by shrillness of sound. Those words 'I am an ex-convict', coming out of Monsieur Fauchelevent's mouth and entering Marius's ear, exceeded the bounds of possibility. He had the feeling that something had just been said to him, but he did not know what. He was left baffled.

Then he noticed that the man speaking to him looked ghastly. Completely absorbed in his own bliss, he had not until that moment noticed that terrible pallor.

Jean Valjean untied the black scarf supporting his right arm, unrolled the bandage around his hand, bared his thumb and showed it to Marius.

'There's nothing wrong with my hand,' he said.

Marius stared at the thumb.

'There never was anything wrong with it,' Jean Valjean went on.

Indeed, there was no trace of any injury.

Jean Valjean continued, 'For respectability's sake, it was better I didn't attend your wedding. I kept away as much as I could. I faked this injury so as to avoid being an impostor, so as not to invalidate the marriage contract in any way, so as not to have to sign anything.'

Marius stammered out, 'What does this mean?'

'It means', replied Jean Valjean, 'that I've been in the prison hulks.'

'You're driving me out of my wits!' cried Marius, appalled.

'Monsieur Pontmercy,' said Jean Valjean, 'I was nineteen years in the prison hulks. For theft. I was then given a life sentence. For theft. For re-offending. At the present moment I'm in breach of parole.'

In vain did Marius attempt to shrink from reality, deny the facts, resist the evidence, it had to be faced. He began to understand and, as always happens in such instances, he understood too much. He shuddered at an horrendous moment of illumination, an idea that made him tremble went through his mind. He discerned for himself in the future a blighted destiny.

'Tell all, tell all!' he cried. 'You're Cosette's father!'

And he stepped back two paces in unutterable horror.

Jean Valjean raised his head with such majesty that he seemed to grow taller and almost reach the ceiling.

'In this, monsieur, you will have to believe me. And although the solemn oath of the likes of us is not accepted in law –' Here he paused, then with a kind of sovereign and sepulchral authority, articulating slowly and dwelling on every syllable, he added: '– you will believe me. I, the father of Cosette! Before God, no. Monsieur le baron Pontmercy, I am a peasant from Faverolles. I used to earn my living by pruning trees. My name is not Fauchelevent, but Jean Valjean. I am not related to Cosette. Rest assured.'

'Who's to prove that to me?' Marius stammered.

'I do. Since I tell you it is so.'

Marius looked at this man. He was dour and calm. No lie could issue from such calm. That which is ice-cold is sincere. There was a sense of truthfulness in that sepulchral chill.

'I believe you,' said Marius.

Jean Valjean bowed his head, as though in acknowledgement, and went on.

'What am I to Cosette? A passer-by. Ten years ago I didn't know of her existence. I love her, it's true. When you've seen a child as a little girl, you love that child, being already old yourself. When you're old, you feel like a grandfather to all little children. You're capable, it seems to me, of imagining that I have something resembling a heart. She was an orphan. Fatherless and motherless. She needed me. That's why I began to love her. Children are so defenceless that the first person that comes along, even a man like me, can be their protector. That was my role with regard to Cosette. I don't think that so little can be called a good deed, but if it is a good deed, then let's say I did it. Put it down as a mitigating factor. Today Cosette goes out of my life. Our two paths separate. From now on I can do no more for her. She is Madame Pontmercy. She has a new guardian angel. And Cosette is the better off for it. All is well. As for the six hundred thousand francs – you haven't mentioned them, but I anticipate your thoughts – they were held in trust. How did they come to be entrusted to me? What does it matter? I've returned what had been entrusted to me. No more can be asked of me. To complete the reversion of the funds I'm declaring my real name. That's something else to do with me. I personally want you to know who I am.'

And Jean Valjean looked Marius straight in the face.

All Marius's feelings were turbulent and incoherent. Certain blasts of destiny create these waves in our souls.

We have all had those moments of distress when everything falls apart inside us. We say the first thing that occurs to us, which is not always exactly what should be said. There are sudden revelations that we cannot bear, that befuddle us like noxious wine. Marius was so astounded by the new situation he was faced with that he spoke to this man almost as if he were angry with him for making his confession.

'For goodness' sake, why are you telling me all this?' he exclaimed. 'What is it that's forcing you to? You could have kept your secret to yourself. You've not been exposed, or hounded, or tracked down. You have some reason for cheerfully coming out with such a revelation. Tell me the rest. There's more to be said. Why are you making this confession? For what motive?'

'For what motive?' replied Jean Valjean in a voice so quiet and subdued that it sounded more as if he were talking to himself than to Marius. 'For what motive, indeed, has this convict just said, "I am a convict"? Well, yes! the motive is a strange one. It's honesty. Listen, the unfortunate thing is the attachment I have in my heart. It is especially when you're old that such attachments are strong. Your whole life collapses around you; they withstand. Had I been able to rip out this attachment, to break it, to undo the knot or cut through it, to go far away, I would have been safe. All I had to do was leave. There are coaches in Rue du Bouloi. You're happy; I go away. I've tried to break this attachment, I've pulled and pulled, it held firm, it didn't break, I was tearing my heart out with it. So I said: "I can't live anywhere else but here. I have to stay." But of course, you're right, I'm a fool, why not just stay? You offer me a room in this house, Madame Pontmercy is fond of me, she said to this armchair, "Reach your arms out to him." Your grandfather asks for nothing better than to have my company, he likes me, we shall all live together, eating at the same table, I shall give my arm to Cosette – sorry, it's just habit – to Madame Pontmercy; we shall have but one roof, one table, one fire, the same place at the fireside in winter, the same walk in summer, that's happiness, that's joy, that's everything. We shall live as a family. As a family!'

At that word Jean Valjean looked fierce. He folded his arms, glared at the floor under his feet as if he would have liked to gouge out an abyss there, and his voice was suddenly thunderous.

'As a family! No. I don't belong to any family. I don't belong to yours. I don't belong to the family of men. In houses where people are at home together, I have no place. There are families, but not for me. I'm the poor wretch. I'm on the outside. Did I have a father and mother? I almost doubt it. The day I gave that child away in marriage, that was the end of it, I saw that she was happy, and with the man she loves, and that here was an old gentleman, two angels married to each other, every happiness in this house, and that all was well, and I said to myself: "You keep out of there." I might have lied, it's true, deceived you all, remained Monsieur Fauchelevent. So long as it was for her sake, I was capable of lying. But now that it would be for my sake, I must not. I had only to remain silent, it's true, and everything would have continued as before. You ask me what it is that forces me to speak? An odd thing: my conscience. Yet to remain silent would have been very easy. I spent the night trying to persuade myself of it. You're hearing my confession, and what I've just told you is so extraordinary, you're entitled to hear it. So yes, I spent the night arguing with myself. And I had some very good arguments. Well, I did my best. But there are two things in which I did not succeed: in breaking the attachment that holds me here, tethered, bound, fastened by the heart, and in silencing someone who speaks softly to me when I'm alone. That's why I've come here to you this morning to confess all. All, or nearly all. There's no point in talking of what is of no concern to anyone else. I keep that to myself. Whatever is of any importance, you know. So I've taken my mystery and brought it to you. And I've laid open my secret before your eyes. It wasn't an easy decision to take. I wrestled all night long. Ah! you think I didn't tell myself that this was no Champmathieu affair, that by concealing my name I wasn't doing anyone any harm, that the name of Fauchelevent was given to me by Fauchelevent himself out of gratitude for something I did for him, and that I could surely keep it, and that I'd be happy in that room you're offering me, that I wouldn't be a nuisance, that I'd be in my own little corner, and that while you had Cosette I'd have the thought of being in the same house as her. Each of us would have had a share of happiness. Continuing to be Monsieur Fauchelevent, that put everything right. Yes, except for my soul. Even with every outward joy, the depths of my soul would have remained black. It's not enough to be happy, you have to be content. So I'd have remained Monsieur Fauchelevent. So I'd have hidden my true face. So amid your plenitude of joy I'd have harboured an enigma. So amid your brightness I'd have harboured darkness. So without any warning I'd have brought the prison hulks right into your home, I'd have sat at your table with the thought that if you knew what I was you'd turn me away, I'd have allowed myself to be waited on by servants who, had they known, would have said, "How dreadful!" I'd have made you rub elbows with one that by rights you'd have nothing to do with, I'd have rooked you of your handshakes! In your house, respect would have been shared between the venerable white-haired and the criminal white-haired. In your most intimate moments, when all hearts thought themselves entirely open to each other, when we four were together, your grandfather, you two, and me, there would have been a stranger present! I'd have been living alongside you – and my sole concern never to shift the lid on my ghastly pit! So I, a dead man, would have imposed myself on you, the living. Her I would have condemned to be with me for ever. All three of us, you and Cosette and I, would have been wearing the green cap! Aren't you shuddering? I'm no more than the most oppressed of men; that would have made me the most monstrous. And that crime I'd have been committing every day! And that lie, I'd have been perpetrating every day! And that face of night I'd have been wearing every day! And my criminal contagion I'd have been passing on to you every day! Every day! To you, my dear ones, you, my children, my innocents! To keep quiet is nothing? To remain silent is simple? No, it's not simple. There's a silence that lies. And my lie, and my fraudulence, and my baseness, and my cowardice, and my treachery and my crime – I'd have drunk drop by drop, spat out, then drunk again, finishing at midnight and starting over again at midday, and my "good morning" would have lied, and my "goodnight" would have lied; and I'd have slept with that, I'd have eaten that with my bread, and I'd have looked Cosette in the face and responded to an angel's smile with the smile of the damned, and I'd have been an abominable villain! Why? For the sake of being happy. I! Happy! Have I any right to be happy? I'm one of life's outcasts, monsieur.'

Jean Valjean broke off. Marius was listening. Such an unfolding of thoughts and anguish cannot be interrupted. Jean Valjean lowered his voice again, but this was no longer a subdued voice, it was a grim voice.

'You ask why I speak of this? I've not been exposed, or hounded, or tracked down, you say. Yes, I have been exposed! Yes, I have been hounded! Yes, I have been tracked down! By whom? By myself. It is I who bar my own way, and I drag myself, and push myself, and arrest myself, and indict myself. And when an individual holds himself, he's firmly held.'

And grabbing at his own coat and pulling it towards Marius, he went on, 'Do you see this hand? Don't you think, the way it holds this collar, it won't let go? Well! this is nothing compared with the grip of conscience! If you want to be happy, monsieur, you must never understand duty. For once you've understood, it's implacable. You'd almost think it punishes you for understanding, but no, it rewards you. For it places you in a hell where you sense God at your side. You've no sooner torn yourself apart than you're at peace with yourself.'

And with heart-rending deliberation he added, 'Monsieur Pontmercy, I am, though not in the accepted sense of the word, an honest man. It is by degrading myself in your eyes that I raise myself in my own. This has already happened to me once before, but it was less painful then. It was nothing. Yes, an honest man. I wouldn't be, if through some fault of mine you continued to respect me, but now that you despise me, I am. It is my sorry fate that, only ever able to command respect that is fraudulently obtained, that respect humiliates me and inwardly oppresses me, and if I'm to have any self-respect others must despise me. Then I hold my head up high. I'm a convicted felon who obeys his conscience. I know how unlikely that is. But what do you expect me to do about it? That's the way it is. I've made promises to myself. I'm keeping them. There are some encounters that bind us, some fortuitous incidents that lay responsibilities on us. You see, Monsieur Pontmercy, things have happened to me in the course of my life.'

Jean Valjean paused again, swallowing his saliva with an effort, as if his words had a bitter after-taste, and went on. 'When you have such a dreadful thing looming over you, you have no right to make others share it without their knowledge, you have no right to pass on to them your disease, you have no right to let them slide into your abyss without their noticing, you have no right to let your red jacket trail over them, you have no right cunningly to foist your own wretchedness on the happiness of others. To go near those who are healthy, and to touch them in the dark with your invisible ulcer, is grotesque. For all that Fauchelevent lent me his name, I have no right to use it. He may have given it to me, I couldn't take it. A name is a personal identity. You see, monsieur, I've thought a bit, I've read a bit, peasant though I am. And I understand things. You see how well I express myself. I've educated myself. So yes, to take someone else's name and to go by that name is dishonest. The letters of the alphabet can be misappropriated like a purse or a watch. To be a false signature in flesh and blood, to be a living skeleton key, to enter the homes of honest people by picking their locks, never more to have a direct gaze, always to be shifty-eyed, to be vile on the inside, no, no, no, no, no! Better to suffer, to bleed, to weep, to tear the skin off your flesh with your fingernails, to spend your nights writhing in anguish, to eat your heart and soul out. That's why I've just told you all this. Cheerfully, as you say.'

He breathed heavily, then uttered these last words: 'In the past I stole a loaf of bread for the sake of living. Today, for the sake of living, I don't want to steal a name.'

'For the sake of living!' Marius broke in. 'Haven't you need of that name if you're to live?'

'Oh, I know what I'm saying,' said Jean Valjean, slowly nodding his head several times in succession.

There was a silence. Neither of them spoke, each lost in unfathomable thoughts. Marius had sat down at a table, and he rested the corner of his mouth on one crooked finger. Jean Valjean paced back and forth. He stopped in front of a mirror and stood there motionless. Then, as though in response to some inward reasoning, gazing at the mirror in which he did not see himself, he said, 'Whereas now I feel relieved!'

He started moving about again, and walked to the other end of the drawing room. As he turned round he noticed that Marius was watching him. Then in an indescribable tone of voice he said, 'I drag my leg a little. Now you understand why!'

Then he turned right round to face Marius. 'And now, monsieur, imagine this: I've said nothing, I've remained Monsieur Fauchelevent, I've taken my place in your house, I'm one of you, I'm in my room, I come to breakfast in the morning in my slippers, in the evening we all three of us go out to the theatre, I accompany Madame Pontmercy to the Tuileries and to Place Royale, we're together, you think of me as one of you. One fine day, there I am, there you are, we're chatting, we're laughing, suddenly you hear a voice call out this name: "Jean Valjean!" And then the dreaded hand of the police emerges from the shadows and rips off my mask!'

Once more he fell silent. Marius had leapt to his feet with a shudder. Jean Valjean spoke again, 'What do you say to that?'

Marius's silence answered for him.

Jean Valjean continued. 'You can surely see that I'm right not to keep quiet. Listen, be happy, be in heaven, be the angel of an angel, be in the sun and content yourself with that, and don't worry about the way some poor devil goes about unburdening his heart and doing his duty. You have before you, monsieur, a miserable wretch.'

Marius slowly walked across the drawing room, and when he was close to Jean Valjean offered him his hand. But Marius had to move forward and take that hand, which was not presented. Jean Valjean was unresponsive, and it seemed to Marius that he shook a hand of marble.

'My grandfather has friends,' said Marius. 'I'll obtain your pardon.'

'There's no point,' replied Jean Valjean. 'I'm believed to be dead, that's enough. The dead aren't kept under surveillance. They're supposed to rot away quietly. Death is the same thing as a pardon.'

And freeing the hand that Marius was holding, he added with a sort of inexorable dignity, 'Besides, doing my duty – that's the friend on whose help I can call. And I need only one pardon – that of my conscience.'

At that moment the door at the other end of the drawing room opened gently a fraction, and Cosette's head appeared. Only her sweet face was visible; she was wonderfully dishevelled, and her eyelids were still swollen from sleep. With the gesture of a bird sticking its head out of the nest, she glanced first at her husband, then at Jean Valjean, and cried out to them, laughing – it was like seeing a smile in the heart of a rose – 'I bet you're talking politics. How silly, when you could be with me!'

Jean Valjean gave a start.

'Cosette!' faltered Marius.

And he fell silent. Two guilty men, you would have thought.

Radiant, Cosette continued to gaze at them both, looking from one to the other. There were in her eyes what might have been glimpses of paradise.

'I've caught you red-handed,' said Cosette. 'I just heard through the door my father Fauchelevent talking about "Conscience . . . Doing your duty . . ." That's politics, that is. I won't have it. It's only the day after – there should be no talk of politics. It's not right.'

'You're wrong, Cosette,' said Marius, 'we're talking business. We're discussing the best way to invest your six hundred thousand francs.'

'That's not the be all and end all,' Cosette interjected. 'I'm here. Am I not wanted?'

And resolutely coming through the door, she entered the drawing room. She wore a loose-fitting white dressing-gown, with wide sleeves and countless pleats, that fell from her neck down to her feet. There are in the golden heavens of old Gothic paintings such charming robes, in which angels are clad.

She studied herself from head to foot in a big mirror, then exclaimed in a burst of inexpressible ecstasy, 'Once upon a time there was a king and a queen. Oh! how happy I am!'

That said, she curtsied to Marius and to Jean Valjean.

'Now,' she said, 'I'm going to settle down beside you in an arm-chair, we're having breakfast in half an hour, you can talk about whatever you like, I know that men have to talk, I'll be very good.'

Marius took her by the arm and said to her lovingly, 'We're talking business.'

'By the way,' replied Cosette, 'I opened my window, a flock of blackcaps just arrived in the garden, birds not maskers. Today's Ash Wednesday, but not for the birds.'

'I tell you, we're talking business, my dear Cosette, so go away and leave us for a while. We're discussing figures. You'll be bored.'

'You're wearing a lovely cravat this morning, Marius. You look very stylish, monseigneur. No, I shan't be bored.'

'I can assure you, you'll be bored.'

'No. Seeing as it's you. I shan't understand, but I shall listen. When you hear the voices of those you love, you don't need to understand the words they say. To be here together, that's all I want. I'm staying with you, so there!'

'My darling Cosette! Out of the question.'

'Out of the question?'

'Yes.'

'Very well,' said Cosette. 'I would have told you some news. I would have told you that my grandfather is still asleep, that your aunt is at mass, that the chimney is smoking in my father Fauchelevent's room, that Nicolette has sent for the chimney-sweep, that Toussaint and Nicolette have already quarrelled, that Nicolette is making fun of Toussaint's stammering. Well, you'll be none the wiser. Ah! so it's out of the question? You'll see, gentlemen, I too will say: "It's out of the question." Who's going to be caught out, then? Please, darling Marius, let me stay here with you two.'

'Truly, we must be left alone.'

'Well, do I count as somone?'

Jean Valjean said not a word.

Cosette turned to him. 'First of all, father, I want you to come and kiss me. What are you doing there, saying nothing instead of standing up for me? Who ever gave me such a father? You see how very unhappily married I am. My husband beats me. Come, kiss me right now.'

Jean Valjean moved towards her.

Cosette turned to Marius. 'As for you, I'm pulling a face at you.'

Then she offered her forehead to Jean Valjean. Jean Valjean took a step closer. Cosette stepped back.

'Father, you're pale. Is your arm hurting you?'

'It's healed,' said Jean Valjean.

'Did you sleep badly?'

'No.'

'Are you sad?'

'No.'

'Kiss me. If you feel well, if you slept well, if you're happy, I shan't scold you.' And again she offered him her forehead.

Jean Valjean kissed that forehead, on which there was a heavenly gleam.

'Smile.'

Jean Valjean obeyed. It was the smile of a ghost.

'Now, defend me against my husband.'

'Cosette!' exclaimed Marius.

'Be cross with him, father. Tell him I must stay. Surely you can talk while I'm here. You really must think me very stupid. What you're saying is quite extraordinary! Business, putting money in a bank, now isn't that complicated! Men behave mysteriously over nothing. I want to stay. I'm very pretty this morning. Look at me, Marius.'

And with an adorable shrug of the shoulders and an indescribably exquisite sulkiness, she looked at Marius. Something like a flash of lightning passed between those two. That someone else was present was of little importance.

'I love you!' said Marius.

'I adore you!' said Cosette.

And they fell irresistibly into each other's arms.

'Now,' said Cosette, adjusting a fold of her dressing-gown with a triumphant little pout, 'I'm staying.'

'That, no,' said Marius imploringly. 'We have something to finish.'

'Still no?'

Marius took on a serious tone of voice. 'I assure you, Cosette, it's out of the question.'

'Ah! you're putting on your manly voice, monsieur. Very well, I'm going. You, father, didn't support me. Gentlemen – husband, papa – you're tyrants. I'm going to tell grandfather. If you think I'm coming back to fawn on you, you're mistaken. I'm proud. From on now I'll wait for you to come to me. You'll see, you're the ones who'll be bored without me. It's just as well that I'm going.'

And she left the room.

Two seconds later, the double doors opened again, her fresh rosy face appeared between them and she called out, 'I'm very cross!'

The door closed again and gloom re-established itself. It was as though, unwittingly, a stray sunbeam had suddenly shone through the dark.

Marius made sure the doors were properly closed.

'Poor Cosette!' he murmured. 'When she finds out . . .'

At these words Jean Valjean trembled in every limb. He stared at Marius with a distraught expression in his eyes.

'Cosette! Of course, it's true, you're going to tell Cosette. It's only right. I hadn't thought of that. A man has the strength for one thing, but not for another. Monsieur, I beseech you, I beg you, monsieur, give me your most solemn word – don't tell her. Isn't it enough that you should know? I could have spoken of it of my own accord without being forced to, I would have told the universe, everybody, it didn't matter to me. But she doesn't know what it means – she'd be appalled. A convicted felon! She'd have to have it explained to her, to be told, "He's a man condemned to penal servitude." One day she saw the chain gang go by. Oh my God!'

He collapsed into an armchair and hid his face in both hands. There was no sound to be heard, but from the shaking of his shoulders you could see that he was weeping. Silent tears, terrible tears.

Sobbing is suffocating. A kind of convulsion seized him, he fell back in the chair as though to catch his breath, letting his arms hang loose and letting Marius see the tears streaming down his face; and Marius heard him murmur, so low that his voice seemed to come from a fathomless depth, 'Oh! I wish I could die!'

'Rest assured,' said Marius, 'I'll keep your secret to myself.'

And less compassionate, perhaps, than he ought to have been, but obliged for the past hour to get used to something dreadful that had been sprung on him, seeing a convicted felon being superimposed little by little, before his very eyes, on Monsieur Fauchelevent; gradually overtaken by that grim reality and led unavoidably by the nature of the situation to recognize the gap that had just opened up between this man and himself, Marius added, 'It's inconceivable that I shouldn't mention what was entrusted to you, which you have so faithfully and honestly handed over. That is an act of integrity. It's fair that you should be given some recompense. Name the sum yourself, and you shall have it. Don't be afraid to set it very high.'

'Thank you, monsieur,' Jean Valjean replied softly.

He remained thoughtful for a moment, unconsciously rubbing the tip of his forefinger across his thumbnail, then, raising his voice, 'Everything's more or less settled. There's one last thing.'

'What's that?'

After what seemed the longest hesitation, his voice failing him, almost unable to breathe, Jean Valjean mumbled rather than said, 'Now that you know, monsieur, you being the master, do you think I oughtn't to see Cosette any more?'

'I think that would be best,' replied Marius coldly.

'I shan't see her ever again,' murmured Jean Valjean.

And he headed towards the door. He put his hand on the door handle, the catch gave, the door stood ajar.

Jean Valjean opened it wide enough to pass through, stood motionless for a second, then closed the door again and turned to Marius.

He was no longer pale, he was ashen. There were in his eyes no tears now, but a kind of tragic intensity. His voice had become strangely calm again.

'Listen, monsieur,' he said, 'with your permission, I'll come and see her. I assure you it's my dearest wish. If I'd not wanted to see Cosette, I wouldn't have made the confession I made to you, I'd have gone away. But wanting to stay where Cosette is and to continue to see her, I honestly had to tell you all. You follow my reasoning, don't you? It's understandable enough. You see, for more than nine years now I've had her with me. We lived first in that tenement on the boulevard, then in the convent, then near the Luxembourg Gardens. That was where you first saw her. You remember her fluffy blue hat? Then we were in the Invalides neighbourhood, where there were railings and a garden, Rue Plumet. I lived in a little back yard from where I could hear her piano. Such was my life. We were never apart. That went on for nine years and a few months. I was like a father to her, and she was my child. I don't know whether you understand, Monsieur Pontmercy, but to go away now, never to see her again, never to speak to her again, to be left with nothing at all, that would be hard. If you think there's no harm in it, I'll come and see Cosette now and again.

I won't come often. I won't stay long. You could say that I'm to be received in the little room downstairs. On the ground floor. I'd be happy to come in by the back door, the servants' entrance, but people might wonder at that. It would be better, I think, if I came in by the same door as everyone else. Truly, monsieur. I'd still very much like to see a little of Cosette. As seldom as you like. Put yourself in my place, it's all I have left. And besides, we must be careful. If I no longer came at all, it would give a bad impression, people would find that odd. For instance, what I could do is come in the evening, when it's beginning to get dark.'

'You shall come every evening,' said Marius, 'and Cosette will be waiting for you.'

'You are kind, monsieur,' said Jean Valjean.

Marius bowed, happiness led despair to the door, and these two men parted.

II
The Obscurities That a Revelation May Contain

Marius was shocked.

The kind of reserve he had always felt with regard to the man he was used to seeing Cosette with was now explained to him. There was something mysterious about this person that his instinct warned him against. This mystery was the most terrible disgrace: penal servitude. This Monsieur Fauchelevent was the convicted felon Jean Valjean.

Suddenly discovering such a secret amid your happiness is like finding a scorpion in a turtle-doves' nest. Was the happiness of Marius and Cosette now condemned to this association? Was it an irreversible state of affairs? Was acceptance of this man attached to the marriage that was now consummated? Was there nothing to be done about it?

Had Marius also married the convict?

It is all very well being crowned with light and joy, all very well enjoying that great purple moment in life, being happy in love – shocks of this kind would compel even the archangel in his ecstasy, even the demigod in his glory, to quake.

As always in such dramatic turnabouts, Marius wondered whether he had anything to blame himself for. Had he lacked discernment? Had he lacked caution? Had he been unintentionally thoughtless? A little, perhaps. Had he embarked on this love affair that had led to his marriage to Cosette without sufficient regard to her circumstances? He acknowledged – so it is, by a series of successive acknowledgements about ourselves to ourselves, that life improves us little by little – the fanciful and visionary side of his nature, a kind of inner haze typical of many constitutions and which, in the paroxysms of passion and of sorrow, expands with the soul's changing temperature and entirely takes over, so that the individual is reduced to no more than a fog-bound consciousness. We have more than once pointed to this trait in Marius's personality. He remembered that in the euphoria of his love, in Rue Plumet, during those six or seven ecstatic weeks, he had not even spoken to Cosette of that puzzling drama in the Gorbeau tenement in which the victim had behaved so strangely, remaining silent during the fighting and taking flight afterwards. How was it that he had not spoken of this to Cosette? Yet it was so recent and so terrible! How was it that he had not even mentioned the Thénardiers' name, and particularly on the day he encountered Éponine? Now he could hardly explain to himself his silence at the time. He was aware of it, though. He remembered his giddiness, his intoxicating passion for Cosette, love absorbing everything, each transporting the other into the realms of the ideal; and perhaps, too, like the little touch of reason mingling with that delightful and intense state of emotion, some underlying instinct to conceal and to blot from his memory that dreadful incident in which he feared any involvement, in which he wanted to play no part, from which he shied away, and of which he could be neither narrator nor witness without also accusing. Besides, those few weeks had gone by in flash. There had been no time for anything except loving each other. In any case, all things considered, weighed up, examined, supposing he had told Cosette about the Gorbeau ambush, supposing he had mentioned the Thénardiers' name to her, whatever the consequences might have been – even if he had discovered that Jean Valjean was a convicted felon – would that have changed him, Marius? Would that have changed Cosette? Would he have backed away? Would he have adored her any the less? Would he have married her any the less? No. Would it have changed anything that happened? No. Nothing to regret, then, nothing for which to reproach himself. Everything was fine. There is a god for those drunkards called lovers. Marius had blindly followed the path he would have chosen had he been able to see clearly. Love had blindfolded him, to lead him where? To paradise.

But this paradise now had a hellish association.

Marius's former reserve with regard to this man, this Fauchelevent who had become Jean Valjean, was now mingled with horror. Admittedly, in his horror there was some pity, and even a certain astonishment.

This thief, this hardened thief, had returned something given to him in trust. Six hundred thousand francs. He was the only person who knew about it. He might have kept it all, he handed it all over.

Furthermore, he had of his own accord revealed his situation. Nothing obliged him to do so. If it was now known who he was, that was his doing. There was in this admission something more than an acceptance of humiliation, there was an acceptance of danger. For a convict, a mask is not a mask, it is a refuge. A false name is safety, and he had rejected that false name. He, the convicted felon, might have been able to hide for ever within a respectable family. He had resisted that temptation. And with what motive? A guilty conscience. He had explained this himself with the convincing ring of truth. In short, whatever this Jean Valjean might be, he was undoubtedly an awakening conscience. Some sort of mysterious rehabilitation had begun in him. And, to all appearances, compunction had long been master of this man. Susceptibility to what is right and what is good is not in the nature of a coarse disposition. Awakening of conscience is grandeur of soul.

Jean Valjean was sincere. This sincerity – visible, palpable, undeniable, evident in the very grief it caused him – made further inquiries unnecessary, and conferred authority on everything this man said. Here, for Marius, was a strange inversion of circumstances. What did Monsieur Fauchelevent excite? Suspicion. What did Jean Valjean inspire? Trust.

Brooding on his assessment of this baffling Jean Valjean, Marius noted assets, he noted liabilities, and he tried to strike the balance. But all this was going on as if in a blizzard. Striving to form a clear idea of the man and pursuing, so to speak, Jean Valjean into the depths of his mind, Marius kept losing him and finding him again, in a relentless fog.

The money held in trust honestly returned, the integrity of his confession – that was good. It created some sort of thinning of the cloud, then the cloud darkened again. Confused as Marius's memories were, some shadow of them came back to him.

What was that incident in the Jondrette garret all about? Why, instead of lodging a complaint when the police arrived, had the man fled? Here Marius found the answer. Because the man was a former convict in breach of his parole.

Another question: why did the man come to the barricade? For now Marius clearly visualized that memory, resurfacing amid this emotional turmoil like invisible ink exposed to heat. This man was at the barricade. He did not take part in the fighting. What had he gone there for? At this question a spectre arose and replied, 'Javert'. Marius now remembered perfectly the grim sight of Jean Valjean dragging Javert, securely bound, outside the barricade, and he could still hear that dreadful pistol-shot from round the corner of the Mondétour alleyway. There was probably no love lost between the police spy and the convict. They got in each other's way. Jean Valjean had gone to the barricade to take his revenge. He had arrived late. It was likely that he knew Javert had been taken prisoner there. The Corsican vendetta has penetrated certain sections of the lower depths and prevails as law there. It is so uncomplicated that it does not surprise even souls that have half repented. And such hearts are so constituted that a criminal who has begun to repent may have scruples about theft, but not about revenge. Jean Valjean had killed Javert. At least, that seemed plain enough.

Then the final question. But to this one there was no answer. Marius was tortured by this question: how was it that Jean Valjean's life had for so long been linked with Cosette's? What sinister game of Providence was it that had put that child in contact with this man? So are coupling manacles forged on high, too, and does God take pleasure in pairing angel with demon? So crime and innocence can be room-mates in the mysterious prison-hulk of wretchedness? In that procession of the condemned called human destiny, is it possible for two beings, one clear-browed, the other fearsome, one bathed through and through in the divine purity of dawn, the other for ever caught in the ghastly glimmer of eternal lightning, to walk side by side? Who could have brought about that unaccountable pairing? How, as a result of what extraordinary circumstances, did that heavenly child and that old criminal come to share each other's life? Who could have bound the lamb to the wolf; and, yet more incomprehensible, the wolf to the lamb? Because the wolf loved the lamb, because that savage creature adored the weak one, because for nine years the angel's stay and support had been the monster. Cosette's childhood and adolescence, her development, her virginal growth towards life and light, had been protected by that anomalous devotion. At this point the questions shed, as it were, like fallen leaves, countless enigmas; abysses opened up at the bottom of abysses, and Marius could no longer focus his mind on Jean Valjean without feeling dizzy. What on earth was this chasm of a man?

The old symbols in Genesis are eternal. In human society as it is now, until the day when a greater light transforms it, there will always be two men, one of the higher order, the other of the lower. The one who embraces good is Abel. The other, who embraces evil, is Cain. Who was this tender-hearted Cain? Who was this villain piously absorbed in the adoration of a virgin, looking after her, raising her, watching over her, honouring her, and, foul as he was, enfolding her in purity? Who was this sink of iniquity who had so venerated this innocence as not to leave a single stain on it? Who was this Jean Valjean who had brought up Cosette? Who was this figure of darkness whose sole concern had been to preserve from every shadow and every cloud the rising of a star?

This was Jean Valjean's secret. It was also God's secret.

Faced with this dual secret, Marius retreated. In a way, the one reassured him about the other. God was as visible in this affair as Jean Valjean was. God has his instruments. He uses whatever tool he chooses. He is not answerable to man. Do we understand the ways of God? Jean Valjean had worked at Cosette. He had somewhat created that soul. This was undeniable. So what? The workman was dreadful, but the work was wonderful. God performs his miracles as he pleases. He had fashioned darling Cosette, and he had employed Jean Valjean to do so. He had chosen for himself this strange collaborator. What justification have we to ask of him? Is this the first time the dung-heap has helped spring to produce the rose?

These were the answers Marius gave himself, and he told himself they were good answers. On all the points we have just raised he dared not – without admitting to himself that he dared not – press Jean Valjean. He adored Cosette, Cosette was his, Cosette was splendidly pure. That was enough for him. What further illumination did he need? Cosette was light. Does light need to be illuminated? He had everything. What more could he want? Everything – is that not enough? Jean Valjean's personal affairs did not concern him. And considering that man's fateful shadow, he clung to the wretch's solemn declaration: 'I'm nothing to Cosette. Ten years ago I didn't know she existed.'

Jean Valjean was an itinerant. He had said so himself. Well, now he was moving on. Whatever he had been, his role had ended. From now on there was Marius to play the part of Cosette's protector. Cosette had looked to the heavens for her own kind – her lover, her husband, her celestial mate. Taking flight, winged and transfigured, Cosette left behind on earth her empty, ugly chrysalis, Jean Valjean.

In whatever mental circles Marius kept turning, he always came back to a certain horror of Jean Valjean. A sacred horror, perhaps, for as we have just mentioned he sensed a *quid divinum* in this man. But for all that anyone could do, and whatever extenuating circumstances might be sought, there was no avoiding the fact: the man was a convicted felon, that is to say, a creature who did not even have a place on the social ladder, being beneath the lowest rung. After the very least of men comes the convicted felon. Among the living, the convict is no longer, so to speak, among his like. The law has dispossessed him of all the humanity of which it can divest a man. On penal matters Marius, although a democrat, still upheld the unforgiving system, and about those whom the law punishes he was at one with the law. Let us say, he had not yet made full progress. He had not yet reached the stage of distinguishing between what is written by man and what is written by God, between law and rightfulness. He had not examined and weighed the right that man asserts to deal in the irrevocable and the irreparable. He was not outraged by the words 'punitive justice'. He found it natural that certain infringements of the written law should entail eternal suffering, and he accepted social damnation as a civilized proceeding. He was still at this stage, although bound to advance later – his nature being good and with the basic potential to progress.

In this climate of thought in his own mind, Jean Valjean appeared to him as hideous and repulsive. He was an outcast. He was a convict. This word was for him like the sound of the trumpet on the Day of Judgement. And after considering Jean Valjean for a long time, his final gesture was to turn his head away. *Vade retro**.

It has to be recognized and even stressed that, although he had interrogated Jean Valjean to the point that Jean Valjean had said, 'You're hearing my confession', there were two or three crucial questions that Marius had not asked him. It was not that they had not occurred to him, but he was afraid of them. The Jondrette garret? The barricade? Javert? Who knows where the revelations might have ended? Jean Valjean did not seem like a man who would falter, and who knows whether Marius, after having urged him on, would not have wanted to restrain him? Have we not all, at certain critical junctures, after having asked a question blocked our ears so as not to hear the answer? It is especially where love is concerned that such cowardice arises. It is not wise to question ominous situations too closely, particularly when the indissoluble side of our own lives is inextricably involved. Some terrible light might be shed by Jean Valjean's desperate explanations, and who knows whether the hideous glare would not have been reflected on Cosette? Who knows whether it would not have left some infernal glimmer on that angel's brow? The diffuse light of sheet lightning is still lightning. Fate creates such fellowships, when innocence itself is stamped with crime by the sombre law of reflected coloration. The purest faces may retain for ever the reflection of some dreadful association. Rightly or wrongly, Marius was afraid. He already knew too much. He sought obliviousness rather than

---

* Latin: Literally, 'Go back'. An allusion to the Catholic formula for exorcism, to repel the presence of evil.

illumination. Frantically, he carried Cosette away in his arms and closed his eyes to Jean Valjean.

That man was darkness, a living and terrible darkness. How could anyone dare fathom it? It is terrifying to question the blackness of night. Who knows what the reply will be? The light of dawn might be darkened for ever by it.

In this state of mind it was an agonizing predicament for Marius to think that this man would have any further contact with Cosette. Those dreadful questions that he had shrunk from asking, and that might have led to a final and implacable decision, he now almost reproached himself for not asking. He considered himself too good, too kind, let us say the word, too weak. This weakness had drawn him into making a rash concession. He had allowed himself to feel sympathy. He had been wrong. He should simply have refused to have anything more to do with Jean Valjean. Jean Valjean was the sacrifice he should have made to save the rest; he should have rid his house of the man. He blamed himself, he blamed the onrush of that whirlwind of emotions that had deafened and blinded him, and led him astray. He was dissatisfied with himself.

What was to be done now? Jean Valjean's visits were deeply objectionable to him. What was the good of having that man in his house? What was to be done? Now he was flummoxed; he did not want to delve, he did not want to probe, he did not want to sound his own depths. He had promised, he had allowed himself to be drawn into promising, Jean Valjean had his promise. Even when given to a convict, especially when given to a convict, a man must keep his word. All the same, his first duty was to Cosette. In short, he felt an overwhelming sense of revulsion.

Marius turned over in his mind all these confused thoughts, passing from one to the other and agitated by all of them. Hence a deep disquiet. It was not easy for him to hide this disquiet from Cosette, but love is a talent, and Marius succeeded.

Besides, he put some seemingly aimless questions to Cosette, she being as white as a dove in her innocent candour and suspecting nothing. He spoke to her about her childhood and her youth, and he became more and more convinced that this convicted felon had been for Cosette everything good, fatherly and respectable that a man can be. Everything that Marius had glimpsed and assumed was real. That vicious nettle had loved and protected this lily.

BOOK EIGHT
THE WANING TWILIGHT

I
The Downstairs Room

The next day at nightfall Jean Valjean knocked at the carriage entrance of the Gillenormand house. It was Basque who let him in. Basque was in the courtyard at that very moment, as if by order. It sometimes happens that a servant will be told, 'Look out for Monsieur So-and-So when he's due to arrive.'

Without waiting for Jean Valjean to come over to him, Basque said, 'Monsieur le baron has told me to ask monsieur whether he wants to go upstairs or remain downstairs?'

'Downstairs,' replied Jean Valjean.

With the utmost respect, it must be said, Basque opened the door to the downstairs room and said, 'I'll go and tell Madame you're here.'

The room Jean Valjean entered was a damp and vaulted room on the ground floor, serving as a storeroom when needed, facing the street, red-tiled, and ill-lit by a window with iron bars over it.

This room was not one of those worried by feather duster, ceiling brush or broom. The dust lay undisturbed there. There were no arrangements for the persecution of spiders. A splendid web, extremely large, very black, adorned with dead flies, hung over one of the window-panes. Small and low-ceilinged, the room was furnished with a stack of empty bottles piled in a corner. The walls, distempered with a yellow-ochre wash, were peeling in large flakes. At one end was a black-painted wooden mantelpiece with a narrow shelf. There was a fire burning in it, which suggested that Jean Valjean had given the reply that had been expected: 'Downstairs.'

Two armchairs stood on either side of the fireplace. Between the chairs, by way of a carpet, lay an old bedside rug, more threadbare than woolly. The room was lit by the fire in the hearth and the half-light coming through the window.

Jean Valjean was tired. He had not eaten or slept for several days. He sank into one of the armchairs. Basque returned, set a lighted candle on the mantelpiece and withdrew. Jean Valjean, his head drooping and his chin resting on his chest, was aware of neither Basque nor the candle.

All of a sudden he rose as if with a start. Cosette was behind him. He did not see her come in, but he sensed it. He turned round. He gazed at her. She was adorably beautiful. But what he looked on with that penetrating gaze was not her beauty but her soul.

'Really!' exclaimed Cosette. 'The idea of it! Father, I knew you were quaint, but I'd never have expected this. Marius tells me it was you who insisted that I see you down here.'

'Yes, it was.'

'I expected that reply. You'd better watch out. I warn you, I'm going to make a scene. First things first. Kiss me, father.'

And she offered him her cheek. Jean Valjean stood stock still.

'You're not moving. I see. Sign of guilt. But never mind, I forgive you. Jesus Christ said: "Turn the other cheek." Here it is.'

And she offered him her other cheek. Jean Valjean did not stir. It was as though his feet were nailed to the ground.

'This is getting serious,' said Cosette. 'What have I done to you? Now I'm upset. You'll have to make it up to me. You must have dinner with us.'

'I've already eaten.'

'That's not true. I'll have Monsieur Gillenormand give you a telling-off. Grandfathers are meant for scolding fathers. Now, come upstairs with me to the drawing room. Right now.'

'Out of the question.'

Cosette lost a little ground here. She stopped giving orders and started questioning. 'But why? And you choose the ugliest room in the house to see me in. It's horrible here.'

'You know –' (Jean Valjean corrected himself) '– madame knows I'm perverse, I have my quirks.'

Cosette clapped her little hands together. ' "Madame knows"! That's new too! What does this mean?'

Jean Valjean turned on her that heart-rending smile in which he sometimes took refuge. 'You wanted to be madame. And you are.'

'Not to you, father.'

'Don't call me "father".'

'What?'

'Call me Monsieur Jean. Jean, if you like.'

'You're not father any more? I'm not Cosette any more? Monsieur Jean? What do you mean by this? But this is revolution! What's happened? Come now, just look me in the face. And you won't live with us! And you don't want my room! What have I done to you? Is there something wrong?'

'Nothing.'

1264

'Well then?'

'Everything's just as usual.'

'Why are you changing your name?'

'Well, you've changed yours.' He smiled again with that same smile and added, 'Since you are Madame Pontmercy, I can surely be Monsieur Jean.'

'I'm at a complete loss to understand. This is all absurd. I shall ask my husband's permission for you to be Monsieur Jean. I hope he won't agree to it. You're making me very unhappy. A person can have his quirks, but not at the cost of upsetting his dearest Cosette. It's wicked. You're a good man, you've no right to be cruel.'

He did not reply. In a movement that brooked no resistance, she snatched both his hands and, raising them towards her face, pressed them to her neck, underneath her chin – which is a deeply affectionate gesture.

'Oh!' she said to him. 'Be good!' And she went on, 'This is what I call being good: being obliging, coming to live here, going for our lovely little walks again – there are birds here, like in Rue Plumet – living with us, leaving that miserable place in Rue de l'Homme-Armé, not giving us puzzles to work out, being like everyone else, having dinner with us, having breakfast with us, being my father.'

He freed his hands.

'You don't need a father any more, you have a husband.'

Cosette flared up. 'I don't need a father any more! Really, to things like that, lacking all common sense, a person just doesn't know what to say!'

'If Toussaint were here,' Jean Valjean went on, like someone having to seek authority and clutching at any straw, 'she would be the first to agree it's true that I've always had my own ways. It's nothing new. I've always loved my own dark corner.'

'But it's cold here. There's not enough light to see. And that's awful, wanting to be Monsieur Jean! I don't want you to stand on ceremony with me.'

'Just now, on my way here,' replied Jean Valjean, 'I saw a piece of furniture in Rue St-Louis. In a cabinet-maker's shop. If I were a pretty woman, I'd treat myself to that piece of furniture. A very nice dressing-table. The latest style. What you call rosewood, I think. It's inlaid. Quite a large looking-glass. It has drawers. It's pretty.'

'Ooh! The nasty bear!' replied Cosette. And with supreme charm, setting her teeth and drawing back her lips, she hissed at Jean Valjean. It was one of the Graces copying a cat.

'I'm furious,' she went on. 'Ever since yesterday, you've all been infuriating me. I'm very upset. I don't understand. You're not defending me against Marius. Marius won't support me against you. I'm all alone. I prepare a room nicely. If I could have put the good Lord in there, I'd have done so. I'm left with an unwanted room on my hands. My tenant lets me down. I order a delightful little dinner from Nicolette. Your dinner's not wanted, madame. And my father Fauchelevent wants me to call him Monsieur Jean and to see him in a horrible old damp and ugly cellar where the walls are mouldy and there are empty bottles for glassware and spiders' webs for curtains! You're quaint, I accept that, it's the way you are, but people who get married are granted some respite. You shouldn't have started being quaint again straight away. So you're going to be perfectly content in your dreadful Rue de l'Homme-Armé. I was truly in despair there myself! What are you holding against me? You're being very unkind. Shame on you!'

And suddenly serious, she gazed intently at Jean Valjean and added, 'Are you angry with me, then, because I'm happy?'

Sometimes, unknowingly, artlessness strikes very deep. This question, simple for Cosette, for Jean Valjean was a penetrating one. Cosette meant to scratch. She tore.

Jean Valjean paled. For a moment he did not reply, then in a tone of voice that no words can describe, and talking to himself, he murmured, 'Her happiness, that was the purpose of my life. God can sign my exit pass now. Cosette, you're happy. I've served my time.'

'Ah, you called me Cosette!' she cried. And she threw her arms around his neck.

Overcome with emotion, Jean Valjean clasped her frantically to his breast. He almost felt that she was his again.

'Thank you, father!' said Cosette.

Her impulsiveness was going to become agonizing for Jean Valjean. He gently freed himself from Cosette's arms, and took his hat.

'Well?' said Cosette.

'I take my leave of you, madame, there are people waiting for you.'

And from the threshold he added, 'I called you Cosette. Tell your husband that won't happen again. Forgive me.'

Jean Valjean left the room, leaving Cosette astounded by this enigmatic farewell.

II
Stepping Further Back

Jean Valjean came the next day, at the same time.

Cosette asked him no questions this time, expressed no astonishment, voiced no protest about feeling cold and made no mention of the drawing room. She avoided saying either 'father' or 'Monsieur Jean'. She allowed herself to be addressed formally as 'madame'. Only, her joyfulness was slightly diminished. She would have been sad, had she been capable of sadness.

It is likely that she and Marius had had one of those conversations between lovers in which the man says what he wants, explains nothing, and the woman is satisfied. Lovers' curiosity does not extend very far beyond their own love.

The downstairs room had been tidied up a little. Basque had removed the bottles, and Nicolette the spiders.

Every following day brought Jean Valjean at the same time. He came every day, not having the strength to take Marius's words other than literally. Marius arranged to be absent when Jean Valjean came. The household became used to Monsieur Fauchelevent's new incarnation. Toussaint was a help in this. 'Monsieur has always been like this,' she kept saying. The grandfather issued this statement: 'He's an eccentric.' And that was that. In any case, at the age of ninety there is no possibility of a new attachment, there is only accidental juxtaposition, a newcomer is bothersome. There is no more room. Habits are already acquired. Monsieur Fauchelevent, Monsieur Tranchelevent – old Gillenormand asked for nothing better than to be spared 'that gentleman'. He added, 'Nothing more commonplace than eccentrics like that. They do all kinds of strange things. For no reason. The Marquis de Canaples was worse. He bought a palace in order to live in the garret. It's the fanciful way that some people behave.'

No one had any insight into the pernicious underside. In any case, who could have guessed such a thing? There are swamps in India – the water looks extraordinary, inexplicable, quivering when there is no wind, agitated where it should be calm. You look on the surface of these turbulences without cause, you do not see the hydra crawling about in the depths.

In the same way, many men have a secret monster, a malady that they nurture, a dragon that gnaws at them, a despair that inhabits their darkness. Such a man looks like any other, going about his business. No one knows that he has inside him a terrible parasitic pain with countless teeth, which lives inside this poor wretch, who is dying of it. No one knows that this man is an abyss. His waters are stagnant but deep. From time to time, a disturbance the onlooker cannot account for occurs on the surface. A mysterious ripple forms, then vanishes, then reappears, an air bubble rises and bursts. It is not much, it is terrifying. It is the breathing of the unknown beast.

Certain strange habits – arriving when others leave, being self-effacing while others show off, on all occasions remaining cloaked in what may be called the wall-coloured mantle, seeking out the lonely path, preferring the deserted street, not getting involved in conversation, avoiding crowds and festivities, appearing to be comfortably off and living frugally, and rich as you are, having your key in your pocket and your candle at the porter's lodge, entering by the side door, going up by the back stairs – all these insignificant oddities, ripples, air bubbles, fleeting ruffles on the surface, often emanate from sinister depths.

Several weeks went by in this way. A new life gradually took over Cosette: the social relationships that marriage creates, visits, domestic responsibilities, those things of great importance – pleasures. Cosette's pleasures were not costly, they numbered but one: being with Marius. The great occupation of her life was to go out with him, to be with him. It was for them always a fresh joy to go arm in arm, out in the sun, out on the street, without hiding themselves, in the presence of everyone, the two of them on their own. Cosette had one vexation. Toussaint could not get on with Nicolette, unity between two old maids being impossible to establish, and she left. The grandfather was in good health. Marius pleaded the occasional court case. Living peacefully with the new couple, as part of the same household, Aunt Gillenormand led that ancillary life that satisfied her. Jean Valjean came every day.

The loss of intimacy, the formality, the 'madame', the 'Monsieur Jean', all this made him different for Cosette. The pains he had himself taken to detach her from him were succeeding. She became more and more cheerful and less and less tender-hearted. Yet she still loved him, and he sensed it. One day she said to him suddenly, 'You used to be my father, you're no longer my father, you used to be my uncle, you're no longer my uncle, you used to be Monsieur Fauchelevent, now you're Jean. So who are you? I don't like all this. If I didn't know how kind-hearted you are, I'd be frightened of you.'

He still lived in Rue de l'Homme-Armé because he could not bring himself to move away from the neighbourhood where Cosette lived.

At first, he stayed only a few minutes with Cosette, and then left. Gradually he got into the habit of making his visits less brief. It was as if the days growing longer gave him the authorization to do so. He arrived earlier and left later.

One day Cosette forgot herself and called him 'father'. A gleam of joy lit up Jean Valjean's dour old face.

He corrected her. 'Call me Jean.'

'Ah! true enough,' she replied with a burst of laughter. 'Monsieur Jean.'

'That's better,' he said.

And he turned away so that she would not see him wipe his eyes.

III
They Remember the Garden in Rue Plumet

That was the last time. After that glimmer, total extinction followed. No more familiarity, no more being greeted with a kiss, never again that word of such sweet intensity: 'Father!' At his own request and with his own collusion, he was driven from his every joy, one after the other. And he suffered the misery, after having lost Cosette entirely in one day, of then having to lose her all over again little by little.

The eye eventually adjusts to dingy light. In short, to see Cosette every day was enough for him. His whole life was concentrated in that one hour. He sat beside her, he gazed at her in silence, or he talked to her of years past, of her childhood, of the convent, of her young friends of that period.

One afternoon – it was one of the first days of April, already warm, still fresh, the sun's moment of great gladness, in the surrounding gardens outside Marius and Cosette's windows were the stirrings of an awakening, the hawthorn was about to blossom, an array of gillyflowers bejewelled the old walls, yawning pink snapdragons poked through cracks between the stones, there were daisies and buttercups starting to spangle the grass, white butterflies were making their first appearance of the year, the wind, that fiddler at the eternal wedding dance, was rehearsing in the trees the first notes of that great dawn symphony which the old poets called the springtide – Marius said to Cosette, 'We said we'd return to see our garden in Rue Plumet. Let's go there. We mustn't forget it.'

And they flew off like two swallows towards springtime. This garden in Rue Plumet was like a dawn to them. Already they had something behind them in life that was, as it were, the springtime of their love. The house in Rue Plumet, taken on a lease, still belonged to Cosette. They went to that garden and to that house. There they rediscovered themselves, there they forgot themselves. That evening, at the usual hour, Jean Valjean came to Rue des Filles-du-Calvaire.

'Madame went out with Monsieur and has not yet returned,' Basque told him.

He sat down in silence and waited an hour. Cosette did not return. He bowed his head and left.

Cosette was so elated with her outing to 'their garden' and so delighted to have 'spent a whole day reliving the past' that she talked of nothing else the next day. She failed to realize that she had not seen Jean Valjean.

'How did you get there?' Jean Valjean asked her.

'On foot.'

'And how did you return?'

'In a cab.'

For some time Jean Valjean had noticed the frugal life led by the young people. He was troubled by it. Marius's frugality was severe, and for Jean Valjean the full meaning of that word applied.

He ventured a question. 'Why haven't you a carriage of your own? A nice coupé would cost you only five hundred francs a month. You're wealthy.'

'I don't know,' replied Cosette.

'It's the same thing with Toussaint,' Jean Valjean went on. 'She's gone. You haven't replaced her. Why not?'

'With Nicolette, I've no need of anyone else.'

'But you ought to have a lady's maid.'

'I have Marius, don't I?'

'You ought to have a house of your own, servants of your own, a carriage, a box at the theatre. Nothing's too good for you. Why not take advantage of being wealthy? Wealth adds to happiness.'

Cosette said nothing.

Jean Valjean's visits did not get any shorter. Far from it. When the heart is on the slippery slope, there is no stopping it.

When Jean Valjean wanted to prolong his visit and for time to be forgotten, he sang Marius's praises. He declared him handsome, noble, courageous, witty, eloquent, kind-hearted. Cosette outsang him. Jean Valjean would start anew. They could go on and on. Marius. That word was inexhaustible. There were volumes in those six letters. In this way Jean Valjean contrived to stay a long while. To see Cosette, to be at her side and to forget – that was so sweet to him! It was the dressing of his wound. It happened several times that Basque came twice to say, 'Monsieur Gillenormand has sent me to remind Madame la Baronne that dinner is served.'

On those days Jean Valjean went home very thoughtful.

So was there any truth in that comparison with the chrysalis that had come to Marius's mind? Was Jean Valjean indeed a chrysalis that would persist, and come visiting its butterfly?

One day he stayed even later than usual. The next day he noticed there was no fire in the hearth. 'Well now!' he thought. 'No fire.' And he gave himself this explanation: 'It's perfectly simple. It's April. The cold weather is over.'

'Heavens! It's so cold down here!' exclaimed Cosette when she came in.

'Not at all,' said Jean Valjean.

'So was it you who told Basque not to light a fire?'

'Yes. It will very soon be May.'

'But we keep the fires going until June. Down here in the cellar you need one all year round.'

'I thought a fire was unnecessary.'

'That's just another of your ideas!' Cosette replied.

The next day there was a fire. But the two armchairs were set by the door at the far end of the room.

'What's the meaning of this?' thought Jean Valjean.

He fetched the armchairs and put them back in their usual position by the fire.

Yet he was encouraged by that relit fire. He kept their little chat going even longer than usual. As he rose to take his leave, Cosette said, 'My husband said a strange thing to me yesterday.'

'What was that?'

'He said to me, "Cosette, we have an income of thirty thousand francs. Twenty-seven that are yours, and three from my grandfather." I replied, "That makes thirty." He went on, "Would you have the heart to live on three thousand?" I replied, "Yes, on nothing. As long as it was with you." And then I asked, "Why do you ask?" He replied, "Just to know."'

Jean Valjean did not say a word. Cosette probably expected some explanation from him. He listened in dejected silence. He returned to Rue de l'Homme-Armé. He was so deeply lost in thought that he went to the wrong entrance, and instead of going into his own building he went into the building next door. It was only when he had almost reached the second floor that he noticed his mistake and went back down again.

His mind was bursting with speculation. It was plain that Marius had his doubts about the origin of those six hundred thousand francs, that he feared some contaminated source. Who knows? He might even have discovered that the money came from him, Jean Valjean; and faced with that suspect fortune, he hesitated and was loath to take it for himself, preferring to remain poor, he and Cosette, rather than be rich on dubious wealth.

Besides, Jean Valjean began vaguely to sense that he was being excluded.

The next day he experienced something of a shock on entering the downstairs room. The armchairs had disappeared. There was no chair of any kind.

'Honestly!' cried Cosette when she came in. 'No armchairs! Where on earth are the armchairs?'

'They're gone,' replied Jean Valjean.

'This is really too much!'

Jean Valjean stammered out, 'It was I who told Basque to remove them.'

'And why was that?'

'I'm staying only a few minutes today.'

'Not staying long is no reason to remain standing.'

'I think Basque needed the chairs for the drawing room.'

'Why?'

'You probably have company this evening.'

'We're not expecting anyone.'

There was nothing more Jean Valjean could say.

Cosette shrugged. 'Asking for the chairs to be removed! The other day you had the fire put out. How peculiar you are!'

'Goodbye!' murmured Jean Valjean. He did not say, 'Goodbye, Cosette.' But it was beyond him to say, 'Goodbye, madame.'

He went away, crushed. This time he had understood. The following day he did not come. Cosette did not realize until later that evening.

'Why,' she said, 'Monsieur Jean didn't come today.' And she felt a slight pang, as it were, but she was hardly aware of it, being immediately distracted by a kiss from Marius.

He did not come the day after. Cosette did not notice, she whiled away her evening and slept through the night as usual, and it occurred to her only when she awoke. She was so happy! She very quickly sent Nicolette to Monsieur Jean's house to find out if he was ill, and why he had not come the day before. Nicolette brought back Monsieur Jean's reply. He was not ill. He was busy. He would come soon. As soon as he could. In fact, he was going away on a short trip. Madame would remember, he was in the habit of going away from time to time. There was no need to worry. They need not be concerned about him.

On being admitted to Monsieur Jean's house, Nicolette had

repeated to him her mistress's exact words. That Madame had sent her to find out why Monsieur Jean had not come the day before.

'I haven't been for two days,' Jean Valjean said softly.

But his remark made no impression on Nicolette, who said nothing about it to Cosette.

IV
Attraction and Extinction

During the last months of spring and the first months of summer 1833, the occasional passer-by in the Marais, shopkeepers, people idling at their doorways, noticed an old man, neatly dressed in black, who every day at the same time, towards nightfall, emerged from Rue de l'Homme-Armé, on the Rue Ste-Croix-de-la-Bretonnerie side, walked past Blancs-Manteaux up to Rue Culture-Ste-Catherine, and at Rue de l'Écharpe turned left into Rue St-Louis.

There he would walk slowly, seeing nothing, hearing nothing, his head straining forward, his eyes fixed undeviatingly on a point, always the same, that seemed for him starry and was none other than the corner of Rue des Filles-du-Calvaire. The nearer he got to that street corner the more his eyes brightened. A kind of joy lit up his gaze like an inner dawn, he had a spellbound look of fondness, his lips moved slightly as if he were talking to someone he could not see, he smiled vaguely, and advanced as slowly as possible. It was as though, while wanting to get there, he was afraid of the moment when he would be very close to his destination. When there were only a few houses between him and the street that seemed to be attracting him, his pace slowed to the point that at times an observer might have thought he was not advancing at all. The shaking of his head and the fixity of his gaze brought to mind the magnetic needle seeking the pole. However long he managed to protract his arrival, arrive he must. He would come to Rue des Filles-du-Calvaire. Then he would stop. He would tremble. With a doleful timidity he would crane his head around the corner of the last house. And he would gaze into that street. And there was in that tragic gaze something that resembled the dazzling brilliance of the impossible and the reflection of an inaccessible paradise. Then a tear that had slowly gathered in the corner of his eye and grown large enough to fall would trickle down his cheek, sometimes stopping at his mouth. The old man tasted its bitterness. So he would remain for several minutes, as if made of stone. Then he would go home by the same route, at the same pace, the light fading from his eyes as he moved away.

Little by little, the old man ceased to go as far as the corner of Rue des Filles-du-Calvaire. He would stop halfway, in Rue St-Louis, sometimes a little further off, sometimes a little closer. One day he stopped at the corner of Rue Culture-Ste-Catherine and looked towards Rue des Filles-du-Calvaire from a distance. Then he silently shook his head, as if denying himself something, and he turned back.

Soon he no longer came even as far as Rue St-Louis. He would arrive at Rue Pavée, shake his head and turn back. Then, he no longer went beyond Rue des Trois-Pavillons. Then, no further than Blancs-Manteaux. He was like the pendulum of a clock that does not get wound, its arc shortening until it stops altogether.

Every day he emerged from his house at the same time, he would set off on the same expedition, but he no longer completed it, and it was perhaps unawares that he kept curtailing it. His whole face expressed this one notion: what's the use? His gaze was dull, no brightness now. The tear, too, was gone; it no longer gathered in the corner of his eye. Those contemplative eyes were dry. The old man's head still strained forward. His chin wobbled occasionally. The folds in his gaunt neck were pitiful. Sometimes, when the weather was bad, he carried an umbrella under his arm, which he did not open. The local women said, 'He's simple-minded.' Children would follow after him, laughing.

BOOK NINE
ULTIMATE DARKNESS,
ULTIMATE DAWN

I
Pity the Unhappy, but Make
Allowances for the Happy

It is a terrible thing to be happy! How it satisfies those who are! How they regard it as enough in itself! How, having attained the false purpose of life, happiness, they forget the true purpose, duty!

Let us say, however, that we would be wrong to blame Marius.

Before his marriage, as we have explained, Marius had asked Monsieur Fauchelevent no questions, and since his marriage he had been afraid to ask Jean Valjean any. He regretted the promise he had let himself be drawn into making. He had told himself time and again that he had been wrong to make that concession to despair. He had contented himself with keeping Jean Valjean away from his house little by little, and causing him to fade as much as possible from Cosette's mind. Somehow he always put himself between Cosette and Jean Valjean, feeling confident that if she did not see him she would not think of him. It was more than just a fading-away, it was an eclipse.

Marius did what he judged to be necessary and right. He thought he had serious reasons, which we have already seen, and others that will become apparent later, for getting rid of Jean Valjean, without harshness, but without weakness either. Chance having brought him into contact with a former employee of the Laffitte banking house during a trial in which he acted as advocate, he had, without searching it out, come by some mysterious information, which in fact he had not been able to investigate out of respect for that very secret he had promised to keep, and out of consideration for Jean Valjean's perilous position. Right then, he believed he had a solemn duty to fulfil: the restitution of those six hundred thousand francs to someone he was searching for with the utmost discretion. In the meantime, he refrained from touching that money.

As for Cosette, she was not party to any of these secrets; but it would be harsh to condemn her either.

Marius exercised an overpowering magnetism over her, which caused her, instinctively and almost automatically, to do what he wanted. Sensing Marius's will with regard to 'Monsieur Jean', she conformed to it. Her husband did not need to say anything to her, she yielded to the undefined but clear pressure of his unspoken intentions, and obeyed blindly. Her obedience in this instance consisted in not remembering what Marius forgot. She did not have to make any effort to do this. Without herself knowing why, and without there being any blame attached to it, her soul had become so much her husband's that what was steeped in shadow in Marius's mind became obscured in hers.

Let us not go too far, however. As regards Jean Valjean, this forgetting about him and letting him fade from her mind were merely superficial. She was being thoughtless rather than forgetful. Essentially, she loved the man she had for so long called her father. But she loved her husband even more. This is what had upset somewhat the balance of her heart, now favouring one side only.

Cosette would sometimes speak of Jean Valjean, and wonder. Then Marius would allay her worries. 'I think he's away. Didn't he say he was going on a trip?'

'That's true,' thought Cosette. He was in the habit of disappearing like this. But not for so long.

Two or three times she sent Nicolette to Rue de l'Homme-Armé to find out whether Monsieur Jean had returned from his journey. Jean Valjean sent back the answer no.

Cosette enquired no further, needing only one thing on earth, Marius. Let us say also that Cosette and Marius too had been away. They had been to Vernon. Marius had taken Cosette to his father's grave.

Marius had gradually withdrawn Cosette from Jean Valjean. Cosette had not resisted.

Besides, what in certain cases is far too harshly called the ingratitude of children is not always something as reprehensible as people believe. It is the ingratitude of nature. Nature, as we have said elsewhere, 'looks ahead'. Nature divides the living into those arriving and those departing. Those departing are turned towards the shadow, those arriving towards the light. Hence, a divergence that for the old is inevitable, and for the young unintentional. This divergence, at first imperceptible, slowly increases, like all separations into branches. Without becoming detached from the trunk, those branches grow away from it. It is not their fault. Youth goes where there is gladness, towards rejoicings, bright lights, love. Old age is directed towards the end. They do not lose sight of each other but they are no longer bound together. Young people feel the chill of life, old people, that of the tomb. Let us not blame these poor children.

II
Last Flickerings of the Lamp without Oil

One day Jean Valjean descended the stairs, went a few steps down the street, sat on a boundary-post, the very same one on which Gavroche had found him lost in thought on the night between the fifth and sixth of June. He remained there a few minutes, then went back up again. That was the last swing of the pendulum. The next day he did not go out of the house. The day after that, he did not get out of bed.

His doorkeeper, who prepared his frugal meals, a little cabbage or a few potatoes with a bit of bacon fat, glanced at the brown earthenware plate and exclaimed, 'But my poor dear man, you didn't eat yesterday!'

'I certainly did,' replied Jean Valjean.

'The plate's untouched.'

'Look at the water jug. It's empty.'

'That proves you drank, it doesn't prove you've eaten.'

'Well,' said Jean Valjean, 'perhaps I was hungry only for water?'

'That's called thirst, and not eating at the same time is called fever.'

'I'll eat tomorrow.'

'Or on St Never's Day. Why not today? Would any reasonable person say, "I'll eat tomorrow"! Fancy leaving the whole plateful without even touching it! And my vitelotte potatoes were so good!'

Jean Valjean took the old woman's hand. 'I promise I'll eat them,' he said in his kindly voice.

'I'm cross with you,' replied the doorkeeper.

Jean Valjean saw hardly any other human being apart from this good woman. There are streets in Paris that no one ever comes along and houses that no one ever visits. He lived in one of those streets and in one of those houses.

In the days when he was still going out he bought from an ironmonger, for just a few sous, a little copper crucifix that he hung on a nail opposite his bed. That gibbet is one that is ever good to behold.

A week went by without Jean Valjean taking so much as a single step in his room. He stayed in bed the whole time.

The doorkeeper said to her husband, 'The old man upstairs isn't getting up any more, he's not eating, he won't last long. That's a case of heartache, that is. No one's going to convince me that his daughter hasn't made a bad marriage.'

Her husband replied, with the ring of marital supremacy in his voice, 'If he's rich, let him see a doctor. If he's not rich, let him go without. If he doesn't see a doctor, he'll die.'

'And if he does see one?'

'He'll die,' said her husband.

The doorkeeper began scratching with an old knife at the weeds growing out of what she called her 'pavement', and as she pulled out the weeds she muttered, 'It's a shame. Such a decent old man! He's as white as a sheet.'

She caught sight of a local doctor going past the end of the street. She took it upon herself to ask him to go upstairs.

'It's on the second floor,' she said. 'You can just walk in. Since the old man doesn't stir from his bed any more, the key's always left in the door.'

The doctor saw Jean Valjean and spoke to him.

When he came downstairs again the doorkeeper questioned him. 'Well, doctor?'

'The poor fellow is very poorly indeed.'

'What's the matter with him?'

'Everything and nothing. He's a man who in all probability has lost a loved one. People die of that.'

'What did he say to you?'

'He told me he was fine.'

'Will you be coming back, doctor?'

'Yes,' replied the doctor. 'But it's another, not I, who had better come back.'

III
A Quill Pen Feels Heavy to the Man Who Lifted Fauchelevent's Cart

One evening Jean Valjean had difficulty raising himself on his elbow. He felt his wrist and could not find his pulse. His breathing was shallow, and now and then stopped. He realized he was weaker than he had ever been. Then, no doubt under the pressure of some preoccupation of paramount importance, he made an effort, sat up, and dressed. He put on his old workman's jacket. Now that he did not go out any more, he had reverted to it and preferred it. He had to pause many times while dressing. Just getting his arms into the sleeves of his jacket left him with sweat trickling from his brow.

Since being on his own he had moved his bed into the antechamber so as to inhabit as little as possible of that deserted apartment.

He opened the case and unpacked Cosette's outfit. He laid it on his bed.

The bishop's candlesticks were in place on the mantelpiece. He took out of a drawer two wax candles and put them in the candlesticks. Then, although it was still broad daylight – it was summer – he lit them. You sometimes see candles lit in broad daylight like that, in rooms where the dead lie.

Every step he took, moving from one piece of furniture to another, tired him, and he had to sit down. This was not ordinary weariness that consumes energy in order to renew it. These were the last of all possible movements, these were the final drops of exhausted life squeezed out in debilitating efforts that will never be renewed.

The chair into which he sank was placed in front of that mirror, so disastrous for him, so providential for Marius, in which he had read on the blotter Cosette's reversed handwriting. He saw himself in this mirror, and did not recognize himself. He was eighty years old. Before Marius's marriage he would have passed for scarcely fifty. The last year had counted for thirty. What he bore on his forehead was no longer the wrinkling of old age, it was the mysterious mark of death. The gouging of that pitiless fingernail could be sensed there. His cheeks sagged. The skin on his face was of a colour to suggest that earth was already upon it. Both corners of his mouth drooped, as in that mask the ancients used to sculpt on tombs. He stared into space with an air of reproach. He looked like one of those great tragic beings who have been wronged by someone.

He was in that state – the last phase of despondency – in which sorrow no longer flows freely. It is, as it were, coagulated. There is a sort of clot of despair in the soul.

Darkness had fallen. Laboriously, he dragged a table and the old armchair over to the fireside, and placed on the table a pen, some ink and some paper.

That done, he fainted. When he regained consciousness, he felt thirsty. Unable to lift the jug, he tilted it with difficulty towards his mouth, and took a gulp.

Then he turned towards the bed, and still seated – for he could not remain standing – he gazed at the little mourning dress and at all those cherished objects. Such contemplations last for hours that seem like minutes. Suddenly he shivered, felt the chill gaining on him. He rested his elbows on the table lit by the bishop's candles, and picked up the pen.

As neither pen nor ink had been used for a long time, the nib was curled over, the ink had dried. He had to get up and put a few drops of water into the ink, which he could not manage without stopping and sitting down two or three times; and he had to write with the back of the pen. From time to time he wiped his brow.

His hand shook. Slowly, he wrote these few lines:

Cosette, I give you my blessing. I'm going to explain. Your husband was right to make me realize that I ought to stay away, although he is a little mistaken in what he believed, but he was right. He is a good man. Always love him dearly after I am dead. Monsieur Pontmercy, always love my darling child. Cosette, someone will find this note, this is what I want to tell you, you will see from the figures, if I have the strength to remember them, listen carefully, that money is rightfully yours. To explain everything: white jet comes from Norway, black jet comes from England, black glass jewellery comes from Germany. Jet is lighter, more precious, more costly. We can make imitation jet in France as in Germany. What is needed is a little anvil two inches square, and a spirit lamp to soften the wax. The wax used to be made with resin and lampblack, and cost four francs a pound. I thought of making it with shellac and turpentine. It costs no more than thirty sous, and is much better. Earrings are made out of violet glass glued with this wax to a little black iron mounting. The glass must be violet for iron-mounted jewellery, and black for gold-mounted jewellery. Spain buys a great deal of it. It is the country of jet—

Here he broke off, the pen fell from his fingers, he was overcome by one of those desperate sobs that at times welled up from the depths of his being; the poor man held his head in both hands, and pondered.

'Oh!' he cried within himself – pitiful cries, heard by God alone. 'It's all over! I'll never see her again. She was for me a passing smile. I'm going into the dark without even another glimpse of her. Oh, for one minute, for one moment, to hear her voice, to touch her dress, to see her, the angel, and then to die! It's nothing to die, what's dreadful is to die without seeing her. If she were to smile at me, if she were to say something to me! Would that do anybody any harm? No, it's over now, that can never be. I'm all alone. My God! My God! I shall never see her again!'

At that moment there was a knock at the door.

IV
The Bottle of Stain-removing Ink

That same day, or to be more precise that same evening, when, after leaving the table, Marius had just retired to his study with a brief to read through, Basque handed him a letter, saying, 'The person who wrote the letter is in the antechamber.'

Cosette had taken his grandfather's arm for a turn around the garden.

A letter, like a man, may have an unprepossessing appearance. Rough paper, crudely folded, the mere sight of certain missives is offensive. The letter that Basque had brought was one of this kind.

Marius took it. It smelled of tobacco. Nothing evokes a memory like a smell. Marius recognized that tobacco. He looked at the address: 'To Monsieur, Monsieur le Baron Pommerci. At home.' Recognizing the tobacco helped him to recognize the handwriting. Astonishment might be said to strike like a thunderbolt. Marius was, as it were, illuminated by one such thunderbolt.

The sense of smell, that mysterious aid to memory, had just revived in him a whole world. It was the same paper, the same way of folding it, the same pallid ink, the same familiar handwriting – above all, it was the same tobacco. The Jondrette garret loomed in his mind.

So, by a strange quirk of fate, one of the two trails he had so avidly sought, the one that only recently he had made such efforts to find and believed was lost for ever, now turned up and presented itself to him of its own accord.

He eagerly unsealed the letter, and read:

Monsieur le Baron,

If the Supreme Being had given me the talent, I might have been baron Thénard, member of the Institute (academy of scienses), but I am not that man. I merely bear his name, happily, if this remembrince recommends me to your excellent munifissince. The asisstance with which you favour me will be ricipricated. I am in posession of a secret conserning an indi-videwal. This individewal conserns you. I hold the secret at your disposal with the desyre that I may have the onor of being useful to you. I will give you the simple means of ridding your onorable family of that individewal who has no entitelment to be associated with it, madame la baronne being of noble birth. The sanctewery of virtue could not cohabit with crime any longer without abdicating.

I await the orders of monsieur le baron in the antichamber.

With respect.

The letter was signed 'THÉNARD'. It was not a false signature. It was merely a little abbreviated.

And the whole rigmarole and the spelling were conclusive in revealing the man's identity. The certificate of origin was complete. There could be absolutely no doubt.

Marius's feelings were intense. After his initial surprise, he felt a thrill of happiness. Now, if only he were to find the other man he was looking for, the man who had saved him, he would have everything he could wish for.

He opened a drawer in his desk, took out several banknotes, put them in his pocket, closed the desk again, and rang for Basque, who opened the door.

'Show the man in,' said Marius.

Basque announced, 'Monsieur Thénard.'

A man entered the room. Yet another surprise for Marius. The man who entered was totally unfamiliar to him.

This man, an old man moreover, had a big nose, a cravat up to his chin, with green spectacles plus a green taffeta eyeshade. His hair was grey, smoothed and plastered down on his forehead and skimming his eyebrows, like the wigs of English high society's coachmen. He was dressed in black from head to foot, a very threadbare black, but clean. A bunch of watch-charms emerging from his fob-pocket suggested a watch inside it. He held an old hat in his hand. He walked with a stoop, and the curve of his back increased with the deepness of his bow.

The first thing that struck the eye was that this individual's coat, although carefully buttoned up, was too loose, and seemed not to have been made for him.

Here a short digression is necessary. There was in Paris at that time, in a disreputable old building in Rue Beautreillis near the Arsenal, a canny Jewish fellow who made a trade out of changing scoundrels into honest men. Not for too long – that might have inconvenienced the scoundrels. The change was in appearance, for a day or two, at the rate of thirty sous a day, by means of a costume that had as far as possible a look of commonplace honesty about it. This hirer-out of costumes was called the Changer. Parisian rogues had given him this name and knew him by no other. He had quite a comprehensive wardrobe. The cast-offs in which he rigged people out were just about passable. He had specialities and categories. On every nail in his shop hung a social station, worn and crumpled. Here, a magistrate's garb; there, that of a clergyman; there, a banker's; in one corner the garb of a retired military man, in another that of a man of letters, and over there, the garb of a statesman. This individual was the costumier of the immense drama staged in Paris by skulduggery. His den was the wings from which theft emerged and into which swindle stepped back again. A ragged rascal would come to this dressing room, pay thirty sous and select the appropriate outfit, depending on the role he wished to play that day; and on going back downstairs that rascal was a somebody. The next day the clothes were faithfully returned, and the Changer, who entrusted everything to those thieves, was never robbed. The clothes had one drawback: they 'weren't quite right'. Not having been made for those who wore them, they were tight on this one, loose on that one, and a good fit for no one. Any crook who was bigger or smaller than the human average was uncomfortable in the Changer's costumes. You had to be neither too fat nor too thin. The Changer provided only for the ordinary man. He had taken as the measure for the entire species the physique of the average rascal who is neither stout nor slight, neither tall nor short. Hence the sometimes difficult accommodations whereby the Changer's clients had to make the best of it. Too bad for any exceptions to the norm! The statesman's coat, for instance, black from top to bottom and therefore respectable, would have been too big for Pitt and too small for Castelcicala. The 'statesman's outfit' was described in the Changer's catalogue, from which we copy, as follows: 'A coat of black cloth, trousers of thick black wool, silk waistcoat, boots and linen'. In the margin was written 'Former ambassador', and a note that we also transcribe: 'In a separate box, a tidily curled wig, green spectacles, watch-charms, and two little quill tips, an inch long, wrapped in cotton'. All this belonged to the statesman, former ambassador. This whole costume was, if the expression may be allowed, on its last legs. The stitching was turning white, a kind of buttonhole was opening up on one of the elbows. Furthermore, one of the coat's breast buttons was missing. But that is a mere trifle. The statesman's hand, having always to be kept inside his coat and over his heart, served to conceal the missing button.

If Marius had been familiar with the arcane institutions of Paris, he would instantly have recognized, on the back of the visitor whom Basque had just ushered in, the statesman's outfit borrowed from the Changer's hand-me-downs stock.

Marius's disappointment on seeing a man other than the one he was expecting to enter the room turned to disfavour towards the newcomer. While this individual bowed exaggeratedly, Marius looked him over from head to toe and asked him curtly, 'What do you want?'

The man replied with a gracious rictus suggestive of a crocodile's affectionate smile, 'I cannot believe that I haven't already had the honour of seeing monsieur le baron in society. Indeed, I think I did meet him personally, several years ago, at the house of Madame la Princesse Bagration and at the receptions of his Lordship the Vicomte Dambray, peer of France.'

It is always a good tactic in double-dealing to pretend to recognize someone you do not know. Marius was alert to the way this man spoke. He paid close attention to his accent and behaviour, but his disappointment increased. This was a nasal delivery, totally different from the harsh, dry sound he expected. He was completely baffled.

'I'm not acquainted with Madame Bagration, or with Monsieur Dambray,' he said. 'I've never in my life set foot in the home of either.'

This was a brusque reply. Nonetheless gracious, the visitor persisted.

'Then it must have been at Chateaubriand's that I saw monsieur! I know Chateaubriand well. He's most amiable. He sometimes says to me, "Thénard, my friend, won't you drink a glass with me?"'

Marius's expression grew more and more severe. 'I've never had the honour of being received by Monsieur de Chateaubriand. Let's be brief. What do you want?'

At this harsher tone, the man bowed lower. 'Monsieur le baron, deign to listen to me. There is in America, somewhere near Panama, a village called La Joya. That village consists of a single house, a large, square, three-storeyed house of sun-baked brick, each side of the square five hundred foot long, each storey set twelve foot back on the storey below so as to leave in front of it a terrace going all round the building, an inside courtyard in the centre where provisions and munitions are kept, no windows but loopholes, no doors but ladders, ladders to get up from the ground floor to the first terrace, and from the first to the second, and from the second to the third, ladders to get down into the inside courtyard, no doors to the rooms but hatchways, no staircases to the rooms but ladders. Come evening, the hatchways are closed, the ladders are withdrawn, carbines and blunderbusses are aimed out of the loopholes. No way of getting inside. A house by day, a fortress by night, eight hundred inhabitants. That's the village. Why so many precautions? Because it's a dangerous place. It's full of cannibals. So why does anyone go there? Because it's a wonderful place: that's where you find gold.'

'What's all this leading up to?' cut in Marius, whose disappointment was giving way to impatience.

'To this, monsieur le baron. I'm a weary former diplomat. The old civilization's worn me out. I want to give the savages a try.'

'So?'

'Monsieur le baron, egoism is the way of the world. The landless peasant woman who works as a day labourer looks up when the carriage goes by, the landowning peasant woman working her own field does not. The poor man's dog barks at the rich man, the rich man's dog barks at the poor man. Every individual for himself. Self-interest, that's the object of mankind. Gold, that's the lodestone.'

'So? Come to the point.'

'I'd like to go and settle in La Joya. There are three of us. I have my wife and my daughter, who's a very beautiful young girl. The journey's long and costly. I need a little money.'

'What has any of this to do with me?' asked Marius.

The stranger stretched his neck out from his cravat, a gesture characteristic of the vulture, and replied with twice as much smiling, 'Monsieur le baron hasn't read my letter?'

This was more or less the truth. The fact is, the contents of the missive had made little impression on Marius. He had seen the writing more than read the letter. He could barely remember anything of it. A moment ago he had been given another hint. He had noted that detail: 'my wife and my daughter'. He fixed a penetrating gaze on the stranger. An examining magistrate could not have eyed him better. He watched him, almost warily. Marius confined himself to replying, 'Be specific.'

The stranger put both hands in his two fob-pockets, raised his head without straightening his backbone, but with the green gaze of his spectacles scrutinizing Marius in return.

'Very well, monsieur le baron. I'll be specific. I've a secret to sell you.'

'A secret?'

'A secret.'

'That concerns me?'

'Indeed.'

'What is this secret?'

As he listened, Marius studied the man ever more closely.

'I begin gratis,' said the stranger. 'You'll see that I'm of interest.'

'Speak.'

'Monsieur le baron, you have in your house a thief and an assassin.'

Marius shuddered.

'In my house? No,' he said.

The stranger brushed his hat with his elbow and went on, unperturbed. 'An assassin and a thief. Mark you, monsieur le baron, I'm not talking about ancient, bygone, non-actionable deeds, which can be erased in the eyes of the law by statute of limitations and in the eyes of God by repentance. I'm talking about recent deeds, actionable deeds, deeds even now unknown to justice. I continue. This man's insinuated himself into your confidence, and almost into your family, under a false name. I'm going to tell you his real name. And tell it to you for nothing.'

'I'm listening.'

'His name's Jean Valjean.'

'I know.'

'I'm going to tell you, this too for nothing, who he is.'

'Speak.'

'He's an ex-convict.'

'I know.'

'You've known ever since I've had the honour of telling you.'

'No. I knew before.'

Marius's coldness of tone, that twofold reply 'I know', his terseness, inimical to dialogue, stirred some smouldering anger in the stranger. He shot a furtive and furious glance at Marius that was instantly quenched. Rapid as it was, that glance was of a kind that, once seen, is recognized. It did not escape Marius. Certain fierinesses can emanate only from certain souls; they blaze in the eye, that window on the mind – spectacles hide nothing, you might as well glass over hell!

The stranger went on, smiling, 'I will not take the liberty of contradicting monsieur le baron. In any case, you must see, I'm well informed. Now what I have to tell you is known to myself alone. It concerns the fortune of madame la baronne. It's an extraordinary secret. It's for sale. It's to you I'm offering it first. Cheap at the price. Twenty thousand francs.'

'I know that secret just as I know the others,' said Marius.

The individual felt the need to lower his price a little. 'Monsieur le baron, make it ten thousand, and I'll talk.'

'I repeat, there's nothing I can learn from you. I know what you want to tell me.'

There was a fresh gleam in the man's eye. He exclaimed, 'But I really must eat today. It's an extraordinary secret, I tell you. Monsieur le baron, I'll talk. I'm ready to talk. Give me twenty francs.'

Marius gazed at him intently. 'I know your extraordinary secret, just as I knew Jean Valjean's name, just as I know your name.'

'My name?'

'Yes.'

'That's not difficult, monsieur le baron. I had the honour of writing it down for you and of telling you. Thénard.'

'Dier.'

'Huh?'

'Thénardier.'

'Who?'

When in danger, the porcupine bristles, the beetle feigns death, the Old Guard forms a square. This man burst out laughing. Then he flicked a speck of dust off the sleeve of his coat.

Marius continued. 'You're also the workman Jondrette, the actor Fabantou, the poet Genflot, the Spaniard Don Alvarez and Balizard's wife.'

'Whose wife?'

'And you used to keep an inn at Montfermeil.'

'An inn! Never.'

'And I tell you that you are Thénardier.'

'I deny it.'

'And that you're a villain. Here.' And drawing a banknote from his pocket, Marius flung it in his face.

'Thank you! Forgive me! Five hundred francs! Monsieur le baron!' And grabbing the banknote, the man examined it, overwhelmed, bowing.

'Five hundred francs!' he repeated in astonishment. And he muttered to himself, 'Serious lucre!'

Then suddenly, 'Very well, then!' he exclaimed. 'Let's make ourselves comfortable.'

And with the deftness of a monkey, tossing back his hair, tearing off his spectacles and removing from his nose and conjuring out of sight the two quill tips mentioned above, which were also encountered on an earlier page in this book, he took off his face as a man takes off his hat.

His eyes glinted. His brow was revealed, uneven, furrowed, with bulges in some places and hideously wrinkled at the top; and his nose again became as sharp as a beak. The shrewd and ferocious profile of the man of prey reappeared.

'Monsieur le baron is unerring,' he said in a clear voice from which all nasal sound had disappeared, 'I am Thénardier.'

And he straightened his stooped back.

Thénardier, for he it was, was strangely surprised. He would have been disconcerted had he been capable of it. He had come to cause astonishment and it was he who was made to feel it. He had been paid five hundred francs for this humiliation, and all things considered he accepted it, but he was nonetheless astounded.

Here he was, seeing this Baron Pontmercy for the first time, and despite his disguise this Baron Pontmercy recognized him, and recognized him thoroughly. And not only did this baron know all about

Thénardier, but he seemed to know all about Jean Valjean. Who was this almost beardless young man, so cold and so generous, who knew people's names, all their names, and opened his purse to them, who dealt with crooks like a judge and who paid them like a fool?

Thénardier, remember, despite having been Marius's next-door neighbour, had never seen him, as often happens in Paris. He had at one time vaguely heard his daughters talking about a very poor young man named Marius who lived in the same house. He had written him that letter we know of, without having met him. There was no possible connection in his mind between that Marius and Monsieur le Baron Pontmercy.

As for the name Pontmercy, remember that on the battlefield of Waterloo he heard only the last two syllables, for which he had always felt the legitimate scorn due to what is a mere expression of thanks.

On the other hand, through his daughter Azelma, whom he had sent to track down the couple who were married on the sixteenth of February, and through his own personal delvings, he had managed to find out a great many things, and he had succeeded in unearthing from the shadows more than one mysterious lead. He had through industrious effort discovered, or at least through a process of intuitive reasoning guessed, who the man was that he had encountered one particular day in the Great Sewer. From the man, he had easily arrived at the name. He knew that Madame la Baronne Pontmercy was Cosette. But in that respect he intended to be discreet. Who was Cosette? He did not know, exactly. He certainly harboured some suspicion of illegitimacy, Fantine's story had always seemed dubious to him. But what was the good of mentioning that? To be paid for his silence? He had, or thought he had, something better than that to sell. And to come to Baron Pontmercy and without any proof to deliver this revelation, 'Your wife is a bastard', would in all likelihood have succeeded only in bringing the husband's boot to meet the revealer's backside.

To Thénardier's way of thinking, the conversation with Marius had not yet begun. He had to retreat, alter his strategy, abandon his position, open up a new front. But nothing essential had as yet been compromised, and he had five hundred francs in his pocket. Moreover, he had something crucial to say, and even against this very well informed and very well armed Baron Pontmercy he felt strong. For men like Thénardier, every dialogue is a battle. In the one that was about to begin, how did he stand? He did not know who he was talking to, but he did know what he was talking about. He rapidly made this inward assessment of his strength, and having said, 'I am Thénardier', he waited.

Marius was left pensive. At last, then, he had got hold of Thénardier. Here was the man he had so much wanted to find. He was now going to be able to honour Colonel Pontmercy's request. He was mortified that this hero should be indebted in any way to this ruffian, and that payment on the letter of credit drawn on him, Marius, by his father from the depths of the grave should not have been made before now. It also seemed to him, in his complex state of mind with regard to Thénardier, that there was a case for avenging the colonel for the misfortune of having been saved by such a villain. Be that as it may, he was content. He was finally going to redeem the colonel's shade from this unworthy creditor, and it seemed to him that he was going to rescue his father's memory from the debtors' prison.

Alongside this duty he had another: to elucidate, if possible, the source of Cosette's fortune. The opportunity seemed to present itself. Perhaps Thénardier knew something. It might be useful to sound the man out. This was his starting-point.

Thénardier had hidden away the 'serious lucre' in his fob-pocket, and was gazing at Marius with an almost affectionate meekness. Marius broke the silence.

'Thénardier, I've told you your name. Now your secret, the knowledge you came to impart – shall I tell you what it is? I have my own sources of information. You'll see, I know more about it than you do. Jean Valjean, as you said, is a murderer and a thief. A thief, because he robbed a wealthy manufacturer, Monsieur Madeleine, and brought about his ruin. A murderer, because he murdered the police officer Javert.'

'I don't understand, monsieur le baron,' said Thénardier.

'I shall explain. Around 1822, in a district of the Pas de Calais, there was a man who'd had some kind of brush with the law in the past, and who under the name of Monsieur Madeleine had overcome that and rehabilitated himself. This individual became a good man in the full sense of the term. By means of industry, the manufacture of black glass beads, he made the fortune of an entire town. As for his personal fortune, he made that too, but incidentally and to some degree unintentionally. He was a foster-father to the poor. He founded hospitals, opened schools, visited the sick, provided young girls with dowries, supported widows, adopted orphans. He was, as it were, the protector of the region. He refused the cross of the Legion of Honour, he was appointed mayor. A freed convict knew the secret of some sentence this man had once served. He denounced him and had him arrested, and took advantage of this arrest to come to Paris and, using a false signature, to have the Laffitte banking house – I have it from the cashier himself – hand over to him the sum of more than half a million francs that belonged to Monsieur Madeleine. This ex-convict who robbed Monsieur Madeleine was Jean Valjean. As for the other crime, you can't tell me anything about that, either, that I don't already know. Jean Valjean killed the policeman Javert. He shot him with a pistol. I, who am speaking to you now, was there at the time.'

Thénardier gave Marius the lordly look of a defeated man who once more has victory in his grasp, and who has just regained in a moment all the ground he had lost. But the smile returned instantly. In triumph over his superior the inferior must cajole. Thénardier contented himself with saying to Marius, 'Monsieur le baron, we're on the wrong track.'

And he emphasized this statement with an expressive whirl of his watch-charms.

'What!' Marius retorted. 'You dispute this? These are facts.'

'They're fantasies. I'm obliged by the favour of monsieur le baron's confidence to tell him so. Above all, truth and justice. I don't like to see people unjustly accused. Monsieur le baron, Jean Valjean did not rob Monsieur Madeleine and Jean Valjean did not kill Javert.'

'Oh indeed! And how can you be so sure?'

'For two reasons.'

'Which reasons? Explain.'

'Here's the first: he did not rob Monsieur Madeleine seeing as Jean Valjean is himself Monsieur Madeleine.'

'What story's this you're telling me?'

'And here's the second: he did not murder Javert seeing as the person who killed Javert was Javert.'

'What do you mean?'

'Javert committed suicide.'

'Prove it! Prove it!' cried Marius, beside himself.

Scanning his sentence as if it were a classic alexandrine line, Thénardier replied, 'Po-lice-officer-Ja-vert-was-found-drowned-under-a-boat-at-the-Pont-au-Change.'

'But go on, prove it!'

Thénardier drew from his pocket a large grey envelope that appeared to contain folded sheets of different sizes.

'I have my records,' he said calmly.

And he added, 'Monsieur le baron, in your interests I wanted to acquire a thorough knowledge of Jean Valjean. I say that Jean Valjean and Monsieur Madeleine are one and the same man, and I say that Javert had no other murderer than Javert, and when I speak, it is because I have evidence. Not handwritten evidence – handwriting is suspect, handwriting is adaptable – but printed evidence.'

As he spoke, Thénardier extracted from the envelope two newspapers, yellowed, faded, and smelling strongly of tobacco. One of these two newspapers, coming apart at every fold and falling away in squares, seemed much older than the other.

'Two facts, two pieces of evidence,' said Thénardier. And he held out to Marius the two unfolded newspapers.

These two newspapers are known to the reader. The older one, a copy of *Le Drapeau Blanc* of the twenty-fifth of July 1823, the text of which we saw on page 328 of this book, identified Monsieur Madeleine as Jean Valjean. The other, *Le Moniteur* of the fifteenth of June 1832, announced the suicide of Javert, adding that it appeared from an oral report Javert had made to the chief of police that, having been taken prisoner inside the Rue de la Chanvrerie barricade, he owed his life to an insurgent who held him at his mercy and instead of blowing his brains out had fired his pistol into the air.

Marius read. Here was evidence, of certain date, irrefutable proof – these two newspapers had not been printed for the express purpose of backing up Thénardier's assertions. The report published in *Le Moniteur* was an official statement issued by police headquarters. Marius could entertain no doubts. The bank clerk's information was wrong, and he himself had been mistaken. Jean Valjean, his stature suddenly enhanced, was emerging from darkness.

Marius could not hold back a cry of joy. 'Well then, this poor wretch is a man to be admired! All that wealth was truly his! He is Madeleine, the salvation of a whole region! He is Jean Valjean, Javert's saviour! He's a hero! He's a saint!'

'He's no saint and he's no hero!' said Thénardier. 'He's a murderer and a thief.' And he added in the tone of a man beginning to feel he has some authority, 'Let's not get excited.'

Thief, murderer, these words that Marius thought had been dispelled, here they were again, dousing him like an ice-cold shower.

'Still!' he said.

'Just the same,' said Thénardier. 'Jean Valjean didn't rob Madeleine, but he's a thief. He didn't kill Javert, but he's a murderer.'

'Are you talking,' said Marius, 'about that paltry theft of forty years ago, expiated, as your newspapers themselves say, by a whole lifetime's repentance, self-sacrifice and virtue?'

'I say murder and theft, monsieur le baron, and I repeat that I'm talking about actual facts. What I have to reveal to you is absolutely unknown.

This is new information. And perhaps you'll find in it the source of that wealth so cunningly offered to madame la baronne by Jean Valjean. I say cunningly because to worm your way, with a gift of this kind, into a respectable household whose comforts you'll then share, and at one stroke to conceal your crime, enjoy the benefits of your thievery, cover up your name and create a family for yourself – that would take some doing.'

'I could interrupt you there,' Marius remarked, 'but go on.'

'Monsieur le baron, I'm going to tell you all, leaving the recompense to your generosity. This secret is worth solid gold. You'll say to me, "Why didn't you go to Jean Valjean?" For a very simple reason. I know he's divested himself, and divested himself in your favour, and I think it's an ingenious device. But now he hasn't got a sou to his name, he'd show me his empty hands, and since I need money for my journey to La Joya, I prefer you, who've got everything, to him, who's got nothing. I'm a bit tired, allow me to take a seat.'

Marius sat down and motioned him to sit down too.

Thénardier settled himself on an upholstered chair, picked up the two newspapers, thrust them back into their envelope, and tapping on *Le Drapeau Blanc* with his fingernail murmured, 'This one was difficult to get hold of.' With that, he crossed his legs and leaned back, an attitude characteristic of people who are sure of what they are saying; then, solemnly dwelling on his words, he began: 'Monsieur le baron, about a year ago, on the sixth of June 1832, the day of the riot, a man was in Paris's Great Sewer, where the drain comes down to the Seine, between the Pont des Invalides and the Pont d'Iéna.'

Marius suddenly pulled his chair closer to Thénardier's. Thénardier noticed this movement, and continued with the deliberation of an orator who holds his audience's attention and senses his adversary trembling at his words: 'Forced into hiding – for reasons that've got nothing to do with politics, as it happens – this man had taken up residence in the sewer and had a key to it. It was, I repeat, the sixth of June. It might've been eight o'clock in the evening. The man heard a sound inside the sewer. Very surprised, he hunkered down and kept watch. It was the sound of footsteps, of someone walking in the dark, of someone coming towards him. Strange to relate, there was another man besides himself in the sewer. The sewer's exit grille wasn't far off. A bit of light coming from it enabled him to recognize the newcomer, and he could see that this man was carrying something on his back. He walked with a stoop. The man walking with a stoop was an ex-convict, and what he was hauling on his shoulders was a corpse. A murder, if ever there was one, in the very act of being committed. As for theft, that goes without saying. No one kills a man for nothing. This convict was on his way to dump that body in the river. One thing worth mentioning is that before reaching the exit grille this ex-convict, who'd come a long way in the sewer, would've had to have encountered a dreadful sink-hole where you'd think he might've left the body, but sewermen working at the sink-hole would've found the murdered man the very next day, and that didn't suit the murderer. He preferred to make his way through that sink-hole with his burden, and it must've cost him the most terrible effort, you couldn't take any greater risk with your life. I don't understand how he came out of it alive.'

Marius's chair moved nearer. Thénardier took the opportunity to take a deep breath. He resumed.

'Monsieur le baron, a sewer is not the Champ de Mars. You've got nothing there, not even space. Two men inside it are bound to meet. That's what happened. The man who'd taken up residence there and the one who was passing through couldn't avoid each other, a matter of regret to both of them. The one passing through said to the other, "You see what I've got on my back, I must get out, you've got the key, give it to me." That convict was a man of tremendous strength. He wasn't to be refused. Yet the man who had the key kept him talking, just to gain time. He took a good look at that dead man but he couldn't see anything, except that he was young, well dressed, rich-looking, and his face all bloodied. While chatting away, the man contrived to tear the murdered man's coat and rip off a piece from behind without the murderer noticing. Incriminating evidence, you understand. A way of retracing things and proving the criminal guilty of his crime. He put this incriminating evidence in his pocket. After that he opened the grille, let the man out with his load on his back, closed the grille again and cleared off, not very keen to get mixed up in the rest of the intrigue and above all not wanting to be there when the murderer threw his victim in the river. You understand now. The one who was carrying the corpse was Jean Valjean. The one who had the key is speaking to you at this very moment. And the fragment of the coat—'

Thénardier completed the sentence by drawing from his pocket and holding up at eye level, pinned between his two thumbs and his two forefingers, a tattered shred of black cloth all darkly stained.

Marius had risen to his feet, pale, scarcely breathing, staring at the fragment of black cloth, and without uttering a word, without taking his eyes off that scrap of material, he backed across the room and with his right hand stretched out behind him groped along the wall for a key in the lock of a cupboard by the chimney. He found this key, opened the cupboard, stuck his arm into it without looking, his bewildered gaze riveted to the scrap that Thénardier held up.

Meanwhile, Thénardier continued. 'Monsieur le baron, I have the strongest grounds for believing that the murdered young man was a wealthy stranger lured into a trap by Jean Valjean, and the bearer of a huge sum of money.'

'That young man was myself, and here's the coat!' cried Marius, and he threw on to the floor an old black coat, all stained with blood.

Then, snatching the fragment from Thénardier's hands, he crouched down over the coat and placed the shred against the ripped edge of the coat. They matched perfectly and the scrap of material supplied the coat's missing piece. Thénardier was thunderstruck. He thought, 'Well, I'm blowed!'

Marius rose to his feet, quivering, frantic, radiant. He fumbled in his pocket and, furious, marched over to Thénardier, holding out towards him and almost pushing in his face a fistful of five-hundred-and one-thousand-franc banknotes.

'You're an infamous wretch! You're a liar, a slanderer, a villain. You came to accuse a man of wrong-doing, you've completely cleared him. You wanted to ruin him, you've succeeded only in crowning him with glory. And you're the one who's a thief! And you're the one who's a murderer! I saw you, Thénardier Jondrette, in that squalid place on Boulevard de l'Hôpital. I know enough about you to have you put in chains, and worse if I chose. Here, that's a thousand francs for you, blackguard that you are!'

And he threw a thousand-franc note at Thénardier.

'Ah! Jondrette Thénardier, you nasty piece of work! Let this be a lesson to you, you peddler of secrets, you mystery-monger, you grubber in the shadows, you wretch! Take these five hundred francs and get out of here! Waterloo is your salvation.'

'Waterloo!' growled Thénardier, pocketing the five hundred francs along with the thousand.

'Yes, murderer! Where you saved the life of a colonel—'

'A general,' said Thénardier, raising his head.

'A colonel!' repeated Marius angrily. 'I wouldn't give a quarter-sou for a general. And you come here to spread slander! I tell you that you're the one guilty of all those crimes. Go away! Disappear! I just hope you're successful. Ah, you monster! Here's another three thousand francs. Take them. You're to leave for America no later than tomorrow, together with your daughter – for your wife is dead, you dreadful liar. I'll be watching to make sure you leave, villain, and at that point I'll pay you twenty thousand francs. Go and get yourself hanged elsewhere!'

'Monsieur le baron,' replied Thénardier, bowing down to the ground, 'my eternal gratitude.' And Thénardier went away understanding nothing, astounded and delighted by this gentle battering with sacks of gold and this storm of banknotes breaking over him.

Thunderstruck he was, but also pleased, and he would have been very annoyed by any lightning rod that had protected him against these particular thunderbolts.

Let us have done with this man once and for all. Two days after the events we are now recounting he set off for America, thanks to Marius, under a false name with his daughter Azelma, equipped with a bill of exchange for twenty thousand francs to be drawn in New York. The moral destitution of Thénardier, that bourgeois manqué, was incurable. He was in America what he had been in Europe. Contact with a wicked man is sometimes enough to corrupt a good deed, and to cause something bad to result from it. With Marius's money Thénardier established himself as a slave-trader.

As soon as Thénardier was out of the house, Marius rushed into the garden, where Cosette was still taking her stroll.

'Cosette! Cosette!' he cried. 'Come! Come quickly! Let's go. Basque, a carriage! Cosette, come. Oh, my God! It was he who saved my life! Let's not waste a minute! Put on your shawl.'

Cosette thought he was mad, and obeyed.

He could not breathe, he put his hand on his heart to curb its palpitations. He strode back and forth, he hugged Cosette.

'Ah! Cosette! What a wretch I am!' he said.

Marius was bewildered. He began to glimpse in Jean Valjean some sad and noble figure. An extraordinary virtuousness became apparent to him, a supreme and gentle virtuousness, humble in its immensity The convict was undergoing a Christ-like transfiguration – Marius was dazzled by this wonder. He did not know exactly what he was seeing, but he saw its greatness.

Within an instant a cab was at the door.

Marius helped Cosette in and jumped in himself.

'Driver,' he said, 'Rue de l'Homme-Armé, number seven.'

The carriage set off.

'Ah, what a pleasure!' said Cosette. 'Rue de l'Homme-Armé, I dared not mention it to you any more. We're going to see Monsieur Jean.'

'Your father, Cosette. Your father more than ever. Cosette, I've worked it out. You told me you'd never received the letter I sent to you with Gavroche. It must have fallen into his hands. Cosette, he went to the barricade to save me. As he can't help but be an angel, while he was about it he saved others too. He saved Javert. He rescued me from that abyss so as to give me to you. He carried me on his back through that dreadful sewer. Ah! I'm an ungrateful monster! Cosette, having been your protector, he was mine. Just imagine, there was a terrible sink-hole where a man could drown a hundred times over, drown in mud. Cosette, he carried me through it. I was unconscious. I saw nothing, I heard nothing, I could know nothing of my own perilous experience. We're going to fetch him, to bring him back with us, no matter what he says, he won't ever leave us again. I only hope he's at home! I only hope we can find him! I shall venerate him for the rest of my life. Yes, that must be it, you see, Cosette? Gavroche must have delivered my letter to him. All is explained. You understand?'

Cosette did not understand a word.

'You're right,' she told him.

Meanwhile, the cab drove on.

V

From Darkness into Light

On hearing the knock at his door, Jean Valjean turned round.

'Come in,' he said weakly.

The door opened. Cosette and Marius appeared. Cosette rushed into the room. Marius remained standing on the threshold, leaning against the doorpost.

'Cosette!' said Jean Valjean, and he straightened up in his chair, his trembling arms outstretched, looking drawn, ashen, in a bad way, with an immense joy in his eyes.

Choked with emotion, Cosette fell on Jean Valjean's breast. 'Father!' she said.

Overwhelmed, Jean Valjean faltered, 'Cosette! Here! You, madame! You, my dear! Oh my God!' And clasped in Cosette's arms, he exclaimed, 'It's you! You've come! So you forgive me!'

Lowering his eyelids to prevent his tears from flowing, Marius took a step forward and, between lips convulsively tightened to check the sobs, he murmured, 'My father!'

'And you too forgive me!' said Jean Valjean.

Marius was at a loss for words, and Jean Valjean added, 'Thank you.'

Cosette threw off her shawl and tossed her hat on to the bed. 'They're getting in my way,' she said.

And sitting on the old man's lap, she brushed back his white hair with an adorable gesture and kissed his brow. Jean Valjean submitted to this in bewilderment.

Cosette, who had only a very confused understanding of the situation, redoubled her caresses, as though she wanted to repay Marius's debt.

Jean Valjean mumbled, 'How stupid! I thought I'd never see her again. Imagine, Monsieur Pontmercy, at the very moment you came in, I was saying to myself, "That's all over. Here's her little dress, I'm a wretched man, I shall never see Cosette again" – I was saying that at the very moment you were climbing the stairs. What a fool I was! That's how foolish you can be! But that's not taking the good Lord into account. The good Lord says, "You think you're going to be abandoned, silly! No, no, it's not going to turn out like that. Look, there's a poor old man in need of an angel." And the angel comes. And he sees his Cosette again! He sees his little Cosette again! Oh, I was so unhappy.'

For a moment he could not speak, then he resumed. 'I really needed to see Cosette for a little while every so often. A heart needs a bone to gnaw on. Yet I was well aware I was unwanted. I reasoned with myself: "They don't need you, keep out of their way, you've no right to outstay your welcome." Oh, thank God, I'm seeing her again! You know, Cosette, your husband is very handsome? Ah! that's a pretty embroidered collar you're wearing. My compliments. I like the pattern. It was your husband who chose it, wasn't it? And you ought to have some cashmere shawls. Monsieur Pontmercy, let me speak to her the way I used to. It won't be for long.'

And Cosette chided him, 'How unkind you were to leave us like that! Where did you go? Why were you away for such a long time? Before, your trips lasted no more than three or four days. I sent Nicolette round, and the answer was always "He's away." When did you get back? Why didn't you let us know? You know, you're much changed? Oh, what a naughty father! He's been ill, and we didn't know! Look, Marius, feel how cold his hand is!'

'So here you are! Monsieur Pontmercy, you forgive me!' Jean Valjean repeated.

At that word, which Jean Valjean had just said again, Marius, giving vent to everything with which his heart was swelling, burst out, 'Cosette, do you hear? He even goes that far! He asks my forgiveness! And do you know what he has done for me, Cosette? He has saved my life. He has done more. He has given you to me. And after having saved me, and after having given you, Cosette, to me, what did he do with himself? He sacrificed himself. Behold the man. And to me, the ungrateful one, to me, the forgetful one, the pitiless one, the guilty one, to me he says thank you! Cosette, if I were to spend my whole life at the feet of this man it would be too little. That barricade, that sewer, that hell-hole, that cesspit, he went through all that for me, for you, Cosette! He carried me through all manner of deaths, deaths that he deflected from me and took on himself. Every courage, every virtue, every heroism, every saintliness – he has them all! Cosette, this man is an angel!'

'Hush! hush!' said Jean Valjean very quietly. 'Why speak of all that?'

'But you!' cried Marius with an anger marked with reverence. 'Why didn't you speak of it? It's your fault, too. You save people's lives, and you conceal it from them! You go even further, professing to expose yourself, you malign yourself. It's appalling.'

'I told the truth,' replied Jean Valjean.

'No,' said Marius, 'the truth is the whole truth, and that you did not tell. You were Monsieur Madeleine, why not say so? You saved Javert, why not say so? I owed my life to you, why not say so?'

'Because I agreed with you. I thought you were right. I had to go away. If you'd known about that matter of the sewer, you'd have made me stay with you. So I had to keep quiet. If I'd spoken, that would have upset everything.'

'Upset what? Upset whom?' replied Marius. 'You think you're going to stay here? We're taking you with us. Ah! my God! when I think that it was only by accident I learned all this. We're taking you with us. You're a part of ourselves. You're her father, and mine. You're not going to spend another day in this ghastly house. Don't imagine that you'll be here tomorrow.'

'Tomorrow,' said Jean Valjean, 'I shan't be here, but I shan't be with you.'

'What do you mean?' replied Marius. 'Now then, we won't allow any more going away. You shan't ever leave us again. You belong to us. We won't let you go.'

'This time it's for good,' added Cosette. 'We have a carriage at the door. I'm kidnapping you. If necessary, I shall use force.' And laughing, she made as if to lift the old man in her arms. 'There's still your room in our house,' she went on. 'If you only knew how pretty the garden is now! The azaleas are doing well. The paths are spread with river gravel – there are tiny purple shells in it. You shall eat some of my strawberries. I water them myself. And no more "madame", no more "Monsieur Jean", we're living in a republic, everybody uses *tu* with each other, don't they, Marius? It's all changed now. If you only knew, father, what a sad thing happened to me, there was a robin that had made its nest in a hole in the wall, and a horrible cat ate it. My poor pretty little robin that used to pop its head out of its window and look at me! I cried over it. I'd have killed the cat! But no one's crying any more. Everyone's laughing, everyone's happy. You're going to come with us. Grandfather will be so pleased! You'll have your own plot in the garden to cultivate, and we'll see whether your strawberries are as splendid as mine. And then I'll do whatever you want, and then you'll do everything I say.'

Jean Valjean listened without taking it in. He heard the music of her voice rather than the sense of her words. One of those big tears, which are the dark pearls of the soul, slowly welled up in his eye.

He murmured, 'The proof that God is good is that she is here.'

'Father!' said Cosette.

Jean Valjean continued, 'It's quite true, it would be delightful to live together. Their trees are full of birds. I'd go for walks with Cosette. It's a pleasure to be among the living, with people who say good morning, who call out to each other in the garden, seeing each other first thing. We'd each cultivate our own little patch. She'd make me eat her strawberries. I'd make her pick my roses. It would be delightful. Only—' He broke off and said softly, 'It's a pity.'

The tear did not fall, it shrank back, and Jean Valjean replaced it with a smile. Cosette took the old man's two hands in hers.

'My goodness,' she said, 'your hands feel even colder. Are you ill? Are you in pain?'

'I? No,' replied Jean Valjean. 'I'm fine. Only—' He paused.

'Only what?'

'I'm going to die soon.'

Cosette and Marius shuddered.

'Die!' cried Marius.

'Yes, but it's nothing,' said Jean Valjean. He breathed in, smiled and went on, 'Cosette, you were talking to me, go on, carry on talking, so your little robin died? Talk, so that I can hear your voice!'

Marius stared at the old man, transfixed.

Cosette gave a heart-rending cry. 'Father! father! you'll live. You're going to live. I want you to live, do you hear?'

Jean Valjean looked up at her adoringly. 'Oh! yes, forbid me to die. Who knows? Perhaps I shall obey. I was dying when you two arrived. That stopped me, I felt as if I was being reborn.'

'You're full of strength and life,' cried Marius. 'Do you think people die just like that? You've suffered heartache, you shan't suffer any more. I'm the one to ask forgiveness of you – and what's more, down on my knees! You're going to live, and to live with us, and to live a long time. We're taking you back. There are two of us here who will have only one thought from now on, your happiness.'

'You see,' said Cosette, in tears, 'Marius says you won't die.'

Jean Valjean continued to smile.

'Even if you were to take me back, Monsieur Pontmercy, would that make me other than I am? No, God agreed with you and me, and he doesn't change his mind. I had better go. Death is a good arrangement. God knows what we need better than we do. That you should be happy, that Monsieur Pontmercy should have Cosette, that youth should wed the morn, that there should be lilacs and nightingales around you, my children, that your life should be a beautiful sunny lawn, that all of heaven's enchantments should fill your souls, and that I, who am good for nothing, should now die – all this is surely right. You see, let's be reasonable, nothing else is possible now, I have the firm feeling that this is the end. And then, last night, I drank all the water out of that jug over there. Your husband is so good, Cosette! You're much better off with him than with me.'

A noise was heard at the door. It was the doctor coming in.

'Hallo and goodbye, doctor,' said Jean Valjean. 'These are my poor children.'

Marius approached the doctor. He said this one word to him: 'Monsieur?' But in the way he said it there was a whole question.

The doctor replied to the question with a telling glance.

'Just because we don't like things,' said Jean Valjean, 'is no reason to be unfair to God.'

There was a silence. All hearts felt heavy. Jean Valjean turned to Cosette. He began to contemplate her as if to capture her for eternity. From as far into the shadows as he had already descended, the sight of Cosette was still capable of inspiring him with ecstasy. The reflection of that sweet face lit up his own pale countenance. There may be wonderment even at death's door.

The doctor felt his pulse. 'Ah! it was you he needed!' he murmured, looking at Cosette and Marius. And bending close to Marius's ear, he added in a very low voice, 'Too late.'

Almost without ceasing to gaze at Cosette, Jean Valjean observed the doctor and Marius serenely. These barely articulated words were heard issuing from his lips, 'It's nothing to die. It's dreadful not to live.'

Suddenly he stood up. Sometimes these very returns of strength are a last sign of life. He walked resolutely to the wall, waved aside Marius and the doctor, who tried to help him, took down from the wall a little copper crucifix hanging there, returned to his seat with all the ease of movement of one in the best of health, and said in a loud voice as he laid the crucifix on the table, 'There's the great martyr.'

Then his chest sank, his head swayed as if he were being overtaken by the intoxication of the tomb, and his two hands, resting on his knees, began to claw at the cloth of his trousers.

Cosette held him by the shoulders, and sobbed, and tried to talk to him, but failed. Among the words lost in the doleful choking that accompanies tears could be distinguished phrases such as these: 'Father, don't leave us. Is it possible that we've found you only to lose you again?'

Dying, it might be said, is a meandering process of coming and going, of advancing towards the grave and turning back towards life. In the throes of death there is a groping for the way.

Jean Valjean rallied after this half-loss of consciousness, shook his head as if to shake the shadows from his brow, and once again became almost completely lucid. He took hold of Cosette's sleeve and kissed it.

'He's coming round again! doctor, he's coming round again!' cried Marius.

'You're kind, both of you,' said Jean Valjean. 'I'll tell you what has hurt me. What has hurt me, Monsieur Pontmercy, is that you haven't wanted to touch that money. That money rightfully belongs to your wife. I'm going to explain to you, children, it's actually for that very reason I'm glad to see you. Black jet comes from England, white jet comes from Norway. It's all written down on this piece of paper for you to read. For bracelets I thought of replacing soldered metal links with metal links pinched together. It's prettier, better and less costly. Imagine all the money that can be saved like that. So Cosette's fortune is rightfully hers. I give you these details to put your minds at rest.'

The doorkeeper had come upstairs and was looking in through the half-open door. The doctor sent her away, but he could not prevent this zealous good woman from calling out to the dying man before she disappeared, 'Would you like a priest?'

'I have one,' replied Jean Valjean. And with his finger he seemed to point to somewhere above his head as if he saw someone there. It is likely that the bishop was indeed present at this hour of death.

Cosette gently slipped a pillow behind his back.

Jean Valjean went on, 'Monsieur Pontmercy, have no fear, I beseech you. The six hundred thousand francs rightfully belong to Cosette. So I'd have wasted my life if you didn't enjoy them! We succeeded very well with that glass jewellery. We were competing with what is called "Berlin jewellery". The fact is, black glass from Germany can't be equalled. A gross, which contains twelve hundred very well cut beads, costs only three francs.'

When someone dear to us is dying, we fix them with a look that fastens on to them and tries to detain them. Despairing and trembling, the two of them, Cosette giving Marius her hand, stood before him, speechless with distress, not knowing what to say to death.

Jean Valjean was failing with every passing moment. He was sinking, he was drawing nearer to the dark horizon. His breathing had become irregular, interspersed with a little rasping. He had difficulty in moving his forearm, his feet had lost all movement, and as his limbs grew ever weaker and his body succumbed, all the majesty of his soul rose to the surface and showed on his brow. The light of the unknown world was already visible in his eyes.

His face paled, and at the same time smiled. The life was gone from him, this was something else. His breathing dwindled, his gaze intensified. Here was a corpse that conveyed a sense of having wings.

He motioned to Cosette, then to Marius, to come closer. This was clearly the last minute of the last hour, and he began to speak to them in a voice so feeble that it seemed to come from afar, and it was as if there were already a wall between them and him.

'Come close, come close, both of you. I love you dearly. Oh, it's good to die like this! And you love me too, my Cosette. I knew you were still fond of your old fellow. How sweet you are to have put that pillow behind my back! You'll grieve for me a little, won't you? Not too much. I don't want you to have any real sorrows. You must have plenty of enjoyment, my children. I forgot to tell you, we made more on the buckles without pins than on all the rest. A gross, twelve dozen, cost ten francs and sold for sixty. It was very good business. So you mustn't be surprised at the six hundred thousand francs, Monsieur Pontmercy. It's honest money. You can be rich with an easy conscience. You must have a carriage, now and again a box at the theatre, and beautiful ball gowns, my Cosette, and also give your friends good dinners, and be very happy. I was writing to Cosette earlier. She'll find my letter. The two candlesticks on the mantelpiece, I leave to her. They're silver, but for me they're gold candlesticks, diamond candlesticks. They turn the ordinary candles placed in them into hallowed candles. I don't know whether the person up there who gave them to me is pleased with me. I've done what I could. My children, you won't forget I'm a pauper, you'll bury me in just any little patch of ground beneath a stone to mark the spot. That's my wish. No name on the stone. If Cosette wants to come occasionally and spend a little time at my grave, that will give me pleasure. You too, Monsieur Pontmercy.

I must admit, I haven't always liked you. For which I ask your forgiveness. Now, she and you are just one to me. I'm very grateful to you. I can see that you make Cosette happy. If you only knew, Monsieur Pontmercy, her pretty rosy cheeks were my delight: whenever I saw her the least bit pale, I was sad. In the chest of drawers there's a five-hundred-franc note. I haven't touched it. It's for the poor. Cosette, you see your little dress there on the bed? Do you recognize it? Yet that was only ten years ago. How time flies! We've been very happy. That's all in the past now. Don't cry, my children, I'm not going very far. I shall see you from there. You'll only have to look up when it's dark, and you'll see me smiling. Cosette, do you remember Montfermeil? You were in the forest, you were very scared. Do you remember when I took hold of the handle on the bucket of water? That was the first time I touched your poor little hand. It was so cold! Ah, your hands were red in those days, mademoiselle, they're very white now. And the big doll! Do you remember? You called her Catherine. You were sorry not to have brought her to the convent! How you made me laugh sometimes, my sweet angel! When it had been raining, you'd set wisps of straw afloat in the gutters and watch them go. One day I gave you a willow racket and a shuttlecock with yellow, blue and green feathers. You don't remember that. You were so mischievous when you were very small! You played. You hung cherries over your ears. Those are things of the past. The forests we passed through together, I and my child, the trees we walked among, the convents where we hid, the games, the happy laughter of childhood, are but shadow now. I imagined all that was mine. That was my foolishness. Those Thénardiers were wicked. You must forgive them. Cosette, now is the time to tell you your mother's name. She was called Fantine. Remember that name: Fantine. Go down on your knees whenever you say it. She suffered a lot. She loved you dearly. There was as much unhappiness in her life as there is happiness in yours. It's God who determines the lot that falls to us. He's up there, he sees us all, and he knows what he's doing among his great stars. So I'm leaving you now, my children. Love each other always. That's about the only thing in the world that matters: loving each other. You'll sometimes spare a thought for the poor old man who died here. Oh my Cosette, believe me, it's not my fault that I haven't seen you in all this time, it broke my heart. I'd go as far as the corner of your street, I must have made a strange impression on the people who saw me pass by, I behaved like a madman, I once went out without a hat. My children, I can't see very well any more, I still had things to say, but never mind. Think of me a little. You are blessed creatures. I don't know what's happening to me, I see

Notes

EPIGRAPH

Hauteville House: Hugo worked extensively on the manuscript of *The Wretched* during a long period of political exile (1851–70) that he spent largely on the island of Guernsey, living at Hauteville House. *The Wretched* was published in instalments between April and June 1862. It was an immediate publishing sensation.

PART ONE: FANTINE

the parliament at Aix: The Provence parliament, dating from 1501 and based in Aix-en-Provence, was the chief judiciary authority and highest court in Provence. Bastions of privilege associated with the *ancien régime*, all the provincial parliaments and the Paris parliament were abolished in the early days of the Revolution.

judicial aristocracy: Before the French Revolution the French aristocracy who owed their rank to their military service were known as the *noblesse d'épée*, 'the nobility of the sword', while those who were ennobled because of their judicial or administrative position were the *noblesse de robe*, 'nobility of the robe', or 'gown'.

the tragic spectacles of '93: Louis XVI was executed on 21 January, Marie-Antoinette on 16 October. The Terror implemented by the Revolutionary government's Committee of Public Safety began in September and continued until the fall of Robespierre in July 1794.

the coronation: Napoleon's coronation as emperor took place on 2 December 1804 at the church of Notre-Dame in Paris, in a ceremony at which Pope Pius VII officiated.

Cardinal Fesch: Joseph Fesch (1763–1839), an uncle of Napoleon, was named archbishop of Lyon in 1802 and created cardinal in 1803; Napoleon appointed him ambassador to Rome that same year.

palabres: Now commonly used in modern French to mean 'interminable discussions', etymologically and historically the word derives from the Spanish *palabra* ('word'), which entered French usage as a result of contacts with Africans who had previously traded with the Spanish. The word came to be associated with notoriously lengthy ritual gift-presentation ceremonies. Hence its southern connotations.

Council of Five Hundred ... 18th Brumaire ... Bigot de Préameneu: On 9 November 1799, 18th Brumaire in the French Republican calendar, Napoleon took part in a coup against the Directory, the French Revolutionary government from November 1795 to November 1799, that led to the introduction of a new constitution under which he became first consul, invested with the powers he needed eventually to become emperor. A rump session of the Council of Five Hundred, the lower house of the bicameral legislature, the Legislative Corps, that formed part of Directory, signed the transfer of political power. Félix-Julien-Jean Bigot de Préameneu (1747–1825), a moderate during the Revolution (and saved from the guillotine by the fall of Robespierre), was a supporter of the Brumaire conspiracy, a member of the committee that prepared Napoleon's Civil Code, and minister of public worship 1808–14. This ministry was created in 1804 to implement the 1801 Concordat with Rome, and had jurisdiction over all religious affairs in France.

Eh bé ... froumage grase: The translations given in the footnotes are translations of the French variants that appear in the text of *Les Misères*, an earlier draft of *The Wretched* (given in Maurice Allen's annotated edition of *Les Misérables* published by Gallimard, 1951, in the Bibliothèque de la Pléiade, p. 1991).

de Maistre ... Beccaria: Joseph de Maistre (1753–1821), an arch-conservative Catholic monarchist who saw the Revolution as divine punishment for the degeneration of society, was the author of a number of works, including *Les Soirées de Saint-Pétersbourg* (St Petersburg Evenings, 1821), in which he celebrated the executioner as protector of the social order and bulwark against chaos. Cesare Beccaria (1738–94) wrote an influential treatise on the reform of criminal justice entitled *Of Crimes and Punishment* (1764), in which he advocated the abolition of capital punishment. Hugo himself championed the abolition of the death penalty in his writings, particularly in his 1829 novel *Le Dernier jour d'un condamné* (Last Day of a Condemned Man) and his short story 'Claude Gueux' (1834), and also took part in public campaigns seeking clemency for those condemned – the American John Brown, for instance, in 1859.

Flavius Josephus ... Onkelos: Flavius Josephus was a Jewish historian (37–c.100), author of *Antiquities of the Jews*, a history of the Jewish people 'from the original creation of man until the twelfth year of the reign of Nero'. Onkelos is the name by which the author of an Aramaic translation of the Jewish scriptures dating from around the third century AD, known as the Targum of Onkelos, is recognized.

Hugo, bishop of Ptolemais: Charles-Hyacinthe Hugo (1667–1739), author of a great many theological and religious works and a history of Lorraine, was appointed titular bishop of Ptolemais in 1728.

Correspondence of Lord Germain: Published in 1784 in the context of the Clinton–Cornwallis controversy, centring on the conflict between the English generals Sir Henry Clinton (1730–95), commander of the British forces in America 1778–82, and Lord Charles Cornwallis (1738–1805), Clinton's second-in-command who surrendered Yorktown in 1781, over the way the war in America had been conducted and lost. Lord George Germain, previously known as Lord Sackville (1716–85), was Britain's Secretary of State for America 1775–82.

solidism ... Tournefort ... natural method ... cotyledons ... Jussieu ... Linnaeus: A mechanistic doctrine of physiology (as opposed to Hippocrates' humoral theory), promoted by the Greek physician Asclepiades to explain the concept of disease, solidism was important to the debate on heredity. Joseph Pitton de Tournefort (1656–1708), a distinguished botanist, author of *Institutiones rei herbariae: sive Elementa Botanices* (1691), a classification of plants based on a so-called artificial system, whereby a single common character of superficial similarity identifies an organism as belonging to a group. Tournefort's system depends chiefly on the corolla. A method of classification whereby organisms with a number of important shared characters are grouped together is a so-called natural method. The classification of flowering plants into the two major groups of monocotyledons and dicotyledons was first published by the English botanist John Ray in 1682. Antoine-Laurent de Jussieu (1748–1836), from a distinguished family of botanists, is the author of *Genera plantarum secundum ordines naturales disposita* (Genera of Plants Arranged according to Their Natural Orders), published in 1789, which laid down the principles for the natural system of plant classification. Carl Linnaeus (1707–78), the Swedish botanist, author of numerous works of natural history, standardized the binomial system of naming plants and introduced a hierarchical classification system. Linnaeus' system of classification was an artificial one defined by the sexual characteristics of plants.

Epicurus: The ancient Greek philosopher Epicurus (341–270 BC), whose advocacy of the pursuit of pleasure has been misinterpreted as a licence for hedonism, was in fact a promoter of moderation and of the social harmony that ensues from living wisely and justly.

Pigault-Lebrun: The work of the playwright and novelist Charles-Antoine-Guillaume Pigault-Lebrun (1753–1835), a prolific writer favoured by Thénardier, is characterized by a coarse zestfulness and a ribald anticlericalism.

Marquis d'Argens ... Pyrrho ... Hobbes: A French philosopher and writer, friend of Voltaire and fierce critic of the Catholic Church, Jean-Baptiste de Boyer, Marquis d'Argens (1704–71) spent most of his adult life outside of France, first in Amsterdam, then at the court of Frederick the Great in Prussia. The Greek philosopher Pyrrho (*c.*360–*c.*270 BC) was the founder of the Greek school of scepticism. The English political philosopher Thomas Hobbes (1588–1679), author of *Leviathan* (written during the English Civil War), famously predicated his development of the social-contract theory on the principle that in the state of nature the life of man is 'solitary, poor, nasty, brutish, and short'.

Monsieur Naigeon ... Diderot: Jacques-André Naigeon (1738–1810), man of letters and self-professed atheist, who frequented radical Enlightenment circles, was a close friend and collaborator of the philosopher and Encyclopaedist Denis Diderot (1713–84), and after Diderot's death his literary executor. Diderot has been described as first a deist, then a sceptic and finally an atheist.

Voltaire ... Needham: John Turberville Needham (1713–81), an English natural scientist, published his observations on the generation of living organisms, based on microscopic studies of tiny worms in blighted wheat grains and also in paste made of flour and water. The great Enlightenment philosopher Voltaire (1694–1778) satirized and ridiculed Needham, identifying in his work an argument for atheism and biological materialism, which he himself as a deist abhorred (in his words, 'If God did not exist, it would be necessary to invent him').

Isis: Ancient Egyptian mother god who continued to be worshipped throughout the Graeco-Roman world.

Tertullian: An early convert to Christianity, after seeing the way that persecuted Christians faced death for their beliefs, Tertullian (*c.*150–229, born in Carthage) is the author of numerous works in Latin, of which thirty-one texts have survived, including *Apologeticum*, a defence of Christians.

Le Moniteur: A newspaper that first appeared in 1789 to publish the debates in the National Assembly, it was declared an official government journal in 1799.

Sardanapalus: The last Assyrian king, notorious for his decadence, who is supposed to have died on a funeral pyre with all his wealth and his entourage in order to avoid falling into the hands of his enemies.

Vincent de Paul: Founder in 1625 of a missionary order now known as the Vincentians or Lazarists, dedicated to working among the poor and the marginalized, and co-founder of the Daughters (or Sisters) of Charity. Vincent de Paul (1581–1660) was canonized in 1737.

Cato . . . Stephen . . . Joan of Arc: A staunch defender of the Republic, Cato the Younger (95–46 BC) left Rome when Caesar marched into Italy with his troops, and after Caesar defeated his opponents in the civil war he committed suicide. The first Christian martyr, St Stephen was stoned to death *c.* AD 34 (Acts of the Apostles 7:55–60). Inspired by divine visions, Joan of Arc (*c.*1412–31) led the French army in important victories against the English in the Hundred Years War, in particular in raising the siege of Orléans. When she fell into the hands of the English, in their attempt to delegitimize the coronation of Charles VII in which she was so instrumental she was tried by an ecclesiastical court for heresy and burned at the stake. Now one of the patron saints of France, she was canonized in 1920.

Telemachus: Telemachus was a character familiar to eighteenth-century readers from Fénelon's *Les Aventures de Télémaque* (1699), a didactic novel satirizing the reign of Louis XIV that became popular all over Europe. The son of Ulysses and Penelope, Telemachus is accompanied in his travels by his tutor Mentor, who turns out to be the goddess Minerva in disguise. Nevertheless, Mademoiselle Baptistine seems to be somewhat innocently confused about the scenes in her paintings.

the Convention: The Revolutionary Assembly that was formed to implement the abolition of the monarchy and to draw up a constitution. It presided over the trial and execution of Louis XVI on 21 January 1793 and was the executive power in France from September 1792 until October 1795, when it was dissolved, to be replaced by the Directory.

that disastrous return of the past: After Napoleon was forced to abdicate in April 1814 and was exiled to Elba, the Bourbon monarchy was restored and Louis XVIII installed as king.

Cartouche: Louis-Dominique Bourguignon, known as Cartouche (1693–1721), was the leader of a criminal gang based in the Cour des Miracles in Paris, guilty of robbery and murder. He was eventually betrayed, then executed.

the grandson of Louis XV: The son of Louis XVI and Marie-Antoinette died of tuberculosis in the Temple prison at the age of ten on 8 June 1795, corroborative evidence of which was provided by DNA tests conducted in 2000 on a child's heart said to have been stolen by the doctor who performed the autopsy at the time of death.

Barabbas . . . Herod: Barabbas is the criminal whom, in all four Gospels, Pontius Pilate, obeying the will of the crowd, releases (rather than Jesus the Messiah, whom they call on Pilate to crucify). Herod was the name of several kings, belonging to the same dynasty, who ruled over the Roman province of Judaea.

Marat: The political theorist and journalist Jean-Paul Marat (1743–93) was one of the leaders of the Revolution; he championed the sovereignty of the people and advocated violent purges of counter-revolutionaries to defend the values of the Revolution.

Bossuet . . . *dragonnades*: Tutor to the Dauphin under Louis XIV, elected to the French Academy in 1671, appointed bishop of Meaux in 1681, an eloquent preacher and a consummate prose stylist, Jacques-Bénigne Bossuet (1627–1704) exercised great political as well as religious influence and was a strong advocate of absolutism and the divine right of kings. The *dragonnades* were the compulsory billetings of royal dragoons on Huguenot households, who had to bear the cost of their board and lodging and suffer the unchecked oppression of their presence – a policy of persecution intended to win converts, who were exempted from this imposition.

Carrier . . . *Montrevel*: As a lawyer and member of the National Convention, Jean-Baptiste Carrier (1756–94) was sent in 1793 to Nantes to deal with counter-revolutionaries. Notoriously, he had hundreds of prisoners drowned in the Loire on scuttled barges; these became known as the *noyades de Nantes* ('the Nantes drownings'). In November 1794 he was brought to trial for mass murder, and guillotined. As commander-in-chief of the army in the Languedoc Nicolas de Montrevel (1636–1716) was responsible for the violent repression of Protestants of the Cévennes region.

Fouquier-Tinville . . . *Lamoignon-Bâville*: Antoine-Quentin Fouquier-Tinville (1746–95) was public prosecutor of the Revolutionary Tribunal of Paris from its creation in 1793 until shortly after the fall of Robespierre in July 1794. He was guillotined in 1795. As governor (*intendant*) of the Languedoc, Nicolas Lamoignon-Bâville (1648–1724) gained a reputation for his severe repression of Protestants.

Maillard . . . *Saulx-Tavannes*: Stanislas Maillard (1763–94) was a National Guardsman who played a leading role in the storming of the Bastille and was believed – by Thomas Carlyle, for instance – to have been partly responsible for the massacre of prisoners in September 1792, although this is disputed. He died of consumption. As lieutenant-general of Burgundy and marshal of France, Gaspard de Saulx-Tavannes (1509–73) was a zealous persecutor of Protestants and is believed to have been one of the chief instigators of the St Bartholomew's Day massacre of Huguenots on 24 August 1572.

Père Duchêne . . . *Père Letellier*: A character that emerged out of popular culture, Père Duchesne was adopted as the title of a radical newspaper published during the Revolution by Jacques Hébert (1757–94); it denounced abuses and injustices in the name of the people in often scurrilous and libellous terms, demonizing its targets such as Marie-Antoinette. Hébert was himself eventually guillotined, but later publications during times of unrest have revived the name of Père Duchesne, or Duchêne. The Jesuit priest Père Letellier (1648–1719) became Louis XIV's confessor in 1709 and was generally believed to have encouraged him in his harsh repression of the Jansenists (see note p. 1351 on *a Jansenist*).

Jourdan-Coupe-Tête . . . *Marquis de Louvois*: Mathieu Jouve Jourdan (1746–94), nicknamed Jourdan-Coupe-Tête (Jourdan the Beheader), played a leading role in a retaliatory massacre of papists that took place at Avignon in 1791 after the lynching of a Revolutionary municipal administrator (the so-called Massacre de La Glacière). He is also believed to have murdered the governor of the Bastille when it was stormed by Revolutionaries in 1789. He was executed in 1794. Louis XIV's minister of war François-Michel Le Tellier, Marquis de Louvois (1641–91), pressed for the complete revocation, in 1685, of the Edict of Nantes, which had previously allowed Protestants some freedom of worship. He was also responsible in 1688 for the wanton destruction of the Palatinate, to which Louis XIV laid claim.

Tantalus torture: In Greek mythology Tantalus was the immortal son of Zeus who committed the heinous crime of serving up his own son at a banquet for the gods, for which he was condemned to the torture of eternal thirst and eternal hunger, with water and fruit apparently within reach but always eluding his grasp. In some versions of the myth Tantalus is condemned to everlasting fear, with the perpetual threat of being crushed by a boulder precariously balanced above his head.

the red cap: Also called 'the Phrygian cap' (possibly because worn by freed Phrygian slaves in the ancient world) and sometimes 'the liberty cap', the red cap was identified with Revolutionaries. The red hat is one of the insignia of a cardinal.

a patriot parish priest: There was an old folksong called 'J'ons un curé patriote' ('I Have a Patriot Parish Priest') to the tune of which many other popular songs were sung.

The arrest of the pope: After Napoleon's coronation by Pope Pius VII in 1804 relations between France and the Vatican gradually deteriorated, Napoleon challenging the pope's temporal authority and independence with the annexation of the papal territories and, in 1808, the occupation of Rome. In June 1809 the pope issued a bull of excommunication against all those who violated the Holy See's temporal sovereignty. This was followed by the arrest of the pope, who was then held by the French for the next five years. Cardinal Fesch was at the time of the arrest French ambassador to the Holy See.

more ultramontane than Gallican: The so-called ultramontanes (from Latin, meaning 'beyond the mountains', i.e. the Alps) recognized the supremacy of papal authority over national, 'Gallican' liberties.

after his return from the island of Elba: Escaping from exile on Elba, Napoleon landed at the Gulf of Juan near Cannes on 28 February 1815 and marched on Paris, gathering support along the way. Louis XVIII fled, leaving Napoleon in control for what is known as the Hundred Days, until his defeat in June at Waterloo.

1812 . . . avert one's gaze: In June 1812 Napoleon launched what was to be his disastrous campaign against Russia, in which he lost some 500,000 men. On 29 December 1813 the Legislative Corps drew up a statement denouncing the continuing war as a reflection of Napoleon's personal ambition and asserting the rights of the people. On 1 April 1814 the Senate appointed a provisional government under Talleyrand (see note p. 1314 on *Talleyrand . . . Abbé Louis*), then on 2 April they declared Napoleon to have been dethroned and the French people and the army released from their oath of loyalty. Under pressure from his own marshals Napoleon was forced to abdicate on 6 April 1814.

Legion of Honour: After all distinctions were abolished during the Revolution, a new system of military distinctions, the so-called arms of honour, was created in December 1799 by the Consulate, which came into being when Bonaparte overthrew the Directory by the coup of 18 Brumaire on 9 November 1799, and he himself became first consul. The Legion of Honour, conceived by Napoleon and established in May 1802, was designed to recognize both military and civilian excellence and to create a body of talent in the service of the state. All those who held the arms-of-honour distinction automatically became members of the Legion. The first awards ceremony was held on 15 July 1804. The Legion of Honour survived the restoration of the monarchy in 1815 and was restructured in 1816, with grades and decorations that survive to this day. Victor Hugo was appointed a member of the Legion of Honour on 19 April 1825.

three toads: Legend has it that under Clovis (482–511), founder of the Merovingian dynasty of French kings, three toads were the insignia of the French monarchy until Clovis's conversion to Christianity, when he adopted the emblem of three lilies, the fleurs-de-lys.

St Francis of Sales: Canonized in 1665 and proclaimed Doctor of the Church in 1877, Francis of Sales (1567–1622), bishop of Geneva at Annecy, was revered for his eloquent preaching, his goodness and his love for the poor.

the Rota ... the pallium: The Rota is the highest ecclesiastical court of the Roman Catholic Church. The pallium is a liturgical vestment worn by the pope and by archbishops.

Perrette with her pot of milk: A reference to La Fontaine's 'La Laitière et le pot au lait' (The Milkmaid and the Pot of Milk), fable 10, bk 7. Thinking to buy a hundred eggs with the money she makes from selling the milk she is carrying to market, Perrette starts counting her chickens before they are hatched. She then drops the milk on her way there.

a spurious Corneille: The French dramatist Jean Galbert de Campistron (1656–1723), whose play *Tiridate*, about the incestuous passion of Tiridates, son of the king of Parthia, for his sister Erinice, was performed in 1691.

a military Prudhomme: Monsieur Prudhomme was the creation of the caricaturist, playwright and actor Henri Monnier (1799–1877). Embodying the archetypal petit-bourgeois, full of pompous and sententious inanity, Prudhomme first appeared in 1830 in *Scènes populaires*; in 1852 came the five-act comedy *Grandeur et Décadence de Monsieur Joseph Prudhomme*, then in 1857 *Les Mémoires de Joseph Prudhomme*.

Mousqueton: Literally, 'blunderbuss', Mousqueton is the name of Porthos's man-servant in Alexandre Dumas's *The Three Musketeers* (1844).

Claudius' bull neck: Suetonius in *The Lives of the Twelve Caesars* describes Claudius as having a majestic appearance and a bull neck ('Claudius', ch. 45).

text from Ecclesiastes: 'Who knoweth the spirit of a man that goeth upward, and the spirit of the beast that goeth downward to the earth?' Ecclesiastes 3:21.

Marcus Aurelius: AD 121–80, emperor of Rome from AD 161: 'As to the animals which have no reason ... do thou, since thou hast reason and they have none, make use of them with a generous and liberal spirit', *The Meditations of Marcus Aurelius*, VI, 23, translated by George Long, 1862.

Gregory XVI: Bartolomeo Alberto Cappellari (1765–1846) was elected Pope Gregory XVI in 1831 on the eve of an uprising of the Papal States against papal authority; the uprising was suppressed. A reactionary who resisted reform and defended papal sovereignty and the principle of papal infallibility, Cappellari, originally a monk, was made a cardinal without having been a bishop.

Swedenborg and Pascal: The writings of Emmanuel Swedenborg (1688–1772), scientist, philosopher and mystic visionary theologian were attacked as those of a lunatic by his contemporary the English theologian John Wesley (1703–91), founder of Methodism. Blaise Pascal (1623–62), mathematician, philosopher and theologian, who in 1654 after a near-fatal accident underwent a visionary religious experience by which he was profoundly influenced. In his *Pensées* (VI: 414), he wrote 'Les hommes sont si nécessairement fous que ce serait être fou par un autre tour de folie de n'être pas fou' ('Men are so necessarily mad that not to be mad would amount to another form of madness', as translated by W. F. Trotter, New York: Collier & Son, 1910).

the folds of Elijah's mantle: An allusion to the ministry of the Old Testament prophet Elijah, which is passed on to Elisha when he takes up the mantle after Elijah is gathered up into heaven by a whirlwind (2 Kings 2:9–15).

St Teresa and St Jerome: St Teresa of Ávila (1515–82) in her writings gives an account of the various stages of contemplative prayer, rising to a state of devotional ecstasy. St Jerome (*c*.347–420) is one of the great scholars of the Church, the most notable of his works being the Latin Vulgate translation of the Bible.

Lucretius, Manu: A Roman poet and philosopher, Lucretius (*c*.99–*c*.55 BC) was the author of the philosophical epic poem *De Rerum Natura* (On the Nature of Things). According to Hindu tradition, Manu is the progenitor of mankind, and author of *The Laws of Manu*, a sacred text dating from between 200 BC and AD 200.

General Drouot: One of Napoleon's most loyal officers, General Drouot (1774–1847), had accompanied his commander-in-chief into exile on Elba, and faithfully served his emperor during the Hundred Days (counted from 20 March, when Napoleon reached Paris, to 18 June, when he was defeated at the battle of Waterloo).

Gulf of Juan proclamation: The proclamation issued by Napoleon on 1 March 1815, when he landed on French soil after his escape from Elba, was addressed to the French people and to French soldiers. It was read out at subsequent stages of his advance on Paris, as he gathered support along the way.

the Guides corps: An élite corps created in 1796 for the personal protection of Napoleon.

General Bertrand: Henri Gatien Bertrand (1773–1844) was Napoleon's aide-de-camp, who had accompanied him to Elba and after the defeat at Waterloo went with him to St Helena, where he wrote his journals (later published). He remained there until Napoleon's death in 1821, then in 1840 returned to St Helena to bring Napoleon's remains back to France. He is buried close to the emperor's tomb at Les Invalides.

gold napoleons: Twenty-franc gold coins bearing the effigy of Napoleon, minted between 1803 and 1815.

the covered rose: In French stick-fencing, which thrived in the early nineteenth century when it became illegal to carry a sword, this was a complicated virtuoso sequence of movements describing a pattern that would look like a many-petalled rose: 'la rose couverte . . . est la plus jolie arabesque dessinée au bâton que l'on puisse voir' ('the "covered rose" . . . is the prettiest arabesque, performed with a stick, that anyone might see'), Théophile Gautier (1811–72) in 'Le maître de chausson' (The Foot-fighting Master), in vol. 5 of *Les Français peints par eux-mêmes: Encyclopédie morale du dix-neuvième siècle* (1840–42).

I'm an ex-convict . . . from Toulon: Before 1748, criminals sentenced to hard labour served as galley slaves in the French Mediterranean fleet. In 1748 the galleys, unable to compete with the firepower of sailing vessels, were replaced. The convict labour was used instead to carry out naval construction work, originally in the arsenal prisons (*les bagnes*) of three ports, Brest, Rochefort and Toulon. The prisoners were housed on prison hulks (*bagnes flottants*), and later in specially constructed buildings around the docks. The term *bagne* derives from the word used in Italian to refer to the prison at Livorno, which was built on the site of ancient baths, *bagno*. The term *galérien* (rower on a galley) continued to be applied to these land-based prisoners. Jean Valjean's original sentence was 'cinq ans de galères', literally, five years in the galleys.

yellow passport: Though briefly abolished after the Revolution, internal passports were reintroduced in February 1792. All French citizens over the age of fifteen wishing to travel outside the local area to which they belonged (and all foreigners travelling in France) were obliged to carry passports issued by the competent authorities. A main argument for their reintroduction was the protection of law-abiding communities from brigandage and vagabondage, and it was for this reason that passports specified an itinerary. The yellow identity document with which released convicts were issued, what Jean Valjean refers to as 'mon passeport jaune', was officially entitled a *congé de forçat* (convict's release paper).

the Medusa: When a French naval vessel, the *Medusa*, ran aground on a reef off the coast of Senegal in 1816, the ship was evacuated. Of the 146 men and women who boarded a raft in an attempt to reach safety, only fifteen were still alive when they were rescued after thirteen days adrift. The ship's surgeon Henri Savigny and his shipmate the geographer Alexandre Corréard, who both survived, wrote an account of their experience, which became an international bestseller and inspired Géricault's famous painting *The Raft of the Medusa*. The captain of the doomed frigate, Jean-Hugues de Chaumareix (1763–1841), was court-martialled, found guilty, cashiered, and sentenced in 1817 to three years' imprisonment.

the red jacket: The convict's uniform included a red jacket of a coarse wool cloth, and trousers that buttoned up the outside leg to facilitate the wearing and the verification of the shackles round his ankle.

the double-chain punishment: The double chain meant confinement night and day, for a period of months if not years, chained to a sleeping-bench.

Montenotte: The battle of Montenotte, 12 April 1796, was General Napoleon Bonaparte's first victory at the beginning of his Italian campaign.

Bicêtre: The buildings at Bicêtre, dating from the seventeenth century, housed at various times an orphanage, a hospice for old soldiers, an hospital for the poor, an asylum for the insane, and a prison. It was the place where the guillotine was first tried out (on the corpses of prisoners) on 17 April 1792, and it was first used in April 1796 as a transit station where convicts sentenced to hard labour were assembled and put in chains.

The naval court: Since the prison hulks were in the Arsenal at Toulon, they fell under naval jurisdiction.

Claude Gueux: In 1834, Victor Hugo published a short story inspired by the case of Claude Gueux, a petty criminal who, like Jean Valjean, stole a loaf of bread, for which he was sentenced to five years' imprisonment. While in prison he committed a murder, in 1831, for which he was executed in June 1832.

Ignorantine friars: '. . . the *Brothers of the Christian Schools* (Christian Brothers) founded by St. Jean-Baptiste de la Salle in 1684 for the general instruction of the poor; they were, and still are often called *Brothers of the Christian Doctrine*, and were, more or less contemptuously referred to as *Ignorantins* by their detractors, as they interested themselves only in vernacular schools of the lower grade . . .', François de La Fontainerie, *French Liberalism and Education in the Eighteenth Century*, New York: McGraw-Hill, 1932, p. 60.

like Dante: 'Abandon all hope, you who enter', the inscription above the gate of Hell in Dante's *Inferno*, III, 9.

Puget's splendid caryatids: Pierre Puget (1622–94), sculptor. The balcony was destroyed in the Second World War.

Guillons cochlearia: A Hugolian invention: Les Guillons is a place on the way to Pontarlier, which here is combined with the name of a four-petalled plant of the Cruciferae family ('cruciferous' meaning cross-bearing).

Savoyard . . . on his back: A Savoyard, meaning a person from Savoy, a term applied not only to poor emigrants from that province but more generally to anyone pursuing an itinerant way of life such as chimney-sweep, chair-mender, knife-grinder, street entertainer with a hurdy-gurdy and a bear or a marmot trained to dance.

Bruguière de Sorsum: A man of letters, Antoine Bruguière de Sorsum (1773–1823) was responsible for numerous translations from English, including works by Shakespeare, Byron and Southey.

Comte Lynch: In March 1814, shortly before the abdication of Napoleon in April that year, Jean-Baptiste Lynch (1749–1835) handed the keys of Bordeaux to the Duc d'Angoulême (1775–1844), who was representing his uncle in exile, the soon to be King Louis XVIII, and was accompanied by English troops.

Napoleon . . . St Helena: After his defeat at the battle of Waterloo, Napoleon was exiled in 1815 to St Helena, an island in the South Atlantic then under the control of the English East India Company, where he died on 5 May 1821.

Pellegrini . . . Bigottini . . . Potier . . . Odry . . . Saqui . . . Forioso: Felice Pellegrini (1774–1832), Italian baritone opera singer. Émilie Bigottini (1784–1858) was a French dancer of Italian origin who made her career at the Paris Opéra. Charles-Gabriel Potier des Cailletières, known as Potier (1774–1838), a noted French actor of noble birth, and comic actor Jacques-Charles Odry (1779–1858) both performed at the Théâtre des Variétés. Madame Saqui (Marguerite-Antoinette Lalanne, 1786–1866) was a noted French tightrope dancer, and Forioso (1769–1846) was another of the great tightrope artists of the day.

Monsieur Delalot: Charles Delalot (1772–1842), who took part in 1795 in the 13 Vendémiaire royalist rising that was quelled by Napoleon, was elected a deputy under the Restoration and was a contributor to the influential Parisian daily newspaper *Journal des Débats*, making a name for himself as a moderate royalist.

Pleignier, Carbonneau and Tolleron: Members of an anti-royalist society called the Patriots of 1816, these three foolhardy working men, manipulated to a considerable extent by the police and by an agent provocateur, were found guilty of conspiracy and lese-majesty. Sentenced to death, they first had their right hands cut off and were then guillotined – the penalty for parricide. Their execution took place in 1816.

Talleyrand . . . Abbé Louis: A consummate politician and diplomat, Charles-Maurice de Talleyrand-Périgord (1754–1838) was an extraordinary survivor. Appointed bishop of Autun by Louis XVI – he resigned from his diocese in 1791 and was excommunicated after taking the oath of loyalty to the civil constitution of the clergy – he held political office during the Revolution, under Napoleon, during the Restoration and under Louis-Philippe, whom he served as ambassador to London until he retired in 1834. He was Grand Chamberlain under Napoleon from 1804 to 1809, and under the Restoration, serving both Louis XVIII and Charles X between 1815 and 1830. Talleyrand was responsible for the selection by the provisional government of Joseph-Dominique Louis (1775–1837) as minister of finance in April 1814, an appointment later confirmed by Louis XVIII. Abbé Louis served five times in this capacity.

Feast of the Federation: Celebrations on the first anniversary of the storming of the Bastille, called the Feast of Federation, took the form of a military parade and an open-air mass held on the Champ de Mars, for which a huge temporary amphitheatre was constructed by volunteers.

Champ de Mai: In emulation of the assemblies held under early Frankish kings, originally in March (called the *champ de mars*), and then in May (the *champ de mai*), Napoleon during the Hundred Days summoned deputies from all over France to a Champ de Mai, ostensibly to vote on a new constitution; but in effect a constitution was being presented to them simply for their endorsement. Because the deputies could not get to Paris in time for the May date originally scheduled, the assembly was postponed until 1 June.

the Austrians bivouacked: In early July 1815 after Napoleon's defeat at Waterloo, Allied troops occupied Paris, the English on the right bank, the Prussians and Austrians on the left. Under the terms of the 1815 Treaty of Paris signed on 20 November, some regions of France would continue to be occupied for up to five years, though by no more than 150,000 Allied troops.

kaiserlicks: The name given during the French Revolution to Prussian or Austrian soldiers (from the German word *kaiserlich*, meaning 'imperial').

Touquet edition . . . snuff-box: In 1821 the Bonapartist publisher Colonel Touquet published a fifteen-volume selection of Voltaire's works. The Charter-engraved snuff-box was one of a series of novelty snuff-boxes invented and sold by the same Colonel Touquet, celebrating the constitutional Charter of 1814, which guaranteed the rights of citizens under the Restoration Bourbon government. A paper edition of the Charter priced at only five centimes was another financially successful venture.

Dautun: Charles Dautun (1780–1815) was tried and found guilty of the murder of his aunt and of his brother, whose dismembered body was found in several different places in Paris. He was guillotined in 1815.

Chaumareix . . . Géricault: See note p. 1313 on *the Medusa*.

Colonel Selves: Joseph Anthelme Selves (or Sève; 1788–1860), a former soldier in Napoleon's army, left France under the Restoration and went to Egypt where, having converted to Islam, he helped to modernize and train the Egyptian army and became known as Suleiman Pasha. He returned to France on several occasions, was awarded the Legion of Honour by Louis-Philippe and eventually died in Cairo, where the present-day Talaat Harb Square was once named after him.

Palais des Thermes: Although proposals were made for establishing a museum of Roman and Gaulish antiquities in this Roman brick building, the project was not carried out until 1836, when ownership was transferred from the city to the national government and it became part of the Cluny Museum.

Messier, the naval astronomer: Charles Messier (1730–1817) worked with a previous astronomer for the navy, Joseph-Nicolas Delisle (1688–1768), who in 1748 established the observatory on the Cluny tower. Messier was appointed naval astronomer in 1771. He identified thirteen new comets during his lifetime.

Duchesse de Duras: Claire de Duras (1777–1828) presided over an influential salon during the Restoration. Her novel *Ourika*, published anonymously in 1823, tells the story of a young black child rescued from slavery and raised in France. Duras herself lived in Martinique for a number of years.

The Ns . . . Louvre: As emperor, Napoleon had his initial emblazoned on the Louvre. These Ns were duly removed under the Restoration. The Ns that currently adorn the Louvre façade celebrate his nephew Napoleon III.

Pont du Jardin du Roi: The Pont d'Austerlitz, so named in celebration of Napoleon's great victory over his Russian–Austrian adversaries in 1805, was known under the Restoration as Pont du Jardin du Roi, the Jardin du Roi itself having been nationalized as part of the Museum of Natural History and renamed the

Jardin des Plantes during the Revolution. The Napoleonic and Revolutionary names are the ones that have survived.

Horace ... Louis XVIII: Louis XVIII was known to be fond of quoting Horace. Alexandre Dumas made much of this in a scene in *The Count of Monte Cristo* (1844), ch. 10. Hugo himself translated poems of Horace.

Mathurin Bruneau: An impostor who claimed to be the son of Louis XVI, Bruneau (1784–1822), a cobbler by trade, was tried in 1818 and imprisoned at Mont St-Michel, where he died.

The French Academy ... through Study: Hugo himself entered this poetry competition, but his entry met with disbelief that it could have been written by one so young.

Monsieur Bellart: Famed for his oratory as a lawyer, Nicolas Bellart (1761–1826), having turned against his former protector Napoleon once the emperor was on the brink of losing power, was appointed Attorney-General at the Royal Court of Paris by Louis XVIII in 1815, in which capacity he played a critical role in the trial of Marshal Ney, who in November that year was sentenced to death for treason for rallying to Napoleon during the Hundred Days.

de Broë ... Courier: Paul-Louis Courier (1772–1825) was prosecuted for the publication in 1821 of an anti-royalist pamphlet, and retaliated with another pamphlet about his trial, ridiculing the public prosecutor Jacques-Nicolas de Broë (1790–1840).

Chateaubriand: Writer and royalist politician René de Chateaubriand (1768–1848), whose autobiographical *Mémoires d'Outre-Tombe* (Memories from beyond the Grave) paint an invaluable portrait of the age, was a leading figure of French Romanticism. Victor Hugo, as a schoolboy, is supposed to have said, 'I want to be Chateaubriand, or nothing!'

Marchangy ... d'Arlincourt: Louis de Marchangy (1782–1826), author of *La Gaule Poétique; ou l'Histoire de France considérée dans ses rapports avec la poésie, l'éloquence et les beaux-arts* (Poetic Gaul; or the History of France in Relation to Poetry, Eloquence and the Fine Arts), was a fervent royalist (also, the ruthless prosecutor of the Four Sergeants of La Rochelle in 1822 – see note p. 1355 on *Sanson ... Montès ... Lacenaire* [etc.]). In his correspondence, Stendhal wrote of *La Gaule Poétique*: 'The style is indebted to that M. de Chateaubriand. If M. de Marchangy wrote novels he would be almost as absurd as M. d'Arlincourt' (cited in a footnote in *Le Vicomte d'Arlincourt, Prince des Romantiques* by Alfred Marquiset, Paris: Hachette, 1909, p. 107). Charles d'Arlincourt (1789–1856), poet, novelist and dramatist, enjoyed a wide readership in his day, but was not so successful with the critics. Of his novel *Le Solitaire* (The Loner), published in 1821, Charles-Marie de Féletz (see note p. 1319 on *Monsieur de Féletz ... Hoffmann ... Z*) is reported to have commented that it 'has been translated into every language except French' (Marquiset, op. cit., p. 107).

Claire d'Albe ... Malek-Adel: Sophie Cottin (1770–1807), a popular writer in her day, was the author of five Romantic novels, of which *Claire d'Albe* (1799) was the first. Malek-Adel is the Muslim hero of her historical novel *Mathilde, or Memories Drawn from the History of the Crusades* (1805), which enjoyed immense popularity in its day and gave rise to a number of operatic works that took the name of its hero for their title.

The Institute ... list of members: The Institut National des Sciences et des Arts (later, the Institut de France) was founded in 1795 to replace the royal academies and to extend their scope to include more disciplines. It was restructured in 1814 under Louis XVIII, who took the opportunity to exclude certain members and to reintroduce the term 'academy' for its constituent sections: the French Academy, the Academy of Inscriptions and Belles-Lettres, the Academy of Sciences, the Academy of Fine Arts, and the Academy of Political and Moral Sciences.

the Duc d'Angoulême: Nephew of Louis XVIII and son of Charles X. The Grand Admiralty was a titular position; Angoulême in the south-west of France is completely landlocked.

Franconi: Antonio Franconi (1737–1836) was an Italian circus impresario whose sons carried on the business when he retired. They called the new theatre they opened the Cirque Olympique.

Paer, author of Agnese . . . Sassenay: The Italian composer Ferdinando Paer (1771–1839), who was taken up by Napoleon and became director of the Théâtre Italien in Paris, was at one time director of music in the Duchesse de Berry's household. He wrote his best-known opera, *Agnese*, in 1809. The Marquis de Sassenay (1760–1840), married to Claudine Bretton des Chapelles (1778–1832), was also a member of the Duchesse de Berry's household.

L'Ermite de St-Avelle . . . Géraud: Edmond Géraud (1775–1831) was a journalist, diarist and poet. His poem, actually entitled 'L'Hermite de Ste-Avelle', tells of a young man complaining of the anguish of love, for which a hermit tells him there is no cure. Published in 1820, it inspired two vaudeville comedies staged in June of the same year under the title that Hugo gives here.

Le Nain Jaune . . . Le Miroir: *Le Nain Jaune* was a literary and political journal founded in 1814 and suppressed in 1815, appearing in Belgium in 1816 as *Le Nain Jaune Réfugié*. *Le Miroir* was a monarchist journal published briefly (1796–7) during the Revolution. Another journal, *Le Miroir des Spectacles, des Lettres, des Moeurs et des Arts*, was published between 1821 and 1823.

Louvel . . . Duc de Berry: The Duc de Berry (1778–1820), nephew of Louis XVI and Louis XVIII and son of the future Charles X, on 17 June 1816 married Marie-Caroline of Naples, Princess of the Two Sicilies (1798–1870). He was murdered outside the Opéra on 13 February 1820 by Louis Louvel (1783–1820), an anti-Bourbonist.

Madame de Staël: Daughter of Louis XVI's finance minister Jacques Necker, Germaine de Staël (1766–1817), novelist and outspoken critic of Napoleon, presided over one of the most influential salons in Paris. Her lovers included Talleyrand and Benjamin Constant (see note p. 1335 on *Benjamin Constant*). She suffered a stroke that paralysed her in February 1817 and died four months later.

Mademoiselle Mars: Anne Boutet (1779–1847), whose stage name was Mademoiselle Mars, was a leading actress and a favourite of Napoleon. After the Restoration this was held against her by some royalist theatre-goers.

freedom of expression: After all censorship was abolished during the Hundred Days, a law passed on 22 February 1817 required newspapers and periodicals to be authorized before publication. This requirement was lifted in 1819, but the assassination of the Duc de Berry in 1820 led to the reimposition of censorship.

Le Constitutionnel . . . La Minerve: Founded during the Hundred Days under the title of *L'Indépendant*, then undergoing subsequent name changes, *Le Constitutionnel* was a paper of liberal anticlerical Bonapartist sentiment. The title ceased publication in 1919. *La Minerve* was a weekly liberal periodical whose principal editor was Benjamin Constant.

Châteaubriant: The town where Victor Hugo's parents met.

exiled in 1815 ... David ... Arnault ... Carnot: An active Revolutionary (he was a member of the Convention and voted for the execution of Louis XVI), Jacques-Louis David (1748–1825), whose *Death of Marat* is perhaps his best-known painting, went into exile in Brussels, and is buried there. Poet, dramatist and politician, Antoine Arnault (1766–1834), minister of public education during the Hundred Days, was exiled in 1816 and his membership of the French Academy withdrawn. He was allowed to return to France in 1819 and was re-elected to the Academy in 1829. A distinguished mathematician and engineer, Lazare Carnot (1753–1823) was also a leading politician. As a member of the Convention he voted for the execution of Louis XVI, then in 1794 contributed to the downfall of Robespierre. He was the great organizer of the French Revolutionary Army, and one of the first five directors of the Directory. Appointed minister of war in 1800 by First Consul Napoleon, he resigned from public office in 1804 after Napoleon was crowned emperor but returned as minister of the interior during the Hundred Days. He was exiled in 1815 and died in Magdeburg.

Soult: Marshal Soult (1769–1851) joined the army in 1785 as a private soldier, and was appointed marshal in 1804. Having rallied to Napoleon during the Hundred Days (he was Napoleon's chief of staff at Waterloo), he went into exile until 1819. Displaying considerable political opportunism, he was made a peer by Charles X and went on to serve under Louis-Philippe as minister of war, minister of foreign affairs, and several times as prime minister. He represented the French government at the coronation of Queen Victoria in 1838.

Descartes: The philosopher René Descartes (1596–1650) went to the Netherlands in 1628 and stayed there for most of the rest of his life, making a few brief visits to France in the 1640s, then at the invitation of Queen Christina in 1649 moving to Sweden, where he died. His self-imposed exile in a Protestant country gave him the greatest possible freedom to pursue his philosophical investigations, without fear of Catholic reprisals and without the distractions of life in Paris.

Buonaparte: It was a studied insult to call the Corsican-born Napoleon by his Italian surname. France took control of Corsica in 1768, and all the family eventually adopted the Gallicized version of their name.

the statue of Henri IV: An equestrian statue of Henri IV was erected at the end of the Pont-Neuf in 1614. It was melted down by Revolutionaries in 1792, and replaced in 1818 with a replica commissioned by Louis XVIII.

write to Bacot: Claude-René Bacot (1782–1853), made a baron in 1816, was an undistinguished politician.

Monsieur ... the Riverside Conspiracy: All those arrested in 1818 for their involvement – supposedly with the encouragement of the king's brother Monsieur, the future Charles X – in the so-called Riverside Conspiracy, including Vicomte Jean-Baptiste Chappedelaine (1741–1830) and Simon de Canuel (1767–1840), were acquitted of any royalist plot. There is no evidence that Jean-François O'Mahony (1772–1842), a French general of Irish origin who rallied to the Bourbons, was in any way connected with this incident.

The Black Pin: A black pin was supposed to identify members of another conspiracy, all former soldiers or army employees, who were brought to trial in 1817 but ultimately acquitted of any wrong-doing.

Delaverderie ... Trogoff: What is known as the 19 August 1820 (or French Bazaar) conspiracy was an alleged military plot to overthrow the government.

Gauthier de Laverderie (1793–1866), then a lieutenant, and Adolphe-Édouard de Trogoff (1788–1830), a captain, were involved. A small number of defendants were found guilty and sentenced to short terms in prison.

Decazes . . . something of a liberal: Appointed Paris prefect of police in 1815, Élie Decazes (1780–1860) was a moderate royalist who went on to become Louis XVIII's minister of the interior and prime minister. After the murder of the Duc de Berry he was ousted by the ultra-royalists, who accused his liberalism of being responsible for the assassination.

Pilorge . . . according to the Charter: In *De la monarchie selon la charte*, a pamphlet in defence of the legitimacy of the 1814 Charter and of a constitutional monarchy, Chateaubriand attacked the dissolution of the notoriously reactionary but constitutionally legitimate Chamber of Deputies. This led to Chateaubriand's fall from favour with the king, and he became a member of the ultra-royalist opposition. Hyacinthe Pilorge (1795–1861) was Chateaubriand's secretary from 1816 to 1843.

Lafon above Talma: François-Joseph Talma (1763–1826), who started out as a dentist, embarked on his glorious career as an actor during the Revolution. The younger actor Pierre Lafon (1773–1846) had to make his way in Talma's shadow, but an announcement of his appearance at the Grand Théâtre, Bordeaux, in 1814, for instance, hailed him as the 'foremost tragic actor on the French stage' (H. Carrington Lancaster in 'Letters of Lafon to Napoleon, Talma and Others', *Modern Language Notes*, vol. 68, no. 6, June 1953, pp. 377–82, Johns Hopkins University Press).

Monsieur de Féletz . . . Hoffmann . . . Z: A churchman who refused to take the oath of loyalty to the civil constitution, Charles-Marie de Féletz (1767–1850) was a journalist, Academician (who voted against Victor Hugo's candidature) and literary critic, who signed his articles A. A review of Hugo's *Nouvelles Odes* in 1824 in the *Journal des Débats*, written by François-Benoît Hoffmann (1760–1828), who signed himself Z, prompted a response from Hugo, challenging the critic's literary criteria and the usefulness of the terms 'classical' and 'Romantic'.

Charles Nodier: The Romantic poet and novelist Charles Nodier (1780–1844), a regular contributor to the *Journal des Débats*, in 1819 published his novel *Thérèse Aubert*, a story set during the insurrectionary wars in the Vendée region against the Revolutionary government (1793–6). Nodier was a friend of Hugo and a prominent supporter of his candidature for a seat in the French Academy.

Divorce was abolished: Divorce legislation was introduced in France in 1792. Over subsequent years the law was reformed and divorce became harder to obtain. It was abolished in 1816.

The lycées . . . colleges: The term *lycée*, introduced with the educational reforms under Napoleon in 1802 and replaced during the Restoration with the pre-Revolutionary name *collège*, was reinstated after the 1848 Revolution.

the king of Rome: The courtesy title of Napoleon's son (1811–32) by the Archduchess Marie-Louise of Austria, whom Napoleon, when he abdicated in 1815, named as his heir. (For this reason the next Bonaparte to occupy the French throne, in 1852, styled himself Napoleon III.)

Her Royal Highness Madame . . . Duc d'Orléans . . . Duc de Berry . . . dragoons: *Son altesse royale* was the honorific title of the wife of the king's brother (later Charles X), Marie Thérèse of Savoy. The future king Louis-Philippe, from a cadet branch of the Bourbons, inherited the title of Duc d'Orléans and the command of the hussars from his father, who was guillotined in 1793. Charles X's younger son, the Duc de Berry, was colonel-general of the lancers, not the dragoons, whose colonel-general was his older brother the Duc d'Angoulême.

Les Invalides: Louis XIV was the founder of Les Invalides, built as a hospital and home for veteran soldiers. The church of the Dome, a private royal chapel within the complex, designed by Jules Hardouin-Mansart (1646–1708), was completed in 1706. Under Napoleon the Dome became the pantheon of France's military heroes. Napoleon's ashes were transferred there in 1840.

Monsieur de Trinquelague: Charles-François de Trinquelague-Dions (1747–1837), a right-wing deputy, in 1815 backed a call for the reintroduction of the gibbet as a more convenient and less complicated instrument of capital punishment than the guillotine. 'Where would one not be able to find a piece of string? Everyone carries one in his pocket, and there is always a nail, a beam or the branch of a tree to which it may be attached.'

Clausel de Montals . . . de Coussergues: Clausel de Montals (1769–1857), bishop of Chartres (1824–53), was chaplain to the Duchesse d'Angoulême. His brother Clausel de Coussergues, a zealous supporter of the Bourbons who accused the moderate prime minister Decazes of being accomplice to the murder of the Duc de Berry, shared his Catholic royalist views.

Monsieur de Salaberry: Charles-Marie d'Irumberry Salaberry (1766–1847) was notoriously intemperate in his views and his language in the Chamber of Deputies. In 1816 he advocated the death penalty for anyone who flew the tricolour flag and in 1826 declared that 'printing was the only plague with which Moses forgot to strike Egypt'.

Picard . . . Les Deux Philibert: Actor, theatre manager and playwright Louis-Benoît Picard (1769–1828), author of *Les Deux Philibert* (The Two Philiberts), a comedy first staged at the Théâtre Royal de l'Odéon in 1816, was elected to the French Academy in 1807. The great comic playwright Molière (1622–73) was never a member.

Cugnet de Montarlot: One of those accused of taking part in the Black Pin conspiracy and in a number of other plots and conspiracies against the government but always eventually acquitted, Claude-François Cugnet de Montarlot (1778–1824) ended up being court-martialled and shot in Spain for his involvement with Spanish revolutionaries.

Fabvier: General Charles-Nicolas Fabvier (1782–1855), who was active in the later campaigns of the Empire, rallied to Louis XVIII, but like many ex-soldiers became disaffected and was involved in the 19 August 1820 conspiracy (see note p. 1318 on *Delaverderie . . . Trogoff*). In 1823 he joined the Greeks in their War of Independence against the Turks.

Bavoux: Initially in favour of the return of the Bourbons, Nicolas Bavoux (1774–1848) was a law professor and judge who in 1819 began to use his lectures as a platform for criticism of the government. He was charged with inciting citizens to disobey the law, but was acquitted.

Voltaire of the French Academy: Voltaire was eventually elected unanimously to the Academy in 1746, having faced strong religious opposition to his candidature earlier in his career.

Charles Loyson: Poet and political essayist Charles Loyson (1791–1820) competed in the same poetry competition as Victor Hugo in 1817 and won a commendation.

Cardinal Fesch: After the Restoration, Fesch retired to Rome and never returned to his archdiocese, which was run in his absence by Archbishop Pins.

the valley of Dappes . . . Dufour: Originally part of the Swiss canton of Vaud, the Dappes valley was annexed by Napoleon, and despite rulings made by the Congress of Vienna in 1815 for its restitution a final settlement was not reached until 1863, when it was divided between Switzerland and France. The Swiss-born Guillaume-Henri Dufour (1787–1875) served under Napoleon, then rejoined the Swiss army as captain in 1817. As general, he was involved in the ratification of the Treaty of Berne by which the Valley of Dappes Settlement was reached.

Saint-Simon: An aristocrat by birth, Claude-Henri de Rouvroy, Comte de Saint-Simon (1760–1825), embraced revolutionary ideals, taking part in the American War of Independence. He held Jacobin views during the French Revolution, but within the context of an ordered society governed by a scientific and industrialist hierarchy working together in the spirit of a new religion that recognized the moral value of economics. His ideas gained influence after his death.

Fourier: The physicist Joseph Fourier (1768–1830), author of *The Analytic Theory of Heat* (1822), was elected to the Academy of Sciences in 1817 and to the French Academy in 1826. He was Napoleon's scientific adviser in Egypt. Charles Fourier (1772–1837), author of *The Theory of Universal Unity* (1841), published after his death (as were most of his writings), like Saint-Simon was a Utopian socialist.

Lord Byron: George Gordon Byron, 6th Baron Byron (1788–1824) is the subject of Victor Hugo's poem 'Dédain' (Disdain), written in 1830 and dedicated 'To Byron in 1811', in which he celebrates the poet whose genius would triumph over the clamour of his detractors. Byron's poetic career began in earnest in 1812 with the publication of *Childe Harold's Pilgrimage* Cantos I and II, continuing with, among other works, his verse tales *The Giaour* (1813), *The Bride of Abydos* (1813) and *The Corsair* (1814), then *Childe Harold* Canto III in 1816. *Don Juan* Cantos I and II were first published, anonymously, in 1819. French translations of extracts of his works appeared from 1816.

Millevoye: The Romantic poet Charles Millevoye (1782–1816), whose best-known poem is 'La Chute des Feuilles' (Falling Leaves), on which the young Charlotte Brontë wrote in one of her early essays. He referred to 'Lord Baron' in a note to his poem 'Alfred, roi d'Angleterre', published in 1815.

David d'Angers: The sculptor David d'Angers (1789–1856) made several busts of Victor Hugo, by whom he was much admired. Like Hugo, he went into exile after the 1851 *coup d'état* by Louis-Napoleon.

Abbé Carron: Guy-Toussaint Carron (1760–1821), an émigré priest who set up charitable foundations for French émigrés first in Jersey, then in London, returned to Paris after the Restoration and ran an orphanage for the children of aristocratic families ruined by the Revolution. He first met Lamennais (see entry below) in London.

Lamennais: Félicité-Robert de Lamennais (1782–1854), ordained as a priest in 1816, was an apologist of ultramontanism as opposed to Gallicanism. He defended this position in numerous journals and periodicals, including *Le Drapeau Blanc*, an ultra-royalist publication, although politically and socially he was a liberal and increasingly radical in his views. He came to regard the papacy as misguided in its support of politically repressive regimes, and his writings were condemned by Pope Gregory XVI. In 1848 he was elected a deputy and allied himself with the democratic socialists. As unpopular with the government as he was with the Roman Catholic Church, he was revered by the common people and admired by Hugo.

steamboat: In August 1816 Jouffroy d'Abbans (1751–1832), who as early as 1783 successfully trialled his invention the pyroscaphe, a prototype steamboat, on the Saône, launched the *Charles-Philippe* steamboat on the Seine. (His was not the first steamboat on the Seine – that honour went in 1803 to the American Robert Fulton, who returned to America and had a successful career designing steamboats and running steamboat services.)

Monsieur de Vaublanc: As minister of the interior under Louis XVIII, the Comte de Vaublanc (1756–1845) was responsible for the restructuring of the French Institute under which the Academies were reinstated as independent bodies within the Institute. He was not himself appointed to the Academy.

the Pavillon de Marsan ... Monsieur Delavau: The Pavillon de Marsan is the part of the Louvre Palace that was occupied after the Restoration by Louis XVIII's brother the arch-royalist Comte d'Artois, later Charles X, and his son the Duc de Berry. The ultra-royalist Guy Delavau (1788–1874) was prefect of police 1821–8.

Dupuytren ... Récamier ... Cuvier: Chief surgeon at the Hôtel-Dieu and professor of clinical surgery, Guillaume Dupuytren (1777–1835), who played an important role in the development of modern surgery, was an alleged atheist. A pioneer in gynaecological and surgical medicine, chief physician at the Hôtel-Dieu, professor at the Faculty of Medicine and at the Collège de France, Joseph Récamier (1774–1852) cultivated a social circle of fellow Catholic intellectuals. A devout Lutheran, Georges Cuvier (1769–1828) was a naturalist and zoologist who made a major contribution to palaeontological research but was critical of contemporary evolutionary theories.

François de Neufchâteau ... Parmentier: President of the National Assembly 1791–2, member of the Directory, twice minister of the interior, president of the Senate and member of the French Academy, François de Neufchâteau (1750–1828) actively promoted industry, organizing the first French industrial exhibition in 1798; after the Bourbon Restoration and his retirement from public life, he devoted himself to the study of agriculture. Inspector-general of the armed forces' health service, Antoine-Augustin Parmentier (1737–1813) is best known as a great promoter of the potato (*pomme de terre*) as a source of nutrition.

Abbé Grégoire: A Republican priest and for ten years (1791–1801) bishop of Blois, Abbé Grégoire (1750–1831) was a member of the National Convention; he proposed the motion for the abolition of the monarchy and demanded that the king be brought to trial, but he would have suspended the death penalty.

Royer-Collard: Elected to the French Academy in 1827, Pierre-Paul Royer-Collard (1763–1845) led a campaign for the suppression of the neologism *baser* ('to base'), which had been accepted as a French word in the *Dictionnaire de l'Académie* of 1798; he threatened to leave the Academy if *baser* were not thrown out: 'S'il entre, je sors' ('If it's in, I'm out'). It was rejected on the grounds that there was no significant difference between *baser* and the preferred word *fonder* (Adolphe Thomas, *Dictionnaire des difficultés de la langue française*, Paris: Larousse, 1988). In Hugo's text the expression to which Royer-Collard takes exception is 'passer à l'état de'.

Pont d'Iéna ... Blücher: When the Allies occupied Paris after the abdication of Napoleon in 1814, the Prussian commander Blücher (whose troops were to play a decisive role in the battle of Waterloo) attempted to blow up the Pont d'Iéna, one of the four bridges in Paris built during the Napoleonic era and named after Napoleon's great victory over the Prussians at Jena in 1806.

Blücher was eventually dissuaded from this attempt to even scores, and the bridge was temporarily renamed the 'Pont des Invalides'. It regained its original name in 1830.

deserters from Ligny and Quatre-Bras: Napoleon's strategy before the battle of Waterloo, fought on 18 June 1815, was to avoid having to face combined Allied forces. So two days before, he launched attacks on the Prussians at Ligny and on the English at Quatre-Bras. The French failed to win a decisive victory at Quatre-Bras; and although the Prussians were defeated, they were able to retreat to a position where they could still play a crucial role in the engagement at Waterloo. There was a considerable number of Prussian deserters, but there are no figures for the French.

Burn for him . . . Oscar approaches . . . Ossian had left his mark: 'Brûlez pour lui les parfums d'Arabie / Oscar s'avance, Oscar, je vais le voir.' Hugo is quoting two lines from an anonymous popular song, 'Il va venir, le sultan que j'adore' ('He is coming, the sultan I adore'), which concludes with the singer expressing her fear that her lover will not be true. Oscar is also the name of a character (the son of Ossian) in James Macpherson's *Poems of Ossian* (1760–62). Purportedly translated from an ancient Scottish manuscript by the Gaelic warrior and bard Ossian, the poems' authenticity was contested at the time and they are now believed to be the work of Macpherson himself. Nevertheless, they enjoyed a phenomenal success, were widely translated and had a huge influence on contemporary literature and music.

the Jungfrau: Snow-white and unattainable, the Jungfrau (literally, 'young woman') is one of the peaks in the Swiss Alps.

grisettes: An archetypal figure of nineteenth-century Parisian life, the grisette is the sexually attractive and available young working woman. More often than not a seamstress or florist, poor but financially independent, she wants to enjoy herself and keeps company with students and artists, with whom she goes dancing and on country weekend outings.

Fécamp . . . St-Cloud: Fécamp, on the Normandy coast, is some 130 miles from Paris; St-Cloud, six.

Tête-Noire . . . Castaing: Dr Edmé Samuel Castaing and Auguste Ballet stayed at the Tête-Noire, where Castaing poisoned Ballet in May 1823, after the two of them had conspired to poison Ballet's brother in October of the previous year.

the Lantern of Diogenes: Napoleon had a square tower built in the grounds of the palace of St-Cloud, from which a light shone when he was in residence. The tower, known as the Lantern of Diogenes (a copy of the monument in Athens), and the palace were destroyed in the Franco-Prussian War in 1870, and the ruins razed to the ground in 1891.

Labouïsse . . . Éléonore: Married in 1802 to Éléonore Musard de St-Michel, Auguste de Labouïsse-Rochefort (1778–1852) dedicated much of his poetry to her, including a collection of elegies entitled *Les Amours*, and *Éléonoriana*, recounting the lives of famous Éléonores. She died in 1833.

keepsakes: Literary albums popular in the nineteenth century. The *Keepsake Annual* was published in England from 1827 until 1856.

Delvincourt . . . Blondeau: Claude Étienne Delvincourt (1762–1831), professor of civil law. Hyacinthe Blondeau (1784–1854), Belgian professor of Roman law.

Ternaux shawl: Imitation Kashmir shawls manufactured in France by Guillaume Ternaux (1763–1833) to satisfy the craze for shawls.

Galatea: In Greek mythology the water nymph Galatea, who is in love with Acis, flees from the jealous Cyclops, Polyphemus. In the pastoral romance *Galatée*

(1784) by Jean-Pierre Claris de Florian (1755–94), the shepherdess Galatea appears on a hill, 'ses longs cheveux blonds flottaient sur ses épaules ... Simple comme la fleur des champs, elle était belle et ne le savait pas' ('her long blonde hair hung loose on her shoulders ... As natural as the flower of the fields, she was lovely and did not know it'). There is an echo of this in the later paragraph beginning 'Fantine was beautiful without really being aware of it.'

Erigone: In Greek mythology, the lovely Erigone is seduced by Bacchus when he turns himself into a bunch of grapes (Ovid, *Metamorphoses*, bk VI). More darkly, she is also the daughter of Icarius, and hangs herself when she finds her father has been murdered – by those to whom he had served wine (made from grapes of the vine given him by Dionysius); they thought the effects of the drink were those of poison. She is then turned into the constellation Virgo.

the Canebière: The commercial thoroughfare that climbs uphill from the port of Marseille, where the southern accent would pronounce *quinze août* (15 August, the date of the big summer festival in honour of the Assumption of the Virgin) as *canezou* (a spencer-like jacket).

Aeginetan Junos: The so-called Aeginetan Marbles, discovered in 1811 on the Greek island of Aegina and now in the Munich Glyptothek, came from a temple at first thought to be dedicated to Zeus Panhellenius and now known from an inscription to be dedicated to Aphaia. The Junos are probably what were later identified as the Athenas.

Coustou: Nicolas (1658–1733) and Guillaume (1677–1746) Coustou, both sculptors, were brothers who sometimes worked together on the same commissions.

Psyche from Venus: The Latin 'novel' *The Golden Ass* by Apuleius (c.123–80) tells the story of Psyche and Cupid. The goddess Venus, jealous of Psyche's beauty, tries to punish her mortal rival; but her plan is thwarted when Cupid falls in love with the girl, who is equally enamoured of him, and through their love for each other Psyche eventually gains immortality.

Barbarossa: The Holy Roman Emperor Frederick I, known as Barbarossa (1122–90), on an expedition to the Holy Land during the Third Crusade took the city of Iconium (modern-day Konya) after the battle of Iconium in May 1190, shortly before he died.

The departure for Cythera: Two famous paintings by the rococo artist Jean-Antoine Watteau (1684–1721) are called *Pèlerinage à l'île de Cythère* (Pilgrimage to the Island of Cythera) and *Embarquement pour Cythère* or *Le retour du pèlerinage à Cythère* (Embarkation for Cythera, or Return of the Pilgrimage to Cythera), which was copied by Watteau's colleague Nicolas Lancret (1690–1743) and entitled *Le départ pour Cythère* (Departure for Cythera).

d'Urfé: Honoré d'Urfé (1568–1625), author of the pastoral novel *L'Astrée* (Astraea), which featured Druids.

Bourguin: Probably an allusion to Louis Bourgain (1752–1837), a Parisian candlemaker who in 1792 bought an estate at Issy and eventually became the owner of one of the largest local property holdings.

Turcaret: Turcaret is the main character in a satirical comedy of the same name by Alain-René Lesage (1668–1747) about an unscrupulous and lovelorn financier.

Abbé de Bernis: Pierre de Bernis (1715–94), poet and Academician (elected in 1744), became a cardinal (1758) and ambassador to Rome (1769).

Greuze: Jean-Baptiste Greuze (1725–1805) was successful as a genre painter, celebrated for sentimental and moralizing depictions of village life and almost provocatively charming portraits of young girls.

the old Galician song: 'I am from Badajoz. / Love calls me. / All my soul / Is in my eyes / Because you are showing / Your legs.'

the Beaujon heights: In 1801 a descendant of the Ruggieri firework-making family took over the running of the extravagant pleasure garden known as the Folie-Beaujon, constructed (close to where the Arc de Triomphe now stands) by the immensely wealthy financier Nicolas Beaujon (1708–86), banker to the court of Louis XVI. An aerial rail-ride, a forerunner of the roller-coaster, was inaugurated there in 1817. The Beaujon estate had been bought in 1796 by the Flemish-born Ignace Vanlerberghe, who made his fortune by supplying the French army.

says Molière: Hugo is slightly misquoting two lines from Act IV, scene iv of Molière's *L'Étourdi* (The Blunderer; 1655).

the Marly horses: The work of Guillaume Coustou, made for the gardens of the Château de Marly and moved in 1795 to the Champs-Élysées, where they were replaced by copies when the originals were transferred to the Louvre in 1984.

The white flag: Also known as the Bourbon banner, 'The White Flag' was taken as the name of the ultra-royalist newspaper *Le Drapeau Blanc*, published 1819–27.

Place Louis XV: Place de la Concorde regained its Revolutionary name after the 1830 Revolution.

the moire ribbon: The Decoration of the Fleur-de-Lys suspended on a white moire ribbon was introduced under the monarchy in 1814 for the National Guard of Paris, then extended throughout the realm beyond those serving in the National Guard. It was replaced in 1816 by the Decoration of Fidelity.

paper caps: A distinctive attribute of the apprentice printer's trade.

Prefect of Police Anglès: Jules Anglès (1778–1828), prefect of police from 1815 to 1821.

tenth of August: The Tuileries Palace was stormed by Parisian Revolutionaries in August 1792 at a time of political stalemate, prompting the king and his family to seek the protection of the Legislative Assembly and effectively bringing the monarchy to an end.

Danton: The Revolutionary leader Georges Danton (1759–94) had a particular charisma that made him very popular with the people. He claimed responsibility for the storming of the Tuileries (see entry above) and played a major role in the early years of the Revolutionary period. He increasingly distanced himself from Revolutionary extremism and eventually fell victim to the Terror.

Caudine Forks ... Rue Greneta: In 321 BC, trapped in the plain between two narrow exits, the Romans were defeated by the Samnites at the mountain pass known as the Caudine Forks. A busy street to the north-east of Les Halles, Rue Greneta was regularly barricaded during popular uprisings in Paris and was the last stronghold of the insurrectionists in the 1839 uprising.

Carmagnole ... Marseillaise: A Revolutionary song that became popular in 1792, the 'Carmagnole' is a celebration of the overthrow of the monarchy. A patriotic song written by Rouget de Lisle (1760–1836) and initially taken up and brought to Paris by revolutionary volunteers from the South, the 'Marseillaise', first declared the 'national song' in July 1795, is a celebration of national identity.

No overeagerness ... Grimod de la Reynière ... Talleyrand: Talleyrand, the great political survivor, may well have owed his political longevity to the dictum he is supposed to have issued to his subordinates, usually quoted as 'Surtout, pas de zèle' ('Above all, no zeal'). Grimod de la Reynière (1758–1837), author of

Manuel des amphitryons (1808), a guide to entertaining at table, is the gastronome who with his *Almanach des Gourmands*, published annually (1803–12), established the role of restaurant and food critic.

Moses . . . Isaac: On being told by God that his ninety-year-old wife Sarah is to bear him a child, Abraham falls on his face and laughs. God then tells him he is to call the child Isaac (Genesis 17:15–19), a name that derives from the Hebrew verb 'to laugh'.

Aeschylus . . . Polynices: In *Seven Against Thebes* Aeschylus makes several references to the literal meaning of the name of the warring brother Polynices, 'man of great strife'.

Cleopatra . . . Octavian: In Plutarch's *Life of Antony*, shortly before Octavian's victory at Actium, Cleopatra plays on the word *toryne* – meaning 'ladle', and the name of the town *Toryne*, occupied by Octavian, who has arrived there at lightning speed – to make a disparaging remark about the threat that Octavian poses, suggesting he is simply stirring his soup-pot.

Amphiaraus: King of Argos, in Aeschylus' play *Seven Against Thebes* Amphiaraus was leader of the Argive attack on the sixth gate of Thebes; renowned for his moderation and prudence, he deplores the vengeful enterprise of Polynices and foresees his own death with resignation.

Caesar's baldness: Suetonius comments on Caesar's baldness in his *Lives of the Twelve Caesars* ('Julius Caesar', ch. 45).

the Parricide: An allusion to Nero, known to have been involved in the murder of his mother Agrippina and probably that of his step-brother Britannicus, *parricidum* meaning 'murder of a close relative'.

Sulla, or Origen: Plutarch tells of Lucius Cornelius Sulla's rise to murderous dictator, followed by his voluntary abdication and retirement in 79 BC, a year before his death. In his *History of the Church* the bishop of Caesarea Eusebius (*c.*263–339) records that so great was the ascetic zeal of the scholar theologian Origen (*c.*185–232) that he castrated himself.

Here's the recipe: What follows is a paraphrase of the remedies listed in the entry for 'Satyriasis' (male hypersexuality) in Diderot and d'Alembert's *Encyclopédie*, vol. 14, 1765.

to win the apple: In Greek mythology, Aphrodite (or Venus, in Roman terms) was awarded the golden apple by Paris for being the goddess of the greatest beauty, in a contest with Hera and Athena.

waistcoat-makers and shoe-stitchers: Two other grisette categories.

Bonaparte's sublime address: Napoleon's proclamation to the army at the beginning of the Italian campaign in March 1796 inspired his troops to great victories: 'Soldiers, you are naked, ill-nourished. The government owes you a great deal, it can give you nothing . . . I want to lead you into the world's most fertile plains. Rich provinces and great cities will be in your power. There you will find honour, glory and riches. Soldiers of Italy, will you lack courage or steadfastness?'

Clermont-Tonnerre: Possibly a reference to Anne-Jules de Clermont-Tonnerre (1749–1830), who as archbishop of Toulouse (1820–30) was engaged in trying to integrate into the post-Revolutionary Church old believers who had never sworn the constitutional oath and refused to recognize the legitimacy of the 1801 Concordat between Napoleon and the papacy.

St John's Day: The feast day of St John the Evangelist is 27 December, traditionally a period of Misrule.

Elleviou: François Elleviou (1769–1842) was a celebrated tenor who sang at the Opéra-Comique, where he commanded huge sums. In 1813, when his financial demands became too great and were refused, he went into retirement and never sang in public again.

silver chin: In his *Chronicles*, a medieval prose narrative about the Hundred Years War, Jean Froissart (*c.*1337–1405) talks of an English squire who had sustained facial injuries in battle having a silver chin made for him. The case of a French gunner, injured at the siege of Antwerp in 1832, whose lower jaw was replaced by a silver mask was reported in the *London Medical Gazette* of 1833.

Désaugiers: The two Désaugiers, father (1742–93) and son (1772–1827), both with the first name Marc-Antoine, were composers of operas and comedies for the stage; the son also gained popularity with his light-hearted and satirical songs.

Ber ... quin ... choux: Arnaud Berquin (1747–91) was a writer of children's literature, most notably *L'Ami des Enfants* (The Children's Friend; 1872–3), which remained popular in France and indeed in Britain and elsewhere well into the nineteenth century. The poet and humorist Joseph Berchoux (1760–1833) wrote a poem about food, published in 1800, entitled 'La gastronomie', thereby introducing a new word into the French language.

Aspasia: Aspasia of Miletus (*c.*470–400 BC) became the consort of the Athenian statesman and general Pericles (*c.*495–429 BC). She is reported by Plutarch (*Life of Pericles*) to have been accused of encouraging him to sail against Samos, which was at war with Miletus. One of Socrates' students, Aeschinus, has left written testimony to her intellectual capabilities.

Manon Lescaut: Manon Lescaut is the faithless young beauty who forsakes her lover for the sake of riches, in the novel of the same title (1733) by Abbé Prévost (1697–1763), which was to enjoy immense popularity and be taken up by other writers and composers.

Prometheus: In Greek mythology, Prometheus is the Titan who fashions man from clay and steals fire from the gods to give it to his creation.

civil code for respectable children: There is an allusion in Hugo's 'le code civil puéril et honnête' to a manual of good manners for children entitled *La Civilité puérile et honnête*, of which twenty editions were published between 1775 and 1846, whose authorship was attributed to a schoolteacher named Mathurin Cordier (?1479–1564), and which was inspired by Erasmus's *De Civilitate Morum Puerilium* (On Good Manners for Boys; 1530).

Laffitte ... Caillard: Jean-Baptiste Laffitte (1775–1849) and Vincent Caillard (1758–1843) in 1828 set up the Messageries Laffitte et Caillard, which became the leading public transport company in France, offering thirty stage-coach routes throughout the country.

Homer ... Polyphemus ... Shakespeare, Caliban: In Homer's *Odyssey*, bk 9, Polyphemus is the man-eating Cyclops who holds Odysseus and his men prisoner inside his cave until they manage to escape by getting him drunk on wine, and blinding him. Caliban, Prospero's slave in Shakespeare's *Tempest*, is 'as disproportioned in his manners as in his shape'.

A warrior so bold and a virgin so bright: From 'The Ballad of Alonzo the Brave and Fair Imogine', published in England in 1796 in Matthew Lewis's seminal Gothic novel *The Monk*: 'A Warrior so bold, and a Virgin so bright / Conversed, as They sat on the green: / They gazed on each other with tender delight; / Alonzo the Brave was the name of the Knight, / The Maid's was the Fair Imogine. // "And Oh!" said the Youth, "since tomorrow I go / To fight in a far distant land, / Your tears for my absence soon leaving to flow, / Some Other will court you, and you will bestow / On a wealthier Suitor your hand."'

The ballad ends gruesomely: 'While They drink out of skulls newly torn from the grave, / Dancing around them the Spectres are seen: / Their liquor is blood, and this horrible Stave / They howl: "To the health of Alonzo the Brave, / And his Consort, the False Imogine!"' First translated and published in Paris in 1797, the ballad was very popular in the nineteenth century, quoted for instance in *La Misère* by Louise Michel and Marguerite Tinayre (1882) and referred to in François Coppée's poem number XI in his collection *Promenades et Intérieurs* (1872). Madame Thénardier sings the first four lines of the French version: 'Il le faut, disait un guerrier / À la belle et tendre Imogine / Il le faut, je suis chevalier / Et je pars pour la Palestine.'

Louis-Philippe: King of France from 1830 to 1848.

Clélie ... Lodoïska ... Scudéry ... Barthélémy-Hadot ... Lafayette ... Bournon-Malarme: A historical novel with a Roman setting, *Clélie*, by Mademoiselle de Scudéry (1607–1701), was published in ten volumes (1654–61), and very soon translated into English. Madame de Lafayette (1634–93) is best known for her novel *La Princesse de Clèves* (1678). Madame Barthélémy-Hadot (1763–1821) and the prolific Madame Bournon-Malarme (1753–1830) wrote sentimental stories that have since fallen into obscurity. Lodoïska is the heroine of the novel *Les Amours du chevalier de Faublas* by the journalist and Revolutionary of the moderate Girondist faction Louvet de Couvrai (1760–97). The Italian composer Luigi Cherubini (1760–1842) and the German composer Simon Mayr (1763–1845) based their operas *Lodoïska* (1791) and *La Lodoïska* (1796), respectively, on his novel.

Pamela ... Megaera: The heroine of Richardson's novel *Pamela, or Virtue Rewarded* (1740) is a lovely young serving-girl who manages to avoid being seduced and eventually marries the squire. Megaera is one of the three Furies of Greek mythology, whose name has come to signify a shrewish woman.

Éponine ... Gulnare: Eponina is the name of a woman famed for her heroic devotion to her husband Julius Sabinus, a Gaul who led a rebellion against the Romans in AD 69. The story is told by Tacitus in his *Histories* and by Plutarch in his *Dialogue on Love*. Gulnare is a name from the *Arabian Nights*, taken up by Byron, for instance, in his poem *The Corsair*.

Ducray-Duminil: François-Guillaume Ducray-Duminil (1761–1819), playwright and songwriter, and author of a number of novels of Gothic inspiration, many of them featuring children as central characters, that were hugely successful in their day.

Dumollard: Martin Dumollard (1810–62) was executed as a serial murderer. His father was executed by the Austrians when Martin was four years old. Hugo mentioned the case in a letter of 1862 in support of the campaign for the abolition of the death penalty in Geneva.

Laffitte: Jacques Laffitte (1767–1844), as a 50 per cent shareholder and director of Perregaux Laffitte, built up what became one of Europe's leading banks. In 1814 he was appointed governor of the Bank of France; he later served as prime minister (1830–31). He was the older brother of Jean-Baptiste Laffitte, of the public transport company Laffitte et Caillard.

Legislative Corps under the Empire: A constituent part of the government apparatus under Napoleon's Consulate and Empire, but with little power.

Fouché: Joseph Fouché (1759–1820), the most opportunist of political operators, served the Republic, the Directory, the Consulate, the Empire and the monarchy for many years as minister of police. Educated by the Oratorians, he took minor clerical vows, but later renounced his religion and as a member of the Convention from 1792 he implemented a policy of radical anticlericalism. He was made Duke of Otranto by Napoleon in 1808 and served as minister of police 1799–1802 and 1804–10.

industrial exhibition: The first Paris Exhibition, the Exposition Publique des Produits de l'Industrie Française, was held in 1798. Others followed at irregular intervals. The one held in 1819 was the fifth.

the cross: The Legion of Honour badge, known as a cross, looks like a five-branched Maltese cross but with ten points instead of eight.

Brutus in Vidocq: Marcus Junius Brutus (85–42 BC), who joined the Ides of March conspiracy to assassinate Julius Caesar in 44 BC, was celebrated in Revolutionary France as the embodiment of Republican integrity, as was the legendary founder of the Roman Republic Lucius Junius Brutus (sixth century BC), who sentenced to death his own sons for conspiring to restore the monarchy, an incident that inspired David's controversial painting of 1789, *The Lictors Bring to Brutus the Bodies of His Sons*. Eugène-François Vidocq (1775–1857) was a reformed criminal, condemned to penal servitude for theft and fraud, who twice escaped prison and eventually joined the police as an informer. He was extraordinarily successful as the head of the police detective force, and after he retired set up his own private detective agency. He published his memoirs, first ghost-written and then rewritten by himself (1828–9). His other publications included a dictionary of slang (1836), a study of thieves (1836) and a novel (1845) about the extortionist bandits known as the *chauffeurs* (see note p. 1410 on *chauffeurs*).

Monsieur de Villèle: The ultra-royalist Jean-Baptiste de Villèle (1773–1854), appointed minister of finance in 1821, was later prime minister (1822–8) and minister of the interior.

Jacobins: The Jacobin Club was the most extreme faction of the Revolutionaries, responsible for the implementation of the Terror, and was so called because its meetings were held at the convent of the Dominicans, known also as the Jacobins; their convent and church in Paris were dedicated to St Jacques.

Bolívar against Morillo: Born in Caracas, Venezuela, Simón Bolívar (1783–1830) was commander of the revolutionary forces in the wars of independence in the South American Spanish colonies. Pablo Morillo (1775–1837) was the Spanish general sent to South America in 1814 to pacify the revolts in the Spanish colonies. (After he returned to Spain he supported the liberal constitution in the Spanish Civil War of 1820–3.)

the wise . . . foolish virgins: Allusion to the parable in Matthew 25:1–13.

Laennec's admirable lead: René Laennec (1781–1826), a Breton doctor who in 1816 first applied the principle of using a stethoscope for diagnosis (he applied a rolled-up tube of paper to a patient's chest), and went on to make major advances in the understanding of pulmonary diseases.

Sicard . . . Massieu: Jean Massieu (1772–1846), pupil, friend and successor of the deaf educator Abbé Sicard (1742–1822), is particularly remembered in the English-speaking world for having taught Laurent Clerc, who became the founding father of deaf education in the United States; a lasting legacy is that French and American sign languages remain close (while British and American are quite dissimilar).

Simplice of Sicily: St Agatha of Catania in Sicily is the Christian martyr commonly associated with the torture of having her breasts torn off rather than renounce her faith. Simplician and Simplicius are the names of a number of Italian saints, all male.

the green cap: The green cap was worn by convicts serving a life sentence.

Monsieur de Conzié: Louis-Hilaire de Conzié (1736–1804), bishop of Arras 1775–95.

Jean-Nicolas Pache: Having been driven from his position as minister of war by the Girondist faction, Jean-Nicolas Pache (1746–1823) was elected mayor of Paris in 1793 (and is responsible for the motto 'Liberty, Equality, Fraternity' being placed on public buildings in the capital). He took his revenge by leading a popular insurrection that resulted in the expulsion from the Convention of Girondist ministers and deputies, who, in a prelude to the Terror, were ordered on 3 June 1793 to be placed under house arrest.

9 June year II: It is the mixture of the Revolutionary and Gregorian calendars that Hugo highlights here as a mistake.

Melpomene: The Greek muse of tragedy.

young Levites: In Numbers 18:1–32 the tribe of Levi is invested by God with the role of the priesthood.

Bénigne Bossuet . . . acquitted himself magnificently: Bossuet's funeral orations were among the most celebrated examples of his rhetorical skills. In the one dedicated to the Princess Palatine Anne de Gonzague de Clèves (1685) he refers to a vision that she had in which the love of Jesus Christ was revealed to her in the image of a mother hen looking after her young.

L'Oriflamme . . . La Quotidienne: L'Oriflamme was a short-lived (July 1824–July 1825) Catholic royalist journal *'de littérature, des sciences et des arts, d'histoire, et de doctrines religieuses et monarchiques'* that took a strong anti-Romantic line, referring to Romantics as 'jeunes Vandales . . . qui se croient sublimes parce qu'ils sont hypocondres' ('young Vandals . . . who think they are sublime because they are hypochondriac'). La Quotidienne was a royalist newspaper founded in 1790 that continued to appear almost uninterrupted until 1847.

Théramène's speech: The famous speech in Racine's tragedy *Phèdre* (Act V, sc. vi) in which Théramène describes to Theseus how his son Hippolyte has died, killed by his own runaway horses that are frightened by a dreadful monster: 'Le ciel avec horreur voit ce monstre sauvage, / La terre s'en émeut, l'air en est infecté' ('The sky sees with horror this ferocious monster, / The earth is appalled by it, the air is poisoned by it'). The disparaging remark about the speech being 'of no use to tragedy' comes from the author of *Hernani*, the play staged in 1830 which provoked the famous brawl between the advocates of classicism and those of Romanticism, marking the moment when the Romantics successfully challenged the traditionalists and forced the establishment theatre to take them seriously.

Mardi Gras: Shrove Tuesday, the last day before the beginning of Lent, celebrated with parades, masquerades and carnival festivities.

the first of March 1815: See note p. 1312 on *Gulf of Juan proclamation*.

St Michael: In the Christian tradition, St Michael is the avenging archangel who leads the fight against Satan.

PART TWO: COSETTE

biscayen bullet: A long-barrelled large-bore musket, dating from the late seventeenth century, that originated in the Spanish province of Biscay, the biscayen gave its name to large bullets or balls used in canister-shot even after the muskets fell out of use.

Hougomont: Often spelled Hougoumont. Hugo's spelling allows him the personal satisfaction of deriving its name from *Hugomons*, for which he is the sole authority.

something that . . . looked like a lion: The statue of a lion, standing on a mound that was constructed after the battle, with earth moved from other parts of the battlefield, is a monument (completed in 1826) erected by King William of the Netherlands to commemorate the bravery of his son the Prince of Orange, who was injured at this spot in the course of the battle.

Villers Abbey: A twelfth-century Cistercian abbey that reached its apogee in the thirteenth century, when it housed a hundred monks and three hundred lay brothers. It was suppressed in 1796.

Cooke: Major-General George Cooke (1768–1837) commanded the British defence of Hougomont.

his brother Jerome: Napoleon's youngest brother (1784–1860) was a division commander at Waterloo, although Napoleon himself had a poor opinion of Jerome's capabilities.

Guilleminot: General Armand-Charles Guilleminot (1774–1840) served as chief of staff to the division commanded by Jerome Bonaparte.

Foy: After Waterloo, at which he commanded an infantry corps, General Maximilien Foy (1775–1825) went on to become a respected and popular liberal politician, greatly mourned when he died.

Bachelu: General Gilbert Bachelu (1777–1849), in command of an infantry division, was wounded in the attack on Hougomont. This was the end of his military career, but during the 1830s he was elected as deputy representing the non-Republican left.

Reille: General Honoré Reille (1775–1860) commanded the army's 2nd Corps at Waterloo. He was named a marshal of France in 1847.

Kellermann: General François-Étienne Kellermann (1770–1835), who made a historic cavalry charge at the battle of Marengo, commanded the 3rd Cavalry Corps at Waterloo.

Bauduin: General Pierre Bauduin (1768–1815), infantry brigade commander at Waterloo. There is a commemorative plaque dedicated to him on Hougomont's exterior wall, at which he fell.

Soye: General Jean-Louis Soye (1774–1832) was an infantry brigade commander at Waterloo.

Legros: Serving under the command of Colonel de Cubières of the 1st Light Infantry, Sous-Lieutenant Legros, known by his fellow soldiers as 'l'Enfonceur' ('the one who breaks through', 'the rammer'), armed with an axe, led a French attack on a gate into the courtyard of Hougomont, and a small doomed band managed to break in. The English fought back and re-closed the gate.

van Kylsom: When Hugo visited in 1861 the name of the family living at Hougomont was van Cutsem. Evidence suggests that the same family was not there in 1815 – see Michel Damiens, *Hougoumont: Une clé de la bataille de Waterloo* (Hougoumont: A key to the battle of Waterloo), http://www.scribd.com/doc/81344169/Hougoumont-une-cle-de-la-bataille-de-Waterloo, pp. 42–4.

Wilda: There is no direct evidence for this anecdote. It is, it seems, a Hugolian conflation of name and of incident.

Le Nôtre: The grandson and son of royal gardeners, the landscape gardener André Le Nôtre (1613–1700) designed the park and gardens at Versailles, Vaux-le-Vicomte and Chantilly.

Major Blackman: Captain John Lucie Blackman (1793–1815) of the Coldstream Guards died at the end of the day's fighting and was buried in the orchard, where there is a gravestone bearing his name, although his body was subsequently moved, in 1890, to the Memorial in the Brussels Cemetery at Evere.

Duplat: Colonel Charles Duplat (1770–1815) commanded the 1st Infantry Brigade of the King's German Legion.

Edict of Nantes: Signed in 1598 by Henri IV, the Huguenot king who converted to Catholicism (with the apocryphal words, 'Paris is well worth a mass') to secure his hold over a unified France; ending the French Wars of Religion (1562–98), the Edict of Nantes guaranteed the civil and religious rights of French Protestants. It was revoked by Louis XIV in 1685, leading to the emigration of over 400,000 Huguenots.

Blücher: The Prussian army fought alongside the Anglo-Dutch-German army in this campaign under the independent command of Field-Marshal Gebhard Leberecht von Blücher (1742–1819); his intervention in the battle late in the day proved decisive.

Aboukir: The battle of Aboukir on 25 July 1799 was a French victory, led by Napoleon (then a general), against the Turks.

Walter Scott, Lamartine, Vaulabelle, Charras, Quinet, Thiers: An early visitor to Waterloo after the battle, Sir Walter Scott (1771–1832) arrived there in August, and published his impressions in a series of imaginary letters entitled *Paul's Letters to His Kinsfolk* (1816). He also treated the subject in poems such as *The Field of Waterloo* (1815), and in 1827 published a *Life of Napoleon Buonaparte*. Alphonse de Lamartine (1790–1869), poet, politician, minister of foreign affairs in 1848 and historian, author of *Histoire de la Restauration* (1851–2); Achille Tenaille de Vaulabelle (1799–1879), a liberal, journalist, politician and historian, author of a number of works relating to the battle of Waterloo; Jean-Baptiste Adolphe Charras (1810–65), Republican, army officer and politician, military historian and author of *Histoire de la campagne de 1815 – Waterloo* (History of the 1815 Campaign – Waterloo; Brussels, 1857), published while he was in exile; Edgard Quinet (1803–75), academic, left-wing politician, political philosopher, poet and historian, author of *La Campagne de 1815* (The 1815 Campaign; Paris, 1862); Adolphe Thiers (1797–1877), politician, president of France 1871–73, prime minister in 1836 and 1840, lawyer, Academician, journalist and historian whose publications include a twenty-volume *Histoire du Consulat et de l'Empire* (History of the Consulate and the Empire; 1843–62) and *Waterloo* (1862).

d'Erlon ... Picton ... Hill: General Drouet d'Erlon (1765–1844) commanded the French 1st Corps. The division led by General Thomas Picton (1758–1815) was part of the reserve under the direct orders of Wellington. General Rowland Hill (1772–1842) was commander of the Allied 2nd Corps.

Brienne Academy: The military preparatory school at Brienne-le-Château where Napoleon spent five and a half years, from 1779 to 1784, and where there is now a museum dedicated to him.

his plaque ... red sash: Legion of Honour decoration.

the Marengo sword: The sword worn by Napoleon at the battle of Marengo, 14 June 1800, when victory was claimed late in the day by the seemingly defeated French.

Babylon ... Alexander: Alexander took Babylon in 331 BC.

Jerusalem ... Titus: When in AD 70 Jerusalem fell to Titus (39–81; Roman emperor for the last two years of his life), all those who had held out in the

Great Temple were slaughtered and the building was razed to the ground; only the western wall, now known as the Wailing Wall, was left standing.

Colville: Lieutenant-General Charles Colville (1770–1843), in charge of the 4th Division, did not actually take part in the battle at Waterloo, being posted at the nearby town of Hal.

Quiot: General Joachim Quiot du Passage (1775–1849) at Waterloo took command of France's 1st Division.

Ney: After a distinguished career in the French Revolutionary and Napeolonic Wars, Marshal Ney (1769–1815) commanded the left wing of the French army at Waterloo, and has been blamed for some poor decisions that contributed to France's defeat. After the battle he was arrested, tried and condemned for treason (to the Bourbon regime, having rallied to Napoleon during the Hundred Days). He was executed by firing squad on 7 December 1815 (although there are those who believe that he survived and fled to safety in America, dying there in 1846).

Perponcher: The Dutch general Count Perponcher Sedlnitsky (1771–1856) commanded the 2nd Netherlands Division at Quatre-Bras and Waterloo.

Kempt: The British general James Kempt (1765–1854) led Wellington's 8th Brigade at Waterloo in Picton's 5th Division, of which he took command after Picton was killed. He later became governor-general of Canada.

Salvator Rosa: Italian painter (1615–73), who enjoyed great popularity with the Romantics; he treated a wide range of subject matter, including battle scenes.

Gribeauval: General and military engineer Jean-Baptiste Vaquette de Gribeauval (1715–89) restructured the artillery corps, reorganized the use of artillery, improved the design and standardized the manufacture of artillery equipment. See note p. 1406 on *Gribeauval's étoile mobile*.

van der Meulen: The Flemish painter Adam Franz van der Meulen (1632–90) accompanied Louis XIV on several of his campaigns to record France's military accomplishments.

Folard . . . Polybius: In a commentary published in 1727 on Polybius' *Histories*, an account by the Greek historian of the rise of Rome and a study of successful warfare, Jean-Charles Folard (1669–1752) developed his own theories of military strategy, most notably building on what Polybius said about the Macedonian phalanx as opposed to the Roman legion and advocating column over line formation.

the foremost boxer in England: John Shaw (1789–1815), a corporal in the Life Guards.

Baring: The Hanoverian officer Major Georg Baring (1773–1848) of the 2nd Light Infantry of the King's German Legion led the heroic defence of La Haie-Sainte.

Alten: Lieutenant-General Sir Charles (also Karl) von Alten (1764–1840), 'the best of the Hanoverians' in Wellington's words, commanded the British 3rd Infantry Division.

Ponsonby: Major-General Sir William Ponsonby (1772–1815) commanded the Union cavalry brigade, including the Scots Greys.

Bro: Colonel Louis Bro (1781–1844) commanded the 4th Regiment of Light Lancers in France's 1st Corps. He later served in Algeria.

Travers: General Travers, Baron de Jever (1765–1827), commanded Napoleon's 2nd Cavalry Brigade of two cuirassier regiments and was wounded at Waterloo. After the battle he settled in Brussels.

Hamilton: Colonel James Inglis Hamilton (1777–1815), in command of the Scots Greys, was killed in the charge that he led.

Mater: Probably a reference to Lieutenant-Colonel Joseph Muter of the 6th (Inniskilling) Dragoons, who assumed command of the Union cavalry brigade after Ponsonby was killed, until he himself was wounded and command passed to Lieutenant-Colonel Arthur Clifton (1780–1879). Shortly after the battle Muter took the name Straton on inheriting from a relative on that side of the family; he died, a lieutenant-general, in 1841.

Gordon: Wellington's aide-de-camp Lieutenant-Colonel Sir Alexander Gordon (1786–1815), whose leg was smashed by a cannon-ball and later amputated, died early the next morning.

Marsh: There was a Corporal William Marsh of the 12th Light Dragoons killed at Waterloo, whose name appears on a plaque in St Joseph's church at Waterloo, but this is possibly a reference to Troop Sergeant-Major Matthew Marshall of the 6th (Inniskilling) Dragoons, who lay on the battlefield for two days and three nights with 19 lance and sabre wounds; he died in 1825.

Chassé: Lieutenant-General David Hendrik Chassé (1765–1849), commander of a Dutch light infantry division, had fought with the French after the Netherlands was annexed by the French in 1810.

Haxo: General Haxo (1774–1838) served at Waterloo as commander-in-chief of the Imperial Guard Engineers, and after the fall of Napoleon continued to serve France as a distinguished military engineer. In 1832 he was made a peer of France by Louis-Philippe.

Vincke: Colonel Ernst von Vincke (1768–1845) commanded the 5th Hanoverian Brigade in Picton's 5th Division.

Clinton: General Henry Clinton (1771–1829), whose father was commander-in-chief of British forces during the American Revolutionary War, led the 2nd Division Waterloo.

Halkett: Major-General Colin Halkett (1774–1856) commanded the 5th Brigade in Alten's 3rd Division. He was later lieutenant governor of Jersey.

Mitchell: Colonel Hugh Henry Mitchell (1770–1817), in command of the 4th Brigade in the 4th Division, was involved in the defence of Hougomont farm.

Maitland: Major-General Sir Peregrine Maitland (1777–1854) at Waterloo commanded the 1st Brigade of Foot Guards. He was later lieutenant governor of Nova Scotia, then governor of the Cape of Good Hope.

Kielmansegge: Major-General Friedrich von Kielmansegge (1768–1851) commanded the 1st Hanoverian Brigade in Alten's 3rd Division.

Ompteda: The Hanoverian officer Baron Christian von Ompteda (1765–1815) commanded the 2nd Brigade of the King's German Legion at Waterloo. His own 5th Line Battalion was virtually destroyed and he himself was shot through the neck and buried near La Haie-Sainte.

The right wing ... behind the centre: The quotation, very slightly amended, is from Charras's *Histoire de la campagne de 1815 – Waterloo* (Brussels: Meline, Cans et Comp.; J. Hetzel et Comp., 1857), ch. 12, p. 284: 'l'aile droite était rabattue derrière le centre.'

the Museum of Waterloo: Probably the Cotton Museum, containing mementoes of the battle and created by a British Waterloo veteran, Sergeant-Major Edward Cotton (1792–1849), who in 1835 opened a hotel and museum (now housing the Waxworks Museum) at the foot of the Lion Mound, and for over twenty years served as guide to the battlefield. He also wrote a guidebook, *A Voice from Waterloo: A History of the Battle Fought on the 18th June 1815*, first published by himself at Mont-St-Jean in 1847, and whose success led him to seek a London publisher (B. L. Green) for a third edition, published in 1849.

Somerset: Major-General Lord Edward Somerset (1776–1842) commanded the Dragoon Guards in the 1st Cavalry Brigade, who distinguished themselves in the battle.

Talavera, Vitoria and Salamanca: Battles fought in the Peninsular War (Talavera 1809, Vitoria 1813, Salamanca 1812).

a painful indisposition: Napoleon is believed to have been suffering from haemorrhoids.

Vivian's brigade: Major-General Sir Richard Hussey Vivian (1775–1842) commanded the 6th Cavalry Brigade, and led his hussars in the final charge of the day. He went on to be elected as a member of parliament in 1820 and was created a peer in 1841.

the Duchess of Richmond: During the ball, held on 15 June and hosted by the duchess, whose husband commanded a reserve force for the protection of the city, news arrived that Napoleon had crossed the border into the Netherlands; thereupon Allied officers attending the party, including Wellington, rejoined their troops to begin the march out of Brussels early on the morning of the 16th. The battle of Quatre-Bras was fought that afternoon. The ball features in Thackeray's *Vanity Fair* (1848).

Chaboulon: Napoleon's secretary during the Hundred Days, Fleury de Chaboulon (1779–1835) was the author of *Les Cents Jours, Mémoires pour servir à l'histoire de la vie privée, du retour, et du règne de Napoléon en 1815* (1820), of which Napoleon was very critical.

Gourgaud: General Gaspar Gourgaud (1783–1852), who had once saved Napoleon's life, accompanied him to St Helena but left the island in 1818. In 1823, with the Comte de Montholon he published Napoleon's *Memoirs*. He was also the author of an account of the 1815 campaign (1818) and a *Réfutation de la vie de Napoléon par Sir Walter Scott* (Refutation of Sir Walter Scott's Life of Napoleon; 1827), in which he defended himself against the charge of spying for the English. He was a member of the commission that went to St Helena to bring Napoleon's ashes back to France.

Benjamin Constant: The Swiss-born Benjamin Constant de Rebecque (1767–1830), who as a profligate and inveterate gambler died in penury, made his mark as a writer, political philosopher and politician. His autobiographical novel *Adolphe*, a thinly disguised account of his protracted affair with Madame de Staël, is an important text in the canon of French Romantic literature and a forerunner of the modern psychological novel. An early Republican sympathizer, Constant was fiercely critical of Napoleon, but during the Hundred Days was recruited by him to work on a new constitution, which led to his marginalization when Napoleon fell. In 1819 he was elected to the Chamber of Deputies and was vocal as both a prolific journalist and a parliamentarian in the liberal opposition.

Lobau: An infantry officer and Napoleon's aide-de-camp, Georges Mouton (1770–1838) was in 1810 given the title Comte de Lobau (having distinguished himself at the battle of Aspern–Essling in 1809, where the isle of Lobau in the Danube served as a French staging-post for crossing the river). At Waterloo he fought valiantly on the right flank against Bülow and his men, but with his own ten thousand was considerably outnumbered and eventually taken prisoner by the English.

Lacoste: A local inhabitant by the name of Jean Decoster (Lacoste is a Gallicization of his Flemish name) during the battle was found in his house at Plancenoit and pressed into service as a guide.

Uxbridge: Lieutenant-General Henry Paget, Lord Uxbridge (1768–1854), later the Marquis of Anglesey, in the heavy calvary charge against d'Erlon's troops took a hit from a cannon that shattered his right leg. He survived the injury and went on to become lord lieutenant of Ireland, while his amputated leg became a tourist attraction in the village of Waterloo, where it was buried.

Piré: General Rosnyvinen de Piré (1778–1850) began his military career as a royalist and joined the Republican army only after the defeat of the counter-revolutionary uprising in the Vendée, in which he took part. At Waterloo he commanded the 2nd Cavalry Division.

Bourgeois: General Baron Charles-François Bourgeois (1759–1821) was commander of the 2nd Brigade of Line Regiments in d'Erlon's 1st Corps.

Donzelot: Governor of the Ionian Islands 1808–14, General Baron François-Xavier Donzelot (1764–1843) was commander of the 1st Corps's 2nd Division.

Durutte: Although General Pierre-François Durutte (1767–1827) had opposed Napoleon's appointment as emperor and his career languished for a while as a result, he returned to favour and fought loyally in subsequent campaigns. At Waterloo, where he was severely wounded, he commanded the 4th Infantry Division in d'Erlon's 1st Corps.

Lieutenant Vieux: Survived the wounds he received at Waterloo, and died in Algeria in 1837, in the taking of Constantine.

Marcognet: Commander of the 3rd Division in d'Erlon's 1st Corps at Waterloo, General Baron Binet de Marcognet (1765–1854) had fought during 1781–3 in the American Revolutionary War.

Best and Pack: Colonel Charles Best (176?–1837) commanded the 4th Hanoverian Brigade and Sir Denis Pack (1774–1823) the 9th Infantry Brigade of Picton's 5th Division.

Prince of Saxe-Weimar: Bernhard of Saxe-Weimar-Eisenach (1792–1862) commanded the 2nd Brigade Allied Forces holding the farms of Papelotte, Frichemont and La Haie.

Grouchy: Emmanuel de Grouchy (1766–1847) was in command of the French army's reserve cavalry, which had been ordered to pursue the retreating Prussian army after the battle of Ligny two days before the battle of Waterloo. His absence at Waterloo was a decisive contributing factor to Napoleon's defeat.

Beresina, Leipzig and Fontainebleau: At the battle of Beresina, fought in November 1812 as the French army retreated after their failed invasion of Russia, Napoleon, threatened with total destruction, managed to get his army across the Beresina River, thanks to the ingenuity and resourcefulness of General Éblé and the Herculean efforts of his engineers, but suffered enormous losses. In October 1813 Napoleon was defeated by the Allies at the battle of Leipzig, also known as the battle of the Nations, and as a result the French army was driven out of Germany and back into France. On 6 April 1814 at Fontainebleau he was forced to abdicate. He was then exiled to the island of Elba.

Crécy, Poitiers, Malplaquet and Ramillies . . . Agincourt: English victories over the French during the Hundred Years War (Crécy 1346, Poitiers 1356, Agincourt 1415) and the War of the Spanish Succession (Ramillies 1706, Malplaquet 1709).

Milhaud: A former member of the National Convention, General Édouard Milhaud (1766–1833) commanded the 4th Cavalry Corps.

Lefebvre-Desnouettes: Wounded at Waterloo, Comte Charles Lefebvre-Desnouettes (1773–1822) after the fall of Napoleon emigrated to the United

1336

States. He went down with the ship that sank on his intended return to France in 1822.

'Veillons au salut de l'empire': 'Let Us Watch Over the Safety of the Empire' was a popular Revolutionary song (the word 'Empire' is used here loosely, to mean 'state'); dating from 1791, it has the refrain: 'Liberté, liberté, que tout mortel te rend hommage, / Tyrans, tremblez, vous allez expier vos forfaits! / Plutôt la mort que l'esclavage, / C'est la devise des Français' ('Liberty, liberty, let every mortal pay homage to you, / Tyrants, tremble, you are going to pay for your crimes, / Death sooner than slavery / Is the motto of the French people').

Bernard: A military engineer, General Simon Bernard (1779–1839) after the battle of Waterloo emigrated to the United States, where he was involved in both military and civil engineering projects. He returned to France in 1830 and served as minister of war.

Wathier: General Pierre Wathier, Comte de St-Alphonse (1770–1846), commanded the 13th Division of Milhaud's 4th Cavalry Corps.

Delort: The cavalry officer General Jacques Delort (1773–1846) distinguished himself on many battlefields and survived the wounds he received at Ligny and Waterloo to serve in Louis-Philippe's government. He was made a peer of the realm in 1837 and sat in the Upper Chamber until his death.

great redoubt at Borodino: At the battle of Borodino in September 1812, a cavalry attack led by Marshal Murat (1767–1815) successfully stormed the crucial Raevsky Redoubt.

Dubois: General Baron Jacques-Charles Dubois (1762–1847) commanded the 1st Brigade of Milhaud's 4th Cavalry Corps.

Dornberg: The Hanoverian Major-General Sir William de Dornberg (1768–1850) led the 3rd Cavalry Brigade of Dragoons and was wounded during the battle.

Trip: Major-General Albert Trip van Zoudtlandt (1776–1835) commanded the Dutch–Belgian heavy cavalry brigade. Although Wellington mentioned him in dispatches, some controversy was raised by an English account of his actions in the battle. He was later appointed commander-in-chief of the Dutch cavalry.

Fuller: Colonel William Fuller (177?–1815), leading the 1st Dragoon Guards in General Somerset's 1st Brigade, was killed in a cavalry charge at Waterloo.

Clinton . . . Badajoz: Clinton commanded an infantry division during the Peninsular War, fighting at the battles of Talavera (1809) and Badajoz (1812).

Dehaze: When Hugo visited Waterloo in 1861 he stayed for two months at the Hotel des Colonnes run by Joseph Dehaze and his brother.

van Kluze: Possibly an allusion to General Baron August von Kruse (1779–1848), who commanded the Nassau infantry brigade. As a client state of France, Nassau had fought against the British in the Peninsular War, but switched allegiance towards the end of 1813.

Lhéritier: General Samuel Lhéritier, Baron de Chézelles (1772–1829), commanded the 11th Cavalry Division.

Colbert: Perhaps Colonel Armand-Louis Gobert (1785–1816), who commanded the 5th Regiment of Cuirassiers in Delort's 14th Cavalry Division; he was seriously wounded at Waterloo and died of his injuries within the year.

Donop: General Frédéric Guillaume de Donop (1773–1815), commander of the 2nd Brigade of the 12th Cavalry Division, died at Waterloo.

Blancard: General Baron Amable-Guy Blancard (1774–1853), commander of the 2nd Cavalry Brigade of the 12th Cavalry Division.

Barnes: As adjutant general, Major-General Sir Edward Barnes (1776–1838) was severely wounded at Waterloo. He was later governor of Ceylon and commander-in-chief in India.

Delancey: Colonel Sir William Delancey (1778–1815) was with Wellington when he was injured on the field of battle, and died of his injuries a week later.

van Merlen: Major-General Baron Jean-Baptiste van Merlen (1773–1815), who as a Dutch army officer had fought alongside the French until the abdication of Napoleon, commanded the 3rd Light Brigade, and died on the battlefield.

Hake: The Hanoverian officer Colonel Georg von Hake (1768–1835) was court-martialled after the battle for having failed in his duty by leaving the battlefield.

Prince de Condé: A member of the Bourbon royal family, Louis Joseph de Bourbon (1736–1818) inherited the title of Prince de Condé on the death of his father in 1740. During the Revolution he established himself at Koblenz, raising an émigré counter-revolutionary army there.

Siborne: English army officer and military historian William Siborne (1797–1849) is the author of *History of the War in France and Belgium in 1815* (1844).

Pringle: Captain John W. Pringle (1790?–1861) served in the Royal Engineers. He was wounded at Waterloo and retired from the army in 1832. His comments on the Waterloo campaign were published as an Appendix to Sir Walter Scott's *Life of Napoleon Buonaparte* (1827): 'perhaps the actual force under the Duke of Wellington at this time, half-past six, did not amount to more than 34,000.'

Vincent: Representing Austria as one of four Allied commissioners at Waterloo, Nicolas-Charles, Baron de Vincent (1757–1834), of Belgian origin, served as Austrian ambassador to Paris 1814–26.

Álava: The Spanish naval officer Don Miguel Ricardo de Álava (1770–1843), attached to Wellington's staff in the Peninsular War, was Spanish commissioner on Wellington's staff at the battle of Waterloo.

Bülow: General Friedrich von Bülow (1755–1816) distinguished himself in the Allied war against Napoleon, and at Waterloo commanded the 4th Corps of Blücher's Prussian army.

Muffling: General Baron Friedrich Karl von Muffling (1775–1851), Prussian commissioner on Wellington's staff, author of a *History of the Campaign of the British, Dutch, Hanoverian and Brunswick Armies under the command of the Duke of Wellington, and of the Prussians under that of Prince Blücher of Wahlstadt in the year of 1815* (1816), among other memoirs and works of military history.

Domon: Lieutenant-General Baron Jean-Simon Domon (1774–1830) commanded the 3rd Cavalry Division of Vandamme's 3rd Corps.

Losthin, Hiller . . . and Ryssel: Prussian Major-General Michael Heinrich von Losthin (1762–1839) commanded the 15th Infantry Brigade in Bülow's 4th Corps; Lieutenant-Colonel August Friedrich Hiller von Gaertringen (1772–1856) the 16th Infantry Brigade; and Major-General Anton Friedrich Karl von Ryssel (1773–1833) the 14th Infantry Brigade.

Prince William of Prussia: After the death of his brother Friedrich Wilhelm IV in 1861, Wilhelm Friedrich (1797–1888), who fought at Waterloo (as Prince William of Prussia) under Blücher's command, would become king of Prussia and from 1871 the first German emperor.

Pirch I: Major-General Georg Dubislav Ludwig von Pirch, known as Pirch I (1763–1838), was commander of the Prussian 2nd Corps. (His younger brother Major-General Otto von Pirch, known as Pirch II (1765–1824), commanded the 2nd Division of Zieten's 1st Corps.)

Zieten: Hans Ernst Karl von Zieten (1770–1848) commanded the Prussian 1st Corps.

Friant, Michel, Roguet, Harlet, Mallet, Poret de Morvan: General Comte Louis Friant (1758–1829), in command of the grenadier division of the Imperial Guard; General Comte Claude-Étienne Michel (1772–1815), second-in-command of the chasseur division, fatally wounded in the battle; General Comte François Roguet (1770–1846), second-in-command of the grenadier division; General Baron Louis Harlet (1772–1853) of the 4th Regiment of Grenadiers; Colonel Chevalier Pierre Antoine-Anselme Mallet (1778–1815), in command of the 3rd Regiment of Chasseurs, fatally wounded at Waterloo; General Baron Paul Poret de Morvan (1777–1834) of the 3rd Regiment of Grenadiers.

Up, Guards, and at 'em: These are the words as recorded by Sir Walter Scott in *Paul's Letters to His Kinsfolk* (Letter VII; 1816); in Amadée Pichot's translation of 1823 'Debout et en avant', while Hugo has 'Debout, gardes, et visez juste!'

Rylandt: Probably an allusion to Major Arthur Rowley Heyland (1781–1815) in command of the 40th Foot. He was buried close to the spot where he died at Waterloo (and close to the hotel where Hugo stayed). In 1820 an individual tomb was erected on his grave, which has since been moved to the Wellington Museum.

Subervie: General Baron Jacques-Gervais Protais Subervie (1776–1856), in command of the 5th Cavalry Division of the 1st Cavalry Reserve Corps, later served as a deputy in the National Assembly and was briefly minister of war in 1848.

Guyot: General Comte Claude Guyot (1768–1837), in command of the heavy cavalry division of the French Imperial Guard, had a horse killed under him and briefly fell into the hands of the enemy before being rescued by his own side.

Duhesme: General Guillaume Philibert Duhesme (1766–1815) commanded the Young Guard division of the Imperial Guard.

Cambronne: General Pierre Cambronne (1770–1842), who had accompanied Napoleon into exile on Elba, commanded an infantry regiment of the Old Guard at Waterloo. He was taken prisoner by Colonel Hugh Halkett, and allowed to return to France in 1816. He never admitted to having said the word that Hugo and others ascribed to him, the expletive *merde*, meaning 'shit'. It is also said that to the invitation to surrender he responded thus: 'La garde meurt et ne se rend pas' ('The Guard dies and does not surrender').

to complement Leonidas with Rabelais: Leonidas was the warrior king of the Spartans who, fighting heroically to the last, made a legendary stand against the Persians at Thermopylae in 480 BC. François Rabelais (1494–1553) left his indelible mark on the French language with his inventive, erudite and earthy display of linguistic creativity in his masterly account of the adventures of the giants Pantagruel and Gargantua.

Kléber: General Jean-Baptiste Kléber (1753–1800) distinguished himself in the French Revolutionary Wars, and in 1793 suppressed a counter-revolutionary uprising in the Vendée region; he played a prominent role in Napoleon's Egyptian campaign (1798–1800) and was left in command when Napoleon returned to France in 1799 to pursue his political ambitions. The following year Kléber was assassinated in Cairo, his death 'an irreparable loss to France and to myself', said Napoleon.

Hugo's footnote . . . Dictées de Ste-Hélène: The quotation comes from the army bulletin dictated by Napoleon on 20 June 1815 at Laon to his secretary Fleury de Chaboulon and published in a special supplement of the newspaper *Le Moniteur* on the 21st. *Dictées de Ste-Hélène* is an informal reference to the memoirs published under the title *Mémoires pour servir à l'histoire de France sous le règne de Napoléon, écrits à Sainte-Hélène, sous sa dictée, par les généraux qui ont partagé sa captivité* (1823–5), and published in English as *Memoirs of the history of France during the reign of Napoleon, dictated by the Emperor at Saint Helena to the generals who shared his captivity.*

Jomini: The Swiss military theorist Antoine-Henri Jomini (1779–1869), who served in both the French and Russian armies, wrote *Vie Politique et Militaire de Napoléon* (Political and Military Life of Napoleon; 1827).

the Barrême of warfare: François Barrême (1638–1703), famous for his calculation tables, is remembered in the French word *barème*, meaning a table, list or schedule. His ready-reckoner *Livre des Comptes Faits*, first published in 1669, was still being reprinted in 1862.

Beaulieu . . . Alvinzi . . . Wurmser . . . Melas . . . Mack: Austrian commanders defeated by Napoleon: General Johan Peter de Beaulieu (1725–1819) was outmanoeuvred at Montenotte in April 1796 and defeated at Borghetto the following month; General Joseph Alvinzi (1735–1810), who after Borghetto took over command from Beaulieu, was defeated at Arcola in November 1796 and at Rivoli in 1797; Field-Marshal Dagobert von Wurmser (1724–97) at the age of seventy-two was defeated by Napoleon at the battle of Castiglione in August 1796, and on 2 February 1797 was forced to surrender Mantua after a six-month siege; General Michael von Melas (1729–1806) was defeated at Marengo on 14 June 1800; General Karl Mack (1752–1828) surrendered his entire army to Napoleon at the battle of Ulm in October 1805.

infamous army: Wellington wrote in a letter to Lord Bathurst on 2 July 1813, 'We have in the service the scum of the earth as common soldiers.' In a letter to Lord Stewart, written on 8 May 1815, he wrote, 'I have got an infamous army; very weak and ill-equipped, and a very inexperienced staff.' He wrote after the battle, from Waterloo on 19 June, to Lord Bathurst, 'There is no officer or description of troops that did not behave well.'

Waterloo memorial: Wellington's Column in Liverpool, on which work began in 1861 and which was completed in 1865, is surmounted by a statue of the duke by sculptor George Anderson Lawson (1832–1904). The commemorative column erected at Wellington's Stratfield Saye House bears a statue of Wellington (1863) by Baron Carlo Marochetti (1805–67), who in 1844 had produced for the city of Glasgow an equestrian statue of Wellington. Originally intended to bear a statue of the duke, the memorial monument in Somerset above the town of Wellington is a three-sided pillar, completed in 1854.

battle of Inkerman . . . Lord Raglan: Fought on 5 November 1854 during the Crimean War, Inkerman is often referred to as 'the soldiers' battle' because of the nature of the conflict, in which troops fought heroically on their own initiative, under no direct higher command. The British Distinguished Conduct Medal was in fact created during the Crimean War, in 1854, to recognize acts of gallantry performed by non-commissioned officers and junior ranks. Younger brother of Lord Edward Somerset, Field-Marshal Fitzroy Somerset (1788–1855), from 1852 Lord Raglan (who had served as Wellington's aide-de-camp at Waterloo, where he had lost his right arm), was in command until June 1855 of British forces in the Crimean War (1854–6).

Bautzen: The battle of Bautzen 1813, a French victory but not as decisive as it might have been.

a coachman on the throne of Naples . . . a sergeant on the throne of Sweden: The son of an innkeeper, Joachim Murat (1767–1815) enlisted in 1787 and by 1798 was commander of the cavalry in the Egyptian campaign. He married Napoleon's sister Caroline in 1800, was made a marshal of France in 1804 and named king of Naples and Sicily in 1808. Jean-Baptiste Bernadotte (1763–1844) was a sergeant at the time of the French Revolution. He served as minister of war in 1798 and became a marshal of France in 1804. In 1810, by a strange combination of circumstances, neither supported nor opposed by Napoleon he was elected heir to the old and childless Swedish king Charles XIII, by whom he was formally adopted and whom he succeeded in 1818 as Charles XIV, founder of the present Swedish dynasty.

Louis XVIII at St-Ouen: After Napoleon's abdication, Louis XVIII (brother of Louis XVI) returned to France from his court in exile at Hartwell House in Buckinghamshire, and on 2 May 1814 signed the Declaration of St-Ouen whereby he committed himself to a restoration of the monarchy under which representative government would be maintained, and to the adoption of a liberal constitution that would guarantee and uphold a number of specific freedoms, rights and principles.

the Declaration of the Rights of Man: Approved by the National Assembly on 26 August 1789, *La Déclaration des droits de l'homme et du citoyen* is the foundation document underlying the Constitution of the post-Revolutionary French state.

Père Élysée . . . the gout-sufferer: Marie-Vincent Talochon (1753–1817), known as Père Élysée, a member of the Congregation of the Brothers of Charity, was personal doctor and surgeon to Louis XVIII, who suffered from gout.

July the eighth: The date of Louis XVIII's return to Paris.

the Béarnais: The Bourbon dynasty was of Béarnais origin.

Bouvines and Fontenoy: Philippe II's victory against the alliance between the Holy Roman Empire, England and Flanders at the battle of Bouvines on 27 July 1214 confirmed the French Crown's sovereignty over Brittany and Normandy. The battle of Fontenoy, 11 May 1745, was a major French victory in the War of the Austrian Succession (from which France ultimately benefited little).

Trestaillon: Jacques Dupont, known as Trestaillon, was the instigator of a 'white terror' – murderous mob violence against Bonapartists and Protestants – for which he was not prosecuted, as recounted by Alexandre Dumas in *Massacres du Midi* (Massacres of the South) *1551–1815* in his *Crimes Célèbres* (Celebrated Crimes; 1839–40).

Arc du Carrousel: Completed in 1808, the triumphal monument built to celebrate Napoleon's military victories, originally surmounted by the four horses from Venice's St Mark's Basilica, which were returned to Venice in 1815.

Duc d'Enghien: Louis-Antoine, Duc d'Enghien (1772–1804), a member of the Bourbon family, grandson of the Prince de Condé, in whose émigré army he served, was in 1804 falsely accused of being involved in a royalist conspiracy against Napoleon (at that time first consul for life), on whose orders he was abducted and arrested. He was then summarily executed at Vincennes in the castle moat and buried there.

Schönbrunn . . . the king of Rome: A summer palace of the Habsburgs (and a childhood home of Marie-Antoinette), Schönbrunn Palace had been Napoleon's headquarters in Vienna and after his fall was where his son, 'the king of Rome', later known as the Duc de Reichstadt, resided until his death from tuberculosis in 1832.

Article 14: Article 14 of the Constitutional Charter of 1814, on which the Restoration was based, recognized the king as the supreme head of state with the power to take whatever measures were necessary for the enforcement of law and the security of the state. It was this article that gave the king the authority to introduce all kinds of censorship measures and limitations on freedom.

Holy Alliance: By a treaty signed in September 1815, Russia, Austria and Prussia united in a 'Holy Alliance', to which France also later committed itself, to uphold and defend Christian values. In the eyes of liberals it represented a statement of reactionary solidarity among Europe's political rulers.

Hudson Lowe . . . Montchenu: Under the terms of the Paris Convention signed on 2 August 1815, Britain was made responsible for the location and conditions of Napoleon's captivity. Sir Hudson Lowe (1769–1844) was appointed governor of the island of St Helena, to which Napoleon was exiled – at Longwood House, where he resided until his death in May 1821 – while Russia, Austria, Prussia and (under a supplementary article) France were entitled to appoint commissioners to assure themselves of Napoleon's continued presence in his place of captivity. France was represented by Marquis Claude-Marin-Henri de Montchenu (1757–1831), who, like Lowe, remained on the island from 1816 to 1821.

Alexander: Tsar Alexander I of Russia (1777–1825).

Marquis de Fervacques . . . Ceresole: Jean de Hautemer IV, Marquis de Fervacques, was found dying on the battlefield of Ceresole in Piedmont in 1544.

Turenne: One of France's most celebrated generals; by winning the battle of Sinzheim in Louis XIV's Dutch War, Marshal Turenne (1611–75) gained control of the Palatinate in 1674 and laid waste to it.

Hoche and Marceau: General Lazare-Louis Hoche (1768–97), who was made responsible for the pacification of the Vendée in that civil conflict, earned a reputation for humanity and tolerance as well as for military excellence. François-Séverin Marceau (1769–96), a general at the age of twenty-four, after his early death as a result of being wounded in battle was saluted by the Austrians he had fought against.

Gazette des Tribunaux: A newspaper specializing in reports of court cases. Although there had been earlier publications under this title, this version began publication in 1825 and survived until 1955.

Journal de Paris: France's first daily newspaper, published from 1777 until 1840.

the patriarch of Ferney: Voltaire, Ferney being the village to which he retired in 1759 and where he remained until the year of his death in 1778. These lines appear in his poem 'Le Pauvre Diable'.

gunpowder . . . Roger Bacon: A Franciscan monk and Oxford professor, Roger Bacon (1214–92/4), in a text dating from the mid thirteenth century, was the first European to give the formula for making gunpowder.

playing-cards . . . Charles VI: An account-book entry dating from 1392 for the household expenses of Charles VI of France (1368–1422) was for a long time the earliest known reference to playing-cards in Europe. There are now known references from across Europe that pre-date this by as much as twenty years.

the Spanish war: In 1823 France intervened on the side of the royalists in the Spanish Civil War (1820–3), with the result that liberal gains were reversed and Ferdinand VII was restored to the throne as absolute monarch.

the hero of Andújar: Commander of the French forces in Spain, the Duc d'Angoulême signed an ordinance in the Andalusian town of Andújar that would have offered some protection to liberals against whom royalist reprisals were being taken, but it was not implemented and 'the white terror' continued.

descamisados: 'Shirtless ones', a name the Spanish royalists gave to their revolutionary enemies, who were defeated when in 1823 France intervened to support the king, a campaign known in France as 'the Spanish expedition'.

Prince of Carignano: Inheriting the title Prince of Carignano from his father in 1800, Carlo Alberto of Savoy (1798–1849) succeeded to the throne of Piedmont-Sardinia in 1831 as Charles Albert, king of Sardinia.

Saragossa: During the Peninsular War (1807–14), having heroically and successfully resisted a first siege in 1808 (15 June–14 August) under the command of the Spanish General Palafox (1780–1847), Saragossa fell in 1809 to a second siege (20 December 1808–20 February 1809) at the cost of great suffering and loss of life to the Saragossans. In his memoirs of the campaigns he fought in Spain, General Suchet (see note p. 1407 on *Suchet . . . Saragossa*) put the number of lives lost in the city at over 40,000, but admitted the siege had also taken its toll on the French – hence Hugo's turn of phrase: 'sur lesquels s'était formidablement écroulée Saragosse' ('on whom Saragossa had fallen mightily').

Rostopchin . . . Ballesteros: Count Rostopchin (1763–1826) was the military governor of Moscow during the French invasion of Russia. General Francisco Ballesteros (1770–1832), who fought against the French in the Peninsular War, sided with the liberals in the Spanish Civil War.

Bonaparte said so: When negotiating the Treaty of Campo Formio in 1797 after his victorious Italian campaign, Napoleon is reported to have objected to the wording used by the Austrian emperor in recognizing the French Republic, saying, 'The French Republic is like the sun, none but the blind can fail to see it.'

manchineel tree: Contact with the leaves, bark and sap of this poisonous tree, found in the Caribbean and Central America, causes blistering and inflammation, and the fruit can be deadly if eaten.

wings and feelers: The words *ailes* ('wings') and *antennes* ('feelers'), used here, can also mean 'sails' and specifically 'lateen sails' (*antennes*).

de Ruyter: Dutch admiral Michiel de Ruyter (1607–76).

Abbé Delille: Poet, classicist, and member of the French Academy from 1774, Jacques Delille (1738–1813) established his reputation with a translation of Virgil's *Georgics* (1770). He was also the translator, notably, of the *Aeneid* (1804) and Milton's *Paradise Lost* (1805). There is a portrait of Delille at the Musée de Blois by Élisabeth Vigée-Lebrun (1755–1842), painted from memory after his death, and an unfinished portrait at the Musée Antoine Lécuyer by Joseph Ducreux (1735–1802).

Raynal: The best-known and most influential of the works of Abbé Raynal (1713–96) is *L'Histoire philosophique et politique des établissements et du commerce des Européens dans les deux Indes* (The Philosophical and Political History of European Settlements and Trade in the Two Indies; 1770), dismissed by Voltaire as being of little substance.

Parny: Much admired in his day for his love poetry, Évariste de Parny (1753–1814) made his name with *La Guerre des Dieux* (1799), satirizing the Church and Christian dogma, and was elected to the French Academy in 1803. Ravel's *Chansons Madécasses* are musical settings of three poems by Parny.

the Champ d'Asile fund: A colony of Bonapartist refugees settled on the Trinity River in Texas in May 1818, but the settlement, called the Champ d'Asile (Field of Asylum), lasted barely six months, partly because they settled in

territory disputed between the United States and Mexico, neither of which
wanted the French there, and they were forced to leave. The *Minerve* newspaper raised funds for the doomed enterprise (whose failure led to controversy
over the destination of those funds).

the Golden Fleece: A Christian chivalric order founded in 1430 by Philippe III of
Burgundy, the Order of the Golden Fleece eventually fell under the control of
the Habsburgs, from whom French kings, including Louis XVIII, accepted
membership.

the cross of St Louis . . . the Holy Spirit silver plaque: The Royal and Military
Order of St Louis was founded in 1693 by Louis XIV. The Order of the Holy
Spirit was founded in 1578, during the French Wars of Religion, by Henri III.
Abolished during the Revolution, both chivalric orders were revived by Louis
XVIII, then definitively abolished by Louis-Philippe in 1830.

the Duc d'Havré: Joseph de Croÿ d'Havré (1744–1839) was a close confidant in
exile of Louis XVIII, who after the Restoration appointed him captain of his
personal bodyguard and made him a peer of the realm. When Louis-Philippe
came to power he retired to Belgium, where he died.

The Two Convicts: A melodrama in three acts by Boirie, Carmouche and Poujol,
Les Deux Forçats was first staged in 1822.

Le Courrier Français: Founded in 1819 under the title *Le Courrier*, as a voice for
constitutional monarchists, in 1820 it became *Le Courrier Français*, surviving
until 1851.

Castlereagh . . . Congress of Vienna: At the Congress of Vienna (September
1814–June 1815), an international conference of European powers who met
to negotiate a post-Napoleonic settlement redefining territorial borders and
exacting compensation from France, Great Britain was represented initially by
Foreign Minister Lord Castlereagh (1769–1822). Under the second Treaty of
Paris (20 November 1815), after the Hundred Days that culminated in Napoleon's defeat at Waterloo, France was required to pay an indemnity of 700
million francs and Britain made a considerable number of territorial gains.

one of the city's boulevards: In 1670, Paris's city walls, no longer needed for
defensive purposes, were razed and their old moats filled in. They were replaced
by broad, elevated promenades, the first Parisian boulevards (the word derives
from the Dutch word *bolwerk* ('bulwark' or 'rampart'), beyond which lay the
faubourgs (originally spelled *faux-bourg*, literally, 'false [or 'mock'] town'). As
the city expanded these so-called *grands boulevards* slowly became an integral
part of the urban fabric. An outer ring of boulevards was constructed after
1860, and the cross-town arteries that cut through the centre of Paris as part
of the major restructuring of the city in the 1850s and 60s under the direction
of Baron Georges-Eugène Haussmann (1809–91) also took the name of
'boulevards'.

the Châtelet: A stronghold of the *ancien régime*, the Châtelet contained law
courts, prisons, a police headquarters and a morgue. It ceased to function as a
law court in 1791 and as a morgue in 1804; it was demolished in 1808.

Cardinal de la Roche-Aymon: Cardinal de la Roche-Aymon (1697–1777) administered last rites to Louis XV in 1774, and having presided over the marriage
of his heir to Marie-Antoinette in 1770 consecrated his successor as king in
1775.

Madame du Barry: The Comtesse du Barry (1743–93) was the last of Louis XV's
official mistresses. She was executed during the Terror.

perimeter wall: This is the Farmers-General (tax collectors) Wall, built in 1784–91, to enable taxes to be imposed on goods entering Paris. Most of these toll-barriers disappeared during the expansion of Paris in 1860.

Ulbach stabbed the goat-girl of Ivry: In May 1827 Aimée Millot, a nineteen-year-old shepherdess, while looking after her goats was stabbed to death by Honoré Ulbach, a young man whose advances she had rejected. He was guillotined for the crime.

St-Jacques toll-gate . . . Place de Grève: The last public execution took place on the Place de Grève in 1830. By a decree of 1832 the guillotine was transferred to the St-Jacques toll-gate, where executions for capital crimes took place until 1851.

the madness of women . . . men: The Salpêtrière Hospital and the Maison de Bicêtre were asylums for the insane, Salpêtrière – where Sigmund Freud later attended lectures by the pioneering neurologist Dr Charcot (1825–93) – for women, and Bicêtre for men.

the Paris–Orléans railway: The Paris–Orléans line was inaugurated in 1843 when the extension to the Paris–Juvisy–Corbeil line, which opened in 1840, was completed. The Paris terminus was located more or less where the Gare d'Austerlitz now stands.

Spanish bonds: As a result of Ferdinand's restoration as absolute monarch in Spain in 1823, all acts of the constitutional government were annulled and Spain defaulted on its debts in May 1824.

the author of this book . . . for many years now: After the *coup d'état* in December 1851 by which Louis-Napoleon, who came to power after the 1848 Revolution, used military force to occupy the National Assembly and overturn the Constitution as a prelude to declaring himself emperor (Napoleon III) in 1852, Hugo, who had long been a vocal critic, fearing for his safety left Paris and went into exile. He did not return to Paris until 1870, after the fall of Napoleon III. In the meantime, Paris underwent enormous physical transformation.

Mazas prison: Considered a model of its kind when it was completed in 1850, the Mazas prison, whose inmates were to be housed in individual cells, was built as a replacement for La Force (see note p. 1381 on *La Force*). A mere fifty years later it was demolished, partly because of concerns about the impression it would make on tourists coming to Paris for the World Fair in 1900 and partly because the cellular regime was proving to be problematic, with very high suicide rates.

the Institut the 'Quatre-Nations' . . . the Opéra-Comique the 'Feydeau': The French statesman Cardinal Mazarin, Louis XIV's chief minister from 1642 until his death in 1661, left provisions in his will for the founding of a college for students from France's newly acquired territories, to be known as the Collège des Quatre-Nations (College of Four Nations) or the Collège Mazarin. Suppressed during the Revolution, it became in 1801 the Palais des Beaux-Arts, and in 1805 the home of the Institut de France. The Théâtre Feydeau merged in 1801 with the Opéra-Comique, which then moved to the Salle Feydeau, where it continued to stage performances as the Opéra-Comique until 1829.

at the sign of Prudence: Printers and publishers addresses were identified by their shop sign, which in many cases took the form of the colophon, or printer's mark, they used to identify their publications, or vice versa. Prudence may have been represented by a snake.

the Conciergerie: Dating back to the Middle Ages the royal palace on the Île de la Cité became known as the Conciergerie after Charles V moved his residence to the Louvre palace in the fourteenth century. It continued to serve as an administrative centre and as a prison. It became notorious as the place where the Revolutionary Tribunal sat and many of the victims of the Revolution were held. It is now part of the Palais de Justice, still serving as a judicial institution.

Duvivier . . . a sorcerer: The entry for hunting (*vénerie*) in Diderot and d'Alembert's *Encyclopédie* (1751–72) alludes to a hunt described by Jacques Espée de Selincourt, author of *Le Parfait Chasseur* (The Perfect Hunter; 1683): 'Le même auteur dit avoir vu un cerf chassé pendant trois jours par trois équipages différens . . . Tous ces messieurs le soir ne savoient que dire, ni Duvivier, Artonge, Desprez, & tous les autres vieux chasseurs crurent tous que c'étoit un sorcier' ('The same author asserts that he has seen a stag hunted for three days by three different packs . . . In the evening none of these gentlemen – Duvivier, Artonge, Desprez – knew what to say, and all the other old huntsmen, every one of them, thought it was a sorcerer'). Jean de Ligniville, another seventeenth-century writer on hunting, is also mentioned.

Attila . . . Hannibal . . . Danton: On coming to power in 450 the Byzantine emperor Marcian (392?–457) refused to continue paying tribute to Attila the Hun (406?–53). At this point, Gibbon tells us in *The Decline and Fall of the Roman Empire* (ch. 35), '[Attila] threatened to chastise the rash successor of Theodosius; but he hesitated, whether he should first direct his invincible arms against the Eastern or the Western Empire' – the latter ruled by the Roman emperor Valentinian (419–55). He chose to attack the West and thereby met his downfall. Hannibal, after defeating the Romans at the battle of Cannae in 216 BC, wintered his troops at Capua, a great mistake according to Livy (*History of Rome*, bk 23, ch. 18) because there they 'fell victims to a prosperity too great and pleasures too attractive for them to withstand', with the result that the Carthaginian general left Capua 'with another army altogether; it did not retain a shred of its former discipline'. Distancing himself from the excesses of the Terror, Danton retired to his native Arcis-sur-Aube and refused to believe he was in danger when told of his imminent arrest. 'Murmuring "They dare not", he goes to sleep as usual' (Carlyle, *The French Revolution*, vol. 3, bk 6, ch. 2).

Martin Verga: An allusion to Dom Martin de Vargas (died 1446), founder in 1425 of the Cisterian Congregation of Castile, at Monte Sion, near Toledo in Spain, with the intention of returning to a more strict observance of the Benedictine Rule.

Clairvaux . . . Cîteaux . . . St Bernard . . . St Benedict: St Benedict of Nursia (*c*.480–*c*.547) is generally recognized as the founder of Western monasticism, and his Rule is a detailed guide to how the religious life should be observed and regulated. He himself founded a number of monasteries, including the one at Monte Cassino, where he died. In 1098 St Robert (*c*.1028–1111), abbot de Molesme, founded a monastery at Cîteaux near Dijon, where it was intended the Rule of St Benedict would be rigorously observed. This community became known as members of the Cistercian Order, and was joined in 1112 by St Bernard (1090–1153), who in 1115 was sent forth by the abbot to found a new house. Bernard founded the monastery at Clairvaux with which he is identified and where the monastic tradition was reformed and revived.

Subiaco . . . temple of Apollo: St Gregory the Great (*c*.540–604; from 590 Pope Gregory I) tells us in his account of St Benedict's life (*Dialogues*, bk 2) that as an aspiring servant of God, Benedict fled from his home (more likely at about the age of nineteen or twenty) to 'a desert place called Subiaco, almost forty miles distant from Rome', where he lived as a hermit, devoting himself to prayer and to overcoming the temptations of the flesh. After a number of years, probably in about 529, he went to Monte Cassino, about eighty miles south of Rome, and there on the site of a temple to Apollo founded the monastery for which he wrote the Benedictine Rule.

the Oratory ... Filippo de' Neri ... Pierre de Bérulle: Founded by the Italian Filippo de' Neri (1515–95), the Congregation of the Oratory received papal recognition in 1575. It is an institution consisting of autonomous communities of priests bound not by monastic vows but by those of the priesthood only, and devoted to prayer and preaching and the celebration of the sacraments. Filippo de' Neri refused a cardinalship (offered by Gregory XIV) and was canonized in 1622. In 1611 Cardinal Pierre de Bérulle (1575–1629) founded a new Congregation in France, recognized by a papal bull in 1613, and differing from the Italian institution mostly in that the houses came under the overall authority of a superior-general and a general assembly. The Oratory was founded in England in 1847 by John Henry Newman (1801–90), cardinal from 1879.

stability: The Benedictine vow of stability (*stabilitas loci*) binds the new member of the order to the particular monastery or convent in which the vows are made, thereby securing the stable communities that St Benedict sought to establish.

lay sisters: In some Catholic orders a distinction is made between lay sisters and choir sisters. The lay sisters, who generally perform household duties, may be bound by the same vows and as strictly enclosed as the choir sisters, but although they may attend the offices they do not sing.

Perrault ... Hecuba ... Little Red Riding Hood's grandmother: Elected to the French Academy in 1671, Charles Perrault (1628–1703) in 1697 published *Contes de Ma Mère l'Oye* (Tales of Mother Goose), which included 'Le Petit Chaperon Rouge' ('Little Red Riding Hood'). Hecuba was the wife of Priam of Troy, the city destroyed by the Greeks in the Trojan War, of which Homer's *Iliad* gives an account. Among her nineteen children were Paris, Hector and Cassandra.

four nations ... Collège Mazarin: See note p. 1345 on *the Institut the 'Quatre-Nations' ... the Opéra-Comique the 'Feydeau'*.

Écouen: In 1805 Napoleon signed a decree providing for the creation of three schools for the daughters (often orphaned) of holders of the Legion of Honour. The first to open, in 1807, was housed in the Château d'Écouen, dating from the sixteenth century, some fifteen miles north of Paris. The school foundation exists to this day, but has not been located at Écouen since 1962. The Château d'Écouen now houses the Musée National de la Renaissance.

White Paternoster: Almost a magic charm rather than a prayer, the White Paternoster is part of medieval folklore, referred to in Chaucer's *Miller's Tale* (line 3485), for instance. (The English prayer rhyme 'Matthew, Mark, Luke and John, / Bless the bed that I lie on' is sometimes called the Black Paternoster.)

St Margaret's cross: St Margaret of Antioch is associated with a number of miraculous incidents, including being swallowed by Satan in the form of a dragon, from which she escaped alive, protected by the cross that she was wearing.

Monsieur de Quélen: Louis de Quélen (1778–1839), archbishop of Paris from 1821, member of the French Academy from 1824.

Monsieur le Duc de Rohan: Auguste de Rohan (1788–1833) in 1815 was widowed when his young wife Armandine de Sérent (1789–1815) died in a tragic accident after her dress caught fire. He then became a priest, was named arch-bishop of Besançon, and in 1830 was made a cardinal.

the king's musketeers: A creation of Louis XIII, this royal cavalry guard, having been revived in 1814, was finally suppressed in 1816.

Magnates mulieres: The formula is taken from 'an ordinance issued in 1245 by Eudes [Odo] de Châteauroux ... canon and chancellor of Notre-Dame' (he was also papal legate to France in 1245), prohibiting outsiders – including the mothers and sisters of the nuns – from staying overnight within the cloister of Notre-Dame, unless they are great ladies *quae sine scandolo evitari non poss-int*', and cited in *The History of Paris from the Earliest Period to the Present Day*, London: Whitaker and Galignani, 1825, vol. 1, p. 32.

My Zétulbé: A song from the popular French comic opera *Le Calife de Bagdad* (first performed in 1800) by François-Adrien Boieldieu (1775–1834) with a libretto by Claude de Saint-Just. In 1817 it was staged in Paris in an Italian version, *Il Califfo di Bagdad*, translated by Andrea Leone Tottola and with a new score by Manuel Garcia (1775–1832). Zétulbé is the young woman of Baghdad wooed by the caliph in disguise.

Madame de Genlis ... L'Intrépide: Félicité du Crest de St-Aubin, Comtesse de Genlis (1746–1830), was entrusted by the Duc de Chartres (from 1785, Duc d'Orléans), whose mistress she was, with the education of his children. The eldest was Louis-Philippe, who inherited the title Duc d'Orléans when his father was guillotined in 1793 and was king of France from 1830 to 1848. Madame de Genlis also made a name for herself as a prolific writer. She wrote historical and pedagogical novels (one of which, *Adelaide and Theodore* in the English translation, is mentioned in Jane Austen's *Emma*, 1816), and received an honorary degree from Oxford University. The journal *L'Intrépide*, in which her intention, as she says in her memoirs, was to correct grammar mistakes made in the daily newspapers, did not survive beyond the first issue in 1820.

Vicomte de Gestas: Gestas is the name of a noble family dating back to the begin-ning of the eleventh century, but they have not held the title of vicomte.

Marguerite de Blemeur: The Benedictine nun Jacqueline Bouette de Blemur (1618–96) is the author of *L'année bénédictine, ou les vies des saints de l'ordre de S. Benoît* (The Benedictine Year, or the Lives of the Saints of the Order of St Benedict), 1667–73.

Madame Dacier: Anne Dacier (1654–1720) was a noted scholar and translator of the classics, including Homer's *Iliad* (1699) and *Odyssey* (1708).

Gauvain ... Drouet ... Cogolludo ... d'Auverney ... Cifuentes ... La Miltière ... Laudinière ... Sigüenza ... Suzon: Hugo has used in this para-graph names connected with his own life: Julienne Gauvain, better known as Juliette Drouet (1806–83), was his mistress and devoted companion from 1833 until her death. During the Peninsular War, Hugo's father was made gen-eral and governor of the central provinces of Spain and given the title count by the then king of Spain Joseph Bonaparte. Cogolludo, Cifuentes and Sigüenza are all towns located in the Spanish central province of Guadalajar, which came under General Hugo's governorship. Hugo's maternal grandfather was born at Auvergné near Nantes; Hugo wrote some of his early articles under the name d'Auverney, and gave the name Auverney to one of the main characters in his first novel, *Bug-Jargal*, written when he was sixteen. La Miltière is the country estate of which l'Audinière was a smaller part, bought by General Hugo and his second wife in 1823, and is where Victor Hugo's first child, Léopold, who died aged three months, was buried. 'Suzette et Suzon' is a poem by Hugo, published posthumously in the collection *Toute la Lyre* (1888 and 1893) and set to music by Saint-Saëns.

Ceracchi: Giuseppe Ceracchi (1751–1801) was an Italian neoclassical sculptor who lived and worked in England, America, Holland, Prussia and Austria, before finally moving to Paris. He was guillotined in 1801 after becoming embroiled in a conspiracy against Napoleon.

Île Bourbon: Claimed as French territory in 1642, this island in the Indian Ocean, named Île Bourbon in 1649, was renamed Île de la Réunion in 1793, retaining that name since 1848.

Chevalier Roze: The nobleman Nicolas Roze (1675–1733) distinguished himself during the epidemic of plague in Marseille in 1720 by his devoted and selfless service, particularly in organizing the burial of the dead. He himself contracted the disease, but survived.

the eleven thousand devils' playground: In his book *William Shakespeare*, Hugo refers (bk 1, ch. 3) to a drinking establishment, founded by the Vicomte de Montauban, called 'le Tripot des onze mille diables'. A gang of bandits who ravaged the Limousin and Auvergne area in the mid sixteenth century were known as the 'eleven thousand devils'. (A leader of the gang, Jean de Cathalando, repented of his misdeeds and became a Franciscan friar at the monastery of Sellières.)

Fontevrault: The huge medieval abbey complex at Fontevrault in Anjou, once housing four communities – of monks, repentant fallen women, lepers and nuns, ruled by the aristocratic women who predominated within the order – was the burial place of the Plantagenet kings Henry II (1133–89) and his sons Richard the Lionheart (1157–99) and John (1167–1216), and also of Henry's wife Eleanor of Aquitaine (1124–1204).

Monsieur de Miromesnil: Armand Thomas Hue (1723–96), Marquis de Miromesnil, Louis XVI's minister of justice (1774–87).

the distinction of inspiring Molière: In Molière's play of 1669, *Monsieur de Pourceaugnac*, the hapless provincial nobleman of the title, who has come to Paris to claim an unwilling bride, is the victim of a comic conspiracy to thwart him, and he ends up at the end of Act I being pursued by an apothecary, doctors and dancing swordsmen, all brandishing syringes.

Julia Alpinula: According to legend, Julia Alpinula was a priestess serving the goddess Aventia in Helvetia when the Roman emperor Galba died in AD 69. Loyal to Galba, her father refused to recognize his successor Vitellius, and when defeated by one of Vitellius' ruthless generals, Aulus Caecina, he was executed despite his daughter's pleas for mercy. She too was executed. Byron alludes to her story in *Childe Harold* (canto 3, stanza 66) and in a footnote gives a fuller version of the epitaph: *Julia Alpinula / Hic jaceo / Infelicis patris infelix proles / Deae Aventiae Sacerdos / Exorare patris necem non potui / Male mori in fatis illi erat / Vixi annos XXIII* ('Julia Alpinula / here I lie / unhappy child of an unhappy father / priestess of the goddess Aventia / I could not avert my father's death by entreaty / he was doomed to die by violence / I lived twenty-three years.') Byron comments: 'I know of no human composition so affecting as this; nor a history of deeper interest: these are names and actions which ought not to perish ...' Even in 1846 the epitaph was considered a forgery and there is no evidence that Julia Alpinula ever existed.

Hortus conclusus: The enclosed garden is a visual theme of devotional art identified with Mary the Mother of God, emerging in the fifteenth century and evoking her perpetual virginity. Its literary origins go back to the Song of Songs

4:12: 'A garden enclosed is my sister, my spouse; a spring shut up, a fountain sealed.'

Voltaire . . . to mock the crucifix: Voltaire was famously outraged by the barbaric torture and execution of a young nobleman, the Chevalier de la Barre, accused of mutilating a crucifix at Abbeville in 1765, a crime which was not proven and which should not in any case have warranted the death penalty. In his *Account of the Death of the Chevalier de la Barre* (1766) he protested against the exposure of crucifixes and religious images on public highways, rather than in the churches where in his view they more properly belonged. In 1761, Voltaire had taken up the case of the Huguenot merchant Jean Calas of Toulouse, who was found guilty of murdering his son in order to prevent or punish his conversion to Catholicism, for which Calas was tortured and executed. As a result of Voltaire's involvement in the campaign to clear his name, the case was reviewed. The conviction was overturned and the family was paid compensation. In his *Treatise on Tolerance* (1763; ch. 23) Voltaire addresses a prayer to an all-embracing God: 'que les petites différences entre les vêtements qui couvrent nos débiles corps, entre tous nos langages insuffisants, entre tous nos usages ridicules, entre toutes nos lois imparfaites, entre toutes nos opinions insensées, entre toutes nos conditions si disproportionnées à nos yeux, et si égales devant toi; que toutes ces petites nuances qui distinguent les atomes appelés *hommes* ne soient pas des signaux de haine et de persécution' ('that the slight differences in the garments that cover our frail bodies, in our insufficient languages, in our ridiculous customs, in our imperfect laws, in our unreasonable opinions, in all our conditions, so incomparable in our eyes and so equal before you; that all these small distinctions that differentiate the atoms called men be not signals for hatred and persecution').

Voltaire . . . Sirven: In 1762 a Huguenot couple named Sirven, accused of murdering their daughter because she wanted to become a Catholic, escaped to Switzerland to avoid arrest. They were sentenced to death *in absentia*, and all their assets confiscated. Voltaire took up their cause, and eventually their conviction was overthrown.

that poor Holofernes: As related in the Book of Judith, Holofernes was the Assyrian general who laid siege to the Jewish city of Bethulia and was beheaded in his sleep by a woman called Judith; it was a popular theme of the Renaissance and Baroque periods, treated by Michelangelo (in the Sistine Chapel) and Caravaggio, among many others.

a black heifer: 'White animals were offered to heavenly deities, black to those of the underworld . . . So at Rome, where the importance and difficulty of getting a white victim for Jupiter led to whitening with pipe clay (Juvenal, Satire 10, line 65, *cretatum bovem*)', *A Dictionary of Greek and Roman Antiquities*, ed. W. Smith, W. Wayte and G. E. Marindin, London: J. Murray, 1890.

metaphysical school of the north: For the German philosopher Arthur Schopenhauer (1788–1860), author of *The World as Will and Representation* (1819), the driving energy is Will; for Descartes it is Force.

a Lyceum: The gymnasium located beyond the walls of ancient Athens, mentioned in Plato's dialogues as a place where Socrates taught, and the site of a later philosophical school founded by Aristotle.

Caiaphas . . . Draco . . . Trimalchio . . . Tiberius: Caiaphas was the Jewish high priest who presided over the court that sought evidence against Christ in order to put him to death (Matthew 26:57–68). He appears in medieval passion plays dressed as a bishop. Draco, the Athenian legislator of the seventh century

BC, established a legal code that was considered particularly harsh, with the death penalty prescribed for even minor offences – hence the term 'draconian'. A debauched parvenu of immense wealth and no morals, Trimalchio is a character in the satirical novel *Satyricon* by the first-century-AD Latin author Petronius. The Roman emperor Tiberius (42 BC–AD 37) is portrayed by the historian Tacitus (56–117) as crafty, cruel, licentious and unprincipled.

Thales: Writing in the third century AD in *Lives and Opinions of Eminent Philosophers*, Diogenes Laertius describes Thales of Miletus (*c.*624–*c.*546 BC) as one attached to a solitary and reclusive life.

We must die . . . La Trappe echoes Horace: Horace, *Odes* II:3: 'moreris / Victima nil miserantis Orci. / Omnes eodem cogimur, omnium / Versatur urna serius ocius / Sors exitura et nos in aeternum / Exilium impositura cumbae' ('you will die, victim of none-sparing Orcus. We are all compelled to go there, a turn of the urn determines the fate of all and sooner or later imposes on us embarkation for eternal exile'). Founded in 1140, the monastery of La Trappe acquired its modern reputation for austerity in the late seventeenth century under the rule of Armand de Rance (1626–1700), nominally abbot from a very young age. For many years he led a dissolute life, but he underwent a conversion in the late 1650s and introduced a strict ascetic rule with which the name of the reformed Cistercian monastery is now synonymous. It was an erroneous popular belief that the monks of La Trappe greeted each other with the words 'Memento mori' and that they daily dug their own graves.

Leibniz: The German mathematician and rationalist philosopher Gottfried von Leibniz (1646–1716), who discovered integral and differential calculus (independently of Isaac Newton), argued that God of necessity must exist and could not but choose the most perfect universe; therefore this world is the best of all possible worlds (a claim satirized by Voltaire in his novel *Candide*, 1759). Leibniz defended prayers as useful 'because the idea or the foreknowledge of our prayers aided the divine understanding when it arranged the universe' (Lloyd Strickland, *The Shorter Leibniz Texts: A Collection of New Translations*, London: Continuum, 2006, p. 102).

Dom Mabillon . . . Merlonus Horstius: In 1641 the Dutch theologian Jacobus Merlonus Horstius – there are numerous variant spellings of this name – (1597–1644) published in Cologne an edition of *The Works of St Bernard*, including letters. The Benedictine monk Jean Mabillon (1632–1707) published an edition of *The Works* in 1667. Mabillon is also the author of a celebrated work entitled *Réflexions sur les prisons des ordres religieux* (Reflections on the Prisons of Religious Orders; written 1690, published 1724), which exposed and condemned the *in pace* as inhuman.

a Jansenist: The Augustinian-inspired teachings of Cornelius Jansen (1585–1638), bishop of Ypres, published after his death, were regarded by the Roman Catholic Church as heretical on the issues of grace and predestination. Fuelled by anti-papalism and an ascetic spirituality, and centred on the Cistercian religious communities of the Port-Royal abbeys, Jansenism attracted influential supporters in France but was vigorously opposed by the Jesuits, the papacy and Louis XIV. By the mid eighteenth century it was in decline, although the spirit of Jansenism persisted into the nineteenth century.

Cardinal de Bérulle: Died of an apoplexy at the altar on 2 October 1629.

St Diodorus . . . Acarus: St Diodorus (died *c.*392) was bishop of Tarsus. *Acarus* means 'tick', 'mite'.

Portus: There is no record of a St Terence who was bishop of Portus.

Bernard Guidonis: Bishop of Tuy in Galicia, then of Lodève; inquisitor of Toulouse against the Albigensians, the Dominican Bernard Guidonis (or Gui; 1261–1331) was born and died in France.

Plantavit de la Fosse: Jean de Plantavit de la Pause (1579–1651) was bishop of Lodève from 1625; Guillaume Plantavit de la Pause (1684–1760), abbot of Margon, retired to a Bernardine abbey and wrote a number of works of religious history.

St Benedict II ... Constantine Pogonatus: St Benedict II (elected to the papacy in 683, died in 685) was pope-elect for eleven months before his position was confirmed by the Byzantine emperor Constantine IV (*c*.652–85).

Constans: The youngest son of the Byzantine emperor Constantine the Great, Constans (*c*.320–50) was emperor of the Western Roman Empire from 337 to 350.

Bernard ... Abelard ... de Bruys ... Henry ... Apostolicals ... Arnold of Brescia ... Radulf ... Porée ... Étoile ... Louis the Young ... Eugenius III ... Templars: At the Council of Sens (1140), the writings and teachings of the scholastic philosopher and theologian Peter Abelard (1079–1142), challenged by Bernard of Clairvaux, were condemned as heretical, and in consequence Abelard was sentenced to monastic isolation. Pierre de Bruys was burned as a heretic in 1126 and his disciple Henry of Lausanne was arrested in 1145/6 and sentenced to life imprisonment. Apostolicals is a designation loosely applied to a twelfth-century heretical grouping with pretensions to an apostolic way of life. Abelard's disciple Arnold of Brescia (*c*.1100–*c*.1155) was eventually executed in Rome. Bernard deplored the anti-Jewish violence to which a Cistercian monk, Radulf, incited the population in the Rhineland at the time of the Second Crusade (1145–9), and took measures to curtail his activities. Gilbert de la Porée, bishop of Poitiers (1070–1154), was censured by the Council of Reims (1148) for some of his teachings about the Trinity, a judgement to which he bowed without protest. A self-appointed messiah, the Breton monk Éon de l'Étoile was deemed insane at the Council of Reims and sentenced to the seclusion of a monastery. Louis VII, known as Louis the Young (1120–80), was prevailed upon by St Bernard to join the Second Crusade (proclaimed by Pope Eugenius III in 1145, the year of his election to the papacy). The first Cistercian to become pope, Eugenius III (died 1153) presided over the Council of Reims. The rule of the Knights Templars, dating from the Council of Troyes in 1128, was inspired by St Bernard.

the Basil of the West: Particularly revered in the Eastern Christian Churches, St Basil the Great (330–79), bishop of Caesarea, was born in Cappadocia. He founded the Basilian monastic order and is regarded as the father of Eastern monasticism, his influence on the monastic tradition extending to the Western Church.

Bernard of the Poor Catholics: Bernard Primus was the first superior of the mendicant Order of the Poor Catholics, founded in 1208 to combat the Albigensian heresy.

Yet César de Bus ... far from blessed: In the French text, 'Pourtant César de Bus est un bienheureaux, et Voltaire est un malheureaux.' A French Catholic priest who founded two religious congregations devoted to the teaching of Christian doctrine, César de Bus (1544–1607) was declared Venerable in 1821. He would not formally have been called Blessed ('bienheureaux') until he was beatified in 1975, but Mère Innocente is using the term a little more loosely, in contrast with the 'malheureux' ('wretched') Voltaire.

Périgord ... Gondren ... Bourgoing ... Senault ... Père de la Ste-Marthe: The churchman Alexandre-Angélique de Talleyrand-Périgord (1736–1821), uncle of Talleyrand the politician, was made cardinal in 1817 and archbishop of Paris later the same year. Father Charles de Gondren was the second superior of the Oratorians; he was succeeded in 1641 by François Bourgoing, who died in 1662. The Belgian theologian Jean-François Senault was Bourgoing's successor, and following his death in 1672 Louis de la Sainte-Marthe (1621–97) became the superior of the order.

Père Coton: Pierre Coton (or Cotton; 1564–1626) and St Francis of Sales (1567–1622) were both strong supporters of the founding of the French Oratorian Congregation by Pierre de Bérulle.

cheated at cards: This accusation is reported (in her vast correspondence, by the German-born Duchesse d'Orléans, Charlotte-Élisabeth, Princess Palatine; 1652–1722) to have been made by Marshal Nicolas de Neufville de Villeroi (1598–1685).

Sagittarius ... Salonius ... Mummulus: Gregory of Tours (539–94) relates in his *History of the Franks* (bk IV) that an incursion into Gaul by the Lombards in the early 570s was defeated by the Comte d'Auxerre, Ennius Mummulus, at the head of a Burgundian army, with the two brother bishops Sagittarius and Salonius taking part in the battle – and, 'what is worse', killing many by their own hand.

St Martin of Tours: St Martin (316–97), born in Hungary, came to Gaul as a soldier, where according to legend he shared his cloak with a beggar and was subsequently baptized. He lived as a monk for many years and about 371, by the will of the people, was made bishop of Tours.

St Leo II: Pope Leo II (died 683) had to wait even longer than his successor St Benedict II for his election to the papacy (in 681) to be confirmed (in 682) by the imperial authority, represented in Italy by the exarch of Ravenna. Spain was at that time ruled by the Visigoths; there are extant some letters that Leo sent to Spain by the notary Peter, one of which is addressed to King Ervig.

Gautier ... Duc de Bourgogne: When Robert de Molesme founded the Cistercian Order in 1098, his new abbey was built on land granted to him by Eudes, sometimes Othon (in various spellings), Duc de Bourgogne; Robert was installed as abbot by Gautier, bishop of Châlons (1080–1121).

Arnold de Wyon, Gabriel Bucelin, Trithemius, Maurolycus ... Luc d'Achéry: Benedictine scholars who wrote about the order and its most illustrious figures: the Flemish Arnold de Wyon (1554–?), author of *Lignum Vitae* (Tree of Life: History of the Order of St Benedict); the German ecclesiastical historian Gabriel Bucelin (1599–1681); the humanist historian Abbot Johannes Trithemius (1462–1516); the Sicilian-born Greek mathematician and astronomer Franciscus Maurolycus (1494–1575); Luc d'Achéry (1609–85), a Benedictine of the Congregation of St-Maur.

Emperor Henry II: Crowned Holy Roman Emperor by Pope Benedict VIII (died 1024) in 1014, Henry II (972–1024) was canonized in 1147. Benedict's election to the papacy in 1012 had been opposed by the antipope Gregory VI, who appealed to Henry for his support but was denied it.

the monk Austin Castillejo ... Charles V ... La Plombes ... the monastery of San Yuste: It is recorded that the emperor Charles V (1500–58) developed a passion for a beautiful young woman, Eliodora de Plombes, from Ratisbon (Regensburg), who became his mistress at Cambrai in 1544; so enamoured of each other were they that she visited him, dressed as a man, while he was on military campaign (Gregorio Leti, *Vita dell' Invittissimo Imperadore Carlo V*, 1700, vol. 3, pp. 157–60). In 1556 Charles abdicated, and retired to the monastery of San Yuste in Extremadura, Spain. Cristóbal de Castillejo (1491–1556) was a Spanish poet and monk, who served as secretary to Charles V's brother Ferdinand. Austin Castillejo is probably an invention of Hugo.

Perronet: Jean-Rodolphe Perronet (1708–94) was an architect and structural engineer who designed many stone bridges all over France, including the Pont Louis XVI, now Pont de la Concorde, in Paris, as well as Paris's main sewer.

Three one-hundred-sou coins: From the adoption of a decimalized currency in 1795 until the sou was withdrawn from circulation in 1947, one sou was worth five centimes.

'step on your foot': A game that schoolchildren play to get warm (*Dictionnaire de l'Académie française*, 1835).

Monsieur de Latil: Jean-Baptiste de Latil (1761–1839), archbishop of Chartres (1817) and of Reims (1824), was made cardinal in 1826. As archbishop of Reims, in 1825 he conducted the coronation of Charles X, who before succeeding to the throne as brother to the king (Louis XVIII) was known as 'Monsieur'.

Leo XII: Annibale della Genga (1760–1829) was elected pope in 1823. Before then, he was briefly papal nuncio in Paris.

Illustrated London News: A weekly illustrated newspaper founded by Herbert Ingram (1811–60), first published 14 May 1842. From 1971 it was no longer able to survive as a weekly and eventually ceased publication in 2003.

royalist banknote of '93 … Chouan counter-revolutionary: Opposition to the Revolution broke out in western France in the Vendée region and in Brittany from 1793, triggered by a levy of conscripts for the Republican army, which rallied peasant support for the royalist Catholic cause. In Brittany the counter-revolutionaries were known as the Chouans. Jean-Nicolas Stofflet (1751–96), major-general of the so-called Armée Catholique et Royale de Vendée, was captured and executed in 1796. This civil war is the subject of Hugo's novel *Quatre-vingt-treize* ('93), published in 1874. It was also the subject of the first novel, entitled *Les Chouans* (1829), in Balzac's *Human Comedy* cycle.

PART THREE: MARIUS

the gamin: Before his consecration by Hugo in the character of Gavroche, the Parisian gamin emerges as a social archetype, both celebrated and deplored by writers and illustrators, from 1830 and the July Revolution onwards. (See Jean-Jacques Yvorel, 'De Delacroix à Poulbot, l'image du gamin de Paris', *Revue d'histoire de l'enfance 'irrégulière'*, no. 4 (2002), pp. 39–72, http://rhei. revues.org/index52.html.)

Homuncio: The term *homuncio*, 'a little man', was used by the later Roman comic playwright Terence (*c*.190–158 BC). Lewis and Short, *A Latin Dictionary*, 1879, also gives references to use of the word by Suetonius and Juvenal, but none by Plautus (*c*.254–184 BC).

Adamastor: The hideously fearsome giant that guards the southern Cape of Africa in the Portuguese epic poem *The Lusiads* (1572) by Luís de Camões (*c*.1524–80).

Fouillou: Jacques Fouillou (1670–1736) was an independent-minded Jansenist theologian, born at La Rochelle, who made his career at the Sorbonne.

Grenelle's ghastly wall: The wall at Grenelle was a place of execution for military and political offenders, where in 1812 General Lahorie, Hugo's mother's lover, met his end, condemned to death for his part in the Malet conspiracy against Napoleon, a failed *coup d'état* staged by General Charles-François de Malet (1754–1812) in October of that year, while Napoleon was in Russia.

the swallows of the Pont d'Arcole: According to legend, the Pont d'Arcole was named not after Napoleon's victory against the Austrians at the Bridge of Arcola in November 1796, but after a young Revolutionary of that name who died on this footbridge, previously called the Passerelle de Grève, during the 1830 Revolution. Over subsequent years the arches beneath the bridge became home to young Parisian vagabonds, referred to as *les hirondelles du Pont d'Arcole*.

Barbier: The chronicler Edmond Barbier (1689–1771) in his *Journal historique et anecdotique du règne de Louis XV* (1847–56, vol. 3) writes of the abduction of children (pp. 124–60) and of bloodbaths (p. 125).

Claude Gueux: In fact the word *gamin* appears in print in earlier texts than Hugo's short story of 1834, not least in Hugo's *Notre-Dame de Paris* (1831, bk II, ch. 5).

Sanson ... Montès ... Lacenaire ... Dautun ... Papavoine ... Tolleron ... Avril ... Louvel ... Delaporte ... Castaing ... Bories ... Martin ... Lecouffé ... Debacker: The Sanson family held the office of public executioner from 1688 until 1847. Abbé Montès was chaplain of the Conciergerie prison, attending those condemned to death, including Pierre-François Lacenaire, who was executed for murder and theft in January 1836, together with his accomplice Victor Avril. While in prison Lacenaire wrote songs, poems and his memoirs (published after his death). He was reincarnated as the criminal poet dandy in Marcel Carné's film *Les Enfants du Paradis*. For details of Lacenaire's role model, the notorious murderer Dautun, see note p. 1315. Louis-Auguste Papavoine was executed in March 1825 for the murder of two children. Edmé-Henri-Charles Tolleron, an engraver, was found guilty of taking part in a seditious plot – orchestrated by agents provocateurs – against the Bourbon monarchy, and was executed in July 1816. François Delaporte was executed, together with two accomplices, in April 1824 for highway robbery. In *Victor Hugo raconté par un témoin de sa vie*, Hugo is said to have seen both Louvel (the Duc de Berry's assassin) and the bald Delaporte ('an old man') on their way to execution (Louvel, in June 1820). Dr Edme-Samuel Castaing was executed in December 1823 for the murder of two brothers (of the first with the complicity of the second, who paid him handsomely for it). Jean-François-Louis-Clair Bories was one of the four young sergeants of La Rochelle (along with Pommier, Raoulx and Goubin) executed for sedition in September 1822, despite Bories's attempt to exculpate his companions. Jean Martin is the name of a parricide referred to in *Victor Hugo raconté par un témoin de sa vie* as having been executed in 1825. In Hugo's 1829 novel *Le Dernier jour d'un condamné*, written in protest against capital punishment, Jean Martin's name appears on the wall of the narrator's prison with the date 1821. However, the only parricide with a name bearing any resemblance to Jean Martin who died during this period of whom there is any record was thirty-three-year-old Pierre-Martin Godefroy, executed along with his brother in 1820 for the murder of their father in 1815. Lecouffé and his mother were executed in January 1824 for the murder of an old woman carried out by Lecouffé at his mother's instigation. Philippe-François Debacker was executed in June 1829 for the murder of his mistress and her employer.

pears on walls . . . a pear on that too: In 1831 Charles Philipon published in his satirical weekly magazine *La Caricature* drawings that established an identification between Louis-Philippe's physiognomy and a pear, which quickly became a national joke. Pears chalked up on walls all over Paris and the provinces were treated by the government as a seditious emblem.

Poquelin: Jean-Baptiste Poquelin (1622–73), better known as Molière.

Beaumarchais: The Paris-born playwright Pierre-Auguste Caron de Beaumarchais (1732–99), a watchmaker like his father, is best known as the author of *The Barber of Seville* (first performed in 1775) and *The Marriage of Figaro* (first performed in 1784).

Camille Desmoulins: A childhood friend of Robespierre and political ally of Danton, the journalist and politician Camille Desmoulins (1760–94) was one of the architects of the French Revolution who, like Danton, perished by it.

Championnet . . . St Genevieve: As commander-in-chief of the French 'army of Rome', sent to protect the infant Roman Republic in 1798, General Jean-Étienne Championnet (1762–1800) succeeded not only in defending Rome against the Neapolitan king but also in capturing Naples. To celebrate the achievement he was determined that the miracle of the liquefaction of the blood of Naples's patron saint Januarius should occur. And it did. St Genevieve is the patron saint of Paris. The church of St-Étienne du Mont houses the relics of St Genevieve and the Rue St-Jean de Beauvais is near by. Championnet was born and brought up in the south-east of France.

the young Theban: An allusion to Herakles (Latinized as Hercules), the son of Zeus by a mortal, who as a baby squeezed to death two snakes sent to kill him by Zeus' jealous wife Hera. As an adult seeking to purify himself, Herakles was required to fulfil Twelve Labours, the first of which was the killing of the Nemean lion. He is usually depicted in Greek art wearing the lion's pelt.

Bara the drummer-boy: Joseph Bara (1779–93) became a Republican hero of mythic stature when he was killed by counter-revolutionaries of the Vendée who stole the horses he was leading. There were even plans for the boy to be buried in the Panthéon, and his death was celebrated in a painting by David, now at the Musée Calvet in Avignon.

Aventine Hill . . . Asinarium . . . Pantheon . . . Via Sacra . . . Tower of the Winds . . . Gemonian Steps: One of the seven hills on which ancient Rome was built, the Aventine Hill lay outside the city's original boundary and, like the Faubourg St-Antoine, was incorporated within its walls at a later date. Amid his celebrations of Paris as a rival to Rome, Hugo aims a gibe at the Sorbonne – an asinarium is a collection of asses. Dating from around 50 BC and designed to serve as a weathervane, sundial and water clock, the Tower of the Winds, also called the Horologion of Andronicus, stands close to the Roman agora in Athens. On the Gemonian Steps, which led past the prison in ancient Rome, the bodies of executed criminals were left exposed before being thrown into the river (see Tacitus, *Annals* 3:14 or *Histories* 3:74).

Dumarsais's thieving harridan . . . Euripides' herb-seller: A repeated taunt in the comedies of the Greek playwright Aristophanes is that the mother of the tragedian Euripides was a herb-seller. For the French grammarian, philosopher and contributor to Diderot and d'Alembert's *Encyclopédie*, César Chesneau, Sieur Dumarsais (1676–1756), life was always a struggle. His father died when he was young and his mother squandered his inheritance, including the library, which had to be sold. Hugo refers to her here as the *poissarde*, a word that came to mean 'fishwife' but has the older meaning of 'thief' (apparently deriving from the word *poisse*, slime left on the hands and clothes of people who handle fish – see R. Anthony Lodge, *A Sociolinguistic History of Parisian French*, Cambridge: Cambridge University Press, 2004, p. 163).

the discus-thrower Vejanus: Horace mentions a celebrated gladiator named Vejanus (Epistles, I:1, lines 4–5). A marble copy of the Greek sculptor Naucydes' *Discobolus* entered the Louvre collection, together with the *Borghese Gladiator* (now described as a *Fighting Warrior*) in 1808, after Napoleon bought these antiquities from his brother-in-law Camillo Borghese.

Therapontigonus Miles . . . Vadeboncoeur: Therapontigonus Miles is the soldier character in Plautus' comedy *Curculio*. In the eighteenth century French soldiers were required to adopt a *nom de guerre* to distinguish them from others in their company with the same surname. Vadeboncoeur (literally, 'Go willingly') was a common choice.

Damasippus: In Horace's *Satires* II:3, lines 18–26, Damasippus describes his passion for buying old statues, and how having lost his own money he now deals on behalf of others.

Vincennes . . . Agora: In 1749 Diderot was imprisoned for over three months in the Château de Vincennes, east of Paris, for having caused offence with the publication of his *Lettre sur les aveugles* (Essay on Blindness). The trial of Socrates took place in the people's court in the Agora.

Curtillus: In Horace's *Satires* II:8, lines 52–3, the dinner-party host Nasidienus, presenting a dish of lamprey to his guests, mentions that Curtillus adds sea urchins because they give a better flavour: 'inlutos Curtillus echinos, / ut melius muria quod testa marina remittat.' *Echinus* means either 'hedgehog' or 'sea urchin' (also called the sea hedgehog).

trapeze: The Spanish Colonel Francisco Amóros (1770–1848) is credited with introducing the trapeze into France as part of his military gymnastic training programme. In the mid nineteenth century the acrobat Thévelin performed on a trapeze suspended from a balloon at the Hippodrome, and the trapeze act continued to evolve as part of the circus repertoire. The reference to Plautus' trapeze is possibly a play on the Latin word *trapezita*, 'banker', of which there are many in Plautus' plays, including *Curculio* (The Forgery).

The sword-eater . . . Poecile Portico: A reference to Apuleius' *Golden Ass*, bk I, ch. 4: 'Et tamen Athenis proxime et ante Poecilen porticum isto gemino obtutu circulatorem aspexi equestrem spatham praeacutam mucrone infesto devorasse' ('And yet at Athens before the porch called the Poecile, I saw a juggler that swallowed a sharply honed sword, with a very keen edge').

Rameau's nephew: The eponymous character of Diderot's posthumously published work (first appearing in a German translation by Goethe, in 1805) with whom the narrator engages in a dialogue satirizing critics of the Enlightenment.

Curculio: Curculio (*curculio*, meaning 'weevil') plays the stock role of the parasitic servant in Plautus' play.

Ergasilus . . . d'Aigrefeuille . . . Cambacérès: Ergasilus the parasite is a character in Plautus' play *Captivi* (The Captives). The lawyer and statesman Jean-Jacques Régis de Cambacérès (1753–1824), president of the committee that drew up the Napoleonic Civil Code, was famous for his gourmet indulgences, which he shared with his close friend the Marquis Toussaint d'Aigrefeuille (1747–1818), who acted as high priest of his gastronomic epicurism.

Rome's four young fops: These are four love-struck Plautine characters: Alcesimarchus in *Cistellaria* (The Casket), Argyrippus and Diabolus in *Asinaria*, and Phaedromus in *Curculio*.

La Courtille: Located beyond the city walls and therefore exempt from the Parisian tax on wine, La Courtille on the heights of Belleville was where Parisians went to enjoy themselves in its many bars, dance halls and restaurants. Mardi Gras festivities continued there throughout the night and the procession of revellers returning to Paris, known as the *descente de la Courtille*, marked the end of Carnival.

Aulus Gellius . . . Congrio . . . Nodier . . . Pulchinello: The Roman author of *Noctes Atticae* (Attic Nights), written in the mid second century AD and consisting of notes on a wide range of subjects, Aulus Gellius cites the works of many Greek and Latin writers (he mentions 275 by name), for some of whom little else or nothing has survived. Congrio is the cook in Plautus' *Aulularia* (The Pot of Gold), and Aulus Gellius was a great admirer of Plautus. The writer Charles Nodier (1780–1844), a patron and friend of Hugo, was enamoured of Pulchinello and wrote an enthusiastic article celebrating the character ('Polichinelle', *Paris, ou le Livre des Cent-et-un*, vol. 2, Ladvocat: Paris, 1831).

Marton . . . Pardalisca: Marton is the beautiful country girl ravished by Sire Robert in Voltaire's verse narrative *Ce qui plaît aux dames* (What Pleases Women; 1764). Pardalisca is the clever slave-girl in Plautus' *Casina*.

Pantolabus . . . Nomentanus: An allusion to two parasitic characters mentioned several times in Horace's *Satires*, Pantolabus as a joker or buffoon (I:2, 8), and Nomentanus as a rake or wastrel (I:1, 2, 8; and as one of the guests at Nasidienus' dinner party, II:8).

Hermogenes: Mentioned as a good singer (*optimus cantor*) in Horace's *Satires* I:3.

Thrasius: An alternative spelling for the Trausius in Horace's Satire on frugality, who is referred to as poor but extravagant, II:2, lines 89–111.

Bobèche: Antoine Mandelard (1791–c.1841), better known as Bobèche, was a French theatre clown who enjoyed great popularity and success under the first Empire and the Restoration.

Désaugier's glassful . . . Balatro's huge goblet: The hugely successful songwriter Marc-Antoine Désaugier (1772–1827) summed up a whole philosophy of life in the refrain of one of his most popular compositions: 'Verse encor / encor, encor, encor, / encor un rouge bord, / Dieu joufflu de la treille! / Verse encor, / encor, encor, encor. / Par toi tout se réveille, / Et sans toi tout est mort' ('Pour another, / and another, and another, / another brimming glass of red, / Chubby-cheeked god of the vine, / Through you everything wakens, / And without you everything is dead'). At Nasidienus' feast (Horace, *Satires* II:8), guests Balatro and his dining companion Vibidius call for larger glasses (lines 34–6) and serve themselves generously (lines 40–1).

Père-Lachaise . . . Esquiline: Paris's Père-Lachaise cemetery was opened in 1804 in what was then an outlying district of the city, and only after the remains of La Fontaine, Molière, Abelard and Héloïse were transferred there in 1817 did it become a fashionable burial ground. The eastern slopes of the Esquiline, one of the seven hills of Rome, was at one time a burial place for paupers (see Horace *Satires* I:8, line 10).

Trophonius' cave . . . Mesmer's tub: Consulting the ancient Greek oracle of Trophonius was a complicated and unnerving experience (as described by Pausanias in his *Description of Greece*, Boeotia, ch. 39), which involved descending into a dark cave. Unable to deal individually with the numbers who flocked to him, the legendary healer Anton Mesmer (1734–1815) developed the *baquet*, a kind of tub around which the patients sat to receive his therapy, based on his theory of animal magnetism. (The commission set up in 1784 to investigate this therapy was headed by Benjamin Franklin, then American ambassador to Paris.)

Ergaphilas . . . Cagliostro: Count Alessandro di Cagliostro (1743–95) was a man whose life was shrouded in mystery and occultism, who has been identified as an Italian adventurer named Giuseppe Balsamo, although Cagliostro himself denied this. He was eventually arrested by spies of the Inquisition and sentenced to death for being a freemason, although this sentence was apparently commuted to life imprisonment. He has enjoyed a long and varied afterlife in numerous literary and musical manifestations. Ergaphilas may be the Athenian general Ergophilus, who shared with Cagliostro the experience of escaping the death sentence (Aristotle, *Rhetoric*, 2.3.13: 'For men grow mild when they have exhausted their anger upon another, as happened in the case of Ergophilus. For although the Athenians were more indignant with him than with Callisthenes, they acquitted him because they had condemned Callisthenes the day before.')

Comte de St-Germain: Another eighteenth-century adventurer and self-mythologizer, the Comte de St-Germain impressed, intrigued, even fascinated all those who encountered him, including Horace Walpole, Casanova and Madame de Pompadour.

St-Médard . . . Umumiye . . . Damascus: The tomb of the saintly Jansenist deacon François de Pâris, buried in St-Médard Cemetery in 1727, became a shrine of devotion and the site of miraculous cures among those who flocked to it, many of whom were seized with strange convulsions, a phenomenon that was first recorded in 1731 and persisted for some fifteen years. The great holy shrine in Damascus is the Ummayad Mosque.

Mayeux: Like Aesop a hunchback critic of humanity, Mayeux is the character of the social outsider speaking for the ordinary citizen, by means of which the political caricaturist Charles Traviès (1804–59) and others satirized the bourgeoisie and the July Monarchy.

Canidia . . . Mademoiselle Lenormand: Canidia is a sorceress who appears in three of Horace's texts (*Epodes* 5, 17; *Satires* I:8). Mademoiselle Lenormand (1772–1843) was a renowned fortune-teller, supposedly consulted by Napoleon and the empress Josephine.

Dodona: The site of an ancient oracle located in north-western Greece, where the oracle's responses were inferred from the rustling leaves of an oak tree (symbol of Zeus) or from the sound of the wind in the bronze tripods standing around the sanctuary.

Messalina: The notoriously promiscuous third wife of the Roman emperor Claudius, Messalina has become synonymous with harlotry.

Chodruc-Duclos: A diehard royalist, Chodruc-Duclos (1780–1842), once an exceptionally handsome young man, outraged not to be given the high military office he thought he deserved when the monarchy was restored, became a familiar figure on the streets of Paris; like the Greek philosopher Diogenes, he lived the life of a tramp for years until his death. He was on several occasions arrested and even imprisoned, but charges against him were hard to uphold: he could not be called a vagrant since he owned property in his native Gascony, and he argued that the small amounts of money he solicited were loans rather than the fruits of begging.

Plutarch: In *De Genio Socratis* (section 6), Plutarch reports 'the excellent answer' that Thales gave when asked by his friends on his return from a long absence abroad what was the most remarkable thing he had seen: 'A tyrant in old age.'

Sulla and Domitian: Having defeated his political opponents on the battlefield, Sulla was appointed dictator of Rome in 82 BC; he instituted a reign of terror, after two years abdicated, re-established consular government, then retired. He died in 78 BC. Domitian (51–96) ruled as emperor for fifteen years and is portrayed by Suetonius as a cruel and avaricious tyrant. After he was assassinated in a conspiracy involving those close to him, the Senate condemned his memory to oblivion.

callipygian beauty is a Hottentot: The *Callipygian Venus* is a Roman marble statue dating from the first century BC, which was rediscovered in Rome in the sixteenth century and is now held in the National Archaeological Museum of Naples. The epithet 'callipygian' is from the Greek, meaning 'with beautiful buttocks'. Sara Baartman, who came to England from South Africa in 1810 (and subsequently travelled to Paris where she later died), became known as 'the Hottentot Venus', her physique – her large buttocks in particular, characteristic of her Khoekhoe origins – attracting immense curiosity and scientific interest. Her remains were finally returned to South Africa in 2002.

hold its nose at Basile: Possibly a reference to Don Basile in Beaumarchais's *Barber of Seville*, as sanctimonious a hypocrite as Molière's character Tartuffe.

Priapus' 'eruption': An allusion to Horace, *Satires* I:8, at the end of which Priapus releases an explosive and what could be interpreted as a flatulent sound to scare off the witches, who run away laughing.

the Bal Mabille . . . Polymnia . . . Janiculum: Originally a dancing institution for the pupils of the dancing-master Jacques Mabille (1772–1845), the Bal Mabille as developed by Mabille's sons became a huge pleasure garden, with music provided by large orchestras and dancing that continued into the night, illuminated by gaslight, in what was still countryside (to the west of Paris). Polymnia was the muse of sacred poetry, and the Janiculum Hill on the west bank of the Tiber, outside the walls of Rome, was a place of sacred woods and shrines.

the purveyor of frippery: Clothes dealers exploited young Parisiennes who bought second-hand finery from them on long-term credit (see Philippe Perrot, *Fashioning the Bourgeoisie: A History of Clothing in the Nineteenth Century*, Princeton: Princeton University Press, 1994).

the procuress Staphyla . . . the virgin Planesium: Planesium is the virgin slave-girl in Plautus' *Curculio*; the old woman Staphyla in *Aulularia* is the slave of a miserly master whose daughter is pregnant out of wedlock.

The Syrian hostess: An allusion to *The Copa*, a Latin poem attributed to Virgil, about a Syrian tavern hostess (*copa*) who invites her clients to enjoy the pleasures of her establishment.

Mère Saguet: Immortalized in the title of a posthumously published collection of essays by the poet and novelist Gérard de Nerval (1808–55), the tavern run by Mère Saguet, on the outskirts of the city close to the Moulin de Beurre, was frequented by writers and artists including Hugo himself.

Charlet: The painter and engraver Nicolas-Toussaint Charlet (1792–1845) specialized in Bonapartist themes celebrating the Napoleonic legend.

Adonai: One of the Hebrew names for God in the Old Testament, generally translated 'Lord'.

Silenus: In Greek mythology, Silenus was companion and tutor to the wine god Dionysus. A Falstaff-like character, he is often depicted riding on an ass.

Ramponneau: Jean Ramponneau (1724–1802) was a wine merchant who ran a celebrated tavern, the Tambour Royal; it was phenomenally successful, partly because he undercut his competitors' prices, and partly because of his own personality, particularly after he broke a contract he had made with a theatre manager, which led to his involvement in a lawsuit that became the talk of the town.

Sybaris: Sybaris was a colony founded in southern Italy in the eighth century BC by the Greeks. Its destruction in the late sixth century BC was proverbially blamed on the citizens' overindulgence in the comforts and luxuries their great prosperity had brought them.

Alexander: Carlyle in his 'Essay on Voltaire' (1829) quotes Alexander the Great as saying, 'O Athenians, what toil do I undergo to please you.'

Tennis Court Oath: On 20 June 1789 the self-declared National Assembly – which the king refused to recognize, also denying it entry to the place where it had previously met as the Third Estate in France's parliamentary body, the Estates General – gathered in a nearby tennis court (*jeu de paume*), where its members took a vow that they would continue their meetings, as the National Constituent Assembly, until they had drawn up a new constitution.

Its night of the fourth of August: The National Constituent Assembly interrupted its debate on the constitution so as to address the unrest that was spreading throughout France after the storming of the Bastille on 14 July. At the end of a sitting that went on through the night of 4 August, legislation was passed abolishing all feudal rights and privileges in the interests of equality, legitimacy and fairness.

Washington, Kosciuszko . . . Botsaris, Riego, Bem, Manin, López, John Brown, Garibaldi: Before he was elected first President of the United States, George Washington (1732–99) was appointed commander-in-chief of the Continental Army during the American Revolutionary War (1775–83). Tadeusz Kosciuszko (1746–1817) was leader of the 1794 uprising against Imperial Russia and the Kingdom of Prussia, having previously served as colonel in the Continental Army in the American Revolutionary War. Markos Botsaris (1788–1823) was a Souliote leader and hero of the Greek War of Independence against the Ottoman Empire. The Spanish general and liberal politician Rafael del Riego (1784–1823) was one of the leaders of the mutiny in the Spanish Civil War of 1820–3 that led to the reinstatement of the 1812 Constitution. General Józef Bem (1794–1850) was a Polish freedom-fighter who took part in uprisings in Poland, Austria and Hungary. The statesman Daniele Manin (1804–57) led the Venetian revolution against the Austrians in 1848–9, and was an early advocate of Italian unity. Antonio López de Santa Anna (1794–1876) fought for the independence of Mexico from Spanish rule, later becoming a presidential dictator. The American abolitionist and folk hero John Brown (1800–59), executed for murder and treason by the state of Virginia, is remembered in 'John Brown's Body', which became a Union marching song during the American Civil War (1861–5). Giuseppe Garibaldi (1807–82) not only fought successfully for the liberation and unification of Italy, but also during exile in South America for the liberation of Uruguay from Argentina.

Boston . . . Isla de León . . . Pest . . . Palermo . . . Harpers Ferry . . . Ancona . . . Gli Archi: The Boston Tea Party was an act of resistance to British rule that was to lead in 1775 to the outbreak of the American Revolutionary War. A military insurgency on Isla de León (now San Fernando) near Cadiz, in which Riego played so decisive a role, marked the beginning of the Spanish Civil War of 1820–3. The Pest Uprising of 1848 was the start of the ultimately doomed Hungarian Revolution. In one of the most dramatic achievements of the Italian

Risorgimento, with a core force of only one thousand men Garibaldi captured Palermo from the Neapolitan Bourbon troops in 1860. He went on to take control of Naples and to hand over his territorial gains in southern Italy to the Piedmontese king Victor Emmanuel II. It was after the attack on the federal armoury and arsenal at Harpers Ferry in 1859, with the intention of arming abolitionists and triggering a slave uprising, that John Brown was tried and executed. Ancona fell to the patriots in September 1860. Gli Archi is a coastal district of Ancona that began to develop outside the walls of the city in the eighteenth century.

Canaris . . . Quiroga . . . Pisacane: A freedom-fighter during the Greek War of Independence, commanding fire boats that set fire to Turkish warships, Constantinos Canaris (1793/5–1877) rose to become an admiral in the Greek navy and was prime minister of Greece when he died. Colonel Antonio Quiroga (1784–1841) was one of the military leaders of the Spanish Revolution of 1820–23. An Italian socialist revolutionary, Carlo Pisacane (1818–57) was killed leading an abortive insurrection in Campania against the Kingdom of Naples.

Byron . . . Missolonghi . . . Mazet . . . Barcelona: Lord Byron (1788–1824) joined the Greeks' revolutionary struggle against Ottoman rule and died at Missolonghi of a fever. Author of *Observations on Yellow Fever, Made at Cadiz in 1819*, Dr André Mazet (1793–1821) himself died of yellow fever when, as a member of a French medical team, he returned to Spain to provide assistance during a later outbreak of the disease in Barcelona.

Mirabeau: Rejected by his fellow aristocrats as a potential delegate to the Estates General in 1788, Mirabeau (1749–91) with his great oratorial and pamphleteering skills was elected as a commoner to the Third Estate and elected president of the National Assembly three months before he died. Buried in the Panthéon, his remains were removed when it became known he had colluded with the king in a failed attempt to establish a constitutional monarchy.

Régnier: Destined by his family for a career in the Church for which he was by nature ill suited, Mathurin Régnier (1573–1613) was a talented poet of satirical and licentious verse.

temple of Theseus . . . 'Crédeville's a thief': In the 1830s two graffiti entered Parisian urban mythology (and French literature, in the texts of numerous writers who, like Hugo, recorded the phenomenon): a huge-nosed caricature identified as Bouginier, and the slogan 'Crédeville voleur', sometimes simply the name 'Crédeville'. Their origins remain obscure, although a number of explanations have been offered. Crédeville, for instance, may have been the name of an escaped convict who left his calling-card, as it were, Pink Panther-like, to taunt the police; or the grieving fiancée of some Crédeville taken before his time may have been communicating in this way with her deceased lover; or some victim of a usurer called Crédeville may have been taking his revenge. Gérard de Nerval writes in *Voyage en Orient* that 'Crédeville voleur' and Bouginier's nose are even to be found scrawled on the Pyramids. Privat d'Anglemont has an anecdotal account of Bouginier's nose being used by the first of two separated parties of travellers to lay a trail between Paris and the Pyramids for those following behind them. (See Pierre Enckell, 'Documents pour servir à l'histoire de Crédeville et de Bouginier', in *Études nervaliennes et romantiques III*, Namur: Presses Universitaires de Namur, 1981.) Possibly one sighting was on the Theseion, now known as the temple of Hephaestus, in

Athens, where many philhellenes killed in the Greek War of Independence (1821-30) were buried.

Montesquieu: One of the great political philosophers of the Enlightenment, Charles-Louis de Secondat, Baron de Montesquieu (1689-1755), was elected to the French Academy in 1728 but remained something of an outsider, his first election to that institution in 1725 having been declared invalid because he was still resident in Bordeaux, where he was president of the criminal division of the local parliament. His two great works are his *Persian Letters* (1721), giving a view of European society through the eyes of two foreigners, and *The Spirit of the Laws* (1748), a study of different types of government and the legal and social institutions on which they rest.

Condorcet: The mathematician, philosopher and political theorist Nicolas de Condorcet (1743-94) was a central figure of the French Enlightenment, who believed in social progress through the power of education and knowledge. He was elected in 1791 to the Legislative Assembly, of which he was briefly president. However, opposed to the death penalty on principle, he voted against the execution of Louis XVI and subsequently defended the Girondists, which led to his own imprisonment. He was found dead in his cell, in circumstances which have never been entirely explained.

Arouet: François-Marie Arouet, who adopted the name Voltaire in 1718.

'Mob!' adds Burke: In his *Reflections on the Revolution in France* the Anglo-Irish politician and political theorist Edmund Burke (1729-97) deplored a Revolutionary government whose authority resided in the mob.

Château-d'Eau: A cast-iron water-tower fountain built in 1811 by Pierre-Simon Girard on the site of what is now Place de la République, it was moved in 1867 to outside the former meat market, now a cultural centre, at La Villette.

Monsieur de Vivonne: The brother of Louis XIV's mistress Madame de Montespan, Louis-Victor de Rochechouart, later Duc de Vivonne (1636-88), was in charge of the galley fleet from 1669 until his death. Prisoners serving on the galleys were allowed to use skills they might have – and a significant number were textile artisans – to earn money working in port during the winter months when the galleys were not sailing.

Jordaens: The Flemish Baroque painter Jacob Jordaens (1593-1678).

Camargo and Sallé: Two leading dancers of the early eighteenth century, Marie-Anne de Cupis de Camargo (1710-70), and Marie Sallé (*c.*1707-56), who began her career in London.

Guimard: Marie-Madeleine Guimard (1743-1816), whose career began at the age of fourteen, was the most celebrated dancer of her age.

her tresses in tightly curled ringlets: Her hair is curled 'en sentiments soutenus'. I am indebted to M. Alain Ducher, an expert on historical hairstyles, for his explanation: 'Les boucles sur le cou [se désignaient sous le nom de] sentiments . . . Les sentiments soutenus sont des boucles où une grande partie de la longueur et la pointe est frisée nerveuse' ('Tresses on the neck were referred to by the name of *sentiments*. *Les sentiments soutenus* are tresses which along most of their length and at the tip are tightly curled').

Madame de Boufflers: The Marquise de Boufflers (1711-87) was the mistress of King Stanislaw I of Poland.

Corbière . . . Humann . . . Périer: Jacques-Joseph Corbière (1766-1853), parliamentary deputy and minister of the interior (1821-8); Jean-Georges Humann (1780-1842), parliamentary deputy and minister of finance (1832-4, 1834-6,

1840–2); Casimir Périer (1777–1832), parliamentary deputy, minister of the interior and prime minister (1831–2).

Duc de Nevers . . . *blue sash*: Louis-Jules Mancini-Mazarini, Duc de Nivernais (1716–98), was a politician, serving as France's ambassador to Rome, Berlin and London, and a man of letters elected to the Academy in 1742. The blue sash – *le cordon bleu* – is that worn by the Knights of the Order of the Holy Spirit, an exclusive body of privileged individuals (and the term *cordon bleu* came by transference to apply to excellence in the culinary field, first appearing in the title of a cookery book in 1827).

partitioning Poland: The signatories to the first partition of Poland in 1772 were Russia (ruled by Catherine the Great), Prussia and Austria.

Bestuchef . . . *elixir of gold*: The elixir, thought to be a tincture of gold and not only to have remedial powers – as a cure for syphilis – but also to prolong life, was a solution of ferric chloride in alcohol. The Russian count Alexis Bestuchef-Rumin was the first to discover this concoction in 1725, but its secret then fell into the hands of General Lamotte, who produced a version of it in Paris, for which he was awarded a pension by Louis XV. Around 1780 the then holders of the secrets of the preparation presented the recipe to Catherine the Great, who paid them 3,000 roubles and ordered the publication of the tincture's composition.

ninety-three a second time: The first time would have been 1793, the year of Louis XVI's execution (January) and the beginning of the Terror (September).

consolidated third of the public debt: By a law of September 1797 the public debt was reduced to one-third and termed 'consolidated', and for the other two-thirds of the debt bonds were issued that immediately became almost worthless, being exchanged in 1800 at 1 per cent of their face value.

Rue Quincampoix: The Scottish economist John Law (1671–1729), appointed controller-general of finances by Louis XV, in 1716 established in Rue Quincampoix the Banque Générale, which developed the use of paper money. Law's career ended, and fortunes were lost, with the collapse of the bank during the Mississippi Bubble of 1720.

Monsieur Virginal . . . *Cardinal Sourdis*: Virginal, Marquis d'Alluye (1584–1602), died without issue by his wife Catherine Hurault. His elder brother François (1574–1628), made cardinal by Pope Clement VIII in 1598, became archbishop of Bordeaux the following year.

Monsieur de Bonald: Louis de Bonald (1754–1840), appointed minister in 1822 and made a peer in 1823, was a critic of the Enlightenment and an advocate of aristocratic institutions.

Monsieur Bengy-Puy-Vallée: A friend of de Bonald, Philippe Bengy-Puy-Vallée (1743–1823), of noble descent, served in the pre-Revolutionary army, fled France as an émigré, then returned under the Consulate.

the federates: The National Guardsmen from the provinces, summoned by the Legislative Assembly in 1792 to celebrate the storming of the Bastille at the Festival of Federation (those from Marseille bringing the 'Marseillaise' with them to Paris), were referred to as 'the federates'. They went on to storm the Tuileries on 10 August.

Damas, Sabran, Gouvion St-Cyr: After a military career Ange Hyacinthe Maxence de Damas de Cormaillon, Baron de Damas (1785–1862) served briefly under the Restoration as minister of war and minister of foreign affairs; Comte Elzéar-Louis-Zozime de Sabran (1764–1847) served in the émigré army and in 1814 was made a general by Louis XVIII; Laurent de Gouvion St-Cyr (1764–

1830) distinguished himself in the Napoleonic Wars but his opposition to Napoleon becoming emperor delayed his promotion to marshal. He served as minister of war under the Restoration and was made marquis in 1817.

Fualdès affair: The brutal murder, in March 1817, of the retired prosecutor Antoine-Bernardin Fualdès (born 1761) and the subsequent trials – the first was declared a mistrial on a legal technicality – created a sensation and were covered widely in the press, both in France and abroad. Indicative of the huge interest is Mary Shelley's request, in a letter from Italy dated 30 April 1818 addressed to Thomas Love Peacock, for a publication about the trial to be sent out to her (*The Letters of Thomas Love Peacock: 1792–1827*, ed. Nicholas A. Joukovsky, Oxford: Oxford University Press, 2001, p. 132). Charles Bastide-Gramont (godson of Fualdès), Joseph Jausion and Jean-Baptiste Collard were executed for the murder. The whole affair remains contentious.

the necklace affair . . . strange amnesties: The involvement of the Comte de Lamothe-Valois (or more usually La Motte; 1755–1831) in the necklace affair, a fraud perpetrated by his wife, who arranged the forging of Marie-Antoinette's signature in order to acquire a diamond necklace for herself – and which was exploited by anti-royalists to discredit the queen – should have made him anathema to this royalist salon.

Marigny . . . La Pompadour . . . Prince de Soubise: Jeanne-Antoinette Poisson, Madame de Pompadour (1721–64), was Louis XV's mistress from 1745 until her death. Her brother Abel became Marquis de Marigny in 1754. The Prince de Soubise, Charles de Rohan (1715–87), was a protégé of Madame de Pompadour, and through her influence was given command of an army during the Seven Years War (1756–63); he suffered a humiliating defeat at the battle of Rossbach in 1757.

Vaubernier . . . du Barry . . . Richelieu: Jean-Baptiste du Barry (1723–94) established as a courtesan Jeanne Vaubernier (1743–93), who attracted the attentions of Armand du Plessis, Maréchal Duc de Richelieu (1696–1788), a renowned libertine. In 1768 du Barry arranged for her to be married to his brother Comte Guillaume du Barry (1732–1811) so that she could become the official mistress of Louis XV.

Mercury . . . Prince de Guéménée . . . A thief: Henri de Rohan, Prince de Guéménée (1745–1809), son-in-law of the Prince de Soubise, declared bankruptcy in 1782, owing the colossal sum of 33 million francs. The Greek god Hermes (Mercury in the Roman pantheon) is characterized in classical literature as a thief, associated in particular with the theft of Apollo's oxen ('of many shifts, blandly cunning, a robber, a cattle driver, a bringer of dreams, a watcher by night, a thief at the gates' – *Homeric Hymn IV, To Hermes*, lines 13–15). He is also the patron of (among others) thieves.

the Valois name: This de Lamothe acquired by his marriage to Jeanne de Valois-St-Rémy (1756–91). The House of Valois was a cadet branch of the French royal family that unexpectedly succeeded to the throne in 1328 – the crisis over the succession precipitated the Hundred Years War (1337–1543) between England and France – and reigned until 1589.

Count von Ruppin: The Hohenzollern dynasty first acquired the title 'Margrave of Brandenburg' in 1415, and early on took over the smaller fiefdom of Ruppin. They were granted the title 'king' in Prussia in 1701, and only in 1772 did Frederick II adopt the title 'King of Prussia'. When travelling, Frederick the Great occasionally made use of the title Count von Ruppin.

a brigand of the Loire: After the defeat of Napoleon at Waterloo and the capitulation of Paris in July 1815, the army under the command of General

Louis-Nicolas Davout (1770–1823) withdrew to the Loire region and was often referred to by royalists as 'the brigands of the Loire'.

that beautiful stone bridge: A medieval construction originally of twenty-five arches of which only eight were still standing in 1830, the stone bridge of Vernon was replaced in 1860 by a new stone bridge, the Pont Napoléon, renamed the Pont Clemenceau in 1930. This bridge was destroyed in 1940, and after a series of temporary replacements a new concrete-built Pont Clemenceau was inaugurated in 1954.

Soulange Bodin: Étienne Soulange-Bodin (1774–1846) was a French horticulturalist, who created a botanical garden of some 170 acres at Fromont, about fifteen miles south-east of Paris. He was a pioneer in breeding hybrid magnolias and has given his name to the *Magnolia X soulangeana*.

Saintonge regiment: The Saintonge regiment fought in the American Revolutionary War as part of the French expeditionary force sent to support the Americans. Its two battalions were absorbed into brigade formations in 1794 and 1796.

Speyer, Worms, Neustadt, Turckheim, Alzey and Mainz ... Andernach ... Marchiennes ... Mont-Palissel: Engagements in the Rhineland and in northern France during the French Revolutionary Wars of 1792–7.

Houchard: General Jean-Nicolas Houchard (1738–1793), a soldier of humble origins, rose through the ranks to a position of command that exceeded his capabilities. Appointed commander-in-chief of the Army of the North in 1793, during the French Revolutionary Wars, he was arrested on charges of cowardice for his failure to pursue the enemy after winning the battle of Hondschoote in September 1793. Despite the many scars of battle that he bore, he was found guilty by the Revolutionary Tribunal and sent to the guillotine.

the Col di Tenda with Joubert: General Barthélemy-Catherine Joubert (1769–99): 'In 1791 [Joubert] enrolled as a volunteer, and served in all the lower ranks, from that of an ordinary grenadier. Having been made an infantry lieutenant, he was charged in September 1793 with the defence of a redoubt on the Col di Tenda: surrounded by five hundred Piedmontese, it was only after a spirited resistance that he was taken prisoner' (Louis-Gabriel Michaud, *Biographie Universelle*, 1843). Joubert was killed at the battle of Novi (15 August 1799).

Berthier ... gunner, trooper and grenadier: Louis-Alexandre Berthier (1753–1815) was Napoleon's chief of staff, serving him in that post from 1794. The words are from a letter of 11 May 1796 written by Napoleon to the Directory, the day after the battle of Lodi, when the bridge held by the Austrians was taken by the French.

Malher ... Günzburg: Jean-Pierre Firmin Malher (1761–1808) was general of division at the battle of Günzburg, in October 1805, where the French succeeded in capturing from the Austrians the bridge over the Danube.

Wertingen ... Maupetit: Colonel Pierre Maupetit distinguished himself as described at the battle of Wertingen on 8 October 1805, and although reported in the army bulletin to have been mortally wounded, he survived. He was named Commander of the Legion of Honour at Austerlitz (2 December 1805), promoted to general of brigade in 1806 after the battle of Jena, and made a baron of the Empire in 1808; he died in 1811.

the 4th Line: The Russian Horse Guards captured from the 4th Line the only French colour that was lost at Austerlitz.

Mortier ... Hamburg: Édouard-Adolphe Mortier (1768–1835) served in the French Revolutionary Wars and was one of the first marshals Napoleon created. He led the occupation of Hamburg on 19 November 1806. Having served under Louis-Philippe as French ambassador to Russia, as minister of war and prime minister, he was killed in Fieschi's attempt on Louis-Philippe's life (see note p. 1386 on *the Fieschi conspiracy*).

Eylau . . . Louis Hugo: Hugo's paternal uncle Louis (1777–1853) was awarded the Legion of Honour for his part in the battle of Eylau, fought against the Russians in East Prussia in February 1807. His defence of the cemetery is told in Victor Hugo's poem 'Le Cimetière d'Eylau', published in the second series of his epic cycle *La Légende des Siècles*, on which he began work in 1862 and which was published in 1877.

Arnay-le-Duc: This perhaps should be Bar-le-Duc, some 130 miles east of Paris, close to St-Dizier, where Napoleon won his last victory on 26 March 1814. Hugo may be referring to events that took place near by at what is referred to as the second battle of Fère-Champenoise on 25 March 1814, in which some 3,500 young and inexperienced National Guardsmen were killed making a heroic stand under General Michel-Marie Pacthod (1764–1830), whose arm was shattered in the fighting. Arnay-le-Duc is 155 miles south-east of Paris, in Burgundy, and not on the route of the retreating army.

Flaminius: The third-century Roman consul Gaius Flaminius was killed at the battle of Lake Trasimene in 217 BC, when the great Carthaginian general Hannibal (247–183 BC) ambushed and destroyed the Roman army during the Second Punic War (218–202 BC), which began on the Iberian peninsula where the Romans may have taken some Carthaginians prisoner.

St George's Day: His father's name-day.

monorhymed odes: Odes in which all the lines have the same end-rhyme.

d'Espinouse: In response to a letter he had received from the Marquis Charles-Louis-Alexandre de Coriolis d'Espinouse (1770–1841) Hugo wrote a poem entitled 'Écrit en 1846' (Written in 1846), published in his collection *Les Contemplations* of 1856: 'Marquis, je m'en souviens, vous veniez chez ma mère, / Vous me faisiez parfois réciter ma grammaire . . .' ('Marquis, I remember, you used to visit my mother, / You sometimes made me recite my grammar . . .').

the 'unfindable' kind: The ultra-royalist Chamber of Deputies elected in August 1815 was referred to by Louis XVIII as 'introuvable' ('unfindable'), meaning that he could not have found a more royalist Chamber if he had tried. When the extremism of the 'introuvable' Chamber became a threat to the survival of the monarchy, the Assembly was dissolved by the king, in September 1816, and new elections returned more moderates.

the famous right-wing taunter: Charles Nicolas Cornet-Dincourt (1773–1852) in 1816 proposed suspending the freedom of the press entirely, and restoring unsold assets to the Church.

the bailiff of Ferrette: The county of Ferrette in Alsace came under the jurisdiction of Austria in 1324 and was ruled by a royal official known as the *bailli* ('bailiff') de Ferrette. In *La Muse du Département*, set in 1820s and 30s, Balzac writes of the bailiff that he was said to be 'l'homme le plus courageux de l'Europe parce qu'il osait marcher sur ses deux jambes' ('the bravest man in Europe for daring to walk on his legs'); and that he was accused 'de mettre du plomb dans ses souliers, pour ne pas être emporté par le vent' ('of putting lead in his shoes to save himself from being blown away').

Aristotle . . . Campaspe: The story arose in the thirteenth century that when the philosopher Aristotle remonstrated with his pupil Alexander the Great for allowing himself to be distracted from more important things by his mistress, she took her revenge by using her charms to make Aristotle fall in love with her, to the point where he allowed her to ride on his back. When challenged about his behaviour, the philosopher replied that he had proved precept by example: if a man of his age and wisdom could be made a fool of by a woman, how much more dangerous must she be to a young man? While Pliny the Elder wrote in his *Natural History* that Campaspe was a favourite mistress of Alexander's, the woman who seduced Aristotle is more usually given the name Phyllis. George Sarton in an article published in 1930 ('Aristotle and Phyllis', *Isis*, vol. 14, no. 1, p. 13) cites a reference to a French parlour game called *le cheval d'Aristote* ('Aristotle's horse'), in which as a forfeit a man is obliged to crawl around the room on all fours with one of the ladies on his back.

Abbé Halma ... *La Foudre*: Nicolas Halma (1755–1828), scholar and translator, notably of the Greek astronomer Ptolemy's *Almageste* (1813). *La Foudre* was a royalist newspaper, founded in 1820 by Emmanuel Théaulon (1787–1841), who had earlier founded another royalist paper, *Le Nain Rose* – whose name perhaps suggested to Hugo the name Monsieur Larose.

Frayssinous: Abbé Denis de Frayssinous (1765–1841), bishop of Hermopolis, in 1822 was elected to the Academy and appointed grand master of the university. In 1824 he became minister of public education and ecclesiastical affairs, and delivered the funeral oration for Louis XVIII. In Flaubert's *Madame Bovary* (pt 1, ch. 6) we read: 'Le soir, avant la prière, on faisait dans l'étude une lecture religieuse. C'était, pendant la semaine, quelque résumé d'Histoire sainte ou les *Conférences* de l'abbé Frayssinous ...' ('In the evening, before prayers, there would be a religious reading in the study. During the week it would be a commentary on some biblical story or Abbé Frayssinous's *Lectures* ...').

the illustrious Liberian basilica: The Basilica of Sta Maria Maggiore in Rome, called 'Liberian' after its original founder, Pope Liberius (352–66).

master of requests: Occupying a high-level position dating back to the Middle Ages, a *maître des requêtes* is a judicial officer whose role originally was to examine petitions (*requêtes*) to the Royal Household. In post-Revolutionary France masters of requests are members of the Council of State, which provides the government with legal advice.

Le Conservateur: A royalist newspaper published from October 1818 to March 1820, with which Chateaubriand was closely associated.

the Encyclopaedia: Compiled and edited by Denis Diderot and Jean d'Alembert (1718–83), the *Encyclopédie, ou Dictionnaire raisonné des sciences, des arts et des métiers* (Encyclopaedia, or Classified Dictionary of the Sciences, Arts and Trades) consisted of 28 volumes and contained over 70,000 entries and over 3,000 illustrations. Published over the years 1751–72 and expanded by successive editors, it was intended to be a comprehensive corpus of world knowledge to be made available to the reading public and to future generations. With signed contributions by some of the greatest minds of the age, it represents one the highest achievements of the Enlightenment.

one of the Forty: The forty members of the Academy included Jean-Armand de Roquelaure (1721–1818), elected in 1771. He was bishop of Senlis from 1754 to 1801; the see of Senlis was then suppressed and absorbed into the see of Beauvais.

Vibraye ... Talaru ... Herbouville ... Dambray ... Valentinois: Anne-Victor-Denis Hurault, Marquis de Vibraye (1767–1843); Louis-Justin-Marie, Marquis de Talaru (1769–1850); Charles-Joseph-Fortuné, Marquis de Herbouville (1756–1829); Charles-Henri, Vicomte Dambray (1760–1829). The title of Duc de Valentinois, awarded to the Grimaldi house of Monaco by Louis XIII in 1642, was held during 1777–1814 by Honoré IV of Monaco (1758–1819).

Comte Beugnot: Jacques-Claude Beugnot (1761–1835) was elected to the Legislative Assembly for 1791–2 and 1816–20.

Epimenides: The third-century-AD biographer of the Greek philosophers Diogenes Laertius tells us that Epimenides of Knossos fell asleep for fifty-seven years, and when he awoke after what he thought was a short nap he was bewildered by the changes that had taken place in the meantime.

Koblenz: Many of the royalist émigrés who fled France after the Revolution gathered in Koblenz in the Rhineland, where Louis XVI's brothers the Comte de Provence (the future Louis XVIII) and the Comte d'Artois (later Charles X) had taken up residence, and where the Prince de Condé commanded an émigré army. In 1794 Koblenz fell to the Revolutionary army in the French Revolutionary Wars.

the sword of Fontenoy: The battle of Fontenoy was a pre-Revolutionary French victory in 1745 during the War of the Austrian Succession (1740–48).

called Bonaparte 'Scapin': A pre-Revolutionary bishop, Napoleon's chaplain, later bishop of Poitiers, then archbishop of Malines and in 1812 Napoleon's ambassador to Warsaw, Abbé de Pradt (1759–1837) in the preface to his post-Restoration *Histoire de l'Ambassade dans le Grand-Duché de Varsovie* (History of the Embassy to the Grand-Duchy of Warsaw; Paris, 1815) associates Napoleon with the trickster in Molière's comedy *Les Fourberies de Scapin* (Scapin's Tricks) by referring to him as 'une espèce de Jupiter-Scapin qui n'avait pas encore paru sur la scène du monde' ('a kind of Jupiter-Scapin never before seen on the world stage').

Martainville: A playwright and journalist of no great distinction, Alphonse Martainville (1776–1830) in 1819 founded the ultra-conservative newspaper *Le Drapeau Blanc*.

Fiévée: A journalist of ultra-royalist opinions, Joseph Fiévée (1767–1839) was also the author of a very successful novel of royalist sentiment, *La Dot de Suzette* (Suzette's Dowry), adapted for the stage within months of publication (1798).

Monsieur Agier: An ardent ultra-royalist in 1816, François-Marie Agier (1780–1848) gradually moved to a more liberal position, and as vice-president of the Chamber of Deputies in 1828 led a group, regarded as defectors by the ultras, that controlled the majority.

Colnet: The journalist and satirist Charles Colnet du Ravel (1768–1832) was an outspoken critic of Napoleon in the many articles that he wrote for a number of journals, and his bookshop, known as his *caverne*, became a meeting-place for other writers who shared his political opinions.

Monsieur le Marquis de Buonaparté: The Jesuit Père Jean-Nicolas Loriquet (1767–1845) was accused of having made this reference to Napoleon in a school textbook that presented an anti-Revolutionary view of French history. There is no evidence that the phrase was ever included in his text, but Loriquet and the Jesuits were discredited as educators as a result of the accusation.

the fifth of September: The Terror was instituted by a decree of 5 September 1793 authorizing the Revolutionary government to eliminate its enemies.

the eighth of July: The restoration of the Bourbon monarchy dates from 8 July 1815 when Louis XVIII made his entry into Paris.

We jeer at Monsieur de Vaublanc: Vaublanc, who had been a well rewarded supporter of Napoleon, enthusiastically welcomed the return of the monarchy and was appointed minister of the interior in September 1815.

Bouvines: Philippe II (1165–1223) won a decisive victory for France at the battle of Bouvines in 1214.

the Congregation: A religious association for clergy and laity; revived in 1814 by the Jesuit Pierre Ronsin (1771–1846) for the defence of Catholicism, the Congregation came to be closely allied with the royalist cause and politically influential.

Mémorial de Ste-Hélène: A journal published in 1823 concerning the private life and conversations of Napoleon as recorded by Emmanuel, Comte de las Cases (1766–1842), who accompanied Napoleon to St Helena and remained there with him until 1816. Las Cases wrote, under the pseudonym Lesage, a historical atlas first published in England in 1801.

Vergniaud: A brilliant defence lawyer who became leader of the moderate Republican Girondist faction, Pierre Vergniaud (1753–93) was the last of the twenty-one Girondists to be guillotined in October 1793.

Saint-Just: Louis de Saint-Just (1767–94), a fierce advocate for the execution of Louis XVI and for the Reign of Terror, was a bold and ruthless ideologue of the Revolution. He was himself guillotined, along with Robespierre, in 1794.

his own sisters' lover: A defamatory rumour that circulated among anti-Bonapartists.

the charlatan . . . Talma: Napoleon took a great interest in the theatre and was a particular admirer of the actor Talma, reportedly offering him advice on how men of power in the great tragedies should move on stage. The rumour that Napoleon was taking lessons in deportment from Talma is reflected in a cartoon of 1814 in which Napoleon is caricatured aping poses struck by the tragedian.

the poisoner of Jaffa: Contemporary rumours, much disputed, had it that when Napoleon withdrew from Jaffa in 1799 after the abortive Syrian campaign, he gave the order that wounded and plague-infected French troops should be administered fatal overdoses of opium, an allegation for which Walter Scott in his *Life of Napoleon Buonaparte* (1827) found 'insufficient evidence'.

Géronte: The stock character of the old man in the comic tradition, as represented for instance in Molière's *Le Médecin Malgré Lui* (1666) or *Les Fourberies de Scapin* (1671).

Werther's melancholy: An allusion to the Romantic hero of Goethe's confessional novel *The Sorrows of Young Werther* (1774).

Argus snored: The hundred-eyed giant, whom the jealous goddess Juno appoints to guard her rival in love Io (see note p. 1375 on *Io . . . Pissevache*), is lulled to sleep by Mercury and then beheaded in order to release Jupiter's paramour from his watchfulness (Ovid, *Metamorphoses*, bk I, lines 622–722).

Tugenbund: A Prussian nationalist movement founded in Königsberg in 1808, the Tugenbund (literally, 'league of virtue') was declared illegal in 1809 but continued to operate as a secret society.

Italian carbonarism: The Carbonari (literally, 'charcoal-burners', the forest-dwelling artisans from whom the movement took its inspiration) were members of secret revolutionary nationalist societies originating in the Kingdom of Naples and Sicily in the early nineteenth century, later spreading to France.

Cougourde: An association of liberals that arose in Aix-en-Provence and spread to other parts of France, but was short-lived. The name means 'gourd'.

Antinous: Of renowned beauty, Antinous (*c*.111–30) was the favourite of the Roman emperor Hadrian (76–138). After the youth, believed to have been his lover, died, Hadrian deified him, and his image abounded in statuary and on coins.

Evadne: The daughter of Poseidon by the nymph Pitane, Evadne was loved by the god Phoebus, by whom she bore a son, Iamos. Evadne was also the name of the wife who, for love of her husband Capaneus, threw herself on his funeral pyre.

Aristogeiton . . . Harmodius: The story of the homosexual couple Aristogeiton and Harmodius who overthrew a tyrant (they are also known as the Tyrannicides) is one of the founding myths of Athenian democracy explored in Thucydides' *History of the Peloponnesian War* (bk VI, chs 54–9).

Ezekiel's awesome cherub: As described in the Book of Ezekiel, chs 1 and 10.

Beaumarchais's gallant Cherubino: The charming young page in *The Marriage of Figaro* who is in love with the Countess Rosina.

Arago: Physicist and astronomer, Dominique-François Arago (1786–1853) was director of the Paris Observatory.

Geoffroy Saint-Hilaire: At the age of only twenty-one, the naturalist Saint-Hilaire (1772–1844) was appointed professor of zoology at the Musée National d'Histoire Naturelle, and in 1809 he became professor of zoology at the University of Paris. He wrote *Philosophie Anatomique* (1818–22).

Puységur and Deleuze: Jacques de Chastenet, Marquis de Puységur (1752–1825), was a disciple of Mesmer who conducted research into hypnotic trances, what he called 'artificial somnambulism'. The naturalist François Deleuze (1755–1835), who became librarian of the Musée National d'Histoire Naturelle, was also an advocate of the theory of animal magnetism.

Montfaucon's lake: Montfaucon was for centuries the site of a gallows where executed criminals were left to hang until their bodies decomposed. It was also an area of gypsum and lime quarries, which, when exhausted, were used for dumping rubbish, including waste from the nearby slaughterhouses, and thousands of square yards were filled with stinking lakes of human excrement that eventually produced fertilizer.

André Chénier: The poet Chénier (1762–94), who initially welcomed the Revolution, was an outspoken critic of its excesses – in 1793 he wrote an 'Ode to Marie-Anne-Charlotte Corday', Marat's assassin. Arrested in March 1794, and held in St-Lazare prison, he was executed on 25 July 1794 (7 Thermidor year II), only a few days before the fall of Robespierre and the end of the Terror.

Agrippa d'Aubigné: The poet Théodore Agrippa d'Aubigné (1552–1630) was also a man of action, who fought with the Protestant army in the Wars of Religion. In 1620 his religious position eventually obliged him to leave France and take refuge in Geneva. Françoise d'Aubigné (1635–1719), the future Madame de Maintenon, mistress and then wife of Louis XIV, was his granddaughter.

Chauvelin . . . Caumartin: An aristocrat who embraced the Revolution, Bernard-François, Marquis de Chauvelin (1766–1832), was elected under the Restoration as a deputy who voted with the extreme left. Imprisoned for several months during the Terror, Jacques Caumartin (1769–1825) served as a liberal deputy 1817–23.

young Lallemand's funeral: In June 1820 parliamentary debate on proposed electoral changes intended to increase conservative representation by means of the 'double vote' (only the most highly taxed would be eligible to vote for a second college of deputies at the *département* level) led to disturbances in Paris in which the medical student Nicolas Lallemand (1787–1820) was killed by a royal guard, further heightening tensions and fuelling protests.

Marquis d'Avaray: When Louis XVI's brother escaped into exile in June 1791, he was escorted by François de Bésiade, Comte d'Avaray (1759–1811), whom he elevated to a dukedom in 1799 on his authority as the future Louis XVIII. Bésiade died without heirs before the restoration of the monarchy, but the title was confirmed in 1817 by Louis XVIII and reverted to his father, the Marquis d'Avaray.

L'Aigle . . . Lesgle . . . Lesgueules: After Napoleon was proclaimed emperor in 1804 he chose the eagle (*l'aigle*), with its associations with Rome and Charlemagne, as the emblem for the imperial coat of arms. He was himself referred to as *l'Aigle*, and his son was known as *l'Aiglon*, 'the young eagle'. *L'aigle* and Lesgle are pronounced exactly the same. An animal's mouth is a *gueule*, and the word is used in various hunting expressions, so the term *les gueules* refers to the hunting dogs.

Loizerolles: The lawyer Jean-Simon Aved de Loizerolles (1733–94), imprisoned during the Terror with his son the poet François-Simon (1771–1845), presented himself when his son was called to face execution, and it was he who went to the guillotine on 26 July 1794, the day before the fall of Robespierre. (It was later established that it was the father, not the son – he had been misidentified because of a copyist's error – who had been accused of taking part in the Conspiracy of the Prisons, and therefore condemned to be executed.)

the younger Robespierre: When the Convention turned against Robespierre and he was arrested on 9 Thermidor year II (27 July 1794), Augustin Robespierre (1763–94) insisted on joining him, and the two brothers were executed the following day.

Pollux, Patroclus, Nisus, Eudamidas, Hephaestion, Pechméja: Castor and Pollux are the heavenly twins of Greek and Roman mythology. An important theme in Homer's *Iliad* is the friendship between Achilles and Patroclus, who is killed in battle by Hector (bk XVI). In the *Aeneid* (bk IX, lines 176–446) Virgil tells of the dangerous mission that the Trojan warriors Nisus and Euryalus embark on to find Aeneas, and how, rather than make good his escape alone, Nisus chooses to die with his friend Euryalus at the hands of their enemies (a theme revisited by Byron). The story of Eudamidas, told by Lucian of Samosata (second century AD), cited by Montaigne in his essay *On Friendship* and depicted in a painting by Poussin that was much admired in the eighteenth century, is that of a man who, being poor, bequeaths in his will to his two friends Aretheus and Charixenus the legacy of taking care of his elderly mother and unmarried daughter. When Alexander the Great's closest friend and companion from childhood Hephaestion died of a fever, classical sources tell us, Alexander was inconsolable. Jean de Pechméja (1741–85), author of *Télephe*, a classically inspired Utopian novel published in 1784, was a childhood friend of Léon Dubreuil (1743–85), doctor to the Marquis de Noailles's household, who fell ill with a contagious disease and asked that only Pechméja should tend him. They died within a few weeks of each other, their mutual devotion hailed by contemporaries as a model of friendship.

Orestes and Pylades: Another classical couple whose friendship, as represented in Aeschylus' *Oresteia* and in plays by Euripides, has become proverbial.

the foundling hospital: Jean-Jacques Rousseau (1712–78), author of *The Social Contract* (1762), which laid the foundations of revolutionary ideology, related

in his *Confessions* (bks VII and VIII) that he had fathered five children by his
mistress Thérèse Levasseur (1721–1801) and consigned all of them to the
foundling hospital: 'Mon troisième enfant fut donc mis aux Enfants-Trouvés,
ainsi que les premiers, et il en fut de même des deux suivants, car j'en ai eu cinq
en tout' ('So my third child was put in the Foundling Hospital, as well as the
first ones, and it was the same with the next two, for I had five in all').

Argand lamp: An oil lamp patented in 1780 by the Swiss physicist and chemist
François-Pierre Aimé Argand (1750–1803), which provided a brighter and
cheaper source of light than candles. They are called *quinquets* in France,
where the pharmacist Antoine Quinquet (1745–1803) in 1783 developed and
commercialized a slightly improved version.

the Heidelberg tun: Built at Heidelberg Castle in 1751 to contain wine paid in
taxes to the Elector Palatine by local wine growers, it has a capacity of over
58,000 gallons. Mark Twain in *A Tramp Abroad* (Appendix B) wrote: 'the
great Heidelberg Tun . . . is a wine-cask as big as a cottage, and some traditions
say it holds eighteen hundred thousand bottles, and other traditions say it
holds eighteen hundred million barrels. I think it likely that one of these statements is a mistake, and the other is a lie. However, the mere matter of capacity
is a thing of no sort of consequence, since the cask is empty, and indeed has
always been empty, history says. An empty cask the size of a cathedral could
excite but little emotion in me. I do not see any wisdom in building a monster
cask to hoard up emptiness in, when you can get a better quality, outside, any
day, free of expense.'

Zero: Could this be a textual error – perhaps an allusion to the Greek philosopher Zeno and his paradoxes?

a woodlouse is a pterygibranchia: The French zoologist Pierre-André Latreille
(1762–1833) was a leading entomologist who made important contributions
to the classification of insects, including that of the woodlouse, a crustacean in
the order of isopoda. Pterygibranchia is a now defunct term for a particular
subclass of isopod crustaceans, and is not to be confused with Pterobranchia,
a class, established in 1877, of worm-like creatures that live on the ocean floor.

Consul Incitatus: According to Suetonius (*Lives of the Twelve Caesars*, 'Caligula',
ch. 55), the Roman emperor Caligula (12–41) intended to make his favourite
horse Incitatus a consul.

Gros: Antoine-Jean Gros (1771–1835) made his reputation with paintings celebrating the achievements of Napoleon. He became professor at the École des
Beaux-Arts in 1816.

Diogenes' cloak: The fourth-century-BC Greek philosopher Diogenes the Cynic
scorned the trappings of the comfortable life and embraced an existence of
ascetic simplicity, housing himself in a tub, with a cloak for sole warmth and
bedding.

Strongylion: An allusion to a reference in Pliny, *Natural History*, bk XXXIV.

the battle of Pydna: A decisive Roman victory over the Macedonians, fought in
168 BC.

Clovis's Tolbiac: When the battle of Tolbiac (496) appeared to be going against
Clovis, king of the Franks, he invoked the God of the Christians and then
triumphed over his German foes, for which deliverance, legend has it, he converted to Christianity.

Phocion, another Coligny: The murder of the Huguenot leader Admiral Gaspard
de Coligny (1515–72), a man of integrity and valour, marked the beginning of
the St Bartholomew's Day massacre of Protestants by Catholics in August

1572, and the subsequent exodus of Huguenots from France. The Athenian general Phocion the Good (c.402–318 BC), described by Plutarch as a good man devoted to the state, was falsely accused of treason, executed, and denied the rites of burial.

Anacephorus: Possibly the ancient Greek historian Ephorus (c.400–330 BC), who wrote a universal history.

Pisistratus: Tyrant of Athens 546–527/8 BC.

Philetas: The Greek poet and literary scholar (340–285 BC) of whose work only fragments survive. The story that he put lead weights in his shoes so as not to be blown away by the wind is in the *Various History* of the second–third-century Roman author Aelian.

Silanion . . . Pliny: A reference to the same paragraph in Pliny's *Natural History,* bk XXXIV, in which the sculptor Strongylion is mentioned.

Brother Jonathan: A term by which the citizen of the pre-Civil War American union was known to himself and to others, as for instance in the title of a book by James Kirke Paulding published in London, 1814: *A brief and humorous history of the political peculiarities of England and America, characterised in John Bull and Brother Jonathan.*

Time is money: A concept with ancient roots, it was first phrased in this way by Benjamin Franklin in 'Advice to a Young Tradesman' (1748).

Cotton is king: An anachronistic reference in 1832, this was the title of a book by David Christy exposing the economics of slavery (1855). The southern American states mistakenly believed that their supply of cotton guaranteed European support in the event of war. In the words of James Henry Hammon of South Carolina, in 1858: 'No, you dare not to make war on cotton. No power on earth dares to make war upon it. Cotton is king.'

Voltaire admired it: Voltaire admired the extraordinary development of Russia over a short period under Peter the Great, of whom he wrote a celebratory biography (1759–63). He also expressed admiration for the achievements of China in *Essai sur les moeurs et l'esprit des nations* (Essay on the Manners and Spirit of Nations), his monumental universal history (1756).

An Alexis beheaded . . . a Paul strangled: Alexis (1690–1718), the eldest son of Peter the Great, was tried as a traitor, tortured, then died in prison, believed to have been beheaded. Paul I (1754–1801), eldest son and heir of Catherine the Great, was assassinated by members of his own court. He is said to have been struck with a sword, or a gold snuff-box, strangled and trampled.

Isabella's dirty shift: The stuff of folklore: Isabella of Castile, it is said, vowed not to change her shift until Granada was taken (the siege lasted from 1491 to 1492); alternatively, Isabella of Austria made the same vow in relation to the siege of Ostend (1601–3). There are written sources from the eighteenth century giving these stories as derivations for the word 'isabella' or 'isabelline', a pale-yellowish colour, applied particularly to the coats of horses.

carpets . . . naked Cleopatra: Plutarch in his *Life of Caesar* relates the story that after being expelled from Egypt Cleopatra gained access to Caesar by having herself rolled up in a 'bedsack' – *stromatodesmon*, often represented as a carpet.

Hippocrates . . . Artaxerxes' trifles: According to biographical tradition, the Greek physician Hippocrates (c.460–c.370 BC) declined untold wealth and honours offered to him by Artaxerxes, king of Persia and enemy of Greece, to come and treat his subjects.

Vaud . . . Gex: The French occupied Vaud in south-west Switzerland in 1798. Contiguous with Vaud is the French district of Gex, the town of Gex lying some five miles west of the southern end of Lake Geneva. After the defeat of Napoleon, the Congress of Vienna debated making Gex part of the Swiss Confederation. Under the final Treaty of Paris, France had to cede the six communes of the Gex region that linked Geneva with Vaud, but retained Gex.

Vignemale ... Cybele: The Vignemale is the highest of the French Pyrenean peaks. Cybele was worshipped by the Phrygians in Asia Minor as a mother goddess, *matar kubileya* ('mother of the mountain'), from which the Greek name Cybele is thought to derive. The cult spread from Phrygia to Rome, and she came to be frequently depicted on Roman coins wearing a turreted city-wall head-dress.

Io ... Pissevache: Io was a priestess seduced by Jupiter, who turned her into a white heifer, hoping to hide and protect her from his jealous wife. The story is told in Ovid's *Metamorphoses* (bk I, lines 567–746). Pissevache, meaning 'pissing cow', hence the connection with Io, is a waterfall in the Swiss Alps. Because waters have been diverted for hydroelectric purposes, it is not quite as dramatic as it used to be when celebrated by Romantic writers, including Goethe.

The 1814 Charter: The charter granted (*octroyée*) by Louis XVIII to his people in 1814 was the legal foundation on which the Restoration and the constitutional monarchy were based. In the 1830 Charter, introduced after the July Revolution, the monarchy was no longer invested with this power to grant, the rights of the people being constitutionally founded.

Desmarets: Nephew of Louis XIV's great finance minister Colbert, Nicolas Desmarets, Marquis de Maillebois (1648–1721), himself became controller-general of finances in 1708. Hugo is basing these calculations on figures given by Voltaire in *The Age of Louis XIV* (1751), ch. 30.

Tilsit: Napoleon's victory at the battle of Friedland in 1807, enshrined in the two Treaties of Tilsit, one made with Russia, whereby the two nations became allies, and a second securing the humiliation of Prussia, marked the apogee of his power.

Laplace: The mathematician and astronomer Pierre-Simon, Marquis de Laplace (1749–1827), was elected to the Academy of Sciences in 1773. Napoleon was himself mathematically gifted. Laplace is supposed to have said to him, 'General, we expected anything of you but lessons in geometry', after Napoleon demonstrated a geometrical theorem.

Merlin: The politician and jurist Philippe-Antoine Merlin de Douai (1754–1838), who served under the Directory as minister of justice and then as one of the Directors (1797–9), was appointed councillor of state in 1806.

Like Cromwell: Cromwell is said to have chided his wife for sewing by the light of two candles instead of one.

If Caesar ... I love my mother more: 'Si César m'avait donné / La gloire et la guerre, / Et qu'il me fallût quitter / L'amour de ma mère, / Je dirais au grand César: / Reprends ton sceptre et ton char, / J'aime mieux ma mère, ô gué! / J'aime mieux ma mère.' This is a recognizable recasting of the song Alceste sings in Molière's *Le Misanthrope* (Act I, sc. ii): 'Si le roi m'avait donné / Paris sa grand' ville / Et qu'il me fallût quitter / L'amour de ma mie / Je dirais au roi Henri / Reprenez votre Paris / J'aime mieux ma mie, ô gué! / J'aime mieux ma mie' ('If the king had offered me / Paris his great capital / But it meant forsaking / My sweetheart's love / I'd tell king Henri / To keep his Paris / I love my sweetheart more, tra-la, / I love my sweetheart more').

Septembrist: One who took part in the September massacres of 1792; the mob violence that broke out in a climate of fear of foreign invasion resulted in the killing of half the prison population of Paris, incarcerated royalists – men, women and children – and clergymen. The ferocious attack on the Princesse de Lamballe, friend of Marie-Antoinette and sister-in-law of the Duc d'Orléans, was particularly notorious.

He removed my cataracts: In 1752 the surgeon Jacques Daviel (1696–1762) published through the Royal Academy of Surgery in Paris *A New Method of Curing Cataract by Extracting the Crystalline Lens*, describing the revolutionary procedure he had followed a few years previously and laying the foundations of the method used today.

an Elzevir edition: Louis Elzevir (1540–1617) was the first of several generations of Dutch printers and booksellers operating between 1583 and 1712 who established themselves as among the foremost publishers in Europe.

the July Revolution: Charles X succeeded his brother Louis XVIII in 1824, and became increasingly unpopular as a result of his attempts to circumvent constitutional limitations on the monarchy that culminated in the introduction, on the basis of Article 14, of the July Ordinances, suppressing the freedom of the press, dissolving the Chamber of Deputies, restricting the franchise and holding new elections (only months after elections had returned an increased liberal majority). This led to a popular uprising known as Les Trois Glorieuses ('the three glorious days') at the end of July 1830. Charles X fled Paris, and in his absence a political consensus was reached whereby the Duc d'Orléans, Louis-Philippe, of a cadet branch of the Bourbon family, was invited to become king.

Austerlitz: A tiny hamlet east of Paris and close to La Salpêtrière, incorporated into the city in 1818.

Comte Pajol: A cavalry officer, Claude-Pierre Pajol (1772–1844) was several times badly wounded in the course of his distinguished and much decorated military career. He also played a decisive role in the July Revolution, and under Louis-Philippe was elevated to the peerage and awarded the Legion of Honour Grand Cross.

Bellavesne . . . Fririon: General Jacques-Nicolas Bellavesne (1770–1826), who lost a leg in an engagement with the Austrians in 1796 and subsequently ran the military academies at Fontainebleau and St-Cyr, and General François-Nicolas Fririon (1766–1840) were friends of Hugo's mother. They were involved in hiding from the police (unsuccessfully, in the end) her lover General Lahorie after he was found guilty of conspiracy against Napoleon (*Victor Hugo raconté par un témoin de sa vie* – the biography, published in 1863, written by Hugo's wife Adèle, ch. 6).

Carnot . . . Fouché: In 1815 the treacherous and self-serving Fouché yet again betrayed his colleagues – in particular, Carnot, the man of integrity – by colluding with the restoration of Louis XVIII. This resulted in Carnot being exiled and Fouché becoming the new minister of police. This exchange is recorded in Fouché's own posthumously published memoirs (1824; authorship is somewhat contested).

Hernani: Hugo's play of 1830, which created a literary revolution – and gave rise to a celebrated 'battle' between rival literary factions on the opening night – by presenting a direct challenge to the old cultural establishment. In the name of the new Romantic sensibility it broke with classical theatrical traditions such as the unities of time, place and action, embracing less formal language and characteristic antitheses – the beautiful and the grotesque, the noble-hearted bandit, the pure love of a fallen woman.

the Apollo Belvedere: This celebrated marble statue, dating from classical antiquity, was brought to Paris by Napoleon from Donato Bramante's Belvedere courtyard in the Vatican; it was placed in the Louvre collection, but was among the artworks later returned to Italy and is now back in the Vatican.

the Venus de' Medici: Shipped to Paris in 1803, the *Venus de' Medici* (from the Villa Medici in Rome) was also returned to Italy after the fall of Napoleon. It is now in the Uffizi in Florence.

Tiercelin: A celebrated comic actor of the period, Tiercelin (1763–1837) excelled in playing drunkards.

Sieyès: Emmanuel-Joseph Sieyès (1748–1836) was a member of the Convention and of the Council of Five Hundred, member and president of the Directory and a consul; under the Empire he was a senator, then president of the Senate, and in 1809 was made a count. He lived in exile during the Restoration, returning to France in 1830.

the antics . . . Tivoli Gardens: Paul de Kock (1793–1871) wrote in his *Memoirs* (published by his son in 1873), ch. 4: 'Il y avait aussi un grimacier. Les grimaciers étaient à la mode alors . . . ne le sont-ils pas toujours? Celui de Tivoli était un grimacier plaisant; il portait une perruque blanche et jouait de la trompette et du violon' ('There was also a man who pulled faces. Face-pullers were in vogue then – are they not always? The Tivoli face-puller was an amusing fellow. He wore a white wig and played the trumpet and violin').

like the monkeys at the tiger's court: Hugo's poem reads: 'Un jour, maigre et sentant un royal appétit, / Un singe d'une peau de tigre se vêtit / . . . Chacun, voyant la peau, croyait au personnage. / Il s'écriait, poussant d'affreux rugissements: / Regardez, ma caverne est pleine d'ossements; / Devant moi tout recule et frémit, tout émigre, / Tout tremble; admirez-moi, voyez, je suis un tigre! / Les bêtes l'admiraient, et fuyaient à grands pas. / Un belluaire vint, le saisit dans ses bras, / Déchira cette peau comme on déchire un linge, / Mit à nu ce vainqueur, et dit: Tu n'es qu'un singe!' ('One day, thin and feeling a royal appetite, / A monkey dressed up in a tiger's skin / . . . Everyone seeing the skin gave credence to the image. / He cried out with terrible roars, / Look, my cave is full of bones, / Everything retreats before me and quakes, everything emigrates, / Everything trembles. Admire me, look, I'm a tiger. / The animals admired him and fled. / A lion-tamer came, grabbed it in his arms, / Tore this skin asunder, as one might tear a sheet, / Stripped this conqueror naked, and said: You're just a monkey!').

the Sicambri: One of the barbarian Germanic tribes the Romans contend with in Caesar's *Gallic Wars* (bks iv and vi).

Jean Goujon: A sculptor who excelled in bas-relief, Jean Goujon (*c.*1510–*c.*1565) is especially noted for his panels on the Fontaine des Nymphes, also known as the Fontaine des Innocents, which were moved to the Louvre in 1824.

The Baccalauréat Manual: The *baccalauréat* was introduced into France under Napoleon in 1808; it was then a university qualification, obtained by oral examination. Written exams were introduced in 1830.

'right in the line of cannon-fire': 'Sous le canon de la place': An allusion to a phrase used in a description of the battle of Carillon (1758) during the Seven Years War (1754–63), published in the widely read *Histoire Philosophique et politique des établissements et du commerce des Européens dans les deux Indes* (1770; published anonymously but known to have been compiled by Abbé Raynal), bk XVI, ch. 21. The English suffered a humiliating defeat in their attack on Fort Carillon, which gained the reputation of being impregnable.

author of the dissertation . . . Obregón . . . passing it off as his own: A reference to an incident in Hugo's own life: in 1817, at the age of fifteen, Hugo did some literary research for the Academician François de Neufchâteau, who was working on an edition of Lesage's novel *Gil Blas*. Neufchâteau included in his preface what the young man had written, with no acknowledgement (see Graham Robb, *Victor Hugo*, 1997, pp. 64–7). Marcos de Obregón is the eponymous hero of a picaresque novel (1618) by the Spanish writer Vicente Martínez de Espinel (1550–1624), born in Ronda, Malaga. Hugo has also conflated the name of Espinel's hero with that of Cherubin de la Ronda, hero of Alain Lesage's *Le Bachelier de Salamanque* (The Bachelor of Salamanca; 1736), a novel greatly inspired by Espinel's work.

Audry de Puyraveau: A left-wing deputy under the Restoration, and a member of the committee that put Louis-Philippe on the throne, Pierre Audry de Puyraveau (1773–1852) was a key player in the July Revolution, which left him with considerable debts (he ran a haulage business which was unable to operate during the disturbances), and very much alive to the impact of taxation on the poor.

Frédérick . . . L'Auberge des Adrets: Frédérick Lemaître (1800–76) was a famous actor who made his name in the role of Robert Macaire in Benjamin Antier's *L'Auberge des Adrets*, first staged in 1823. He is also a character in Marcel Carné's film *Les Enfants du Paradis*, inspired by Antier's play.

Quicherat's dictionaries: The Latin scholar Louis Quicherat (1799–1884) was the author of a number of dictionaries and works on prosody and versification. He became a member of the Legion of Honour in 1844.

the Gladiator: A copy of a classical statue, made in 1765 by the French artist Laurent Guiard (1723–88).

Prairial breeze: Prairial in the Revolutionary calendar extends from 20/21 May to 19/20 June.

Theocritus: A pastoral poet of the third century BC.

Bartolo: A character who first appears in Beaumarchais's *The Barber of Seville* as Rosina's guardian. His plots to marry her off are thwarted by Figaro, and he reappears, seeking revenge, in *The Marriage of Figaro*. Figaro turns out to be his son. In a double wedding Bartolo marries Figaro's mother Marcellina when Figaro marries Susanna.

ordinary soldier's St Louis cross: Louis XV in 1771 created a veterans' medal, usually called the *Médaillon de Vétérance*, awarded for twenty-four years' service. It was an oval medallion with two crossed swords and a red ribbon; after the Revolution it was issued with a tricolour ribbon. The military Order of St Louis, awarded to officers, was created in 1693 by Louis XIV.

'the third level down': Honoré de Balzac, in *Splendeurs et Misères des Courtisanes*, pt 4, in the chapter entitled 'Essai philosophique, linguistique et littéraire sur l'argot, les filles et les voleurs' (Philosophical, Linguistic and Literary Essay on Slang, Prostitutes and Thieves), writes: 'Le Troisième-Dessous est la dernière cave pratiquée sous les planches de l'Opéra, pour en receler les machines, les machinistes, la rampe, les apparitions, les diables bleus que vomit l'enfer . . .' ('The third level down is the deepest cellar under the Opéra for concealing the stage effects, the stage hands, the footlights, the apparitions, the blue devils that hell vomits forth . . .'). Proust has this term in mind when he makes a joke about social standing in *À la Recherche du temps perdu*, vol. 5, *La Prisonnière*: 'Les Montesquiou descendent d'une ancienne famille, qu'est-ce que ça prouverait, même si c'était prouvé? Ils descendent tellement qu'ils sont dans le

quatorzième dessous' ('The Montesquious descend from an ancient family, and what would that prove, even if it were proved? They descend so far they're at the fourteenth level down').

Socinus: Laelius Socinus (1525–62), born Lelio Sozzini in Siena, was generally supported by Calvin; but Calvin did challenge his anti-trinitarian views, and Socinus fell back into line.

Jan Hus: Born in Bohemia, Jan Hus (*c.*1371–1415) was a priest and professor of theology whose challenge to the authority of the Church, and in particular to the authority of the pope, led to his being found guilty of heresy and burned at the stake.

Babeuf: A political journalist of the Revolutionary period, François 'Gracchus' Babeuf (1760–97), an advocate of a form of communism, was involved in a conspiracy to overthrow the Directory by an armed uprising of the masses. The so-called 'conspiracy for equality' was exposed and Babeuf was executed. Other conspirators were sentenced to deportation.

Owen: The cotton-mill manager and owner Robert Owen (1771–1858) was a pioneering social reformer in England, and a source of inspiration to the Co-operative Movement.

Ugolino: Count Ugolino appears in Dante's *Inferno*, cantos 32–3, in the ninth circle of hell, gnawing at the neck of his co-conspirator Archbishop Ruggieri. Imprisoned for treachery along with his children, he is supposed to have eaten his children after they had starved to death (canto 33, line 75, 'Poscia, più che il dolor, potè il digiuno', 'Then fasting had more power than grief', in J. A. Carlyle's translation of 1867).

Schinderhannes: Johannes Bückler (1778–1803) was a German highwayman-robber known as Schinderhannes, who was eventually caught and tried in Mainz, found guilty and executed along with nineteen other members of his band.

Arche-Marion sewer: One of the main sewer outlets into the Seine.

Farnese Hercules: A massive classical statue of a muscular Hercules, which was recovered from the Caracalla Baths in 1546 and became part of Cardinal Farnese's collection in Rome. Many sketches, engravings and replicas of it were made by artists from all over Europe. The copy in the gardens of Versailles, dating from 1684–8, is by Jean Cornu (1650–1710).

Marshal Brune: After the return of Louis XVIII in 1815 a white terror was unleashed, and Marshal Guillaume Brune (1763–1815), who rallied to Napoleon during the Hundred Days, was one of its victims. Isolated in Avignon from any military support, he was murdered in his hotel room by a porter named Guidon and a silkworker named Farge, who attempted to exculpate themselves by saying he had committed suicide. However, Brune's widow was determined to obtain justice, and eventually in 1821 they were tried *in absentia* and found guilty of the murder.

Bobino: The professional name of a popular entertainer – comedian, acrobat, clown – turned theatrical entrepreneur, who opened a small variety theatre near the Luxembourg Gardens called the Théâtre Bobino, or Théâtre du Luxembourg, demolished in 1868.

Le Messager: Founded in 1828 by the centre-right Vicomte de Martignac (1778–1832), who was briefly prime minister under Charles X, this daily newspaper changed proprietor several times until it ceased publication in 1846.

Coco-Lacour: Barthélemy Coco-Latour was a convicted thief whom Vidocq, as he recalls in his *Memoirs*, recruited into the police service and who was to succeed Vidocq after he retired.

La Chaumière . . . public dance at Sceaux: La Chaumière on the Boulevard Montparnasse was a pleasure garden, with dancing on Sundays, Mondays and Thursdays, favoured by students. It opened in 1787 and closed in 1853. First published in 1830, *Le Bal de Sceaux* is the title of *Scenes from Private Life*, bk 2, vol. 1, in Honoré de Balzac's *La Comédie humaine* (*The Human Comedy*); he gives a vivid description of the scene at this weekend public dance in the country on the outskirts of Paris.

Mathieu Laensberg: The name (with various spellings) under which was published in Liège an almanac popular in the eighteenth and nineteenth centuries. There is a reference to one lying on the mantelpiece in the wet-nurse's cottage in *Madame Bovary*, pt II, ch. 2, for instance.

ghouls: The word *goule* first appeared in the French translation (published 1704–17) of *The Arabian Nights* by Antoine Galland (1646–1715), its first European translator. 'Ghoul' first appeared in English in 1786 in William Beckford's novel *Vatek*, referring to the creature of Arabian folklore.

if you don't like it . . . you curs: Quoted in French ('Crevez chiens, si vous n'êtes pas contents') in Dostoevsky's *Crime and Punishment* (1866), pt III, ch. 3.

MARINGO . . . ELOT: Phoneticized spellings of Marengo, Austerlitz, Jena, Wagram and Eylau, to reflect French pronunciation.

Lavater: Johann Caspar Lavater (1741–1801), the Swiss author of *Physiognomische Fragmente* (1775–8; translated into English as *Essays on Physiognomy*), much admired in its day, particularly for its fine illustrations. It promoted the pseudoscientific theory that moral character is disclosed in the cast of an individual's facial features.

GOD . . . DUCRAY-DUMINIL: François-Guillaume Ducray-Duminil (1761–1819), author of popular novels in which virtue always triumphs. His novel *Dieu, le Roi et la Patrie* (God, King and Country) was published in 1814. A novel entitled *Dieu, l'Honneur et les Dames* (God, Honour and the Ladies) by Jean Edme Paccard (1777–1844) had been published in 1813.

Rothschild: The Rothschild family first came to prominence in Frankfurt, where they built up their money-lending and investment business in the latter half of the eighteenth century. In 1798 the family established a branch in England, and in 1812 opened a banking house in Paris run by James (originally Jacob) Rothschild (1792–1868). The financial stability of the July Monarchy relied on loans provided by the Rothschild bank.

Mademoiselle Mars: See note p. 1317 on *Mademoiselle Mars*. Mars was associated with two roles in particular, both in plays by Molière: Célimène the young coquette in *Le Misanthrope*, and Elmire the virtuous wife in *Tartuffe*. She had a house on the corner of Rue de la Tour-des-Dames, which she bought in 1824.

give alms to Belisarius: Belisarius (c.505–65) was commander of the Byzantine army under the emperor Justinian, but his success and popularity made him suspect, and he was eventually accused of involvement in a plot against Justinian which led to his disgrace. Legend has it that the emperor ordered his eyes to be put out and that he was reduced to living as a beggar. The theme of the noble commander rejected by an ungrateful sovereign had great resonance in eighteenth-century France and was a popular subject with painters. David's *Belisarius Begging for Alms* (1781) is a notable example.

La Palisse: Jacques de Chabannes (1470–1525), Seigneur de la Palice (or La Palisse), died heroically on the battlefield at Pavia during the Italian War of 1521–6. His death was to give rise to numerous versions of a comic song, characterized by the kind of ridiculous tautologous truths that came to be referred to in French as *palissades*, such as the following: 'Hélas! La Palice est mort. / Il est mort devant Pavie. / Hélas! S'il n'était pas mort / Il serait encore en vie' ('Alas! La Palice is dead. / He died outside Pavia. / Alas! If he hadn't died / He would still be alive').

La Force: Opened in 1782 under Louis XVI, La Force prison is where many of the victims of the Terror were incarcerated, including the Princesse de Lamballe. (It is also the place where Charles Darnay is confined in Dickens's *Tale of Two Cities*.) One of the courtyards, the Cour St-Bernard, was supposed to be where the most dangerous inmates gathered and was nicknamed the Lions' Den.

A whole week of love ... for ever: A song, set to an English tune arranged by Alexandre Doche (1799–1849), from Act II sc. i of the vaudeville comedy *Le Hussard de Felsheim* – based on the novel *Les Barons de Felsheim* (1798) by Pigault-Lebrun (1753–1835) – first performed in 1827. 'Nos amours ont duré toute une semaine, / mais que du bonheur les instants sont courts! / S'adorer huit jours, c'était bien la peine! / Le temps des amours devrait durer toujours! / Devrait durer toujours! Devrait durer toujours!' The next verse is 'Ah! que son regard était doux et tendre! / Sans qu'il dit un mot, je savais l'entendre! / Mais lorsque ces murs sont entre nous deux / Comment à présent nous parler des yeux?' ('Oh, so sweet and tender was his gaze! / Though he spoke not a word, I understood him! / But with these walls between us / How are our eyes to speak?').

You're leaving me ... follows: In his *Impressions de Voyage: En Suisse* (Travel Impressions in Switzerland; 1834), Alexandre Dumas (1802–70) gives an account in the chapter entitled 'Une ex-reine' ('A Former Queen') of his meeting with the Duchesse de St-Leu, daughter of Napoleon's first wife Josephine, in which she explains that she composed the music for this song with words written by the Comte de Ségur (1753–1830) at the request of her mother, before Napoleon left for Wagram amid rumours of the imminent divorce: 'Vous me quittez pour aller à la gloire, / Mon triste coeur suivra partout vos pas.'

coronation of Charles X: The coronation, which took place at Reims cathedral on 29 May 1825, was intended to underline the monarchy's historical credentials, and was criticized for being a very theatrical affair. Hugo was invited to mark the event in celebratory verse – see his 'Ode sur le Sacre de Charles X' (Ode on the Coronation of Charles X). It was at this time that a Legion of Honour knighthood was conferred on him.

the Bourbe: The Hospice de la Maternité on Rue de la Bourbe, originally the Port-Royal Abbey that was suppressed in 1790, served briefly as a prison (the Prison de la Bourbe), and was transformed in 1796 into a maternity and foundling hospital.

New Year gifts: Until the end of the nineteenth century it was the custom to exchange gifts not at Christmas but at New Year.

like the Rhône: In the nineteenth century the disappearance of the Rhône, which used to occur near Vanchy where the waters were funnelled underground by the erosion of the riverbed, was an awesome tourist spectacle. The location of this geological phenomenon is now the site of a reservoir behind the first dam to be built across the river, at Génissiat in 1948.

Sakoski: 'The celebrated artist in leather – for the term shoemaker is too ignoble for Sakoski – thus the German poet Heinrich Heine eulogized the master bootmaker when he died aged eighty-eight in 1840. Sakoski had an address in the Palais-Royal, parts of which were developed as a shopping and entertainment complex under Louis-Philippe.

Engineer Chevallier: Member of a renowned family of optical instrument manufacturers established from 1765 on Quai de l'Horloge, Jean-Gabriel Chevallier (1778-1848), optician to Louis-Philippe and known as Ingénieur Chevallier, opened his establishment on the corner of the Pont-Neuf in the late 1830s. The thermometer and a crowd gathered in front of it are depicted in a lithograph by Honoré Daumier (1808-79), published in *Le Charivari* in 1845 (see the Benjamin A. and Julia M. Trustman Collection of Honoré Daumier Lithographs at Brandeis University).

the Benvenuto Cellinis: In his autobiography (first published in the eighteenth century) the Florentine goldsmith and sculptor Benvenuto Cellini (1500-71), who was at one time employed in the papal mint at Rome creating the dies for coins and medals, tells not only of how he acquired and practised his craftsman's skills but also of his brawling, duelling and fighting in battle (killing several men), and of being imprisoned for his crimes.

Villons of the language: The poet, robber and murderer François Villon (1431-63) suffered imprisonment, torture and banishment for his crimes, and was sentenced to be hanged before this was commuted to ten years' banishment. He left a small but highly influential body of work including his masterpiece *Le Testament*, in which he expresses regret for his misspent youth and meditates on the brevity of life and the inevitability of death in language that is lively, lyrical and colloquial.

the wet finger: Those drawing lots have to choose which finger is the one that has been wetted underneath, as described in Dumas's *Ascanio* (inspired by Benvenuto Cellini's autobiography), ch. 10.

Frederick II . . . Potsdam parade: The great military commander of his age, Frederick the Great (1712-86) of Prussia built up Potsdam as a military garrison town and royal seat where he built two palaces, the grand New Palace (1763-9) and the more intimate Sans Souci retreat (1745-7).

St-Lazare: Originally a leper hospital (hence the name) built in the eleventh century, then from 1632 the mother house of St Vincent de Paul's Congregation of the Mission. It was sacked for its grain stores on the eve of the storming of the Bastille, confiscated by the state in 1792, and in 1794 became a prison where those to be tried by the Revolutionary Tribunal were held. From the end of that year until 1932 it served as a women's prison.

Les Madelonnettes: A convent whose mission was to reform fallen women, Les Madelonnettes was suppressed in 1790 and became a prison in 1793. By 1795 it was operating as an annexe to St-Lazare, taking in women prisoners only.

PART FOUR: THE RUE PLUMET IDYLL AND THE RUE ST-DENIS EPIC

'resistance' and 'movement': The terms used to refer to the two main political tendencies, the Resistance being the more conservative and right-wing, the Movement the more liberal. Louis-Philippe first entrusted his government to the banker Jacques Laffitte, leader of the Movement, but replaced him in February 1831 with Casimir Périer, leader of the Resistance. Périer died in the outbreak of cholera that swept through Paris in 1832.

Prusias: Prusias, of Bithynia in Asia Minor where Hannibal had sought asylum, was the treacherous king who, after Hannibal had served him well militarily, was prepared to betray the Carthaginian commander to his Roman enemies. Hannibal committed suicide rather than fall into their hands.

the king of Yvetot: Yvetot was a tiny kingdom in feudal Normandy whose existence would have been long forgotten but for the hugely popular and successful songwriter Pierre-Jean de Béranger (1780–1857), who in 1813 wrote a song entitled 'The King of Yvetot', which told the tale of a king who liked to tipple and otherwise lived a simple and harmless life, much beloved of his people. 'What a good little king was he!' is the refrain. Some of Béranger's later songs were bitingly satirical and politically subversive, glorifying the Napoleonic past and ridiculing the monarchy.

the Stuarts after the Protector: An allusion to the restoration of the monarchy in England in 1660, with the return of the Stuart king Charles II after the Protectorate of Oliver Cromwell, who died in 1658.

Louis XVII . . . Marengo: Louis XVII was never crowned king. His father Louis XVI was executed in January 1793, and he himself died at the age of ten in June 1795. The 9th Thermidor in the Revolutionary calendar was 27 July 1794, the date that marked the fall of Robespierre. Louis XVIII came to the throne in 1814 after the abdication of Napoleon, who won the battle of Marengo in 1800 when France was ruled by the Consulate.

Charles I: Charles I of England was executed in 1649. After the Restoration, in 1661, he was canonized by the Church of England, and is known as King Charles the Martyr.

a round table . . . a square one: The story of Charles X insisting on having a table refashioned because for a king of France to eat at a round table was a violation of protocol is related from hearsay by Charles Beslay (1795–1878) in his *Memoirs 1830–1848–1870* (1873). In a pamphlet published in 1830 after the July Revolution entitled *Histoire scandaleuse, politique, anecdotique et bigote de Charles X*, the king has to settle for a round table, no other being available.

Guillaume du Vair . . . day of the barricades: The rising by the Paris populace against Henri III on 12 May 1588, known as the Day of the Barricades, which forced the king to flee the city, was a demonstration of Paris's hostility towards Protestantism, of the king's political vulnerability, of the strength of the Catholic League and the ambitions of its leader, the Duc de Guise. Magistrate, cleric and moral philosopher, Guillaume du Vair (1556–1621) held the positions of president of the parliament of Aix and minister of justice, and in 1617 was made bishop of Lisieux.

Machiavelli: Italian political philosopher and author of political, historical and fictional works as well as of *The Prince*, a political treatise that justifies ruthlessness and treachery in a ruler and for which he is best known, Niccolò Machiavelli (1469–1527) devoted himself to writing after being charged with conspiracy in 1513 and forced into retirement.

Iturbide: A royalist military officer who championed Mexican independence, Augustín de Iturbide (1783–1824) was proclaimed emperor of Mexico by his army supporters in May 1822. His election was never officially recognized and in 1823 he was forced into exile. When he returned to Mexico in 1824 he was tried and executed.

House of Brunswick: Under the terms of the English Act of Settlement of 1701, designed to ensure a Protestant succession, the granddaughter of James I,

Sophia Electress of Hanover (1630–1714), who had married into the House of Brunswick, was named next in line to the throne. Sophia, however, did not outlive the childless Queen Anne (1665–1714), so it was Sophia's eldest son Georg Ludwig, Duke of Brunswick and Elector of Hanover, who succeeded as King George I of England and Scotland.

although–because: For the left, Louis-Philippe, although a Bourbon, was an acceptable replacement as head of state; and because he was a Bourbon, he was also acceptable to the right.

The two hundred and twenty-one: The liberal majority in Charles X's Chamber of Deputies, who voted to defend the Charter whose terms Charles was in the process of breaching; this led to the dissolution of the Assembly, new elections, an increased liberal majority and the July Revolution.

Lafayette: Gilbert de Motier, Marquis de Lafayette (1757–1834), made his name under George Washington fighting for the American Revolution, and successfully lobbied the French government to recognize the independence of the United States. In Revolutionary France he was a reformist in the National Constituent Assembly, but as an upholder of order he lost the support of the people and had to flee the country. Elected to the Chamber of Deputies during the Hundred Days in 1815, he presented the motion requiring Napoleon to abdicate after the defeat at Waterloo. Again as a deputy, he was a key player in the July Revolution: effectively head of the provisional government, the preferred candidate of some permanently to replace Charles X, he gave his public support at the Hôtel de Ville to Louis-Philippe, wrapping him in a tricolour flag and embracing him. In the words of Chateaubriand, 'Le baiser républicain de La Fayette fit un roi' ('Lafayette's Republican kiss created a king'; *Mémoires d'Outre-Tombe*, bk 32, ch. 15). Although Lafayette denied having said that Louis-Philippe was 'la meilleure des républiques' ('the best of republics'), he was popularly believed by his contemporaries to have done so, as recorded for instance by the anarchist sociologist Pierre-Joseph Proudhon (1809–65) in his *Du Principe Fédératif* (1863; published in English as *The Principle of Federation*), pt I, ch. 4.

a father . . . worthy of blame: Louis-Philippe's father the Duc d'Orléans, Louis-Philippe II (1747–93), embraced Revolutionary and Enlightenment ideas and was one of the nobles who joined the National Assembly in June 1789; he changed his name to Philippe Égalité and voted in favour of the execution of Louis XVI. However, he was himself arrested and executed in 1793. In his private life he was something of a libertine and had numerous mistresses.

Ancona: When in 1831 Austria intervened against revolutionists in Bologna at the invitation of the pope, to defend the authority of the papacy, France interpreted this as an act of aggression by Austria and seized Ancona, refusing to leave until the Austrians left Bologna, which did not happen until 1838.

determined . . . Spain: In the 1830s and 40s England and France, although allies, vied for influence in the Iberian peninsula. Their rivalry culminated in the Spanish Marriages Affair, in which the two powers favoured different marriage alliances for the Spanish queen and her sister, who in 1846 married the French choice of candidates.

bombarding Antwerp: The Belgian Revolution in 1830 led to the establishment of a new Belgian state, independent of the United Kingdom of the Netherlands, of which it had been made part by the Congress of Vienna in 1815. The former Dutch ruler, William I of the Netherlands (1772–1843), refused to recognize its independence and launched a military campaign to retake the provinces.

The French intervened and the Dutch withdrew, leaving a garrison in Antwerp, to which the French laid siege during 28 November–24 December 1832, firing some sixty-five thousand shells and cannon-balls.

paying off Pritchard: British consul and missionary in Tahiti, George Pritchard (1796–1883) was first imprisoned and then expelled from the island by French forces, who annexed the territory to France. France was obliged to pay an indemnity to Pritchard.

Valmy . . . Jemappes: Louis-Philippe, the Duc d'Orléans, fought at the battle of Valmy in September 1792, the first victory won by the French Revolutionary army, and at the battle of Jemappes in November 1792, before defecting.

a bit of a builder . . . gardener . . . doctor: A number of building restoration projects were carried out under Louis-Philippe, on the Louvre, the Tuileries and Versailles (1833–7), in which the king took a close on-site interest. He was also interested in his gardens, and appointed the distinguished rose-breeder Antoine Jacques (1782–1866) as his head gardener. There are accounts of Louis-Philippe seen bleeding himself after being involved in an accident with runaway horses in Carlisle, Pennsylvania, in 1797, and as a result being offered a job as a doctor by the local inhabitants (see for instance the American journalist Benjamin Perley Poore's *The rise and fall of Louis Philippe, ex-king of the French*, 1848, pp. 98–9). Other accounts give his brother the Duc de Montpensier, with whom he was travelling, as the one who bled himself.

Rue Transnonain: When rioting broke out in Paris in April 1834, shots were supposedly fired from a house in Rue Transnonain and the troops were ordered to retaliate. Twelve civilians were killed, and men, women and children injured. The event was recorded in a celebrated lithograph by Honoré Daumier, *Rue Transnonain, le 15 avril 1834*.

Belgium refused: Having freed itself from the Dutch rule of the royal House of Orange-Nassau, the newly independent state of Belgium offered the crown to the Duc de Nemours, second son of Louis-Philippe. This was unacceptable to the British, who feared French annexation of Belgium; the offer was declined and the English choice of candidate, Prince Leopold of Saxe-Coburg, who later married Louis-Philippe's daughter Louise, became Leopold I, king of the Belgians.

Algeria . . . Abd al-Qader: French troops invaded Algeria in June 1830, before the July Revolution, but the conquest and colonization of Algeria continued under Louis-Philippe. The Algerian Islamic scholar Abd al-Qader (1808–83) was an able leader of national resistance against France, but his initially successful attempts to establish a functioning Muslim state in Algeria were eventually thwarted by the French, who reneged on a treaty they had signed with him, and to whom he surrendered in 1847.

Blaye, Deutz bribed: Simon Deutz (1802–44) was the paid informer who betrayed to the authorities the Duchesse de Berry, wife of the son of Charles X. She was imprisoned in the fortress at Blaye for plotting against the July Monarchy in the name of her young son, pretender to the throne.

Marie d'Orléans: For Marie d'Orléans (1813–39), second daughter of Louis-Philippe, Joan of Arc was a favourite theme: the small body of work completed before her early death included a number of small statues of Joan, on horseback or standing, listening to her voices.

Charles d'Orléans: Author of ballads, songs of courtly love, poems of exile and hymns to nature, the medieval poet and nobleman Charles d'Orléans (1394–1465) was taken prisoner at the battle of Agincourt (1415) and held captive in

England for twenty-four years before he was finally allowed to return to France. He is believed to be the author of translations of his own French poems into English.

Metternich: The Austrian diplomat and statesman Prince Klemens Wenzel von Metternich (1773–1859), who served as Austria's ambassador to France 1806–9, throughout his long career was associated with a policy of conservatism and anti-liberalism, and of preserving peace in Europe through a balance of power. He greeted the news of the July Revolution with dismay.

Prince Equality: During the Revolution Philippe Égalité's son was known as Citoyen ('Citizen') Orléans, or Égalité *fils* ('son'). When in 1797 Louis-Philippe, in exile in America with his two brothers, called on George Washington at Mount Vernon, the doorman is supposed to have announced them as 'three Equalities at the door'.

Reichenau: In 1793 Louis-Philippe deserted the French army with his commander General Charles-François Dumouriez (1739–1823), thereby exposing himself, his father and the Girondists to Jacobin accusations of conspiracy against the Republic. He took refuge at Reichenau in Switzerland, where for some months he was employed as a tutor under an assumed name.

Mont-St-Michel: Louis XI (1423–83) is supposed to have had the treasonous Cardinal La Balue (*c.*1421–91) confined in an iron cage in the prison at Mont-St-Michel (1469–80). Madame de Genlis reports a visit to the prison with her young royal charges, who destroyed the cage – made of wood – the Duc de Chartres (the young Louis-Philippe) striking the first blow with an axe. Notoriously, the pamphleteer Victor de la Castaigne, alias Henri Dubourg, (1715–46) was imprisoned and died here under Louis XV (1710–74).

Capet: After Louis XVI was deposed, he was known to the Revolutionaries as Citoyen Louis Capet (the House of Capet, from whom the Valois and Bourbons are directly descended, being the dynasty that succeeded the Carolingians in 987), and it was under this name that he was tried, sentenced and executed.

the September laws: These were repressive measures adopted in 1835 in response to an assassination attempt against the king and his sons, known as the Fieschi plot – see note below. Supported by a clear majority in parliament, they included restrictions on press freedom.

Louis Blanc: The socialist historian and politician Louis Blanc (1811–82) in 1841 published his *Histoire de dix ans 1830–1840*, critical of the July Monarchy. Elected a deputy in 1848, he voted against the banishment of the Orléans family, shortly before he himself was forced into exile. Remaining in England until 1870, on his return to France he was re-elected to the Chamber of Deputies.

the Fieschi conspiracy: Giuseppe Fieschi (1790–1836) was the chief conspirator in the plot to assassinate Louis-Philippe by exploding an 'infernal machine' designed and built by Fieschi, using twenty-five gun barrels. It claimed the lives of nineteen people, including Marshal Mortier. He was tried and executed along with two of his co-conspirators, Théodore Pépin (1800–36) and Pierre Morey (1774–1836), members of the Société des Droits de l'Homme.

a political activist: A reference to Armand Barbès (1809–70), a political revolutionary, arrested after a failed insurrection in May 1839 in which he was accused of having shot and killed a National Guardsman (a charge he vigorously denied) and condemned to death. Victor Hugo was one of those who petitioned the king for a pardon. Barbès's sentence was commuted to life imprisonment. He was freed in 1848 after the February Revolution, and elected a deputy in the April. Imprisoned again in 1849 for his part in further political disturbances, he was released in 1854 and went into exile, where he died.

Lafayette . . . to defend Polignac: After the July Revolution, Prince Jules de Polignac (1780–1847), Charles X's prime minister, along with other members of his cabinet held responsible for the July Ordinances that led to the overthrow of his government and of the Bourbon monarchy, was arrested and tried for treason. They had to be protected from the angry Parisian populace by Lafayette, general-in-chief of the National Guard. Lafayette was able to maintain order without bloodshed even after a sentence of life imprisonment (rather than the death sentence) was delivered. The prisoners were released in 1836.

the last Prince de Condé: Louis Henri de Bourbon (1756–1830), son of Louis-Joseph and father of the Duc d'Enghien Louis-Antoine, was found hanged by the neck from the window of his room. The prince's confessor was not the only one to reject the explanation of suicide. Given that one of the main beneficiaries of his death was the son of Louis-Philippe, there were accusations in some circles of assassination with the complicity of the Orléans family and with that of another beneficiary, his mistress the Irishwoman Sophie Dawes, Baronesse de Feuchères. But no proof of murder was established.

two demons of the south: The last decade of the rule of Ferdinand VII of Spain (1784–1833) was one of anti-liberal repression, but in 1830, with no direct male heir, he decreed a change in the law of succession in favour of his infant daughter Isabella. This led to civil war, with supporters of his brother, the even more reactionary Carlos, fighting to establish his claim. Carlos took refuge in Portugal with Dom Miguel, also an enemy of liberalism, whose usurpation of the Portuguese throne led to civil war in that country, at the end of which Miguel was forced to abdicate and went into exile.

Poland back into her coffin: By late 1831, after the November Uprising in 1830, rebellion in Russian-controlled Poland was again crushed, Warsaw falling that September.

the peerage . . . four guilty men: Under the Restoration and the July Monarchy the French parliament consisted of two chambers, the *chambre des pairs* (Chamber of Peers, or Lords), whose members were hereditary and appointed peers, and the elected *chambre des députés* (Chamber of Deputies). The *chambre des pairs* served as a high court of justice, dealing with crimes of treason and conspiracy against the security of the state. The four guilty men were Polignac and his ministers Charles-Ignace Peyronnet (1778–1854), minister of the interior, Jean de Chantelauze (1787–1859), minister of justice, and Guernon de Ranville (1787–1866), minister of ecclesiastical affairs and education.

'servile war': An allusion to the slave uprisings in the late Roman Empire, 135–132 BC, 104–100 BC and (led by Spartacus) 73–71 BC. There was major industrial unrest in Lyon in 1831 and 1834, when the silk workers took to the streets – with the slogan 'Live working or die fighting' – to press their claim for higher wages and to defend their democratic rights.

Quénisset: François Quénisset, who went by the name of Jean-Nicolas Papart, was found guilty along with nineteen others of involvement in a plot to foment revolution, organized by a secret society called the Travailleurs Égalitaires. On 13 September 1841 he had fired shots at a regimental parade led by Louis-Philippe's youngest son, the Duc d'Aumale, with his brothers the Duc d'Orléans and the Duc de Nemours in attendance. The shots that Quénisset fired hit two horses. His death sentence was commuted to deportation.

The recent collapse . . . cotton trade: Some of these snippets are more or less direct quotations from documents cited in the report of the judicial inquiry conducted by the Court of Lords into the events of April 1834 that led to the deaths in Rue Transnonain, *Affaire du mois d'avril 1834: Rapport fait à la cour par Monsieur Girod (de l'Ain)*, published by the Imprimerie Royale in 1834: 'La débâcle qui vient d'avoir lieu dans les cotons nous a convertis plusieurs juste-milieu . . . L'avenir des peuples fermente et s'élabore dans nos rangs obscurs . . . Toutes les questions étaient posées lorsque nous nous sommes réunis et une fois encore les termes étaient ceux-ci: *action* ou *réaction*, *révolution* ou *contre-révolution*; car à notre époque on ne croit plus ni à l'inaction ni à l'immuabilité. Pour le peuple ou contre le peuple, c'est la question, et il n'y en a pas d'autre . . . Le jour où nous ne vous conviendrons plus, cassez-nous, mais jusque-là aidez-nous à marcher . . .'

Gisquet: Joseph-Henri Gisquet (1792–1866), politician, banker and industrialist, was prefect of police 1831–6.

jacquerie: The name given to the peasants' revolt of 1358 in north-east France, any peasant at that time being referred to as 'Jacques'.

The committee . . . these strange documents: Also cited and reproduced in the *Affaire du mois d'avril 1834* judicial report (see note above on *The recent collapse . . . cotton trade*): 'il faut que le comité prenne des mesures pour enpêcher le recrutement dans les sections pour les différantes socites, en autres cel dite d'*Ation* [*sic*] . . . Nous avons apris qu'il y avait des fusils, rue du Faubourg-Poissonniére, no. 5 (bis), au nombre de cinq ou six mil, chez un armurié dans cette cour. La section ne possède point d'armes [*sic*] . . .'. Also in the report are the tabulated document, an explanation of the code, and the section names of which Hugo gives a sample, with typical entries alongside them.

Populaire: This radical newssheet was founded in 1833 (closed down in 1835 and later revived) by the socialist politician and deputy Étienne Cabet (1788–1856). 'Tilly, street seller of *Le Populaire*' appears among the entries listed (for a different section) in a document reproduced in the *Affaire du mois d'avril 1834* judicial report (see note above on *The recent collapse . . . cotton trade*).

Saltpetre 12 ounces . . . Water 2 ounces: This recipe was one of the pieces of evidence produced in the trial against Quénisset and his accomplices in October 1841 and referred to in the report of the judicial inquiry into that affair (*Attentat du 13 Septembre 1841: Procédure: Déposition de Témoins, Paris 1841*).

Lahautière: The lawyer and poet Richard Lahautière (1813–82) was a left-wing political journalist who contributed to a number of socialist newspapers and in 1841 founded his own, *La Fraternité* (Brotherhood).

a certain Pardon: Contained in the *Affaire du mois d'avril 1834* judicial report (see note above on *The recent collapse . . . cotton trade*): 'Perdon [*sic*], sectionnaire du sixième arrondissement, de la section Barricade Méry. Ces quatorze homme tués, ou morts plus tard des suites de leur blessures, étaient tous porteurs d'armes et de munitions.'

Siamese skittles: A variant of skittles that features 'a thick wooden wheel-like disc known technically, for obvious reasons, as the "cheese". Cut obliquely on its rim, the cheese would move in a circular or spiral path when rolled, and the pins would therefore be set up in a circle or spiral round the king at the centre – the object of the game being to overturn them all in a sequence with a single roll', Mark J. Zucker, 'An Allegory of Renaissance Politics in a Contemporary Italian Engraving', *Journal of the Warburg and Courtauld Institutes*, vol. 52 (1989), p. 237.

A certain Gallais: Contained in the *Affaire du mois d'avril 1834* judicial report (see note p. 1388 on *The recent collapse . . . cotton trade*): 'Gallais, tué le 14 avril rue Beaubourg . . . une perquisition faite chez lui a fait saisir sept cents cartouches et vingt-quatre pierres à fusils . . .'

The government one day . . . four hours: Cited in the *Affaire du mois d'avril 1834* judicial report (see note p. 1388 on *The recent collapse . . . cotton trade*): 'La semaine dernière il a été distribué des armes et deux cent mille cartouches; le Gouvernement le sait et ne peut en découvrir aucune. Hier, trente-deux mille autres cartouches ont encore été distribuées, aujourd'hui il va en être distribué, j'en sais pas le nombre. Mais je sais que le jour n'est pas éloigné et qu'en quatre heures d'horloge quatre-vingt mille républicains seront sur les armes . . .'

the genius of Venice: A reference to the complicated voting system developed in the Venetian Republic to ensure that power was never concentrated in the hands of any individual.

Where was this meeting . . . central committee: This question-and-answer dialogue is cited in the *Affaire du mois d'avril 1834* judicial report (see note p. 1388 on *The recent collapse . . . cotton trade*): 'D [question]: Où se tint cette réunion? R [answer]: Dans la rue de la Paix. D: Chez qui? R: Dans la rue même. D: Quelles sections parurent à cette réunion? R: Il n'y avait que la section Manuel. D: Quel était le chef de la réunion ce soir-là? R: C'est moi. D: Vous êtes trop jeune pour avoir ce jour-là, de votre propre mouvement, pris un parti semblable: d'où vous venaient vos instructions? R: Du comité central.'

Mount Aventine . . . sibyl's cave . . . tripods: The sibyl's cave with poisonous exhalations emanating from it that Virgil speaks of (*Aeneid*, bk VI, lines 237–42) was at Lake Avernus in Campania. Tripods were important sacred furniture at oracular sites, sometimes sat upon by the priestess at the shrine, who would deliver her prophecies in a state of trance, probably induced by narcotic gases that emanated from the ground underneath the tripod.

Ennius: A Latin poet whose most famous work, of which only a fragment survives, was an epic poem in eighteen books relating to the history of Rome. Ennius (*c*.239–*c*.169 BC) had a reputation for consuming liberal quantities of wine.

I've read Prudhomme: During the Revolutionary period, the journalist Louis Prudhomme (1752–1830) was associated with the newspaper *Révolutions de Paris*. He was also the author of a history of the Revolution, *Histoire générale et impartiale des erreurs, des fautes et des crimes commis pendant la Révolution française* (General and Impartial History of the Errors, Mistakes and Crimes Committed during the French Revolution; 1796–7).

Social Contract: The title of Jean-Jacques Rousseau's treatise published in 1762, in which the terms of the political debate surrounding the Revolution are to be found.

constitution of the year II: There is no constitution of year II, but there are constitutions of year I (24 June 1793) and year III (22 August 1795). The principle that Grantaire appears to be citing is not a direct quotation but a paraphrase of Article 4 of the 1789 Declaration of the Rights of Man and of the Citizen ('Liberty consists in being entitled to do whatever causes no injury to others'), Article 6 of the 1793 constitution ('Liberty is the inherent right of man to do whatever causes no injury to the rights of others'), and Article 2 (under Rights) of the 1795 constitution ('Liberty consists in being entitled to do that which causes no injury to the rights of others').

Hébertist: See note p. 1309 on *Père Duchêne . . . Père Letellier*.

St-Anne marble: A darkish-grey marble with white veining, commonly used for Paris café tables.

Escousse and Lebras: Victor Escousse (1813–32) was a young playwright who enjoyed a little success but not enough to satisfy him, and Auguste Lebras (1811–32), a young poet, his collaborator on his last play *Raymond*. The two men suffocated themselves with the vapour of burning charcoal in a suicide pact that made a great impression on contemporaries and was widely reported and commented on in the press.

Ruysdael: The Dutch artist Salomon van Ruysdael (1600/03–70) painted mainly riverscapes.

the tree of the Deaf-Mutes School: In the courtyard of the Deaf-Mutes School, transferred in 1791 to the Faubourg St-Jacques, was an elm tree thought to have been planted in 1605 and with a circumference of over sixteen feet at its base.

a Némorin: Némorin is the name of the young lover in the pastoral novel *Estelle et Némorin*, published in 1788 by Jean-Pierre Claris de Florian, which was the inspiration of Berlioz's opera of the same name.

at the Salon: The official art exhibition of the Académie des Beaux Arts was first held in 1725 and opened to the public in 1737. A jury was first appointed in 1748.

Pedro de Medina: First published in Spanish in 1545, *The Art of Navigation* by the Spanish mathematician and royal cosmographer Pedro de Medina (1493–1567) became a standard manual on nautical science, and was translated into many languages and published in many editions.

Judge Delancre: In 1612 Pierre Delancre (1553–1631), a magistrate of the Bordeaux parliament, published his *Tableau de l'Inconstance des Mauvais Anges et Démons* (published in English as *On the Inconstancy of Witches*), the result of an investigation into witchcraft practices in the Basque region of France.

the quarto volume . . . Rubaudière: Both book and author are invented.

the Gans–Savigny controversy: The German legal theorists Friedrich Karl von Savigny (1779–1861) and Eduard Gans (1797–1839) disagreed over the issue of property rights and the rights of succession. Gans attacked the basis of Savigny's notion of ownership as propounded in his *Das Recht des Besitzes* (The Right of Possession; 1803) in his own major work *Das Erbrecht in weltgeschichtlicher Entwicklung* (Historical Development of Inheritance Law; 1824–35).

Combat des Animaux: Figuring on some eighteenth-century maps, this was where dogs were set to fight all kinds of other animals – bulls, boars, wolves, bears and even lions and tigers. The Pantin toll-gate was better known as the Combat toll-gate, taking the name from this form of public entertainment that was staged nearby.

the Mansart style: Characteristic of the architecture of François Mansart (1598–1666) are the steep double-sloped roofs that became known as 'mansard roofs'.

Comte de Lobau: In 1830 Lobau was appointed commander of the National Guard, and was responsible for putting down the insurrections of 1832 and 1834.

During Floréal: Eighth month of the year in the Revolutionary calendar, late April–late May.

geometric point: In Euclidean geometry, 'that which has no part', i.e. the smallest indivisible constituent element of geometric space.

Paphos: City-kingdom of Cyprus, where the Greek goddess Aphrodite, associated with the arts of love and seduction, was by tradition born of the sea-foam near by.

Lamoignon: The most famous of a dynasty of Parisian magistrates was Chrétien-Guillaume de Lamoignon de Malesherbes (1721–94), better known simply as Malesherbes, who defended Louis XVI at his trial and was himself guillotined.

Le Nôtre: The grandson and son of royal gardeners, the landscape gardener André Le Nôtre (1613–1700) designed the park and gardens at Versailles, Vaux-le-Vicomte and Chantilly.

Coutard: Having risen through the ranks during the Revolutionary and Napoleonic Wars, General Louis-François Coutard (1769–1852) welcomed the return of the Bourbons. In 1816 he was made count, and in 1822 appointed military commander of the 1st Division, based in Paris.

a then famous medley: Marc-Antoine Désaugiers (1772–1827) wrote light-hearted parodies of well-known operas of the day. His *Cadet Buteux à l'opéra de La Vestale* consists of a medley of tunes (*pot-pourri*) from the opera *La Vestale* (first performed in December 1807) by the Italian composer Gaspare Spontini (1774–1851) with a French libretto by Étienne de Jouy (1764–1846).

facial angles: The Dutch anatomist and scientific illustrator Petrus Camper (1722–89) in the course of his physiognomical investigations developed his theory of the 'facial angle', by which human types could be differentiated. He delivered a lecture on this theory in Paris in 1777. His work has subsequently been associated with theories of relative racial superiority.

patent-leather: The process for making highly glossed leather dates back to the late eighteenth century; various methods were subsequently patented, as demand for what came to be called 'patent leather' for dress wear grew.

Euryanthe: Cosette plays and sings the 'Huntsmen's Chorus' from the opera *Euryanthe* by Carl Maria von Weber (1786–1826), which premiered in Vienna in 1823 and was first staged in Paris, in French, as *Euriante*, in 1831. The chorus, which Hugo cites in French, 'Chasseurs égarés dans les bois' ('Hunters lost in the woods'), opens in German 'Die Thale dampfen, die Höhen glühn' ('The valleys are misty, the heights are sunlit').

the Maréchale de La Mothe-Houdancourt: Louise de Prie (1624–1709) was governess to the children of Louis XIV and to those of Louis XIV's eldest son and grandson. By her marriage to Philippe de La Mothe-Houdancourt she had three daughters: the Duchesses d'Aumont, de la Ferté, and de Ventadour; the last was governess to Louis XV and to his children (1727–35).

the coins . . . Mars's diamonds: After a trial that excited enormous public interest, Mademoiselle Mars's chambermaid Françoise Constance Richard and her husband were in 1828 found guilty of the theft from her home in Paris of the actress's diamonds and jewellery, and were sentenced to ten years' hard labour. In November 1831 a major robbery took place at the Cabinet des Médailles at the Bibliothèque Nationale. Countless gold coins and much of Childeric's treasure, which was also housed there, were lost for ever; some of the stolen objects were recovered only after they had been melted down.

the blast of cholera: The cholera epidemic of 1832, which broke out in Paris in March and subsided in September, left some 18,000 dead in the capital and over 100,000 across the whole country.

Windsor soaps: Despite the embargo on English goods, Napoleon is reputed to have favoured this English soap; some was found in his carriage that was captured at Waterloo. Subsequently bought by William Bullock (1773–1849), the carriage and its contents were displayed in the Egyptian Hall, a building on Piccadilly in London, commissioned by Bullock to house his collection of curiosities

(Rev. Joseph Nightingale, *London and Middlesex*, vol. 3, pt 2, pp. 643–53, London, 1815).

Faust . . . on the Brocken: The Brocken is the highest peak in the Harz Mountains in Germany. An optical effect of meteorological conditions on the peak are spectre-like shadows that have contributed to the mountain's reputation as the haunt of witches, which Goethe draws on in the text of *Faust* (1808).

Callot: The printmaker and draughtsman Jacques Callot (1592–1635) was a master of his art, capturing low-life characters in all their vitality but also treating grander subjects, including religious figures.

member of the Institute: Napoleon was at his own request elected to the Institut National des Sciences et des Arts in December 1797, after his successes in the Italian campaign. As commander-in-chief of the Egyptian campaign of 1798 he was responsible for the foundation of the Institut d'Égypte, which ceased to exist after the French were forced to withdraw from Egypt.

It was an elephant . . . spectre of the Bastille: The Bastille prison ('the sombre fortress with its nine towers'), stormed by Revolutionaries on 14 July 1789, was demolished almost immediately afterwards. Napoleon's projected elephant cast in bronze that was to have stood in a fountain on the site of the old prison was never realized. The plaster model, by the sculptor Bridan (1766–1836), was completed in 1813 and remained *in situ* until 1846, when it was deemed structurally unsound and dismantled.

the gigantic stove: Standing where Napoleon's elephant fountain was to have been sited, the July Column, commissioned by Louis-Philippe to celebrate the July Revolution, was initially entrusted to the architect Jean-Antoine Alavoine (1777–1834) and completed after his death by Joseph-Louis Duc (1802–79), with the addition of a gilded bronze statue representing the spirit of Liberty by the sculptor Auguste Dumont (1801–84) on top of it. The column was finally inaugurated in 1840, to the accompaniment of Berlioz's *Symphonie funèbre et triomphale*.

the Fumade lighter: A shopkeeper on the Pont-Neuf by the name of Fumade sold phosphorus-box lighters, into which sulphur-tipped matches were dipped to ignite them.

Paul de Kock: One of the most celebrated writers of his day, a prolific novelist whose popularity has since declined.

the Ambigu: The Ambigu-Comique, which was founded in 1769 by the actor-playwright Nicolas-Médard Audinot, burned down in a fire in 1827, which was started when the effect of a firework was being tried out for one of the melodramas for which this theatre was famous. The theatre was rebuilt on a different site and reopened in 1829. This building was eventually demolished in 1966.

Berquin: Arnaud Berquin (1749–91) wrote books and plays for children, including a French adaptation (1786–7) of the first two parts of Thomas Day's *Sandford and Merton* (1783–9), a moralizing educational work for children that enjoyed huge popularity in both countries throughout the nineteenth century.

Desrues: Antoine Desrues (1744–77) was found guilty of murder and executed, having poisoned a mother and son in a fraudulent attempt to acquire a property.

Sleep-inducers: Louis-Sébastien Mercier (1740–1814), author of *Tableau de Paris*, a detailed and lively multi-volume portrait of the city (1781–8), in vol. 2 (1781) writes: 'Chaque année offre une race nouvelle de voleurs & de scélérats qui ont un caractère différent: l'an passé c'étoient des empoisonneurs, connus sous le nom d'*endormeurs*, qui mêloient dans le tabac & dans les boissons un venin assoupissant, dangereux & mortel . . .' ('Every year presents a new race of thieves and scoundrels of a different character: last year they were poisoners, known by the name of "sleep-inducers", who mixed into tobacco and drinks a soporific, dangerous and lethal poison . . .').

Balzac and Eugène Sue: Honoré de Balzac (1799–1850) in his sequence of novels collectively entitled *La Comédie Humaine* (*The Human Comedy*) sought to portray French society as a whole, including the criminal world, which featured most notably in *Splendeurs et Misères des Courtisanes* (*Splendours and Miseries of Courtesans*, also translated as *A Harlot High and Low*), first published in serial form, 1838–47. Author of *Les Mystères de Paris*, which explored the Parisian underworld and gave voice to a class previously little heard in literature, Eugène Sue (1804–57) was one of the most successful writers of his age. Well connected (his godmother was the empress Josephine), the son of a distinguished surgeon, he became a socialist in his political sympathies, and served briefly as a left-wing deputy in the National Assembly, before going into exile after Louis-Napoleon's *coup d'état* in 1851.

the Hôtel de Rambouillet: Madame de Rambouillet (1588–1665) hosted this seventeenth-century Parisian salon of greatest renown; it was closely identified with the *précieuses*, the society ladies who constituted an influential cultural and literary phenomenon, advocating refinement of language and feeling, and whom Molière satirized in his early play, *Les Précieuses Ridicules* (1659).

the Cour des Miracles: A 'court of miracles' came to be a general term applied to any place that housed a gathering of beggars, who when plying their trade by day were afflicted with all sorts of ailments and disabilities that miraculously disappeared when they retired to their underworld citadels at night. Hugo is referring to one here, in Paris's second *arrondissement*, that figures large in his novel *Notre-Dame de Paris* (*The Hunchback of Notre-Dame*).

Pomona: The story of how the Roman wood nymph Pomona, whose sole delight is to nurture her orchards, is wooed by the god Vertumnus is told in Ovid's *Metamorphoses*, bk 14, lines 622–771.

Bellona: The Roman goddess of war, described as the sister, or sometimes the wife or daughter, of Mars.

Bart . . . Duquesne . . . Suffren . . . Duperré: Of humble birth, and so not eligible to serve as an officer in the French navy, the Flemish-born Jean Bart (1650–1702) through his naval exploits as a privateer became a national hero in France. In 1694, against the odds, he famously recaptured a convoy of over a hundred ships carrying cargoes of grain destined for France that had been hijacked by a Dutch fleet. In the same year he was ennobled for his services to his country. Admiral Abraham Duquesne (1610–88), a Huguenot, served with distinction in both the Swedish and French navies. Admiral Pierre-André de Suffren (1729–88) fought against the English in the Seven Years War, in the American War of Independence and in the East Indies. Admiral Victor-Guy Duperré (1775–1846), after a brilliant naval career, was three times naval minister.

Plautus: An allusion to Plautus' play *Poenulus, or The Young Carthaginian*, Act V, sc. ii, in which Punic, the Phoenician dialect of Carthage, is spoken by one character to another, who claims an understanding that he does not have.

Mandrin: Leader of a band of brigands, guilty of murder, extortion and smuggling on a grand scale, Louis Mandrin (1725–55) was regarded by the peasantry as something of a Robin Hood. He was eventually caught, tried and brutally executed.

Thunes: A deformation of the place-name Tunis, the *roi de Thunes* ('king of Tunis') being one of the titles taken by the chief of the beggar underworld, also known as *le Grand Coesre* ('a word surely linked to Caesar', Jonathon Green, http://jonathongreen.co.uk/taking-slang-seriously-iii/).

the Maltese galleys: The Knights of Rhodes relocated with their fleet to Malta in 1530; in the sixteenth century their galleys were elite fighting vessels of unmatched capability with relatively well paid pilots and senior crewmen.

lansquenets: Fifteenth- and sixteenth-century German mercenary footsoldiers serving in France (from the German *Landsknecht*).

Montgomery: Gabriel de Lorges, Comte de Montgomery (1530–74), captain of the King's Scots Guard under Henri II, whom he killed by accident in a jousting tournament in which the king obliged him to take part; however, Henri II's widow Catherine de' Medici was determined to exact revenge. Montgomery subsequently converted to Protestantism and fought repeatedly against the royal army in northern France, at one point escaping, after defeat, in a galley. He was eventually taken prisoner, brought to trial and executed.

Poulailler . . . Voltaire . . . Langleviel La Beaumelle: A cobbler by trade, Jean Chevalier, known by various other names including Poulailler, was a house-breaker and horse-stealer in the 1770s and 80s. He was eventually brought to trial and hanged in 1786. Laurent Angliviel de la Beaumelle – Hugo's spelling is slightly different – (1726–73) was a Protestant man of letters who made an enemy of Voltaire with attacks on both his integrity and his work. While Voltaire certainly used the word *camouflet* in his letters (in one dated 14 July 1767 to d'Alembert, for instance, and another of 19 July 1776 to the Comte d'Argental), I have not traced the wording that Hugo cites.

Andromeda: In Greek mythology, the innocent princess Andromeda was chained naked to a rock to be sacrificed to a sea-monster, but was rescued by Perseus, who slew the monster; as related in bk 4, lines 663–804 of Ovid's *Metamorphoses*.

physiocrats led by Turgot: The physiocrats were economic theorists who in the mid eighteenth century combined a revolutionary scientific approach to economics with a conservative emphasis on the importance of land as the paramount source of wealth. Their views were to some extent represented by Jacques Turgot (1727–81), who towards the end of his career as a financial administrator served as Louis XV's finance minister (1774–6), but he failed to get his reforms accepted and was dismissed.

philosophes: The term *philosophe* applies not only to philosophers but extends to all intellectuals of the Enlightenment in eighteenth-century France who placed their faith in the supremacy of reason. All four names that Hugo cites – Diderot, Turgot and Rousseau, as well as Voltaire – would be considered *philosophes*.

sponsored by a prince: An allusion to the Prince de Conti (1717–76), a great-grandson of Louis XIV and cousin of Louis XV, with whom he had difficult relations which in 1756 resulted in a total rift between the two men. The prince became actively engaged in opposition to Louis XV; no longer welcome at Versailles, he held his own court in Paris, hosting one of the great salons of the eighteenth century where he cultivated Enlightenment philosophers, offering asylum and patronage to Rousseau, and built up an important art collection.

Restif de la Bretonne: A printer by trade, Nicolas-Edmé Restif (1734–1806), also known as Rétif de la Bretonne and who has been called *le Rousseau du ruisseau* ('the Rousseau of the gutter'), was a prolific writer in many literary forms, a chronicler of life at the lower end of the social scale, an analyst of sexual relations, a pornographer and a political radical.

Schiller: In 1781 the German poet and philosopher Friedrich Schiller (1759–1805) published his first play, *Die Räuber* (*The Robbers*), a complex and melodramatic investigation into notions of good and evil, moral responsibility and personal and social freedom, which created a sensation when it was performed the following year.

the Tuileries: Protests in favour of electoral reform came to a head in February 1848, forcing the abdication of Louis-Philippe, who fled from the Tuileries Palace to take refuge in England, and leading to the proclamation of the Second Republic.

the Regent diamond: Now displayed in the Louvre, the Regent diamond was bought by the Duc d'Orléans (1674–1723), Regent of France before Louis XV came of age, and set in the crown used for the coronation of Louis XV in 1722.

great red spectre: An allusion to a pamphlet by Auguste Romieu (1800–55), *Le spectre rouge de 1852*, published in Paris in 1851 and justifying in advance the *coup d'état* of 1851 by which Louis-Napoleon became sole ruler of France and that prompted Hugo and his family to go into exile. In December 1852 France ceased to be a republic and Louis-Napoleon was proclaimed emperor as Napoleon III.

Briareus: A mythological giant with fifty heads and a hundred hands, mentioned by Homer in the *Iliad* (bk I, lines 402–6) as intervening to help Zeus assert his authority over the gods.

the field ... encamped: Livy in his *History of Rome*, bk 26, ch. 11, recounts that when Hannibal came to lay siege to Rome the land on which he was camped with his troops outside the city had that day been sold at its full price, so little did the Romans fear him and so little regard had they for his right of conquest.

the imams ... Great Pyramid: It was reported on 27 November 1798 in *Le Moniteur* that on 12 August, accompanied by some army officers and members of the Cairo Institute, Napoleon had been shown round the Great Pyramid by several imams and muftis.

the nets at St-Cloud: It is generally believed that nets were hung from the bridge at St-Cloud to catch debris, and in particular the corpses of suicides, carried downstream. There seems little evidence of nets placed there officially, but bodies were certainly caught in what were probably fishermen's nets, an image that has captured the public imagination.

Those bygone days ... my winning ways: In the French text, 'Mon bras si dodu, / Ma jambe bien faite, / Et le temps perdu' (literally, 'My arm so plump, / My well turned leg, / And the time gone by', or 'wasted'), from the refrain of 'Ma Grand'mère' ('My Gran'mother'), a song by Béranger about a grandmother remembering with nostalgia her youthful charms and the lovers she had before she married. (It is delightfully sung by the bevy of girls from a brothel taken to a first communion celebration in the country, in Max Ophuls' *Le Plaisir* of 1952, based on three short stories by Guy de Maupassant, including 'La Maison Tellier', published in 1881, in which this episode occurs.)

the Faublas: An allusion to the hero of a novel about the amorous adventures of a libertine provincial, *Les Amours du Chevalier de Faublas* by Jean-Baptiste Louvet de Couvray (1760–97).

Busiris: In Greek mythology, Busiris was a king of Egypt and the son of Poseidon; he made sacrificial victims of all strangers to his country, and was slain by Herakles when he too was taken to the altar to be sacrificed.

Humblot-Conté: A tradesman in origin, Arnould Humblot-Conté (1776–1845) married into the Conté family, who in 1795 had obtained a patent for the manufacture of artificial black-lead pencils, which made their fortune. From 1817 Humblot-Conté ran this family business. He was three times elected to the Chamber of Deputies as a member of the liberal opposition. Having failed to win election after the July Revolution, which he welcomed, he was made a peer in 1832.

Garat: A baritone and later singing-master at the Paris Conservatory, Pierre-Jean Garat (1762–1823) was a well known dandy of royalist sympathies, and like Monsieur Gillenormand one who dressed in the style of the *incroyables*.

the attack on the Louvre: The Louvre was stormed by the Paris mob on 29 July 1830, during the three days of the July Revolution.

a fountain . . . Duc de Berry: A mausoleum planned for the Duc de Berry was to have been erected on the site of the opera house where he died. After the July Revolution the monument was not completed, and in 1844 a fountain designed by Louis Visconti (1791–1853) took its place. The funerary sculpture intended to be housed in the mausoleum now stands behind the basilica of St Denis.

A Pamela: An allusion to Pamela, the eponymous heroine of Samuel Richardson's novel published in England in 1740 and in a French translation by Abbé Prévost in 1742. It tells the story of a servant-maid whose charms attract unwanted attentions but who manages nevertheless to preserve her virtue and to win the love of a gentleman who offers her marriage.

'Lightly touch and quickly go': The verse to which Hugo alludes here, by the poet and librettist Pierre-Charles Roy (1683–1764), appeared beneath an engraving by Nicolas Larmessin *fils* (1684–1755) of a winter scene with a group of skaters: 'Sur un mince cristal, l'hiver conduit leurs pas. / Le précipice est sous la glace. / Telle est de nos plaisirs la légère surface: / Glissez, mortels, n'appuyez pas' ('Over thin crystal, winter guides their steps. / The precipice is beneath the ice. / Such is the fragile surface of our pleasures: / Glide lightly, mortals, do not rest your weight'). Hester Piozzi in *Anecdotes of the Late Samuel Johnson* (1786) gives Johnson's translation and relates the circumstances in which he produced it: 'O'er ice the rapid skater flies, / With sport above and death below; / Where mischief lurks in gay disguise, / Thus lightly touch and quickly go.' Johnson's translation captures the ring that the French line has, and strikes the right tone for Monsieur Gillenormand.

Pépin or Morey: See note p. 1386 on *the Fieschi conspiracy*).

Candide: Candide is the innocent young man of Voltaire's satirical novel of 1759, attacking Leibnizian optimism and its blindness to the harsh realities of life.

General Lamarque's funeral: After distinguished service in the Napoleonic campaigns, General Jean-Maximilien Lamarque (1770–1832) was named governor of Paris during the Hundred Days and was in command of the suppression of the Vendean uprising in 1815. In 1828 he was elected to the Chamber of Deputies and won considerable popularity by his oratorial skill in addressing military matters. He died in the cholera epidemic of 1832 and his funeral on 5 June was the catalyst for an insurrection in Paris that led to the introduction of martial law.

Philinte as opposed to Alceste: Philinte is the more politic friend of the uncompromising Alceste in Molière's play *Le Misanthrope* (1622).

Chouan: Jean Chouan (1757–94), as he was known – his real name was Jean Cottereau – was one of the leaders of the counter-revolutionary royalist insurrection in the west of France.

Jeanne: The name of the leader of the St-Merry barricade during the rioting that took place on 5 and 6 June 1832. He was one of twenty-two who were tried in October that year for offences relating to the defence of the barricade, and was sentenced to transportation – thought by many at the time to be a brutally harsh punishment for a young man of thirty-two whose integrity and heroism were much admired. See *Procès des vingt-deux accusés du cloître St-Merry, événements des 5 et 6 juin 1832*, Rouanet: Paris, 1832.

School clashed with legion: The legion was a unit of the National Guard made up of four battalions.

Securing the throne for Philip V: The War of the Spanish Succession (1701–14) was fought by France to defend the Bourbon claim of Louis XIV's grandson, Philip, the Duc d'Anjou, to the Spanish throne. Other European powers feared this would lead to the union of Spain and France. The war ended with Philip's renunciation of his claim to the French throne. (The island of Gibraltar was ceded to Great Britain under the terms of the Treaty of Utrecht of 1713, concluded at the end of the war.)

The same cannon . . . Vendémiaire: In the tenth of August attack on the Tuileries a great many of the king's Swiss Guard were killed. The fourteenth of Vendémiaire is an allusion to Napoleon's action on 5 October 1795 (actually, 13 Vendémiaire year IV) when royalist rebels attacked the Tuileries, where the National Convention were sitting. A junior officer at the time, Napoleon gave the order for cannons to be fired against the royalists, and restored order. (The Republican calendar became law on 14 Vendémiaire year II, i.e. 5 October 1793 – this may account for the slip.)

Terray . . . Turgot: Abbé Terray (1715–78) served as Louis XV's minister of finance for five years from 1769. His financial reforms were efficient but antiliberal. Turgot (see note p. 1394 on *physiocrats led by Turgot*) tried to suppress the imposition of tariffs on the circulation of grain so as to ensure its general availability at reasonable prices, but was thwarted by the landowners and speculators who benefited by the tariffs; when he tried to introduce a tax on landowners, he was dismissed from office.

Ramus . . . by students . . . Rousseau . . . riot: The humanist scholar and academic reformist Petrus Ramus (1515–72), a Huguenot convert from Catholicism, was murdered during the St Bartholomew's Day massacre in August 1572, possibly by students. Rousseau had fled to Switzerland after the publication and condemnation of *The Social Contract* and *Émile* in 1762, but there too he met with opposition and condemnation. His house at Môtiers was stoned in September 1765, and in 1766 he left Switzerland, travelling to England with the Scottish philosopher David Hume.

Israel . . . Moses . . . Rome . . . Scipio: The Israelites blamed Moses for the hardship they suffered after he had led them out of the land of Egypt (Exodus 16:2, Numbers 14:2). Publius Cornelius Scipio Africanus (235–183 BC) was the Roman general who defeated Hannibal. His political enemies, fearful of his popularity, tried unsuccessfully to bring him to trial for bribery and corruption. He retired to Liternum, and Livy tells us (*History of Rome*, bk 38, ch. 53) that 'on his deathbed he gave orders that he should be buried . . . there, so that there might be no funeral rites performed for him by his ungrateful country'.

soldiers against Alexander, sailors against Christopher Columbus: In 326 BC Alexander the Great was forced to abandon his designs on India because at the Hyphasis River his troops mutinied and refused to go any further. In October

1492 Christopher Columbus faced the prospect of mutiny among his crew, who wanted to turn back, before eventually sighting land.

salt smugglers: Jean Chouan and many of his co-insurrectionists were salt smugglers, able to make a living out of smuggling salt from Brittany, where it was not taxed, to neighbouring provinces where it was. Jean Chouan was alleged to have murdered a customs agent, but legend has it that his mother made a personal appeal to the king and won his pardon.

Miquelets, Verdets, Cadenettes, Companions of Jehu, Knights of the Armband: Various royalist sympathizers: Miquelets, originally a name given to Pyrenean bandits, was a term used for a Catalonian irregular militia who fought in the Peninsular War against Napoleon; the Verdets were so called because they wore green (the archaic *verdet* meaning 'light green'), thus identifying themselves as supporters of the Comte d'Artois (later Charles X), whose livery was green; Cadenettes indicated their royalist allegiance with a particular hairstyle – the long lock of hair hanging on either side of the face, called *une cadenette*. The Companions of Jehu were counter-revolutionary gangs who after the fall of Robespierre in 1794 unleashed a white terror in the south of France. A special decoration, the Brassard de Bordeaux ('the Bordeaux armband'), was created by the Duc d'Angoulême (son of the Comte d'Artois) for those who had formed his guard when he returned from exile and landed at Bordeaux after the abdication of Napoleon in 1814.

as Lafayette says: Addressing the National Assembly on 20 February 1790, Lafayette said: 'Pour la Révolution il a fallu des désordres; l'ordre ancien n'était que servitude, et dans ce cas l'insurrection est le plus saint des devoirs' ('For the sake of the Revolution, disorder was necessary; the old order was mere servitude, and in such circumstances insurrection is the most sacred of duties').

author of the Annals: An allusion to Tacitus (56–117) and his last work, not all of which survives. In this history of the Roman Empire, Tacitus regrets the free institutions of the Republic and deplores the dynastic system. He is a fierce critic of Nero, whose persecution of the Christians he is the first secular historian to record. The *Annals* cover the period after Augustus Caesar, dealing with the emperor Tiberius and his successors Caligula, Claudius and Nero.

Patmos exile: John the Divine, author of the Book of Revelation (the Apocalypse of St John), which was written in Hellenistic Greek, is traditionally believed to have been exiled to Patmos under the rule of Domitian (81–96).

Verres: The provincial governor of Sicily, Caius Verres (*c.*120–43 BC), was brought to trial in 70 BC and successfully prosecuted for abuse of his powers by Cicero (106–43 BC). Cicero made a strong enough case that Verres fled into exile before the end of the trial.

Rubicon: When Caesar crossed the Rubicon with armed troops under his command in 49 BC he was violating the integrity of the Roman Republic in a challenge to its authority, which signalled the beginning of a civil war that lasted until 45 BC.

Vitellius: In the Year of the Four Emperors, Vitellius (15–69) was the third, reigning for eight months before he was killed by the soldiers of Vespasian, who succeeded him. Suetonius describes Vitellius' greed and cruelty.

Caracalla ... Commodus ... Heliogabalus: Caracalla (188–217) was Roman emperor from 198 to 217; Commodus (161–92), from 180 to 192; and Heliogabalus (*c.*203–22), from 218 to 222. All were reviled for their cruelty or depravity.

Masaniello: Tommaso Aniello (1620–47), known as Masaniello, was a Neapolitan fisherman who led a popular revolt against the levying of a tax on fruit as a tribute demanded by Naples's Spanish rulers. His initial success went to his head and he alienated his supporters, who may even have been his assassins. *La Muette de Portici* (The Mute Girl of Portici), an opera by Daniel Auber (1782–1871) based on the story of Masaniello, was first performed in Paris in 1828. It was thought by Richard Wagner to have influenced the July Revolution.

Gaster: Rabelais, 'l'Eschyle de la mangeaille', as Victor Hugo referred to him ('the Aeschylus of belly-fodder'), first used the term *Messer Gaster* to denote the stomach in *The Fourth Book of Pantagruel*, ch. VII. It was used also by La Fontaine in fable 2, bk 3, 'Les Membres et l'Estomac' (The Limbs and the Stomach), in which the stomach is proved to be not always wrong.

as at Buzançais: In 1847 during a period of famine several grain carts passing through the small town of Buzançais in central France were intercepted. In the course of the rioting that followed, several killings took place. Government repression was merciless: five of the rioters were condemned to death, and harsh sentences were passed on others.

his predecessor Foy: Foy was the younger of the two but was elected a deputy before Lamarque; he also predeceased him.

Gérard and Drouet: Napoleon's Generals Étienne-Maurice Gérard (1773–1852) and Jean-Baptiste Drouet (1765–1844), who both rallied to him during the Hundred Days and whom he had intended to appoint as marshals (*in petto*), were both made marshals by Louis-Philippe, Gérard in 1830 and Drouet in 1843. Gérard was elected a deputy in 1822 and during the July Revolution became minister for war. Drouet was made governor of Algeria in 1834.

Duc de Reichstadt: Napoleon's son by Marie-Louise of Austria was given this title in 1818 by his grandfather Emperor Francis of Austria. Born in 1811, he was four when Napoleon abdicated in his favour after the battle of Waterloo. Although his claim to the succession was never recognized – and in 1832 he died of tuberculosis – his cousin Louis-Napoleon, when declared emperor in 1852, styled himself Napoleon III.

Vendôme column: A victory monument to commemorate the achievements of the Grand Army, the Vendôme column was covered with bronze plaques made of melted-down Austrian and Russian cannons captured by the French, on which were depicted the major episodes in the campaigns the army had fought. The column was completed in 1810.

Duc de Fitzjames: Édouard de Fitzjames (1776–1838) was an outspoken ultra-royalist. He was a descendant of the Duke of Berwick, James Fitzjames, the illegitimate son of James II of England, who sought refuge in France after James II was driven from the throne in 1688 and on whom Louis XIV conferred the title Duc de Fitzjames in 1710.

the Gallic cockerel: The cockerel as a symbol of France has a long history dating back to the Roman empire, *gallus* in Latin meaning 'cockerel' and evoking the word *Gallia* ('Gaul'). Napoleon preferred the eagle, and the Bourbons the fleur-de-lys, which was officially replaced by the Gallic cockerel as the national emblem after the July Revolution.

Exelmans: Rémy Exelmans (1775–1852) joined the army as a sixteen-year-old volunteer and rose through the ranks during the Revolutionary and Napoleonic Wars, becoming a general and a peer of France. After the Bourbon restoration he went into exile, but was able to return in 1819. In 1828 he was appointed inspector-general of cavalry and in 1851 he became a marshal of France.

Ludwig Snyder: John Ludwig Snyder (1746–1860) is buried in New Washington Cemetery in Pennsylvania.

Île Louviers: It was in 1847 that the branch of the Seine that flowed between the Île Louviers and the right bank was filled in.

Bugeaud: After a distinguished military career in the Napoleonic campaigns and the Peninsular War, Thomas-Robert Bugeaud de la Piconnerie (1784–1849) was elected to the Chamber of Deputies in 1831. In command of a brigade deployed to suppress the rioting in 1834, he was accused of having provoked the massacre of Rue Transnonain by ordering his soldiers to give no quarter. In 1840 he was made governor-general of Algeria.

Marshal Soult: Soult was at this time (1830–4) minister of war.

twelfth of May . . . 1839: The leaders of this insurrection were Auguste Blanqui (1805–81) and Armand Barbès (1809–70), lifelong left-wing activists. The killing of a soldier in the uprising led to death sentences being passed on both leaders (Blanqui having evaded arrest for six months), but these were commuted, Hugo famously appealing in a poem addressed to Louis-Philippe, recently bereaved of his daughter, to pardon Barbès in her name. The insurrection was quickly suppressed. Barbès felt he had been deserted by Blanqui and the two men became enemies. Both were later elected to the Chamber of Deputies, Barbès in 1848 and Blanqui in 1879, but neither held his position as deputy for more than a few months.

Armand Carrel: An army officer of liberal sympathies, Armand Carrel (1800–36) in 1823 joined the Spanish Foreign Legion and fought for the constitutional cause in Spain against the French, for which he was court-martialled and initially condemned to death. His army career over, he distinguished himself as a journalist of political insight and integrity, and co-founded the authoritative *National* newspaper, supporting conservative Republicanism. While not endorsing the 1832 insurrection, he reminded the government that it was itself born of a popular insurrection. He died after a duel with a rival editor.

Marshal Clauzel: One of General Lamarque's pallbearers (so too was Lafayette); a volunteer recruit in 1791, Bertrand Clauzel (1772–1842), who had rallied to Napoleon during the Hundred Days, after the Restoration went into exile in the United States, but was able to return to France in 1820. In 1829 he was elected to the Chamber of Deputies and in 1830 appointed commander-in-chief of the army in Algeria. He was made a marshal of France in 1831. Recalled to take command in Algeria in 1835, his military career ended after the failure of the siege of Constantine in 1836.

that Ann Radcliffe element: The Gothic novels of Ann Radcliffe (1764–1823) were translated into French soon after their publication in English (*The Mysteries of Udolpho* of 1794 was published in France in 1797; *The Italian* of 1797, in the same year) and had considerable influence on popular fiction across the Channel.

Rue de Paris: So called because this was the antechamber to execution at the hands of the executioner, who was known as Monsieur de Paris.

Lagrange: Charles Lagrange (1804–57), Parisian by birth and a member of the Society of the Rights of Man, was one of the leaders of the silkworkers' six-day uprising in Lyon in 1834 that triggered the Paris disturbances in April of that year. Brought to trial, he was sentenced to twenty years' imprisonment but was amnestied in 1839. He took an active part in the Revolution of 1848 that resulted in the end of Louis-Philippe's reign and the introduction of the Second Republic, and was elected to the Chamber of Deputies. After the 1851 *coup d'état* he went into exile and died in the Netherlands.

It's dark . . . Toodle-toot: Gavroche sings a ditty invented by Hugo but with the refrain 'Tutu chapeau pointu', which goes back to the Middle Ages. The *tutu* is onomatopoeic, sometimes extended to *turlututu*, mimicking the sound of a flute or similar instrument. The *chapeau pointu* ('pointed hat') is childish nonsense, to rhyme with *tutu*.

Baour-Lormian, one of the Forty: That is, one of the forty members of the French Academy. Elected in 1815, Pierre-Marie-François Baour-Lormian (1770–1854) was an undistinguished poet who voted against Hugo's election to the Academy (he was elected in 1841 after two unsuccessful attempts).

Duc de Bordeaux: Henri d'Artois (1820–83), the posthumous son of the Duc de Berry, was regarded by royalist legitimists as the rightful heir to Charles X, but he never succeeded (as Henri V) to the throne and died in exile without issue.

where the veal comes from: According to the *Dictionnaire de Cuisine et d'Économie Ménagère* by Monsieur Burnet (Paris, 1836), it was commonly but erroneously believed in Paris that the best veal came from Pontoise. Burnet says, however, that there is very little veal bred around Pontoise and that the veal supplied to Paris from Pontoise actually comes from Normandy.

Prudhomme: See note p. 1311 on *a military Prudhomme*.

I noticed his mount . . . fifteen hands: I am grateful to Monsieur Philippe Osché for confirming that the description Hugo gives here very closely matches that given in the register of horses in Napoleon's stable, conserved in the French National Archives, for Napoleon's horse Désirée, a grey mare, which he rode at Waterloo.

Pindaric tones: An allusion to the ancient Greek poet Pindar (c.522–443 BC), admired for his eloquence and the elegance of his language, whose Pythian odes celebrate Greek military victories against foreign invaders.

old Théophile: An allusion to the poet Théophile de Viau (1590–1626), whose licentious verse almost led to his being burned at the stake; instead, he was imprisoned and died at thirty-six, shortly after being released from captivity. In fact these lines are from a celebrated poem, 'La Solitude', written around 1619 by his contemporary Gérard de Saint-Amant (1594–1661): 'Là branle le squelette horrible / D'un pauvre amant qui se pendit.'

the worthy Natoire: The artist Charles-Joseph Natoire (1700–71) in 1751 was appointed director of the French Academy in Rome, where he painted the ceiling of the French church of St Louis-des-Français. He enjoyed a successful career but was soon forgotten after his death.

Laigle of the funeral oration: An allusion to the famous funeral orations of Laigle's namesake, Bossuet.

Du Breul . . . Sauval . . . Abbé Lebeuf: Jacques Du Breul (1528–1614): *Le Théâtre des antiquitez de Paris* (1612); Henri Sauval (1623–76), *Histoire et Recherches des Antiquités de la ville de Paris*, completed by others after the author's death and published in 1724; Abbé Lebeuf (1687–1760): *Histoire de la ville et de tout le diocèse de Paris* (1754–8).

the big public library: The Bibliothèque Nationale, formerly the Bibliothèque du Roi, which was nationalized after the Revolution, has occupied premises in Rue de Richelieu since 1721, and some of its collections are still housed there. In 1720 it was decreed that the library should be open to the public, for two hours, one day a week. The reference to 'a pile of oyster-shells' is puzzling. However, in *Le Rhin: Lettres à un ami* (1842), an epistolary fiction inspired by his own travels on the Rhine, Hugo writes: 'La bibliothèque de Bâle est assez mal tenue; les objets y sont rangés comme des écailles d'huîtres. J'ai vu sur un

bahut un petit tableau de Rubens qui est posé debout contre une pile de bou-
quins, et qui a déjà dû tomber bien des fois, car le cadre est tout brisé' ('Basle
Library is rather ill-cared for; the objects in it are disposed like oyster-shells. I
saw propped up against a pile of books on a chest a little Rubens painting that
must have fallen over many times already, for the frame is all broken').

Gauls ... Brennus ... Sabines: Brennus was the chieftain of the Gauls who in
391 BC besieged Clusium in Etruria. The intervention of the Romans in
defence of Clusium led eventually to the fall of Rome itself to the Gauls. In his
History of Rome, Livy relates (bk 5, ch. 48) that after a ransom had been
agreed, which the Romans were to pay the Gauls for the siege of the Capitoline
Hill to be lifted, the Romans protested at the Gauls' use of unjust weights to
measure the gold. Brennus added insult to injury by tossing his sword on to the
scale, with the words *Vae victis!*, 'Woe to the vanquished!' or 'Tough luck for
the loser!' Alba, Fidenae, the Aequi, the Volsci and the Sabines were all conquered by Rome.

lean cockerel ... canton of Glarus: According to legend, the Swiss cantons of
Glarus and Uri agreed to settle a dispute over where the border between them
lay, by having a race. A runner from each place was to set off at cock-crow, and
wherever they met would define the boundary of their respective territories.
The inhabitants of Uri deliberately omitted to feed their cockerel, which therefore woke earlier than the well fed cockerel of Glarus, so the runner from Uri
got off to a head start, giving Uri the territorial advantage.

the comet of 1811: The Great Comet of 1811 was a particularly spectacular
phenomenon.

sleeping Psyche: An allusion to the story of Cupid and Psyche, in Apuleius' *Golden
Ass* (see note p. 1324 on *Psyche from Venus*). When Psyche opens the box,
supposedly containing beauty, that Venus sends her down into the Underworld
to fetch, she releases an infernal sleep that overcomes her.

a Gothic Pygmalion: Pygmalion is the legendary sculptor in Ovid's *Metamorphoses*, bk 10, who falls in love with his statue of a woman, who in answer to
his prayers comes to life.

Titian's mistress: An allusion to the painting in the Salon Carré of the Louvre,
now known as *Alfonso I of Ferrara and Laura Dianti* and previously called
Titian's Mistress after the Life.

fifteen intermediate acids: An allusion to the work of France's foremost chemist
Jean-Baptiste Dumas (1800–84), *Essai de Statique Chimique* (An Essay on
Chemical Statics), published in 1842 but previously delivered as lectures at the
Sorbonne.

official magistrate and master of poetry: Grantaire is alluding to a poetry competition held by the Academy of Toulouse, sponsored by the municipality; the official
magistrates of Toulouse were called *capitouls*, and particularly distinguished
practitioners of the art were awarded honorary membership of the Academy and
the title *maître ès jeux floraux*. Hugo himself first won this competition in 1819
at the age of seventeen. In 1820, after winning again, he was named *maître ès
jeux floraux* (see Graham Robb, *Victor Hugo*, 1997, pp. 71–2).

Drogheda with Cromwell: Defended by English royalists and Irish Catholics,
Drogheda, north of Dublin on the east coast of Ireland, fell to Cromwell's
troops in 1649. When those who had taken refuge in the church of St Peter
refused to surrender, Cromwell gave orders for the church to be set on fire, and
they were burned alive. A massacre followed the taking of the city, in which
some 3,000–4,000 were killed.

king's name-day festivities: The first day of May was the feast of St Philip. Although this was celebrated under the July Monarchy, it was not made an official holiday.

Manuel, proud and wise: Jacques-Antoine Manuel (1775–1827) served as an eloquent left-wing representative in the Chamber of Deputies (1815 and 1818–23) until he was famously expelled after being accused by the right-wing majority of justifying regicide in his arguments against French intervention in Spain in support of Ferdinand.

the map of Tenderness: An allusion to a fanciful sentimental guide, the invention of Mademoiselle de Scudéry as described in her novel *Clélie*. Charles Dickens wrote a comprehensive description of this 'allegorical shadowland' in an article entitled 'About Some Allegorical Books', published in the weekly *All Year Round*, 26 October 1889.

Malebranche: Nicolas Malebranche (1638–1715) was an Oratorian priest and moral philosopher whose Cartesian philosophy was informed by the writings of St Augustine. Among his own writings is a *Treatise on the Love of God* (1698).

ancient Themis: In ancient mythology Themis was the daughter of Uranus, goddess of law and order, depicted with the sword of justice in one hand and the scales in the other.

Montmirail or Champaubert: Two Napoleonic victories in February 1814.

Timoleon against the tyrant: As recounted in Plutarch's *Lives*, the Corinthian general Timoleon (411–336 BC) delivered Syracuse from its own tyranny and saved it from the Carthaginians.

brand with infamy . . . Marcel . . . Blankenheim: Étienne Marcel (1302/10–58) was provost of the merchants of Paris and led the populace of the city in an invasion of the Estates General in 1358 to press for reform. In Liège in 1312, Arnould von Blankenheim championed the cause of the people against the nobles in the conflict known as the Mal de St Martin, in which he died.

Ambiorix . . . Artevelde . . . Marnix . . . Pelagius: Ambiorix was the barbarian leader of the Germanic Eburones tribe, who waged war against the Romans and whose initial successes were punished by Caesar with the total annihilation of his people. Jacob van Artevelde (c.1290–1345) was a Flemish leader in the early phase of the Hundred Years War (1337–1453), striving with considerable success to preserve Flemish independence of both France and England. Philips van Marnix (1538–98) was a Flemish Calvinist who fought in the revolt against the Spanish rule of Philip II in the Netherlands. After rebelling against Spain's Arab rulers, Pelagius (c.685–737), a Visigoth nobleman, founded the Kingdom of Asturias in Spain.

Prometheus Bound: The ancient Greek play *Prometheus Bound* (whose attribution to Aeschylus is now disputed) opens with the Titan Prometheus being chained to a rock as punishment for his rebellious independence in saving men from destruction by Zeus and championing their cause, and in particular giving them fire.

Thrasybulus: Thrasybulus (d. 388 BC) was the leader of democratic resistance to the oligarchic regimes in Athens of the late fifth and early fourth centuries BC, after the collapse of the Athenian Empire and defeat by Sparta in the Peloponnesian War.

'Au clair de la lune': The earliest known recording of the human voice, discovered in 2008 and made in 1860, pre-dating Edison's phonograph by nearly two decades, is of someone singing the well-known folksong 'Au clair de la lune'.

the Commendatore's statue: An allusion to Mozart's opera *Don Giovanni*, in which the statue of the man Don Giovanni has murdered when trying to seduce his daughter, comes after his unrepentant killer and drags him down to hell.

Barneville: On the west coast of the Cotentin peninsula opposite Guernsey (where Hugo in exile returned to the manuscript of what was to become *The Wretched*, which he had set aside in 1848 at more or less this point, having reached the end of the previous chapter).

Monsieur Orfila: Professor of forensic medicine, dean of the faculty of medicine at the University of Paris and physician to Louis-Philippe, the Spanish-born Mateu Orfila (1787–1853) was a celebrated toxicologist.

Auvergnat: Migrants from the Auvergne in Paris often started out as wood- and coal-carriers (sometimes having arrived in Paris on their own coal barges), water-carriers and wine-carriers. They were poor and hard-working.

PART FIVE: JEAN VALJEAN

Scylla . . . Charybdis: An allusion to the sea monsters in Homer's *Odyssey* (bk 12) who prey on seafarers from either side of a narrow channel of water, Scylla dwelling in a jagged cliff-face on one side and Charybdis under a whirlpool on the other. To steer a course between the two has become a proverbial metaphor for navigating difficulties.

the fateful insurrection: On 22 June 1848 there was an insurrection of Parisian workers against the provisional government that had replaced Louis-Philippe after the February Revolution of that year. The workers were reacting to the abandonment by the new government of radical initiatives in their favour. By 26 June the insurgency had been crushed.

Sisyphus: In Greek mythology Sisyphus was punished everlastingly for his hubris, by being condemned to roll a huge stone uphill that would always roll back down again as soon as it reached the top.

Job his pot shard: 'So Satan went forth from the presence of the Lord, and smote Job with sore boils from the sole of his foot unto his crown. And he took him a potsherd to scrape himself withal', Book of Job 2:7–8.

Ossa on Pelion: In Greek mythology, the giants who waged war against the immortals piled mountains on top of each other in an attempt to reach the realm of the gods, in some sources heaping Mount Ossa on Pelion (e.g., Virgil, *Georgics*, bk I), in others (e.g., Homer, *Odyssey*, bk 11) Pelion on Ossa, in what has become a proverbially strenuous but fruitless effort.

eighteenth of Brumaire . . . twenty-first of January: Respectively, Napoleon's *coup d'état* against the Directory (1799) and the execution of Louis XVI (1793).

Vendémiaire on Prairial: In 1795 there was a popular uprising in May (Prairial in the Revolutionary calendar), with women clamouring for bread and Jacobins for the implementation of their democratic constitution – 'St-Antoine rages, "Bread and Constitution!"', wrote Carlyle in his *History of the French Revolution*. And October (Vendémiaire) saw an armed attack against the Convention by royalists and counter-revolutionaries, in which Napoleon distinguished himself with 'a whiff of grapeshot', Carlyle tells us.

Sinai: It was on Mount Sinai that Moses heard the voice of God and received the Ten Commandments, as related in Exodus.

Porcelain, that is: Prized for its hardness and fineness, porcelain, previously imported from China, was first manufactured in Europe in the early eighteenth century.

Zaatcha . . . Constantine: In their conquest of Algeria, which began in 1830, the French twice laid siege to the city of Constantine, in 1836 and then successfully in 1837. The siege of Zaatcha in 1849 ended in ruthless reprisals against the civilian population.

Barthélemy: Emmanuel Barthélemy, a mechanic from Sceaux, was a radical activist who ended up in 1849 as an émigré in London, where in 1855 he was hanged for the murder of two Englishmen. His effigy subsequently appeared in Madame Tussaud's exhibition.

Cournet: Frédéric-Constant Cournet (1801–52), a retired Breton naval officer, was elected to the National Assembly in 1850. He then took part in the unsuccessful insurrection that followed Louis-Napoleon's *coup d'état* in December 1851, and fled to London, where he was killed in a duel by fellow barricadist Emmanuel Barthélemy.

Chaerea: As recounted by Suetonius in his *Lives of the Twelve Caesars*, Cassius Chaerea was the conspirator who struck the first blow in the assassination of the emperor Caligula in AD 41 ('Caligula', ch. 56–8). Claudius, who succeeded Caligula, ordered the execution of Chaerea and his co-conspirators 'because he knew that they had also demanded his own death' ('Claudius', ch. 11).

Stephanus: The steward who murdered the emperor Domitian in AD 96. Cassius Dio in the Epitome of bk LXVII, 17, of his *Roman History* recounts: 'Not only was Domitian murdered, but Stephanus, too, perished when those who had not shared in the conspiracy made a concerted rush upon him.'

Charlotte Corday: Corday (1768–93) murdered Jean-Paul Marat by stabbing him with a knife in his bath on 13 July 1793; she was tried and convicted by the Revolutionary Tribunal, and guillotined on 17 July.

Sand: The assassination in 1819 of the dramatist (and alleged Russian spy and German traitor) August von Kotzebue by Karl Ludwig Sand (1795–1820), a young German nationalist, 'whom kings regarded as an assassin, judges as a fanatic, and the youth of Germany as a hero' (Alexandre Dumas, *Celebrated Crimes*), gave the authorities the justification they needed for the repression of radical nationalist groups. Sand was subsequently executed.

translators of the Georgics: Abbé Delille (1738–1813; translation of 1770), Jacques-Charles-Louis Clinchamp de Malfilâtre (1732–67; posthumous publication of his translations of Virgil, 1810), J.-F. Raux (translation of 1802), Antoine de Cournand (1742–1814; translation of 1804).

portents at Caesar's death: As described in Virgil's *Georgics*, bk I, lines 461–97.

Zoilus . . . Maevius: A Greek scholar of the fourth century BC, Zoilus made a name for himself as a critic of Homer's writings. Ridiculed in verse by Virgil (*Eclogue* 3) and Horace (*Epode* 10), the Augustan poet Maevius is now remembered only as a critic of better writers than himself.

Visé insults Molière: Playwright and journalist, Jean Donneau de Visé (1638–1710) was highly critical of Molière's *School for Wives* (1662), but later became a warm admirer of his talents as a playwright and an actor, and wrote for his acting troupe.

Pope insults Shakespeare: Pope's admiration for Shakespeare was by no means uncritical: 'It must be own'd that with all these great excellencies he has almost as great defects; and that as he has certainly written better so he has perhaps written worse than any other.' From Pope's *Preface to Shakespeare* (1725).

Fréron insults Voltaire: Élie Fréron (1718–76) used *L'Année Littéraire*, the successful journal that he founded, to launch a conservative rearguard attack on the luminaries of the Enlightenment. Voltaire defended himself against this relentless critic with scathing satire.

Eutropius: Flavius Eutropius, the fourth-century-AD Roman historian, wrote: 'As [Caesar] disposed, therefore, at his own pleasure, of those honours, which were before conferred by the people and did not even rise up when the senate approached him, and exercised regal or almost tyrannical power in other respects [*aliaque regia et paene tyrannica faceret*], a conspiracy was formed against him by sixty or more Roman senators and knights' (*Breviarium Historiae Romanae*, bk VI, 25, as translated by the Rev. John Selby Watson).

Cydathenaeum . . . Aedapteon: Cydathenaeum, Myrrhinus, Probalinthus, Laurium and Aedapteon are ancient Greek towns in Attica. The Aeantis, named after the Greek warrior Ajax, were one of the ten tribes of Attica.

Anacharsis Cloots: Cloots (1755–94), a Prussian nobleman who arrived in Paris in 1776, became a member of the Jacobin Club, adopted French citizenship and was elected to the Convention in 1792; he was a fervent revolutionary internationalist. His patriotism and revolutionary credentials were questioned by Robespierre, who like Saint-Just distrusted cosmopolitan and universalist ambitions. Cloots was guillotined.

amphictyons: Delegates to a 'league of neighbours', a form of alliance dating back to the early history of ancient Greece.

Gribeauval's étoile mobile: Gribeauval invented a portable calibre gauge for verifying the regularity of the inner bore of a cannon, called an *étoile mobile* ('mobile star').

Light . . . a second: In 1728 James Bradley estimated the speed of light to be 185,000 miles per second (301,000 kps). In 1849 the French physicist Hippolyte Fizeau obtained a measurement of 313,300 kps, and in 1862 his compatriot Léon Foucault, refining Fizeau's method, increased the accuracy to 299,796 kps. The accepted modern measurement is 299,792.458 kps, or 186,282.397 mps.

A fireman . . . lookout: After a catastrophic fire broke out at a ball held in July 1810 by the Austrian ambassador to celebrate Napoleon's marriage to the Austrian Archduchess Marie-Louise, Napoleon in September 1811 created a military corps of professional fire-fighters.

Pantin . . . Des Vertus . . . La Cunette: What used to be outlying areas of Paris: Pantin lies to the north, Des Vertus in the Marais to the east, and La Cunette on the left bank to the west.

Lacedaemonian fervour: The fighting spirit of the Lacedaemonians, or Spartans, who so distinguished themselves at Thermopylae, was legendary.

Henri Fonfrède: A political journalist who spent most of his career in Bordeaux, Fonfrède (1788–1841) was a liberal conservative advocate of the July Monarchy.

Lynch law: While its precise origins are disputed, the term, most commonly associated with the actions of Charles Lynch (1736–96) of Virginia in implementing local justice, is first recorded in the early nineteenth century and appears in standard dictionaries from the mid nineteenth century.

Paul-Aimé Garnier: Under the pseudonym Paul Zéro, Garnier (1820–46) wrote a parody, entitled *Les Barbus-Graves* (The Solemn Bearded Ones), of Victor Hugo's last play (1843), the epic verse drama *Les Burgraves* (The Burgraves).

Place Royale . . . number six: After their home had been invaded by insurgents during the rioting in 1848, Hugo and his family moved out of 6 Place Royale, where they had lived since 1832. Place Royale reverted in 1848 to what had been its Revolutionary name until the Restoration, Place des Vosges. It was again renamed Place Royale from 1852 to 1870, and has been Place des Vosges ever since.

quid divinum: The element of the divine, first mentioned with reference to Waterloo. With the storming of the Tuileries, 10 August 1792 saw the end of Louis XVI's reign, and 29 July 1830 was the last of 'the three glorious days' (*les Trois Glorieuses*) of revolution against the Restoration that ended with the overthrow of Bourbon rule and the abdication of Charles X.

Cavaignac de Baragne: Jacques-Marie Cavaignac (1774–1855) served in the Napoleonic campaigns and under the Restoration. He was inspector-general of cavalry 1830–9 and was made a peer in 1839.

Suchet ... Saragossa: Louis-Gabriel Suchet, Duc d'Albufera (1770–1826), was one of Napoleon's greatest generals. He distinguished himself during the Peninsular War, where he gained the marshal's baton for both his military achievements and his administrative skills in overcoming local hostility as commander of Aragon after the fall of Saragossa.

Madame Scarron: Françoise d'Aubigné Scarron (1635–1719), better known as Madame de Maintenon, was unofficially married to Louis XIV.

Orlando ... Angelica: An allusion to Ariosto's *Orlando Furioso*, the early-sixteenth-century Italian epic poem about the knight Orlando's unrequited love for the princess Angelica.

For that blame ...: The two refrains, blaming Voltaire and Rousseau, had been used by two songwriters before Hugo, Béranger and the Swiss journalist and poet Jean-François Chaponnière (1769–1856). Their songs were satirical responses to a notice that was read out in French Catholic churches in February 1817 abhorring the publication of cheap new editions of the works of the two philosophers held responsible in conservative and clerical circles for the horrors of the Revolution. The songs enjoyed huge popularity.

Antaeus: The giant with whom Hercules has to wrestle in order to take the golden apples from the Hesperides derives his strength from contact with the ground, and therefore rises again every time he is overthrown. To defeat him Hercules has to hold him up in the air (Apollodorus, *Library*, bk 2, ch. 5, section 11).

Aldebaran: One of the brightest stars in the night sky, in the constellation Taurus, in which it makes the celestial Bull's eye.

Marie de' Medici: The Palais du Luxembourg with its Italianate gardens was built in 1612–27 for the then queen mother and regent (1575–1642).

The cadet branch: The House of Orléans, to which Louis-Philippe belonged, had replaced the senior Bourbons.

Epidotes: A purifying spirit, worshipped by the Spartans when wishing to avert divine punishment for murder (Pausanias, *Description of Greece*, bk 3, ch. 17, lines 8–9).

Clermont-Tonnerre: Aimé-Marie Gaspard, Duc de Clermont-Tonnerre (1779–1865), minister of the navy and colonies 1821–4, and minister of war 1824–8.

Gérard de Nerval: One of the forerunners of modern French poetry, Nerval (1806–55) took from the German Romantic writer Jean Paul (1763–1825) as the epigram for his sonnet sequence 'Le Christ aux Oliviers' (1844): 'Dieu est mort! le ciel est vide – Pleurez! enfants, vous n'avez plus de père' ('God is dead! Heaven is empty – Weep! children, you no longer have a father'). Nerval met Hugo in 1829 and was prominent among his supporters when *Hernani* was first staged.

Corinth: The Peloponnesian city of Corinth, which had enjoyed great wealth, was later destroyed by the Romans, but rose again to become once more a thriving trading centre.

Missouri ... South Carolina: Under the terms of the so-called Missouri Compromise (1820), Missouri entered the United States Union in 1821 as a slave
state. South Carolina was the first state to secede from the Union, on 20
December 1860.

those salamanders: Salamanders were believed to be able to resist fire and even
to extinguish it. Pliny refers to this in his *Natural History* (bk 10, ch. 94), and
in his autobiography (bk 1, ch. 4) Benvenuto Cellini wrote of seeing a salamander in the fire.

the Veda ... Forest of Swords: Asipatravana, meaning 'the sword-leafed forest',
is a state of hell described in the ancient Hindu texts.

François I at Marignano: The battle of Marignano in 1515 was a protracted and
bloody engagement between France and the Swiss Confederation, from which
the young François I, who distinguished himself on the battlefield, emerged
victorious, winning control of Milan.

Esplandian: The knight errant hero of book 5 of a fifteenth-century Hispanic chivalric romance by Garci Rodríguez de Montalvo, *Las Sergas de Esplandián*.

Phyleus ... lord of men, Euphetes: A reference to the *Iliad*, bk 15, lines 518-35
(with a slight misreading: Phyleus was not in fact the father of Polydamas but
of Meges, who in this passage attacks Polydamas in retaliation for killing Otus
of Cyllene, 'comrade of Phyleus' son').

Megaryon ... mighty Ajax: The Lycians are allies of the Trojans in the war in
which their king, Sarpedon, is killed by Patroclus. He is succeeded by Megaryon. Ajax is one of the Greek heroes of the war.

gates of Thebes: The story of the impregnable seven-gated city of Thebes is told
in the *Thebaid*, one of the earliest epics of ancient Greek literature, of which
only fragments survive, and retold in Aeschylus' play of the fifth century BC,
Seven Against Thebes.

the houses of Saragossa: '[T]he crossing of the large streets divided the town into
certain small districts or islands of houses. To gain possession of these, it was
necessary not only to mine, but to fight for each house', W. F. P Napier, *History
of the War in the Peninsula* (1828-40), bk 5, ch. 3

When Suchet ... Palafox: Louis-Gabriel Suchet was a divisional commander
under Marshal Édouard-Adolphe Mortier at the second siege of Saragossa, but
it was actually General Jean-Antoine Verdier, commanding the first siege of
Saragossa, who offered peace and capitulation to José de Palafox, who famously replied, 'Guerra a cuchillo!' ('War to the knife'). Shortly afterwards,
Verdier lifted the siege.

Greek fire ... Archimedes: The Greek inventor of the third century BC Archimedes
designed a number of war machines that were used to great defensive effect when
the Romans besieged his home town of Syracuse in 214-212 BC. However, there
is no classical source for his having used or invented so-called Greek fire, an
incendiary weapon used by the Byzantine Empire from the seventh century,
although Leonardo da Vinci attributes to him the invention of a steam cannon.

boiling pitch ... Bayard: Pierre Terrail LeVieux, seigneur de Bayard, known
simply as Bayard (1473-1524), was recognized by his contemporaries as both
a valorous soldier and the epitome of the chivalrous knight – François I chose
to be knighted by Bayard after the battle of Marignano – but Bayard also distinguished himself in what had been regarded as the far from chivalrous art of
siege warfare.

Ekeberg: The Swedish seaman and explorer Carl Gustav Ekeberg (1716-84),
author of books based on his travels and a member of the Swedish Academy

of Science, made numerous visits to China and in particular wrote *An Account of Chinese Husbandry*.

parasitisms: In Hugo's last novel, *Quatre-vingt-treize* (1874), the idealist Gauvain, when challenged to explain his new economy, says, 'd'abord supprimez les parasitismes: le parasitisme du prêtre, le parasitisme du juge, le parasitisme du soldat' ('first of all, eliminate parasitisms: the parasitism of the priest, the parasitism of the judge, the parasitism of the soldier').

Fokien: Now known as Fujian, a famously fertile and agriculturally productive southern maritime province of China.

Liebig: Justus von Liebig (1803–73), German chemist, who pioneered the use of chemical fertilizers in agriculture.

Lutetia: The Roman name for Paris, which possibly derives from the Latin word *lutum*, mud.

Bacon: The English Renaissance intellectual Francis Bacon (1561–1626) was much admired as a philosopher of science and for his scientific method, based on inductive reasoning and experiment, by the great *philosophe* of the French Enlightenment, Denis Diderot.

vermin pit of Benares: 'Qu'un brahmine / Se fasse à Benarès manger par la vermine, / C'est pour le paradis et cela se comprend' ('It is for the sake of paradise that a Brahmin allows himself to be eaten by vermin in Benares, and that is understandable'), from Hugo's 'Août 1870', *L'Année terrible* (1872).

lions' den of Babylon: Into which the prophet Daniel was cast and from which he was delivered (Book of Daniel 6).

Tiglath-Pileser . . . Nineveh: The ancient Assyrian city of Nineveh was ruled by Tiglath-Pileser I in the eleventh century BC, by Tiglath-Pileser II in the tenth century BC, and by Tiglath Pileser III in the eighth century BC.

Jan van Leiden: A radical Anabaptist, Jan van Leiden (*c*.1509–36) was one of the leaders of the 1534 Münster Rebellion. He was declared king of the city and ruled for a year and a half, instituting polygamy and communizing property. When the former bishop of Münster recaptured the town, he was sentenced to death and horribly tortured.

Mokanna . . . Khorassan: Thomas Moore's phenomenally successful Oriental romance *Lalla Rookh* (1817), reviewed in *Le Conservateur littéraire* (the review founded by Victor Hugo and his brother Abel) in 1820, is a prose narrative linking four poems, including 'The Veiled Prophet of Khorassan' (another, 'Paradise and the Peri', inspired Robert Schumann's 1843 work of the same name). In Moore's retelling of the story of Mokanna, the eighth-century founder of a religious sect in Persia, the veil, which Mokanna's followers believe he wears to cover the dazzling radiance of his countenance, in reality hides his monstrous hideousness. In Moore's version, and according to the French seventeenth-century Orientalist D'Herbelot, Mokanna is able by his wicked arts to conjure up the brightness of the moon out of 'Neksheb's Holy Well'.

Maillotins: Participants in a Parisian uprising against increased taxation in 1382 (during the reign of Charles VI), so called because they were armed with iron *maillets* ('mallets'), tools of their trade.

Morin's visionaries: In his 'Commentary' on Beccaria's *Essay on Crimes and Punishments* Voltaire tells the story of Simon Morin, who believed 'he was sent from God, and that he was incorporated with Jesus Christ'. Initially treated as a madman, Morin was burned at the stake in 1663. His followers were branded and condemned to penal servitude for life.

chauffeurs: Extortionist bandits rife in the late eighteenth century, so called because they were reputed to scorch their victims' feet to compel them to reveal where valuables were hidden. The most famous of this type of bandit was Johannes Bückler, known as Schinderhannes or John the Scorcher, who was active in the Rhine area.

Basil's mask . . . Scapin's false nose: Scapino, a stock servant character of the Italian *commedia dell'arte*, often portrayed with a hooked nose, was Gallicized by Molière in *Les Fourberies de Scapin* (1671), while Don Basile in Beaumarchais's *The Barber of Seville* (1775) wears an invisible mask of hypocrisy.

Caiaphas's spittle: Having established his guilt to their satisfaction, Christ's interrogators, of whom Caiaphas is one, spit in his face.

Louis XI . . . Tristan: Even in his lifetime, Louis XI was called the 'universal spider' because of the guile and patience he applied in overcoming his enemies. Louis Tristan l'Hermite (dates unknown) is described in Michaud's *Biographie Universelle* (1826) as 'the cruellest agent of our most ruthless king'. Hugo gives a masterly portrayal of the two operating together in *The Hunchback of Notre-Dame*, bk X, ch. 5.

François I . . . Duprat: Cardinal-archbishop and chancellor, Antoine Duprat (1463–1535) – 'the most vicious of bipeds', in the words of a contemporary – was intransigent in the persecution of heretics and vindictive in the persecution of his enemies; and while François I was initially more lenient in his attitude towards Reformist scholars, his position against heretics hardened, culminating in the Edict of Fontainebleau (1540) directed against the Huguenots. In Hugo's play *Le Roi s'amuse* (1832), on which Verdi based the plot of *Rigoletto*, François is depicted as a debauched philanderer abusing his power.

Charles IX . . . his mother: Catherine de' Medici (1519–89) became regent when her son Charles (1550–74) inherited the throne in 1561. The reign of Charles IX was dominated by the Wars of Religion, culminating in the St Bartholomew's Day Massacre of August 1572, for which the queen mother was widely held responsible; it began in Paris and spread throughout the country, resulting in the deaths of thousands of Huguenots.

Richelieu . . . Louis XIII: Cardinal Richelieu (1585–1642) was for nearly twenty years the ruthless power behind the throne during the reign of Louis XIII. Hugo's play *Marion de Lorme* (1829) was initially banned because of its portrayal of this relationship, and performed only after the 1830 Revolution.

Judengasse . . . Ghetto: Districts of the cities of Frankfurt and Venice in which their Jewish populations were confined.

Bruneseau: Pierre-Emmanuel Bruneseau (1751–1819), inspector of public works in Paris, whose contribution to the modernization of Paris's sewer system has been immortalized in this novel by Hugo.

Mercier: In his *Tableau de Paris*, Mercier bewails the state of the riverbanks, which for want of proper provision of public latrines are used as a public convenience, and describes how open sewers, once built over, are no longer cleaned and are left to poison the atmosphere with their stench.

Behemoth: The creature described in the Book of Job 40:15–24, which (in the words of the English Revised Version) 'he only that made him can make his sword to approach unto him'.

Sainte-Foix: Possibly a misspelled reference to Germain-François Poulain de Saint-Foix (1698–1776), playwright and author of a collection of *Essais historiques sur Paris* (Historical Essays on Paris; 1754–7), who had a reputation for quarrelsomeness and for duelling.

Marmousets: The disparagingly named Marmousets, so called because of their humble origins (the term is first recorded by the medieval chronicler Jean Froissart), were the political faction favoured by Charles VI on reaching his majority. When Charles went mad, the Marmousets lost power and some were imprisoned, although not murdered as Hugo suggests.

Fagon: Doctor and botanist, Guy Fagon (1638–1718) was Louis XIV's chief physician from 1693 until the king's death in 1715.

barathrum: A notorious pit or ravine on the outskirts of ancient Athens, where the bodies of criminals were thrown.

some Decrès or Crétet: Denis Decrès (1761–1820) was vice-admiral, and minister for the navy and the colonies 1801–14. Emmanuel Crétet (1747–1809), appointed first governor of the Bank of France in 1806, served as minister of the interior from 1807 until October 1809.

Escaut: The French name for the River Scheldt.

Fleurus balloonists: At the battle of Fleurus on 26 June 1794, won by the French during the French Revolutionary Wars, the French Aerostatic Corps, founded in April 1794, used balloons to monitor the movements of the opposing Austrian army.

Junot's cannon-ball: At the siege of Toulon in 1793, Napoleon had just finished dictating orders to a young sergeant, Jean-Androche Junot (1771–1813), when a cannon-ball fell between the two men, scattering dust over the sheet of paper on which Junot had been writing. Junot's quip that thanks to the dust he would not need to blot the ink with sand won him favour with Napoleon.

Zuyderzee: Trapped by ice in the Zuyderzee, the Dutch fleet was taken by a French cavalry regiment on 30 January 1795, marking the fall of the Dutch Republic in the Flanders campaign during the French Revolutionary Wars.

Fourcroy: Antoine-François Fourcroy (1755–1809) was a chemist and politician who played a significant role in the development of public education after the Revolution and in the reform and reorganization of medical studies.

Philibert Delorme: Author of the only comprehensive French Renaissance treatise on architecture, Delorme (*c.*1514–70) designed Diane de Poitiers's château at Anet, and the first plans for the Tuileries Palace for Catherine de' Medici.

Gros-Jean . . . Lebel: 'Gros-Jean' is a standard name for a rustic simpleton, as used by Rabelais in *The Fourth Book of Pantagruel* and La Fontaine (fable 10, bk 7). Dominique Lebel (1696–1768) was chief valet to Louis XV.

orang-utan: Edgar Allan Poe's 'Murders in the Rue Morgue', featuring an escaped orang-utan, was published in 1841 and appeared in French in 1848.

Laubespine: The Revolutionary leader Jean-Paul Marat, who first practised medicine in Britain, treated the Marquise de l'Aubespine in 1777 and as a result of her recommendation was appointed doctor to the Comte d'Artois's household.

Friend of the People: *L'Ami du Peuple* was the name of a Revolutionary newspaper founded by Marat in 1789.

Tartuffe after confession: In Molière's play, Tartuffe's confession in Act III will allow the scheming hypocrite to persist in his depravity.

Grenelle well: The first artesian well successfully opened in Paris to provide badly needed drinking water was located in the Grenelle slaughterhouse. The works, conducted by engineer Louis-Georges Mulot (1792–1872) and started in 1833, first delivered water in 1841.

bousingot: A term describing young men of radical opinions and affecting a casual style of dress, often including the *bousingot* hat. A volume of *Contes du*

Bouzingo, advertised in 1832 and 1833 and for which Gérard de Nerval wrote 'La Main de Gloire', never materialized. See http://haquelebac.wordpress. com/2010/03/07/bousingot-not-in-your-dictionaries/

François I's house: A Renaissance façade of a house thought to have been built by François I for his mistress was bought by Colonel Brack, a property developer, who had it transported from near Fontainebleau to Paris and rebuilt in the Champs-Élysées area that he was trying to develop. The Paris house was demolished in 1956 and the façade returned to Moret-sur-Loing.

butt of malmsey . . . Clarence: George, Duke of Clarence (1449–78), was sentenced to death for treason against his brother King Edward IV. Even as early as the 1480s, he was reported to have been drowned in a butt of malmsey. See John Webster Spargo, 'Clarence in the Malmsey-butt', *Modern Language Notes*, vol. 51, no. 3 (March 1936), pp. 166–73.

Lerida: In 1647 during the Thirty Years War (1618–48), when the French under the command of the Grand Condé (Louis II de Bourbon-Condé, 1621–86) laid siege to Lerida, they were accompanied in their action by twenty-four violins (Hugo elsewhere says thirty-six).

Hero . . . Leander: Ovid (*Heroides*, 18–19) and the sixth-century Byzantine poet Musaeus Grammaticus tell the story of Leander, who drowns swimming across the Hellespont to join his lover Hero, who then throws herself from her tower in grief.

Thisbe . . . Pyramus: Ovid in the *Metamorphoses* (bk 4, lines 55–167) tells the story of the two lovers who commit suicide, he, thinking that his mistress has been killed by a lion, and she, on finding his dead body.

Gros-Caillou: This district of Paris, which in the early nineteenth century was still semi-rural, takes its name from a boundary-stone that marked the city limits in the seventeenth century.

the good angel: In Alexandre Dumas's 1836 play *Don Juan de Marana, ou La Chute d'un Ange* (The Fall of an Angel) a good angel, who descends from heaven, taking on the human appearance of a nun, vies for the soul of Don Juan with a bad angel, who emerges from the ground.

Tirecuir de Corcelles: Colonel of the National Guard during the Hundred Days, Claude Tirguy de Corcelles (1768–1843) was a liberal politician who served in the National Assembly and the Chamber of Deputies. His family name – Tirguy, sometimes Tircuy – is satirically mispronounced by Monsieur Gillenormand (*tirer* meaning 'to pull' and *cuir*, 'leather').

clubbist: A reference to the Revolutionary political clubs that flourished before and after the Revolution.

Pontius Pilate's basin: An allusion to Matthew 27:24, in which the Roman governor of Judaea, Pontius Pilate, washes his hands, disclaiming responsibility for the spilling of Christ's blood.

the Fampoux of a rectilinear conscience: Fampoux in Pas-de-Calais was the scene of a train disaster on 8 July 1846, shortly after the inauguration of the new Paris–Lille line, when a derailment led to the death of fourteen people.

pin-cushion box: The writer and poet Joseph Poisle Desgranges (1823–79) gives a detailed description of the pin-cushion box (*la grimace*) on his desk in chapter 32 of his humorous novel *Voyage à mon Bureau* (Journey to my Office; 1861).

Tityrus: Virgil's *Eclogue* 1 opens with a description of the shepherd Tityrus lying under the canopy of a spreading beech tree.

scandalous Gisquet decree: Henri Gisquet gives an account of this 'still-born' decree issued on 9 June 1832, which met with universal condemnation and was never enforced, in *Mémoires de M. Gisquet, ancien préfet de police*, Paris, 1840, pp. 267–73.

Regency: From the death of Louis XIV (1715) until his great-grandson and heir came of age (1723), Louis XIV's nephew Philippe, Duc d'Orléans, was regent. Grandfather Gillenormand is slightly exaggerating his age, but claiming spiritual association with a period that represented the values he cherishes.

Dorante . . . Géronte: Names that frequently occur in a literary context to denote a young man and an old man. In Corneille's *Le Menteur* (The Liar; 1644), for instance, Géronte is the father of the young lover Dorante.

Chénier: André Chénier's poem 'Le Jeune Malade' tells of a young man pining away because of his undeclared love, and ends with his beloved coming to his bedside to cure him.

Boulard: Antoine-Marie-Henri Boulard (1754–1825), a famous book collector whose library on his death numbered several hundred thousand volumes.

de Birague's fountain: Dating back to the sixteenth century, then rebuilt in 1707 by Jean Beausire, it was destroyed in 1856.

Mère Gigogne: A puppet character, dating from 1602, who shares with the Old Woman Who Lived in a Shoe the characteristic of having many children, and who has gained archetypal status as mother of a large family. 'Gigogne' is probably a deformation of *cigogne*, meaning 'stork'.

bridal gift-basket: A key element of the marriage transaction in the nineteenth century, given by the groom to his bride in exchange for her dowry. See Susan Hiner, *Accessories to Modernity: Fashion and the Feminine in Nineteenth-century France*, ch. 2, 'Unpacking the *Corbeille de Mariage*', Philadelphia: University of Pennsylvania Press, 2010.

Cato and Phocion: Plutarch in his *Lives* draws a parallel between the Athenian statesman and general Phocion and the Roman statesman and general Cato the Younger, in respect of their probity and devotion to the state.

Strasbourg . . . a clock: Strasbourg Cathedral's astrological clock, dating originally from the mid fourteenth century, was an astonishingly complex and elaborate device, rich in decoration, showing the position of the stars and planets, including the sun and moon (Phoebus and Phoebe). It was rebuilt in the sixteenth century and a new mechanism was installed in the nineteenth, when the earlier geocentric stereographic projection of the stars and planets was replaced with a Copernican heliocentric model.

Sarmatians: The ancient Sarmatians were a nomadic and warlike tribal people from whom Poles in the fifteenth century began to claim descent. During the Enlightenment this cultural 'Sarmatism' came to be regarded as backward and provincial.

Cujas . . . Camacho: Jacques Cujas (1520–90) was a celebrated French jurist and scholar with a profound knowledge of Roman law. Camacho, a character in Cervantes' *Don Quixote*, serves a vast amount of food at his wedding, and his name has come to signify in French a person who likes to eat well and in very large quantity. *Les Noces de Gamache* (Gamache's Wedding) is the title of a ballet-pantomime inspired by the Quixote incident, written by Louis Milon with music by François-Charlemagne Lefebvre, first performed at the Paris Opéra in 1801, and of a comic opera by Thomas Sauvage and Jean-Henri Dupin with music by Saverio Mercadante, first performed at the Théâtre Royal de l'Odéon in 1825. Mendelssohn's comic opera *Die Hochzeit des Camacho* (Camacho's Wedding) was first performed in Berlin in 1827.

captain of dragoons . . . Florian: The pastoral poet Jean-Pierre Claris de Florian held a captain's commission in a dragoon regiment.

Les Indes Galantes: An opera-ballet, set in exotic locations and on the theme of love, by Rameau, first performed in 1735.

rigadoon: A sprightly dance that became fashionable in the eighteenth century and involved jumping on the spot.

pagoda of Chanteloup: Built by the Duc de Choiseul in 1775 in the grounds of his now demolished château at Chanteloup in the Loire, the pagoda is a charming, some 140-foot-high folly still standing today.

Argyraspides: The Greek name, meaning 'silver shields', of an elite corps of Macedonian infantry under Alexander the Great.

Prince Aldobrandini: Possibly Francesco Borghese, Prince Aldobrandini (1776–1839), who married Ade de la Rochefoucauld (1793–1877) in France in 1809. This might also be an oblique reference to the so-called Aldobrandini wedding fresco, a first-century BC Roman work recovered in 1601, which came into the possession of Cardinal Cinzio Aldobrandini, from whom it took its name. It is now in the Vatican.

Amphitrite: A sea goddess, wife of Poseidon, mother of Triton.

Duchesse d'Anville ... at La Roche-Guyon: In 1821 Hugo was a guest of Cardinal de Rohan at La Roche-Guyon, which previously belonged to the cardinal's great-grandmother Marie-Louise-Nicole-Élisabeth de la Rochefoucauld, Duchesse d'Anville (1716–97), who undertook considerable decorative works on the château.

the postilion of Lonjumeau: Le Postillon de Lonjumeau is the title of a comic opera by Adolphe Adam (who also wrote the ballet *Giselle*) with a libretto by de Leuven and Brunswick, first performed in Paris in 1836. The leading role is that of a coachman who abandons his bride to become an opera singer.

in memory of Churchill: John Churchill, first Duke of Marlborough (1650–1722), married Sarah Jennings (1660–1744) in 1677, a marriage at first opposed by his parents as she brought no money to it, but her close friendship with Princess Anne, daughter of King James II, gained her enormous influence when Anne became queen in 1702.

Paillasse, Pantaloon and Gille: French stock characters based on the *commedia dell'arte* characters Pagliaccio, Pantalone and Pedrolino, also associated with the Pierrot character in France, with which Gille (or Gilles) is closely identified: the name is said to have been that of an actor who played this role about 1640.

Lord Seymour ... a vulgar nickname: Lord Henry Seymour (1805–59), who was born and died in Paris, was probably the illegitimate son of the 3rd Marquess of Hertford. He passed for something of an eccentric Englishman, and attracted the nickname Milord Arsouille (Lord Crapulous). Some of his notoriety results from a confusion of identity with another eccentric of dubious birth, Charles de la Battut (1806–35), who had a penchant for disguise and carnival high-jinks, and was the 'real' Milord Arsouille. Seymour was the founder of the Paris Jockey Club.

Thespis' wagon ... Vadé's hackney cab: The Greek poet Thespis of the sixth century BC is associated with the origins of Greek tragedy. Horace refers to Thespis going on theatrical tours with a cart or wagon (*Ars Poetica*, lines 275–7). Jean-Joseph Vadé (1720–57), poet, playwright and songwriter, made his name with comic-realist writing inspired by the colourfully robust language of the common people, for which he was jokingly hailed in his day as 'the Corneille of Les Halles'.

minted at Tours: Tours, which was incorporated into the Kingdom of France in 1205 by Philippe-Auguste (1165–1223), minted its own currency. Louis IX (1214–70) established the supremacy of the royal currency, minted either at

Tours or Paris, restricting the circulation of other, local currencies minted by individual barons and prelates. Louis XI (1423–83) established his court at Plessis-les-Tours, effectively making Tours the capital of his kingdom.

Collé, Panard and Piron: Playwrights for the popular theatre, parodists and songwriters, Charles Collé (1709–83), Charles-François Panard (1689–1765) and Alexis Piron (1689–1773) were three founder members of a famous dining society called the Caveau, established in 1729, that brought together many prominent figures of Paris's theatrical and musical world.

fishwives' catechism: The fishwives, *les poissardes* of Les Halles, were notorious for their coarse language and rough manners, hence the use of the adjective *poissard* to mean 'low-class' or 'popular', and applied to the style of comic writing associated with Vadé, Collé, Panard and Piron.

Roquelaure: Gaston-Jean-Baptiste, Duc de Roquelaure (1617–83), a celebrated wit and a favourite of Louis XIV.

Cadran-Bleu: A fashionable eating establishment on Boulevard du Temple, where the leaders of the insurrection of 10 August 1792 are known to have met. It was demolished in 1860.

Barras: Paul, Vicomte de Barras (1755–1829), was a member of the Convention from its inception in 1792, and of the Committee of Public Safety, where he was instrumental in the downfall of Robespierre. He went on to become a powerful member of the Directory from 1795 until Napoleon's coup of 18 Brumaire (9 November 1799), when his political career ended. (Joséphine de Beauharnais, later to become Napoleon's wife, was for a time his mistress.)

the Sancy diamond: Bought in Constantinople in 1570 by the French ambassador Nicolas de Harlay, Sieur de Sancy (1546–1629), the Sancy, a 55-carat diamond, has passed through many hands – James I of England and Lady Astor were among those who once owned it. It is now in the Louvre, which acquired it in 1976.

Louis the Great: Louis XIV, the Sun King (1638–1715).

bourrée . . . cachucha: The *bourrée* is a traditional Auvergne folk dance, adopted as a court dance in the sixteenth century. The *cachucha* is a Spanish dance dating from the early nineteenth; the celebrated Austrian dancer Fanny Elssler created a sensation when she danced it at the Paris Opéra in 1836 in Jean Coralli's ballet-pantomime *Le Diable Boiteux*.

Célimène . . . Alceste: Alceste is the protagonist of Molière's *The Misanthrope*, who despite his moralistic rigidity cannot help but fall in love with Célimène, the charming young woman who represents everything to which he is opposed.

Daphnis and Chloe . . . Philemon and Baucis: A prose romance by the Greek classical writer Longus, *Daphnis and Chloe* tells the story of young love that overcomes all obstacles. Philemon and Baucis, in Ovid's *Metamorphoses*, bk VIII, lines 612–727, exemplify devoted love enduring into old age. There is a retelling of their story by La Fontaine: fable 25, bk 12, 'Philémon et Baucis'.

Ventre-saint-gris: Gilles Henry in his *Dictionnaire des expressions nées de l'histoire* (Paris: Tallandier, 1992) suggests that this was a construing of *Ventre sangue Christi* ('The belly and blood of Christ') by Parisians unused to Henri's oaths and his Gascon accent. It has also been explained as a deformation of *Vendredi Saint* ('Good Friday') or *Ventre de St-Denis* ('St Denis's belly').

THE LAST DROP IN THE CHALICE: An allusion to Christ's agony in the Garden of Gethsemane (Matthew 26:39, Mark 14:36, Luke 22:42).

The Seventh Circle and the Eighth Heaven: Dante's seventh circle of Hell (*Inferno*, cantos 12–17) is where those guilty of violence – against others, against themselves and against God – are condemned to be punished. How-ever, in *Actes et Paroles* (1875) Hugo writes: 'chômage, maladie, travail au rabais, exploitation, marchandage, parasitisme, misère, il [Bony] avait traversé les sept cercles de l'enfer du prolétaire' ('unemployment, sickness, underpaid work, exploitation, illegal subcontraction of labour, parasitism, destitution, he [Bony] had been through the proletariat's seven circles of hell'). The eighth heaven (Dante's *Paradiso*, cantos 23–7) is an affirmation of faith, hope and love that brings the soul closer to the light of God.

Captain Cook . . . by Vancouver: Captain James Cook (1728–79) in 1777 pub-lished his *Voyage towards the South Pole and Round the World in HMS Resolution and HMS Adventure in 1772, 1773, 1774 and 1775*. Captain George Vancouver (1758–98), who served under Captain Cook earlier in his career, wrote an account of his own explorations, *A Voyage of Discovery to the North Pacific Ocean and Round the World*, published shortly after his death.

on St Never's Day: In the French: 'à la Trinité'. The expression *à Pâques ou à la Trinité* ('at Easter or on Trinity Sunday') was widely disseminated through a folk song about the Duke of Marlborough in which the duke fails to come home from war (against the French in the War of the Spanish Succession, 1701–14) either by Easter or by Trinity Sunday, because he has been killed in battle. The song became immensely popular in the late eighteenth century, and there is a translation of it by the American poet Longfellow. The expression may derive from references to the king's debts in thirteenth-century docu-ments: when payment fell due, it appears, these due dates came and went and the debts remained unpaid.

Thénard: Louis-Jacques Thénard (1777–1857), a distinguished chemist who rose from a humble background eventually to become chancellor of the University of Paris, published a chemistry textbook that was used for many years through-out Europe; he also discovered hydrogen peroxide, and gave his name to a pigment used in the making of Sèvres porcelain. He was made a baron in 1825.

green taffetta eyeshade: In Flaubert's *Dictionnaire des Idées Reçues*, under the head-ing 'Institute': 'The members are all old men who wear green silk eyeshades.'

big for Pitt . . . small for Castelcicala: William Pitt the Younger (1759–1806), British prime minister 1783–1801 and 1804–6, was a distinctively thin man – said to have given him an unfair advantage when he fought a duel with his more robust fellow parliamentarian George Tierney on 27 May 1798. Fabrizio Ruffo (1763–1832), Prince of Castelcicala from 1768, served as Neapolitan ambassador in London and subsequently in Paris. He is depicted by Thomas Rowlandson in a pen-and-ink caricature (1816, Courtauld Institute, London) entitled *A Neapolitan Ambassador – Prince Castelcicala* as a very fat man.

la Princesse Bagration . . . Vicomte Dambray: Great-niece of Catherine the Great's lover Prince Grigory Potemkin and widow of the war hero Prince Petr Ivanovich Bagration, who was killed at the battle of Borodino, Catherine Skavronskaya (1783–1857) was known as 'the White Pussycat' (alabaster skin, blue eyes) or 'the Naked Angel' (due to her taste for see-through dresses). She was at one time the mistress of Metternich, by whom she had a child. Emmanuel Dambray (1785–1868) was elevated to the peerage in 1815. He retired from public life after the July Revolution of 1830, refusing to serve under the new regime. His father Charles-Henri (1760–1829) served as lord chancellor under Louis XVIII.